# CONTENTS

# CONTENTS

# Introduction

## BY MARK SCHORER

When Sinclair Lewis published *Main Street* in 1920, he was the author of five earlier novels which, while they had been generally well-received, caused no great excitement on the American literary scene and enjoyed only the most modest sales. Lewis had earned his living first by working in publishing houses and then by selling with alarming regularity story after slick story to the magazines of largest circulation. These stories, more often than not, perpetuated an old and favorite notion in American fiction about life in the small town: here was America at its heart, at its kindest, its friendliest, its best. In the early novels, too, and especially in the worst of them, *The Innocents,* this same theme appears, but in the novels it appears in the context of a larger optimism and perhaps a larger sentimentality about American life in general. It is an optimism derived in part from England, particularly from the H. G. Wells of novels like *The History of Mr. Polly* and from Dickens in his more superficial moods, in part from a prevailing view in American thought in the years before World War I, a view most effectively presented in Herbert Croly's *The Promise of American Life* of 1909.

The amalgamation came out in the early Lewis novels as a liberal individualism that proclaimed the possibility of an adventurous freedom from social convention and class demands for even the humblest person if only he himself was adventurous enough to run the risk of being free; and as an implied national flexibility that suggested the potentiality within American life of an almost endless extension of democratic relaxation, innocence, amiable eccentricity, intelligence without pretension, discovery of the beautiful and the simply real. When the work that embodied this view was praised, it was chiefly for what seemed then a remarkable blending of realistic observation with "romance," a combination that seemed to cut neatly between the saccharine sentimentalities of popular fiction and the melodramatic brutalities of naturalism.

From this general view emerged a plot pattern that appeared over and over in Lewis's work, both long and short: of a person, usually young, who glimpses a vision of a fuller life beyond the stultifying environment within which he exists, who tries to actualize that vision, and who, in one degree or another, succeeds or fails. "Rebellious optimism" was Lewis's phrase for it, and the success of his short stories in the commercial market enabled him to break out of the stultifying environment of commercial New York and take to the adventurous highway, a rebellious optimist himself. That highway led him back, presently, to his own earliest environment—Sauk Centre, Minnesota—and to a long visit there.

It led him back, too, in memory, to a hot summer of eleven years before when all that was most odious and most exasperating in that environment as he had known it for the first twenty years of his life threatened to drive him out of his wits. He had been an incompetent and unhappy boy in an environment where skill at hunting and fishing and active sports alone made for a boy's happiness. His pleasures were the solitary pleasures of walking and reading. As he was the laughingstock and the butt of cruel jokes among his male contemporaries, so he was an object of derision among young females and a noisy eccentric to the respectable adults who made up the bulk of the population in that conventional small town. It no doubt seemed worse to him than it was. And yet, when he left it for a brief college-preparatory term at Oberlin and then for college itself at New Haven, nothing much improved. He was more than ever the outsider, the ever more raucous eccentric. From chilly Yale he could look back on Sauk Centre as warm and friendly. But every time that he returned to it, he discovered again that it was smotheringly provincial in those fixed conventions and smug complacencies that somehow excluded everything that he aspired to. It was some kind of poisonous disease from which the village suffered, he decided in that summer of 1905, and he found a name for it, "the village virus," and he determined that some day he would write a novel about it. Visiting it again, then, in 1916 with his young and chic New York wife, he recalled not only all his own frustrations but he saw the present village, as she has said, through her eyes. What if a woman such as she were suddenly doomed to live out her life there? The novel *Main Street* was born at last after its long gestation, and Sinclair Lewis had found at last his métier in a broadly satirical assault on the provincial types of hinterland America.

The delay from 1916 to 1920 was fortunate. Nineteen-sixteen might have been just a little too early, but the publication of *Main Street* in 1920 seems to have hit almost to the day the moment at which American readers were most receptive to precisely such an attack on the small town, and this whether in the larger group that praised it as the truest novel ever written about America or in the sensitively defiant group that damned it as untrue. The result was one of the most explosive events in the history of American publishing, and it led Robert Littell to observe that "If *Main Street* lives, it will probably be not as a novel but as an incident in American life."

Beside that long sentimental tradition, so dear to the Hoosier school of writers best represented by Booth Tarkington and Meredith Nicholson, the tradition of the warm generosity of small-town life, of Zona Gale's *Friendship Village*, there ran a thinner, harsher, and briefer tradition of the narrow cruelty of small-town life, but somehow this tradition, going back perhaps no further than the 1870's of Edward Eggleston and the 1880's of E. W. Howe, coming up through Hamlin Garland and Harold Frederic, then finding new force in poetry in Edgar Lee Masters's *Spoon River Anthology* of 1915 and in more novels after that—those of the early Sherwood Anderson,

Floyd Dell, a later Zona Gale—somehow that second tradition had never been strong enough to provide a second stereotype or even to challenge the strength of the first one. *Main Street* did that singlehandedly, and the American small town today is still most generally seen as Sinclair Lewis saw it.

It seemed, too, to most readers who knew Lewis's earlier work, to mark a total change in him. Gone now was the "romance," and what was left was the "realism" alone. It was a "realism" that embodied in all the densely observed details of fiction the more abstract invective of H. L. Mencken against the limitations of the American middle class and the stupid provinciality that these engendered, and the invective of Mencken, like the satire of Sinclair Lewis, was to mount in influence as the 1920's began to unroll. Together, they perfectly met the mood of a postwar, disillusioned American people, and they seemed to characterize most strikingly a new national mood of self-criticism and even of self-disgust.

Most of Lewis's readers did not read him closely enough to see that in fact he was a very different man from H. L. Mencken. Mencken's assault was directed not only against the bourgeois character of American life but against the whole notion of a democratic society. Sinclair Lewis's assault was on the false values that an unenlightened *bourgeoisie* pursued, forgetting or smugly neglecting the real promises of democratic life. And thus the familiar pattern of his fiction appears here in *Main Street* as it had earlier: of the eager young creature who has intimations of a fuller life beyond the environment in which she finds herself and of her attempts to make these intimations real. That she must sharply compromise with her aspirations in the end means for a reader today only that her aspirations were not good enough, that they themselves were the moon-calf gropings of the silliest "romanticism."

Today, Carol Kennicott seems like a fool, and so she did to Sinclair Lewis long before his career as a novelist had come to an end. But in 1920 she did not seem so. Like Lewis himself, like a "culture"-hungry America, she wanted to bring "culture" to Gopher Prairie, or, that failing, to find it elsewhere. Had she been able, she would have done what Sinclair Lewis presently did—joined the searching American trek to Europe to find it there; but she could not get so far in search of it and was in the end forced back to Gopher Prairie. The strength of *Main Street* lies not in the portrait of the shrilly discontented Carol but in that of the obdurate citizenry that would have none of her nonsense. But the issues that the novel presents are by no means so clear, stemming as they do from Lewis's own unsettled discontents. From the point of view of Sauk Centre, New Haven had looked good; from the point of view of New Haven, Sauk Centre had looked good. The cold rebuff of "culture" to the provincial; the no-nonsense rejection of "culture" by the province: as an individual, Sinclair Lewis had no way of adjusting this impasse. And his novel ends in irresolution, with Carol, whose yearnings were his as much as hers, yearning still, but with the last word given to downright "Doc" Kennicott, who, worrying about storm windows, embodies all of Sinclair Lewis's provincial inheritance.

Such considerations the novel raises today, but if they were raised in 1920 they were the cause of no wavering in his career. He had found in his special brand of satire and its special subject the means of addressing himself to an enormous audience. He had succeeded in giving America its new image of the small town in all its drab meanness. He would proceed at once to give it its new image of the medium-sized city, but personalized now, in a way that *Main Street* was not, in the enormously overdrawn portrait of its chief inhabitant, the small businessman. ". . . and two years from now we'll have them talking of Babbittry." The expectation was too mild. *Babbitt,* even more than *Main Street,* rocked literary America, and the figure of Babbitt himself, it is probably safe to say, became more nearly the equivalent of the American character itself than any literary figure created either before or since.

There had been many novels about American businessmen before *Babbitt,* but they were always about extraordinary businessmen—tycoons, great overlords, great overreachers. Sinclair Lewis, pursuing a new method of literary "research," devoted his study, his observation, above all, his ear, to a different kind of businessman—the raconteur of the Pullman car, the boasting salesman of the side-street hotel, the enterprising real-estate man of Rotary and the Chamber of Commerce, the noisy brotherhood of the Athletic Club— and made such a compilation of notes on his interests, his manners, his lingo, that what emerged in his novel seemed at once archetypal and final. *Here* was the middling businessman who gave American life its peculiar coloration and quality; *here* was the source of our gross materialism and our choking commercialism; *here* was the bigotry, the hypocrisy, the boneheaded complacency that drove every sensitive American to Europe and that made Europe retch. But here, too, was the great American buffoonery, the circus no less than the inferno, the clowning no less than the cloaca. And besides all that, here was pathos! How could this book, in 1922, have been anything but a stupendous success, and Babbitt himself anything but a monstrous if inverted icon? America had been discovered.

The pathos takes us back to the familiar Lewis pattern—to the glimmer, beyond the gauche *décor* of the Athletic Club, of something truly golden. To the discomfited Paul Riesling this vision is granted, and for Riesling, Babbitt feels a peculiar affection, and in that friendship, his one source of those truly human satisfactions that the prevailing "fellowship" of Zenith does not admit. Riesling is driven to suicide. Another kind of vision is given to Seneca Doane, the liberal lawyer, and he is defeated. For Babbitt, the vision takes the form of sexual fantasies about a "fairy child," of a fumbling ideal of friendship, of a sentimental conception of the life of the outdoors, and, finally, of a vague expectation that illicit love will illuminate his dreary days. But at last he is routed, too, relinquishes his timorous divagations from the code of the "fellowship," scurries gladly back into the hell of his middle-class security, albeit with the final realization that "I've never done a single thing I've wanted to in my whole life!" As Carol lets her hopes devolve on the future of her child, so Babbitt lets his come to rest in the future of his unpromising son.

The two books share a fault. In neither can Lewis find adequate forms for the expression of that optimistic idealism that lies at the basis of his satire, and as a result, in the end, the negatives of the satire far outweigh the positives of the idealism, even as that idealism, because of its sentimental character, threatens to blur the edges of the satire. If he himself recognized this situation and was dissatisfied with his achievement because of it, he did not say so; but he did say that in his next novel he wanted to write something that was "heroic."

Medicine had long attracted him as a subject, chiefly because of its considerable importance in his family background. For his father and his brother, both of whom were doctors, he had always felt an overwhelming respect, but in a large way he had given expression to his respect for their professional fidelities in the person of Will Kennicott. Yet Kennicott was hardly "heroic." Rather accidentally, Lewis met a man who had had close experience with a more impressive area of medicine than a country medical practice. This was Paul de Kruif, a bacteriologist recently associated with the Rockefeller Institute. The "research materials" for *Main Street* Lewis had found in his own past; those for *Babbitt* he assiduously collected through his observations of life in the cities of the Middle West. Why not go one step further in approaching this new and less-familiar material and "employ," so to speak, a research assistant who was already in command of the subject, and who could serve as guide while the novelist worked out his fiction? Thus, although the writing was Lewis's own, Paul de Kruif became his indispensable collaborator.

The new subject gave Lewis, for the first time, a proper focus for his idealistic strain in the person of a scientist who dedicates himself to the pursuit of truth in spite of every social and commercial pressure to compromise it. In some ways, it was the subject most perfectly calculated to unify the double nature of his talent: here was opportunity to exploit in satire all the grubbiness, the shams, the follies of the commercial spirit in American life and at the same time to exalt the nobility of spirit and the devotion to high ends that America had always promised. This is the subject that brings the younger Lewis of the five early novels into his maturity, and it is not surprising that it should have become his own favorite among his novels. Now the terms of the pattern reach some balance—the stifling environment and the possibilities beyond it—and in the end, the possibilities, this time, can triumph. Only H. L. Mencken was disappointed. Was Sinclair Lewis not, after all, the chief exemplar in fiction of the derisive spirit of the 1920's? Perhaps not. Was he not, in fact, rather old-fashioned, speaking for a time that was past? Perhaps. But at this moment, in 1925, the general audience was not yet prepared to ask these questions or to answer them positively. It would require a long succession of other novels to make a positive answer certain, and in the meantime, while less fantastically successful than either of the two preceding novels, *Arrowsmith* commanded again an enormous audience, and was called by some the most American novel in American literature.

Whether he was an artist, not many people asked. That question was rather beside the point. What he had done in these three novels was to help Americans, at precisely the moment when they wanted this help, to see themselves as they had never seen themselves before, and his creations slipped easily into the receptive American imagination itself, and there, sometimes to our discomfort because of our inability to transcend and thereby to expel them, they endure.

# Main Street

*To*
*James Branch Cabell*
*and*
*Joseph Hergesheimer*

*This is America—a town of a few thousand, in a region of wheat and corn and dairies and little groves.*

*The town is, in our tale, called "Gopher Prairie, Minnesota." But its Main Street is the continuation of Main Streets everywhere. The story would be the same in Ohio or Montana, in Kansas or Kentucky or Illinois, and not very differently would it be told Up York State or in the Carolina hills.*

*Main Street is the climax of civilization. That this Ford car might stand in front of the Bon Ton Store, Hannibal invaded Rome and Erasmus wrote in Oxford cloisters. What Ole Jenson the grocer says to Ezra Stowbody the banker is the new law for London, Prague, and the unprofitable isles of the sea; whatsoever Ezra does not know and sanction, that thing is heresy, worthless for knowing and wicked to consider.*

*Our railway station is the final aspiration of architecture. Sam Clark's annual hardware turnover is the envy of the four counties which constitute God's Country. In the sensitive art of the Rosebud Movie Palace there is a Message, and humor strictly moral.*

*Such is our comfortable tradition and sure faith. Would he not betray himself an alien cynic who should otherwise portray Main Street, or distress the citizens by speculating whether there may not be other faiths?*

# 1

On a hill by the Mississippi where Chippewas camped two generations ago, a girl stood in relief against the cornflower blue of Northern sky. She saw no Indians now; she saw flour-mills and the blinking windows of skyscrapers in Minneapolis and St. Paul. Nor was she thinking of squaws and portages, and the Yankee fur-traders whose shadows were all about her. She was meditating upon walnut fudge, the plays of Brieux, the reasons why heels run over, and the fact that the chemistry instructor had stared at the new coiffure which concealed her ears.

A breeze which had crossed a thousand miles of wheat-lands bellied her taffeta skirt in a line so graceful, so full of animation and moving beauty, that the heart of a chance watcher on the lower road tightened to wistfulness over her quality of suspended freedom. She lifted her arms, she leaned back against the wind, her skirt dipped and flared, a lock blew wild. A girl on a hilltop; credulous, plastic, young; drinking the air as she longed to drink life. The eternal aching comedy of expectant youth.

It is Carol Milford, fleeing for an hour from Blodgett College.

The days of pioneering, of lassies in sunbonnets, and bears killed with

axes in piney clearings, are deader now than Camelot; and a rebellious girl
is the spirit of that bewildered empire called the American Middlewest.

II

Blodgett College is on the edge of Minneapolis. It is a bulwark of sound
religion. It is still combating the recent heresies of Voltaire, Darwin, and
Robert Ingersoll. Pious families in Minnesota, Iowa, Wisconsin, the Dakotas
send their children thither, and Blodgett protects them from the wickedness
of the universities. But it secretes friendly girls, young men who sing, and
one lady instructress who really likes Milton and Carlyle. So the four years
which Carol spent at Blodgett were not altogether wasted. The smallness of
the school, the fewness of rivals, permitted her to experiment with her
perilous versatility. She played tennis, gave chafing-dish parties, took a graduate seminar in the drama, went "twosing," and joined half a dozen societies
for the practise of the arts or the tense stalking of a thing called General
Culture.

In her class there were two or three prettier girls, but none more eager.
She was noticeable equally in the classroom grind and at dances, though
out of the three hundred students of Blodgett, scores recited more accurately
and dozens Bostoned more smoothly. Every cell of her body was alive—thin
wrists, quince-blossom skin, ingénue eyes, black hair.

The other girls in her dormitory marveled at the slightness of her body
when they saw her in sheer negligée, or darting out wet from a shower-bath.
She seemed then but half as large as they had supposed; a fragile child who
must be cloaked with understanding kindness. "Psychic," the girls whispered,
and "spiritual." Yet so radioactive were her nerves, so adventurous her trust
in rather vaguely conceived sweetness and light, that she was more energetic
than any of the hulking young women who, with calves bulging in heavy-
ribbed woolen stockings beneath decorous blue serge bloomers, thuddingly
galloped across the floor of the "gym" in practise for the Blodgett Ladies'
Basket-Ball Team.

Even when she was tired her dark eyes were observant. She did not yet
know the immense ability of the world to be casually cruel and proudly
dull, but if she should ever learn those dismaying powers, her eyes would
never become sullen or heavy or rheumily amorous.

For all her enthusiasms, for all the fondness and the "crushes" which she
inspired, Carol's acquaintances were shy of her. When she was most ardently
singing hymns or planning deviltry she yet seemed gently aloof and critical.
She was credulous, perhaps; a born hero-worshipper; yet she did question
and examine unceasingly. Whatever she might become she would never be
static.

Her versatility ensnared her. By turns she hoped to discover that she had
an unusual voice, a talent for the piano, the ability to act, to write, to manage
organizations. Always she was disappointed, but always she effervesced anew
—over the Student Volunteers, who intended to become missionaries, over

painting scenery for the dramatic club, over soliciting advertisements for the college magazine.

She was on the peak that Sunday afternoon when she played in chapel. Out of the dusk her violin took up the organ theme, and the candle-light revealed her in a straight golden frock, her arm arched to the bow, her lips serious. Every man fell in love then with religion and Carol.

Throughout Senior year she anxiously related all her experiments and partial successes to a career. Daily, on the library steps or in the hall of the Main Building, the co-eds talked of "What shall we do when we finish college?" Even the girls who knew that they were going to be married pretended to be considering important business positions; even they who knew that they would have to work hinted about fabulous suitors. As for Carol, she was an orphan; her only near relative was a vanilla-flavored sister married to an optician in St. Paul. She had used most of the money from her father's estate. She was not in love—that is, not often, nor ever long at a time. She would earn her living.

But how she was to earn it, how she was to conquer the world—almost entirely for the world's own good—she did not see. Most of the girls who were not betrothed meant to be teachers. Of these there were two sorts: careless young women who admitted that they intended to leave the "beastly classroom and grubby children" the minute they had a chance to marry; and studious, sometimes bulbous-browed and popeyed maidens who at class prayer-meetings requested God to "guide their feet along the paths of greatest usefulness." Neither sort tempted Carol. The former seemed insincere (a favorite word of hers at this era). The earnest virgins were, she fancied, as likely to do harm as to do good by their faith in the value of parsing Cæsar.

At various times during Senior year Carol finally decided upon studying law, writing motion-picture scenarios, professional nursing, and marrying an unidentified hero.

Then she found a hobby in sociology.

The sociology instructor was new. He was married, and therefore taboo, but he had come from Boston, he had lived among poets and socialists and Jews and millionaire uplifters at the University Settlement in New York, and he had a beautiful white strong neck. He led a giggling class through the prisons, the charity bureaus, the employment agencies of Minneapolis and St. Paul. Trailing at the end of the line Carol was indignant at the prodding curiosity of the others, their manner of staring at the poor as at a Zoo. She felt herself a great liberator. She put her hand to her mouth, her forefinger and thumb quite painfully pinching her lower lip, and frowned, and enjoyed being aloof.

A classmate named Stewart Snyder, a competent bulky young man in a gray flannel shirt, a rusty black bow tie, and the green-and-purple class cap, grumbled to her as they walked behind the others in the muck of the South St. Paul stock-yards, "These college chumps make me tired. They're so top-lofty. They ought to of worked on the farm, the way I have. These workmen put it all over them."

"I just love common workmen," glowed Carol.

"Only you don't want to forget that common workmen don't think they're common!"

"You're right! I apologize!" Carol's brows lifted in the astonishment of emotion, in a glory of abasement. Her eyes mothered the world. Stewart Snyder peered at her. He rammed his large red fists into his pockets, he jerked them out, he resolutely got rid of them by clenching his hands behind him, and he stammered:

"I know. You *get* people. Most of these darn co-eds—— Say, Carol, you could do a lot for people."

"How?"

"Oh—oh well—you know—sympathy and everything—if you were—say you were a lawyer's wife. You'd understand his clients. I'm going to be a lawyer. I admit I fall down in sympathy sometimes. I get so dog-gone impatient with people that can't stand the gaff. You'd be good for a fellow that was too serious. Make him more—more—*you* know—sympathetic!"

His slightly pouting lips, his mastiff eyes, were begging her to beg him to go on. She fled from the steam-roller of his sentiment. She cried, "Oh, see those poor sheep—millions and millions of them." She darted on.

Stewart was not interesting. He hadn't a shapely white neck, and he had never lived among celebrated reformers. She wanted, just now, to have a cell in a settlement-house, like a nun without the bother of a black robe, and be kind, and read Bernard Shaw, and enormously improve a horde of grateful poor.

The supplementary reading in sociology led her to a book on village-improvement—tree-planting, town pageants, girls' clubs. It had pictures of greens and garden-walls in France, New England, Pennsylvania. She had picked it up carelessly, with a slight yawn which she patted down with her finger-tips as delicately as a cat.

She dipped into the book, lounging on her window-seat, with her slim, lisle-stockinged legs crossed, and her knees up under her chin. She stroked a satin pillow while she read. About her was the clothy exuberance of a Blodgett College room: cretonne-covered window-seat, photographs of girls, a carbon print of the Coliseum, a chafing-dish, and a dozen pillows embroidered or beaded or pyrographed. Shockingly out of place was a miniature of the Dancing Bacchante. It was the only trace of Carol in the room. She had inherited the rest from generations of girl students.

It was as a part of all this commonplaceness that she regarded the treatise on village-improvement. But she suddenly stopped fidgeting. She strode into the book. She had fled half-way through it before the three o'clock bell called her to the class in English history.

She sighed, "That's what I'll do after college! I'll get my hands on one of these prairie towns and make it beautiful. Be an inspiration. I suppose I'd better become a teacher then, but—I won't be that kind of a teacher.

I won't drone. Why should they have all the garden suburbs on Long Island? Nobody has done anything with the ugly towns here in the Northwest except hold revivals and build libraries to contain the Elsie books. I'll make 'em put in a village green, and darling cottages, and a quaint Main Street!"

Thus she triumphed through the class, which was a typical Blodgett contest between a dreary teacher and unwilling children of twenty, won by the teacher because his opponents had to answer his questions, while their treacherous queries he could counter by demanding, "Have you looked that up in the library? Well then, suppose you do!"

The history instructor was a retired minister. He was sarcastic today. He begged of sporting young Mr. Charley Holmberg, "Now Charles, would it interrupt your undoubtedly fascinating pursuit of that malevolent fly if I were to ask you to tell us that you do not know anything about King John?" He spent three delightful minutes in assuring himself of the fact that no one exactly remembered the date of Magna Charta.

Carol did not hear him. She was completing the roof of a half-timbered town hall. She had found one man in the prairie village who did not appreciate her picture of winding streets and arcades, but she had assembled the town council and dramatically defeated him.

III

Though she was Minnesota-born Carol was not an intimate of the prairie villages. Her father, the smiling and shabby, the learned and teasingly kind, had come from Massachusetts, and through all her childhood he had been a judge in Mankato, which is not a prairie town, but in its garden-sheltered streets and aisles of elms is white and green New England reborn. Mankato lies between cliffs and the Minnesota River, hard by Traverse des Sioux, where the first settlers made treaties with the Indians, and the cattle-rustlers once came galloping before hell-for-leather posses.

As she climbed along the banks of the dark river Carol listened to its fables about the wide land of yellow waters and bleached buffalo bones to the West; the Southern levees and singing darkies and palm trees toward which it was forever mysteriously gliding; and she heard again the startled bells and thick puffing of high-stacked river steamers wrecked on sand-reefs sixty years ago. Along the decks she saw missionaries, gamblers in tall pot hats, and Dakota chiefs with scarlet blankets. . . . Far off whistles at night, round the river bend, plunking paddles re-echoed by the pines, and a glow on black sliding waters.

Carol's family were self-sufficient in their inventive life, with Christmas a rite full of surprises and tenderness, and "dressing-up parties" spontaneous and joyously absurd. The beasts in the Milford hearth-mythology were not the obscene Night Animals who jump out of closets and eat little girls, but beneficent and bright-eyed creatures—the tam htab, who is woolly and blue and lives in the bathroom, and runs rapidly to warm small feet; the ferruginous oil stove, who purrs and knows stories; and the skitamarigg, who

will play with children before breakfast if they spring out of bed and close
the window at the very first line of the song about puellas which father
sings while shaving.

Judge Milford's pedagogical scheme was to let the children read whatever
they pleased, and in his brown library Carol absorbed Balzac and Rabelais
and Thoreau and Max Müller. He gravely taught them the letters on the
backs of the encyclopedias, and when polite visitors asked about the mental
progress of the "little ones," they were horrified to hear the children earnestly
repeating A-And, And-Aus, Aus-Bis, Bis-Cal, Cal-Cha.

Carol's mother died when she was nine. Her father retired from the
judiciary when she was eleven, and took the family to Minneapolis. There
he died, two years after. Her sister, a busy proper advisory soul, older than
herself, had become a stranger to her even when they lived in the same
house.

From those early brown and silver days and from her independence of
relatives Carol retained a willingness to be different from brisk efficient
book-ignoring people; an instinct to observe and wonder at their bustle even
when she was taking part in it. But, she felt approvingly, as she discovered
her career of town-planning, she was now roused to being brisk and efficient
herself.

### IV

In a month Carol's ambition had clouded. Her hesitancy about becoming
a teacher had returned. She was not, she worried, strong enough to endure
the routine, and she could not picture herself standing before grinning children and pretending to be wise and decisive. But the desire for the creation
of a beautiful town remained. When she encountered an item about small-
town women's clubs or a photograph of a straggling Main Street, she was
homesick for it, she felt robbed of her work.

It was the advice of the professor of English which led her to study
professional library-work in a Chicago school. Her imagination carved and
colored the new plan. She saw herself persuading children to read charming
fairy tales, helping young men to find books on mechanics, being ever so
courteous to old men who were hunting for newspapers—the light of the
library, an authority on books, invited to dinners with poets and explorers,
reading a paper to an association of distinguished scholars.

### V

The last faculty reception before commencement. In five days they would
be in the cyclone of final examinations.

The house of the president had been massed with palms suggestive of
polite undertaking parlors, and in the library, a ten-foot room with a globe
and the portraits of Whittier and Martha Washington, the student orchestra
was playing "Carmen" and "Madame Butterfly." Carol was dizzy with music
and the emotions of parting. She saw the palms as a jungle, the pink-shaded

electric globes as an opaline haze, and the eye-glassed faculty as Olympians. She was melancholy at sight of the mousey girls with whom she had "always intended to get acquainted," and the half dozen young men who were ready to fall in love with her.

But it was Stewart Snyder whom she encouraged. He was so much manlier than the others; he was an even warm brown, like his new ready-made suit with its padded shoulders. She sat with him, and with two cups of coffee and a chicken patty, upon a pile of presidential overshoes in the coat-closet under the stairs, and as the thin music seeped in, Stewart whispered:

"I can't stand it, this breaking up after four years! The happiest years of life."

She believed it. "Oh, I know! To think that in just a few days we'll be parting, and we'll never see some of the bunch again!"

"Carol, you got to listen to me! You always duck when I try to talk seriously to you, but you got to listen to me. I'm going to be a big lawyer, maybe a judge, and I need you, and I'd protect you——"

His arm slid behind her shoulders. The insinuating music drained her independence. She said mournfully, "Would you take care of me?" She touched his hand. It was warm, solid.

"You bet I would! We'd have, Lord, we'd have bully times in Yankton, where I'm going to settle——"

"But I want to do something with life."

"What's better than making a comfy home and bringing up some cute kids and knowing nice homey people?"

It was the immemorial male reply to the restless woman. Thus to the young Sappho spake the melon-venders; thus the captains to Zenobia; and in the damp cave over gnawed bones the hairy suitor thus protested to the woman advocate of matriarchy. In the dialect of Blodgett College but with the voice of Sappho was Carol's answer:

"Of course. I know. I suppose that's so. Honestly, I do love children. But there's lots of women that can do housework, but I—well, if you *have* got a college education, you ought to use it for the world."

"I know, but you can use it just as well in the home. And gee, Carol, just think of a bunch of us going out on an auto picnic, some nice spring evening."

"Yes."

"And sleigh-riding in winter, and going fishing——"

Blarrrrrr! The orchestra had crashed into the "Soldiers' Chorus"; and she was protesting, "No! No! You're a dear, but I want to do things. I don't understand myself but I want—everything in the world! Maybe I can't sing or write, but I know I can be an influence in library work. Just suppose I encouraged some boy and he became a great artist! I will! I will do it! Stewart dear, I can't settle down to nothing but dish-washing!"

Two minutes later—two hectic minutes—they were disturbed by an embarrassed couple also seeking the idyllic seclusion of the overshoe-closet.

After graduation she never saw Stewart Snyder again. She wrote to him once a week—for one month.

VI

A year Carol spent in Chicago. Her study of library-cataloguing, recording, books of reference, was easy and not too somniferous. She reveled in the Art Institute, in symphonies and violin recitals and chamber music, in the theater and classic dancing. She almost gave up library work to become one of the young women who dance in cheese-cloth in the moonlight. She was taken to a certified Studio Party, with beer, cigarettes, bobbed hair, and a Russian Jewess who sang the Internationale. It cannot be reported that Carol had anything significant to say to the Bohemians. She was awkward with them, and felt ignorant, and she was shocked by the free manners which she had for years desired. But she heard and remembered discussions of Freud, Romain Rolland, syndicalism, the Confédération Générale du Travail, feminism vs. haremism, Chinese lyrics, nationalization of mines, Christian Science, and fishing in Ontario.

She went home, and that was the beginning and end of her Bohemian life.

The second cousin of Carol's sister's husband lived in Winnetka, and once invited her out to Sunday dinner. She walked back through Wilmette and Evanston, discovered new forms of suburban architecture, and remembered her desire to re-create villages. She decided that she would give up library work and, by a miracle whose nature was not very clearly revealed to her, turn a prairie town into Georgian houses and Japanese bungalows.

The next day in library class she had to read a theme on the use of the *Cumulative Index*, and she was taken so seriously in the discussion that she put off her career of town-planning—and in the autumn she was in the public library of St. Paul.

VII

Carol was not unhappy and she was not exhilarated, in the St. Paul Library. She slowly confessed that she was not visibly affecting lives. She did, at first, put into her contact with the patrons a willingness which should have moved worlds. But so few of these stolid worlds wanted to be moved. When she was in charge of the magazine room the readers did not ask for suggestions about elevated essays. They grunted, "Wanta find the *Leather Goods Gazette* for last February." When she was giving out books the principal query was, "Can you tell me of a good, light, exciting love story to read? My husband's going away for a week."

She was fond of the other librarians; proud of their aspirations. And by the chance of propinquity she read scores of books unnatural to her gay white littleness: volumes of anthropology with ditches of foot-notes filled with heaps of small dusty type, Parisian imagistes, Hindu recipes for curry, voyages to the Solomon Isles, theosophy with modern American improvements, treatises upon success in the real-estate business. She took walks, and was sensible about shoes and diet. And never did she feel that she was living.

She went to dances and suppers at the houses of college acquaintances. Sometimes she one-stepped demurely; sometimes, in dread of life's slipping past, she turned into a bacchanal, her tender eyes excited, her throat tense, as she slid down the room.

During her three years of library work several men showed diligent interest in her—the treasurer of a fur-manufacturing firm, a teacher, a newspaper reporter, and a petty railroad official. None of them made her more than pause in thought. For months no male emerged from the mass. Then, at the Marburys', she met Dr. Will Kennicott.

# 2

It was a frail and blue and lonely Carol who trotted to the flat of the Johnson Marburys for Sunday evening supper. Mrs. Marbury was a neighbor and friend of Carol's sister; Mr. Marbury a traveling representative of an insurance company. They made a specialty of sandwich-salad-coffee lap suppers, and they regarded Carol as their literary and artistic representative. She was the one who could be depended upon to appreciate the Caruso phonograph record, and the Chinese lantern which Mr. Marbury had brought back as his present from San Francisco. Carol found the Marburys admiring and therefore admirable.

This September Sunday evening she wore a net frock with a pale pink lining. A nap had soothed away the faint lines of tiredness beside her eyes. She was young, naive, stimulated by the coolness. She flung her coat at the chair in the hall of the flat, and exploded into the green-plush living-room. The familiar group were trying to be conversational. She saw Mr. Marbury, a woman teacher of gymnastics in a high school, a chief clerk from the Great Northern Railway offices, a young lawyer. But there was also a stranger, a thick tall man of thirty-six or -seven, with stolid brown hair, lips used to giving orders, eyes which followed everything good-naturedly, and clothes which you could never quite remember.

Mr. Marbury boomed, "Carol, come over here and meet Doc Kennicott— Dr. Will Kennicott of Gopher Prairie. He does all our insurance-examining up in that neck of the woods, and they do say he's some doctor!"

As she edged toward the stranger and murmured nothing in particular, Carol remembered that Gopher Prairie was a Minnesota wheat-prairie town of something over three thousand people.

"Pleased to meet you," stated Dr. Kennicott. His hand was strong; the palm soft, but the back weathered, showing golden hairs against firm red skin.

He looked at her as though she was an agreeable discovery. She tugged her hand free and fluttered, "I must go out to the kitchen and help Mrs. Marbury." She did not speak to him again till, after she had heated the rolls and passed the paper napkins, Mr. Marbury captured her with a loud, "Oh, quit fussing now. Come over here and sit down and tell us how's tricks." He herded her to a sofa with Dr. Kennicott, who was rather vague about the eyes, rather drooping of bulky shoulder, as though he was wondering what he was expected to do next. As their host left them, Kennicott awoke:

"Marbury tells me you're a high mogul in the public library. I was surprised. Didn't hardly think you were old enough. I thought you were a girl, still in college maybe."

"Oh, I'm dreadfully old. I expect to take to a lip-stick, and to find a gray hair any morning now."

"Huh! You must be frightfully old—prob'ly too old to be my grand-daughter, I guess!"

Thus in the Vale of Arcady nymph and satyr beguiled the hours; precisely thus, and not in honeyed pentameters, discoursed Elaine and the worn Sir Launcelot in the pleached alley.

"How do you like your work?" asked the doctor.

"It's pleasant, but sometimes I feel shut off from things—the steel stacks, and the everlasting cards smeared all over with red rubber stamps."

"Don't you get sick of the city?"

"St. Paul? Why, don't you like it? I don't know of any lovelier view than when you stand on Summit Avenue and look across Lower Town to the Mississippi cliffs and the upland farms beyond."

"I know but—— Of course I've spent nine years around the Twin Cities—took my B.A. and M.D. over at the U., and had my internship in a hospital in Minneapolis, but still, oh well, you don't get to know folks here, way you do up home. I feel I've got something to say about running Gopher Prairie, but you take it in a big city of two-three hundred thousand, and I'm just one flea on the dog's back. And then I like country driving, and the hunting in the fall. Do you know Gopher Prairie at all?"

"No, but I hear it's a very nice town."

"Nice? Say honestly—— Of course I may be prejudiced, but I've seen an awful lot of towns—one time I went to Atlantic City for the American Medical Association meeting, and I spent practically a week in New York! But I never saw a town that had such up-and-coming people as Gopher Prairie. Bresnahan—you know—the famous auto manufacturer—he comes from Gopher Prairie. Born and brought up there! And it's a darn pretty town. Lots of fine maples and box-elders, and there's two of the dandiest lakes you ever saw, right near town! And we've got seven miles of cement walks already, and building more every day! Course a lot of these towns still put up with plank walks, but not for us, you bet!"

"Really?"

(Why was she thinking of Stewart Snyder?)

"Gopher Prairie is going to have a great future. Some of the best dairy and wheat land in the state right near there—some of it selling right now at one-fifty an acre, and I bet it will go up to two and a quarter in ten years!"

"Is—— Do you like your profession?"

"Nothing like it. Keeps you out, and yet you have a chance to loaf in the office for a change."

"I don't mean that way. I mean—it's such an opportunity for sympathy."

Dr. Kennicott launched into a heavy, "Oh, these Dutch farmers don't want sympathy. All they need is a bath and a good dose of salts."

Carol must have flinched, for instantly he was urging, "What I mean is— I don't want you to think I'm one of these old salts-and-quinine peddlers, but I mean: so many of my patients are husky farmers that I suppose I get kind of casehardened."

"It seems to me that a doctor could transform a whole community, if he wanted to—if he saw it. He's usually the only man in the neighborhood who has any scientific training, isn't he?"

"Yes, that's so, but I guess most of us get rusty. We land in a rut of obstetrics and typhoid and busted legs. What we need is women like you to jump on us. It'd be you that would transform the town."

"No, I couldn't. Too flighty. I did used to think about doing just that, curiously enough, but I seem to have drifted away from the idea. Oh, I'm a fine one to be lecturing you!"

"No! You're just the one. You have ideas without having lost feminine charm. Say! Don't you think there's a lot of these women that go out for all these movements and so on that sacrifice——"

After his remarks upon suffrage he abruptly questioned her about herself. His kindliness and the firmness of his personality enveloped her and she accepted him as one who had a right to know what she thought and wore and ate and read. He was positive. He had grown from a sketched-in stranger to a friend, whose gossip was important news. She noticed the healthy solidity of his chest. His nose, which had seemed irregular and large, was suddenly virile.

She was jarred out of this serious sweetness when Marbury bounced over to them and with horrible publicity yammered, "Say, what do you two think you're doing? Telling fortunes or making love? Let me warn you that the doc is a frisky bacheldore, Carol. Come on now, folks, shake a leg. Let's have some stunts or a dance or something."

She did not have another word with Dr. Kennicott until their parting:

"Been a great pleasure to meet you, Miss Milford. May I see you some time when I come down again? I'm here quite often—taking patients to hospitals for majors, and so on."

"Why——"

"What's your address?"

"You can ask Mr. Marbury next time you come down—if you really want to know!"

"Want to know? Say, you wait!"

## II

Of the love-making of Carol and Will Kennicott there is nothing to be told which may not be heard on every summer evening, on every shadowy block.

They were biology and mystery; their speech was slang phrases and flares of poetry; their silences were contentment, or shaky crises when his arm took her shoulder. All the beauty of youth, first discovered when it is passing—and all the commonplaceness of a well-to-do unmarried man encountering a pretty girl at the time when she is slightly weary of her employment and sees no glory ahead nor any man she is glad to serve.

They liked each other honestly—they were both honest. She was disappointed by his devotion to making money, but she was sure that he did not lie to patients, and that he did keep up with the medical magazines. What aroused her to something more than liking was his boyishness when they went tramping.

They walked from St. Paul down the river to Mendota, Kennicott more elastic-seeming in a cap and a soft crêpe shirt, Carol youthful in a tam-o'-shanter of mole velvet, a blue serge suit with an absurdly and agreeably broad turn-down linen collar, and frivolous ankles above athletic shoes. The High Bridge crosses the Mississippi, mounting from low banks to a palisade of cliffs. Far down beneath it on the St. Paul side, upon mud flats, is a wild settlement of chicken-infested gardens and shanties patched together from discarded sign-boards, sheets of corrugated iron, and planks fished out of the river. Carol leaned over the rail of the bridge to look down at this Yang-tse village; in delicious imaginary fear she shrieked that she was dizzy with the height; and it was an extremely human satisfaction to have a strong male snatch her back to safety, instead of having a logical woman teacher or librarian sniff, "Well, if you're scared, why don't you get away from the rail, then?"

From the cliffs across the river Carol and Kennicott looked back at St. Paul on its hills; an imperial sweep from the dome of the cathedral to the dome of the state capitol.

The river road led past rocky field slopes, deep glens, woods flamboyant now with September, to Mendota, white walls and a spire among trees beneath a hill, old-world in its placid ease. And for this fresh land, the place is ancient. Here is the bold stone house which General Sibley, the king of fur-traders, built in 1835, with plaster of river mud, and ropes of twisted grass for laths. It has an air of centuries. In its solid rooms Carol and Kennicott found prints from other days which the house had seen—tail-coats of robin's-egg blue, clumsy Red River carts laden with luxurious furs, whiskered Union soldiers in slant forage caps and rattling sabers.

It suggested to them a common American past, and it was memorable because they had discovered it together. They talked more trustingly, more personally, as they trudged on. They crossed the Minnesota River in a rowboat ferry. They climbed the hill to the round stone tower of Fort Snelling.

They saw the junction of the Mississippi and the Minnesota, and recalled the men who had come here eighty years ago—Maine lumbermen, York traders, soldiers from the Maryland hills.

"It's a good country, and I'm proud of it. Let's make it all that those old boys dreamed about," the unsentimental Kennicott was moved to vow.

"Let's!"

"Come on. Come to Gopher Prairie. Show us. Make the town—well—make it artistic. It's mighty pretty, but I'll admit we aren't any too darn artistic. Probably the lumber-yard isn't as scrumptious as all these Greek temples. But go to it! Make us change!"

"I would like to. Some day!"

"Now! You'd love Gopher Prairie. We've been doing a lot with lawns and gardening the past few years, and it's so homey—the big trees and—— And the best people on earth. And keen. I bet Luke Dawson——"

Carol but half listened to the names. She could not fancy their ever becoming important to her.

"I bet Luke Dawson has got more money than most of the swells on Summit Avenue; and Miss Sherwin in the high school is a regular wonder—reads Latin like I do English; and Sam Clark, the hardware man, he's a corker—not a better man in the state to go hunting with; and if you want culture, besides Vida Sherwin there's Reverend Warren, the Congregational preacher, and Professor Mott, the superintendent of schools, and Guy Pollock, the lawyer—they say he writes regular poetry and—and Raymie Wutherspoon, he's not such an awful boob when you get to *know* him, and he sings swell. And —— And there's plenty of others. Lym Cass. Only of course none of them have your finesse, you might call it. But they don't make 'em any more appreciative and so on. Come on! We're ready for you to boss us!"

They sat on the bank below the parapet of the old fort, hidden from observation. He circled her shoulder with his arm. Relaxed after the walk, a chill nipping her throat, conscious of his warmth and power, she leaned gratefully against him.

"You know I'm in love with you, Carol!"

She did not answer, but she touched the back of his hand with an exploring finger.

"You say I'm so darn materialistic. How can I help it, unless I have you to stir me up?"

She did not answer. She could not think.

"You say a doctor could cure a town the way he does a person. Well, you cure the town of whatever ails it, if anything does, and I'll be your surgical kit."

She did not follow his words, only the burring resoluteness of them.

She was shocked, thrilled, as he kissed her cheek and cried, "There's no use saying things and saying things and saying things. Don't my arms talk to you—now?"

"Oh, please, please!" She wondered if she ought to be angry, but it was a drifting thought, and she discovered that she was crying.

Then they were sitting six inches apart, pretending that they had never been nearer, while she tried to be impersonal:

"I would like to—would like to see Gopher Prairie."

"Trust me! Here she is! Brought some snapshots down to show you."

Her cheek near his sleeve, she studied a dozen village pictures. They were streaky; she saw only trees, shrubbery, a porch indistinct in leafy shadows. But she exclaimed over the lakes: dark water reflecting wooded bluffs, a flight of ducks, a fisherman in shirt sleeves and a wide straw hat, holding up a string of croppies. One winter picture of the edge of Plover Lake had the air of an etching: lustrous slide of ice, snow in the crevices of a boggy bank, the mound of a muskrat house, reeds in thin black lines, arches of frosty grasses. It was an impression of cool clear vigor.

"How'd it be to skate there for a couple of hours, or go zinging along on a fast ice-boat, and skip back home for coffee and some hot wienies?" he demanded.

"It might be—fun."

"But here's the picture. Here's where you come in."

A photograph of a forest clearing: pathetic new furrows straggling among stumps, a clumsy log cabin chinked with mud and roofed with hay. In front of it a sagging woman with tight-drawn hair, and a baby bedraggled, smeary, glorious-eyed.

"Those are the kind of folks I practise among, good share of the time. Nels Erdstrom, fine clean young Svenska. He'll have a corking farm in ten years, but now—— I operated his wife on a kitchen table, with my driver giving the anesthetic. Look at that scared baby! Needs some woman with hands like yours. Waiting for you! Just look at that baby's eyes, look how he's begging——"

"Don't! They hurt me. Oh, it would be sweet to help him—so sweet."

As his arms moved toward her she answered all her doubts with "Sweet, so sweet."

# 3

Under the rolling clouds of the prairie a moving mass of steel. An irritable clank and rattle beneath a prolonged roar. The sharp scent of oranges cutting the soggy smell of unbathed people and ancient baggage.

Towns as planless as a scattering of pasteboard boxes on an attic floor. The stretch of faded gold stubble broken only by clumps of willows encircling white houses and red barns.

No. 7, the way train, grumbling through Minnesota, imperceptibly climbing the giant tableland that slopes in a thousand-mile rise from hot Mississippi bottoms to the Rockies.

It is September, hot, very dusty.

There is no smug Pullman attached to the train, and the day coaches of the East are replaced by free chair cars, with each seat cut into two adjustable plush chairs, the head-rests covered with doubtful linen towels. Halfway down the car is a semi-partition of carved oak columns, but the aisle is of bare, splintery, grease-blackened wood. There is no porter, no pillows, no provision for beds, but all today and all tonight they will ride in this long steel box—farmers with perpetually tired wives and children who seem all to be of the same age; workmen going to new jobs; traveling salesmen with derbies and freshly shined shoes.

They are parched and cramped, the lines of their hands filled with grime; they go to sleep curled in distorted attitudes, heads against the window-panes or propped on rolled coats on seat-arms, and legs thrust into the aisle. They do not read; apparently they do not think. They wait. An early-wrinkled, young-old mother, moving as though her joints were dry, opens a suit-case in which are seen creased blouses, a pair of slippers worn through at the toes, a bottle of patent medicine, a tin cup, a paper-covered book about dreams which the news-butcher has coaxed her into buying. She brings out a graham cracker which she feeds to a baby lying flat on a seat and wailing hopelessly. Most of the crumbs drop on the red plush of the seat, and the woman sighs and tries to brush them away, but they leap up impishly and fall back on the plush.

A soiled man and woman munch sandwiches and throw the crusts on the floor. A large brick-colored Norwegian takes off his shoes, grunts in relief, and props his feet in their thick gray socks against the seat in front of him.

An old woman whose toothless mouth shuts like a mud-turtle's, and whose hair is not so much white as yellow like moldy linen, with bands of pink skull apparent between the tresses, anxiously lifts her bag, opens it, peers in, closes it, puts it under the seat, and hastily picks it up and opens it and hides it all over again. The bag is full of treasures and of memories: a leather buckle, an ancient band-concert program, scraps of ribbon, lace, satin. In the aisle beside her is an extremely indignant parrakeet in a cage.

Two facing seats, overflowing with a Slovene iron-miner's family, are littered with shoes, dolls, whisky bottles, bundles wrapped in newspapers, a sewing bag. The oldest boy takes a mouth-organ out of his coat pocket, wipes the tobacco crumbs off, and plays "Marching through Georgia" till every head in the car begins to ache.

The news-butcher comes through selling chocolate bars and lemon drops. A girl-child ceaselessly trots down to the water-cooler and back to her seat. The stiff paper envelope which she uses for a cup drips in the aisle as she goes, and on each trip she stumbles over the feet of a carpenter, who grunts, "Ouch! Look out!"

The dust-caked doors are open, and from the smoking-car drifts back a visible blue line of stinging tobacco smoke, and with it a crackle of laughter over the story which the young man in the bright blue suit and lavender tie and light yellow shoes has just told to the squat man in garage overalls. The smell grows constantly thicker, more stale.

## II

To each of the passengers his seat was his temporary home, and most of the passengers were slatternly housekeepers. But one seat looked clean and deceptively cool. In it were an obviously prosperous man and a black-haired, fine-skinned girl whose pumps rested on an immaculate horsehide bag.

They were Dr. Will Kennicott and his bride, Carol.

They had been married at the end of a year of conversational courtship, and they were on their way to Gopher Prairie after a wedding journey in the Colorado mountains.

The hordes of the way-train were not altogether new to Carol. She had seen them on trips from St. Paul to Chicago. But now that they had become her own people, to bathe and encourage and adorn, she had an acute and uncomfortable interest in them. They distressed her. They were so stolid. She had always maintained that there is no American peasantry, and she sought now to defend her faith by seeing imagination and enterprise in the young Swedish farmers, and in a traveling man working over his order-blanks. But the older people, Yankees as well as Norwegians, Germans, Finns, Canucks, had settled into submission to poverty. They were peasants, she groaned.

"Isn't there any way of waking them up? What would happen if they understood scientific agriculture?" she begged of Kennicott, her hand groping for his.

It had been a transforming honeymoon. She had been frightened to discover how tumultuous a feeling could be roused in her. Will had been lordly —stalwart, jolly, impressively competent in making camp, tender and understanding through the hours when they had lain side by side in a tent pitched among pines high up on a lonely mountain spur.

His hand swallowed hers as he started from thoughts of the practise to which he was returning. "These people? Wake 'em up? What for? They're happy."

"But they're so provincial. No, that isn't what I mean. They're—oh, so sunk in the mud."

"Look here, Carrie. You want to get over your city idea that because a man's pants aren't pressed, he's a fool. These farmers are mighty keen and up-and-coming."

"I know! That's what hurts. Life seems so hard for them—these lonely farms and this gritty train."

"Oh, they don't mind it. Besides, things are changing. The auto, the telephone, rural free delivery; they're bringing the farmers in closer touch with the town. Takes time, you know, to change a wilderness like this was fifty years ago. But already, why, they can hop into the Ford or the Overland and get in to the movies on Saturday evening quicker than you could get down to 'em by trolley in St. Paul."

"But if it's these towns we've been passing that the farmers run to for relief from their bleakness—— Can't you understand? Just *look* at them!"

Kennicott was amazed. Ever since childhood he had seen these towns from trains on this same line. He grumbled, "Why, what's the matter with 'em? Good hustling burgs. It would astonish you to know how much wheat and rye and corn and potatoes they ship in a year."

"But they're so ugly."

"I'll admit they aren't comfy like Gopher Prairie. But give 'em time."

"What's the use of giving them time unless some one has desire and training enough to plan them? Hundreds of factories trying to make attractive motor cars, but these towns—left to chance. No! That can't be true. It must have taken genius to make them so scrawny!"

"Oh, they're not so bad," was all he answered. He pretended that his hand was the cat and hers the mouse. For the first time she tolerated him rather than encouraged him. She was staring out at Schoenstrom, a hamlet of perhaps a hundred and fifty inhabitants, at which the train was stopping.

A bearded German and his pucker-mouthed wife tugged their enormous imitation-leather satchel from under a seat and waddled out. The station agent hoisted a dead calf aboard the baggage-car. There were no other visible activities in Schoenstrom. In the quiet of the halt, Carol could hear a horse kicking his stall, a carpenter shingling a roof.

The business-center of Schoenstrom took up one side of one block, facing the railroad. It was a row of one-story shops covered with galvanized iron, or with clapboards painted red and bilious yellow. The buildings were as ill-assorted, as temporary-looking, as a mining-camp street in the motion-pictures. The railroad station was a one-room frame box, a mirey cattle-pen on one side and a crimson wheat-elevator on the other. The elevator, with its cupola on the ridge of a shingled roof, resembled a broad-shouldered man with a small, vicious, pointed head. The only habitable structures to be seen were the florid red-brick Catholic church and rectory at the end of Main Street.

Carol picked at Kennicott's sleeve. "You wouldn't call this a not-so-bad town, would you?"

"These Dutch burgs *are* kind of slow. Still, at that—— See that fellow coming out of the general store there, getting into the big car? I met him once. He owns about half the town, besides the store. Rauskukle, his name is. He owns a lot of mortgages, and he gambles in farm-lands. Good nut on him, that fellow. Why, they say he's worth three or four hundred thousand dollars! Got a dandy great big yellow brick house with tiled walks and a garden and everything, other end of town—can't see it from here—I've gone past it when I've driven through here. Yes sir!"

"Then, if he has all that, there's no excuse whatever for this place! If his three hundred thousand went back into the town, where it belongs, they could burn up these shacks, and build a dream-village, a jewel! Why do the farmers and the townpeople let the Baron keep it?"

"I must say I don't quite get you sometimes, Carrie. Let him? They can't help themselves! He's a dumm old Dutchman, and probably the priest can twist him around his finger, but when it comes to picking good farming land, he's a regular wiz!"

"I see. He's their symbol of beauty. The town erects him, instead of erecting buildings."

"Honestly, don't know what you're driving at. You're kind of played out, after this long trip. You'll feel better when you get home and have a good bath, and put on the blue negligée. That's some vampire costume, you witch!"

He squeezed her arm, looked at her knowingly.

They moved on from the desert stillness of the Schoenstrom station. The train creaked, banged, swayed. The air was nauseatingly thick. Kennicott turned her face from the window, rested her head on his shoulder. She was coaxed from her unhappy mood. But she came out of it unwillingly, and when Kennicott was satisfied that he had corrected all her worries and had opened a magazine of saffron detective stories, she sat upright.

Here—she meditated—is the newest empire of the world; the Northern Middlewest; a land of dairy herds and exquisite lakes, of new automobiles and tar-paper shanties and silos like red towers, of clumsy speech and a hope that is boundless. An empire which feeds a quarter of the world—yet its work is merely begun. They are pioneers, these sweaty wayfarers, for all their telephones and bank-accounts and automatic pianos and co-operative leagues. And for all its fat richness, theirs is a pioneer land. What is its future? she wondered. A future of cities and factory smut where now are loping empty fields? Homes universal and secure? Or placid châteaux ringed with sullen huts? Youth free to find knowledge and laughter? Willingness to sift the sanctified lies? Or creamy-skinned fat women, smeared with grease and chalk, gorgeous in the skins of beasts and the bloody feathers of slain birds, playing bridge with puffy pink-nailed jeweled fingers, women who after much expenditure of labor and bad temper still grotesquely resemble their own flatulent lap-dogs? The ancient stale inequalities, or something different in history, unlike the tedious maturity of other empires? What future and what hope?

Carol's head ached with the riddle.

She saw the prairie, flat in giant patches or rolling in long hummocks. The width and bigness of it, which had expanded her spirit an hour ago, began to frighten her. It spread out so; it went on so uncontrollably; she could never know it. Kennicott was closeted in his detective story. With the loneliness which comes most depressingly in the midst of many people she tried to forget problems, to look at the prairie objectively.

The grass beside the railroad had been burnt over; it was a smudge prickly with charred stalks of weeds. Beyond the undeviating barbed-wire fences were clumps of golden rod. Only this thin hedge shut them off from the plains—shorn wheat-lands of autumn, a hundred acres to a field, prickly and gray near-by but in the blurred distance like tawny velvet stretched over dipping hillocks. The long rows of wheat-shocks marched like soldiers in worn yellow tabards. The newly plowed fields were black banners fallen on the distant slope. It was a martial immensity, vigorous, a little harsh, unsoftened by kindly gardens.

The expanse was relieved by clumps of oaks with patches of short wild grass; and every mile or two was a chain of cobalt slews, with the flicker of blackbirds' wings across them.

All this working land was turned into exuberance by the light. The sunshine was dizzy on open stubble; shadows from immense cumulus clouds were forever sliding across low mounds; and the sky was wider and loftier and more resolutely blue than the sky of cities . . . she declared.

"It's a glorious country; a land to be big in," she crooned.

Then Kennicott startled her by chuckling, "D' you realize the town after the next is Gopher Prairie? Home!"

### III

That one word—home—it terrified her. Had she really bound herself to live, inescapably, in this town called Gopher Prairie? And this thick man beside her, who dared to define her future, he was a stranger! She turned in her seat, stared at him. Who was he? Why was he sitting with her? He wasn't of her kind! His neck was heavy; his speech was heavy; he was twelve or thirteen years older than she; and about him was none of the magic of shared adventures and eagerness. She could not believe that she had ever slept in his arms. That was one of the dreams which you had but did not officially admit.

She told herself how good he was, how dependable and understanding. She touched his ear, smoothed the plane of his solid jaw, and, turning away again, concentrated upon liking his town. It wouldn't be like these barren settlements. It couldn't be! Why, it had three thousand population. That was a great many people. There would be six hundred houses or more. And —— The lakes near it would be so lovely. She'd seen them in the photographs. They had looked charming . . . hadn't they?

As the train left Wahkeenyan she began nervously to watch for the lakes —the entrance to all her future life. But when she discovered them, to the left of the track, her only impression of them was that they resembled the photographs.

A mile from Gopher Prairie the track mounts a curving low ridge, and she could see the town as a whole. With a passionate jerk she pushed up the window, looked out, the arched fingers of her left hand trembling on the sill, her right hand at her breast.

And she saw that Gopher Prairie was merely an enlargement of all the hamlets which they had been passing. Only to the eyes of a Kennicott was it exceptional. The huddled low wooden houses broke the plains scarcely more than would a hazel thicket. The fields swept up to it, past it. It was unprotected and unprotecting; there was no dignity in it nor any hope of greatness. Only the tall red grain-elevator and a few tinny church-steeples rose from the mass. It was a frontier camp. It was not a place to live in, not possibly, not conceivably.

The people—they'd be as drab as their houses, as flat as their fields. She couldn't stay here. She would have to wrench loose from this man, and flee.

She peeped at him. She was at once helpless before his mature fixity, and touched by his excitement as he sent his magazine skittering along the aisle, stooped for their bags, came up with flushed face, and gloated, "Here we are!"

She smiled loyally, and looked away. The train was entering town. The houses on the outskirts were dusky old red mansions with wooden frills, or gaunt frame shelters like grocery boxes, or new bungalows with concrete foundations imitating stone.

Now the train was passing the elevator, the grim storage-tanks for oil, a creamery, a lumber-yard, a stock-yard muddy and trampled and stinking. Now they were stopping at a squat red frame station, the platform crowded with unshaven farmers and with loafers—unadventurous people with dead eyes. She was here. She could not go on. It was the end—the end of the world. She sat with closed eyes, longing to push past Kennicott, hide somewhere in the train, flee on toward the Pacific.

Something large arose in her soul and commanded, "Stop it! Stop being a whining baby!" She stood up quickly; she said, "Isn't it wonderful to be here at last!"

He trusted her so. She would make herself like the place. And she was going to do tremendous things——

She followed Kennicott and the bobbing ends of the two bags which he carried. They were held back by the slow line of disembarking passengers. She reminded herself that she was actually at the dramatic moment of the bride's home-coming. She ought to feel exalted. She felt nothing at all except irritation at their slow progress toward the door.

Kennicott stooped to peer through the windows. He shyly exulted:

"Look! Look! There's a bunch come down to welcome us! Sam Clark and the missus and Dave Dyer and Jack Elder, and, yes sir, Harry Haydock and Juanita, and a whole crowd! I guess they see us now. Yuh, yuh sure, they see us! See 'em waving!"

She obediently bent her head to look out at them. She had hold of herself. She was ready to love them. But she was embarrassed by the heartiness of the cheering group. From the vestibule she waved to them, but she clung a second to the sleeve of the brakeman who helped her down before she had the courage to dive into the cataract of hand-shaking people, people whom she could not tell apart. She had the impression that all the men had coarse voices, large damp hands, toothbrush mustaches, bald spots, and Masonic watch-charms.

She knew that they were welcoming her. Their hands, their smiles, their shouts, their affectionate eyes overcame her. She stammered, "Thank you, oh, thank you!"

One of the men was clamoring at Kennicott, "I brought my machine down to take you home, doc."

"Fine business, Sam!" cried Kennicott; and, to Carol, "Let's jump in. That big Paige over there. Some boat, too, believe me! Sam can show speed to any of these Marmons from Minneapolis!"

Only when she was in the motor car did she distinguish the three people who were to accompany them. The owner, now at the wheel, was the essence of decent self-satisfaction; a baldish, largish, level-eyed man, rugged of neck but sleek and round of face—face like the back of a spoon bowl. He was chuckling at her, "Have you got us all straight yet?"

"Course she has! Trust Carrie to get things straight and get 'em darn quick! I bet she could tell you every date in history!" boasted her husband.

But the man looked at her reassuringly and with a certainty that he was a person whom she could trust she confessed, "As a matter of fact I haven't got anybody straight."

"Course you haven't, child. Well, I'm Sam Clark, dealer in hardware, sporting goods, cream separators, and almost any kind of heavy junk you can think of. You can call me Sam—anyway, I'm going to call you Carrie, seein' 's you've been and gone and married this poor fish of a bum medic that we keep round here." Carol smiled lavishly, and wished that she called people by their given names more easily. "The fat cranky lady back there beside you, who is pretending that she can't hear me giving her away, is Mrs. Sam'l Clark; and this hungry-looking squirt up here beside me is Dave Dyer, who keeps his drug store running by not filling your hubby's prescriptions right—fact you might say he's the guy that put the 'shun' in 'prescription.' So! Well, leave us take the bonny bride home. Say, doc, I'll sell you the Candersen place for three thousand plunks. Better be thinking about building a new home for Carrie. Prettiest *Frau* in G. P., if you asks me!"

Contentedly Sam Clark drove off, in the heavy traffic of three Fords and the Minniemashie House Free 'Bus.

"I shall like Mr. Clark . . . . I *can't* call him 'Sam'! They're all so friendly." She glanced at the houses; tried not to see what she saw; gave way in: "Why do these stories lie so? They always make the bride's home-coming a bower of roses. Complete trust in noble spouse. Lies about marriage. I'm *not* changed. And this town—O my God! I can't go through with it. This junkheap!"

Her husband bent over her. "You look like you were in a brown study. Scared? I don't expect you to think Gopher Prairie is a paradise, after St. Paul. I don't expect you to be crazy about it, at first. But you'll come to like it so much—life's so free here and best people on earth."

She whispered to him (while Mrs. Clark considerately turned away), "I love you for understanding. I'm just—I'm beastly over-sensitive. Too many books. It's my lack of shoulder-muscles and sense. Give me time, dear."

"You bet! All the time you want!"

She laid the back of his hand against her cheek, snuggled near him. She was ready for her new home.

Kennicott had told her that, with his widowed mother as housekeeper, he had occupied an old house, "but nice and roomy, and well-heated, best furnace I could find on the market." His mother had left Carol her love, and gone back to Lac-qui-Meurt.

It would be wonderful, she exulted, not to have to live in Other People's Houses, but to make her own shrine. She held his hand tightly and stared ahead as the car swung round a corner and stopped in the street before a prosaic frame house in a small parched lawn.

IV

A concrete sidewalk with a "parking" of grass and mud. A square smug brown house, rather damp. A narrow concrete walk up to it. Sickly yellow leaves in a windrow with dried wings of box-elder seeds and snags of wool from the cottonwoods. A screened porch with pillars of thin painted pine surmounted by scrolls and brackets and bumps of jigsawed wood. No shrubbery to shut off the public gaze. A lugubrious bay-window to the right of the porch. Window curtains of starched cheap lace revealing a pink marble table with a conch shell and a Family Bible.

"You'll find it old-fashioned—what do you call it?—Mid-Victorian. I left it as is, so you could make any changes you felt were necessary." Kennicott sounded doubtful for the first time since he had come back to his own.

"It's a real home!" She was moved by his humility. She gaily motioned good-by to the Clarks. He unlocked the door—he was leaving the choice of a maid to her, and there was no one in the house. She jiggled while he turned the key, and scampered in. . . . It was next day before either of them remembered that in their honeymoon camp they had planned that he should carry her over the sill.

In hallway and front parlor she was conscious of dinginess and lugubriousness and airlessness, but she insisted, "I'll make it all jolly." As she followed Kennicott and the bags up to their bedroom she quavered to herself the song of the fat little gods of the hearth:

> I have my own home,
> To do what I please with,
> To do what I please with,
> My den for me and my mate and my cubs,
> My own!

She was close in her husband's arms; she clung to him; whatever of strangeness and slowness and insularity she might find in him, none of that mattered so long as she could slip her hands beneath his coat, run her fingers over the warm smoothness of the satin back of his waistcoat, seem almost to creep into his body, find in him strength, find in the courage and kindness of her man a shelter from the perplexing world.

"Sweet, so sweet," she whispered.

# 4

"The Clarks have invited some folks to their house to meet us, tonight," said Kennicott, as he unpacked his suit-case.

"Oh, that is nice of them!"

"You bet. I told you you'd like 'em. Squarest people on earth. Uh, Carrie—— Would you mind if I sneaked down to the office for an hour, just to see how things are?"

"Why, no. Of course not. I know you're keen to get back to work."

"Sure you don't mind?"

"Not a bit. Out of my way. Let me unpack."

But the advocate of freedom in marriage was as much disappointed as a drooping bride at the alacrity with which he took that freedom and escaped to the world of men's affairs. She gazed about their bedroom, and its full dismalness crawled over her: the awkward knuckly L-shape of it; the black walnut bed with apples and spotty pears carved on the headboard; the imitation maple bureau, with pink-daubed scent-bottles and a petticoated pincushion on a marble slab uncomfortably like a gravestone; the plain pine washstand and the garlanded water-pitcher and bowl. The scent was of horsehair and plush and Florida Water.

"How could people ever live with things like this?" she shuddered. She saw the furniture as a circle of elderly judges, condemning her to death by smothering. The tottering brocade chair squeaked, "Choke her—choke her—smother her." The old linen smelled of the tomb. She was alone in this house, this strange still house, among the shadows of dead thoughts and haunting repressions. "I hate it! I hate it!" she panted. "Why did I ever——"

She remembered that Kennicott's mother had brought these family relics from the old home in Lac-qui-Meurt. "Stop it! They're perfectly comfortable things. They're—comfortable. Besides—— Oh, they're horrible! We'll change them, right away."

Then, "But of course he *has* to see how things are at the office——"

She made a pretense of busying herself with unpacking. The chintz-lined, silver-fitted bag which had seemed so desirable a luxury in St. Paul was an extravagant vanity here. The daring black chemise of frail chiffon and lace was a hussy at which the deep-bosomed bed stiffened in disgust, and she hurled it into a bureau drawer, hid it beneath a sensible linen blouse.

She gave up unpacking. She went to the window, with a purely literary thought of village charm—hollyhocks and lanes and apple-cheeked cottagers. What she saw was the side of the Seventh-Day Adventist Church—a plain clapboard wall of a sour liver color; the ash-pile back of the church; an unpainted stable; and an alley in which a Ford delivery-wagon had been stranded. This was the terraced garden below her boudoir; this was to be her scenery for——

"I mustn't! I mustn't! I'm nervous this afternoon. Am I sick? . . . Good Lord, I hope it isn't that! Not now! How people lie! How these stories lie! They say the bride is always so blushing and proud and happy when she finds that out, but—I'd hate it! I'd be scared to death! Some day but—— Please, dear nebulous Lord, not now! Bearded sniffy old men sitting and demanding that we bear children. If *they* had to bear them——! I wish they did have to! Not now! Not till I've got hold of this job of liking the ash-pile out there! . . . I must shut up. I'm mildly insane. I'm going out for a walk. I'll see the town by myself. My first view of the empire I'm going to conquer!"

She fled from the house.

She stared with seriousness at every concrete crossing, every hitching-post, every rake for leaves; and to each house she devoted all her speculation. What would they come to mean? How would they look six months from now? In which of them would she be dining? Which of these people whom she passed, now mere arrangements of hair and clothes, would turn into intimates, loved or dreaded, different from all the other people in the world?

As she came into the small business-section she inspected a broad-beamed grocer in an alpaca coat who was bending over the apples and celery on a slanted platform in front of his store. Would she ever talk to him? What would he say if she stopped and stated, "I am Mrs. Dr. Kennicott. Some day I hope to confide that a heap of extremely dubious pumpkins as a window-display doesn't exhilarate me much."

(The grocer was Mr. Frederick F. Ludelmeyer, whose market is at the corner of Main Street and Lincoln Avenue. In supposing that only she was observant Carol was ignorant, misled by the indifference of cities. She fancied that she was slipping through the streets invisible; but when she had passed, Mr. Ludelmeyer puffed into the store and coughed at his clerk, "I seen a young woman, she come along the side street. I bet she iss Doc Kennicott's new bride, good-looker, nice legs, but she wore a hell of a plain suit, no style, I wonder will she pay cash, I bet she goes to Howland & Gould's more as she does here, what you done with the poster for Fluffed Oats?")

## II

When Carol had walked for thirty-two minutes she had completely covered the town, east and west, north and south; and she stood at the corner of Main Street and Washington Avenue and despaired.

Main Street with its two-story brick shops, its story-and-a-half wooden residences, its muddy expanse from concrete walk to walk, its huddle of Fords and lumber-wagons, was too small to absorb her. The broad, straight, unenticing gashes of the streets let in the grasping prairie on every side. She realized the vastness and the emptiness of the land. The skeleton iron wind-mill on the farm a few blocks away, at the north end of Main Street, was like the ribs of a dead cow. She thought of the coming of the Northern winter, when the unprotected houses would crouch together in terror of storms galloping out of that wild waste. They were so small and weak, the little brown houses. They were shelters for sparrows, not homes for warm laughing people.

She told herself that down the street the leaves were a splendor. The maples were orange; the oaks a solid tint of raspberry. And the lawns had been nursed with love. But the thought would not hold. At best the trees resembled a thinned woodlot. There was no park to rest the eyes. And since not Gopher Prairie but Wakamin was the county-seat, there was no court-house with its grounds.

She glanced through the fly-specked windows of the most pretentious building in sight, the one place which welcomed strangers and determined their opinion of the charm and luxury of Gopher Prairie—the Minnie-mashie House. It was a tall lean shabby structure, three stories of yellow-streaked wood, the corners covered with sanded pine slabs purporting to symbolize stone. In the hotel office she could see a stretch of bare unclean floor, a line of rickety chairs with brass cuspidors between, a writing-desk with advertisements in mother-of-pearl letters upon the glass-covered back. The dining-room beyond was a jungle of stained table-cloths and catsup bottles.

She looked no more at the Minniemashie House.

A man in cuffless shirt-sleeves with pink arm-garters, wearing a linen collar but no tie, yawned his way from Dyer's Drug Store across to the hotel. He leaned against the wall, scratched a while, sighed, and in a bored way gos-siped with a man tilted back in a chair. A lumber-wagon, its long green box filled with large spools of barbed-wire fencing, creaked down the block. A Ford, in reverse, sounded as though it were shaking to pieces, then recovered and rattled away. In the Greek candy-store was the whine of a peanut-roaster, and the oily smell of nuts.

There was no other sound nor sign of life.

She wanted to run, fleeing from the encroaching prairie, demanding the security of a great city. Her dreams of creating a beautiful town were ludi-crous. Oozing out from every drab wall, she felt a forbidding spirit which she could never conquer.

She trailed down the street on one side, back on the other, glancing into the cross streets. It was a private Seeing Main Street tour. She was within ten minutes beholding not only the heart of a place called Gopher Prairie, but ten thousand towns from Albany to San Diego:

Dyer's Drug Store, a corner building of regular and unreal blocks of arti-ficial stone. Inside the store, a greasy marble soda-fountain with an electric lamp of red and green and curdled-yellow mosaic shade. Pawed-over heaps of toothbrushes and combs and packages of shaving-soap. Shelves of soap-cartons, teething-rings, garden-seeds, and patent medicines in yellow pack-ages—nostrums for consumption, for "women's diseases"—notorious mixtures of opium and alcohol, in the very shop to which her husband sent patients for the filling of prescriptions.

From a second-story window the sign "W. P. Kennicott, Phys. & Surgeon," gilt on black sand.

A small wooden motion-picture theater called "The Rosebud Movie Palace." Lithographs announcing a film called "Fatty in Love."

Howland & Gould's Grocery. In the display window, black, overripe bananas and lettuce on which a cat was sleeping. Shelves lined with red crêpe paper which was now faded and torn and concentrically spotted. Flat against the wall of the second story the signs of lodges—the Knights of Pythias, the Maccabees, the Woodmen, the Masons.

Dahl & Oleson's Meat Market—a reek of blood.

A jewelry shop with tinny-looking wrist-watches for women. In front of it, at the curb, a huge wooden clock which did not go.

A fly-buzzing saloon with a brilliant gold and enamel whisky sign across the front. Other saloons down the block. From them a stink of stale beer, and thick voices bellowing pidgin German or trolling out dirty songs—vice gone feeble and unenterprising and dull—the delicacy of a mining-camp minus its vigor. In front of the saloons, farmwives sitting on the seats of wagons, waiting for their husbands to become drunk and ready to start home.

A tobacco shop called "The Smoke House," filled with young men shaking dice for cigarettes. Racks of magazines, and pictures of coy fat prostitutes in striped bathing-suits.

A clothing store with a display of "ox-blood-shade Oxfords with bull-dog toes." Suits which looked worn and glossless while they were still new, flabbily draped on dummies like corpses with painted cheeks.

The Bon Ton Store—Haydock & Simons'—the largest shop in town. The first-story front of clear glass, the plates cleverly bound at the edges with brass. The second story of pleasant tapestry brick. One window of excellent clothes for men, interspersed with collars of floral piqué which showed mauve daisies on a saffron ground. Newness and an obvious notion of neatness and service. Haydock & Simons. Haydock. She had met a Haydock at the station; Harry Haydock; an active person of thirty-five. He seemed great to her, now, and very like a saint. His shop was clean!

Axel Egge's General Store, frequented by Scandinavian farmers. In the shallow dark window-space heaps of sleazy sateens, badly woven galateas, canvas shoes designed for women with bulging ankles, steel and red glass buttons upon cards with broken edges, a cottony blanket, a granite-ware frying pan reposing on a sun-faded crêpe blouse.

Sam Clark's Hardware Store. An air of frankly metallic enterprise. Guns and churns and barrels of nails and beautiful shiny butcher knives.

Chester Dashaway's House Furnishing Emporium. A vista of heavy oak rockers with leather seats, asleep in a dismal row.

Billy's Lunch. Thick handleless cups on the wet oilcloth-covered counter.

An odor of onions and the smoke of hot lard. In the doorway a young man audibly sucking a toothpick.

The warehouse of the buyer of cream and potatoes. The sour smell of a dairy.

The Ford Garage and the Buick Garage, competent one-story brick and cement buildings opposite each other. Old and new cars on grease-blackened concrete floors. Tire advertisements. The roaring of a tested motor; a racket which beat at the nerves. Surly young men in khaki union-overalls. The most energetic and vital places in town.

A large warehouse for agricultural implements. An impressive barricade of green and gold wheels, of shafts and sulky seats, belonging to machinery of which Carol knew nothing—potato-planters, manure-spreaders, silage-cutters, disk-harrows, breaking-plows.

A feed store, its windows opaque with the dust of bran, a patent medicine advertisement painted on its roof.

Ye Art Shoppe, Prop. Mrs. Mary Ellen Wilks, Christian Science Library open daily free. A touching fumble at beauty. A one-room shanty of boards recently covered with rough stucco. A show-window delicately rich in error: vases starting out to imitate tree-trunks but running off into blobs of gilt—an aluminum ash-tray labeled "Greetings from Gopher Prairie"—a Christian Science magazine—a stamped sofa-cushion portraying a large ribbon tied to a small poppy, the correct skeins of embroidery-silk lying on the pillow. Inside the shop, a glimpse of bad carbon prints of bad and famous pictures, shelves of phonograph records and camera films, wooden toys, and in the midst an anxious small woman sitting in a padded rocking chair.

A barber shop and pool room. A man in shirt sleeves, presumably Del Snafflin the proprietor, shaving a man who had a large Adam's apple.

Nat Hicks's Tailor Shop, on a side street off Main. A one-story building. A fashion-plate showing human pitchforks in garments which looked as hard as steel plate.

On another side street a raw red-brick Catholic Church with a varnished yellow door.

The post-office—merely a partition of glass and brass shutting off the rear of a mildewed room which must once have been a shop. A tilted writing-shelf against a wall rubbed black and scattered with official notices and army recruiting-posters.

The damp, yellow-brick schoolbuilding in its cindery grounds.

The State Bank, stucco masking wood.

The Farmers' National Bank. An Ionic temple of marble. Pure, exquisite, solitary. A brass plate with "Ezra Stowbody, Pres't."

A score of similar shops and establishments.

Behind them and mixed with them, the houses, meek cottages or large, comfortable, soundly uninteresting symbols of prosperity.

In all the town not one building save the Ionic bank which gave pleasure to Carol's eyes; not a dozen buildings which suggested that, in the fifty years of Gopher Prairie's existence, the citizens had realized that it was either desirable or possible to make this, their common home, amusing or attractive.

It was not only the unsparing unapologetic ugliness and the rigid straightness which overwhelmed her. It was the planlessness, the flimsy temporariness of the buildings, their faded unpleasant colors. The street was cluttered with electric-light poles, telephone poles, gasoline pumps for motor cars, boxes of goods. Each man had built with the most valiant disregard of all the others. Between a large new "block" of two-story brick shops on one side, and the fire-brick Overland garage on the other side, was a one-story cottage turned into a millinery shop. The white temple of the Farmers' Bank was elbowed back by a grocery of glaring yellow brick. One store-building had a patchy galvanized iron cornice; the building beside it was crowned with battlements and pyramids of brick capped with blocks of red sandstone.

She escaped from Main Street, fled home.

She wouldn't have cared, she insisted, if the people had been comely. She had noted a young man loafing before a shop, one unwashed hand holding the cord of an awning; a middle-aged man who had a way of staring at women as though he had been married too long and too prosaically; an old farmer, solid, wholesome, but not clean—his face like a potato fresh from the earth. None of them had shaved for three days.

"If they can't build shrines, out here on the prairie, surely there's nothing to prevent their buying safety-razors!" she raged.

She fought herself: "I must be wrong. People do live here. It *can't* be as ugly as—as I know it is! I must be wrong. But I can't do it. I can't go through with it."

She came home too seriously worried for hysteria; and when she found Kennicott waiting for her, and exulting, "Have a walk? Well, like the town? Great lawns and trees, eh?" she was able to say, with a self-protective maturity new to her, "It's very interesting."

III

The train which brought Carol to Gopher Prairie also brought Miss Bea Sorenson.

Miss Bea was a stalwart, corn-colored, laughing young woman, and she was bored by farm-work. She desired the excitements of city-life, and the way to enjoy city-life was, she had decided, to "go get a yob as hired girl in Gopher Prairie." She contentedly lugged her pasteboard telescope from the station to her cousin, Tina Malmquist, maid of all work in the residence of Mrs. Luke Dawson.

"Vell, so you come to town," said Tina.

"Ya. Ay get a yob," said Bea.

"Vell. . . . You got a fella now?"

"Ya. Yim Yacobson."

"Vell. I'm glat to see you. How much you vant a veek?"

"Sex dollar."

"There ain't nobody pay dat. Vait! Dr. Kennicott, I t'ink he marry a girl from de Cities. Maybe she pay dat. Vell. You go take a valk."

"Ya," said Bea.

So it chanced that Carol Kennicott and Bea Sorenson were viewing Main Street at the same time.

Bea had never before been in a town larger than Scandia Crossing, which has sixty-seven inhabitants.

As she marched up the street she was meditating that it didn't hardly seem like it was possible there could be so many folks all in one place at the same time. My! It would take years to get acquainted with them all. And swell people, too! A fine big gentleman in a new pink shirt with a diamond, and not no washed-out blue denim working-shirt. A lovely lady in a longery dress (but it must be an awful hard dress to wash). And the stores!

Not just three of them, like there were at Scandia Crossing, but more than four whole blocks!

The Bon Ton Store—big as four barns—my! it would simply scare a person to go in there, with seven or eight clerks all looking at you. And the men's suits, on figures just like human. And Axel Egge's, like home, lots of Swedes and Norskes in there, and a card of dandy buttons, like rubies.

A drug store with a soda fountain that was just huge, awful long, and all lovely marble; and on it there was a great big lamp with the biggest shade you ever saw—all different kinds colored glass stuck together; and the soda spouts, they were silver, and they came right out of the bottom of the lampstand! Behind the fountain there were glass shelves, and bottles of new kinds of soft drinks, that nobody ever heard of. Suppose a fella took you *there!*

A hotel, awful high, higher than Oscar Tollefson's new red barn; three stories, one right on top of another; you had to stick your head back to look clear up to the top. There was a swell traveling man in there—probably been to Chicago, lots of times.

Oh, the dandiest people to know here! There was a lady going by, you wouldn't hardly say she was any older than Bea herself; she wore a dandy new gray suit and black pumps. She almost looked like she was looking over the town, too. But you couldn't tell what she thought. Bea would like to be that way—kind of quiet, so nobody would get fresh. Kind of—oh, elegant.

A Lutheran Church. Here in the city there'd be lovely sermons, and church twice on Sunday, *every* Sunday!

And a movie show!

A regular theater, just for movies. With the sign "Change of bill every evening." Pictures every evening!

There were movies in Scandia Crossing, but only once every two weeks, and it took the Sorensons an hour to drive in—papa was such a tightwad he wouldn't get a Ford. But here she could put on her hat any evening, and in three minutes' walk be to the movies, and see lovely fellows in dress-suits and Bill Hart and everything!

How could they have so many stores? Why! There was one just for tobacco alone, and one (a lovely one—the Art Shoppy it was) for pictures and vases and stuff, with oh, the dandiest vase made so it looked just like a tree trunk!

Bea stood on the corner of Main Street and Washington Avenue. The roar of the city began to frighten her. There were five automobuls on the street all at the same time—and one of 'em was a great big car that must of cost two thousand dollars—and the 'bus was starting for a train with five elegant-dressed fellows, and a man was pasting up red bills with lovely pictures of washing-machines on them, and the jeweler was laying out bracelets and wrist-watches and *everything* on real velvet.

What did she care if she got six dollars a week? Or two! It was worth while working for nothing, to be allowed to stay here. And think how it would be in the evening, all lighted up—and not with no lamps, but with electrics! And maybe a gentleman friend taking you to the movies and buying you a strawberry ice cream soda!

Bea trudged back.

"Vell? You lak it?" said Tina.

"Ya. Ay lak it. Ay t'ink maybe Ay stay here," said Bea.

IV

The recently built house of Sam Clark, in which was given the party to welcome Carol, was one of the largest in Gopher Prairie. It had a clean sweep of clapboards, a solid squareness, a small tower, and a large screened porch. Inside, it was as shiny, as hard, and as cheerful as a new oak upright piano.

Carol looked imploringly at Sam Clark as he rolled to the door and shouted, "Welcome, little lady! The keys of the city are yourn!"

Beyond him, in the hallway and the living-room, sitting in a vast prim circle as though they were attending a funeral, she saw the guests. They were *waiting* so! They were waiting for her! The determination to be all one pretty flowerlet of appreciation leaked away. She begged of Sam, "I don't dare face them! They expect so much. They'll swallow me in one mouthful—glump!—like that!"

"Why, sister, they're going to love you—same as I would if I didn't think the doc here would beat me up!"

"B-but—— I don't dare! Faces to the right of me, faces in front of me, volley and wonder!"

She sounded hysterical to herself; she fancied that to Sam Clark she sounded insane. But he chuckled, "Now you just cuddle under Sam's wing, and if anybody rubbers at you too long, I'll shoo 'em off. Here we go! Watch my smoke—Sam'l, the ladies' delight and the bridegrooms' terror!"

His arm about her, he led her in and bawled, "Ladies and worser halves, the bride! We won't introduce her round yet, because she'll never get your bum names straight anyway. Now bust up this star-chamber!"

They tittered politely, but they did not move from the social security of their circle, and they did not cease staring.

Carol had given creative energy to dressing for the event. Her hair was demure, low on her forehead with a parting and a coiled braid. Now she wished that she had piled it high. Her frock was an ingénue slip of lawn, with a wide gold sash and a low square neck, which gave a suggestion of throat and molded shoulders. But as they looked her over she was certain that it was all wrong. She wished alternately that she had worn a spinsterish high-necked dress, and that she had dared to shock them with a violent brick-red scarf which she had bought in Chicago.

She was led about the circle. Her voice mechanically produced safe remarks:

"Oh, I'm sure I'm going to like it here ever so much," and "Yes, we did have the best time in Colorado—mountains," and "Yes, I lived in St. Paul several years. Euclid P. Tinker? No, I don't *remember* meeting him, but I'm pretty sure I've heard of him."

Kennicott took her aside and whispered, "Now I'll introduce you to them, one at a time."

"Tell me about them first."

"Well, the nice-looking couple over there are Harry Haydock and his wife, Juanita. Harry's dad owns most of the Bon Ton, but it's Harry who runs it and gives it the pep. He's a hustler. Next to him is Dave Dyer the druggist—you met him this afternoon—mighty good duck-shot. The tall husk beyond him is Jack Elder—Jackson Elder—owns the planing-mill, and the Minniemashie House, and quite a share in the Farmers' National Bank. Him and his wife are good sports—him and Sam and I go hunting together a lot. The old cheese there is Luke Dawson, the richest man in town. Next to him is Nat Hicks, the tailor."

"Really? A tailor?"

"Sure. Why not? Maybe we're slow, but we are democratic. I go hunting with Nat same as I do with Jack Elder."

"I'm glad. I've never met a tailor socially. It must be charming to meet one and not have to think about what you owe him. And do you—— Would you go hunting with your barber, too?"

"No but—— No use running this democracy thing into the ground. Besides, I've known Nat for years, and besides, he's a mighty good shot and—— That's the way it is, see? Next to Nat is Chet Dashaway. Great fellow for chinning. He'll talk your arm off, about religion or politics or books or anything."

Carol gazed with a polite approximation to interest at Mr. Dashaway, a tan person with a wide mouth. "Oh, I know! He's the furniture-store man!" She was much pleased with herself.

"Yump, and he's the undertaker. You'll like him. Come shake hands with him."

"Oh no, no! He doesn't—he doesn't do the embalming and all that—himself? I couldn't shake hands with an undertaker!"

"Why not? You'd be proud to shake hands with a great surgeon, just after he'd been carving up people's bellies."

She sought to regain her afternoon's calm of maturity. "Yes. You're right.

I want—oh, my dear, do you know how much I want to like the people you like? I want to see people as they are."

"Well, don't forget to see people as other folks see them as they are! They have the stuff. Did you know that Percy Bresnahan came from here? Born and brought up here!"

"Bresnahan?"

"Yes—you know—president of the Velvet Motor Company of Boston, Mass. —make the Velvet Twelve—biggest automobile factory in New England."

"I think I've heard of him."

"Sure you have. Why, he's a millionaire several times over! Well, Perce comes back here for the black-bass fishing almost every summer, and he says if he could get away from business, he'd rather live here than in Boston or New York or any of those places. *He* doesn't mind Chet's undertaking."

"Please! I'll—I'll like everybody! I'll be the community sunbeam!"

He led her to the Dawsons.

Luke Dawson, lender of money on mortgages, owner of Northern cut-over land, was a hesitant man in unpressed soft gray clothes, with bulging eyes in a milky face. His wife had bleached cheeks, bleached hair, bleached voice, and a bleached manner. She wore her expensive green frock, with its passementeried bosom, bead tassels, and gaps between the buttons down the back, as though she had bought it secondhand and was afraid of meeting the former owner. They were shy. It was "Professor" George Edwin Mott, superintendent of schools, a Chinese mandarin turned brown, who held Carol's hand and made her welcome.

When the Dawsons and Mr. Mott had stated that they were "pleased to meet her," there seemed to be nothing else to say, but the conversation went on automatically.

"Do you like Gopher Prairie?" whimpered Mrs. Dawson.

"Oh, I'm sure I'm going to be ever so happy."

"There's so many nice people." Mrs. Dawson looked to Mr. Mott for social and intellectual aid. He lectured:

"There's a fine class of people. I don't like some of these retired farmers who come here to spend their last days—especially the Germans. They hate to pay school-taxes. They hate to spend a cent. But the rest are a fine class of people. Did you know that Percy Bresnahan came from here? Used to go to school right at the old building!"

"I heard he did."

"Yes. He's a prince. He and I went fishing together, last time he was here."

The Dawsons and Mr. Mott teetered upon weary feet, and smiled at Carol with crystallized expressions. She went on:

"Tell me, Mr. Mott: Have you ever tried any experiments with any of the new educational systems? The modern kindergarten methods or the Gary system?"

"Oh. Those. Most of these would-be reformers are simply notoriety-seekers. I believe in manual training, but Latin and mathematics always will be the backbone of sound Americanism, no matter what these faddists advocate

—heaven knows what they do want—knitting, I suppose, and classes in wiggling the ears!"

The Dawsons smiled their appreciation of listening to a savant. Carol waited till Kennicott should rescue her. The rest of the party waited for the miracle of being amused.

Harry and Juanita Haydock, Rita Simons and Dr. Terry Gould—the young smart set of Gopher Prairie. She was led to them. Juanita Haydock flung at her in a high, cackling, friendly voice:

"Well, this is so nice to have you here. We'll have some good parties—dances and everything. You'll have to join the Jolly Seventeen. We play bridge and we have a supper once a month. You play, of course?"

"N-no, I don't."

"Really? In St. Paul?"

"I've always been such a book-worm."

"We'll have to teach you. Bridge is half the fun of life." Juanita had become patronizing, and she glanced disrespectfully at Carol's golden sash, which she had previously admired.

Harry Haydock said politely, "How do you think you're going to like the old burg?"

"I'm sure I shall like it tremendously."

"Best people on earth here. Great hustlers, too. Course I've had lots of chances to go live in Minneapolis, but we like it here. Real he-town. Did you know that Percy Bresnahan came from here?"

Carol perceived that she had been weakened in the biological struggle by disclosing her lack of bridge. Roused to nervous desire to regain her position she turned on Dr. Terry Gould, the young and pool-playing competitor of her husband. Her eyes coquetted with him while she gushed:

"I'll learn bridge. But what I really love most is the outdoors. Can't we all get up a boating party, and fish, or whatever you do, and have a picnic supper afterwards?"

"Now you're talking!" Dr. Gould affirmed. He looked rather too obviously at the cream-smooth slope of her shoulder. "Like fishing? Fishing is my middle name. I'll teach you bridge. Like cards at all?"

"I used to be rather good at bezique."

She knew that bezique was a game of cards—or a game of something else. Roulette, possibly. But her lie was a triumph. Juanita's handsome, high-colored, horsey face showed doubt. Harry stroked his nose and said humbly, "Bezique? Used to be great gambling game, wasn't it?"

While others drifted to her group, Carol snatched up the conversation. She laughed and was frivolous and rather brittle. She could not distinguish their eyes. They were a blurry theater-audience before which she self-consciously enacted the comedy of being the Clever Little Bride of Doc Kennicott:

"These-here celebrated Open Spaces, that's what I'm going out for. I'll never read anything but the sporting-page again. Will converted me on our Colorado trip. There were so many mousey tourists who were afraid to get out of the motor 'bus that I decided to be Annie Oakley, the Wild Western Wampire, and I bought oh! a vociferous skirt which revealed my perfectly nice ankles to the Presbyterian glare of all the Ioway schoolma'ams, and I leaped from peak to peak like the nimble chamoys, and—— You may think that Herr Doctor Kennicott is a Nimrod, but you ought to have seen me daring him to strip to his B. V. D.'s and go swimming in an icy mountain brook."

She knew that they were thinking of becoming shocked, but Juanita Haydock was admiring, at least. She swaggered on:

"I'm sure I'm going to ruin Will as a respectable practitioner—— Is he a good doctor, Dr. Gould?"

Kennicott's rival gasped at this insult to professional ethics, and he took an appreciable second before he recovered his social manner. "I'll tell you, Mrs. Kennicott." He smiled at Kennicott, to imply that whatever he might say in the stress of being witty was not to count against him in the commercio-medical warfare. "There's some people in town that say the doc is a fair to middlin' diagnostician and prescription-writer, but let me whisper this to you —but for heaven's sake don't tell him I said so—don't you ever go to him for anything more serious than a pendectomy of the left ear or a strabismus of the cardiograph."

No one save Kennicott knew exactly what this meant, but they laughed, and Sam Clark's party assumed a glittering lemon-yellow color of brocade panels and champagne and tulle and crystal chandeliers and sporting duchesses. Carol saw that George Edwin Mott and the blanched Mr. and Mrs. Dawson were not yet hypnotized. They looked as though they wondered whether they ought to look as though they disapproved. She concentrated on them:

"But I know whom I wouldn't have dared to go to Colorado with! Mr. Dawson there! I'm sure he's a regular heartbreaker. When we were introduced he held my hand and squeezed it frightfully."

"Haw! Haw! Haw!" The entire company applauded. Mr. Dawson was beatified. He had been called many things—loan-shark, skinflint, tightwad, pussyfoot—but he had never before been called a flirt.

"He is wicked, isn't he, Mrs. Dawson? Don't you have to lock him up?"

"Oh no, but maybe I better," attempted Mrs. Dawson, a tint on her pallid face.

For fifteen minutes Carol kept it up. She asserted that she was going to stage a musical comedy, that she preferred café parfait to beefsteak, that she hoped Dr. Kennicott would never lose his ability to make love to charming women, and that she had a pair of gold stockings. They gaped for more. But she could not keep it up. She retired to a chair behind Sam Clark's bulk. The smile-wrinkles solemnly flattened out in the faces of all the other collaborators in having a party, and again they stood about hoping but not expecting to be amused.

Carol listened. She discovered that conversation did not exist in Gopher Prairie. Even at this affair, which brought out the young smart set, the hunting squire set, the respectable intellectual set, and the solid financial set, they sat up with gaiety as with a corpse.

Juanita Haydock talked a good deal in her rattling voice but it was invariably of personalities: the rumor that Raymie Wutherspoon was going to send for a pair of patent leather shoes with gray buttoned tops; the rheumatism of Champ Perry; the state of Guy Pollock's grippe; and the dementia of Jim Howland in painting his fence salmon-pink.

Sam Clark had been talking to Carol about motor cars, but he felt his duties as host. While he droned, his brows popped up and down. He interrupted himself, "Must stir 'em up." He worried at his wife, "Don't you think I better stir 'em up?" He shouldered into the center of the room, and cried:

"Let's have some stunts, folks."

"Yes, let's!" shrieked Juanita Haydock.

"Say, Dave, give us that stunt about the Norwegian catching a hen."

"You bet; that's a slick stunt; do that, Dave!" cheered Chet Dashaway.

Mr. Dave Dyer obliged.

All the guests moved their lips in anticipation of being called on for their own stunts.

"Ella, came on and recite 'Old Sweetheart of Mine,' for us," demanded Sam.

Miss Ella Stowbody, the spinster daughter of the Ionic bank, scratched her dry palms and blushed. "Oh, you don't want to hear that old thing again."

"Sure we do! You bet!" asserted Sam.

"My voice is in terrible shape tonight."

"Tut! Come on!"

Sam loudly explained to Carol, "Ella is our shark at elocuting. She's had professional training. She studied singing and oratory and dramatic art and shorthand for a year, in Milwaukee."

Miss Stowbody was reciting. As encore to "An Old Sweetheart of Mine," she gave a peculiarly optimistic poem regarding the value of smiles.

There were four other stunts: one Jewish, one Irish, one juvenile, and Nat Hicks's parody of Mark Antony's funeral oration.

During the winter Carol was to hear Dave Dyer's hen-catching impersonation seven times, "An Old Sweetheart of Mine" nine times, the Jewish story and the funeral oration twice; but now she was ardent and, because she did so want to be happy and simple-hearted, she was as disappointed as the others when the stunts were finished, and the party instantly sank back into coma.

They gave up trying to be festive; they began to talk naturally, as they did at their shops and homes.

The men and women divided, as they had been tending to do all evening. Carol was deserted by the men, left to a group of matrons who steadily pattered of children, sickness, and cooks—their own shop-talk. She was piqued. She remembered visions of herself as a smart married woman in a drawing-room, fencing with clever men. Her dejection was relieved by speculation as to what the men were discussing, in the corner between the piano and the

phonograph. Did they rise from these housewifely personalities to a larger
world of abstractions and affairs?

She made her best curtsy to Mrs. Dawson; she twittered, "I won't have
my husband leaving me so soon! I'm going over and pull the wretch's ears."
She rose with a *jeune fille* bow. She was self-absorbed and self-approving
because she had attained that quality of sentimentality. She proudly dipped
across the room and, to the interest and commendation of all beholders, sat
on the arm of Kennicott's chair.

He was gossiping with Sam Clark, Luke Dawson, Jackson Elder of the
planing-mill, Chet Dashaway, Dave Dyer, Harry Haydock, and Ezra Stowbody, president of the Ionic bank.

Ezra Stowbody was a troglodyte. He had come to Gopher Prairie in 1865.
He was a distinguished bird of prey—swooping thin nose, turtle mouth, thick
brows, port-wine cheeks, floss of white hair, contemptuous eyes. He was not
happy in the social changes of thirty years. Three decades ago, Dr. Westlake,
Julius Flickerbaugh the lawyer, Merriman Peedy the Congregational pastor
and himself had been the arbiters. That was as it should be; the fine arts—
medicine, law, religion, and finance—recognized as aristocratic; four Yankees democratically chatting with but ruling the Ohioans and Illini and
Swedes and Germans who had ventured to follow them. But Westlake was
old, almost retired; Julius Flickerbaugh had lost much of his practise to
livelier attorneys; Reverend (not The Reverend) Peedy was dead; and nobody was impressed in this rotten age of automobiles by the "spanking grays"
which Ezra still drove. The town was as heterogeneous as Chicago. Norwegians and Germans owned stores. The social leaders were common merchants. Selling nails was considered as sacred as banking. These upstarts—
the Clarks, the Haydocks—had no dignity. They were sound and conservative
in politics, but they talked about motor cars and pump-guns and heaven
only knew what new-fangled fads. Mr. Stowbody felt out of place with them.
But his brick house with the mansard roof was still the largest residence in
town, and he held his position as squire by occasionally appearing among the
younger men and reminding them by a wintry eye that without the banker
none of them could carry on their vulgar businesses.

As Carol defied decency by sitting down with the men, Mr. Stowbody
was piping to Mr. Dawson, "Say, Luke, when was't Biggins first settled in
Winnebago Township? Wa'n't it in 1879?"

"Why no 'twa'n't!" Mr. Dawson was indignant. "He come out from Vermont in 1867—no, wait, in 1868, it must have been—and took a claim on
the Rum River, quite a ways above Anoka."

"He did not!" roared Mr. Stowbody. "He settled first in Blue Earth County,
him and his father!"

("What's the point at issue?" Carol whispered to Kennicott.

("Whether this old duck Biggins had an English setter or a Llewellyn.
They've been arguing it all evening!")

Dave Dyer interrupted to give tidings, "D' tell you that Clara Biggins was in town couple days ago? She bought a hot-water bottle—expensive one, too —two dollars and thirty cents!"

"Yaaaaaah!" snarled Mr. Stowbody. "Course. She's just like her grandad was. Never save a cent. Two dollars and twenty—thirty, was it?—two dollars and thirty cents for a hot-water bottle! Brick wrapped up in a flannel petticoat just as good, anyway!"

"How's Ella's tonsils, Mr. Stowbody?" yawned Chet Dashaway.

While Mr. Stowbody gave a somatic and psychic study of them, Carol reflected, "Are they really so terribly interested in Ella's tonsils, or even in Ella's esophagus? I wonder if I could get them away from personalities? Let's risk damnation and try."

"There hasn't been much labor trouble around here, has there, Mr. Stowbody?" she asked innocently.

"No, ma'am, thank God, we've been free from that, except maybe with hired girls and farm-hands. Trouble enough with these foreign farmers; if you don't watch these Swedes they turn socialist or populist or some fool thing on you in a minute. Of course, if they have loans you can make 'em listen to reason. I just have 'em come into the bank for a talk, and tell 'em a few things. I don't mind their being democrats, so much, but I won't stand having socialists around. But thank God, we ain't got the labor trouble they have in these cities. Even Jack Elder here gets along pretty well, in the planing-mill, don't you, Jack?"

"Yep. Sure. Don't need so many skilled workmen in my place, and it's a lot of these cranky, wage-hogging, half-baked skilled mechanics that start trouble—reading a lot of this anarchist literature and union papers and all."

"Do you approve of union labor?" Carol inquired of Mr. Elder.

"Me? I should say not! It's like this: I don't mind dealing with my men if they think they've got any grievances—though Lord knows what's come over workmen, nowadays—don't appreciate a good job. But still, if they come to me honestly, as man to man, I'll talk things over with them. But I'm not going to have any outsider, any of these walking delegates, or whatever fancy names they call themselves now—bunch of rich grafters, living on the ignorant workmen! Not going to have any of those fellows butting in and telling *me* how to run *my* business!"

Mr. Elder was growing more excited, more belligerent and patriotic. "I stand for freedom and constitutional rights. If any man don't like my shop, he can get up and git. Same way, if I don't like him, he gits. And that's all there is to it. I simply can't understand all these complications and hoop-te-doodles and government reports and wage-scales and God knows what all that these fellows are balling up the labor situation with, when it's all perfectly simple. They like what I pay 'em, or they get out. That's all there is to it!"

"What do you think of profit-sharing?" Carol ventured.

Mr. Elder thundered his answer, while the others nodded, solemnly and in tune, like a shop-window of flexible toys, comic mandarins and judges and ducks and clowns, set quivering by a breeze from the open door:

"All this profit-sharing and welfare work and insurance and old-age pen-sion is simply poppycock. Enfeebles a workman's independence—and wastes a lot of honest profit. The half-baked thinker that isn't dry behind the ears yet, and these suffragettes and God knows what all buttinskis there are that are trying to tell a business man how to run his business, and some of these college professors are just about as bad, the whole kit and bilin' of 'em are nothing in God's world but socialism in disguise! And it's my bounden duty as a producer to resist every attack on the integrity of American industry to the last ditch. Yes—SIR!"

Mr. Elder wiped his brow.

Dave Dyer added, "Sure! You bet! What they ought to do is simply to hang every one of these agitators, and that would settle the whole thing right off. Don't you think so, doc?"

"You bet," agreed Kennicott.

The conversation was at last relieved of the plague of Carol's intrusions and they settled down to the question of whether the justice of the peace had sent that hobo drunk to jail for ten days or twelve. It was a matter not readily determined. Then Dave Dyer communicated his carefree adventures on the gipsy trail:

"Yep. I get good time out of the flivver. 'Bout a week ago I motored down to New Wurttemberg. That's forty-three—— No, let's see: It's seventeen miles to Belldale, and 'bout six and three-quarters, call it seven, to Torgenquist, and it's a good nineteen miles from there to New Wurttemberg—seventeen and seven and nineteen, that makes, uh, let me see: seventeen and seven 's twenty-four, plus nineteen, well say plus twenty, that makes forty-four, well anyway, say about forty-three or -four miles from here to New Wurttemberg. We got started about seven-fifteen, prob'ly seven-twenty, because I had to stop and fill the radiator, and we ran along, just keeping up a good steady gait——"

Mr. Dyer did finally, for reasons and purposes admitted and justified, attain to New Wurttemberg.

Once—only once—the presence of the alien Carol was recognized. Chet Dashaway leaned over and said asthmatically, "Say, uh, have you been reading this serial 'Two Out' in *Tingling Tales?* Corking yarn! Gosh, the fellow that wrote it certainly can sling baseball slang!"

The others tried to look literary. Harry Haydock offered, "Juanita is a great hand for reading high-class stuff, like 'Mid the Magnolias' by this Sara Hetwiggin Butts, and 'Riders of Ranch Reckless.' Books. But me," he glanced about importantly, as one convinced that no other hero had ever been in so strange a plight, "I'm so darn busy I don't have much time to read."

"I never read anything I can't check against," said Sam Clark.

Thus ended the literary portion of the conversation, and for seven minutes Jackson Elder outlined reasons for believing that the pike-fishing was better on the west shore of Lake Minniemashie than on the east—though it was indeed quite true that on the east shore Nat Hicks had caught a pike altogether admirable.

The talk went on. It did go on! Their voices were monotonous, thick, emphatic. They were harshly pompous, like men in the smoking-compartments of Pullman cars. They did not bore Carol. They frightened her. She panted, "They will be cordial to me, because my man belongs to their tribe. God help me if I were an outsider!"

Smiling as changelessly as an ivory figurine she sat quiescent, avoiding thought, glancing about the living-room and hall, noting their betrayal of unimaginative commercial prosperity. Kennicott said, "Dandy interior, eh? My idea of how a place ought to be furnished. Modern." She looked polite, and observed the oiled floors, hard-wood staircase, unused fireplace with tiles which resembled brown linoleum, cut-glass vases standing upon doilies, and the barred, shut, forbidding unit bookcases that were half filled with swashbuckler novels and unread-looking sets of Dickens, Kipling, O. Henry, and Elbert Hubbard.

She perceived that even personalities were failing to hold the party. The room filled with hesitancy as with a fog. People cleared their throats, tried to choke down yawns. The men shot their cuffs and the women stuck their combs more firmly into their back hair.

Then a rattle, a daring hope in every eye, the swinging of a door, the smell of strong coffee, Dave Dyer's mewing voice in a triumphant, "The eats!" They began to chatter. They had something to do. They could escape from themselves. They fell upon the food—chicken sandwiches, maple cake, drugstore ice cream. Even when the food was gone they remained cheerful. They could go home, any time now, and go to bed!

They went, with a flutter of coats, chiffon scarfs, and good-bys.

Carol and Kennicott walked home.

"Did you like them?" he asked.

"They were terribly sweet to me."

"Uh, Carrie—— You ought to be more careful about shocking folks. Talking about gold stockings, and about showing your ankles to schoolteachers and all!" More mildly: "You gave 'em a good time, but I'd watch out for that, 'f I were you. Juanita Haydock is such a damn cat. I wouldn't give her a chance to criticize me."

"My poor effort to lift up the party! Was I wrong to try to amuse them?"

"No! No! Honey, I didn't mean—— You were the only up-and-coming person in the bunch. I just mean—— Don't get onto legs and all that immoral stuff. Pretty conservative crowd."

She was silent, raw with the shameful thought that the attentive circle might have been criticizing her, laughing at her.

"Don't, please don't worry!" he pleaded.

Silence.

"Gosh, I'm sorry I spoke about it. I just meant—— But they were crazy about you. Sam said to me, 'That little lady of yours is the slickest thing that ever came to this town,' he said; and Ma Dawson—I didn't hardly know whether she'd like you or not, she's such a dried-up old bird, but she said, 'Your bride is so quick and bright, I declare, she just wakes me up.'"

Carol liked praise, the flavor and fatness of it, but she was so energetically being sorry for herself that she could not taste this commendation.

"Please! Come on! Cheer up!" His lips said it, his anxious shoulder said it, his arm about her said it, as they halted on the obscure porch of their house.

"Do you care if they think I'm flighty, Will?"

"Me? Why, I wouldn't care if the whole world thought you were this or that or anything else. You're my—well, you're my soul!"

He was an undefined mass, as solid-seeming as rock. She found his sleeve, pinched it, cried, "I'm glad! It's sweet to be wanted! You must tolerate my frivolousness. You're all I have!"

He lifted her, carried her into the house, and with her arms about his neck she forgot Main Street.

# 5

"We'll steal the whole day, and go hunting. I want you to see the country round here," Kennicott announced at breakfast. "I'd take the car—want you to see how swell she runs since I put in a new piston. But we'll take a team, so we can get right out into the fields. Not many prairie chickens left now, but we might just happen to run onto a small covey."

He fussed over his hunting-kit. He pulled his hip boots out to full length and examined them for holes. He feverishly counted his shotgun shells, lecturing her on the qualities of smokeless powder. He drew the new hammerless shotgun out of its heavy tan leather case and made her peep through the barrels to see how dazzlingly free they were from rust.

The world of hunting and camping-outfits and fishing-tackle was unfamiliar to her, and in Kennicott's interest she found something creative and joyous. She examined the smooth stock, the carved hard rubber butt of the gun. The shells, with their brass caps and sleek green bodies and hieroglyphics on the wads, were cool and comfortably heavy in her hands.

Kennicott wore a brown canvas hunting-coat with vast pockets lining the inside, corduroy trousers which bulged at the wrinkles, peeled and scarred shoes, a scarecrow felt hat. In this uniform he felt virile. They clumped out to the livery buggy, they packed the kit and the box of lunch into the back, crying to each other that it was a magnificent day.

Kennicott had borrowed Jackson Elder's red and white English setter, a complacent dog with a waving tail of silver hair which flickered in the sunshine. As they started, the dog yelped, and leaped at the horses' heads, till Kennicott took him into the buggy, where he nuzzled Carol's knees and leaned out to sneer at farm mongrels.

The grays clattered out on the hard dirt road with a pleasant song of hoofs: "Ta ta ta rat! Ta ta ta rat!" It was early and fresh, the air whistling, frost bright on the golden rod. As the sun warmed the world of stubble into a welter of yellow they turned from the highroad, through the bars of a farmer's gate, into a field, slowly bumping over the uneven earth. In a hollow of the rolling prairie they lost sight even of the country road. It was warm and placid. Locusts trilled among the dry wheat-stalks, and brilliant little flies hurtled across the buggy. A buzz of content filled the air. Crows loitered and gossiped in the sky.

The dog had been let out and after a dance of excitement he settled down to a steady quartering of the field, forth and back, forth and back, his nose down.

"Pete Rustad owns this farm, and he told me he saw a small covey of chickens in the west forty, last week. Maybe we'll get some sport after all," Kennicott chuckled blissfully.

She watched the dog in suspense, breathing quickly every time he seemed to halt. She had no desire to slaughter birds, but she did desire to belong to Kennicott's world.

The dog stopped, on the point, a forepaw held up.

"By golly! He's hit a scent! Come on!" squealed Kennicott. He leaped from the buggy, twisted the reins about the whip-socket, swung her out, caught up his gun, slipped in two shells, stalked toward the rigid dog, Carol pattering after him. The setter crawled ahead, his tail quivering, his belly close to the stubble. Carol was nervous. She expected clouds of large birds to fly up instantly. Her eyes were strained with staring. But they followed the dog for a quarter of a mile, turning, doubling, crossing two low hills, kicking through a swale of weeds, crawling between the strands of a barbed-wire fence. The walking was hard on her pavement-trained feet. The earth was lumpy, the stubble prickly and lined with grass, thistles, abortive stumps of clover. She dragged and floundered.

She heard Kennicott gasp, "Look!" Three gray birds were starting up from the stubble. They were round, dumpy, like enormous bumble bees. Kennicott was sighting, moving the barrel. She was agitated. Why didn't he fire? The birds would be gone! Then a crash, another, and two birds turned somersaults in the air, plumped down.

When he showed her the birds she had no sensation of blood. These heaps of feathers were so soft and unbruised—there was about them no hint of death. She watched her conquering man tuck them into his inside pocket, and trudged with him back to the buggy.

They found no more prairie chickens that morning.

At noon they drove into her first farmyard, a private village, a white house with no porches save a low and quite dirty stoop at the back, a crimson barn with white trimmings, a glazed brick silo, an ex-carriage-shed, now the garage of a Ford, an unpainted cow-stable, a chicken-house, a pig-pen, a corncrib, a granary, the galvanized-iron skeleton tower of a windmill. The dooryard was of packed yellow clay, treeless, barren of grass, littered with rusty plowshares and wheels of discarded cultivators. Hardened trampled mud, like lava, filled the pig-pen. The doors of the house were grime-rubbed, the corners and eaves were rusted with rain, and the child who stared at them from the kitchen window was smeary-faced. But beyond the barn was a clump of scarlet geraniums; the prairie breeze was sunshine in motion; the flashing metal blades of the windmill revolved with a lively hum; a horse neighed, a rooster crowed, martins flew in and out of the cow-stable.

A small spare woman with flaxen hair trotted from the house. She was twanging a Swedish patois—not in monotone, like English, but singing it, with a lyrical whine:

"Pete he say you kom pretty soon hunting, doctor. My, dot's fine you kom. Is dis de bride? Ohhhh! Ve yoost say las' night, ve hope maybe ve see her som day. My, soch a pretty lady!" Mrs. Rustad was shining with welcome. "Vell, vell! Ay hope you lak dis country! Von't you stay for dinner, doctor?"

"No, but I wonder if you wouldn't like to give us a glass of milk?" condescended Kennicott.

"Vell Ay should say Ay vill! You vait har a second and Ay run on de milk-house!" She nervously hastened to a tiny red building beside the windmill; she came back with a pitcher of milk from which Carol filled the thermos bottle.

As they drove off Carol admired, "She's the dearest thing I ever saw. And she adores you. You are the Lord of the Manor."

"Oh no," much pleased, "but still they do ask my advice about things. Bully people, these Scandinavian farmers. And prosperous, too. Helga Rustad, she's still scared of America, but her kids will be doctors and lawyers and governors of the state and any darn thing they want to."

"I wonder——" Carol was plunged back into last night's *Weltschmerz*. "I wonder if these farmers aren't bigger than we are? So simple and hard-working. The town lives on them. We townies are parasites, and yet we feel superior to them. Last night I heard Mr. Haydock talking about 'hicks.' Apparently he despises the farmers because they haven't reached the social heights of selling thread and buttons."

"Parasites? Us? Where'd the farmers be without the town? Who lends them money? Who—why, we supply them with everything!"

"Don't you find that some of the farmers think they pay too much for the services of the towns?"

"Oh, of course there's a lot of cranks among the farmers same as there are among any class. Listen to some of these kickers, a fellow'd think that the farmers ought to run the state and the whole shooting-match—probably if they had their way they'd fill up the legislature with a lot of farmers in manure-covered boots—yes, and they'd come tell me I was hired on a salary now, and couldn't fix my fees! That'd be fine for you, wouldn't it!"

"But why shouldn't they?"

"Why? That bunch of—— Telling *me*—— Oh, for heaven's sake, let's quit arguing. All this discussing may be all right at a party but—— Let's forget it while we're hunting."

"I know. The Wonderlust—probably it's a worse affliction than the Wanderlust. I just wonder——"

She told herself that she had everything in the world. And after each self-rebuke she stumbled again on "I just wonder——"

They ate their sandwiches by a prairie slew: long grass reaching up out of clear water, mossy bogs, red-winged blackbirds, the scum a splash of gold-green. Kennicott smoked a pipe while she leaned back in the buggy and let her tired spirit be absorbed in the Nirvana of the incomparable sky.

They lurched to the highroad and awoke from their sun-soaked drowse at the sound of the clopping hoofs. They paused to look for partridges in a rim of woods, little woods, very clean and shiny and gay, silver birches and poplars with immaculate green trunks, encircling a lake of sandy bottom, a splashing seclusion demure in the welter of hot prairie.

Kennicott brought down a fat red squirrel and at dusk he had a dramatic shot at a flight of ducks whirling down from the upper air, skimming the lake, instantly vanishing.

They drove home under the sunset. Mounds of straw, and wheat-stacks like bee-hives, stood out in startling rose and gold, and the green-tufted stubble glistened. As the vast girdle of crimson darkened, the fulfilled land became autumnal in deep reds and browns. The black road before the buggy turned to a faint lavender, then was blotted to uncertain grayness. Cattle came in a long line up to the barred gates of the farmyards, and over the resting land was a dark glow.

Carol had found the dignity and greatness which had failed her in Main Street.

II

Till they had a maid they took noon dinner and six o'clock supper at Mrs. Gurrey's boarding-house.

Mrs. Elisha Gurrey, relict of Deacon Gurrey the dealer in hay and grain, was a pointed-nosed, simpering woman with iron-gray hair drawn so tight that it resembled a soiled handkerchief covering her head. But she was unexpectedly cheerful, and her dining-room, with its thin tablecloth on a long pine table, had the decency of clean bareness.

In the line of unsmiling, methodically chewing guests, like horses at a manger, Carol came to distinguish one countenance: the pale, long, spectacled face and sandy pompadour hair of Mr. Raymond P. Wutherspoon, known as "Raymie," professional bachelor, manager and one half the sales-force in the shoe-department of the Bon Ton Store.

"You will enjoy Gopher Prairie very much, Mrs. Kennicott," petitioned Raymie. His eyes were like those of a dog waiting to be let in out of the cold. He passed the stewed apricots effusively. "There are a great many bright cultured people here. Mrs. Wilks, the Christian Science reader, is a very bright woman—though I am not a Scientist myself, in fact I sing in the Episcopal choir. And Miss Sherwin of the high school—she is such a pleasing, bright girl—I was fitting her to a pair of tan gaiters yesterday, I declare, it really was a pleasure."

"Gimme the butter, Carrie," was Kennicott's comment. She defied him by encouraging Raymie:

"Do you have amateur dramatics and so on here?"

"Oh yes! The town's just full of talent. The Knights of Pythias put on a dandy minstrel show last year."

"It's nice you're so enthusiastic."

"Oh, do you really think so? Lots of folks jolly me for trying to get up shows and so on. I tell them they have more artistic gifts than they know. Just yesterday I was saying to Harry Haydock: if he would read poetry, like Longfellow, or if he would join the band—I get so much pleasure out of playing the cornet, and our band-leader, Del Snafflin, is such a good musician, I often say he ought to give up his barbering and become a professional musician, he could play the clarinet in Minneapolis or New York or anywhere, but—but I couldn't get Harry to see it at all and—I hear you and the doctor went out hunting yesterday. Lovely country, isn't it. And did you make some calls? The mercantile life isn't inspiring like medicine. It must be wonderful to see how patients trust you, doctor."

"Huh. It's me that's got to do all the trusting. Be damn sight more wonderful 'f they'd pay their bills," grumbled Kennicott and, to Carol, he whispered something which sounded like "gentleman hen."

But Raymie's pale eyes were watering at her. She helped him with, "So you like to read poetry?"

"Oh yes, so much—though to tell the truth, I don't get much time for reading, we're always so busy at the store and—— But we had the dandiest professional reciter at the Pythian Sisters sociable last winter."

Carol thought she heard a grunt from the traveling salesman at the end of the table, and Kennicott's jerking elbow was a grunt embodied. She persisted:

"Do you get to see many plays, Mr. Wutherspoon?"

He shone at her like a dim blue March moon, and sighed, "No, but I do love the movies. I'm a real fan. One trouble with books is that they're not so thoroughly safeguarded by intelligent censors as the movies are, and when you drop into the library and take out a book you never know what you're wasting your time on. What I like in books is a wholesome, really improving story, and sometimes—— Why, once I started a novel by this fellow Balzac that you read about, and it told how a lady wasn't living with her husband, I mean she wasn't his wife. It went into details, disgustingly! And the English was real poor. I spoke to the library about it, and they took it off the shelves. I'm not narrow, but I must say I don't see any use in this deliberately dragging in immorality! Life itself is so full of temptations that in literature one wants only that which is pure and uplifting."

"What's the name of that Balzac yarn? Where can I get hold of it?" giggled the traveling salesman.

Raymie ignored him. "But the movies, they are mostly clean, and their humor—— Don't you think that the most essential quality for a person to have is a sense of humor?"

"I don't know. I really haven't much," said Carol.

He shook his finger at her. "Now, now, you're too modest. I'm sure we can all see that you have a perfectly corking sense of humor. Besides, Dr. Kennicott wouldn't marry a lady that didn't have. We all know how he loves his fun!"

"You bet. I'm a jokey old bird. Come on, Carrie; let's beat it," remarked Kennicott.

Raymie implored, "And what is your chief artistic interest, Mrs. Kennicott?"

"Oh——" Aware that the traveling salesman had murmured, "Dentistry," she desperately hazarded, "Architecture."

"That's a real nice art. I've always said—when Haydock & Simons were finishing the new front on the Bon Ton building, the old man came to me, you know, Harry's father, 'D. H.,' I always call him, and he asked me how I liked it, and I said to him, 'Look here, D. H.,' I said—you see, he was going to leave the front plain, and I said to him, 'It's all very well to have modern lighting and a big display-space,' I said, 'but when you get that in, you want to have some architecture, too,' I said, and he laughed and said he guessed maybe I was right, and so he had 'em put on a cornice."

"Tin!" observed the traveling salesman.

Raymie bared his teeth like a belligerent mouse. "Well, what if it is tin? That's not my fault. I told D. H. to make it polished granite. You make me tired!"

"Leave us go! Come on, Carrie, leave us go!" from Kennicott.

Raymie waylaid them in the hall and secretly informed Carol that she musn't mind the traveling salesman's coarseness—he belonged to the hwa pollwa.

Kennicott chuckled, "Well, child, how about it? Do you prefer an artistic guy like Raymie to stupid boobs like Sam Clark and me?"

"My dear! Let's go home, and play pinochle, and laugh, and be foolish, and slip up to bed, and sleep without dreaming. It's beautiful to be just a solid citizeness!"

III

From the *Gopher Prairie Weekly Dauntless:*

One of the most charming affairs of the season was held Tuesday evening at the handsome new residence of Sam and Mrs. Clark, when many of our most prominent citizens gathered to greet the lovely new bride of our popular local physician, Dr. Will Kennicott. All present spoke of the many charms of the bride, formerly Miss Carol Milford of St. Paul. Games and stunts were the order of the day, with merry talk and conversation. At a late hour dainty refreshments were served, and the party broke up with many expressions of pleasure at the pleasant affair. Among those present were Mesdames Kennicott, Elder——

\* \* \*

Dr. Will Kennicott, for the past several years one of our most popular and skilful physicians and surgeons, gave the town a delightful surprise when he returned from an extended honeymoon tour in Colorado this week with his charming bride, née Miss Carol Milford of St. Paul, whose family are socially prominent in Minneapolis and Mankato. Mrs. Kennicott is a lady of manifold charms, not only of striking charm of appearance but is also a distinguished graduate of a school in the East and has for the past year been prominently connected in an important position of responsibility with the St. Paul Public Library, in which city Dr. "Will" had the good fortune to meet her. The city of Gopher Prairie welcomes her to our midst and prophesies for her many happy years in the energetic city of the twin lakes and the future. The Dr. and Mrs. Kennicott will reside for the present at the Doctor's home on Poplar Street which his charming mother has been keeping for him who has now returned to her own home at Lac-qui-Meurt leaving a host of friends who regret her absence and hope to see her soon with us again.

## IV

She knew that if she was ever to effect any of the "reforms" which she had pictured, she must have a starting-place. What confused her during the three or four months after her marriage was not lack of perception that she must be definite, but sheer careless happiness of her first home.

In the pride of being a housewife she loved every detail—the brocade armchair with the weak back, even the brass water-cock on the hot-water reservoir, when she had become familiar with it by trying to scour it to brilliance.

She found a maid—plump radiant Bea Sorenson from Scandia Crossing. Bea was droll in her attempt to be at once a respectful servant and a bosom friend. They laughed together over the fact that the stove did not draw, over the slipperiness of fish in the pan.

Like a child playing Grandma in a trailing skirt, Carol paraded uptown for her marketing, crying greetings to housewives along the way. Everybody bowed to her, strangers and all, and made her feel that they wanted her, that she belonged here. In city shops she was merely A Customer—a hat, a voice to bore a harassed clerk. Here she was Mrs. Doc Kennicott, and her preferences in grape-fruit and manners were known and remembered and worth discussing. . . . even if they weren't worth fulfilling.

Shopping was a delight of brisk conferences. The very merchants whose droning she found the dullest at the two or three parties which were given to welcome her were the pleasantest confidants of all when they had something to talk about—lemons or cotton voile or floor-oil. With that skip-jack Dave Dyer, the druggist, she conducted a long mock-quarrel. She pretended that he cheated her in the price of magazines and candy; he pretended she was a detective from the Twin Cities. He hid behind the prescription-counter, and when she stamped her foot he came out wailing, "Honest, I haven't done nothing crooked today—not yet."

She never recalled her first impression of Main Street; never had precisely the same despair at its ugliness. By the end of two shopping-tours everything had changed proportions. As she never entered it, the Minniemashie House ceased to exist for her. Clark's Hardware Store, Dyer's Drug Store, the groceries of Ole Jenson and Frederick Ludelmeyer and Howland & Gould, the meat markets, the notions shop—they expanded, and hid all other structures. When she entered Mr. Ludelmeyer's store and he wheezed, "Goot mornin', Mrs. Kennicott. Vell, dis iss a fine day," she did not notice the dustiness of the shelves nor the stupidity of the girl clerk; and she did not remember the mute colloquy with him on her first view of Main Street.

She could not find half the kinds of food she wanted, but that made shopping more of an adventure. When she did contrive to get sweetbreads at Dahl & Oleson's Meat Market the triumph was so vast that she buzzed with excitement and admired the strong wise butcher, Mr. Dahl.

She appreciated the homely ease of village life. She liked the old men, farmers, G.A.R. veterans, who when they gossiped sometimes squatted on their heels on the sidewalk, like resting Indians, and reflectively spat over the curb.

She found beauty in the children.

She had suspected that her married friends exaggerated their passion for children. But in her work in the library, children had become individuals to her, citizens of the State with their own rights and their own senses of humor. In the library she had not had much time to give them, but now she knew the luxury of stopping, gravely asking Bessie Clark whether her doll had yet recovered from its rheumatism, and agreeing with Oscar Martinsen that it would be Good Fun to go trapping "mushrats."

She touched the thought, "It would be sweet to have a baby of my own. I do want one. Tiny—— No! Not yet! There's so much to do. And I'm still tired from the job. It's in my bones."

She rested at home. She listened to the village noises common to all the world, jungle or prairie; sounds simple and charged with magic—dogs barking, chickens making a gurgling sound of content, children at play, a man beating a rug, wind in the cottonwood trees, a locust fiddling, a footstep on the walk, jaunty voices of Bea and a grocer's boy in the kitchen, a clinking anvil, a piano—not too near.

Twice a week, at least, she drove into the country with Kennicott, to hunt ducks in lakes enameled with sunset, or to call on patients who looked up to her as the squire's lady and thanked her for toys and magazines. Evenings she went with her husband to the motion pictures and was boisterously greeted by every other couple; or, till it became too cold, they sat on the porch, bawling to passers-by in motors, or to neighbors who were raking the leaves. The dust became golden in the low sun; the street was filled with the fragrance of burning leaves.

v

But she hazily wanted some one to whom she could say what she thought.

On a slow afternoon when she fidgeted over sewing and wished that the telephone would ring, Bea announced Miss Vida Sherwin.

Despite Vida Sherwin's lively blue eyes, if you had looked at her in detail you would have found her face slightly lined, and not so much sallow as with the bloom rubbed off; you would have found her chest flat, and her fingers rough from needle and chalk and penholder; her blouses and plain cloth skirts undistinguished; and her hat worn too far back, betraying a dry forehead. But you never did look at Vida Sherwin in detail. You couldn't. Her electric activity veiled her. She was as energetic as a chipmunk. Her fingers fluttered; her sympathy came out in spurts; she sat on the edge of a chair in eagerness to be near her auditor, to send her enthusiasms and optimism across.

She rushed into the room pouring out: "I'm afraid you'll think the teachers have been shabby in not coming near you, but we wanted to give you a chance to get settled. I am Vida Sherwin, and I try to teach French and English and a few other things in the high school."

"I've been hoping to know the teachers. You see, I was a librarian——"

"Oh, you needn't tell me. I know all about you! Awful how much I know—this gossipy village. We need you so much here. It's a dear loyal town (and isn't loyalty the finest thing in the world!) but it's a rough diamond, and we need you for the polishing, and we're ever so humble——" She stopped for breath and finished her compliment with a smile.

"If I *could* help you in any way—— Would I be committing the unpardonable sin if I whispered that I think Gopher Prairie is a tiny bit ugly?"

"Of course it's ugly. Dreadfully! Though I'm probably the only person in town to whom you could safely say that. (Except perhaps Guy Pollock the lawyer—have you met him?—oh, you *must!*—he's simply a darling—intelligence and culture and so gentle.) But I don't care so much about the ugliness. That will change. It's the spirit that gives me hope. It's sound. Wholesome. But afraid. It needs live creatures like you to awaken it. I shall slave-drive you!"

"Splendid. What shall I do? I've been wondering if it would be possible to have a good architect come here to lecture."

"Ye-es, but don't you think it would be better to work with existing agencies? Perhaps it will sound slow to you, but I was thinking—— It would be lovely if we could get you to teach Sunday School."

Carol had the empty expression of one who finds that she has been affectionately bowing to a complete stranger. "Oh yes. But I'm afraid I wouldn't be much good at that. My religion is so foggy."

"I know. So is mine. I don't care a bit for dogma. Though I do stick firmly

to the belief in the fatherhood of God and the brotherhood of man and the
leadership of Jesus. As you do, of course."

Carol looked respectable and thought about having tea.

"And that's all you need teach in Sunday School. It's the personal influence. Then there's the library-board. You'd be so useful on that. And of
course there's our women's study club—the Thanatopsis Club."

"Are they doing anything? Or do they read papers made out of the
Encyclopedia?"

Miss Sherwin shrugged. "Perhaps. But still, they are so earnest. They will
respond to your fresher interest. And the Thanatopsis does do a good social
work—they've made the city plant ever so many trees, and they run the
rest-room for farmers' wives. And they do take such an interest in refinement
and culture. So—in fact, so very unique."

Carol was disappointed—by nothing very tangible. She said politely, "I'll
think them all over. I must have a while to look around first."

Miss Sherwin darted to her, smoothed her hair, peered at her. "Oh, my
dear, don't you suppose I know? These first tender days of marriage—they're
sacred to me. Home, and children that need you, and depend on you to keep
them alive, and turn to you with their wrinkly little smiles. And the hearth
and——" She hid her face from Carol as she made an activity of patting the
cushion of her chair, but she went on with her former briskness:

"I mean, you must help us when you're ready. . . . I'm afraid you'll think
I'm conservative. I am! So much to conserve. All this treasure of American
ideals. Sturdiness and democracy and opportunity. Maybe not at Palm Beach.
But, thank heaven, we're free from such social distinctions in Gopher Prairie.
I have only one good quality—overwhelming belief in the brains and hearts
of our nation, our state, our town. It's so strong that sometimes I do have
a tiny effect on the haughty ten-thousandaires. I shake 'em up and make 'em
believe in ideals—yes, in themselves. But I get into a rut of teaching. I need
young critical things like you to punch me up. Tell me, what are you
reading?"

"I've been re-reading 'The Damnation of Theron Ware.' Do you know it?"

"Yes. It was clever. But hard. Man wanted to tear down, not build up.
Cynical. Oh, I do hope I'm not a sentimentalist. But I can't see any use in
this high-art stuff that doesn't encourage us day-laborers to plod on."

Ensued a fifteen-minute argument about the oldest topic in the world:
It's art but is it pretty? Carol tried to be eloquent regarding honesty of
observation. Miss Sherwin stood out for sweetness and a cautious use of the
uncomfortable properties of light. At the end Carol cried:

"I don't care how much we disagree. It's a relief to have somebody talk
something besides crops. Let's make Gopher Prairie rock to its foundations:
let's have afternoon tea instead of afternoon coffee."

The delighted Bea helped her bring out the ancestral folding sewing-table,
whose yellow and black top was scarred with dotted lines from a dressmaker's
tracing-wheel, and to set it with an embroidered lunch-cloth, and the mauve-
glazed Japanese tea-set which she had brought from St. Paul. Miss Sherwin

confided her latest scheme—moral motion pictures for country districts, with light from a portable dynamo hitched to a Ford engine. Bea was twice called to fill the hot-water pitcher and to make cinnamon toast.

When Kennicott came home at five he tried to be courtly, as befits the husband of one who has afternoon tea. Carol suggested that Miss Sherwin stay for supper, and that Kennicott invite Guy Pollock, the much-praised lawyer, the poetic bachelor.

Yes, Pollock could come. Yes, he was over the grippe which had prevented his going to Sam Clark's party.

Carol regretted her impulse. The man would be an opinionated politician, heavily jocular about The Bride. But at the entrance of Guy Pollock she discovered a personality. Pollock was a man of perhaps thirty-eight, slender, still, deferential. His voice was low. "It was very good of you to want me," he said, and he offered no humorous remarks, and did not ask her if she didn't think Gopher Prairie was "the livest little burg in the state."

She fancied that his even grayness might reveal a thousand tints of lavender and blue and silver.

At supper he hinted his love for Sir Thomas Browne, Thoreau, Agnes Repplier, Arthur Symons, Claude Washburn, Charles Flandrau. He presented his idols diffidently, but he expanded in Carol's bookishness, in Miss Sherwin's voluminous praise, in Kennicott's tolerance of any one who amused his wife.

Carol wondered why Guy Pollock went on digging at routine law-cases; why he remained in Gopher Prairie. She had no one whom she could ask. Neither Kennicott nor Vida Sherwin would understand that there might be reasons why a Pollock should not remain in Gopher Prairie. She enjoyed the faint mystery. She felt triumphant and rather literary. She already had a Group. It would be only a while now before she provided the town with fanlights and a knowledge of Galsworthy. She was doing things! As she served the emergency dessert of cocoanut and sliced oranges, she cried to Pollock, "Don't you think we ought to get up a dramatic club?"

# 6

When the first dubious November snow had filtered down, shading with white the bare clods in the plowed fields, when the first small fire had been started in the furnace, which is the shrine of a Gopher Prairie home, Carol began to make the house her own. She dismissed the parlor furniture—the golden oak table with brass knobs, the moldy brocade chairs, the picture of "The Doctor." She went to Minneapolis, to scamper through department stores and small Tenth Street shops devoted to ceramics and high thought.

She had to ship her treasures, but she wanted to bring them back in her arms.

Carpenters had torn out the partition between front parlor and back parlor, thrown it into a long room on which she lavished yellow and deep blue; a Japanese obi with an intricacy of gold thread on stiff ultramarine tissue, which she hung as a panel against the maize wall; a couch with pillows of sapphire velvet and gold bands; chairs which, in Gopher Prairie, seemed flippant. She hid the sacred family phonograph in the dining-room, and replaced its stand with a square cabinet on which was a squat blue jar between yellow candles.

Kennicott decided against a fireplace. "We'll have a new house in a couple of years, anyway."

She decorated only one room. The rest, Kennicott hinted, she'd better leave till he "made a ten-strike."

The brown cube of a house stirred and awakened; it seemed to be in motion; it welcomed her back from shopping; it lost its mildewed repression.

The supreme verdict was Kennicott's "Well, by golly, I was afraid the new junk wouldn't be so comfortable, but I must say this divan, or whatever you call it, is a lot better than that bumpy old sofa we had, and when I look around—— Well, it's worth all it cost, I guess."

Every one in town took an interest in the refurnishing. The carpenters and painters who did not actually assist crossed the lawn to peer through the windows and exclaim, "Fine! Looks swell!" Dave Dyer at the drug store, Harry Haydock and Raymie Wutherspoon at the Bon Ton, repeated daily, "How's the good work coming? I hear the house is getting to be real classy."

Even Mrs. Bogart.

Mrs. Bogart lived across the alley from the rear of Carol's house. She was a widow, and a Prominent Baptist, and a Good Influence. She had so painfully reared three sons to be Christian gentlemen that one of them had become an Omaha bartender, one a professor of Greek, and one, Cyrus N. Bogart, a boy of fourteen who was still at home, the most brazen member of the toughest gang in Boytown.

Mrs. Bogart was not the acid type of Good Influence. She was the soft, damp, fat, sighing, indigestive, clinging, melancholy, depressingly hopeful kind. There are in every large chicken-yard a number of old and indignant hens who resemble Mrs. Bogart, and when they are served at Sunday noon dinner, as fricasseed chicken with thick dumplings, they keep up the resemblance.

Carol had noted that Mrs. Bogart from her side window kept an eye upon the house. The Kennicotts and Mrs. Bogart did not move in the same sets—which meant precisely the same in Gopher Prairie as it did on Fifth Avenue or in Mayfair. But the good widow came calling.

She wheezed in, sighed, gave Carol a pulpy hand, sighed, glanced sharply at the revelation of ankles as Carol crossed her legs, sighed, inspected the new blue chairs, smiled with a coy sighing sound, and gave voice:

"I've wanted to call on you so long, dearie, you know we're neighbors,

but I thought I'd wait till you got settled, you must run in and see me,
how much did that big chair cost?"

"Seventy-seven dollars!"

"Sev—— Sakes alive! Well, I suppose it's all right for them that can afford
it, though I do sometimes think—— Of course as our pastor said once, at
Baptist Church—— By the way, we haven't seen you there yet, and of course
your husband was raised up a Baptist, and I do hope he won't drift away
from the fold, of course we all know there isn't anything, not cleverness or
gifts of gold or anything, that can make up for humility and the inward grace
and they can say what they want to about the P. E. church, but of course
there's no church that has more history or has stayed by the true principles
of Christianity better than the Baptist Church and—— In what church were
you raised, Mrs. Kennicott?"

"W-why, I went to Congregational, as a girl in Mankato, but my college
was Universalist."

"Well—— But of course as the Bible says, is it the Bible, at least I know
I have heard it in church and everybody admits it, it's proper for the little
bride to take her husband's vessel of faith, so we all hope we shall see you
at the Baptist Church and—— As I was saying, of course I agree with Reverend
Zitterel in thinking that the great trouble with this nation today is lack of
spiritual faith—so few going to church, and people automobiling on Sunday
and heaven knows what all. But still I do think that one trouble is this
terrible waste of money, people feeling that they've got to have bath-tubs
and telephones in their houses—— I heard you were selling the old furniture
cheap."

"Yes!"

"Well—of course you know your own mind, but I can't help thinking, when
Will's ma was down here keeping house for him—*she* used to run in to *see*
me, real *often!*—it was good enough furniture for her. But there, there, I
mustn't croak, I just wanted to let you know that when you find you can't
depend on a lot of these gadding young folks like the Haydocks and the
Dyers—and heaven only knows how much money Juanita Haydock blows in
in a year—why then you may be glad to know that slow old Aunty Bogart is
always right there, and heaven knows——" A portentous sigh. "—I *hope* you
and your husband won't have any of the troubles, with sickness and quarreling and wasting money and all that so many of these young couples do have
and—— But I must be running along now, dearie. It's been such a pleasure
and—— Just run in and see me any time. I hope Will is well? I thought he
looked a wee mite peaked."

It was twenty minutes later when Mrs. Bogart finally oozed out of the
front door. Carol ran back into the living-room and jerked open the windows.
"That woman has left damp finger-prints in the air," she said.

II

Carol was extravagant, but at least she did not try to clear herself of blame by going about whimpering, "I know I'm terribly extravagant but I don't seem to be able to help it."

Kennicott had never thought of giving her an allowance. His mother had never had one! As a wage-earning spinster Carol had asserted to her fellow librarians that when she was married, she was going to have an allowance and be business-like and modern. But it was too much trouble to explain to Kennicott's kindly stubbornness that she was a practical housekeeper as well as a flighty playmate. She bought a budget-plan account book and made her budgets as exact as budgets are likely to be when they lack budgets.

For the first month it was a honeymoon jest to beg prettily, to confess, "I haven't a cent in the house, dear," and to be told, "You're an extravagant little rabbit." But the budget book made her realize how inexact were her finances. She became self-conscious; occasionally she was indignant that she should always have to petition him for the money with which to buy his food. She caught herself criticizing his belief that, since his joke about trying to keep her out of the poorhouse had once been accepted as admirable humor, it should continue to be his daily *bon mot*. It was a nuisance to have to run down the street after him because she had forgotten to ask him for money at breakfast.

But she couldn't "hurt his feelings," she reflected. He liked the lordliness of giving largess.

She tried to reduce the frequency of begging by opening accounts and having the bills sent to him. She had found that staple groceries, sugar, flour, could be most cheaply purchased at Axel Egge's rustic general store. She said sweetly to Axel:

"I think I'd better open a charge account here."

"I don't do no business except for cash," grunted Axel.

She flared, "Do you know who I am?"

"Yuh, sure, I know. The doc is good for it. But that's yoost a rule I made. I make low prices. I do business for cash."

She stared at his red impassive face, and her fingers had the undignified desire to slap him, but her reason agreed with him. "You're quite right. You shouldn't break your rule for me."

Her rage had not been lost. It had been transferred to her husband. She wanted ten pounds of sugar in a hurry, but she had no money. She ran up the stairs to Kennicott's office. On the door was a sign advertising a headache cure and stating, "The doctor is out, back at——" Naturally, the blank space was not filled out. She stamped her foot. She ran down to the drug store— the doctor's club.

As she entered she heard Mrs. Dyer demanding, "Dave, I've got to have some money."

Carol saw that her husband was there, and two other men, all listening in amusement.

Dave Dyer snapped, "How much do you want? Dollar be enough?"

"No, it won't! I've got to get some underclothes for the kids."

"Why, good Lord, they got enough now to fill the closet so I couldn't find my hunting boots, last time I wanted them."

"I don't care. They're all in rags. You got to give me ten dollars——"

Carol perceived that Mrs. Dyer was accustomed to this indignity. She perceived that the men, particularly Dave, regarded it as an excellent jest. She waited—she knew what would come—it did. Dave yelped, "Where's that ten dollars I gave you last year?" and he looked to the other men to laugh. They laughed.

Cold and still, Carol walked up to Kennicott and commanded, "I want to see you upstairs."

"Why—something the matter?"

"Yes!"

He clumped after her, up the stairs, into his barren office. Before he could get out a query she stated:

"Yesterday, in front of a saloon, I heard a German farmwife beg her husband for a quarter, to get a toy for the baby—and he refused. Just now I've heard Mrs. Dyer going through the same humiliation. And I—I'm in the same position! I have to beg you for money. Daily! I have just been informed that I couldn't have any sugar because I hadn't the money to pay for it!"

"Who said that? By God, I'll kill any——"

"Tut. It wasn't his fault. It was yours. And mine. I now humbly beg you to give me the money with which to buy meals for you to eat. And hereafter to remember it. The next time, I sha'n't beg. I shall simply starve. Do you understand? I can't go on being a slave——"

Her defiance, her enjoyment of the rôle, ran out. She was sobbing against his overcoat, "How can you shame me so?" and he was blubbering, "Dog-gone it, I meant to give you some, and I forgot it. I swear I won't again. By golly I won't!"

He pressed fifty dollars upon her, and after that he remembered to give her money regularly. . . . sometimes.

Daily she determined, "But I must have a stated amount—be business-like. System. I must do something about it." And daily she didn't do anything about it.

III

Mrs. Bogart had, by the simpering viciousness of her comments on the new furniture, stirred Carol to economy. She spoke judiciously to Bea about left-overs. She read the cookbook again and, like a child with a picture-book, she studied the diagram of the beef which gallantly continues to browse though it is divided into cuts.

But she was a deliberate and joyous spendthrift in her preparations for her first party, the housewarming. She made lists on every envelope and laundry-slip in her desk. She sent orders to Minneapolis "fancy grocers." She pinned patterns and sewed. She was irritated when Kennicott was jocular about "these frightful big doings that are going on." She regarded the affair as an attack on Gopher Prairie's timidity in pleasure. "I'll make 'em lively, if nothing else. I'll make 'em stop regarding parties as committee-meetings."

Kennicott usually considered himself the master of the house. At his desire, she went hunting, which was his symbol of happiness, and she ordered porridge for breakfast, which was his symbol of morality. But when he came home on the afternoon before the housewarming he found himself a slave, an intruder, a blunderer. Carol wailed, "Fix the furnace so you won't have to touch it after supper. And for heaven's sake take that horrible old door-mat off the porch. And put on your nice brown and white shirt. Why did you come home so late? Would you mind hurrying? Here it is almost suppertime, and those fiends are just as likely as not to come at seven instead of eight. *Please* hurry!"

She was as unreasonable as an amateur leading woman on a first night, and he was reduced to humility. When she came down to supper, when she stood in the doorway, he gasped. She was in a silver sheath, the calyx of a lily, her piled hair like black glass; she had the fragility and costliness of a Viennese goblet; and her eyes were intense. He was stirred to rise from the table and to hold the chair for her; and all through supper he ate his bread dry because he felt that she would think him common if he said "Will you hand me the butter?"

IV

She had reached the calmness of not caring whether her guests liked the party or not, and a state of satisfied suspense in regard to Bea's technique in serving, before Kennicott cried from the bay-window in the living-room, "Here comes somebody!" and Mr. and Mrs. Luke Dawson faltered in, at a quarter to eight. Then in a shy avalanche arrived the entire aristocracy of Gopher Prairie: all persons engaged in a profession, or earning more than twenty-five hundred dollars a year, or possessed of grandparents born in America.

Even while they were removing their overshoes they were peeping at the new decorations. Carol saw Dave Dyer secretively turn over the gold pillows to find a price-tag, and heard Mr. Julius Flickerbaugh, the attorney, gasp, "Well, I'll be switched," as he viewed the vermilion print hanging against the Japanese obi. She was amused. But her high spirits slackened as she beheld them form in dress parade, in a long, silent, uneasy circle clear round the living-room. She felt that she had been magically whisked back to her first party, at Sam Clark's.

"Have I got to lift them, like so many pigs of iron? I don't know that I can make them happy, but I'll make them hectic."

A silver flame in the darkling circle, she whirled around, drew them with her smile, and sang, "I want my party to be noisy and undignified! This is the christening of my house, and I want you to help me have a bad influence on it, so that it will be a giddy house. For me, won't you all join in an old-fashioned square dance? And Mr. Dyer will call."

She had a record on the phonograph; Dave Dyer was capering in the center of the floor, loose-jointed, lean, small, rusty-headed, pointed of nose, clapping his hands and shouting, "Swing y' pardners—alamun lef!"

Even the millionaire Dawsons and Ezra Stowbody and "Professor" George Edwin Mott danced, looking only slightly foolish; and by rushing about the room and being coy and coaxing to all persons over forty-five, Carol got them into a waltz and a Virginia Reel. But when she left them to disenjoy themselves in their own way Harry Haydock put a one-step record on the phonograph, the younger people took the floor, and all the elders sneaked back to their chairs, with crystallized smiles which meant, "Don't believe I'll try this one myself, but I do enjoy watching the youngsters dance."

Half of them were silent; half resumed the discussions of that afternoon in the store. Ezra Stowbody hunted for something to say, hid a yawn, and offered to Lyman Cass, the owner of the flour-mill, "How d' you folks like the new furnace, Lym? Huh? So."

"Oh, let them alone. Don't pester them. They must like it, or they wouldn't do it," Carol warned herself. But they gazed at her so expectantly when she flickered past that she was reconvinced that in their debauches of respectability they had lost the power of play as well as the power of impersonal thought. Even the dancers were gradually crushed by the invisible force of fifty perfectly pure and well-behaved and negative minds; and they sat down, two by two. In twenty minutes the party was again elevated to the decorum of a prayer-meeting.

"We're going to do something exciting," Carol exclaimed to her new confidante, Vida Sherwin. She saw that in the growing quiet her voice had carried across the room. Nat Hicks, Ella Stowbody, and Dave Dyer were abstracted, fingers and lips slightly moving. She knew with a cold certainty that Dave was rehearsing his "stunt" about the Norwegian catching the hen, Ella running over the first lines of "An Old Sweetheart of Mine," and Nat thinking of his popular parody on Mark Antony's oration.

"But I will not have anybody use the word 'stunt' in my house," she whispered to Miss Sherwin.

"That's good. I tell you: why not have Raymond Wutherspoon sing?"

"Raymie? Why, my dear, he's the most sentimental yearner in town!"

"See here, child! Your opinions on house-decorating are sound, but your opinions of people are rotten! Raymie does wag his tail. But the poor dear—— Longing for what he calls 'self-expression' and no training in anything except selling shoes. But he can sing. And some day when he gets away from Harry Haydock's patronage and ridicule, he'll do something fine."

Carol apologized for her superciliousness. She urged Raymie, and warned the planners of "stunts," "We all want you to sing, Mr. Wutherspoon. You're the only famous actor I'm going to let appear on the stage tonight."

While Raymie blushed and admitted, "Oh, they don't want to hear me," he was clearing his throat, pulling his clean handkerchief farther out of his breast pocket, and thrusting his fingers between the buttons of his vest.

In her affection for Raymie's defender, in her desire to "discover artistic talent," Carol prepared to be delighted by the recital.

Raymie sang "Fly as a Bird," "Thou Art My Dove," and "When the Little Swallow Leaves Its Tiny Nest," all in a reasonably bad offertory tenor.

Carol was shuddering with the vicarious shame which sensitive people feel when they listen to an "elocutionist" being humorous, or to a precocious child publicly doing badly what no child should do at all. She wanted to laugh at the gratified importance in Raymie's half-shut eyes; she wanted to weep over the meek ambitiousness which clouded like an aura his pale face, flap ears, and sandy pompadour. She tried to look admiring, for the benefit of Miss Sherwin, that trusting admirer of all that was or conceivably could be the good, the true, and the beautiful.

At the end of the third ornithological lyric Miss Sherwin roused from her attitude of inspired vision and breathed to Carol, "My! That was sweet! Of course Raymond hasn't an unusually good voice, but don't you think he puts such a lot of feeling into it?"

Carol lied blackly and magnificently, but without originality: "Oh yes, I do think he has so much *feeling!*"

She saw that after the strain of listening in a cultured manner the audience had collapsed; had given up their last hope of being amused. She cried, "Now we're going to play an idiotic game which I learned in Chicago. You will have to take off your shoes, for a starter! After that you will probably break your knees and shoulder-blades."

Much attention and incredulity. A few eyebrows indicating a verdict that Doc Kennicott's bride was noisy and improper.

"I shall choose the most vicious, like Juanita Haydock and myself, as the shepherds. The rest of you are wolves. Your shoes are the sheep. The wolves go out into the hall. The shepherds scatter the sheep through this room, then turn off all the lights, and the wolves crawl in from the hall and in the darkness they try to get the shoes away from the shepherds—who are permitted to do anything except bite and use blackjacks. The wolves chuck the captured shoes out into the hall. No one excused! Come on! Shoes off!"

Every one looked at every one else and waited for every one else to begin.

Carol kicked off her silver slippers, and ignored the universal glance at her arches. The embarrassed but loyal Vida Sherwin unbuttoned her high black shoes. Ezra Stowbody cackled, "Well, you're a terror to old folks. You're like the gals I used to go horseback-riding with, back in the sixties. Ain't much accustomed to attending parties barefoot, but here goes!" With a whoop and a gallant jerk Ezra snatched off his elastic-sided Congress shoes.

The others giggled and followed.

When the sheep had been penned up, in the darkness the timorous wolves crept into the living-room, squealing, halting, thrown out of their habit of stolidity by the strangeness of advancing through nothingness toward a waiting foe, a mysterious foe which expanded and grew more menacing. The wolves peered to make out landmarks, they touched gliding arms which did not seem to be attached to a body, they quivered with a rapture of fear. Reality had vanished. A yelping squabble suddenly rose, then Juanita Haydock's high titter, and Guy Pollock's astonished, "Ouch! Quit! You're scalping me!"

Mrs. Luke Dawson galloped backward on stiff hands and knees into the safety of the lighted hallway, moaning, "I declare, I nev' was so upset in my life!" But the propriety was shaken out of her, and she delightedly continued to ejaculate "Nev' in my *life*" as she saw the living-room door opened by invisible hands and shoes hurling through it, as she heard from the darkness beyond the door a squawling, a bumping, a resolute "Here's a lot of shoes. Come on, you wolves. Ow! Y' would, would you!"

When Carol abruptly turned on the lights in the embattled living-room, half of the company were sitting back against the walls, where they had craftily remained throughout the engagement, but in the middle of the floor Kennicott was wrestling with Harry Haydock—their collars torn off, their hair in their eyes; and the owlish Mr. Julius Flickerbaugh was retreating from Juanita Haydock, and gulping with unaccustomed laughter. Guy Pollock's discreet brown scarf hung down his back. Young Rita Simons's net blouse had lost two buttons, and betrayed more of her delicious plump shoulder than was regarded as pure in Gopher Prairie. Whether by shock, disgust, joy of combat, or physical activity, all the party were freed from their years of social decorum. George Edwin Mott giggled; Luke Dawson twisted his beard; Mrs. Clark insisted, "I did too, Sam—I got a shoe—I never knew I could fight so terrible!"

Carol was certain that she was a great reformer.

She mercifully had combs, mirrors, brushes, needle and thread ready. She permitted them to restore the divine decency of buttons.

The grinning Bea brought down-stairs a pile of soft thick sheets of paper with designs of lotos blossoms, dragons, apes, in cobalt and crimson and gray, and patterns of purple birds flying among sea-green trees in the valleys of Nowhere.

"These," Carol announced, "are real Chinese masquerade costumes. I got them from an importing shop in Minneapolis. You are to put them on over your clothes, and please forget that you are Minnesotans, and turn into mandarins and coolies and—and samurai (isn't it?), and anything else you can think of."

While they were shyly rustling the paper costumes she disappeared. Ten minutes after she gazed down from the stairs upon grotesquely ruddy Yankee heads above Oriental robes, and cried to them, "The Princess Winky Poo salutes her court!"

As they looked up she caught their suspense of admiration. They saw an airy figure in trousers and coat of green brocade edged with gold; a high gold collar under a proud chin; black hair pierced with jade pins; a languid peacock fan in an outstretched hand; eyes uplifted to a vision of pagoda towers. When she dropped her pose and smiled down she discovered Kenni-

cott apoplectic with domestic pride—and gray Guy Pollock staring beseechingly. For a second she saw nothing in all the pink and brown mass of their
faces save the hunger of the two men.

She shook off the spell and ran down. "We're going to have a real Chinese
concert. Messrs. Pollock, Kennicott, and, well, Stowbody are drummers; the
rest of us sing and play the fife."

The fifes were combs with tissue paper; the drums were tabourets and the
sewing-table. Loren Wheeler, editor of the *Dauntless*, led the orchestra, with
a ruler and a totally inaccurate sense of rhythm. The music was a reminiscence of tom-toms heard at circus fortune-telling tents or at the Minnesota
State Fair, but the whole company pounded and puffed and whined in a
sing-song, and looked rapturous.

Before they were quite tired of the concert Carol led them in a dancing
procession to the dining-room, to blue bowls of chow mein, with Lichee nuts
and ginger preserved in syrup.

None of them save that city-rounder Harry Haydock had heard of any
Chinese dish except chop sooey. With agreeable doubt they ventured through
the bamboo shoots into the golden fried noodles of the chow mein; and
Dave Dyer did a not very humorous Chinese dance with Nat Hicks; and
there was hubbub and contentment.

Carol relaxed, and found that she was shockingly tired. She had carried
them on her thin shoulders. She could not keep it up. She longed for her
father, that artist at creating hysterical parties. She thought of smoking a
cigarette, to shock them, and dismissed the obscene thought before it was
quite formed. She wondered whether they could for five minutes be coaxed
to talk about something besides the winter top of Knute Stamquist's Ford,
and what Al Tingley had said about his mother-in-law. She sighed, "Oh, let
'em alone. I've done enough." She crossed her trousered legs, and snuggled
luxuriously above her saucer of ginger; she caught Pollock's congratulatory
still smile, and thought well of herself for having thrown a rose light on
the pallid lawyer; repented the heretical supposition that any male save her
husband existed; jumped up to find Kennicott and whisper, "Happy, my
lord? . . . No, it didn't cost much!"

"Best party this town ever saw. Only—— Don't cross your legs in that
costume. Shows your knees too plain."

She was vexed. She resented his clumsiness. She returned to Guy Pollock
and talked of Chinese religions—not that she knew anything whatever about
Chinese religions, but he had read a book on the subject as, on lonely evenings in his office, he had read at least one book on every subject in the
world. Guy's thin maturity was changing in her vision to flushed youth and
they were roaming an island in the yellow sea of chatter when she realized
that the guests were beginning that cough which indicated, in the universal
instinctive language, that they desired to go home and go to bed.

While they asserted that it had been "the nicest party they'd ever seen—
my! so clever and original," she smiled tremendously, shook hands, and cried
many suitable things regarding children, and being sure to wrap up warmly,

and Raymie's singing and Juanita Haydock's prowess at games. Then she turned wearily to Kennicott in a house filled with quiet and crumbs and shreds of Chinese costumes.

He was gurgling, "I tell you, Carrie, you certainly are a wonder, and guess you're right about waking folks up. Now you've showed 'em how, they won't go on having the same old kind of parties and stunts and everything. Here! Don't touch a thing! Done enough. Pop up to bed, and I'll clear up."

His wise surgeon's-hands stroked her shoulder, and her irritation at his clumsiness was lost in his strength.

## V

From the *Weekly Dauntless*:

One of the most delightful social events of recent months was held Wednesday evening in the housewarming of Dr. and Mrs. Kennicott, who have completely redecorated their charming home on Poplar Street, and is now extremely nifty in modern color scheme. The doctor and his bride were at home to their numerous friends and a number of novelties in diversions were held, including a Chinese orchestra in original and genuine Oriental costumes, of which Ye Editor was leader. Dainty refreshments were served in true Oriental style, and one and all voted a delightful time.

## VI

The week after, the Chet Dashaways gave a party. The circle of mourners kept its place all evening, and Dave Dyer did the "stunt" of the Norwegian and the hen.

# 7

Gopher Prairie was digging in for the winter. Through late November and all December it snowed daily; the thermometer was at zero and might drop to twenty below, or thirty. Winter is not a season in the North Middlewest; it is an industry. Storm sheds were erected at every door. In every block the householders, Sam Clark, the wealthy Mr. Dawson, all save asthmatic Ezra Stowbody who extravagantly hired a boy, were seen perilously staggering up ladders, carrying storm windows and screwing them to second-story jambs. While Kennicott put up his windows Carol danced inside the bedrooms and begged him not to swallow the screws, which he held in his mouth like an extraordinary set of external false teeth.

The universal sign of winter was the town handyman—Miles Bjornstam, a tall, thick, red-mustached bachelor, opinionated atheist, general-store arguer, cynical Santa Claus. Children loved him, and he sneaked away from work to tell them improbable stories of sea-faring and horse-trading and bears. The children's parents either laughed at him or hated him. He was the one democrat in town. He called both Lyman Cass the miller and the Finn homesteader from Lost Lake by their first names. He was known as "The Red Swede," and considered slightly insane.

Bjornstam could do anything with his hands—solder a pan, weld an automobile spring, soothe a frightened filly, tinker a clock, carve a Gloucester schooner which magically went into a bottle. Now, for a week, he was commissioner general of Gopher Prairie. He was the only person besides the repairman at Sam Clark's who understood plumbing. Everybody begged him to look over the furnace and the water-pipes. He rushed from house to house till after bedtime—ten o'clock. Icicles from burst water-pipes hung along the skirt of his brown dogskin overcoat; his plush cap, which he never took off in the house, was a pulp of ice and coal-dust; his red hands were cracked to rawness; he chewed the stub of a cigar.

But he was courtly to Carol. He stooped to examine the furnace flues; he straightened, glanced down at her, and hemmed, "Got to fix your furnace, no matter what else I do."

The poorer houses of Gopher Prairie, where the services of Miles Bjornstam were a luxury—which included the shanty of Miles Bjornstam—were banked to the lower windows with earth and manure. Along the railroad the sections of snow fence, which had been stacked all summer in romantic wooden tents occupied by roving small boys, were set up to prevent drifts from covering the track.

The farmers came into town in home-made sleighs, with bedquilts and hay piled in the rough boxes.

Fur coats, fur caps, fur mittens, overshoes buckling almost to the knees, gray knitted scarfs ten feet long, thick woolen socks, canvas jackets lined with fluffy yellow wool like the plumage of ducklings, moccasins, red flannel wristlets for the blazing chapped wrists of boys—these protections against winter were busily dug out of moth-ball-sprinkled drawers and tar-bags in closets, and all over town small boys were squealing, "Oh, there's my mittens!" or "Look at my shoe-packs!" There is so sharp a division between the panting summer and the stinging winter of the Northern plains that they rediscovered with surprise and a feeling of heroism this armor of an Arctic explorer.

Winter garments surpassed even personal gossip as the topic at parties. It was good form to ask, "Put on your heavies yet?" There were as many distinctions in wraps as in motor cars. The lesser sort appeared in yellow and black dogskin coats, but Kennicott was lordly in a long raccoon ulster and a new seal cap. When the snow was too deep for his motor he went off on country calls in a shiny, floral, steel-tipped cutter, only his ruddy nose and his cigar emerging from the fur.

Carol herself stirred Main Street by a loose coat of nutria. Her finger-tips loved the silken fur.

Her liveliest activity now was organizing outdoor sports in the motor-paralyzed town.

The automobile and bridge-whist had not only made more evident the social divisions in Gopher Prairie but they had also enfeebled the love of activity. It was so rich-looking to sit and drive—and so easy. Skiing and sliding were "stupid" and "old-fashioned." In fact, the village longed for the elegance of city recreations almost as much as the cities longed for village sports; and Gopher Prairie took as much pride in neglecting coasting as St. Paul—or New York—in going coasting. Carol did inspire a successful skating-party in mid-November. Plover Lake glistened in clear sweeps of gray-green ice, ringing to the skates. On shore the ice-tipped reeds clattered in the wind, and oak twigs with stubborn last leaves hung against a milky sky. Harry Haydock did figure-eights, and Carol was certain that she had found the perfect life. But when snow had ended the skating and she tried to get up a moonlight sliding party, the matrons hesitated to stir away from their radiators and their daily bridge-whist imitations of the city. She had to nag them. They scooted down a long hill on a bob-sled, they upset and got snow down their necks, they shrieked that they would do it again immediately—and they did not do it again at all.

She badgered another group into going skiing. They shouted and threw snowballs, and informed her that it was *such* fun, and they'd have another skiing expedition right away, and they jollily returned home and never thereafter left their manuals of bridge.

Carol was discouraged. She was grateful when Kennicott invited her to go rabbit-hunting in the woods. She waded down stilly cloisters between burnt stump and icy oak, through drifts marked with a million hieroglyphics of rabbit and mouse and bird. She squealed as he leaped on a pile of brush and fired at the rabbit which ran out. He belonged there, masculine in reefer and sweater and high-laced boots. That night she ate prodigiously of steak and fried potatoes; she produced electric sparks by touching his ear with her finger-tip; she slept twelve hours; and awoke to think how glorious was this brave land.

She rose to a radiance of sun on snow. Snug in her furs she trotted up-town. Frosted shingles smoked against a sky colored like flax-blossoms, sleigh-bells clinked, shouts of greeting were loud in the thin bright air, and everywhere was a rhythmic sound of wood-sawing. It was Saturday, and the neighbors' sons were getting up the winter fuel. Behind walls of corded wood in back yards their sawbucks stood in depressions scattered with canary-yellow flakes of sawdust. The frames of their buck-saws were cherry-red, the blades blued steel, and the fresh cut ends of the sticks—poplar, maple, ironwood, birch—were marked with engraved rings of growth. The boys wore shoe-packs, blue flannel shirts with enormous pearl buttons, and mackinaws of crimson, lemon yellow, and foxy brown.

Carol cried "Fine day!" to the boys; she came in a glow to Howland & Gould's grocery, her collar white with frost from her breath; she bought a can of tomatoes as though it were Orient fruit; and returned home planning to surprise Kennicott with an omelet creole for dinner.

So brilliant was the snow-glare that when she entered the house she saw the door-knobs, the newspaper on the table, every white surface as dazzling mauve, and her head was dizzy in the pyrotechnic dimness. When her eyes had recovered she felt expanded, drunk with health, mistress of life. The world was so luminous that she sat down at her rickety little desk in the living-room to make a poem. (She got no farther than "The sky is bright, the sun is warm, there ne'er will be another storm.")

In the mid-afternoon of this same day Kennicott was called into the country. It was Bea's evening out—her evening for the Lutheran Dance. Carol was alone from three till midnight. She wearied of reading pure love stories in the magazines and sat by a radiator, beginning to brood.

Thus she chanced to discover that she had nothing to do.

## II

She had, she meditated, passed through the novelty of seeing the town and meeting people, of skating and sliding and hunting. Bea was competent; there was no household labor except sewing and darning and gossipy assistance to Bea in bed-making. She couldn't satisfy her ingenuity in planning meals. At Dahl & Oleson's Meat Market you didn't give orders—you wofully inquired whether there was anything today besides steak and pork and ham. The cuts of beef were not cuts. They were hacks. Lamb chops were as exotic as sharks' fins. The meat-dealers shipped their best to the city, with its higher prices.

In all the shops there was the same lack of choice. She could not find a glass-headed picture-nail in town; she did not hunt for the sort of veiling she wanted—she took what she could get; and only at Howland & Gould's was there such a luxury as canned asparagus. Routine care was all she could devote to the house. Only by such fussing as the Widow Bogart's could she make it fill her time.

She could not have outside employment. To the village doctor's wife it was taboo.

She was a woman with a working brain and no work.

There were only three things which she could do: Have children; start her career of reforming; or become so definitely a part of the town that she would be fulfilled by the activities of church and study-club and bridge-parties.

Children, yes, she wanted them, but—— She was not quite ready. She had been embarrassed by Kennicott's frankness, but she agreed with him that in the insane condition of civilization, which made the rearing of citizens more costly and perilous than any other crime, it was inadvisable to have children till he had made more money. She was sorry—— Perhaps he had made all the mystery of love a mechanical cautiousness but—— She fled from the thought with a dubious, "Some day."

Her "reforms," her impulses toward beauty in raw Main Street, they had become indistinct. But she would set them going now. She would! She swore it with soft fist beating the edges of the radiator. And at the end of all her vows she had no notion as to when and where the crusade was to begin.

Become an authentic part of the town? She began to think with unpleasant lucidity. She reflected that she did not know whether the people liked her. She had gone to the women at afternoon-coffees, to the merchants in their stores, with so many outpouring comments and whimsies that she hadn't given them a chance to betray their opinions of her. The men smiled—but did they like her? She was lively among the women—but was she one of them? She could not recall many times when she had been admitted to the whispering of scandal which is the secret chamber of Gopher Prairie conversation.

She was poisoned with doubt, as she drooped up to bed.

Next day, through her shopping, her mind sat back and observed. Dave Dyer and Sam Clark were as cordial as she had been fancying; but wasn't there an impersonal abruptness in the "H' are yuh?" of Chet Dashaway? Howland the grocer was curt. Was that merely his usual manner?

"It's infuriating to have to pay attention to what people think. In St. Paul I didn't care. But here I'm spied on. They're watching me. I mustn't let it make me self-conscious," she coaxed herself—overstimulated by the drug of thought, and offensively on the defensive.

### III

A thaw which stripped the snow from the sidewalks; a ringing iron night when the lakes could be heard booming; a clear roistering morning. In tam o'shanter and tweed skirt Carol felt herself a college junior going out to play hockey. She wanted to whoop, her legs ached to run. On the way home from shopping she yielded, as a pup would have yielded. She galloped down a block and as she jumped from a curb across a welter of slush, she gave a student "Yippee!"

She saw that in a window three old women were gasping. Their triple glare was paralyzing. Across the street, at another window, the curtain had secretively moved. She stopped, walked on sedately, changed from the girl Carol into Mrs. Dr. Kennicott.

She never again felt quite young enough and defiant enough and free enough to run and halloo in the public streets; and it was as a Nice Married Woman that she attended the next weekly bridge of the Jolly Seventeen.

### IV

The Jolly Seventeen (the membership of which ranged from fourteen to twenty-six) was the social cornice of Gopher Prairie. It was the country club, the diplomatic set, the St. Cecilia, the Ritz oval room, the Club de Vingt. To belong to it was to be "in." Though its membership partly coincided with that of the Thanatopsis study club, the Jolly Seventeen as a separate entity guffawed at the Thanatopsis, and considered it middle-class and even "highbrow."

Most of the Jolly Seventeen were young married women, with their husbands as associate members. Once a week they had a women's afternoon-bridge; once a month the husbands joined them for supper and evening-bridge; twice a year they had dances at I. O. O. F. Hall. Then the town exploded. Only at the annual balls of the Firemen and of the Eastern Star was there such prodigality of chiffon scarfs and tangoing and heart-burnings, and these rival institutions were not select—hired girls attended the Firemen's Ball, with section-hands and laborers. Ella Stowbody had once gone to a Jolly Seventeen Soirée in the village hack, hitherto confined to chief mourners at funerals; and Harry Haydock and Dr. Terry Gould always appeared in the town's only specimens of evening clothes.

The afternoon-bridge of the Jolly Seventeen which followed Carol's lonely doubting was held at Juanita Haydock's new concrete bungalow, with its door of polished oak and beveled plate-glass, jar of ferns in the plastered hall, and in the living-room, a fumed oak Morris chair, sixteen color-prints, and a square varnished table with a mat made of cigar-ribbons on which was one Illustrated Gift Edition and one pack of cards in a burnt-leather case.

Carol stepped into a sirocco of furnace heat. They were already playing. Despite her flabby resolves she had not yet learned bridge. She was winningly apologetic about it to Juanita, and ashamed that she should have to go on being apologetic.

Mrs. Dave Dyer, a sallow woman with a thin prettiness, devoted to experiments in religious cults, illnesses, and scandal-bearing, shook her finger at Carol and trilled, "You're a naughty one! I don't believe you appreciate the honor, when you got into the Jolly Seventeen so easy!"

Mrs. Chet Dashaway nudged her neighbor at the second table. But Carol kept up the appealing bridal manner so far as possible. She twittered, "You're perfectly right. I'm a lazy thing. I'll make Will start teaching me this very evening." Her supplication had all the sound of birdies in the nest, and Easter church-bells, and frosted Christmas cards. Internally she snarled, "That ought to be saccharine enough." She sat in the smallest rocking-chair, a model of Victorian modesty. But she saw or she imagined that the women who had gurgled at her so welcomingly when she had first come to Gopher Prairie were nodding at her brusquely.

During the pause after the first game she petitioned Mrs. Jackson Elder, "Don't you think we ought to get up another bob-sled party soon?"

"It's so cold when you get dumped in the snow," said Mrs. Elder, indifferently.

"I hate snow down my neck," volunteered Mrs. Dave Dyer, with an unpleasant look at Carol and, turning her back, she bubbled at Rita Simons, "Dearie, won't you run in this evening? I've got the loveliest new Butterick pattern I want to show you."

Carol crept back to her chair. In the fervor of discussing the game they ignored her. She was not used to being a wallflower. She struggled to keep from oversensitiveness, from becoming unpopular by the sure method of believing that she was unpopular; but she hadn't much reserve of patience, and at the end of the second game, when Ella Stowbody sniffily asked her, "Are you going to send to Minneapolis for your dress for the next soirée—heard you were," Carol said "Don't know yet" with unnecessary sharpness.

She was relieved by the admiration with which the *jeune fille* Rita Simons looked at the steel buckles on her pumps; but she resented Mrs. Howland's tart demand, "Don't you find that new couch of yours is too broad to be practical?" She nodded, then shook her head, and touchily left Mrs. Howland to get out of it any meaning she desired. Immediately she wanted to make peace. She was close to simpering in the sweetness with which she addressed Mrs. Howland: "I think that is the prettiest display of beef-tea your husband has in his store."

"Oh yes, Gopher Prairie isn't so much behind the times," gibed Mrs. Howland. Some one giggled.

Their rebuffs made her haughty; her haughtiness irritated them to franker rebuffs; they were working up to a state of painfully righteous war when they were saved by the coming of food.

Though Juanita Haydock was highly advanced in the matters of finger-bowls, doilies, and bath-mats, her "refreshments" were typical of all the afternoon-coffees. Juanita's best friends, Mrs. Dyer and Mrs. Dashaway, passed large dinner plates, each with a spoon, a fork, and a coffee cup without saucer. They apologized and discussed the afternoon's game as they passed through the thicket of women's feet. Then they distributed hot buttered rolls, coffee poured from an enamel-ware pot, stuffed olives, potato salad, and angel's-food cake. There was, even in the most strictly conforming Gopher Prairie circles, a certain option as to collations. The olives need not be stuffed. Doughnuts were in some houses well thought of as a substitute for the hot buttered rolls. But there was in all the town no heretic save Carol who omitted angel's-food.

They ate enormously. Carol had a suspicion that the thriftier housewives made the afternoon treat do for evening supper.

She tried to get back into the current. She edged over to Mrs. McGanum. Chunky, amiable, young Mrs. McGanum, with her breast and arms of a milkmaid, and her loud delayed laugh which burst startlingly from a sober face, was the daughter of old Dr. Westlake, and the wife of Westlake's partner, Dr. McGanum. Kennicott asserted that Westlake and McGanum and their contaminated families were tricky, but Carol had found them gracious. She asked for friendliness by crying to Mrs. McGanum, "How is the baby's throat now?" and she was attentive while Mrs. McGanum rocked and knitted and placidly described symptoms.

Vida Sherwin came in after school, with Miss Ethel Villets, the town librarian. Miss Sherwin's optimistic presence gave Carol more confidence. She talked. She informed the circle, "I drove almost down to Wahkeenyan with Will, a few days ago. Isn't the country lovely! And I do admire the Scandinavian farmers down there so: their big red barns and silos and milking-machines and everything. Do you all know that lonely Lutheran church, with the tin-covered spire, that stands out alone on a hill? It's so bleak; somehow it seems so brave. I do think the Scandinavians are the hardiest and best people——"

"Oh, do you *think* so?" protested Mrs. Jackson Elder. "My husband says the Svenskas that work in the planing-mill are perfectly terrible—so silent and cranky, and so selfish, the way they keep demanding raises. If they had their way they'd simply ruin the business."

"Yes, and they're simply *ghastly* hired girls!" wailed Mrs. Dave Dyer. "I swear, I work myself to skin and bone trying to please my hired girls—when I can get them! I do everything in the world for them. They can have their gentleman friends call on them in the kitchen any time, and they get just the same to eat as we do, if there's any left over, and I practically never jump on them."

Juanita Haydock rattled, "They're ungrateful, all that class of people. I do think the domestic problem is simply becoming awful. I don't know what the country's coming to, with these Scandahoofian clodhoppers demanding every cent you can save, and so ignorant and impertinent, and on my word, demanding bath-tubs and everything—as if they weren't mighty good and lucky at home if they got a bath in the wash-tub."

They were off, riding hard. Carol thought of Bea and waylaid them:

"But isn't it possibly the fault of the mistresses if the maids are ungrateful? For generations we've given them the leavings of food, and holes to live in. I don't want to boast, but I must say I don't have much trouble with Bea. She's so friendly. The Scandinavians are sturdy and honest——"

Mrs. Dave Dyer snapped, "Honest? Do you call it honest to hold us up for every cent of pay they can get? I can't say that I've had any of them steal anything (though you might call it stealing to eat so much that a roast of beef hardly lasts three days), but just the same I don't intend to let them think they can put anything over on *me!* I always make them pack and unpack their trunks down-stairs, right under my eyes, and then I know they aren't being tempted to dishonesty by any slackness on *my* part!"

"How much do the maids get here?" Carol ventured.

Mrs. B. J. Gougerling, wife of the banker, stated in a shocked manner, "Any place from three-fifty to five-fifty a week! I know positively that Mrs. Clark, after swearing that she wouldn't weaken and encourage them in their outrageous demands, went and paid five-fifty—think of it! practically a dollar a day for unskilled work and, of course, her food and room and a chance to do her own washing right in with the rest of the wash. *How much do you pay, Mrs. Kennicott?*"

"Yes! How much do you pay?" insisted half a dozen.

"W-why, I pay six a week," she feebly confessed.

They gasped. Juanita protested, "Don't you think it's hard on the rest of us when you pay so much?" Juanita's demand was re-inforced by the universal glower.

Carol was angry. "I don't care! A maid has one of the hardest jobs on earth. She works from ten to eighteen hours a day. She has to wash slimy dishes and dirty clothes. She tends the children and runs to the door with wet chapped hands and——"

Mrs. Dave Dyer broke into Carol's peroration with a furious, "That's all very well, but believe me, I do those things myself when I'm without a maid —and that's a good share of the time for a person that isn't willing to yield and pay exorbitant wages!"

Carol was retorting, "But a maid does it for strangers, and all she gets out of it is the pay——"

Their eyes were hostile. Four of them were talking at once. Vida Sherwin's dictatorial voice cut through, took control of the revolution:

"Tut, tut, tut, tut! What angry passions—and what an idiotic discussion! All of you getting too serious. Stop it! Carol Kennicott, you're probably right, but you're too much ahead of the times. Juanita, quit looking so belligerent. What is this, a card party or a hen fight? Carol, you stop admiring yourself as the Joan of Arc of the hired girls, or I'll spank you. You come over here and talk libraries with Ethel Villets. Boooooo! If there's any more pecking, I'll take charge of the hen roost myself!"

They all laughed artificially, and Carol obediently "talked libraries."

A small-town bungalow, the wives of a village doctor and a village dry-goods merchant, a provincial teacher, a colloquial brawl over paying a servant a dollar more a week. Yet this insignificance echoed cellar-plots and cabinet meetings and labor conferences in Persia and Prussia, Rome and Boston, and the orators who deemed themselves international leaders were but the raised voices of a billion Juanitas denouncing a million Carols, with a hundred thousand Vida Sherwins trying to shoo away the storm.

Carol felt guilty. She devoted herself to admiring the spinsterish Miss Villets—and immediately committed another offense against the laws of decency.

"We haven't seen you at the library yet," Miss Villets reproved.

"I've wanted to run in so much but I've been getting settled and—— I'll probably come in so often you'll get tired of me! I hear you have such a nice library."

"There are many who like it. We have two thousand more books than Wakamin."

"Isn't that fine. I'm sure you are largely responsible. I've had some experience, in St. Paul."

"So I have been informed. Not that I entirely approve of library methods in these large cities. So careless, letting tramps and all sorts of dirty persons practically sleep in the reading-rooms."

"I know, but the poor souls—— Well, I'm sure you will agree with me in one thing: The chief task of a librarian is to get people to read."

"You feel so? My feeling, Mrs. Kennicott, and I am merely quoting the librarian of a very large college, is that the first duty of the *conscientious* librarian is to preserve the books."

"Oh!" Carol repented her "Oh." Miss Villets stiffened, and attacked:

"It may be all very well in cities, where they have unlimited funds, to let nasty children ruin books and just deliberately tear them up, and fresh young men take more books out than they are entitled to by the regulations, but I'm never going to permit it in this library!"

"What if some children are destructive? They learn to read. Books are cheaper than minds."

"Nothing is cheaper than the minds of some of these children that come in and bother me simply because their mothers don't keep them home where they belong. Some librarians may choose to be so wishy-washy and turn their libraries into nursing-homes and kindergartens, but as long as I'm in charge, the Gopher Prairie library is going to be quiet and decent, and the books well kept!"

Carol saw that the others were listening, waiting for her to be objectionable. She flinched before their dislike. She hastened to smile in agreement with Miss Villets, to glance publicly at her wrist-watch, to warble that it was "so late—have to hurry home—husband—such nice party—maybe you were right about maids, prejudiced because Bea so nice—such perfectly divine angel's-food, Mrs. Haydock must give me the recipe—good-by, such happy party——"

She walked home. She reflected, "It was my fault. I was touchy. And I opposed them so much. Only—— I can't! I can't be one of them if I must damn all the maids toiling in filthy kitchens, all the ragged hungry children. And these women are to be my arbiters, the rest of my life!"

She ignored Bea's call from the kitchen; she ran up-stairs to the unfrequented guest-room; she wept in terror, her body a pale arc as she knelt beside a cumbrous black-walnut bed, beside a puffy mattress covered with a red quilt, in a shuttered and airless room.

# 8

"Don't I, in looking for things to do, show that I'm not attentive enough to Will? Am I impressed enough by his work? I will be. Oh, I will be. If I can't be one of the town, if I must be an outcast——"

When Kennicott came home she bustled, "Dear, you must tell me a lot more about your cases. I want to know. I want to understand."

"Sure. You bet." And he went down to fix the furnace.

At supper she asked, "For instance, what did you do today?"

"Do today? How do you mean?"

"Medically. I want to understand——"

"Today? Oh, there wasn't much of anything: couple chumps with belly-aches, and a sprained wrist, and a fool woman that thinks she wants to kill herself because her husband doesn't like her and—— Just routine work."

"But the unhappy woman doesn't sound routine!"

"Her? Just case of nerves. You can't do much with these marriage mix-ups."

"But dear, *please*, will you tell me about the next case that you do think is interesting?"

"Sure. You bet. Tell you about anything that—— Say, that's pretty good salmon. Get it at Howland's?"

II

Four days after the Jolly Seventeen débâcle Vida Sherwin called and casually blew Carol's world to pieces.

"May I come in and gossip a while?" she said, with such excess of bright innocence that Carol was uneasy. Vida took off her furs with a bounce, she sat down as though it were a gymnasium exercise, she flung out:

"Feel disgracefully good, this weather! Raymond Wutherspoon says if he had my energy he'd be a grand opera singer. I always think this climate is the finest in the world, and my friends are the dearest people in the world, and my work is the most essential thing in the world. Probably I fool myself. But I know one thing for certain: You're the pluckiest little idiot in the world."

"And so you are about to flay me alive." Carol was cheerful about it.

"Am I? Perhaps. I've been wondering—I know that the third party to a squabble is often the most to blame: the one who runs between A and B having a beautiful time telling each of them what the other has said. But I want you to take a big part in vitalizing Gopher Prairie and so—— Such a very unique opportunity and—— Am I silly?"

"I know what you mean. I was too abrupt at the Jolly Seventeen."

"It isn't that. Matter of fact, I'm glad you told them some wholesome truths about servants. (Though perhaps you were just a bit tactless.) It's bigger than that. I wonder if you understand that in a secluded community like this every newcomer is on test? People cordial to her but watching her all the time. I remember when a Latin teacher came here from Wellesley, they resented her broad A. Were sure it was affected. Of course they have discussed you——"

"Have they talked about me much?"

"My dear!"

"I always feel as though I walked around in a cloud, looking out at others but not being seen. I feel so inconspicuous and so normal—so normal that there's nothing about me to discuss. I can't realize that Mr. and Mrs. Haydock must gossip about me." Carol was working up a small passion of distaste. "And I don't like it. It makes me crawly to think of their daring to talk over all I do and say. Pawing me over! I resent it. I hate——"

"Wait, child! Perhaps they resent some things in you. I want you to try and be impersonal. They'd paw over anybody who came in new. Didn't you, with newcomers in College?"

"Yes."

"Well then! Will you be impersonal? I'm paying you the compliment of supposing that you can be. I want you to be big enough to help me make this town worth while."

"I'll be as impersonal as cold boiled potatoes. (Not that I shall ever be able to help you 'make the town worth while.') What do they say about me? Really. I want to know."

"Of course the illiterate ones resent your references to anything farther away than Minneapolis. They're so suspicious—that's it, suspicious. And some think you dress too well."

"Oh, they do, do they! Shall I dress in gunny-sacking to suit them?"

"Please! Are you going to be a baby?"

"I'll be good," sulkily.

"You certainly will, or I won't tell you one single thing. You must understand this: I'm not asking you to change yourself. Just want you to know what they think. You must do that, no matter how absurd their prejudices are, if you're going to handle them. Is it your ambition to make this a better town, or isn't it?"

"I don't know whether it is or not!"

"Why—why—— Tut, tut, now, of course it is! Why, I depend on you. You're a born reformer."

"I am not—not any more!"

"Of course you are."

"Oh, if I really could help—— So they think I'm affected?"

"My lamb, they do! Now don't say they're nervy. After all, Gopher Prairie standards are as reasonable to Gopher Prairie as Lake Shore Drive standards are to Chicago. And there's more Gopher Prairies than there are Chicagos. Or Londons. And—— I'll tell you the whole story: They think you're showing off when you say 'American' instead of 'Ammurrican.' They think you're too frivolous. Life's so serious to them that they can't imagine any kind of laughter except Juanita's snortling. Ethel Villets was sure you were patronizing her when——"

"Oh, I was not!"

"——you talked about encouraging reading; and Mrs. Elder thought you were patronizing when you said she had 'such a pretty little car.' She thinks it's an enormous car! And some of the merchants say you're too flip when you talk to them in the store and——"

"Poor me, when I was trying to be friendly!"

"——every housewife in town is doubtful about your being so chummy with your Bea. All right to be kind, but they say you act as though she were your cousin. (Wait now! There's plenty more.) And they think you were eccentric in furnishing this room—they think the broad couch and that Japanese dingus are absurd. (Wait! I know they're silly.) And I guess I've heard a dozen criticize you because you don't go to church oftener and——"

"I can't stand it—I can't bear to realize that they've been saying all these things while I've been going about so happily and liking them. I wonder if you ought to have told me? It will make me self-conscious."

"I wonder the same thing. Only answer I can get is the old saw about knowledge being power. And some day you'll see how absorbing it is to have power, even here; to control the town—— Oh, I'm a crank. But I do like to see things moving."

"It hurts. It makes these people seem so beastly and treacherous, when I've been perfectly natural with them. But let's have it all. What did they say about my Chinese housewarming party?"

"Why, uh——"

"Go on. Or I'll make up worse things than anything you can tell me."

"They did enjoy it. But I guess some of them felt you were showing off—pretending that your husband is richer than he is."

"I can't—— Their meanness of mind is beyond any horrors I could imagine. They really thought that I—— And you want to 'reform' people like that when dynamite is so cheap? Who dared to say that? The rich or the poor?"

"Fairly well assorted."

"Can't they at least understand me well enough to see that though I might be affected and culturine, at least I simply couldn't commit that other kind of vulgarity? If they must know, you may tell them, with my compliments, that Will makes about four thousand a year, and the party cost half of what they probably thought it did. Chinese things are not very expensive, and I made my own costume——"

"Stop it! Stop beating me! I know all that. What they meant was: they felt you were starting dangerous competition by giving a party such as most people here can't afford. Four thousand is a pretty big income for this town."

"I never thought of starting competition. Will you believe that it was in all love and friendliness that I tried to give them the gayest party I could? It was foolish; it was childish and noisy. But I did mean it so well."

"I know, of course. And it certainly is unfair of them to make fun of your having that Chinese food—chow men, was it?—and to laugh about your wearing those pretty trousers——"

Carol sprang up, whimpering, "Oh, they didn't do that! They didn't poke fun at my feast, that I ordered so carefully for them! And my little Chinese costume that I was so happy making—I made it secretly, to surprise them. And they've been ridiculing it, all this while!"

She was huddled on the couch.

Vida was stroking her hair, muttering, "I shouldn't——"

Shrouded in shame, Carol did not know when Vida slipped away. The clock's bell, at half past five, aroused her. "I must get hold of myself before Will comes. I hope he never knows what a fool his wife is. . . . Frozen, sneering, horrible hearts."

Like a very small, very lonely girl she trudged up-stairs, slow step by step, her feet dragging, her hand on the rail. It was not her husband to whom she wanted to run for protection—it was her father, her smiling understanding father, dead these twelve years.

### III

Kennicott was yawning, stretched in the largest chair, between the radiator and a small kerosene stove.

Cautiously, "Will dear, I wonder if the people here don't criticize me sometimes? They must. I mean: if they ever do, you mustn't let it bother you."

"Criticize you? Lord, I should say not. They all keep telling me you're the swellest girl they ever saw."

"Well, I've just fancied—— The merchants probably think I'm too fussy about shopping. I'm afraid I bore Mr. Dashaway and Mr. Howland and Mr. Ludelmeyer."

"I can tell you how that is. I didn't want to speak of it, but since you've brought it up: Chet Dashaway probably resents the fact that you got this new furniture down in the Cities instead of here. I didn't want to raise any objection at the time but—— After all, I make my money here and they naturally expect me to spend it here."

"If Mr. Dashaway will kindly tell me how any civilized person can furnish a room out of the mortuary pieces that he calls——" She remembered. She said meekly, "But I understand."

"And Howland and Ludelmeyer—— Oh, you've probably handed 'em a few roasts for the bum stocks they carry, when you just meant to jolly 'em. But rats, what do we care! This is an independent town, not like these Eastern holes where you have to watch your step all the time, and live up to fool demands and social customs, and a lot of old tabbies always busy criticizing. Everybody's free here to do what he wants to." He said it with a flourish, and Carol perceived that he believed it. She turned her breath of fury into a yawn.

"By the way, Carrie, while we're talking of this: Of course I like to keep independent, and I don't believe in this business of binding yourself to trade with the man that trades with you unless you really want to, but same time: I'd be just as glad if you dealt with Jenson or Ludelmeyer as much as you can, instead of Howland & Gould, who go to Dr. Gould every last time, and the whole tribe of 'em the same way. I don't see why I should be paying out my good money for groceries and having them pass it on to Terry Gould!"

"I've gone to Howland & Gould because they're better, and cleaner."

"I know. I don't mean cut them out entirely. Course Jenson is tricky—give you short weight—and Ludelmeyer is a shiftless old Dutch hog. But same time, I mean let's keep the trade in the family whenever it is convenient, see how I mean?"

"I see."

"Well, guess it's about time to turn in."

He yawned, went out to look at the thermometer, slammed the door, patted her head, unbuttoned his waistcoat, yawned, wound the clock, went down to look at the furnace, yawned, and clumped up-stairs to bed, casually scratching his thick woolen undershirt.

Till he bawled, "Aren't you ever coming up to bed?" she sat unmoving.

# 9

She had tripped into the meadow to teach the lambs a pretty educational dance and found that the lambs were wolves. There was no way out between their pressing gray shoulders. She was surrounded by fangs and sneering eyes.

She could not go on enduring the hidden derision. She wanted to flee. She wanted to hide in the generous indifference of cities. She practised saying to Kennicott, "Think perhaps I'll run down to St. Paul for a few days." But she could not trust herself to say it carelessly; could not abide his certain questioning.

Reform the town? All she wanted was to be tolerated!

She could not look directly at people. She flushed and winced before citizens who a week ago had been amusing objects of study, and in their good-mornings she heard a cruel sniggering.

She encountered Juanita Haydock at Ole Jenson's grocery. She besought, "Oh, how do you do! Heavens, what beautiful celery that is!"

"Yes, doesn't it look fresh. Harry simply has to have his celery on Sunday, drat the man!"

Carol hastened out of the shop exulting, "She didn't make fun of me. . . . Did she?"

In a week she had recovered from consciousness of insecurity, of shame and whispering notoriety, but she kept her habit of avoiding people. She walked the streets with her head down. When she spied Mrs. McGanum or Mrs. Dyer ahead she crossed over with an elaborate pretense of looking at a billboard. Always she was acting, for the benefit of every one she saw—and for the benefit of the ambushed leering eyes which she did not see.

She perceived that Vida Sherwin had told the truth. Whether she entered a store, or swept the back porch, or stood at the bay-window in the living-room, the village peeped at her. Once she had swung along the street triumphant in making a home. Now she glanced at each house, and felt, when she was safely home, that she had won past a thousand enemies armed with ridicule. She told herself that her sensitiveness was preposterous, but daily she was thrown into panic. She saw curtains slide back into innocent smoothness. Old women who had been entering their houses slipped out again to stare at her—in the wintry quiet she could hear them tiptoeing on their porches. When she had for a blessed hour forgotten the searchlight, when she was scampering through a chill dusk, happy in yellow windows against gray night, her heart checked as she realized that a head covered with a shawl was thrust up over a snow-tipped bush to watch her.

She admitted that she was taking herself too seriously; that villagers gape at every one. She became placid, and thought well of her philosophy. But next morning she had a shock of shame as she entered Ludelmeyer's. The grocer, his clerk, and neurotic Mrs. Dave Dyer had been giggling about something. They halted, looked embarrassed, babbled about onions. Carol felt guilty. That evening when Kennicott took her to call on the crotchety Lyman Casses, their hosts seemed flustered at their arrival. Kennicott jovially hooted, "What makes you so hang-dog, Lym?" The Casses tittered feebly.

Except Dave Dyer, Sam Clark, and Raymie Wutherspoon, there were no merchants of whose welcome Carol was certain. She knew that she read mockery into greetings but she could not control her suspicion, could not rise from her psychic collapse. She alternately raged and flinched at the superiority of the merchants. They did not know that they were being rude, but they meant to have it understood that they were prosperous and "not scared of no doctor's wife." They often said, "One man's as good as another—and a darn sight better." This motto, however, they did not commend to farmer customers who had had crop failures. The Yankee merchants were crabbed; and Ole Jenson, Ludelmeyer, and Gus Dahl, from the "Old Country," wished to be taken for Yankees. James Madison Howland, born in New Hampshire, and Ole Jenson, born in Sweden, both proved that they were free American citizens by grunting, "I don't know whether I got any or not," or "Well, you can't expect me to get it delivered by noon."

It was good form for the customers to fight back. Juanita Haydock cheerfully jabbered, "You have it there by twelve or I'll snatch that fresh delivery-boy bald-headed." But Carol had never been able to play the game of friendly rudeness; and now she was certain that she never would learn it. She formed the cowardly habit of going to Axel Egge's.

Axel was not respectable and rude. He was still a foreigner, and he expected to remain one. His manner was heavy and uninterrogative. His establishment was more fantastic than any cross-roads store. No one save Axel himself could find anything. A part of the assortment of children's stockings was under a blanket on a shelf, a part in a tin ginger-snap box, the rest heaped like a nest of black-cotton snakes upon a flour-barrel which was surrounded by brooms, Norwegian Bibles, dried cod for *ludfisk*, boxes of apricots, and a pair and a half of lumbermen's rubber-footed boots. The place was crowded with Scandinavian farmwives, standing aloof in shawls and ancient fawn-colored leg o' mutton jackets, awaiting the return of their lords. They spoke Norwegian or Swedish, and looked at Carol uncomprehendingly. They were a relief to her—they were not whispering that she was a poseur.

But what she told herself was that Axel Egge's was "so picturesque and romantic."

It was in the matter of clothes that she was most self-conscious.

When she dared to go shopping in her new checked suit with the black-

embroidered sulphur collar, she had as good as invited all of Gopher Prairie
(which interested itself in nothing so intimately as in new clothes and the
cost thereof) to investigate her. It was a smart suit with lines unfamiliar to
the dragging yellow and pink frocks of the town. The Widow Bogart's stare,
from her porch, indicated, "Well I never saw anything like that before!"
Mrs. McGanum stopped Carol at the notions shop to hint, "My, that's a
nice suit—wasn't it terribly expensive?" The gang of boys in front of the drug
store commented, "Hey, Pudgie, play you a game of checkers on that dress."
Carol could not endure it. She drew her fur coat over the suit and hastily
fastened the buttons, while the boys snickered.

II

No group angered her quite so much as these staring young roués.

She had tried to convince herself that the village, with its fresh air, its
lakes for fishing and swimming, was healthier than the artificial city. But she
was sickened by glimpses of the gang of boys from fourteen to twenty who
loafed before Dyer's Drug Store, smoking cigarettes, displaying "fancy" shoes
and purple ties and coats of diamond-shaped buttons, whistling the Hoochi-
Koochi and catcalling, "Oh, you baby-doll" at every passing girl.

She saw them playing pool in the stinking room behind Del Snafflin's
barber shop, and shaking dice in "The Smoke House," and gathered in a
snickering knot to listen to the "juicy stories" of Bert Tybee, the bartender
of the Minniemashie House. She heard them smacking moist lips over every
love-scene at the Rosebud Movie Palace. At the counter of the Greek Con-
fectionery Parlor, while they ate dreadful messes of decayed bananas, acid
cherries, whipped cream, and gelatinous ice-cream, they screamed to one another, "Hey, lemme 'lone," "Quit dog-gone you, looka what you went and
done, you almost spilled my glass swater," "Like hell I did," "Hey, gol darn
your hide, don't you go sticking your coffin nail in my i-scream," "Oh you
Batty, how juh like dancing with Tillie McGuire, last night? Some squeezing,
heh, kid?"

By diligent consultation of American fiction she discovered that this was
the only virile and amusing manner in which boys could function; that boys
who were not compounded of the gutter and the mining-camp were molly-
coddles and unhappy. She had taken this for granted. She had studied the
boys pityingly, but impersonally. It had not occurred to her that they might
touch her.

Now she was aware that they knew all about her; that they were waiting
for some affectation over which they could guffaw. No schoolgirl passed their
observation-posts more flushingly than did Mrs. Dr. Kennicott. In shame
she knew that they glanced appraisingly at her snowy overshoes, speculating
about her legs. Theirs were not young eyes—there was no youth in all the
town, she agonized. They were born old, grim and old and spying and censorious.

She cried again that their youth was senile and cruel on the day when she overheard Cy Bogart and Earl Haydock.

Cyrus N. Bogart, son of the righteous widow who lived across the alley, was at this time a boy of fourteen or fifteen. Carol had already seen quite enough of Cy Bogart. On her first evening in Gopher Prairie Cy had appeared at the head of a "charivari," banging immensely upon a discarded automobile fender. His companions were yelping in imitation of coyotes. Kennicott had felt rather complimented; had gone out and distributed a dollar. But Cy was a capitalist in charivaris. He returned with an entirely new group, and this time there were three automobile fenders and a carnival rattle. When Kennicott again interrupted his shaving, Cy piped, "Naw, you got to give us two dollars," and he got it. A week later Cy rigged a tic-tac to a window of the living-room, and the tattoo out of the darkness frightened Carol into screaming. Since then, in four months, she had beheld Cy hanging a cat, stealing melons, throwing tomatoes at the Kennicott house, and making ski-tracks across the lawn, and had heard him explaining the mysteries of generation, with great audibility and dismaying knowledge. He was, in fact, a museum specimen of what a small town, a well-disciplined public school, a tradition of hearty humor, and a pious mother could produce from the material of a courageous and ingenious mind.

Carol was afraid of him. Far from protesting when he set his mongrel on a kitten, she worked hard at not seeing him.

The Kennicott garage was a shed littered with paint-cans, tools, a lawn-mower, and ancient wisps of hay. Above it was a loft which Cy Bogart and Earl Haydock, young brother of Harry, used as a den, for smoking, hiding from whippings, and planning secret societies. They climbed to it by a ladder on the alley side of the shed.

This morning of late January, two or three weeks after Vida's revelations, Carol had gone into the stable-garage to find a hammer. Snow softened her step. She heard voices in the loft above her:

"Ah gee, lez—oh, lez go down the lake and swipe some mushrats out of somebody's traps," Cy was yawning.

"And get our ears beat off!" grumbled Earl Haydock.

"Gosh, these cigarettes are dandy. 'Member when we were just kids, and used to smoke corn-silk and hayseed?"

"Yup. Gosh!"

Spit. Silence.

"Say Earl, ma says if you chew tobacco you get consumption."

"Aw rats, your old lady is a crank."

"Yuh, that's so." Pause. "But she says she knows a fella that did."

"Aw, gee whiz, didn't Doc Kennicott used to chew tobacco all the time before he married this-here girl from the Cities? He used to spit—— Gee! Some shot! He could hit a tree ten feet off."

This was news to the girl from the Cities.

"Say, how is she?" continued Earl.

"Huh? How's who?"

"You know who I mean, smarty."

A tussle, a thumping of loose boards, silence, weary narration from Cy:

"Mrs. Kennicott? Oh, she's all right, I guess." Relief to Carol, below. "She gimme a hunk o' cake, one time. But Ma says she's stuck-up as hell. Ma's always talking about her. Ma says if Mrs. Kennicott thought as much about the doc as she does about her clothes, the doc wouldn't look so peaked."

Spit. Silence.

"Yuh. Juanita's always talking about her, too," from Earl. "She says Mrs. Kennicott thinks she knows it all. Juanita says she has to laugh till she almost busts every time she sees Mrs. Kennicott peerading along the street with that 'take a look—I'm a swell skirt' way she's got. But gosh, I don't pay no attention to Juanita. She's meaner 'n a crab."

"Ma was telling somebody that she heard that Mrs. Kennicott claimed she made forty dollars a week when she was on some job in the Cities, and Ma says she knows posolutely that she never made but eighteen a week—Ma says that when she's lived here a while she won't go round making a fool of herself, pulling that bighead stuff on folks that know a whole lot more than she does. They're all laughing up their sleeves at her."

"Say, jever notice how Mrs. Kennicott fusses around the house? Other evening when I was coming over here, she'd forgot to pull down the curtain, and I watched her for ten minutes. Jeeze, you'd 'a' died laughing. She was there all alone, and she must 'a' spent five minutes getting a picture straight. It was funny as hell the way she'd stick out her finger to straighten the picture—deedle-dee, see my tunnin' 'ittle finger, oh my, ain't I cute, what a fine long tail my cat's got!"

"But say, Earl, she's some good-looker, just the same, and O Ignatz! the glad rags she must of bought for her wedding. Jever notice these low-cut dresses and these thin shimmy-shirts she wears? I had a good squint at 'em when they were out on the line with the wash. And some ankles she's got, heh?"

Then Carol fled.

In her innocence she had not known that the whole town could discuss even her garments, her body. She felt that she was being dragged naked down Main Street.

The moment it was dusk she pulled down the window-shades, all the shades, flush with the sill, but beyond them she felt moist fleering eyes.

III

She remembered, and tried to forget, and remembered more sharply the vulgar detail of her husband's having observed the ancient customs of the land by chewing tobacco. She would have preferred a prettier vice—gambling or a mistress. For these she might have found a luxury of forgiveness. She could not remember any fascinatingly wicked hero of fiction who chewed tobacco. She asserted that it proved him to be a man of the bold free West. She tried to align him with the hairy-chested heroes of the motion-pictures.

She curled on the couch, a pallid softness in the twilight, and fought herself, and lost the battle. Spitting did not identify him with rangers riding the buttes; it merely bound him to Gopher Prairie—to Nat Hicks the tailor and Bert Tybee the bartender.

"But he gave it up for me. Oh, what does it matter! We're all filthy in some things. I think of myself as so superior, but I do eat and digest, I do wash my dirty paws and scratch. I'm not a cool slim goddess on a column. There aren't any! He gave it up for me. He stands by me, believing that every one loves me. He's the Rock of Ages—in a storm of meanness that's driving me mad. . . . it will drive me mad."

All evening she sang Scotch ballads to Kennicott, and when she noticed that he was chewing an unlighted cigar she smiled maternally at his secret.

She could not escape asking (in the exact words and mental intonations which a thousand million women, dairy wenches and mischief-making queens, had used before her, and which a million million women will know hereafter), "Was it all a horrible mistake, my marrying him?" She quieted the doubt—without answering it.

IV

Kennicott had taken her north to Lac-qui-Meurt, in the Big Woods. It was the entrance to a Chippewa Indian reservation, a sandy settlement among Norway pines on the shore of a huge snow-glaring lake. She had her first sight of his mother, except the glimpse at the wedding. Mrs. Kennicott had a hushed and delicate breeding which dignified her woodeny overscrubbed cottage with its worn hard cushions in heavy rockers. She had never lost the child's miraculous power of wonder. She asked questions about books and cities. She murmured:

"Will is a dear hard-working boy but he's inclined to be too serious, and you've taught him how to play. Last night I heard you both laughing about the old Indian basket-seller, and I just lay in bed and enjoyed your happiness."

Carol forgot her misery-hunting in this solidarity of family life. She could depend upon them; she was not battling alone. Watching Mrs. Kennicott flit about the kitchen she was better able to translate Kennicott himself. He was matter-of-fact, yes, and incurably mature. He didn't really play; he let Carol play with him. But he had his mother's genius for trusting, her disdain for prying, her sure integrity.

From the two days at Lac-qui-Meurt Carol drew confidence in herself, and she returned to Gopher Prairie in a throbbing calm like those golden drugged seconds when, because he is for an instant free from pain, a sick man revels in living.

A bright hard winter day, the wind shrill, black and silver clouds booming across the sky, everything in panicky motion during the brief light. They struggled against the surf of wind, through deep snow. Kennicott was cheerful. He hailed Loren Wheeler, "Behave yourself while I been away?" The editor bellowed, "B' gosh you stayed so long that all your patients have got well!" and importantly took notes for the *Dauntless* about their journey. Jackson Elder cried, "Hey, folks! How's tricks up North?" Mrs. McGanum waved to them from her porch.

"They're glad to see us. We mean something here. These people are satisfied. Why can't I be? But can I sit back all my life and be satisfied with 'Hey, folks'? They want shouts on Main Street, and I want violins in a paneled room. Why——?"

### v

Vida Sherwin ran in after school a dozen times. She was tactful, torrentially anecdotal. She had scuttled about town and plucked compliments: Mrs. Dr. Westlake had pronounced Carol a "very sweet, bright, cultured young woman," and Brad Bemis, the tinsmith at Clark's Hardware Store, had declared that she was "easy to work for and awful easy to look at."

But Carol could not yet take her in. She resented this outsider's knowledge of her shame. Vida was not too long tolerant. She hinted, "You're a great brooder, child. Buck up now. The town's quit criticizing you, almost entirely. Come with me to the Thanatopsis Club. They have some of the *best* papers, and current-events discussions—*so* interesting."

In Vida's demands Carol felt a compulsion, but she was too listless to obey.

It was Bea Sorenson who was really her confidante.

However charitable toward the Lower Classes she may have thought herself, Carol had been reared to assume that servants belong to a distinct and inferior species. But she discovered that Bea was extraordinarily like girls she had loved in college, and as a companion altogether superior to the young matrons of the Jolly Seventeen. Daily they became more frankly two girls playing at housework. Bea artlessly considered Carol the most beautiful and accomplished lady in the country; she was always shrieking, "My, dot's a swell hat!" or, "Ay t'ink all dese ladies yoost die when dey see how elegant you do your hair!" But it was not the humbleness of a servant, nor the hypocrisy of a slave; it was the admiration of Freshman for Junior.

They made out the day's menus together. Though they began with propriety, Carol sitting by the kitchen table and Bea at the sink or blacking the stove, the conference was likely to end with both of them by the table, while Bea gurgled over the ice-man's attempt to kiss her, or Carol admitted, "Everybody knows that the doctor is lots more clever than Dr. McGanum." When Carol came in from marketing, Bea plunged into the hall to take off her coat, rub her frosted hands, and ask, "Vos dere lots of folks up-town today?"

This was the welcome upon which Carol depended.

### VI

Through her weeks of cowering there was no change in her surface life. No one save Vida was aware of her agonizing. On her most despairing days

she chatted to women on the street, in stores. But without the protection of
Kennicott's presence she did not go to the Jolly Seventeen; she delivered herself to the judgment of the town only when she went shopping and on the
ritualistic occasions of formal afternoon calls, when Mrs. Lyman Cass or
Mrs. George Edwin Mott, with clean gloves and minute handkerchiefs and
sealskin card-cases and countenances of frozen approbation, sat on the edges
of chairs and inquired, "Do you find Gopher Prairie pleasing?" When they
spent evenings of social profit-and-loss at the Haydocks' or the Dyers' she hid
behind Kennicott, playing the simple bride.

Now she was unprotected. Kennicott had taken a patient to Rochester for
an operation. He would be away for two or three days. She had not minded;
she would loosen the matrimonial tension and be a fanciful girl for a time.
But now that he was gone the house was listeningly empty. Bea was out this
afternoon—presumably drinking coffee and talking about "fellows" with her
cousin Tina. It was the day for the monthly supper and evening-bridge of the
Jolly Seventeen, but Carol dared not go.

She sat alone.

# 10

The house was haunted, long before evening. Shadows slipped down the
walls and waited behind every chair.

Did that door move?

No. She wouldn't go to the Jolly Seventeen. She hadn't energy enough to
caper before them, to smile blandly at Juanita's rudeness. Not today. But
she did want a party. Now! If some one would come in this afternoon,
some one who liked her—Vida or Mrs. Sam Clark or old Mrs. Champ Perry
or gentle Mrs. Dr. Westlake. Or Guy Pollock! She'd telephone——

No. That wouldn't be it. They must come of themselves.

Perhaps they would.

Why not?

She'd have tea ready, anyway. If they came—splendid. If not—what did she
care? She wasn't going to yield to the village and let down; she was going
to keep up a belief in the rite of tea, to which she had always looked forward
as the symbol of a leisurely fine existence. And it would be just as much
fun, even if it was so babyish, to have tea by herself and pretend that she
was entertaining clever men. It would!

She turned the shining thought into action. She bustled to the kitchen,
stoked the wood-range, sang Schumann while she boiled the kettle, warmed
up raisin cookies on a newspaper spread on the rack in the oven. She scampered up-stairs to bring down her filmiest tea-cloth. She arranged a silver
tray. She proudly carried it into the living-room and set it on the long cherry-

wood table, pushing aside a hoop of embroidery, a volume of Conrad from the library, copies of the *Saturday Evening Post*, the *Literary Digest*, and Kennicott's *National Geographic Magazine*.

She moved the tray back and forth and regarded the effect. She shook her head. She busily unfolded the sewing-table, set it in the bay-window, patted the tea-cloth to smoothness, moved the tray. "Some time I'll have a mahogany tea-table," she said happily.

She had brought in two cups, two plates. For herself, a straight chair, but for the guest the big wing-chair, which she pantingly tugged to the table.

She had finished all the preparations she could think of. She sat and waited. She listened for the door-bell, the telephone. Her eagerness was stilled. Her hands drooped.

Surely Vida Sherwin would hear the summons.

She glanced through the bay-window. Snow was sifting over the ridge of the Howland house like sprays of water from a hose. The wide yards across the street were gray with moving eddies. The black trees shivered. The roadway was gashed with ruts of ice.

She looked at the extra cup and plate. She looked at the wing-chair. It was so empty.

The tea was cold in the pot. With wearily dipping finger-tip she tested it. Yes. Quite cold. She couldn't wait any longer.

The cup across from her was icily clean, glisteningly empty.

Simply absurd to wait. She poured her own cup of tea. She sat and stared at it. What was it she was going to do now? Oh yes; how idiotic; take a lump of sugar.

She didn't want the beastly tea.

She was springing up. She was on the couch, sobbing.

II

She was thinking more sharply than she had for weeks.

She reverted to her resolution to change the town—awaken it, prod it, "reform" it. What if they were wolves instead of lambs? They'd eat her all the sooner if she was meek to them. Fight or be eaten. It was easier to change the town completely than to conciliate it! She could not take their point of view; it was a negative thing; an intellectual squalor; a swamp of prejudices and fears. She would have to make them take hers. She was not a Vincent de Paul, to govern and mold a people. What of that? The tiniest change in their distrust of beauty would be the beginning of the end; a seed to sprout and some day with thickening roots to crack their wall of mediocrity. If she could not, as she desired, do a great thing nobly and with laughter, yet she need not be content with village nothingness. She would plant one seed in the blank wall.

Was she just? Was it merely a blank wall, this town which to three thousand and more people was the center of the universe? Hadn't she, returning from Lac-qui-Meurt, felt the heartiness of their greetings? No. The ten thousand Gopher Prairies had no monopoly of greetings and friendly hands. Sam Clark was no more loyal than girl librarians she knew in St. Paul, the people she had met in Chicago. And those others had so much that Gopher Prairie complacently lacked—the world of gaiety and adventure, of music and the integrity of bronze, of remembered mists from tropic isles and Paris nights and the walls of Bagdad, of industrial justice and a God who spake not in doggerel hymns.

One seed. Which seed it was did not matter. All knowledge and freedom were one. But she had delayed so long in finding that seed. Could she do something with this Thanatopsis Club? Or should she make her house so charming that it would be an influence? She'd make Kennicott like poetry. That was it, for a beginning! She conceived so clear a picture of their bending over large fair pages by the fire (in a non-existent fireplace) that the spectral presences slipped away. Doors no longer moved; curtains were not creeping shadows but lovely dark masses in the dusk; and when Bea came home Carol was singing at the piano which she had not touched for many days.

Their supper was the feast of two girls. Carol was in the dining-room, in a frock of black satin edged with gold, and Bea, in blue gingham and an apron, dined in the kitchen; but the door was open between, and Carol was inquiring, "Did you see any ducks in Dahl's window?" and Bea chanting, "No, ma'am. Say, ve have a svell time, dis afternoon. Tina she have coffee and *knäckebröd*, and her fella vos dere, and ve yoost laughed and laughed, and her fella say he vos president and he going to make me queen of Finland, and Ay stick a fedder in may hair and say Ay bane going to go to var—oh, ve vos so foolish and ve *laugh* so!"

When Carol sat at the piano again she did not think of her husband but of the book-drugged hermit, Guy Pollock. She wished that Pollock would come calling.

"If a girl really kissed him, he'd creep out of his den and be human. If Will were as literate as Guy, or Guy were as executive as Will, I think I could endure even Gopher Prairie.

"It's so hard to mother Will. I could be maternal with Guy. Is that what I want, something to mother, a man or a baby or a town? I *will* have a baby. Some day. But to have him isolated here all his receptive years——

"And so to bed.

"Have I found my real level in Bea and kitchen-gossip?

"Oh, I do miss you, Will. But it will be pleasant to turn over in bed as often as I want to, without worrying about waking you up.

"Am I really this settled thing called a 'married woman'? I feel so unmarried tonight. So free. To think that there was once a Mrs. Kennicott who let herself worry over a town called Gopher Prairie when there was a whole world outside it!

"Of course Will is going to like poetry."

### III

A black February day. Clouds hewn of ponderous timber weighing down on the earth; an irresolute dropping of snow specks upon the trampled wastes. Gloom but no veiling of angularity. The lines of roofs and sidewalks sharp and inescapable.

The second day of Kennicott's absence.

She fled from the creepy house for a walk. It was thirty below zero; too cold to exhilarate her. In the spaces between houses the wind caught her. It stung, it gnawed at nose and ears and aching cheeks, and she hastened from shelter to shelter, catching her breath in the lee of a barn, grateful for the protection of a billboard covered with ragged posters showing layer under layer of paste-smeared green and streaky red.

The grove of oaks at the end of the street suggested Indians, hunting, snow-shoes, and she struggled past the earth-banked cottages to the open country, to a farm and a low hill corrugated with hard snow. In her loose nutria coat, seal toque, virginal cheeks unmarked by lines of village jealousies, she was as out of place on this dreary hillside as a scarlet tanager on an ice-floe. She looked down on Gopher Prairie. The snow, stretching without break from streets to devouring prairie beyond, wiped out the town's pretense of being a shelter. The houses were black specks on a white sheet. Her heart shivered with that still loneliness as her body shivered with the wind.

She ran back into the huddle of streets, all the while protesting that she wanted a city's yellow glare of shop-windows and restaurants, or the primitive forest with hooded furs and a rifle, or a barnyard warm and steamy, noisy with hens and cattle, certainly not these dun houses, these yards choked with winter ash-piles, these roads of dirty snow and clotted frozen mud. The zest of winter was gone. Three months more, till May, the cold might drag on, with the snow ever filthier, the weakened body less resistant. She wondered why the good citizens insisted on adding the chill of prejudice, why they did not make the houses of their spirits more warm and frivolous, like the wise chatterers of Stockholm and Moscow.

She circled the outskirts of the town and viewed the slum of "Swede Hollow." Wherever as many as three houses are gathered there will be a slum of at least one house. In Gopher Prairie, the Sam Clarks boasted, "you don't get any of this poverty that you find in cities—always plenty of work—no need of charity—man got to be blame shiftless if he don't get ahead." But now that the summer mask of leaves and grass was gone, Carol discovered misery and dead hope. In a shack of thin boards covered with tar-paper she saw the washerwoman, Mrs. Steinhof, working in gray steam. Outside, her six-year-old boy chopped wood. He had a torn jacket, muffler of a blue like skimmed milk. His hands were covered with red mittens through which protruded his chapped raw knuckles. He halted to blow on them, to cry disinterestedly.

A family of recently arrived Finns were camped in an abandoned stable. A man of eighty was picking up lumps of coal along the railroad.

She did not know what to do about it. She felt that these independent citizens, who had been taught that they belonged to a democracy, would resent her trying to play Lady Bountiful.

She lost her loneliness in the activity of the village industries—the rail-road-yards with a freight-train switching, the wheat-elevator, oil-tanks, a slaughter-house with blood-marks on the snow, the creamery with the sleds of farmers and piles of milk-cans, an unexplained stone hut labeled "Danger —Powder Stored Here." The jolly tombstone-yard, where a utilitarian sculptor in a red calfskin overcoat whistled as he hammered the shiniest of granite headstones. Jackson Elder's small planing-mill, with the smell of fresh pine shavings and the burr of circular saws. Most important, the Gopher Prairie Flour and Milling Company, Lyman Cass president. Its windows were blanketed with flour-dust, but it was the most stirring spot in town. Workmen were wheeling barrels of flour into a box-car; a farmer sitting on sacks of wheat in a bob-sled argued with the wheat-buyer; machinery within the mill boomed and whined; water gurgled in the ice-freed mill-race.

The clatter was a relief to Carol after months of smug houses. She wished that she could work in the mill; that she did not belong to the caste of pro-fessional-man's-wife.

She started for home, through the small slum. Before a tar-paper shack, at a gateless gate, a man in rough brown dogskin coat and black plush cap with lappets was watching her. His square face was confident, his foxy mustache was picaresque. He stood erect, his hands in his side-pockets, his pipe puffing slowly. He was forty-five or -six, perhaps.

"How do, Mrs. Kennicott," he drawled.

She recalled him—the town handyman, who had repaired their furnace at the beginning of winter.

"Oh, how do you do," she fluttered.

"My name 's Bjornstam. 'The Red Swede' they call me. Remember? Always thought I'd kind of like to say howdy to you again."

"Ye—yes—— I've been exploring the outskirts of town."

"Yump. Fine mess. No sewage, no street cleaning, and the Lutheran min-ister and the priest represent the arts and sciences. Well, thunder, we sub-merged tenth down here in Swede Hollow are no worse off than you folks. Thank God, we don't have to go and purr at Juanity Haydock at the Jolly Old Seventeen."

The Carol who regarded herself as completely adaptable was uncomforta-ble at being chosen as comrade by a pipe-reeking odd-job man. Probably he was one of her husband's patients. But she must keep her dignity.

"Yes, even the Jolly Seventeen isn't always so exciting. It's very cold again today, isn't it. Well——"

Bjornstam was not respectfully valedictory. He showed no signs of pulling a forelock. His eyebrows moved as though they had a life of their own. With a subgrin he went on:

"Maybe I hadn't ought to talk about Mrs. Haydock and her Solemcholy Seventeen in that fresh way. I suppose I'd be tickled to death if I was invited to sit in with that gang. I'm what they call a pariah, I guess. I'm the town badman, Mrs. Kennicott: town atheist, and I suppose I must be an anarchist, too. Everybody who doesn't love the bankers and the Grand Old Republican Party is an anarchist."

Carol had unconsciously slipped from her attitude of departure into an attitude of listening, her face full toward him, her muff lowered. She fumbled:

"Yes, I suppose so." Her own grudges came in a flood. "I don't see why you shouldn't criticize the Jolly Seventeen if you want to. They aren't sacred."

"Oh yes, they are! The dollar-sign has chased the crucifix clean off the map. But then, I've got no kick. I do what I please, and I suppose I ought to let them do the same."

"What do you mean by saying you're a pariah?"

"I'm poor, and yet I don't decently envy the rich. I'm an old bach. I make enough money for a stake, and then I sit around by myself, and shake hands with myself, and have a smoke, and read history, and I don't contribute to the wealth of Brother Elder or Daddy Cass."

"You—— I fancy you read a good deal."

"Yep. In a hit-or-a-miss way. I'll tell you: I'm a lone wolf. I trade horses, and saw wood, and work in lumber-camps—I'm a first-rate swamper. Always wished I could go to college. Though I s'pose I'd find it pretty slow, and they'd probably kick me out."

"You really are a curious person, Mr.——"

"Bjornstam. Miles Bjornstam. Half Yank and half Swede. Usually known as 'that damn lazy big-mouthed calamity-howler that ain't satisfied with the way we run things.' No, I ain't curious—whatever you mean by that! I'm just a bookworm. Probably too much reading for the amount of digestion I've got. Probably half-baked. I'm going to get in 'half-baked' first, and beat you to it, because it's dead sure to be handed to a radical that wears jeans!"

They grinned together. She demanded:

"You say that the Jolly Seventeen is stupid. What makes you think so?"

"Oh, trust us borers into the foundation to know about your leisure class. Fact, Mrs. Kennicott, I'll say that far as I can make out, the only people in this man's town that do have any brains—I don't mean ledger-keeping brains or duck-hunting brains or baby-spanking brains, but real imaginative brains—are you and me and Guy Pollock and the foreman at the flour-mill. He's a socialist, the foreman. (Don't tell Lym Cass that! Lym would fire a socialist quicker than he would a horse-thief!)"

"Indeed no, I sha'n't tell him."

"This foreman and I have some great set-to's. He's a regular old-line party-member. Too dogmatic. Expects to reform everything from deforestation to nosebleed by saying phrases like 'surplus value.' Like reading the prayer-book. But same time, he's a Plato J. Aristotle compared with people like Ezry Stowbody or Professor Mott or Julius Flickerbaugh."

"It's interesting to hear about him."

He dug his toe into a drift, like a schoolboy. "Rats. You mean I talk too much. Well, I do, when I get hold of somebody like you. You probably want to run along and keep your nose from freezing."

"Yes, I must go, I suppose. But tell me: Why did you leave Miss Sherwin, of the high school, out of your list of the town intelligentsia?"

"I guess maybe she does belong in it. From all I can hear she's in everything and behind everything that looks like a reform—lot more than most folks realize. She lets Mrs. Reverend Warren, the president of this-here Thanatopsis Club, think she's running the works, but Miss Sherwin is the secret boss, and nags all the easy-going dames into doing something. But way I figure it out—— You see, I'm not interested in these dinky reforms. Miss Sherwin's trying to repair the holes in this barnacle-covered ship of a town by keeping busy bailing out the water. And Pollock tries to repair it by reading poetry to the crew! Me, I want to yank it up on the ways, and fire the poor bum of a shoemaker that built it so it sails crooked, and have it rebuilt right, from the keel up."

"Yes—that—that would be better. But I must run home. My poor nose is nearly frozen."

"Say, you better come in and get warm, and see what an old bach's shack is like."

She looked doubtfully at him, at the low shanty, the yard that was littered with cord-wood, moldy planks, a hoopless wash-tub. She was disquieted, but Bjornstam did not give her the opportunity to be delicate. He flung out his hand in a welcoming gesture which assumed that she was her own counselor, that she was not a Respectable Married Woman but fully a human being. With a shaky, "Well, just a moment, to warm my nose," she glanced down the street to make sure that she was not spied on, and bolted toward the shanty.

She remained for one hour, and never had she known a more considerate host than the Red Swede.

He had but one room: bare pine floor, small work-bench, wall bunk with amazingly neat bed, frying-pan and ash-stippled coffee-pot on the shelf behind the pot-bellied cannon-ball stove, backwoods chairs—one constructed from half a barrel, one from a tilted plank—and a row of books incredibly assorted; Byron and Tennyson and Stevenson, a manual of gas-engines, a book by Thorstein Veblen, and a spotty treatise on "The Care, Feeding, Diseases, and Breeding of Poultry and Cattle."

There was but one picture—a magazine color-plate of a steep-roofed village in the Harz Mountains which suggested kobolds and maidens with golden hair.

Bjornstam did not fuss over her. He suggested, "Might throw open your coat and put your feet up on the box in front of the stove." He tossed his dogskin coat into the bunk, lowered himself into the barrel chair, and droned on:

"Yeh, I'm probably a yahoo, but by gum I do keep my independence by doing odd jobs, and that's more 'n these polite cusses like the clerks in the banks do. When I'm rude to some slob, it may be partly because I don't know better (and God knows I'm not no authority on trick forks and what pants you wear with a Prince Albert), but mostly it's because I mean something. I'm about the only man in Johnson County that remembers the joker in the Declaration of Independence about Americans being supposed to have the right to 'life, liberty, and the pursuit of happiness.'

"I meet old Ezra Stowbody on the street. He looks at me like he wants me to remember he's a highmuckamuck and worth two hundred thousand dollars, and he says, 'Uh, Bjornquist——'

"'Bjornstam's my name, Ezra,' I says. He knows my name, all rightee.

"'Well, whatever your name is,' he says, 'I understand you have a gasoline saw. I want you to come around and saw up four cords of maple for me,' he says.

"'So you like my looks, eh?' I says, kind of innocent.

"'What difference does that make? Want you to saw that wood before Saturday,' he says, real sharp. Common workman going and getting fresh with a fifth of a million dollars all walking around in a hand-me-down fur coat!

"'Here's the difference it makes,' I says, just to devil him. 'How do you know I like *your* looks?' Maybe he didn't look sore! 'Nope,' I says, 'thinking it all over, I don't like your application for a loan. Take it to another bank, only there ain't any,' I says, and I walks off on him.

"Sure. Probably I was surly—and foolish. But I figured there had to be *one* man in town independent enough to sass the banker!"

He hitched out of his chair, made coffee, gave Carol a cup, and talked on, half defiant and half apologetic, half wistful for friendliness and half amused by her surprise at the discovery that there was a proletarian philosophy.

At the door, she hinted:

"Mr. Bjornstam, if you were I, would you worry when people thought you were affected?"

"Huh? Kick 'em in the face! Say, if I were a sea-gull, and all over silver, think I'd care what a pack of dirty seals thought about my flying?"

It was not the wind at her back, it was the thrust of Bjornstam's scorn which carried her through town. She faced Juanita Haydock, cocked her head at Maud Dyer's brief nod, and came home to Bea radiant. She telephoned Vida Sherwin to "run over this evening." She lustily played Tschaikowsky— the virile chords an echo of the red laughing philosopher of the tar-paper shack.

(When she hinted to Vida, "Isn't there a man here who amuses himself by being irreverent to the village gods— Bjornstam, some such a name?" the reform-leader said "Bjornstam? Oh yes. Fixes things. He's awfully impertinent.")

IV

Kennicott had returned at midnight. At breakfast he said four several times that he had missed her every moment.

On her way to market Sam Clark hailed her, "The top o' the mornin' to yez! Going to stop and pass the time of day mit Sam'l? Warmer, eh? What'd the doc's thermometer say it was? Say, you folks better come round and visit with us, one of these evenings. Don't be so dog-gone proud, staying by your-selves."

Champ Perry the pioneer, wheat-buyer at the elevator, stopped her in the post-office, held her hand in his withered paws, peered at her with faded eyes, and chuckled, "You are so fresh and blooming, my dear. Mother was saying t'other day that a sight of you was better 'n a dose of medicine."

In the Bon Ton Store she found Guy Pollock tentatively buying a modest gray scarf. "We haven't seen you for so long," she said. "Wouldn't you like to come in and play cribbage, some evening?" As though he meant it, Pollock begged, "May I, really?"

While she was purchasing two yards of malines the vocal Raymie Wutherspoon tiptoed up to her, his long sallow face bobbing, and he be-sought, "You've just got to come back to my department and see a pair of patent leather slippers I set aside for you."

In a manner of more than sacerdotal reverence he unlaced her boots, tucked her skirt about her ankles, slid on the slippers. She took them.

"You're a good salesman," she said.

"I'm not a salesman at all! I just like elegant things. All this is so in-artistic." He indicated with a forlornly waving hand the shelves of shoe-boxes, the seat of thin wood perforated in rosettes, the display of shoe-trees and tin boxes of blacking, the lithograph of a smirking young woman with cherry cheeks who proclaimed in the exalted poetry of advertising, "My tootsies never got hep to what pedal perfection was till I got a pair of clever classy Cleopatra Shoes."

"But sometimes," Raymie sighed, "there is a pair of dainty little shoes like these, and I set them aside for some one who will appreciate. When I saw these I said right away, 'Wouldn't it be nice if they fitted Mrs. Kenni-cott,' and I meant to speak to you first chance I had. I haven't forgotten our jolly talks at Mrs. Gurrey's!"

That evening Guy Pollock came in and, though Kennicott instantly im-pressed him into a cribbage game, Carol was happy again.

v

She did not, in recovering something of her buoyancy, forget her deter-mination to begin the liberalizing of Gopher Prairie by the easy and agree-able propaganda of teaching Kennicott to enjoy reading poetry in the lamplight. The campaign was delayed. Twice he suggested that they call on neighbors; once he was in the country. The fourth evening he yawned pleas-antly, stretched, and inquired, "Well, what'll we do tonight? Shall we go to the movies?"

"I know exactly what we're going to do. Now don't ask questions! Come and sit down by the table. There, are you comfy? Lean back and forget you're a practical man, and listen to me."

It may be that she had been influenced by the managerial Vida Sherwin; certainly she sounded as though she was selling culture. But she dropped it when she sat on the couch, her chin in her hands, a volume of Yeats on her knees, and read aloud.

Instantly she was released from the homely comfort of a prairie town. She was in the world of lonely things—the flutter of twilight linnets, the aching call of gulls along a shore to which the netted foam crept out of darkness, the island of Aengus and the elder gods and the eternal glories that never were, tall kings and women girdled with crusted gold, the woful incessant chanting and the——

"Heh-cha-cha!" coughed Dr. Kennicott. She stopped. She remembered that he was the sort of person who chewed tobacco. She glared, while he uneasily petitioned, "That's great stuff. Study it in college? I like poetry fine— James Whitcomb Riley and some of Longfellow—this 'Hiawatha.' Gosh, I wish I could appreciate that highbrow art stuff. But I guess I'm too old a dog to learn new tricks."

With pity for his bewilderment, and a certain desire to giggle, she consoled him, "Then let's try some Tennyson. You've read him?"

"Tennyson? You bet. Read him in school. There's that:

> And let there be no (what is it?) of farewell
> When I put out to sea,
> But let the——

Well, I don't remember all of it but—— Oh, sure! And there's that 'I met a little country boy who——' I don't remember exactly how it goes, but the chorus ends up, 'We are seven.'"

"Yes. Well—— Shall we try 'The Idylls of the King?' They're so full of color."

"Go to it. Shoot." But he hastened to shelter himself behind a cigar.

She was not transported to Camelot. She read with an eye cocked on him, and when she saw how much he was suffering she ran to him, kissed his forehead, cried, "You poor forced tube-rose that wants to be a decent turnip!"

"Look here now, that ain't——"

"Anyway, I sha'n't torture you any longer."

She could not quite give up. She read Kipling, with a great deal of emphasis:

> There's a REGIMENT a-COMING down the
> GRAND Trunk ROAD.

He tapped his foot to the rhythm; he looked normal and reassured. But when he complimented her, "That was fine. I don't know but what you can elocute just as good as Ella Stowbody," she banged the book and suggested that they were not too late for the nine o'clock show at the movies.

That was her last effort to harvest the April wind, to teach divine un-happiness by a correspondence course, to buy the lilies of Avalon and the sunsets of Cockaigne in tin cans at Ole Jenson's Grocery.

But the fact is that at the motion-pictures she discovered herself laughing as heartily as Kennicott at the humor of an actor who stuffed spaghetti down a woman's evening frock. For a second she loathed her laughter; mourned for the day when on her hill by the Mississippi she had walked the battle-ments with queens. But the celebrated cinema jester's conceit of dropping toads into a soup-plate flung her into unwilling tittering, and the afterglow faded, the dead queens fled through darkness.

VI

She went to the Jolly Seventeen's afternoon bridge. She had learned the elements of the game from the Sam Clarks. She played quietly and reason-ably badly. She had no opinions on anything more polemic than woolen union-suits, a topic on which Mrs. Howland discoursed for five minutes. She smiled frequently, and was the complete canary-bird in her manner of thanking the hostess, Mrs. Dave Dyer.

Her only anxious period was during the conference on husbands.

The young matrons discussed the intimacies of domesticity with a frank-ness and a minuteness which dismayed Carol. Juanita Haydock communi-cated Harry's method of shaving, and his interest in deer-shooting. Mrs. Gougerling reported fully, and with some irritation, her husband's inappre-ciation of liver and bacon. Maud Dyer chronicled Dave's digestive disorders; quoted a recent bedtime controversy with him in regard to Christian Sci-ence, socks and the sewing of buttons upon vests; announced that she "simply wasn't going to stand his always pawing girls when he went and got crazy-jealous if a man just danced with her"; and rather more than sketched Dave's varieties of kisses.

So meekly did Carol give attention, so obviously was she at last desirous of being one of them, that they looked on her fondly, and encouraged her to give such details of her honeymoon as might be of interest. She was embarrassed rather than resentful. She deliberately misunderstood. She talked of Kennicott's overshoes and medical ideals till they were thoroughly bored. They regarded her as agreeable but green.

Till the end she labored to satisfy the inquisition. She bubbled at Juanita, the president of the club, that she wanted to entertain them. "Only," she said, "I don't know that I can give you any refreshments as nice as Mrs. Dyer's salad, or that simply delicious angel's-food we had at your house, dear."

"Fine! We need a hostess for the seventeenth of March. Wouldn't it be awfully original if you made it a St. Patrick's Day bridge! I'll be tickled to death to help you with it. I'm glad you've learned to play bridge. At first I didn't hardly know if you were going to like Gopher Prairie. Isn't it dandy that you've settled down to being homey with us! Maybe we aren't as high-

brow as the Cities, but we do have the daisiest times and—oh, we go swimming in summer, and dances and—oh, lots of good times. If folks will just
take us as we are, I think we're a pretty good bunch!"

"I'm sure of it. Thank you so much for the idea about having a St. Patrick's
Day bridge."

"Oh, that's nothing. I always think the Jolly Seventeen are so good at
original ideas. If you knew these other towns, Wakamin and Joralemon and
all, you'd find out and realize that G. P. is the liveliest, smartest town in
the state. Did you know that Percy Bresnahan, the famous auto manufacturer, came from here and—— Yes, I think that a St. Patrick's Day party
would be awfully cunning and original, and yet not too queer or freaky or
anything."

# 11

She had often been invited to the weekly meetings of the Thanatopsis, the
women's study club, but she had put it off. The Thanatopsis was, Vida
Sherwin promised, "such a cozy group, and yet it puts you in touch with all
the intellectual thoughts that are going on everywhere."

Early in March Mrs. Westlake, wife of the veteran physician, marched
into Carol's living-room like an amiable old pussy and suggested, "My dear,
you really must come to the Thanatopsis this afternoon. Mrs. Dawson is
going to be leader and the poor soul is frightened to death. She wanted me
to get you to come. She says she's sure you will brighten up the meeting
with your knowledge of books and writings. (English poetry is our topic
today.) So shoo! Put on your coat!"

"English poetry? Really? I'd love to go. I didn't realize you were reading
poetry."

"Oh, we're not so slow!"

Mrs. Luke Dawson, wife of the richest man in town, gaped at them pite-
ously when they appeared. Her expensive frock of beaver-colored satin with
rows, plasters, and pendants of solemn brown beads was intended for a
woman twice her size. She stood wringing her hands in front of nineteen
folding chairs, in her front parlor with its faded photograph of Minnehaha
Falls in 1890, its "colored enlargement" of Mr. Dawson, its bulbous lamp
painted with sepia cows and mountains and standing on a mortuary marble
column.

She creaked, "O Mrs. Kennicott, I'm in such a fix. I'm supposed to lead
the discussion, and I wondered would you come and help?"

"What poet do you take up today?" demanded Carol, in her library tone
of "What book do you wish to take out?"

"Why, the English ones."

"Not all of them?"

"W-why yes. We're learning all of European Literature this year. The club gets such a nice magazine, *Culture Hints*, and we follow its programs. Last year our subject was Men and Women of the Bible, and next year we'll probably take up Furnishings and China. My, it does make a body hustle to keep up with all these new culture subjects, but it is improving. So will you help us with the discussion today?"

On her way over Carol had decided to use the Thanatopsis as the tool with which to liberalize the town. She had immediately conceived enormous enthusiasm; she had chanted, "These are the real people. When the housewives, who bear the burdens, are interested in poetry, it means something. I'll work with them—for them—anything!"

Her enthusiasm had become watery even before thirteen women resolutely removed their overshoes, sat down meatily, ate peppermints, dusted their fingers, folded their hands, composed their lower thoughts, and invited the naked muse of poetry to deliver her most improving message. They had greeted Carol affectionately, and she tried to be a daughter to them. But she felt insecure. Her chair was out in the open, exposed to their gaze, and it was a hard-slatted, quivery, slippery church-parlor chair, likely to collapse publicly and without warning. It was impossible to sit on it without folding the hands and listening piously.

She wanted to kick the chair and run. It would make a magnificent clatter.

She saw that Vida Sherwin was watching her. She pinched her wrist, as though she were a noisy child in church, and when she was decent and cramped again, she listened.

Mrs. Dawson opened the meeting by sighing, "I'm sure I'm glad to see you all here today, and I understand that the ladies have prepared a number of very interesting papers, this is such an interesting subject, the poets, they have been an inspiration for higher thought, in fact wasn't it Reverend Benlick who said that some of the poets have been as much an inspiration as a good many of the ministers, and so we shall be glad to hear——"

The poor lady smiled neuralgically, panted with fright, scrabbled about the small oak table to find her eye-glasses, and continued, "We will first have the pleasure of hearing Mrs. Jenson on the subject 'Shakespeare and Milton.'"

Mrs. Ole Jenson said that Shakespeare was born in 1564 and died 1616. He lived in London, England, and in Stratford-on-Avon, which many American tourists loved to visit, a lovely town with many curios and old houses well worth examination. Many people believed that Shakespeare was the greatest playwright who ever lived, also a fine poet. Not much was known about his life, but after all that did not really make so much difference, because they loved to read his numerous plays, several of the best known of which she would now criticize.

Perhaps the best known of his plays was "The Merchant of Venice," having a beautiful love story and a fine appreciation of a woman's brains, which a woman's club, even those who did not care to commit themselves on the question of suffrage, ought to appreciate. (Laughter.) Mrs. Jenson was sure that she, for one, would love to be like Portia. The play was about a Jew named Shylock, and he didn't want his daughter to marry a Venice gentleman named Antonio——

Mrs. Leonard Warren, a slender, gray, nervous woman, president of the Thanatopsis and wife of the Congregational pastor, reported the birth and death dates of Byron, Scott, Moore, Burns; and wound up:

"Burns was quite a poor boy and he did not enjoy the advantages we enjoy today, except for the advantages of the fine old Scotch kirk where he heard the Word of God preached more fearlessly than even in the finest big brick churches in the big and so-called advanced cities of today, but he did not have our educational advantages and Latin and the other treasures of the mind so richly strewn before the, alas, too ofttimes inattentive feet of our youth who do not always sufficiently appreciate the privileges freely granted to every American boy rich or poor. Burns had to work hard and was sometimes led by evil companionship into low habits. But it is morally instructive to know that he was a good student and educated himself, in striking contrast to the loose ways and so-called aristocratic society-life of Lord Byron, on which I have just spoken. And certainly though the lords and earls of his day may have looked down upon Burns as a humble person, many of us have greatly enjoyed his pieces about the mouse and other rustic subjects, with their message of humble beauty—I am so sorry I have not got the time to quote some of them."

Mrs. George Edwin Mott gave ten minutes to Tennyson and Browning.

Mrs. Nat Hicks, a wry-faced, curiously sweet woman, so awed by her betters that Carol wanted to kiss her, completed the day's grim task by a paper on "Other Poets." The other poets worthy of consideration were Coleridge, Wordsworth, Shelley, Gray, Mrs. Hemans, and Kipling.

Miss Ella Stowbody obliged with a recital of "The Recessional" and extracts from "Lalla Rookh." By request, she gave "An Old Sweetheart of Mine" as encore.

Gopher Prairie had finished the poets. It was ready for the next week's labor: English Fiction and Essays.

Mrs. Dawson besought, "Now we will have a discussion of the papers, and I am sure we shall all enjoy hearing from one who we hope to have as a new member, Mrs. Kennicott, who with her splendid literary training and all should be able to give us many pointers and—many helpful pointers."

Carol had warned herself not to be so "beastly supercilious." She had insisted that in the belated quest of these work-stained women was an aspiration which ought to stir her tears. "But they're so self-satisfied. They think they're doing Burns a favor. They don't believe they have a 'belated quest.' They're sure that they have culture salted and hung up." It was out of this stupor of doubt that Mrs. Dawson's summons roused her. She was in a panic. How could she speak without hurting them?

Mrs. Champ Perry leaned over to stroke her hand and whisper, "You look tired, dearie. Don't you talk unless you want to."

Affection flooded Carol; she was on her feet, searching for words and courtesies:

"The only thing in the way of suggestion—— I know you are following a definite program, but I do wish that now you've had such a splendid introduction, instead of going on with some other subject next year you could return and take up the poets more in detail. Especially actual quotations—even though their lives are so interesting and, as Mrs. Warren said, so morally instructive. And perhaps there are several poets not mentioned today whom it might be worth while considering—Keats, for instance, and Matthew Arnold and Rossetti and Swinburne. Swinburne would be such a—well, that is, such a contrast to life as we all enjoy it in our beautiful Middlewest——"

She saw that Mrs. Leonard Warren was not with her. She captured her by innocently continuing:

"Unless perhaps Swinburne tends to be, uh, more outspoken than you, than we really like. What do you think, Mrs. Warren?"

The pastor's wife decided, "Why, you've caught my very thoughts, Mrs. Kennicott. Of course I have never *read* Swinburne, but years ago, when he was in vogue, I remember Mr. Warren saying that Swinburne (or was it Oscar Wilde? but anyway:) he said that though many so-called intellectual people posed and pretended to find beauty in Swinburne, there can never be genuine beauty without the message from the heart. But at the same time I do think you have an excellent idea, and though we have talked about Furnishings and China as the probable subject for next year, I believe that it would be nice if the program committee would try to work in another day entirely devoted to English poetry! In fact, Madame Chairman, I so move you."

When Mrs. Dawson's coffee and angel's-food had helped them to recover from the depression caused by thoughts of Shakespeare's death they all told Carol that it was a pleasure to have her with them. The membership committee retired to the sitting-room for three minutes and elected her a member.

And she stopped being patronizing.

She wanted to be one of them. They were so loyal and kind. It was they who would carry out her aspiration. Her campaign against village sloth was actually begun! On what specific reform should she first loose her army? During the gossip after the meeting Mrs. George Edwin Mott remarked that the city hall seemed inadequate for the splendid modern Gopher Prairie. Mrs. Nat Hicks timidly wished that the young people could have free dances there—the lodge dances were so exclusive. The city hall. That was it! Carol hurried home.

She had not realized that Gopher Prairie was a city. From Kennicott she discovered that it was legally organized with a mayor and city-council and wards. She was delighted by the simplicity of voting one's self a metropolis. Why not?

She was a proud and patriotic citizen, all evening.

II

She examined the city hall, next morning. She had remembered it only as a bleak inconspicuousness. She found it a liver-colored frame coop half a block from Main Street. The front was an unrelieved wall of clapboards and dirty windows. It had an unobstructed view of a vacant lot and Nat Hicks's tailor shop. It was larger than the carpenter shop beside it, but not so well built.

No one was about. She walked into the corridor. On one side was the municipal court, like a country school; on the other, the room of the volunteer fire company, with a Ford hose-cart and the ornamental helmets used in parades; at the end of the hall, a filthy two-cell jail, now empty but smelling of ammonia and ancient sweat. The whole second story was a large unfinished room littered with piles of folding chairs, a lime-crusted mortar-mixing box, and the skeletons of Fourth of July floats covered with decomposing plaster shields and faded red, white, and blue bunting. At the end was an abortive stage. The room was large enough for the community dances which Mrs. Nat Hicks advocated. But Carol was after something bigger than dances.

In the afternoon she scampered to the public library.

The library was open three afternoons and four evenings a week. It was housed in an old dwelling, sufficient but unattractive. Carol caught herself picturing pleasanter reading-rooms, chairs for children, an art collection, a librarian young enough to experiment.

She berated herself, "Stop this fever of reforming everything! I *will* be satisfied with the library! The city hall is enough for a beginning. And it's really an excellent library. It's—it isn't so bad. . . . Is it possible that I am to find dishonesties and stupidity in every human activity I encounter? In schools and business and government and everything? Is there never any contentment, never any rest?"

She shook her head as though she were shaking off water, and hastened into the library, a young, light, amiable presence, modest in unbuttoned fur coat, blue suit, fresh organdy collar, and tan boots roughened from scuffling snow. Miss Villets stared at her, and Carol purred, "I was so sorry not to see you at the Thanatopsis yesterday. Vida said you might come."

"Oh. You went to the Thanatopsis. Did you enjoy it?"

"So much. Such good papers on the poets." Carol lied resolutely. "But I did think they should have had you give one of the papers on poetry!"

"Well—— Of course I'm not one of the bunch that seem to have the time to take and run the club, and if they prefer to have papers on literature by other ladies who have no literary training—after all, why should I complain? What am I but a city employee!"

"You're not! You're the one person that does—that does—oh, you do so much. Tell me, is there, uh—— Who are the people who control the club?"

Miss Villets emphatically stamped a date in the front of "Frank on the

Lower Mississippi" for a small flaxen boy, glowered at him as though she were stamping a warning on his brain, and sighed:

"I wouldn't put myself forward or criticize any one for the world, and Vida is one of my best friends, and such a splendid teacher, and there is no one in town more advanced and interested in all movements, but I must say that no matter who the president or the committees are, Vida Sherwin seems to be behind them all the time, and though she is always telling me about what she is pleased to call my 'fine work in the library,' I notice that I'm not often called on for papers, though Mrs. Lyman Cass once volunteered and told me that she thought my paper on 'The Cathedrals of England' was the most interesting paper we had, the year we took up English and French travel and architecture. But—— And of course Mrs. Mott and Mrs. Warren are very important in the club, as you might expect of the wives of the superintendent of schools and the Congregational pastor, and indeed they are both very cultured, but—— No, you may regard me as entirely unimportant. I'm sure what I say doesn't matter a bit!"

"You're much too modest, and I'm going to tell Vida so, and, uh, I wonder if you can give me just a teeny bit of your time and show me where the magazine files are kept?"

She had won. She was profusely escorted to a room like a grandmother's attic, where she discovered periodicals devoted to house-decoration and town-planning, with a six-year file of the *National Geographic*. Miss Villets blessedly left her alone. Humming, fluttering pages with delighted fingers, Carol sat cross-legged on the floor, the magazines in heaps about her.

She found pictures of New England streets: the dignity of Falmouth, the charm of Concord, Stockbridge and Farmington and Hillhouse Avenue. The fairy-book suburb of Forest Hills on Long Island. Devonshire cottages and Essex manors and a Yorkshire High Street and Port Sunlight. The Arab village of Djeddah—an intricately chased jewel-box. A town in California which had changed itself from the barren brick fronts and slatternly frame sheds of a Main Street to a way which led the eye down a vista of arcades and gardens.

Assured that she was not quite mad in her belief that a small American town might be lovely, as well as useful in buying wheat and selling plows, she sat brooding, her thin fingers playing a tattoo on her cheeks. She saw in Gopher Prairie a Georgian city hall: warm brick walls with white shutters, a fanlight, a wide hall and curving stair. She saw it the common home and inspiration not only of the town but of the country about. It should contain the court-room (she couldn't get herself to put in a jail), public library, a collection of excellent prints, rest-room and model kitchen for farmwives, theater, lecture room, free community ballroom, farm-bureau, gymnasium. Forming about it and influenced by it, as mediæval villages gathered about the castle, she saw a new Georgian town as graceful and beloved as Annapolis or that bowery Alexandria to which Washington rode.

All this the Thanatopsis Club was to accomplish with no difficulty whatever, since its several husbands were the controllers of business and politics. She was proud of herself for this practical view.

She had taken only half an hour to change a wire-fenced potato-plot into a walled rose-garden. She hurried out to apprize Mrs. Leonard Warren, as president of the Thanatopsis, of the miracle which had been worked.

### III

At a quarter to three Carol had left home; at half-past four she had created the Georgian town; at a quarter to five she was in the dignified poverty of the Congregational parsonage, her enthusiasm pattering upon Mrs. Leonard Warren like summer rain upon an old gray roof; at two minutes to five a town of demure courtyards and welcoming dormer windows had been erected; and at two minutes past five the entire town was as flat as Babylon.

Erect in a black William and Mary chair against gray and speckly-brown volumes of sermons and Biblical commentaries and Palestine geographies upon long pine shelves, her neat black shoes firm on a rag-rug, herself as correct and low-toned as her background, Mrs. Warren listened without comment till Carol was quite through, then answered delicately:

"Yes, I think you draw a very nice picture of what might easily come to pass—some day. I have no doubt that such villages will be found on the prairie—some day. But if I might make just the least little criticism: it seems to me that you are wrong in supposing either that the city hall would be the proper start, or that the Thanatopsis would be the right instrument. After all, it's the churches, isn't it, that are the real heart of the community. As you may possibly know, my husband is prominent in Congregational circles all through the state for his advocacy of church-union. He hopes to see all the evangelical denominations joined in one strong body, opposing Catholicism and Christian Science, and properly guiding all movements that make for morality and prohibition. Here, the combined churches could afford a splendid club-house, maybe a stucco and half-timber building with gargoyles and all sorts of pleasing decorations on it, which, it seems to me, would be lots better to impress the ordinary class of people than just a plain old-fashioned colonial house, such as you describe. And that would be the proper center for all educational and pleasurable activities, instead of letting them fall into the hands of the politicians."

"I don't suppose it will take more than thirty or forty years for the churches to get together?" Carol said innocently.

"Hardly that long even; things are moving so rapidly. So it would be a mistake to make any other plans."

Carol did not recover her zeal till two days after, when she tried Mrs. George Edwin Mott, wife of the superintendent of schools.

Mrs. Mott commented, "Personally, I am terribly busy with dressmaking and having the seamstress in the house and all, but it would be splendid to have the other members of the Thanatopsis take up the question. Except for one thing: First and foremost, we must have a new schoolbuilding. Mr. Mott says they are terribly cramped."

Carol went to view the old building. The grades and the high school were combined in a damp yellow-brick structure with the narrow windows of an antiquated jail—a hulk which expressed hatred and compulsory training. She conceded Mrs. Mott's demand so violently that for two days she dropped her own campaign. Then she built the school and city hall together, as the center of the reborn town.

She ventured to the lead-colored dwelling of Mrs. Dave Dyer. Behind the mask of winter-stripped vines and a wide porch only a foot above the ground, the cottage was so impersonal that Carol could never visualize it. Nor could she remember anything that was inside it. But Mrs. Dyer was personal enough. With Carol, Mrs. Howland, Mrs. McGanum, and Vida Sherwin she was a link between the Jolly Seventeen and the serious Thanatopsis (in contrast to Juanita Haydock, who unnecessarily boasted of being a "lowbrow" and publicly stated that she would "see herself in jail before she'd write any darned old club papers"). Mrs. Dyer was superfeminine in the kimono in which she received Carol. Her skin was fine, pale, soft, suggesting a weak voluptuousness. At afternoon-coffees she had been rude but now she addressed Carol as "dear," and insisted on being called Maud. Carol did not quite know why she was uncomfortable in this talcum-powder atmosphere, but she hastened to get into the fresh air of her plans.

Maud Dyer granted that the city hall wasn't "so very nice," yet, as Dave said, there was no use doing anything about it till they received an appropriation from the state and combined a new city hall with a national guard armory. Dave had given verdict, "What these mouthy youngsters that hang around the pool-room need is universal military training. Make men of 'em."

Mrs. Dyer removed the new schoolbuilding from the city hall:

"Oh, so Mrs. Mott has got you going on her school craze! She's been dinging at that till everybody's sick and tired. What she really wants is a big office for her dear bald-headed Gawge to sit around and look important in. Of course I admire Mrs. Mott, and I'm very fond of her, she's so brainy, even if she does try to butt in and run the Thanatopsis, but I must say we're sick of her nagging. The old building was good enough for us when we were kids! I hate these would-be women politicians, don't you?"

## IV

The first week of March had given promise of spring and stirred Carol with a thousand desires for lakes and fields and roads. The snow was gone except for filthy woolly patches under trees; the thermometer leaped in a day from wind-bitten chill to itchy warmth. As soon as Carol was convinced that even in this imprisoned North, spring could exist again, the snow came down as abruptly as a paper storm in a theater; the northwest gale flung it up in a half-blizzard; and with her hope of a glorified town went hope of summer meadows.

But a week later, though the snow was everywhere in slushy heaps, the promise was unmistakable. By the invisible hints in air and sky and earth which had aroused her every year through ten thousand generations she knew that spring was coming. It was not a scorching, hard, dusty day like the treacherous intruder of a week before, but soaked with languor, softened with a milky light. Rivulets were hurrying in each alley; a calling robin appeared by magic on the crab-apple tree in the Howlands' yard. Everybody chuckled, "Looks like winter is going," and "This 'll bring the frost out of the roads—have the autos out pretty soon now—wonder what kind of bass-fishing we'll get this summer—ought to be good crops this year."

Each evening Kennicott repeated, "We better not take off our Heavy Underwear or the storm windows too soon—might be 'nother spell of cold—got to be careful 'bout catching cold—wonder if the coal will last through?"

The expanding forces of life within her choked the desire for reforming. She trotted through the house, planning the spring cleaning with Bea. When she attended her second meeting of the Thanatopsis she said nothing about remaking the town. She listened respectably to statistics on Dickens, Thackeray, Jane Austen, George Eliot, Scott, Hardy, Lamb, De Quincey, and Mrs. Humphry Ward, who, it seemed, constituted the writers of English Fiction and Essays.

Not till she inspected the rest-room did she again become a fanatic. She had often glanced at the store-building which had been turned into a refuge in which farmwives could wait while their husbands transacted business. She had heard Vida Sherwin and Mrs. Warren caress the virtue of the Thanatopsis in establishing the rest-room and in sharing with the city council the expense of maintaining it. But she had never entered it till this March day.

She went in impulsively; nodded at the matron, a plump worthy widow named Nodelquist, and at a couple of farmwomen who were meekly rocking. The rest-room resembled a second-hand store. It was furnished with discarded patent rockers, lopsided reed chairs, a scratched pine table, a gritty straw mat, old steel engravings of milkmaids being morally amorous under willow-trees, faded chromos of roses and fish, and a kerosene stove for warming lunches. The front window was darkened by torn net curtains and by a mound of geraniums and rubber-plants.

While she was listening to Mrs. Nodelquist's account of how many thousands of farmers' wives used the rest-room every year, and how much they "appreciated the kindness of the ladies in providing them with this lovely place, and all free," she thought, "Kindness nothing! The kind-ladies' husbands get the farmers' trade. This is mere commercial accommodation. And it's horrible. It ought to be the most charming room in town, to comfort women sick of prairie kitchens. Certainly it ought to have a clear window, so that they can see the metropolitan life go by. Some day I'm going to make a better rest-room—a club-room. Why! I've already planned that as part of my Georgian town hall!"

So it chanced that she was plotting against the peace of the Thanatopsis at her third meeting (which covered Scandinavian, Russian, and Polish Literature, with remarks by Mrs. Leonard Warren on the sinful paganism of the Russian so-called church). Even before the entrance of the coffee and hot rolls Carol seized on Mrs. Champ Perry, the kind and ample-bosomed pioneer woman who gave historic dignity to the modern matrons of the Thanatopsis. She poured out her plans. Mrs. Perry nodded and stroked Carol's hand, but at the end she sighed:

"I wish I could agree with you, dearie. I'm sure you're one of the Lord's anointed (even if we don't see you at the Baptist Church as often as we'd like to)! But I'm afraid you're too tender-hearted. When Champ and I came here we teamed-it with an ox-cart from Sauk Centre to Gopher Prairie, and there was nothing here then but a stockade and a few soldiers and some log cabins. When we wanted salt pork and gunpowder, we sent out a man on horseback, and probably he was shot dead by the Injuns before he got back. We ladies—of course we were all farmers at first—we didn't expect any rest-room in those days. My, we'd have thought the one they have now was simply elegant! My house was roofed with hay and it leaked something terrible when it rained—only dry place was under a shelf.

"And when the town grew up we thought the new city hall was real fine. And I don't see any need for dance-halls. Dancing isn't what it was, anyway. We used to dance modest, and we had just as much fun as all these young folks do now with their terrible Turkey Trots and hugging and all. But if they must neglect the Lord's injunction that young girls ought to be modest, then I guess they manage pretty well at the K. P. Hall and the Oddfellows', even if some of the lodges don't always welcome a lot of these foreigners and hired help to all their dances. And I certainly don't see any need of a farm-bureau or this domestic science demonstration you talk about. In my day the boys learned to farm by honest sweating, and every gal could cook, or her ma learned her how across her knee! Besides, ain't there a county agent at Wakamin? He comes here once a fortnight, maybe. That's enough monkeying with this scientific farming—Champ says there's nothing to it anyway.

"And as for a lecture hall—haven't we got the churches? Good deal better to listen to a good old-fashioned sermon than a lot of geography and books and things that nobody needs to know—more 'n enough heathen learning right here in the Thanatopsis. And as for trying to make a whole town in this Colonial architecture you talk about—— I do love nice things; to this day I run ribbons into my petticoats, even if Champ Perry does laugh at me, the old villain! But just the same I don't believe any of us old-timers would like to see the town that we worked so hard to build being tore down to make a place that wouldn't look like nothing but some Dutch story-book and not a bit like the place we loved. And don't you think it's sweet now? All the trees and lawns? And such comfy houses, and hot-water heat and electric lights and telephones and cement walks and everything? Why, I thought everybody from the Twin Cities always said it was such a beautiful town!"

Carol forswore herself; declared that Gopher Prairie had the color of Algiers and the gaiety of Mardi Gras.

Yet the next afternoon she was pouncing on Mrs. Lyman Cass, the hook-nosed consort of the owner of the flour-mill.

Mrs. Cass's parlor belonged to the crammed-Victorian school, as Mrs. Luke Dawson's belonged to the bare-Victorian. It was furnished on two principles: First, everything must resemble something else. A rocker had a back like a lyre, a near-leather seat imitating tufted cloth, and arms like Scotch Presbyterian lions; with knobs, scrolls, shields, and spear-points on unexpected portions of the chair. The second principle of the crammed-Victorian school was that every inch of the interior must be filled with useless objects.

The walls of Mrs. Cass's parlor were plastered with "handpainted" pictures, "buckeye" pictures, of birch-trees, newsboys, puppies, and church-steeples on Christmas Eve; with a plaque depicting the Exposition Building in Minneapolis, burntwood portraits of Indian chiefs of no tribe in particular, a pansy-decked poetic motto, a Yard of Roses, and the banners of the educational institutions attended by the Casses' two sons—Chicopee Falls Business College and McGillicuddy University. One small square table contained a card-receiver of painted china with a rim of wrought and gilded lead, a Family Bible, Grant's Memoirs, the latest novel by Mrs. Gene Stratton Porter, a wooden model of a Swiss chalet which was also a bank for dimes, a polished abalone shell holding one black-headed pin and one empty spool, a velvet pin-cushion in a gilded metal slipper with "Souvenir of Troy, N. Y." stamped on the toe, and an unexplained red glass dish which had warts.

Mrs. Cass's first remark was, "I must show you all my pretty things and art objects."

She piped, after Carol's appeal:

"I see. You think the New England villages and Colonial houses are so much more cunning than these Middlewestern towns. I'm glad you feel that way. You'll be interested to know I was born in Vermont."

"And don't you think we ought to try to make Gopher Prai——"

"My gracious no! We can't afford it. Taxes are much too high as it is. We ought to retrench, and not let the city council spend another cent. Uh—— Don't you think that was a grand paper Mrs. Westlake read about Tolstoy? I was so glad she pointed out how all his silly socialistic ideas failed."

What Mrs. Cass said was what Kennicott said, that evening. Not in twenty years would the council propose or Gopher Prairie vote the funds for a new city hall.

v

Carol had avoided exposing her plans to Vida Sherwin. She was shy of the big-sister manner; Vida would either laugh at her or snatch the idea and change it to suit herself. But there was no other hope. When Vida came in to tea Carol sketched her Utopia.

Vida was soothing but decisive:

"My dear, you're all off. I would like to see it: a real gardeny place to shut out the gales. But it can't be done. What could the clubwomen accomplish?"

"Their husbands are the most important men in town. They *are* the town!"

"But the town as a separate unit is not the husband of the Thanatopsis. If you knew the trouble we had in getting the city council to spend the money and cover the pumping-station with vines! Whatever you may think of Gopher Prairie women, they're twice as progressive as the men."

"But can't the men see the ugliness?"

"They don't think it's ugly. And how can you prove it? Matter of taste. Why should they like what a Boston architect likes?"

"What they like is to sell prunes!"

"Well, why not? Anyway, the point is that you have to work from the inside, with what we have, rather than from the outside, with foreign ideas. The shell ought not to be forced on the spirit. It can't be! The bright shell has to grow out of the spirit, and express it. That means waiting. If we keep after the city council for another ten years they *may* vote the bonds for a new school."

"I refuse to believe that if they saw it the big men would be too tight-fisted to spend a few dollars each for a building—think!—dancing and lectures and plays, all done co-operatively!"

"You mention the word 'co-operative' to the merchants and they'll lynch you! The one thing they fear more than mail-order houses is that farmers' co-operative movements may get started."

"The secret trails that lead to scared pocket-books! Always, in everything! And I don't have any of the fine melodrama of fiction: the dictagraphs and speeches by torchlight. I'm merely blocked by stupidity. Oh, I know I'm a fool. I dream of Venice, and I live in Archangel and scold because the Northern seas aren't tender-colored. But at least they sha'n't keep me from loving Venice, and sometime I'll run away—— All right. No more."

She flung out her hands in a gesture of renunciation.

### VI

Early May; wheat springing up in blades like grass; corn and potatoes being planted; the land humming. For two days there had been steady rain. Even in town the roads were a furrowed welter of mud, hideous to view and difficult to cross. Main Street was a black swamp from curb to curb; on residence streets the grass parking beside the walks oozed gray water. It was prickly hot, yet the town was barren under the bleak sky. Softened neither by snow nor by waving boughs the houses squatted and scowled, revealed in their unkempt harshness.

As she dragged homeward Carol looked with distaste at her clay-loaded rubbers, the smeared hem of her skirt. She passed Lyman Cass's pinnacled, dark-red, hulking house. She waded a streaky yellow pool. This morass was not her home, she insisted. Her home, and her beautiful town, existed in her mind. They had already been created. The task was done. What she really had been questing was some one to share them with her. Vida would not; Kennicott could not.

Some one to share her refuge.

Suddenly she was thinking of Guy Pollock.

She dismissed him. He was too cautious. She needed a spirit as young and unreasonable as her own. And she would never find it. Youth would never come singing. She was beaten.

Yet that same evening she had an idea which solved the rebuilding of Gopher Prairie.

Within ten minutes she was jerking the old-fashioned bell-pull of Luke Dawson. Mrs. Dawson opened the door and peered doubtfully about the edge of it. Carol kissed her cheek, and frisked into the lugubrious sitting-room.

"Well, well, you're a sight for sore eyes!" chuckled Mr. Dawson, dropping his newspaper, pushing his spectacles back on his forehead.

"You seem so excited," sighed Mrs. Dawson.

"I am! Mr. Dawson, aren't you a millionaire?"

He cocked his head, and purred, "Well, I guess if I cashed in on all my securities and farm-holdings and my interests in iron on the Mesaba and in Northern timber and cut-over lands, I could push two million dollars pretty close, and I've made every cent of it by hard work and having the sense to not go out and spend every——"

"I think I want most of it from you!"

The Dawsons glanced at each other in appreciation of the jest; and he chirped, "You're worse than Reverend Benlick! He don't hardly ever strike me for more than ten dollars—at a time!"

"I'm not joking. I mean it! Your children in the Cities are grown-up and well-to-do. You don't want to die and leave your name unknown. Why not do a big, original thing? Why not rebuild the whole town? Get a great architect, and have him plan a town that would be suitable to the prairie. Perhaps he'd create some entirely new form of architecture. Then tear down all these shambling buildings——"

Mr. Dawson had decided that she really did mean it. He wailed, "Why, that would cost at least three or four million dollars!"

"But you alone, just one man, have two of those millions!"

"Me? Spend all my hard-earned cash on building houses for a lot of shift-less beggars that never had the sense to save their money? Not that I've ever been mean. Mama could always have a hired girl to do the work—when we could find one. But her and I have worked our fingers to the bone and—spend it on a lot of these rascals——?"

"Please! Don't be angry! I just mean—I mean—— Oh, not spend all of it, of course, but if you led off the list, and the others came in, and if they heard you talk about a more attractive town——"

"Why now, child, you've got a lot of notions. Besides, what's the matter with the town? Looks good to me. I've had people that have traveled all over the world tell me time and again that Gopher Prairie is the prettiest place in the Middlewest. Good enough for anybody. Certainly good enough for Mama and me. Besides! Mama and me are planning to go out to Pasadena and buy a bungalow and live there."

### VII

She had met Miles Bjornstam on the street. For the second of welcome encounter this workman with the bandit mustache and the muddy overalls seemed nearer than any one else to the credulous youth which she was seeking to fight beside her, and she told him, as a cheerful anecdote, a little of her story.

He grunted, "I never thought I'd be agreeing with Old Man Dawson, the penny-pinching old land-thief—and a fine briber he is, too. But you got the wrong slant. You aren't one of the people—yet. You want to do something for the town. I don't! I want the town to do something for itself. We don't want old Dawson's money—not if it's a gift, with a string. We'll take it away from him, because it belongs to us. You got to get more iron and cussedness into you. Come join us cheerful bums, and some day—when we educate ourselves and quit being bums—we'll take things and run 'em straight."

He had changed from her friend to a cynical man in overalls. She could not relish the autocracy of "cheerful bums."

She forgot him as she tramped the outskirts of town.

She had replaced the city hall project by an entirely new and highly exhilarating thought of how little was done for these unpicturesque poor.

### VIII

The spring of the plains is not a reluctant virgin but brazen and soon away. The mud roads of a few days ago are powdery dust and the puddles beside them have hardened into lozenges of black sleek earth like cracked patent leather.

Carol was panting as she crept to the meeting of the Thanatopsis program committee which was to decide the subject for next fall and winter.

Madam Chairman (Miss Ella Stowbody in an oyster-colored blouse) asked if there was any new business.

Carol rose. She suggested that the Thanatopsis ought to help the poor of the town. She was ever so correct and modern. She did not, she said, want charity for them, but a chance of self-help; an employment bureau, direction in washing babies and making pleasing stews, possibly a municipal fund for home-building. "What do you think of my plans, Mrs. Warren?" she concluded.

Speaking judiciously, as one related to the church by marriage, Mrs. Warren gave verdict:

"I'm sure we're all heartily in accord with Mrs. Kennicott in feeling that wherever genuine poverty is encountered, it is not only *noblesse oblige* but a joy to fulfil our duty to the less fortunate ones. But I must say it seems to me we should lose the whole point of the thing by not regarding it as charity. Why, that's the chief adornment of the true Christian and the church! The Bible has laid it down for our guidance. 'Faith, Hope, and *Charity*,' it says, and, 'The poor ye have with ye always,' which indicates that there never can be anything to these so-called scientific schemes for abolishing charity, never! And isn't it better so? I should hate to think of a world in which we were deprived of all the pleasure of giving. Besides, if these shiftless folks realize they're getting charity, and not something to which they have a right, they're so much more grateful."

"Besides," snorted Miss Ella Stowbody, "they've been fooling you, Mrs. Kennicott. There isn't any real poverty here. Take that Mrs. Steinhof you speak of: I send her our washing whenever there's too much for our hired girl—I must have sent her ten dollars' worth the past year alone! I'm sure Papa would never approve of a city home-building fund. Papa says these folks are fakers. Especially all these tenant farmers that pretend they have so much trouble getting seed and machinery. Papa says they simply won't pay their debts. He says he's sure he hates to foreclose mortgages, but it's the only way to make them respect the law."

"And then think of all the clothes we give these people!" said Mrs. Jackson Elder.

Carol intruded again. "Oh yes. The clothes. I was going to speak of that. Don't you think that when we give clothes to the poor, if we do give them old ones, we ought to mend them first and make them as presentable as we can? Next Christmas when the Thanatopsis makes its distribution, wouldn't it be jolly if we got together and sewed on the clothes, and trimmed hats, and made them——"

"Heavens and earth, they have more time than we have! They ought to be mighty good and grateful to get anything, no matter what shape it's in. I know I'm not going to sit and sew for that lazy Mrs. Vopni, with all I've got to do!" snapped Ella Stowbody.

They were glaring at Carol. She reflected that Mrs. Vopni, whose husband had been killed by a train, had ten children.

But Mrs. Mary Ellen Wilks was smiling. Mrs. Wilks was the proprietor of Ye Art Shoppe and Magazine and Book Store, and the reader of the small Christian Science church. She made it all clear:

"If this class of people had an understanding of Science and that we are the children of God and nothing can harm us, they wouldn't be in error and poverty."

Mrs. Jackson Elder confirmed, "Besides, it strikes me the club is already doing enough, with tree-planting and the anti-fly campaign and the responsibility for the rest-room—to say nothing of the fact that we've talked of trying to get the railroad to put in a park at the station!"

"I think so too!" said Madam Chairman. She glanced uneasily at Miss Sherwin. "But what do you think, Vida?"

Vida smiled tactfully at each of the committee, and announced, "Well, I don't believe we'd better start anything more right now. But it's been a privilege to hear Carol's dear generous ideas, hasn't it! Oh! There is one thing we must decide on at once. We must get together and oppose any move on the part of the Minneapolis clubs to elect another State Federation president from the Twin Cities. And this Mrs. Edgar Potbury they're putting forward—I know there are people who think she's a bright interesting speaker, but I regard her as very shallow. What do you say to my writing to the Lake Ojibawasha Club, telling them that if their district will support Mrs. Warren for second vice-president, we'll support their Mrs. Hagelton (and such a dear, lovely, cultivated woman, too) for president."

"Yes! We ought to show up those Minneapolis folks!" Ella Stowbody said acidly. "And oh, by the way, we must oppose this movement of Mrs. Potbury's to have the state clubs come out definitely in favor of woman suffrage. Women haven't any place in politics. They would lose all their daintiness and charm if they became involved in these horrid plots and log-rolling and all this awful political stuff about scandal and personalities and so on."

All—save one—nodded. They interrupted the formal business-meeting to discuss Mrs. Edgar Potbury's husband, Mrs. Potbury's income, Mrs. Potbury's sedan, Mrs. Potbury's residence, Mrs. Potbury's oratorical style, Mrs. Potbury's mandarin evening coat, Mrs. Potbury's coiffure, and Mrs. Potbury's altogether reprehensible influence on the State Federation of Women's Clubs.

Before the program committee adjourned they took three minutes to decide which of the subjects suggested by the magazine *Culture Hints*, Furnishings and China, or The Bible as Literature, would be better for the coming year. There was one annoying incident. Mrs. Dr. Kennicott interfered and showed off again. She commented, "Don't you think that we already get enough of the Bible in our churches and Sunday Schools?"

Mrs. Leonard Warren, somewhat out of order but much more out of temper, cried, "Well upon my word! I didn't suppose there was any one who felt that we could get enough of the Bible! I guess if the Grand Old Book has withstood the attacks of infidels for these two thousand years it is worth our *slight* consideration!"

"Oh, I didn't mean——" Carol begged. Inasmuch as she did mean, it was hard to be extremely lucid. "But I wish, instead of limiting ourselves either to the Bible, or to anecdotes about the Brothers Adam's wigs, which *Culture Hints* seems to regard as the significant point about furniture, we could study some of the really stirring ideas that are springing up today—whether it's chemistry or anthropology or labor problems—the things that are going to mean so terribly much."

Everybody cleared her polite throat.

Madam Chairman inquired, "Is there any other discussion? Will some one make a motion to adopt the suggestion of Vida Sherwin—to take up Furnishings and China?"

It was adopted, unanimously.

"Checkmate!" murmured Carol, as she held up her hand.

Had she actually believed that she could plant a seed of liberalism in the

blank wall of mediocrity? How had she fallen into the folly of trying to
plant anything whatever in a wall so smooth and sun-glazed, and so satisfying to the happy sleepers within?

# 12

One week of authentic spring, one rare sweet week of May, one tranquil
moment between the blast of winter and the charge of summer. Daily Carol
walked from town into flashing country hysteric with new life.

One enchanted hour when she returned to youth and a belief in the possibility of beauty.

She had walked northward toward the upper shore of Plover Lake, taking
to the railroad track, whose directness and dryness make it the natural highway for pedestrians on the plains. She stepped from tie to tie, in long strides.
At each road-crossing she had to crawl over a cattle-guard of sharpened
timbers. She walked the rails, balancing with arms extended, cautious heel
before toe. As she lost balance her body bent over, her arms revolved wildly,
and when she toppled she laughed aloud.

The thick grass beside the track, coarse and prickly with many burnings,
hid canary-yellow buttercups and the mauve petals and woolly sage-green
coats of the pasque flowers. The branches of the kinnikinic brush were red
and smooth as lacquer on a saki bowl.

She ran down the gravelly embankment, smiled at children gathering
flowers in a little basket, thrust a handful of the soft pasque flowers into
the bosom of her white blouse. Fields of springing wheat drew her from the
straight propriety of the railroad and she crawled through the rusty barbed-
wire fence. She followed a furrow between low wheat blades and a field of
rye which showed silver lights as it flowed before the wind. She found a
pasture by the lake. So sprinkled was the pasture with rag-baby blossoms
and the cottony herb of Indian tobacco that it spread out like a rare old
Persian carpet of cream and rose and delicate green. Under her feet the rough
grass made a pleasant crunching. Sweet winds blew from the sunny lake beside her, and small waves sputtered on the meadowy shore. She leaped a
tiny creek bowered in pussy-willow buds. She was nearing a frivolous grove
of birch and poplar and wild plum trees.

The poplar foliage had the downiness of a Corot arbor; the green and
silver trunks were as candid as the birches, as slender and lustrous as the
limbs of a Pierrot. The cloudy white blossoms of the plum trees filled the
grove with a springtime mistiness which gave an illusion of distance.

She ran into the wood, crying out for joy of freedom regained after winter.
Choke-cherry blossoms lured her from the outer sun-warmed spaces to depths
of green stillness, where a submarine light came through the young leaves.

She walked pensively along an abandoned road. She found a moccasin-flower beside a lichen-covered log. At the end of the road she saw the open acres —dipping rolling fields bright with wheat.

"I believe! The woodland gods still live! And out there, the great land. It's beautiful as the mountains. What do I care for Thanatopsises?"

She came out on the prairie, spacious under an arch of boldly cut clouds. Small pools glittered. Above a marsh red-winged blackbirds chased a crow in a swift melodrama of the air. On a hill was silhouetted a man following a drag. His horse bent its neck and plodded, content.

A path took her to the Corinth road, leading back to town. Dandelions glowed in patches amidst the wild grass by the way. A stream galloped through a concrete culvert beneath the road. She trudged in healthy weariness.

A man in a bumping Ford rattled up beside her, hailed, "Give you a lift, Mrs. Kennicott?"

"Thank you. It's awfully good of you, but I'm enjoying the walk."

"Great day, by golly. I seen some wheat that must of been five inches high. Well, so long."

She hadn't the dimmest notion who he was, but his greeting warmed her. This countryman gave her a companionship which she had never (whether by her fault or theirs or neither) been able to find in the matrons and commercial lords of the town.

Half a mile from town, in a hollow between hazelnut bushes and a brook, she discovered a gipsy encampment: a covered wagon, a tent, a bunch of pegged-out horses. A broad-shouldered man was squatted on his heels, holding a frying-pan over a camp-fire. He looked toward her. He was Miles Bjornstam.

"Well, well, what you doing out here?" he roared. "Come have a hunk o' bacon. Pete! Hey, Pete!"

A tousled person came from behind the covered wagon.

"Pete, here's the one honest-to-God lady in my bum town. Come on, crawl in and set a couple minutes, Mrs. Kennicott. I'm hiking off for all summer."

The Red Swede staggered up, rubbed his cramped knees, lumbered to the wire fence, held the strands apart for her. She unconsciously smiled at him as she went through. Her skirt caught on a barb; he carefully freed it.

Beside this man in blue flannel shirt, baggy khaki trousers, uneven suspenders, and vile felt hat, she was small and exquisite.

The surly Pete set out an upturned bucket for her. She lounged on it, her elbows on her knees. "Where are you going?" she asked.

"Just starting off for the summer, horse-trading." Bjornstam chuckled. His red mustache caught the sun. "Regular hoboes and public benefactors we are. Take a hike like this every once in a while. Sharks on horses. Buy 'em from farmers and sell 'em to others. We're honest—frequently. Great time. Camp along the road. I was wishing I had a chance to say good-by to you before I ducked out but—— Say, you better come along with us."

"I'd like to."

"While you're playing mumblety-peg with Mrs. Lym Cass, Pete and me will be rambling across Dakota, through the Bad Lands, into the butte country, and when fall comes, we'll be crossing over a pass of the Big Horn Mountains, maybe, and camp in a snow-storm, quarter of a mile right straight up above a lake. Then in the morning we'll lie snug in our blankets and look up through the pines at an eagle. How'd it strike you? Heh? Eagle soaring and soaring all day—big wide sky——"

"Don't! Or I will go with you, and I'm afraid there might be some slight scandal. Perhaps some day I'll do it. Good-by."

Her hand disappeared in his blackened leather glove. From the turn in the road she waved at him. She walked on more soberly now, and she was lonely.

But the wheat and grass were sleek velvet under the sunset; the prairie clouds were tawny gold; and she swung happily into Main Street.

II

Through the first days of June she drove with Kennicott on his calls. She identified him with the virile land; she admired him as she saw with what respect the farmers obeyed him. She was out in the early chill, after a hasty cup of coffee, reaching open country as the fresh sun came up in that unspoiled world. Meadow larks called from the tops of thin split fence-posts. The wild roses smelled clean.

As they returned in late afternoon the low sun was a solemnity of radial bands, like a heavenly fan of beaten gold; the limitless circle of the grain was a green sea rimmed with fog, and the willow wind-breaks were palmy isles.

Before July the close heat blanketed them. The tortured earth cracked. Farmers panted through corn-fields behind cultivators and the sweating flanks of horses. While she waited for Kennicott in the car, before a farm-house, the seat burned her fingers and her head ached with the glare on fenders and hood.

A black thunder-shower was followed by a dust storm which turned the sky yellow with the hint of a coming tornado. Impalpable black dust far-borne from Dakota covered the inner sills of the closed windows.

The July heat was ever more stifling. They crawled along Main Street by day; they found it hard to sleep at night. They brought mattresses down to the living-room, and thrashed and turned by the open window. Ten times a night they talked of going out to soak themselves with the hose and wade through the dew, but they were too listless to take the trouble. On cool evenings, when they tried to go walking, the gnats appeared in swarms which peppered their faces and caught in their throats.

She wanted the Northern pines, the Eastern sea, but Kennicott declared that it would be "kind of hard to get away, just *now.*" The Health and Improvement Committee of the Thanatopsis asked her to take part in the anti-fly campaign, and she toiled about town persuading householders to use the fly-traps furnished by the club, or giving out money prizes to fly-swatting children. She was loyal enough but not ardent, and without ever quite intending to, she began to neglect the task as heat sucked at her strength.

Kennicott and she motored North and spent a week with his mother—that is, Carol spent it with his mother, while he fished for bass.

The great event was their purchase of a summer cottage, down on Lake Minniemashie.

Perhaps the most amiable feature of life in Gopher Prairie was the summer cottages. They were merely two-room shanties, with a seepage of broken-down chairs, peeling veneered tables, chromos pasted on wooden walls, and inefficient kerosene stoves. They were so thin-walled and so close together that you could—and did—hear a baby being spanked in the fifth cottage off. But they were set among elms and lindens on a bluff which looked across the lake to fields of ripened wheat sloping up to green woods.

Here the matrons forgot social jealousies, and sat gossiping in gingham; or, in old bathing-suits, surrounded by hysterical children, they paddled for hours. Carol joined them; she ducked shrieking small boys, and helped babies construct sand-basins for unfortunate minnows. She liked Juanita Haydock and Maud Dyer when she helped them make picnic-supper for the men, who came motoring out from town each evening. She was easier and more natural with them. In the debate as to whether there should be veal loaf or poached egg on hash, she had no chance to be heretical and oversensitive.

They danced sometimes, in the evening; they had a minstrel show, with Kennicott surprisingly good as end-man; always they were encircled by children wise in the lore of woodchucks and gophers and rafts and willow whistles.

If they could have continued this normal barbaric life Carol would have been the most enthusiastic citizen of Gopher Prairie. She was relieved to be assured that she did not want bookish conversation alone; that she did not expect the town to become a Bohemia. She was content now. She did not criticize.

But in September, when the year was at its richest, custom dictated that it was time to return to town; to remove the children from the waste occupation of learning the earth, and send them back to lessons about the number of potatoes which (in a delightful world untroubled by commission-houses or shortages in freight-cars) William sold to John. The women who had cheerfully gone bathing all summer looked doubtful when Carol begged, "Let's keep up an outdoor life this winter, let's slide and skate." Their hearts shut again till spring, and the nine months of cliques and radiators and dainty refreshments began all over.

III

Carol had started a salon.

Since Kennicott, Vida Sherwin, and Guy Pollock were her only lions, and since Kennicott would have preferred Sam Clark to all the poets and radicals in the entire world, her private and self-defensive clique did not get beyond

one evening dinner for Vida and Guy, on her first wedding anniversary; and
that dinner did not get beyond a controversy regarding Raymie Wutherspoon's yearnings.

Guy Pollock was the gentlest person she had found here. He spoke of her
new jade and cream frock naturally, not jocosely; he held her chair for her
as they sat down to dinner; and he did not, like Kennicott, interrupt her to
shout, "Oh say, speaking of that, I heard a good story today." But Guy was
incurably hermit. He sat late and talked hard, and did not come again.

Then she met Champ Perry in the post-office—and decided that in the
history of the pioneers was the panacea for Gopher Prairie, for all of America.
We have lost their sturdiness, she told herself. We must restore the last of the
veterans to power and follow them on the backward path to the integrity of
Lincoln, to the gaiety of settlers dancing in a saw-mill.

She read in the records of the Minnesota Territorial Pioneers that only
sixty years ago, not so far back as the birth of her own father, four cabins
had composed Gopher Prairie. The log stockade which Mrs. Champ Perry
was to find when she trekked in was built afterward by the soldiers as a defense against the Sioux. The four cabins were inhabited by Maine Yankees
who had come up the Mississippi to St. Paul and driven north over virgin
prairie into virgin woods. They ground their own corn; the men-folks shot
ducks and pigeons and prairie chickens; the new breakings yielded the tur-
nip-like rutabagas, which they ate raw and boiled and baked and raw again.
For treat they had wild plums and crab-apples and tiny wild strawberries.

Grasshoppers came darkening the sky, and in an hour ate the farmwife's
garden and the farmer's coat. Precious horses, painfully brought from Illinois,
were drowned in bogs or stampeded by the fear of blizzards. Snow blew
through the chinks of new-made cabins, and Eastern children, with flowery
muslin dresses, shivered all winter and in summer were red and black with
mosquito bites. Indians were everywhere; they camped in dooryards, stalked
into kitchens to demand doughnuts, came with rifles across their backs into
schoolhouses and begged to see the pictures in the geographies. Packs of
timber-wolves treed the children; and the settlers found dens of rattlesnakes,
killed fifty, a hundred, in a day.

Yet it was a buoyant life. Carol read enviously in the admirable Minnesota
chronicles called "Old Rail Fence Corners" the reminiscence of Mrs. Mahlon
Black, who settled in Stillwater in 1848:

"There was nothing to parade over in those days. We took it as it came
and had happy lives. . . . We would all gather together and in about two
minutes would be having a good time—playing cards or dancing. . . . We
used to waltz and dance contra dances. None of these new jigs and not wear
any clothes to speak of. We covered our hides in those days; no tight skirts
like now. You could take three or four steps inside our skirts and then not
reach the edge. One of the boys would fiddle a while and then some one
would spell him and he could get a dance. Sometimes they would dance and
fiddle too."

She reflected that if she could not have ballrooms of gray and rose and crystal, she wanted to be swinging across a puncheon-floor with a dancing fiddler. This smug in-between town, which had exchanged "Money Musk" for phonographs grinding out ragtime, it was neither the heroic old nor the sophisticated new. Couldn't she somehow, some yet unimagined how, turn it back to simplicity?

She herself knew two of the pioneers: the Perrys. Champ Perry was the buyer at the grain-elevator. He weighed wagons of wheat on a rough plat-form-scale, in the cracks of which the kernels sprouted every spring. Between times he napped in the dusty peace of his office.

She called on the Perrys at their rooms above Howland & Gould's grocery.

When they were already old they had lost the money, which they had invested in an elevator. They had given up their beloved yellow brick house and moved into these rooms over a store, which were the Gopher Prairie equivalent of a flat. A broad stairway led from the street to the upper hall, along which were the doors of a lawyer's office, a dentist's, a photographer's "studio," the lodge-rooms of the Affiliated Order of Spartans and, at the back, the Perrys' apartment.

They received her (their first caller in a month) with aged fluttering ten-derness. Mrs. Perry confided, "My, it's a shame we got to entertain you in such a cramped place. And there ain't any water except that ole iron sink outside in the hall, but still, as I say to Champ, beggars can't be choosers. 'Sides, the brick house was too big for me to sweep, and it was way out, and it's nice to be living down here among folks. Yes, we're glad to be here. But —— Some day, maybe we can have a house of our own again. We're saving up—— Oh, dear, if we could have our own home! But these rooms are real nice, ain't they!"

As old people will, the world over, they had moved as much as possible of their familiar furniture into this small space. Carol had none of the superi-ority she felt toward Mrs. Lyman Cass's plutocratic parlor. She was at home here. She noted with tenderness all the makeshifts: the darned chair-arms, the patent rocker covered with sleazy cretonne, the pasted strips of paper mending the birch-bark napkin-rings labeled "Papa" and "Mama."

She hinted of her new enthusiasm. To find one of the "young folks" who took them seriously, heartened the Perrys, and she easily drew from them the principles by which Gopher Prairie should be born again—should again be-come amusing to live in.

This was their philosophy complete . . . in the era of aeroplanes and syndicalism:

The Baptist Church (and, somewhat less, the Methodist, Congregational, and Presbyterian Churches) is the perfect, the divinely ordained standard in music, oratory, philanthropy, and ethics. "We don't need all this new-fangled science, or this terrible Higher Criticism that's ruining our young men in colleges. What we need is to get back to the true Word of God, and a good sound belief in hell, like we used to have it preached to us."

The Republican Party, the Grand Old Party of Blaine and McKinley, is the agent of the Lord and of the Baptist Church in temporal affairs.

All socialists ought to be hanged.

"Harold Bell Wright is a lovely writer, and he teaches such good morals in his novels, and folks say he's made prett' near a million dollars out of 'em."

People who make more than ten thousand a year or less than eight hundred are wicked.

Europeans are still wickeder.

It doesn't hurt any to drink a glass of beer on a warm day, but anybody who touches wine is headed straight for hell.

Virgins are not so virginal as they used to be.

Nobody needs drug-store ice cream; pie is good enough for anybody.

The farmers want too much for their wheat.

The owners of the elevator-company expect too much for the salaries they pay.

There would be no more trouble or discontent in the world if everybody worked as hard as Pa did when he cleared our first farm.

IV

Carol's hero-worship dwindled to polite nodding, and the nodding dwindled to a desire to escape, and she went home with a headache.

Next day she saw Miles Bjornstam on the street.

"Just back from Montana. Great summer. Pumped my lungs chuck-full of Rocky Mountain air. Now for another whirl at sassing the bosses of Gopher Prairie." She smiled at him, and the Perrys faded, the pioneers faded, till they were but daguerreotypes in a black walnut cupboard.

# 13

She tried, more from loyalty than from desire, to call upon the Perrys on a November evening when Kennicott was away. They were not at home.

Like a child who has no one to play with she loitered through the dark hall. She saw a light under an office door. She knocked. To the person who opened she murmured, "Do you happen to know where the Perrys are?" She realized that it was Guy Pollock.

"I'm awfully sorry, Mrs. Kennicott, but I don't know. Won't you come in and wait for them?"

"W-why——" she observed, as she reflected that in Gopher Prairie it is not decent to call on a man; as she decided that no, really, she wouldn't go in; and as she went in.

"I didn't know your office was up here."

"Yes, office, town-house, and château in Picardy. But you can't see the château and town-house (next to the Duke of Sutherland's). They're beyond that inner door. They are a cot and a wash-stand and my other suit and the blue crêpe tie you said you liked."

"You remember my saying that?"

"Of course. I always shall. Please try this chair."

She glanced about the rusty office—gaunt stove, shelves of tan law-books, desk-chair filled with newspapers so long sat upon that they were in holes and smudged to grayness. There were only two things which suggested Guy Pollock. On the green felt of the table-desk, between legal blanks and a clotted inkwell, was a cloisonné vase. On a swing shelf was a row of books unfamiliar to Gopher Prairie: Mosher editions of the poets, black and red German novels, a Charles Lamb in crushed levant.

Guy did not sit down. He quartered the office, a grayhound on the scent; a grayhound with glasses tilted forward on his thin nose, and a silky indecisive brown mustache. He had a golf jacket of jersey, worn through at the creases in the sleeves. She noted that he did not apologize for it, as Kennicott would have done.

He made conversation: "I didn't know you were a bosom friend of the Perrys. Champ is the salt of the earth but somehow I can't imagine him joining you in symbolic dancing, or making improvements on the Diesel engine."

"No. He's a dear soul, bless him, but he belongs in the National Museum, along with General Grant's sword, and I'm—— Oh, I suppose I'm seeking for a gospel that will evangelize Gopher Prairie."

"Really? Evangelize it to what?"

"To anything that's definite. Seriousness or frivolousness or both. I wouldn't care whether it was a laboratory or a carnival. But it's merely safe. Tell me, Mr. Pollock, what *is* the matter with Gopher Prairie?"

"Is anything the matter with it? Isn't there perhaps something the matter with you and me? (May I join you in the honor of having something the matter?)"

"(Yes, thanks.) No, I think it's the town."

"Because they enjoy skating more than biology?"

"But I'm not only more interested in biology than the Jolly Seventeen, but also in skating! I'll skate with them, or slide, or throw snowballs, just as gladly as talk with you."

("Oh no!")

("Yes!) But they want to stay home and embroider."

"Perhaps. I'm not defending the town. It's merely—— I'm a confirmed doubter of myself. (Probably I'm conceited about my lack of conceit!) Anyway, Gopher Prairie isn't particularly bad. It's like all villages in all countries. Most places that have lost the smell of earth but not yet acquired the smell of patchouli—or of factory-smoke—are just as suspicious and righteous. I wonder if the small town isn't, with some lovely exceptions, a social appendix? Some day these dull market-towns may be as obsolete as monasteries. I can imagine the farmer and his local store-manager going by monorail, at the of the day, into a city more charming than any William Morris Utopia —music, a university, clubs for loafers like me. (Lord, how I'd like to have a real club!)"

She asked impulsively, "You, why do you stay here?"

"I have the Village Virus."

"It sounds dangerous."

"It is. More dangerous than the cancer that will certainly get me at fifty unless I stop this smoking. The Village Virus is the germ which—it's extraordinarily like the hook-worm—it infects ambitious people who stay too long in the provinces. You'll find it epidemic among lawyers and doctors and ministers and college-bred merchants—all these people who have had a glimpse of the world that thinks and laughs, but have returned to their swamp. I'm a perfect example. But I sha'n't pester you with my dolors."

"You won't. And do sit down, so I can see you."

He dropped into the slatcking desk-chair. He looked squarely at her; she was conscious of the pupils of his eyes; of the fact that he was a man, and lonely. They were embarrassed. They elaborately glanced away, and were relieved as he went on:

"The diagnosis of my Village Virus is simple enough. I was born in an Ohio town about the same size as Gopher Prairie, and much less friendly. It'd had more generations in which to form an oligarchy of respectability. Here, a stranger is taken in if he is correct, if he likes hunting and motoring and God and our Senator. There, we didn't take in even our own till we had contemptuously got used to them. It was a red-brick Ohio town, and the trees made it damp, and it smelled of rotten apples. The country wasn't like our lakes and prairie. There were small stuffy corn-fields and brick-yards and greasy oil-wells.

"I went to a denominational college and learned that since dictating the Bible, and hiring a perfect race of ministers to explain it, God has never done much but creep around and try to catch us disobeying it. From college I went to New York, to the Columbia Law School. And for four years I lived. Oh, I won't rhapsodize about New York. It was dirty and noisy and breathless and ghastly expensive. But compared with the moldy academy in which I had been smothered——! I went to symphonies twice a week. I saw Irving and Terry and Duse and Bernhardt, from the top gallery. I walked in Gramercy Park. And I read, oh, everything.

"Through a cousin I learned that Julius Flickerbaugh was sick and needed a partner. I came here. Julius got well. He didn't like my way of loafing five hours and then doing my work (really not so badly) in one. We parted.

"When I first came here I swore I'd 'keep up my interests.' Very lofty! I read Browning, and went to Minneapolis for the theaters. I thought I was 'keeping up.' But I guess the Village Virus had me already. I was reading four copies of cheap fiction-magazines to one poem. I'd put off the Minneapolis trips till I simply had to go there on a lot of legal matters.

"A few years ago I was talking to a patent lawyer from Chicago, and I realized that—— I'd always felt so superior to people like Julius Flickerbaugh, but I saw that I was as provincial and behind-the-times as Julius. (Worse! Julius plows through the *Literary Digest* and the *Outlook* faithfully, while I'm turning over pages of a book by Charles Flandrau that I already know by heart.)

"I decided to leave here. Stern resolution. Grasp the world. Then I found that the Village Virus had me, absolute: I didn't want to face new streets and younger men—real competition. It was too easy to go on making out conveyances and arguing ditching cases. So—— That's all of the biography of a living dead man, except the diverting last chapter, the lies about my having been 'a tower of strength and legal wisdom' which some day a preacher will spin over my lean dry body."

He looked down at his table-desk, fingering the starry enameled vase.

She could not comment. She pictured herself running across the room to pat his hair. She saw that his lips were firm, under his soft faded mustache. She sat still, and maundered, "I know. The Village Virus. Perhaps it will get me. Some day I'm going—— Oh, no matter. At least, I am making you talk! Usually you have to be polite to my garrulousness, but now I'm sitting at your feet."

"It would be rather nice to have you literally sitting at my feet, by a fire."

"Would you have a fireplace for me?"

"Naturally! Please don't snub me now! Let the old man rave. How old are you, Carol?"

"Twenty-six, Guy."

"Twenty-six! I was just leaving New York, at twenty-six. I heard Patti sing, at twenty-six. And now I'm forty-seven. I feel like a child, yet I'm old enough to be your father. So it's decently paternal to imagine you curled at my feet. . . . Of course I hope it isn't, but we'll reflect the morals of Gopher Prairie by officially announcing that it is! . . . These standards that you and I live up to! There's one thing that's the matter with Gopher Prairie, at least with the ruling-class (there is a ruling-class, despite all our professions of democracy). And the penalty we tribal rulers pay is that our subjects watch us every minute. We can't get wholesomely drunk and relax. We have to be so correct about sex morals, and inconspicuous clothes, and doing our commercial trickery only in the traditional ways, that none of us can live up to it, and we become horribly hypocritical. Unavoidably. The widow-robbing deacon of fiction can't help being hypocritical. The widows themselves demand it! They admire his unctuousness. And look at me. Suppose I did dare to make love to—some exquisite married woman. I wouldn't admit it to myself. I giggle with the most revolting salaciousness over *La Vie Parisienne*, when I get hold of one in Chicago, yet I shouldn't even try to hold your hand. I'm broken. It's the historical Anglo-Saxon way of making life miserable. . . . Oh, my dear, I haven't talked to anybody about myself and all ourselves for years."

"Guy! Can't we do something with the town? Really?"

"No, we can't!" He disposed of it like a judge ruling out an improper objection; returned to matters less uncomfortably energetic: "Curious. Most troubles are unnecessary. We have Nature beaten; we can make her grow wheat; we can keep warm when she sends blizzards. So we raise the devil just for pleasure—wars, politics, race-hatreds, labor-disputes. Here in Gopher Prairie we've cleared the fields, and become soft, so we make ourselves unhappy artificially, at great expense and exertion: Methodists disliking Episcopalians, the man with the Hudson laughing at the man with the flivver. The worst is the commercial hatred—the grocer feeling that any man who doesn't deal with him is robbing him. What hurts me is that it applies to lawyers and doctors (and decidedly to their wives!) as much as to grocers. The doctors—you know about that—how your husband and Westlake and Gould dislike one another."

"No! I won't admit it!"

He grinned.

"Oh, maybe once or twice, when Will has positively known of a case where Doctor—where one of the others has continued to call on patients longer than necessary, he has laughed about it, but——"

He still grinned.

"No, *really!* And when you say the wives of the doctors share these jealousies—— Mrs. McGanum and I haven't any particular crush on each other; she's so stolid. But her mother, Mrs. Westlake—nobody could be sweeter."

"Yes, I'm sure she's very bland. But I wouldn't tell her my heart's secrets if I were you, my dear. I insist that there's only one professional-man's wife in this town who doesn't plot, and that is you, you blessed, credulous outsider!"

"I won't be cajoled! I won't believe that medicine, the priesthood of healing, can be turned into a penny-picking business."

"See here: Hasn't Kennicott ever hinted to you that you'd better be nice to some old woman because she tells her friends which doctor to call in? But I oughtn't to——"

She remembered certain remarks which Kennicott had offered regarding the Widow Bogart. She flinched, looked at Guy beseechingly.

He sprang up, strode to her with a nervous step, smoothed her hand. She wondered if she ought to be offended by his caress. Then she wondered if he liked her hat, the new Oriental turban of rose and silver brocade.

He dropped her hand. His elbow brushed her shoulder. He flitted over to the desk-chair, his thin back stooped. He picked up the cloisonné vase. Across it he peered at her with such loneliness that she was startled. But his eyes faded into impersonality as he talked of the jealousies of Gopher Prairie. He stopped himself with a sharp, "Good Lord, Carol, you're not a jury. You are within your legal rights in refusing to be subjected to this summing-up. I'm a tedious old fool analyzing the obvious, while you're the spirit of rebellion. Tell me your side. What is Gopher Prairie to you?"

"A bore!"

"Can I help?"

"How could you?"

"I don't know. Perhaps by listening. I haven't done that tonight. But normally—— Can't I be the confidant of the old French plays, the tiring-maid with the mirror and the loyal ears?"

"Oh, what is there to confide? The people are savorless and proud of it. And even if I liked you tremendously, I couldn't talk to you without twenty old hexes watching, whispering."

"But you will come talk to me, once in a while?"

"I'm not sure that I shall. I'm trying to develop my own large capacity for dullness and contentment. I've failed at every positive thing I've tried. I'd better 'settle down,' as they call it, and be satisfied to be—nothing."

"Don't be cynical. It hurts me, in you. It's like blood on the wing of a humming-bird."

"I'm not a humming-bird. I'm a hawk; a tiny leashed hawk, pecked to death by these large, white, flabby, wormy hens. But I am grateful to you for confirming me in the faith. And I'm going home!"

"Please stay and have some coffee with me."

"I'd like to. But they've succeeded in terrorizing me. I'm afraid of what people might say."

"I'm not afraid of that. I'm only afraid of what you might say!" He stalked to her; took her unresponsive hand. "Carol! You have been happy here to-night? (Yes. I'm begging!)"

She squeezed his hand quickly, then snatched hers away. She had but little of the curiosity of the flirt, and none of the intrigante's joy in furtiveness. If she was the naive girl, Guy Pollock was the clumsy boy. He raced about the office; he rammed his fists into his pockets. He stammered, "I—I—I—— Oh, the devil! Why do I awaken from smooth dustiness to this jagged rawness? I'll make—— I'm going to trot down the hall and bring in the Dillons, and we'll all have coffee or something."

"The Dillons?"

"Yes. Really quite a decent young pair—Harvey Dillon and his wife. He's a dentist, just come to town. They live in a room behind his office, same as I do here. They don't know much of anybody——"

"I've heard of them. And I've never thought to call. I'm horribly ashamed. Do bring them——"

She stopped, for no very clear reason, but his expression said, her faltering admitted, that they wished they had never mentioned the Dillons. With spurious enthusiasm he said, "Splendid! I will." From the door he glanced at her, curled in the peeled leather chair. He slipped out, came back with Dr. and Mrs. Dillon.

The four of them drank rather bad coffee which Pollock made on a kerosene burner. They laughed, and spoke of Minneapolis, and were tremendously tactful; and Carol started for home, through the November wind.

# 14

She was marching home.

"No. I couldn't fall in love with him. I like him, very much. But he's too much of a recluse. Could I kiss him? No! No! Guy Pollock at twenty-six —— I could have kissed him then, maybe, even if I were married to some one else, and probably I'd have been glib in persuading myself that 'it wasn't really wrong.'

"The amazing thing is that I'm not more amazed at myself. I, the virtuous young matron. Am I to be trusted? If the Prince Charming came——

"A Gopher Prairie housewife, married a year, and yearning for a 'Prince Charming' like a bachfisch of sixteen! They say that marriage is a magic change. But I'm not changed. But——

"No! I wouldn't want to fall in love, even if the Prince did come. I wouldn't want to hurt Will. I am fond of Will. I am! He doesn't stir me, not any longer. But I depend on him. He is home and children.

"I wonder when we will begin to have children? I do want them.

"I wonder whether I remembered to tell Bea to have hominy tomorrow, instead of oatmeal? She will have gone to bed by now. Perhaps I'll be up early enough——

"Ever so fond of Will. I wouldn't hurt him, even if I had to lose the mad love. If the Prince came I'd look once at him, and run. Darn fast! Oh, Carol, you are not heroic nor fine. You are the immutable vulgar young female.

"But I'm not the faithless wife who enjoys confiding that she's 'misunderstood.' Oh, I'm not, I'm not!

"Am I?

"At least I didn't whisper to Guy about Will's faults and his blindness to my remarkable soul. I didn't! Matter of fact, Will probably understands me perfectly! If only—if he would just back me up in rousing the town.

"How many, how incredibly many wives there must be who tingle over the first Guy Pollock who smiles at them. No! I will not be one of that herd of yearners! The coy virgin brides. Yet probably if the Prince were young and dared to face life——

"I'm not half as well oriented as that Mrs. Dillon. So obviously adoring her dentist! And seeing Guy only as an eccentric fogy.

"They weren't silk, Mrs. Dillon's stockings. They were lisle. Her legs are nice and slim. But no nicer than mine. I hate cotton tops on silk stockings. . . . Are my ankles getting fat? I will *not* have fat ankles!

"No. I am fond of Will. His work—one farmer he pulls through diphtheria is worth all my yammering for a castle in Spain. A castle with baths.

"This hat is so tight. I must stretch it. Guy liked it.

"There's the house. I'm awfully chilly. Time to get out the fur coat. I wonder if I'll ever have a beaver coat? Nutria is *not* the same thing! Beaver— glossy. Like to run my fingers over it. Guy's mustache like beaver. How utterly absurd!

"I am, I *am* fond of Will, and—— Can't I ever find another word than 'fond'?

"He's home. He'll think I was out late.

"Why can't he ever remember to pull down the shades? Cy Bogart and all the beastly boys peeping in. But the poor dear, he's absent-minded about minute—minush—whatever the word is. He has so much worry and work, while I do nothing but jabber to Bea.

"I *mustn't* forget the hominy——"

She was flying into the hall. Kennicott looked up from the *Journal of the American Medical Society.*

"Hello! What time did you get back?" she cried.

"About nine. You been gadding. Here it is past eleven!" Good-natured yet not quite approving.

"Did it feel neglected?"

"Well, you didn't remember to close the lower draft in the furnace."

"Oh, I'm so sorry. But I don't often forget things like that, do I?"

She dropped into his lap and (after he had jerked back his head to save his eye-glasses, and removed the glasses, and settled her in a position less cramping to his legs, and casually cleared his throat) he kissed her amiably, and remarked:

"Nope, I must say you're fairly good about things like that. I wasn't kicking. I just meant I wouldn't want the fire to go out on us. Leave that draft open and the fire might burn up and go out on us. And the nights are beginning to get pretty cold again. Pretty cold on my drive. I put the side-curtains up, it was so chilly. But the generator is working all right now."

"Yes. It is chilly. But I feel fine after my walk."

"Go walking?"

"I went up to see the Perrys." By a definite act of will she added the truth: "They weren't in. And I saw Guy Pollock. Dropped into his office."

"Why, you haven't been sitting and chinning with him till eleven o'clock?"

"Of course there were some other people there and—— Will! What do you think of Dr. Westlake?"

"Westlake? Why?"

"I noticed him on the street today."

"Was he limping? If the poor fish would have his teeth X-rayed, I'll bet nine and a half cents he'd find an abscess there. 'Rheumatism' he calls it. Rheumatism, hell! He's behind the times. Wonder he doesn't bleed himself! Wellllllll——" A profound and serious yawn. "I hate to break up the party, but it's getting late, and a doctor never knows when he'll be routed out before morning." (She remembered that he had given this explanation, in these words, not less than thirty times in the year.) "I guess we better be trotting up to bed. I've wound the clock and looked at the furnace. Did you lock the front door when you came in?"

They trailed up-stairs, after he had turned out the lights and twice tested the front door to make sure it was fast. While they talked they were preparing for bed. Carol still sought to maintain privacy by undressing behind the screen of the closet door. Kennicott was not so reticent. Tonight, as every night, she was irritated by having to push the old plush chair out of the way before she could open the closet door. Every time she opened the door she shoved the chair. Ten times an hour. But Kennicott liked to have the chair in the room, and there was no place for it except in front of the closet.

She pushed it, felt angry, hid her anger. Kennicott was yawning, more portentously. The room smelled stale. She shrugged and became chatty:

"You were speaking of Dr. Westlake. Tell me—you've never summed him up: Is he really a good doctor?"

"Oh yes, he's a wise old coot."

("There! You see there is no medical rivalry. Not in my house!" she said triumphantly to Guy Pollock.)

She hung her silk petticoat on a closet hook, and went on, "Dr. Westlake is so gentle and scholarly——"

"Well, I don't know as I'd say he was such a whale of a scholar. I've always had a suspicion he did a good deal of four-flushing about that. He likes to have people think he keeps up his French and Greek and Lord knows what all; and he's always got an old Dago book lying around the sitting-room, but I've got a hunch he reads detective stories 'bout like the rest of us. And I don't know where he'd ever learn so dog-gone many languages anyway! He kind of lets people assume he went to Harvard or Berlin or Oxford or somewhere, but I looked him up in the medical register, and he graduated from a hick college in Pennsylvania, 'way back in 1861!"

"But this is the important thing: Is he an honest doctor?"

"How do you mean 'honest'? Depends on what you mean."

"Suppose you were sick. Would you call him in? Would you let me call him in?"

"Not if I were well enough to cuss and bite, I wouldn't! No, *sir*! I wouldn't have the old fake in the house. Makes me tired, his everlasting palavering and soft-soaping. He's all right for an ordinary bellyache or holding some fool woman's hand, but I wouldn't call him in for an honest-to-God illness, not much I wouldn't, *no*-sir! You know I don't do much backbiting, but same time—— I'll tell you, Carrie: I've never got over being sore at Westlake for the way he treated Mrs. Jonderquist. Nothing the matter with her, what she really needed was a rest, but Westlake kept calling on her and calling on her for weeks, almost every day, and he sent her a good big fat bill, too, you can bet! I never did forgive him for that. Nice decent hard-working people like the Jonderquists!"

In her batiste nightgown she was standing at the bureau engaged in the invariable rites of wishing that she had a real dressing-table with a triple mirror, of bending toward the streaky glass and raising her chin to inspect a pin-head mole on her throat, and finally of brushing her hair. In rhythm to the strokes she went on:

"But, Will, there isn't any of what you might call financial rivalry between you and the partners—Westlake and McGanum—is there?"

He flipped into bed with a solemn back-somersault and a ludicrous kick of his heels as he tucked his legs under the blankets. He snorted, "Lord no! I never begrudge any man a nickel he can get away from me—fairly."

"But is Westlake fair? Isn't he sly?"

"Sly is the word. He's a fox, that boy!"

She saw Guy Pollock's grin in the mirror. She flushed.

Kennicott, with his arms behind his head, was yawning:

"Yump. He's smooth, too smooth. But I bet I make prett' near as much as Westlake and McGanum both together, though I've never wanted to grab more than my just share. If anybody wants to go to the partners instead of to me, that's his business. Though I must say it makes me tired when Westlake gets hold of the Dawsons. Here Luke Dawson had been coming to me for every toeache and headache and a lot of little things that just wasted my time, and then when his grandchild was here last summer and had summer-complaint, I suppose, or something like that, probably—you know, the time you and I drove up to Lac-qui-Meurt—why, Westlake got hold of Ma Dawson, and scared her to death, and made her think the kid had appendicitis, and, by golly, if he and McGanum didn't operate, and holler their heads off about the terrible adhesions they found, and what a regular Charley and Will Mayo they were for classy surgery. They let on that if they'd waited two hours more the kid would have developed peritonitis, and God knows what all; and then they collected a nice fat hundred and fifty dollars. And probably they'd have charged three hundred, if they hadn't been afraid of me! I'm no hog, but I certainly do hate to give old Luke ten dollars' worth of advice for a dollar and a half, and then see a hundred and fifty go glimmering. And if I can't do a better 'pendectomy than either Westlake or McGanum, I'll eat my hat!"

As she crept into bed she was dazzled by Guy's blazing grin. She experimented:

"But Westlake is cleverer than his son-in-law, don't you think?"

"Yes, Westlake may be old-fashioned and all that, but he's got a certain amount of intuition, while McGanum goes into everything bull-headed, and butts his way through like a damn yahoo, and tries to argue his patients into having whatever he diagnoses them as having! About the best thing Mac can do is to stick to baby-snatching. He's just about on a par with this bone-pounding chiropractor female, Mrs. Mattie Gooch."

"Mrs. Westlake and Mrs. McGanum, though—they're nice. They've been awfully cordial to me."

"Well, no reason why they shouldn't be, is there? Oh, they're nice enough —though you can bet your bottom dollar they're both plugging for their husbands all the time, trying to get the business. And I don't know as I call it so damn cordial in Mrs. McGanum when I holler at her on the street and she nods back like she had a sore neck. Still, she's all right. It's Ma Westlake that makes the mischief, pussyfooting around all the time. But I wouldn't trust any Westlake out of the whole lot, and while Mrs. McGanum *seems* square enough, you don't never want to forget that she's Westlake's daughter. You bet!"

"What about Dr. Gould? Don't you think he's worse than either Westlake or McGanum? He's so cheap—drinking, and playing pool, and always smoking cigars in such a cocky way——"

"That's all right now! Terry Gould is a good deal of a tinhorn sport, but he knows a lot about medicine, and don't you forget it for one second!"

She stared down Guy's grin, and asked more cheerfully, "Is he honest, too?"

"Ooooooooooo! Gosh I'm sleepy!" He burrowed beneath the bedclothes in a luxurious stretch, and came up like a diver, shaking his head, as he complained, "How's that? Who? Terry Gould honest? Don't start me laughing— I'm too nice and sleepy! I didn't say he was honest. I said he had savvy enough to find the index in 'Gray's Anatomy,' which is more than McGanum can do! But I didn't say anything about his being honest. He isn't. Terry is crooked as a dog's hind leg. He's done me more than one dirty trick. He told Mrs. Glorbach, seventeen miles out, that I wasn't up-to-date in obstetrics. Fat lot of good it did him! She came right in and told me! And Terry's lazy. He'd let a pneumonia patient choke rather than interrupt a poker game."

"Oh no. I can't believe——"

"Well now, I'm telling you!"

"Does he play much poker? Dr. Dillon told me that Dr. Gould wanted him to play——"

"Dillon told you what? Where'd you meet Dillon? He's just come to town."

"He and his wife were at Mr. Pollock's tonight."

"Say, uh, what'd you think of them? Didn't Dillon strike you as pretty light-waisted?"

"Why no. He seemed intelligent. I'm sure he's much more wide-awake than our dentist."

"Well now, the old man is a good dentist. He knows his business. And Dillon—— I wouldn't cuddle up to the Dillons too close, if I were you. All right for Pollock, and that's none of our business, but we—— I think I'd just give the Dillons the glad hand and pass 'em up."

"But why? He isn't a rival."

"That's—all—right!" Kennicott was aggressively awake now. "He'll work right in with Westlake and McGanum. Matter of fact, I suspect they were largely responsible for his locating here. They'll be sending him patients, and he'll send all that he can get hold of to them. I don't trust anybody that's too much hand-in-glove with Westlake. You give Dillon a shot at some fellow that's just bought a farm here and drifts into town to get his teeth looked at, and after Dillon gets through with him, you'll see him edging around to Westlake and McGanum, every time!"

Carol reached for her blouse, which hung on a chair by the bed. She draped it about her shoulders, and sat up studying Kennicott, her chin in her hands. In the gray light from the small electric bulb down the hall she could see that he was frowning.

"Will, this is—I must get this straight. Some one said to me the other day that in towns like this, even more than in cities, all the doctors hate each other, because of the money——"

"Who said that?"

"It doesn't matter."

"I'll bet a hat it was your Vida Sherwin. She's a brainy woman, but she'd be a damn sight brainier if she kept her mouth shut and didn't let so much of her brains ooze out that way."

"Will! O Will! That's horrible! Aside from the vulgarity—— Some ways, Vida is my best friend. Even if she *had* said it. Which, as a matter of fact, she didn't."

He reared up his thick shoulders, in absurd pink and green flannelette pajamas. He sat straight, and irritatingly snapped his fingers, and growled:

"Well, if she didn't say it, let's forget her. Doesn't make any difference who said it, anyway. The point is that you believe it. God! To think you don't understand me any better than that! Money!"

("This is the first real quarrel we've ever had," she was agonizing.)

He thrust out his long arm and snatched his wrinkly vest from a chair. He took out a cigar, a match. He tossed the vest on the floor. He lighted the cigar and puffed savagely. He broke up the match and snapped the fragments at the foot-board.

She suddenly saw the foot-board of the bed as the footstone of the grave of love.

The room was drab-colored and ill-ventilated—Kennicott did not "believe in opening the windows so darn wide that you heat all outdoors." The stale air seemed never to change. In the light from the hall they were two lumps of bedclothes with shoulders and tousled heads attached.

She begged, "I didn't mean to wake you up, dear. And please don't smoke. You've been smoking so much. Please go back to sleep. I'm sorry."

"Being sorry 's all right, but I'm going to tell you one or two things. This falling for anybody's say-so about medical jealousy and competition is simply part and parcel of your usual willingness to think the worst you possibly can of us poor dubs in Gopher Prairie. Trouble with women like you is, you always want to *argue*. Can't take things the way they are. Got to argue. Well, I'm not going to argue about this in any way, shape, manner, or form. Trouble with you is, you don't make any effort to appreciate us. You're so damned superior, and think the city is such a hell of a lot finer place, and you want us to do what *you* want, all the time——"

"That's not true! It's I who make the effort. It's they—it's you—who stand back and criticize. I have to come over to the town's opinion; I have to devote myself to their interests. They can't even *see* my interests, to say nothing of adopting them. I get ever so excited about their old Lake Minniemashie and the cottages, but they simply guffaw (in that lovely friendly way you advertise so much) if I speak of wanting to see Taormina also."

"Sure, Tormina, whatever that is—some nice expensive millionaire colony, I suppose. Sure; that's the idea; champagne taste and beer income; and make sure that we never will have more than a beer income, too!"

"Are you by any chance implying that I am not economical?"

"Well, I hadn't intended to, but since you bring it up yourself, I don't mind saying the grocery bills are about twice what they ought to be."

"Yes, they probably are. I'm not economical. I can't be. Thanks to you!"

"Where d' you get that 'thanks to you'?"

"Please don't be quite so colloquial—or shall I say *vulgar?*"

"I'll be as damn colloquial as I want to. How do you get that 'thanks to you'? Here about a year ago you jump me for not remembering to give you money. Well, I'm reasonable. I didn't blame you, and I *said* I was to blame. But have I ever forgotten it since—practically?"

"No. You haven't—practically! But that isn't it. I ought to have an allow-- ance. I will, too! I must have an agreement for a regular stated amount, every month."

"Fine idea! Of course a doctor gets a regular stated amount! Sure! A thousand one month—and lucky if he makes a hundred the next."

"Very well then, a percentage. Or something else. No matter how much you vary, you can make a rough average for——"

"But what's the idea? What are you trying to get at? Mean to say I'm unreasonable? Think I'm so unreliable and tightwad that you've got to tie me down with a contract? By God, that hurts! I thought I'd been pretty generous and decent, and I took a lot of pleasure—thinks I, 'she'll be tickled when I hand her over this twenty'—or fifty, or whatever it was; and now seems you been wanting to make it a kind of alimony. Me, like a poor fool, thinking I was liberal all the while, and you——"

"Please stop pitying yourself! You're having a beautiful time feeling injured. I admit all you say. Certainly. You've given me money both freely and amiably. Quite as if I were your mistress!"

"Carrie!"

"I mean it! What was a magnificent spectacle of generosity to you was humiliation to me. You *gave* me money—gave it to your mistress, if she was complaisant, and then you——"

"Carrie!"

"(Don't interrupt me!)—then you felt you'd discharged all obligation. Well, hereafter I'll refuse your money, as a gift. Either I'm your partner, in charge of the household department of our business, with a regular budget for it, or else I'm nothing. If I'm to be a mistress, I shall choose my lovers. Oh, I hate it—I hate it—this smirking and hoping for money—and then not even spending it on jewels as a mistress has a right to, but spending it on double-boilers and socks for you! Yes indeed! You're generous! You give me a dollar, right out—the only proviso is that I must spend it on a tie for you! And you give it when and as you wish. How can I be anything but uneconomical?"

"Oh well, of course, looking at it that way——"

"I can't shop around, can't buy in large quantities, have to stick to stores where I have a charge account, good deal of the time, can't plan because I don't know how much money I can depend on. That's what I pay for your charming sentimentalities about giving so generously. You make me——"

"Wait! Wait! You know you're exaggerating. You never thought about that mistress stuff till just this minute! Matter of fact, you never have 'smirked and hoped for money.' But all the same, you may be right. You ought to run the household as a business. I'll figure out a definite plan tomorrow, and hereafter you'll be on a regular amount or percentage, with your own checking account."

"Oh, that *is* decent of you!" She turned toward him, trying to be affectionate. But his eyes were pink and unlovely in the flare of the match with which he lighted his dead and malodorous cigar. His head drooped, and a ridge of flesh scattered with pale small bristles bulged out under his chin.

She sat in abeyance till he croaked:

"No. 'Tisn't especially decent. It's just fair. And God knows I want to be fair. But I expect others to be fair, too. And you're so high and mighty about people. Take Sam Clark; best soul that ever lived, honest and loyal and a damn good fellow——"

("Yes, and a good shot at ducks, don't forget that!")

("Well, and he is a good shot, too!) Sam drops around in the evening to sit and visit, and by golly just because he takes a dry smoke and rolls his cigar around in his mouth, and maybe spits a few times, you look at him as if he was a hog. Oh, you didn't know I was onto you, and I certainly hope Sam hasn't noticed it, but I never miss it."

"I have felt that way. Spitting—ugh! But I'm sorry you caught my thoughts. I tried to be nice; I tried to hide them."

"Maybe I catch a whole lot more than you think I do!"

"Yes, perhaps you do."

"And d' you know why Sam doesn't light his cigar when he's here?"

"Why?"

"He's so darn afraid you'll be offended if he smokes. You scare him. Every time he speaks of the weather you jump him because he ain't talking about poetry or Gertie–Goethe?–or some other highbrow junk. You've got him so leery he scarcely dares to come here."

"Oh, I *am* sorry. (Though I'm sure it's you who are exaggerating now.")

"Well now, I don't know as I am! And I can tell you one thing: if you keep on you'll manage to drive away every friend I've got."

"That would be horrible of me. You *know* I don't mean to—— Will, what is it about me that frightens Sam–if I do frighten him."

"Oh, you do, all right! 'Stead of putting his legs up on another chair, and unbuttoning his vest, and telling a good story or maybe kidding me about something, he sits on the edge of his chair and tries to make conversation

about politics, and he doesn't even cuss, and Sam's never real comfortable
unless he can cuss a little!"

"In other words, he isn't comfortable unless he can behave like a peasant
in a mud hut!"

"Now that'll be about enough of that! You want to know how you scare
him? First you deliberately fire some question at him that you know darn
well he can't answer—any fool could see you were experimenting with him—
and then you shock him by talking of mistresses or something, like you were
doing just now——"

"Of course the pure Samuel never speaks of such erring ladies in his private
conversations!"

"Not when there's ladies around! You can bet your life on that!"

"So the impurity lies in failing to pretend that——"

"Now we won't go into all that—eugenics or whatever damn fad you choose
to call it. As I say, first you shock him, and then you become so darn flighty
that nobody can follow you. Either you want to dance, or you bang the piano,
or else you get moody as the devil and don't want to talk or anything else.
If you must be temperamental, why can't you be that way by yourself?"

"My dear man, there's nothing I'd like better than to be by myself occasionally! To have a room of my own! I suppose you expect me to sit here
and dream delicately and satisfy my 'temperamentality' while you wander in
from the bathroom with lather all over your face, and shout, 'Seen my brown
pants?'"

"Huh!" He did not sound impressed. He made no answer. He turned out
of bed, his feet making one solid thud on the floor. He marched from the
room, a grotesque figure in baggy union-pajamas. She heard him drawing a
drink of water at the bathroom tap. She was furious at the contemptuousness of his exit. She snuggled down in bed, and looked away from him as he
returned. He ignored her. As he flumped into bed he yawned, and casually
stated:

"Well, you'll have plenty of privacy when we build a new house."

"When!"

"Oh, I'll build it all right, don't you fret! But of course I don't expect any
credit for it."

Now it was she who grunted "Huh!" and ignored him, and felt independent
and masterful as she shot up out of bed, turned her back on him, fished a
lone and petrified chocolate out of her glove-box in the top right-hand drawer
of the bureau, gnawed at it, found that it had cocoanut filling, said "Damn!"
wished that she had not said it, so that she might be superior to his col-
loquialism, and hurled the chocolate into the wastebasket, where it made an
evil and mocking clatter among the débris of torn linen collars and tooth-
paste box. Then, in great dignity and self-dramatization, she returned to bed.

All this time he had been talking on, embroidering his assertion that he
"didn't expect any credit." She was reflecting that he was a rustic, that she
hated him, that she had been insane to marry him, that she had married him
only because she was tired of work, that she must get her long gloves cleaned,

that she would never do anything more for him, and that she mustn't forget his hominy for breakfast. She was roused to attention by his storming:

"I'm a fool to think about a new house. By the time I get it built you'll probably have succeeded in your plan to get me completely in Dutch with every friend and every patient I've got."

She sat up with a bounce. She said coldly, "Thank you very much for revealing your real opinion of me. If that's the way you feel, if I'm such a hindrance to you, I can't stay under this roof another minute. And I am perfectly well able to earn my own living. I will go at once, and you may get a divorce at your pleasure! What you want is a nice sweet cow of a woman who will enjoy having your dear friends talk about the weather and spit on the floor!"

"Tut! Don't be a fool!"

"You will very soon find out whether I'm a fool or not! I mean it! Do you think I'd stay here one second after I found out that I was injuring you? At least I have enough sense of justice not to do that."

"Please stop flying off at tangents, Carrie. This——"

"Tangents? *Tangents!* Let me tell you——"

"——isn't a theater-play; it's a serious effort to have us get together on fundamentals. We've both been cranky, and said a lot of things we didn't mean. I wish we were a couple o' bloomin' poets and just talked about roses and moonshine, but we're human. All right. Let's cut out jabbing at each other. Let's admit we both do fool things. See here: You *know* you feel superior to folks. You're not as bad as I say, but you're not as good as you say—not by a long shot! What's the reason you're so superior? Why can't you take folks as they are?"

Her preparations for stalking out of the Doll's House were not yet visible. She mused:

"I think perhaps it's my childhood." She halted. When she went on her voice had an artificial sound, her words the bookish quality of emotional meditation. "My father was the tenderest man in the world, but he did feel superior to ordinary people. Well, he was! And the Minnesota Valley—— I used to sit there on the cliffs above Mankato for hours at a time, my chin in my hand, looking way down the valley, wanting to write poems. The shiny tilted roofs below me, and the river, and beyond it the level fields in the mist, and the rim of palisades across—— It held my thoughts in. I *lived*, in the valley. But the prairie—all my thoughts go flying off into the big space. Do you think it might be that?"

"Um, well, maybe, but—— Carrie, you always talk so much about getting all you can out of life, and not letting the years slip by, and here you deliberately go and deprive yourself of a lot of real good home pleasure by not enjoying people unless they wear frock coats and trot out——"

("Morning clothes. Oh. Sorry. Didn't mean t' interrupt you.")

"——to a lot of tea-parties. Take Jack Elder. You think Jack hasn't got any ideas about anything but manufacturing and the tariff on lumber. But do you know that Jack is nutty about music? He'll put a grand-opera record on the phonograph and sit and listen to it and close his eyes—— Or you take Lym Cass. Ever realize what a well-informed man he is?"

"But *is* he? Gopher Prairie calls anybody 'well-informed' who's been through the State Capitol and heard about Gladstone."

"Now I'm telling you! Lym reads a lot—solid stuff—history. Or take Mart Mahoney, the garageman. He's got a lot of Perry prints of famous pictures in his office. Or old Bingham Playfair, that died here 'bout a year ago—lived seven miles out. He was a captain in the Civil War, and knew General Sherman, and they say he was a miner in Nevada right alongside of Mark Twain. You'll find these characters in all these small towns, and a pile of savvy in every single one of them, if you just dig for it."

"I know. And I do love them. Especially people like Champ Perry. But I can't be so very enthusiastic over the smug cits like Jack Elder."

"Then I'm a smug cit, too, whatever that is."

"No, you're a scientist. Oh, I will try and get the music out of Mr. Elder. Only, why can't he let it *come* out, instead of being ashamed of it, and always talking about hunting dogs? But I will try. Is it all right now?"

"Sure. But there's one other thing. You might give me some attention, too!"

"That's unjust! You have everything I am!"

"No, I haven't. You think you respect me—you always hand out some spiel about my being so 'useful.' But you never think of me as having ambitions, just as much as you have!"

"Perhaps not. I think of you as being perfectly satisfied."

"Well, I'm not, not by a long shot! I don't want to be a plug general practitioner all my life, like Westlake, and die in harness because I can't get out of it, and have 'em say, 'He was a good fellow, but he couldn't save a cent.' Not that I care a whoop what they say, after I've kicked in and can't hear 'em, but I want to put enough money away so you and I can be independent some day, and not have to work unless I feel like it, and I want to have a good house—by golly, I'll have as good a house as anybody in *this* town!—and if we want to travel and see your Tormina or whatever it is, why we can do it, with enough money in our jeans so we won't have to take anything off anybody, or fret about our old age. You never worry about what might happen if we got sick and didn't have a good fat wad salted away, do you!"

"I don't suppose I do."

"Well then, I have to do it for you. And if you think for one moment I want to be stuck in this burg all my life, and not have a chance to travel and see the different points of interest and all that, then you simply don't get me. I want to have a squint at the world, much's you do. Only, I'm practical about it. First place, I'm going to make the money—I'm investing in good safe farmlands. Do you understand why now?"

"Yes."

"Will you try and see if you can't think of me as something more than just a dollar-chasing roughneck?"

"Oh, my dear, I haven't been just! I *am* difficile. And I won't call on the Dillons! And if Dr. Dillon is working for Westlake and McGanum, I hate him!"

# 15

That December she was in love with her husband.

She romanticized herself not as a great reformer but as the wife of a country physician. The realities of the doctor's household were colored by her pride.

Late at night, a step on the wooden porch, heard through her confusion of sleep; the storm-door opened; fumbling over the inner door-panels; the buzz of the electric bell. Kennicott muttering "Gol darn it," but patiently creeping out of bed, remembering to draw the covers up to keep her warm, feeling for slippers and bathrobe, clumping down-stairs.

From below, half-heard in her drowsiness, a colloquy in the pidgin-German of the farmers who have forgotten the Old Country language without learning the new:

"Hello, Barney, *wass willst du?*"

"*Morgen*, doctor. *Die Frau ist ja* awful sick. All night she been having an awful pain in de belly."

"How long she been this way? *Wie lang*, eh?"

"I dunno, maybe two days."

"Why didn't you come for me yesterday, instead of waking me up out of a sound sleep? Here it is two o'clock! So *spät—warum*, eh?"

"*Nun aber*, I know it, but she got soch a lot vorse last evening. I t'ought maybe all de time it go avay, but it got a lot vorse."

"Any fever?"

"Vell *ja*, I t'ink she got fever."

"Which side is the pain on?"

"Huh?"

"*Das Schmertz—die Weh*—which side is it on? Here?"

"So. Right here it is."

"Any rigidity there?"

"Huh?"

"Is it rigid—stiff—I mean, does the belly feel hard to the fingers?"

"I dunno. She ain't said yet."

"What she been eating?"

"Vell, I t'ink about vot ve alwis eat, maybe corn beef and cabbage and sausage, *und so weiter*. Doc, *sie weint immer*, all the time she holler like hell. I vish you come."

"Well, all right, but you call me earlier, next time. Look here, Barney,

Germen

you better install a 'phone—telephone *haben*. Some of you Dutchmen will be dying one of these days before you can fetch the doctor."

The door closing. Barney's wagon—the wheels silent in the snow, but the wagon-body rattling. Kennicott clicking the receiver-hook to rouse the night telephone-operator, giving a number, waiting, cursing mildly, waiting again, and at last growling, "Hello, Gus, this is the doctor. Say, uh, send me up a team. Guess snow's too thick for a machine. Going eight miles south. All right. Huh? The hell I will! Don't *you* go back to sleep. Huh? Well, that's all right now, you didn't wait so very darn long. All right, Gus; shoot her along. By!"

His step on the stairs; his quiet moving about the frigid room while he dressed; his abstracted and meaningless cough. She was supposed to be asleep; she was too exquisitely drowsy to break the charm by speaking. On a slip of paper laid on the bureau—she could hear the pencil grinding against the marble slab—he wrote his destination. He went out, hungry, chilly, unprotesting; and she, before she fell asleep again, loved him for his sturdiness, and saw the drama of his riding by night to the frightened household on the distant farm; pictured children standing at a window, waiting for him. He suddenly had in her eyes the heroism of a wireless operator on a ship in a collision; of an explorer, fever-clawed, deserted by his bearers, but going on—jungle—going——

At six, when the light faltered in as through ground glass and bleakly identified the chairs as gray rectangles, she heard his step on the porch; heard him at the furnace: the rattle of shaking the grate, the slow grinding removal of ashes, the shovel thrust into the coal-bin, the abrupt clatter of the coal as it flew into the fire-box, the fussy regulation of drafts—the daily sounds of a Gopher Prairie life, now first appealing to her as something brave and enduring, many-colored and free. She visioned the fire-box: flames turned to lemon and metallic gold as the coal-dust sifted over them; thin twisty flutters of purple, ghost flames which gave no light, slipping up between the dark banked coals.

It was luxurious in bed, and the house would be warm for her when she rose, she reflected. What a worthless cat she was! What were her aspirations beside his capability?

She awoke again as he dropped into bed.

"Seems just a few minutes ago that you started out!"

"I've been away four hours. I've operated a woman for appendicitis, in a Dutch kitchen. Came awful close to losing her, too, but I pulled her through all right. Close squeak. Barney says he shot ten rabbits last Sunday."

He was instantly asleep—one hour of rest before he had to be up and ready for the farmers who came in early. She marveled that in what was to her but a night-blurred moment, he should have been in a distant place, have taken charge of a strange house, have slashed a woman, saved a life.

What wonder he detested the lazy Westlake and McGanum! How could the easy Guy Pollock understand this skill and endurance?

Then Kennicott was grumbling, "Seven-fifteen! Aren't you ever going to get up for breakfast?" and he was not a hero-scientist but a rather irritable and commonplace man who needed a shave. They had coffee, griddle-cakes, and sausages, and talked about Mrs. McGanum's atrocious alligator-hide belt. Night witchery and morning disillusion were alike forgotten in the march of realities and days.

### II

Familiar to the doctor's wife was the man with an injured leg, driven in from the country on a Sunday afternoon and brought to the house. He sat in a rocker in the back of a lumber-wagon, his face pale from the anguish of the jolting. His leg was thrust out before him, resting on a starch-box and covered with a leather-bound horse-blanket. His drab courageous wife drove the wagon, and she helped Kennicott support him as he hobbled up the steps, into the house.

"Fellow cut his leg with an ax—pretty bad gash—Halvor Nelson, nine miles out," Kennicott observed.

Carol fluttered at the back of the room, childishly excited when she was sent to fetch towels and a basin of water. Kennicott lifted the farmer into a chair and chuckled, "There we are, Halvor! We'll have you out fixing fences and drinking *aquavit* in a month." The farmwife sat on the couch, expressionless, bulky in a man's dogskin coat and unplumbed layers of jackets. The flowery silk handkerchief which she had worn over her head now hung about her seamed neck. Her white wool gloves lay in her lap.

Kennicott drew from the injured leg the thick red "German sock," the innumerous other socks of gray and white wool, then the spiral bandage. The leg was of an unwholesome dead white, with the black hairs feeble and thin and flattened, and the scar a puckered line of crimson. Surely, Carol shuddered, this was not human flesh, the rosy shining tissue of the amorous poets.

Kennicott examined the scar, smiled at Halvor and his wife, chanted, "Fine, b' gosh! Couldn't be better!"

The Nelsons looked deprecating. The farmer nodded a cue to his wife and she mourned:

"Vell, how much ve going to owe you, doctor?"

"I guess it'll be—— Let's see: one drive out and two calls. I guess it'll be about eleven dollars in all, Lena."

"I dunno ve can pay you yoost a little w'ile, doctor."

Kennicott lumbered over to her, patted her shoulder, roared, "Why, Lord love you, sister, I won't worry if I never get it! You pay me next fall, when you get your crop. . . . Carrie! Suppose you or Bea could shake up a cup of coffee and some cold lamb for the Nelsons? They got a long cold drive ahead."

### III

He had been gone since morning; her eyes ached with reading; Vida Sherwin could not come to tea. She wandered through the house, empty as the bleary street without. The problem of "Will the doctor be home in time for supper, or shall I sit down without him?" was important in the household. Six was the rigid, the canonical supper-hour, but at half-past six he had not come. Much speculation with Bea: Had the obstetrical case taken longer than he had expected? Had he been called somewhere else? Was the snow much heavier out in the country, so that he should have taken a buggy, or even a cutter, instead of the car? Here in town it *had* melted a lot, but still——

A honking, a shout, the motor engine raced before it was shut off.

She hurried to the window. The car was a monster at rest after furious adventures. The headlights blazed on the clots of ice in the road so that the tiniest lumps gave mountainous shadows, and the taillight cast a circle of ruby on the snow behind. Kennicott was opening the door, crying, "Here we are, old girl! Got stuck couple times, but we made it, by golly, we made it, and here we be! Come on! Food! Eatin's!"

She rushed to him, patted his fur coat, the long hairs smooth but chilly to her fingers. She joyously summoned Bea, "All right! He's here! We'll sit right down!"

### IV

There were, to inform the doctor's wife of his successes, no clapping audiences nor book-reviews nor honorary degrees. But there was a letter written by a German farmer recently moved from Minnesota to Saskatchewan:

> Dear sor, as you haf bin treading mee for a fue Weaks dis Somer and seen wat is rong wit mee so in Regarding to dat i wont to tank you. the Doctor heir say wat shot bee rong wit mee and day give mee som Madsin but it diten halp mee like wat you dit. Now day glaim dat i Woten Neet aney Madsin ad all wat you tink?
>
> Well i haven ben tacking aney ting for about one &½ Mont but i dont get better so i like to heir Wat you tink about it i feel like dis Disconfebil feeling around the Stomac after eating and dat Pain around Heard and down the arm and about 3 to 3½ Hour after Eating i feel weeak like and dissy and a dull Hadig. Now you gust lett mee know Wat you tink about mee, i do Wat you say.

### V

She encountered Guy Pollock at the drug store. He looked at her as though he had a right to; he spoke softly, "I haven't seen you, the last few days."

"No. I've been out in the country with Will several times. He's so—— Do you know that people like you and me can never understand people like him? We're a pair of hypercritical loafers, you and I, while he quietly goes and does things."

She nodded and smiled and was very busy about purchasing boric acid. He stared after her, and slipped away.

When she found that he was gone she was slightly disconcerted.

She could—at times—agree with Kennicott that the shaving-and-corsets familiarity of married life was not dreary vulgarity but a wholesome frankness; that artificial reticences might merely be irritating. She was not much disturbed when for hours he sat about the living-room in his honest socks. But she would not listen to his theory that "all this romance stuff is simply moonshine—elegant when you're courting, but no use busting yourself keeping it up all your life."

She thought of surprises, games, to vary the days. She knitted an astounding purple scarf, which she hid under his supper plate. (When he discovered it he looked embarrassed, and gasped, "Is today an anniversary or something? Gosh, I'd forgotten it!")

Once she filled a thermos bottle with hot coffee, a corn-flakes box with cookies just baked by Bea, and bustled to his office at three in the afternoon. She hid her bundles in the hall and peeped in.

The office was shabby. Kennicott had inherited it from a medical predecessor, and changed it only by adding a white enameled operating-table, a sterilizer, a Roentgen-ray apparatus, and a small portable typewriter. It was a suite of two rooms: a waiting-room with straight chairs, shaky pine table, and those coverless and unknown magazines which are found only in the offices of dentists and doctors. The room beyond, looking on Main Street, was business-office, consulting-room, operating-room, and, in an alcove, bacteriological and chemical laboratory. The wooden floors of both rooms were bare; the furniture was brown and scaly.

Waiting for the doctor were two women, as still as though they were paralyzed, and a man in a railroad brakeman's uniform, holding his bandaged right hand with his tanned left. They stared at Carol. She sat modestly in a stiff chair, feeling frivolous and out of place.

Kennicott appeared at the inner door, ushering out a bleached man with a trickle of wan beard, and consoling him, "All right, Dad. Be careful about the sugar, and mind the diet I gave you. Get the prescription filled, and come in and see me next week. Say, uh, better, uh, better not drink too much beer. All right, Dad."

His voice was artificially hearty. He looked absently at Carol. He was a medical machine now, not a domestic machine. "What is it, Carrie?" he droned.

"No hurry. Just wanted to say hello."

"Well——"

Self-pity because he did not divine that this was a surprise party rendered her sad and interesting to herself, and she had the pleasure of the martyrs in saying bravely to him, "It's nothing special. If you're busy long I'll trot home."

While she waited she ceased to pity and began to mock herself. For the first time she observed the waiting-room. Oh yes, the doctor's family had to have obi panels and a wide couch and an electric percolator, but any hole was good enough for sick tired common people who were nothing but the one means and excuse for the doctor's existing! No. She couldn't blame Kennicott. He was satisfied by the shabby chairs. He put up with them as his patients did. It was her neglected province—she who had been going about talking of rebuilding the whole town!

When the patients were gone she brought in her bundles.

"What's those?" wondered Kennicott.

"Turn your back! Look out of the window!"

He obeyed—not very much bored. When she cried "Now!" a feast of cookies and small hard candies and hot coffee was spread on the roll-top desk in the inner room.

His broad face lightened. "That's a new one on me! Never was more surprised in my life! And, by golly, I believe I am hungry. Say, this is fine."

When the first exhilaration of the surprise had declined she demanded, "Will! I'm going to refurnish your waiting-room!"

"What's the matter with it? It's all right."

"It is not! It's hideous. We can afford to give your patients a better place. And it would be good business." She felt tremendously politic.

"Rats! I don't worry about the business. You look here now: As I told you—— Just because I like to tuck a few dollars away, I'll be switched if I'll stand for your thinking I'm nothing but a dollar-chasing——"

"Stop it! Quick! I'm not hurting your feelings! I'm not criticizing! I'm the adoring least one of thy harem. I just mean——"

Two days later, with pictures, wicker chairs, a rug, she had made the waiting-room habitable; and Kennicott admitted, "Does look a lot better. Never thought much about it. Guess I need being bullied."

She was convinced that she was gloriously content in her career as doctor's-wife.

## VII

She tried to free herself from the speculation and disillusionment which had been twitching at her; sought to dismiss all the opinionation of an insurgent era. She wanted to shine upon the veal-faced bristly-bearded Lyman Cass as much as upon Miles Bjornstam or Guy Pollock. She gave a reception for the Thanatopsis Club. But her real acquiring of merit was in calling upon that Mrs. Bogart whose gossipy good opinion was so valuable to a doctor.

Though the Bogart house was next door she had entered it but three times. Now she put on her new moleskin cap, which made her face small and innocent, she rubbed off the traces of a lip-stick—and fled across the alley before her admirable resolution should sneak away.

The age of houses, like the age of men, has small relation to their years. The dull-green cottage of the good Widow Bogart was twenty years old, but it had the antiquity of Cheops, and the smell of mummy-dust. Its neatness rebuked the street. The two stones by the path were painted yellow; the outhouse was so overmodestly masked with vines and lattice that it was not concealed at all; the last iron dog remaining in Gopher Prairie stood among whitewashed conch-shells upon the lawn. The hallway was dismayingly scrubbed; the kitchen was an exercise in mathematics, with problems worked out in equidistant chairs.

The parlor was kept for visitors. Carol suggested, "Let's sit in the kitchen. Please don't trouble to light the parlor stove."

"No trouble at all! My gracious, and you coming so seldom and all, and the kitchen is a perfect sight, I try to keep it clean, but Cy will track mud all over it, I've spoken to him about it a hundred times if I've spoken once, no, you sit right there, dearie, and I'll make a fire, no trouble at all, practically no trouble at all."

Mrs. Bogart groaned, rubbed her joints, and repeatedly dusted her hands while she made the fire, and when Carol tried to help she lamented, "Oh, it doesn't matter; guess I ain't good for much but toil and workin' anyway; seems as though that's what a lot of folks think."

The parlor was distinguished by an expanse of rag carpet from which, as they entered, Mrs. Bogart hastily picked one sad dead fly. In the center of the carpet was a rug depicting a red Newfoundland dog, reclining in a green and yellow daisy field and labeled "Our Friend." The parlor organ, tall and thin, was adorned with a mirror partly circular, partly square, and partly diamond-shaped, and with brackets holding a pot of geraniums, a mouth-organ, and a copy of "The Oldtime Hymnal." On the center table was a Sears-Roebuck mail-order catalogue, a silver frame with photographs of the Baptist Church and of an elderly clergyman, and an aluminum tray containing a rattlesnake's rattle and a broken spectacle-lens.

Mrs. Bogart spoke of the eloquence of the Reverend Mr. Zitterel, the coldness of cold days, the price of poplar wood, Dave Dyer's new hair-cut, and Cy Bogart's essential piety. "As I said to his Sunday School teacher, Cy may be a little wild, but that's because he's got so much better brains than a lot of these boys, and this farmer that claims he caught Cy stealing 'beggies, is a liar, and I ought to have the law on him."

Mrs. Bogart went thoroughly into the rumor that the girl waiter at Billy's Lunch was not all she might be—or, rather, was quite all she might be.

"My lands, what can you expect when everybody knows what her mother was? And if these traveling salesmen would let her alone she would be all right, though I certainly don't believe she ought to be allowed to think she can pull the wool over our eyes. The sooner she's sent to the school for incorrigible girls down at Sauk Centre, the better for all and—— Won't you just have a cup of coffee, Carol dearie, I'm sure you won't mind old Aunty Bogart calling you by your first name when you think how long I've known Will, and I was such a friend of his dear lovely mother when she lived here and—was that fur cap expensive? But—— Don't you think it's awful, the way folks talk in this town?"

Mrs. Bogart hitched her chair nearer. Her large face, with its disturbing collection of moles and lone black hairs, wrinkled cunningly. She showed her decayed teeth in a reproving smile, and in the confidential voice of one who scents stale bedroom scandal she breathed:

"I just don't see how folks can talk and act like they do. You don't know the things that go on under cover. This town—why it's only the religious training I've given Cy that's kept him so innocent of—things. Just the other day—— I never pay no attention to stories, but I heard it mighty good and straight that Harry Haydock is carrying on with a girl that clerks in a store down in Minneapolis, and poor Juanita not knowing anything about it— though maybe it's the judgment of God, because before she married Harry she acted up with more than one boy—— Well, I don't like to say it, and maybe I ain't up-to-date, like Cy says, but I always believed a lady shouldn't even give names to all sorts of dreadful things, but just the same I know there was at least one case where Juanita and a boy—well, they were just dreadful. And—and—— Then there's that Ole Jenson the grocer, that thinks he's so plaguey smart, and I know he made up to a farmer's wife and—— And this awful man Bjornstam that does chores, and Nat Hicks and——"

There was, it seemed, no person in town who was not living a life of shame except Mrs. Bogart, and naturally she resented it.

She knew. She had always happened to be there. Once, she whispered, she was going by when an indiscreet window-shade had been left up a couple of inches. Once she had noticed a man and woman holding hands, and right at a Methodist sociable!

"Another thing—— Heaven knows I never want to start trouble, but I can't help what I see from my back steps, and I notice your hired girl Bea carrying on with the grocery boys and all——"

"Mrs. Bogart! I'd trust Bea as I would myself!"

"Oh, dearie, you don't understand me! I'm sure she's a good girl. I mean she's green, and I hope that none of these horrid young men that there are around town will get her into trouble! It's their parents' fault, letting them run wild and hear evil things. If I had my way there wouldn't be none of them, not boys nor girls neither, allowed to know anything about—about things till they was married. It's terrible the bald way that some folks talk. It just shows and gives away what awful thoughts they got inside them, and there's nothing can cure them except coming right to God and kneeling down like I do at prayer-meeting every Wednesday evening, and saying, 'O God, I would be a miserable sinner except for thy grace.'

"I'd make every last one of these brats go to Sunday School and learn to think about nice things 'stead of about cigarettes and goings-on—and these dances they have at the lodges are the worst thing that ever happened to this town, lot of young men squeezing girls and finding out—— Oh, it's dreadful. I've told the mayor he ought to put a stop to them and—— There was one boy in this town, I don't want to be suspicious or uncharitable but——"

It was half an hour before Carol escaped.

She stopped on her own porch and thought viciously:

"If that woman is on the side of the angels, then I have no choice; I must be on the side of the devil. But—isn't she like me? She too wants to 'reform the town'! She too criticizes everybody! She too thinks the men are vulgar and limited! *Am I like her?* This is ghastly!"

That evening she did not merely consent to play cribbage with Kennicott; she urged him to play; and she worked up a hectic interest in land-deals and Sam Clark.

VIII

In courtship days Kennicott had shown her a photograph of Nels Erdstrom's baby and log cabin, but she had never seen the Erdstroms. They had become merely "patients of the doctor." Kennicott telephoned her on a mid-December afternoon, "Want to throw your coat on and drive out to Erdstrom's with me? Fairly warm. Nels got the jaundice."

"Oh yes!" She hastened to put on woolen stockings, high boots, sweater, muffler, cap, mittens.

The snow was too thick and the ruts frozen too hard for the motor. They drove out in a clumsy high carriage. Tucked over them was a blue woolen cover, prickly to her wrists, and outside of it a buffalo robe, humble and moth-eaten now, used ever since the bison herds had streaked the prairie a few miles to the west.

The scattered houses between which they passed in town were small and desolate in contrast to the expanse of huge snowy yards and wide street. They crossed the railroad tracks, and instantly were in the farm country. The big piebald horses snorted clouds of steam, and started to trot. The carriage squeaked in rhythm. Kennicott drove with clucks of "There boy, take it easy!" He was thinking. He paid no attention to Carol. Yet it was he who commented, "Pretty nice, over there," as they approached an oak-grove where shifty winter sunlight quivered in the hollow between two snow-drifts.

They drove from the natural prairie to a cleared district which twenty years ago had been forest. The country seemed to stretch unchanging to the North Pole: low hill, brush-scraggly bottom, reedy creek, muskrat mound, fields with frozen brown clods thrust up through the snow.

Her ears and nose were pinched; her breath frosted her collar; her fingers ached.

"Getting colder," she said.

"Yup."

That was all their conversation for three miles. Yet she was happy.

They reached Nels Erdstrom's at four, and with a throb she recognized the courageous venture which had lured her to Gopher Prairie: the cleared fields, furrows among stumps, a log cabin chinked with mud and roofed with dry hay. But Nels had prospered. He used the log cabin as a barn; and a new house reared up, a proud, unwise, Gopher Prairie house, the more naked and ungraceful in its glossy white paint and pink trimmings. Every tree had been cut down. The house was so unsheltered, so battered by the wind, so bleakly thrust out into the harsh clearing, that Carol shivered. But they were welcomed warmly enough in the kitchen, with its crisp new plaster, its black and nickel range, its cream separator in a corner.

Mrs. Erdstrom begged her to sit in the parlor, where there was a phono-graph and an oak and leather davenport, the prairie farmer's proofs of social progress, but she dropped down by the kitchen stove and insisted, "Please don't mind me." When Mrs. Erdstrom had followed the doctor out of the room Carol glanced in a friendly way at the grained pine cupboard, the framed Lutheran *Konfirmations Attest*, the traces of fried eggs and sausages on the dining table against the wall, and a jewel among calendars, presenting not only a lithographic young woman with cherry lips, and a Swedish ad-vertisement of Axel Egge's grocery, but also a thermometer and a match-holder.

She saw that a boy of four or five was staring at her from the hall; a boy in gingham shirt and faded corduroy trousers, but large-eyed, firm-mouthed, wide-browed. He vanished, then peeped in again, biting his knuckles, turning his shoulder toward her in shyness.

Didn't she remember—what was it?—Kennicott sitting beside her at Fort Snelling, urging, "See how scared that baby is. Needs some woman like you."

Magic had fluttered about her then—magic of sunset and cool air and the curiosity of lovers. She held out her hands as much to that sanctity as to the boy.

He edged into the room, doubtfully sucking his thumb.

"Hello," she said. "What's your name?"

"Hee, hee, hee!"

"You're quite right. I agree with you. Silly people like me always ask chil-dren their names."

"Hee, hee, hee!"

"Come here and I'll tell you the story of—well, I don't know what it will be about, but it will have a slim heroine and a Prince Charming."

He stood stoically while she spun nonsense. His giggling ceased. She was winning him. Then the telephone bell—two long rings, one short.

Mrs. Erdstrom galloped into the room, shrieked into the transmitter, "Vell? Yes, yes, dis is Erdstrom's place! Heh? Oh, you vant de doctor?"

Kennicott appeared, growled into the telephone:

"Well, what do you want? Oh, hello Dave; what do you want? Which Morgenroth's? Adolph's? All right. Amputation? Yuh, I see. Say, Dave, get Gus to harness up and take my surgical kit down there—and have him take some chloroform. I'll go straight down from here. May not get home tonight. You can get me at Adolph's. Huh? No, Carrie can give the anesthetic, I guess. G'-by. Huh? No; tell me about that tomorrow—too damn many people al-ways listening in on this farmers' line."

He turned to Carol. "Adolph Morgenroth, farmer ten miles southwest of town, got his arm crushed—fixing his cow-shed and a post caved in on him —smashed him up pretty bad—may have to amputate, Dave Dyer says. Afraid we'll have to go right from here. Darn sorry to drag you clear down there with me——"

"Please do. Don't mind me a bit."

"Think you could give the anesthetic? Usually have my driver do it."

"If you'll tell me how."

"All right. Say, did you hear me putting one over on these goats that are always rubbering in on party-wires? I hope they heard me! Well. . . . Now, Bessie, don't you worry about Nels. He's getting along all right. Tomorrow you or one of the neighbors drive in and get this prescription filled at Dyer's. Give him a teaspoonful every four hours. Good-by. Hel-lo! Here's the little fellow! My Lord, Bessie, it ain't possible this is the fellow that used to be so sickly? Why, say, he's a great big strapping Svenska now—going to be bigger 'n his daddy!"

Kennicott's bluffness made the child squirm with a delight which Carol could not evoke. It was a humble wife who followed the busy doctor out to the carriage, and her ambition was not to play Rachmaninoff better, nor to build town halls, but to chuckle at babies.

The sunset was merely a flush of rose on a dome of silver, with oak twigs and thin poplar branches against it, but a silo on the horizon changed from a red tank to a tower of violet misted over with gray. The purple road vanished, and without lights, in the darkness of a world destroyed, they swayed on—toward nothing.

It was a bumpy cold way to the Morgenroth farm, and she was asleep when they arrived.

Here was no glaring new house with a proud phonograph, but a low whitewashed kitchen smelling of cream and cabbage. Adolph Morgenroth was lying on a couch in the rarely used dining-room. His heavy work-scarred wife was shaking her hands in anxiety.

Carol felt that Kennicott would do something magnificent and startling. But he was casual. He greeted the man, "Well, well, Adolph, have to fix you up, eh?" Quietly, to the wife, "*Hat die* drug store my *schwartze* bag *hier geschickt? So—schön. Wie viel Uhr ist 's? Sieben? Nun, lassen uns ein wenig* supper *zuerst haben.* Got any of that good beer left—*giebt 's noch Bier?*"

He had supped in four minutes. His coat off, his sleeves rolled up, he was scrubbing his hands in a tin basin in the sink, using the bar of yellow kitchen soap.

Carol had not dared to look into the farther room while she labored over the supper of beer, rye bread, moist corn-beef and cabbage, set on the kitchen table. The man in there was groaning. In her one glance she had seen that his blue flannel shirt was open at a corded tobacco-brown neck, the hollows of which were sprinkled with thin black and gray hairs. He was covered with a sheet, like a corpse, and outside the sheet was his right arm, wrapped in towels stained with blood.

But Kennicott strode into the other room gaily, and she followed him. With surprising delicacy in his large fingers he unwrapped the towels and revealed an arm which, below the elbow, was a mass of blood and raw flesh. The man bellowed. The room grew thick about her; she was very seasick; she fled to a chair in the kitchen. Through the haze of nausea she heard Kennicott grumbling, "Afraid it will have to come off, Adolph. What did you do? Fall on a reaper blade? We'll fix it right up. Carrie! *Carol!*"

She couldn't—she couldn't get up. Then she was up, her knees like water, her stomach revolving a thousand times a second, her eyes filmed, her ears full of roaring. She couldn't reach the dining-room. She was going to faint. Then she was in the dining-room, leaning against the wall, trying to smile, flushing hot and cold along her chest and sides, while Kennicott mumbled, "Say, help Mrs. Morgenroth and me carry him in on the kitchen table. No, first go out and shove those two tables together, and put a blanket on them and a clean sheet."

It was salvation to push the heavy tables, to scrub them, to be exact in placing the sheet. Her head cleared; she was able to look calmly in at her husband and the farmwife while they undressed the wailing man, got him into a clean nightgown, and washed his arm. Kennicott came to lay out his instruments. She realized that, with no hospital facilities, yet with no worry about it, her husband—*her husband*—was going to perform a surgical operation, that miraculous boldness of which one read in stories about famous surgeons.

She helped them to move Adolph into the kitchen. The man was in such a funk that he would not use his legs. He was heavy, and smelled of sweat and the stable. But she put her arm about his waist, her sleek head by his chest; she tugged at him; she clicked her tongue in imitation of Kennicott's cheerful noises.

When Adolph was on the table Kennicott laid a hemispheric steel and cotton frame on his face; suggested to Carol, "Now you sit here at his head and keep the ether dripping—about this fast, see? I'll watch his breathing. Look who's here! Real anesthetist! Ochsner hasn't got a better one! Class, eh? . . . Now, now, Adolph, take it easy. This won't hurt you a bit. Put you all nice and asleep and it won't hurt a bit. *Schweig' mal! Bald schlaft man grat wie ein Kind. So! So! Bald geht's besser!*"

As she let the ether drip, nervously trying to keep the rhythm that Kennicott had indicated, Carol stared at her husband with the abandon of hero-worship.

He shook his head. "Bad light—bad light. Here, Mrs. Morgenroth, you stand right here and hold this lamp. *Hier, und dieses—dieses* lamp *halten—so!*"

By that streaky glimmer he worked, swiftly, at ease. The room was still. Carol tried to look at him, yet not look at the seeping blood, the crimson slash, the vicious scalpel. The ether fumes were sweet, choking. Her head seemed to be floating away from her body. Her arm was feeble.

It was not the blood but the grating of the surgical saw on the living bone that broke her, and she knew that she had been fighting off nausea, that she was beaten. She was lost in dizziness. She heard Kennicott's voice:

"Sick? Trot outdoors couple minutes. Adolph will stay under now."

She was fumbling at a door-knob which whirled in insulting circles; she was on the stoop, gasping, forcing air into her chest, her head clearing. As she returned she caught the scene as a whole: the cavernous kitchen, two milk-cans a leaden patch by the wall, hams dangling from a beam, bars of light at the stove door, and in the center, illuminated by a small glass lamp held by a frightened stout woman, Dr. Kennicott bending over a body which was humped under a sheet—the surgeon, his bare arms daubed with blood, his hands, in pale-yellow rubber gloves, loosening the tourniquet, his face without emotion save when he threw up his head and clucked at the farm-wife, "Hold that light steady just a second more—*noch blos ein wenig.*"

"He speaks a vulgar, common, incorrect German of life and death and birth and the soil. I read the French and German of sentimental lovers and Christmas garlands. And I thought that it was I who had the culture!" she worshiped as she returned to her place.

After a time he snapped, "That's enough. Don't give him any more ether." He was concentrated on tying an artery. His gruffness seemed heroic to her.

As he shaped the flap of flesh she murmured, "Oh, you *are* wonderful!"

He was surprised. "Why, this is a cinch. Now if it had been like last week—— Get me some more water. Now last week I had a case with an ooze in the peritoneal cavity, and by golly if it wasn't a stomach ulcer that I hadn't suspected and—— There. Say, I certainly am sleepy. Let's turn in here. Too late to drive home. And tastes to me like a storm coming."

### IX

They slept on a feather bed with their fur coats over them; in the morning they broke ice in the pitcher—the vast flowered and gilt pitcher.

Kennicott's storm had not come. When they set out it was hazy and growing warmer. After a mile she saw that he was studying a dark cloud in the north. He urged the horses to the run. But she forgot his unusual haste in wonder at the tragic landscape. The pale snow, the prickles of old stubble, and the clumps of ragged brush faded into a gray obscurity. Under the hillocks were cold shadows. The willows about a farmhouse were agitated by the rising wind, and the patches of bare wood where the bark had peeled away were white as the flesh of a leper. The snowy slews were of a harsh flatness. The whole land was cruel, and a climbing cloud of slate-edged blackness dominated the sky.

"Guess we're about in for a blizzard," speculated Kennicott. "We can make Ben McGonegal's, anyway."

"Blizzard? Really? Why—— But still we used to think they were fun when I was a girl. Daddy had to stay home from court, and we'd stand at the window and watch the snow."

"Not much fun on the prairie. Get lost. Freeze to death. Take no chances." He chirruped at the horses. They were flying now, the carriage rocking on the hard ruts.

The whole air suddenly crystallized into large damp flakes. The horses and the buffalo robe were covered with snow; her face was wet; the thin butt of the whip held a white ridge. The air became colder. The snowflakes were harder; they shot in level lines, clawing at her face.

She could not see a hundred feet ahead.

Kennicott was stern. He bent forward, the reins firm in his coonskin gauntlets. She was certain that he would get through. He always got through things.

Save for his presence, the world and all normal living disappeared. They were lost in the boiling snow. He leaned close to bawl, "Letting the horses have their heads. They'll get us home."

With a terrifying bump they were off the road, slanting with two wheels in the ditch, but instantly they were jerked back as the horses fled on. She gasped. She tried to, and did not, feel brave as she pulled the woolen robe up about her chin.

They were passing something like a dark wall on the right. "I know that barn!" he yelped. He pulled at the reins. Peeping from the covers she saw his teeth pinch his lower lip, saw him, scowl as he slackened and sawed and jerked sharply again at the racing horses.

They stopped.

"Farmhouse there. Put robe around you and come on," he cried.

It was like diving into icy water to climb out of the carriage, but on the ground she smiled at him, her face little and childish and pink above the buffalo robe over her shoulders. In a swirl of flakes which scratched at their eyes like a maniac darkness, he unbuckled the harness. He turned and plodded back, a ponderous furry figure, holding the horses' bridles, Carol's hand dragging at his sleeve.

They came to the cloudy bulk of a barn whose outer wall was directly upon the road. Feeling along it, he found a gate, led them into a yard, into the barn. The interior was warm. It stunned them with its languid quiet.

He carefully drove the horses into stalls.

Her toes were coals of pain. "Let's run for the house," she said.

"Can't. Not yet. Might never find it. Might get lost ten feet away from it. Sit over in this stall, near the horses. We'll rush for the house when the blizzard lifts."

"I'm so stiff! I can't walk!"

He carried her into the stall, stripped off her overshoes and boots, stopping to blow on his purple fingers as he fumbled at her laces. He rubbed her feet, and covered her with the buffalo robe and horse-blankets from the pile on the feed-box. She was drowsy, hemmed in by the storm. She sighed:

"You're so strong and yet so skilful and not afraid of blood or storm or——"

"Used to it. Only thing that's bothered me was the chance the ether fumes might explode, last night."

"I don't understand."

"Why, Dave, the darn fool, sent me ether, instead of chloroform like I told him, and you know ether fumes are mighty inflammable, especially with that lamp right by the table. But I had to operate, of course—wound chuck-full of barnyard filth that way."

"You knew all the time that—— Both you and I might have been blown up? You knew it while you were operating?"

"Sure. Didn't you? Why, what's the matter?"

# 16

Kennicott was heavily pleased by her Christmas presents, and he gave her a diamond bar-pin. But she could not persuade herself that he was much interested in the rites of the morning, in the tree she had decorated, the three stockings she had hung, the ribbons and gilt seals and hidden messages. He said only:

"Nice way to fix things, all right. What do you say we go down to Jack Elder's and have a game of five hundred this afternoon?"

She remembered her father's Christmas fantasies: the sacred old rag doll at the top of the tree, the score of cheap presents, the punch and carols, the roast chestnuts by the fire, and the gravity with which the judge opened the children's scrawly notes and took cognizance of demands for sled-rides, for opinions upon the existence of Santa Claus. She remembered him reading out a long indictment of himself for being a sentimentalist, against the peace and dignity of the State of Minnesota. She remembered his thin legs twinkling before their sled——

She muttered unsteadily, "Must run up and put on my shoes—slippers so cold." In the not very romantic solitude of the locked bathroom she sat on the slippery edge of the tub and wept.

## II

Kennicott had five hobbies: medicine, land-investment, Carol, motoring, and hunting. It is not certain in what order he preferred them. Solid though his enthusiasms were in the matter of medicine—his admiration of this city surgeon, his condemnation of that for tricky ways of persuading country practitioners to bring in surgical patients, his indignation about fee-splitting, his pride in a new X-ray apparatus—none of these beatified him as did motoring.

He nursed his two-year-old Buick even in winter, when it was stored in the stable-garage behind the house. He filled the grease-cups, varnished a fender, removed from beneath the back seat the débris of gloves, copper washers, crumpled maps, dust, and greasy rags. Winter noons he wandered out and stared owlishly at the car. He became excited over a fabulous "trip we might take next summer." He galloped to the station, brought home railway maps, and traced motor-routes from Gopher Prairie to Winnipeg or Des Moines or Grand Marais, thinking aloud and expecting her to be effusive about such academic questions as "Now I wonder if we could stop at Baraboo and break the jump from La Crosse to Chicago?"

To him motoring was a faith not to be questioned, a high-church cult, with electric sparks for candles, and piston-rings possessing the sanctity of altar-vessels. His liturgy was composed of intoned and metrical road-comments: "They say there's a pretty good hike from Duluth to International Falls."

Hunting was equally a devotion, full of metaphysical concepts veiled from Carol. All winter he read sporting-catalogues, and thought about remarkable past shots: "'Member that time when I got two ducks on a long chance, just at sunset?" At least once a month he drew his favorite repeating shotgun, his "pump gun," from its wrapper of greased canton flannel; he oiled the trigger, and spent silent ecstatic moments aiming at the ceiling. Sunday mornings Carol heard him trudging up to the attic and there, an hour later, she found him turning over boots, wooden duck-decoys, lunch-boxes, or reflectively squinting at old shells, rubbing their brass caps with his sleeve and shaking his head as he thought about their uselessness.

He kept the loading-tools he had used as a boy: a capper for shot-gun shells, a mold for lead bullets. When once, in a housewifely frenzy for getting rid of things, she raged, "Why don't you give these away?" he solemnly defended them, "Well, you can't tell; they might come in handy some day."

She flushed. She wondered if he was thinking of the child they would have when, as he put it, they were "sure they could afford one."

Mysteriously aching, nebulously sad, she slipped away, half-convinced but only half-convinced that it was horrible and unnatural, this postponement of release of mother-affection, this sacrifice to her opinionation and to his cautious desire for prosperity.

"But it would be worse if he were like Sam Clark—insisted on having children," she considered; then, "If Will were the Prince, wouldn't I *demand* his child?"

Kennicott's land-deals were both financial advancement and favorite game. Driving through the country, he noticed which farms had good crops; he heard the news about the restless farmer who was "thinking about selling out here and pulling his freight for Alberta." He asked the veterinarian about the value of different breeds of stock; he inquired of Lyman Cass whether or not Einar Gyseldson really had had a yield of forty bushels of wheat to the acre. He was always consulting Julius Flickerbaugh, who handled more real estate than law, and more law than justice. He studied township maps, and read notices of auctions.

Thus he was able to buy a quarter-section of land for one hundred and fifty dollars an acre, and to sell it in a year or two, after installing a cement floor in the barn and running water in the house, for one hundred and eighty or even two hundred.

He spoke of these details to Sam Clark. . . . rather often.

In all his games, cars and guns and land, he expected Carol to take an interest. But he did not give her the facts which might have created interest. He talked only of the obvious and tedious aspects; never of his aspirations in finance, nor of the mechanical principles of motors.

This month of romance she was eager to understand his hobbies. She shivered in the garage while he spent half an hour in deciding whether to put alcohol or patent non-freezing liquid into the radiator, or to drain out the water entirely. "Or no, then I wouldn't want to take her out if it turned warm —still, of course, I could fill the radiator again—wouldn't take so awful long— just take a few pails of water—still, if it turned cold on me again before I drained it—— Course there's some people that put in kerosene, but they say it rots the hose-connections and—— Where did I put that lug-wrench?"

It was at this point that she gave up being a motorist and retired to the house.

In their new intimacy he was more communicative about his practise; he informed her, with the invariable warning not to tell, that Mrs. Sunderquist had another baby coming, that the "hired girl at Howland's was in trouble." But when she asked technical questions he did not know how to answer; when she inquired, "Exactly what is the method of taking out the tonsils?" he yawned, "Tonsilectomy? Why you just—— If there's pus, you operate. Just take 'em out. Seen the newspaper? What the devil did Bea do with it?"

She did not try again.

### III

They had gone to the "movies." The movies were almost as vital to Kennicott and the other solid citizens of Gopher Prairie as land-speculation and guns and automobiles.

The feature film portrayed a brave young Yankee who conquered a South American republic. He turned the natives from their barbarous habits of singing and laughing to the vigorous sanity, the Pep and Punch and Go, of the North; he taught them to work in factories, to wear Klassy Kollege Klothes, and to shout, "Oh, you baby doll, watch me gather in the mazuma." He changed nature itself. A mountain which had borne nothing but lilies and cedars and loafing clouds was by his Hustle so inspirited that it broke out in long wooden sheds, and piles of iron ore to be converted into steamers to carry iron ore to be converted into steamers to carry iron ore.

The intellectual tension induced by the master film was relieved by a livelier, more lyric and less philosophical drama: Mack Schnarken and the Bathing Suit Babes in a comedy of manners entitled "Right on the Coco." Mr. Schnarken was at various high moments a cook, a life-guard, a burlesque actor, and a sculptor. There was a hotel hallway up which policemen charged, only to be stunned by plaster busts hurled upon them from the innumerous doors. If the plot lacked lucidity, the dual motif of legs and pie was clear and sure. Bathing and modeling were equally sound occasions for legs; the wedding-scene was but an approach to the thunderous climax when Mr. Schnarken slipped a piece of custard pie into the clergyman's rear pocket.

The audience in the Rosebud Movie Palace squealed and wiped their eyes; they scrambled under the seats for overshoes, mittens, and mufflers, while the screen announced that next week Mr. Schnarken might be seen in a new, riproaring, extra-special superfeature of the Clean Comedy Corporation entitled, "Under Mollie's Bed."

"I'm glad," said Carol to Kennicott as they stooped before the northwest gale which was torturing the barren street, "that this is a moral country. We don't allow any of these beastly frank novels."

"Yump. Vice Society and Postal Department won't stand for them. The American people don't like filth."

"Yes. It's fine. I'm glad we have such dainty romances as 'Right on the Coco' instead."

"Say what in heck do you think you're trying to do? Kid me?"

He was silent. She awaited his anger. She meditated upon his gutter patois, the Bœotian dialect characteristic of Gopher Prairie. He laughed puzzlingly. When they came into the glow of the house he laughed again. He condescended:

"I've got to hand it to you. You're consistent, all right. I'd of thought that after getting this look-in at a lot of good decent farmers, you'd get over this high-art stuff, but you hang right on."

"Well——" To herself: "He takes advantage of my trying to be good."

"Tell you, Carrie: There's just three classes of people: folks that haven't got any ideas at all; and cranks that kick about everything; and Regular Guys, the fellows with sticktuitiveness, that boost and get the world's work done."

"Then I'm probably a crank." She smiled negligently.

"No. I won't admit it. You do like to talk, but at a show-down you'd prefer Sam Clark to any damn long-haired artist."

"Oh—well——"

"Oh well!" mockingly. "My, we're just going to change everything, aren't we! Going to tell fellows that have been making movies for ten years how to direct 'em; and tell architects how to build towns; and make the magazines publish nothing but a lot of highbrow stories about old maids, and about wives that don't know what they want. Oh, we're a terror! . . . Come on now, Carrie; come out of it; wake up! You've got a fine nerve, kicking about a movie because it shows a few legs! Why, you're always touting these Greek dancers, or whatever they are, that don't even wear a shimmy!"

"But, dear, the trouble with that film—it wasn't that it got in so many legs, but that it giggled coyly and promised to show more of them, and then didn't keep the promise. It was Peeping Tom's idea of humor."

"I don't get you. Look here now——"

She lay awake, while he rumbled with sleep.

"I must go on. My 'crank ideas,' he calls them. I thought that adoring him, watching him operate, would be enough. It isn't. Not after the first thrill.

"I don't want to hurt him. But I must go on.

"It isn't enough, to stand by while he fills an automobile radiator and chucks me bits of information.

"If I stood by and admired him long enough, I would be content. I would become a 'nice little woman.' The Village Virus. Already—— I'm not reading anything. I haven't touched the piano for a week. I'm letting the days drown in worship of 'a good deal, ten plunks more per acre.' I won't! I won't succumb!

"How? I've failed at everything: the Thanatopsis, parties, pioneers, city hall, Guy and Vida. But—— It doesn't *matter!* I'm not trying to 'reform the town' now. I'm not trying to organize Browning Clubs, and sit in clean white kids yearning up at lecturers with ribbony eyeglasses. I am trying to save my soul.

"Will Kennicott, asleep there, trusting me, thinking he holds me. And I'm leaving him. All of me left him when he laughed at me. It wasn't enough for him that I admired him; I must change myself and grow like him. He takes advantage. No more. It's finished. I will go on."

### IV

Her violin lay on top of the upright piano. She picked it up. Since she had last touched it the dried strings had snapped, and upon it lay a gold and crimson cigar-band.

### V

She longed to see Guy Pollock, for the confirming of the brethren in the faith. But Kennicott's dominance was heavy upon her. She could not determine whether she was checked by fear or him, or by inertia—by dislike of the emotional labor of the "scenes" which would be involved in asserting independence. She was like the revolutionist at fifty: not afraid of death, but bored by the probability of bad steaks and bad breaths and sitting up all night on windy barricades.

The second evening after the movies she impulsively summoned Vida Sherwin and Guy to the house for pop-corn and cider. In the living-room Vida and Kennicott debated "the value of manual training in grades below the eighth," while Carol sat beside Guy at the dining table, buttering pop-corn. She was quickened by the speculation in his eyes. She murmured:

"Guy, do you want to help me?"

"My dear! How?"

"I don't know!"

He waited.

"I think I want you to help me find out what has made the darkness of the women. Gray darkness and shadowy trees. We're all in it, ten million women, young married women with good prosperous husbands, and business women in linen collars, and grandmothers that gad out to teas, and wives of underpaid miners, and farmwives who really like to make butter and go to church. What is it we want—and need? Will Kennicott there would say that we need lots of children and hard work. But it isn't that. There's the same discontent in women with eight children and one more coming—always one more coming! And you find it in stenographers and wives who scrub, just as much as in girl college-graduates who wonder how they can escape their kind parents. What do we want?"

"Essentially, I think, you are like myself, Carol; you want to go back to an age of tranquillity and charming manners. You want to enthrone good taste again."

"Just good taste? Fastidious people? Oh—no! I believe all of us want the same things—we're all together, the industrial workers and the women and the farmers and the negro race and the Asiatic colonies, and even a few of the Respectables. It's all the same revolt, in all the classes that have waited and taken advice. I think perhaps we want a more conscious life. We're tired of drudging and sleeping and dying. We're tired of seeing just a few people able to be individualists. We're tired of always deferring hope till the next generation. We're tired of hearing the politicians and priests and cautious reformers (and the husbands!) coax us, 'Be calm! Be patient! Wait! We have the plans for a Utopia already made; just give us a bit more time and we'll produce it; trust us; we're wiser than you.' For ten thousand years they've said that. We want our Utopia *now*—and we're going to try our hands at it. All we want is—everything for all of us! For every housewife and every longshoreman and every Hindu nationalist and every teacher. We want everything. We sha'n't get it. So we sha'n't ever be content——"

She wondered why he was wincing. He broke in:

"See here, my dear, I certainly hope you don't class yourself with a lot of trouble-making labor-leaders! Democracy is all right theoretically, and I'll admit there are industrial injustices, but I'd rather have them than see the world reduced to a dead level of mediocrity. I refuse to believe that you have anything in common with a lot of laboring men rowing for bigger wages so that they can buy wretched flivvers and hideous player-pianos and——"

At this second, in Buenos Ayres, a newspaper editor broke his routine of being bored by exchanges to assert, "Any injustice is better than seeing the world reduced to a gray level of scientific dullness." At this second a clerk standing at the bar of a New York saloon stopped milling his secret fear of his nagging office-manager long enough to growl at the chauffeur beside him, "Aw, you socialists make me sick! I'm an individualist. I ain't going to be nagged by no bureaus and take orders off labor-leaders. And mean to say a hobo's as good as you and me?"

At this second Carol realized that for all Guy's love of dead elegances his timidity was as depressing to her as the bulkiness of Sam Clark. She realized that he was not a mystery, as she had excitedly believed; not a romantic messenger from the World Outside on whom she could count for escape. He belonged to Gopher Prairie, absolutely. She was snatched back from a dream of far countries, and found herself on Main Street.

He was completing his protest, "You don't want to be mixed up in all this orgy of meaningless discontent?"

She soothed him. "No, I don't. I'm not heroic. I'm scared by all the fighting that's going on in the world. I want nobility and adventure, but perhaps I want still more to curl on the hearth with some one I love."

"Would you——"

He did not finish it. He picked up a handful of pop-corn, let it run through his fingers, looked at her wistfully.

With the loneliness of one who has put away a possible love Carol saw that he was a stranger. She saw that he had never been anything but a frame on which she had hung shining garments. If she had let him diffidently make love to her, it was not because she cared, but because she did not care, because it did not matter.

She smiled at him with the exasperating tactfulness of a woman checking a flirtation; a smile like an airy pat on the arm. She sighed, "You're a dear to let me tell you my imaginary troubles." She bounced up, and trilled, "Shall we take the pop-corn in to them now?"

Guy looked after her desolately.

While she teased Vida and Kennicott she was repeating, "I must go on."

## VI

Miles Bjornstam, the pariah "Red Swede," had brought his circular saw and portable gasoline engine to the house, to cut the cords of poplar for the kitchen range. Kennicott had given the order; Carol knew nothing of it till she heard the ringing of the saw, and glanced out to see Bjornstam, in black leather jacket and enormous ragged purple mittens, pressing sticks against the whirling blade, and flinging the stove-lengths to one side. The red irritable motor kept up a red irritable "tip-tip-tip-tip-tip-tip." The whine of the saw rose till it simulated the shriek of a fire-alarm whistle at night, but always at the end it gave a lively metallic clang, and in the stillness she heard the flump of the cut stick falling on the pile.

She threw a motor robe over her, ran out. Bjornstam welcomed her, "Well, well, well! Here's old Miles, fresh as ever. Well say, that's all right; he ain't even begun to be cheeky yet; next summer he's going to take you out on his horse-trading trip, clear into Idaho."

"Yes, and I may go!"

"How's tricks? Crazy about the town yet?"

"No, but I probably shall be, some day."

"Don't let 'em get you. Kick 'em in the face!"

He shouted at her while he worked. The pile of stove-wood grew astonishingly. The pale bark of the poplar sticks was mottled with lichens of sage-green and dusty gray; the newly sawed ends were fresh-colored, with the agreeable roughness of a woolen muffler. To the sterile winter air the wood gave a scent of March sap.

Kennicott telephoned that he was going into the country. Bjornstam had not finished his work at noon, and she invited him to have dinner with Bea in the kitchen. She wished that she were independent enough to dine with these her guests. She considered their friendliness, she sneered at "social distinctions," she raged at her own taboos—and she continued to regard them as retainers and herself as a lady. She sat in the dining-room and listened through the door to Bjornstam's booming and Bea's giggles. She was the more absurd to herself in that, after the rite of dining alone, she could go out to the kitchen, lean against the sink, and talk to them.

They were attracted to each other; a Swedish Othello and Desdemona, more useful and amiable than their prototypes. Bjornstam told his scapes:

selling horses in a Montana mining-camp, breaking a log-jam, being impertinent to a "two-fisted" millionaire lumberman. Bea gurgled "Oh my!" and
kept his coffee cup filled.

He took a long time to finish the wood. He had frequently to go into the
kitchen to get warm. Carol heard him confiding to Bea, "You're a darn nice
Swede girl. I guess if I had a woman like you I wouldn't be such a sorehead.
Gosh, your kitchen is clean; makes an old bach feel sloppy. Say, that's nice
hair you got. Huh? Me fresh? Saaaay, girl, if I ever do get fresh, you'll know
it. Why, I could pick you up with one finger, and hold you in the air long
enough to read Robert J. Ingersoll clean through. Ingersoll? Oh, he's a religious writer. Sure. You'd like him fine."

When he drove off he waved to Bea; and Carol, lonely at the window above,
was envious of their pastoral.

"And I—— But I will go on."

# 17

They were driving down the lake to the cottages that moonlit January night,
twenty of them in the bob-sled. They sang "Toy Land" and "Seeing Nelly
Home"; they leaped from the low back of the sled to race over the slippery
snow ruts; and when they were tired they climbed on the runners for a lift.
The moon-tipped flakes kicked up by the horses settled over the revelers
and dripped down their necks, but they laughed, yelped, beat their leather
mittens against their chests. The harness rattled, the sleigh-bells were frantic,
Jack Elder's setter sprang beside the horses, barking.

For a time Carol raced with them. The cold air gave fictive power. She
felt that she could run on all night, leap twenty feet at a stride. But the
excess of energy tired her, and she was glad to snuggle under the comforters
which covered the hay in the sled-box.

In the midst of the babel she found enchanted quietude.

Along the road the shadows from oak-branches were inked on the snow like
bars of music. Then the sled came out on the surface of Lake Minniemashie.
Across the thick ice was a veritable road, a short-cut for farmers. On the glaring expanse of the lake—levels of hard crust, flashes of green ice blown clear,
chains of drifts ribbed like the sea-beach—the moonlight was overwhelming.
It stormed on the snow, it turned the woods ashore into crystals of fire. The
night was tropical and voluptuous. In that drugged magic there was no difference between heavy heat and insinuating cold.

Carol was dream-strayed. The turbulent voices, even Guy Pollock being
connotative beside her, were nothing. She repeated:

> Deep on the convent-roof the snows
> Are sparkling to the moon.

The words and the light blurred into one vast indefinite happiness, and she believed that some great thing was coming to her. She withdrew from the clamor into a worship of incomprehensible gods. The night expanded, she was conscious of the universe, and all mysteries stooped down to her.

She was jarred out of her ecstasy as the bob-sled bumped up the steep road to the bluff where stood the cottages.

They dismounted at Jack Elder's shack. The interior walls of unpainted boards, which had been grateful in August, were forbidding in the chill. In fur coats and mufflers tied over caps they were a strange company, bears and walruses talking. Jack Elder lighted the shavings waiting in the belly of a cast-iron stove which was like an enlarged bean-pot. They piled their wraps high on a rocker, and cheered the rocker as it solemnly tipped over backward.

Mrs. Elder and Mrs. Sam Clark made coffee in an enormous blackened tin pot; Vida Sherwin and Mrs. McGanum unpacked doughnuts and ginger-bread; Mrs. Dave Dyer warmed up "hot dogs"—frankfurters in rolls; Dr. Terry Gould, after announcing, "Ladies and gents, prepare to be shocked; shock line forms on the right," produced a bottle of bourbon whisky.

The others danced, muttering "Ouch!" as their frosted feet struck the pine planks. Carol had lost her dream. Harry Haydock lifted her by the waist and swung her. She laughed. The gravity of the people who stood apart and talked made her the more impatient for frolic.

Kennicott, Sam Clark, Jackson Elder, young Dr. McGanum, and James Madison Howland, teetering on their toes near the stove, conversed with the sedate pomposity of the commercialist. In details the men were unlike, yet they said the same things in the same hearty monotonous voices. You had to look at them to see which was speaking.

"Well, we made pretty good time coming up," from one—any one.

"Yump, we hit it up after we struck the good going on the lake."

"Seems kind of slow though, after driving an auto."

"Yump, it does, at that. Say, how'd you make out with that Sphinx tire you got?"

"Seems to hold out fine. Still, I don't know's I like it any better than the Roadeater Cord."

"Yump, nothing better than a Roadeater. Especially the cord. The cord's lots better than the fabric."

"Yump, you said something—— Roadeater's a good tire."

"Say, how'd you come out with Pete Garsheim on his payments?"

"He's paying up pretty good. That's a nice piece of land he's got."

"Yump, that's a dandy farm."

"Yump, Pete's got a good place there."

They glided from these serious topics into the jocose insults which are the wit of Main Street. Sam Clark was particularly apt at them. "What's this wild-eyed sale of summer caps you think you're trying to pull off?" he clamored at Harry Haydock. "Did you steal 'em, or are you just overcharging us, as usual? . . . Oh say, speaking about caps, d'I ever tell you the good one I've got on Will? The doc thinks he's a pretty good driver, fact, he thinks

he's almost got human intelligence, but one time he had his machine out
in the rain, and the poor fish, he hadn't put on chains, and thinks I——"

Carol had heard the story rather often. She fled back to the dancers, and
at Dave Dyer's masterstroke of dropping an icicle down Mrs. McGanum's
back she applauded hysterically.

They sat on the floor, devouring the food. The men giggled amiably as
they passed the whisky bottle, and laughed, "There's a real sport!" when
Juanita Haydock took a sip. Carol tried to follow; she believed that she desired to be drunk and riotous; but the whisky choked her and as she saw
Kennicott frown she handed the bottle on repentantly. Somewhat too late
she remembered that she had given up domesticity and repentance.

"Let's play charades!" said Raymie Wutherspoon.

"Oh yes, do let us," said Ella Stowbody.

"That's the caper," sanctioned Harry Haydock.

They interpreted the word "making" as May and King. The crown was a
red flannel mitten cocked on Sam Clark's broad pink bald head. They forgot
they were respectable. They made-believe. Carol was stimulated to cry:

"Let's form a dramatic club and give a play! Shall we? It's been so much
fun tonight!"

They looked affable.

"Sure," observed Sam Clark loyally.

"Oh, do let us! I think it would be lovely to present 'Romeo and Juliet'!"
yearned Ella Stowbody.

"Be a whale of a lot of fun," Dr. Terry Gould granted.

"But if we did," Carol cautioned, "it would be awfully silly to have amateur theatricals. We ought to paint our own scenery and everything, and really do something fine. There'd be a lot of hard work. Would you—would
we all be punctual at rehearsals, do you suppose?"

"You bet!" "Sure." "That's the idea." "Fellow ought to be prompt at rehearsals," they all agreed.

"Then let's meet next week and form the Gopher Prairie Dramatic Association!" Carol sang.

She drove home loving these friends who raced through moonlit snow, had
Bohemian parties, and were about to create beauty in the theater. Everything was solved. She would be an authentic part of the town, yet escape the
coma of the Village Virus. . . . She would be free of Kennicott again, without hurting him, without his knowing.

She had triumphed.

The moon was small and high now, and unheeding.

II

Though they had all been certain that they longed for the privilege of
attending committee meetings and rehearsals, the dramatic association as
definitely formed consisted only of Kennicott, Carol, Guy Pollock, Vida
Sherwin, Ella Stowbody, the Harry Haydocks, the Dave Dyers, Raymie

Wutherspoon, Dr. Terry Gould, and four new candidates: flirtatious Rita Simons, Dr. and Mrs. Harvey Dillon and Myrtle Cass, an uncomely but intense girl of nineteen. Of these fifteen only seven came to the first meeting. The rest telephoned their unparalleled regrets and engagements and illnesses, and announced that they would be present at all other meetings through eternity.

Carol was made president and director.

She had added the Dillons. Despite Kennicott's apprehension the dentist and his wife had not been taken up by the Westlakes but had remained as definitely outside really smart society as Willis Woodford, who was teller, bookkeeper, and janitor in Stowbody's bank. Carol had noted Mrs. Dillon dragging past the house during a bridge of the Jolly Seventeen, looking in with pathetic lips at the splendor of the accepted. She impulsively invited the Dillons to the dramatic association meeting, and when Kennicott was brusque to them she was unusually cordial, and felt virtuous.

That self-approval balanced her disappointment at the smallness of the meeting, and her embarrassment during Raymie Wutherspoon's repetitions of "The stage needs uplifting," and "I believe that there are great lessons in some plays."

Ella Stowbody, who was a professional, having studied elocution in Milwaukee, disapproved of Carol's enthusiasm for recent plays. Miss Stowbody expressed the fundamental principle of the American drama: the only way to be artistic is to present Shakespeare. As no one listened to her she sat back and looked like Lady Macbeth.

### III

The Little Theaters, which were to give piquancy to American drama three or four years later, were only in embryo. But of this fast coming revolt Carol had premonitions. She knew from some lost magazine article that in Dublin were innovators called The Irish Players. She knew confusedly that a man named Gordon Craig had painted scenery—or had he written plays? She felt that in the turbulence of the drama she was discovering a history more important than the commonplace chronicles which dealt with senators and their pompous puerilities. She had a sensation of familiarity; a dream of sitting in a Brussels café and going afterward to a tiny gay theater under a cathedral wall.

The advertisement in the Minneapolis paper leaped from the page to her eyes:

> The Cosmos School of Music, Oratory, and
> Dramatic Art announces a program of four
> one-act plays by Schnitzler, Shaw, Yeats, and
> Lord Dunsany.

She had to be there! She begged Kennicott to "run down to the Cities" with her.

"Well, I don't know. Be fun to take in a show, but why the deuce do you want to see those darn foreign plays, given by a lot of amateurs? Why don't you wait for a regular play, later on? There's going to be some corkers coming: 'Lottie of Two-Gun Rancho,' and 'Cops and Crooks'—real Broadway stuff, with the New York casts. What's this junk you want to see? Hm. 'How He Lied to Her Husband.' That doesn't listen so bad. Sounds racy. And, uh, well, I could go to the motor show, I suppose. I'd like to see this new Hup roadster. Well——"

She never knew which attraction made him decide.

She had four days of delightful worry—over the hole in her one good silk petticoat, the loss of a string of beads from her chiffon and brown velvet frock, the catsup stain on her best georgette crêpe blouse. She wailed, "I haven't a single solitary thing that's fit to be seen in," and enjoyed herself very much indeed.

Kennicott went about casually letting people know that he was "going to run down to the Cities and see some shows."

As the train plodded through the gray prairie, on a windless day with the smoke from the engine clinging to the fields in giant cotton-rolls, in a low and writhing wall which shut off the snowy fields, she did not look out of the window. She closed her eyes and hummed, and did not know that she was humming.

She was the young poet attacking fame and Paris.

In the Minneapolis station the crowd of lumberjacks, farmers, and Swedish families with innumerable children and grandparents and paper parcels, their foggy crowding and their clamor confused her. She felt rustic in this once familiar city, after a year and a half of Gopher Prairie. She was certain that Kennicott was taking the wrong trolley-car. By dusk, the liquor warehouses, Hebraic clothing-shops, and lodging-houses on lower Hennepin Avenue were smoky, hideous, ill-tempered. She was battered by the noise and shuttling of the rush-hour traffic. When a clerk in an overcoat too closely fitted at the waist stared at her, she moved nearer to Kennicott's arm. The clerk was flippant and urban. He was a superior person, used to this tumult. Was he laughing at her?

For a moment she wanted the secure quiet of Gopher Prairie.

In the hotel-lobby she was self-conscious. She was not used to hotels; she remembered with jealousy how often Juanita Haydock talked of the famous hotels in Chicago. She could not face the traveling salesmen, baronial in large leather chairs. She wanted people to believe that her husband and she were accustomed to luxury and chill elegance; she was faintly angry at him for the vulgar way in which, after signing the register "Dr. W. P. Kennicott & wife," he bellowed at the clerk, "Got a nice room with bath for us, old man?" She gazed about haughtily, but as she discovered that no one was interested in her she felt foolish, and ashamed of her irritation.

She asserted, "This silly lobby is too florid," and simultaneously she admired it: the onyx columns with gilt capitals, the crown-embroidered velvet curtains at the restaurant door, the silk-roped alcove where pretty girls perpetually waited for mysterious men, the two-pound boxes of candy and the variety of magazines at the news-stand. The hidden orchestra was lively. She saw a man who looked like a European diplomat, in a loose top-coat and a Homburg hat. A woman with a broadtail coat, a heavy lace veil, pearl earrings, and a close black hat entered the restaurant. "Heavens! That's the first really smart woman I've seen in a year!" Carol exulted. She felt metropolitan.

But as she followed Kennicott to the elevator the coat-check girl, a confident young woman, with cheeks powdered like lime, and a blouse low and thin and furiously crimson, inspected her, and under that supercilious glance Carol was shy again. She unconsciously waited for the bellboy to precede her into the elevator. When he snorted "Go ahead!" she was mortified. He thought she was a hayseed, she worried.

The moment she was in their room, with the bellboy safely out of the way, she looked critically at Kennicott. For the first time in months she really saw him.

His clothes were too heavy and provincial. His decent gray suit, made by Nat Hicks of Gopher Prairie, might have been of sheet iron; it had no distinction of cut, no easy grace like the diplomat's Burberry. His black shoes were blunt and not well polished. His scarf was a stupid brown. He needed a shave.

But she forgot her doubt as she realized the ingenuities of the room. She ran about, turning on the taps of the bathtub, which gushed instead of dribbling like the taps at home, snatching the new wash-rag out of its envelope of oiled paper, trying the rose-shaded light between the twin beds, pulling out the drawers of the kidney-shaped walnut desk to examine the engraved stationery, planning to write on it to every one she knew, admiring the claret-colored velvet arm-chair and the blue rug, testing the ice-water tap, and squealing happily when the water really did come out cold. She flung her arms about Kennicott, kissed him.

"Like it, old lady?"

"It's adorable. It's so amusing. I love you for bringing me. You really are a dear!"

He looked blankly indulgent, and yawned, and condescended, "That's a pretty slick arrangement on the radiator, so you can adjust it at any temperature you want. Must take a big furnace to run this place. Gosh, I hope Bea remembers to turn off the drafts tonight."

Under the glass cover of the dressing-table was a menu with the most enchanting dishes: breast of guinea hen De Vitresse, pommes de terre à la Russe, meringue Chantilly, gâteaux Bruxelles.

"Oh, let's—— I'm going to have a hot bath, and put on my new hat with the wool flowers, and let's go down and eat for hours, and we'll have a cocktail!" she chanted.

While Kennicott labored over ordering it was annoying to see him permit the waiter to be impertinent, but as the cocktail elevated her to a bridge among colored stars, as the oysters came in—not canned oysters in the Gopher Prairie fashion, but on the half-shell—she cried, "If you only knew how wonderful it is not to have had to plan this dinner, and order it at the butcher's and fuss and think about it, and then watch Bea cook it! I feel so free. And to have new kinds of food, and different patterns of dishes and linen, and not worry about whether the pudding is being spoiled! Oh, this is a great moment for me!"

IV

They had all the experiences of provincials in a metropolis. After breakfast Carol bustled to a hair-dresser's, bought gloves and a blouse, and importantly met Kennicott in front of an optician's, in accordance with plans laid down, revised, and verified. They admired the diamonds and furs and frosty silverware and mahogany chairs and polished morocco sewing-boxes in shop-windows, and were abashed by the throngs in the department-stores, and were bullied by a clerk into buying too many shirts for Kennicott, and gaped at the "clever novelty perfumes—just in from New York." Carol got three books on the theater, and spent an exultant hour in warning herself that she could not afford this rajah-silk frock, in thinking how envious it would make Juanita Haydock, in closing her eyes, and buying it. Kennicott went from shop to shop, earnestly hunting down a felt-covered device to keep the windshield of his car clear of rain.

They dined extravagantly at their hotel at night, and next morning sneaked round the corner to economize at a Childs' Restaurant. They were tired by three in the afternoon, and dozed at the motion-pictures and said they wished they were back in Gopher Prairie—and by eleven in the evening they were again so lively that they went to a Chinese restaurant that was frequented by clerks and their sweethearts on pay-days. They sat at a teak and marble table eating Eggs Fooyung, and listened to a brassy automatic piano, and were altogether cosmopolitan.

On the street they met people from home—the McGanums. They laughed, shook hands repeatedly, and exclaimed, "Well, this is quite a coincidence!" They asked when the McGanums had come down, and begged for news of the town they had left two days before. Whatever the McGanums were at home, here they stood out as so superior to all the undistinguishable strangers absurdly hurrying past that the Kennicotts held them as long as they could. The McGanums said good-by as though they were going to Tibet instead of to the station to catch No. 7 north.

They explored Minneapolis. Kennicott was conversational and technical regarding gluten and cockle-cylinders and No. 1 Hard, when they were shown through the gray stone hulks and new cement elevators of the largest flour-mills in the world. They looked across Loring Park and the Parade to the towers of St. Mark's and the Procathedral, and the red roofs of houses climbing Kenwood Hill. They drove about the chain of garden-circled lakes, and viewed the houses of the millers and lumbermen and real estate peers—the potentates of the expanding city. They surveyed the small eccentric bungalows with pergolas, the houses of pebbledash and tapestry brick with sleeping-porches above sun-parlors, and one vast incredible château fronting the Lake of the Isles. They tramped through a shining-new section of apartment-houses; not the tall bleak apartments of Eastern cities but low structures of cheerful yellow brick, in which each flat had its glass-enclosed porch with swinging couch and scarlet cushions and Russian brass bowls. Between a waste of tracks and a raw gouged hill they found poverty in staggering shanties.

They saw miles of the city which they had never known in their days of absorption in college. They were distinguished explorers, and they remarked, in great mutual esteem, "I bet Harry Haydock's never seen the City like this! Why, he'd never have sense enough to study the machinery in the mills, or go through all these outlying districts. Wonder folks in Gopher Prairie wouldn't use their legs and explore, the way *we* do!"

They had two meals with Carol's sister, and were bored, and felt that intimacy which beatifies married people when they suddenly admit that they equally dislike a relative of either of them.

So it was with affection but also with weariness that they approached the evening on which Carol was to see the plays at the dramatic school. Kennicott suggested not going. "So darn tired from all this walking; don't know but what we better turn in early and get rested up." It was only from duty that Carol dragged him and herself out of the warm hotel, into a stinking trolley, up the brownstone steps of the converted residence which lugubriously housed the dramatic school.

v

They were in a long whitewashed hall with a clumsy draw-curtain across the front. The folding chairs were filled with people who looked washed and ironed: parents of the pupils, girl students, dutiful teachers.

"Strikes me it's going to be punk. If the first play isn't good, let's beat it," said Kennicott hopefully.

"All right," she yawned. With hazy eyes she tried to read the lists of characters, which were hidden among lifeless advertisements of pianos, music-dealers, restaurants, candy.

She regarded the Schnitzler play with no vast interest. The actors moved and spoke stiffly. Just as its cynicism was beginning to rouse her village-dulled frivolity, it was over.

"Don't think a whale of a lot of that. How about taking a sneak?" petitioned Kennicott.

"Oh, let's try the next one, 'How He Lied to Her Husband.'"

The Shaw conceit amused her, and perplexed Kennicott:

"Strikes me it's darn fresh. Thought it would be racy. Don't know as I think much of a play where a husband actually claims he wants a fellow to make love to his wife. No husband ever did that! Shall we shake a leg?"

"I want to see this Yeats thing, 'Land of Heart's Desire.' I used to love it in college." She was awake now, and urgent. "I know you didn't care so much for Yeats when I read him aloud to you, but you just see if you don't adore him on the stage."

Most of the cast were as unwieldy as oak chairs marching, and the setting was an arty arrangement of batik scarfs and heavy tables, but Maire Bruin was slim as Carol, and larger-eyed, and her voice was a morning bell. In her, Carol lived, and on her lifting voice was transported from this sleepy small-town husband and all the rows of polite parents to the stilly loft of a thatched cottage where in a green dimness, beside a window caressed by linden branches, she bent over a chronicle of twilight women and the ancient gods.

"Well—gosh—nice kid played that girl—good-looker," said Kennicott. "Want to stay for the last piece? Heh?"

She shivered. She did not answer.

The curtain was again drawn aside. On the stage they saw nothing but long green curtains and a leather chair. Two young men in brown robes like furniture-covers were gesturing vacuously and droning cryptic sentences full of repetitions.

It was Carol's first hearing of Dunsany. She sympathized with the restless Kennicott as he felt in his pocket for a cigar and unhappily put it back.

Without understanding when or how, without a tangible change in the stilted intoning of the stage-puppets, she was conscious of another time and place.

Stately and aloof among vainglorious tiring-maids, a queen in robes that murmured on the marble floor, she trod the gallery of a crumbling palace. In the courtyard, elephants trumpeted, and swart men with beards dyed crimson stood with blood-stained hands folded upon their hilts, guarding the caravan from El Sharnak, the camels with Tyrian stuffs of topaz and cinnabar. Beyond the turrets of the outer wall the jungle glared and shrieked, and the sun was furious above drenched orchids. A youth came striding through the steel-bossed doors, the sword-bitten doors that were higher than ten tall men. He was in flexible mail, and under the rim of his planished morion were amorous curls. His hand was out to her; before she touched it she could feel its warmth——

"Gosh all hemlock! What the dickens is all this stuff about, Carrie?"

She was no Syrian queen. She was Mrs. Dr. Kennicott. She fell with a jolt into a whitewashed hall and sat looking at two scared girls and a young man in wrinkled tights.

Kennicott fondly rambled as they left the hall:

"What the deuce did that last spiel mean? Couldn't make head or tail of it. If that's highbrow drama, give me a cowpuncher movie, every time! Thank God, that's over, and we can get to bed. Wonder if we wouldn't make time by walking over to Nicollet to take a car? One thing I will say for that dump: they had it warm enough. Must have a big hot-air furnace, I guess. Wonder how much coal it takes to run 'em through the winter?"

In the car he affectionately patted her knee, and he was for a second the striding youth in armor; then he was Doc Kennicott of Gopher Prairie, and she was recaptured by Main Street. Never, not all her life, would she behold jungles and the tombs of kings. There were strange things in the world, they really existed; but she would never see them.

She would re-create them in plays!

She would make the dramatic association understand her aspiration. They would, surely they would——

She looked doubtfully at the impenetrable reality of yawning trolley conductor and sleepy passengers and placards advertising soap and underwear.

# 18

She hurried to the first meeting of the play-reading committee. Her jungle romance had faded, but she retained a religious fervor, a surge of half-formed thought about the creation of beauty by suggestion.

A Dunsany play would be too difficult for the Gopher Prairie association. She would let them compromise on Shaw—on "Androcles and the Lion," which had just been published.

The committee was composed of Carol, Vida Sherwin, Guy Pollock, Raymie Wutherspoon, and Juanita Haydock. They were exalted by the picture of themselves as being simultaneously business-like and artistic. They were entertained by Vida in the parlor of Mrs. Elisha Gurrey's boarding-house, with its steel engraving of Grant at Appomattox, its basket of stereoscopic views, and its mysterious stains on the gritty carpet.

Vida was an advocate of culture-buying and efficiency-systems. She hinted that they ought to have (as at the committee-meetings of the Thanatopsis) a "regular order of business," and "the reading of the minutes," but as there were no minutes to read, and as no one knew exactly what was the regular order of the business of being literary, they had to give up efficiency.

Carol, as chairman, said politely, "Have you any ideas about what play we'd better give first?" She waited for them to look abashed and vacant, so that she might suggest "Androcles."

Guy Pollock answered with disconcerting readiness, "I'll tell you: since we're going to try to do something artistic, and not simply fool around, I believe we ought to give something classic. How about 'The School for Scandal'?"

"Why—— Don't you think that has been done a good deal?"

"Yes, perhaps it has."

Carol was ready to say, "How about Bernard Shaw?" when he treacherously went on, "How would it be then to give a Greek drama—say 'Œdipus Tyrannus'?"

"Why, I don't believe——"

Vida Sherwin intruded, "I'm sure that would be too hard for us. Now I've brought something that I think would be awfully jolly."

She held out, and Carol incredulously took, a thin gray pamphlet entitled

"McGinerty's Mother-in-law." It was the sort of farce which is advertised in "school entertainment" catalogues as:

> Riproaring knock-out, 5 m. 3 f., time 2 hrs., interior set, popular with churches and all high-class occasions.

Carol glanced from the scabrous object to Vida, and realized that she was not joking.

"But this is—this is—why, it's just a—— Why, Vida, I thought you appreciated—well—appreciated art."

Vida snorted, "Oh. Art. Oh yes. I do like art. It's very nice. But after all, what does it matter what kind of play we give as long as we get the association started? The thing that matters is something that none of you have spoken of, that is: what are we going to do with the money, if we make any? I think it would be awfully nice if we presented the high school with a full set of Stoddard's travel-lectures!"

Carol moaned, "Oh, but Vida dear, do forgive me but this farce—— Now what I'd like us to give is something distinguished. Say Shaw's 'Androcles.' Have any of you read it?"

"Yes. Good play," said Guy Pollock.

Then Raymie Wutherspoon astoundingly spoke up:

"So have I. I read through all the plays in the public library, so's to be ready for this meeting. And—— But I don't believe you grasp the irreligious ideas in this 'Androcles,' Mrs. Kennicott. I guess the feminine mind is too innocent to understand all these immoral writers. I'm sure I don't want to criticize Bernard Shaw; I understand he is very popular with the highbrows in Minneapolis; but just the same—— As far as I can make out, he's downright improper! The things he *says*—— Well, it would be a very risky thing for our young folks to see. It seems to me that a play that doesn't leave a nice taste in the mouth and that hasn't any message is nothing but—nothing but—— Well, whatever it may be, it isn't art. So—— Now I've found a play that is clean, and there's some awfully funny scenes in it, too. I laughed out loud, reading it. It's called 'His Mother's Heart,' and it's about a young man in college who gets in with a lot of freethinkers and boozers and everything, but in the end his mother's influence——"

Juanita Haydock broke in with a derisive, "Oh rats, Raymie! Can the mother's influence! I say let's give something with some class to it. I bet we could get the rights to 'The Girl from Kankakee,' and that's a real show. It ran for eleven months in New York!"

"That would be lots of fun, if it wouldn't cost too much," reflected Vida.

Carol's was the only vote cast against "The Girl from Kankakee."

II

She disliked "The Girl from Kankakee" even more than she had expected. It narrated the success of a farm-lassie in clearing her brother of a charge of forgery. She became secretary to a New York millionaire and social counselor to his wife; and after a well-conceived speech on the discomfort of having money, she married his son.

There was also a humorous office-boy.

Carol discerned that both Juanita Haydock and Ella Stowbody wanted the lead. She let Juanita have it. Juanita kissed her and in the exuberant manner of a new star presented to the executive committee her theory, "What we want in a play is humor and pep. There's where American playwrights put it all over these darn old European glooms."

As selected by Carol and confirmed by the committee, the persons of the play were:

| | |
|---|---|
| John Grimm, a millionaire . . . . . | Guy Pollock |
| His wife . . . . . . . . . . | Miss Vida Sherwin |
| His son . . . . . . . . . . | Dr. Harvey Dillon |
| His business rival . . . . . . . | Raymond T. Wutherspoon |
| Friend of Mrs. Grimm . . . . . . | Miss Ella Stowbody |
| The girl from Kankakee . . . . . . | Mrs. Harold C. Haydock |
| Her brother . . . . . . . . . | Dr. Terence Gould |
| Her mother . . . . . . . . . | Mrs. David Dyer |
| Stenographer . . . . . . . . | Miss Rita Simons |
| Office-boy . . . . . . . . | Miss Myrtle Cass |
| Maid in the Grimms' home . . . . . | Mrs. W. P. Kennicott |

Direction of Mrs. Kennicott

Among the minor lamentations was Maud Dyer's "Well of course I suppose I look old enough to be Juanita's mother, even if Juanita is eight months older than I am, but I don't know as I care to have everybody noticing it and——"

Carol pleaded, "Oh, my *dear!* You two look exactly the same age. I chose you because you have such a darling complexion, and you know with powder and a white wig, anybody looks twice her age, and I want the mother to be sweet, no matter who else is."

Ella Stowbody, the professional, perceiving that it was because of a conspiracy of jealousy that she had been given a small part, alternated between lofty amusement and Christian patience.

Carol hinted that the play would be improved by cutting, but as every actor except Vida and Guy and herself wailed at the loss of a single line, she was defeated. She told herself that, after all, a great deal could be done with direction and settings.

Sam Clark had boastfully written about the dramatic association to his schoolmate, Percy Bresnahan, president of the Velvet Motor Company of Boston. Bresnahan sent a check for a hundred dollars; Sam added twenty-five and brought the fund to Carol, fondly crying, "There! That'll give you a start for putting the thing across swell!"

She rented the second floor of the city hall for two months. All through the spring the association thrilled to its own talent in that dismal room. They cleared out the bunting, ballot-boxes, handbills, legless chairs. They attacked the stage. It was a simple-minded stage. It was raised above the floor, and it did have a movable curtain, painted with the advertisement of a druggist dead these ten years, but otherwise it might not have been recognized as a stage. There were two dressing-rooms, one for men, one for women, on either side. The dressing-room doors were also the stage-entrances, opening from the house, and many a citizen of Gopher Prairie had for his first glimpse of romance the bare shoulders of the leading woman.

There were three sets of scenery: a woodland, a Poor Interior, and a Rich Interior, the last also useful for railway stations, offices, and as a background for the Swedish Quartette from Chicago. There were three gradations of lighting: full on, half on, and entirely off.

This was the only theater in Gopher Prairie. It was known as the "op'ra house." Once, strolling companies had used it for performances of "The Two Orphans," and "Nellie the Beautiful Cloak Model," and "Othello" with specialties between acts, but now the motion-pictures had ousted the gipsy drama.

Carol intended to be furiously modern in constructing the office-set, the drawing-room for Mr. Grimm, and the Humble Home near Kankakee. It was the first time that any one in Gopher Prairie had been so revolutionary as to use enclosed scenes with continuous side-walls. The rooms in the op'ra house sets had separate wing-pieces for sides, which simplified dramaturgy, as the villain could always get out of the hero's way by walking out through the wall.

The inhabitants of the Humble Home were supposed to be amiable and intelligent. Carol planned for them a simple set with warm color. She could see the beginning of the play: all dark save the high settles and the solid wooden table between them, which were to be illuminated by a ray from off-stage. The high light was a polished copper pot filled with primroses. Less clearly she sketched the Grimm drawing-room as a series of cool high white arches.

As to how she was to produce these effects she had no notion.

She discovered that, despite the enthusiastic young writers, the drama was not half so native and close to the soil as motor cars and telephones. She discovered that simple arts require sophisticated training. She discovered that to produce one perfect stage-picture would be as difficult as to turn all of Gopher Prairie into a Georgian garden.

She read all she could find regarding staging; she bought paint and light wood; she borrowed furniture and drapes unscrupulously; she made Kennicott turn carpenter. She collided with the problem of lighting. Against the protest of Kennicott and Vida she mortgaged the association by sending to Minneapolis for a baby spotlight, a strip light, a dimming device, and blue and amber bulbs; and with the gloating rapture of a born painter first turned loose among colors, she spent absorbed evenings in grouping, dimming—painting with lights.

Only Kennicott, Guy, and Vida helped her. They speculated as to how flats could be lashed together to form a wall; they hung crocus-yellow curtains at the windows; they blacked the sheet-iron stove; they put on aprons and swept. The rest of the association dropped into the theater every evening, and were literary and superior. They had borrowed Carol's manuals of play-production and had become extremely stagey in vocabulary.

Juanita Haydock, Rita Simons, and Raymie Wutherspoon sat on a saw-horse, watching Carol try to get the right position for a picture on the wall in the first scene.

"I don't want to hand myself anything but I believe I'll give a swell performance in this first act," confided Juanita. "I wish Carol wasn't so bossy though. She doesn't understand clothes. I want to wear, oh, a dandy dress I have—all scarlet—and I said to her, 'When I enter wouldn't it knock their eyes out if I just stood there at the door in this straight scarlet thing?' But she wouldn't let me."

Young Rita agreed, "She's so much taken up with her old details and carpentering and everything that she can't see the picture as a whole. Now I thought it would be lovely if we had an office-scene like the one in 'Little, But Oh My!' Because I *saw* that, in Duluth. But she simply wouldn't listen at all."

Juanita sighed, "I wanted to give one speech like Ethel Barrymore would, if she was in a play like this. (Harry and I heard her one time in Minneapolis —we had dandy seats, in the orchestra—I just know I could imitate her.) Carol didn't pay any attention to my suggestion. I don't want to criticize but I guess Ethel knows more about acting than Carol does!"

"Say, do you think Carol has the right dope about using a strip light behind the fireplace in the second act? I told her I thought we ought to use a bunch," offered Raymie. "And I suggested it would be lovely if we used a cyclorama outside the window in the first act, and what do you think she said? 'Yes, and it would be lovely to have Eleanora Duse play the lead,' she said, 'and aside from the fact that it's evening in the first act, you're a great technician,' she said. I must say I think she was pretty sarcastic. I've been reading up, and I know I could build a cyclorama, if she didn't want to run everything."

"Yes, and another thing, I think the entrance in the first act ought to be L. U. E., not L. 3 E.," from Juanita.

"And why does she just use plain white tormenters?"

"What's a tormenter?" blurted Rita Simons.

The savants stared at her ignorance.

### III

Carol did not resent their criticisms, she didn't very much resent their sudden knowledge, so long as they let her make pictures. It was at rehearsals that the quarrels broke. No one understood that rehearsals were as real engagements as bridge-games or sociables at the Episcopal Church. They gaily came in half an hour late, or they vociferously came in ten minutes early, and they were so hurt that they whispered about resigning when Carol protested. They telephoned, "I don't think I'd better come out; afraid the damp-ness might start my toothache," or "Guess can't make it tonight; Dave wants me to sit in on a poker game."

When, after a month of labor, as many as nine-elevenths of the cast were often present at a rehearsal; when most of them had learned their parts and some of them spoke like human beings, Carol had a new shock in the realiza-tion that Guy Pollock and herself were very bad actors, and that Raymie Wutherspoon was a surprisingly good one. For all her visions she could not control her voice, and she was bored by the fiftieth repetition of her few lines as maid. Guy pulled his soft mustache, looked self-conscious, and turned Mr. Grimm into a limp dummy. But Raymie, as the villain, had no repres-sions. The tilt of his head was full of character; his drawl was admirably vicious.

There was an evening when Carol hoped she was going to make a play; a rehearsal during which Guy stopped looking abashed.

From that evening the play declined.

They were weary. "We know our parts well enough now; what's the use of getting sick of them?" they complained. They began to skylark; to play with the sacred lights; to giggle when Carol was trying to make the sentimental Myrtle Cass into a humorous office-boy; to act everything but "The Girl from Kankakee." After loafing through his proper part Dr. Terry Gould had great applause for his burlesque of "Hamlet." Even Raymie lost his simple faith, and tried to show that he could do a vaudeville shuffle.

Carol turned on the company. "See here, I want this nonsense to stop. We've simply got to get down to work."

Juanita Haydock led the mutiny: "Look here, Carol, don't be so bossy. After all, we're doing this play principally for the fun of it, and if we have fun out of a lot of monkeyshines, why then——"

"Ye-es," feebly.

"You said one time that folks in G. P. didn't get enough fun out of life. And now we are having a circus, you want us to stop!"

Carol answered slowly: "I wonder if I can explain what I mean? It's the difference between looking at the comic page and looking at Manet. I want fun out of this, of course. Only—— I don't think it would be less fun, but more, to produce as perfect a play as we can." She was curiously exalted; her voice was strained; she stared not at the company but at the grotesques scrawled on the backs of wing-pieces by forgotten stage-hands. "I wonder if you can understand the 'fun' of making a beautiful thing, the pride and satisfaction of it, and the holiness!"

The company glanced doubtfully at one another. In Gopher Prairie it is not good form to be holy except at a church, between ten-thirty and twelve on Sunday.

"But if we want to do it, we've got to work; we must have self-discipline."

They were at once amused and embarrassed. They did not want to affront this mad woman. They backed off and tried to rehearse. Carol did not hear

Juanita, in front, protesting to Maud Dyer, "If she calls it fun and holiness to sweat over her darned old play—well, I don't!"

IV

Carol attended the only professional play which came to Gopher Prairie that spring. It was a "tent show, presenting snappy new dramas under canvas." The hard-working actors doubled in brass, and took tickets; and between acts sang about the moon in June, and sold Dr. Wintergreen's Surefire Tonic for Ills of the Heart, Lungs, Kidneys, and Bowels. They presented "Sunbonnet Nell: A Dramatic Comedy of the Ozarks," with J. Witherbee Boothby wringing the soul by his resonant "Yuh ain't done right by mah little gal, Mr. City Man, but yer a-goin' to find that back in these-yere hills there's honest folks and good shots!"

The audience, on planks beneath the patched tent, admired Mr. Boothby's beard and long rifle; stamped their feet in the dust at the spectacle of his heroism; shouted when the comedian aped the City Lady's use of a lorgnon by looking through a doughnut stuck on a fork; wept visibly over Mr. Boothby's Little Gal Nell, who was also Mr. Boothby's legal wife Pearl, and when the curtain went down, listened respectfully to Mr. Boothby's lecture on Dr. Wintergreen's Tonic as a cure for tape-worms, which he illustrated by horrible pallid objects curled in bottles of yellowing alcohol.

Carol shook her head. "Juanita is right. I'm a fool. Holiness of the drama! Bernard Shaw! The only trouble with 'The Girl from Kankakee' is that it's too subtle for Gopher Prairie!"

She sought faith in spacious banal phrases, taken from books: "the instinctive nobility of simple souls," "need only the opportunity, to appreciate fine things," and "sturdy exponents of democracy." But these optimisms did not sound so loud as the laughter of the audience at the funny-man's line, "Yes, by heckelum, I'm a smart fella." She wanted to give up the play, the dramatic association, the town. As she came out of the tent and walked with Kennicott down the dusty spring street, she peered at this straggling wooden village and felt that she could not possibly stay here through all of tomorrow.

It was Miles Bjornstam who gave her strength—he and the fact that every seat for "The Girl from Kankakee" had been sold.

Bjornstam was "keeping company" with Bea. Every night he was sitting on the back steps. Once when Carol appeared he grumbled, "Hope you're going to give this burg one good show. If you don't, reckon nobody ever will."

V

It was the great night; it was the night of the play. The two dressing-rooms were swirling with actors, panting, twitchy, pale. Del Snafflin the barber, who was as much a professional as Ella, having once gone on in a mob scene at a stock-company performance in Minneapolis, was making them up, and showing his scorn for amateurs with, "Stand still! For the love o' Mike, how do you expect me to get your eyelids dark if you keep a-wigglin'?" The actors were beseeching, "Hey, Del, put some red in my nostrils—you put some in Rita's—gee, you didn't hardly do anything to my face."

They were enormously theatric. They examined Del's make-up box, they sniffed the scent of grease-paint, every minute they ran out to peep through the hole in the curtain, they came back to inspect their wigs and costumes, they read on the whitewashed walls of the dressing-rooms the pencil inscriptions: "The Flora Flanders Comedy Company," and "This is a bum theater," and felt that they were companions of these vanished troupers.

Carol, smart in maid's uniform, coaxed the temporary stagehands to finish setting the first act, wailed at Kennicott, the electrician, "Now for heaven's sake remember the change in cue for the ambers in Act Two," slipped out to ask Dave Dyer, the ticket-taker, if he could get some more chairs, warned the frightened Myrtle Cass to be sure to upset the waste-basket when John Grimm called, "Here you, Reddy."

Del Snafflin's orchestra of piano, violin, and cornet began to tune up and every one behind the magic line of the proscenic arch was frightened into paralysis. Carol wavered to the hole in the curtain. There were so many people out there, staring so hard——

In the second row she saw Miles Bjornstam, not with Bea but alone. He really wanted to see the play! It was a good omen. Who could tell? Perhaps this evening would convert Gopher Prairie to conscious beauty.

She darted into the women's dressing-room, roused Maud Dyer from her fainting panic, pushed her to the wings, and ordered the curtain up.

It rose doubtfully, it staggered and trembled, but it did get up without catching—this time. Then she realized that Kennicott had forgotten to turn off the houselights. Some one out front was giggling.

She galloped round to the left wing, herself pulled the switch, looked so ferociously at Kennicott that he quaked, and fled back.

Mrs. Dyer was creeping out on the half-darkened stage. The play was begun.

And with that instant Carol realized that it was a bad play abominably acted.

Encouraging them with lying smiles, she watched her work go to pieces. The settings seemed flimsy, the lighting commonplace. She watched Guy Pollock stammer and twist his mustache when he should have been a bullying magnate; Vida Sherwin, as Grimm's timid wife, chatter at the audience as though they were her class in high-school English; Juanita, in the leading rôle, defy Mr. Grimm as though she were repeating a list of things she had to buy at the grocery this morning; Ella Stowbody remark "I'd like a cup of tea" as though she were reciting "Curfew Shall Not Ring Tonight"; and Dr. Gould, making love to Rita Simons, squeak, "My—my—you—are—a—won'erful—girl."

Myrtle Cass, as the office-boy, was so much pleased by the applause of her relatives, then so much agitated by the remarks of Cy Bogart, in the back row, in reference to her wearing trousers, that she could hardly be got off the stage. Only Raymie was so unsociable as to devote himself entirely to acting.

That she was right in her opinion of the play Carol was certain when Miles Bjornstam went out after the first act, and did not come back.

VI

Between the second and third acts she called the company together, and supplicated, "I want to know something, before we have a chance to separate. Whether we're doing well or badly tonight, it is a beginning. But will we take it as merely a beginning? How many of you will pledge yourselves to start in with me, right away, tomorrow, and plan for another play, to be given in September?"

They stared at her; they nodded at Juanita's protest: "I think one's enough for a while. It's going elegant tonight, but another play—— Seems to me it'll be time enough to talk about that next fall. Carol! I hope you don't mean to hint and suggest we're not doing fine tonight? I'm sure the applause shows the audience think it's just dandy!"

Then Carol knew how completely she had failed.

As the audience seeped out she heard B. J. Gougerling the banker say to Howland the grocer, "Well, I think the folks did splendid; just as good as professionals. But I don't care much for these plays. What I like is a good movie, with auto accidents and hold-ups, and some git to it, and not all this talky-talk."

Then Carol knew how certain she was to fail again.

She wearily did not blame them, company nor audience. Herself she blamed for trying to carve intaglios in good wholesome jack-pine.

"It's the worst defeat of all. I'm beaten. By Main Street. 'I must go on.' But I can't!"

She was not vastly encouraged by the *Gopher Prairie Dauntless:*

. . . would be impossible to distinguish among the actors when all gave such fine account of themselves in difficult rôles of this well-known New York stage play. Guy Pollock as the old millionaire could not have been bettered for his fine impersonation of the gruff old millionaire; Mrs. Harry Haydock as the young lady from the West who so easily showed the New York four-flushers where they got off was a vision of loveliness and with fine stage presence. Miss Vida Sherwin the ever popular teacher in our high school pleased as Mrs. Grimm, Dr. Gould was well suited in the rôle of young lover—girls you better look out, remember the doc is a bachelor. The local Four Hundred also report that he is a great hand at shaking the light fantastic tootsies in the dance. As the stenographer Rita Simons was pretty as a picture, and Miss Ella Stowbody's long and intensive study of the drama and kindred arts in Eastern schools was seen in the fine finish of her part.

. . . to no one is greater credit to be given than to Mrs. Will Kennicott on whose capable shoulders fell the burden of directing.

"So kindly," Carol mused, "so well meant, so neighborly—and so confoundedly untrue. Is it really my failure, or theirs?"

She sought to be sensible; she elaborately explained to herself that it was hysterical to condemn Gopher Prairie because it did not foam over the drama. Its justification was in its service as a market-town for farmers. How bravely and generously it did its work, forwarding the bread of the world, feeding and healing the farmers!

Then, on the corner below her husband's office, she heard a farmer holding forth:

"Sure. Course I was beaten. The shipper and the grocers here wouldn't pay us a decent price for our potatoes, even though folks in the cities were howling for 'em. So we says, well, we'll get a truck and ship 'em right down to Minneapolis. But the commission merchants there were in cahoots with the local shipper here; they said they wouldn't pay us a cent more than he would, not even if they was nearer to the market. Well, we found we could get higher prices in Chicago, but when we tried to get freight cars to ship there, the railroads wouldn't let us have 'em—even though they had cars standing empty right here in the yards. There you got it—good market, and these towns keeping us from it. Gus, that's the way these towns work all the time. They pay what they want to for our wheat, but we pay what they want us to for their clothes. Stowbody and Dawson foreclose every mortgage they can, and put in tenant farmers. The *Dauntless* lies to us about the Nonpartisan League, the lawyers sting us, the machinery-dealers hate to carry us over bad years, and then their daughters put on swell dresses and look at us as if we were a bunch of hoboes. Man, I'd like to burn this town!"

Kennicott observed, "There's that old crank Wes Brannigan shooting off his mouth again. Gosh, but he loves to hear himself talk! They ought to run that fellow out of town!"

## VII

She felt old and detached through high-school commencement week, which is the fête of youth in Gopher Prairie; through baccalaureate sermon, senior parade, junior entertainment, commencement address by an Iowa clergyman who asserted that he believed in the virtue of virtuousness, and the procession of Decoration Day, when the few Civil War veterans followed Champ Perry, in his rusty forage-cap, along the spring-powdered road to the cemetery. She met Guy; she found that she had nothing to say to him. Her head ached in an aimless way. When Kennicott rejoiced, "We'll have a great time this summer; move down to the lake early and wear old clothes and act natural," she smiled, but her smile creaked.

In the prairie heat she trudged along unchanging ways, talked about nothing to tepid people, and reflected that she might never escape from them.

She was startled to find that she was using the word "escape."

Then, for three years which passed like one curt paragraph, she ceased to find anything interesting save the Bjornstams and her baby.

# 19

In three years of exile from herself Carol had certain experiences chronicled as important by the *Dauntless*, or discussed by the Jolly Seventeen, but the event unchronicled, undiscussed, and supremely controlling, was her slow admission of longing to find her own people.

II

Bea and Miles Bjornstam were married in June, a month after "The Girl from Kankakee." Miles had turned respectable. He had renounced his criticisms of state and society; he had given up roving as horse-trader, and wearing red mackinaws in lumber-camps; he had gone to work as engineer in Jackson Elder's planing-mill; he was to be seen upon the streets endeavoring to be neighborly with suspicious men whom he had taunted for years.

Carol was the patroness and manager of the wedding. Juanita Haydock mocked, "You're a chump to let a good hired girl like Bea go. Besides! How do you know it's a good thing, her marrying a sassy bum like this awful Red Swede person? Get wise! Chase the man off with a mop, and hold onto your Svenska while the holding's good. Huh? Me go to their Scandahoofian wedding? Not a chance!"

The other matrons echoed Juanita. Carol was dismayed by the casualness of their cruelty, but she persisted. Miles had exclaimed to her, "Jack Elder says maybe he'll come to the wedding! Gee, it would be nice to have Bea meet the Boss as a reg'lar married lady. Some day I'll be so well off that Bea can play with Mrs. Elder—and you! Watch us!"

There was an uneasy knot of only nine guests at the service in the unpainted Lutheran Church—Carol, Kennicott, Guy Pollock, and the Champ Perrys, all brought by Carol; Bea's frightened rustic parents, her cousin Tina, and Pete, Miles's ex-partner in horse-trading, a surly, hairy man who had bought a black suit and come twelve hundred miles from Spokane for the event.

Miles continuously glanced back at the church door. Jackson Elder did not appear. The door did not once open after the awkward entrance of the first guests. Miles's hand closed on Bea's arm.

He had, with Carol's help, made his shanty over into a cottage with white curtains and a canary and a chintz chair.

Carol coaxed the powerful matrons to call on Bea. They half scoffed, half promised to go.

Bea's successor was the oldish, broad, silent Oscarina, who was suspicious of her frivolous mistress for a month, so that Juanita Haydock was able to crow, "There, smarty, I told you you'd run into the Domestic Problem!" But Oscarina adopted Carol as a daughter, and with her as faithful to the kitchen as Bea had been, there was nothing changed in Carol's life.

III

She was unexpectedly appointed to the town library-board by Ole Jenson, the new mayor. The other members were Dr. Westlake, Lyman Cass, Julius Flickerbaugh the attorney, Guy Pollock, and Martin Mahoney, former livery-stable keeper and now owner of a garage. She was delighted. She went to the first meeting rather condescendingly, regarding herself as the only one besides Guy who knew anything about books or library methods. She was planning to revolutionize the whole system.

Her condescension was ruined and her humility wholesomely increased when she found the board, in the shabby room on the second floor of the house which had been converted into the library, not discussing the weather and longing to play checkers, but talking about books. She discovered that amiable old Dr. Westlake read everything in verse and "light fiction"; that Lyman Cass, the veal-faced, bristly-bearded owner of the mill, had tramped through Gibbon, Hume, Grote, Prescott, and the other thick historians; that he could repeat pages from them—and did. When Dr. Westlake whispered to her, "Yes, Lym is a very well-informed man, but he's modest about it," she felt uninformed and immodest, and scolded at herself that she had missed the human potentialities in this vast Gopher Prairie. When Dr. Westlake quoted the "Paradiso," "Don Quixote," "Wilhelm Meister," and the Koran, she reflected that no one she knew, not even her father, had read all four.

She came diffidently to the second meeting of the board. She did not plan to revolutionize anything. She hoped that the wise elders might be so tolerant as to listen to her suggestions about changing the shelving of the juveniles.

Yet after four sessions of the library-board she was where she had been before the first session. She had found that for all their pride in being reading men, Westlake and Cass and even Guy had no conception of making the library familiar to the whole town. They used it, they passed resolutions about it, and they left it as dead as Moses. Only the Henty books and the Elsie books and the latest optimisms by moral female novelists and virile clergymen were in general demand, and the board themselves were interested only in old, stilted volumes. They had no tenderness for the noisiness of youth discovering great literature.

If she was egotistic about her tiny learning, they were at least as much so regarding theirs. And for all their talk of the need of additional library-tax none of them was willing to risk censure by battling for it, though they now had so small a fund that, after paying for rent, heat, light, and Miss Villets's salary, they had only a hundred dollars a year for the purchase of books.

The Incident of the Seventeen Cents killed her none too enduring interest. She had come to the board-meeting singing with a plan. She had made a list of thirty European novels of the past ten years, with twenty important books on psychology, education, and economics which the library lacked. She had made Kennicott promise to give fifteen dollars. If each of the board would contribute the same, they could have the books.

Lym Cass looked alarmed, scratched himself, and protested, "I think it would be a bad precedent for the board-members to contribute money—uh—not that I mind, but it wouldn't be fair—establish precedent. Gracious! They don't pay us a cent for our services! Certainly can't expect us to pay for the privilege of serving!"

Only Guy looked sympathetic, and he stroked the pine table and said nothing.

The rest of the meeting they gave to a bellicose investigation of the fact that there was seventeen cents less than there should be in the Fund. Miss Villets was summoned; she spent half an hour in explosively defending herself; the seventeen cents were gnawed over, penny by penny; and Carol, glancing at the carefully inscribed list which had been so lovely and exciting an hour before, was silent, and sorry for Miss Villets, and sorrier for herself.

She was reasonably regular in attendance till her two years were up and Vida Sherwin was appointed to the board in her place, but she did not try to be revolutionary. In the plodding course of her life there was nothing changed, and nothing new.

IV

Kennicott made an excellent land-deal, but as he told her none of the details, she was not greatly exalted or agitated. What did agitate her was his announcement, half whispered and half blurted, half tender and half coldly medical, that they "ought to have a baby, now they could afford it." They had so long agreed that "perhaps it would be just as well not to have any children for a while yet," that childlessness had come to be natural. Now, she feared and longed and did not know; she hesitatingly assented, and wished that she had not assented.

As there appeared no change in their drowsy relations, she forgot all about it, and life was planless.

V

Idling on the porch of their summer cottage at the lake, on afternoons when Kennicott was in town, when the water was glazed and the whole air languid, she pictured a hundred escapes: Fifth Avenue in a snow-storm, with limousines, golden shops, a cathedral spire. A reed hut on fantastic piles above the mud of a jungle river. A suite in Paris, immense high grave rooms, with lambrequins and a balcony. The Enchanted Mesa. An ancient stone mill in Maryland, at the turn of the road, between rocky brook and

abrupt hills. An upland moor of sheep and flitting cool sunlight. A clanging
dock where steel cranes unloaded steamers from Buenos Ayres and Tsingtao.
A Munich concert-hall, and a famous 'cellist playing—playing to her.

One scene had a persistent witchery:

She stood on a terrace overlooking a boulevard by the warm sea. She
was certain, though she had no reason for it, that the place was Mentone.
Along the drive below her swept barouches, with a mechanical tlot-tlot, tlot-
tlot, tlot-tlot, and great cars with polished black hoods and engines quiet as
the sigh of an old man. In them were women erect, slender, enameled, and
expressionless as marionettes, their small hands upon parasols, their unchanging eyes always forward, ignoring the men beside them, tall men with gray
hair and distinguished faces. Beyond the drive were painted sea and painted
sands, and blue and yellow pavilions. Nothing moved except the gliding
carriages, and the people were small and wooden, spots in a picture drenched
with gold and hard bright blues. There was no sound of sea or winds; no
softness of whispers nor of falling petals; nothing but yellow and cobalt and
staring light, and the never-changing tlot-tlot, tlot-tlot——

She startled. She whimpered. It was the rapid ticking of the clock which
had hypnotized her into hearing the steady hoofs. No aching color of the sea
and pride of supercilious people, but the reality of a round-bellied nickel
alarm-clock on a shelf against a fuzzy unplaned pine wall, with a stiff gray
wash-rag hanging above it and a kerosene-stove standing below.

A thousand dreams governed by the fiction she had read, drawn from the
pictures she had envied, absorbed her drowsy lake afternoons, but always
in the midst of them Kennicott came out from town, drew on khaki trousers
which were plastered with dry fish-scales, asked, "Enjoying yourself?" and
did not listen to her answer.

And nothing was changed, and there was no reason to believe that there
ever would be change.

### VI

Trains!

At the lake cottage she missed the passing of the trains. She realized that
in town she had depended upon them for assurance that there remained a
world beyond.

The railroad was more than a means of transportation to Gopher Prairie.
It was a new god; a monster of steel limbs, oak ribs, flesh of gravel, and a
stupendous hunger for freight; a deity created by man that he might keep
himself respectful to Property, as elsewhere he had elevated and served as
tribal gods the mines, cotton-mills, motor-factories, colleges, army.

The East remembered generations when there had been no railroad, and
had no awe of it; but here the railroads had been before time was. The
towns had been staked out on barren prairie as convenient points for future
train-halts; and back in 1860 and 1870 there had been much profit, much
opportunity to found aristocratic families, in the possession of advance
knowledge as to where the towns would arise.

If a town was in disfavor, the railroad could ignore it, cut it off from commerce, slay it. To Gopher Prairie the tracks were eternal verities, and boards of railroad directors an omnipotence. The smallest boy or the most secluded grandam could tell you whether No. 32 had a hot-box last Tuesday, whether No. 7 was going to put on an extra day-coach; and the name of the president of the road was familiar to every breakfast table.

Even in this new era of motors the citizens went down to the station to see the trains go through. It was their romance; their only mystery besides mass at the Catholic Church; and from the trains came lords of the outer world— traveling salesmen with piping on their waistcoats, and visiting cousins from Milwaukee.

Gopher Prairie had once been a "division-point." The roundhouse and repair-shops were gone, but two conductors still retained residence, and they were persons of distinction, men who traveled and talked to strangers, who wore uniforms with brass buttons, and knew all about these crooked games of con-men. They were a special caste, neither above nor below the Hay-docks, but apart, artists and adventurers.

The night telegraph-operator at the railroad station was the most melo-dramatic figure in town: awake at three in the morning, alone in a room hectic with clatter of the telegraph key. All night he "talked" to operators twenty, fifty, a hundred miles away. It was always to be expected that he would be held up by robbers. He never was, but round him was a suggestion of masked faces at the window, revolvers, cords binding him to a chair, his struggle to crawl to the key before he fainted.

During blizzards everything about the railroad was melodramatic. There were days when the town was completely shut off, when they had no mail, no express, no fresh meat, no newspapers. At last the rotary snow-plow came through, bucking the drifts, sending up a geyser, and the way to the Out-side was open again. The brakemen, in mufflers and fur caps, running along the tops of ice-coated freight-cars; the engineers scratching frost from the cab windows and looking out, inscrutable, self-contained, pilots of the prairie sea—they were heroism, they were to Carol the daring of the quest in a world of groceries and sermons.

To the small boys the railroad was a familiar playground. They climbed the iron ladders on the sides of the box-cars; built fires behind piles of old ties; waved to favorite brakemen. But to Carol it was magic.

She was motoring with Kennicott, the car lumping through darkness, the lights showing mud-puddles and ragged weeds by the road. A train coming! A rapid chuck-a-chuck, chuck-a-chuck, chuck-a-chuck. It was hurling past—the Pacific Flyer, an arrow of golden flame. Light from the fire-box splashed the under side of the trailing smoke. Instantly the vision was gone; Carol was back in the long darkness; and Kennicott was giving his version of that fire and wonder: "No. 19. Must be 'bout ten minutes late."

In town, she listened from bed to the express whistling in the cut a mile north. Uuuuuuu!—faint, nervous, distrait, horn of the free night riders journeying to the tall towns where were laughter and banners and the sound of bells—Uuuuu! Uuuuu!—the world going by—Uuuuuuu!—fainter, more wistful, gone.

Down here there were no trains. The stillness was very great. The prairie encircled the lake, lay round her, raw, dusty, thick. Only the train could cut it. Some day she would take a train; and that would be a great taking.

### VII

She turned to the Chautauqua as she had turned to the dramatic association, to the library-board.

Besides the permanent Mother Chautauqua, in New York, there are, all over these States, commercial Chautauqua companies which send out to every smallest town troupes of lecturers and "entertainers" to give a week of culture under canvas. Living in Minneapolis, Carol had never encountered the ambulant Chautauqua, and the announcement of its coming to Gopher Prairie gave her hope that others might be doing the vague things which she had attempted. She pictured a condensed university course brought to the people. Mornings when she came in from the lake with Kennicott she saw placards in every shop-window, and strung on a cord across Main Street, a line of pennants alternately worded "The Boland Chautauqua COMING!" and "A solid week of inspiration and enjoyment!" But she was disappointed when she saw the program. It did not seem to be a tabloid university; it did not seem to be any kind of a university; it seemed to be a combination of vaudeville performance, Y. M. C. A. lecture, and the graduation exercises of an elocution class.

She took her doubt to Kennicott. He insisted, "Well, maybe it won't be so awful darn intellectual, the way you and I might like it, but it's a whole lot better than nothing." Vida Sherwin added, "They have some splendid speakers. If the people don't carry off so much actual information, they do get a lot of new ideas, and that's what counts."

During the Chautauqua Carol attended three evening meetings, two afternoon meetings, and one in the morning. She was impressed by the audience: the sallow women in skirts and blouses, eager to be made to think, the men in vests and shirt-sleeves, eager to be allowed to laugh, and the wriggling children, eager to sneak away. She liked the plain benches, the portable stage under its red marquee, the great tent over all, shadowy above strings of incandescent bulbs at night and by day casting an amber radiance on the patient crowd. The scent of dust and trampled grass and sun-baked wood gave her an illusion of Syrian caravans; she forgot the speakers while she listened to noises outside the tent: two farmers talking hoarsely, a wagon creaking down Main Street, the crow of a rooster. She was content. But it was the contentment of the lost hunter stopping to rest.

For from the Chautauqua itself she got nothing but wind and chaff and heavy laughter, the laughter of yokels at old jokes, a mirthless and primitive sound like the cries of beasts on a farm.

These were the several instructors in the condensed university's seven-day course:

Nine lecturers, four of them ex-ministers, and one an ex-congressman, all of them delivering "inspirational addresses." The only facts or opinions which Carol derived from them were: Lincoln was a celebrated president of the United States, but in his youth extremely poor. James J. Hill was the best-known railroad-man of the West, and in his youth extremely poor. Honesty and courtesy in business are preferable to boorishness and exposed trickery, but this is not to be taken personally, since all persons in Gopher Prairie are known to be honest and courteous. London is a large city. A distinguished statesman once taught Sunday School.

Four "entertainers" who told Jewish stories, Irish stories, German stories, Chinese stories, and Tennessee mountaineer stories, most of which Carol had heard.

A "lady elocutionist" who recited Kipling and imitated children.

A lecturer with motion-pictures of an Andean exploration; excellent pictures and a halting narrative.

Three brass-bands, a company of six opera-singers, a Hawaiian sextette, and four youths who played saxophones and guitars disguised as wash-boards. The most applauded pieces were those, such as the "Lucia" inevitability, which the audience had heard most often.

The local superintendent, who remained through the week while the other enlighteners went to other Chautauquas for their daily performances. The superintendent was a bookish, underfed man who worked hard at rousing artificial enthusiasm, at trying to make the audience cheer by dividing them into competitive squads and telling them that they were intelligent and made splendid communal noises. He gave most of the morning lectures, droning with equal unhappy facility about poetry, the Holy Land, and the injustice to employers in any system of profit-sharing.

The final item was a man who neither lectured, inspired, nor entertained; a plain little man with his hands in his pockets. All the other speakers had confessed, "I cannot keep from telling the citizens of your beautiful city that none of the talent on this circuit have found a more charming spot or more enterprising and hospitable people." But the little man suggested that the architecture of Gopher Prairie was haphazard, and that it was sottish to let the lake-front be monopolized by the cinder-heaped wall of the railroad embankment. Afterward the audience grumbled, "Maybe that guy's got the right dope, but what's the use of looking on the dark side of things all the time? New ideas are first-rate, but not all this criticism. Enough trouble in life without looking for it!"

Thus the Chautauqua, as Carol saw it. After it, the town felt proud and educated.

VIII

Two weeks later the Great War smote Europe.

For a month Gopher Prairie had the delight of shuddering, then, as the war settled down to a business of trench-fighting, they forgot.

When Carol talked about the Balkans, and the possibility of a German revolution, Kennicott yawned, "Oh yes, it's a great old scrap, but it's none of our business. Folks out here are too busy growing corn to monkey with any fool war that those foreigners want to get themselves into."

It was Miles Bjornstam who said, "I can't figure it out. I'm opposed to wars, but still, seems like Germany has got to be licked because them Junkers stands in the way of progress."

She was calling on Miles and Bea, early in autumn. They had received her with cries, with dusting of chairs, and a running to fetch water for coffee. Miles stood and beamed at her. He fell often and joyously into his old irreverence about the lords of Gopher Prairie, but always—with a certain difficulty—he added something decorous and appreciative.

"Lots of people have come to see you, haven't they?" Carol hinted.

"Why, Be's cousin Tina comes in right along, and the foreman at the mill, and—— Oh, we have good times. Say, take a look at that Bea! Wouldn't you think she was a canary-bird, to listen to her, and to see that Scanda-hoofian towhead of hers? But say, know what she is? She's a mother hen! Way she fusses over me—way she makes old Miles wear a necktie! Hate to spoil her by letting her hear it, but she's one pretty darn nice—nice—— Hell! What do we care if none of the dirty snobs come and call? We've got each other."

Carol worried about their struggle, but she forgot it in the stress of sickness and fear. For that autumn she knew that a baby was coming, that at last life promised to be interesting in the peril of the great change.

# 20

The baby was coming. Each morning she was nauseated, chilly, bedraggled, and certain that she would never again be attractive; each twilight she was afraid. She did not feel exalted, but unkempt and furious. The period of daily sickness crawled into an endless time of boredom. It became difficult for her to move about, and she raged that she, who had been slim and light-footed, should have to lean on a stick, and be heartily commented upon by street gossips. She was encircled by greasy eyes. Every matron hinted, "Now that you're going to be a mother, dearie, you'll get over all these ideas of yours and settle down." She felt that willy-nilly she was being initiated into the assembly of housekeepers; with the baby for hostage, she would never escape; presently she would be drinking coffee and rocking and talking about diapers.

"I could stand fighting them. I'm used to that. But this being taken in, being taken as a matter of course, I can't stand it—and I must stand it!"

She alternately detested herself for not appreciating the kindly women, and detested them for their advice: lugubrious hints as to how much she would suffer in labor, details of baby-hygiene based on long experience and total misunderstanding, superstitious cautions about the things she must eat and read and look at in prenatal care for the baby's soul, and always a pest of simpering baby-talk. Mrs. Champ Perry bustled in to lend "Ben Hur," as a preventive of future infant immorality. The Widow Bogart appeared trailing pinkish exclamations, "And how is our lovely 'ittle muzzy today! My, ain't it just like they always say: being in a Family Way does make the girlie so lovely, just like a Madonna. Tell me—" Her whisper was tinged with salaciousness—"does oo feel the dear itsy one stirring, the pledge of love? I remember with Cy, of course he was so big——"

"I do not look lovely, Mrs. Bogart. My complexion is rotten, and my hair is coming out, and I look like a potato-bag, and I think my arches are falling, and he isn't a pledge of love, and I'm afraid he *will* look like us, and I don't believe in mother-devotion, and the whole business is a confounded nuisance of a biological process," remarked Carol.

Then the baby was born, without unusual difficulty: a boy with straight back and strong legs. The first day she hated him for the tides of pain and hopeless fear he had caused; she resented his raw ugliness. After that she loved him with all the devotion and instinct at which she had scoffed. She marveled at the perfection of the miniature hands as noisily as did Kennicott; she was overwhelmed by the trust with which the baby turned to her; passion for him grew with each unpoetic irritating thing she had to do for him.

He was named Hugh, for her father.

Hugh developed into a thin healthy child with a large head and straight delicate hair of a faint brown. He was thoughtful and casual—a Kennicott.

For two years nothing else existed. She did not, as the cynical matrons had prophesied, "give up worrying about the world and other folks' babies soon as she got one of her own to fight for." The barbarity of that willingness to sacrifice other children so that one child might have too much was impossible to her. But she would sacrifice herself. She understood consecration—she who answered Kennicott's hints about having Hugh christened: "I refuse to insult my baby and myself by asking an ignorant young man in a frock coat to sanction him, to permit me to have him! I refuse to subject him to any devil-chasing rites! If I didn't give my baby—*my baby*—enough sanctification in those nine hours of hell, then he can't get any more out of the Reverend Mr. Zitterel!"

"Well, Baptists hardly ever christen kids. I was kind of thinking more about Reverend Warren," said Kennicott.

Hugh was her reason for living, promise of accomplishment in the future, shrine of adoration—and a diverting toy. "I thought I'd be a dilettante mother, but I'm as dismayingly natural as Mrs. Bogart," she boasted.

For two years Carol was a part of the town; as much one of Our Young Mothers as Mrs. McGanum. Her opiniation seemed dead; she had no apparent desire for escape; her brooding centered on Hugh. While she wondered at the pearl texture of his ear she exulted, "I feel like an old woman, with a skin like sandpaper, beside him, and I'm glad of it! He is perfect. He shall have everything. He sha'n't always stay here in Gopher Prairie. . . . I wonder which is really the best, Harvard or Yale or Oxford?"

II

The people who hemmed her in had been brilliantly reinforced by Mr. and Mrs Whittier N. Smail—Kennicott's Uncle Whittier and Aunt Bessie.

The true Main Streetite defines a relative as a person to whose house you go uninvited, to stay as long as you like. If you hear that Lym Cass on his journey East has spent all his time "visiting" in Oyster Center, it does not mean that he prefers that village to the rest of New England, but that he has relatives there. It does not mean that he has written to the relatives these many years, nor that they have ever given signs of a desire to look upon him. But "you wouldn't expect a man to go and spend good money at a hotel in Boston, when his own third cousins live right in the same state, would you?"

When the Smails sold their creamery in North Dakota they visited Mr. Smail's sister, Kennicott's mother, at Lac-qui-Meurt, then plodded on to Gopher Prairie to stay with their nephew. They appeared unannounced, before the baby was born, took their welcome for granted, and immediately began to complain of the fact that their room faced north.

Uncle Whittier and Aunt Bessie assumed that it was their privilege as relatives to laugh at Carol, and their duty as Christians to let her know how absurd her "notions" were. They objected to the food, to Oscarina's lack of friendliness, to the wind, the rain, and the immodesty of Carol's maternity gowns. They were strong and enduring; for an hour at a time they could go on heaving questions about her father's income, about her theology, and about the reason why she had not put on her rubbers when she had gone across the street. For fussy discussion they had a rich, full genius, and their example developed in Kennicott a tendency to the same form of affectionate flaying.

If Carol was so indiscreet as to murmur that she had a small headache, instantly the two Smails and Kennicott were at it. Every five minutes, every time she sat down or rose or spoke to Oscarina, they twanged, "Is your head better now? Where does it hurt? Don't you keep hartshorn in the house? Didn't you walk too far today? Have you tried hartshorn? Don't you keep some in the house so it will be handy? Does it feel better now? How does it feel? Do your eyes hurt, too? What time do you usually get to bed? As late as *that*? Well! How does it feel now?"

In her presence Uncle Whittier snorted at Kennicott, "Carol get these headaches often? Huh? Be better for her if she didn't go gadding around to all these bridge-whist parties, and took some care of herself once in a while!"

They kept it up, commenting, questioning, commenting, questioning, till her determination broke and she bleated, "For heaven's *sake*, don't dis-*cuss* it! My head 's all *right!*"

She listened to the Smails and Kennicott trying to determine by dialectics whether the copy of the *Dauntless*, which Aunt Bessie wanted to send to her sister in Alberta, ought to have two or four cents postage on it. Carol would have taken it to the drug store and weighed it, but then she was a dreamer, while they were practical people (as they frequently admitted). So they sought to evolve the postal rate from their inner consciousnesses, which, combined with entire frankness in thinking aloud, was their method of settling all problems.

The Smails did not "believe in all this nonsense" about privacy and reticence. When Carol left a letter from her sister on the table, she was astounded to hear from Uncle Whittier, "I see your sister says her husband is doing fine. You ought to go see her oftener. I asked Will and he says you don't go see her very often. My! You ought to go see her oftener!"

If Carol was writing a letter to a classmate, or planning the week's menus, she could be certain that Aunt Bessie would pop in and titter, "Now don't let me disturb you, I just wanted to see where you were, don't stop, I'm not going to stay only a second. I just wondered if you could possibly have thought that I didn't eat the onions this noon because I didn't think they were properly cooked, but that wasn't the reason at all, it wasn't because I didn't think they were well cooked, I'm sure that everything in your house is always very dainty and nice, though I do think that Oscarina is careless about some things, she doesn't appreciate the big wages you pay her, and she is so cranky, all these Swedes are so cranky, I don't really see why you have a Swede, but—— But that wasn't it, I didn't eat them not because I didn't think they weren't cooked proper, it was just—I find that onions don't agree with me, it's very strange, ever since I had an attack of biliousness one time, I have found that onions, either fried onions or raw ones, and Whittier does love raw onions with vinegar and sugar on them——"

It was pure affection.

Carol was discovering that the one thing that can be more disconcerting than intelligent hatred is demanding love.

She supposed that she was being gracefully dull and standardized in the Smails' presence, but they scented the heretic, and with forward-stooping delight they sat and tried to drag out her ludicrous concepts for their amusement. They were like the Sunday-afternoon mob staring at monkeys in the Zoo, poking fingers and making faces and giggling at the resentment of the more dignified race.

With a loose-lipped, superior, village smile Uncle Whittier hinted, "What's this I hear about your thinking Gopher Prairie ought to be all tore down and rebuilt, Carrie? I don't know where folks get these new-fangled ideas. Lots of farmers in Dakota getting 'em these days. About co-operation. Think they can run stores better 'n storekeepers! Huh!"

"Whit and I didn't need no co-operation as long as we was farming!" triumphed Aunt Bessie. "Carrie, tell your old auntie now: don't you ever go to church on Sunday? You do go sometimes? But you ought to go every Sunday! When you're as old as I am, you'll learn that no matter how smart folks think they are, God knows a whole lot more than they do, and then you'll realize and be glad to go and listen to your pastor!"

In the manner of one who has just beheld a two-headed calf they repeated that they had "never *heard* such funny ideas!" They were staggered to learn that a real tangible person, living in Minnesota, and married to their own flesh-and-blood relation, could apparently believe that divorce may not always be immoral; that illegitimate children do not bear any special and guaranteed form of curse; that there are ethical authorities outside of the Hebrew Bible; that men have drunk wine yet not died in the gutter; that the capitalistic system of distribution and the Baptist wedding-ceremony were not known in the Garden of Eden; that mushrooms are as edible as corn-beef hash; that the word "dude" is no longer frequently used; that there are Ministers of the Gospel who accept evolution; that some persons of apparent intelligence and business ability do not always vote the Republican ticket straight; that it is not a universal custom to wear scratchy flannels next the skin in winter; that a violin is not inherently more immoral than a chapel organ; that some poets do not have long hair; and that Jews are not always pedlers or pants-makers.

"Where does she get all them the'ries?" marveled Uncle Whittier Smail; while Aunt Bessie inquired, "Do you suppose there's many folks got notions like hers? My! If there are," and her tone settled the fact that there were not, "I just don't know what the world's coming to!"

Patiently—more or less—Carol awaited the exquisite day when they would announce departure. After three weeks Uncle Whittier remarked, "We kinda like Gopher Prairie. Guess maybe we'll stay here. We'd been wondering what we'd do, now we've sold the creamery and my farms. So I had a talk with Ole Jenson about his grocery, and I guess I'll buy him out and storekeep for a while."

He did.

Carol rebelled. Kennicott soothed her: "Oh, we won't see much of them. They'll have their own house."

She resolved to be so chilly that they would stay away. But she had no talent for conscious insolence. They found a house, but Carol was never safe from their appearance with a hearty, "Thought we'd drop in this evening and keep you from being lonely. Why, you ain't had them curtains washed yet!" Invariably, whenever she was touched by the realization that it was they who were lonely, they wrecked her pitying affection by comments—questions—comments—advice.

They immediately became friendly with all of their own race, with the Luke Dawsons, the Deacon Piersons, and Mrs. Bogart; and brought them along in the evening. Aunt Bessie was a bridge over whom the older women, bearing gifts of counsel and the ignorance of experience, poured into Carol's island of reserve. Aunt Bessie urged the good Widow Bogart, "Drop in and see Carrie real often. Young folks today don't understand housekeeping like we do."

Mrs. Bogart showed herself perfectly willing to be an associate relative.

Carol was thinking up protective insults when Kennicott's mother came down to stay with Brother Whittier for two months. Carol was fond of Mrs. Kennicott. She could not carry out her insults.

She felt trapped.

She had been kidnaped by the town. She was Aunt Bessie's niece, and she was to be a mother. She was expected, she almost expected herself, to sit forever talking of babies, cooks, embroidery stitches, the price of potatoes, and the tastes of husbands in the matter of spinach.

She found a refuge in the Jolly Seventeen. She suddenly understood that they could be depended upon to laugh with her at Mrs. Bogart, and she now saw Juanita Haydock's gossip not as vulgarity but as gaiety and remarkable analysis.

Her life had changed, even before Hugh appeared. She looked forward to the next bridge of the Jolly Seventeen, and the security of whispering with her dear friends Maud Dyer and Juanita and Mrs. McGanum.

She was part of the town. Its philosophy and its feuds dominated her.

III

She was no longer irritated by the cooing of the matrons, nor by their opinion that diet didn't matter so long as the Little Ones had plenty of lace and moist kisses, but she concluded that in the care of babies as in politics, intelligence was superior to quotations about pansies. She liked best to talk about Hugh to Kennicott, Vida, and the Bjornstams. She was happily domestic when Kennicott sat by her on the floor, to watch baby make faces. She was delighted when Miles, speaking as one man to another, admonished Hugh, "I wouldn't stand them skirts if I was you. Come on. Join the union and strike. Make 'em give you pants."

As a parent, Kennicott was moved to establish the first child-welfare week held in Gopher Prairie. Carol helped him weigh babies and examine their throats, and she wrote out the diets for mute German and Scandinavian mothers.

The aristocracy of Gopher Prairie, even the wives of the rival doctors, took part, and for several days there was community spirit and much uplift. But this reign of love was overthrown when the prize for Best Baby was awarded not to decent parents but to Bea and Miles Bjornstam! The good matrons glared at Olaf Bjornstam, with his blue eyes, his honey-colored hair, and magnificent back, and they remarked, "Well, Mrs. Kennicott, maybe that Swede brat is as healthy as your husband says he is, but let me tell you I hate to think of the future that awaits any boy with a hired girl for a mother and an awful irreligious socialist for a pa!"

She raged, but so violent was the current of their respectability, so persistent was Aunt Bessie in running to her with their blabber, that she was embarrassed when she took Hugh to play with Olaf. She hated herself for it, but she hoped that no one saw her go into the Bjornstam shanty. She hated herself and the town's indifferent cruelty when she saw Bea's radiant devotion to both babies alike; when she saw Miles staring at them wistfully.

He had saved money, had quit Elder's planing-mill and started a dairy on a vacant lot near his shack. He was proud of his three cows and sixty chickens, and got up nights to nurse them.

"I'll be a big farmer before you can bat an eye! I tell you that young fellow Olaf is going to go East to college along with the Haydock kids. Uh—— Lots of folks dropping in to chin with Bea and me now. Say! Ma Bogart come in one day! She was—— I liked the old lady fine. And the mill foreman comes in right along. Oh, we got lots of friends. You bet!"

IV

Though the town seemed to Carol to change no more than the surrounding fields, there was a constant shifting, these three years. The citizen of the prairie drifts always westward. It may be because he is the heir of ancient migrations—and it may be because he finds within his own spirit so little adventure that he is driven to seek it by changing his horizon. The towns remain unvaried, yet the individual faces alter like classes in college. The Gopher Prairie jeweler sells out, for no discernible reason, and moves on to Alberta or the state of Washington, to open a shop precisely like his former one, in a town precisely like the one he has left. There is, except among professional men and the wealthy, small permanence either of residence or occupation. A man becomes farmer, grocer, town policeman, garageman, restaurant-owner, postmaster, insurance-agent, and farmer all over again, and the community more or less patiently suffers from his lack of knowledge in each of his experiments.

Ole Jenson the grocer and Dahl the butcher moved on to South Dakota and Idaho. Luke and Mrs. Dawson picked up ten thousand acres of prairie soil, in the magic portable form of a small check book, and went to Pasadena, to a bungalow and sunshine and cafeterias. Chet Dashaway sold his furniture and undertaking business and wandered to Los Angeles, where, the *Dauntless* reported, "Our good friend Chester has accepted a fine position with a real-estate firm, and his wife has in the charming social circles of the Queen City of the Southwestland that same popularity which she enjoyed in our own society sets."

Rita Simons was married to Terry Could, and rivaled Juanita Haydock as the gayest of the Young Married Set. But Juanita also acquired merit. Harry's father died, Harry became senior partner in the Bon Ton Store, and Juanita was more acidulous and shrewd and cackling than ever. She bought an evening frock, and exposed her collar-bone to the wonder of the Jolly Seventeen, and talked of moving to Minneapolis.

To defend her position against the new Mrs. Terry Gould she sought to attach Carol to her faction by giggling that "*some* folks might call Rita innocent, but I've got a hunch that she isn't half as ignorant of things as brides are supposed to be—and of course Terry isn't one-two-three as a doctor alongside of your husband."

Carol herself would gladly have followed Mr. Ole Jenson, and migrated even to another Main Street; flight from familiar tedium to new tedium would have for a time the outer look and promise of adventure. She hinted to Kennicott of the probable medical advantages of Montana and Oregon. She knew that he was satisfied with Gopher Prairie, but it gave her vicarious hope to think of going, to ask for railroad folders at the station, to trace the maps with a restless forefinger.

Yet to the casual eye she was not discontented, she was not an abnormal and distressing traitor to the faith of Main Street.

The settled citizen believes that the rebel is constantly in a stew of complaining and, hearing of a Carol Kennicott, he gasps, "What an awful person! She must be a Holy Terror to live with! Glad *my* folks are satisfied with things way they are!" Actually, it was not so much as five minutes a day that Carol devoted to lonely desires. It is probable that the agitated citizen has within his circle at least one inarticulate rebel with aspirations as wayward as Carol's.

The presence of the baby had made her take Gopher Prairie and the brown house seriously, as natural places of residence. She pleased Kennicott by being friendly with the complacent maturity of Mrs. Clark and Mrs. Elder, and when she had often enough been in conference upon the Elders' new Cadillac car, or the job which the oldest Clark boy had taken in the office of the flour-mill, these topics became important, things to follow up day by day.

With nine-tenths of her emotion concentrated upon Hugh, she did not criticize shops, streets, acquaintances . . . this year or two. She hurried to Uncle Whittier's store for a package of corn-flakes, she abstractedly listened to Uncle Whittier's denunciation of Martin Mahoney for asserting that the wind last Tuesday had been south and not southwest, she came back along streets that held no surprises nor the startling faces of strangers. Thinking of Hugh's teething all the way, she did not reflect that this store, these drab blocks, made up all her background. She did her work, and she triumphed over winning from the Clarks at five hundred.

v

The most considerable event of the two years after the birth of Hugh occurred when Vida Sherwin resigned from the high school and was married. Carol was her attendant, and as the wedding was at the Episcopal Church, all the women wore new kid slippers and long white kid gloves, and looked refined.

For years Carol had been little sister to Vida, and had never in the least known to what degree Vida loved her and hated her and in curious strained ways was bound to her.

# 21

Gray steel that seems unmoving because it spins so fast in the balanced flywheel, gray snow in an avenue of elms, gray dawn with the sun behind it—this was the gray of Vida Sherwin's life at thirty-six.

She was small and active and sallow; her yellow hair was faded, and looked dry; her blue silk blouses and modest lace collars and high black shoes and sailor hats were as literal and uncharming as a schoolroom desk; but her eyes determined her appearance, revealed her as a personage and a force, indicated her faith in the goodness and purpose of everything. They were blue, and they were never still; they expressed amusement, pity, enthusiasm. If she had been seen in sleep, with the wrinkles beside her eyes stilled and the creased lids hiding the radiant irises, she would have lost her potency.

She was born in a hill-smothered Wisconsin village where her father was a prosy minister; she labored through a sanctimonious college; she taught for two years in an iron-range town of blurry-faced Tatars and Montenegrins, and wastes of ore, and when she came to Gopher Prairie, its trees and the shining spaciousness of the wheat prairie made her certain that she was in paradise.

She admitted to her fellow-teachers that the schoolbuilding was slightly damp, but she insisted that the rooms were "arranged so conveniently—and then that bust of President McKinley at the head of the stairs, it's a lovely art-work, and isn't it an inspiration to have the brave, honest, martyr president to think about!" She taught French, English, and history, and the Sophomore Latin class, which dealt in matters of a metaphysical nature called Indirect Discourse and the Ablative Absolute. Each year she was re-convinced that the pupils were beginning to learn more quickly. She spent four winters in building up the Debating Society, and when the debate really was lively one Friday afternoon, and the speakers of pieces did not forget their lines, she felt rewarded.

She lived an engrossed useful life, and seemed as cool and simple as an apple. But secretly she was creeping among fears, longing, and guilt. She knew what it was, but she dared not name it. She hated even the sound of the word "sex." When she dreamed of being a woman of the harem, with great white warm limbs, she awoke to shudder, defenseless in the dusk of her room. She prayed to Jesus, always to the Son of God, offering him the terrible power of her adoration, addressing him as the eternal lover, growing passionate, exalted, large, as she contemplated his splendor. Thus she mounted to endurance and surcease.

By day, rattling about in many activities, she was able to ridicule her blazing nights of darkness. With spurious cheerfulness she announced everywhere, "I guess I'm a born spinster," and "No one will ever marry a plain schoolma'am like me," and "You men, great big noisy bothersome creatures, we women wouldn't have you round the place, dirtying up nice clean rooms, if it wasn't that you have to be petted and guided. We just ought to say 'Scat!' to all of you!"

But when a man held her close at a dance, even when "Professor" George Edwin Mott patted her hand paternally as they considered the naughtinesses of Cy Bogart, she quivered, and reflected how superior she was to have kept her virginity.

In the autumn of 1911, a year before Dr. Will Kennicott was married, Vida was his partner at a five-hundred tournament. She was thirty-four then; Kennicott about thirty-six. To her he was a superb, boyish, diverting creature; all the heroic qualities in a manly magnificent body. They had been helping the hostess to serve the Waldorf salad and coffee and gingerbread. They were in the kitchen, side by side on a bench, while the others ponderously supped in the room beyond.

Kennicott was masculine and experimental. He stroked Vida's hand, he put his arm carelessly about her shoulder.

"Don't!" she said sharply.

"You're a cunning thing," he offered, patting the back of her shoulder in an exploratory manner.

While she strained away, she longed to move nearer to him. He bent over, looked at her knowingly. She glanced down at his left hand as it touched her knee. She sprang up, started noisily and needlessly to wash the dishes. He helped her. He was too lazy to adventure further—and too used to women in his profession. She was grateful for the impersonality of his talk. It enabled her to gain control. She knew that she had skirted wild thoughts.

A month after, on a sleighing-party, under the buffalo robes in the bob-sled, he whispered, "You pretend to be a grown-up schoolteacher, but you're nothing but a kiddie." His arm was about her. She resisted.

"Don't you like the poor lonely bachelor?" he yammered in a fatuous way.

"No, I don't! You don't care for me in the least. You're just practising on me."

"You're so mean! I'm terribly fond of you."

"I'm not of you. And I'm not going to let myself be fond of you, either."

He persistently drew her toward him. She clutched his arm. Then she threw off the robe, climbed out of the sled, raced after it with Harry Haydock. At the dance which followed the sleigh-ride Kennicott was devoted to the watery prettiness of Maud Dyer, and Vida was noisily interested in getting up a Virginia Reel. Without seeming to watch Kennicott, she knew that he did not once look at her.

That was all of her first love-affair.

He gave no sign of remembering that he was "terribly fond." She waited for him; she reveled in longing, and in a sense of guilt because she longed.

She told herself that she did not want part of him; unless he gave her all his devotion she would never let him touch her; and when she found that she was probably lying, she burned with scorn. She fought it out in prayer. She knelt in a pink flannel nightgown, her thin hair down her back, her forehead as full of horror as a mask of tragedy, while she identified her love for the Son of God with her love for a mortal, and wondered if any other woman had ever been so sacrilegious. She wanted to be a nun and observe perpetual adoration. She bought a rosary, but she had been so bitterly reared as a Protestant that she could not bring herself to use it.

Yet none of her intimates in the school and in the boarding-house knew of her abyss of passion. They said she was "so optimistic."

When she heard that Kennicott was to marry a girl, pretty, young, and imposingly from the Cities, Vida despaired. She congratulated Kennicott; carelessly ascertained from him the hour of marriage. At that hour, sitting in her room, Vida pictured the wedding in St. Paul. Full of an ecstasy which horrified her, she followed Kennicott and the girl who had stolen her place, followed them to the train, through the evening, the night.

She was relieved when she had worked out a belief that she wasn't really shameful, that there was a mystical relation between herself and Carol, so that she was vicariously yet veritably with Kennicott, and had the right to be.

She saw Carol during the first five minutes in Gopher Prairie. She stared at the passing motor, at Kennicott and the girl beside him. In that fog world of transference of emotion Vida had no normal jealousy but a conviction that, since through Carol she had received Kennicott's love, then Carol was a part of her, an astral self, a heightened and more beloved self. She was glad of the girl's charm, of the smooth black hair, the airy head and young shoulders. But she was suddenly angry. Carol glanced at her for a quarter-second, but looked past her, at an old roadside barn. If she had made the great sacrifice, at least she expected gratitude and recognition, Vida raged, while her conscious schoolroom mind fussily begged her to control this insanity.

During her first call half of her wanted to welcome a fellow reader of books; the other half itched to find out whether Carol knew anything about Kennicott's former interest in herself. She discovered that Carol was not aware that he had ever touched another woman's hand. Carol was an amusing, naive, curiously learned child. While Vida was most actively describing the glories of the Thanatopsis, and complimenting this librarian on her training as a worker, she was fancying that this girl was the child born of herself and Kennicott; and out of that symbolizing she had a comfort she had not known for months.

When she came home, after supper with the Kennicotts and Guy Pollock, she had a sudden and rather pleasant backsliding from devotion. She bustled into her room, she slammed her hat on the bed, and chattered, "I don't *care!* I'm a lot like her—except a few years older. I'm light and quick, too, and I can talk just as well as she can, and I'm sure—— Men are such fools. I'd be ten times as sweet to make love to as that dreamy baby. And I *am* as good-looking!"

But as she sat on the bed and stared at her thin thighs, defiance oozed away. She mourned:

"No. I'm not. Dear God, how we fool ourselves! I pretend I'm 'spiritual,' I pretend my legs are graceful. They aren't. They're skinny. Old-maidish. I hate it! I hate that impertinent young woman! A selfish cat, taking his love for granted. . . . No, she's adorable. . . . I don't think she ought to be so friendly with Guy Pollock."

For a year Vida loved Carol, longed to and did not pry into the details of her relations with Kennicott, enjoyed her spirit of play as expressed in child-ish tea-parties, and, with the mystic bond between them forgotten, was healthily vexed by Carol's assumption that she was a sociological messiah come to save Gopher Prairie. This last facet of Vida's thought was the one which, after a year, was most often turned to the light. In a testy way she brooded, "These people that want to change everything all of a sudden with-out doing any work, make me tired! Here I have to go and work for four years, picking out the pupils for debates, and drilling them, and nagging at them to get them to look up references, and begging them to choose their own subjects—four years, to get up a couple of good debates! And she comes rushing in, and expects in one year to change the whole town into a lollypop paradise with everybody stopping everything else to grow tulips and drink tea. And it's a comfy homey old town, too!"

She had such an outburst after each of Carol's campaigns—for better Thanatopsis programs, for Shavian plays, for more human schools—but she never betrayed herself, and always she was penitent.

Vida was, and always would be, a reformer, a liberal. She believed that details could excitingly be altered, but that things-in-general were comely and kind and immutable. Carol was, without understanding or accepting it, a revolutionist, a radical, and therefore possessed of "constructive ideas," which only the destroyer can have, since the reformer believes that all the essential constructing has already been done. After years of intimacy it was this unexpressed opposition more than the fancied loss of Kennicott's love which held Vida irritably fascinated.

But the birth of Hugh revived the transcendental emotion. She was in-dignant that Carol should not be utterly fulfilled in having borne Kennicott's child. She admitted that Carol seemed to have affection and immaculate care for the baby, but she began to identify herself now with Kennicott, and in this phase to feel that she had endured quite too much from Carol's instability.

She recalled certain other women who had come from the Outside and had not appreciated Gopher Prairie. She remembered the rector's wife who had been chilly to callers and who was rumored throughout the town to have said, "Re-ah-ly I cawn't endure this bucolic heartiness in the responses." The woman was positively known to have worn handkerchiefs in her bodice as padding—oh, the town had simply roared at her. Of course the rector and she were got rid of in a few months.

Then there was the mysterious woman with the dyed hair and penciled eyebrows, who wore tight English dresses, like basques, who smelled of stale musk, who flirted with the men and got them to advance money for her expenses in a lawsuit, who laughed at Vida's reading at a school-entertainment, and went off owing a hotel-bill and the three hundred dollars she had borrowed.

Vida insisted that she loved Carol, but with some satisfaction she compared her to these traducers of the town.

II

Vida had enjoyed Raymie Wutherspoon's singing in the Episcopal choir; she had thoroughly reviewed the weather with him at Methodist sociables and in the Bon Ton. But she did not really know him till she moved to Mrs. Gurrey's boarding-house. It was five years after her affair with Kennicott. She was thirty-nine, Raymie perhaps a year younger.

She said to him, and sincerely, "My! You can do anything, with your brains and tact and that heavenly voice. You were so good in 'The Girl from Kankakee.' You made me feel terribly stupid. If you'd gone on the stage, I believe you'd be just as good as anybody in Minneapolis. But still, I'm not sorry you stuck to business. It's such a constructive career."

"Do you really think so?" yearned Raymie, across the apple-sauce.

It was the first time that either of them had found a dependable intellectual companionship. They looked down on Willis Woodford the bank-clerk, and his anxious babycentric wife, the silent Lyman Casses, the slangy traveling man, and the rest of Mrs. Gurrey's unenlightened guests. They sat opposite, and they sat late. They were exhilarated to find that they agreed in confession of faith:

"People like Sam Clark and Harry Haydock aren't earnest about music and pictures and eloquent sermons and really refined movies, but then, on the other hand, people like Carol Kennicott put too much stress on all this art. Folks ought to appreciate lovely things, but just the same, they got to be practical and—they got to look at things in a practical way."

Smiling, passing each other the pressed-glass pickle-dish, seeing Mrs. Gurrey's linty supper-cloth irradiated by the light of intimacy, Vida and Raymie talked about Carol's rose-colored turban, Carol's sweetness, Carol's new low shoes, Carol's erroneous theory that there was no need of strict discipline in school, Carol's amiability in the Bon Ton, Carol's flow of wild ideas, which, honestly, just simply made you nervous trying to keep track of them;

About the lovely display of gents' shirts in the Bon Ton window as dressed by Raymie, about Raymie's offertory last Sunday, the fact that there weren't any of these new solos as nice as "Jerusalem the Golden," and the way Raymie stood up to Juanita Haydock when she came into the store and tried to run things and he as much as told her that she was so anxious to have folks think she was smart and bright that she said things she didn't mean, and anyway, Raymie was running the shoe-department, and if Juanita, or Harry either, didn't like the way he ran things, they could go get another man;

About Vida's new jabot which made her look thirty-two (Vida's estimate) or twenty-two (Raymie's estimate), Vida's plan to have the high-school Debating Society give a playlet, and the difficulty of keeping the younger boys well behaved on the playground when a big lubber like Cy Bogart acted up so;

About the picture post-card which Mrs. Dawson had sent to Mrs. Cass from Pasadena, showing roses growing right outdoors in February, the change in time on No. 4, the reckless way Dr. Gould always drove his auto, the reckless way almost all these people drove their autos, the fallacy of supposing that these socialists could carry on a government for as much as six months if they ever did have a chance to try out their theories, and the crazy way in which Carol jumped from subject to subject.

Vida had once beheld Raymie as a thin man with spectacles, mournful drawn-out face, and colorless stiff hair. Now she noted that his jaw was square, that his long hands moved quickly and were bleached in a refined manner, and that his trusting eyes indicated that he had "led a clean life." She began to call him "Ray," and to bounce in defense of his unselfishness and thoughtfulness every time Juanita Haydock or Rita Gould giggled about him at the Jolly Seventeen.

On a Sunday afternoon of late autumn they walked down to Lake Minnie-mashie. Ray said that he would like to see the ocean; it must be a grand sight; it must be much grander than a lake, even a great big lake. Vida had seen it, she stated modestly; she had seen it on a summer trip to Cape Cod.

"Have you been clear to Cape Cod? Massachusetts? I knew you'd traveled, but I never realized you'd been that far!"

Made taller and younger by his interest she poured out, "Oh my yes. It was a wonderful trip. So many points of interest through Massachusetts—historical. There's Lexington where we turned back the redcoats, and Long-fellow's home at Cambridge, and Cape Cod—just everything—fishermen and whaleships and sand-dunes and everything."

She wished that she had a little cane to carry. He broke off a willow branch.

"My, you're strong!" she said.

"No, not very. I wish there was a Y. M. C. A. here, so I could take up regular exercise. I used to think I could do pretty good acrobatics, if I had a chance."

"I'm sure you could. You're unusually lithe, for a large man."

"Oh no, not so very. But I wish we had a Y. M. It would be dandy to have lectures and everything, and I'd like to take a class in improving the memory —I believe a fellow ought to go on educating himself and improving his mind even if he is in business, don't you, Vida—I guess I'm kind of fresh to call you 'Vida'!"

"I've been calling you 'Ray' for weeks!"

He wondered why she sounded tart.

He helped her down the bank to the edge of the lake but dropped her hand abruptly, and as they sat on a willow log and he brushed her sleeve, he delicately moved over and murmured, "Oh, excuse me—accident."

She stared at the mud-browned chilly water, the floating gray reeds.

"You look so thoughtful," he said.

She threw out her hands. "I am! Will you kindly tell me what's the use of —anything! Oh, don't mind me. I'm a moody old hen. Tell me about your plan for getting a partnership in the Bon Ton. I do think you're right: Harry Haydock and that mean old Simons ought to give you one."

He hymned the old unhappy wars in which he had been Achilles and the mellifluous Nestor, yet gone his righteous ways unheeded by the cruel kings. . . . "Why, if I've told 'em once, I've told 'em a dozen times to get in a side-line of light-weight pants for gents' summer wear, and of course here they go and let a cheap kike like Rifkin beat them to it and grab the trade right off 'em, and then Harry said—you know how Harry is, maybe he don't mean to be grouchy, but he's such a sore-head——"

He gave her a hand to rise. "If you don't *mind*. I think a fellow is awful if a lady goes on a walk with him and she can't trust him and he tries to flirt with her and all."

"I'm sure you're highly trustworthy!" she snapped, and she sprang up without his aid. Then, smiling excessively, "Uh—don't you think Carol sometimes fails to appreciate Dr. Will's ability?"

### III

Ray habitually asked her about his window-trimming, the display of the new shoes, the best music for the entertainment at the Eastern Star, and (though he was recognized as a professional authority on what the town called "gents' furnishings") about his own clothes. She persuaded him not to wear the small bow ties which made him look like an elongated Sunday School scholar. Once she burst out:

"Ray, I could shake you! Do you know you're too apologetic? You always appreciate other people too much. You fuss over Carol Kennicott when she has some crazy theory that we all ought to turn anarchists or live on figs and nuts or something. And you listen when Harry Haydock tries to show off and talk about turnovers and credits and things you know lots better than he does. Look folks in the eye! Glare at 'em! Talk deep! You're the smartest man in town, if you only knew it. You *are*!"

He could not believe it. He kept coming back to her for confirmation. He practised glaring and talking deep, but he circuitously hinted to Vida that when he had tried to look Harry Haydock in the eye, Harry had inquired, "What's the matter with you, Raymie? Got a pain?" But afterward Harry had asked about Kantbeatum socks in a manner which, Ray felt, was somehow different from his former condescension.

They were sitting on the squat yellow satin settee in the boarding-house parlor. As Ray reannounced that he simply wouldn't stand it many more years if Harry didn't give him a partnership, his gesticulating hand touched Vida's shoulders.

"Oh, excuse me!" he pleaded.

"It's all right. Well, I think I must be running up to my room. Headache," she said briefly.

## IV

Ray and she had stopped in at Dyer's for a hot chocolate on their way home from the movies, that March evening. Vida speculated, "Do you know that I may not be here next year?"

"What do you mean?"

With her fragile narrow nails she smoothed the glass slab which formed the top of the round table at which they sat. She peeped through the glass at the perfume-boxes of black and gold and citron in the hollow table. She looked about at shelves of red rubber water-bottles, pale yellow sponges, wash-rags with blue borders, hair-brushes of polished cherry backs. She shook her head like a nervous medium coming out of a trance, stared at him unhappily, demanded:

"Why should I stay here? And I must make up my mind. Now. Time to renew our teaching-contracts for next year. I think I'll go teach in some other town. Everybody here is tired of me. I might as well go. Before folks come out and *say* they're tired of me. I have to decide tonight. I might as well—— Oh, no matter. Come. Let's skip. It's late."

She sprang up, ignoring his wail of "Vida! Wait! Sit down! Gosh! I'm flabbergasted! Gee! Vida!" She marched out. While he was paying his check she got ahead. He ran after her, blubbering, "Vida! Wait!" In the shade of the lilacs in front of the Gougerling house he came up with her, stayed her flight by a hand on her shoulder.

"Oh, don't! Don't! What does it matter?" she begged. She was sobbing, her soft wrinkly lids soaked with tears. "Who cares for my affection or help? I might as well drift on, forgotten. O Ray, please don't hold me. Let me go. I'll just decide not to renew my contract here, and—and drift—way off——"

His hand was steady on her shoulder. She dropped her head, rubbed the back of his hand with her cheek.

They were married in June.

## V

They took the Ole Jenson house. "It's small," said Vida, "but it's got the dearest vegetable garden, and I love having time to get near to Nature for once."

Though she became Vida Wutherspoon technically, and though she certainly had no ideals about the independence of keeping her name, she continued to be known as Vida Sherwin.

She had resigned from the school, but she kept up one class in English. She bustled about on every committee of the Thanatopsis; she was always popping into the rest-room to make Mrs. Nodelquist sweep the floor; she was appointed to the library-board to succeed Carol; she taught the Senior Girls' Class in the Episcopal Sunday School, and tried to revive the King's Daughters. She exploded into self-confidence and happiness; her draining thoughts were by marriage turned into energy. She became daily and visibly more plump, and though she chattered as eagerly, she was less obviously admiring of marital bliss, less sentimental about babies, sharper in demanding that the entire town share her reforms—the purchase of a park, the compulsory cleaning of back-yards.

She penned Harry Haydock at his desk in the Bon Ton; she interrupted his joking; she told him that it was Ray who had built up the shoe-department and men's department; she demanded that he be made a partner. Before Harry could answer she threatened that Ray and she would start a rival shop. "I'll clerk behind the counter myself, and a Certain Party is all ready to put up the money."

She rather wondered who the Certain Party was.

Ray was made a one-sixth partner.

He became a glorified floor-walker, greeting the men with new poise, no longer coyly subservient to pretty women. When he was not affectionately coercing people into buying things they did not need, he stood at the back of the store, glowing, abstracted, feeling masculine as he recalled the tempestuous surprises of love revealed by Vida.

The only remnant of Vida's identification of herself with Carol was a jealousy when she saw Kennicott and Ray together, and reflected that some people might suppose that Kennicott was his superior. She was sure that Carol thought so, and she wanted to shriek, "You needn't try to gloat! I wouldn't have your pokey old husband. He hasn't one single bit of Ray's spiritual nobility."

# 22

The greatest mystery about a human being is not his reaction to sex or praise, but the manner in which he contrives to put in twenty-four hours a day. It is this which puzzles the longshoreman about the clerk, the Londoner about the bushman. It was this which puzzled Carol in regard to the married Vida. Carol herself had the baby, a larger house to care for, all the telephone calls for Kennicott when he was away; and she read everything, while Vida was satisfied with newspaper headlines.

But after detached brown years in boarding-houses, Vida was hungry for housework, for the most pottering detail of it. She had no maid, nor wanted one. She cooked, baked, swept, washed supper-cloths, with the triumph of a chemist in a new laboratory. To her the hearth was veritably the altar. When she went shopping she hugged the cans of soup, and she bought a mop or a side of bacon as though she were preparing for a reception. She knelt beside a bean sprout and crooned, "I raised this with my own hands—I brought this new life into the world."

"I love her for being so happy," Carol brooded. "I ought to be that way. I worship the baby, but the housework—— Oh, I suppose I'm fortunate; so much better off than farmwomen on a new clearing, or people in a slum."

It has not yet been recorded that any human being has gained a very large or permanent contentment from meditation upon the fact that he is better off than others.

In Carol's own twenty-four hours a day she got up, dressed the baby, had breakfast, talked to Oscarina about the day's shopping, put the baby on the porch to play, went to the butcher's to choose between steak and pork chops, bathed the baby, nailed up a shelf, had dinner, put the baby to bed for a nap, paid the iceman, read for an hour, took the baby out for a walk, called on Vida, had supper, put the baby to bed, darned socks, listened to Kennicott's yawning comment on what a fool Dr. McGanum was to try to use that cheap X-ray outfit of his on an epithelioma, repaired a frock, drowsily heard Kennicott stoke the furnace, tried to read a page of Thorstein Veblen—and the day was gone.

Except when Hugh was vigorously naughty, or whiney, or laughing, or saying "I like my chair" with thrilling maturity, she was always enfeebled by loneliness. She no longer felt superior about that misfortune. She would gladly have been converted to Vida's satisfaction in Gopher Prairie and mopping the floor.

II

Carol drove through an astonishing number of books from the public library and from city shops. Kennicott was at first uncomfortable over her disconcerting habit of buying them. A book was a book, and if you had several thousand of them right here in the library, free, why the dickens should you spend your good money? After worrying about it for two or three years, he decided that this was one of the Funny Ideas which she had caught as a librarian and from which she would never entirely recover.

The authors whom she read were most of them frightfully annoyed by the Vida Sherwins. They were young American sociologists, young English realists, Russian horrorists; Anatole France, Rolland, Nexo, Wells, Shaw, Key, Edgar Lee Masters, Theodore Dreiser, Sherwood Anderson, Henry Mencken, and all the other subversive philosophers and artists whom women were consulting everywhere, in batik-curtained studios in New York, in Kansas farmhouses, San Francisco drawing-rooms, Alabama schools for negroes. From them she got the same confused desire which the million other women felt;

the same determination to be class-conscious without discovering the class of which she was to be conscious.

Certainly her reading precipitated her observations of Main Street, of Gopher Prairie and of the several adjacent Gopher Prairies which she had seen on drives with Kennicott. In her fluid thought certain convictions appeared, jaggedly, a fragment of an impression at a time, while she was going to sleep, or manicuring her nails, or waiting for Kennicott.

These convictions she presented to Vida Sherwin—Vida Wutherspoon—beside a radiator, over a bowl of not very good walnuts and pecans from Uncle Whittier's grocery, on an evening when both Kennicott and Raymie had gone out of town with the other officers of the Ancient and Affiliated Order of Spartans, to inaugurate a new chapter at Wakamin. Vida had come to the house for the night. She helped in putting Hugh to bed, sputtering the while about his soft skin. Then they talked till midnight.

What Carol said that evening, what she was passionately thinking, was also emerging in the minds of women in ten thousand Gopher Prairies. Her formulations were not pat solutions but visions of a tragic futility. She did not utter them so compactly that they can be given in her words; they were roughened with "Well, you see" and "if you get what I mean" and "I don't know that I'm making myself clear." But they were definite enough, and indignant enough.

III

In reading popular stories and seeing plays, asserted Carol, she had found only two traditions of the American small town. The first tradition, repeated in scores of magazines every month, is that the American village remains the one sure abode of friendship, honesty, and clean sweet marriageable girls. Therefore all men who succeed in painting in Paris or in finance in New York at last become weary of smart women, return to their native towns, assert that cities are vicious, marry their childhood sweethearts and, presumably, joyously abide in those towns until death.

The other tradition is that the significant features of all villages are whiskers, iron dogs upon lawns, gold bricks, checkers, jars of gilded cat-tails, and shrewd comic old men who are known as "hicks" and who ejaculate "Waal I swan." This altogether admirable tradition rules the vaudeville stage, facetious illustrators, and syndicated newspaper humor, but out of actual life it passed forty years ago. Carol's small town thinks not in hoss-swapping but in cheap motor cars, telephones, ready-made clothes, silos, alfalfa, kodaks, phonographs, leather-upholstered Morris chairs, bridge-prizes, oilstocks, motion-pictures, land-deals, unread sets of Mark Twain, and a chaste version of national politics.

With such a small-town life a Kennicott or a Champ Perry is content, but there are also hundreds of thousands, particularly women and young men, who are not at all content. The more intelligent young people (and the fortunate widows!) flee to the cities with agility and, despite the fictional tradition, resolutely stay there, seldom returning even for holidays. The most protesting patriots of the towns leave them in old age, if they can afford it, and go to live in California or in the cities.

The reason, Carol insisted, is not a whiskered rusticity. It is nothing so amusing!

It is an unimaginatively standardized background, a sluggishness of speech and manners, a rigid ruling of the spirit by the desire to appear respectable. It is contentment . . . the contentment of the quiet dead, who are scornful of the living for their restless walking. It is negation canonized as the one positive virtue. It is the prohibition of happiness. It is slavery self-sought and self-defended. It is dullness made God.

A savorless people, gulping tasteless food, and sitting afterward, coatless and thoughtless, in rocking-chairs prickly with inane decorations, listening to mechanical music, saying mechanical things about the excellence of Ford automobiles, and viewing themselves as the greatest race in the world.

## IV

She had inquired as to the effect of this dominating dullness upon foreigners. She remembered the feeble exotic quality to be found in the first-generation Scandinavians; she recalled the Norwegian Fair at the Lutheran Church, to which Bea had taken her. There, in the *bondestue*, the replica of a Norse farm kitchen, pale women in scarlet jackets embroidered with gold thread and colored beads, in black skirts with a line of blue, green-striped aprons, and ridged caps very pretty to set off a fresh face, had served *rommegrod og lefse*—sweet cakes and sour milk pudding spiced with cinnamon. For the first time in Gopher Prairie Carol had found novelty. She had reveled in the mild foreignness of it.

But she saw these Scandinavian women zealously exchanging their spiced puddings and red jackets for fried pork chops and congealed white blouses, trading the ancient Christmas hymns of the fjords for "She's My Jazzland Cutie," being Americanized into uniformity, and in less than a generation losing in the grayness whatever pleasant new customs they might have added to the life of the town. Their sons finished the process. In ready-made clothes and ready-made high-school phrases they sank into propriety, and the sound American customs had absorbed without one trace of pollution another alien invasion.

And along with these foreigners, she felt herself being ironed into glossy mediocrity, and she rebelled, in fear.

The respectability of the Gopher Prairies, said Carol, is reinforced by vows of poverty and chastity in the matter of knowledge. Except for half a dozen in each town the citizens are proud of that achievement of ignorance which it is so easy to come by. To be "intellectual" or "artistic" or, in their own word, to be "highbrow," is to be priggish and of dubious virtue.

Large experiments in politics and in co-operative distribution, ventures requiring knowledge, courage, and imagination, do originate in the West and Middlewest, but they are not of the towns, they are of the farmers. If these heresies are supported by the townsmen it is only by occasional teachers, doctors, lawyers, the labor unions, and workmen like Miles Bjornstam, who are punished by being mocked as "cranks," as "half-baked parlor socialists." The editor and the rector preach at them. The cloud of serene ignorance submerges them in unhappiness and futility.

v

Here Vida observed, "Yes—well—— Do you know, I've always thought that Ray would have made a wonderful rector. He has what I call an essentially religious soul. My! He'd have read the service beautifully! I suppose it's too late now, but as I tell him, he can also serve the world by selling shoes and—— I wonder if we oughtn't to have family-prayers?"

vi

Doubtless all small towns, in all countries, in all ages, Carol admitted, have a tendency to be not only dull but mean, bitter, infested with curiosity. In France or Tibet quite as much as in Wyoming or Indiana these timidities are inherent in isolation.

But a village in a country which is taking pains to become altogether standardized and pure, which aspires to succeed Victorian England as the chief mediocrity of the world, is no longer merely provincial, no longer downy and restful in its leaf-shadowed ignorance. It is a force seeking to dominate the earth, to drain the hills and sea of color, to set Dante at boosting Gopher Prairie, and to dress the high gods in Klassy Kollege Klothes. Sure of itself, it bullies other civilizations, as a traveling salesman in a brown derby conquers the wisdom of China and tacks advertisements of cigarettes over arches for centuries dedicated to the sayings of Confucius.

Such a society functions admirably in the large production of cheap automobiles, dollar watches, and safety razors. But it is not satisfied until the entire world also admits that the end and joyous purpose of living is to ride in flivvers, to make advertising-pictures of dollar watches, and in the twilight to sit talking not of love and courage but of the convenience of safety razors.

And such a society, such a nation, is determined by the Gopher Prairies. The greatest manufacturer is but a busier Sam Clark, and all the rotund senators and presidents are village lawyers and bankers grown nine feet tall.

Though a Gopher Prairie regards itself as a part of the Great World, compares itself to Rome and Vienna, it will not acquire the scientific spirit, the international mind, which would make it great. It picks at information which will visibly procure money or social distinction. Its conception of a community ideal is not the grand manner, the noble aspiration, the fine aristocratic pride, but cheap labor for the kitchen and rapid increase in the price of land. It plays at cards on greasy oilcloth in a shanty, and does not know that prophets are walking and talking on the terrace.

If all the provincials were as kindly as Champ Perry and Sam Clark there would be no reason for desiring the town to seek great traditions. It is the Harry Haydocks, the Dave Dyers, the Jackson Elders, small busy men crushingly powerful in their common purpose, viewing themselves as men of the world but keeping themselves men of the cash-register and the comic film, who make the town a sterile oligarchy.

VII

She had sought to be definite in analyzing the surface ugliness of the Gopher Prairies. She asserted that it is a matter of universal similarity; of flimsiness of construction, so that the towns resemble frontier camps; of neglect of natural advantages, so that the hills are covered with brush, the lakes shut off by railroads, and the creeks lined with dumping-grounds; of depressing sobriety of color; rectangularity of buildings; and excessive breadth and straightness of the gashed streets, so that there is no escape from gales and from sight of the grim sweep of land, nor any windings to coax the loiterer along, while the breadth which would be majestic in an avenue of palaces makes the low shabby shops creeping down the typical Main Street the more mean by comparison.

The universal similarity—that is the physical expression of the philosophy of dull safety. Nine-tenths of the American towns are so alike that it is the completest boredom to wander from one to another. Always, west of Pittsburg, and often, east of it, there is the same lumber yard, the same railroad station, the same Ford garage, the same creamery, the same box-like houses and two-story shops. The new, more conscious houses are alike in their very attempts at diversity: the same bungalows, the same square houses of stucco or tapestry brick. The shops show the same standardized, nationally advertised wares; the newspapers of sections three thousand miles apart have the same "syndicated features"; the boy in Arkansas displays just such a flamboyant ready-made suit as is found on just such a boy in Delaware, both of them iterate the same slang phrases from the same sporting-pages, and if one of them is in college and the other is a barber, no one may surmise which is which.

If Kennicott were snatched from Gopher Prairie and instantly conveyed to a town leagues away, he would not realize it. He would go down apparently the same Main Street (almost certainly it would be called Main Street); in the same drug store he would see the same young man serving the same ice-cream soda to the same young woman with the same magazines and phonograph records under her arm. Not till he had climbed to his office and found another sign on the door, another Dr. Kennicott inside, would he understand that something curious had presumably happened.

Finally, behind all her comments, Carol saw the fact that the prairie towns no more exist to serve the farmers who are their reason of existence than do the great capitals; they exist to fatten on the farmers, to provide for the townsmen large motors and social preferment; and, unlike the capitals, they do not give to the district in return for usury a stately and permanent center, but only this ragged camp. It is a "parasitic Greek civilization"—minus the civilization.

"There we are then," said Carol. "The remedy? Is there any? Criticism, perhaps, for the beginning of the beginning. Oh, there's nothing that attacks the Tribal God Mediocrity that doesn't help a little . . . and probably there's nothing that helps very much. Perhaps some day the farmers will build and own their market-towns. (Think of the club they could have!) But I'm afraid I haven't any 'reform program.' Not any more! The trouble is spiritual, and no League or Party can enact a preference for gardens rather than dumping-grounds. . . . There's my confession. *Well?*"

"In other words, all you want is perfection?"

"Yes! Why not?"

"How you hate this place! How can you expect to do anything with it if you haven't any sympathy?"

"But I have! And affection. Or else I wouldn't fume so. I've learned that Gopher Prairie isn't just an eruption on the prairie, as I thought first, but as large as New York. In New York I wouldn't know more than forty or fifty people, and I know that many here. Go on! Say what you're thinking."

"Well, my dear, if I *did* take all your notions seriously, it would be pretty discouraging. Imagine how a person would feel, after working hard for years and helping to build up a nice town, to have you airily flit in and simply say 'Rotten!' Think that's fair?"

"Why not? It must be just as discouraging for the Gopher Prairieite to see Venice and make comparisons."

"It would not! I imagine gondolas are kind of nice to ride in, but we've got better bath-rooms! But—— My dear, you're not the only person in this town who has done some thinking for herself, although (pardon my rudeness) I'm afraid you think so. I'll admit we lack some things. Maybe our theater isn't as good as shows in Paris. All right! I don't want to see any foreign culture suddenly forced on us—whether it's street-planning or table-manners or crazy communistic ideas."

Vida sketched what she termed "practical things that will make a happier and prettier town, but that do belong to our life, that actually are being done." Of the Thanatopsis Club she spoke; of the rest-room, the fight against mosquitos, the campaign for more gardens and shade-trees and sewers—matters not fantastic and nebulous and distant, but immediate and sure.

Carol's answer was fantastic and nebulous enough:

"Yes. . . . Yes. . . . I know. They're good. But if I could put through all those reforms at once, I'd still want startling, exotic things. Life is comfortable and clean enough here already. And so secure. What it needs is to be less secure, more eager. The civic improvements which I'd like the Thanatopsis to advocate are Strindberg plays, and classic dancers—exquisite legs beneath tulle—and (I can see him so clearly!) a thick, black-bearded, cynical Frenchman who would sit about and drink and sing opera and tell bawdy stories and laugh at our proprieties and quote Rabelais and not be ashamed to kiss my hand!"

"Huh! Not sure about the rest of it but I guess that's what you and all the other discontented young women really want: some stranger kissing your hand!" At Carol's gasp, the old squirrel-like Vida darted out and cried, "Oh, my dear, don't take that too seriously. I just meant——"

"I know. You just meant it. Go on. Be good for my soul. Isn't it funny: here we all are—me trying to be good for Gopher Prairie's soul, and Gopher Prairie trying to be good for my soul. What are my other sins?"

"Oh, there's plenty of them. Possibly some day we shall have your fat cynical Frenchman (horrible, sneering, tobacco-stained object, ruining his brains and his digestion with vile liquor!) but, thank heaven, for a while we'll manage to keep busy with our lawns and pavements! You see, these things really are coming! The Thanatopsis is getting somewhere. And you——" Her tone italicized the words—"to my great disappointment, are doing less, not more, than the people you laugh at! Sam Clark, on the school-board, is working for better school ventilation. Ella Stowbody (whose elocuting you always think is so absurd) has persuaded the railroad to share the expense of a parked space at the station, to do away with that vacant lot.

"You sneer so easily. I'm sorry, but I do think there's something essentially cheap in your attitude. Especially about religion.

"If you must know, you're not a sound reformer at all. You're an impossibilist. And you give up too easily. You gave up on the new city hall, the anti-fly campaign, club papers, the library-board, the dramatic association—just because we didn't graduate into Ibsen the very first thing. You want perfection all at once. Do you know what the finest thing you've done is—aside from bringing Hugh into the world? It was the help you gave Dr. Will during baby-welfare week. You didn't demand that each baby be a philosopher and artist before you weighed him, as you do with the rest of us.

"And now I'm afraid perhaps I'll hurt you. We're going to have a new schoolbuilding in this town—in just a few years—and we'll have it without one bit of help or interest from you!

"Professor Mott and I and some others have been dinging away at the moneyed men for years. We didn't call on you because you would never stand the pound-pound-pounding year after year without one bit of encouragement. And we've won! I've got the promise of everybody who counts that just as soon as war-conditions permit, they'll vote the bonds for the schoolhouse. And we'll have a wonderful building—lovely brown brick, with big windows, and agricultural and manual-training departments. When we get it, that'll be my answer to all your theories!"

"I'm glad. And I'm ashamed I haven't had any part in getting it. But——Please don't think I'm unsympathetic if I ask one question: Will the teachers in the hygienic new building go on informing the children that Persia is a yellow spot on the map, and 'Cæsar' the title of a book of grammatical puzzles?"

VIII

Vida was indignant; Carol was apologetic; they talked for another hour, the eternal Mary and Martha—an immoralist Mary and a reformist Martha. It was Vida who conquered.

The fact that she had been left out of the campaign for the new school-building disconcerted Carol. She laid her dreams of perfection aside. When Vida asked her to take charge of a group of Camp Fire Girls, she obeyed, and had definite pleasure out of the Indian dances and ritual and costumes. She went more regularly to the Thanatopsis. With Vida as lieutenant and unofficial commander she campaigned for a village nurse to attend poor families, raised the fund herself, saw to it that the nurse was young and strong and amiable and intelligent,

Yet all the while she beheld the burly cynical Frenchman and the diaphanous dancers as clearly as the child sees its air-born playmates; she relished the Camp Fire Girls not because, in Vida's words, "this Scout training will help so much to make them Good Wives," but because she hoped that the Sioux dances would bring subversive color into their dinginess.

She helped Ella Stowbody to set out plants in the tiny triangular park at the railroad station; she squatted in the dirt, with a small curved trowel and the most decorous of gardening gauntlets; she talked to Ella about the public-spiritedness of fuchsias and cannas; and she felt that she was scrubbing a temple deserted by the gods and empty even of incense and the sound of chanting. Passengers looking from trains saw her as a village woman of fading prettiness, incorruptible virtue, and no abnormalities; the baggageman heard her say, "Oh yes, I do think it will be a good example for the children"; and all the while she saw herself running garlanded through the streets of Babylon.

Planting led her to botanizing. She never got much farther than recognizing the tiger lily and the wild rose, but she rediscovered Hugh. "What does the buttercup say, mummy?" he cried, his hand full of straggly grasses, his cheek gilded with pollen. She knelt to embrace him; she affirmed that he made life more than full; she was altogether reconciled . . . for an hour.

But she awoke at night to hovering death. She crept away from the hump of bedding that was Kennicott; tiptoed into the bathroom and, by the mirror in the door of the medicine-cabinet, examined her pallid face.

Wasn't she growing visibly older in ratio as Vida grew plumper and younger? Wasn't her nose sharper? Wasn't her neck granulated? She stared and choked. She was only thirty. But the five years since her marriage—had they not gone by as hastily and stupidly as though she had been under ether; would time not slink past till death? She pounded her fist on the cool enameled rim of the bathtub and raged mutely against the indifferent gods:

"I don't care! I won't endure it! They lie so—Vida and Will and Aunt Bessie—they tell me I ought to be satisfied with Hugh and a good home and planting seven nasturtiums in a station garden! I am I! When I die the world will be annihilated, as far as I'm concerned. I am I! I'm not content to leave the sea and the ivory towers to others. I want them for me! Damn Vida! Damn all of them! Do they think they can make me believe that a display of potatoes at Howland & Gould's is enough beauty and strangeness?"

# 23

When America entered the Great European War, Vida sent Raymie off to an officers' training-camp—less than a year after her wedding. Raymie was diligent and rather strong. He came out a first lieutenant of infantry, and was one of the earliest sent abroad.

Carol grew definitely afraid of Vida as Vida transferred the passion which had been released in marriage to the cause of the war; as she lost all tolerance. When Carol was touched by the desire for heroism in Raymie and tried tactfully to express it, Vida made her feel like an impertinent child.

By enlistment and draft, the sons of Lyman Cass, Nat Hicks, Sam Clark joined the army. But most of the soldiers were the sons of German and Swedish farmers unknown to Carol. Dr. Terry Gould and Dr. McGanum became captains in the medical corps, and were stationed at camps in Iowa and Georgia. They were the only officers, besides Raymie, from the Gopher Prairie district. Kennicott wanted to go with them, but the several doctors of the town forgot medical rivalry and, meeting in council, decided that he would do better to wait and keep the town well till he should be needed. Kennicott was forty-two now; the only youngish doctor left in a radius of eighteen miles. Old Dr. Westlake, who loved comfort like a cat, protestingly rolled out at night for country calls, and hunted through his collar-box for his G. A. R. button.

Carol did not quite know what she thought about Kennicott's going. Certainly she was no Spartan wife. She knew that he wanted to go; she knew that this longing was always in him, behind his unchanged trudging and remarks about the weather. She felt for him an admiring affection—and she was sorry that she had nothing more than affection.

Cy Bogart was the spectacular warrior of the town. Cy was no longer the weedy boy who had sat in the loft speculating about Carol's egotism and the mysteries of generation. He was nineteen now, tall, broad, busy, the "town sport," famous for his ability to drink beer, to shake dice, to tell undesirable stories, and, from his post in front of Dyer's drug store, to embarrass the girls by "jollying" them as they passed. His face was at once peach-bloomed and pimply.

Cy was to be heard publishing it abroad that if he couldn't get the Widow Bogart's permission to enlist, he'd run away and enlist without it. He shouted that he "hated every dirty Hun; by gosh, if he could just poke a bayonet into one big fat Heinie and learn him some decency and democracy, he'd die happy." Cy got much reputation by whipping a farmboy named Adolph Pochbauer for being a "damn hyphenated German." . . . This was the younger Pochbauer, who was killed in the Argonne, while he was trying to bring the body of his Yankee captain back to the lines. At this time Cy Bogart was still dwelling in Gopher Prairie and planning to go to war.

## II

Everywhere Carol heard that the war was going to bring a basic change in psychology, to purify and uplift everything from marital relations to national politics, and she tried to exult in it. Only she did not find it. She saw the women who made bandages for the Red Cross giving up bridge, and laughing at having to do without sugar, but over the surgical-dressings they did not speak of God and the souls of men, but of Miles Bjornstam's impudence, of Terry Gould's scandalous carryings-on with a farmer's daughter four years ago, of cooking cabbage, and of altering blouses. Their references to the war touched atrocities only. She herself was punctual, and efficient at making dressings, but she could not, like Mrs. Lyman Cass and Mrs. Bogart, fill the dressings with hate for enemies.

When she protested to Vida, "The young do the work while these old ones sit around and interrupt us and gag with hate because they're too feeble to do anything but hate," then Vida turned on her:

"If you can't be reverent, at least don't be so pert and opinionated, now when men and women are dying. Some of us—we have given up so much, and we're glad to. At least we expect that you others sha'n't try to be witty at our expense."

There was weeping.

Carol did desire to see the Prussian autocracy defeated; she did persuade herself that there were no autocracies save that of Prussia; she did thrill to motion-pictures of troops embarking in New York; and she was uncomfortable when she met Miles Bjornstam on the street and he croaked:

"How's tricks? Things going fine with me; got two new cows. Well, have you become a patriot? Eh? Sure, they'll bring democracy—the democracy of death. Yes, sure, in every war since the Garden of Eden the workmen have gone out to fight each other for perfectly good reasons—handed to them by their bosses. Now me, I'm wise. I'm so wise that I know I don't know anything about the war."

It was not a thought of the war that remained with her after Miles's declamation but a perception that she and Vida and all of the good-intentioners who wanted to "do something for the common people" were insignificant, because the "common people" were able to do things for themselves, and highly likely to, as soon as they learned the fact. The conception of millions of workmen like Miles taking control frightened her, and she scuttled rapidly away from the thought of a time when she might no longer retain the position of Lady Bountiful to the Bjornstams and Beas and Oscarinas whom she loved—and patronized.

### III

It was in June, two months after America's entrance into the war, that the momentous event happened—the visit of the great Percy Bresnahan, the millionaire president of the Velvet Motor Car Company of Boston, the one native son who was always to be mentioned to strangers.

For two weeks there were rumors. Sam Clark cried to Kennicott, "Say, I hear Perce Bresnahan is coming! By golly it'll be great to see the old scout, eh?" Finally the *Dauntless* printed, on the front page with a No. 1 head, a letter from Bresnahan to Jackson Elder:

DEAR JACK:

Well, Jack, I find I can make it. I'm to go to Washington as a dollar a year man for the government, in the aviation motor section, and tell them how much I don't know about carburetors. But before I start in being a hero I want to shoot out and catch me a big black bass and cuss out you and Sam Clark and Harry Haydock and Will Kennicott and the rest of you pirates. I'll land in G.P. on June 7, on No. 7 from Mpls. Shake a day-day. Tell Bert Tybee to save me a glass of beer.
                        Sincerely yours,
                                        PERCE.

All members of the social, financial, scientific, literary, and sporting sets were at No. 7 to meet Bresnahan; Mrs. Lyman Cass was beside Del Snafflin the barber, and Juanita Haydock almost cordial to Miss Villets the librarian. Carol saw Bresnahan laughing down at them from the train vestibule—big, immaculate, overjawed, with the eye of an executive. In the voice of the professional Good Fellow he bellowed, "Howdy, folks!" As she was introduced to him (not he to her) Bresnahan looked into her eyes, and his handshake was warm, unhurried.

He declined the offers of motors; he walked off, his arm about the shoulder of Nat Hicks the sporting tailor, with the elegant Harry Haydock carrying one of his enormous pale leather bags, Del Snafflin the other, Jack Elder bearing an overcoat, and Julius Flickerbaugh the fishing-tackle. Carol noted that though Bresnahan wore spats and a stick, no small boy jeered. She decided, "I must have Will get a double-breasted blue coat and a wing collar and a dotted bow-tie like his."

That evening, when Kennicott was trimming the grass along the walk with sheep-shears, Bresnahan rolled up, alone. He was now in corduroy trousers, khaki shirt open at the throat, a white boating hat, and marvelous canvas-and-leather shoes. "On the job there, old Will! Say, my Lord, this is living, to come back and get into a regular man-sized pair of pants. They can talk all they want to about the city, but my idea of a good time is to loaf around and see you boys and catch a gamey bass!"

He hustled up the walk and blared at Carol, "Where's that little fellow? I hear you've got one fine big he-boy that you're holding out on me!"

"He's gone to bed," rather briefly.

"I know. And rules are rules, these days. Kids get routed through the shop like a motor. But look here, sister; I'm one great hand at busting rules. Come on now, let Uncle Perce have a look at him. Please now, sister?"

He put his arm about her waist; it was a large, strong, sophisticated arm, and very agreeable; he grinned at her with a devastating knowingness, while Kennicott glowed inanely. She flushed; she was alarmed by the ease with which the big-city man invaded her guarded personality. She was glad, in retreat, to scamper ahead of the two men up-stairs to the hall-room in which Hugh slept. All the way Kennicott muttered, "Well, well, say, gee whittakers but it's good to have you back, certainly is good to see you!"

Hugh lay on his stomach, making an earnest business of sleeping. He burrowed his eyes in the dwarf blue pillow to escape the electric light, then sat up abruptly, small and frail in his woolly nightdrawers, his floss of brown hair wild, the pillow clutched to his breast. He wailed. He stared at the stranger, in a manner of patient dismissal. He explained confidentially to Carol, "Daddy wouldn't let it be morning yet. What does the pillow say?"

Bresnahan dropped his arm caressingly on Carol's shoulder; he pronounced, "My Lord, you're a lucky girl to have a fine young husk like that. I figure Will knew what he was doing when he persuaded you to take a chance on an old bum like him! They tell me you come from St. Paul. We're going to get you to come to Boston some day." He leaned over the bed. "Young man, you're the slickest sight I've seen this side of Boston. With your permission, may we present you with a slight token of our regard and appreciation of your long service?"

He held out a red rubber Pierrot. Hugh remarked, "Gimme it," hid it under the bedclothes, and stared at Bresnahan as though he had never seen the man before.

For once Carol permitted herself the spiritual luxury of not asking "Why, Hugh dear, what do you say when some one gives you a present?" The great man was apparently waiting. They stood in inane suspense till Bresnahan led them out, rumbling, "How about planning a fishing-trip, Will?"

He remained for half an hour. Always he told Carol what a charming person she was; always he looked at her knowingly.

"Yes. He probably would make a woman fall in love with him. But it wouldn't last a week. I'd get tired of his confounded buoyancy. His hypocrisy. He's a spiritual bully. He makes me rude to him in self-defense. Oh yes, he is glad to be here. He does like us. He's so good an actor that he convinces his own self. . . . I'd *hate* him in Boston. He'd have all the obvious big-city things. Limousines. Discreet evening-clothes. Order a clever dinner at a smart restaurant. Drawing-room decorated by the best firm—but the pictures giving him away. I'd rather talk to Guy Pollock in his dusty office. . . . How I lie! His arm coaxed my shoulder and his eyes dared me not to admire him. I'd be afraid of him. I hate him! . . . Oh, the inconceivable egotistic imagination of women! All this stew of analysis about a man, a good, decent, friendly, efficient man, because he was kind to me, as Will's wife!"

iv

The Kennicotts, the Elders, the Clarks, and Bresnahan went fishing at Red Squaw Lake. They drove forty miles to the lake in Elder's new Cadillac. There was much laughter and bustle at the start, much storing of lunch-baskets and jointed poles, much inquiry as to whether it would *really* bother Carol to sit with her feet up on a roll of shawls. When they were ready to go Mrs. Clark lamented, "Oh, Sam, I forgot my magazine," and Bresnahan bullied, "Come on now, if you women think you're going to be literary, you can't go with us tough guys!" Every one laughed a great deal, and as they drove on Mrs. Clark explained that though probably she would not have read it, still, she might have wanted to, while the other girls had a nap in the afternoon, and she was right in the middle of a serial—it was an awfully exciting story—it seems that this girl was a Turkish dancer (only she was really the daughter of an American lady and a Russian prince) and men kept running after her, just disgustingly, but she remained pure, and there was a scene——

While the men floated on the lake, casting for black bass, the women prepared lunch and yawned. Carol was a little resentful of the manner in which the men assumed that they did not care to fish. "I don't want to go with them, but I would like the privilege of refusing."

The lunch was long and pleasant. It was a background for the talk of the great man come home, hints of cities and large imperative affairs and famous people, jocosely modest admissions that, yes, their friend Perce was doing about as well as most of these "Boston swells that think so much of themselves because they come from rich old families and went to college and everything. Believe me, it's us new business men that are running Beantown today, and not a lot of fussy old bucks snoozing in their clubs!"

Carol realized that he was not one of the sons of Gopher Prairie who, if they do not actually starve in the East, are invariably spoken of as "highly successful"; and she found behind his too incessant flattery a genuine affection for his mates. It was in the matter of the war that he most favored and thrilled them. Dropping his voice while they bent nearer (there was no one within two miles to overhear), he disclosed the fact that in both Boston and Washington he'd been getting a lot of inside stuff on the war—right straight from headquarters—he was in touch with some men—couldn't name them but they were darn high up in both the War and State Departments—and he would say—only for Pete's sake they mustn't breathe one word of this; it was strictly on the Q.T. and not generally known outside of Washington—but just between ourselves—and they could take this for gospel—Spain had finally decided to join the Entente allies in the Grand Scrap. Yes, sir, there'd be two million fully equipped Spanish soldiers fighting with us in France in one month now. Some surprise for Germany, all right!

"How about the prospects for revolution in Germany?" reverently asked Kennicott.

The authority grunted, "Nothing to it. The one thing you can bet on is that no matter what happens to the German people, win or lose, they'll stick by the Kaiser till hell freezes over. I got that absolutely straight, from a fellow who's on the inside of the inside in Washington. No, sir! I don't pretend to know much about international affairs but one thing you can put down as settled is that Germany will be a Hohenzollern empire for the next forty years. At that, I don't know as it's so bad. The Kaiser and the Junkers keep a firm hand on a lot of these red agitators who'd be worse than a king if they could get control."

"I'm terribly interested in this uprising that overthrew the Czar in Russia," suggested Carol. She had finally been conquered by the man's wizard knowledge of affairs.

Kennicott apologized for her: "Carrie's nuts about this Russian revolution. Is there much to it, Perce?"

"There is not!" Bresnahan said flatly. "I can speak by the book there. Carol, honey, I'm surprised to find you talking like a New York Russian Jew, or one of these long-hairs! I can tell you, only you don't need to let every one in on it, this is confidential, I got it from a man who's close to the State Department, but as a matter of fact the Czar will be back in power before the end of the year. You read a lot about his retiring and about his being killed, but I know he's got a big army back of him, and he'll show these damn agitators, lazy beggars hunting for a soft berth bossing the poor goats that fall for 'em, he'll show 'em where they get off!"

Carol was sorry to hear that the Czar was coming back, but she said nothing. The others had looked vacant at the mention of a country so far away as Russia. Now they edged in and asked Bresnahan what he thought about the Packard car, investments in Texas oil-wells, the comparative merits of young men born in Minnesota and in Massachusetts, the question of prohibition, the future cost of motor tires, and wasn't it true that American aviators put it all over these Frenchmen?

They were glad to find that he agreed with them on every point.

As she heard Bresnahan announce, "We're perfectly willing to talk to any committee the men may choose, but we're not going to stand for some outside agitator butting in and telling us how we're going to run our plant!" Carol remembered that Jackson Elder (now meekly receiving New Ideas) had said the same thing in the same words.

While Sam Clark was digging up from his memory a long and immensely detailed story of the crushing things he had said to a Pullman porter, named George, Bresnahan hugged his knees and rocked and watched Carol. She wondered if he did not understand the laboriousness of the smile with which she listened to Kennicott's account of the "good one he had on Carrie," that marital, coyly improper, ten-times-told tale of how she had forgotten to attend to Hugh because she was "all het up pounding the box"—which may be translated as "eagerly playing the piano." She was certain that Bresnahan saw through her when she pretended not to hear Kennicott's invitation to join a game of cribbage. She feared the comments he might make; she was irritated by her fear.

She was equally irritated, when the motor returned through Gopher Prairie, to find that she was proud of sharing in Bresnahan's kudos as people waved, and Juanita Haydock leaned from a window. She said to herself, "As though I cared whether I'm seen with this fat phonograph!" and simultaneously, "Everybody has noticed how much Will and I are playing with Mr. Bresnahan."

The town was full of his stories, his friendliness, his memory for names, his clothes, his trout-flies, his generosity. He had given a hundred dollars to Father Klubok the priest, and a hundred to the Reverend Mr. Zitterel the Baptist minister, for Americanization work.

At the Bon Ton, Carol heard Nat Hicks the tailor exulting:

"Old Perce certainly pulled a good one on this fellow Bjornstam that always is shooting off his mouth. He's supposed to of settled down since he got married, but Lord, those fellows that think they know it all, they never change. Well, the Red Swede got the grand razz handed to him, all right. He had the nerve to breeze up to Perce, at Dave Dyer's, and he said, he said to Perce, 'I've always wanted to look at a man that was so useful that folks would pay him a million dollars for existing,' and Perce gave him the once-over and come right back, 'Have, eh?' he says. 'Well,' he says, 'I've been looking for a man so useful sweeping floors that I could pay him four dollars a day. Want the job, my friend?' Ha, ha, ha! Say, you know how lippy Bjornstam is? Well for once he didn't have a thing to say. He tried to get fresh, and tell what a rotten town this is, and Perce come right back at him, 'If you don't like this country, you better get out of it and go back to Germany, where you belong!' Say, maybe us fellows didn't give Bjornstam the horse-laugh though! Oh, Perce is the white-haired boy in this burg, all rightee!"

### V

Bresnahan had borrowed Jackson Elder's motor; he stopped at the Kennicotts'; he bawled at Carol, rocking with Hugh on the porch, "Better come for a ride."

She wanted to snub him. "Thanks so much, but I'm being maternal."

"Bring him along! Bring him along!" Bresnahan was out of the seat, stalking up the sidewalk, and the rest of her protests and dignities were feeble.

She did not bring Hugh along.

Bresnahan was silent for a mile, in words, but he looked at her as though he meant her to know that he understood everything she thought.

She observed how deep was his chest.

"Lovely fields over there," he said.

"You really like them? There's no profit in them."

He chuckled. "Sister, you can't get away with it. I'm onto you. You consider me a big bluff. Well, maybe I am. But so are you, my dear—and pretty enough so that I'd try to make love to you, if I weren't afraid you'd slap me."

"Mr. Bresnahan, do you talk that way to your wife's friends? And do you call them 'sister'?"

"As a matter of fact, I do! And I make 'em like it. Score two!" But his chuckle was not so rotund, and he was very attentive to the ammeter.

In a moment he was cautiously attacking: "That's a wonderful boy, Will Kennicott. Great work these country practitioners are doing. The other day, in Washington, I was talking to a big scientific shark, a professor in Johns Hopkins medical school, and he was saying that no one has ever sufficiently appreciated the general practitioner and the sympathy and help he gives folks. These crack specialists, the young scientific fellows, they're so cocksure and so wrapped up in their laboratories that they miss the human element. Except in the case of a few freak diseases that no respectable human being would waste his time having, it's the old doc that keeps a community well, mind and body. And strikes me that Will is one of the steadiest and clearest-headed country practitioners I've ever met. Eh?"

"I'm sure he is. He's a servant of reality."

"Come again? Um. Yes. All of that, whatever that is. . . . Say, child, you don't care a whole lot for Gopher Prairie, if I'm not mistaken."

"Nope."

"There's where you're missing a big chance. There's nothing to these cities. Believe me, I *know!* This is a good town, as they go. You're lucky to be here. I wish I could stay on!"

"Very well, why don't you?"

"Huh? Why—Lord—can't get away fr——"

"You don't have to stay. I do! So I want to change it. Do you know that men like you, prominent men, do quite a reasonable amount of harm by insisting that your native towns and native states are perfect? It's you who encourage the denizens not to change. They quote you, and go on believing that they live in paradise, and——" She clenched her fist. "The incredible dullness of it!"

"Suppose you were right. Even so, don't you think you waste a lot of thundering on one poor scared little town? Kind of mean!"

"I tell you it's dull. *Dull!*"

"The folks don't find it dull. These couples like the Haydocks have a high old time; dances and cards——"

"They don't. They're bored. Almost every one here is. Vacuousness and bad manners and spiteful gossip—that's what I hate."

"Those things—course they're here. So are they in Boston! And every place else! Why, the faults you find in this town are simply human nature, and never will be changed."

"Perhaps. But in a Boston all the good Carols (I'll admit I have no faults) can find one another and play. But here—I'm alone, in a stale pool—except as it's stirred by the great Mr. Bresnahan!"

"My Lord, to hear you tell it, a fellow 'd think that all the denizens, as you impolitely call 'em, are so confoundedly unhappy that it's a wonder they don't all up and commit suicide. But they seem to struggle along somehow!"

"They don't know what they miss. And anybody can endure anything. Look at men in mines and in prisons."

He drew up on the south shore of Lake Minniemashie. He glanced across the reeds reflected on the water, the quiver of wavelets like crumpled tinfoil, the distant shores patched with dark woods, silvery oats and deep yellow wheat. He patted her hand. "Sis—— Carol, you're a darling girl, but you're difficult. Know what I think?"

"Yes."

"Humph. Maybe you do, but—— My humble (not too humble!) opinion is that you like to be different. You like to think you're peculiar. Why, if you knew how many tens of thousands of women, especially in New York, say just what you do, you'd lose all the fun of thinking you're a lone genius and you'd be on the band-wagon whooping it up for Gopher Prairie and a good decent family life. There's always about a million young women just out of college who want to teach their grandmothers how to suck eggs."

"How proud you are of that homely rustic metaphor! You use it at 'banquets' and directors' meetings, and boast of your climb from a humble homestead."

"Huh! You may have my number. I'm not telling. But look here: You're so prejudiced against Gopher Prairie that you overshoot the mark; you antagonize those who might be inclined to agree with you in some particulars but—— Great guns, the town can't be all wrong!"

"No, it isn't. But it could be. Let me tell you a fable. Imagine a cavewoman complaining to her mate. She doesn't like one single thing; she hates the damp cave, the rats running over her bare legs, the stiff skin garments, the eating of half-raw meat, her husband's bushy face, the constant battles, and the worship of the spirits who will hoodoo her unless she gives the priests her best claw necklace. Her man protests, 'But it can't all be wrong!' and he thinks he has reduced her to absurdity. Now you assume that a world which produces a Percy Bresnahan and a Velvet Motor Company must be civilized. It is? Aren't we only about half-way along in barbarism? I suggest Mrs. Bogart as a test. And we'll continue in barbarism just as long as people as nearly intelligent as you continue to defend things as they are because they are."

"You're a fair spieler, child. But, by golly, I'd like to see you try to design a new manifold, or run a factory and keep a lot of your fellow reds from Czech-slovenski-magyar-godknowswheria on the job! You'd drop your theories so darn quick! I'm not any defender of things as they are. Sure. They're rotten. Only I'm sensible."

He preached his gospel: love of outdoors, Playing the Game, loyalty to friends. She had the neophyte's shock of discovery that, outside of tracts, conservatives do not tremble and find no answer when an iconoclast turns on them, but retort with agility and confusing statistics.

He was so much the man, the worker, the friend, that she liked him when she most tried to stand out against him; he was so much the successful exec-

utive that she did not want him to despise her. His manner of sneering at
what he called "parlor socialists" (though the phrase was not overwhelmingly
new) had a power which made her wish to placate his company of well-fed,
speed-loving administrators. When he demanded, "Would you like to associate with nothing but a lot of turkey-necked, horn-spectacled nuts that
have adenoids and need a hair-cut, and that spend all their time kicking
about 'conditions' and never do a lick of work?" she said, "No, but just the
same——" When he asserted, "Even if your cavewoman was right in knocking
the whole works, I bet some red-blooded Regular Fellow, some real He-
man, found her a nice dry cave, and not any whining criticizing radical,"
she wriggled her head feebly, between a nod and a shake.

His large hands, sensual lips, easy voice supported his self-confidence. He
made her feel young and soft—as Kennicott had once made her feel. She had
nothing to say when he bent his powerful head and experimented, "My dear,
I'm sorry I'm going away from this town. You'd be a darling child to play
with. You *are* pretty! Some day in Boston I'll show you how we buy a lunch.
Well, hang it, got to be starting back."

The only answer to his gospel of beef which she could find, when she was
home, was a wail of "But just the same——"

She did not see him again before he departed for Washington.

His eyes remained. His glances at her lips and hair and shoulders had revealed to her that she was not a wife-and-mother alone, but a girl; that there
still were men in the world, as there had been in college days.

That admiration led her to study Kennicott, to tear at the shroud of intimacy, to perceive the strangeness of the most familiar.

# 24

All that midsummer month Carol was sensitive to Kennicott. She recalled a
hundred grotesqueries: her comic dismay at his having chewed tobacco, the
evening when she had tried to read poetry to him; matters which had seemed
to vanish with no trace or sequence. Always she repeated that he had been
heroically patient in his desire to join the army. She made much of her consoling affection for him in little things. She liked the homeliness of his tinkering about the house; his strength and handiness as he tightened the hinges of
a shutter; his boyishness when he ran to her to be comforted because he had
found rust in the barrel of his pump-gun. But at the highest he was to her
another Hugh, without the glamor of Hugh's unknown future.

There was, late in June, a day of heat-lightning.

Because of the work imposed by the absence of the other doctors the Kennicotts had not moved to the lake cottage but remained in town, dusty and

irritable. In the afternoon, when she went to Oleson & McGuire's (formerly Dahl & Oleson's), Carol was vexed by the assumption of the youthful clerk, recently come from the farm, that he had to be neighborly and rude. He was no more brusquely familiar than a dozen other clerks of the town, but her nerves were heat-scorched.

When she asked for codfish, for supper, he grunted, "What d'you want that darned old dry stuff for?"

"I like it!"

"Punk! Guess the doc can afford something better than that. Try some of the new wienies we got in. Swell. The Haydocks use 'em."

She exploded. "My dear young man, it is not your duty to instruct me in housekeeping, and it doesn't particularly concern me what the Haydocks condescend to approve!"

He was hurt. He hastily wrapped up the leprous fragment of fish; he gaped as she trailed out. She lamented, "I shouldn't have spoken so. He didn't mean anything. He doesn't know when he is being rude."

Her repentance was not proof against Uncle Whittier when she stopped in at his grocery for salt and a package of safety matches. Uncle Whittier, in a shirt collarless and soaked with sweat in a brown streak down his back, was whining at a clerk, "Come on now, get a hustle on and lug that pound cake up to Mis' Cass's. Some folks in this town think a storekeeper ain't got nothing to do but chase out 'phone-orders. . . . Hello, Carrie. That dress you got on looks kind of low in the neck to me. May be decent and modest— I suppose I'm old-fashioned—but I never thought much of showing the whole town a woman's bust! Hee, hee, hee! . . . Afternoon, Mrs. Hicks. Sage? Just out of it. Lemme sell you some other spices. Heh?" Uncle Whittier was nasally indignant. "*Certainly!* Got *plenty* other spices jus' good as sage for any purp'se whatever! What's the matter with—well, with allspice?" When Mrs. Hicks had gone, he raged, "Some folks don't know what they want!"

"Sweating sanctimonious bully—my husband's uncle!" thought Carol.

She crept into Dave Dyer's. Dave held up his arms with, "Don't shoot! I surrender!" She smiled, but it occurred to her that for nearly five years Dave had kept up this game of pretending that she threatened his life.

As she went dragging through the prickly-hot street she reflected that a citizen of Gopher Prairie does not have jests—he has a jest. Every cold morning for five winters Lyman Cass had remarked, "Fair to middlin' chilly—get worse before it gets better." Fifty times had Ezra Stowbody informed the public that Carol had once asked, "Shall I indorse this check on the back?" Fifty times had Sam Clark called to her, "Where'd you steal that hat?" Fifty times had the mention of Barney Cahoon, the town drayman, like a nickel in a slot produced from Kennicott the apocryphal story of Barney's directing a minister, "Come down to the depot and get your case of religious books—they're leaking!"

She came home by the unvarying route. She knew every house-front, every street-crossing, every billboard, every tree, every dog. She knew every blackened banana-skin and empty cigarette-box in the gutters. She knew every greeting. When Jim Howland stopped and gaped at her there was no possibility that he was about to confide anything but his grudging, "Well, haryuh t'day?"

All her future life, this same red-labeled bread-crate in front of the bakery, this same thimble-shaped crack in the sidewalk a quarter of a block beyond Stowbody's granite hitching-post——

She silently handed her purchases to the silent Oscarina. She sat on the porch, rocking, fanning, twitchy with Hugh's whining.

Kennicott came home, grumbled, "What the devil is the kid yapping about?"

"I guess you can stand it ten minutes if I can stand it all day!"

He came to supper in his shirt sleeves, his vest partly open, revealing discolored suspenders.

"Why don't you put on your nice Palm Beach suit, and take off that hideous vest?" she complained.

"Too much trouble. Too hot to go up-stairs."

She realized that for perhaps a year she had not definitely looked at her husband. She regarded his table-manners. He violently chased fragments of fish about his plate with a knife and licked the knife after gobbling them. She was slightly sick. She asserted, "I'm ridiculous. What do these things matter! Don't be so simple!" But she knew that to her they did matter, these solecisms and mixed tenses of the table.

She realized that they found little to say; that, incredibly, they were like the talked-out couples whom she had pitied at restaurants.

Bresnahan would have spouted in a lively, exciting, unreliable manner. . . .

She realized that Kennicott's clothes were seldom pressed. His coat was wrinkled; his trousers would flap at the knees when he arose. His shoes were unblacked, and they were of an elderly shapelessness. He refused to wear soft hats; cleaved to a hard derby, as a symbol of virility and prosperity; and sometimes he forgot to take it off in the house. She peeped at his cuffs. They were frayed in prickles of starched linen. She had turned them once; she clipped them every week; but when she had begged him to throw the shirt away, last Sunday morning at the crisis of the weekly bath, he had uneasily protested, "Oh, it'll wear quite a while yet."

He was shaved (by himself or more socially by Del Snafflin) only three times a week. This morning had not been one of the three times.

Yet he was vain of his new turn-down collars and sleek ties; he often spoke of the "sloppy dressing" of Dr. McGanum; and he laughed at old men who wore detachable cuffs or Gladstone collars.

Carol did not care much for the creamed codfish that evening.

She noted that his nails were jagged and ill-shaped from his habit of cutting them with a pocket-knife and despising a nail-file as effeminate and urban. That they were invariably clean, that his were the scoured fingers of the surgeon, made his stubborn untidiness the more jarring. They were wise hands, kind hands, but they were not the hands of love.

She remembered him in the days of courtship. He had tried to please her, then; had touched her by sheepishly wearing a colored band on his straw hat. Was it possible that those days of fumbling for each other were gone so completely? He had read books, to impress her; had said (she recalled it ironically) that she was to point out his every fault; had insisted once, as they sat in the secret place beneath the walls of Fort Snelling——

She shut the door on her thoughts. That was sacred ground. But it *was* a shame that——

She nervously pushed away her cake and stewed apricots.

After supper, when they had been driven in from the porch by mosquitos, when Kennicott had for the two-hundredth time in five years commented, "We must have a new screen on the porch—lets all the bugs in," they sat reading, and she noted, and detested herself for noting, and noted again his habitual awkwardness. He slumped down in one chair, his legs up on another, and he explored the recesses of his left ear with the end of his little finger—she could hear the faint smack—he kept it up—he kept it up——

He blurted, "Oh. Forgot tell you. Some of the fellows coming in to play poker this evening. Suppose we could have some crackers and cheese and beer?"

She nodded.

"He might have mentioned it before. Oh well, it's his house."

The poker-party straggled in: Sam Clark, Jack Elder, Dave Dyer, Jim Howland. To her they mechanically said, " 'Devenin'," but to Kennicott, in a heroic male manner, "Well, well, shall we start playing? Got a hunch I'm going to lick somebody real bad." No one suggested that she join them. She told herself that it was her own fault, because she was not more friendly; but she remembered that they never asked Mrs. Sam Clark to play.

Bresnahan would have asked her.

She sat in the living-room, glancing across the hall at the men as they humped over the dining table.

They were in shirt sleeves; smoking, chewing, spitting incessantly; lowering their voices for a moment so that she did not hear what they said and afterward giggling hoarsely; using over and over the canonical phrases: "Three to dole," "I raise you a finif," "Come on now, ante up; what do you think this is, a pink tea?" The cigar-smoke was acrid and pervasive. The firmness with which the men mouthed their cigars made the lower part of their faces expressionless, heavy, unappealing. They were like politicians cynically dividing appointments.

How could they understand her world?

Did that faint and delicate world exist? Was she a fool? She doubted her world, doubted herself, and was sick in the acid, smoke-stained air.

She slipped back into brooding upon the habituality of the house.

Kennicott was as fixed in routine as an isolated old man. At first he had amorously deceived himself into liking her experiments with food—the one medium in which she could express imagination—but now he wanted only his round of favorite dishes: steak, roast beef, boiled pig's-feet, oatmeal, baked apples. Because at some more flexible period he had advanced from oranges to grape-fruit he considered himself an epicure.

During their first autumn she had smiled over his affection for his hunting-coat, but now that the leather had come unstitched in dribbles of pale yellow thread, and tatters of canvas, smeared with dirt of the fields and grease from gun-cleaning, hung in a border of rags, she hated the thing.

Wasn't her whole life like that hunting-coat?

She knew every nick and brown spot on each piece of the set of china purchased by Kennicott's mother in 1895—discreet china with a pattern of washed-out forget-me-nots, rimmed with blurred gold: the gravy-boat, in a saucer which did not match, the solemn and evangelical covered vegetable-dishes, the two platters.

Twenty times had Kennicott sighed over the fact that Bea had broken the other platter—the medium-sized one.

The kitchen.

Damp black iron sink, damp whitey-yellow drain-board with shreds of dis-colored wood which from long scrubbing were as soft as cotton thread, warped table, alarm clock, stove bravely blackened by Oscarina but an abomination in its loose doors and broken drafts and oven that never would keep an even heat.

Carol had done her best by the kitchen: painted it white, put up curtains, replaced a six-year-old calendar by a color print. She had hoped for tiling, and a kerosene range for summer cooking, but Kennicott always postponed these expenses.

She was better acquainted with the utensils in the kitchen than with Vida Sherwin or Guy Pollock. The can-opener, whose soft gray metal handle was twisted from some ancient effort to pry open a window, was more pertinent to her than all the cathedrals in Europe; and more significant than the future of Asia was the never-settled weekly question as to whether the small kitchen knife with the unpainted handle or the second-best buckhorn carving-knife was better for cutting up cold chicken for Sunday supper.

II

She was ignored by the males till midnight. Her husband called, "Suppose we could have some eats, Carrie?" As she passed through the dining-room the men smiled on her, belly-smiles. None of them noticed her while she was serving the crackers and cheese and sardines and beer. They were determining the exact psychology of Dave Dyer in standing pat, two hours before.

When they were gone she said to Kennicott, "Your friends have the manners of a barroom. They expect me to wait on them like a servant. They're not so much interested in me as they would be in a waiter, because they don't have to tip me. Unfortunately! Well, good night."

So rarely did she nag in this petty, hot-weather fashion that he was astonished rather than angry. "Hey! Wait! What's the idea? I must say I don't get you. The boys—— Barroom? Why, Perce Bresnahan was saying there isn't a finer bunch of royal good fellows anywhere than just the crowd that were here tonight!"

They stood in the lower hall. He was too shocked to go on with his duties of locking the front door and winding his watch and the clock.

"Bresnahan! I'm sick of him!" She meant nothing in particular.

"Why, Carrie, he's one of the biggest men in the country! Boston just eats out of his hand!"

"I wonder if it does? How do we know but that in Boston, among well-bred people, he may be regarded as an absolute lout? The way he calls women 'Sister,' and the way——"

"Now look here! That'll do! Of course I know you don't mean it—you're simply hot and tired, and trying to work off your peeve on me. But just the same, I won't stand your jumping on Perce. You—— It's just like your attitude toward the war—so darn afraid that America will become militaristic——"

"But you are the pure patriot!"

"By God, I am!"

"Yes, I heard you talking to Sam Clark tonight about ways of avoiding the income tax!"

He had recovered enough to lock the door; he clumped up-stairs ahead of her, growling, "You don't know what you're talking about. I'm perfectly willing to pay my full tax—fact, I'm in favor of the income tax—even though I do think it's a penalty on frugality and enterprise—fact, it's an unjust, darn-fool tax. But just the same, I'll pay it. Only, I'm not idiot enough to pay more than the government makes me pay, and Sam and I were just figuring out whether all automobile expenses oughtn't to be exemptions. I'll take a lot off you, Carrie, but I don't propose for one second to stand your saying I'm not patriotic. You know mighty well and good that I've tried to get away and join the army. And at the beginning of the whole fracas I said—I've said right along—that we ought to have entered the war the minute Germany invaded Belgium. You don't get me at all. You can't appreciate a man's work. You're abnormal. You've fussed so much with these fool novels and books and all this highbrow junk—— You like to argue!"

It ended, a quarter of an hour later, in his calling her a "neurotic" before he turned away and pretended to sleep.

For the first time they had failed to make peace.

"There are two races of people, only two, and they live side by side. His calls mine 'neurotic'; mine calls his 'stupid.' We'll never understand each other, never; and it's madness for us to debate—to lie together in a hot bed in a creepy room—enemies, yoked."

### III

It clarified in her the longing for a place of her own.

"While it's so hot, I think I'll sleep in the spare room," she said next day.

"Not a bad idea." He was cheerful and kindly.

The room was filled with a lumbering double bed and a cheap pine bureau.

She stored the bed in the attic; replaced it by a cot which, with a denim cover, made a couch by day; put in a dressing-table, a rocker transformed by a cretonne cover; had Miles Bjornstam build book-shelves.

Kennicott slowly understood that she meant to keep up her seclusion. In his queries, "Changing the whole room?" "Putting your books in there?" she caught his dismay. But it was so easy, once her door was closed, to shut out his worry. That hurt her—the ease of forgetting him.

Aunt Bessie Smail sleuthed out this anarchy. She yammered, "Why, Carrie, you ain't going to sleep all alone by yourself? I don't believe in that. Married folks should have the same room, of course! Don't go getting silly notions. No telling what a thing like that might lead to. Suppose I up and told your Uncle Whit that I wanted a room of my own!"

Carol spoke of recipes for corn-pudding.

But from Mrs. Dr. Westlake she drew encouragement. She had made an afternoon call on Mrs. Westlake. She was for the first time invited up-stairs, and found the suave old woman sewing in a white and mahogany room with a small bed.

"Oh, do you have your own royal apartments, and the doctor his?" Carol hinted.

"Indeed I do! The doctor says it's bad enough to have to stand my temper at meals. Do——" Mrs. Westlake looked at her sharply. "Why, don't you do the same thing?"

"I've been thinking about it." Carol laughed in an embarrassed way. "Then you wouldn't regard me as a complete hussy if I wanted to be by myself now and then?"

"Why, child, every woman ought to get off by herself and turn over her thoughts—about children, and God, and how bad her complexion is, and the way men don't really understand her, and how much work she finds to do in the house, and how much patience it takes to endure some things in a man's love."

"Yes!" Carol said it in a gasp, her hands twisted together. She wanted to confess not only her hatred for the Aunt Bessies but her covert irritation toward those she best loved: her alienation from Kennicott, her disappointment in Guy Pollock, her uneasiness in the presence of Vida. She had enough self-control to confine herself to, "Yes. Men! The dear blundering souls, we do have to get off and laugh at them."

"Of course we do. Not that you have to laugh at Dr. Kennicott so much, but *my* man, heavens, now there's a rare old bird! Reading story-books when he ought to be tending to business! 'Marcus Westlake,' I say to him, 'you're a romantic old fool.' And does he get angry? He does not! He chuckles and says, 'Yes, my beloved, folks do say that married people grow to resemble each other!' Drat him!" Mrs. Westlake laughed comfortably.

After such a disclosure what could Carol do but return the courtesy by remarking that as for Kennicott, he wasn't romantic enough—the darling. Before she left she had babbled to Mrs. Westlake her dislike for Aunt Bessie, the fact that Kennicott's income was now more than five thousand a year, her view of the reason why Vida had married Raymie (which included some thoroughly insincere praise of Raymie's "kind heart"), her opinion of the library-board, just what Kennicott had said about Mrs. Carthal's diabetes, and what Kennicott thought of the several surgeons in the Cities.

She went home soothed by confession, inspirited by finding a new friend.

IV

The tragicomedy of the "domestic situation."

Oscarina went back home to help on the farm, and Carol had a succession of maids, with gaps between. The lack of servants was becoming one of the most cramping problems of the prairie town. Increasingly the farmers' daughters rebelled against village dullness, and against the unchanged attitude of the Juanitas toward "hired girls." They went off to city kitchens, or to city shops and factories, that they might be free and even human after hours.

The Jolly Seventeen were delighted at Carol's desertion by the loyal Oscarina. They reminded her that she had said, "I don't have any trouble with maids; see how Oscarina stays on."

Between incumbencies of Finn maids from the North Woods, Germans from the prairies, occasional Swedes and Norwegians and Icelanders, Carol did her own work—and endured Aunt Bessie's skittering in to tell her how to dampen a broom for fluffy dust, how to sugar doughnuts, how to stuff a goose. Carol was deft, and won shy praise from Kennicott, but as her shoulder blades began to sting, she wondered how many millions of women had lied to themselves during the death-rimmed years through which they had pretended to enjoy the puerile methods persisting in housework.

She doubted the convenience and, as a natural sequent, the sanctity of the monogamous and separate home which she had regarded as the basis of all decent life.

She considered her doubts vicious. She refused to remember how many of the women of the Jolly Seventeen nagged their husbands and were nagged by them.

She energetically did not whine to Kennicott. But her eyes ached; she was not the girl in breeches and a flannel shirt who had cooked over a camp-fire in the Colorado mountains five years ago. Her ambition was to get to bed at nine; her strongest emotion was resentment over rising at half-past six to care for Hugh. The back of her neck ached as she got out of bed. She was cynical about the joys of a simple laborious life. She understood why workmen and workmen's wives are not grateful to their kind employers.

At mid-morning, when she was momentarily free from the ache in her neck and back, she was glad of the reality of work. The hours were living and nimble. But she had no desire to read the eloquent little newspaper essays in praise of labor which are daily written by the white-browed journalistic prophets. She felt independent and (though she hid it) a bit surly.

In cleaning the house she pondered upon the maid's-room. It was a slant-roofed, small-windowed hole above the kitchen, oppressive in summer, frigid in winter. She saw that while she had been considering herself an unusually good mistress, she had been permitting her friends Bea and Oscarina to live in a sty. She complained to Kennicott. "What's the matter with it?" he growled, as they stood on the perilous stairs dodging up from the kitchen. She commented upon the sloping roof of unplastered boards stained in brown rings by the rain, the uneven floor, the cot and its tumbled discouraged-looking quilts, the broken rocker, the distorting mirror.

"Maybe it ain't any Hotel Radisson parlor, but still, it's so much better than anything these hired girls are accustomed to at home that they think it's fine. Seems foolish to spend money when they wouldn't appreciate it."

But that night he drawled, with the casualness of a man who wishes to be surprising and delightful, "Carrie, don't know but what we might begin to think about building a new house, one of these days. How'd you like that?"

"W-why——"

"I'm getting to the point now where I feel we can afford one—and a corker! I'll show this burg something like a real house! We'll put one over on Sam and Harry! Make folks sit up an' take notice!"

"Yes," she said.

He did not go on.

Daily he returned to the subject of the new house, but as to time and mode he was indefinite. At first she believed. She babbled of a low stone house with lattice windows and tulip-beds, of colonial brick, of a white frame cottage with green shutters and dormer windows. To her enthusiasms he answered, "Well, ye-es, might be worth thinking about. Remember where I put my pipe?" When she pressed him he fidgeted, "I don't know; seems to me those kind of houses you speak of have been overdone."

It proved that what he wanted was a house exactly like Sam Clark's, which was exactly like every third new house in every town in the country: a square, yellow stolidity with immaculate clapboards, a broad screened porch, tidy grass-plots, and concrete walks; a house resembling the mind of a merchant who votes the party ticket straight and goes to church once a month and owns a good car.

He admitted, "Well, yes, maybe it isn't so darn artistic but—— Matter of fact, though, I don't want a place just like Sam's. Maybe I would cut off that fool tower he's got, and I think probably it would look better painted a nice cream color. That yellow on Sam's house is too kind of flashy. Then there's another kind of house that's mighty nice and substantial-looking, with shingles, in a nice brown stain, instead of clapboards—seen some in Minneapolis. You're way off your base when you say I only like one kind of house!"

Uncle Whittier and Aunt Bessie came in one evening when Carol was sleepily advocating a rose-garden cottage.

"You've had a lot of experience with housekeeping, aunty, and don't you think," Kennicott appealed, "that it would be sensible to have a nice square house, and pay more attention to getting a crackajack furnace than to all this architecture and doodads?"

Aunt Bessie worked her lips as though they were an elastic band. "Why of course! I know how it is with young folks like you, Carrie; you want towers and bay-windows and pianos and heaven knows what all, but the thing to get is closets and a good furnace and a handy place to hang out the washing, and the rest don't matter."

Uncle Whittier dribbled a little, put his face near to Carol's, and sputtered, "Course it don't! What d'you care what folks think about the outside of your house? It's the inside you're living in. None of my business, but I must say you young folks that'd rather have cakes than potatoes get me riled."

She reached her room before she became savage. Below, dreadfully near, she could hear the broom-swish of Aunt Bessie's voice, and the mop-pounding of Uncle Whittier's grumble. She had a reasonless dread that they would intrude on her, then a fear that she would yield to Gopher Prairie's conception of duty toward an Aunt Bessie and go down-stairs to be "nice." She felt the demand for standardized behavior coming in waves from all the citizens who sat in their sitting-rooms watching her with respectable eyes, waiting, demanding, unyielding. She snarled, "Oh, all right, I'll go!" She powdered her nose, straightened her collar, and coldly marched down-stairs. The three elders ignored her. They had advanced from the new house to agreeable general fussing. Aunt Bessie was saying, in a tone like the munching of dry toast:

"I do think Mr. Stowbody ought to have had the rain-pipe fixed at our store right away. I went to see him on Tuesday morning before ten, no, it was couple minutes after ten, but anyway, it was long before noon—I know because I went right from the bank to the meat market to get some steak—my! I think it's outrageous, the prices Oleson & McGuire charge for their meat, and it isn't as if they gave you a good cut either, but just any old thing, and I had time to get it, and I stopped in at Mrs. Bogart's to ask about her rheumatism——"

Carol was watching Uncle Whittier. She knew from his taut expression that he was not listening to Aunt Bessie but herding his own thoughts, and that he would interrupt her bluntly. He did:

"Will, where c'n I get an extra pair of pants for this coat and vest? D' want to pay too much."

"Well, guess Nat Hicks could make you up a pair. But if I were you, I'd drop into Ike Rifkin's—his prices are lower than the Bon Ton's."

"Humph. Got the new stove in your office yet?"

"No, been looking at some at Sam Clark's but——"

"Well, y' ought get 't in. Don't do to put off getting a stove all summer, and then have it come cold on you in the fall."

Carol smiled upon them ingratiatingly. "Do you dears mind if I slip up to bed? I'm rather tired—cleaned the up-stairs today."

She retreated. She was certain that they were discussing her, and foully forgiving her. She lay awake till she heard the distant creak of a bed which indicated that Kennicott had retired. Then she felt safe.

It was Kennicott who brought up the matter of the Smails at breakfast.

With no visible connection he said, "Uncle Whit is kind of clumsy, but just the same, he's a pretty wise old coot. He's certainly making good with the store."

Carol smiled, and Kennicott was pleased that she had come to her senses. "As Whit says, after all the first thing is to have the inside of a house right, and darn the people on the outside looking in!"

It seemed settled that the house was to be a sound example of the Sam Clark school.

Kennicott made much of erecting it entirely for her and the baby. He spoke of closets for her frocks, and "a comfy sewing-room." But when he drew on a leaf from an old account-book (he was a paper-saver and a string-picker) the plans for the garage, he gave much more attention to a cement floor and a work-bench and a gasoline-tank than he had to sewing-rooms.

She sat back and was afraid.

In the present rookery there were odd things—a step up from the hall to the dining-room, a picturesqueness in the shed and bedraggled lilac bush. But the new place would be smooth, standardized, fixed. It was probable, now that Kennicott was past forty, and settled, that this would be the last venture he would ever make in building. So long as she stayed in this ark, she would always have a possibility of change, but once she was in the new house, there she would sit for all the rest of her life—there she would die. Desperately she wanted to put it off, against the chance of miracles. While Kennicott was chattering about a patent swing-door for the garage she saw the swing-doors of a prison.

She never voluntarily returned to the project. Aggrieved, Kennicott stopped drawing plans, and in ten days the new house was forgotten.

v

Every year since their marriage Carol had longed for a trip through the East. Every year Kennicott had talked of attending the American Medical Association convention, "and then afterwards we could do the East up brown. I know New York clean through—spent pretty near a week there—but I would like to see New England and all these historic places and have some sea-food." He talked of it from February to May, and in May he invariably decided that coming confinement-cases or land-deals would prevent his "getting away from home-base for very long *this* year—and no sense going till we can do it right."

The weariness of dish-washing had increased her desire to go. She pictured herself looking at Emerson's manse, bathing in a surf of jade and ivory, wearing a *trottoir* and a summer fur, meeting an aristocratic Stranger. In the spring Kennicott had pathetically volunteered, "S'pose you'd like to get in a good long tour this summer, but with Gould and Mac away and so many patients depending on me, don't see how I can make it. By golly, I feel like a tightwad though, not taking you." Through all this restless July after she had tasted Bresnahan's disturbing flavor of travel and gaiety, she wanted to go, but she said nothing. They spoke of and postponed a trip to the Twin Cities. When she suggested, as though it were a tremendous joke, "I think baby and I might up and leave you, and run off to Cape Cod by ourselves!" his only reaction was "Golly, don't know but what you may almost have to do that, if we don't get in a trip next year."

Toward the end of July he proposed, "Say, the Beavers are holding a convention in Joralemon, street fair and everything. We might go down tomorrow. And I'd like to see Dr. Calibree about some business. Put in the whole day. Might help some to make up for our trip. Fine fellow, Dr. Calibree."

Joralemon was a prairie town of the size of Gopher Prairie.

Their motor was out of order, and there was no passenger-train at an early hour. They went down by freight-train, after the weighty and conversational business of leaving Hugh with Aunt Bessie. Carol was exultant over this irregular jaunting. It was the first unusual thing, except the glance of Bresnahan, that had happened since the weaning of Hugh. They rode in the caboose, the small red cupola-topped car jerked along at the end of the train. It was a roving shanty, the cabin of a land schooner, with black oilcloth seats along the side, and for desk, a pine board to be let down on hinges. Kennicott played seven-up with the conductor and two brakemen. Carol liked the blue silk kerchiefs about the brakemen's throats; she liked their welcome to her, and their air of friendly independence. Since there were no sweating passengers crammed in beside her, she reveled in the train's slowness. She was part of these lakes and tawny wheat-fields. She liked the smell of hot earth and clean grease; and the leisurely chug-a-chug, chug-a-chug of the trucks was a song of contentment in the sun.

She pretended that she was going to the Rockies. When they reached Joralemon she was radiant with holiday-making.

Her eagerness began to lessen the moment they stopped at a red frame station exactly like the one they had just left at Gopher Prairie, and Kennicott yawned, "Right on time. Just in time for dinner at the Calibrees'. I 'phoned the doctor from G. P. that we'd be here. 'We'll catch the freight that gets in before twelve,' I told him. He said he'd meet us at the depot and take us right up to the house for dinner. Calibree is a good man, and you'll find his wife is a mighty brainy little woman, bright as a dollar. By golly, there he is."

Dr. Calibree was a squat, clean-shaven, conscientious-looking man of forty. He was curiously like his own brown-painted motor car, with eye-glasses for windshield. "Want you to meet my wife, doctor—Carrie, make you 'quainted with Dr. Calibree," said Kennicott. Calibree bowed quietly and shook her hand, but before he had finished shaking it he was concentrating upon Kennicott with, "Nice to see you, doctor. Say, don't let me forget to ask you about what you did in that exopthalmic goiter case—that Bohemian woman at Wahkeenyan."

The two men, on the front seat of the car, chanted goiters and ignored her. She did not know it. She was trying to feed her illusion of adventure

by staring at unfamiliar houses. . . . drab cottages, artificial stone bungalows, square painty stolidities with immaculate clapboards and broad
screened porches and tidy grass-plots.

Calibree handed her over to his wife, a thick woman who called her
"dearie," and asked if she was hot and, visibly searching for conversation,
produced, "Let's see, you and the doctor have a Little One, haven't you?"
At dinner Mrs. Calibree served the corned beef and cabbage and looked
steamy, looked like the steamy leaves of cabbage. The men were oblivious
of their wives as they gave the social passwords of Main Street, the orthodox
opinions on weather, crops, and motor cars, then flung away restraint and
gyrated in the debauch of shop-talk. Stroking his chin, drawling in the
ecstasy of being erudite, Kennicott inquired, "Say, doctor, what success have
you had with thyroid for treatment of pains in the legs before child-birth?"

Carol did not resent their assumption that she was too ignorant to be
admitted to masculine mysteries. She was used to it. But the cabbage and
Mrs. Calibree's monotonous "I don't know what we're coming to with all this
difficulty getting hired girls" were gumming her eyes with drowsiness. She
sought to clear them by appealing to Calibree, in a manner of exaggerated
liveliness, "Doctor, have the medical societies in Minnesota ever advocated
legislation for help to nursing mothers?"

Calibree slowly revolved toward her. "Uh—I've never—uh—never looked
into it. I don't believe much in getting mixed up in politics." He turned
squarely from her and, peering earnestly at Kennicott, resumed, "Doctor,
what's been your experience with unilateral pyelonephritis? Buckburn of
Baltimore advocates decapsulation and nephrotomy, but seems to me——"

Not till after two did they rise. In the lee of the stonily mature trio Carol
proceeded to the street fair which added mundane gaiety to the annual rites
of the United and Fraternal Order of Beavers. Beavers, human Beavers, were
everywhere: thirty-second degree Beavers in gray sack suits and decent derbies, more flippant Beavers in crash summer coats and straw hats, rustic Beavers in shirt sleeves and frayed suspenders; but whatever his caste-symbols,
every Beaver was distinguished by an enormous shrimp-colored ribbon
lettered in silver, "Sir Knight and Brother, U. F. O. B., Annual State Convention." On the motherly shirtwaist of each of their wives was a badge,
"Sir Knight's Lady." The Duluth delegation had brought their famous Beaver
amateur band, in Zouave costumes of green velvet jacket, blue trousers, and
scarlet fez. The strange thing was that beneath their scarlet pride the
Zouaves' faces remained those of American business-men, pink, smooth, eye-
glassed; and as they stood playing in a circle, at the corner of Main Street
and Second, as they tootled on fifes or with swelling cheeks blew into cornets,
their eyes remained as owlish as though they were sitting at desks under the
sign "This Is My Busy Day."

Carol had supposed that the Beavers were average citizens organized for
the purposes of getting cheap life-insurance and playing poker at the lodge-
rooms every second Wednesday, but she saw a large poster which proclaimed:

BEAVERS

U. F. O. B.

The greatest influence for good citizenship in the
country. The jolliest aggregation of red-blooded, open-
handed, hustle-em-up good fellows in the world.

Joralemon welcomes you to her hospitable city.

Kennicott read the poster and to Calibree admired, "Strong lodge, the
Beavers. Never joined. Don't know but what I will."

Calibree adumbrated, "They're a good bunch. Good strong lodge. See
that fellow there that's playing the snare drum? He's the smartest wholesale
grocer in Duluth, they say. Guess it would be worth joining. Oh say, are you
doing much insurance examining?"

They went on to the street fair.

Lining one block of Main Street were the "attractions"—two hot-dog
stands, a lemonade and pop-corn stand, a merry-go-round, and booths in
which balls might be thrown at rag dolls, if one wished to throw balls at
rag dolls. The dignified delegates were shy of the booths, but country boys
with brick-red necks and pale-blue ties and bright-yellow shoes, who had
brought sweethearts into town in somewhat dusty and listed Fords, were
wolfing sandwiches, drinking strawberry pop out of bottles, and riding the
revolving crimson and gold horses. They shrieked and giggled; peanut-
roasters whistled; the merry-go-round pounded out monotonous music; the
barkers bawled, "Here's your chance—here's your chance—come on here, boy
—come on here—give that girl a good time—give her a swell time—here's
your chance to win a genuwine gold watch for five cents, half a dime, the
twentieth part of a dollah!" The prairie sun jabbed the unshaded street
with shafts that were like poisonous thorns; the tinny cornices above the
brick stores were glaring; the dull breeze scattered dust on sweaty Beavers
who crawled along in tight scorching new shoes, up two blocks and back,
up two blocks and back, wondering what to do next, working at having a
good time.

Carol's head ached as she trailed behind the unsmiling Calibrees along
the block of booths. She chirruped at Kennicott, "Let's be wild! Let's ride
on the merry-go-round and grab a gold ring!"

Kennicott considered it, and mumbled to Calibree, "Think you folks would
like to stop and try a ride on the merry-go-round?"

Calibree considered it, and mumbled to his wife, "Think you'd like to
stop and try a ride on the merry-go-round?"

Mrs. Calibree smiled in a washed-out manner, and sighed, "Oh no, I don't
believe I care to much, but you folks go ahead and try it."

Calibree stated to Kennicott, "No, I don't believe we care to a whole lot,
but you folks go ahead and try it."

Kennicott summarized the whole case against wildness: "Let's try it some
other time, Carrie."

She gave it up. She looked at the town. She saw that in adventuring from

Main Street, Gopher Prairie, to Main Street, Joralemon, she had not stirred. There were the same two-story brick groceries with lodge-signs above the awnings; the same one-story wooden millinery shop; the same fire-brick garages; the same prairie at the open end of the wide street; the same people wondering whether the levity of eating a hot-dog sandwich would break their taboos.

They reached Gopher Prairie at nine in the evening.

"You look kind of hot," said Kennicott.

"Yes."

"Joralemon is an enterprising town, don't you think so?"

She broke. "No! I think it's an ash-heap."

"Why, Carrie!"

He worried over it for a week. While he ground his plate with his knife as he energetically pursued fragments of bacon, he peeped at her.

# 25

"Carrie's all right. She's finicky, but she'll get over it. But I wish she'd hurry up about it! What she can't understand is that a fellow practising medicine in a small town like this has got to cut out the highbrow stuff, and not spend all his time going to concerts and shining his shoes. (Not but what he might be just as good at all these intellectual and art things as some other folks, if he had the time for it!)" Dr. Will Kennicott was brooding in his office, during a free moment toward the end of the summer afternoon. He hunched down in his tilted desk-chair, undid a button of his shirt, glanced at the state news in the back of the *Journal of the American Medical Association*, dropped the magazine, leaned back with his right thumb hooked in the arm-hole of his vest and his left thumb stroking the back of his hair.

"By golly, she's taking an awful big chance, though. You'd expect her to learn by and by that I won't be a parlor lizard. She says we try to 'make her over.' Well, she's always trying to make me over, from a perfectly good M. D. into a damn poet with a socialist necktie! She'd have a fit if she knew how many women would be willing to cuddle up to Friend Will and comfort him, if he'd give 'em the chance! There's still a few dames that think the old man isn't so darn unattractive! I'm glad I've ducked all that woman-game since I've been married but—— Be switched if sometimes I don't feel tempted to shine up to some girl that has sense enough to take life as it is; some frau that doesn't want to talk Longfellow all the time, but just hold my hand and say, 'You look all in, honey. Take it easy, and don't try to talk.'

"Carrie thinks she's such a whale at analyzing folks. Giving the town the once-over. Telling us where we get off. Why, she'd simply turn up her toes and croak if she found out how much she doesn't know about the high old times a wise guy could have in this burg on the Q.T., if he wasn't faithful to his wife. But I am. At that, no matter what faults she's got, there's nobody here, no, nor in Minn'aplus either, that's as nice-looking and square and bright as Carrie. She ought to of been an artist or a writer or one of those things. But once she took a shot at living here, she ought to stick by it. Pretty—— Lord yes. But cold. She simply doesn't know what passion is. She simply hasn't got an i-dea how hard it is for a full-blooded man to go on pretending to be satisfied with just being endured. It gets awful tiresome, having to feel like a criminal just because I'm normal. She's getting so she doesn't even care for my kissing her. Well——

"I guess I can weather it, same as I did earning my way through school and getting started in practise. But I wonder how long I can stand being an outsider in my own home?"

He sat up at the entrance of Mrs. Dave Dyer. She slumped into a chair and gasped with the heat. He chuckled, "Well, well, Maud, this is fine. Where's the subscription-list? What cause do I get robbed for, this trip?"

"I haven't any subscription-list, Will. I want to see you professionally."

"And you a Christian Scientist? Have you given that up? What next? New Thought or Spiritualism?"

"No, I have not given it up!"

"Strikes me it's kind of a knock on the sisterhood, your coming to see a doctor!"

"No, it isn't. It's just that my faith isn't strong enough yet. So there now! And besides, you *are* kind of consoling, Will. I mean as a man, not just as a doctor. You're so strong and placid."

He sat on the edge of his desk, coatless, his vest swinging open with the thick gold line of his watch-chain across the gap, his hands in his trousers pockets, his big arms bent and easy. As she purred he cocked an interested eye. Maud Dyer was neurotic, religiocentric, faded; her emotions were moist, and her figure was unsystematic—splendid thighs and arms, with thick ankles, and a body that was bulgy in the wrong places. But her milky skin was delicious, her eyes were alive, her chestnut hair shone, and there was a tender slope from her ears to the shadowy place below her jaw.

With unusual solicitude he uttered his stock phrase, "Well, what seems to be the matter, Maud?"

"I've got such a backache all the time. I'm afraid the organic trouble that you treated me for is coming back."

"Any definite signs of it?"

"N-no, but I think you'd better examine me."

"Nope. Don't believe it's necessary, Maud. To be honest, between old friends, I think your troubles are mostly imaginary. I can't really advise you to have an examination."

She flushed, looked out of the window. He was conscious that his voice was not impersonal and even.

She turned quickly. "Will, you always say my troubles are imaginary. Why can't you be scientific? I've been reading an article about these new nerve-specialists, and they claim that lots of 'imaginary' ailments, yes, and lots of real pain, too, are what they call psychoses, and they order a change in a woman's way of living so she can get on a higher plane——"

"Wait! Wait! Whoa-up! Wait now! Don't mix up your Christian Science and your psychology! They're two entirely different fads! You'll be mixing in socialism next! You're as bad as Carrie, with your 'psychoses.' Why, Good Lord, Maud, I could talk about neuroses and psychoses and inhibitions and repressions and complexes just as well as any damn specialist, if I got paid for it, if I was in the city and had the nerve to charge the fees that those fellows do. If a specialist stung you for a hundred-dollar consultation-fee and told you to go to New York to duck Dave's nagging, you'd do it, to save the hundred dollars! But you know me—I'm your neighbor—you see me mowing the lawn—you figure I'm just a plug general practitioner. If I said, 'Go to New York,' Dave and you would laugh your heads off and say, 'Look at the airs Will is putting on. What does he think he is?'

"As a matter of fact, you're right. You have a perfectly well-developed case of repression of sex instinct, and it raises the old Ned with your body. What you need is to get away from Dave and travel, yes, and go to every dog-gone kind of New Thought and Bahai and Swami and Hooptedoodle meeting you can find. I know it, well 's you do. But how can I advise it? Dave would be up here taking my hide off. I'm willing to be family physician and priest and lawyer and plumber and wet-nurse, but I draw the line at making Dave loosen up on money. Too hard a job in weather like this! So, savvy, my dear? Believe it will rain if this heat keeps——"

"But, Will, he'd never give it to me on *my* say-so. He'd never let me go away. You know how Dave is: so jolly and liberal in society, and oh, just *loves* to match quarters, and such a perfect sport if he loses! But at home he pinches a nickel till the buffalo drips blood. I have to nag him for every single dollar."

"Sure, I know, but it's your fight, honey. Keep after him. He'd simply resent my butting in."

He crossed over and patted her shoulder. Outside the window, beyond the fly-screen that was opaque with dust and cottonwood lint, Main Street was hushed except for the impatient throb of a standing motor car. She took his firm hand, pressed his knuckles against her cheek.

"O Will, Dave is so mean and little and noisy—the shrimp! You're so calm. When he's cutting up at parties I see you standing back and watching him—the way a mastiff watches a terrier."

He fought for professional dignity with, "Dave 's not a bad fellow."

Lingeringly she released his hand. "Will, drop round by the house this evening and scold me. Make me be good and sensible. And I'm so lonely."

"If I did, Dave would be there, and we'd have to play cards. It's his evening off from the store."

"No. The clerk just got called to Corinth—mother sick. Dave will be in the store till midnight. Oh, come on over. There's some lovely beer on the ice, and we can sit and talk and be all cool and lazy. That wouldn't be wrong of us, *would* it!"

"No, no, course it wouldn't be wrong. But still, oughtn't to——" He saw Carol, slim black and ivory, cool, scornful of intrigue.

"All right. But I'll be so lonely."

Her throat seemed young, above her loose blouse of muslin and machine-lace.

"Tell you, Maud: I'll drop in just for a minute, if I happen to be called down that way."

"If you'd like," demurely. "O Will, I just want comfort. I know you're all married, and my, such a proud papa, and of course now—— If I could just sit near you in the dusk, and be quiet, and forget Dave! You *will* come?"

"Sure I will!"

"I'll expect you. I'll be lonely if you don't come! Good-by."

He cursed himself: "Darned fool, what 'd I promise to go for? I'll have to keep my promise, or she'll feel hurt. She's a good, decent, affectionate girl, and Dave's a cheap skate, all right. She's got more life to her than Carol has. All my fault, anyway. Why can't I be more cagey, like Calibree and McGanum and the rest of the doctors? Oh, I am, but Maud's such a demanding idiot. Deliberately bamboozling me into going up there tonight. Matter of principle: ought not to let her get away with it. I won't go. I'll call her up and tell her I won't go. Me, with Carrie at home, finest little woman in the world, and a messy-minded female like Maud Dyer—no, *sir!* Though there's no need of hurting her feelings. I may just drop in for a second, to tell her I can't stay. All my fault anyway; ought never to have started in and jollied Maud along in the old days. If it's my fault, I've got no right to punish Maud. I could just drop in for a second and then pretend I had a country call and beat it. Damn nuisance, though, having to fake up excuses. Lord, why can't the women let you alone? Just because once or twice, seven hundred million years ago, you were a poor fool, why can't they let you forget it? Maud's own fault. I'll stay strictly away. Take Carrie to the movies, and forget Maud. . . . But it would be kind of hot at the movies tonight."

He fled from himself. He rammed on his hat, threw his coat over his arm, banged the door, locked it, tramped down-stairs. "I won't go!" he said sturdily and, as he said it, he would have given a good deal to know whether he was going.

He was refreshed, as always, by the familiar windows and faces. It restored his soul to have Sam Clark trustingly bellow, "Better come down to the lake this evening and have a swim, doc. Ain't you going to open your cottage at all, this summer? By golly, we miss you." He noted the progress on the new garage. He had triumphed in the laying of every course of bricks; in them he had seen the growth of the town. His pride was ushered back to its throne by the respectfulness of Oley Sunderquist: "Evenin', doc! The woman is a lot better. That was swell medicine you gave her." He was calmed by the me-

chanicalness of the tasks at home: burning the gray web of a tent-worm on
the wild cherry tree, sealing with gum a cut in the right front tire of the
car, sprinkling the road before the house. The hose was cool to his hands.
As the bright arrows fell with a faint puttering sound, a crescent of blackness
was formed in the gray dust.

Dave Dyer came along.

"Where going, Dave?"

"Down to the store. Just had supper."

"But Thursday 's your night off."

"Sure, but Pete went home. His mother 's supposed to be sick. Gosh,
these clerks you get nowadays—overpay 'em and then they won't work!"

"That's tough, Dave. You'll have to work clear up till twelve, then."

"Yup. Better drop in and have a cigar, if you're downtown."

"Well, I may, at that. May have to go down and see Mrs Champ Perry.
She's ailing. So long, Dave."

Kennicott had not yet entered the house. He was conscious that Carol was
near him, that she was important, that he was afraid of her disapproval; but
he was content to be alone. When he had finished sprinkling he strolled into
the house, up to the baby's room, and cried to Hugh, "Story-time for the
old man, eh?"

Carol was in a low chair, framed and haloed by the window behind her,
an image in pale gold. The baby curled in her lap, his head on her arm,
listening with gravity while she sang from Gene Field:

> 'Tis little Luddy-Dud in the morning—
> 'Tis little Luddy-Dud at night:
> And all day long
> 'Tis the same dear song,
> Of that growing, crowing, knowing little sprite.

Kennicott was enchanted.

"Maud Dyer? I should say not!"

When the current maid bawled up-stairs, "Supper on de table!" Kennicott
was upon his back, flapping his hands in the earnest effort to be a seal,
thrilled by the strength with which his son kicked him. He slipped his arm
about Carol's shoulder; he went down to supper rejoicing that he was
cleansed of perilous stuff. While Carol was putting the baby to bed he sat
on the front steps. Nat Hicks, tailor and roué, came to sit beside him. Between waves of his hand as he drove off mosquitos, Nat whispered, "Say,
doc, you don't feel like imagining you're a bacheldore again, and coming out
for a Time tonight, do you?"

"As how?"

"You know this new dressmaker, Mrs. Swiftwaite?—swell dame with
blondine hair? Well, she's a pretty good goer. Me and Harry Haydock are
going to take her and that fat wren that works in the Bon Ton—nice kid, too
—on an auto ride tonight. Maybe we'll drive down to that farm Harry bought.
We're taking some beer, and some of the smoothest rye you ever laid tongue

to. I'm not predicting none, but if we don't have a picnic, I'll miss my guess."

"Go to it. No skin off my ear, Nat. Think I want to be fifth wheel in the coach?"

"No, but look here: The little Swiftwaite has a friend with her from Winona, dandy looker and some gay bird, and Harry and me thought maybe you'd like to sneak off for one evening."

"No—no——"

"Rats now, doc, forget your everlasting dignity. You used to be a pretty good sport yourself, when you were foot-free."

It may have been the fact that Mrs. Swiftwaite's friend remained to Kennicott an ill-told rumor, it may have been Carol's voice, wistful in the pallid evening as she sang to Hugh, it may have been natural and commendable virtue, but certainly he was positive:

"Nope. I'm married for keeps. Don't pretend to be any saint. Like to get out and raise Cain and shoot a few drinks. But a fellow owes a duty—— Straight now, won't you feel like a sneak when you come back to the missus after your jamboree?"

"Me? My moral in life is, 'What they don't know won't hurt 'em none.' The way to handle wives, like the fellow says, is to catch 'em early, treat 'em rough, and tell 'em nothing!"

"Well, that's your business, I suppose. But I can't get away with it. Besides that—way I figure it, this illicit love-making is the one game that you always lose at. If you do lose, you feel foolish; and if you win, as soon as you find out how little it is that you've been scheming for, why then you lose worse than ever. Nature stinging us, as usual. But at that, I guess a lot of wives in this burg would be surprised if they knew everything that goes on behind their backs, eh, Nattie?"

"*Would* they! Say, boy! If the good wives knew what some of the boys get away with when they go down to the Cities, why, they'd throw a fit! Sure you won't come, doc? Think of getting all cooled off by a good long drive, and then the lov-e-ly Swiftwaite's white hand mixing you a good stiff highball!"

"Nope. Nope. Sorry. Guess I won't," grumbled Kennicott.

He was glad that Nat showed signs of going. But he was restless. He heard Carol on the stairs. "Come have a seat—have the whole earth!" he shouted jovially.

She did not answer his joviality. She sat on the porch, rocked silently, then sighed, "So many mosquitos out here. You haven't had the screen fixed."

As though he was testing her he said quietly, "Head aching again?"

"Oh, not much, but—— This maid is *so* slow to learn. I have to show her everything. I had to clean most of the silver myself. And Hugh was so bad all afternoon. He whined so. Poor soul, he was hot, but he did wear me out."

"Uh—— You usually want to get out. Like to walk down to the lake shore? (The girl can stay home.) Or go to the movies? Come on, let's go to the movies! Or shall we jump in the car and run out to Sam's, for a swim?"

"If you don't mind, dear, I'm afraid I'm rather tired."

"Why don't you sleep down-stairs tonight, on the couch? Be cooler. I'm going to bring down my mattress. Come on! Keep the old man company. Can't tell—I might get scared of burglars. Lettin' little fellow like me stay all alone by himself!"

"It's sweet of you to think of it, but I like my own room so much. But you go ahead and do it, dear. Why don't you sleep on the couch, instead of putting your mattress on the floor? Well—— I believe I'll run in and read for just a second—want to look at the last *Vogue*—and then perhaps I'll go by-by. Unless you want me, dear? Of course if there's anything you really *want* me for——?"

"No. No. . . . Matter of fact, I really ought to run down and see Mrs. Champ Perry. She's ailing. So you skip in and—— May drop in at the drug store. If I'm not home when you get sleepy, don't wait up for me."

He kissed her, rambled off, nodded to Jim Howland, stopped indifferently to speak to Mrs. Terry Gould. But his heart was racing, his stomach was constricted. He walked more slowly. He reached Dave Dyer's yard. He glanced in. On the porch, sheltered by a wild-grape vine, was the figure of a woman in white. He heard the swing-couch creak as she sat up abruptly, peered, then leaned back and pretended to relax.

"Be nice to have some cool beer. Just drop in for a second," he insisted, as he opened the Dyer gate.

## II

Mrs. Bogart was calling upon Carol, protected by Aunt Bessie Smail.

"Have you heard about this awful woman that's supposed to have come here to do dressmaking—a Mrs. Swiftwaite—awful peroxide blonde?" moaned Mrs. Bogart. "They say there's some of the awfullest goings-on at her house —mere boys and old gray-headed rips sneaking in there evenings and drinking licker and every kind of goings-on. We women can't never realize the carnal thoughts in the hearts of men. I tell you, even though I been acquainted with Will Kennicott almost since he was a mere boy, seems like, I wouldn't trust even him! Who knows what designin' women might tempt him! Especially a doctor, with women rushin' in to see him at his office and all! You know I never hint around, but haven't you felt that——"

Carol was furious. "I don't pretend that Will has no faults. But one thing I do know: He's as simple-hearted about what you call 'goings-on' as a babe. And if he ever were such a sad dog as to look at another woman, I certainly hope he'd have spirit enough to do the tempting, and not be coaxed into it, as in your depressing picture!"

"Why, what a wicked thing to say, Carrie!" from Aunt Bessie.

"No, I mean it! Oh, of course, I don't mean it! But—— I know every thought in his head so well that he couldn't hide anything even if he wanted to. Now this morning—— He was out late, last night; he had to go see Mrs. Perry, who is ailing, and then fix a man's hand, and this morning he was so quiet and thoughtful at breakfast and——" She leaned forward, breathed dramatically to the two perched harpies, "What do you suppose he was thinking of?"

"What?" trembled Mrs. Bogart.

"Whether the grass needs cutting, probably! There, there! Don't mind my naughtiness. I have some fresh-made raisin cookies for you."

# 26

Carol's liveliest interest was in her walks with the baby. Hugh wanted to know what the box-elder tree said, and what the Ford garage said, and what the big cloud said, and she told him, with a feeling that she was not in the least making up stories, but discovering the souls of things. They had an especial fondness for the hitching-post in front of the mill. It was a brown post, stout and agreeable; the smooth leg of it held the sunlight, while its neck, grooved by hitching-straps, tickled one's fingers. Carol had never been awake to the earth except as a show of changing color and great satisfying masses; she had lived in people and in ideas about having ideas; but Hugh's questions made her attentive to the comedies of sparrows, robins, blue jays, yellowhammers; she regained her pleasure in the arching flight of swallows, and added to it a solicitude about their nests and family squabbles.

She forgot her seasons of boredom. She said to Hugh, "We're two fat disreputable old minstrels roaming round the world," and he echoed her, "Roamin' round—roamin' round."

The high adventure, the secret place to which they both fled joyously, was the house of Miles and Bea and Olaf Bjornstam.

Kennicott steadily disapproved of the Bjornstams. He protested, "What do you want to talk to that crank for?" He hinted that a former "Swede hired girl" was low company for the son of Dr. Will Kennicott. She did not explain. She did not quite understand it herself; did not know that in the Bjornstams she found her friends, her club, her sympathy, and her ration of blessed cynicism. For a time the gossip of Juanita Haydock and the Jolly Seventeen had been a refuge from the droning of Aunt Bessie, but the relief had not continued. The young matrons made her nervous. They talked so loud, always so loud. They filled a room with clashing cackle; their jests and gags they repeated nine times over. Unconsciously, she had discarded the Jolly Seventeen, Guy Pollock, Vida, and every one save Mrs. Dr. Westlake and the friends whom she did not clearly know as friends—the Bjornstams.

To Hugh, the Red Swede was the most heroic and powerful person in the world. With unrestrained adoration he trotted after while Miles fed the cows, chased his one pig—an animal of lax and migratory instincts—or dramatically slaughtered a chicken. And to Hugh, Olaf was lord among mortal men, less stalwart than the old monarch, King Miles, but more understanding of the relations and values of things, of small sticks, lone playing-cards, and irretrievably injured hoops.

Carol saw, though she did not admit, that Olaf was not only more beautiful than her own dark child, but more gracious. Olaf was a Norse chieftain: straight, sunny-haired, large-limbed, resplendently amiable to his subjects. Hugh was a vulgarian; a bustling business man. It was Hugh that bounced and said "Let's play"; Olaf that opened luminous blue eyes and agreed "All right," in condescending gentleness. If Hugh batted him—and Hugh did bat him—Olaf was unafraid but shocked. In magnificent solitude he marched toward the house, while Hugh bewailed his sin and the overclouding of august favor.

The two friends played with an imperial chariot which Miles had made out of a starch-box and four red spools; together they stuck switches into a mouse-hole, with vast satisfaction though entirely without known results.

Bea, the chubby and humming Bea, impartially gave cookies and scoldings to both children, and if Carol refused a cup of coffee and a wafer of buttered *knäckebröd*, she was desolated.

Miles had done well with his dairy. He had six cows, two hundred chickens, a cream separator, a Ford truck. In the spring he had built a two-room addition to his shack. That illustrious building was to Hugh a carnival. Uncle Miles did the most spectacular, unexpected things: ran up the ladder; stood on the ridge-pole, waving a hammer and singing something about "To arms, my citizens"; nailed shingles faster than Aunt Bessie could iron handkerchiefs; and lifted a two-by-six with Hugh riding on one end and Olaf on the other. Uncle Miles's most ecstatic trick was to make figures not on paper but right on a new pine board, with the broadest softest pencil in the world. There was a thing worth seeing!

The tools! In his office Father had tools fascinating in their shininess and curious shapes, but they were sharp, they were something called sterilized, and they distinctly were not for boys to touch. In fact it was a good dodge to volunteer "I must not touch," when you looked at the tools on the glass shelves in Father's office. But Uncle Miles, who was a person altogether superior to Father, let you handle all his kit except the saws. There was a hammer with a silver head; there was a metal thing like a big L; there was a magic instrument, very precious, made out of costly red wood and gold, with a tube which contained a drop—no, it wasn't a drop, it was a nothing, which lived in the water, but the nothing *looked* like a drop, and it ran in a frightened way up and down the tube, no matter how cautiously you tilted the magic instrument. And there were nails, very different and clever—big valiant spikes, middle-sized ones which were not very interesting, and shingle-nails much jollier than the fussed-up fairies in the yellow book.

II

While he had worked on the addition Miles had talked frankly to Carol. He admitted now that so long as he stayed in Gopher Prairie he would remain a pariah. Bea's Lutheran friends were as much offended by his agnostic gibes as the merchants by his radicalism. "And I can't seem to keep my mouth shut. I think I'm being a baa-lamb, and not springing any theories wilder than 'c-a-t spells cat,' but when folks have gone, I re'lize I've been stepping on their pet religious corns. Oh, the mill foreman keeps dropping in, and that Danish shoemaker, and one fellow from Elder's factory, and a few Svenskas, but you know Be: big good-hearted wench like her wants a lot of folks around—likes to fuss over 'em—never satisfied unless she tiring herself out making coffee for somebody.

"Once she kidnapped me and drug me to the Methodist Church. I goes in, pious as Widow Bogart, and sits still and never cracks a smile while the preacher is favoring us with his misinformation on evolution. But afterwards, when the old stalwarts were pumphandling everybody at the door and calling 'em 'Brother' and 'Sister,' they let me sail right by with nary a clinch. They figure I'm the town badman. Always will be, I guess. It'll have to be Olaf who goes on. And sometimes—— Blamed if I don't feel like coming out and saying, 'I've been conservative. Nothing to it. Now I'm going to start something in these rotten one-horse lumber-camps west of town.' But Be's got me hynotized. Lord, Mrs. Kennicott, do you re'lize what a jolly, square, faithful woman she is? And I love Olaf—— Oh well, I won't go and get sentimental on you.

"Course I've had thoughts of pulling up stakes and going West. Maybe if they didn't know it beforehand, they wouldn't find out I'd ever been guilty of trying to think for myself. But—oh, I've worked hard, and built up this dairy business, and I hate to start all over again, and move Be and the kid into another one-room shack. That's how they get us! Encourage us to be thrifty and own our own houses, and then, by golly, they've got us; they know we won't dare risk everything by committing lez—what is it? lez majesty?—I mean they know we won't be hinting around that if we had a co-operative bank, we could get along without Stowbody. Well—— As long as I can sit and play pinochle with Be, and tell whoppers to Olaf about his daddy's adventures in the woods, and how he snared a wapaloosie and knew Paul Bunyan, why, I don't mind being a bum. It's just for them that I mind. Say! Say! Don't whisper a word to Be, but when I get this addition done, I'm going to buy her a phonograph!"

He did.

While she was busy with the activities her work-hungry muscles found—washing, ironing, mending, baking, dusting, preserving, plucking a chicken, painting the sink; tasks which, because she was Miles's full partner, were exciting and creative—Bea listened to the phonograph records with rapture like that of cattle in a warm stable. The addition gave her a kitchen with a bedroom above. The original one-room shack was now a living-room, with the phonograph, a genuine leather-upholstered golden-oak rocker, and a picture of Governor John Johnson.

In late July Carol went to the Bjornstams' desirous of a chance to express her opinion of Beavers and Calibrees and Joralemons. She found Olaf abed, restless from a slight fever, and Bea flushed and dizzy but trying to keep up her work. She lured Miles aside and worried:

"They don't look at all well. What's the matter?"

"Their stomachs are out of whack. I wanted to call in Doc Kennicott, but Be thinks the doc doesn't like us—she thinks maybe he's sore because you come down here. But I'm getting worried."

"I'm going to call the doctor at once."

She yearned over Olaf. His lambent eyes were stupid, he moaned, he rubbed his forehead.

"Have they been eating something that's been bad for them?" she fluttered to Miles.

"Might be bum water. I'll tell you: We used to get our water at Oscar Eklund's place, over across the street, but Oscar kept dinging at me, and hinting I was a tightwad not to dig a well of my own. One time he said, 'Sure, you socialists are great on divvying up other folks' money—and water!' I knew if he kept it up there'd be a fuss, and I ain't safe to have around, once a fuss starts; I'm likely to forget myself and let loose with a punch in the snoot. I offered to pay Oscar but he refused—he'd rather have the chance to kid me. So I starts getting water down at Mrs. Fageros's, in the hollow there, and I don't believe it's real good. Figuring to dig my own well this fall."

One scarlet word was before Carol's eyes while she listened. She fled to Kennicott's office. He gravely heard her out, nodded, said, "Be right over."

He examined Bea and Olaf. He shook his head. "Yes. Looks to me like typhoid."

"Golly, I've seen typhoid in lumber-camps," groaned Miles, all the strength dripping out of him. "Have they got it very bad?"

"Oh, we'll take good care of them," said Kennicott, and for the first time in their acquaintance he smiled on Miles and clapped his shoulder.

"Won't you need a nurse?" demanded Carol.

"Why——" To Miles, Kennicott hinted, "Couldn't you get Bea's cousin, Tina?"

"She's down at the old folks', in the country."

"Then let me do it!" Carol insisted. "They need some one to cook for them, and isn't it good to give them sponge baths, in typhoid?"

"Yes. All right." Kennicott was automatic; he was the official, the physician. "I guess probably it would be hard to get a nurse here in town just now. Mrs. Stiver is busy with an obstetrical case, and that town nurse of yours is off on vacation, ain't she? All right, Bjornstam can spell you at night."

All week, from eight each morning till midnight, Carol fed them, bathed them, smoothed sheets, took temperatures. Miles refused to let her cook. Terrified, pallid, noiseless in stocking feet, he did the kitchen work and the sweeping, his big red hands awkwardly careful. Kennicott came in three times a day, unchangingly tender and hopeful in the sick-room, evenly polite to Miles.

Carol understood how great was her love for her friends. It bore her through; it made her arm steady and tireless to bathe them. What exhausted her was the sight of Bea and Olaf turned into flaccid invalids, uncomfortably flushed after taking food, begging for the healing of sleep at night.

During the second week Olaf's powerful legs were flabby. Spots of a viciously delicate pink came out on his chest and back. His cheeks sank. He looked frightened. His tongue was brown and revolting. His confident voice dwindled to a bewildered murmur, ceaseless and racking.

Bea had stayed on her feet too long at the beginning. The moment Kennicott had ordered her to bed she had begun to collapse. One early evening she startled them by screaming, in an intense abdominal pain, and within half an hour she was in a delirium. Till dawn Carol was with her, and not all of Bea's groping through the blackness of half-delirious pain was so pitiful to Carol as the way in which Miles silently peered into the room from the top of the narrow stairs. Carol slept three hours next morning, and ran back. Bea was altogether delirious but she muttered nothing save, "Olaf—ve have such a good time——"

At ten, while Carol was preparing an ice-bag in the kitchen, Miles answered a knock. At the front door she saw Vida Sherwin, Maud Dyer, and Mrs. Zitterel, wife of the Baptist pastor. They were carrying grapes, and women's-magazines, magazines with high-colored pictures and optimistic fiction.

"We just heard your wife was sick. We've come to see if there isn't something we can do," chirruped Vida.

Miles looked steadily at the three woman. "You're too late. You can't do nothing now. Bea's always kind of hoped that you folks would come see her. She wanted to have a chance and be friends. She used to sit waiting for somebody to knock. I've seen her sitting here, waiting. Now—— Oh, you ain't worth God-damning." He shut the door.

All day Carol watched Olaf's strength oozing. He was emaciated. His ribs were grim clear lines, his skin was clammy, his pulse was feeble but terrifyingly rapid. It beat—beat—beat in a drum-roll of death. Late that afternoon he sobbed, and died.

Bea did not know it. She was delirious. Next morning, when she went, she did not know that Olaf would no longer swing his lath sword on the door-step, no longer rule his subjects of the cattle-yard; that Miles's son would not go East to college.

Miles, Carol, Kennicott were silent. They washed the bodies together, their eyes veiled.

"Go home now and sleep. You're pretty tired. I can't ever pay you back for what you done," Miles whispered to Carol.

"Yes. But I'll be back here tomorrow. Go with you to the funeral," she said laboriously.

When the time for the funeral came, Carol was in bed, collapsed. She assumed that neighbors would go. They had not told her that word of Miles's rebuff to Vida had spread through town, a cyclonic fury.

It was only by chance that, leaning on her elbow in bed, she glanced through the window and saw the funeral of Bea and Olaf. There was no music, no carriages. There was only Miles Bjornstam, in his black wedding-suit, walking quite alone, head down, behind the shabby hearse that bore the bodies of his wife and baby.

An hour after, Hugh came into her room crying, and when she said as cheerily as she could, "What is it, dear?" he besought, "Mummy, I want to go play with Olaf."

That afternoon Juanita Haydock dropped in to brighten Carol. She said, "Too bad about this Bea that was your hired girl. But I don't waste any sympathy on that man of hers. Everybody says he drank too much, and treated his family awful, and that's how they got sick."

# 27

A letter from Raymie Wutherspoon, in France, said that he had been sent to the front, been slightly wounded, been made a captain. From Vida's pride Carol sought to draw a stimulant to rouse her from depression.

Miles had sold his dairy. He had several thousand dollars. To Carol he said good-by with a mumbled word, a harsh hand-shake, "Going to buy a farm in northern Alberta—far off from folks as I can get." He turned sharply away, but he did not walk with his former spring. His shoulders seemed old.

It was said that before he went he cursed the town. There was talk of arresting him, of riding him on a rail. It was rumored that at the station old Champ Perry rebuked him, "You better not come back here. We've got respect for your dead, but we haven't got any for a blasphemer and a traitor that won't do anything for his country and only bought one Liberty Bond."

Some of the people who had been at the station declared that Miles made some dreadful seditious retort: something about loving German workmen more than American bankers; but others asserted that he couldn't find one word with which to answer the veteran; that he merely sneaked up on the platform of the train. He must have felt guilty, everybody agreed, for as the train left town, a farmer saw him standing in the vestibule and looking out.

His house—with the addition which he had built four months ago—was very near the track on which his train passed.

When Carol went there, for the last time, she found Olaf's chariot with its red spool wheel standing in the sunny corner beside the stable. She wondered if a quick eye could have noticed it from a train.

That day and that week she went reluctantly to Red Cross work; she stitched and packed silently, while Vida read the war bulletins. And she said nothing at all when Kennicott commented, "From what Champ says, I guess Bjornstam was a bad egg, after all. In spite of Bea, don't know but what the citizens' committee ought to have forced him to be patriotic—let on like they could send him to jail if he didn't volunteer and come through for bonds and the Y. M. C. A. They've worked that stunt fine with all these German farmers."

II

She found no inspiration but she did find a dependable kindness in Mrs. Westlake, and at last she yielded to the old woman's receptivity and had relief in sobbing the story of Bea.

Guy Pollock she often met on the street, but he was merely a pleasant voice which said things about Charles Lamb and sunsets.

Her most positive experience was the revelation of Mrs. Flickerbaugh, the tall, thin, twitchy wife of the attorney. Carol encountered her at the drug store.

"Walking?" snapped Mrs. Flickerbaugh.

"Why, yes."

"Humph. Guess you're the only female in this town that retains the use of her legs. Come home and have a cup o' tea with me."

Because she had nothing else to do, Carol went. But she was uncomfortable in the presence of the amused stares which Mrs. Flickerbaugh's raiment drew. Today, in reeking early August, she wore a man's cap, a skinny fur like a dead cat, a necklace of imitation pearls, a scabrous satin blouse, and a thick cloth skirt hiked up in front.

"Come in. Sit down. Stick the baby in that rocker. Hope you don't mind the house looking like a rat's nest. You don't like this town. Neither do I," said Mrs. Flickerbaugh.

"Why——"

"Course you don't!"

"Well then, I don't! But I'm sure that some day I'll find some solution. Probably I'm a hexagonal peg. Solution: find the hexagonal hole." Carol was very brisk.

"How do you know you ever will find it?"

"There's Mrs. Westlake. She's naturally a big-city woman—she ought to have a lovely old house in Philadelphia or Boston—but she escapes by being absorbed in reading."

"You be satisfied to never do anything but read?"

"No, but—— Heavens, one can't go on hating a town always!"

"Why not? I can! I've hated it for thirty-two years. I'll die here—and I'll hate it till I die. I ought to have been a business woman. I had a good deal of talent for tending to figures. All gone now. Some folks think I'm crazy.

Guess I am. Sit and grouch. Go to church and sing hymns. Folks think I'm religious. Tut! Trying to forget washing and ironing and mending socks. Want an office of my own, and sell things. Julius never hear of it. Too late."

Carol sat on the gritty couch, and sank into fear. Could this drabness of life keep up forever, then? Would she some day so despise herself and her neighbors that she too would walk Main Street an old skinny eccentric woman in a mangy cat's-fur? As she crept home she felt that the trap had finally closed. She went into the house, a frail small woman, still winsome but hopeless of eye as she staggered with the weight of the drowsy boy in her arms.

She sat alone on the porch, that evening. It seemed that Kennicott had to make a professional call on Mrs. Dave Dyer.

Under the stilly boughs and the black gauze of dusk the street was meshed in silence. There was but the hum of motor tires crunching the road, the creak of a rocker on the Howlands' porch, the slap of a hand attacking a mosquito, a heat-weary conversation starting and dying, the precise rhythm of crickets, the thud of moths against the screen—sounds that were a distilled silence. It was a street beyond the end of the world, beyond the boundaries of hope. Though she should sit here forever, no brave procession, no one who was interesting, would be coming by. It was tediousness made tangible, a street builded of lassitude and of futility.

Myrtle Cass appeared, with Cy Bogart. She giggled and bounced when Cy tickled her ear in village love. They strolled with the half-dancing gait of lovers, kicking their feet out sideways or shuffling a dragging jig, and the concrete walk sounded to the broken two-four rhythm. Their voices had a dusky turbulence. Suddenly, to the woman rocking on the porch of the doctor's house, the night came alive, and she felt that everywhere in the darkness panted an ardent quest which she was missing as she sank back to wait for—— There must be something.

# 28

It was at a supper of the Jolly Seventeen in August that Carol heard of "Elizabeth," from Mrs. Dave Dyer.

Carol was fond of Maud Dyer, because she had been particularly agreeable lately; had obviously repented of the nervous distaste which she had once shown. Maud patted her hand when they met, and asked about Hugh.

Kennicott said that he was "kind of sorry for the girl, some ways; she's too darn emotional, but still, Dave is sort of mean to her." He was polite to poor Maud when they all went down to the cottages for a swim. Carol was proud of that sympathy in him, and now she took pains to sit with their new friend.

Mrs. Dyer was bubbling, "Oh, have you folks heard about this young fellow that's just come to town that the boys call 'Elizabeth'? He's working in Nat Hicks's tailor shop. I bet he doesn't make eighteen a week, but my! isn't he the perfect lady though! He talks so refined, and oh, the lugs he puts on—belted coat, and piqué collar with a gold pin, and socks to match his necktie, and honest—you won't believe this, but I got it straight—this fellow, you know he's staying at Mrs. Gurrey's punk old boarding-house, and they say he asked Mrs. Gurrey if he ought to put on a dress-suit for supper! Imagine! Can you beat that? And him nothing but a Swede tailor —Erik Valborg his name is. But he used to be in a tailor shop in Minneapolis (they do say he's a smart needle-pusher, at that) and he tries to let on that he's a regular city fellow. They say he tries to make people think he's a poet —carries books around and pretends to read 'em. Myrtle Cass says she met him at a dance, and he was mooning around all over the place, and he asked her did she like flowers and poetry and music and everything; he spieled like he was a regular United States Senator; and Myrtle—she's a devil, that girl, ha! ha!—she kidded him along, and got him going, and honest, what d'you think he said? He said he didn't find any intellectual companionship in this town. Can you *beat* it? Imagine! And him a Swede tailor! My! And they say he's the most awful mollycoddle—looks just like a girl. The boys call him 'Elizabeth,' and they stop him and ask about the books he lets on to have read, and he goes and tells them, and they take it all in and jolly him terribly, and he never gets onto the fact they're kidding him. Oh, I think it's just *too* funny!"

The Jolly Seventeen laughed, and Carol laughed with them. Mrs. Jack Elder added that this Erik Valborg had confided to Mrs. Gurrey that he would "love to design clothes for women." Imagine! Mrs. Harvey Dillon had had a glimpse of him, but honestly, she'd thought he was awfully handsome. This was instantly controverted by Mrs. B. J. Gougerling, wife of the banker. Mrs. Gougerling had had, she reported, a good look at this Valborg fellow. She and B. J. had been motoring, and passed "Elizabeth" out by McGruder's Bridge. He was wearing the awfullest clothes, with the waist pinched in like a girl's. He was sitting on a rock doing nothing, but when he heard the Gougerling car coming he snatched a book out of his pocket, and as they went by he pretended to be reading it, to show off. And he wasn't really good-looking —just kind of soft, as B. J. had pointed out.

When the husbands came they joined in the exposé. "My name is Elizabeth. I'm the celebrated musical tailor. The skirts fall for me by the thou. Do I get some more veal loaf?" merrily shrieked Dave Dyer. He had some admirable stories about the tricks the town youngsters had played on Valborg. They had dropped a decaying perch into his pocket. They had pinned on his back a sign, "I'm the prize boob, kick me."

Glad of any laughter, Carol joined the frolic, and surprised them by crying,

"Dave, I do think you're the dearest thing since you got your hair cut!" That was an excellent sally. Everybody applauded. Kennicott looked proud.

She decided that sometime she really must go out of her way to pass Hicks's shop and see this freak.

II

She was at Sunday morning service at the Baptist Church, in a solemn row with her husband, Hugh, Uncle Whittier, Aunt Bessie.

Despite Aunt Bessie's nagging the Kennicotts rarely attended church. The doctor asserted, "Sure, religion is a fine influence—got to have it to keep the lower classes in order—fact, it's the only thing that appeals to a lot of those fellows and makes 'em respect the rights of property. And I guess this theology is O.K.; lot of wise old coots figured it all out, and they knew more about it than we do." He believed in the Christian religion, and never thought about it; he believed in the church, and seldom went near it; he was shocked by Carol's lack of faith, and wasn't quite sure what was the nature of the faith that she lacked.

Carol herself was an uneasy and dodging agnostic.

When she ventured to Sunday School and heard the teachers droning that the genealogy of Shamsherai was a valuable ethical problem for children to think about; when she experimented with Wednesday prayer-meeting and listened to store-keeping elders giving their unvarying weekly testimony in primitive erotic symbols and such gory Chaldean phrases as "washed in the blood of the lamb" and "a vengeful God"; when Mrs. Bogart boasted that through his boyhood she had made Cy confess nightly upon the basis of the Ten Commandments; then Carol was dismayed to find the Christian religion, in America, in the twentieth century, as abnormal as Zoroastrianism —without the splendor. But when she went to church suppers and felt the friendliness, saw the gaiety with which the sisters served cold ham and scalloped potatoes; when Mrs. Champ Perry cried to her, on an afternoon call, "My dear, if you just knew how happy it makes you to come into abiding grace," then Carol found the humanness behind the sanguinary and alien theology. Always she perceived that the churches—Methodist, Baptist, Congregational, Catholic, all of them—which had seemed so unimportant to the judge's home in her childhood, so isolated from the city struggle in St. Paul, were still, in Gopher Prairie, the strongest of the forces compelling respectability.

This August Sunday she had been tempted by the announcement that the Reverend Edmund Zitterel would preach on the topic "America, Face Your Problems!" With the great war, workmen in every nation showing a desire to control industries, Russia hinting a leftward revolution against Kerensky, woman suffrage coming, there seemed to be plenty of problems for the Reverend Mr. Zitterel to call on America to face. Carol gathered her family and trotted off behind Uncle Whittier.

The congregation faced the heat with informality. Men with highly plastered hair, so painfully shaved that their faces looked sore, removed their coats, sighed, and unbuttoned two buttons of their uncreased Sunday vests. Large-bosomed, white-bloused, hot-necked, spectacled matrons—the Mothers in Israel, pioneers and friends of Mrs. Champ Perry—waved their palm-leaf fans in a steady rhythm. Abashed boys slunk into the rear pews and giggled, while milky little girls, up front with their mothers, self-consciously kept from turning around.

The church was half barn and half Gopher Prairie parlor. The streaky brown wallpaper was broken in its dismal sweep only by framed texts, "Come unto Me" and "The Lord is My Shepherd," by a list of hymns, and by a crimson and green diagram, staggeringly drawn upon hemp-colored paper, indicating the alarming ease with which a young man may descend from Palaces of Pleasure and the House of Pride to Eternal Damnation. But the varnished oak pews and the new red carpet and the three large chairs on the platform, behind the bare reading-stand, were all of a rocking-chair comfort.

Carol was civic and neighborly and commendable today. She beamed and bowed. She trolled out with the others the hymn:

> How pleasant 'tis on Sabbath morn
> To gather in the church,
> And there I'll have no carnal thoughts,
> Nor sin shall me besmirch.

With a rustle of starched linen skirts and stiff shirt-fronts, the congregation sat down, and gave heed to the Reverend Mr. Zitterel. The priest was a thin, swart, intense young man with a bang. He wore a black sack suit and a lilac tie. He smote the enormous Bible on the reading-stand, vociferated, "Come, let us reason together," delivered a prayer informing Almighty God of the news of the past week, and began to reason.

It proved that the only problems which America had to face were Mormonism and Prohibition:

"Don't let any of these self-conceited fellows that are always trying to stir up trouble deceive you with the belief that there's anything to all these smart-aleck movements to let the unions and the Farmers' Nonpartisan League kill all our initiative and enterprise by fixing wages and prices. There isn't any movement that amounts to a whoop without it's got a moral background. And let me tell you that while folks are fussing about what they call 'economics' and 'socialism' and 'science' and a lot of things that are nothing in the world but a disguise for atheism, the Old Satan is busy spreading his secret net and tentacles out there in Utah, under his guise of Joe Smith or Brigham Young or whoever their leaders happen to be today, it doesn't make any difference, and they're making game of the Old Bible that has led this American people through its manifold trials and tribulations to its firm position as the fulfilment of the prophecies and the recognized leader of all nations. 'Sit thou on my right hand till I make thine enemies the footstool of my feet,' said the Lord of Hosts, Acts II, the thirty-fourth verse—and let me tell you right now, you got to get up a good deal earlier in the morning than you get up even when you're going fishing, if you want to be smarter than the Lord, who has shown us the straight and narrow way, and he that passeth therefrom is in eternal peril and, to return to this vital and terrible subject of Mormonism—and as I say, it is terrible to realize how little attention is given to this evil right here in our midst and on our very doorstep, as it were—it's a shame and a disgrace that the Congress of these United States spends all its time talking about inconsequential financial matters that ought to be left to the Treasury Department, as I understand it, instead of arising in their might and passing a law that any one admitting he is a Mormon shall simply be deported and as it were kicked out of this free country in which we haven't got any room for polygamy and the tyrannies of Satan.

"And, to digress for a moment, especially as there are more of them in this state than there are Mormons, though you never can tell what will happen with this vain generation of young girls, that think more about wearing silk stockings than about minding their mothers and learning to bake a good loaf of bread, and many of them listening to these sneaking Mormon missionaries—and I actually heard one of them talking right out on a street-corner in Duluth, a few years ago, and the officers of the law not protesting —but still, as they are a smaller but more immediate problem, let me stop for just a moment to pay my respects to these Seventh-Day Adventists. Not that they are immoral, I don't mean, but when a body of men go on insisting that Saturday is the Sabbath, after Christ himself has clearly indicated the new dispensation, then I think the legislature ought to step in——"

At this point Carol awoke.

She got through three more minutes by studying the face of a girl in the pew across: a sensitive unhappy girl whose longing poured out with intimidating self-revelation as she worshiped Mr. Zitterel. Carol wondered who the girl was. She had seen her at church suppers. She considered how many of the three thousand people in the town she did not know; to how many of them the Thanatopsis and the Jolly Seventeen were icy social peaks; how many of them might be toiling through boredom thicker than her own—with greater courage.

She examined her nails. She read two hymns. She got some satisfaction out of rubbing an itching knuckle. She pillowed on her shoulder the head of the baby who, after killing time in the same manner as his mother, was so fortunate as to fall asleep. She read the introduction, title-page, and acknowledgment of copyrights, in the hymnal. She tried to evolve a philosophy which would explain why Kennicott could never tie his scarf so that it would reach the top of the gap in his turn-down collar.

There were no other diversions to be found in the pew. She glanced back at the congregation. She thought that it would be amiable to bow to Mrs. Champ Perry.

Her slow turning head stopped, galvanized.

Across the aisle, two rows back, was a strange young man who shone among the cud-chewing citizens like a visitant from the sun—amber curls, low forehead, fine nose, chin smooth but not raw from Sabbath shaving. His lips startled her. The lips of men in Gopher Prairie are flat in the face, straight and grudging. The stranger's mouth was arched, the upper lip short. He wore a brown jersey coat, a delft-blue bow, a white silk shirt, white flannel trousers. He suggested the ocean beach, a tennis court, anything but the sun-blistered utility of Main Street.

A visitor from Minneapolis, here for business? No. He wasn't a business man. He was a poet. Keats was in his face, and Shelley, and Arthur Upson, whom she had once seen in Minneapolis. He was at once too sensitive and too sophisticated to touch business as she knew it in Gopher Prairie.

With restrained amusement he was analyzing the noisy Mr. Zitterel. Carol was ashamed to have this spy from the Great World hear the pastor's maundering. She felt responsible for the town. She resented his gaping at their private rites. She flushed, turned away. But she continued to feel his presence.

How could she meet him? She must! For an hour of talk. He was all that she was hungry for. She could not let him get away without a word—and she would have to. She pictured, and ridiculed, herself as walking up to him and remarking, "I am sick with the Village Virus. Will you please tell me what people are saying and playing in New York?" She pictured, and groaned over, the expression of Kennicott if she should say, "Why wouldn't it be reasonable for you, my soul, to ask that complete stranger in the brown jersey coat to come to supper tonight?"

She brooded, not looking back. She warned herself that she was probably exaggerating; that no young man could have all these exalted qualities. Wasn't he too obviously smart, too glossy-new? Like a movie actor. Probably he was a traveling salesman who sang tenor and fancied himself in imitations of Newport clothes and spoke of "the swellest business proposition that ever came down the pike." In a panic she peered at him. No! This was no hustling salesman, this boy with the curving Grecian lips and the serious eyes.

She rose after the service, carefully taking Kennicott's arm and smiling at him in a mute assertion that she was devoted to him no matter what happened. She followed the Mystery's soft brown jersey shoulders out of the church.

Fatty Hicks, the shrill and puffy son of Nat, flapped his hand at the beautiful stranger and jeered, "How's the kid? All dolled up like a plush horse today, ain't we!"

Carol was exceeding sick. Her herald from the outside was Erik Valborg, "Elizabeth." Apprentice tailor! Gasoline and hot goose! Mending dirty jackets! Respectfully holding a tape-measure about a paunch!

And yet, she insisted, this boy was also himself.

### III

They had Sunday dinner with the Smails, in a dining-room which centered about a fruit and flower piece and a crayon-enlargement of Uncle Whittier.

Carol did not heed Aunt Bessie's fussing in regard to Mrs. Robert B. Schminke's bead necklace and Whittier's error in putting on the striped pants, day like this. She did not taste the shreds of roast pork. She said vacuously:

"Uh—Will, I wonder if that young man in the white flannel trousers, at church this morning, was this Valborg person that they're all talking about?"

"Yump. That's him. Wasn't that the darndest get-up he had on!" Kennicott scratched at a white smear on his hard gray sleeve.

"It wasn't so bad. I wonder where he comes from? He seems to have lived in cities a good deal. Is he from the East?"

"The East? Him? Why, he comes from a farm right up north here, just this side of Jefferson. I know his father slightly—Adolph Valborg—typical cranky old Swede farmer."

"Oh, really?" blandly.

"Believe he has lived in Minneapolis for quite some time, though. Learned his trade there. And I will say he's bright, some ways. Reads a lot. Pollock says he takes more books out of the library than anybody else in town. Huh! He's kind of like you in that!"

The Smails and Kennicott laughed very much at this sly jest. Uncle Whittier seized the conversation. "That fellow that's working for Hicks? Milksop, that's what he is. Makes me tired to see a young fellow that ought to be in the war, or anyway out in the fields earning his living honest, like I done when I was young, doing a woman's work and then come out and dress up like a show-actor! Why, when I was his age——"

Carol reflected that the carving-knife would make an excellent dagger with which to kill Uncle Whittier. It would slide in easily. The headlines would be terrible.

Kennicott said judiciously, "Oh, I don't want to be unjust to him. I believe he took his physical examination for military service. Got varicose veins—not bad, but enough to disqualify him. Though I will say he doesn't look like a fellow that would be so awful darn crazy to poke his bayonet into a Hun's guts."

"Will! *Please!*"

"Well, he don't. Looks soft to me. And they say he told Del Snafflin, when he was getting a hair-cut on Saturday, that he wished he could play the piano."

"Isn't it wonderful how much we all know about one another in a town like this," said Carol innocently.

Kennicott was suspicious, but Aunt Bessie, serving the floating island pudding, agreed, "Yes, it is wonderful. Folks can get away with all sorts of meannesses and sins in these terrible cities, but they can't here. I was noticing this tailor fellow this morning, and when Mrs. Riggs offered to share her hymn-book with him, he shook his head, and all the while we was singing he just stood there like a bump on a log and never opened his mouth. Everybody says he's got an idea that he's got so much better manners and

all than what the rest of us have, but if that's what he calls good manners,
I want to know!"

Carol again studied the carving-knife. Blood on the whiteness of a tablecloth might be gorgeous.

Then:

"Fool! Neurotic impossibilist! Telling yourself orchard fairy-tales—at
thirty. . . . Dear Lord, am I really *thirty?* That boy can't be more than
twenty-five."

IV

She went calling.

Boarding with the Widow Bogart was Fern Mullins, a girl of twenty-two
who was to be teacher of English, French, and gymnastics in the high school
this coming session. Fern Mullins had come to town early, for the six-weeks
normal course for country teachers. Carol had noticed her on the street, had
heard almost as much about her as about Erik Valborg. She was tall, weedy,
pretty, and incurably rakish. Whether she wore a low middy collar or dressed
reticently for school in a black suit with a high-necked blouse, she was airy,
flippant. "She looks like an absolute totty," said all the Mrs. Sam Clarks,
disapprovingly, and all the Juanita Haydocks, enviously.

That Sunday evening, sitting in baggy canvas lawn-chairs beside the house,
the Kennicotts saw Fern laughing with Cy Bogart who, though still a junior
in high school, was now a lump of a man, only two or three years younger
than Fern. Cy had to go downtown for weighty matters connected with the
pool-parlor. Fern drooped on the Bogart porch, her chin in her hands.

"She looks lonely," said Kennicott.

"She does, poor soul. I believe I'll go over and speak to her. I was introduced to her at Dave's but I haven't called." Carol was slipping across the
lawn, a white figure in the dimness, faintly brushing the dewy grass. She
was thinking of Erik and of the fact that her feet were wet, and she was casual
in her greeting: "Hello! The doctor and I wondered if you were lonely."

Resentfully, "I am!"

Carol concentrated on her. "My dear, you sound so! I know how it is. I
used to be tired when I was on the job—I was a librarian. What was your
college? I was Blodgett."

More interestedly, "I went to the U." Fern meant the University of Minnesota.

"You must have had a splendid time. Blodgett was a bit dull."

"Where were you a librarian?" challengingly.

"St. Paul—the main library."

"Honest? Oh dear, I wish I was back in the Cities! This is my first year
of teaching, and I'm scared stiff. I did have the best time in college: dramatics and basket-ball and fussing and dancing—I'm simply crazy about
dancing. And here, except when I have the kids in gymnasium class, or when
I'm chaperoning the basket-ball team on a trip out-of-town, I won't dare to
move above a whisper. I guess they don't care much if you put any pep into

teaching or not, as long as you look like a Good Influence out of school-hours
—and that means never doing anything you want to. This normal course is
bad enough, but the regular school will be *fierce!* If it wasn't too late to
get a job in the Cities, I swear I'd resign here. I bet I won't dare to go to a
single dance all winter. If I cut loose and danced the way I like to, they'd
think I was a perfect hellion—poor harmless me! Oh, I oughtn't to be talking
like this. Fern, you never could be cagey!"

"Don't be frightened, my dear! . . . Doesn't that sound atrociously old
and kind! I'm talking to you the way Mrs. Westlake talks to me! That's
having a husband and a kitchen range, I suppose. But I feel young, and I
want to dance like a—like a hellion?—too. So I sympathize."

Fern made a sound of gratitude. Carol inquired, "What experience did
you have with college dramatics? I tried to start a kind of Little Theater
here. It was dreadful. I must tell you about it——"

Two hours later, when Kennicott came over to greet Fern and to yawn,
"Look here, Carrie, don't you suppose you better be thinking about turning
in? I've got a hard day tomorrow," the two were talking so intimately that
they constantly interrupted each other.

As she went respectably home, convoyed by a husband, and decorously
holding up her skirts, Carol rejoiced, "Everything has changed! I have two
friends, Fern and—— But who's the other? That's queer; I thought there
was—— Oh, how absurd!"

V

She often passed Erik Valborg on the street; the brown jersey coat became
unremarkable. When she was driving with Kennicott, in early evening, she
saw him on the lake shore, reading a thin book which might easily have
been poetry. She noted that he was the only person in the motorized town
who still took long walks.

She told herself that she was the daughter of a judge, the wife of a doctor,
and that she did not care to know a capering tailor. She told herself that
she was not responsive to men . . . not even to Percy Bresnahan. She told
herself that a woman of thirty who heeded a boy of twenty-five was ridiculous. And on Friday, when she had convinced herself that the errand was
necessary, she went to Nat Hicks's shop, bearing the not very romantic burden of a pair of her husband's trousers. Hicks was in the back room. She
faced the Greek god who, in a somewhat ungodlike way, was stitching a
coat on a scaly sewing-machine, in a room of smutted plaster walls.

She saw that his hands were not in keeping with a Hellenic face. They
were thick, roughened with needle and hot iron and plow-handle. Even in
the shop he persisted in his finery. He wore a silk shirt, a topaz scarf, thin
tan shoes.

This she absorbed while she was saying curtly, "Can I get these pressed,
please?"

Not rising from the sewing-machine he stuck out his hand, mumbled,
"When do you want them?"

"Oh, Monday."

The adventure was over. She was marching out.

"What name?" he called after her.

He had risen and, despite the farcicality of Dr. Will Kennicott's bulgy trousers draped over his arm, he had the grace of a cat.

"Kennicott."

"Kennicott. Oh! Oh say, you're Mrs. Dr. Kennicott then, aren't you?"

"Yes." She stood at the door. Now that she had carried out her preposterous impulse to see what he was like, she was cold, she was as ready to detect familiarities as the virtuous Miss Ella Stowbody.

"I've heard about you. Myrtle Cass was saying you got up a dramatic club and gave a dandy play. I've always wished I had a chance to belong to a Little Theater, and give some European plays, or whimsical like Barrie, or a pageant."

He pronounced it "pagent"; he rhymed "pag" with "rag."

Carol nodded in the manner of a lady being kind to a tradesman, and one of her selves sneered, "Our Erik is indeed a lost John Keats."

He was appealing, "Do you suppose it would be possible to get up another dramatic club this coming fall?"

"Well, it might be worth thinking of." She came out of her several conflicting poses, and said sincerely, "There's a new teacher, Miss Mullins, who might have some talent. That would make three of us for a nucleus. If we could scrape up half a dozen we might give a real play with a small cast. Have you had any experience?"

"Just a bum club that some of us got up in Minneapolis when I was working there. We had one good man, an interior decorator—maybe he was kind of sis and effeminate, but he really was an artist, and we gave one dandy play. But I—— Of course I've always had to work hard, and study by myself, and I'm probably sloppy, and I'd love it if I had training in rehearsing—I mean, the crankier the director was, the better I'd like it. If you didn't want to use me as an actor, I'd love to design the costumes. I'm crazy about fabrics— textures and colors and designs."

She knew that he was trying to keep her from going, trying to indicate that he was something more than a person to whom one brought trousers for pressing. He besought:

"Some day I hope I can get away from this fool repairing, when I have the money saved up. I want to go East and work for some big dressmaker, and study art drawing, and become a high-class designer. Or do you think that's a kind of fiddlin' ambition for a fellow? I was brought up on a farm. And then monkeyin' round with silks! I don't know. What do you think? Myrtle Cass says you're awfully educated."

"I am. Awfully. Tell me: Have the boys made fun of your ambition?"

She was seventy years old, and sexless, and more advisory than Vida Sherwin.

"Well, they have, at that. They've jollied me a good deal, here and Minneapolis both. They say dressmaking is ladies' work. (But I was willing to get

drafted for the war! I tried to get in. But they rejected me. But I did try!)
I thought some of working up in a gents' furnishings store, and I had a chance
to travel on the road for a clothing house, but somehow—I hate this tailoring,
but I can't seem to get enthusiastic about salesmanship. I keep thinking
about a room in gray oatmeal paper with prints in very narrow gold frames—
or would it be better in white enamel paneling?—but anyway, it looks out on
Fifth Avenue, and I'm designing a sumptuous——" He made it "sump-too-
ous"—"robe of linden green chiffon over cloth of gold! You know—tileul. It's
elegant. . . . What do you think?"

"Why not? What do you care for the opinion of city rowdies, or a lot of
farm boys? But you mustn't, you really mustn't, let casual strangers like me
have a chance to judge you."

"Well—— You aren't a stranger, one way. Myrtle Cass—Miss Cass, should
say—she's spoken about you so often. I wanted to call on you—and the doctor
—but I didn't quite have the nerve. One evening I walked past your house,
but you and your husband were talking on the porch, and you looked so
chummy and happy I didn't dare butt in."

Maternally, "I think it's extremely nice of you to want to be trained in—
in enunciation by a stage-director. Perhaps I could help you. I'm a thoroughly sound and uninspired schoolma'am by instinct; quite hopelessly mature."

"Oh, you aren't *either!*"

She was not very successful at accepting his fervor with the air of amused
woman of the world, but she sounded reasonably impersonal: "Thank you.
Shall we see if we really can get up a new dramatic club? I'll tell you: Come
to the house this evening, about eight. I'll ask Miss Mullins to come over,
and we'll talk about it."

VI

"He has absolutely no sense of humor. Less than Will. But hasn't he——
What is a 'sense of humor'? Isn't the thing he lacks the back-slapping
jocosity that passes for humor here? Anyway—— Poor lamb, coaxing me to
stay and play with him! Poor lonely lamb! If he could be free from Nat
Hickses, from people who say 'dandy' and 'bum,' would he develop?

"I wonder if Whitman didn't use Brooklyn back-street slang, as a boy?

"No. Not Whitman. He's Keats—sensitive to silken things. 'Innumerable of
stains and splendid dyes as are the tiger-moth's deep-damask'd wings.' Keats,
here! A bewildered spirit fallen on Main Street. And Main Street laughs till
it aches, giggles till the spirit doubts his own self and tries to give up the
use of wings for the correct uses of a 'gents' furnishings store.' Gopher
Prairie with its celebrated eleven miles of cement walk. . . . I wonder how
much of the cement is made out of the tombstones of John Keatses?"

VII

Kennicott was cordial to Fern Mullins, teased her, told her he was a "great hand for running off with pretty schoolteachers," and promised that if the school-board should object to her dancing, he would "bat 'em one over the head and tell 'em how lucky they were to get a girl with some go to her, for once."

But to Erik Valborg he was not cordial. He shook hands loosely, and said, "H' are yuh."

Nat Hicks was socially acceptable; he had been here for years, and owned his shop; but this person was merely Nat's workman, and the town's principle of perfect democracy was not meant to be applied indiscriminately.

The conference on a dramatic club theoretically included Kennicott, but he sat back, patting yawns, conscious of Fern's ankles, smiling amiably on the children at their sport.

Fern wanted to tell her grievances; Carol was sulky every time she thought of "The Girl from Kankakee"; it was Erik who made suggestions. He had read with astounding breadth, and astounding lack of judgment. His voice was sensitive to liquids, but he overused the word "glorious." He mispronounced a tenth of the words he had from books, but he knew it. He was insistent, but he was shy.

When he demanded, "I'd like to stage 'Suppressed Desires,' by Cook and Miss Glaspell," Carol ceased to be patronizing. He was not the yearner: he was the artist, sure of his vision. "I'd make it simple. Use a big window at the back, with a cyclorama of a blue that would simply hit you in the eye, and just one tree-branch, to suggest a park below. Put the breakfast table on a dais. Let the colors be kind of arty and tea-roomy—orange chairs, and orange and blue table, and blue Japanese breakfast set, and some place, one big flat smear of black—bang! Oh. Another play I wish we could do is Tennyson Jesse's 'The Black Mask.' I've never seen it but—— Glorious ending, where this woman looks at the man with his face all blown away, and she just gives one horrible scream."

"Good God, is that your idea of a glorious ending?" bayed Kennicott.

"That sounds fierce! I do love artistic things, but not the horrible ones," moaned Fern Mullins.

Erik was bewildered; glanced at Carol. She nodded loyally.

At the end of the conference they had decided nothing.

## 29

She had walked up the railroad track with Hugh, this Sunday afternoon.

She saw Erik Valborg coming, in an ancient highwater suit, tramping sullenly and alone, striking at the rails with a stick. For a second she unreasoningly wanted to avoid him, but she kept on, and she serenely talked about God, whose voice, Hugh asserted, made the humming in the telegraph wires. Erik stared, straightened. They greeted each other with "Hello."

"Hugh, say how-do-you-do to Mr. Valborg."

"Oh, dear me, he's got a button unbuttoned," worried Erik, kneeling. Carol frowned, then noted the strength with which he swung the baby in the air.

"May I walk along a piece with you?"

"I'm tired. Let's rest on those ties. Then I must be trotting back."

They sat on a heap of discarded railroad ties, oak logs spotted with cinnamon-colored dry-rot and marked with metallic brown streaks where iron plates had rested. Hugh learned that the pile was the hiding-place of Injuns; he went gunning for them while the elders talked of uninteresting things.

The telegraph wires thrummed, thrummed, thrummed above them; the rails were glaring hard lines; the goldenrod smelled dusty. Across the track was a pasture of dwarf clover and sparse lawn cut by earthy cow-paths; beyond its placid narrow green, the rough immensity of new stubble, jagged with wheat-stacks like huge pineapples.

Erik talked of books; flamed like a recent convert to any faith. He exhibited as many titles and authors as possible, halting only to appeal, "Have you read his last book? Don't you think he's a terribly strong writer?"

She was dizzy. But when he insisted, "You've been a librarian; tell me; do I read too much fiction?" she advised him loftily, rather discursively. He had, she indicated, never studied. He had skipped from one emotion to another. Especially—she hesitated, then flung it at him—he must not guess at pronunciations; he must endure the nuisance of stopping to reach for the dictionary.

"I'm talking like a cranky teacher," she sighed.

"No! And I will study! Read the damned dictionary right through." He crossed his legs and bent over, clutching his ankle with both hands. "I know what you mean. I've been rushing from picture to picture, like a kid let loose in an art gallery for the first time. You see, it's so awful recent that I've found there was a world—well, a world where beautiful things counted. I was on the farm till I was nineteen. Dad is a good farmer, but nothing else. Do you know why he first sent me off to learn tailoring? I wanted to study drawing, and he had a cousin that'd made a lot of money tailoring out in Dakota, and he said tailoring was a lot like drawing, so he sent me down to a punk hole called Curlew, to work in a tailor shop. Up to that time I'd only had three months' schooling a year—walked to school two miles, through snow up to my knees—and Dad never would stand for my having a single book except schoolbooks.

"I never read a novel till I got 'Dorothy Vernon of Haddon Hall' out of the library at Curlew. I thought it was the loveliest thing in the world! Next I read 'Barriers Burned Away' and then Pope's translation of Homer. Some combination, all right! When I went to Minneapolis, just two years ago, I guess I'd read pretty much everything in that Curlew library, but I'd never heard of Rossetti or John Sargent or Balzac or Brahms. But—— Yump, I'll study. Look here! Shall I get out of this tailoring, this pressing and repairing?"

"I don't see why a surgeon should spend very much time cobbling shoes."

"But what if I find I can't really draw and design? After fussing around in New York or Chicago, I'd feel like a fool if I had to go back to work in a gents' furnishings store!"

"Please say 'haberdashery.'"

"Haberdashery? All right. I'll remember." He shrugged and spread his fingers wide.

She was humbled by his humility; she put away in her mind, to take out and worry over later, a speculation as to whether it was not she who was naive. She urged, "What if you do have to go back? Most of us do! We can't all be artists—myself, for instance. We have to darn socks, and yet we're not content to think of nothing but socks and darning-cotton. I'd demand all I could get—whether I finally settled down to designing frocks or building temples or pressing pants. What if you do drop back? You'll have had the adventure. Don't be too meek toward life! Go! You're young, you're unmarried. Try everything! Don't listen to Nat Hicks and Sam Clark and be a 'steady young man'—in order to help them make money. You're still a blessed innocent. Go and play till the Good People capture you!"

"But I don't just want to play. I want to make something beautiful. God! And I don't know enough. Do you get it? Do you understand? Nobody else ever has! Do you understand?"

"Yes."

"And so—— But here's what bothers me: I like fabrics; dinky things like that; little drawings and elegant words. But look over there at those fields. Big! New! Don't it seem kind of a shame to leave this and go back to the East and Europe, and do what all those people have been doing so long? Being careful about words, when there's millions of bushels of wheat here! Reading this fellow Pater, when I've helped Dad to clear fields!"

"It's good to clear fields. But it's not for you. It's one of our favorite American myths that broad plains necessarily make broad minds, and high mountains make high purpose. I thought that myself, when I first came to the prairie. 'Big-new.' Oh, I don't want to deny the prairie future. It will be magnificent. But equally I'm hanged if I want to be bullied by it, go to war on behalf of Main Street, be bullied and *bullied* by the faith that the future is already here in the present, and that all of us must stay and worship wheat-stacks and insist that this is 'God's Country'—and never, of course, do anything original or gay-colored that would help to make that future! Anyway, you don't belong here. Sam Clark and Nat Hicks, that's what our big newness has produced. Go! Before it's too late, as it has been for—for some of us. Young man, go East and grow up with the revolution! Then perhaps you may come back and tell Sam and Nat and me what to do with the land we've been clearing—if we'll listen—if we don't lynch you first!"

He looked at her reverently. She could hear him saying, "I've always wanted to know a woman who would talk to me like that."

Her hearing was faulty. He was saying nothing of the sort. He was saying: "Why aren't you happy with your husband?"

"I—you——"

"He doesn't care for the 'blessed innocent' part of you, does he!"

"Erik, you mustn't——"

"First you tell me to go and be free, and then you say that I 'mustn't'!"

"I know. But you mustn't—— You must be more impersonal!"

He glowered at her like a downy young owl. She wasn't sure but she thought that he muttered, "I'm damned if I will." She considered with wholesome fear the perils of meddling with other people's destinies, and she said timidly, "Hadn't we better start back now?"

He mused, "You're younger than I am. Your lips are for songs about rivers in the morning and lakes at twilight. I don't see how anybody could ever hurt you. . . . Yes. We better go."

He trudged beside her, his eyes averted. Hugh experimentally took his thumb. He looked down at the baby seriously. He burst out, "All right. I'll do it. I'll stay here one year. Save. Not spend so much money on clothes. And then I'll go East, to art-school. Work on the side—tailor shop, dressmaker's. I'll learn what I'm good for: designing clothes, stage-settings, illustrating, or selling collars to fat men. All settled." He peered at her, unsmiling.

"Can you stand it here in town for a year?"

"With you to look at?"

"Please! I mean: Don't the people here think you're an odd bird? (They do me, I assure you!)"

"I don't know. I never notice much. Oh, they do kid me about not being in the army—especially the old warhorses, the old men that aren't going themselves. And this Bogart boy. And Mr. Hicks's son—he's a horrible brat. But probably he's licensed to say what he thinks about his father's hired man!"

"He's beastly!"

They were in town. They passed Aunt Bessie's house. Aunt Bessie and Mrs. Bogart were at the window, and Carol saw that they were staring so intently that they answered her wave only with the stiffly raised hands of automatons. In the next block Mrs. Dr. Westlake was gaping from her porch. Carol said with an embarrassed quaver:

"I want to run in and see Mrs. Westlake. I'll say good-by here."

She avoided his eyes.

Mrs. Westlake was affable. Carol felt that she was expected to explain; and while she was mentally asserting that she'd be hanged if she'd explain, she was explaining:

"Hugh captured that Valborg boy up the track. They became such good friends. And I talked to him for a while. I'd heard he was eccentric, but really, I found him quite intelligent. Crude, but he reads—reads almost the way Dr. Westlake does."

"That's fine. Why does he stick here in town? What's this I hear about his being interested in Myrtle Cass?"

"I don't know. Is he? I'm sure he isn't! He said he was quite lonely! Besides, Myrtle is a babe in arms!"

"Twenty-one if she's a day!"

"Well—— Is the doctor going to do any hunting this fall?"

## II

The need of explaining Erik dragged her back into doubting. For all his ardent reading, and his ardent life, was he anything but a small-town youth bred on an illiberal farm and in cheap tailor shops? He had rough hands. She had been attracted only by hands that were fine and suave, like those of her father. Delicate hands and resolute purpose. But this boy—powerful seamed hands and flabby will.

"It's not appealing weakness like his, but sane strength that will animate the Gopher Prairies. Only—— Does that mean anything? Or am I echoing Vida? The world has always let 'strong' statesmen and soldiers—the men with strong voices—take control, and what have the thundering boobies done? What is 'strength'?

"This classifying of people! I suppose tailors differ as much as burglars or kings.

"Erik frightened me when he turned on me. Of course he didn't mean anything, but I mustn't let him be so personal.

"Amazing impertinence!

"But he didn't mean to be.

"His hands are *firm*. I wonder if sculptors don't have thick hands, too?

"Of course if there really is anything I can do to *help* the boy——

"Though I despise these people who interfere. He must be independent."

## III

She wasn't altogether pleased, the week after, when Erik was independent and, without asking for her inspiration, planned the tennis tournament. It proved that he had learned to play in Minneapolis; that, next to Juanita Haydock, he had the best serve in town. Tennis was well spoken of in Gopher Prairie and almost never played. There were three courts: one belonging to

Harry Haydock, one to the cottages at the lake, and one, a rough field on the outskirts, laid out by a defunct tennis association.

Erik had been seen in flannels and an imitation panama hat, playing on the abandoned court with Willis Woodford, the clerk in Stowbody's bank. Suddenly he was going about proposing the reorganization of the tennis association, and writing names in a fifteen-cent note-book bought for the purpose at Dyer's. When he came to Carol he was so excited over being an organizer that he did not stop to talk of himself and Aubrey Beardsley for more than ten minutes. He begged, "Will you get some of the folks to come in?" and she nodded agreeably.

He proposed an informal exhibition match to advertise the association; he suggested that Carol and himself, the Haydocks, the Woodfords, and the Dillons play doubles, and that the association be formed from the gathered enthusiasts. He had asked Harry Haydock to be tentative president. Harry, he reported, had promised, "All right. You bet. But you go ahead and arrange things, and I'll O.K. 'em." Erik planned that the match should be held Saturday afternoon, on the old public court at the edge of town. He was happy in being, for the first time, part of Gopher Prairie.

Through the week Carol heard how select an attendance there was to be. Kennicott growled that he didn't care to go.

Had he any objections to her playing with Erik?

No; sure not; she needed the exercise.

Carol went to the match early. The court was in a meadow out on the New Antonia road. Only Erik was there. He was dashing about with a rake, trying to make the court somewhat less like a plowed field. He admitted that he had stage-fright at the thought of the coming horde. Willis and Mrs. Woodford arrived, Willis in home-made knickers and black sneakers through at the toe; then Dr. and Mrs. Harvey Dillon, people as harmless and grateful as the Woodfords.

Carol was embarrassed and excessively agreeable, like the bishop's lady trying not to feel out of place at a Baptist bazaar.

They waited.

The match was scheduled for three. As spectators there assembled one youthful grocery clerk, stopping his Ford delivery wagon to stare from the seat, and one solemn small boy, tugging a smaller sister who had a careless nose.

"I wonder where the Haydocks are? They ought to show up, at least," said Erik.

Carol smiled confidently at him, and peered down the empty road toward town. Only heat-waves and dust and dusty weeds.

At half-past three no one had come, and the grocery boy reluctantly got out, cranked his Ford, glared at them in a disillusioned manner, and rattled away. The small boy and his sister ate grass and sighed.

The players pretended to be exhilarated by practising service, but they startled at each dust-cloud from a motor car. None of the cars turned into the meadow—none till a quarter to four, when Kennicott drove in.

Carol's heart swelled. "How loyal he is! Depend on him! He'd come, if nobody else did. Even though he doesn't care for the game. The old darling!"

Kennicott did not alight. He called out, "Carrie! Harry Haydock 'phoned me that they've decided to hold the tennis matches, or whatever you call 'em, down at the cottages at the lake, instead of here. The bunch are down there now: Haydocks and Dyers and Clarks and everybody. Harry wanted to know if I'd bring you down. I guess I can take the time—come right back after supper."

Before Carol could sum it all up, Erik stammered, "Why, Haydock didn't say anything to me about the change. Of course he's the president, but——"

Kennicott looked at him heavily, and grunted, "I don't know a thing about it. . . . Coming, Carrie?"

"I am not! The match was to be here, and it will be here! You can tell Harry Haydock that he's beastly rude!" She rallied the five who had been left out, who would always be left out. "Come on! We'll toss to see which four of us play the Only and Original First Annual Tennis Tournament of Forest Hills, Del Monte, and Gopher Prairie!"

"Don't know as I blame you," said Kennicott. "We'll have supper at home then?" He drove off.

She hated him for his composure. He had ruined her defiance. She felt much less like Susan B. Anthony as she turned to her huddled followers.

Mrs. Dillon and Willis Woodford lost the toss. The others played out the game, slowly, painfully, stumbling on the rough earth, muffing the easiest shots, watched only by the small boy and his sniveling sister. Beyond the court stretched the eternal stubble-fields. The four marionettes, awkwardly going through exercises, insignificant in the hot sweep of contemptuous land, were not heroic; their voices did not ring out in the score, but sounded apologetic; and when the game was over they glanced about as though they were waiting to be laughed at.

They walked home. Carol took Erik's arm. Through her thin linen sleeve she could feel the crumply warmth of his familiar brown jersey coat. She observed that there were purple and red-gold threads interwoven with the brown. She remembered the first time she had seen it.

Their talk was nothing but improvisations on the theme: "I never did like this Haydock. He just considers his own convenience." Ahead of them, the Dillons and Woodfords spoke of the weather and B. J. Gougerling's new bungalow. No one referred to their tennis tournament. At her gate Carol shook hands firmly with Erik and smiled at him.

Next morning, Sunday morning, when Carol was on the porch, the Haydocks drove up.

"We didn't mean to be rude to you, dearie!" implored Juanita. "I wouldn't have you think that for anything. We planned that Will and you should come down and have supper at our cottage."

"No. I'm sure you didn't mean to be." Carol was superneighborly. "But I do think you ought to apologize to poor Erik Valborg. He was terribly hurt."

"Oh. Valborg. I don't care so much what he thinks," objected Harry. "He's nothing but a conceited buttinsky. Juanita and I kind of figured he was trying to run this tennis thing too darn much anyway."

"But you asked him to make arrangements."

"I know, but I don't like him. Good Lord, you couldn't hurt his feelings! He dresses up like a chorus man—and, by golly, he looks like one!—but he's nothing but a Swede farm boy, and these foreigners, they all got hides like a covey of rhinoceroses."

"But he *is* hurt!"

"Well—— I don't suppose I ought to have gone off half-cocked, and not jollied him along. I'll give him a cigar. He'll——"

Juanita had been licking her lips and staring at Carol. She interrupted her husband, "Yes, I do think Harry ought to fix it up with him. You *like* him, *don't* you, Carol?"

Over and through Carol ran a frightened cautiousness. "Like him? I haven't an i-dea. He seems to be a very decent young man. I just felt that when he'd worked so hard on the plans for the match, it was a shame not to be nice to him."

"Maybe there's something to that," mumbled Harry; then, at sight of Kennicott coming round the corner tugging the red garden hose by its brass nozzle, he roared in relief, "What d' you think you're trying to do, doc?"

While Kennicott explained in detail all that he thought he was trying to do, while he rubbed his chin and gravely stated, "Struck me the grass was looking kind of brown in patches—didn't know but what I'd give it a sprinkling," and while Harry agreed that this was an excellent idea, Juanita made friendly noises and, behind the gilt screen of an affectionate smile, watched Carol's face.

### IV

She wanted to see Erik. She wanted some one to play with! There wasn't even so dignified and sound an excuse as having Kennicott's trousers pressed; when she inspected them, all three pairs looked discouragingly neat. She probably would not have ventured on it had she not spied Nat Hicks in the pool-parlor, being witty over bottle-pool. Erik was alone! She fluttered toward the tailor shop, dashed into its slovenly heat with the comic fastidiousness of a humming bird dipping into a dry tiger-lily. It was after she had entered that she found an excuse.

Erik was in the back room, cross-legged on a long table, sewing a vest. But he looked as though he were doing this eccentric thing to amuse himself.

"Hello. I wonder if you couldn't plan a sports-suit for me?" she said breathlessly.

He stared at her; he protested, "No, I won't! God! I'm not going to be a tailor with you!"

"Why, Erik!" she said, like a mildly shocked mother.

It occurred to her that she did not need a suit, and that the order might have been hard to explain to Kennicott.

He swung down from the table. "I want to show you something." He rummaged in the roll-top desk on which Nat Hicks kept bills, buttons, calendars, buckles, thread-channeled wax, shotgun shells, samples of brocade for "fancy vests," fishing-reels, pornographic post-cards, shreds of buckram lining. He pulled out a blurred sheet of Bristol board and anxiously gave it to her. It was a sketch for a frock. It was not well drawn; it was too finicking; the pillars in the background were grotesquely squat. But the frock had an original back, very low, with a central triangular section from the waist to a string of jet beads at the neck.

"It's stunning. But how it would shock Mrs. Clark!"

"Yes, wouldn't it!"

"You must let yourself go more when you're drawing."

"Don't know if I can. I've started kind of late. But listen! What do you think I've done this two weeks? I've read almost clear through a Latin grammar, and about twenty pages of Cæsar."

"Splendid! You are lucky. You haven't a teacher to make you artificial."

"You're my teacher!"

There was a dangerous edge of personality to his voice. She was offended and agitated. She turned her shoulder on him, stared through the back window, studying this typical center of a typical Main Street block, a vista hidden from casual strollers. The backs of the chief establishments in town surrounded a quadrangle neglected, dirty, and incomparably dismal. From the front, Howland & Gould's grocery was smug enough, but attached to the rear was a lean-to of storm-streaked pine lumber with a sanded tar roof—a staggering doubtful shed behind which was a heap of ashes, splintered packing-boxes, shreds of excelsior, crumpled straw-board, broken olive-bottles, rotten fruit, and utterly disintegrated vegetables: orange carrots turning black, and potatoes with ulcers. The rear of the Bon Ton Store was grim with blistered black-painted iron shutters, under them a pile of once glossy red shirt-boxes, now a pulp from recent rain.

As seen from Main Street, Oleson & McGuire's Meat Market had a sanitary and virtuous expression with its new tile counter, fresh sawdust on the floor, and a hanging veal cut in rosettes. But she now viewed a back room with a home-made refrigerator of yellow smeared with black grease. A man in an apron spotted with dry blood was hoisting out a hard slab of meat.

Behind Billy's Lunch, the cook, in an apron which must long ago have been white, smoked a pipe and spat at the pest of sticky flies. In the center of the block, by itself, was the stable for the three horses of the drayman, and beside it a pile of manure.

The rear of Ezra Stowbody's bank was whitewashed, and back of it was a concrete walk and a three-foot square of grass, but the window was barred, and behind the bars she saw Willis Woodford cramped over figures in pompous books. He raised his head, jerkily rubbed his eyes, and went back to the eternity of figures.

The backs of the other shops were an impressionistic picture of dirty grays, drained browns, writhing heaps of refuse.

"Mine is a back-yard romance—with a journeyman tailor!"

She was saved from self-pity as she began to think through Erik's mind. She turned to him with an indignant, "It's disgusting that this is all you have to look at."

He considered it. "Outside there? I don't notice much. I'm learning to look inside. Not awful easy!"

"Yes. . . . I must be hurrying."

As she walked home—without hurrying—she remembered her father saying to a serious ten-year-old Carol, "Lady, only a fool thinks he's superior to beautiful bindings, but only a double-distilled fool reads nothing but bindings."

She was startled by the return of her father, startled by a sudden conviction that in this flaxen boy she had found the gray reticent judge who was divine love, perfect understanding. She debated it, furiously denied it, reaffirmed it, ridiculed it. Of one thing she was unhappily certain: there was nothing of the beloved father image in Will Kennicott.

v

She wondered why she sang so often, and why she found so many pleasant things—lamplight seen though trees on a cool evening, sunshine on brown wood, morning sparrows, black sloping roofs turned to plates of silver by moonlight. Pleasant things, small friendly things, and pleasant places—a field of goldenrod, a pasture by the creek—and suddenly a wealth of pleasant people. Vida was lenient to Carol at the surgical-dressing class; Mrs. Dave Dyer flattered her with questions about her health, baby, cook, and opinions on the war.

Mrs. Dyer seemed not to share the town's prejudice against Erik. "He's a nice-looking fellow; we must have him go on one of our picnics some time." Unexpectedly, Dave Dyer also liked him. The tight-fisted little farceur had a confused reverence for anything that seemed to him refined or clever. He answered Harry Haydock's sneers, "That's all right now! Elizabeth may doll himself up too much, but he's smart, and don't you forget it! I was asking round trying to find out where this Ukraine is, and darn if he didn't tell me. What's the matter with his talking so polite? Hell's bells, Harry, no harm in being polite. There's some regular he-men that are just as polite as women, prett' near."

Carol found herself going about rejoicing, "How neighborly the town is!" She drew up with a dismayed "Am I falling in love with this boy? That's ridiculous! I'm merely interested in him. I like to think of helping him to succeed."

But as she dusted the living-room, mended a collar-band, bathed Hugh, she was picturing herself and a young artist—an Apollo nameless and evasive —building a house in the Berkshires or in Virginia; exuberantly buying a chair with his first check; reading poetry together, and frequently being earnest over valuable statistics about labor; tumbling out of bed early for a Sunday walk, and chattering (where Kennicott would have yawned) over bread and butter by a lake. Hugh was in her pictures, and he adored the young artist, who made castles of chairs and rugs for him. Beyond these playtimes she saw the "things I could do for Erik"—and she admitted that Erik did partly make up the image of her altogether perfect artist.

In panic she insisted on being attentive to Kennicott, when he wanted to be left alone to read the newspaper.

### VI

She needed new clothes. Kennicott had promised, "We'll have a good trip down to the Cities in the fall, and take plenty of time for it, and you can get your new glad-rags then." But as she examined her wardrobe she flung her ancient black velvet frock on the floor and raged, "They're disgraceful. Everything I have is falling to pieces."

There was a new dressmaker and milliner, a Mrs. Swiftwaite. It was said that she was not altogether an elevating influence in the way she glanced at men; that she would as soon take away a legally appropriated husband as not; that if there *was* any Mr. Swiftwaite, "it certainly was strange that nobody seemed to know anything about him!" But she had made for Rita Gould an organdy frock and hat to match universally admitted to be "too cunning for words," and the matrons went cautiously, with darting eyes and excessive politeness, to the rooms which Mrs. Swiftwaite had taken in the old Luke Dawson house, on Floral Avenue.

With none of the spiritual preparation which normally precedes the buying of new clothes in Gopher Prairie, Carol marched into Mrs. Swiftwaite's, and demanded, "I want to see a hat, and possibly a blouse."

In the dingy old front parlor which she had tried to make smart with a pier glass, covers from fashion magazines, anemic French prints, Mrs. Swiftwaite moved smoothly among the dress-dummies and hat-rests, spoke smoothly as she took up a small black and red turban. "I am sure the lady will find this extremely attractive."

"It's dreadfully tabby and small-towny," thought Carol, while she soothed, "I don't believe it quite goes with me."

"It's the choicest thing I have, and I'm sure you'll find it suits you beautifully. It has a great deal of *chic*. Please try it on," said Mrs. Swiftwaite, more smoothly than ever.

Carol studied the woman. She was as imitative as a glass diamond. She was the more rustic in her effort to appear urban. She wore a severe high-collared blouse with a row of small black buttons, which was becoming to her low-breasted slim neatness, but her skirt was hysterically checkered, her cheeks were too highly roughed, her lips too sharply penciled. She was magnificently a specimen of the illiterate divorcée of forty made up to look thirty, clever, and alluring.

While she was trying on the hat Carol felt very condescending. She took it off, shook her head, explained with the kind smile for inferiors, "I'm afraid it won't do, though it's unusually nice for so small a town as this."

"But it's really absolutely New-Yorkish."

"Well, it——"

"You see, I know my New York styles. I lived in New York for years, besides almost a year in Akron!"

"You did?" Carol was polite, and edged away, and went home unhappily. She was wondering whether her own airs were as laughable as Mrs. Swiftwaite's. She put on the eye-glasses which Kennicott had recently given to her for reading, and looked over a grocery bill. She went hastily up to her room, to her mirror. She was in a mood of self-depreciation. Accurately or not, this was the picture she saw in the mirror:

Neat rimless eye-glasses. Black hair clumsily tucked under a mauve straw hat which would have suited a spinster. Cheeks clear, bloodless. Thin nose. Gentle mouth and chin. A modest voile blouse with an edging of lace at the neck. A virginal sweetness and timorousness—no flare of gaiety, no suggestion of cities, music, quick laughter.

"I have become a small-town woman. Absolute. Typical. Modest and moral and safe. Protected from life. *Genteel!* The Village Virus—the village virtuousness. My hair—just scrambled together. What can Erik see in that wedded spinster there? He does like me! Because I'm the only woman who's decent to him! How long before he'll wake up to me? . . . I've waked up to myself. . . . Am I as old as—as old as I am?

"Not really old. Become careless. Let myself look tabby.

"I want to chuck every stitch I own. Black hair and pale cheeks—they'd go with a Spanish dancer's costume—rose behind my ear, scarlet mantilla over one shoulder, the other bare."

She seized the rouge sponge, daubed her cheeks, scratched at her lips with the vermilion pencil until they stung, tore open her collar. She posed with her thin arms in the attitude of the fandango. She dropped them sharply. She shook her head. "My heart doesn't dance," she said. She flushed as she fastened her blouse.

"At least I'm much more graceful than Fern Mullins.

"Heavens! When I came here from the Cities, girls imitated me. Now I'm trying to imitate a city girl."

# 30

Fern Mullins rushed into the house on a Saturday morning early in September and shrieked at Carol, "School starts next Tuesday. I've got to have one more spree before I'm arrested. Let's get up a picnic down the lake for this afternoon. Won't you come, Mrs. Kennicott, and the doctor? Cy Bogart wants to go—he's a brat but he's lively."

"I don't think the doctor can go," sedately. "He said something about having to make a country call this afternoon. But I'd love to."

"That's dandy! Who can we get?"

"Mrs. Dyer might be chaperon. She's been so nice. And maybe Dave, if he could get away from the store."

"How about Erik Valborg? I think he's got lots more style than these town boys. You like him all right, don't you?"

So the picnic of Carol, Fern, Erik, Cy Bogart, and the Dyers was not only moral but inevitable.

They drove to the birch grove on the south shore of Lake Minniemashie. Dave Dyer was his most clownish self. He yelped, jigged, wore Carol's hat, dropped an ant down Fern's back, and when they went swimming (the women modestly changing in the car with the side curtains up, the men undressing behind the bushes, constantly repeating, "Gee, hope we don't run into poison ivy"), Dave splashed water on them and dived to clutch his wife's ankle. He infected the others. Erik gave an imitation of the Greek dancers he had seen in vaudeville, and when they sat down to picnic supper spread on a lap-robe on the grass, Cy climbed a tree to throw acorns at them.

But Carol could not frolic.

She had made herself young, with parted hair, sailor blouse and large blue bow, white canvas shoes and short linen skirt. Her mirror had asserted that she looked exactly as she had in college, that her throat was smooth, her collar-bone not very noticeable. But she was under restraint. When they swam she enjoyed the freshness of the water but she was irritated by Cy's tricks, by Dave's excessive good spirits. She admired Erik's dance; he could never betray bad taste, as Cy did, and Dave. She waited for him to come to her. He did not come. By his joyousness he had apparently endeared himself to the Dyers. Maud watched him and, after supper, cried to him, "Come sit down beside me, bad boy!" Carol winced at his willingness to be a bad boy and come and sit, at his enjoyment of a not very stimulating game in which Maud, Dave, and Cy snatched slices of cold tongue from one another's plates. Maud, it seemed, was slightly dizzy from the swim. She remarked publicly, "Dr. Kennicott has helped me so much by putting me on a diet," but it was to Erik alone that she gave the complete version of her peculiarity in being so sensitive, so easily hurt by the slightest cross word, that she simply had to have nice cheery friends.

Erik was nice and cheery.

Carol assured herself, "Whatever faults I may have, I certainly couldn't ever be jealous. I do like Maud; she's always so pleasant. But I wonder if she isn't just a bit fond of fishing for men's sympathy? Playing with Erik, and her married—— Well—— But she looks at him in that languishing, swooning, mid-Victorian way. Disgusting!"

Cy Bogart lay between the roots of a big birch, smoking his pipe and teasing Fern, assuring her that a week from now, when he was again a high-school boy and she his teacher, he'd wink at her in class. Maud Dyer wanted Erik to "come down to the beach to see the darling little minnies." Carol was

left to Dave, who tried to entertain her with humorous accounts of Ella
Stowbody's fondness for chocolate peppermints. She watched Maud Dyer put
her hand on Erik's shoulder to steady herself.

"Disgusting!" she thought.

Cy Bogart covered Fern's nervous hand with his red paw, and when she
bounced with half-anger and shrieked, "Let go, I tell you!" he grinned and
waved his pipe—a gangling twenty-year-old satyr.

"Disgusting!"

When Maud and Erik returned and the grouping shifted, Erik muttered
at Carol, "There's a boat on shore. Let's skip off and have a row."

"What will they think?" she worried. She saw Maud Dyer peer at Erik
with moist possessive eyes. "Yes! Let's!" she said.

She cried to the party, with the canonical amount of sprightliness,
"Good-by, everybody. We'll wireless you from China."

As the rhythmic oars plopped and creaked, as she floated on an unreality
of delicate gray over which the sunset was poured out thin, the irritation
of Cy and Maud slipped away. Erik smiled at her proudly. She considered
him—coatless, in white thin shirt. She was conscious of his male differentness,
of his flat masculine sides, his thin thighs, his easy rowing. They talked of
the library, of the movies. He hummed and she softly sang "Swing Low,
Sweet Chariot." A breeze shivered across the agate lake. The wrinkled water
was like armor damascened and polished. The breeze flowed round the boat
in a chill current. Carol drew the collar of her middy blouse over her bare
throat.

"Getting cold. Afraid we'll have to go back," she said.

"Let's not go back to them yet. They'll be cutting up. Let's keep along
the shore."

"But you enjoy the 'cutting up!' Maud and you had a beautiful time."

"Why! We just walked on the shore and talked about fishing!"

She was relieved, and apologetic to her friend Maud. "Of course. I was
joking."

"I'll tell you! Let's land here and sit on the shore—that bunch of hazel-
brush will shelter us from the wind—and watch the sunset. It's like melted
lead. Just a short while! We don't want to go back and listen to them!"

"No, but——" She said nothing while he sped ashore. The keel clashed on
the stones. He stood on the forward seat, holding out his hand. They were
alone, in the ripple-lapping silence. She rose slowly, slowly stepped over the
water in the bottom of the old boat. She took his hand confidently. Unspeaking they sat on a bleached log, in a russet twilight which hinted of
autumn. Linden leaves fluttered about them.

"I wish—— Are you cold now?" he whispered.

"A little." She shivered. But it was not with cold.

"I wish we could curl up in the leaves there, covered all up, and lie looking
out at the dark."

"I wish we could." As though it was comfortably understood that he did
not mean to be taken seriously.

"Like what all the poets say—brown nymph and faun."

"No. I can't be a nymph any more. Too old—— Erik, am I old? Am I faded and small-towny?"

"Why, you're the youngest—— Your eyes are like a girl's. They're so—well, I mean, like you believed everything. Even if you do teach me, I feel a thousand years older than you, instead of maybe a year younger."

"Four or five years younger!"

"Anyway, your eyes are so innocent and your cheeks so soft—— Damn it, it makes me want to cry, somehow, you're so defenseless; and I want to protect you and—— There's nothing to protect you against!"

"Am I young? Am I? Honestly? Truly?" She betrayed for a moment the childish, mock-imploring tone that comes into the voice of the most serious woman when an agreeable man treats her as a girl; the childish tone and childish pursed-up lips and shy lift of the cheek.

"Yes, you are!"

"You're dear to believe it, Will—*Erik!*"

"Will you play with me? A lot?"

"Perhaps."

"Would you really like to curl in the leaves and watch the stars swing by overhead?"

"I think it's rather better to be sitting here!" He twined his fingers with hers. "And—— Erik, we must go back."

"Why?"

"It's somewhat late to outline all the history of social custom!"

"I know. We must. Are you glad we ran away though?"

"Yes." She was quiet, perfectly simple. But she rose.

He circled her waist with a brusque arm. She did not resist. She did not care. He was neither a peasant tailor, a potential artist, a social complication, nor a peril. He was himself, and in him, in the personality flowing from him, she was unreasoningly content. In his nearness she caught a new view of his head; the last light brought out the planes of his neck, his flat ruddied cheeks, the side of his nose, the depression of his temples. Not as coy or uneasy lovers but as companions they walked to the boat, and he lifted her up on the prow.

She began to talk intently, as he rowed: "Erik, you've got to work! You ought to be a personage. You're robbed of your kingdom. Fight for it! Take one of these correspondence courses in drawing—they mayn't be any good in themselves, but they'll make you try to draw and——"

As they reached the picnic ground she perceived that it was dark, that they had been gone for a long time.

"What will they say?" she wondered.

The others greeted them with the inevitable storm of humor and slight vexation: "Where the deuce do you think you've been?" "You're a fine pair, you are!" Erik and Carol looked self-conscious; failed in their effort to be witty. All the way home Carol was embarrassed. Once Cy winked at her. That Cy, the Peeping Tom of the garage-loft, should consider her a fellow-sinner—— She was furious and frightened and exultant by turns, and in all her moods certain that Kennicott would read her adventuring in her face.

She came into the house awkwardly defiant.

Her husband, half asleep under the lamp, greeted her, "Well, well, have nice time?"

She could not answer. He looked at her. But his look did not sharpen. He began to wind his watch, yawning the old "Wellllll, guess it's about time to turn in."

That was all. Yet she was not glad. She was almost disappointed.

II

Mrs. Bogart called next day. She had a hen-like, crumb-pecking, diligent appearance. Her smile was too innocent. The pecking started instantly:

"Cy says you had lots of fun at the picnic yesterday. Did you enjoy it?"

"Oh yes. I raced Cy at swimming. He beat me badly. He's so strong, isn't he!"

"Poor boy, just crazy to get into the war, too, but—— This Erik Valborg was along, wa'n't he?"

"Yes."

"I think he's an awful handsome fellow, and they say he's smart. Do you like him?"

"He seems very polite."

"Cy says you and him had a lovely boat-ride. My, that must have been pleasant."

"Yes, except that I couldn't get Mr. Valborg to say a word. I wanted to ask him about the suit Mr. Hicks is making for my husband. But he insisted on singing. Still, it was restful, floating around on the water and singing. So happy and innocent. Don't you think it's a shame, Mrs. Bogart, that people in this town don't do more nice clean things like that, instead of all this horrible gossiping?"

"Yes. . . . Yes."

Mrs. Bogart sounded vacant. Her bonnet was awry; she was incomparably dowdy. Carol stared at her, felt contemptuous, ready at last to rebel against the trap, and as the rusty goodwife fished again, "Plannin' some more picnics?" she flung out, "I haven't the slightest idea! Oh. Is that Hugh crying? I must run up to him."

But up-stairs she remembered that Mrs. Bogart had seen her walking with Erik from the railroad track into town, and she was chilly with disquietude.

At the Jolly Seventeen, two days after, she was effusive to Maud Dyer, to Juanita Haydock. She fancied that every one was watching her, but she could not be sure, and in rare strong moments she did not care. She could rebel against the town's prying now that she had something, however indistinct, for which to rebel.

In a passionate escape there must be not only a place from which to flee but a place to which to flee. She had known that she would gladly leave

Gopher Prairie, leave Main Street and all that it signified, but she had had no destination. She had one now. That destination was not Erik Valborg and the love of Erik. She continued to assure herself that she wasn't in love with him but merely "fond of him, and interested in his success." Yet in him she had discovered both her need of youth and the fact that youth would welcome her. It was not Erik to whom she must escape, but universal and joyous youth, in class-rooms, in studios, in offices, in meetings to protest against Things in General. . . . But universal and joyous youth rather resembled Erik.

All week she thought of things she wished to say to him. High, improving things. She began to admit that she was lonely without him. Then she was afraid.

It was at the Baptist church supper, a week after the picnic, that she saw him again. She had gone with Kennicott and Aunt Bessie to the supper, which was spread on oilcloth-covered and trestle-supported tables in the church basement. Erik was helping Myrtle Cass to fill coffee cups for the waitresses. The congregation had doffed their piety. Children tumbled under the tables, and Deacon Pierson greeted the women with a rolling, "Where's Brother Jones, sister, where's Brother Jones? Not going to be with us to-night? Well, you tell Sister Perry to hand you a plate, and make 'em give you enough oyster pie!"

Erik shared in the cheerfulness. He laughed with Myrtle, jogged her elbow when she was filling cups, made deep mock bows to the waitresses as they came up for coffee. Myrtle was enchanted by his humor. From the other end of the room, a matron among matrons, Carol observed Myrtle, and hated her, and caught herself at it. "To be jealous of a wooden-faced village girl!" But she kept it up. She detested Erik; gloated over his gaucheries—his "breaks," she called them. When he was too expressive, too much like a Russian dancer, in saluting Deacon Pierson, Carol had the ecstasy of pain in seeing the deacon's sneer. When, trying to talk to three girls at once, he dropped a cup and effeminately wailed, "Oh dear!" she sympathized with—and ached over—the insulting secret glances of the girls.

From meanly hating him she rose to compassion as she saw that his eyes begged every one to like him. She perceived how inaccurate her judgments could be. At the picnic she had fancied that Maud Dyer looked upon Erik too sentimentally, and she had snarled, "I hate these married women who cheapen themselves and feed on boys." But at the supper Maud was one of the waitresses; she bustled with platters of cake, she was pleasant to old women; and to Erik she gave no attention at all. Indeed, when she had her own supper, she joined the Kennicotts, and how ludicrous it was to suppose that Maud was a gourmet of emotions Carol saw in the fact that she talked not to one of the town beaux but to the safe Kennicott himself!

When Carol glanced at Erik again she discovered that Mrs. Bogart had an eye on her. It was a shock to know that at last there was something which could make her afraid of Mrs. Bogart's spying.

"What am I doing? Am I in love with Erik? Unfaithful? *I*? I want youth but I don't want him—I mean, I don't want youth—enough to break up my life. I must get out of this. Quick."

She said to Kennicott on their way home, "Will! I want to run away for a few days. Wouldn't you like to skip down to Chicago?"

"Still be pretty hot there. No fun in a big city till winter. What do you want to go for?"

"People! To occupy my mind. I want stimulus."

"Stimulus?" He spoke good-naturedly. "Who's been feeding you meat? You got that 'stimulus' out of one of these fool stories about wives that don't know when they're well off. Stimulus! Seriously, though, to cut out the jollying, I can't get away."

"Then why don't I run off by myself?"

"Why—— 'Tisn't the money, you understand. But what about Hugh?"

"Leave him with Aunt Bessie. It would be just for a few days."

"I don't think much of this business of leaving kids around. Bad for 'em."

"So you don't think——"

"I'll tell you: I think we better stay put till after the war. Then we'll have a dandy long trip. No, I don't think you better plan much about going away now."

So she was thrown at Erik.

### III

She awoke at ebb-time, at three of the morning, woke sharply and fully; and sharply and coldly as her father pronouncing sentence on a cruel swindler she gave judgment:

"A pitiful and tawdry love-affair.

"No splendor, no defiance. A self-deceived little woman whispering in corners with a pretentious little man.

"No, he is not. He is fine. Aspiring. It's not his fault. His eyes are sweet when he looks at me. Sweet, so sweet."

She pitied herself that her romance should be pitiful; she sighed that in this colorless hour, to this austere self, it should seem tawdry.

Then, in a very great desire of rebellion and unleashing of all her hatreds, "The pettier and more tawdry it is, the more blame to Main Street. It shows how much I've been longing to escape. Any way out! Any humility so long as I can flee. Main Street has done this to me. I came here eager for nobilities, ready for work, and now—— Any way out.

"I came trusting them. They beat me with rods of dullness. They don't know, they don't understand how agonizing their complacent dullness is. Like ants and August sun on a wound.

"Tawdry! Pitiful! Carol—the clean girl that used to walk so fast!—sneaking and tittering in dark corners, being sentimental and jealous at church suppers!"

At breakfast-time her agonies were night-blurred, and persisted only as a nervous irresolution.

IV

Few of the aristocrats of the Jolly Seventeen attended the humble folk-meets of the Baptist and Methodist church suppers, where the Willis Woodfords, the Dillons, the Champ Perrys, Oleson the butcher, Brad Bemis the tinsmith, and Deacon Pierson found release from loneliness. But all of the smart set went to the lawn-festivals of the Episcopal Church, and were reprovingly polite to outsiders.

The Harry Haydocks gave the last lawn-festival of the season; a splendor of Japanese lanterns and card-tables and chicken patties and Neapolitan ice-cream. Erik was no longer entirely an outsider. He was eating his ice-cream with a group of the people most solidly "in"—the Dyers, Myrtle Cass, Guy Pollock, the Jackson Elders. The Haydocks themselves kept aloof, but the others tolerated him. He would never, Carol fancied, be one of the town pillars, because he was not orthodox in hunting and motoring and poker. But he was winning approbation by his liveliness, his gaiety—the qualities least important in him.

When the group summoned Carol she made several very well-taken points in regard to the weather.

Myrtle cried to Erik, "Come on! We don't belong with these old folks. I want to make you 'quainted with the jolliest girl, she comes from Wakamin, she's staying with Mary Howland."

Carol saw him being profuse to the guest from Wakamin. She saw him confidentially strolling with Myrtle. She burst out to Mrs. Westlake, "Valborg and Myrtle seem to have quite a crush on each other."

Mrs. Westlake glanced at her curiously before she mumbled, "Yes, don't they."

"I'm mad, to talk this way," Carol worried.

She had regained a feeling of social virtue by telling Juanita Haydock "how darling her lawn looked with the Japanese lanterns" when she saw that Erik was stalking her. Though he was merely ambling about with his hands in his pockets, though he did not peep at her, she knew that he was calling her. She sidled away from Juanita. Erik hastened to her. She nodded coolly (she was proud of her coolness).

"Carol! I've got a wonderful chance! Don't know but what some ways it might be better than going East to take art. Myrtle Cass says—— I dropped in to say howdy to Myrtle last evening, and had quite a long talk with her father, and he said he was hunting for a fellow to go to work in the flour mill and learn the whole business, and maybe become general manager. I know something about wheat from my farming, and I worked a couple of months in the flour mill at Curlew when I got sick of tailoring. What do you think? You said any work was artistic if it was done by an artist. And flour is so important. What do you think?"

"Wait! Wait!"

This sensitive boy would be very skilfully stamped into conformity by Lyman Cass and his sallow daughter; but did she detest the plan for this reason? "I must be honest. I mustn't tamper with his future to please my vanity." But she had no sure vision. She turned on him:

"How can I decide? It's up to you. Do you want to become a person like Lym Cass, or do you want to become a person like—yes, like me! Wait! Don't be flattering. Be honest. This is important."

"I know. I am a person like you now! I mean, I want to rebel."

"Yes. We're alike," gravely.

"Only I'm not sure I can put through my schemes. I really can't draw much. I guess I have pretty fair taste in fabrics, but since I've known you I don't like to think about fussing with dress-designing. But as a miller, I'd have the means—books, piano, travel."

"I'm going to be frank and beastly. Don't you realize that it isn't just because her papa needs a bright young man in the mill that Myrtle is amiable to you? Can't you understand what she'll do to you when she has you, when she sends you to church and makes you become respectable?"

He glared at her. "I don't know. I suppose so."

"You are thoroughly unstable!"

"What if I am? Most fish out of water are! Don't talk like Mrs. Bogart! How can I be anything but 'unstable'—wandering from farm to tailor shop to books, no training, nothing but trying to make books talk to me! Probably I'll fail. Oh, I know it; probably I'm uneven. But I'm not unstable in thinking about this job in the mill—and Myrtle. I know what I want. I want you!"

"Please, please, oh, please!"

"I do. I'm not a schoolboy any more. I want you. If I take Myrtle, it's to forget you."

"Please, please!"

"It's you that are unstable! You talk at things and play at things, but you're scared. Would I mind it if you and I went off to poverty, and I had to dig ditches? I would not! But you would. I think you would come to like me, but you won't admit it. I wouldn't have said this, but when you sneer at Myrtle and the mill—— If I'm not to have good sensible things like those, d' you think I'll be content with trying to become a damn dressmaker, after *you*? Are you fair? Are you?"

"No, I suppose not."

"Do you like me? Do you?"

"Yes—— No! Please! I can't talk any more."

"Not here. Mrs. Haydock is looking at us."

"No, nor anywhere. O Erik, I am fond of you, but I'm afraid."

"What of?"

"Of Them! Of my rulers—Gopher Prairie. . . . My dear boy, we are talking very foolishly. I am a normal wife and a good mother, and you are—oh, a college freshman."

"You do like me! I'm going to make you love me!"

She looked at him once, recklessly, and walked away with a serene gait that was a disordered flight.

Kennicott grumbled on their way home, "You and this Valborg fellow seem quite chummy."

"Oh, we are. He's interested in Myrtle Cass, and I was telling him how nice she is."

In her room she marveled, "I have become a liar. I'm snarled with lies and foggy analyses and desires—I who was clear and sure."

She hurried into Kennicott's room, sat on the edge of his bed. He flapped a drowsy welcoming hand at her from the expanse of quilt and dented pillows.

"Will, I really think I ought to trot off to St. Paul or Chicago or some place."

"I thought we settled all that, few nights ago! Wait till we can have a real trip." He shook himself out of his drowsiness. "You might give me a good-night kiss."

She did—dutifully. He held her lips against his for an intolerable time. "Don't you like the old man any more?" he coaxed. He sat up and shyly fitted his palm about the slimness of her waist.

"Of course. I like you very much indeed." Even to herself it sounded flat. She longed to be able to throw into her voice the facile passion of a light woman. She patted his cheek.

He sighed, "I'm sorry you're so tired. Seems like—— But of course you aren't very strong."

"Yes. . . . Then you don't think—you're quite sure I ought to stay here in town?"

"I told you so! I certainly do!"

She crept back to her room, a small timorous figure in white.

"I can't face Will down—demand the right. He'd be obstinate. And I can't even go off and earn my living again. Out of the habit of it. He's driving me—— I'm afraid of what he's driving me to. Afraid.

"That man in there, snoring in stale air, my husband? Could any ceremony make him my husband?

"No. I don't want to hurt him. I want to love him. I can't, when I'm thinking of Erik. Am I too honest—a funny topsy-turvy honesty—the faithfulness of unfaith? I wish I had a more compartmental mind, like men. I'm too monogamous—toward Erik!—my child Erik, who needs me.

"Is an illicit affair like a gambling debt—demands stricter honor than the legitimate debt of matrimony, because it's not legally enforced?

"That's nonsense! I don't care in the least for Erik! Not for any man. I want to be let alone, in a woman world—a world without Main Street, or politicians, or business men, or men with that sudden beastly hungry look, that glistening unfrank expression that wives know——

"If Erik were here, if he would just sit quiet and kind and talk, I could be still, I could go to sleep.

"I am so tired. If I could sleep——"

# 31

Their night came unheralded.

Kennicott was on a country call. It was cool but Carol huddled on the porch, rocking, meditating, rocking. The house was lonely and repellent, and though she sighed, "I ought to go in and read—so many things to read—ought to go in," she remained. Suddenly Erik was coming, turning in, swinging open the screen door, touching her hand.

"Erik!"

"Saw your husband driving out of town. Couldn't stand it."

"Well—— You mustn't stay more than five minutes."

"Couldn't stand not seeing you. Every day, towards evening, felt I had to see you—pictured you so clear. I've been good though, staying away, haven't I!"

"And you must go on being good."

"Why must I?"

"We better not stay here on the porch. The Howlands across the street are such window-peepers, and Mrs. Bogart——"

She did not look at him but she could divine his tremulousness as he stumbled indoors. A moment ago the night had been coldly empty; now it was incalculable, hot, treacherous. But it is women who are the calm realists once they discard the fetishes of the premarital hunt. Carol was serene as she murmured, "Hungry? I have some little honey-colored cakes. You may have two, and then you must skip home."

"Take me up and let me see Hugh asleep."

"I don't believe——"

"Just a glimpse!"

"Well——"

She doubtfully led the way to the hallroom-nursery. Their heads close, Erik's curls pleasant as they touched her cheek, they looked in at the baby. Hugh was pink with slumber. He had burrowed into his pillow with such energy that it was almost smothering him. Beside it was a celluloid rhinoceros; tight in his hand a torn picture of Old King Cole.

"Shhh!" said Carol, quite automatically. She tiptoed in to pat the pillow. As she returned to Erik she had a friendly sense of his waiting for her. They smiled at each other. She did not think of Kennicott, the baby's father. What she did think was that some one rather like Erik, an older and surer Erik, ought to be Hugh's father. The three of them would play—incredible imaginative games.

"Carol! You've told me about your own room. Let me peep in at it."

"But you mustn't stay, not a second. We must go down-stairs."

"Yes."

"Will you be good?"

"R-reasonably!" He was pale, large-eyed, serious.

"You've got to be more than reasonably good!" She felt sensible and superior; she was energetic about pushing open the door.

Kennicott had always seemed out of place there but Erik surprisingly harmonized with the spirit of the room as he stroked the books, glanced at the prints. He held out his hands. He came toward her. She was weak, betrayed to a warm softness. Her head was tilted back. Her eyes were closed. Her thoughts were formless but many-colored. She felt his kiss, diffident and reverent, on her eyelid.

Then she knew that it was impossible.

She shook herself. She sprang from him. "Please!" she said sharply.

He looked at her unyielding.

"I am fond of you," she said. "Don't spoil everything. Be my friend."

"How many thousands and millions of women must have said that! And now you! And it doesn't spoil everything. It glorifies everything."

"Dear, I do think there's a tiny streak of fairy in you—whatever you do with it. Perhaps I'd have loved that once. But I won't. It's too late. But I'll keep a fondness for you. Impersonal—I will be impersonal! It needn't be just a thin talky fondness. You do need me, don't you? Only you and my son need me. I've wanted so to be wanted! Once I wanted love to be given to me. Now I'll be content if I can give. . . . Almost content!

"We women, we like to do things for men. Poor men! We swoop on you when you're defenseless and fuss over you and insist on reforming you. But it's so pitifully deep in us. You'll be the one thing in which I haven't failed. Do something definite! Even if it's just selling cottons. Sell beautiful cottons —caravans from China——"

"Carol! Stop! You do love me!"

"I do not! It's just—— Can't you understand? Everything crushes in on me so, all the gaping dull people, and I look for a way out—— Please go. I can't stand any more. Please!"

He was gone. And she was not relieved by the quiet of the house. She was empty and the house was empty and she needed him. She wanted to go on talking, to get this threshed out, to build a sane friendship. She wavered down to the living-room, looked out of the bay-window. He was not to be seen. But Mrs. Westlake was. She was walking past, and in the light from the corner arc-lamp she quickly inspected the porch, the windows. Carol dropped the curtain, stood with movement and reflection paralyzed. Automatically, without reasoning, she mumbled, "I will see him again soon and make him understand we must be friends. But—— The house is so empty. It echoes so."

II

Kennicott had seemed nervous and absent-minded through that supper-hour, two evenings after. He prowled about the living-room, then growled:

"What the dickens have you been saying to Ma Westlake?"

Carol's book rattled. "What do you mean?"

"I told you that Westlake and his wife were jealous of us, and here you been chumming up to them and—— From what Dave tells me, Ma Westlake has been going around town saying you told her that you hate Aunt Bessie, and that you fixed up your own room because I snore, and you said Bjornstam was too good for Bea, and then, just recent, that you were sore on the town because we don't all go down on our knees and beg this Valborg fellow to come take supper with us. God only knows what else she says you said."

"It's not true, any of it! I did like Mrs. Westlake, and I've called on her, and apparently she's gone and twisted everything I've said——"

"Sure. Of course she would. Didn't I tell you she would? She's an old cat, like her pussyfooting, hand-holding husband. Lord, if I was sick, I'd rather have a faith-healer than Westlake, and she's another slice off the same bacon. What I can't understand though——"

She waited, taut.

"——is whatever possessed you to let her pump you, bright a girl as you are. I don't care what you told her—we all get peeved sometimes and want to blow off steam, that's natural—but if you wanted to keep it dark, why didn't you advertise it in the *Dauntless*, or get a megaphone and stand on top of the hotel and holler, or do anything besides spill it to her!"

"I know. You told me. But she was so motherly. And I didn't have any woman—— Vida 's become so married and proprietary."

"Well, next time you'll have better sense."

He patted her head, flumped down behind his newspaper, said nothing more.

Enemies leered through the windows, stole on her from the hall. She had no one save Erik. This kind good man Kennicott—he was an elder brother. It was Erik, her fellow outcast, to whom she wanted to run for sanctuary. Through her storm she was, to the eye, sitting quietly with her fingers between the pages of a baby-blue book on home-dressmaking. But her dismay at Mrs. Westlake's treachery had risen to active dread. What had the woman said of her and Erik? What did she know? What had she seen? Who else would join in the baying hunt? Who else had seen her with Erik? What had she to fear from the Dyers, Cy Bogart, Juanita, Aunt Bessie? What precisely had she answered to Mrs. Bogart's questioning?

All next day she was too restless to stay home, yet as she walked the streets on fictitious errands she was afraid of every person she met. She waited for them to speak; waited with foreboding. She repeated, "I mustn't ever see Erik again." But the words did not register. She had no ecstatic indulgence in the sense of guilt which is, to the women of Main Street, the surest escape from blank tediousness.

At five, crumpled in a chair in the living-room, she started at the sound of the bell. Some one opened the door. She waited, uneasy. Vida Sherwin charged into the room. "Here's the one person I can trust!" Carol rejoiced.

Vida was serious but affectionate. She bustled at Carol with, "Oh, there you are, dearie, so glad t' find you in, sit down, want to talk to you."

Carol sat, obedient.

Vida fussily tugged over a large chair and launched out:

"I've been hearing vague rumors you were interested in this Erik Valborg. I knew you couldn't be guilty, and I'm surer than ever of it now. Here we are, as blooming as a daisy."

"How does a respectable matron look when she feels guilty?"

Carol sounded resentful.

"Why—— Oh, it would show! Besides! I know that you, of all people, are the one that can appreciate Dr. Will."

"What have you been hearing?"

"Nothing, really. I just heard Mrs. Bogart say she'd seen you and Valborg walking together a lot." Vida's chirping slackened. She looked at her nails. "But—— I suspect you do like Valborg. Oh, I don't mean in any wrong way. But you're young; you don't know what an innocent liking might drift into. You always pretend to be so sophisticated and all, but you're a baby. Just because you are so innocent, you don't know what evil thoughts may lurk in that fellow's brain."

"You don't suppose Valborg could actually think about making love to me?"

Her rather cheap sport ended abruptly as Vida cried, with contorted face, "What do you know about the thoughts in hearts? You just play at reforming the world. You don't know what it means to suffer."

There are two insults which no human being will endure: the assertion that he hasn't a sense of humor, and the doubly impertinent assertion that he has never known trouble. Carol said furiously, "You think I don't suffer? You think I've always had an easy——"

"No, you don't. I'm going to tell you something I've never told a living soul, not even Ray." The dam of repressed imagination which Vida had builded for years, which now, with Raymie off at the wars, she was building again, gave way. "I was—I liked Will terribly well. One time at a party—oh, before he met you, of course—but we held hands, and we were so happy. But I didn't feel I was really suited to him. I let him go. Please don't think I still love him! I see now that Ray was predestined to be my mate. But because I liked him, I know how sincere and pure and noble Will is, and his thoughts never straying from the path of rectitude, and—— If I gave him up to you, at least you've got to appreciate him! We danced together and laughed so, and I gave him up, but—— This *is* my affair! I'm *not* intruding! I see the whole thing as he does, because of all I've told you. Maybe it's shameless to bare my heart this way, but I do it for him—for him and you!"

Carol understood that Vida believed herself to have recited minutely and brazenly a story of intimate love; understood that, in alarm, she was trying to cover her shame as she struggled on, "Liked him in the most honorable way—simply can't help it if I still see things through his eyes—— If I gave him up, I certainly am not beyond my rights in demanding that you take care to avoid even the appearance of evil and——" She was weeping; an insignificant, flushed, ungracefully weeping woman.

Carol could not endure it. She ran to Vida, kissed her forehead, comforted her with a murmur of dove-like sounds, sought to reassure her with worn and hastily assembled gifts of words: "Oh, I appreciate it so much," and "You are so fine and splendid," and "Let me assure you there isn't a thing to what you've heard," and "Oh, indeed, I do know how sincere Will is, and as you say, so—so sincere."

Vida believed that she had explained many deep and devious matters. She came out of her hysteria like a sparrow shaking off rain-drops. She sat up, and took advantage of her victory:

"I don't want to rub it in, but you can see for yourself now, this is all a result of your being so discontented and not appreciating the dear good people here. And another thing: People like you and me, who want to reform things, have to be particularly careful about appearances. Think how much better you can criticize conventional customs if you yourself live up to them, scrupulously. Then people can't say you're attacking them to excuse your own infractions."

To Carol was given a sudden great philosophical understanding, an explanation of half the cautious reforms in history. "Yes. I've heard that plea. It's a good one. It sets revolts aside to cool. It keeps strays in the flock. To word it differently: 'You must live up to the popular code if you believe in it; but if you don't believe in it, then you *must* live up to it!'"

"I don't think so at all," said Vida vaguely. She began to look hurt, and Carol let her be oracular.

### III

Vida had done her a service; had made all agonizing seem so fatuous that she ceased writhing and saw that her whole problem was simple as mutton: she was interested in Erik's aspiration; interest gave her a hesitating fondness for him; and the future would take care of the event. . . . But at night, thinking in bed, she protested, "I'm not a falsely accused innocent, though! If it were some one more resolute than Erik, a fighter, an artist with bearded surly lips—— They're only in books. Is that the real tragedy, that I never shall know tragedy, never find anything but blustery complications that turn out to be a farce?

"No one big enough or pitiful enough to sacrifice for. Tragedy in neat blouses; the eternal flame all nice and safe in a kerosene stove. Neither heroic faith nor heroic guilt. Peeping at love from behind lace curtains—on Main Street!"

Aunt Bessie crept in next day, tried to pump her, tried to prime the pump by again hinting that Kennicott might have his own affairs. Carol snapped, "Whatever I may do, I'll have you to understand that Will is only too safe!" She wished afterward that she had not been so lofty. How much would Aunt Bessie make of "Whatever I may do?"

When Kennicott came home he poked at things, and hemmed, and brought out, "Saw aunty, this afternoon. She said you weren't very polite to her."

Carol laughed. He looked at her in a puzzled way and fled to his news-paper.

IV

She lay sleepless. She alternately considered ways of leaving Kennicott, and remembered his virtues, pitied his bewilderment in face of the subtle cor-roding sicknesses which he could not dose nor cut out. Didn't he perhaps need her more than did the book-solaced Erik? Suppose Will were to die, suddenly. Suppose she never again saw him at breakfast, silent but amiable, listening to her chatter. Suppose he never again played elephant for Hugh. Suppose—— A country call, a slippery road, his motor skidding, the edge of the road crumbling, the car turning turtle, Will pinned beneath, suffering, brought home maimed, looking at her with spaniel eyes—or waiting for her, calling for her, while she was in Chicago, knowing nothing of it. Suppose he were sued by some vicious shrieking woman for malpractice. He tried to get witnesses; Westlake spread lies; his friends doubted him; his self-confidence was so broken that it was horrible to see the indecision of the decisive man; he was convicted, handcuffed, taken on a train——

She ran to his room. At her nervous push the door swung sharply in, struck a chair. He awoke, gasped, then in a steady voice: "What is it, dear? Any-thing wrong?" She darted to him, fumbled for the familiar harsh bristly cheek. How well she knew it, every seam, and hardness of bone, and roll of fat! Yet when he sighed, "This is a nice visit," and dropped his hand on her thin-covered shoulder, she said, too cheerily, "I thought I heard you moaning. So silly of me. Good night, dear."

V

She did not see Erik for a fortnight, save once at church and once when she went to the tailor shop to talk over the plans, contingencies, and strategy of Kennicott's annual campaign for getting a new suit. Nat Hicks was there, and he was not so deferential as he had been. With unnecessary jauntiness he chuckled, "Some nice flannels, them samples, heh?" Needlessly he touched her arm to call attention to the fashion-plates, and humorously he glanced from her to Erik. At home she wondered if the little beast might not be suggesting himself as a rival to Erik, but that abysmal bedragglement she would not consider.

She saw Juanita Haydock slowly walking past the house—as Mrs. Westlake had once walked past.

She met Mrs. Westlake in Uncle Whittier's store, and before that alert stare forgot her determination to be rude, and was shakily cordial.

She was sure that all the men on the street, even Guy Pollock and Sam Clark, leered at her in an interested hopeful way, as though she were a no-torious divorcée. She felt as insecure as a shadowed criminal. She wished to see Erik, and wished that she had never seen him. She fancied that Kenni-cott was the only person in town who did not know all—know incomparably more than there was to know—about herself and Erik. She crouched in her chair as she imagined men talking of her, thick-voiced, obscene, in barber shops and the tobacco-stinking pool parlor.

Through early autumn Fern Mullins was the only person who broke the suspense. The frivolous teacher had come to accept Carol as of her own youth, and though school had begun she rushed in daily to suggest dances, welsh-rabbit parties.

Fern begged her to go as chaperon to a barn-dance in the country, on a Saturday evening. Carol could not go. The next day, the storm crashed.

# 32

Carol was on the back porch, tightening a bolt on the baby's go-cart, this Sunday afternoon. Through an open window of the Bogart house she heard a screeching, heard Mrs. Bogart's haggish voice:

". . . did too, and there's no use your denying it . . . no you don't, you march yourself right straight out of the house . . . never in my life heard of such . . . never had nobody talk to me like . . . walk in the ways of sin and nastiness . . . leave your clothes here, and heaven knows that's more than you deserve . . . any of your lip or I'll call the policeman."

The voice of the other interlocutor Carol did not catch, nor, though Mrs. Bogart was proclaiming that he was her confidant and present assistant, did she catch the voice of Mrs. Bogart's God.

"Another row with Cy," Carol inferred.

She trundled the go-cart down the back steps and tentatively wheeled it across the yard, proud of her repairs. She heard steps on the sidewalk. She saw not Cy Bogart but Fern Mullins, carrying a suit-case, hurrying up the street with her head low. The widow, standing on the porch with buttery arms akimbo, yammered after the fleeing girl:

"And don't you dare show your face on this block again. You can send the drayman for your trunk. My house has been contaminated long enough. Why the Lord should afflict me——"

Fern was gone. The righteous widow glared, banged into the house, came out poking at her bonnet, marched away. By this time Carol was staring in a manner not visibly to be distinguished from the window-peeping of the rest of Gopher Prairie. She saw Mrs. Bogart enter the Howland house, then the Casses'. Not till suppertime did she reach the Kennicotts. The doctor answered her ring, and greeted her, "Well, well, how's the good neighbor?"

The good neighbor charged into the living-room, waving the most unctuous of black kid gloves and delightedly sputtering:

"You may well ask how I am! I really do wonder how I could go through the awful scenes of this day—and the impudence I took from that woman's tongue, that ought to be cut out——"

"Whoa! Whoa! Hold up!" roared Kennicott. "Who's the hussy, Sister Bogart? Sit down and take it cool and tell us about it."

"I can't sit down, I must hurry home, but I couldn't devote myself to my own selfish cares till I'd warned you, and heaven knows I don't expect any thanks for trying to warn the town against her, there's always so much evil in the world that folks simply won't see or appreciate your trying to safeguard them—— And forcing herself in here to get in with you and Carrie, many 's the time I've seen her doing it, and, thank heaven, she was found out in time before she could do any more harm, it simply breaks my heart and prostrates me to think what she may have done already, even if some of us that understand and know about things——"

"Whoa-up! Who are you talking about?"

"She's talking about Fern Mullins," Carol put in, not pleasantly.

"Huh?"

Kennicott was incredulous.

"I certainly am!" flourished Mrs. Bogart, "and good and thankful you may be that I found her out in time, before she could get *you* into something, Carol; because even if you are my neighbor and Will's wife and a cultured lady, let me tell you right now, Carol Kennicott, that you ain't always as respectful to—you ain't as reverent—you don't stick by the good old ways like they was laid down for us by God in the Bible, and while of course there ain't a bit of harm in having a good laugh, and I know there ain't any real wickedness in you, yet just the same you don't fear God and hate the transgressors of his commandments like you ought to, and you may be thankful I found out this serpent I nourished in my bosom—and oh yes! oh yes indeed! my lady must have two eggs every morning for breakfast, and eggs sixty cents a dozen, and wa'n't satisfied with one, like most folks—what did she care how much they cost or if a person couldn't make hardly nothing on her board and room, in fact I just took her in out of charity and I might have known from the kind of stockings and clothes that she sneaked into my house in her trunk——"

Before they got her story she had five more minutes of obscene wallowing. The gutter comedy turned into high tragedy, with Nemesis in black kid gloves. The actual story was simple, depressing, and unimportant. As to details Mrs. Bogart was indefinite, and angry that she should be questioned.

Fern Mullins and Cy had, the evening before, driven alone to a barn-dance in the country. (Carol brought out the admission that Fern had tried to get a chaperon.) At the dance Cy had kissed Fern—she confessed that. Cy had obtained a pint of whisky; he said that he didn't remember where he had got it; Mrs. Bogart implied that Fern had given it to him; Fern herself insisted that he had stolen it from a farmer's overcoat—which, Mrs. Bogart raged, was obviously a lie. He had become soggily drunk. Fern had driven him home; deposited him, retching and wabbling, on the Bogart porch.

Never before had her boy been drunk, shrieked Mrs. Bogart. When Kennicott grunted, she owned, "Well, maybe once or twice I've smelled licker on his breath." She also, with an air of being only too scrupulously exact, granted that sometimes he did not come home till morning. But he couldn't ever have been drunk, for he always had the best excuses: the other boys had tempted him to go down the lake spearing pickerel by torchlight, or he had been out in a "machine that ran out of gas." Anyway, never before had her boy fallen into the hands of a "designing woman."

"What do you suppose Miss Mullins could design to do with him?" insisted Carol.

Mrs. Bogart was puzzled, gave it up, went on. This morning, when she had faced both of them, Cy had manfully confessed that all of the blame was on Fern, because the teacher—his own teacher—had dared him to take a drink. Fern had tried to deny it.

"Then," gabbled Mrs. Bogart, "then that woman had the impudence to say to me, 'What purpose could I have in wanting the filthy pup to get drunk?' That's just what she called him—pup. 'I'll have no such nasty language in my house,' I says, 'and you pretending and pulling the wool over people's eyes and making them think you're educated and fit to be a teacher and look out for young people's morals—you're worse 'n any street-walker!' I says. I let her have it good. I wa'n't going to flinch from my bounden duty and let her think that decent folks had to stand for her vile talk. 'Purpose?' I says, 'Purpose? I'll tell you what purpose you had! Ain't I seen you making up to everything in pants that'd waste time and pay attention to your impert'nence? Ain't I seen you showing off your legs with them short skirts of yours, trying to make out like you was so girlish and la-de-da, running along the street?'"

Carol was very sick at this version of Fern's eager youth, but she was sicker as Mrs. Bogart hinted that no one could tell what had happened between Fern and Cy before the drive home. Without exactly describing the scene, by her power of lustful imagination the woman suggested dark country places apart from the lanterns and rude fiddling and banging dance-steps in the barn, then madness and harsh hateful conquest. Carol was too sick to interrupt. It was Kennicott who cried, "Oh, for God's sake quit it! You haven't any idea what happened. You haven't given us a single proof yet that Fern is anything but a rattle-brained youngster."

"I haven't, eh? Well, what do you say to this? I come straight out and I says to her, 'Did you or did you not taste the whisky Cy had?' and she says, 'I think I did take one sip—Cy made me,' she said. She owned up to that much, so you can imagine——"

"Does that prove her a prostitute?" asked Carol.

"Carrie! Don't you never use a word like that again!" wailed the outraged Puritan.

"Well, does it prove her to be a bad woman, that she took a taste of whisky? I've done it myself!"

"That's different. Not that I approve your doing it. What do the Scriptures tell us? 'Strong drink is a mocker'! But that's entirely different from a teacher drinking with one of her own pupils."

"Yes, it does sound bad. Fern was silly, undoubtedly. But as a matter of fact she's only a year or two older than Cy, and probably a good many years younger in experience of vice."

"That's—not—true! She is plenty old enough to corrupt him!"

"The job of corrupting Cy was done by your sinless town, five years ago!"

Mrs. Bogart did not rage in return. Suddenly she was hopeless. Her head drooped. She patted her black kid gloves, picked at a thread of her faded brown skirt, and sighed, "He's a good boy, and awful affectionate if you treat him right. Some thinks he's terrible wild, but that's because he's young. And he's so brave and truthful—why, he was one of the first in town that wanted to enlist for the war, and I had to speak real sharp to him to keep him from running away. I didn't want him to get into no bad influences round these camps—and then," Mrs. Bogart rose from her pitifulness, recovered her pace, "then I go and bring into my own house a woman that's worse, when all's said and done, than any bad woman he could have met. You say this Mullins woman is too young and inexperienced to corrupt Cy. Well then, she's too young and inexperienced to teach him, too, one or t'other, you can't have your cake and eat it! So it don't make no difference which reason they fire her for, and that's practically almost what I said to the school-board."

"Have you been telling this story to the members of the school-board?"

"I certainly have! Every one of 'em! And their wives I says to them, ' 'Tain't my affair to decide what you should or should not do with your teachers,' I says, 'and I ain't presuming to dictate in any way, shape, manner, or form. I just want to know,' I says, 'whether you're going to go on record as keeping here in our schools, among a lot of innocent boys and girls, a woman that drinks, smokes, curses, uses bad language, and does such dreadful things as I wouldn't lay tongue to but you know what I mean,' I says, 'and if so, I'll just see to it that the town learns about it.' And that's what I told Professor Mott, too, being superintendent—and he's a righteous man, not going autoing on the Sabbath like the school-board members. And the professor as much as admitted he was suspicious of the Mullins woman himself."

II

Kennicott was less shocked and much less frightened than Carol, and more articulate in his description of Mrs. Bogart, when she had gone.

Maud Dyer telephoned to Carol and, after a rather improbable question about cooking lima beans with bacon, demanded, "Have you heard the scandal about this Miss Mullins and Cy Bogart?"

"I'm sure it's a lie."

"Oh, probably is." Maud's manner indicated that the falsity of the story was an insignificant flaw in its general delightfulness.

Carol crept to her room, sat with hands curled tight together as she listened to a plague of voices. She could hear the town yelping with it, every soul of them, gleeful at new details, panting to win importance by having details of their own to add. How well they would make up for what they had been afraid to do by imagining it in another! They who had not been entirely afraid (but merely careful and sneaky), all the barber-shop roués and millinery-parlor mondaines, how archly they were giggling (this second—she could hear them at it); with what self-commendation they were cackling their suavest wit: "You can't tell *me* she ain't a gay bird; I'm wise!"

And not one man in town to carry out their pioneer tradition of superb and contemptuous cursing, not one to verify the myth that their "rough chivalry" and "rugged virtues" were more generous than the petty scandal-picking of older lands, not one dramatic frontiersman to thunder, with fantastic and fictional oaths, "What are you hinting at? What are you snickering at? What facts have you? What are these unheard-of sins you condemn so much—and like so well?"

No one to say it. Not Kennicott nor Guy Pollock nor Champ Perry.

Erik? Possibly. He would sputter uneasy protest.

She suddenly wondered what subterranean connection her interest in Erik had with this affair. Wasn't it because they had been prevented by her caste from bounding on her own trail that they were howling at Fern?

### III

Before supper she found, by half a dozen telephone calls, that Fern had fled to the Minniemashie House. She hastened there, trying not to be self-conscious about the people who looked at her on the street. The clerk said indifferently that he "guessed" Miss Mullins was up in Room 37, and left Carol to find the way. She hunted along the stale-smelling corridors with their wallpaper of cerise daisies and poison-green rosettes, streaked in white spots from spilled water, their frayed red and yellow matting, and rows of pine doors painted a sickly blue. She could not find the number. In the darkness at the end of a corridor she had to feel the aluminum figures on the door-panels. She was startled once by a man's voice: "Yep? Whadyuh want?" and fled. When she reached the right door she stood listening. She made out a long sobbing. There was no answer till her third knock; then an alarmed "Who is it? Go away!"

Her hatred of the town turned resolute as she pushed open the door.

Yesterday she had seen Fern Mullins in boots and tweed skirt and canary-yellow sweater, fleet and self-possessed. Now she lay across the bed, in crumpled lavender cotton and shabby pumps, very feminine, utterly cowed. She lifted her head in stupid terror. Her hair was in tousled strings and her face was sallow, creased. Her eyes were a blur from weeping.

"I didn't! I didn't!" was all she would say at first, and she repeated it while Carol kissed her cheek, stroked her hair, bathed her forehead. She rested then, while Carol looked about the room—the welcome to strangers, the sanctuary of hospitable Main Street, the lucrative property of Kennicott's friend, Jackson Elder. It smelled of old linen and decaying carpet and ancient tobacco smoke. The bed was rickety, with a thin knotty mattress; the sand-colored walls were scratched and gouged; in every corner, under everything, were fluffy dust and cigar ashes; on the tilted wash-stand was a nicked and squatty pitcher; the only chair was a grim straight object of spotty varnish; but there was an altogether splendid gilt and rose cuspidor.

She did not try to draw out Fern's story; Fern insisted on telling it.

She had gone to the party, not quite liking Cy but willing to endure him for the sake of dancing, of escaping from Mrs. Bogart's flow of moral comments, of relaxing after the first strained weeks of teaching. Cy "promised to be good." He was, on the way out. There were a few workmen from Gopher Prairie at the dance, with many young farm-people. Half a dozen squatters from a degenerate colony in a brush-hidden hollow, planters of potatoes, suspected thieves, came in noisily drunk. They all pounded the floor of the barn in old-fashioned square dances, swinging their partners, skipping, laughing, under the incantations of Del Snafflin the barber, who fiddled and called the figures. Cy had two drinks from pocket-flasks. Fern saw him fumbling among the overcoats piled on the feedbox at the far end of the barn; soon after she heard a farmer declaring that some one had stolen his bottle. She taxed Cy with the theft; he chuckled, "Oh, it's just a joke; I'm going to give it back." He demanded that she take a drink. Unless she did, he wouldn't return the bottle.

"I just brushed my lips with it, and gave it back to him," moaned Fern. She sat up, glared at Carol. "Did you ever take a drink?"

"I have. A few. I'd love to have one right now! This contact with righteousness has about done me up!"

Fern could laugh then. "So would I! I don't suppose I've had five drinks in my life, but if I meet just one more Bogart and Son—— Well, I didn't really touch that bottle—horrible raw whisky—though I'd have loved some wine. I felt so jolly. The barn was almost like a stage scene—the high rafters, and the dark stalls, and tin lanterns swinging, and a silage-cutter up at the end like some mysterious kind of machine. And I'd been having lots of fun dancing with the nicest young farmer, so strong and nice, and awfully intelligent. But I got uneasy when I saw how Cy was. So I doubt if I touched two drops of the beastly stuff. Do you suppose God is punishing me for even wanting wine?"

"My dear, Mrs. Bogart's god may be—Main Street's god. But all the courageous intelligent people are fighting him . . . though he slay us."

Fern danced again with the young farmer; she forgot Cy while she was talking with a girl who had taken the University agricultural course. Cy could not have returned the bottle; he came staggering toward her—taking time to make himself offensive to every girl on the way and to dance a jig. She insisted on their returning. Cy went with her, chuckling and jigging. He kissed her, outside the door. . . . "And to think I used to think it was interesting to have men kiss you at a dance!" . . . She ignored the kiss, in the need of getting him home before he started a fight. A farmer helped her harness the buggy, while Cy snored in the seat. He awoke before they set out; all the way home he alternately slept and tried to make love to her.

"I'm almost as strong as he is. I managed to keep him away while I drove—such a rickety buggy. I didn't feel like a girl; I felt like a scrubwoman—no, I guess I was too scared to have any feelings at all. It was terribly dark. I got home, somehow. But it was hard, the time I had to get out, and it was quite muddy, to read the sign-post—I lit matches that I took from Cy's coat pocket, and he followed me—he fell off the buggy step into the mud, and got up and tried to make love to me, and—— I was scared. But I hit him. Quite hard. And got in, and so he ran after the buggy, crying like a baby, and I let him in again, and right away again he was trying—— But no matter. I got him home. Up on the porch. Mrs. Bogart was waiting up. . . .

"You know, it was funny; all the time she was—oh, talking to me—and Cy was being terribly sick—I just kept thinking, 'I've still got to drive the buggy down to the livery stable. I wonder if the livery man will be awake?' But I got through somehow. I took the buggy down to the stable, and got to my room. I locked my door, but Mrs. Bogart kept saying things, outside the door. Stood out there saying things about me, dreadful things, and rattling the knob. And all the while I could hear Cy in the back yard—being sick. I don't think I'll ever marry any man. And then today——

"She drove me right out of the house. She wouldn't listen to me, all morning. Just to Cy. I suppose he's over his headache now. Even at breakfast he thought the whole thing was a grand joke. I suppose right this minute he's going around town boasting about his 'conquest.' You understand—oh, *don't* you understand? I *did* keep him away! But I don't see how I can face my school. They say country towns are fine for bringing up boys in, but—— I can't believe this is me, lying here and saying this. I don't *believe* what happened last night.

"Oh. This was curious: When I took off my dress last night—it was a darling dress, I loved it so, but of course the mud had spoiled it. I cried over it and—— No matter. But my white silk stockings were all torn, and the strange thing is, I don't know whether I caught my legs in the briers when I got out to look at the sign-post, or whether Cy scratched me when I was fighting him off."

IV

Sam Clark was president of the school-board. When Carol told him Fern's story Sam looked sympathetic and neighborly, and Mrs. Clark sat by cooing, "Oh, isn't that too bad." Carol was interrupted only when Mrs. Clark begged, "Dear, don't speak so bitter about 'pious' people. There's lots of sincere practising Christians that are real tolerant. Like the Champ Perrys."

"Yes. I know. Unfortunately there are enough kindly people in the churches to keep them going."

When Carol had finished, Mrs. Clark breathed, "Poor girl; I don't doubt her story a bit," and Sam rumbled, "Yuh, sure. Miss Mullins is young and reckless, but everybody in town, except Ma Bogart, knows what Cy is. But Miss Mullins was a fool to go with him."

"But not wicked enough to pay for it with disgrace?"

"N-no, but——" Sam avoided verdicts, clung to the entrancing horrors of the story. "Ma Bogart cussed her out all morning, did she? Jumped her neck, eh? Ma certainly is one hell-cat."

"Yes, you know how she is; so vicious."

"Oh no, her best style ain't her viciousness. What she pulls in our store is to come in smiling with Christian Fortitude and keep a clerk busy for one hour while she picks out half a dozen fourpenny nails. I remember one time——"

"Sam!" Carol was uneasy. "You'll fight for Fern, won't you? When Mrs. Bogart came to see you did she make definite charges?"

"Well, yes, you might say she did."

"But the school-board won't act on them?"

"Guess we'll more or less have to."

"But you'll exonerate Fern?"

"I'll do what I can for the girl personally, but you know what the board is. There's Reverend Zitterel; Sister Bogart about half runs his church, so of course he'll take her say-so; and Ezra Stowbody, as a banker he has to be all hell for morality and purity. Might 's well admit it, Carrie; I'm afraid there'll be a majority of the board against her. Not that any of us would believe a word Cy said, not if he swore it on a stack of Bibles, but still, after all this gossip, Miss Mullins wouldn't hardly be the party to chaperon our basket-ball team when it went out of town to play other high schools, would she!"

"Perhaps not, but couldn't some one else?"

"Why, that's one of the things she was hired for." Sam sounded stubborn.

"Do you realize that this isn't just a matter of a job, and hiring and firing; that it's actually sending a splendid girl out with a beastly stain on her, giving all the other Bogarts in the world a chance at her? That's what will happen if you discharge her."

Sam moved uncomfortably, looked at his wife, scratched his head, sighed, said nothing.

"Won't you fight for her on the board? If you lose, won't you, and who-ever agrees with you, make a minority report?"

"No reports made in a case like this. Our rule is to just decide the thing and announce the final decision, whether it's unanimous or not."

"Rules! Against a girl's future! Dear God! Rules of a school-board! Sam! Won't you stand by Fern, and threaten to resign from the board if they try to discharge her?"

Rather testy, tired of so many subtleties, he complained, "Well, I'll do what I can, but I'll have to wait till the board meets."

And "I'll do what I can," together with the secret admission "Of course you and I know what Ma Bogart is," was all Carol could get from Superin-tendent George Edwin Mott, Ezra Stowbody, the Reverend Mr. Zitterel or any other member of the school-board.

Afterward she wondered whether Mr. Zitterel could have been referring to herself when he observed, "There's too much license in high places in this town, though, and the wages of sin is death—or anyway, bein' fired." The holy leer with which the priest said it remained in her mind.

She was at the hotel before eight next morning. Fern longed to go to school, to face the tittering, but she was too shaky. Carol read to her all day and, by reassuring her, convinced her own self that the school-board would be just. She was less sure of it that evening when, at the motion pictures, she heard Mrs. Gougerling exclaim to Mrs. Howland, "She may be so innocent and all, and I suppose she probably is, but still, if she drank a whole bottle of whisky at that dance, the way everybody says she did, she may have forgotten she was so innocent! Hee, hee, hee!" Maud Dyer, leaning back from her seat, put in, "That's what I've said all along. I don't want to roast anybody, but have you noticed the way she looks at men?"

"When will they have me on the scaffold?" Carol speculated.

Nat Hicks stopped the Kennicotts on their way home. Carol hated him for his manner of assuming that they two had a mysterious understanding. Without quite winking he seemed to wink at her as he gurgled, "What do you folks think about this Mullins woman? I'm not strait-laced, but I tell you we got to have decent women in our schools. D' you know what I heard? They say whatever she may of done afterwards, this Mullins dame took two quarts of whisky to the dance with her, and got stewed before Cy did! Some tank, that wren! Ha, ha, ha!"

"Rats, I don't believe it," Kennicott muttered.

He got Carol away before she was able to speak.

She saw Erik passing the house, late, alone, and she stared after him, longing for the lively bitterness of the things he would say about the town. Kennicott had nothing for her but "Oh, course, ev'body likes a juicy story, but they don't intend to be mean."

She went up to bed proving to herself that the members of the school-board were superior men.

It was Tuesday afternoon before she learned that the board had met at ten in the morning and voted to "accept Miss Fern Mullins's resignation." Sam Clark telephoned the news to her. "We're not making any charges. We're just letting her resign. Would you like to drop over to the hotel and ask her to write the resignation, now we've accepted it? Glad I could get the board to put it that way. It's thanks to you."

"But can't you see that the town will take this as proof of the charges?"

"We're—not—making—no—charges—whatever!" Sam was obviously finding it hard to be patient.

Fern left town that evening.

Carol went with her to the train. The two girls elbowed through a silent lip-licking crowd. Carol tried to stare them down but in face of the impishness of the boys and the bovine gaping of the men, she was embarrassed. Fern did not glance at them. Carol felt her arm tremble, though she was tearless, listless, plodding. She squeezed Carol's hand, said something unintelligible, stumbled up into the vestibule.

Carol remembered that Miles Bjornstam had also taken a train. What would be the scene at the station when she herself took departure?

She walked up-town behind two strangers.

One of them was giggling, "See that good-looking wench that got on here? The swell kid with the small black hat? She's some charmer! I was here yesterday, before my jump to Ojibway Falls, and I heard all about her. Seems she was a teacher, but she certainly was a high-roller—O boy!—high, wide, and fancy! Her and couple of other skirts bought a whole case of whisky and went on a tear, and one night, darned if this bunch of cradle-robbers didn't get hold of some young kids, just small boys, and they all got lit up like a White Way, and went out to a roughneck dance, and they say——"

The narrator turned, saw a woman near and, not being a common person nor a coarse workman but a clever salesman and a householder, lowered his voice for the rest of the tale. During it the other man laughed hoarsely.

Carol turned off on a side-street.

She passed Cy Bogart. He was humorously narrating some achievement to a group which included Nat Hicks, Del Snafflin, Bert Tybee the bartender, and A. Tennyson O'Hearn the shyster lawyer. They were men far older than Cy but they accepted him as one of their own, and encouraged him to go on.

It was a week before she received from Fern a letter of which this was a part:

. . . & of course my family did not really believe the story but as they were sure I must have done something wrong they just lectured me generally, in fact jawed me till I have gone to live at a boarding house. The teachers' agencies must know the story, man at one almost slammed the door in my face when I went to ask about a job, & at another the woman in charge was beastly. Don't know what I will do. Don't seem to feel very well. May marry a fellow that's in love with me but he's so stupid that he makes me *scream*.

Dear Mrs. Kennicott you were the only one that believed me. I guess it's a joke on me, I was such a simp, I felt quite heroic while I was driving the buggy back that night & keeping Cy away from me. I guess I expected the people in Gopher Prairie to admire me. I did use to be admired for my athletics at the U.—just five months ago.

# 33

For a month which was one suspended moment of doubt she saw Erik only casually, at an Eastern Star dance, at the shop, where, in the presence of Nat Hicks, they conferred with immense particularity on the significance of having one or two buttons on the cuff of Kennicott's New Suit. For the benefit of beholders they were respectably vacuous.

Thus barred from him, depressed in the thought of Fern, Carol was suddenly and for the first time convinced that she loved Erik.

She told herself a thousand inspiriting things which he would say if he had the opportunity; for them she admired him, loved him. But she was afraid to summon him. He understood, he did not come. She forgot her every doubt of him, and her discomfort in his background. Each day it seemed impossible to get through the desolation of not seeing him. Each morning, each afternoon, each evening was a compartment divided from all other units of time, distinguished by a sudden "Oh! I want to see Erik!" which was as devastating as though she had never said it before.

There were wretched periods when she could not picture him. Usually he stood out in her mind in some little moment—glancing up from his preposterous pressing-iron, or running on the beach with Dave Dyer. But sometimes he had vanished; he was only an opinion. She worried then about his appearance: Weren't his wrists too large and red? Wasn't his nose a snub, like so many Scandinavians? Was he at all the graceful thing she had fancied? When she encountered him on the street she was as much reassuring herself as rejoicing in his presence. More disturbing than being unable to visualize him was the darting remembrance of some intimate aspect: his face as they had walked to the boat together at the picnic; the ruddy light on his temples, neck-cords, flat cheeks.

On a November evening when Kennicott was in the country she answered the bell and was confused to find Erik at the door, stooped, imploring, his hands in the pockets of his topcoat. As though he had been rehearsing his speech he instantly besought:

"Saw your husband driving away. I've got to see you. I can't stand it. Come for a walk. I know! People might see us. But they won't if we hike into the country. I'll wait for you by the elevator. Take as long as you want to—oh, come quick!"

"In a few minutes," she promised.

She murmured, "I'll just talk to him for a quarter of an hour and come home." She put on her tweed coat and rubber overshoes, considering how honest and hopeless are rubbers, how clearly their chaperonage proved that she wasn't going to a lovers' tryst.

She found him in the shadow of the grain-elevator, sulkily kicking at a rail of the side-track. As she came toward him she fancied that his whole body expanded. But he said nothing, nor she; he patted her sleeve, she returned the pat, and they crossed the railroad tracks, found a road, clumped toward open country.

"Chilly night, but I like this melancholy gray," he said.

"Yes."

They passed a moaning clump of trees and splashed along the wet road. He tucked her hand into the side-pocket of his overcoat. She caught his thumb and, sighing, held it exactly as Hugh held hers when they went walking. She thought about Hugh. The current maid was in for the evening, but was it safe to leave the baby with her? The thought was distant and elusive.

Erik began to talk, slowly, revealingly. He made for her a picture of his work in a large tailor shop in Minneapolis: the steam and heat, and the drudgery; the men in darned vests and crumpled trousers, men who "rushed growlers of beer" and were cynical about women, who laughed at him and played jokes on him. "But I didn't mind, because I could keep away from them outside. I used to go to the Art Institute and the Walker Gallery, and tramp clear around Lake Harriet, or hike out to the Gates house and imagine it was a château in Italy and I lived in it. I was a marquis and collected tapestries—that was after I was wounded in Padua. The only really bad time was when a tailor named Finkelfarb found a diary I was trying to keep and he read it aloud in the shop—it was a bad fight." He laughed. "I got fined five dollars. But that's all gone now. Seems as though you stand between me and the gas stoves—the long flames with mauve edges, licking up around the irons and making that sneering sound all day—aaaaah!"

Her fingers tightened about his thumb as she perceived the hot low room, the pounding of pressing-irons, the reek of scorched cloth, and Erik among giggling gnomes. His finger-tip crept through the opening of her glove and smoothed her palm. She snatched her hand away, stripped off her glove, tucked her hand back into his.

He was saying something about a "wonderful person." In her tranquillity she let the words blow by and heeded only the beating wings of his voice.

She was conscious that he was fumbling for impressive speech.

"Say, uh—Carol, I've written a poem about you."

"That's nice. Let's hear it."

"Damn it, don't be so casual about it! Can't you take me seriously?"

"My dear boy, if I took you seriously——! I don't want us to be hurt more than—more than we will be. Tell me the poem. I've never had a poem written about me!"

"It isn't really a poem. It's just some words that I love because it seems to me they catch what you are. Of course probably they won't seem so to anybody else, but—— Well——

> Little and tender and merry and wise
> With eyes that meet my eyes.

Do you get the idea the way I do?"

"Yes! I'm terribly grateful!" And she was grateful—while she impersonally noted how bad a verse it was.

She was aware of the haggard beauty in the lowering night. Monstrous tattered clouds sprawled round a forlorn moon; puddles and rocks glistened with inner light. They were passing a grove of scrub poplars, feeble by day but looming now like a menacing wall. She stopped. They heard the branches dripping, the wet leaves sullenly plumping on the soggy earth.

"Waiting—waiting—everything is waiting," she whispered. She drew her hand from his, pressed her clenched fingers against her lips. She was lost in the somberness. "I am happy—so we must go home, before we have time to become unhappy. But can't we sit on a log for a minute and just listen?"

"No. Too wet. But I wish we could build a fire, and you could sit on my overcoat beside it. I'm a grand fire-builder! My cousin Lars and me spent a week one time in a cabin way up in the Big Woods, snowed in. The fireplace was filled with a dome of ice when we got there, but we chopped it out, and jammed the thing full of pine-boughs. Couldn't we build a fire back here in the woods and sit by it for a while?"

She pondered, half-way between yielding and refusal. Her head ached faintly. She was in abeyance. Everything, the night, his silhouette, the cautious-treading future, was as undistinguishable as though she were drifting bodiless in a Fourth Dimension. While her mind groped, the lights of a motor car swooped round a bend in the road, and they stood farther apart. "What ought I to do?" she mused. "I think—— Oh, I won't be robbed! I *am* good! If I'm so enslaved that I can't sit by the fire with a man and talk, then I'd better be dead!"

The lights of the thrumming car grew magically; were upon them; abruptly stopped. From behind the dimness of the windshield a voice, annoyed, sharp: "Hello there!"

She realized that it was Kennicott.

The irritation in his voice smoothed out. "Having a walk?"

They made schoolboyish sounds of assent.

"Pretty wet, isn't it? Better ride back. Jump up in front here, Valborg."

His manner of swinging open the door was a command. Carol was conscious that Erik was climbing in, that she was apparently to sit in the back, and that she had been left to open the rear door for herself. Instantly the wonder which had flamed to the gusty skies was quenched, and she was Mrs. W. P. Kennicott of Gopher Prairie, riding in a squeaking old car, and likely to be lectured by her husband.

She feared what Kennicott would say to Erik. She bent toward them. Kennicott was observing, "Going to have some rain before the night's over, all right."

"Yes," said Erik.

"Been funny season this year, anyway. Never saw it with such a cold October and such a nice November. 'Member we had a snow way back on October ninth! But it certainly was nice up to the twenty-first, this month—as I remember it, not a flake of snow in November so far, has there been?

But I shouldn't wonder if we'd be having some snow 'most any time now."

"Yes, good chance of it," said Erik.

"Wish I'd had more time to go after the ducks this fall. By golly, what do you think?" Kennicott sounded appealing. "Fellow wrote me from Man Trap Lake that he shot seven mallards and couple of canvas-back in one hour!"

"That must have been fine," said Erik.

Carol was ignored. But Kennicott was blustrously cheerful. He shouted to a farmer, as he slowed up to pass the frightened team, "There we are—*schon gut!*" She sat back, neglected, frozen, unheroic heroine in a drama insanely undramatic. She made a decision resolute and enduring. She would tell Kennicott—— What would she tell him? She could not say that she loved Erik. *Did* she love him? But she would have it out. She was not sure whether it was pity for Kennicott's blindness, or irritation at his assumption that he was enough to fill any woman's life, which prompted her, but she knew that she was out of the trap, that she could be frank; and she was exhilarated with the adventure of it . . . while in front he was entertaining Erik:

"Nothing like an hour on a duck-pass to make you relish your victuals and—— Gosh, this machine hasn't got the power of a fountain pen. Guess the cylinders are jam-cram-full of carbon again. Don't know but what maybe I'll have to put in another set of piston-rings."

He stopped on Main Street and clucked hospitably, "There, that'll give you just a block to walk. G' night."

Carol was in suspense. Would Erik sneak away?

He stolidly moved to the back of the car, thrust in his hand, muttered, "Good night—Carol. I'm glad we had our walk." She pressed his hand. The car was flapping on. He was hidden from her—by a corner drug store on Main Street!

Kennicott did not recognize her till he drew up before the house. Then he condescended, "Better jump out here and I'll take the boat around back. Say, see if the back door is unlocked, will you?" She unlatched the door for him. She realized that she still carried the damp glove she had stripped off for Erik. She drew it on. She stood in the center of the living-room, unmoving, in damp coat and muddy rubbers. Kennicott was as opaque as ever. Her task wouldn't be anything so lively as having to endure a scolding, but only an exasperating effort to command his attention so that he would understand the nebulous things she had to tell him, instead of interrupting her by yawning, winding the clock, and going up to bed. She heard him shoveling coal into the furnace. He came through the kitchen energetically, but before he spoke to her he did stop in the hall, did wind the clock.

He sauntered into the living-room and his glance passed from her drenched hat to her smeared rubbers. She could hear—she could hear, see, taste, smell, touch—his "Better take your coat off, Carrie; looks kind of wet." Yes, there it was:

"Well, Carrie, you better——" He chucked his own coat on a chair, stalked to her, went on with a rising tingling voice, "——you better cut it out now. I'm not going to do the outraged husband stunt. I like you and I respect you, and I'd probably look like a boob if I tried to be dramatic. But I think it's about time for you and Valborg to call a halt before you get in Dutch, like Fern Mullins did."

"Do you——"

"Course. I know all about it. What d' you expect in a town that's as filled with busybodies, that have plenty of time to stick their noses into other folks' business, as this is? Not that they've had the nerve to do much tattling to *me*, but they've hinted around a lot, and anyway, I could see for myself that you liked him. But of course I knew how cold you were, I knew you wouldn't stand it even if Valborg did try to hold your hand or kiss you, so I didn't worry. But same time, I hope you don't suppose this husky young Swede farmer is as innocent and Platonic and all that stuff as you are! Wait now, don't get sore! I'm not knocking him. He isn't a bad sort. And he's young and likes to gas about books. Course you like him. That isn't the real rub. But haven't you just seen what this town can do, once it goes and gets moral on you, like it did with Fern? You probably think that two young folks making love are alone if anybody ever is, but there's nothing in this town that you don't do in company with a whole lot of uninvited but awful interested guests. Don't you realize that if Ma Westlake and a few others got started they'd drive you up a tree, and you'd find yourself so well advertised as being in love with this Valborg fellow that you'd *have* to be, just to spite 'em!"

"Let me sit down," was all Carol could say. She drooped on the couch, wearily, without elasticity.

He yawned, "Gimme your coat and rubbers," and while she stripped them off he twiddled his watch-chain, felt the radiator, peered at the thermometer. He shook out her wraps in the hall, hung them up with exactly his usual care. He pushed a chair near to her and sat bolt up. He looked like a physician about to give sound and undesired advice.

Before he could launch into his heavy discourse she desperately got in, "Please! I want you to know that I was going to tell you everything, tonight."

"Well, I don't suppose there's really much to tell."

"But there is. I'm fond of Erik. He appeals to something in here." She touched her breast. "And I admire him. He isn't just a 'young Swede farmer.' He's an artist——"

"Wait now! He's had a chance all evening to tell you what a whale of a fine fellow he is. Now it's my turn. I can't talk artistic, but—— Carrie, do you understand my work?" He leaned forward, thick capable hands on thick sturdy thighs, mature and slow, yet beseeching. "No matter even if you are cold, I like you better than anybody in the world. One time I said that you were my soul. And that still goes. You're all the things that I see in a sunset when I'm driving in from the country, the things that I like but can't make poetry of. Do you realize what my job is? I go round twenty-four hours a day, in mud and blizzard, trying my damnedest to heal everybody, rich or poor. You—that 're always spieling about how scientists ought to rule the world, instead of a bunch of spread-eagle politicians—can't you see that I'm all the science there is here? And I can stand the cold and the bumpy roads and the lonely rides at night. All I need is to have you here at home to welcome me. I don't expect you to be passionate—not any more I don't—but I do expect you to appreciate my work. I bring babies into the world, and save lives, and make cranky husbands quit being mean to their wives. And then you go and moon over a Swede tailor because he can talk about how to put ruchings on a skirt! Hell of a thing for a man to fuss over!"

She flew out at him: "You make your side clear. Let me give mine. I admit all you say—except about Erik. But is it only you, and the baby, that want me to back you up, that demand things from me? They're all on me, the whole town! I can feel their hot breaths on my neck! Aunt Bessie and that horrible slavering old Uncle Whittier and Juanita and Mrs. Westlake and Mrs. Bogart and all of them. And you welcome them, you encourage them to drag me down into their cave! I won't stand it! Do you hear? Now, right now, I'm done. And it's Erik who gives me the courage. You say he just thinks about ruches (which do not usually go on skirts, by the way!). I tell you he thinks about God, the God that Mrs. Bogart covers up with greasy gingham wrappers! Erik will be a great man some day, and if I could contribute one tiny bit to his success——"

"Wait, wait, wait now! Hold up! You're assuming that your Erik will make good. As a matter of fact, at my age he'll be running a one-man tailor shop in some burg about the size of Schoenstrom."

"He will not!"

"That's what he's headed for now all right, and he's twenty-five or -six and—— What's he done to make you think he'll ever be anything but a pants-presser?"

"He has sensitiveness and talent——"

"Wait now! What has he actually done in the art line? Has he done one first-class picture or—sketch, d' you call it? Or one poem, or played the piano, or anything except gas about what he's going to do?"

She looked thoughtful.

"Then it's a hundred to one shot that he never will. Way I understand it, even these fellows that do something pretty good at home and get to go to art school, there ain't more than one out of ten of 'em, maybe one out of a hundred, that ever get above grinding out a bum living—about as artistic as plumbing. And when it comes down to this tailor, why, can't you see—you that take on so about psychology—can't you see that it's just by contrast with folks like Doc McGanum or Lym Cass that this fellow seems artistic? Suppose you'd met up with him first in one of these reg'lar New York studios! You wouldn't notice him any more 'n a rabbit!"

She huddled over folded hands like a temple virgin shivering on her knees before the thin warmth of a brazier. She could not answer.

Kennicott rose quickly, sat on the couch, took both her hands. "Suppose he fails—as he will! Suppose he goes back to tailoring, and you're his wife.

Is that going to be this artistic life you've been thinking about? He's in some bum shack, pressing pants all day, or stooped over sewing, and having to be polite to any grouch that blows in and jams a dirty stinking old suit in his face and says, 'Here you, fix this, and be blame quick about it.' He won't even have enough savvy to get him a big shop. He'll pike along doing his own work—unless you, his wife, go help him, go help him in the shop, and stand over a table all day, pushing a big heavy iron. Your complexion will look fine after about fifteen years of baking that way, won't it! And you'll be humped over like an old hag. And probably you'll live in one room back of the shop. And then at night—oh, you'll have your artist—sure! He'll come in stinking of gasoline, and cranky from hard work, and hinting around that if it hadn't been for you, he'd of gone East and been a great artist. Sure! And you'll be entertaining his relatives—— Talk about Uncle Whit! You'll be having some old Axel Axelberg coming in with manure on his boots and sitting down to supper in his socks and yelling at you, 'Hurry up now, you vimmin make me sick!' Yes, and you'll have a squalling brat every year, tugging at you while you press clothes, and you won't love 'em like you do Hugh up-stairs, all downy and asleep——"

"Please! Not any more!"

Her face was on his knee.

He bent to kiss her neck. "I don't want to be unfair. I guess love is a great thing, all right. But think it would stand much of that kind of stuff? Oh, honey, am I so bad? Can't you like me at all? I've—I've been so fond of you!"

She snatched up his hand, she kissed it. Presently she sobbed, "I won't ever see him again. I can't, now. The hot living-room behind the tailor shop—— I don't love him enough for that. And you are—— Even if I were sure of him, sure he was the real thing, I don't think I could actually leave you. This marriage, it weaves people together. It's not easy to break, even when it ought to be broken."

"And do you want to break it?"

"No!"

He lifted her, carried her up-stairs, laid her on her bed, turned to the door.

"Come kiss me," she whimpered.

He kissed her lightly and slipped away. For an hour she heard him moving about his room, lighting a cigar, drumming with his knuckles on a chair. She felt that he was a bulwark between her and the darkness that grew thicker as the delayed storm came down in sleet.

II

He was cheery and more casual than ever at breakfast. All day she tried to devise a way of giving Erik up. Telephone? The village central would unquestionably "listen in." A letter? It might be found. Go to see him? Impossible. That evening Kennicott gave her, without comment, an envelope. The letter was signed "E. V."

I know I can't do anything but make trouble for you, I think. I am going to Minneapolis tonight and from there as soon as I can either to New York or Chicago. I will do as big things as I can. I      I can't write I love you too much      God keep you.

Until she heard the whistle which told her that the Minneapolis train was leaving town, she kept herself from thinking, from moving. Then it was all over. She had no plan nor desire for anything.

When she caught Kennicott looking at her over his newspaper she fled to his arms, thrusting the paper aside, and for the first time in years they were lovers. But she knew that she still had no plan in life, save always to go along the same streets, past the same people, to the same shops.

### III

A week after Erik's going the maid startled her by announcing, "There's a Mr. Valborg down-stairs say he vant to see you."

She was conscious of the maid's interested stare, angry at this shattering of the calm in which she had hidden. She crept down, peeped into the living-room. It was not Erik Valborg who stood there; it was a small, gray-bearded, yellow-faced man in mucky boots, canvas jacket, and red mittens. He glowered at her with shrewd red eyes.

"You de doc's wife?"

"Yes."

"I'm Adolph Valborg, from up by Jefferson. I'm Erik's father."

"Oh!" He was a monkey-faced little man, and not gentle.

"What you done wit' my son?"

"I don't think I understand you."

"I t'ink you're going to understand before I get t'rough! Where is he?"

"Why, really—— I presume that he's in Minneapolis."

"You presume!" He looked through her with a contemptuousness such as she could not have imagined. Only an insane contortion of spelling could portray his lyric whine, his mangled consonants. He clamored, "Presume! Dot's a fine word! I don't want no fine words and I don't want no more lies! I want to know what you *know*!"

"See here, Mr. Valborg, you may stop this bullying right now. I'm not one of your farmwomen. I don't know where your son is, and there's no reason why I should know." Her defiance ran out in face of his immense flaxen stolidity. He raised his fist, worked up his anger with the gesture, and sneered:

"You dirty city women wit' your fine ways and fine dresses! A father come here trying to save his boy from wickedness, and you call him a bully! By God, I don't have to take nothin' off you nor your husband! I ain't one of your hired men. For one time a woman like you is going to hear de trut' about what you are, and no fine city words to it, needer."

"Really, Mr. Valborg——"

"What you done wit' him? Heh? I'll yoost tell you what you done! He was a good boy, even if he was a damn fool. I want him back on de farm. He don't make enough money tailoring. And I can't get me no hired man! I want to take him back on de farm. And you butt in and fool wit' him and make love wit' him, and get him to run away!"

"You are lying! It's not true that—— It's not true, and if it were, you would have no right to speak like this."

"Don't talk foolish. I know. Ain't I heard from a fellow dot live right here in town how you been acting wit' de boy? I know what you done! Walking wit' him in de country! Hiding in de woods wit' him! Yes and I guess you talk about religion in de woods! Sure! Women like you—you're worse dan street-walkers! Rich women like you, wit' fine husbands and no decent work to do—and me, look at my hands, look how I work, look at those hands! But you, oh God no, you mustn't work, you're too fine to do decent work. You got to play wit' young fellows, younger as you are, laughing and rolling around and acting like de animals! You let my son alone, d' you hear?" He was shaking his fist in her face. She could smell the manure and sweat. "It ain't no use talkin' to women like you. Get no trut' out of you. But next time I go by your husband!"

He was marching into the hall. Carol flung herself on him, her clenching hand on his hayseed-dusty shoulder. "You horrible old man, you've always tried to turn Erik into a slave, to fatten your pocketbook! You've sneered at him, and overworked him, and probably you've succeeded in preventing his ever rising above your muck-heap! And now because you can't drag him back, you come here to vent—— Go tell my husband, go tell him, and don't blame me when he kills you, when my husband kills you—he will kill you——"

The man grunted, looked at her impassively, said one word, and walked out.

She heard the word very plainly.

She did not quite reach the couch. Her knees gave way, she pitched forward. She heard her mind saying, "You haven't fainted. This is ridiculous. You're simply dramatizing yourself. Get up." But she could not move. When Kennicott arrived she was lying on the couch. His step quickened. "What's happened, Carrie? You haven't got a bit of blood in your face."

She clutched his arm. "You've got to be sweet to me, and kind! I'm going to California—mountains, sea. Please don't argue about it, because I'm going."

Quietly, "All right. We'll go. You and I. Leave the kid here with Aunt Bessie."

"Now!"

"Well yes, just as soon as we can get away. Now don't talk any more. Just imagine you've already started." He smoothed her hair, and not till after supper did he continue: "I meant it about California. But I think we better wait three weeks or so, till I get hold of some young fellow released from the medical corps to take my practise. And if people are gossiping, you don't want to give them a chance by running away. Can you stand it and face 'em for three weeks or so?"

"Yes," she said emptily.

IV

People covertly stared at her on the street. Aunt Bessie tried to catechize her about Erik's disappearance, and it was Kennicott who silenced the woman with a savage, "Say, are you hinting that Carrie had anything to do with that fellow's beating it? Then let me tell you, and you can go right out and tell the whole bloomin' town, that Carrie and I took Val—took Erik riding, and he asked me about getting a better job in Minneapolis, and I advised him to go to it. . . . Getting much sugar in at the store now?"

Guy Pollock crossed the street to be pleasant apropos of California and new novels. Vida Sherwin dragged her to the Jolly Seventeen. There, with every one rigidly listening, Maud Dyer shot at Carol, "I hear Erik has left town."

Carol was amiable. "Yes, so I hear. In fact, he called me up—told me he had been offered a lovely job in the city. So sorry he's gone. He would have been valuable if we'd tried to start the dramatic association again. Still, I wouldn't be here for the association myself, because Will is all in from work, and I'm thinking of taking him to California. Juanita—you know the Coast so well—tell me: would you start in at Los Angeles or San Francisco, and what are the best hotels?"

The Jolly Seventeen looked disappointed, but the Jolly Seventeen liked to give advice, the Jolly Seventeen liked to mention the expensive hotels at which they had stayed. (A meal counted as a stay.) Before they could question her again Carol escorted in with drum and fife the topic of Raymie Wutherspoon. Vida had news from her husband. He had been gassed in the trenches, had been in a hospital for two weeks, had been promoted to major, was learning French.

V

She left Hugh with Aunt Bessie.

But for Kennicott she would have taken him. She hoped that in some miraculous way yet unrevealed she might find it possible to remain in California. She did not want to see Gopher Prairie again.

The Smails were to occupy the Kennicott house, and quite the hardest thing to endure in the month of waiting was the series of conferences between Kennicott and Uncle Whittier in regard to heating the garage and having the furnace flues cleaned.

Did Carol, Kennicott inquired, wish to stop in Minneapolis to buy new clothes?

"No! I want to get as far away as I can as soon as I can. Let's wait till Los Angeles."

"Sure, sure! Just as you like. Cheer up! We're going to have a large wide time, and everything 'll be different when we come back."

VI

Dusk on a snowy December afternoon. The sleeper which would connect at Kansas City with the California train rolled out of St. Paul with a chick-a-chick, chick-a-chick, chick-a-chick as it crossed the other tracks. It bumped through the factory belt, gained speed. Carol could see nothing but gray fields, which had closed in on her all the way from Gopher Prairie. Ahead was darkness.

"For an hour, in Minneapolis, I must have been near Erik. He's still there, somewhere. He'll be gone when I come back. I'll never know where he has gone."

As Kennicott switched on the seat-light she turned drearily to the illustrations in a motion-picture magazine.

# 34

They journeyed for three and a half months. They saw the Grand Canyon, the adobe walls of Santa Fe and, in a drive from El Paso into Mexico, their first foreign land. They jogged from San Diego and La Jolla to Los Angeles, Pasadena, Riverside, through towns with bell-towered missions and orange-groves; they viewed Monterey and San Francisco and a forest of sequoias. They bathed in the surf and climbed foothills and danced, they saw a polo game and the making of motion-pictures, they sent one hundred and seventeen souvenir post-cards to Gopher Prairie, and once, on a dune by a foggy sea when she was walking alone, Carol found an artist, and he looked up at her and said, "Too damned wet to paint; sit down and talk," and so for ten minutes she lived in a romantic novel.

Her only struggle was in coaxing Kennicott not to spend all his time with the tourists from the ten thousand other Gopher Prairies. In winter, California is full of people from Iowa and Nebraska, Ohio and Oklahoma, who, having traveled thousands of miles from their familiar villages, hasten to secure an illusion of not having left them. They hunt for people from their own states to stand between them and the shame of naked mountains; they talk steadily, in Pullmans, on hotel porches, at cafeterias and motion-picture shows, about the motors and crops and county politics back home. Kennicott discussed land-prices with them, he went into the merits of the several sorts of motor cars with them, he was intimate with train porters, and he insisted on seeing the Luke Dawsons at their flimsy bungalow in Pasadena, where Luke sat and yearned to go back and make some more money. But Kennicott gave promise of learning to play. He shouted in the pool at the

Coronado, and he spoke of (though he did nothing more radical than speak of) buying evening-clothes. Carol was touched by his efforts to enjoy picture galleries, and the dogged way in which he accumulated dates and dimensions when they followed monkish guides through missions.

She felt strong. Whenever she was restless she dodged her thoughts by the familiar vagabond fallacy of running away from them, of moving on to a new place, and thus she persuaded herself that she was tranquil. In March she willingly agreed with Kennicott that it was time to go home. She was longing for Hugh.

They left Monterey on April first, on a day of high blue skies and poppies and a summer sea.

As the train struck in among the hills she resolved, "I'm going to love the fine Will Kennicott quality that there is in Gopher Prairie. The nobility of good sense. It will be sweet to see Vida and Guy and the Clarks. And I'm going to see my baby! All the words he'll be able to say now! It's a new start. Everything will be different!"

Thus on April first, among dappled hills and the bronze of scrub oaks, while Kennicott seesawed on his toes and chuckled, "Wonder what Hugh'll say when he sees us?"

Three days later they reached Gopher Prairie in a sleet storm.

## II

No one knew that they were coming; no one met them; and because of the icy roads, the only conveyance at the station was the hotel 'bus, which they missed while Kennicott was giving his trunk-check to the station agent —the only person to welcome them. Carol waited for him in the station, among huddled German women with shawls and umbrellas, and ragged-bearded farmers in corduroy coats; peasants mute as oxen, in a room thick with the steam of wet coats, the reek of the red-hot stove, the stench of sawdust boxes which served as cuspidors. The afternoon light was as reluctant as a winter dawn.

"This is a useful market-center, an interesting pioneer post, but it is not a home for me," meditated the stranger Carol.

Kennicott suggested, "I'd 'phone for a flivver but it'd take quite a while for it to get here. Let's walk."

They stepped uncomfortably from the safety of the plank platform and, balancing on their toes, taking cautious strides, ventured along the road. The sleety rain was turning to snow. The air was stealthily cold. Beneath an inch of water was a layer of ice, so that as they wavered with their suit-cases they slid and almost fell. The wet snow drenched their gloves; the water underfoot splashed their itching ankles. They scuffled inch by inch for three blocks. In front of Harry Haydock's Kennicott sighed:

"We better stop in here and 'phone for a machine."

She followed him like a wet kitten.

The Haydocks saw them laboring up the slippery concrete walk, up the perilous front steps, and came to the door chanting:

"Well, well, well, back again, eh? Say, this is fine! Have a fine trip? My, you look like a rose, Carol. How did you like the coast, doc? Well, well, well! Where-all did you go?"

But as Kennicott began to proclaim the list of places achieved, Harry interrupted with an account of how much he himself had seen, two years ago. When Kennicott boasted, "We went through the mission at Santa Barbara," Harry broke in, "Yeh, that's an interesting old mission. Say, I'll never forget that hotel there, doc. It was swell. Why, the rooms were made just like these old monasteries. Juanita and I went from Santa Barbara to San Luis Obispo. You folks go to San Luis Obispo?"

"No, but——"

"Well you ought to gone to San Luis Obispo. And then we went from there to a ranch, least they called it a ranch——"

Kennicott got in only one considerable narrative, which began:

"Say, I never knew—did you, Harry?—that in the Chicago district the Kutz Kar sells as well as the Overland? I never thought much of the Kutz. But I met a gentleman on the train—it was when we were pulling out of Albuquerque, and I was sitting on the back platform of the observation car, and this man was next to me and he asked me for a light, and we got to talking, and come to find out, he came from Aurora, and when he found out I came from Minnesota he asked me if I knew Dr. Clemworth of Red Wing, and of course, while I've never met him, I've heard of Clemworth lots of times, and seems he's this man's brother! Quite a coincidence! Well, we got to talking, and we called the porter—that was a pretty good porter on that car—and we had a couple bottles of ginger ale, and I happened to mention the Kutz Kar, and this man—seems he's driven a lot of different kinds of cars—he's got a Franklin now—and he said that he'd tried the Kutz and liked it first-rate. Well, when we got into a station—I don't remember the name of it—Carrie, what the deuce was the name of that first stop we made the other side of Albuquerque?—well, anyway, I guess we must have stopped there to take on water, and this man and I got out to stretch our legs, and darned if there wasn't a Kutz drawn right up at the depot platform, and he pointed out something I'd never noticed, and I was glad to learn about it: seems that the gear lever in the Kutz is an inch longer——"

Even this chronicle of voyages Harry interrupted, with remarks on the advantages of the ball-gear-shift.

Kennicott gave up hope of adequate credit for being a traveled man, and telephoned to a garage for a Ford taxicab, while Juanita kissed Carol and made sure of being the first to tell the latest, which included seven distinct and proven scandals about Mrs. Swiftwaite, and one considerable doubt as to the chastity of Cy Bogart.

They saw the Ford sedan making its way over the waterlined ice, through the snow-storm, like a tug-boat in a fog. The driver stopped at a corner. The car skidded, it turned about with comic reluctance, crashed into a tree, and stood tilted on a broken wheel.

The Kennicotts refused Harry Haydock's not too urgent offer to take them home in his car "if I can manage to get it out of the garage—terrible day—stayed home from the store—but if you say so, I'll take a shot at it." Carol gurgled, "No, I think we'd better walk; probably make better time, and I'm just crazy to see my baby." With their suit-cases they waddled on. Their coats were soaked through.

Carol had forgotten her facile hopes. She looked about with impersonal eyes. But Kennicott, through rain-blurred lashes, caught the glory that was Back Home.

She noted bare tree-trunks, black branches, the spongy brown earth between patches of decayed snow on the lawns. The vacant lots were full of tall dead weeds. Stripped of summer leaves the houses were hopeless—temporary shelters.

Kennicott chuckled, "By golly, look down there! Jack Elder must have painted his garage. And look! Martin Mahoney has put up a new fence around his chicken yard. Say, that's a good fence, eh? Chicken-tight and dog-tight. That's certainly a dandy fence. Wonder how much it cost a yard? Yes, sir, they been building right along, even in winter. Got more enterprise than these Californians. Pretty good to be home, eh?"

She noted that all winter long the citizens had been throwing garbage into their back yards, to be cleaned up in spring. The recent thaw had disclosed heaps of ashes, dog-bones, torn bedding, clotted paint-cans, all half covered by the icy pools which filled the hollows of the yards. The refuse had stained the water to vile colors of waste: thin red, sour yellow, streaky brown.

Kennicott chuckled, "Look over there on Main Street! They got the feed store all fixed up, and a new sign on it, black and gold. That'll improve the appearance of the block a lot."

She noted that the few people whom they passed wore their raggedest coats for the evil day. They were scarecrows in a shanty town. . . . "To think," she marveled, "of coming two thousand miles, past mountains and cities, to get off here, and to plan to stay here! What conceivable reason for choosing this particular place?"

She noted a figure in a rusty coat and a cloth cap.

Kennicott chuckled, "Look who's coming! It's Sam Clark! Gosh, all rigged out for the weather."

The two men shook hands a dozen times and, in the Western fashion, bumbled, "Well, well, well, well, you old hell-hound, you old devil, how are you, anyway? You old horse-thief, maybe it ain't good to see you again!" While Sam nodded at her over Kennicott's shoulder, she was embarrassed.

"Perhaps I should never have gone away. I'm out of practise in lying. I wish they would get it over! Just a block more and—my baby!"

They were home. She brushed past the welcoming Aunt Bessie and knelt by Hugh. As he stammered, "O mummy, mummy, don't go away! Stay with me, mummy!" she cried, "No, I'll never leave you again!"

He volunteered, "That's daddy."

"By golly, he knows us just as if we'd never been away!" said Kennicott. "You don't find any of these California kids as bright as he is, at his age!"

When the trunk came they piled about Hugh the bewhiskered little wooden men fitting one inside another, the miniature junk, and the Oriental drum, from San Francisco Chinatown; the blocks carved by the old Frenchman in San Diego; the lariat from San Antonio.

"Will you forgive mummy for going away? Will you?" she whispered.

Absorbed in Hugh, asking a hundred questions about him—had he had any colds? did he still dawdle over his oatmeal? what about unfortunate morning incidents?—she viewed Aunt Bessie only as a source of information, and was able to ignore her hint, pointed by a coyly shaken finger, "Now that you've had such a fine long trip and spent so much money and all, I hope you're going to settle down and be satisfied and not——"

"Does he like carrots yet?" replied Carol.

She was cheerful as the snow began to conceal the slatternly yards. She assured herself that the streets of New York and Chicago were as ugly as Gopher Prairie in such weather; she dismissed the thought, "But they do have charming interiors for refuge." She sang as she energetically looked over Hugh's clothes.

The afternoon grew old and dark. Aunt Bessie went home. Carol took the baby into her own room. The maid came in complaining, "I can't get no extra milk to make chipped beef for supper." Hugh was sleepy, and he had been spoiled by Aunt Bessie. Even to a returned mother, his whining and his trick of seven times snatching her silver brush were fatiguing. As a background, behind the noises of Hugh and the kitchen, the house reeked with a colorless stillness.

From the window she heard Kennicott greeting the Widow Bogart as he had always done, always, every snowy evening: "Guess this 'll keep up all night." She waited. There they were, the furnace sounds, unalterable, eternal: removing ashes, shoveling coal.

Yes. She was back home! Nothing had changed. She had never been away. California? Had she seen it? Had she for one minute left this scraping sound of the small shovel in the ash-pit of the furnace? But Kennicott preposterously supposed that she had. Never had she been quite so far from going away as now when he believed she had just come back. She felt oozing through the walls the spirit of small houses and righteous people. At that instant she knew that in running away she had merely hidden her doubts behind the officious stir of travel.

"Dear God, don't let me begin agonizing again!" she sobbed. Hugh wept with her.

"Wait for mummy a second!" She hastened down to the cellar, to Kennicott.

He was standing before the furnace. However inadequate the rest of the house, he had seen to it that the fundamental cellar should be large and clean, the square pillars whitewashed, and the bins for coal and potatoes and trunks convenient. A glow from the drafts fell on the smooth gray cement floor at his feet. He was whistling tenderly, staring at the furnace with eyes which saw the black-domed monster as a symbol of home and of the beloved routine to which he had returned—his gipsying decently accomplished, his duty of viewing "sights" and "curios" performed with thoroughness. Unconscious of her, he stooped and peered in at the blue flames among the coals. He closed the door briskly, and made a whirling gesture with his right hand, out of pure bliss.

He saw her. "Why, hello, old lady! Pretty darn good to be back, eh?"

"Yes," she lied, while she quaked, "Not now. I can't face the job of explaining now. He's been so good. He trusts me. And I'm going to break his heart!"

She smiled at him. She tidied his sacred cellar by throwing an empty bluing bottle into the trash bin. She mourned, "It's only the baby that holds me. If Hugh died——" She fled upstairs in panic and made sure that nothing had happened to Hugh in these four minutes.

She saw a pencil-mark on a window-sill. She had made it on a September day when she had been planning a picnic for Fern Mullins and Erik. Fern and she had been hysterical with nonsense, had invented mad parties for all the coming winter. She glanced across the alley at the room which Fern had occupied. A rag of a gray curtain masked the still window.

She tried to think of some one to whom she wanted to telephone. There was no one.

The Sam Clarks called that evening and encouraged her to describe the missions. A dozen times they told her how glad they were to have her back.

"It is good to be wanted," she thought. "It will drug me. But—— Oh, is all life, always, an unresolved But?"

# 35

She tried to be content, which was a contradiction in terms. She fanatically cleaned house all April. She knitted a sweater for Hugh. She was diligent at Red Cross work. She was silent when Vida raved that though America hated war as much as ever, we must invade Germany and wipe out every man, because it was now proven that there was no soldier in the German army who was not crucifying prisoners and cutting off babies' hands.

Carol was volunteer nurse when Mrs. Champ Perry suddenly died of pneumonia.

In her funeral procession were the eleven people left out of the Grand Army and the Territorial Pioneers, old men and women, very old and weak, who a few decades ago had been boys and girls of the frontier, riding broncos through the rank windy grass of this prairie. They hobbled behind a band made up of business men and high-school boys, who straggled along without uniforms or ranks or leader, trying to play Chopin's Funeral March—a shabby group of neighbors with grave eyes, stumbling through the slush under a solemnity of faltering music.

Champ was broken. His rheumatism was worse. The rooms over the store were silent. He could not do his work as buyer at the elevator. Farmers coming in with sled-loads of wheat complained that Champ could not read the scale, that he seemed always to be watching some one back in the darkness of the bins. He was seen slipping through alleys, talking to himself, trying to avoid observation, creeping at last to the cemetery. Once Carol followed him and found the coarse, tobacco-stained, unimaginative old man lying on the snow of the grave, his thick arms spread out across the raw mound as if to protect her from the cold, her whom he had carefully covered up every night for sixty years, who was alone there now, uncared for.

The elevator company, Ezra Stowbody president, let him go. The company, Ezra explained to Carol, had no funds for giving pensions.

She tried to have him appointed to the postmastership, which, since all the work was done by assistants, was the one sinecure in town, the one reward for political purity. But it proved that Mr. Bert Tybee, the former bartender, desired the postmastership.

At her solicitation Lyman Cass gave Champ a warm berth as night watchman. Small boys played a good many tricks on Champ when he fell asleep at the mill.

II

She had vicarious happiness in the return of Major Raymond Wutherspoon. He was well, but still weak from having been gassed; he had been discharged and he came home as the first of the war veterans. It was rumored that he surprised Vida by coming unannounced, that Vida fainted when she saw him, and for a night and day would not share him with the town. When Carol saw them Vida was hazy about everything except Raymie, and never went so far from him that she could not slip her hand under his. Without understanding why, Carol was troubled by this intensity. And Raymie—surely this was not Raymie, but a sterner brother of his, this man with the tight blouse, the shoulder emblems, the trim legs in boots. His face seemed different, his lips more tight. He was not Raymie; he was Major Wutherspoon; and Kennicott and Carol were grateful when he divulged that Paris wasn't half as pretty as Minneapolis, that all of the American soldiers had been distinguished by their morality when on leave. Kennicott was respectful as he inquired whether the Germans had good aeroplanes, and what a salient was, and a cootie, and Going West.

In a week Major Wutherspoon was made full manager of the Bon Ton. Harry Haydock was going to devote himself to the half-dozen branch stores which he was establishing at crossroads hamlets. Harry would be the town's rich man in the coming generation, and Major Wutherspoon would rise with him, and Vida was jubilant, though she was regretful at having to give up most of her Red Cross work. Ray still needed nursing, she explained.

When Carol saw him with his uniform off, in a pepper-and-salt suit and a new gray felt hat, she was disappointed. He was not Major Wutherspoon; he was Raymie.

For a month small boys followed him down the street, and everybody called him Major, but that was presently shortened to Maje, and the small boys did not look up from their marbles as he went by.

### III

The town was booming, as a result of the war price of wheat.

The wheat money did not remain in the pockets of the farmers; the towns existed to take care of all that. Iowa farmers were selling their land at four hundred dollars an acre and coming into Minnesota. But whoever bought or sold or mortgaged, the townsmen invited themselves to the feast—millers, real-estate men, lawyers, merchants, and Dr. Will Kennicott. They bought land at a hundred and fifty, sold it next day at a hundred and seventy, and bought again. In three months Kennicott made seven thousand dollars, which was rather more than four times as much as society paid him for healing the sick.

In early summer began a "campaign of boosting." The Commercial Club decided that Gopher Prairie was not only a wheat-center but also the perfect site for factories, summer cottages, and state institutions. In charge of the campaign was Mr. James Blausser, who had recently come to town to speculate in land. Mr. Blausser was known as a Hustler. He liked to be called Honest Jim. He was a bulky, gauche, noisy, humorous man, with narrow eyes, a rustic complexion, large red hands, and brilliant clothes. He was attentive to all women. He was the first man in town who had not been sensitive enough to feel Carol's aloofness. He put his arm about her shoulder while he condescended to Kennicott, "Nice lil wifey, I'll say, doc," and when she answered, not warmly, "Thank you very much for the *imprimatur*," he blew on her neck, and did not know that he had been insulted.

He was a layer-on of hands. He never came to the house without trying to paw her. He touched her arm, let his fist brush her side. She hated the man, and she was afraid of him. She wondered if he had heard of Erik, and was taking advantage. She spoke ill of him at home and in public places, but Kennicott and the other powers insisted, "Maybe he is kind of a roughneck, but you got to hand it to him; he's got more git-up-and-git than any fellow that ever hit this burg. And he's pretty cute, too. Hear what he said to old Ezra? Chucked him in the ribs and said, 'Say, boy, what do you want to go to Denver for? Wait 'll I get time and I'll move the mountains here. Any mountain will be tickled to death to locate here once we get the White Way in!'"

The town welcomed Mr. Blausser as fully as Carol snubbed him. He was the guest of honor at the Commercial Club Banquet at the Minniemashie

House, an occasion for menus printed in gold (but injudiciously proof-read),
for free cigars, soft damp slabs of Lake Superior whitefish served as fillet of
sole, drenched cigar-ashes gradually filling the saucers of coffee cups, and
oratorical references to Pep, Punch, Go, Vigor, Enterprise, Red Blood, He-
Men, Fair Women, God's Country, James J. Hill, the Blue Sky, the Green
Fields, the Bountiful Harvest, Increasing Population, Fair Return on Investments, Alien Agitators Who Threaten the Security of Our Institutions, the
Hearthstone the Foundation of the State, Senator Knute Nelson, One Hundred Per Cent. Americanism, and Pointing with Pride.

Harry Haydock, as chairman, introduced Honest Jim Blausser. "And I am
proud to say, my fellow citizens, that in his brief stay here Mr. Blausser has
become my warm personal friend as well as my fellow booster, and I advise
you all to very carefully attend to the hints of a man who knows how to
achieve."

Mr. Blausser reared up like an elephant with a camel's neck—red faced,
red eyed, heavy fisted, slightly belching—a born leader, divinely intended to
be a congressman but deflected to the more lucrative honors of real-estate.
He smiled on his warm personal friends and fellow boosters, and boomed:

"I certainly was astonished in the streets of our lovely little city, the other
day. I met the meanest kind of critter that God ever made—meaner than the
horned toad or the Texas lallapaluza! (Laughter.) And do you know what
the animile was? He was a knocker! (Laughter and applause.)

"I want to tell you good people, and it's just as sure as God made little
apples, the thing that distinguishes our American commonwealth from the
pikers and tin-horns in other countries is our Punch. You take a genuwine,
honest-to-God homo Americanibus and there ain't anything he's afraid to
tackle. Snap and speed are his middle name! He'll put her across if he has
to ride from hell to breakfast, and believe me, I'm mighty good and sorry
for the boob that's so unlucky as to get in his way, because that poor slob
is going to wonder where he was at when Old Mr. Cyclone hit town! (Laughter.)

"Now, frien's, there's some folks so yellow and small and so few in the
pod that they go to work and claim that those of us that have the big vision
are off our trolleys. They say we can't make Gopher Prairie, God bless her!
just as big as Minneapolis or St. Paul or Duluth. But lemme tell you right
here and now that there ain't a town under the blue canopy of heaven that's
got a better chance to take a running jump and go scooting right up into the
two-hundred-thousand class than little old G. P.! And if there's anybody
that's got such cold kismets that he's afraid to tag after Jim Blausser on the
Big Going Up, then we don't want him here! Way I figger it, you folks are
just patriotic enough so that you ain't going to stand for any guy sneering
and knocking his own town, no matter how much of a smart Aleck he is—
and just on the side I want to add that this Farmers' Nonpartisan League
and the whole bunch of socialists are right in the same category, or, as the
fellow says, in the same scategory, meaning This Way Out, Exit, Beat It

While the Going's Good, This Means You, for all knockers of prosperity and the rights of property!

"Fellow citizens, there's a lot of folks, even right here in this fair state, fairest and richest of all the glorious union, that stand up on their hind legs and claim that the East and Europe put it all over the golden Northwestland. Now let me nail that lie right here and now. 'Ah-ha,' says they, 'so Jim Blausser is claiming that Gopher Prairie is as good a place to live in as London and Rome and—and all the rest of the Big Burgs, is he? How does the poor fish know?' says they. Well, I'll tell you how I know! I've seen 'em! I've done Europe from soup to nuts! They can't spring that stuff on Jim Blausser and get away with it! And let me tell you that the only live thing in Europe is our boys that are fighting there now! London—I spent three days, sixteen straight hours a day, giving London the once-over, and let me tell you that it's nothing but a bunch of fog and out-of-date buildings that no live American burg would stand for one minute. You may not believe it, but there ain't one first-class skyscraper in the whole works. And the same thing goes for that crowd of crabs and snobs Down East, and next time you hear some zob from Yahooville-on-the-Hudson chewing the rag and bulling and trying to get your goat, you tell him that no two-fisted enterprising Westerner would have New York for a gift!

"Now the point of this is: I'm not only insisting that Gopher Prairie is going to be Minnesota's pride, the brightest ray in the glory of the North Star State, but also and furthermore that it is right now, and still more shall be, as good a place to live in, and love in, and bring up the Little Ones in, and it's got as much refinement and culture, as any burg on the whole bloomin' expanse of God's Green Footstool, and that goes, get me, that goes!"

Half an hour later Chairman Haydock moved a vote of thanks to Mr. Blausser.

The boosters' campaign was on.

The town sought that efficient and modern variety of fame which is known as "publicity." The band was reorganized, and provided by the Commercial Club with uniforms of purple and gold. The amateur baseball-team hired a semi-professional pitcher from Des Moines, and made a schedule of games with every town for fifty miles about. The citizens accompanied it as "rooters," in a special car, with banners lettered "Watch Gopher Prairie Grow," and with the band playing "Smile, Smile, Smile." Whether the team won or lost the *Dauntless* loyally shrieked, "Boost, Boys, and Boost Together—Put Gopher Prairie on the Map—Brilliant Record of Our Matchless Team."

Then, glory of glories, the town put in a White Way. White Ways were in fashion in the Middlewest. They were composed of ornamented posts with clusters of high-powered electric lights along two or three blocks on Main Street. The *Dauntless* confessed: "White Way Is Installed—Town Lit Up Like Broadway—Speech by Hon. James Blausser—Come On You Twin Cities—Our Hat Is In the Ring."

The Commercial Club issued a booklet prepared by a great and expensive literary person from a Minneapolis advertising agency, a red-headed young man who smoked cigarettes in a long amber holder. Carol read the booklet with a certain wonder. She learned that Plover and Minniemashie Lakes were world-famed for their beauteous wooded shores and gamey pike and bass not to be equalled elsewhere in the entire country; that the residences of Gopher Prairie were models of dignity, comfort, and culture, with lawns and gardens known far and wide; that the Gopher Prairie schools and public library, in its neat and commodious building, were celebrated throughout the state; that the Gopher Prairie mills made the best flour in the country; that the surrounding farm lands were renowned, where'er men ate bread and butter, for their incomparable No. 1 Hard Wheat and Holstein-Friesian cattle; and that the stores in Gopher Prairie compared favorably with Minneapolis and Chicago in their abundance of luxuries and necessities and the ever-courteous attention of the skilled clerks. She learned, in brief, that this was the one Logical Location for factories and wholesale houses.

"*There's* where I want to go; to that model town Gopher Prairie," said Carol.

Kennicott was triumphant when the Commercial Club did capture one small shy factory which planned to make wooden automobile-wheels, but when Carol saw the promoter she could not feel that his coming much mattered—and a year after, when he failed, she could not be very sorrowful.

Retired farmers were moving into town. The price of lots had increased a third. But Carol could discover no more pictures nor interesting food nor gracious voices nor amusing conversation nor questing minds. She could, she asserted, endure a shabby but modest town; the town shabby and egomaniac she could not endure. She could nurse Champ Perry, and warm to the neighborliness of Sam Clark, but she could not sit applauding Honest Jim Blausser. Kennicott had begged her, in courtship days, to convert the town to beauty. If it was now as beautiful as Mr. Blausser and the *Dauntless* said, then her work was over, and she could go.

# 36

Kennicott was not so inhumanly patient that he could continue to forgive Carol's heresies, to woo her as he had on the venture to California. She tried to be inconspicuous, but she was betrayed by her failure to glow over the boosting. Kennicott believed in it; demanded that she say patriotic things about the White Way and the new factory. He snorted, "By golly, I've done all I could, and now I expect you to play the game. Here you been complaining for years about us being so poky, and now when Blausser comes along and does stir up excitement and beautify the town like you've always wanted somebody to, why, you say he's a roughneck, and you won't jump on the band-wagon."

Once, when Kennicott announced at noon-dinner, "What do you know about this! They say there's a chance we may get another factory—cream-separator works!" he added, "You might try to look interested, even if you ain't!" The baby was frightened by the Jovian roar; ran wailing to hide his face in Carol's lap; and Kennicott had to make himself humble and court both mother and child. The dim injustice of not being understood even by his son left him irritable. He felt injured.

An event which did not directly touch them brought down his wrath.

In the early autumn, news came from Wakamin that the sheriff had forbidden an organizer for the National Nonpartisan League to speak anywhere in the county. The organizer had defied the sheriff, and announced that in a few days he would address a farmers' political meeting. That night, the news ran, a mob of a hundred business men led by the sheriff—the tame village street and the smug village faces ruddled by the light of bobbing lanterns, the mob flowing between the squatty rows of shops—had taken the organizer from his hotel, ridden him on a fence-rail, put him on a freight train, and warned him not to return.

The story was threshed out in Dave Dyer's drug store, with Sam Clark, Kennicott, and Carol present.

"That's the way to treat those fellows—only they ought to have lynched him!" declared Sam, and Kennicott and Dave Dyer joined in a proud "You bet!"

Carol walked out hastily, Kennicott observing her.

Through supper-time she knew that he was bubbling and would soon boil over. When the baby was abed, and they sat composedly in canvas chairs on the porch, he experimented, "I had a hunch you thought Sam was kind of hard on that fellow they kicked out of Wakamin."

"Wasn't Sam rather needlessly heroic?"

"All these organizers, yes, and a whole lot of the German and Squarehead farmers themselves, they're seditious as the devil—disloyal, non-patriotic, pro-German pacifists, that's what they are!"

"Did this organizer say anything pro-German?"

"Not on your life! They didn't give him a chance!" His laugh was stagey.

"So the whole thing was illegal—and led by the sheriff! Precisely how do you expect these aliens to obey your law if the officer of the law teaches them to break it? Is it a new kind of logic?"

"Maybe it wasn't exactly regular, but what's the odds? They knew this fellow would try to stir up trouble. Whenever it comes right down to a question of defending Americanism and our constitutional rights, it's justifiable to set aside ordinary procedure."

"What editorial did he get that from?" she wondered, as she protested, "See here, my beloved, why can't you Tories declare war honestly? You don't oppose this organizer because you think he's seditious but because you're afraid that the farmers he is organizing will deprive you townsmen of the money you make out of mortgages and wheat and shops. Of course, since we're at war with Germany, anything that any one of us doesn't like is 'pro-German,' whether it's business competition or bad music. If we were fighting England, you'd call the radicals 'pro-English.' When this war is over, I suppose you'll be calling them 'red anarchists.' What an eternal art it is—such a glittery delightful art—finding hard names for our opponents! How we do sanctify our efforts to keep them from getting the holy dollars we want for ourselves! The churches have always done it, and the political orators—and I suppose I do it when I call Mrs. Bogart a 'Puritan' and Mr. Stowbody a 'capitalist.' But you business men are going to beat all the rest of us at it, with your simple-hearted, energetic, pompous——"

She got so far only because Kennicott was slow in shaking off respect for her. Now he bayed:

"That'll be about all from you! I've stood for your sneering at this town, and saying how ugly and dull it is. I've stood for your refusing to appreciate good fellows like Sam. I've even stood for your ridiculing our Watch Gopher Prairie Grow campaign. But one thing I'm not going to stand: I'm not going to stand my own wife being seditious. You can camouflage all you want to, but you know darn well that these radicals, as you call 'em, are opposed to the war, and let me tell you right here and now, and you and all these long-haired men and short-haired women can beef all you want to, but we're going to take these fellows, and if they ain't patriotic, we're going to make them be patriotic. And—Lord knows I never thought I'd have to say this to my own wife—but if you go defending these fellows, then the same thing applies to you! Next thing, I suppose you'll be yapping about free speech. Free speech! There's too much free speech and free gas and free beer and free love and all the rest of your damned mouthy freedom, and if I had my way I'd make you folks live up to the established rules of decency even if I had to take you——"

"Will!" She was not timorous now. "Am I pro-German if I fail to throb to Honest Jim Blausser, too? Let's have my whole duty as a wife!"

He was grumbling, "The whole thing's right in line with the criticism you've always been making. Might have known you'd oppose any decent constructive work for the town or for——"

"You're right. All I've done has been in line. I don't belong to Gopher Prairie. That isn't meant as a condemnation of Gopher Prairie, and it may be a condemnation of me. All right! I don't care! I don't belong here, and I'm going. I'm not asking permission any more. I'm simply going."

He grunted. "Do you mind telling me, if it isn't too much trouble, how long you're going for?"

"I don't know. Perhaps for a year. Perhaps for a lifetime."

"I see. Well, of course, I'll be tickled to death to sell out my practise and go anywhere you say. Would you like to have me go with you to Paris and study art, maybe, and wear velveteen pants and a woman's bonnet, and live on spaghetti?"

"No, I think we can save you that trouble. You don't quite understand. I am going—I really am—and alone! I've got to find out what my work is——"

"Work? Work? Sure! That's the whole trouble with you! You haven't got enough work to do. If you had five kids and no hired girl, and had to help with the chores and separate the cream, like these farmers' wives, then you wouldn't be so discontented."

"I know. That's what most men—and women—like you *would* say. That's how they would explain all I am and all I want. And I shouldn't argue with them. These business men, from their crushing labors of sitting in an office seven hours a day, would calmly recommend that I have a dozen children. As it happens, I've done that sort of thing. There've been a good many times when we hadn't a maid, and I did all the housework, and cared for Hugh, and went to Red Cross, and did it all very efficiently. I'm a good cook and a good sweeper, and you don't dare say I'm not!"

"N-no, you're——"

"But was I more happy when I was drudging? I was not. I was just bedraggled and unhappy. It's work—but not my work. I could run an office or a library, or nurse and teach children. But solitary dish-washing isn't enough to satisfy me—or many other women. We're going to chuck it. We're going to wash 'em by machinery, and come out and play with you men in the offices and clubs and politics you've cleverly kept for yourselves! Oh, we're hopeless, we dissatisfied women! Then why do you want to have us about the place, to fret you? So it's for your sake that I'm going!"

"Of course a little thing like Hugh makes no difference!"

"Yes, all the difference. That's why I'm going to take him with me."

"Suppose I refuse?"

"You won't!"

Forlornly, "Uh—— Carrie, what the devil is it you want, anyway?"

"Oh, conversation! No, it's much more than that. I think it's a greatness of life—a refusal to be content with even the healthiest mud."

"Don't you know that nobody ever solved a problem by running away from it?"

"Perhaps. Only I choose to make my own definition of 'running away.' I don't call—— Do you realize how big a world there is beyond this Gopher Prairie where you'd keep me all my life? It may be that some day I'll come back, but not till I can bring something more than I have now. And even if I am cowardly and run away—all right, call it cowardly, call me anything you want to! I've been ruled too long by fear of being called things. I'm going away to be quiet and think. I'm—I'm going! I have a right to my own life."

"So have I to mine!"

"Well?"

"I have a right to my life—and you're it, you're my life! You've made yourself so. I'm damned if I'll agree to all your freak notions, but I will say I've got to depend on you. Never thought of that complication, did you, in this 'off to Bohemia, and express yourself, and free love, and live your own life' stuff!"

"You have a right to me if you can keep me. Can you?"

He moved uneasily.

## II

For a month they discussed it. They hurt each other very much, and sometimes they were close to weeping, and invariably he used banal phrases about her duties and she used phrases quite as banal about freedom, and through it all, her discovery that she really could get away from Main Street was as sweet as the discovery of love. Kennicott never consented definitely. At most he agreed to a public theory that she was "going to take a short trip and see what the East was like in wartime."

She set out for Washington in October—just before the war ended.

She had determined on Washington because it was less intimidating than the obvious New York, because she hoped to find streets in which Hugh could play, and because in the stress of war-work, with its demand for thousands of temporary clerks, she could be initiated into the world of offices. Hugh was to go with her, despite the wails and rather extensive comments of Aunt Bessie.

She wondered if she might not encounter Erik in the East, but it was a chance thought, soon forgotten.

## III

The last thing she saw on the station platform was Kennicott, faithfully waving his hand, his face so full of uncomprehending loneliness that he could not smile but only twitch up his lips. She waved to him as long as she could, and when he was lost she wanted to leap from the vestibule and run back to him. She thought of a hundred tendernesses she had neglected. She had her freedom, and it was empty. The moment was not the highest of her life, but the lowest and most desolate, which was altogether excellent, for instead of slipping downward she began to climb.

She sighed, "I couldn't do this if it weren't for Will's kindness, his giving me money." But a second after: "I wonder how many women would always stay home if they had the money?"

Hugh complained, "Notice me, mummy!" He was beside her on the red plush seat of the day-coach; a boy of three and a half. "I'm tired of playing train. Let's play something else. Let's go see Auntie Bogart."

"Oh, no! Do you really like Mrs. Bogart?"

"Yes. She gives me cookies and she tells me about the Dear Lord. You never tell me about the Dear Lord. Why don't you tell me about the Dear Lord? Auntie Bogart says I'm going to be a preacher. Can I be a preacher? Can I preach about the Dear Lord?"

"Oh, please wait till my generation has stopped rebelling before yours starts in!"

"What's a generation?"

"It's a ray in the illumination of the spirit."

"That's foolish." He was a serious and literal person, and rather humorless. She kissed his frown, and marveled:

"I am running away from my husband, after liking a Swedish ne'er-do-well and expressing immoral opinions, just as in a romantic story. And my own son reproves me because I haven't given him religious instruction. But the story doesn't go right. I'm neither groaning nor being dramatically saved. I keep on running away, and I enjoy it. I'm mad with joy over it. Gopher Prairie is lost back there in the dust and stubble, and I look forward——"

She continued it to Hugh: "Darling, do you know what mother and you are going to find beyond the blue horizon rim?"

"What?" flatly.

"We're going to find elephants with golden howdahs from which peep young maharanees with necklaces of rubies, and a dawn sea colored like the breast of a dove, and a white and green house filled with books and silver tea-sets."

"And cookies?"

"Cookies? Oh, most decidedly cookies. We've had enough of bread and porridge. We'd get sick on too many cookies, but ever so much sicker on no cookies at all."

"That's foolish."

"It is, O male Kennicott!"

"Huh!" said Kennicott II, and went to sleep on her shoulder.

IV

The theory of the *Dauntless* regarding Carol's absence:

Mrs. Will Kennicott and son Hugh left on No. 24 on Saturday last for a stay of some months in Minneapolis, Chicago, New York, and Washington. Mrs. Kennicott confided to Ye Scribe that she will be connected with one of the multifarious war activities now centering in the Nation's Capital for a brief period before returning. Her countless friends who appreciate her splendid labors with the local Red Cross realize how valuable she will be to any war board with which she chooses to become connected. Gopher Prairie thus adds another shining star to its service flag, and without wishing to knock any neighboring communities, we would like to know any town of anywheres near our size in the state that has such a sterling war record. Another reason why you'd better Watch Gopher Prairie Grow.

\* \* \*

Mr. and Mrs. David Dyer, Mrs. Dyer's sister, Mrs. Jennie Dayborn of Jackrabbit, and Dr. Will Kennicott drove to Minniemashie on Tuesday for a delightful picnic.

# 37

She found employment in the Bureau of War Risk Insurance. Though the armistice with Germany was signed a few weeks after her coming to Washington, the work of the bureau continued. She filed correspondence all day; then she dictated answers to letters of inquiry. It was an endurance of monotonous details, yet she asserted that she had found "real work."

Disillusions she did have. She discovered that in the afternoon, office routine stretches to the grave. She discovered that an office is as full of cliques and scandals as a Gopher Prairie. She discovered that most of the women in the government bureaus lived unhealthfully, dining on snatches in their crammed apartments. But she also discovered that business women may have friendships and enmities as frankly as men, and may revel in a bliss which no housewife attains—a free Sunday. It did not appear that the Great World needed her inspiration, but she felt that her letters, her contact with the anxieties of men and women all over the country, were a part of vast affairs, not confined to Main Street and a kitchen, but linked with Paris, Bangkok, Madrid.

She perceived that she could do office work without losing any of the putative feminine virtue of domesticity; that cooking and cleaning, when divested of the fussing of an Aunt Bessie, take but a tenth of the time which, in a Gopher Prairie, it is but decent to devote to them.

Not to have to apologize for her thoughts to the Jolly Seventeen, not to have to report to Kennicott at the end of the day all that she had done or might do, was a relief which made up for the office weariness. She felt that she was no longer one-half of a marriage but the whole of a human being.

II

Washington gave her all the graciousness in which she had had faith: white columns seen across leafy parks, spacious avenues, twisty alleys. Daily she passed a dark square house with a hint of magnolias and a courtyard behind it, and a tall curtained second-story window through which a woman was always peering. The woman was mystery, romance, a story which told itself differently every day; now she was a murderess, now the neglected wife of an ambassador. It was mystery which Carol had most lacked in Gopher Prairie, where every house was open to view, where every person was but too easy to meet, where there were no secret gates opening upon moors over which one might walk by moss-deadened paths to strange high adventures in an ancient garden.

As she flitted up Sixteenth Street after a Kreisler recital, given late in the afternoon for the government clerks, as the lamps kindled in spheres of soft fire, as the breeze flowed into the street, fresh as prairie winds and kindlier, as she glanced up the elm alley of Massachusetts Avenue, as she was rested by the integrity of the Scottish Rite Temple, she loved the city as she loved no one save Hugh. She encountered negro shanties turned into studios, with orange curtains and pots of mignonette; marble houses on New Hampshire Avenue, with butlers and limousines; and men who looked like fictional explorers and aviators. Her days were swift, and she knew that in her folly of running away she had found the courage to be wise.

She had a dispiriting first month of hunting lodgings in the crowded city. She had to roost in a hall-room in a moldy mansion conducted by an indignant decayed gentlewoman, and leave Hugh to the care of a doubtful nurse. But later she made a home.

III

Her first acquaintances were the members of the Tincomb Methodist Church, a vast red-brick tabernacle. Vida Sherwin had given her a letter to an earnest woman with eye-glasses, plaid silk waist, and a belief in Bible Classes, who introduced her to the Pastor and the Nicer Members of Tincomb. Carol recognized in Washington as she had in California a transplanted and guarded Main Street. Two-thirds of the churchmembers had come from Gopher Prairies. The church was their society and their standard; they went to Sunday service, Sunday School, Christian Endeavor, missionary lectures, church suppers, precisely as they had at home; they agreed that ambassadors and flippant newspapermen and infidel scientists of the bureaus were equally wicked and to be avoided; and by cleaving to Tincomb Church they kept their ideals from all contamination.

They welcomed Carol, asked about her husband, gave her advice regarding colic in babies, passed her the gingerbread and scalloped potatoes at church suppers, and in general made her very unhappy and lonely, so that she wondered if she might not enlist in the militant suffrage organization and be allowed to go to jail.

Always she was to perceive in Washington (as doubtless she would have perceived in New York or London) a thick streak of Main Street. The cautious dullness of a Gopher Prairie appeared in boarding-houses where ladylike bureau-clerks gossiped to polite young army officers about the movies; a thousand Sam Clarks and a few Widow Bogarts were to be identified in the Sunday motor procession, in theater parties, and at the dinners of State Societies, to which the emigrés from Texas or Michigan surged that they might confirm themselves in the faith that their several Gopher Prairies were notoriously "a whole lot peppier and chummier than this stuck-up East."

But she found a Washington which did not cleave to Main Street.

Guy Pollock wrote to a cousin, a temporary army captain, a confiding and buoyant lad who took Carol to tea-dances, and laughed, as she had always wanted some one to laugh, about nothing in particular. The captain introduced her to the secretary of a congressman, a cynical young widow with many acquaintances in the navy. Through her Carol met commanders and majors, newspapermen, chemists and geographers and fiscal experts from the bureaus, and a teacher who was a familiar of the militant suffrage headquarters. The teacher took her to headquarters. Carol never became a prominent suffragist. Indeed her only recognized position was as an able addresser of envelopes. But she was casually adopted by this family of friendly women who, when they were not being mobbed or arrested, took dancing lessons or went picnicking up the Chesapeake Canal or talked about the politics of the American Federation of Labor.

With the congressman's secretary and the teacher Carol leased a small flat. Here she found home, her own place and her own people. She had, though it absorbed most of her salary, an excellent nurse for Hugh. She herself put him to bed and played with him on holidays. There were walks with him, there were motionless evenings of reading, but chiefly Washington was associated with people, scores of them, sitting about the flat, talking, talking, talking, not always wisely but always excitedly. It was not at all the "artist's studio" of which, because of its persistence in fiction, she had dreamed. Most of them were in offices all day, and thought more in card-catalogues or statistics than in mass and color. But they played, very simply, and they saw no reason why anything which exists cannot also be acknowledged.

She was sometimes shocked quite as she had shocked Gopher Prairie by these girls with their cigarettes and elfish knowledge. When they were most eager about soviets or canoeing, she listened, longed to have some special learning which would distinguish her, and sighed that her adventure had come so late. Kennicott and Main Street had drained her self-reliance; the presence of Hugh made her feel temporary. Some day—oh, she'd have to take him back to open fields and the right to climb about hay-lofts.

But the fact that she could never be eminent among these scoffing enthusiasts did not keep her from being proud of them, from defending them in imaginary conversations with Kennicott, who grunted (she could hear his voice), "They're simply a bunch of wild impractical theorists sittin' round chewing the rag," and "I haven't got the time to chase after a lot of these fool fads; I'm too busy putting aside a stake for our old age."

Most of the men who came to the flat, whether they were army officers or radicals who hated the army, had the easy gentleness, the acceptance of women without embarrassed banter, for which she had longed in Gopher Prairie. Yet they seemed to be as efficient as the Sam Clarks. She concluded that it was because they were of secure reputation, not hemmed in by the fire of provincial jealousies. Kennicott had asserted that the villager's lack of courtesy is due to his poverty. "We're no millionaire dudes," he boasted. Yet these army and navy men, these bureau experts, and organizers of multitudinous leagues, were cheerful on three or four thousand a year, while Kennicott had, outside of his land speculations, six thousand or more, and Sam had eight.

Nor could she upon inquiry learn that many of this reckless race died in the poorhouse. That institution is reserved for men like Kennicott who, after devoting fifty years to "putting aside a stake," incontinently invest the stake in spurious oil-stocks.

### IV

She was encouraged to believe that she had not been abnormal in viewing Gopher Prairie as unduly tedious and slatternly. She found the same faith not only in girls escaped from domesticity but also in demure old ladies who, tragically deprived of esteemed husbands and huge old houses, yet managed to make a very comfortable thing of it by living in small flats and having time to read.

But she also learned that by comparison Gopher Prairie was a model of daring color, clever planning, and frenzied intellectuality. From her teacher-housemate she had a sardonic description of a Middlewestern railroad-division town, of the same size as Gopher Prairie but devoid of lawns and trees, a town where the tracks sprawled along the cinder-scabbed Main Street, and the railroad shops, dripping soot from eaves and doorway, rolled out smoke in greasy coils.

Other towns she came to know by anecdote: a prairie village where the wind blew all day long, and the mud was two feet thick in spring, and in summer the flying sand scarred new-painted houses and dust covered the few flowers set out in pots. New England mill-towns with the hands living in rows of cottages like blocks of lava. A rich farming-center in New Jersey, off the railroad, furiously pious, ruled by old men, unbelievably ignorant old men, sitting about the grocery talking of James G. Blaine. A Southern town, full of the magnolias and white columns which Carol had accepted as proof of romance, but hating the negroes, obsequious to the Old Families. A Western mining-settlement like a tumor. A booming semi-city with parks and clever architects, visited by famous pianists and unctuous lecturers, but irritable from a struggle between union labor and the manufacturers' association, so that in even the gayest of the new houses there was a ceaseless and intimidating heresy-hunt.

### V

The chart which plots Carol's progress is not easy to read. The lines are broken and uncertain of direction; often instead of rising they sink in wavering scrawls; and the colors are watery blue and pink and the dim gray of rubbed pencil marks. A few lines are traceable.

Unhappy women are given to protecting their sensitiveness by cynical gossip, by whining, by high-church and new-thought religions, or by a fog of vagueness. Carol had hidden in none of these refuges from reality, but she, who was tender and merry, had been made timorous by Gopher Prairie. Even her flight had been but the temporary courage of panic. The thing she gained in Washington was not information about office-systems and labor unions but renewed courage, that amiable contempt called poise. Her glimpse of tasks involving millions of people and a score of nations reduced Main

Street from bloated importance to its actual pettiness. She could never again
be quite so awed by the power with which she herself had endowed the
Vidas and Blaussers and Bogarts.

From her work and from her association with women who had organized
suffrage associations in hostile cities, or had defended political prisoners,
she caught something of an impersonal attitude; saw that she had been as
touchily personal as Maud Dyer.

And why, she began to ask, did she rage at individuals? Not individuals
but institutions are the enemies, and they most afflict the disciples who
the most generously serve them. They insinuate their tyranny under a hundred guises and pompous names, such as Polite Society, the Family, the
Church, Sound Business, the Party, the Country, the Superior White Race;
and the only defense against them, Carol beheld, is unembittered laughter.

# 38

She had lived in Washington for a year. She was tired of the office. It was
tolerable, far more tolerable than housework, but it was not adventurous.

She was having tea and cinnamon toast, alone at a small round table on
the balcony of Rauscher's Confiserie. Four débutantes clattered in. She had
felt young and dissipated, had thought rather well of her black and leaf-
green suit, but as she watched them, thin of ankle, soft under the chin,
seventeen or eighteen at most, smoking cigarettes with the correct ennui and
talking of "bedroom farces" and their desire to "run up to New York and
see something racy," she became old and rustic and plain, and desirous of
retreating from these hard brilliant children to a life easier and more sympathetic. When they flickered out and one child gave orders to a chauffeur,
Carol was not a defiant philosopher but a faded government clerk from
Gopher Prairie, Minnesota.

She started dejectedly up Connecticut Avenue. She stopped, her heart
stopped. Coming toward her were Harry and Juanita Haydock. She ran to
them, she kissed Juanita, while Harry confided, "Hadn't expected to come
to Washington—had to go to New York for some buying—didn't have your
address along—just got in this morning—wondered how in the world we
could get hold of you."

She was definitely sorry to hear that they were to leave at nine that evening, and she clung to them as long as she could. She took them to St.
Mark's for dinner. Stooped, her elbows on the table, she heard with excitement that "Cy Bogart had the 'flu, but of course he was too gol-darn mean to
die of it."

"Will wrote me that Mr. Blausser has gone away. How did he get on?"

"Fine! Fine! Great loss to the town. There was a real public-spirited fellow, all right!"

She discovered that she now had no opinions whatever about Mr. Blausser, and she said sympathetically, "Will you keep up the town-boosting campaign?"

Harry fumbled, "Well, we've dropped it just temporarily, but—sure you bet! Say, did the doc write you about the luck B. J. Gougerling had hunting ducks down in Texas?"

When the news had been told and their enthusiasm had slackened she looked about and was proud to be able to point out a senator, to explain the cleverness of the canopied garden. She fancied that a man with dinner-coat and waxed mustache glanced superciliously at Harry's highly form-fitting bright-brown suit and Juanita's tan silk frock, which was doubtful at the seams. She glared back, defending her own, daring the world not to appreciate them.

Then, waving to them, she lost them down the long train shed. She stood reading the list of stations: Harrisburg, Pittsburg, Chicago. Beyond Chicago——? She saw the lakes and stubble fields, heard the rhythm of insects and the creak of a buggy, was greeted by Sam Clark's "Well, well, how's the little lady?"

Nobody in Washington cared enough for her to fret about her sins as Sam did.

But that night they had at the flat a man just back from Finland.

## II

She was on the Powhatan roof with the captain. At a table, somewhat vociferously buying improbable "soft drinks" for two fluffy girls, was a man with a large familiar back.

"Oh! I think I know him," she murmured.

"Who? There? Oh, Bresnahan, Percy Bresnahan."

"Yes. You've met him? What sort of a man is he?"

"He's a good-hearted idiot. I rather like him, and I believe that as a salesman of motors he's a wonder. But he's a nuisance in the aeronautic section. Tries so hard to be useful but he doesn't know anything—he doesn't know anything. Rather pathetic: rich man poking around and trying to be useful. Do you want to speak to him?"

"No—no—I don't think so."

## III

She was at a motion-picture show. The film was a highly advertised and abysmal thing smacking of simpering hairdressers, cheap perfume, red-plush suites on the back streets of tenderloins, and complacent fat women chewing gum. It pretended to deal with the life of studios. The leading man did a portrait which was a masterpiece. He also saw visions in pipe-smoke, and was very brave and poor and pure. He had ringlets, and his masterpiece was strangely like an enlarged photograph.

Carol prepared to leave.

On the screen, in the rôle of a composer, appeared an actor called Eric Valour.

She was startled, incredulous, then wretched. Looking straight out at her, wearing a beret and a velvet jacket, was Erik Valborg.

He had a pale part, which he played neither well nor badly. She speculated, "I could have made so much of him——" She did not finish her speculation.

She went home and read Kennicott's letters. They had seemed stiff and undetailed, but now there strode from them a personality, a personality unlike that of the languishing young man in the velvet jacket playing a dummy piano in a canvas room.

IV

Kennicott first came to see her in November, thirteen months after her arrival in Washington. When he announced that he was coming she was not at all sure that she wished to see him. She was glad that he had made the decision himself.

She had leave from the office for two days.

She watched him marching from the train, solid, assured, carrying his heavy suit-case, and she was diffident—he was such a bulky person to handle. They kissed each other questioningly, and said at the same time, "You're looking fine; how's the baby?" and "You're looking awfully well, dear; how is everything?"

He grumbled, "I don't want to butt in on any plans you've made or your friends or anything, but if you've got time for it, I'd like to chase around Washington, and take in some restaurants and shows and stuff, and forget work for a while."

She realized, in the taxicab, that he was wearing a soft gray suit, a soft easy hat, a flippant tie.

"Like the new outfit? Got 'em in Chicago. Gosh, I hope they're the kind you like."

They spent half an hour at the flat, with Hugh. She was flustered, but he gave no sign of kissing her again.

As he moved about the small rooms she realized that he had had his new tan shoes polished to a brassy luster. There was a recent cut on his chin. He must have shaved on the train just before coming into Washington.

It was pleasant to feel how important she was, how many people she recognized, as she took him to the Capitol, as she told him (he asked and she obligingly guessed) how many feet it was to the top of the dome, as she pointed out Senator LaFollette and the vice-president, and at lunch-time showed herself an habitué by leading him through the catacombs to the senate restaurant.

She realized that he was slightly more bald. The familiar way in which his hair was parted on the left side agitated her. She looked down at his hands, and the fact that his nails were as ill-treated as ever touched her more than his pleading shoe-shine.

"You'd like to motor down to Mount Vernon this afternoon, wouldn't you?" she said.

It was the one thing he had planned. He was delighted that it seemed to be a perfectly well bred and Washingtonian thing to do.

He shyly held her hand on the way, and told her the news: they were excavating the basement for the new schoolbuilding, Vida "made him tired the way she always looked at the Maje," poor Chet Dashaway had been killed in a motor accident out on the Coast. He did not coax her to like him. At Mount Vernon he admired the paneled library and Washington's dental tools.

She knew that he would want oysters, that he would have heard of Harvey's apropos of Grant and Blaine, and she took him there. At dinner his hearty voice, his holiday enjoyment of everything, turned into nervousness in his desire to know a number of interesting matters, such as whether they still were married. But he did not ask questions, and he said nothing about her returning. He cleared his throat and observed, "Oh say, been trying out the old camera. Don't you think these are pretty good?"

He tossed over to her thirty prints of Gopher Prairie and the country about. Without defense, she was thrown into it. She remembered that he had lured her with photographs in courtship days; she made a note of his sameness, his satisfaction with the tactics which had proved good before; but she forgot it in the familiar places. She was seeing the sun-speckled ferns among birches on the shore of Minniemashie, wind-rippled miles of wheat, the porch of their own house where Hugh had played, Main Street where she knew every window and every face.

She handed them back, with praise for his photography, and he talked of lenses and time-exposures.

Dinner was over and they were gossiping of her friends at the flat, but an intruder was with them, sitting back, persistent, inescapable. She could not endure it. She stammered:

"I had you check your bag at the station because I wasn't quite sure where you'd stay. I'm dreadfully sorry we haven't room to put you up at the flat. We ought to have seen about a room for you before. Don't you think you better call up the Willard or the Washington now?"

He peered at her cloudily. Without words he asked, without speech she answered, whether she was also going to the Willard or the Washington. But she tried to look as though she did not know that they were debating anything of the sort. She would have hated him had he been meek about it. But he was neither meek nor angry. However impatient he may have been with her blandness he said readily:

"Yes, guess I better do that. Excuse me a second. Then how about grabbing a taxi (Gosh, isn't it the limit the way these taxi shuffers skin around a corner? Got more nerve driving than I have!) and going up to your flat for a while? Like to meet your friends—must be fine women—and I might take a look and see how Hugh sleeps. Like to know how he breathes. Don't think he has adenoids, but I better make sure, eh?" He patted her shoulder.

At the flat they found her two housemates and a girl who had been to jail for suffrage. Kennicott fitted in surprisingly. He laughed at the girl's story of the humors of a hunger-strike; he told the secretary what to do when her eyes were tired from typing; and the teacher asked him—not as the husband of a friend but as a physician—whether there was "anything to this inoculation for colds."

His colloquialisms seemed to Carol no more lax than their habitual slang.

Like an older brother he kissed her good-night in the midst of the company.

"He's terribly nice," said her housemates, and waited for confidences. They got none, nor did her own heart. She could find nothing definite to agonize about. She felt that she was no longer analyzing and controlling forces, but swept on by them.

He came to the flat for breakfast, and washed the dishes. That was her only occasion for spite. Back home he never thought of washing dishes!

She took him to the obvious "sights"—the Treasury, the Monument, the Corcoran Gallery, the Pan-American Building, the Lincoln Memorial, with the Potomac beyond it and the Arlington hills and the columns of the Lee Mansion. For all his willingness to play there was over him a melancholy which piqued her. His normally expressionless eyes had depths to them now, and strangeness. As they walked through Lafayette Square, looking past the Jackson statue at the lovely tranquil façade of the White House, he sighed, "I wish I'd had a shot at places like this. When I was in the U., I had to earn part of my way, and when I wasn't doing that or studying, I guess I was roughhousing. My gang were a great bunch for bumming around and raising Cain. Maybe if I'd been caught early and sent to concerts and all that—— Would I have been what you call intelligent?"

"Oh, my dear, don't be humble! You are intelligent! For instance, you're the most thorough doctor——"

He was edging about something he wished to say. He pounced on it: "You did like those pictures of G. P. pretty well, after all, didn't you!"

"Yes, of course."

"Wouldn't be so bad to have a glimpse of the old town, would it!"

"No, it wouldn't. Just as I was terribly glad to see the Haydocks. But please understand me! That doesn't mean that I withdraw all my criticisms. The fact that I might like a glimpse of old friends hasn't any particular relation to the question of whether Gopher Prairie oughtn't to have festivals and lamb chops."

Hastily, "No, no! Sure not. I und'stand."

"But I know it must have been pretty tiresome to have to live with anybody as perfect as I was."

He grinned. She liked his grin.

V

He was thrilled by old negro coachmen, admirals, aeroplanes, the building to which his income tax would eventually go, a Rolls-Royce, Lynnhaven oysters, the Supreme Court Room, a New York theatrical manager down for the try-out of a play, the house where Lincoln died, the cloaks of Italian officers, the barrows at which clerks buy their box-lunches at noon, the barges on the Chesapeake Canal, and the fact that District of Columbia cars had both District and Maryland licenses.

She resolutely took him to her favorite white and green cottages and Georgian houses. He admitted that fanlights, and white shutters against rosy brick, were more homelike than a painty wooden box. He volunteered, "I see how you mean. They make me think of these pictures of an old-fashioned Christmas. Oh, if you keep at it long enough you'll have Sam and me reading poetry and everything. Oh say, d' I tell you about this fierce green Jack Elder's had his machine painted?"

VI

They were at dinner.

He hinted, "Before you showed me those places today, I'd already made up my mind that when I built the new house we used to talk about, I'd fix it the way you wanted it. I'm pretty practical about foundations and radiation and stuff like that, but I guess I don't know a whole lot about architecture."

"My dear, it occurs to me with a sudden shock that I don't either!"

"Well—anyway—you let me plan the garage and the plumbing, and you do the rest, if you ever—I mean—if you ever want to."

Doubtfully, "That's sweet of you."

"Look here, Carrie; you think I'm going to ask you to love me. I'm not. And I'm not going to ask you to come back to Gopher Prairie!"

She gaped.

"It's been a whale of a fight. But I guess I've got myself to see that you won't ever stand G. P. unless you *want* to come back to it. I needn't say I'm crazy to have you. But I won't ask you. I just want you to know how I wait for you. Every mail I look for a letter, and when I get one I'm kind of scared to open it, I'm hoping so much that you're coming back. Evenings—— You know I didn't open the cottage down at the lake at all, this past summer. Simply couldn't stand all the others laughing and swimming, and you not there. I used to sit on the porch, in town, and I—I couldn't get over the feeling that you'd simply run up to the drug store and would be right back, and till after it got dark I'd catch myself watching, looking up the street, and you never came, and the house was so empty and still that I didn't like to go in. And sometimes I fell asleep there, in my chair, and didn't wake up till after midnight, and the house—— Oh, the devil! Please get me, Carrie.

I just want you to know how welcome you'll be if you ever do come. But I'm not asking you to."

"You're— It's awfully——"

"'Nother thing. I'm going to be frank. I haven't always been absolutely, uh, absolutely, proper. I've always loved you more than anything else in the world, you and the kid. But sometimes when you were chilly to me I'd get lonely and sore, and pike out and—— Never intended——"

She rescued him with a pitying, "It's all right. Let's forget it."

"But before we were married you said if your husband ever did anything wrong, you'd want him to tell you."

"Did I? I can't remember. And I can't seem to think. Oh, my dear, I do know how generously you're trying to make me happy. The only thing is—— I can't think. I don't know what I think."

"Then listen! Don't think! Here's what I want you to do! Get a two weeks leave from your office. Weather's beginning to get chilly here. Let's run down to Charleston and Savannah and maybe Florida."

"A second honeymoon?" indecisively.

"No. Don't even call it that. Call it a second wooing. I won't ask anything. I just want the chance to chase around with you. I guess I never appreciated how lucky I was to have a girl with imagination and lively feet to play with. So—— Could you maybe run away and see the South with me? If you wanted to, you could just—you could just pretend you were my sister and—— I'll get an extra nurse for Hugh! I'll get the best dog-gone nurse in Washington!"

### VII

It was in the Villa Margherita, by the palms of the Charleston Battery and the metallic harbor, that her aloofness melted.

When they sat on the upper balcony, enchanted by the moon glitter, she cried, "Shall I go back to Gopher Prairie with you? Decide for me. I'm tired of deciding and undeciding."

"No. You've got to do your own deciding. As a matter of fact, in spite of this honeymoon, I don't think I want you to come home. Not yet."

She could only stare.

"I want you to be satisfied when you get there. I'll do everything I can to keep you happy, but I'll make lots of breaks, so I want you to take time and think it over."

She was relieved. She still had a chance to seize splendid indefinite freedoms. She might go—oh, she'd see Europe, somehow, before she was recaptured. But she also had a firmer respect for Kennicott. She had fancied that her life might make a story. She knew that there was nothing heroic or obviously dramatic in it, no magic of rare hours, nor valiant challenge, but it seemed to her that she was of some significance because she was commonplaceness, the ordinary life of the age, made articulate and protesting. It had not occurred to her that there was also a story of Will Kennicott, into which she entered only so much as he entered into hers; that he had bewilderments and concealments as intricate as her own, and soft treacherous desires for sympathy.

Thus she brooded, looking at the amazing sea, holding his hand.

### VIII

She was in Washington; Kennicott was in Gopher Prairie, writing as dryly as ever about water-pipes and goose-hunting and Mrs. Fageros's mastoid.

She was talking at dinner to a generalissima of suffrage. Should she return? The leader spoke wearily:

"My dear, I'm perfectly selfish. I can't quite visualize the needs of your husband, and it seems to me that your baby will do quite as well in the schools here as in your barracks at home."

"Then you think I'd better not go back?" Carol sounded disappointed.

"It's more difficult than that. When I say that I'm selfish I mean that the only thing I consider about women is whether they're likely to prove useful in building up real political power for women. And you? Shall I be frank? Remember when I say 'you' I don't mean you alone. I'm thinking of thousands of women who come to Washington and New York and Chicago every year, dissatisfied at home and seeking a sign in the heavens—women of all sorts, from timid mothers of fifty in cotton gloves, to girls just out of Vassar who organize strikes in their own fathers' factories! All of you are more or less useful to me, but only a few of you can take my place, because I have one virtue (only one): I have given up father and mother and children for the love of God.

"Here's the test for you: Do you come to 'conquer the East,' as people say, or do you come to conquer yourself?

"It's so much more complicated than any of you know—so much more complicated than I knew when I put on Ground Grippers and started out to reform the world. The final complication in 'conquering Washington' or 'conquering New York' is that the conquerors must beyond all things not conquer! It must have been so easy in the good old days when authors dreamed only of selling a hundred thousand volumes, and sculptors of being fêted in big houses, and even the Uplifters like me had a simple-hearted ambition to be elected to important offices and invited to go round lecturing. But we meddlers have upset everything. Now the one thing that is disgraceful to any of us is obvious success. The Uplifter who is very popular with wealthy patrons can be pretty sure that he has softened his philosophy to please them, and the author who is making lots of money—poor things, I've heard 'em apologizing for it to the shabby bitter-enders; I've seen 'em ashamed of the sleek luggage they got from movie rights.

"Do you want to sacrifice herself in such a topsy-turvy world, where popularity makes you unpopular with the people you love, and the only failure is cheap success, and the only individualist is the person who gives up all his individualism to serve a jolly ungrateful proletariat which thumbs its nose at him?"

Carol smiled ingratiatingly, to indicate that she was indeed one who desired to sacrifice, but she sighed, "I don't know; I'm afraid I'm not heroic. I certainly wasn't out home. Why didn't I do big effective——"

"Not a matter of heroism. Matter of endurance. Your Middlewest is double-Puritan—prairie Puritan on top of New England Puritan; bluff frontiersman on the surface, but in its heart it still has the ideal of Plymouth Rock in a sleet-storm. There's one attack you can make on it, perhaps the only kind that accomplishes much anywhere: you can keep on looking at one thing after another in your home and church and bank, and ask why it is, and who first laid down the law that it had to be that way. If enough of us do this impolitely enough, then we'll become civilized in merely twenty thousand years or so, instead of having to wait the two hundred thousand years that my cynical anthropologist friends allow. . . . Easy, pleasant, lucrative home-work for wives: asking people to define their jobs. That's the most dangerous doctrine I know!"

Carol was meditating, "I will go back! I will go on asking questions. I've always done it, and always failed at it, and it's all I can do. I'm going to ask Ezra Stowbody why he's opposed to the nationalization of railroads, and ask Dave Dyer why a druggist always is pleased when he's called 'doctor,' and maybe ask Mrs. Bogart why she wears a widow's veil that looks like a dead crow."

The woman leader straightened. "And you have one thing. You have a baby to hug. That's my temptation. I dream of babies—of a baby—and I sneak around parks to see them playing. (The children in Dupont Circle are like a poppy-garden.) And the antis call me 'unsexed'!"

Carol was thinking, in panic, "Oughtn't Hugh to have country air? I won't let him become a yokel. I can guide him away from street-corner loafing. . . . I think I can."

On her way home: "Now that I've made a precedent, joined the union and gone out on one strike and learned personal solidarity, I won't be so afraid. Will won't always be resisting my running away. Some day I really will go to Europe with him . . . or without him.

"I've lived with people who are not afraid to go to jail. I could invite a Miles Bjornstam to dinner without being afraid of the Haydocks . . . I think I could.

"I'll take back the sound of Yvette Guilbert's songs and Elman's violin. They'll be only the lovelier against the thrumming of crickets in the stubble on an autumn day.

"I can laugh now and be serene . . . I think I can."

Though she should return, she said, she would not be utterly defeated. She was glad of her rebellion. The prairie was no longer empty land in the sun-glare; it was the living tawny beast which she had fought and made beautiful by fighting; and in the village streets were shadows of her desires and the sound of her marching and the seeds of mystery and greatness.

### IX

Her active hatred of Gopher Prairie had run out. She saw it now as a toiling new settlement. With sympathy she remembered Kennicott's defense of its citizens as "a lot of pretty good folks, working hard and trying to bring up their families the best they can." She recalled tenderly the young awkwardness of Main Street and the makeshifts of the little brown cottages; she pitied their shabbiness and isolation; had compassion for their assertion of culture, even as expressed in Thanatopsis papers, for their pretense of greatness, even as trumpeted in "boosting." She saw Main Street in the dusty prairie sunset, a line of frontier shanties with solemn lonely people waiting for her, solemn and lonely as an old man who has outlived his friends. She remembered that Kennicott and Sam Clark had listened to her songs, and she wanted to run to them and sing.

"At last," she rejoiced, "I've come to a fairer attitude toward the town. I can love it, now."

She was, perhaps, rather proud of herself for having acquired so much tolerance.

She awoke at three in the morning, after a dream of being tortured by Ella Stowbody and the Widow Bogart.

"I've been making the town a myth. This is how people keep up the tradition of the perfect home-town, the happy boyhood, the brilliant college friends. We forget so. I've been forgetting that Main Street doesn't think it's in the least lonely and pitiful. It thinks it's God's Own Country. It isn't waiting for me. It doesn't care."

But the next evening she again saw Gopher Prairie as her home, waiting for her in the sunset, rimmed round with splendor.

### X

She did not return for five months more; five months crammed with greedy accumulation of sounds and colors to take back for the long still days.

She had spent nearly two years in Washington.

When she departed for Gopher Prairie, in June, her second baby was stirring within her.

# 39

She wondered all the way home what her sensations would be. She wondered about it so much that she had every sensation she had imagined. She was excited by each familiar porch, each hearty "Well, well!" and flattered to be, for a day, the most important news of the community. She bustled about, making calls. Juanita Haydock bubbled over their Washington encounter, and took Carol to her social bosom. This ancient opponent seemed likely to be her most intimate friend, for Vida Sherwin, though she was cordial, stood back and watched for imported heresies.

In the evening Carol went to the mill. The mystical Om-Om-Om of the dynamos in the electric-light plant behind the mill was louder in the darkness. Outside sat the night watchman, Champ Perry. He held up his stringy hands and squeaked, "We've all missed you terrible."

Who in Washington would miss her?

Who in Washington could be depended upon like Guy Pollock? When she saw him on the street, smiling as always, he seemed an eternal thing, a part of her own self.

After a week she decided that she was neither glad nor sorry to be back. She entered each day with the matter-of-fact attitude with which she had gone to her office in Washington. It was her task; there would be mechanical details and meaningless talk; what of it?

The only problem which she had approached with emotion proved insignificant. She had, on the train, worked herself up to such devotion that she was willing to give up her own room, to try to share all of her life with Kennicott.

He mumbled, ten minutes after she had entered the house, "Say, I've kept your room for you like it was. I've kind of come round to your way of thinking. Don't see why folks need to get on each other's nerves just because they're friendly. Darned if I haven't got so I like a little privacy and mulling things over by myself."

## II

She had left a city which sat up nights to talk of universal transition; of European revolution, guild socialism, free verse. She had fancied that all the world was changing.

She found that it was not.

In Gopher Prairie the only ardent new topics were prohibition, the place in Minneapolis where you could get whisky at thirteen dollars a quart, recipes for home-made beer, the "high cost of living," the presidential election, Clark's new car, and not very novel foibles of Cy Bogart. Their problems were exactly what they had been two years ago, what they had been twenty years ago, and what they would be for twenty years to come. With the world a possible volcano, the husbandmen were plowing at the base of the mountain. A volcano does occasionally drop a river of lava on even the best of agriculturists, to their astonishment and considerable injury, but their cousins inherit the farms and a year or two later go back to the plowing.

She was unable to rhapsodize much over the seven new bungalows and the two garages which Kennicott had made to seem so important. Her intensest thought about them was, "Oh yes, they're all right I suppose." The change which she did heed was the erection of the schoolbuilding, with its cheerful brick walls, broad windows, gymnasium, classrooms for agriculture and cooking. It indicated Vida's triumph, and it stirred her to activity—any activity. She went to Vida with a jaunty, "I think I shall work for you. And I'll begin at the bottom."

She did. She relieved the attendant at the rest-room for an hour a day. Her only innovation was painting the pine table a black and orange rather shocking to the Thanatopsis. She talked to the farmwives and soothed their babies and was happy.

Thinking of them she did not think of the ugliness of Main Street as she hurried along it to the chatter of the Jolly Seventeen.

She wore her eye-glasses on the street now. She was beginning to ask Kennicott and Juanita if she didn't look young, much younger than thirty-three. The eye-glasses pinched her nose. She considered spectacles. They would make her seem older, and hopelessly settled. No! She would not wear spectacles yet. But she tried on a pair at Kennicott's office. They really were much more comfortable.

III

Dr. Westlake, Sam Clark, Nat Hicks, and Del Snafflin were talking in Del's barber shop.

"Well, I see Kennicott's wife is taking a whirl at the rest-room, now," said Dr. Westlake. He emphasized the "now."

Del interrupted the shaving of Sam and, with his brush dripping lather, he observed jocularly:

"What'll she be up to next? They say she used to claim this burg wasn't swell enough for a city girl like her, and would we please tax ourselves about thirty-seven point nine and fix it all up pretty, with tidies on the hydrants and statoos on the lawns——"

Sam irritably blew the lather from his lips, with milky small bubbles, and snorted, "Be a good thing for most of us roughnecks if we did have a smart woman to tell us how to fix up the town. Just as much to her kicking as there was to Jim Blausser's gassing about factories. And you can bet Mrs. Kennicott is smart, even if she is skittish. Glad to see her back."

Dr. Westlake hastened to play safe. "So was I! So was I! She's got a nice way about her, and she knows a good deal about books—or fiction anyway. Of course she's like all the rest of these women—not solidly founded—not scholarly—doesn't know anything about political economy—falls for every new idea that some windjamming crank puts out. But she's a nice woman. She'll probably fix up the rest-room, and the rest-room is a fine thing, brings a lot of business to town. And now that Mrs. Kennicott's been away, maybe she's got over some of her fool ideas. Maybe she realizes that folks simply laugh at her when she tries to tell us how to run everything."

"Sure. She'll take a tumble to herself," said Nat Hicks, sucking in his lips judicially. "As far as I'm concerned, I'll say she's as nice a looking skirt as there is in town. But yow!" His tone electrified them. "Guess she'll miss that Swede Valborg that used to work for me! They was a pair! Talking poetry and moonshine! If they could of got away with it, they'd of been so darn lovey-dovey——"

Sam Clark interrupted, "Rats, they never even thought about making love. Just talking books and all that junk. I tell you, Carrie Kennicott's a smart woman, and these smart educated women all get funny ideas, but they get over 'em after they've had three or four kids. You'll see her settled down one of these days, and teaching Sunday School and helping at sociables and behaving herself, and not trying to butt into business and politics. Sure!"

After only fifteen minutes of conference on her stockings, her son, her separate bedroom, her music, her ancient interest in Guy Pollock, her probable salary in Washington, and every remark which she was known to have made since her return, the supreme council decided that they would permit Carol Kennicott to live, and they passed on to a consideration of Nat Hicks's New One about the traveling salesman and the old maid.

IV

For some reason which was totally mysterious to Carol, Maud Dyer seemed to resent her return. At the Jolly Seventeen Maud giggled nervously, "Well, I suppose you found war-work a good excuse to stay away and have a swell time. Juanita! Don't you think we ought to make Carrie tell us about the officers she met in Washington?"

They rustled and stared. Carol looked at them. Their curiosity seemed natural and unimportant.

"Oh yes, yes indeed, have to do that some day," she yawned.

She no longer took Aunt Bessie Smail seriously enough to struggle for independence. She saw that Aunt Bessie did not mean to intrude; that she wanted to do things for all the Kennicotts. Thus Carol hit upon the tragedy of old age, which is not that it is less vigorous than youth, but that it is not needed by youth; that its love and prosy sageness, so important a few years ago, so gladly offered now, are rejected with laughter. She divined that when Aunt Bessie came in with a jar of wild-grape jelly she was waiting in hope of being asked for the recipe. After that she could be irritated but she could not be depressed by Aunt Bessie's simoom of questioning.

She wasn't depressed even when she heard Mrs. Bogart observe, "Now we've got prohibition it seems to me that the next problem of the country ain't so much abolishing cigarettes as it is to make folks observe the Sabbath and arrest these law-breakers that play baseball and go to the movies and all on the Lord's Day."

Only one thing bruised Carol's vanity. Few people asked her about Washington. They who had most admiringly begged Percy Bresnahan for his opinions were least interested in her facts. She laughed at herself when she saw that she had expected to be at once a heretic and a returned hero; she was very reasonable and merry about it; and it hurt just as much as ever.

V

Her baby, born in August, was a girl. Carol could not decide whether she was to become a feminist leader or marry a scientist or both, but did settle on Vassar and a tricolette suit with a small black hat for her Freshman year.

VI

Hugh was loquacious at breakfast. He desired to give his impressions of owls and F Street.

"Don't make so much noise. You talk too much," growled Kennicott.

Carol flared. "Don't speak to him that way! Why don't you listen to him? He has some very interesting things to tell."

"What's the idea? Mean to say you expect me to spend all my time listening to his chatter?"

"Why not?"

"For one thing, he's got to learn a little discipline. Time for him to start getting educated."

"I've learned much more discipline, I've had much more education, from him than he has from me."

"What's this? Some new-fangled idea of raising kids you got in Washington?"

"Perhaps. Did you ever realize that children are people?"

"That's all right. I'm not going to have him monopolizing the conversation."

"No, of course. We have our rights, too. But I'm going to bring him up as a human being. He has just as many thoughts as we have, and I want him to develop them, not take Gopher Prairie's version of them. That's my biggest work now—keeping myself, keeping you, from 'educating' him."

"Well, let's not scrap about it. But I'm not going to have him spoiled."

Kennicott had forgotten it in ten minutes; and she forgot it—this time.

VII

The Kennicotts and the Sam Clarks had driven north to a duck-pass between two lakes, on an autumn day of blue and copper.

Kennicott had given her a light twenty-gauge shotgun. She had a first lesson in shooting, in keeping her eyes open, not wincing, understanding that the bead at the end of the barrel really had something to do with pointing the gun. She was radiant; she almost believed Sam when he insisted that it was she who had shot the mallard at which they had fired together.

She sat on the bank of the reedy lake and found rest in Mrs. Clark's drawling comments on nothing. The brown dusk was still. Behind them were dark marshes. The plowed acres smelled fresh. The lake was garnet and silver. The voices of the men, waiting for the last flight, were clear in the cool air.

"Mark left!" sang Kennicott, in a long-drawn call.

Three ducks were swooping down in a swift line. The guns banged, and a duck fluttered. The men pushed their light boat out on the burnished lake, disappeared beyond the reeds. Their cheerful voices and the slow splash and clank of oars came back to Carol from the dimness. In the sky a fiery plain sloped down to a serene harbor. It dissolved; the lake was white marble; and Kennicott was crying, "Well, old lady, how about hiking out for home? Supper taste pretty good, eh?"

"I'll sit back with Ethel," she said, at the car.

It was the first time she had called Mrs. Clark by her given name; the first time she had willingly sat back, a woman of Main Street.

"I'm hungry. It's good to be hungry," she reflected, as they drove away.

She looked across the silent fields to the west. She was conscious of an unbroken sweep of land to the Rockies, to Alaska; a dominion which will rise to unexampled greatness when other empires have grown senile. Before that time, she knew, a hundred generations of Carols will aspire and go down in tragedy devoid of palls and solemn chanting, the humdrum inevitable tragedy of struggle against inertia.

"Let's all go to the movies tomorrow night. Awfully exciting film," said Ethel Clark.

"Well, I was going to read a new book but—— All right, let's go," said Carol.

VIII

"They're too much for me," Carol sighed to Kennicott. "I've been thinking about getting up an annual Community Day, when the whole town would forget feuds and go out and have sports and a picnic and a dance. But Bert Tybee (why did you ever elect him mayor?)—he's kidnapped my idea. He wants the Community Day, but he wants to have some politician 'give an address.' That's just the stilted sort of thing I've tried to avoid. He asked Vida, and of course she agreed with him."

Kennicott considered the matter while he wound the clock and they tramped up-stairs.

"Yes, it would jar you to have Bert butting in," he said amiably. "Are you going to do much fussing over this Community stunt? Don't you ever get tired of fretting and stewing and experimenting?"

"I haven't even started. Look!" She led him to the nursery door, pointed at the fuzzy brown head of her daughter. "Do you see that object on the pillow? Do you know what it is? It's a bomb to blow up smugness. If you Tories were wise, you wouldn't arrest anarchists; you'd arrest all these children while they're asleep in their cribs. Think what that baby will see and meddle with before she dies in the year 2000! She may see an industrial union of the whole world, she may see aeroplanes going to Mars."

"Yump, probably be changes all right," yawned Kennicott.

She sat on the edge of his bed while he hunted through his bureau for a collar which ought to be there and persistently wasn't.

"I'll go on, always. And I am happy. But this Community Day makes me see how thoroughly I'm beaten."

"That darn collar certainly is gone for keeps," muttered Kennicott and, louder, "Yes, I guess you—— I didn't quite catch what you said, dear."

She patted his pillows, turned down his sheets, as she reflected:

"But I have won in this: I've never excused my failures by sneering at my aspirations, by pretending to have gone beyond them. I do not admit that Main Street is as beautiful as it should be! I do not admit that Gopher Prairie is greater or more generous than Europe! I do not admit that dish-washing is enough to satisfy all women! I may not have fought the good fight, but I have kept the faith."

"Sure. You bet you have," said Kennicott. "Well, good night. Sort of feels to me like it might snow tomorrow. Have to be thinking about putting up the storm-windows pretty soon. Say, did you notice whether the girl put that screwdriver back?"

# Babbitt

*To*
*Edith Wharton*

# 1

The towers of Zenith aspired above the morning mist; austere towers of steel and cement and limestone, sturdy as cliffs and delicate as silver rods. They were neither citadels nor churches, but frankly and beautifully office-buildings.

The mist took pity on the fretted structures of earlier generations: the Post Office with its shingle-tortured mansard, the red brick minarets of hulking old houses, factories with stingy and sooted windows, wooden tenements colored like mud. The city was full of such grotesqueries, but the clean towers were thrusting them from the business center, and on the farther hills were shining new houses, homes—they seemed—for laughter and tranquillity.

Over a concrete bridge fled a limousine of long sleek hood and noiseless engine. These people in evening clothes were returning from an all-night rehearsal of a Little Theater play, an artistic adventure considerably illuminated by champagne. Below the bridge curved a railroad, a maze of green and crimson lights. The New York Flyer boomed past, and twenty lines of polished steel leaped into the glare.

In one of the skyscrapers the wires of the Associated Press were closing down. The telegraph operators wearily raised their celluloid eye-shades after a night of talking with Paris and Peking. Through the building crawled the scrubwomen, yawning, their old shoes slapping. The dawn mist spun away. Cues of men with lunch-boxes clumped toward the immensity of new factories, sheets of glass and hollow tile, glittering shops where five thousand men worked beneath one roof, pouring out the honest wares that would be sold up the Euphrates and across the veldt. The whistles rolled out in greeting a chorus cheerful as the April dawn; the song of labor in a city built—it seemed—for giants.

## II

There was nothing of the giant in the aspect of the man who was beginning to awaken on the sleeping-porch of a Dutch Colonial house in that residential district of Zenith known as Floral Heights.

His name was George F. Babbitt. He was forty-six years old now, in April, 1920, and he made nothing in particular, neither butter nor shoes nor poetry, but he was nimble in the calling of selling houses for more than people could afford to pay.

His large head was pink, his brown hair thin and dry. His face was babyish in slumber, despite his wrinkles and the red spectacle-dents on the slopes of his nose. He was not fat but he was exceedingly well fed; his cheeks were pads, and the unroughened hand which lay helpless upon the khaki-colored blanket was slightly puffy. He seemed prosperous, extremely married and unromantic; and altogether unromantic appeared this sleeping-porch, which looked on one sizable elm, two respectable grass-plots, a cement driveway, and a corrugated iron garage. Yet Babbitt was again dreaming of the fairy child, a dream more romantic than scarlet pagodas by a silver sea.

For years the fairy child had come to him. Where others saw but Georgie Babbitt, she discerned gallant youth. She waited for him, in the darkness beyond mysterious groves. When at last he could slip away from the crowded house he darted to her. His wife, his clamoring friends, sought to follow, but he escaped, the girl fleet beside him, and they crouched together on a shadowy hillside. She was so slim, so white, so eager! She cried that he was gay and valiant, that she would wait for him, that they would sail—

Rumble and bang of the milk-truck.

Babbitt moaned, turned over, struggled back toward his dream. He could see only her face now, beyond misty waters. The furnace-man slammed the basement door. A dog barked in the next yard. As Babbitt sank blissfully into a dim warm tide, the paper-carrier went by whistling, and the rolled-up *Advocate* thumped the front door. Babbitt roused, his stomach constricted with alarm. As he relaxed, he was pierced by the familiar and irritating rattle of some one cranking a Ford: snap-ah-ah, snap-ah-ah, snap-ah-ah. Himself a pious motorist, Babbitt cranked with the unseen driver, with him waited through taut hours for the roar of the starting engine, with him agonized as the roar ceased and again began the infernal patient snap-ah-ah —a round, flat sound, a shivering cold-morning sound, a sound infuriating and inescapable. Not till the rising voice of the motor told him that the Ford was moving was he released from the panting tension. He glanced once at his favorite tree, elm twigs against the gold patina of sky, and fumbled for sleep as for a drug. He who had been a boy very credulous of life was no longer greatly interested in the possible and improbable adventures of each new day.

He escaped from reality till the alarm-clock rang, at seven-twenty.

### III

It was the best of nationally advertised and quantitatively produced alarm-clocks, with all modern attachments, including cathedral chime, intermittent alarm, and a phosphorescent dial. Babbitt was proud of being awakened by such a rich device. Socially it was almost as creditable as buying expensive cord tires.

He sulkily admitted now that there was no more escape, but he lay and detested the grind of the real-estate business, and disliked his family, and disliked himself for disliking them. The evening before, he had played poker at Vergil Gunch's till midnight, and after such holidays he was irritable before breakfast. It may have been the tremendous home-brewed beer of the prohibition-era and the cigars to which that beer enticed him; it may have been resentment of return from this fine, bold man-world to a restricted region of wives and stenographers, and of suggestions not to smoke so much.

From the bedroom beside the sleeping-porch, his wife's detestably cheerful "Time to get up, Georgie boy," and the itchy sound, the brisk and scratchy sound, of combing hairs out of a stiff brush.

He grunted; he dragged his thick legs, in faded baby-blue pajamas, from under the khaki blanket; he sat on the edge of the cot, running his fingers through his wild hair, while his plump feet mechanically felt for his slippers. He looked regretfully at the blanket—forever a suggestion to him of freedom and heroism. He had bought it for a camping trip which had never come off. It symbolized gorgeous loafing, gorgeous cursing, virile flannel shirts.

He creaked to his feet, groaning at the waves of pain which passed behind his eyeballs. Though he waited for their scorching recurrence, he looked blurrily out at the yard. It delighted him, as always; it was the neat yard of a successful business man of Zenith, that is, it was perfection, and made him also perfect. He regarded the corrugated iron garage. For the three-hundred-and-sixty-fifth time in a year he reflected, "No class to that tin shack. Have to build me a frame garage. But by golly it's the only thing on the place that isn't up-to-date!" While he stared he thought of a community garage for his acreage development, Glen Oriole. He stopped puffing and jiggling. His arms were akimbo. His petulant, sleep-swollen face was set in harder lines. He suddenly seemed capable, an official, a man to contrive, to direct, to get things done.

On the vigor of his idea he was carried down the hard, clean, unused-looking hall into the bathroom.

Though the house was not large it had, like all houses on Floral Heights, an altogether royal bathroom of porcelain and glazed tile and metal sleek as silver. The towel-rack was a rod of clear glass set in nickel. The tub was long enough for a Prussian Guard, and above the set bowl was a sensational exhibit of tooth-brush holder, shaving-brush holder, soap-dish, sponge-dish, and medicine-cabinet, so glittering and so ingenious that they resembled an electrical instrument-board. But the Babbitt whose god was Modern Appliances was not pleased. The air of the bathroom was thick with the smell of a heathen toothpaste. "Verona been at it again! 'Stead of sticking to Lilidol, like I've re-peat-ed-ly asked her, she's gone and gotten some confounded stinkum stuff that makes you sick!"

The bath-mat was wrinkled and the floor was wet. (His daughter Verona eccentrically took baths in the morning, now and then.) He slipped on the mat, and slid against the tub. He said "Damn!" Furiously he snatched up his tube of shaving-cream, furiously he lathered, with a belligerent slapping of the unctuous brush, furiously he raked his plump cheeks with a safety-razor. It pulled. The blade was dull. He said, "Damn—oh—oh—damn it!"

He hunted through the medicine-cabinet for a packet of new razor-blades (reflecting, as invariably, "Be cheaper to buy one of these dinguses and strop your own blades,") and when he discovered the packet, behind the round box of bicarbonate of soda, he thought ill of his wife for putting it there and very well of himself for not saying "Damn." But he did say it, immediately afterward, when with wet and soap-slippery fingers he tried to remove the horrible little envelope and crisp clinging oiled paper from the new blade.

Then there was the problem, oft-pondered, never solved, of what to do with the old blade, which might imperil the fingers of his young. As usual, he tossed it on top of the medicine-cabinet, with a mental note that some day he must remove the fifty or sixty other blades that were also temporarily, piled up there. He finished his shaving in a growing testiness increased by his spinning headache and by the emptiness in his stomach. When he was done, his round face smooth and streamy and his eyes stinging from soapy water, he reached for a towel. The family towels were wet, wet and clammy and vile, all of them wet, he found, as he blindly snatched them—his own face-towel, his wife's, Verona's, Ted's, Tinka's, and the lone bath-towel with the huge welt of initial. Then George F. Babbitt did a dismaying thing. He wiped his face on the guest-towel! It was a pansy-embroidered trifle which always hung there to indicate that the Babbitts were in the best Floral Heights society. No one had ever used it. No guest had ever dared to. Guests secretively took a corner of the nearest regular towel.

He was raging, "By golly, here they go and use up all the towels, every doggone one of 'em, and they use 'em and get 'em all wet and sopping, and never put out a dry one for me—of course, I'm the goat!—and then I want one and— I'm the only person in the doggone house that's got the slightest doggone bit of consideration for other people and thoughtfulness and consider there may be others that may want to use the doggone bathroom after me and consider—"

He was pitching the chill abominations into the bath-tub, pleased by the vindictiveness of that desolate flapping sound; and in the midst his wife serenely trotted in, observed serenely, "Why Georgie dear, what are you doing? Are you going to wash out the towels? Why, you needn't wash out the towels. Oh, Georgie, you didn't go and use the guest-towel, did you?"

It is not recorded that he was able to answer.

For the first time in weeks he was sufficiently roused by his wife to look at her.

IV

Myra Babbitt—Mrs. George F. Babbitt—was definitely mature. She had creases from the corners of her mouth to the bottom of her chin, and her plump neck bagged. But the thing that marked her as having passed the line was that she no longer had reticences before her husband, and no longer worried about not having reticences. She was in a petticoat now, and corsets which bulged, and unaware of being seen in bulgy corsets. She had become so dully habituated to married life that in her full matronliness she was as sexless as an anemic nun. She was a good woman, a kind woman, a diligent woman, but no one, save perhaps Tinka her ten-year-old, was at all interested in her or entirely aware that she was alive.

After a rather thorough discussion of all the domestic and social aspects of towels she apologized to Babbitt for his having an alcoholic headache; and he recovered enough to endure the search for a B.V.D. undershirt which had, he pointed out, malevolently been concealed among his clean pajamas.

He was fairly amiable in the conference on the brown suit.

"What do you think, Myra?" He pawed at the clothes hunched on a chair in their bedroom, while she moved about mysteriously adjusting and patting her petticoat and, to his jaundiced eye, never seeming to get on with her dressing. "How about it? Shall I wear the brown suit another day?"

"Well, it looks awfully nice on you."

"I know, but gosh, it needs pressing."

"That's so. Perhaps it does."

"It certainly could stand being pressed, all right."

"Yes, perhaps it wouldn't hurt it to be pressed."

"But gee, the coat doesn't need pressing. No sense in having the whole darn suit pressed, when the coat doesn't need it."

"That's so."

"But the pants certainly need it, all right. Look at them—look at those wrinkles—the pants certainly do need pressing."

"That's so. Oh, Georgie, why couldn't you wear the brown coat with the blue trousers we were wondering what we'd do with them?"

"Good Lord! Did you ever in all my life know me to wear the coat of one suit and the pants of another? What do you think I am? A busted book-keeper?"

"Well, why don't you put on the dark gray suit to-day, and stop in at the tailor and leave the brown trousers?"

"Well, they certainly need— Now where the devil is that gray suit? Oh, yes, here we are."

He was able to get through the other crises of dressing with comparative resoluteness and calm.

His first adornment was the sleeveless dimity B.V.D. undershirt, in which he resembled a small boy humorlessly wearing a cheesecloth tabard at a civic pageant. He never put on B.V.D.'s without thanking the God of Progress that he didn't wear tight, long, old-fashioned undergarments, like his father-in-law and partner, Henry Thompson. His second embellishment was combing and slicking back his hair. It gave him a tremendous forehead, arching up two inches beyond the former hair-line. But most wonder-working of all was the donning of his spectacles.

There is character in spectacles—the pretentious tortoise-shell, the meek pince-nez of the school teacher, the twisted silver-framed glasses of the old villager. Babbitt's spectacles had huge, circular, frameless lenses of the very best glass; the ear-pieces were thin bars of gold. In them he was the modern business man; one who gave orders to clerks and drove a car and played occasional golf and was scholarly in regard to Salesmanship. His head suddenly appeared not babyish but weighty, and you noted his heavy, blunt nose, his straight mouth and thick, long upper lip, his chin overfleshy but strong; with respect you beheld him put on the rest of his uniform as a Solid Citizen.

The gray suit was well cut, well made, and completely undistinguished. It was a standard suit. White piping on the V of the vest added a flavor of law and learning. His shoes were black laced boots, good boots, honest boots, standard boots, extraordinarily uninteresting boots. The only frivolity was in his purple knitted scarf. With considerable comment on the matter to Mrs. Babbitt (who, acrobatically fastening the back of her blouse to her skirt with a safety-pin, did not hear a word he said), he chose between the purple scarf and a tapestry effect with stringless brown harps among blown palms, and into it he thrust a snake-head pin with opal eyes.

A sensational event was changing from the brown suit to the gray the contents of his pockets. He was earnest about these objects. They were of eternal importance, like baseball or the Republican Party. They included a fountain pen and a silver pencil (always lacking a supply of new leads) which belonged in the righthand upper vest pocket. Without them he would have felt naked. On his watch-chain were a gold penknife, silver cigar-cutter, seven keys (the use of two of which he had forgotten), and inciden-tally a good watch. Depending from the chain was a large, yellowish elk's-tooth—proclamation of his membership in the Brotherly and Protective Order of Elks. Most significant of all was his loose-leaf pocket note-book, that modern and efficient note-book which contained the addresses of people whom he had forgotten, prudent memoranda of postal money-orders which had reached their destinations months ago, stamps which had lost their muci-lage, clippings of verses by T. Cholmondeley Frink and of the newspaper editorials from which Babbitt got his opinions and his polysyllables, notes to be sure and do things which he did not intend to do, and one curious inscription—D.S.S.D.M.Y.P.D.F.

But he had no cigarette-case. No one had ever happened to give him one, so he hadn't the habit, and people who carried cigarette-cases he regarded as effeminate.

Last, he stuck in his lapel the Boosters' Club button. With the concise-ness of great art the button displayed two words: "Boosters—Pep!" It made Babbitt feel loyal and important. It associated him with Good Fellows, with men who were nice and human, and important in business circles. It was his V.C., his Legion of Honor ribbon, his Phi Beta Kappa key.

With the subtleties of dressing ran other complex worries. "I feel kind of punk this morning," he said. "I think I had too much dinner last evening. You oughtn't to serve those heavy banana fritters."

"But you asked me to have some."

"I know, but— I tell you, when a fellow gets past forty he has to look after his digestion. There's a lot of fellows that don't take proper care of them-selves. I tell you at forty a man's a fool or his doctor—I mean, his own doctor. Folks don't give enough attention to this matter of dieting. Now I think—

Course a man ought to have a good meal after the day's work, but it would be a good thing for both of us if we took lighter lunches."

"But Georgie, here at home I always do have a light lunch."

"Mean to imply I make a hog of myself, eating down-town? Yes, sure! You'd have a swell time if you had to eat the truck that new steward hands out to us at the Athletic Club! But I certainly do feel out of sorts, this morning. Funny, got a pain down here on the left side—but no, that wouldn't be appendicitis, would it? Last night, when I was driving over to Verg Gunch's, I felt a pain in my stomach, too. Right here it was—kind of a sharp shooting pain. I— Where'd that dime go to? Why don't you serve more prunes at breakfast? Of course I eat an apple every evening—an apple a day keeps the doctor away—but still, you ought to have more prunes, and not all these fancy doodads."

"The last time I had prunes you didn't eat them."

"Well, I didn't feel like eating 'em, I suppose. Matter of fact, I think I did eat some of 'em. Anyway— I tell you it's mighty important to— I was saying to Verg Gunch, just last evening, most people don't take sufficient care of their diges—"

"Shall we have the Gunches for our dinner, next week?"

"Why sure; you bet."

"Now see here, George: I want you to put on your nice dinner-jacket that evening."

"Rats! The rest of 'em won't want to dress."

"Of course they will. You remember when you didn't dress for the Little-fields' supper-party, and all the rest did, and how embarrassed you were."

"Embarrassed, hell! I wasn't embarrassed. Everybody knows I can put on as expensive a Tux. as anybody else, and I should worry if I don't happen to have it on sometimes. All a darn nuisance, anyway. All right for a woman, that stays around the house all the time, but when a fellow's worked like the dickens all day, he doesn't want to go and hustle his head off getting into the soup-and-fish for a lot of folks that he's seen in just reg'lar ordinary clothes that same day."

"You know you enjoy being seen in one. The other evening you admitted you were glad I'd insisted on your dressing. You said you felt a lot better for it. And oh, Georgie, I do wish you wouldn't say 'Tux.' It's 'dinner-jacket.'"

"Rats, what's the odds?"

"Well, it's what all the nice folks say. Suppose Lucile McKelvey heard you calling it a 'Tux.'"

"Well, that's all right now! Lucile McKelvey can't pull anything on me! Her folks are common as mud, even if her husband and her dad are million-aires! I suppose you're trying to rub in *your* exalted social position! Well, let me tell you that your revered paternal ancestor, Henry T., doesn't even call it a 'Tux.'! He calls it a 'bobtail jacket for a ringtail monkey,' and you couldn't get him into one unless you chloroformed him!"

"Now don't be horrid, George."

"Well, I don't want to be horrid, but Lord! you're getting as fussy as Verona. Ever since she got out of college she's been too rambunctious to live with—doesn't know what she wants—well, I know what she wants!—all she wants is to marry a millionaire, and live in Europe, and hold some preacher's hand, and simultaneously at the same time stay right here in Zenith and be some blooming kind of a socialist agitator or boss charity-worker or some damn thing! Lord, and Ted is just as bad! He wants to go to college, and he doesn't want to go to college. Only one of the three that knows her own mind is Tinka. Simply can't understand how I ever came to have a pair of shillyshallying children like Rone and Ted. I may not be any Rockefeller or James J. Shakespeare, but I certainly do know my own mind, and I do keep right on plugging along in the office and— Do you know the latest? Far as I can figure out, Ted's new bee is he'd like to be a movie actor and— And here I've told him a hundred times, if he'll go to college and law-school and make good, I'll set him up in business and— Verona just exactly as bad. Doesn't know what she wants. Well, well, come on! Aren't you ready yet? The girl rang the bell three minutes ago."

v

Before he followed his wife, Babbitt stood at the westernmost window of their room. This residential settlement, Floral Heights, was on a rise; and though the center of the city was three miles away—Zenith had between three and four hundred thousand inhabitants now—he could see the top of the Second National Tower, an Indiana limestone building of thirty-five stories.

Its shining walls rose against April sky to a simple cornice like a streak of white fire. Integrity was in the tower, and decision. It bore its strength lightly as a tall soldier. As Babbitt stared, the nervousness was soothed from his face, his slack chin lifted in reverence. All he articulated was "That's one lovely sight!" but he was inspired by the rhythm of the city; his love of it renewed. He beheld the tower as a temple-spire of the religion of business, a faith passionate, exalted, surpassing common men; and as he clumped down to breakfast he whistled the ballad "Oh, by gee, by gosh, by jingo" as though it were a hymn melancholy and noble.

2

Relieved of Babbitt's bumbling and the soft grunts with which his wife expressed the sympathy she was too experienced to feel and much too experienced not to show, their bedroom settled instantly into impersonality.

It gave on the sleeping-porch. It served both of them as dressing-room, and on the coldest nights Babbitt luxuriously gave up the duty of being manly and retreated to the bed inside, to curl his toes in the warmth and laugh at the January gale.

The room displayed a modest and pleasant color-scheme, after one of the best standard designs of the decorator who "did the interiors" for most of the speculative-builders' houses in Zenith. The walls were gray, the wood-work white, the rug a serene blue; and very much like mahogany was the furniture—the bureau with its great clear mirror, Mrs. Babbitt's dressing-table with toilet-articles of almost solid silver, the plain twin beds, between them a small table holding a standard electric bedside lamp, a glass for water, and a standard bedside book with colored illustrations—what particu-lar book it was cannot be ascertained, since no one had ever opened it. The mattresses were firm but not hard, triumphant modern mattresses which had cost a great deal of money; the hot-water radiator was of exactly the proper scientific surface for the cubic contents of the room. The win-dows were large and easily opened, with the best catches and cords, and Holland roller-shades guaranteed not to crack. It was a masterpiece among bedrooms, right out of Cheerful Modern Houses for Medium Incomes. Only it had nothing to do with the Babbitts, nor with any one else. If people had ever lived and loved here, read thrillers at midnight and lain in beautiful indolence on a Sunday morning, there were no signs of it. It had the air of being a very good room in a very good hotel. One expected the chamber-maid to come in and make it ready for people who would stay but one night, go without looking back, and never think of it again.

Every second house in Floral Heights had a bedroom precisely like this.

The Babbitts' house was five years old. It was all as competent and glossy as this bedroom. It had the best of taste, the best of inexpensive rugs, a simple and laudable architecture, and the latest conveniences. Throughout, electricity took the place of candles and slatternly hearth-fires. Along the bedroom baseboard were three plugs for electric lamps, concealed by little brass doors. In the halls were plugs for the vacuum cleaner, and in the living-room plugs for the piano lamp, for the electric fan. The trim dining-room (with its admirable oak buffet, its leaded-glass cupboard, its creamy plaster walls, its modest scene of a salmon expiring upon a pile of oysters) had plugs which supplied the electric percolator and the electric toaster.

In fact there was but one thing wrong with the Babbitt house: It was not a home.

## II

Often of a morning Babbitt came bouncing and jesting in to breakfast. But things were mysteriously awry to-day. As he pontifically tread the upper hall he looked into Verona's bedroom and protested, "What's the use of giving the family a high-class house when they don't appreciate it and tend to business and get down to brass tacks?"

He marched upon them: Verona, a dumpy brown-haired girl of twenty-two, just out of Bryn Mawr, given to solicitudes about duty and sex and

God and the unconquerable bagginess of the gray sports-suit she was now wearing. Ted—Theodore Roosevelt Babbitt—a decorative boy of seventeen. Tinka—Katherine—still a baby at ten, with radiant red hair and a thin skin which hinted of too much candy and too many ice cream sodas. Babbitt did not show his vague irritation as he tramped in. He really disliked being a family tyrant, and his nagging was as meaningless as it was frequent. He shouted at Tinka, "Well, kittiedoolie!" It was the only pet name in his vocabulary, except the "dear" and "hon." with which he recognized his wife, and he flung it at Tinka every morning.

He gulped a cup of coffee in the hope of pacifying his stomach and his soul. His stomach ceased to feel as though it did not belong to him, but Verona began to be conscientious and annoying, and abruptly there returned to Babbitt the doubts regarding life and families and business which had clawed at him when his dream-life and the slim fairy girl had fled.

Verona had for six months been filing-clerk at the Gruensberg Leather Company offices, with a prospect of becoming secretary to Mr. Gruensberg and thus, as Babbitt defined it, "getting some good out of your expensive college education till you're ready to marry and settle down."

But now said Verona: "Father! I was talking to a classmate of mine that's working for the Associated Charities—oh, Dad, there's the sweetest little babies that come to the milk-station there!—and I feel as though I ought to be doing something worth while like that."

"What do you mean 'worth while'? If you get to be Gruensberg's secretary —and maybe you would, if you kept up your shorthand and didn't go sneaking off to concerts and talk-fests every evening—I guess you'll find thirty-five or forty bones a week worth while!"

"I know, but—oh, I want to—contribute— I wish I were working in a settlement-house. I wonder if I could get one of the department-stores to let me put in a welfare-department with a nice rest-room and chintzes and wicker chairs and so on and so forth. Or I could—"

"Now you look here! The first thing you got to understand is that all this uplift and flipflop and settlement-work and recreation is nothing in God's world but the entering wedge for socialism. The sooner a man learns he isn't going to be coddled, and he needn't expect a lot of free grub and, uh, all these free classes and flipflop and doodads for his kids unless he earns 'em, why, the sooner he'll get on the job and produce—produce—produce! That's what the country needs, and not all this fancy stuff that just enfeebles the will-power of the working man and gives his kids a lot of notions above their class. And you—if you'd tend to business instead of fooling and fussing— All the time! When I was a young man I made up my mind what I wanted to do, and stuck to it through thick and thin, and that's why I'm where I am to-day, and—Myra! What do you let the girl chop the toast up into these dinky little chunks for? Can't get your fist onto 'em. Half cold, anyway!"

Ted Babbitt, junior in the great East Side High School, had been making hiccup-like sounds of interruption. He blurted now, "Say, Rone, you going to—"

Verona whirled. "Ted! Will you kindly not interrupt us when we're talking about serious matters!"

"Aw punk," said Ted judicially. "Ever since somebody slipped up and let you out of college, Ammonia, you been pulling these nut conversations about what-nots and so-on-and-so-forths. Are you going to— I want to use the car to-night."

Babbitt snorted, "Oh, you do! May want it myself!" Verona protested, "Oh, you do, Mr. Smarty! I'm going to take it myself!" Tinka wailed, "Oh, papa, you said maybe you'd drive us down to Rosedale!" and Mrs. Babbitt, "Careful, Tinka, your sleeve is in the butter." They glared, and Verona hurled, "Ted, you're a perfect pig about the car!"

"Course you're not! Not a-tall!" Ted could be maddeningly bland. "You just want to grab it off, right after dinner, and leave it in front of some skirt's house all evening while you sit and gas about lite'ature and the highbrows you're going to marry—if they only propose!"

"Well, Dad oughtn't to *ever* let you have it! You and those beastly Jones boys drive like maniacs. The idea of your taking the turn on Chautauqua Place at forty miles an hour!"

"Aw, where do you get that stuff! You're so darn scared of the car that you drive up-hill with the emergency brake on!"

"I do not! And you— Always talking about how much you know about motors, and Eunice Littlefield told me you said the battery fed the generator!"

"You—why, my good woman, you don't know a generator from a differential." Not unreasonably was Ted lofty with her. He was a natural mechanic, a maker and tinkerer of machines; he lisped in blueprints for the blueprints came.

"That'll do now!" Babbitt flung in mechanically, as he lighted the gloriously satisfying first cigar of the day and tasted the exhilarating drug of the *Advocate-Times* headlines.

Ted negotiated: "Gee, honest, Rone, I don't want to take the old boat, but I promised couple o' girls in my class I'd drive 'em down to the rehearsal of the school chorus, and, gee, I don't want to, but a gentleman's got to keep his social engagements."

"Well, upon my word! You and your social engagements! In high school!"

"Oh, ain't we select since we went to that hen college! Let me tell you there isn't a private school in the state that's got as swell a bunch as we got in Gamma Digamma this year. There's two fellows that their dads are millionaires. Say, gee, I ought to have a car of my own, like lots of the fellows."

Babbitt almost rose. "A car of your own! Don't you want a yacht, and a house and lot? That pretty nearly takes the cake! A boy that can't pass his Latin examinations, like any other boy ought to, and he expects me to give him a motor-car, and I suppose a chauffeur, and an areoplane maybe, as a reward for the hard work he puts in going to the movies with Eunice Littlefield! Well, when you see me giving you—"

Somewhat later, after diplomacies, Ted persuaded Verona to admit that she was merely going to the Armory, that evening, to see the dog and cat show. She was then, Ted planned, to park the car in front of the candy-store across from the Armory and he would pick it up. There were masterly arrangements regarding leaving the key, and having the gasoline tank filled; and passionately, devotees of the Great God Motor, they hymned the patch on the spare inner-tube, and the lost jack-handle.

Their truce dissolving, Ted observed that her friends were "a scream of a bunch—stuck-up gabby four-flushers." His friends, she indicated, were "disgusting imitation sports, and horrid little shrieking ignorant girls." Further: "It's disgusting of you to smoke cigarettes, and so on and so forth, and those clothes you've got on this morning, they're too utterly ridiculous—honestly, simply disgusting."

Ted balanced over to the low beveled mirror in the buffet, regarded his charms, and smirked. His suit, the latest thing in Old Eli Togs, was skin-tight, with skimpy trousers to the tops of his glaring tan boots, a chorus-man waistline, pattern of an agitated check, and across the back a belt which belted nothing. His scarf was an enormous black silk wad. His flaxen hair was ice-smooth, pasted back without parting. When he went to school he would add a cap with a long vizor like a shovel-blade. Proudest of all was his waistcoat, saved for, begged for, plotted for; a real Fancy Vest of fawn with polka dots of a decayed red, the points astoundingly long. On the lower edge of it he wore a high-school button, a class button, and a fraternity pin.

And none of it mattered. He was supple and swift and flushed; his eyes (which he believed to be cynical) were candidly eager. But he was not over-gentle. He waved his hand at poor dumpy Verona and drawled: "Yes, I guess we're pretty ridiculous and disgusticulus, and I rather guess our new necktie is some smear!"

Babbitt barked: "It is! And while you're admiring yourself, let me tell you it might add to your manly beauty if you wiped some of that egg off your mouth!"

Verona giggled, momentary victor in the greatest of Great Wars, which is the family war. Ted looked at her hopelessly, then shrieked at Tinka: "For the love o' Pete, quit pouring the whole sugar bowl on your corn flakes!"

When Verona and Ted were gone and Tinka upstairs, Babbitt groaned to his wife: "Nice family, I must say! I don't pretend to be any baa-lamb, and maybe I'm a little cross-grained at breakfast sometimes, but the way they go on jab-jab-jabbering, I simply can't stand it. I swear, I feel like going off some place where I can get a little peace. I do think after a man's spent his lifetime trying to give his kids a chance and a decent education, it's pretty discouraging to hear them all the time scrapping like a bunch of hyenas and never—and never— Curious; here in the paper it says— Never silent for one mom— Seen the morning paper yet?"

"No, dear." In twenty-three years of married life, Mrs. Babbitt had seen the paper before her husband just sixty-seven times.

"Lots of news. Terrible big tornado in the South. Hard luck, all right. But this, say, this is corking! Beginning of the end for those fellows! New York Assembly has passed some bills that ought to completely outlaw the socialists! And there's an elevator-runners' strike in New York and a lot of college boys are taking their places. That's the stuff! And a mass-meeting in Birmingham's demanded that this Mick agitator, this fellow De Valera, be deported. Dead right, by golly! All these agitators paid with German gold anyway. And we got no business interfering with the Irish or any other foreign government. Keep our hands strictly off. And there's another well-authenticated rumor from Russia that Lenin is dead. That's fine. It's beyond me why we don't just step in there and kick those Bolshevik cusses out."

"That's so," said Mrs. Babbitt.

"And it says here a fellow was inaugurated mayor in overalls—a preacher, too! What do you think of that!"

"Humph! Well!"

He searched for an attitude, but neither as a Republican, a Presbyterian, an Elk, nor a real-estate broker did he have any doctrine about preacher-mayors laid down for him, so he grunted and went on. She looked sympathetic and did not hear a word. Later she would read the headlines, the society columns, and the department-store advertisements.

"What do you know about this! Charley McKelvey still doing the sassiety stunt as heavy as ever. Here's what that gushy woman reporter says about last night:

> Never is Society with the big, big S more flattered than when they are bidden to partake of good cheer at the distinguished and hospitable residence of Mr. and Mrs. Charles L. McKelvey as they were last night. Set in its spacious lawns and landscaping, one of the notable sights crowning Royal Ridge, but merry and homelike despite its mighty stone walls and its vast rooms famed for their decoration, their home was thrown open last night for a dance in honor of Mrs. McKelvey's notable guest, Miss J. Sneeth of Washington. The wide hall is so generous in its proportions that it made a perfect ballroom, its hardwood floor reflecting the charming pageant above its polished surface. Even the delights of dancing paled before the alluring opportunities for tête-à-têtes that invited the soul to loaf in the long library before the baronial fireplace, or in the drawing-room with its deep comfy armchairs, its shaded lamps just made for a sly whisper of pretty nothings all a deux; or even in the billiard room where one could take a cue and show a prowess at still another game than that sponsored by Cupid and Terpsichore."

There was more, a great deal more, in the best urban journalistic style of Miss Elnora Pearl Bates, the popular society editor of the *Advocate-Times*. But Babbitt could not abide it. He grunted. He wrinkled the newspaper. He protested: "Can you beat it! I'm willing to hand a lot of credit to Charley McKelvey. When we were in college together, he was just as hard up as any of us, and he's made a million good bucks out of contracting and hasn't been any dishonester or bought any more city councils than was necessary. And that's a good house of his—though it ain't any 'mighty stone walls' and it ain't worth the ninety thousand it cost him. But when it comes to talking as though Charley McKelvey and all that booze-hoisting set of his are any blooming bunch of of, of Vanderbilts, why, it makes me tired!"

Timidly from Mrs. Babbitt: "I would like to see the inside of their house though. It must be lovely. I've never been inside."

"Well, I have! Lots of—couple of times. To see Chaz about business deals, in the evening. It's not so much. I wouldn't *want* to go there to dinner with that gang of, of highbinders. And I'll bet I make a whole lot more money than some of those tin-horns that spend all they got on dress-suits and haven't got a decent suit of underwear to their name! Hey! What do you think of this!"

Mrs. Babbitt was strangely unmoved by the tidings from the Real Estate and Building column of the *Advocate-Times*:

> Ashtabula Street, 496—J. K. Dawson to
> Thomas Mullally, April 17, 15.7 × 112.2,
> mtg. $4000 . . . . . . . . . . . . . . . . . . . .Nom.

And this morning Babbitt was too disquieted to entertain her with items from Mechanics' Liens, Mortgages Recorded, and Contracts Awarded. He rose. As he looked at her his eyebrows seemed shaggier than usual. Suddenly:

"Yes, maybe— Kind of shame to not keep in touch with folks like the McKelveys. We might try inviting them to dinner, some evening. Oh, thunder, let's not waste our good time thinking about 'em! Our little bunch has a lot liver times than all those plutes. Just compare a real human like you with these neurotic birds like Lucile McKelvey—all highbrow talk and dressed up like a plush horse! You're a great old girl, hon.!"

He covered his betrayal of softness with a complaining: "Say, don't let Tinka go and eat any more of that poison nut-fudge. For Heaven's sake, try to keep her from ruining her digestion. I tell you, most folks don't appreciate how important it is to have a good digestion and regular habits. Be back 'bout usual time, I guess."

He kissed her—he didn't quite kiss her—he laid unmoving lips against her unflushing cheek. He hurried out to the garage, muttering: "Lord, what a family! And now Myra is going to get pathetic on me because we don't train with this millionaire outfit. Oh, Lord, sometimes I'd like to quit the whole game. And the office worry and detail just as bad. And I act cranky and— I don't mean to, but I get— So darn tired!"

# 3

To George F. Babbitt, as to most prosperous citizens of Zenith, his motor car was poetry and tragedy, love and heroism. The office was his pirate ship but the car his perilous excursion ashore.

Among the tremendous crises of each day none was more dramatic than starting the engine. It was slow on cold mornings; there was the long, anxious whirr of the starter; and sometimes he had to drip ether into the cocks of the cylinders, which was so very interesting that at lunch he would chronicle it drop by drop, and orally calculate how much each drop had cost him.

This morning he was darkly prepared to find something wrong, and he felt belittled when the mixture exploded sweet and strong, and the car didn't even brush the door-jamb, gouged and splintery with many bruisings by fenders, as he backed out of the garage. He was confused. He shouted "Morning!" to Sam Doppelbrau with more cordiality than he had intended.

Babbitt's green and white Dutch Colonial house was one of three in that block on Chatham Road. To the left of it was the residence of Mr. Samuel Doppelbrau, secretary of an excellent firm of bathroom-fixture jobbers. His was a comfortable house with no architectural manners whatever; a large wooden box with a squat tower, a broad porch, and glossy paint yellow as a yolk. Babbitt disapproved of Mr. and Mrs. Doppelbrau as "Bohemian." From their house came midnight music and obscene laughter; there were neighborhood rumors of bootlegged whisky and fast motor rides. They furnished Babbitt with many happy evenings of discussion, during which he announced firmly, "I'm not strait-laced, and I don't mind seeing a fellow throw in a drink once in a while, but when it comes to deliberately trying to get away with a lot of hell-raising all the while like the Doppelbraus do, it's too rich for my blood!"

On the other side of Babbitt lived Howard Littlefield, Ph.D., in a strictly modern house whereof the lower part was dark red tapestry brick, with a leaded oriel, the upper part of pale stucco like spattered clay, and the roof red-tiled. Littlefield was the Great Scholar of the neighborhood; the authority on everything in the world except babies, cooking, and motors. He was a Bachelor of Arts of Blodgett College, and a Doctor of Philosophy in economics of Yale. He was the employment-manager and publicity-counsel of the Zenith Street Traction Company. He could, on ten hours' notice, appear before the board of aldermen or the state legislature and prove, absolutely, with figures all in rows and with precedents from Poland and New Zealand, that the street-car company loved the Public and yearned over its employees; that all its stock was owned by Widows and Orphans; and that whatever it desired to do would benefit property-owners by increasing rental values, and help the poor by lowering rents. All his acquaintances turned to Littlefield when they desired to know the date of the battle of Saragossa, the definition of the word "sabotage," the future of the German mark, the translation of "*hinc illæ lachrimæ*," or the number of products of coal tar. He awed Babbitt by confessing that he often sat up till midnight reading the figures and footnotes in Government reports, or skimming (with amusement at the author's mistakes) the latest volumes of chemistry, archeology, and ichthyology.

But Littlefield's great value was as a spiritual example. Despite his strange learnings he was as strict a Presbyterian and as firm a Republican as George F. Babbitt. He confirmed the business men in the faith. Where they knew only by passionate instinct that their system of industry and manners was perfect, Dr. Howard Littlefield proved it to them, out of history, economics, and the confessions of reformed radicals.

Babbitt had a good deal of honest pride in being the neighbor of such a savant, and in Ted's intimacy with Eunice Littlefield. At sixteen Eunice was interested in no statistics save those regarding the ages and salaries of motion-picture stars, but—as Babbitt definitively put it—"she was her father's daughter."

The difference between a light man like Sam Doppelbrau and a really fine character like Littlefield was revealed in their appearances. Doppelbrau was disturbingly young for a man of forty-eight. He wore his derby on the back of his head, and his red face was wrinkled with meaningless laughter. But Littlefield was old for a man of forty-two. He was tall, broad, thick; his gold-rimmed spectacles were engulfed in the folds of his long face; his hair was a tossed mass of greasy blackness; he puffed and rumbled as he talked; his Phi Beta Kappa key shone against a spotty black vest; he smelled of old pipes; he was altogether funereal and archidiaconal; and to real-estate brokerage and the jobbing of bathroom-fixtures he added an aroma of sanctity.

This morning he was in front of his house, inspecting the grass parking between the curb and the broad cement sidewalk. Babbitt stopped his car and leaned out to shout "Mornin'!" Littlefield lumbered over and stood with one foot up on the running-board.

"Fine morning," said Babbitt, lighting—illegally early—his second cigar of the day.

"Yes, it's a mighty fine morning," said Littlefield.

"Spring coming along fast now."

"Yes, it's real spring now, all right," said Littlefield.

"Still cold nights, though. Had to have a couple blankets, on the sleeping-porch last night."

"Yes, it wasn't any too warm last night," said Littlefield.

"But I don't anticipate we'll have any more real cold weather now."

"No, but still, there was snow at Tiflis, Montana, yesterday," said the Scholar, "and you remember the blizzard they had out West three days ago

—thirty inches of snow at Greeley, Colorado—and two years ago we had a snow-squall right here in Zenith on the twenty-fifth of April."

"Is that a fact! Say, old man, what do you think about the Republican candidate? Who'll they nominate for president? Don't you think it's about time we had a real business administration?"

"In my opinion, what the country needs, first and foremost, is a good, sound, business-like conduct of its affairs. What we need is—a business administration!" said Littlefield.

"I'm glad to hear you say that! I certainly am glad to hear you say that! I didn't know how you'd feel about it, with all your associations with colleges and so on, and I'm glad you feel that way. What the country needs—just at this present juncture—is neither a college president nor a lot of monkeying with foreign affairs, but a good—sound—economical—business—administration, that will give us a chance to have something like a decent turnover."

"Yes. It isn't generally realized that even in China the schoolmen are giving way to more practical men, and of course you can see what that implies."

"Is that a fact! Well, well!" breathed Babbitt, feeling much calmer, and much happier about the way things were going in the world. "Well, it's been nice to stop and parleyvoo a second. Guess I'll have to get down to the office now and sting a few clients. Well, so long, old man. See you to-night. So long."

## II

They had labored, these solid citizens. Twenty years before, the hill on which Floral Heights was spread, with its bright roofs and immaculate turf and amazing comfort, had been a wilderness of rank second-growth elms and oaks and maples. Along the precise streets were still a few wooded vacant lots, and the fragment of an old orchard. It was brilliant to-day; the apple boughs were lit with fresh leaves like torches of green fire. The first white of cherry blossoms flickered down a gully, and robins clamored.

Babbitt sniffed the earth, chuckled at the hysteric robins as he would have chuckled at kittens or at a comic movie. He was, to the eye, the perfect office-going executive—a well-fed man in a correct brown soft hat and frameless spectacles, smoking a large cigar, driving a good motor along a semi-suburban parkway. But in him was some genius of authentic love for his neighborhood, his city, his clan. The winter was over; the time was come for the building, the visible growth, which to him was glory. He lost his dawn depression; he was ruddily cheerful when he stopped on Smith Street to leave the brown trousers, and to have the gasoline-tank filled.

The familiarity of the rite fortified him: the sight of the tall red iron gasoline-pump, the hollow-tile and terra-cotta garage, the window full of the most agreeable accessories—shiny casings, spark-plugs with immaculate porcelain jackets, tire-chains of gold and silver. He was flattered by the friendliness with which Sylvester Moon, dirtiest and most skilled of motor mechanics, came out to serve him. "Mornin', Mr. Babbitt!" said Moon, and Babbitt felt himself a person of importance, one whose name even busy garagemen remembered—not one of these cheap-sports flying around in flivvers. He admired the ingenuity of the automatic dial, clicking off gallon by gallon; admired the smartness of the sign: "A fill in time saves getting stuck —gas to-day 31 cents"; admired the rhythmic gurgle of the gasoline as it flowed into the tank, and the mechanical regularity with which Moon turned the handle.

"How much we takin' to-day?" asked Moon, in a manner which combined the independence of the great specialist, the friendliness of a familiar gossip, and respect for a man of weight in the community, like George F. Babbitt.

"Fill 'er up."

"Who you rootin' for for Republican candidate, Mr. Babbitt?"

"It's too early to make any predictions yet. After all, there's still a good month and two weeks—no, three weeks—must be almost three weeks—well, there's more than six weeks in all before the Republican convention, and I feel a fellow ought to keep an open mind and give all the candidates a show —look 'em all over and size 'em up, and then decide carefully."

"That's a fact, Mr. Babbitt."

"But I'll tell you—and my stand on this is just the same as it was four years ago, and eight years ago, and it'll be my stand four years from now —yes, and eight years from now! What I tell everybody, and it can't be too generally understood, is that what we need first, last, and all the time is a good, sound business administration!"

"By golly, that's right!"

"How do those front tires look to you?"

"Fine! Fine! Wouldn't be much work for garages if everybody looked after their car the way you do."

"Well, I do try and have some sense about it." Babbitt paid his bill, said adequately, "Oh, keep the change," and drove off in an ecstasy of honest self-appreciation. It was with the manner of a Good Samaritan that he shouted at a respectable-looking man who was waiting for a trolley car, "Have a lift?" As the man climbed in Babbitt condescended, "Going clear down-town? Whenever I see a fellow waiting for a trolley, I always make it a practice to give him a lift—unless, of course, he looks like a bum."

"Wish there were more folks that were so generous with their machines," dutifully said the victim of benevolence.

"Oh, no, 'tain't a question of generosity, hardly. Fact, I always feel— I was saying to my son just the other night—it's a fellow's duty to share the good things of this world with his neighbors, and it gets my goat when a fellow gets stuck on himself and goes around tooting his horn merely because he's charitable."

The victim seemed unable to find the right answer. Babbitt boomed on:

"Pretty punk service the Company giving us on these car-lines. Nonsense to only run the Portland Road cars once every seven minutes. Fellow gets mighty cold on a winter morning, waiting on a street corner with the wind nipping at his ankles."

"That's right. The Street Car Company don't care a damn what kind of a deal they give us. Something ought to happen to 'em."

Babbitt was alarmed. "But still, of course it won't do to just keep knocking the Traction Company and not realize the difficulties they're operating under, like these cranks that want municipal ownership. The way these workmen hold up the Company for high wages is simply a crime, and of course the burden falls on you and me that have to pay a seven-cent fare! Fact, there's remarkable service on all their lines—considering."

"Well—" uneasily.

"Darn fine morning," Babbitt explained. "Spring coming along fast."

"Yes, it's real spring now."

The victim had no originality, no wit, and Babbitt fell into a great silence and devoted himself to the game of beating trolley cars to the corner: a spurt, a tail-chase, nervous speeding between the huge yellow side of the trolley and the jagged row of parked motors, shooting past just as the trolley stopped—a rare game and valiant.

And all the while he was conscious of the loveliness of Zenith. For weeks together he noticed nothing but clients and the vexing To Rent signs of rival brokers. To-day, in mysterious malaise, he raged or rejoiced with equal nervous swiftness, and to-day the light of spring was so winsome that he lifted his head and saw.

He admired each district along his familiar route to the office: The bungalows and shrubs and winding irregular driveways of Floral Heights. The one-story shops on Smith Street, a glare of plate-glass and new yellow brick; groceries and laundries and drug-stores to supply the more immediate needs of East Side housewives. The market gardens in Dutch Hollow, their shanties patched with corrugated iron and stolen doors. Billboards with crimson goddesses nine feet tall advertising cinema films, pipe tobacco, and talcum powder. The old "mansions" along Ninth Street, S.E., like aged dandies in filthy linen; wooden castles turned into boarding-houses, with muddy walks and rusty hedges, jostled by fast-intruding garages, cheap apartment-houses, and fruit-stands conducted by bland, sleek Athenians. Across the belt of railroad-tracks, factories with high-perched water-tanks and tall stacks—factories producing condensed milk, paper boxes, lighting-fixtures, motor cars. Then the business center, the thickening darting traffic, the crammed trolleys unloading, and high doorways of marble and polished granite.

It was big—and Babbitt respected bigness in anything; in mountains, jewels, muscles, wealth, or words. He was, for a spring-enchanted moment, the lyric and almost unselfish lover of Zenith. He thought of the outlying factory suburbs; of the Chaloosa River with its strangely eroded banks; of the orchard-dappled Tonawanda Hills to the North, and all the fat dairy land and big barns and comfortable herds. As he dropped his passenger he cried, "Gosh, I feel pretty good this morning!"

Epochal as starting the car was the drama of parking it before he entered his office. As he turned from Oberlin Avenue round the corner into Third Street, N.E., he peered ahead for a space in the line of parked cars. He angrily just missed a space as a rival driver slid into it. Ahead, another car was leaving the curb, and Babbitt slowed up, holding out his hand to the cars pressing on him from behind, agitatedly motioning an old woman to go ahead, avoiding a truck which bore down on him from one side. With front wheels nicking the wrought-steel bumper of the car in front, he stopped, feverishly cramped his steering-wheel, slid back into the vacant space and, with eighteen inches of room, manœuvcred to bring the car level with the curb. It was a virile adventure masterfully executed. With satisfaction he locked a thief-proof steel wedge on the front wheel, and crossed the street to his real-estate office on the ground floor of the Reeves Building.

The Reeves Building was as fireproof as a rock and as efficient as a type-writer; fourteen stories of yellow pressed brick, with clean, upright, un-ornamented lines. It was filled with the offices of lawyers, doctors, agents for machinery, for emery wheels, for wire fencing, for mining-stock. Their gold signs shone on the windows. The entrance was too modern to be flam-boyant with pillars; it was quiet, shrewd, neat. Along the Third Street side were a Western Union Telegraph Office, the Blue Delft Candy Shop, Shot-well's Stationery Shop, and the Babbitt-Thompson Realty Company.

Babbitt could have entered his office from the street, as customers did, but it made him feel an insider to go through the corridor of the building and enter by the back door. Thus he was greeted by the villagers.

The little unknown people who inhabited the Reeves Building corridors —elevator-runners, starter, engineers, superintendent, and the doubtful-looking lame man who conducted the news and cigar stand—were in no way city-dwellers. They were rustics, living in a constricted valley, interested only in one another and in The Building. Their Main Street was the entrance hall, with its stone floor, severe marble ceiling, and the inner windows of the shops. The liveliest place on the street was the Reeves Building Barber Shop, but this was also Babbitt's one embarrassment. Himself, he patronized the glittering Pompeian Barber Shop in the Hotel Thornleigh, and every time he passed the Reeves shop—ten times a day, a hundred times—he felt untrue to his own village.

Now, as one of the squirearchy, greeted with honorable salutations by the villagers, he marched into his office, and peace and dignity were upon him, and the morning's dissonances all unheard.

They were heard again, immediately.

Stanley Graff, the outside salesman, was talking on the telephone with tragic lack of that firm manner which disciplines clients: "Say, uh, I think I got just the house that would suit you—the Percival House, in Linton. . . .

Oh, you've seen it. Well, how'd it strike you? . . . Huh? . . . Oh," irresolutely, "oh, I see."

As Babbitt marched into his private room, a coop with semipartition of oak and frosted glass, at the back of the office, he reflected how hard it was to find employees who had his own faith that he was going to make sales.

There were nine members of the staff, besides Babbitt and his partner and father-in-law, Henry Thompson, who rarely came to the office. The nine were Stanley Graff, the outside salesman—a youngish man given to cigarettes and the playing of pool; old Mat Penniman, general utility man, collector of rents and salesman of insurance—broken, silent, gray; a mystery, reputed to have been a "crack" real-estate man with a firm of his own in haughty Brooklyn; Chester Kirby Laylock, resident salesman out at the Glen Oriole acreage development—an enthusiastic person with a silky mustache and much family; Miss Theresa McGoun, the swift and rather pretty stenographer; Miss Wilberta Bannigan, the thick, slow, laborious accountant and file-clerk; and four freelance part-time commission salesmen.

As he looked from his own cage into the main room Babbitt mourned, "McGoun's a good stenog., smart's a whip, but Stan Graff and all those bums—" The zest of the spring morning was smothered in the stale office air.

Normally he admired the office, with a pleased surprise that he should have created this sure lovely thing; normally he was stimulated by the clean newness of it and the air of bustle; but to-day it seemed flat—the tiled floor, like a bathroom, the ocher-colored metal ceiling, the faded maps on the hard plaster walls, the chairs of varnished pale oak, the desks and filing-cabinets of steel painted in olive drab. It was a vault, a steel chapel where loafing and laughter were raw sin.

He hadn't even any satisfaction in the new water-cooler! And it was the very best of water-coolers, up-to-date, scientific, and right-thinking. It had cost a great deal of money (in itself a virtue). It possessed a non-conducting fiber ice-container, a porcelain water-jar (guaranteed hygienic), a dripless non-clogging sanitary faucet, and machine-painted decorations in two tones of gold. He looked down the relentless stretch of tiled floor at the water-cooler, and assured himself that no tenant of the Reeves Building had a more expensive one, but he could not recapture the feeling of social superiority it had given him. He astoundingly grunted, "I'd like to beat it off to the woods right now. And loaf all day. And go to Gunch's again to-night, and play poker, and cuss as much as I feel like, and drink a hundred and nine-thousand bottles of beer."

He sighed; he read through his mail; he shouted "Msgoun," which meant "Miss McGoun"; and began to dictate.

This was his own version of his first letter:

"Omar Gribble, send it to his office, Miss McGoun, yours of twentieth to hand and in reply would say look here, Gribble, I'm awfully afraid if we go on shilly-shallying like this we'll just naturally lose the Allen sale, I had Allen up on carpet day before yesterday and got right down to cases and think I can assure you—uh, uh, no, change that: all my experience indicates he is all right, means to do business, looked into his financial record which is fine—that sentence seems to be a little balled up, Miss McGoun; make a couple sentences out of it if you have to, period, new paragraph.

"He is perfectly willing to pro rate the special assessment and strikes me, am dead sure there will be no difficulty in getting him to pay for title insurance, so now for heaven's sake let's get busy—no, make that: so now let's go to it and get down—no, that's enough—you can tie those sentences up a little better when you type 'em, Miss McGoun—your sincerely, etcetera."

This is the version of his letter which he received, typed, from Miss Mc-Goun that afternoon:

BABBITT-THOMPSON REALTY CO.
Homes for Folks
Reeves Bldg., Oberlin Avenue & 3d St., N.E.
Zenith

Omar Gribble, Esq.,
576 North American Building,
Zenith.
Dear Mr. Gribble:

Your letter of the twentieth to hand. I must say I'm awfully afraid that if we go on shilly-shallying like this we'll just naturally lose the Allen sale. I had Allen up on the carpet day before yesterday, and got right down to cases. All my experience indicates that he means to do business. I have also looked into his financial record, which is fine.

He is perfectly willing to pro rate the special assessment and there will be no difficulty in getting him to pay for title insurance.

*So let's go!*

Yours sincerely,

As he read and signed it, in his correct flowing business-college hand, Babbitt reflected, "Now that's a good, strong letter, and clear's a bell. Now what the— I never told McGoun to make a third paragraph there! Wish she'd quit trying to improve on my dictation! But what I can't understand is: why can't Stan Graff or Chet Laylock write a letter like that? With punch! With a kick!"

The most important thing he dictated that morning was the fortnightly form-letter, to be mimeographed and sent out to a thousand "prospects." It was diligently imitative of the best literary models of the day; of heart-to-heart-talk advertisements, "sales-pulling" letters, discourses on the "development of Will-power," and hand-shaking house-organs, as richly poured forth by the new school of Poets of Business. He had painfully written out a first draft, and he intoned it now like a poet delicate and distrait:

SAY, OLD MAN!

I just want to know can I do you a whaleuva favor? Honest! No kidding! I know you're interested in getting a house, not merely a place where you hang up the old bonnet but a love-nest for the wife and kiddies—and maybe for the flivver out beyant (be sure and spell that b-e-y-a-n-t, Miss McGoun) the spud garden. Say, did you ever stop to think that we're here to save you trouble? That's how we make a living—folks don't pay us for our lovely beauty! Now take a look:

Sit right down at the handsome carved mahogany escritoire and shoot us in a line telling us just what you want, and if we can find it we'll come hopping down your lane with the good tidings, and if we can't, we won't bother you. To save your time, just fill out the blank enclosed. On request will also send blank regarding store properties in Floral Heights, Silver Grove, Linton, Bellevue, and all East Side residential districts.

Yours for service,

P.S.—Just a hint of some plums we can pick for you—some genuine bargains that came in to-day:

SILVER GROVE.—Cute four-room California bungalow, a.m.i., garage, dandy shade tree, swell neighborhood, handy car line. $3700, $780 down and balance liberal, Babbitt-Thompson terms, cheaper than rent.

DORCHESTER.—A corker! Artistic two-family house, all oak trim, parquet floors, lovely gas log, big porches, colonial, HEATED ALL-WEATHER GARAGE, a bargain at $11,250.

Dictation over, with its need of sitting and thinking instead of bustling around and making a noise and really doing something, Babbitt sat creakily back in his revolving desk-chair and beamed on Miss McGoun. He was conscious of her as a girl, of black bobbed hair against demure cheeks. A longing which was indistinguishable from loneliness enfeebled him. While she waited, tapping a long, precise pencil-point on the desk-tablet, he half identified her with the fairy girl of his dreams. He imagined their eyes meeting with terrifying recognition; imagined touching her lips with frightened reverence and— She was chirping, "Any more, Mist' Babbitt?" He grunted, "That winds it up, I guess," and turned heavily away.

For all his wandering thoughts, they had never been more intimate than this. He often reflected, "Nev' forget how old Jake Offutt said a wise bird never goes love-making in his own office or his own home. Start trouble. Sure. But—"

In twenty-three years of married life he had peered uneasily at every graceful ankle, every soft shoulder; in thought he had treasured them; but not once had he hazarded respectability by adventuring. Now, as he calculated the cost of repapering the Styles house, he was restless again, discontented about nothing and everything, ashamed of his discontentment, and lonely for the fairy girl.

# 4

It was a morning of artistic creation. Fifteen minutes after the purple prose of Babbitt's form-letter, Chester Kirby Laylock, the resident salesman at Glen Oriole, came in to report a sale and submit an advertisement. Babbitt disapproved of Laylock, who sang in choirs and was merry at home over games of Hearts and Old Maid. He had a tenor voice, wavy chestnut hair, and a mustache like a camel's-hair brush. Babbitt considered it excusable in a family-man to growl, "Seen this new picture of the kid—husky little devil, eh?" But Laylock's domestic confidences were as bubbling as a girl's.

"Say, I think I got a peach of an ad for the Glen, Mr. Babbitt. Why don't we try something in poetry? Honest, it'd have wonderful pulling-power. Listen:

> 'Mid pleasures and palaces,
> Wherever you may roam,
> You just provide the little bride
> And we'll provide the home.

Do you get it? See—like 'Home Sweet Home.' Don't you—"

"Yes, yes, yes, hell yes, of course I get it. But— Oh, I think we'd better use something more dignified and forceful, like 'We lead, others follow,' or 'Eventually, why not now?' Course I believe in using poetry and humor and all that junk when it turns the trick, but with a high-class restricted development like the Glen we better stick to the more dignified approach, see how I mean? Well, I guess that's all, this morning, Chet."

## II

By a tragedy familiar to the world of art, the April enthusiasm of Chet Laylock served only to stimulate the talent of the older craftsman, George F. Babbitt. He grumbled to Stanley Graff, "That tan-colored voice of Chet's gets on my nerves," yet he was aroused and in one swoop he wrote:

## DO YOU RESPECT YOUR LOVED ONES?

When the last sad rites of bereavement are over, do you know for certain that you have done your best for the Departed? You haven't unless they lie in the Cemetery Beautiful

### LINDEN LANE

the only strictly up-to-date burial place in or near

Zenith, where exquisitely gardened plots look from daisy-dotted hill-slopes across the smiling fields of Dorchester.

Sole agents

**BABBITT-THOMPSON REALTY COMPANY**

Reeves Building

He rejoiced, "I guess that'll show Chan Mott and his weedy old Wildwood Cemetery something about modern merchandizing!"

III

He sent Mat Penniman to the recorder's office to dig out the names of the owners of houses which were displaying For Rent signs of other brokers; he talked to a man who desired to lease a store-building for a pool-room; he ran over the list of home-leases which were about to expire; he sent Thomas Bywaters, a street-car conductor who played at real estate in spare time, to call on side-street "prospects" who were unworthy the strategies of Stanley Graff. But he had spent his credulous excitement of creation, and these routine details annoyed him. One moment of heroism he had, in discovering a new way of stopping smoking.

He stopped smoking at least once a month. He went through with it like the solid citizen he was: admitted the evils of tobacco, courageously made resolves, laid out plans to check the vice, tapered off his allowance of cigars, and expounded the pleasures of virtuousness to every one he met. He did everything, in fact, except stop smoking.

Two months before, by ruling out a schedule, noting down the hour and minute of each smoke, and ecstatically increasing the intervals between smokes, he had brought himself down to three cigars a day. Then he had lost the schedule.

A week ago he had invented a system of leaving his cigar-case and cigarette-box in an unused drawer at the bottom of the correspondence-file, in the outer office. "I'll just naturally be ashamed to go poking in there all day long, making a fool of myself before my own employees!" he reasoned. By the end of three days he was trained to leave his desk, walk to the file, take out and light a cigar, without knowing that he was doing it.

This morning it was revealed to him that it had been too easy to open the file. Lock it, that was the thing! Inspired, he rushed out and locked up his cigars, his cigarettes, and even his box of safety matches; and the key to the file drawer he hid in his desk. But the crusading passion of it made him so tobacco-hungry that he immediately recovered the key, walked with forbidding dignity to the file, took out a cigar and a match—"but only one match; if ole cigar goes out, it'll by golly have to stay out!" Later, when the cigar did go out, he took one more match from the file, and when a buyer and a seller came in for a conference at eleven-thirty, naturally he had to offer them cigars. His conscience protested, "Why, you're smoking with them!"

but he bullied it, "Oh, shut up! I'm busy now. Of course by-and-by—" There was no by-and-by, yet his belief that he had crushed the unclean habit made him feel noble and very happy. When he called up Paul Riesling he was, in his moral splendor, unusually eager.

He was fonder of Paul Riesling than of any one on earth except himself and his daughter Tinka. They had been classmates, roommates, in the State University, but always he thought of Paul Riesling, with his dark slimness, his precisely parted hair, his nose-glasses, his hesitant speech, his moodiness, his love of music, as a younger brother, to be petted and protected. Paul had gone into his father's business, after graduation; he was now a wholesaler and small manufacturer of prepared-paper roofing. But Babbitt strenuously believed and lengthily announced to the world of Good Fellows that Paul could have been a great violinist or painter or writer. "Why say, the letters that boy sent me on his trip to the Canadian Rockies, they just absolutely make you see the place as if you were standing there. Believe me, he could have given any of these bloomin' authors a whale of a run for their money!"

Yet on the telephone they said only:

"South 343. No, no, no! I said *South*—South 343. Say, operator, what the dickens is the trouble? Can't you get me South 343? Why certainly they'll answer. Oh, Hello, 343? Wanta speak Mist' Riesling, Mist' Babbitt talking. . . . 'Lo, Paul?"

"Yuh."

" 'S George speaking."

"Yuh."

"How's old socks?"

"Fair to middlin'. How 're you?"

"Fine, Paulibus. Well, what do you know?"

"Oh, nothing much."

"Where you been keepin' yourself?"

"Oh, just stickin' round. What's up, Georgie?"

"How 'bout lil lunch 's noon?"

"Be all right with me, I guess. Club?"

"Yuh. Meet you there twelve-thirty."

"A' right. Twelve-thirty. S' long, Georgie."

IV

His morning was not sharply marked into divisions. Interwoven with correspondence and advertisement-writing were a thousand nervous details: calls from clerks who were incessantly and hopefully seeking five furnished rooms and bath at sixty dollars a month; advice to Mat Penniman on getting money out of tenants who had no money.

Babbitt's virtues as a real-estate broker—as the servant of society in the department of finding homes for families and shops for distributors of food —were steadiness and diligence. He was conventionally honest, he kept his records of buyers and sellers complete, he had experience with leases and titles and an excellent memory for prices. His shoulders were broad enough, his voice deep enough, his relish of hearty humor strong enough, to establish him as one of the ruling caste of Good Fellows. Yet his eventual importance to mankind was perhaps lessened by his large and complacent ignorance of all architecture save the types of houses turned out by speculative builders; all landscape gardening save the use of curving roads, grass, and six ordinary shrubs; and all the commonest axioms of economics. He serenely believed that the one purpose of the real-estate business was to make money for George F. Babbitt. True, it was a good advertisement at Boosters' Club lunches, and all the varieties of Annual Banquets to which Good Fellows were invited, to speak sonorously of Unselfish Public Service, the Broker's Obligation to Keep Inviolate the Trust of His Clients, and a thing called Ethics, whose nature was confusing but if you had it you were a High-class Realtor and if you hadn't you were a shyster, a piker, and a fly-by-night. These virtues awakened Confidence, and enabled you to handle Bigger Propositions. But they didn't imply that you were to be impractical and refuse to take twice the value of a house if a buyer was such an idiot that he didn't jew you down on the asking-price.

Babbitt spoke well—and often—at these orgies of commercial righteousness about the "realtor's function as a seer of the future development of the community, and as a prophetic engineer clearing the pathway for inevitable changes"—which meant that a real-estate broker could make money by guessing which way the town would grow. This guessing he called Vision.

In an address at the Boosters' Club he had admitted, "It is at once the duty and the privilege of the realtor to know everything about his own city and its environs. Where a surgeon is a specialist on every vein and mysterious cell of the human body, and the engineer upon electricity in all its phases, or every bolt of some great bridge majestically arching o'er a mighty flood, the realtor must know his city, inch by inch, and all its faults and virtues."

Though he did know the market-price, inch by inch, of certain districts of Zenith, he did not know whether the police force was too large or too small, or whether it was in alliance with gambling and prostitution. He knew the means of fireproofing buildings and the relation of insurance-rates to fireproofing, but he did not know how many firemen there were in the city, how they were trained and paid, or how complete their apparatus. He sang eloquently the advantages of proximity of school-buildings to rentable homes, but he did not know—he did not know that it was worth while to know— whether the city schoolrooms were properly heated, lighted, ventilated, furnished; he did not know how the teachers were chosen; and though he chanted "One of the boasts of Zenith is that we pay our teachers adequately," that was because he had read the statement in the *Advocate-Times*. Himself, he could not have given the average salary of teachers in Zenith or anywhere else.

He had heard it said that "conditions" in the County Jail and the Zenith

City Prison were not very "scientific;" he had, with indignation at the criticism of Zenith, skimmed through a report in which the notorious pessimist
Seneca Doane, the radical lawyer, asserted that to throw boys and young
girls into a bull-pen crammed with men suffering from syphilis, delirium
tremens, and insanity was not the perfect way of educating them. He had
controverted the report by growling, "Folks that think a jail ought to be a
bloomin' Hotel Thornleigh make me sick. If people don't like a jail, let 'em
behave 'emselves and keep out of it. Besides, these reform cranks always
exaggerate." That was the beginning and quite completely the end of his
investigations into Zenith's charities and corrections; and as to the "vice districts" he brightly expressed it, "Those are things that no decent man monkeys with. Besides, 'smatter fact, I'll tell you confidentially: it's a protection
to our daughters and to decent women to have a district where tough nuts
can raise Cain. Keeps 'em away from our own homes."

As to industrial conditions, however, Babbitt had thought a great deal,
and his opinions may be coördinated as follows:

"A good labor union is of value because it keeps out radical unions, which
would destroy property. No one ought to be forced to belong to a union,
however. All labor agitators who try to force men to join a union should be
hanged. In fact, just between ourselves, there oughtn't to be any unions allowed at all; and as it's the best way of fighting the unions, every business
man ought to belong to an employers'-association and to the Chamber of
Commerce. In union there is strength. So any selfish hog who doesn't join
the Chamber of Commerce ought to be forced to."

In nothing—as the expert on whose advice families moved to new neigh-
borhoods to live there for a generation—was Babbitt more splendidly innocent than in the science of sanitation. He did not know a malaria-bearing
mosquito from a bat; he knew nothing about tests of drinking water; and in
the matters of plumbing and sewage he was as unlearned as he was voluble.
He often referred to the excellence of the bathrooms in the houses he sold.
He was fond of explaining why it was that no European ever bathed. Some
one had told him, when he was twenty-two, that all cesspools were unhealthy,
and he still denounced them. If a client impertinently wanted him to sell a
house which had a cesspool, Babbitt always spoke about it—before accepting
the house and selling it.

When he laid out the Glen Oriole acreage development, when he ironed
woodland and dipping meadow into a glenless, orioleless, sunburnt flat
prickly with small boards displaying the names of imaginary streets, he righteously put in a complete sewage-system. It made him feel superior; it enabled him to sneer privily at the Martin Lumsen development, Avonlea,
which had a cesspool; and it provided a chorus for the full-page advertisements in which he announced the beauty, convenience, cheapness, and su-
pererogatory healthfulness of Glen Oriole. The only flaw was that the Glen
Oriole sewers had insufficient outlet, so that waste remained in them, not
very agreeably, while the Avonlea cesspool was a Waring septic tank.

The whole of the Glen Oriole project was a suggestion that Babbitt, though he really did hate men recognized as swindlers, was not too unreasonably honest. Operators and buyers prefer that brokers should not be in competition with them as operators and buyers themselves, but attend to their clients' interests only. It was supposed that the Babbitt-Thompson Company were merely agents for Glen Oriole, serving the real owner, Jake Offutt, but the fact was that Babbitt and Thompson owned sixty-two per cent. of the Glen, the president and purchasing agent of the Zenith Street Traction Company owned twenty-eight per cent., and Jake Offutt (a gang-politician, a small manufacturer, a tobacco-chewing old farceur who enjoyed dirty politics, business diplomacy, and cheating at poker) had only ten per cent., which Babbitt and the Traction officials had given to him for "fixing" health inspectors and fire inspectors and a member of the State Transportation Commission.

But Babbitt was virtuous. He advocated, though he did not practise, the prohibition of alcohol; he praised, though he did not obey, the laws against motor-speeding; he paid his debts; he contributed to the church, the Red Cross, and the Y.M.C.A.; he followed the custom of his clan and cheated only as it was sanctified by precedent; and he never descended to trickery—though, as he explained to Paul Riesling:

"Course I don't mean to say that every ad I write is literally true or that I always believe everything I say when I give some buyer a good strong selling-spiel. You see—you see it's like this: In the first place, maybe the owner of the property exaggerated when he put it into my hands, and it certainly isn't my place to go proving my principal a liar! And then most folks are so darn crooked themselves that they expect a fellow to do a little lying, so if I was fool enough to never whoop the ante I'd get the credit for lying anyway! In self-defense I got to toot my own horn, like a lawyer defending a client—his bounden duty, ain't it, to bring out the poor dub's good points? Why, the Judge himself would bawl out a lawyer that didn't, even if they both knew the guy was guilty! But even so, I don't pad out the truth like Cecil Rountree or Thayer or the rest of these realtors. Fact, I think a fellow that's willing to deliberately up and profit by lying ought to be shot!"

Babbitt's value to his clients was rarely better shown than this morning, in the conference at eleven-thirty between himself, Conrad Lyte, and Archibald Purdy.

## v

Conrad Lyte was a real-estate speculator. He was a nervous speculator. Before he gambled he consulted bankers, lawyers, architects, contracting builders, and all of their clerks and stenographers who were willing to be cornered and give him advice. He was a bold entrepreneur, and he desired nothing more than complete safety in his investments, freedom from attention to details, and the thirty or forty per cent. profit which, according to all authorities, a pioneer deserves for his risks and foresight. He was a stubby man with a cap-like mass of short gray curls and clothes which, no matter how well cut, seemed shaggy. Below his eyes were semicircular hollows, as though silver dollars had been pressed against them and had left an imprint.

Particularly and always Lyte consulted Babbitt, and trusted in his slow cautiousness.

Six months ago Babbitt had learned that one Archibald Purdy, a grocer in the indecisive residential district known as Linton, was talking of opening a butcher shop beside his grocery. Looking up the ownership of adjoining parcels of land, Babbitt found that Purdy owned his present shop but did not own the one available lot adjoining. He advised Conrad Lyte to purchase this lot, for eleven thousand dollars, though an appraisal on a basis of rents did not indicate its value as above nine thousand. The rents, declared Babbitt, were too low; and by waiting they could make Purdy come to their price. (This was Vision.) He had to bully Lyte into buying. His first act as agent for Lyte was to increase the rent of the battered store-building on the lot. The tenant said a number of rude things, but he paid.

Now, Purdy seemed ready to buy, and his delay was going to cost him ten thousand extra dollars—the reward paid by the community to Mr. Conrad Lyte for the virtue of employing a broker who had Vision and who understood Talking Points, Strategic Values, Key Situations, Underappraisals, and the Psychology of Salesmanship.

Lyte came to the conference exultantly. He was fond of Babbitt, this morning, and called him "old hoss." Purdy, the grocer, a long-nosed man and solemn, seemed to care less for Babbitt and for Vision, but Babbitt met him at the street door of the office and guided him toward the private room with affectionate little cries of "This way, Brother Purdy!" He took from the correspondence-file the entire box of cigars and forced them on his guests. He pushed their chairs two inches forward and three inches back, which gave an hospitable note, then leaned back in his desk-chair and looked plump and jolly. But he spoke to the weakling grocer with firmness.

"Well, Brother Purdy, we been having some pretty tempting offers from butchers and a slew of other folks for that lot next to your store, but I persuaded Brother Lyte that we ought to give you a shot at the property first. I said to Lyte, 'It'd be a rotten shame,' I said, 'if somebody went and opened a combination grocery and meat market right next door and ruined Purdy's nice little business.' Especially—" Babbitt leaned forward, and his voice was harsh, "—it would be hard luck if one of these cash-and-carry chain-stores got in there and started cutting prices below cost till they got rid of competition and forced you to the wall!"

Purdy snatched his thin hands from his pockets, pulled up his trousers, thrust his hands back into his pockets, tilted in the heavy oak chair, and tried to look amused, as he struggled:

"Yes, they're bad competition. But I guess you don't realize the Pulling Power that Personality has in a neighborhood business."

The great Babbitt smiled. "That's so. Just as you feel, old man. We thought we'd give you first chance. All right then—"

"Now look here!" Purdy wailed. "I know f'r a fact that a piece of property 'bout same size right near, sold for less 'n eighty-five hundred, 'twa'n't two years ago, and here you fellows are asking me twenty-four thousand dollars! Why, I'd have to mortgage— I wouldn't mind so much paying twelve thousand but— Why good God, Mr. Babbitt, you're asking more 'n twice its value! And threatening to ruin me if I don't take it!"

"Purdy, I don't like your way of talking! I don't like it one little bit! Supposing Lyte and I were stinking enough to want to ruin any fellow human, don't you suppose we know it's to our own selfish interest to have everybody in Zenith prosperous? But all this is beside the point. Tell you what we'll do: We'll come down to twenty-three thousand—five thousand down and the rest on mortgage—and if you want to wreck the old shack and rebuild, I guess I can get Lyte here to loosen up for a building-mortgage on good liberal terms. Heavens, man, we'd be glad to oblige you! We don't like these foreign grocery trusts any better 'n you do! But it isn't reasonable to expect us to sacrifice eleven thousand or more just for neighborliness, *is* it! How about it, Lyte? You willing to come down?"

By warmly taking Purdy's part, Babbitt persuaded the benevolent Mr. Lyte to reduce his price to twenty-one thousand dollars. At the right moment Babbitt snatched from a drawer the agreement he had had Miss McGoun type out a week ago and thrust it into Purdy's hands. He genially shook his fountain pen to make certain that it was flowing, handed it to Purdy, and approvingly watched him sign.

The work of the world was being done. Lyte had made something over nine thousand dollars, Babbitt had made a four-hundred-and-fifty dollar commission, Purdy had, by the sensitive mechanism of modern finance, been provided with a business-building, and soon the happy inhabitants of Linton would have meat lavished upon them at prices only a little higher than those down-town.

It had been a manly battle, but after it Babbitt drooped. This was the only really amusing contest he had been planning. There was nothing ahead save details of leases, appraisals, mortgages.

He muttered, "Makes me sick to think of Lyte carrying off most of the profit when I did all the work, the old skinflint! And— What else have I got to do to-day? . . . Like to take a good long vacation. Motor trip. Something."

He sprang up, rekindled by the thought of lunching with Paul Riesling.

# 5

Babbitt's preparations for leaving the office to its feeble self during the hour and a half of his lunch-period were somewhat less elaborate than the plans for a general European war.

He fretted to Miss McGoun, "What time you going to lunch? Well, make sure Miss Bannigan is in then. Explain to her that if Wiedenfeldt calls up, she's to tell him I'm already having the title traced. And oh, b' the way, remind me to-morrow to have Penniman trace it. Now if anybody comes in looking for a cheap house, remember we got to shove that Bangor Road place off onto somebody. If you need me, I'll be at the Athletic Club. And —uh— And—uh— I'll be back by two."

He dusted the cigar-ashes off his vest. He placed a difficult unanswered letter on the pile of unfinished work, that he might not fail to attend to it that afternoon. (For three noons, now, he had placed the same letter on the unfinished pile.) He scrawled on a sheet of yellow backing-paper the memorandum: "See abt apt h drs," which gave him an agreeable feeling of having already seen about the apartment-house doors.

He discovered that he was smoking another cigar. He threw it away, protesting, "Darn it, I thought you'd quit this darn smoking!" He courageously returned the cigar-box to the correspondence-file, locked it up, hid the key in a more difficult place, and raged, "Ought to take care of myself. And need more exercise—walk to the club, every single noon—just what I'll do—every noon—cut out this motoring all the time."

The resolution made him feel exemplary. Immediately after it he decided that this noon it was too late to walk.

It took but little more time to start his car and edge it into the traffic than it would have taken to walk the three and a half blocks to the club.

## II

As he drove he glanced with the fondness of familiarity at the buildings.

A stranger suddenly dropped into the business-center of Zenith could not have told whether he was in a city of Oregon or Georgia, Ohio or Maine, Oklahoma or Manitoba. But to Babbitt every inch was individual and stirring. As always he noted that the California Building across the way was three stories lower, therefore three stories less beautiful, than his own Reeves Building. As always when he passed the Parthenon Shoe Shine Parlor, a one-story hut which beside the granite and red-brick ponderousness of the old California Building resembled a bath-house under a cliff, he commented, "Gosh, ought to get my shoes shined this afternoon. Keep forgetting it." At the Simplex Office Furniture Shop, the National Cash Register Agency, he yearned for a dictaphone, for a typewriter which would add and multiply, as a poet yearns for quartos or a physician for radium.

At the Nobby Men's Wear Shop he took his left hand off the steering-wheel to touch his scarf, and thought well of himself as one who bought expensive ties "and could pay cash for 'em, too, by golly;" and at the United Cigar Store, with its crimson and gold alertness, he reflected, "Wonder if I need some cigars—idiot—plumb forgot—going t' cut down my fool smoking." He looked at his bank, the Miners' and Drovers' National, and considered how clever and solid he was to bank with so marbled an establishment. His high moment came in the clash of traffic when he was halted at the corner beneath the lofty Second National Tower. His car was banked with four others in a line of steel restless as cavalry, while the cross-town traffic, limousines and enormous moving-vans and insistent motor-cycles, poured by; on the farther corner, pneumatic riveters rang on the sun-plated skeleton of a new building; and out of this tornado flashed the inspiration of a familiar face, and a fellow Booster shouted, "H' are you, George!" Babbitt waved in neighborly affection, and slid on with the traffic as the policeman lifted his hand. He noted how quickly his car picked up. He felt superior and powerful, like a shuttle of polished steel darting in a vast machine.

As always he ignored the next two blocks, decayed blocks not yet reclaimed from the grime and shabbiness of the Zenith of 1885. While he was passing the five-and-ten-cent store, the Dakota Lodging House, Concordia Hall with its lodge-rooms and the offices of fortune-tellers and chiropractors, he thought of how much money he made, and he boasted a little and worried a little and did old familiar sums:

"Four hundred fifty plunks this morning from the Lyte deal. But taxes due. Let's see: I ought to pull out eight thousand net this year, and save fifteen hundred of that—no, not if I put up garage and— Let's see: six hundred and forty clear last month, and twelve times six-forty makes—makes—let see: six times twelve is seventy-two hundred and— Oh rats, anyway, I'll make eight thousand—gee now, that's not so bad; mighty few fellows pulling down eight thousand dollars a year—eight thousand good hard iron dollars—bet there isn't more than five per cent. of the people in the whole United States that make more than Uncle George does, by golly! Right up at the top of the heap! But— Way expenses are— Family wasting gasoline, and always dressed like millionaires, and sending that eighty a month to Mother— And all these stenographers and salesmen gouging me for every cent they can get—"

The effect of his scientific budget-planning was that he felt at once triumphantly wealthy and perilously poor, and in the midst of these dissertations he stopped his car, rushed into a small news-and-miscellany shop, and bought the electric cigar-lighter which he had coveted for a week. He dodged his conscience by being jerky and noisy, and by shouting at the clerk, "Guess this will prett' near pay for itself in matches, eh?"

It was a pretty thing, a nickeled cylinder with an almost silvery socket, to be attached to the dashboard of his car. It was not only, as the placard on the counter observed, "a dandy little refinement, lending the last touch of class to a gentleman's auto," but a priceless time-saver. By freeing him from halting the car to light a match, it would in a month or two easily save ten minutes.

As he drove on he glanced at it. "Pretty nice. Always wanted one," he said wistfully. "The one thing a smoker needs, too."

Then he remembered that he had given up smoking.

"Darn it!" he mourned. "Oh well, I suppose I'll hit a cigar once in a while. And— Be a great convenience for other folks. Might make just the difference in getting chummy with some fellow that would put over a sale. And— Certainly looks nice there. Certainly is a mighty clever little jigger. Gives the last touch of refinement and class. I— By golly, I guess I can afford it if I want to! Not going to be the only member of this family that never has a single doggone luxury!"

Thus, laden with treasure, after three and a half blocks of romantic adventure, he drove up to the club.

The Zenith Athletic Club is not athletic and it isn't exactly a club, but it is Zenith in perfection. It has an active and smoke-misted billiard room, it is represented by baseball and football teams, and in the pool and the gymnasium a tenth of the members sporadically try to reduce. But most of its three thousand members use it as a café in which to lunch, play cards, tell stories, meet customers, and entertain out-of-town uncles at dinner. It is the largest club in the city, and its chief hatred is the conservative Union Club, which all sound members of the Athletic call "a rotten, snobbish, dull, expensive old hole—not one Good Mixer in the place—you couldn't hire me to join." Statistics show that no member of the Athletic has ever refused election to the Union, and of those who are elected, sixty-seven per cent. resign from the Athletic and are thereafter heard to say, in the drowsy sanctity of the Union lounge, "The Athletic would be a pretty good hotel, if it were more exclusive."

The Athletic Club building is nine stories high, yellow brick with glassy roof-garden above and portico of huge limestone columns below. The lobby, with its thick pillars of porous Caen stone, its pointed vaulting, and a brown glazed-tile floor like well-baked bread-crust, is a combination of cathedral-crypt and rathskeller. The members rush into the lobby as though they were shopping and hadn't much time for it. Thus did Babbitt enter, and to the group standing by the cigar-counter he whooped, "How's the boys? How's the boys? Well, well, fine day!"

Jovially they whooped back—Vergil Gunch, the coal-dealer, Sidney Finkelstein, the ladies'-ready-to-wear buyer for Parcher & Stein's department-store, and Professor Joseph K. Pumphrey, owner of the Riteway Business College and instructor in Public Speaking, Business English, Scenario Writing, and Commercial Law. Though Babbitt admired this savant, and appreciated Sidney Finkelstein as "a mighty smart buyer and a good liberal spender," it was to Vergil Gunch that he turned with enthusiasm. Mr. Gunch was president of the Boosters' Club, a weekly lunch-club, local chapter of a national organization which promoted sound business and friendliness among Regular Fellows. He was also no less an official than Esteemed Leading Knight in the Benevolent and Protective Order of Elks, and it was rumored that at the next election he would be a candidate for Exalted Ruler. He was a jolly man, given to oratory and to chumminess with the arts. He called on the famous actors and vaudeville artists when they came to town, gave them cigars, addressed them by their first names, and—sometimes—succeeded in bringing them to the Boosters' lunches to give The Boys a Free Entertainment. He was a large man with hair *en brosse,* and he knew the latest jokes, but he played poker close to the chest. It was at his party that Babbitt had sucked in the virus of to-day's restlessness.

Gunch shouted, "How's the old Bolsheviki? How do you feel, the morning after the night before?"

"Oh, boy! Some head! That was a regular party you threw, Verg! Hope you haven't forgotten I took that last cute little jack-pot!" Babbitt bellowed. (He was three feet from Gunch.)

"That's all right now! What I'll hand you next time, Georgie! Say, juh notice in the paper the way the New York Assembly stood up to the Reds?"

"You bet I did. That was fine, eh? Nice day to-day."

"Yes, it's one mighty fine spring day, but nights still cold."

"Yeh, you're right they are! Had to have coupla blankets last night, out on the sleeping-porch. Say, Sid," Babbitt turned to Finkelstein, the buyer, "got something wanta ask you about. I went out and bought me an electric cigar-lighter for the car, this noon, and—"

"Good hunch!" said Finkelstein, while even the learned Professor Pumphrey, a bulbous man with a pepper-and-salt cutaway and a pipe-organ voice, commented, "That makes a dandy accessory. Cigar-lighter gives tone to the dashboard."

"Yep, finally decided I'd buy me one. Got the best on the market, the clerk said it was. Paid five bucks for it. Just wondering if I got stuck. What do they charge for 'em at the store, Sid?"

Finkelstein asserted that five dollars was not too great a sum, not for a really high-class lighter which was suitably nickeled and provided with connections of the very best quality. "I always say—and believe me, I base it on a pretty fairly extensive mercantile experience—the best is the cheapest in the long run. Of course if a fellow wants to be a Jew about it, he can get cheap junk, but in the long *run*, the cheapest thing is—the best you can get! Now you take here just th' other day: I got a new top for my old boat and some upholstery, and I paid out a hundred and twenty-six fifty, and of course a lot of fellows would say that was too much—Lord, if the Old Folks—they live in one of these hick towns up-state and they simply can't get onto the way a city fellow's mind works, and then, of course, they're Jews, and they'd lie right down and die if they knew Sid had anted up a hundred and twenty-six bones. But I don't figure I was stuck, George, not a bit. Machine looks brand new now—not that it's so darned old, of course; had it less 'n three years, but I give it hard service; never drive less 'n a hundred miles on Sunday and, uh— Oh, I don't really think you got stuck, George. In the *long* run, the best is, you might say, it's unquestionably the cheapest."

"That's right," said Vergil Gunch. "That's the way I look at it. If a fellow is keyed up to what you might call intensive living, the way you get it here in Zenith—all the hustle and mental activity that's going on with a bunch of live-wires like the Boosters and here in the Z.A.C., why, he's got to save his nerves by having the best."

Babbitt nodded his head at every fifth word in the roaring rhythm; and by the conclusion, in Gunch's renowned humorous vein, he was enchanted:

"Still, at that, George, don't know's you can afford it. I've heard your business has been kind of under the eye of the gov'ment since you stole the tail of Eathorne Park and sold it!"

"Oh, you're a great little josher, Verg. But when it comes to kidding, how about this report that you stole the black marble steps off the post-office and sold 'em for high-grade coal!" In delight Babbitt patted Gunch's back, stroked his arm.

"That's all right, but what I want to know is: who's the real-estate shark that bought that coal for his apartment-houses?"

"I guess that'll hold you for a while, George!" said Finkelstein. "I'll tell you, though, boys, what I did hear: George's missus went into the gents' wear department at Parcher's to buy him some collars, and before she could give his neck-size the clerk slips her some thirteens. 'How juh know the size?' says Mrs. Babbitt, and the clerk says, 'Men that let their wives buy collars for 'em always wear thirteen, madam.' How's that! That's pretty good, eh? How's that, eh? I guess that'll about fix you, George!"

"I—I—" Babbitt sought for amiable insults in answer. He stopped, stared at the door. Paul Riesling was coming in. Babbitt cried, "See you later, boys," and hastened across the lobby. He was, just then, neither the sulky child of the sleeping-porch, the domestic tyrant of the breakfast table, the crafty money-changer of the Lyte-Purdy conference, nor the blaring Good Fellow, the Josher and Regular Guy, of the Athletic Club. He was an older brother to Paul Riesling, swift to defend him, admiring him with a proud and credulous love passing the love of women. Paul and he shook hands solemnly; they smiled as shyly as though they had been parted three years, not three days—and they said:

"How's the old horse-thief?"

"All right, I guess. How're you, you poor shrimp?"

"I'm first-rate, you second-hand hunk o' cheese."

Reassured thus of their high fondness, Babbitt grunted, "You're a fine guy, you are! Ten minutes late!" Riesling snapped, "Well, you're lucky to have a chance to lunch with a gentleman!" They grinned and went into the Neronian washroom, where a line of men bent over the bowls inset along a prodigious slab of marble as in religious prostration before their own images in the massy mirror. Voices thick, satisfied, authoritative, hurtled along the marble walls, bounded from the ceiling of lavender-bordered milky tiles, while the lords of the city, the barons of insurance and law and fertilizers and motor tires, laid down the law for Zenith; announced that the day was warm—indeed, indisputably of spring; that wages were too high and the interest on mortgages too low; that Babe Ruth, the eminent player of baseball, was a noble man; and that "those two nuts at the Climax Vaudeville Theater this week certainly are a slick pair of actors." Babbitt, though ordinarily his voice was the surest and most episcopal of all, was silent. In the presence of the slight dark reticence of Paul Riesling, he was awkward, he desired to be quiet and firm and deft.

The entrance lobby of the Athletic Club was Gothic, the washroom

Roman Imperial, the lounge Spanish Mission, and the reading-room in Chinese Chippendale, but the gem of the club was the dining-room, the masterpiece of Ferdinand Reitman, Zenith's busiest architect. It was lofty and half-timbered, with Tudor leaded casements, an oriel, a somewhat musicianless musicians'-gallery, and tapestries believed to illustrate the granting of Magna Charta. The open beams had been hand-adzed at Jake Offutt's car-body works, the hinges were of hand-wrought iron, the wainscot studded with hand-made wooden pegs, and at one end of the room was a heraldic and hooded stone fireplace which the club's advertising-pamphlet asserted to be not only larger than any of the fireplaces in European castles but of a draught incomparably more scientific. It was also much cleaner, as no fire had ever been built in it.

Half of the tables were mammoth slabs which seated twenty or thirty men. Babbitt usually sat at the one near the door, with a group including Gunch, Finkelstein, Professor Pumphrey, Howard Littlefield, his neighbor, T. Cholmondeley Frink, the poet and advertising-agent, and Orville Jones, whose laundry was in many ways the best in Zenith. They composed a club within the club, and merrily called themselves "The Roughnecks." To-day as he passed their table the Roughnecks greeted him, "Come on, sit in! You 'n' Paul too proud to feed with poor folks? Afraid somebody might stick you for a bottle of Bevo, George? Strikes me you swells are getting awful darn exclusive!"

He thundered, "You bet! We can't afford to have our reps ruined by being seen with you tightwads!" and guided Paul to one of the small tables beneath the musicians'-gallery. He felt guilty. At the Zenith Athletic Club, privacy was very bad form. But he wanted Paul to himself.

That morning he had advocated lighter lunches and now he ordered nothing but English mutton chop, radishes, peas, deep-dish apple pie, a bit of cheese, and a pot of coffee with cream, adding, as he did invariably, "And uh— Oh, and you might give me an order of French fried potatoes." When the chop came he vigorously peppered it and salted it. He always peppered and salted his meat, and vigorously, before tasting it.

Paul and he took up the spring-like quality of the spring, the virtues of the electric cigar-lighter, and the action of the New York State Assembly. It was not till Babbitt was thick and disconsolate with mutton grease that he flung out:

"I wound up a nice little deal with Conrad Lyte this morning that put five hundred good round plunks in my pocket. Pretty nice—pretty nice! And yet— I don't know what's the matter with me to-day. Maybe it's an attack of spring fever, or staying up too late at Verg Gunch's, or maybe it's just the winter's work piling up, but I've felt kind of down in the mouth all day long. Course I wouldn't beef about it to the fellows at the Roughnecks' Table there, but you— Ever feel that way, Paul? Kind of comes over me: here I've pretty much done all the things I ought to; supported my family, and got a good house and a six-cylinder car, and built up a nice little business, and I haven't any vices 'specially, except smoking—and I'm practically cutting that out, by the way. And I belong to the church, and play enough golf to keep in trim, and I only associate with good decent fellows. And yet, even so, I don't know that I'm entirely satisfied!"

It was drawled out, broken by shouts from the neighboring tables, by mechanical love-making to the waitress, by stertorous grunts as the coffee filled him with dizziness and indigestion. He was apologetic and doubtful, and it was Paul, with his thin voice, who pierced the fog:

"Good Lord, George, you don't suppose it's any novelty to me to find that we hustlers, that think we're so all-fired successful, aren't getting much out of it? You look as if you expected me to report you as seditious! You know what my own life's been."

"I know, old man."

"I ought to have been a fiddler, and I'm a pedler of tar-roofing! And Zilla— Oh, I don't want to squeal, but you know as well as I do about how inspiring a wife she is. . . . Typical instance last evening: We went to the movies. There was a big crowd waiting in the lobby, us at the tail-end. She began to push right through it with her 'Sir, how dare you?' manner— Honestly, sometimes when I look at her and see how she's always so made up and stinking of perfume and looking for trouble and kind of always yelping, "I tell yuh I'm a lady, damn yuh!'—why, I want to kill her! Well, she keeps elbowing through the crowd, me after her, feeling good and ashamed, till she's almost up to the velvet rope and ready to be the next let in. But there was a little squirt of a man there—probably been waiting half an hour—I kind of admired the little cuss—and he turns on Zilla and says, perfectly polite, 'Madam, why are you trying to push past me?' And she simply—God, I was so ashamed!—she rips out at him, 'You're no gentleman,' and she drags me into it and hollers, 'Paul, this person insulted me!' and the poor skate he got ready to fight.

"I made out I hadn't heard them—sure! same as you wouldn't hear a boiler-factory!—and I tried to look away—I can tell you exactly how every tile looks in the ceiling of that lobby; there's one with brown spots on it like the face of the devil—and all the time the people there—they were packed in like sardines—they kept making remarks about us, and Zilla went right on talking about the little chap, and screeching that 'folks like him oughtn't to be admitted in a place that's *supposed* to be for ladies and gentlemen,' and 'Paul, will you kindly call the manager, so I can report this dirty rat?' and— Oof! Maybe I wasn't glad when I could sneak inside and hide in the dark!

"After twenty-four years of that kind of thing, you don't expect me to fall down and foam at the mouth when you hint that this sweet, clean, respectable, moral life isn't all it's cracked up to be, do you? I can't even talk about it, except to you, because anybody else would think I was yellow. Maybe I am. Don't care any longer. . . . Gosh, you've had to stand a lot of whining from me, first and last, Georgie!"

"Rats, now, Paul, you've never really what you could call whined. Sometimes— I'm always blowing to Myra and the kids about what a whale of a realtor I am, and yet sometimes I get a sneaking idea I'm not such a Pierpont Morgan as I let on to be. But if I ever do help by jollying you along, old Paulski, I guess maybe Saint Pete may let me in after all!"

"Yuh, you're an old blow-hard, Georgie, you cheerful cutthroat, but you've certainly kept me going."

"Why don't you divorce Zilla?"

"Why don't I! If I only could! If she'd just give me the chance! You couldn't hire her to divorce me, no, nor desert me. She's too fond of her three squares and a few pounds of nut-center chocolates in between. If she'd only be what they call unfaithful to me! George, I don't want to be too much of a stinker; back in college I'd 've thought a man who could say that ought to be shot at sunrise. But honestly, I'd be tickled to death if she'd really go making love with somebody. Fat chance! Of course she'll flirt with anything—you know how she holds hands and laughs—that laugh—that horrible brassy laugh—the way she yaps, 'You naughty man, you better be careful or my big husband will be after you!'—and the guy looking me over and thinking, 'Why, you cute little thing, you run away now or I'll spank you!' And she'll let him go just far enough so she gets some excitement out of it and then she'll begin to do the injured innocent and have a beautiful time wailing, 'I didn't think you were that kind of a person.' They talk about these *demi-vierges* in stories—"

"These *whats?*"

"—but the wise, hard, corseted, old married women like Zilla are worse than any bobbed-haired girl that ever went boldly out into this-here storm of life—and kept her umbrella slid up her sleeve! But rats, you know what Zilla is. How she nags—nags—nags. How she wants everything I can buy her, and a lot that I can't, and how absolutely unreasonable she is, and when I get sore and try to have it out with her she plays the Perfect Lady so well that even I get fooled and get all tangled up in a lot of 'Why did you say's' and 'I didn't mean's.' I'll tell you, Georgie: You know my tastes are pretty fairly simple—in the matter of food, at least. Course, as you're always complaining, I do like decent cigars—not those Flor de Cabagos you're smoking—"

"That's all right now! That's a good two-for. By the way, Paul, did I tell you I decided to practically cut out smok—"

"Yes you— At the same time, if I can't get what I like, why, I can do without it. I don't mind sitting down to burnt steak, with canned peaches and store cake for a thrilling little dessert afterwards, but I do draw the line at having to sympathize with Zilla because she's so rotten bad-tempered that the cook has quit, and she's been so busy sitting in a dirty lace negligée all afternoon, reading about some brave manly Western hero, that she hasn't had time to do any cooking. You're always talking about 'morals'—meaning monogamy, I suppose. You've been the rock of ages to me, all right, but you're essentially a simp. You—"

"Where d' you get that 'simp,' little man? Let me tell you—"

"—love to look earnest and inform the world that it's the 'duty of responsible business men to be strictly moral, as an example to the community.' In fact you're so earnest about morality, old Georgie, that I hate to think how essentially immoral you must be underneath. All right, you can—"

"Wait, wait now! What's—"

"—talk about morals all you want to, old thing, but believe me, if it hadn't been for you and an occasional evening playing the violin to Terrill O'Farrell's 'cello, and three or four darling girls that let me forget this beastly joke they call 'respectable life,' I'd 've killed myself years ago.

"And business! The roofing business! Roofs for cowsheds! Oh, I don't mean I haven't had a lot of fun out of the Game; out of putting it over on the labor unions, and seeing a big check coming in, and the business increasing. But what's the use of it? You know, my business isn't distributing roofing—it's principally keeping my competitors from distributing roofing. Same with you. All we do is cut each other's throats and make the public pay for it!"

"Look here now, Paul! You're pretty darn near talking socialism!"

"Oh yes, of course I don't really exactly mean that—I s'pose. Course—competition—brings out the best—survival of the fittest—but— But I mean: Take all these fellows we know, the kind right here in the club now, that seem to be perfectly content with their home-life and their businesses, and that boost Zenith and the Chamber of Commerce and holler for a million population. I bet if you could cut into their heads you'd find that one-third of 'em are sure-enough satisfied with their wives and kids and friends and their offices; and one-third feel kind of restless but won't admit it; and one-third are miserable and know it. They hate the whole peppy, boosting, go-ahead game, and they're bored by their wives and think their families are fools—at least when they come to forty or forty-five they're bored—and they hate business, and they'd go— Why do you suppose there's so many 'mysterious' suicides? Why do you suppose so many Substantial Citizens jumped right into the war? Think it was all patriotism?"

Babbitt snorted, "What do you expect? Think we were sent into the world to have a soft time and—what is it?—'float on flowery beds of ease'? Think Man was just made to be happy?"

"Why not? Though I've never discovered anybody that knew what the deuce Man really was made for!"

"Well we know—not just in the Bible alone, but it stands to reason—a man who doesn't buckle down and do his duty, even if it does bore him sometimes, is nothing but a—well, he's simply a weakling. Mollycoddle, in fact! And what do you advocate? Come down to cases! If a man is bored by his wife, do you seriously mean he has a right to chuck her and take a sneak, or even kill himself?"

"Good Lord, I don't know what 'rights' a man has! And I don't know the solution of boredom. If I did, I'd be the one philosopher that had the cure for living. But I do know that about ten times as many people find their lives dull, and unnecessarily dull, as ever admit it; and I do believe that if we busted out and admitted it sometimes, instead of being nice and patient and loyal for sixty years, and then nice and patient and dead for the rest of eternity, why, maybe, possibly, we might make life more fun."

They drifted into a maze of speculation. Babbitt was elephantishly uneasy. Paul was bold, but not quite sure about what he was being bold. Now and then Babbitt suddenly agreed with Paul in an admission which contradicted all his defense of duty and Christian patience, and at each admission he had a curious reckless joy. He said at last:

"Look here, old Paul, you do a lot of talking about kicking things in the face, but you never kick. Why don't you?"

"Nobody does. Habit too strong. But— Georgie, I've been thinking of one mild bat—oh, don't worry, old pillar of monogamy; it's highly proper. It seems to be settled now, isn't it—though of course Zilla keeps rooting for a nice expensive vacation in New York and Atlantic City, with the bright lights and the bootlegged cocktails and a bunch of lounge-lizards to dance with—but the Babbitts and the Rieslings are sure-enough going to Lake Sunasquam, aren't we? Why couldn't you and I make some excuse—say business in New York—and get up to Maine four or five days before they do, and just loaf by ourselves and smoke and cuss and be natural?"

"Great! Great idea!" Babbitt admired.

Not for fourteen years had he taken a holiday without his wife, and neither of them quite believed they could commit this audacity. Many members of the Athletic Club did go camping without their wives, but they were officially dedicated to fishing and hunting, whereas the sacred and unchangeable sports of Babbitt and Paul Riesling were golfing, motoring, and bridge. For either the fishermen or the golfers to have changed their habits would have been an infraction of their self-imposed discipline which would have shocked all right-thinking and regularized citizens.

Babbitt blustered, "Why don't we just put our foot down and say, 'We're going on ahead of you, and that's all there is to it!' Nothing criminal in it. Simply say to Zilla—"

"You don't say anything to Zilla simply. Why, Georgie, she's almost as much of a moralist as you are, and if I told her the truth she'd believe we were going to meet some dames in New York. And even Myra—she never nags you, the way Zilla does, but she'd worry. She'd say, 'Don't you *want* me to go to Maine with you? I shouldn't dream of going unless you wanted me;' and you'd give in to save her feelings. Oh, the devil! Let's have a shot at duck-pins."

During the game of duck-pins, a juvenile form of bowling, Paul was silent. As they came down the steps of the club, not more than half an hour after the time at which Babbitt had sternly told Miss McGoun he would be back, Paul sighed, "Look here, old man, oughtn't to talked about Zilla way I did."

"Rats, old man, it lets off steam."

"Oh, I know! After spending all noon sneering at the conventional stuff, I'm conventional enough to be ashamed of saving my life by busting out with my fool troubles!"

"Old Paul, your nerves are kind of on the bum. I'm going to take you away. I'm going to rig this thing. I'm going to have an important deal in New York and—and sure, of course!—I'll need you to advise me on the roof of the building! And the ole deal will fall through, and there'll be nothing for us but to go on ahead to Maine. I—Paul, when it comes right down to it, I don't care whether you bust loose or not. I do like having a rep for being one of the Bunch, but if you ever needed me I'd chuck it and come out for you every time! Not of course but what you're—course I don't mean you'd ever do anything what would put—that would put a decent position on the fritz but— See how I mean? I'm kind of a clumsy old codger, and I need your fine Eyetalian hand. We— Oh, hell, I can't stand here gassing all day! On the job! S' long! Don't take any wooden money, Paulibus! See you soon! S' long!"

# 6

He forgot Paul Riesling in an afternoon of not unagreeable details. After a return to his office, which seemed to have staggered on without him, he drove a "prospect" out to view a four-flat tenement in the Linton district. He was inspired by the customer's admiration of the new cigar-lighter. Thrice its novelty made him use it, and thrice he hurled half-smoked cigarettes from the car, protesting, "I *got* to quit smoking so blame much!"

Their ample discussion of every detail of the cigar-lighter led them to speak of electric flat-irons and bed-warmers. Babbitt apologized for being so shabbily old-fashioned as still to use a hot-water bottle, and he announced that he would have the sleeping-porch wired at once. He had enormous and poetic admiration, though very little understanding, of all mechanical devices. They were his symbols of truth and beauty. Regarding each new intricate mechanism—metal lathe, two-jet carburetor, machine gun, oxyacetylene welder—he learned one good realistic-sounding phrase, and used it over and over, with a delightful feeling of being technical and initiated.

The customer joined him in the worship of machinery, and they came buoyantly up to the tenement and began that examination of plastic slate roof, kalamein doors, and seven-eights-inch blind-nailed flooring, began those diplomacies of hurt surprise and readiness to be persuaded to do something they had already decided to do, which would some day result in a sale.

On the way back Babbitt picked up his partner and father-in-law, Henry T. Thompson, at his kitchen-cabinet works, and they drove through South Zenith, a high-colored, banging, exciting region: new factories of hollow tile with gigantic wire-glass windows, surly old red-brick factories stained with tar, high-perched water-tanks, big red trucks like locomotives, and, on a score of hectic side-tracks, far-wandering freight-cars from the New York Central and apple orchards, the Great Northern and wheat-plateaus, the Southern Pacific and orange groves.

They talked to the secretary of the Zenith Foundry Company about an interesting artistic project—a cast-iron fence for Linden Lane Cemetery. They drove on to the Zeeco Motor Company and interviewed the sales-manager, Noël Ryland, about a discount on a Zeeco car for Thompson. Babbitt and Ryland were fellow-members of the Boosters' Club, and no Booster felt right if he bought anything from another Booster without receiving a discount. But Henry Thompson growled, "Oh, t' hell with 'em! I'm not going to crawl around mooching discounts, not from nobody." It was one of the differences between Thompson, the old-fashioned, lean Yankee, rugged, traditional, stage type of American business man, and Babbitt, the plump, smooth, efficient, up-to-the-minute and otherwise perfected modern. Whenever Thompson twanged, "Put your John Hancock on that line," Babbitt was as much amused by the antiquated provincialism as any proper Englishman by any American. He knew himself to be of a breeding altogether more esthetic and sensitive than Thompson's. He was a college graduate, he played golf, he often smoked cigarettes instead of cigars, and when he went to Chicago he took a room with a private bath. "The whole thing is," he explained to Paul Riesling, "these old codgers lack the subtlety that you got to have to-day."

This advance in civilization could be carried too far, Babbitt perceived. Noël Ryland, sales-manager of the Zeeco, was a frivolous graduate of Princeton, while Babbitt was a sound and standard ware from that great department-store, the State University. Ryland wore spats, he wrote long letters about City Planning and Community Singing, and, though he was a Booster, he was known to carry in his pocket small volumes of poetry in a foreign language. All this was going too far. Henry Thompson was the extreme of insularity, and Noël Ryland the extreme of frothiness, while between them, supporting the state, defending the evangelical churches and domestic brightness and sound business, were Babbitt and his friends.

With this just estimate of himself—and with the promise of a discount on Thompson's car—he returned to his office in triumph.

But as he went through the corridor of the Reeves Building he sighed, "Poor old Paul! I got to— Oh, damn Noël Ryland! Damn Charley McKelvey! Just because they make more money than I do, they think they're so superior. I wouldn't be found dead in their stuffy old Union Club! I— Somehow, to-day, I don't feel like going back to work. Oh well—"

## II

He answered telephone calls, he read the four o'clock mail, he signed his morning's letters, he talked to a tenant about repairs, he fought with Stanley Graff.

Young Graff, the outside salesman, was always hinting that he deserved an increase of commission, and to-day he complained, "I think I ought to get a bonus if I put through the Heiler sale. I'm chasing around and working on it every single evening, almost."

Babbitt frequently remarked to his wife that it was better to "con your office-help along and keep 'em happy 'stead of jumping on 'em and poking 'em up—get more work out of 'em that way," but this unexampled lack of appreciation hurt him, and he turned on Graff:

"Look here, Stan; let's get this clear. You've got an idea somehow that it's you that do all the selling. Where d' you get that stuff? Where d' you think you'd be if it wasn't for our capital behind you, and our lists of properties, and all the prospects we find for you? All you got to do is follow up our tips and close the deal. The hall-porter could sell Babbitt-Thompson listings! You say you're engaged to a girl, but have to put in your evenings chasing after buyers. Well, why the devil shouldn't you? What do you want to do? Sit around holding her hand? Let me tell you, Stan, if your girl is worth her salt, she'll be glad to know you're out hustling, making some money to furnish the home-nest, instead of doing the lovey-dovey. The kind of fellow that kicks about working overtime, that wants to spend his evenings reading trashy novels or spooning and exchanging a lot of nonsense and foolishness with some girl, he ain't the kind of upstanding, energetic young man, with a future—and with Vision!—that we want here. How about it? What's your Ideal, anyway? Do you want to make money and be a responsible member of the community, or do you want to be a loafer, with no Inspiration or Pep?"

Graff was not so amenable to Vision and Ideals as usual. "You bet I want to make money! That's why I want that bonus! Honest, Mr. Babbitt, I don't want to get fresh, but this Heiler house is a terror. Nobody'll fall for it. The flooring is rotten and the walls are full of cracks."

"That's exactly what I mean! To a salesman with a love for his profession, it's hard problems like that that inspire him to do his best. Besides, Stan—Matter o' fact, Thompson and I are against bonuses, as a matter of principle. We like you, and we want to help you so you can get married, but we can't be unfair to the others on the staff. If we start giving you bonuses, don't you see we're going to hurt the feeling and be unjust to Penniman and Laylock? Right's right, and discrimination is unfair, and there ain't going to be any of it in this office! Don't get the idea, Stan, that because during the war salesmen were hard to hire, now, when there's a lot of men out of work, there aren't a slew of bright young fellows that would be glad to step in and enjoy your opportunities, and not act as if Thompson and I were his enemies and not do any work except for bonuses. How about it, heh? How about it?"

"Oh—well—gee—of course—" sighed Graff, as he went out, crabwise.

Babbitt did not often squabble with his employees. He liked to like the people about him; he was dismayed when they did not like him. It was only when they attacked the sacred purse that he was frightened into fury, but then, being a man given to oratory and high principles, he enjoyed the sound of his own vocabulary and the warmth of his own virtue. To-day he had so passionately indulged in self-approval that he wondered whether he had been entirely just:

"After all, Stan isn't a boy any more. Oughtn't to call him so hard. But rats, got to haul folks over the coals now and then for their own good. Unpleasant duty, but— I wonder if Stan is sore? What's he saying to McGoun out there?"

So chill a wind of hatred blew from the outer office that the normal comfort of his evening home-going was ruined. He was distressed by losing that approval of his employees to which an executive is always slave. Ordinarily he left the office with a thousand enjoyable fussy directions to the effect that there would undoubtedly be important tasks to-morrow, and Miss McGoun and Miss Bannigan would do well to be there early, and for heaven's sake remind him to call up Conrad Lyte soon 's he came in. To-night he departed with feigned and apologetic liveliness. He was as afraid of his still-faced clerks—of the eyes focused on him, Miss McGoun staring with head lifted from her typing, Miss Bannigan looking over her ledger, Mat Penniman craning around at his desk in the dark alcove, Stanley Graff sullenly expressionless—as a parvenu before the bleak propriety of his butler. He hated to expose his back to their laughter, and in his effort to be casually merry he stammered and was raucously friendly and oozed wretchedly out of the door.

But he forgot his misery when he saw from Smith Street the charms of Floral Heights; the roofs of red tile and green slate, the shining new sun-parlors, and the stainless walls.

### III

He stopped to inform Howard Littlefield, his scholarly neighbor, that though the day had been springlike the evening might be cold. He went in to shout "Where are you?" at his wife, with no very definite desire to know where she was. He examined the lawn to see whether the furnace-man had raked it properly. With some satisfaction and a good deal of discussion of the matter with Mrs. Babbitt, Ted, and Howard Littlefield, he concluded that the furnace-man had not raked it properly. He cut two tufts of wild grass with his wife's largest dressmaking-scissors; he informed Ted that it was all nonsense having a furnace-man—"big husky fellow like you ought to do all the work around the house;" and privately he meditated that it was agreeable to have it known throughout the neighborhood that he was so prosperous that his son never worked around the house.

He stood on the sleeping-porch and did his day's exercises: arms out sidewise for two minutes, up for two minutes, while he muttered, "Ought take more exercise; keep in shape;" then went in to see whether his collar needed changing before dinner. As usual it apparently did not.

The Lettish-Croat maid, a powerful woman, beat the dinner-gong.

The roast of beef, roasted potatoes, and string beans were excellent this evening and, after an adequate sketch of the day's progressive weather-states, his four-hundred-and-fifty-dollar fee, his lunch with Paul Riesling, and the proven merits of the new cigar-lighter, he was moved to a benign, "Sort o' thinking about buying a new car. Don't believe we'll get one till next year, but still, we might."

Verona, the older daughter, cried, "Oh, Dad, if you do, why don't you get a sedan? That would be perfectly slick! A closed car is so much more comfy than an open one."

"Well now, I don't know about that. I kind of like an open car. You get more fresh air that way."

"Oh, shoot, that's just because you never tried a sedan. Let's get one. It's got a lot more class," said Ted.

"A closed car does keep the clothes nicer," from Mrs. Babbitt; "You don't get your hair blown all to pieces," from Verona; "It's a lot sportier," from Ted; and from Tinka, the youngest, "Oh, let's have a sedan! Mary Ellen's father has got one." Ted wound up, "Oh, everybody's got a closed car now, except us!"

Babbitt faced them: "I guess you got nothing very terrible to complain about! Anyway, I don't keep a car just to enable you children to look like millionaires! And I like an open car, so you can put the top down on summer evenings and go out for a drive and get some good fresh air. Besides— A closed car costs more money."

"Aw, gee whiz, if the Doppelbraus can afford a closed car, I guess we can!" prodded Ted.

"Humph! I make eight thousand a year to his seven! But I don't blow it all in and waste it and throw it around, the way he does! Don't believe in this business of going and spending a whole lot of money to show off and—"

They went, with ardor and some thoroughness, into the matters of stream-line bodies, hill-climbing power, wire wheels, chrome steel, ignition systems, and body colors. It was much more than a study of transportation. It was an aspiration for knightly rank. In the city of Zenith, in the barbarous twentieth century, a family's motor indicated its social rank as precisely as the grades of the peerage determined the rank of an English family—indeed, more precisely, considering the opinion of old county families upon newly created brewery barons and woolen-mill viscounts. The details of precedence were never officially determined. There was no court to decide whether the second son of a Pierce Arrow limousine should go in to dinner before the first son of a Buick roadster, but of their respective social importance there was no doubt; and where Babbitt as a boy had aspired to the presidency, his son Ted aspired to a Packard twin-six and an established position in the motored gentry.

The favor which Babbitt had won from his family by speaking of a new car evaporated as they realized that he didn't intend to buy one this year. Ted lamented, "Oh, punk! The old boat looks as if it'd had fleas and been scratching its varnish off." Mrs. Babbitt said abstractedly, "Snoway talkcher father." Babbitt raged, "If you're too much of a high-class gentleman, and you belong to the *bon ton* and so on, why, you needn't take the car out this evening." Ted explained, "I didn't mean—" and dinner dragged on with normal domestic delight to the inevitable point at which Babbitt protested,

"Come, come now, we can't sit here all evening. Give the girl a chance to clear away the table."

He was fretting, "What a family! I don't know how we all get to scrapping this way. Like to go off some place and be able to hear myself think. . . . Paul . . . Maine . . . Wear old pants, and loaf, and cuss." He said cautiously to his wife, "I've been in correspondence with a man in New York—wants me to see him about a real-estate trade—may not come off till summer. Hope it doesn't break just when we and the Rieslings get ready to go to Maine. Be a shame if we couldn't make the trip there together. Well, no use worrying now."

Verona escaped, immediately after dinner, with no discussion save an automatic "Why don't you ever stay home?" from Babbitt.

In the living-room, in a corner of the davenport, Ted settled down to his Home Study; plane geometry, Cicero, and the agonizing metaphors of Comus.

"I don't see why they give us this old-fashioned junk by Milton and Shakespeare and Wordsworth and all these has-beens," he protested. "Oh, I guess I could stand it to see a show by Shakespeare, if they had swell scenery and put on a lot of dog, but to sit down in cold blood and *read* 'em— These teachers—how do they get that way?"

Mrs. Babbitt, darning socks, speculated, "Yes, I wonder why. Of course I don't want to fly in the face of the professors and everybody, but I do think there's things in Shakespeare—not that I read him much, but when I was young the girls used to show me passages that weren't, really, they weren't at all nice."

Babbitt looked up irritably from the comic strips in the *Evening Advocate.* They composed his favorite literature and art, these illustrated chronicles in which Mr. Mutt hit Mr. Jeff with a rotten egg, and Mother corrected Father's vulgarisms by means of a rolling-pin. With the solemn face of a devotee, breathing heavily through his open mouth, he plodded nightly through every picture, and during the rite he detested interruptions. Furthermore, he felt that on the subject of Shakespeare he wasn't really an authority. Neither the *Advocate-Times,* the *Evening Advocate,* nor the *Bulletin of the Zenith Chamber of Commerce* had ever had an editorial on the matter, and until one of them had spoken he found it hard to form an original opinion. But even at risk of floundering in strange bogs, he could not keep out of an open controversy.

"I'll tell you why you have to study Shakespeare and those. It's because they're required for college entrance, and that's all there is to it! Personally, I don't see myself why they stuck 'em into an up-to-date high-school system like we have in this state. Be a good deal better if you took Business English, and learned how to write an ad, or letters that would pull. But there it is, and there's no talk, argument, or discussion about it! Trouble with you, Ted, is you always want to do something different! If you're going to law-school— and you are!—I never had a chance to, but I'll see that you do—why, you'll want to lay in all the English and Latin you can get."

"Oh punk. I don't see what's the use of law-school—or even finishing high school. I don't want to go to college 'specially. Honest, there's lot of fellows that have graduated from colleges that don't begin to make as much money as fellows that went to work early. Old Shimmy Peters, that teaches Latin in the High, he's a what-is-it from Columbia and he sits up all night reading a lot of greasy books and he's always spieling about the 'value of languages,' and the poor soak doesn't make but eighteen hundred a year, and no traveling salesman would think of working for that. I know what I'd like to do. I'd like to be an aviator, or own a corking big garage, or else—a fellow was telling me about it yesterday—I'd like to be one of these fellows that the Standard Oil Company sends out to China, and you live in a compound and don't have to do any work, and you get to see the world and pagodas and the ocean and everything! And then I could take up correspondence-courses. That's the real stuff! You don't have to recite to some frosty-faced old dame that's trying to show off to the principal, and you can study any subject you want to. Just listen to these! I clipped out the ads of some swell courses."

He snatched from the back of his geometry half a hundred advertisements of those home-study courses which the energy and foresight of American commerce have contributed to the science of education. The first displayed the portrait of a young man with a pure brow, an iron jaw, silk socks, and hair like patent leather. Standing with one hand in his trousers-pocket and the other extended with chiding forefinger, he was bewitching an audience of men with gray beards, paunches, bald heads, and every other sign of wisdom and prosperity. Above the picture was an inspiring educational symbol—no antiquated lamp or torch or owl of Minerva, but a row of dollar signs. The text ran:

$   $   $   $   $   $   $   $

## POWER AND PROSPERITY IN PUBLIC SPEAKING

### A Yarn Told at the Club

Who do you think I ran into the other evening at the De Luxe Restaurant? Why, old Freddy Durkee, that used to be a dead-or-alive shipping clerk in my old place—Mr. Mouse-Man we used to laughingly call the dear fellow. One time he was so timid he was plumb scared of the Super, and never got credit for the dandy work he did. Him at the De Luxe! And if he wasn't ordering a tony feed with all the "fixings" from celery to nuts! And instead of being embarrassed by the waiters, like he used to be at the little dump where we lunched in Old Lang Syne, he was bossing them around like he was a millionaire!

I cautiously asked him what he was doing. Freddy laughed and said, "Say, old chum, I guess you're wondering what's come over me. You'll be glad to know I'm now Assistant Super at the old shop, and right on the High Road

to Prosperity and Domination, and I look forward with confidence to a twelve-cylinder car,
and the wife is making things hum in the best
society and the kiddies getting a first-class education.

"Here's how it happened. I ran across an ad
of a course that claimed to teach people how
to talk easily and on their feet, how to answer complaints, how to lay a proposition before the Boss, how to hit a bank for a loan,
how to hold a big audience spellbound with
wit, humor, anecdote, inspiration, etc. It was
compiled by the Master Orator, Prof. Waldo
F. Peet. I was
skeptical, too, but
I wrote (just *on
a postcard*, with
name and ad-
dress) to the pub-
lisher for the les-
sons—sent On
Trial, money back
if you are not ab-
solutely satisfied.

There were eight simple lessons in plain language anybody could understand, and I studied
them just a few hours a night, then started
practising on the wife. Soon found I could talk
right up to the Super and get due credit for all
the good work I did. They began to appreciate
me and advance me fast, and say, old doggo,
what do you think they're paying me now?
$6,500 per year! And say, I find I can keep a
big audience fascinated, speaking on any topic.
As a friend, old boy, I advise you to send for
circular (no obligation) and valuable free Art
Picture to:—

Babbitt was again without a canon which would enable him to speak with
authority. Nothing in motoring or real estate had indicated what a Solid

Citizen and Regular Fellow ought to think about culture by mail. He began with hesitation:

"Well—sounds as if it covered the ground. It certainly is a fine thing to be able to orate. I've sometimes thought I had a little talent that way myself, and I know darn well that one reason why a fourflushing old back-number like Chan Mott can get away with it in real estate is just because he can make a good talk, even when he hasn't got a doggone thing to say! And it certainly is pretty cute the way they get out all these courses on various topics and subjects nowadays. I'll tell you, though: No need to blow in a lot of good money on this stuff when you can get a first-rate course in eloquence and English and all that right in your own school—and one of the biggest school buildings in the entire country!"

"That's so," said Mrs. Babbitt comfortably, while Ted complained:

"Yuh, but Dad, they just teach a lot of old junk that isn't any practical use—except the manual training and typewriting and basketball and dancing —and in these correspondence-courses, gee, you can get all kinds of stuff that would come in handy. Say, listen to this one:

### CAN YOU PLAY A MAN'S PART?

If you are walking with your mother, sister or best girl and some one passes a slighting remark or uses improper language, won't you be ashamed if you can't take her part? Well, can you?

We teach boxing and self-defense by mail. Many pupils have written saying that after a few lessons they've outboxed bigger and heavier opponents. The lessons start with simple movements practised before your mirror—holding out your hand for a coin, the breast-stroke in swimming, etc. Before you realize it you are striking scientifically, ducking, guarding and feinting, just as if you had a real opponent before you.

"Oh, baby, maybe I wouldn't like that!" Ted chanted. "I'll tell the world! Gosh, I'd like to take one fellow I know in school that's always shooting off his mouth, and catch him alone—"

"Nonsense! The idea! Most useless thing I ever heard of!" Babbitt fulminated.

"Well, just suppose I was walking with Mama or Rone, and somebody passed a slighting remark or used improper language. What would I do?"

"Why, you'd probably bust the record for the hundred-yard dash!"

"I *would* not! I'd stand right up to any mucker that passed a slighting remark on *my* sister and I'd show him—"

"Look here, young Dempsey! If I ever catch you fighting I'll whale the everlasting daylights out of you—and I'll do it without practising holding out my hand for a coin before the mirror, too!"

"Why, Ted dear," Mrs. Babbitt said placidly, "it's not at all nice, your talking of fighting this way!"

"Well, gosh almighty, that's a fine way to appreciate— And then suppose I was walking with *you*, Ma, and somebody passed a slighting remark—"

"Nobody's going to pass no slighting remarks on nobody," Babbitt observed, "not if they stay home and study their geometry and mind their own affairs instead of hanging around a lot of poolrooms and soda-fountains and places where nobody's got any business to be!"

"But goooooooosh, Dad, if they DID!"

Mrs. Babbitt chirped, "Well, if they did, I wouldn't do them the honor of paying any attention to them! Besides, they never do. You always hear about these women that get followed and insulted and all, but I don't believe a word of it, or it's their own fault, the way some women look at a person. I certainly never 've been insulted by—"

"Aw shoot, Mother, just suppose you *were* sometime! Just *suppose*! Can't you suppose something? Can't you imagine things?"

"Certainly I can imagine things! The idea!"

"Certainly your mother can imagine things—and suppose things! Think you're the only member of this household that's got an imagination?" Babbitt demanded. "But what's the use of a lot of supposing? Supposing never gets you anywhere. No sense supposing when there's a lot of real facts to take into considera—"

"Look here, Dad. Suppose—I mean, just—just suppose you were in your office and some rival real-estate man—"

"Realtor!"

"—some realtor that you hated came in—"

"I don't hate any realtor."

"But suppose you *did*!"

"I don't intend to suppose anything of the kind! There's plenty of fellows in my profession that stoop and hate their competitors, but if you were a little older and understood business, instead of always going to the movies and running around with a lot of fool girls with their dresses up to their knees and powdered and painted and rouged and God knows what all as if they were chorus-girls, then you'd know—and you'd suppose—that if there's any one thing that I stand for in the real-estate circles of Zenith, it is that we ought to always speak of each other only in the friendliest terms and institute a spirit of brotherhood and coöperation, and so I certainly can't suppose and I can't imagine my hating any realtor, not even that dirty, fourflushing society sneak, Cecil Rountree!"

"But—"

"And there's no If, And or But about it! But if I *were* going to lambaste somebody, I wouldn't require any fancy ducks or swimming-strokes before a mirror, or any of these doodads and flipflops! Suppose you were out some place and a fellow called you vile names. Think you'd want to box and jump around like a dancing-master? You'd just lay him out cold (at least I certainly hope any son of mine would!) and then you'd dust off your hands and go on about your business, and that's all there is to it, and you aren't going to have any boxing-lessons by mail, either!"

"Well but— Yes— I just wanted to show how many different kinds of correspondence-courses there are, instead of all the camembert they teach us in the High."

"But I thought they taught boxing in the school gymnasium."

"That's different. They stick you up there and some big stiff amuses himself pounding the stuffin's out of you before you have a chance to learn. Hunka! Not any! But anyway— Listen to some of these others."

The advertisements were truly philanthropic. One of them bore the rousing headline: "Money! Money!! Money!!!" The second announced that "Mr. P. R., formerly making only eighteen a week in a barber shop, writes to us that since taking our course he is now pulling down $5,000 as an Osteovitalic Physician;" and the third that "Miss J. L., recently a wrapper in a store, is now getting Ten Real Dollars a day teaching our Hindu System of Vibratory Breathing and Mental Control."

Ted had collected fifty or sixty announcements, from annual referencebooks, from Sunday School periodicals, fiction-magazines, and journals of discussion. One benefactor implored, "Don't be a Wallflower—Be More Popular and Make More Money—You Can Ukulele or Sing Yourself into Society! By the secret principles of a Newly Discovered System of Music Teaching, any one—man, lady or child—can, without tiresome exercises, special training or long drawn out study, and without waste of time, money or energy, learn to play by note, piano, banjo, cornet, clarinet, saxophone, violin or drum, and learn sight-singing."

The next, under the wistful appeal "Finger Print Detectives Wanted— Big Incomes!" confided: "YOU red-blooded men and women—this is the PROFESSION you have been looking for. There's MONEY in it, BIG money, and that rapid change of scene, that entrancing and compelling interest and fascination, which your active mind and adventurous spirit crave. Think of being the chief figure and directing factor in solving strange mysteries and baffling crimes. This wonderful profession brings you into contact with influential men on the basis of equality, and often calls upon you to travel everywhere, maybe to distant lands—all expenses paid. NO SPECIAL EDUCATION REQUIRED."

"Oh, boy! I guess that wins the fire-brick necklace! Wouldn't it be swell to travel everywhere and nab some famous crook!" whooped Ted.

"Well, I don't think much of that. Doggone likely to get hurt. Still, that music-study stunt might be pretty fair, though. There's no reason why, if efficiency-experts put their minds to it the way they have to routing products in a factory, they couldn't figure out some scheme so a person wouldn't have to monkey with all this practising and exercises that you get in music." Babbitt was impressed, and he had a delightful parental feeling that they two, the men of the family, understood each other.

He listened to the notices of mail-box universities which taught Shortstory Writing and Improving the Memory, Motion-picture-acting and Developing the Soul-power, Banking and Spanish, Chiropody and Photography, Electrical Engineering and Window-trimming, Poultry-raising and Chemistry.

"Well—well—" Babbitt sought for adequate expression of his admiration. "I'm a son of a gun! I knew this correspondence-school business had become a mighty profitable game—makes suburban real-estate look like two cents!—but I didn't realize it'd got to be such a reg'lar key-industry! Must rank right up with groceries and movies. Always figured somebody'd come along with the brains to not leave education to a lot of bookworms and impractical theorists but make a big thing out of it. Yes, I can see how a lot of these courses might interest you. I must ask the fellows at the Athletic if they ever realized— But same time, Ted, you know how advertisers, I mean some advertisers, exaggerate. I don't know as they'd be able to jam you through these courses as fast as they claim they can."

"Oh sure, Dad; of course." Ted had the immense and joyful maturity of a boy who is respectfully listened to by his elders. Babbitt concentrated on him with grateful affection:

"I can see what an influence these courses might have on the whole educational works. Course I'd never admit it publicly—fellow like myself, a State U. graduate, it's only decent and patriotic for him to blow his horn and boost the Alma Mater—but 'smatter of fact, there's a whole lot of valuable time lost even at the U., studying poetry and French and subjects that never brought in anybody a cent. I don't know but what maybe these correspondence-courses might prove to be one of the most important American inventions.

"Trouble with a lot of folks is: they're so blame material; they don't see the spiritual and mental side of American supremacy; they think that inventions like the telephone and the areoplane and wireless—no, that was a Wop invention, but anyway: they think these mechanical improvements are all that we stand for; whereas to a real thinker, he sees that spiritual and, uh, dominating movements like Efficiency, and Rotarianism, and Prohibition, and Democracy are what compose our deepest and truest wealth. And maybe this new principle in education-at-home may be another—may be another factor. I tell you, Ted, we've got to have Vision—"

"I think those correspondence-courses are terrible!"

The philosophers gasped. It was Mrs. Babbitt who had made this discord in their spiritual harmony, and one of Mrs. Babbitt's virtues was that, except during dinner-parties, when she was transformed into a raging hostess, she took care of the house and didn't bother the males by thinking. She went on firmly:

"It sounds awful to me, the way they coax those poor young folks to think they're learning something, and nobody 'round to help them and— You two learn so quick, but me, I always was slow. But just the same—"

Babbitt attended to her: "Nonsense! Get just as much, studying at home. You don't think a fellow learns any more because he blows in his father's hard-earned money and sits around in Morris chairs in a swell Harvard dormitory with pictures and shields and table-covers and those doodads, do you? I tell you, I'm a college man—I *know!* There is one objection you might make though. I certainly do protest against any effort to get a lot of fellows out of barber shops and factories into the professions. They're too crowded already, and what'll we do for workmen if all those fellows go and get educated?"

Ted was leaning back, smoking a cigarette without reproof. He was, for the moment, sharing the high thin air of Babbitt's speculation as though he were Paul Riesling or even Dr. Howard Littlefield. He hinted:

"Well, what do you think then, Dad? Wouldn't it be a good idea if I could go off to China or some peppy place, and study engineering or something by mail?"

"No, and I'll tell you why, son. I've found out it's a mighty nice thing to be able to say you're a B.A. Some client that doesn't know what you are and thinks you're just a plug business man, he gets to shooting off his mouth about economics or literature or foreign trade conditions, and you just ease in something like, 'When I was in college—course I got my B.A. in sociology and all that junk—' Oh, it puts an awful crimp in their style! But there wouldn't be any class to saying 'I got the degree of Stamp-licker from the Bezuzus Mail-order University!' You see— My dad was a pretty good old coot, but he never had much style to him, and I had to work darn hard to earn my way through college. Well, it's been worth it, to be able to associate with the finest gentlemen in Zenith, at the clubs and so on, and I wouldn't want you to drop out of the gentlemen class—the class that are just as red-blooded as the Common People but still have power and personality. It would kind of hurt me if you did that, old man!"

"I know, Dad! Sure! All right. I'll stick to it. Say! Gosh! Gee whiz! I forgot all about those kids I was going to take to the chorus rehearsal. I'll have to duck!"

"But you haven't done all your home-work."

"Do it first thing in the morning."

"Well—"

Six times in the past sixty days Babbitt had stormed, "You will not 'do it first thing in the morning'! You'll do it right now!" but to-night he said, "Well, better hustle," and his smile was the rare shy radiance he kept for Paul Riesling.

### IV

"Ted's a good boy," he said to Mrs. Babbitt.

"Oh, he is!"

"Who's these girls he's going to pick up? Are they nice decent girls?"

"I don't know. Oh dear, Ted never tells me anything any more. I don't understand what's come over the children of this generation. I used to have to tell Papa and Mama everything, but seems like the children to-day have just slipped away from all control."

"I hope they're decent girls. Course Ted's no longer a kid, and I wouldn't want him to, uh, get mixed up and everything."

"George: I wonder if you oughtn't to take him aside and tell him about— Things!" She blushed and lowered her eyes.

"Well, I don't know. Way I figure it, Myra, no sense suggesting a lot of Things to a boy's mind. Think up enough devilment by himself. But I wonder— It's kind of a hard question. Wonder what Littlefield thinks about it?"

"Course Papa agrees with you. He says all this Instruction—is— He says 'tisn't decent."

"Oh, he does, does he! Well, let me tell you that whatever Henry T. Thompson thinks—about morals, I mean, though course you can't beat the old duffer—"

"Why, what a way to talk of Papa!"

"—simply can't beat him at getting in on the ground floor of a deal, but let me tell you whenever he springs any ideas about higher things and education, then I know I think just the opposite. You may not regard me as any great brain-shark, but believe me, I'm a regular college president, compared with Henry T.! Yes sir, by golly, I'm going to take Ted aside and tell him why I lead a strictly moral life."

"Oh, will you? When?"

"When? When? What's the use of trying to pin me down to When and Why and Where and How and When? That's the trouble with women, that's why they don't make high-class executives; they haven't any sense of diplomacy. When the proper opportunity and occasion arises so it just comes in natural, why then I'll have a friendly little talk with him and—and— Was that Tinka hollering up-stairs? She ought to been asleep, long ago."

He prowled through the living-room, and stood in the sun-parlor, that glass-walled room of wicker chairs and swinging couch in which they loafed on Sunday afternoons. Outside, only the lights of Doppelbrau's house and the dim presence of Babbitt's favorite elm broke the softness of April night.

"Good visit with the boy. Getting over feeling cranky, way I did this morning. And restless. Though, by golly, I will have a few days alone with Paul in Maine! . . . That devil Zilla! . . . But . . . Ted's all right. Whole family all right. And good business. Not many fellows make four hundred and fifty bucks, practically half of a thousand dollars, easy as I did to-day! Maybe when we all get to rowing it's just as much my fault as it is theirs. Oughtn't to get grouchy like I do. But— Wish I'd been a pioneer, same as my grand-dad. But then, wouldn't have a house like this. I— Oh, gosh, *I don't know!*"

He thought moodily of Paul Riesling, of their youth together, of the girls they had known.

When Babbitt had graduated from the State University, twenty-four years ago, he had intended to be a lawyer. He had been a ponderous debater in college; he felt that he was an orator; he saw himself becoming governor of the state. While he read law he worked as a real-estate salesman. He saved money, lived in a boarding-house, supped on poached egg on hash. The lively Paul Riesling (who was certainly going off to Europe to study violin, next month or next year) was his refuge till Paul was bespelled by Zilla

Colbeck, who laughed and danced and drew men after her plump and gaily wagging finger.

Babbitt's evenings were barren then, and he found comfort only in Paul's second cousin, Myra Thompson, a sleek and gentle girl who showed her capacity by agreeing with the ardent young Babbitt that of course he was going to be governor some day. Where Zilla mocked him as a country boy, Myra said indignantly that he was ever so much solider than the young dandies who had been born in the great city of Zenith—an ancient settlement in 1897, one hundred and five years old, with two hundred thousand population, the queen and wonder of all the state and, to the Catawba boy, George Babbitt, so vast and thunderous and luxurious that he was flattered to know a girl ennobled by birth in Zenith.

Of love there was no talk between them. He knew that if he was to study law he could not marry for years; and Myra was distinctly a Nice Girl—one didn't kiss her, one didn't "think about her that way at all" unless one was going to marry her. But she was a dependable companion. She was always ready to go skating, walking; always content to hear his discourses on the great things he was going to do, the distressed poor whom he would defend against the Unjust Rich, the speeches he would make at Banquets, the inexactitudes of popular thought which he would correct.

One evening when he was weary and soft-minded, he saw that she had been weeping. She had been left out of a party given by Zilla. Somehow her head was on his shoulder and he was kissing away the tears—and she raised her head to say trustingly, "Now that we're engaged, shall we be married soon or shall we wait?"

Engaged? It was his first hint of it. His affection for this brown tender woman thing went cold and fearful, but he could not hurt her, could not abuse her trust. He mumbled something about waiting, and escaped. He walked for an hour, trying to find a way of telling her that it was a mistake. Often, in the month after, he got near to telling her, but it was pleasant to have a girl in his arms, and less and less could he insult her by blurting that he didn't love her. He himself had no doubt. The evening before his marriage was an agony, and the morning wild with the desire to flee.

She made him what is known as a Good Wife. She was loyal, industrious, and at rare times merry. She passed from a feeble disgust at their closer relations into what promised to be ardent affection, but it drooped into bored routine. Yet she existed only for him and for the children, and she was as sorry, as worried as himself, when he gave up the law and trudged on in a rut of listing real estate.

"Poor kid, she hasn't had much better time than I have," Babbitt reflected, standing in the dark sun-parlor. "But— I wish I could 've had a whirl at law and politics. Seen what I could do. Well— Maybe I've made more money as it is."

He returned to the living-room but before he settled down he smoothed his wife's hair, and she glanced up, happy and somewhat surprised.

# 7

He solemnly finished the last copy of the *American Magazine*, while his wife sighed, laid away her darning, and looked enviously at the lingerie designs in a women's magazine. The room was very still.

It was a room which observed the best Floral Heights standards. The gray walls were divided into artificial paneling by strips of white-enameled pine. From the Babbitts' former house had come two much-carved rocking-chairs, but the other chairs were new, very deep and restful, upholstered in blue and gold-striped velvet. A blue velvet davenport faced the fireplace, and behind it was a cherrywood table and a tall piano-lamp with a shade of golden silk. (Two out of every three houses in Floral Heights had before the fireplace a davenport, a mahogany table real or imitation, and a piano-lamp or a reading-lamp with a shade of yellow or rose silk.)

On the table was a runner of gold-threaded Chinese fabric, four magazines, a silver box containing cigarette-crumbs, and three "gift-books"—large, expensive editions of fairy-tales illustrated by English artists and as yet unread by any Babbitt save Tinka.

In a corner by the front windows was a large cabinet Victrola. (Eight out of every nine Floral Heights houses had a cabinet phonograph.)

Among the pictures, hung in the exact center of each gray panel, were a red and black imitation English hunting-print, an anemic imitation boudoir-print with a French caption of whose morality Babbitt had always been rather suspicious, and a "hand-colored" photograph of a Colonial room—rag rug, maiden spinning, cat demure before a white fireplace. (Nineteen out of every twenty houses in Floral Heights had either a hunting-print, a *Madame Fait la Toilette* print, a colored photograph of a New England house, a photograph of a Rocky Mountain, or all four.)

It was a room as superior in comfort to the "parlor" of Babbitt's boyhood as his motor was superior to his father's buggy. Though there was nothing in the room that was interesting, there was nothing that was offensive. It was as neat, and as negative, as a block of artificial ice. The fireplace was unsoftened by downy ashes or by sooty brick; the brass fire-irons were of immaculate polish; and the grenadier andirons were like samples in a shop, desolate, unwanted, lifeless things of commerce.

Against the wall was a piano, with another piano-lamp, but no one used it save Tinka. The hard briskness of the phonograph contented them; their store of jazz records made them feel wealthy and cultured; and all they knew of creating music was the nice adjustment of a bamboo needle. The books on the table were unspotted and laid in rigid parallels; not one corner of the carpet-rug was curled; and nowhere was there a hockey-stick, a torn picture-book, an old cap, or a gregarious and disorganizing dog.

II

At home, Babbitt never read with absorption. He was concentrated enough at the office but here he crossed his legs and fidgeted. When his story was interesting he read the best, that is the funniest, paragraphs to his wife; when it did not hold him he coughed, scratched his ankles and his right ear, thrust his left thumb into his vest pocket, jingled his silver, whirled the cigar-cutter and the keys on one end of his watch-chain, yawned, rubbed his nose, and found errands to do. He went upstairs to put on his slippers—his elegant slippers of seal-brown, shaped like medieval shoes. He brought up an apple from the barrel which stood by the trunk-closet in the basement.

"An apple a day keeps the doctor away," he enlightened Mrs. Babbitt, for quite the first time in fourteen hours.

"That's so."

"An apple is Nature's best regulator."

"Yes, it—"

"Trouble with women is, they never have sense enough to form regular habits."

"Well, I—"

"Always nibbling and eating between meals."

"George!" She looked up from her reading. "Did you have a light lunch to-day, like you were going to? I did!"

This malicious and unprovoked attack astounded him. "Well, maybe it wasn't as light as— Went to lunch with Paul and didn't have much chance to diet. Oh, you needn't to grin like a chessy cat! If it wasn't for me watching out and keeping an eye on our diet— I'm the only member of this family that appreciates the value of oatmeal for breakfast. I—"

She stooped over her story while he piously sliced and gulped down the apple, discoursing:

"One thing I've done: cut down my smoking.

"Had kind of a run-in with Graff in the office. He's getting too darn fresh. I'll stand for a good deal, but once in a while I got to assert my authority, and I jumped him. 'Stan,' I said— Well, I told him just exactly where he got off.

"Funny kind of a day. Makes you feel restless.

"Welllllllll, uh—" That sleepiest sound in the world, the terminal yawn. Mrs. Babbitt yawned with it, and looked grateful as he droned, "How about going to bed, eh? Don't suppose Rone and Ted will be in till all hours. Yep, funny kind of a day; not terribly warm but yet— Gosh, I'd like— Some day I'm going to take a long motor trip."

"Yes, we'd enjoy that," she yawned.

He looked away from her as he realized that he did not wish to have her go with him. As he locked doors and tried windows and set the heat regulator so that the furnace-drafts would open automatically in the morning, he sighed a little, heavy with a lonely feeling which perplexed and frightened him. So absent-minded was he that he could not remember which window-catches he had inspected, and through the darkness, fumbling at unseen perilous chairs, he crept back to try them all over again. His feet were loud on the steps as he clumped up-stairs at the end of this great and treacherous day of veiled rebellions.

III

Before breakfast he always reverted to up-state village boyhood, and shrank from the complex urban demands of shaving, bathing, deciding whether the current shirt was clean enough for another day. Whenever he stayed home in the evening he went to bed early, and thriftily got ahead in those dismal duties. It was his luxurious custom to shave while sitting snugly in a tubful of hot water. He may be viewed to-night as a plump, smooth, pink, baldish, podgy goodman, robbed of the importance of spectacles, squatting in breast-high water, scraping his lather-smeared cheeks with a safety-razor like a tiny lawn-mower, and with melancholy dignity clawing through the water to recover a slippery and active piece of soap.

He was lulled to dreaming by the caressing warmth. The light fell on the inner surface of the tub in a pattern of delicate wrinkled lines which slipped with a green sparkle over the curving porcelain as the clear water trembled. Babbitt lazily watched it; noted that along the silhouette of his legs against the radiance on the bottom of the tub, the shadows of the air-bubbles clinging to the hairs were reproduced as strange jungle mosses. He patted the water, and the reflected light capsized and leaped and volleyed. He was content and childish. He played. He shaved a swath down the calf of one plump leg.

The drain-pipe was dripping, a dulcet and lively song: drippety drip drip dribble, drippety drip drip drip. He was enchanted by it. He looked at the solid tub, the beautiful nickel taps, the tiled walls of the room, and felt virtuous in the possession of this splendor.

He roused himself and spoke gruffly to his bath-things. "Come here! You've done enough fooling!" he reproved the treacherous soap, and defied the scratchy nail-brush with "Oh, you would, would you!" He soaped himself, and rinsed himself, and austerely rubbed himself; he noted a hole in the Turkish towel, and meditatively thrust a finger through it, and marched back to the bedroom, a grave and unbending citizen.

There was a moment of gorgeous abandon, a flash of melodrama such as he found in traffic-driving, when he laid out a clean collar, discovered that it was frayed in front, and tore it up with a magnificent yeeeeeing sound.

Most important of all was the preparation of his bed and the sleeping-porch.

It is not known whether he enjoyed his sleeping-porch because of the fresh air or because it was the standard thing to have a sleeping-porch.

Just as he was an Elk, a Booster, and a member of the Chamber of Commerce, just as the priests of the Presbyterian Church determined his every religious belief and the senators who controlled the Republican Party decided in little smoky rooms in Washington what he should think about disarmament, tariff, and Germany, so did the large national advertisers fix the surface of his life, fix what he believed to be his individuality. These standard advertised wares—toothpastes, socks, tires, cameras, instantaneous hot-water heaters—were his symbols and proofs of excellence; at first the signs, then the substitutes, for joy and passion and wisdom.

But none of these advertised tokens of financial and social success was more significant than a sleeping-porch with a sun-parlor below.

The rites of preparing for bed were elaborate and unchanging. The blankets had to be tucked in at the foot of his cot. (Also, the reason why the maid hadn't tucked in the blankets had to be discussed with Mrs. Babbitt.) The rag rug was adjusted so that his bare feet would strike it when he arose in the morning. The alarm clock was wound. The hot-water bottle was filled and placed precisely two feet from the bottom of the cot.

These tremendous undertakings yielded to his determination; one by one they were announced to Mrs. Babbitt and smashed through to accomplishment. At last his brow cleared, and in his "Gnight!" rang virile power. But there was yet need of courage. As he sank into sleep, just at the first exquisite relaxation, the Doppelbrau car came home. He bounced into wakefulness, lamenting, "Why the devil can't some people never get to bed at a reasonable hour?" So familiar was he with the process of putting up his own car that he awaited each step like an able executioner condemned to his own rack.

The car insultingly cheerful on the driveway. The car door opened and banged shut, then the garage door slid open, grating on the sill, and the car door again. The motor raced for the climb up into the garage and raced once more, explosively, before it was shut off. A final opening and slamming of the car door. Silence then, a horrible silence filled with waiting, till the leisurely Mr. Doppelbrau had examined the state of his tires and had at last shut the garage door. Instantly, for Babbitt, a blessed state of oblivion.

IV

At that moment in the city of Zenith, Horace Updike was making love to Lucile McKelvey in her mauve drawing-room on Royal Ridge, after their return from a lecture by an eminent English novelist. Updike was Zenith's professional bachelor; a slim-waisted man of forty-six with an effeminate voice and taste in flowers, cretonnes, and flappers. Mrs. McKelvey was red-haired, creamy, discontented, exquisite, rude, and honest. Updike tried his invariable first maneuver—touching her nervous wrist.

"Don't be an idiot!" she said.

"Do you mind awfully?"

"No! That's what I mind!"

He changed to conversation. He was famous at conversation. He spoke reasonably of psychoanalysis, Long Island polo, and the Ming platter he had found in Vancouver. She promised to meet him in Deauville, the coming summer, "though," she sighed, "it's becoming too dreadfully banal; nothing but Americans and frowsy English baronesses."

And at that moment in Zenith, a cocaine-runner and a prostitute were drinking cocktails in Healey Hanson's saloon on Front Street. Since national prohibition was now in force, and since Zenith was notoriously law-abiding, they were compelled to keep the cocktails innocent by drinking them out of tea-cups. The lady threw her cup at the cocaine-runner's head. He worked his revolver out of the pocket in his sleeve, and casually murdered her.

At that moment in Zenith, two men sat in a laboratory. For thirty-seven hours now they had been working on a report of their investigations of synthetic rubber.

At that moment in Zenith, there was a conference of four union officials as to whether the twelve thousand coal-miners within a hundred miles of the city should strike. Of these men one resembled a testy and prosperous grocer, one a Yankee carpenter, one a soda-clerk, and one a Russian Jewish actor. The Russian Jew quoted Kautsky, Gene Debs, and Abraham Lincoln.

At that moment a G. A. R. veteran was dying. He had come from the Civil War straight to a farm which, though it was officially within the city-limits of Zenith, was primitive as the backwoods. He had never ridden in a motor car, never seen a bath-tub, never read any book save the Bible, Mc-Guffey's readers, and religious tracts; and he believed that the earth is flat, that the English are the Lost Ten Tribes of Israel, and that the United States is a democracy.

At that moment the steel and cement town which composed the factory of the Pullmore Tractor Company of Zenith was running on night shift to fill an order of tractors for the Polish army. It hummed like a million bees, glared through its wide windows like a volcano. Along the high wire fences, searchlights played on cinder-lined yards, switch-tracks, and armed guards on patrol.

At that moment Mike Monday was finishing a meeting. Mr. Monday, the distinguished evangelist, the best-known Protestant pontiff in America, had once been a prize-fighter. Satan had not dealt justly with him. As a prize-fighter he gained nothing but his crooked nose, his celebrated vocabulary, and his stage-presence. The service of the Lord had been more profitable. He was about to retire with a fortune. It had been well earned, for, to quote his last report, "Rev. Mr. Monday, the Prophet with a Punch, has shown that he is the world's greatest salesman of salvation, and that by efficient organization the overhead of spiritual regeneration may be kept down to an unprecedented rock-bottom basis. He has converted over two hundred thousand lost and priceless souls at an average cost of less than ten dollars a head."

Of the larger cities of the land, only Zenith had hesitated to submit its vices to Mike Monday and his expert reclamation corps. The more enterprising organizations of the city had voted to invite him—Mr. George F. Babbitt had once praised him in a speech at the Boosters' Club. But there was opposition from certain Episcopalian and Congregationalist ministers, those renegades whom Mr. Monday so finely called "a bunch of gospelpushers with dish-water instead of blood, a gang of squealers that need more dust on the knees of their pants and more hair on their skinny old chests." This opposition had been crushed when the secretary of the Chamber of Commerce had reported to a committee of manufacturers that in every city where he had appeared, Mr. Monday had turned the minds of workmen from wages and hours to higher things, and thus averted strikes. He was immediately invited.

An expense fund of forty thousand dollars had been underwritten; out on the County Fair Grounds a Mike Monday Tabernacle had been erected, to seat fifteen thousand people. In it the prophet was at this moment concluding his message:

"There's a lot of smart college professors and tea-guzzling slobs in this burg that say I'm a roughneck and a never-wuzzer and my knowledge of history is not-yet. Oh, there's a gang of woolly-whiskered book-lice that think they know more than Almighty God, and prefer a lot of Hun science and smutty German criticism to the straight and simple Word of God. Oh, there's a swell bunch of Lizzie boys and lemon-suckers and pie-faces and infidels and beer-bloated scribblers that love to fire off their filthy mouths and yip that Mike Monday is vulgar and full of mush. Those pups are saying now that I hog the gospel-show, that I'm in it for the coin. Well, now listen, folks! I'm going to give those birds a chance! They can stand right up here and tell me to my face that I'm a galoot and a liar and a hick! Only if they do—if they do!—don't faint with surprise if some of those rum-dumm liars get one good swift poke from Mike, with all the kick of God's Flaming Righteousness behind the wallop! Well, come on, folks! Who says it? Who says Mike Monday is a fourflush and a yahoo? Huh? Don't I see anybody standing up? Well, there you are! Now I guess the folks in this man's town will quit listening to all this kyoodling from behind the fence; I guess you'll quit listening to the guys that pan and roast and kick and beef, and vomit out filthy atheism; and all of you 'll come in, with every grain of pep and reverence you got, and boost all together for Jesus Christ and his everlasting mercy and tenderness!"

v

At that moment Seneca Doane, the radical lawyer, and Dr. Kurt Yavitch, the histologist (whose report on the destruction of epithelial cells under radium had made the name of Zenith known in Munich, Prague, and Rome), were talking in Doane's library.

"Zenith's a city with gigantic power—gigantic buildings, gigantic machines, gigantic transportation," meditated Doane.

"I hate your city. It has standardized all the beauty out of life. It is one big railroad station—with all the people taking tickets for the best cemeteries," Dr. Yavitch said placidly.

Doane roused. "I'm hanged if it is! You make me sick, Kurt, with your perpetual whine about 'standardization.' Don't you suppose any other nation is 'standardized?' Is anything more standardized than England, with every house that can afford it having the same muffins at the same tea-hour, and every retired general going to exactly the same evensong at the same gray stone church with a square tower, and every golfing prig in Harris tweeds saying 'Right you are!' to every other prosperous ass? Yet I love England. And for standardization—just look at the sidewalk cafés in France and the love-making in Italy!

"Standardization is excellent, *per se*. When I buy an Ingersoll watch or a Ford, I get a better tool for less money, and I know precisely what I'm getting, and that leaves me more time and energy to be individual in. And— I remember once in London I saw a picture of an American suburb, in a toothpaste ad on the back of the *Saturday Evening Post*—an elm-lined snowy street of these new houses, Georgian some of 'em, or with low raking roofs and— The kind of street you'd find here in Zenith, say in Floral Heights. Open. Trees. Grass. And I was homesick! There's no other country in the world that has such pleasant houses. And I don't care if they *are* standardized. It's a corking standard!

"No, what I fight in Zenith is standardization of thought, and, of course, the traditions of competition. The real villains of the piece are the clean, kind, industrious Family Men who use every known brand of trickery and cruelty to insure the prosperity of their cubs. The worst thing about these fellows is that they're so good and, in their work at least, so intelligent. You can't hate them properly, and yet their standardized minds are the enemy.

"Then this boosting— Sneakingly I have a notion that Zenith is a better place to live in than Manchester or Glasgow or Lyons or Berlin or Turin—"

"It is not, and I have lift in most of them," murmured Dr. Yavitch.

"Well, matter of taste. Personally, I prefer a city with a future so unknown that it excites my imagination. But what I particularly want—"

"You," said Dr. Yavitch, "are a middle-road liberal, and you haven't the slightest idea what you want. I, being a revolutionist, know exactly what I want—and what I want now is a drink."

## VI

At that moment in Zenith, Jake Offutt, the politician, and Henry T. Thompson were in conference. Offutt suggested, "The thing to do is to get your fool son-in-law, Babbitt, to put it over. He's one of these patriotic guys. When he grabs a piece of property for the gang, he makes it look like we were dyin' of love for the dear peepul, and I do love to buy respectability— reasonable. Wonder how long we can keep it up, Hank? We're safe as long as the good little boys like George Babbitt and all the nice respectable labor-leaders think you and me are rugged patriots. There's swell pickings for an honest politician here, Hank: a whole city working to provide cigars and fried chicken and dry martinis for us, and rallying to our banner with indignation, oh, fierce indignation, whenever some squealer like this fellow Seneca Doane comes along! Honest, Hank, a smart codger like me ought to be ashamed of himself if he didn't milk cattle like them, when they come around mooing for it! But the Traction gang can't get away with grand larceny like it used to. I wonder when— Hank, I wish we could fix some way to run this fellow Seneca Doane out of town. It's him or us!"

At that moment in Zenith, three hundred and forty or fifty thousand Ordinary People were asleep, a vast unpenetrated shadow. In the slum beyond the railroad tracks, a young man who for six months had sought work turned on the gas and killed himself and his wife.

At that moment Lloyd Mallam, the poet, owner of the Hafiz Book Shop, was finishing a rondeau to show how diverting was life amid the feuds of medieval Florence, but how dull it was in so obvious a place as Zenith.

And at that moment George F. Babbitt turned ponderously in bed—the last turn, signifying that he'd had enough of this worried business of falling asleep and was about it in earnest.

Instantly he was in the magic dream. He was somewhere among unknown people who laughed at him. He slipped away, ran down the paths of a midnight garden, and at the gate the fairy child was waiting. Her dear and tranquil hand caressed his cheek. He was gallant and wise and well-beloved; warm ivory were her arms; and beyond perilous moors the brave sea glittered.

# 8

The great events of Babbitt's spring were the secret buying of real-estate options in Linton for certain street-traction officials, before the public announcement that the Linton Avenue Car Line would be extended, and a dinner which was, as he rejoiced to his wife, not only "a regular society spread but a real sure-enough highbrow affair, with some of the keenest intellects and the brightest bunch of little women in town." It was so absorbing an occasion that he almost forgot his desire to run off to Maine with Paul Riesling.

Though he had been born in the village of Catawba, Babbitt had risen to that metropolitan social plane on which hosts have as many as four people at dinner without planning it for more than an evening or two. But a dinner of twelve, with flowers from the florist's and all the cut-glass out, staggered even the Babbitts.

For two weeks they studied, debated, and arbitrated the list of guests.

Babbitt marveled, "Of course we're up-to-date ourselves, but still, think of us entertaining a famous poet like Chum Frink, a fellow that on nothing but a poem or so every day and just writing a few advertisements pulls down fifteen thousand berries a year!"

"Yes, and Howard Littlefield. Do you know, the other evening Eunice told me her papa speaks three languages!" said Mrs. Babbitt.

"Huh! That's nothing! So do I—American, baseball, and poker!"

"I don't think it's nice to be funny about a matter like that. Think how wonderful it must be to speak three languages, and so useful and— And with people like that, I don't see why we invite the Orville Joneses."

"Well now, Orville is a mighty up-and-coming fellow!"

"Yes, I know, but— A laundry!"

"I'll admit a laundry hasn't got the class of poetry or real estate, but just the same, Orvy is mighty deep. Ever start him spieling about gardening? Say, that fellow can tell you the name of every kind of tree, and some of their Greek and Latin names too! Besides, we owe the Joneses a dinner. Besides, gosh, we got to have some boob for audience, when a bunch of hot-air artists like Frink and Littlefield get going."

"Well, dear—I meant to speak of this—I do think that as host you ought to sit back and listen, and let your guests have a chance to talk once in a while!"

"Oh, you do, do you! Sure! I talk all the time! And I'm just a business man—oh sure!—I'm no Ph.D. like Littlefield, and no poet, and I haven't anything to spring! Well, let me tell you, just the other day your darn Chum Frink comes up to me at the club begging to know what I thought about the Springfield school-bond issue. And who told him? I did! You bet your life I told him! Little me! I certainly did! He came up and asked me, and I told him all about it! You bet! And he was darn glad to listen to me and— Duty as a host! I guess I know my duty as a host and let me tell you—"

In fact, the Orville Joneses were invited.

## II

On the morning of the dinner, Mrs. Babbitt was restive.

"Now, George, I want you to be sure and be home early to-night. Remember, you have to dress."

"Uh-huh. I see by the *Advocate* that the Presbyterian General Assembly has voted to quit the Interchurch World Movement. That—"

"George! Did you hear what I said? You must be home in time to dress to-night."

"Dress? Hell! I'm dressed now! Think I'm going down to the office in my B.V.D.'s?"

"I will not have you talking indecently before the children! And you do have to put on your dinner-jacket!"

"I guess you mean my Tux. I tell you, of all the doggone nonsensical nuisances that was ever invented—"

Three minutes later, after Babbitt had wailed, "Well, I don't know whether I'm going to dress or *not*" in a manner which showed that he was going to dress, the discussion moved on.

"Now, George, you mustn't forget to call in at Vecchia's on the way home and get the ice cream. Their delivery-wagon is broken down, and I don't want to trust them to send it by—"

"All right! You told me that before breakfast!"

"Well, I don't want you to forget. I'll be working my head off all day long, training the girl that's to help with the dinner—"

"All nonsense, anyway, hiring an extra girl for the feed. Matilda could perfectly well—"

"—and I have to go out and buy the flowers, and fix them, and set the table, and order the salted almonds, and look at the chickens, and arrange for the children to have their supper upstairs and— And I simply must depend on you to go to Vecchia's for the ice cream."

"All riiiiight! Gosh, I'm going to get it!"

"All you have to do is to go in and say you want the ice cream that Mrs. Babbitt ordered yesterday by 'phone, and it will be all ready for you."

At ten-thirty she telephoned to him not to forget the ice cream from Vecchia's.

He was surprised and blasted then by a thought. He wondered whether Floral Heights dinners were worth the hideous toil involved. But he repented the sacrilege in the excitement of buying the materials for cocktails.

Now this was the manner of obtaining alcohol under the reign of righteousness and prohibition:

He drove from the severe rectangular streets of the modern business center into the tangled byways of Old Town—jagged blocks filled with sooty warehouses and lofts; on into The Arbor, once a pleasant orchard but now a morass of lodging-houses, tenements, and brothels. Exquisite shivers chilled his spine and stomach, and he looked at every policeman with intense innocence, as one who loved the law, and admired the Force, and longed to stop and play with them. He parked his car a block from Healey Hanson's saloon, worrying, "Well, rats, if anybody did see me, they'd think I was here on business."

He entered a place curiously like the saloons of ante-prohibition days, with a long greasy bar with sawdust in front and streaky mirror behind, a pine table at which a dirty old man dreamed over a glass of something which resembled whisky, and with two men at the bar, drinking something which resembled beer, and giving that impression of forming a large crowd which two men always give in a saloon. The bartender, a tall pale Swede with a diamond in his lilac scarf, stared at Babbitt as he stalked plumply up to the bar and whispered, "I'd, uh— Friend of Hanson's sent me here. Like to get some gin."

The bartender gazed down on him in the manner of an outraged bishop. "I guess you got the wrong place, my friend. We sell nothing but soft drinks here." He cleaned the bar with a rag which would itself have done with a little cleaning, and glared across his mechanically moving elbow.

The old dreamer at the table petitioned the bartender, "Say, Oscar, listen."

Oscar did not listen.

"Aw, say, Oscar, listen, will yuh? Say, lis-sen!"

The decayed and drowsy voice of the loafer, the agreeable stink of beer-dregs, threw a spell of inanition over Babbitt. The bartender moved grimly toward the crowd of two men. Babbitt followed him as delicately as a cat, and wheedled, "Say, Oscar, I want to speak to Mr. Hanson."

"Whajuh wanta see him for?"

"I just want to talk to him. Here's my card."

It was a beautiful card, an engraved card, a card in the blackest black and the sharpest red, announcing that Mr. George F. Babbitt was Estates, Insurance, Rents. The bartender held it as though it weighed ten pounds, and read it as though it were a hundred words long. He did not bend from his episcopal dignity, but he growled, "I'll see if he's around."

From the back room he brought an immensely old young man, a quiet sharp-eyed man, in tan silk shirt, checked vest hanging open, and burning brown trousers—Mr. Healey Hanson. Mr. Hanson said only "Yuh?" but his implacable and contemptuous eyes queried Babbitt's soul, and he seemed not at all impressed by the new dark-gray suit for which (as he had admitted to every acquaintance at the Athletic Club) Babbitt had paid a hundred and twenty-five dollars.

"Glad meet you, Mr. Hanson. Say, uh— I'm George Babbitt of the Babbitt-Thompson Realty Company. I'm a great friend of Jake Offutt's."

"Well, what of it?"

"Say, uh, I'm going to have a party, and Jake told me you'd be able to fix me up with a little gin." In alarm, in obsequiousness, as Hanson's eyes grew more bored, "You telephone to Jake about me, if you want to."

Hanson answered by jerking his head to indicate the entrance to the back room, and strolled away. Babbitt melodramatically crept into an apartment containing four round tables, eleven chairs, a brewery calendar, and a smell. He waited. Thrice he saw Healey Hanson saunter through, humming, hands in pockets, ignoring him.

By this time Babbitt had modified his valiant morning vow, "I won't pay one cent over seven dollars a quart" to "I might pay ten." On Hanson's next weary entrance he besought, "Could you fix that up?" Hanson scowled, and grated, "Just a minute—Pete's sake—just a min-ute!" In growing meekness Babbitt went on waiting till Hanson casually reappeared with a quart of gin —what is euphemistically known as a quart—in his disdainful long white hands.

"Twelve bucks," he snapped.

"Say, uh, but say, cap'n, Jake thought you'd be able to fix me up for eight or nine a bottle."

"Nup. Twelve. This is the real stuff, smuggled from Canada. This is none o' your neutral spirits with a drop of juniper extract," the honest merchant said virtuously. "Twelve bones—if you want it. Course y' understand I'm just doing this anyway as a friend of Jake's."

"Sure! Sure! I understand!" Babbitt gratefully held out twelve dollars.

He felt honored by contact with greatness as Hanson yawned, stuffed the bills, uncounted, into his radiant vest, and swaggered away.

He had a number of titillations out of concealing the gin-bottle under his coat and out of hiding it in his desk. All afternoon he snorted and chuckled and gurgled over his ability to "give the Boys a real shot in the arm to-night." He was, in fact, so exhilarated that he was within a block of his house before he remembered that there was a certain matter, mentioned by his wife, of fetching ice cream from Vecchia's. He explained, "Well, darn it—" and drove back.

Vecchia was not a caterer, he was The Caterer of Zenith. Most coming-out parties were held in the white and gold ballroom of the Maison Vecchia; at all nice teas the guests recognized the five kinds of Vecchia sandwiches and the seven kinds of Vecchia cakes; and all really smart dinners ended, as on a resolving chord, in Vecchia Neapolitan ice cream in one of the three reliable molds—the melon mold, the round mold like a layer cake, and the long brick.

Vecchia's shop had pale blue woodwork, tracery of plaster roses, attendants in frilled aprons, and glass shelves of "kisses" with all the refinement that inheres in whites of eggs. Babbitt felt heavy and thick amid this professional daintiness, and as he waited for the ice cream he decided, with hot prickles at the back of his neck, that a girl customer was giggling at him. He went home in a touchy temper. The first thing he heard was his wife's agitated:

"George! *Did* you remember to go to Vecchia's and get the ice cream?"

"Say! Look here! Do I ever forget to do things?"

"Yes! Often!"

"Well now, it's darn seldom I do, and it certainly makes me tired, after going into a pink-tea joint like Vecchia's and having to stand around looking at a lot of half-naked young girls, all rouged up like they were sixty and eating a lot of stuff that simply ruins their stomachs—"

"Oh, it's too bad about you! I've noticed how you hate to look at pretty girls!"

With a jar Babbitt realized that his wife was too busy to be impressed by that moral indignation with which males rule the world, and he went humbly up-stairs to dress. He had an impression of a glorified dining-room, of cut-glass, candles, polished wood, lace, silver, roses. With the awed swelling of the heart suitable to so grave a business as giving a dinner, he slew the temptation to wear his plaited dress-shirt for a fourth time, took out an entirely fresh one, tightened his black bow, and rubbed his patent-leather pumps with a handkerchief. He glanced with pleasure at his garnet and silver studs. He smoothed and patted his ankles, transformed by silk socks from the sturdy shanks of George Babbitt to the elegant limbs of what is called a Clubman. He stood before the pier-glass, viewing his trim dinner-coat, his beautiful triple-braided trousers; and murmured in lyric beatitude, "By golly, I don't look so bad. I certainly don't look like Catawba. If the hicks back home could see me in this rig, they'd have a fit!"

He moved majestically down to mix the cocktails. As he chipped ice, as he squeezed oranges, as he collected vast stores of bottles, glasses, and spoons at the sink in the pantry, he felt as authoritative as the bartender at Healey Hanson's saloon. True, Mrs. Babbitt said he was under foot, and Matilda and the maid hired for the evening brushed by him, elbowed him, shrieked "Pleasopn door," as they tottered through with trays, but in this high moment he ignored them.

Besides the new bottle of gin, his cellar consisted of one half-bottle of Bourbon whisky, a quarter of a bottle of Italian vermouth, and approximately one hundred drops of orange bitters. He did not possess a cocktail-shaker. A shaker was proof of dissipation, the symbol of a Drinker, and Babbitt disliked being known as a Drinker even more than he liked a Drink. He mixed by pouring from an ancient gravy-boat into a handleless pitcher; he poured with a noble dignity, holding his alembics high beneath the powerful Mazda globe, his face hot, his shirt-front a glaring white, the copper sink a scoured red-gold.

He tasted the sacred essence. "Now, by golly, if that isn't pretty near one fine old cocktail! Kind of a Bronx, and yet like a Manhattan. Ummmmmm! Hey, Myra, want a little nip before the folks come?"

Bustling into the dining-room, moving each glass a quarter of an inch, rushing back with resolution implacable on her face, her gray and silver-lace party frock protected by a denim towel, Mrs. Babbitt glared at him, and rebuked him, "Certainly not!"

"Well," in a loose, jocose manner, "I think the old man will!"

The cocktail filled him with a whirling exhilaration behind which he was aware of devastating desires—to rush places in fast motors, to kiss girls, to sing, to be witty. He sought to regain his lost dignity by announcing to Matilda:

"I'm going to stick this pitcher of cocktails in the refrigerator. Be sure you don't upset any of 'em."

"Yeh."

"Well, be sure now. Don't go putting anything on this top shelf."

"Yeh."

"Well, be—" He was dizzy. His voice was thin and distant. "Whee!" With enormous impressiveness he commanded, "Well, be sure now," and minced into the safety of the living-room. He wondered whether he could persuade "as slow a bunch as Myra and the Littlefields to go some place aft' dinner and raise Cain and maybe dig up smore booze." He perceived that he had gifts of profligacy which had been neglected.

By the time the guests had come, including the inevitable late couple for whom the others waited with painful amiability, a great gray emptiness had replaced the purple swirling in Babbitt's head, and he had to force the tumultuous greetings suitable to a host on Floral Heights.

The guests were Howard Littlefield, the doctor of philosophy who furnished publicity and comforting economics to the Street Traction Company; Vergil Gunch, the coal-dealer, equally powerful in the Elks and in the Boosters' Club; Eddie Swanson, the agent for the Javelin Motor Car, who lived across the street; and Orville Jones, owner of the Lily White Laundry, which justly announced itself "the biggest, busiest, bulliest cleanerie shoppe in Zenith." But, naturally, the most distinguished of all was T. Cholmondeley Frink, who was not only the author of "Poemulations," which, syndicated daily in sixty-seven leading newspapers, gave him one of the largest audiences of any poet in the world, but also an optimistic lecturer and the creator of "Ads that Add." Despite the searching philosophy and high morality of his verses, they were humorous and easily understood by any child of twelve; and it added a neat air of pleasantry to them that they were set not as verse but as prose. Mr. Frink was known from Coast to Coast as "Chum."

With them were six wives, more or less—it was hard to tell, so early in the evening, as at first glance they all looked alike, and as they all said, "Oh, *isn't this nice!*" in the same tone of determined liveliness. To the eye, the men were less similar: Littlefield, a hedge-scholar, tall and horse-faced; Chum Frink, a trifle of a man with soft and mouse-like hair, advertising his profession as poet by a silk cord on his eye-glasses; Vergil Gunch, broad, with coarse black hair *en brosse*; Eddie Swanson, a bald and bouncing young man who showed his taste for elegance by an evening waistcoat of figured black silk with glass buttons; Orville Jones, a steady-looking, stubby, not very memorable person, with a hemp-colored toothbrush mustache. Yet they were all so well fed and clean, they all shouted " 'Evenin', Georgie!" with such robustness, that they seemed to be cousins, and the strange thing is that the longer one knew the women, the less alike they seemed; while the longer one knew the men, the more alike their bold patterns appeared.

The drinking of the cocktails was as canonical a rite as the mixing. The company waited, uneasily, hopefully, agreeing in a strained manner that the weather had been rather warm and slightly cold, but still Babbitt said nothing about drinks. They became despondent. But when the late couple (the Swansons) had arrived, Babbitt hinted, "Well, folks, do you think you could stand breaking the law a little?"

They looked at Chum Frink, the recognized lord of language. Frink pulled at his eye-glass cord as at a bell-rope, he cleared his throat and said that which was the custom:

"I'll tell you, George: I'm a law-abiding man, but they do say Verg Gunch is a regular yegg, and of course he's bigger 'n I am, and I just can't figure out what I'd do if he tried to force me into anything criminal!"

Gunch was roaring, "Well, I'll take a chance—" when Frink held up his hand and went on, "So if Verg and you insist, Georgie, I'll park my car on the wrong side of the street, because I take it for granted that's the crime you're hinting at!"

There was a great deal of laughter. Mrs. Jones asserted, "Mr. Frink is simply too killing! You'd think he was so innocent!"

Babbitt clamored, "How did you guess it, Chum? Well, you-all just wait a moment while I go out and get the—keys to your cars!" Through a froth of merriment he brought the shining promise, the mighty tray of glasses with the cloudy yellow cocktails in the glass pitcher in the center. The men babbled, "Oh, gosh, have a look!" and "This gets me right where I live!" and "Let me at it!" But Chum Frink, a traveled man and not unused to woes, was stricken by the thought that the potion might be merely fruit-juice with a little neutral spirits. He looked timorous as Babbitt, a moist and ecstatic almoner, held out a glass, but as he tasted it he piped, "Oh, man, let me dream on! It ain't true, but don't waken me! Jus' lemme slumber!"

Two hours before, Frink had completed a newspaper lyric beginning:

*I sat alone and groused and thunk, and scratched my head and sighed and wunk, and groaned, "There still are boobs, alack, who'd like the old-time gin-mill back; that den that makes a sage a loon, the vile and smelly old saloon!" I'll never miss their poison booze, whilst I the bubbling spring can use, that leaves my head at merry morn as clear as any babe new-born!*

Babbitt drank with the others; his moment's depression was gone; he perceived that these were the best fellows in the world; he wanted to give them a thousand cocktails. "Think you could stand another?" he cried. The wives refused, with giggles, but the men, speaking in a wide, elaborate, enjoyable manner, gloated, "Well, sooner than have you get sore at me, Georgie—"

"You got a little dividend coming," said Babbitt to each of them, and each intoned, "Squeeze it, Georgie, squeeze it!"

When, beyond hope, the pitcher was empty, they stood and talked about prohibition. The men leaned back on their heels, put their hands in their trousers-pockets, and proclaimed their views with the booming profundity of a prosperous male repeating a thoroughly hackneyed statement about a matter of which he knows nothing whatever.

"Now, I'll tell you," said Vergil Gunch; "way I figure it is this, and I can speak by the book, because I've talked to a lot of doctors and fellows that ought to know, and the way I see it is that it's a good thing to get rid of the saloon, but they ought to let a fellow have beer and light wines."

Howard Littlefield observed, "What isn't generally realized is that it's a dangerous prop'sition to invade the rights of personal liberty. Now, take this for instance: The King of—Bavaria? I think it was Bavaria—yes, Bavaria, it was—in 1862, March, 1862, he issued a proclamation against public grazing of live-stock. The peasantry had stood for overtaxation without the slightest complaint, but when this proclamation came out, they rebelled. Or it may have been Saxony. But it just goes to show the dangers of invading the rights of personal liberty."

"That's it—no one got a right to invade personal liberty," said Orville Jones.

"Just the same, you don't want to forget prohibition is a mighty good thing for the working-classes. Keeps 'em from wasting their money and lowering their productiveness," said Vergil Gunch.

"Yes, that's so. But the trouble is the manner of enforcement," insisted Howard Littlefield. "Congress didn't understand the right system. Now, if I'd been running the thing, I'd have arranged it so that the drinker himself

was licensed, and then we could have taken care of the shiftless workman—
kept him from drinking—and yet not 've interfered with the rights—with the
personal liberty—of fellows like ourselves."

They bobbed their heads, looked admiringly at one another, and stated,
"That's so, that would be the stunt."

"The thing that worries me is that a lot of these guys will take to cocaine,"
sighed Eddie Swanson.

They bobbed more violently, and groaned, "That's so, there is a danger
of that."

Chum Frink chanted, "Oh, say, I got hold of a swell new receipt for
home-made beer the other day. You take—"

Gunch interrupted, "Wait! Let me tell you mine!" Littlefield snorted,
"Beer! Rats! Thing to do is to ferment cider!" Jones insisted, "I've got the
receipt that does the business!" Swanson begged, "Oh, say, lemme tell you
the story—" But Frink went on resolutely, "You take and save the shells from
peas, and pour six gallons of water on a bushel of shells and boil the mixture
till—"

Mrs. Babbitt turned toward them with yearning sweetness; Frink hastened
to finish even his best beer-recipe; and she said gaily, "Dinner is served."

There was a good deal of friendly argument among the men as to which
should go in last, and while they were crossing the hall from the living-room
to the dining-room Vergil Gunch made them laugh by thundering, "If I
can't sit next to Myra Babbitt and hold her hand under the table, I won't
play—I'm goin' home." In the dining-room they stood embarrassed while
Mrs. Babbitt fluttered, "Now, let me see— Oh, I was going to have some
nice hand-painted place-cards for you but— Oh, let me see; Mr. Frink, you
sit there."

The dinner was in the best style of women's-magazine art, whereby the
salad was served in hollowed apples, and everything but the invincible fried
chicken resembled something else.

Ordinarily the men found it hard to talk to the women; flirtation was an
art unknown on Floral Heights, and the realms of offices and of kitchens
had no alliances. But under the inspiration of the cocktails, conversation
was violent. Each of the men still had a number of important things to say
about prohibition, and now that each had a loyal listener in his dinner-
partner he burst out:

"I found a place where I can get all the hootch I want at eight a quart—"

"Did you read about this fellow that went and paid a thousand dollars
for ten cases of red-eye that proved to be nothing but water? Seems this
fellow was standing on the corner and fellow comes up to him—"

"They say there's a whole raft of stuff being smuggled across at Detroit—"

"What I always say is—what a lot of folks don't realize about prohibition—"

"And then you get all this awful poison stuff—wood alcohol and everything—"

"Course I believe in it on principle, but I don't propose to have anybody
telling me what I got to think and do. No American 'll ever stand for that!"

But they all felt that it was rather in bad taste for Orville Jones—and he not recognized as one of the wits of the occasion anyway—to say, "In fact, the whole thing about prohibition is this: it isn't the initial cost, it's the humidity."

Not till the one required topic had been dealt with did the conversation become general.

It was often and admiringly said of Vergil Gunch, "Gee, that fellow can get away with murder! Why, he can pull a Raw One in mixed company and all the ladies 'll laugh their heads off, but me, gosh, if I crack anything that's just the least bit off color I get the razz for fair!" Now Gunch delighted them by crying to Mrs. Eddie Swanson, youngest of the women, "Louetta! I managed to pinch Eddie's doorkey out of his pocket, and what say you and me sneak across the street when the folks aren't looking? Got something," with a gorgeous leer, "awful important to tell you!"

The women wriggled, and Babbitt was stirred to like naughtiness. "Say, folks, I wished I dared show you a book I borrowed from Doc Patten!"

"Now, George! The idea!" Mrs. Babbitt warned him.

"This book—racy isn't the word! It's some kind of an anthropological report about—about Customs, in the South Seas, and what it doesn't *say*! It's a book you can't buy. Verg, I'll lend it to you."

"Me first!" insisted Eddie Swanson. "Sounds spicy!"

Orville Jones announced, "Say, I heard a Good One the other day about a coupla Swedes and their wives," and, in the best Jewish accent, he resolutely carried the Good One to a slightly disinfected ending. Gunch capped it. But the cocktails waned, the seekers dropped back into cautious reality.

Chum Frink had recently been on a lecture-tour among the small towns, and he chuckled, "Awful good to get back to civilization! I certainly been seeing some hick towns! I mean— Course the folks there are the best on earth, but, gee whiz, those Main Street burgs are slow, and you fellows can't hardly appreciate what it means to be here with a bunch of live ones!"

"You bet!" exulted Orville Jones. "They're the best folks on earth, those small-town folks, but, oh, mama! what conversation! Why, say, they can't talk about anything but the weather and the ne-oo Ford, by heckalorum!"

"That's right. They all talk about just the same things," said Eddie Swanson.

"Don't they, though! They just say the same things over and over," said Vergil Gunch.

"Yes, it's really remarkable. They seem to lack all power of looking at things impersonally. They simply go over and over the same talk about Fords and the weather and so on," said Howard Littlefield.

"Still, at that, you can't blame 'em. They haven't got any intellectual stimulus such as you get up here in the city," said Chum Frink.

"Gosh, that's right," said Babbitt. "I don't want you highbrows to get stuck on yourselves but I must say it keeps a fellow right up on his toes to sit in with a poet and with Howard, the guy that put the con in economics! But these small-town boobs, with nobody but each other to talk to, no wonder they get so sloppy and uncultured in their speech, and so balled-up in their thinking!"

Orville Jones commented, "And, then take our other advantages—the movies, frinstance. These Yapville sports think they're all-get-out if they have one change of bill a week, where here in the city you got your choice of a dozen diff'rent movies any evening you want to name!"

"Sure, and the inspiration we get from rubbing up against high-class hustlers every day and getting jam full of ginger," said Eddie Swanson.

"Same time," said Babbitt, "no sense excusing these rube burgs too easy. Fellow's own fault if he doesn't show the initiative to up and beat it to the city, like we done—did. And, just speaking in confidence among friends, they're jealous as the devil of a city man. Every time I go up to Catawba I have to go around apologizing to the fellows I was brought up with because I've more or less succeeded and they haven't. And if you talk natural to 'em, way we do here, and show finesse and what you might call a broad point of view, why, they think you're putting on side. There's my own half-brother Martin—runs the little ole general store my Dad used to keep. Say, I'll bet he don't know there is such a thing as a Tux.—as a dinner-jacket. If he was to come in here now, he'd think we were a bunch of—of— Why, gosh, I swear, he wouldn't know what to think! Yes, sir, they're jealous!"

Chum Frink agreed, "That's so. But what I mind is their lack of culture and appreciation of the Beautiful—if you'll excuse me for being highbrow. Now, I like to give a high-class lecture, and read some of my best poetry— not the newspaper stuff but the magazine things. But say, when I get out in the tall grass, there's nothing will take but a lot of cheesy old stories and slang and junk that if any of us were to indulge in it here, he'd get the gate so fast it would make his head swim."

Vergil Gunch summed it up: "Fact is, we're mighty lucky to be living among a bunch of city-folks, that recognize artistic things and business-punch equally. We'd feel pretty glum if we got stuck in some Main Street burg and tried to wise up the old codgers to the kind of life we're used to here. But, by golly, there's this you got to say for 'em: Every small American town is trying to get population and modern ideals. And darn if a lot of 'em don't put it across! Somebody starts panning a rube crossroads, telling how he was there in 1900 and it consisted of one muddy street, count 'em, one, and nine hundred human clams. Well, you go back there in 1920, and you find pavements and a swell little hotel and a first-class ladies' ready-to-wear shop—real perfection, in fact! You don't want to just look at what these small towns are, you want to look at what they're aiming to become, and they all got an ambition that in the long run is going to make 'em the finest spots on earth—they all want to be just like Zenith!"

III

However intimate they might be with T. Cholmondeley Frink as a neighbor, as a borrower of lawn-mowers and monkey-wrenches, they knew that he was also a Famous Poet and a distinguished advertising-agent; that behind his easiness were sultry literary mysteries which they could not penetrate. But to-night, in the gin-evolved confidence, he admitted them to the arcanum:

"I've got a literary problem that's worrying me to death. I'm doing a series of ads for the Zeeco Car and I want to make each of 'em a real little gem —reg'lar stylistic stuff. I'm all for this theory that perfection is the stunt, or nothing at all, and these are as tough things as I ever tackled. You might think it'd be harder to do my poems—all these Heart Topics: home and fireside and happiness—but they're cinches. You can't go wrong on 'em; you know what sentiments any decent go-ahead fellow must have if he plays the game, and you stick right to 'em. But the poetry of industrialism, now there's a literary line where you got to open up new territory. Do you know the fellow who's really *the* American genius? The fellow who you don't know his name and I don't either, but his work ought to be preserved so's future generations can judge our American thought and originality to-day? Why, the fellow that writes the Prince Albert Tobacco ads! Just listen to this:

It's P.A. that jams such joy in jimmy pipes. Say—bet you've often bent-an-ear to that spill-of-speech about hopping from five to f-i-f-t-y p-e-r by "stepping on her a bit!" Guess that's going some, all right—BUT— just among ourselves, you better start a rapidwhiz system to keep tabs as to how fast you'll buzz from low smoke spirits to *tip-top-high*—once you line up behind a jimmy pipe that's all aglow with that peach-of-a-pal, Prince Albert.

Prince Albert is john-on-the-job—always joy'usly more-*ish* in flavor; always delightfully cool and fragrant! For a fact, you never hooked such double-decked, copper-riveted, two-fisted smoke enjoyment!

Go to a pipe—speed-o-quick like you light on a good thing! Why— packed with Prince Albert you can play a joy'us jimmy straight across the boards! *And you know what that means!*"

"Now that," caroled the motor agent, Eddie Swanson, "that's what I call he-literature! That Prince Albert fellow—though, gosh, there can't be just one fellow that writes 'em; must be a big board of classy ink-slingers in conference, but anyway: now, him, he doesn't write for long-haired pikers, he writes for Regular Guys, he writes for *me*, and I tip my benny to him! The only thing is: I wonder if it sells the goods? Course, like all these poets, this Prince Albert fellow lets his idea run away with him. It makes elegant reading, but it don't say nothing. I'd never go out and buy Prince Albert Tobacco after reading it, because it doesn't tell me anything about the stuff. It's just a bunch of fluff."

Frink faced him: "Oh, you're crazy! Have I got to sell you the idea of Style? Anyway, that's the kind of stuff I'd like to do for the Zeeco. But I simply can't. So I decided to stick to the straight poetic, and I took a shot at a highbrow ad for the Zeeco. How do you like this:

The long white trail is calling—calling—and it's over the hills and far away for every man or woman that has red blood in his veins and on his lips the ancient song of the buccaneers. It's away with dull drudging, and a fig for care. Speed—glorious Speed—it's more than just a moment's exhilaration—it's Life for you and me! This great new truth the makers of the Zeeco Car have considered as much as price and style. It's fleet as the antelope, smooth as the glide of a swallow, yet powerful as the charge of a bull-elephant. Class breathes in every line. Listen, brother! You'll never know what the high art of hiking is till you TRY LIFE'S ZIPPINGEST ZEST—THE ZEECO!

"Yes," Frink mused, "that's got an elegant color to it, if I do say so, but it ain't got the originality of 'spill-of-speech!'"

The whole company sighed with sympathy and admiration.

# 9

Babbitt was fond of his friends, he loved the importance of being host and shouting, "Certainly, you're going to have smore chicken—the idea!" and he appreciated the genius of T. Cholmondeley Frink, but the vigor of the cocktails was gone, and the more he ate the less joyful he felt. Then the amity of the dinner was destroyed by the nagging of the Swansons.

In Floral Heights and the other prosperous sections of Zenith, especially in the "young married set," there were many women who had nothing to do. Though they had few servants, yet with gas stoves, electric ranges and dish-washers and vacuum cleaners, and tiled kitchen walls, their houses were so convenient that they had little housework, and much of their food came from bakeries and delicatessens. They had but two, one, or no children; and despite the myth that the Great War had made work respectable, their husbands objected to their "wasting time and getting a lot of crank ideas" in unpaid social work, and still more to their causing a rumor, by earning money, that they were not adequately supported. They worked perhaps two hours a day, and the rest of the time they ate chocolates, went to the motion-pictures, went window-shopping, went in gossiping twos and threes to card-parties, read magazines, thought timorously of the lovers who never appeared, and accumulated a splendid restlessness which they got rid of by nagging their husbands. The husbands nagged back.

Of these naggers the Swansons were perfect specimens.

Throughout the dinner Eddie Swanson had been complaining, publicly, about his wife's new frock. It was, he submitted, too short, too low, too immodestly thin, and much too expensive. He appealed to Babbitt:

"Honest, George, what do you think of that rag Louetta went and bought? Don't you think it's the limit?"

"What's eating you, Eddie? I call it a swell little dress."

"Oh, it is, Mr. Swanson. It's a sweet frock," Mrs. Babbitt protested.

"There now, do you see, smarty! You're such an authority on clothes!" Louetta raged, while the guests ruminated and peeped at her shoulders.

"That's all right now," said Swanson. "I'm authority enough so I know it was a waste of money, and it makes me tired to see you not wearing out a whole closetful of clothes you got already. I've expressed my idea about this before, and you know good and well you didn't pay the least bit of attention. I have to camp on your trail to get you to do anything—"

There was much more of it, and they all assisted, all but Babbitt. Everything about him was dim except his stomach, and that was a bright scarlet disturbance. "Had too much grub; oughtn't to eat this stuff," he groaned— while he went on eating, while he gulped down a chill and glutinous slice of the ice-cream brick, and cocoanut cake as oozy as shaving-cream. He felt as though he had been stuffed with clay; his body was bursting, his throat was bursting, his brain was hot mud; and only with agony did he continue to smile and shout as became a host on Floral Heights.

He would, except for his guests, have fled outdoors and walked off the intoxication of food, but in the haze which filled the room they sat forever, talking, talking, while he agonized, "Darn fool to be eating all this—not 'nother mouthful," and discovered that he was again tasting the sickly welter of melted ice cream on his plate. There was no magic in his friends; he was not uplifted when Howard Littlefield produced from his treasure-house of scholarship the information that the chemical symbol for raw rubber is $C_{10}H_{16}$, which turns into isoprene, or $2C_5H_8$. Suddenly, without precedent, Babbitt was not merely bored but admitting that he was bored. It was ecstasy to escape from the table, from the torture of a straight chair, and loll on the davenport in the living-room.

The others, from their fitful unconvincing talk, their expressions of being slowly and painfully smothered, seemed to be suffering from the toil of social life and the horror of good food as much as himself. All of them accepted with relief the suggestion of bridge.

Babbitt recovered from the feeling of being boiled. He won at bridge. He was again able to endure Vergil Gunch's inexorable heartiness. But he pictured loafing with Paul Riesling beside a lake in Maine. It was as overpowering and imaginative as homesickness. He had never seen Maine, yet he beheld the shrouded mountains, the tranquil lake of evening. "That boy Paul's worth all these ballyhooing highbrows put together," he muttered; and, "I'd like to get away from—everything."

Even Louetta Swanson did not rouse him.

Mrs. Swanson was pretty and pliant. Babbitt was not an analyst of women, except as to their tastes in Furnished Houses to Rent. He divided them into Real Ladies, Working Women, Old Cranks, and Fly Chickens. He mooned over their charms but he was of opinion that all of them (save the women of his own family) were "different" and "mysterious." Yet he had known by instinct that Louetta Swanson could be approached. Her eyes and lips were moist. Her face tapered from a broad forehead to a pointed chin, her mouth was thin but strong and avid, and between her brows were two out-curving and passionate wrinkles. She was thirty, perhaps, or younger. Gossip had never touched her, but every man naturally and instantly rose to flirta-tiousness when he spoke to her, and every woman watched her with stilled blankness.

Between games, sitting on the davenport, Babbitt spoke to her with the requisite gallantry, that sonorous Floral Heights gallantry which is not flirta-tion but a terrified flight from it:

"You're looking like a new soda-fountain to-night, Louetta."

"Am I?"

"Ole Eddie kind of on the rampage."

"Yes. I get so sick of it."

"Well, when you get tired of hubby, you can run off with Uncle George."

"If I ran away— Oh, well—"

"Anybody ever tell you your hands are awful pretty?"

She looked down at them, she pulled the lace of her sleeves over them, but otherwise she did not heed him. She was lost in unexpressed imaginings.

Babbitt was too languid this evening to pursue his duty of being a captivat-ing (though strictly moral) male. He ambled back to the bridge-tables. He was not much thrilled when Mrs. Frink, a small twittering woman, proposed that they "try and do some spiritualism and table-tipping—you know Chum can make the spirits come—honest, he just scares me!"

The ladies of the party had not emerged all evening, but now, as the sex given to things of the spirit while the men warred against base things ma-terial, they took command and cried, "Oh, let's!" In the dimness the men were rather solemn and foolish, but the goodwives quivered and adored as they sat about the table. They laughed, "Now, you be good or I'll tell!" when the men took their hands in the circle.

Babbitt tingled with a slight return of interest in life as Louetta Swan-son's hand closed on his with quiet firmness.

All of them hunched over, intent. They startled as some one drew a strained breath. In the dusty light from the hall they looked unreal, they felt disembodied. Mrs. Gunch squeaked, and they jumped with unnatural jocularity, but at Frink's hiss they sank into subdued awe. Suddenly, in-credibly, they heard a knocking. They stared at Frink's half-revealed hands and found them lying still. They wriggled, and pretended not to be impressed.

Frink spoke with gravity: "Is some one there?" A thud. "Is one knock to be the sign for 'yes'?" A thud. "And two for 'no'?" A thud.

"Now, ladies and gentlemen, shall we ask the guide to put us into com-munication with the spirit of some great one passed over?" Frink mumbled.

Mrs. Orville Jones begged, "Oh, let's talk to Dante! We studied him at the Reading Circle. You know who he was, Orvy."

"Certainly I know who he was! The Wop poet. Where do you think I was raised?" from her insulted husband.

"Sure—the fellow that took the Cook's Tour to Hell. I've never waded through his po'try, but we learned about him in the U.," said Babbitt.

"Page Mr. Dannnnnty!" intoned Eddie Swanson.

"You ought to get him easy, Mr. Frink, you and he being fellow-poets," said Louetta Swanson.

"Fellow-poets, rats! Where d' you get that stuff?" protested Vergil Gunch. "I suppose Dante showed a lot of speed for an old-timer—not that I've actually read him, of course—but to come right down to hard facts, he wouldn't stand one-two-three if he had to buckle down to practical literature and turn out a poem for the newspaper-syndicate every day, like Chum does!"

"That's so," from Eddie Swanson. "Those old birds could take their time. Judas Priest, I could write poetry myself if I had a whole year for it, and just wrote about that old-fashioned junk like Dante wrote about."

Frink demanded, "Hush, now! I'll call him. . . . O, Laughing Eyes, emerge forth into the, uh, the ultimates and bring hither the spirit of Dante, that we mortals may list to his words of wisdom."

"You forgot to give um the address: 1658 Brimstone Avenue, Fiery Heights, Hell," Gunch chuckled, but the others felt that this was irreligious. And besides—"probably it was just Chum making the knocks, but still, if there did happen to be something to all this, be exciting to talk to an old fellow belonging to—way back in early times—"

A thud. The spirit of Dante had come to the parlor of George F. Babbitt.

He was, it seemed, quite ready to answer their questions. He was "glad to be with them, this evening."

Frink spelled out the messages by running through the alphabet till the spirit interpreter knocked at the right letter.

Littlefield asked, in a learned tone, "Do you like it in the Paradiso, Messire?"

"We are very happy on the higher plane, Signor. We are glad that you are studying this great truth of spiritualism," Dante replied.

The circle moved with an awed creaking of stays and shirt-fronts. "Suppose—suppose there were something to this?"

Babbitt had a different worry. "Suppose Chum Frink was really one of these spiritualists! Chum had, for a literary fellow, always seemed to be a Regular Guy; he belonged to the Chatham Road Presbyterian Church and went to the Boosters' lunches and liked cigars and motors and racy stories. But suppose that secretly— After all, you never could tell about these darn highbrows; and to be an out-and-out spiritualist would be almost like being a socialist!"

No one could long be serious in the presence of Vergil Gunch. "Ask Dant' how Jack Shakespeare and old Verg'—the guy they named after me—are gettin' along, and don't they wish they could get into the movie game!" he blared, and instantly all was mirth. Mrs. Jones shrieked, and Eddie Swanson desired to know whether Dante didn't catch cold with nothing on but his wreath.

The pleased Dante made humble answer.

But Babbitt—the curst discontent was torturing him again, and heavily, in the impersonal darkness, he pondered, "I don't— We're all so flip and think we're so smart. There'd be— A fellow like Dante— I wish I'd read some of his pieces. I don't suppose I ever will, now."

He had, without explanation, the impression of a slaggy cliff and on it, in silhouette against menacing clouds, a lone and austere figure. He was dismayed by a sudden contempt for his surest friends. He grasped Louetta Swanson's hand, and found the comfort of human warmth. Habit came, a veteran warrior; and he shook himself. "What the deuce is the matter with me, this evening?"

He patted Louetta's hand, to indicate that he hadn't meant anything improper by squeezing it, and demanded of Frink, "Say, see if you can get old Dant' to spiel us some of his poetry. Talk up to him. Tell him, '*Buena giorna, señor, com sa va, wie geht's? Keskersaykersa* a little pome, *señor?*'"

## II

The lights were switched on; the women sat on the fronts of their chairs in that determined suspense whereby a wife indicates that as soon as the present speaker has finished, she is going to remark brightly to her husband, "Well, dear, I think per-*haps* it's about time for us to be saying good-night." For once Babbitt did not break out in blustering efforts to keep the party going. He had—there was something he wished to think out— But the psychical research had started them off again. ("Why didn't they go home! Why didn't they go home!") Though he was impressed by the profundity of the statement, he was only half-enthusiastic when Howard Littlefield lectured, "The United States is the only nation in which the government is a Moral Ideal and not just a social arrangement." ("True—true—weren't they *ever* going home?") He was usually delighted to have an "inside view" of the momentous world of motors but to-night he scarcely listened to Eddie Swanson's revelation: "If you want to go above the Javelin class, the Zeeco is a mighty good buy. Couple weeks ago, and mind you, this was a fair, square test, they took a Zeeco stock touring-car and they slid up the Tonawanda hill on high, and fellow told me—" ("Zeeco—good boat but— Were they planning to stay all night?")

They really were going, with a flutter of "We did have the best time!" Most aggressively friendly of all was Babbitt, yet as he burbled he was reflecting, "I got through it, but for a while there I didn't hardly think I'd last out." He prepared to taste that most delicate pleasure of the host: making fun of his guests in the relaxation of midnight. As the door closed he yawned voluptuously, chest out, shoulders wriggling, and turned cynically to his wife.

She was beaming. "Oh, it was nice, wasn't it! I know they enjoyed every minute of it. Don't you think so?"

He couldn't do it. He couldn't mock. It would have been like sneering at a happy child. He lied ponderously: "You bet! Best party this year, by a long shot."

"Wasn't the dinner good! And honestly I thought the fried chicken was delicious!"

"You bet! Fried to the Queen's taste. Best fried chicken I've tasted for a coon's age."

"Didn't Matilda fry it beautifully! And don't you think the soup was simply delicious?"

"It certainly was! It was corking! Best soup I've tasted since Heck was a pup!" But his voice was seeping away. They stood in the hall, under the electric light in its square box-like shade of red glass bound with nickel. She stared at him.

"Why, George, you don't sound—you sound as if you hadn't really enjoyed it."

"Sure I did! Course I did!"

"George! What is it?"

"Oh, I'm kind of tired, I guess. Been pounding pretty hard at the office. Need to get away and rest up a little."

"Well, we're going to Maine in just a few weeks now, dear."

"Yuh—" Then he was pouring it out nakedly, robbed of reticence. "Myra: I think it'd be a good thing for me to get up there early."

"But you have this man you have to meet in New York about business."

"What man? Oh, sure. Him. Oh, that's all off. But I want to hit Maine early—get in a little fishing, catch me a big trout, by golly!" A nervous, artificial laugh.

"Well, why don't we do it? Verona and Matilda can run the house between them, and you and I can go any time, if you think we can afford it."

"But that's— I've been feeling so jumpy lately, I thought maybe it might be a good thing if I kind of got off by myself and sweat it out of me."

"George! Don't you *want* me to go along?" She was too wretchedly in earnest to be tragic, or gloriously insulted, or anything save dumpy and defenseless and flushed to the red steaminess of a boiled beet.

"Of course I do! I just meant—" Remembering that Paul Riesling had predicted this, he was as desperate as she. "I mean, sometimes it's a good thing for an old grouch like me to go off and get it out of his system." He tried to sound paternal. "Then when you and the kids arrive—I figured maybe I might skip up to Maine just a few days ahead of you—I'd be ready for a real bat, see how I mean?" He coaxed her with large booming sounds, with affable smiles, like a popular preacher blessing an Easter congregation, like a humorous lecturer completing his stint of eloquence, like all perpetrators of masculine wiles.

She stared at him, the joy of festival drained from her face. "Do I bother you when we go on vacations? Don't I add anything to your fun?"

He broke. Suddenly, dreadfully, he was hysterical, he was a yelping baby. "Yes, yes, yes! Hell, yes! But can't you understand I'm shot to pieces? I'm all in! I got to take care of myself! I tell you, I got to— I'm sick of everything and everybody! I got to—"

It was she who was mature and protective now. "Why, of course! You shall run off by yourself! Why don't you get Paul to go along, and you boys just fish and have a good time?" She patted his shoulder—reaching up to it—while he shook with palsied helplessness, and in that moment was not merely by habit fond of her but clung to her strength.

She cried cheerily, "Now up-stairs you go, and pop into bed. We'll fix it all up. I'll see to the doors. Now skip!"

For many minutes, for many hours, for a bleak eternity, he lay awake, shivering, reduced to primitive terror, comprehending that he had won freedom, and wondering what he could do with anything so unknown and so embarrassing as freedom.

# 10

---

No apartment-house in Zenith had more resolutely experimented in condensation than the Revelstoke Arms, in which Paul and Zilla Riesling had a flat. By sliding the beds into low closets the bedrooms were converted into living-rooms. The kitchens were cupboards each containing an electric range, a copper sink, a glass refrigerator, and, very intermittently, a Balkan maid. Everything about the Arms was excessively modern, and everything was compressed—except the garages.

The Babbitts were calling on the Rieslings at the Arms. It was a speculative venture to call on the Rieslings; interesting and sometimes disconcerting. Zilla was an active, strident, full-blown, high-bosomed blonde. When she condescended to be good-humored she was nervously amusing. Her comments on people were saltily satiric and penetrative of accepted hypocrisies. "That's so!" you said, and looked sheepish. She danced wildly, and called on the world to be merry, but in the midst of it she would turn indignant. She was always becoming indignant. Life was a plot against her, and she exposed it furiously.

She was affable to-night. She merely hinted that Orville Jones wore a toupé, that Mrs. T. Cholmondeley Frink's singing resembled a Ford going into high, and that the Hon. Otis Deeble, mayor of Zenith and candidate for Congress, was a flatulent fool (which was quite true). The Babbitts and Rieslings sat doubtfully on stone-hard brocade chairs in the small living-room of the flat, with its mantel unprovided with a fireplace, and its strip of heavy gilt fabric upon a glaring new player-piano, till Mrs. Riesling shrieked,

"Come on! Let's put some pep in it! Get out your fiddle, Paul, and I'll try to make Georgie dance decently."

The Babbitts were in earnest. They were plotting for the escape to Maine. But when Mrs. Babbitt hinted with plump smilingness, "Does Paul get as tired after the winter's work as Georgie does?" then Zilla remembered an injury; and when Zilla Riesling remembered an injury the world stopped till something had been done about it.

"Does he get tired? No, he doesn't get tired, he just goes crazy, that's all! You think Paul is so reasonable, oh, yes, and he loves to make out he's a little lamb, but he's stubborn as a mule. Oh, if you had to live with him—! You'd find out how sweet he is! He just pretends to be meek so he can have his own way. And me, I get the credit for being a terrible old crank, but if I didn't blow up once in a while and get something started, we'd die of dry-rot. He never wants to go any place and— Why, last evening, just because the car was out of order—and that was his fault, too, because he ought to have taken it to the service-station and had the battery looked at—and he didn't want to go down to the movies on the trolley. But we went, and then there was one of those impudent conductors, and Paul wouldn't do a thing.

"I was standing on the platform waiting for the people to let me into the car, and this beast, this conductor, hollered at me, 'Come on, you, move up!' Why, I've never had anybody speak to me that way in all my life! I was so astonished I just turned to him and said—I thought there must be some mistake, and so I said to him, perfectly pleasant, 'Were you speaking to me?' and he went on and bellowed at me, 'Yes, I was! You're keeping the whole car from starting!' he said, and then I saw he was one of these dirty ill-bred hogs that kindness is wasted on, and so I stopped and looked right at him, and I said, 'I—beg—your—pardon, I am not doing anything of the kind,' I said, 'it's the people ahead of me, who won't move up,' I said, 'and furthermore, let me tell you, young man, that you're a low-down, foul-mouthed, impertinent skunk,' I said, 'and you're no gentleman! I certainly intend to report you, and we'll see,' I said, 'whether a lady is to be insulted by any drunken bum that chooses to put on a ragged uniform, and I'd thank you,' I said, 'to keep your filthy abuse to yourself.' And then I waited for Paul to show he was half a man and come to my defense, and he just stood there and pretended he hadn't heard a word, and so I said to him, 'Well,' I said—"

"Oh, cut it, cut it, Zil!" Paul groaned. "We all know I'm a mollycoddle, and you're a tender bud, and let's let it go at that."

"Let it go?" Zilla's face was wrinkled like the Medusa, her voice was a dagger of corroded brass. She was full of the joy of righteousness and bad temper. She was a crusader and, like every crusader, she exulted in the opportunity to be vicious in the name of virtue. "Let it go? If people knew how many things I've let go—"

"Oh, quit being such a bully."

"Yes, a fine figure you'd cut if I didn't bully you! You'd lie abed till noon and play your idiotic fiddle till midnight! You're born lazy, and you're born shiftless, and you're born cowardly, Paul Riesling—"

"Oh, now, don't say that, Zilla; you don't mean a word of it!" protested Mrs. Babbitt.

"I will say that, and I mean every single last word of it!"

"Oh, now, Zilla, the idea!" Mrs. Babbitt was maternal and fussy. She was no older than Zilla, but she seemed so—at first. She was placid and puffy and mature, where Zilla, at forty-five, was so bleached and tight-corseted that you knew only that she was older than she looked. "The idea of talking to poor Paul like that!"

"Poor Paul is right! We'd both be poor, we'd be in the poorhouse, if I didn't jazz him up!"

"Why, now, Zilla, Georgie and I were just saying how hard Paul's been working all year, and we were thinking it would be lovely if the Boys could run off by themselves. I've been coaxing George to go up to Maine ahead of the rest of us, and get the tired out of his system before we come, and I think it would be lovely if Paul could manage to get away and join him."

At this exposure of his plot to escape, Paul was startled out of impassivity. He rubbed his fingers. His hands twitched.

Zilla bayed, "Yes! You're lucky! You can let George go, and not have to watch him. Fat old Georgie! Never peeps at another woman! Hasn't got the spunk!"

"The hell I haven't!" Babbitt was fervently defending his priceless immorality when Paul interrupted him—and Paul looked dangerous. He rose quickly; he said gently to Zilla:

"I suppose you imply I have a lot of sweethearts."

"Yes, I do!"

"Well, then, my dear, since you ask for it— There hasn't been a time in the last ten years when I haven't found some nice little girl to comfort me, and as long as you continue your amiability I shall probably continue to deceive you. It isn't hard. You're so stupid."

Zilla gibbered; she howled; words could not be distinguished in her slaver of abuse.

Then the bland George F. Babbitt was transformed. If Paul was dangerous, if Zilla was a snake-locked fury, if the neat emotions suitable to the Revelstoke Arms had been slashed into raw hatreds, it was Babbitt who was the most formidable. He leaped up. He seemed very large. He seized Zilla's shoulder. The cautions of the broker were wiped from his face, and his voice was cruel:

"I've had enough of all this damn nonsense! I've known you for twenty-five years, Zil, and I never knew you to miss a chance to take your disappointments out on Paul. You're not wicked. You're worse. You're a fool. And let me tell you that Paul is the finest boy God ever made. Every decent person is sick and tired of your taking advantage of being a woman and springing every mean innuendo you can think of. Who the hell are you that a person like Paul should have to ask your *permission* to go with me? You act like you were a combination of Queen Victoria and Cleopatra. You fool, can't you see how people snicker at you, and sneer at you?"

Zilla was sobbing, "I've never—I've never—nobody ever talked to me like this in all my life!"

"No, but that's the way they talk behind your back! Always! They say you're a scolding old woman. Old, by God!"

That cowardly attack broke her. Her eyes were blank. She wept. But Babbitt glared stolidly. He felt that he was the all-powerful official in charge; that Paul and Mrs. Babbitt looked on him with awe; that he alone could handle this case.

Zilla writhed. She begged, "Oh, they don't!"

"They certainly do!"

"I've been a bad woman! I'm terribly sorry! I'll kill myself! I'll do anything. Oh, I'll— What do you want?"

She abased herself completely. Also, she enjoyed it. To the connoisseur of scenes, nothing is more enjoyable than a thorough, melodramatic, egoistic humility.

"I want you to let Paul beat it off to Maine with me," Babbitt demanded.

"How can I help his going? You've just said I was an idiot and nobody paid any attention to me."

"Oh, you can help it, all right, all right! What you got to do is to cut out hinting that the minute he gets out of your sight, he'll go chasing after some petticoat. Matter fact, that's the way you start the boy off wrong. You ought to have more sense—"

"Oh, I will, honestly, I will, George. I know I was bad. Oh, forgive me, all of you, forgive me—"

She enjoyed it.

So did Babbitt. He condemned magnificently and forgave piously, and as he went parading out with his wife he was grandly explanatory to her:

"Kind of a shame to bully Zilla, but course it was the only way to handle her. Gosh, I certainly did have her crawling!"

She said calmly, "Yes. You were horrid. You were showing off. You were having a lovely time thinking what a great fine person you were!"

"Well, by golly! Can you beat it! Of course I might of expected you to not stand by me! I might of expected you'd stick up for your own sex!"

"Yes. Poor Zilla, she's so unhappy. She takes it out on Paul. She hasn't a single thing to do, in that little flat. And she broods too much. And she used to be so pretty and gay, and she resents losing it. And you were just as nasty and mean as you could be. I'm not a bit proud of you—or of Paul, boasting about his horrid love-affairs!"

He was sulkily silent; he maintained his bad temper at a high level of outraged nobility all the four blocks home. At the door he left her, in self-approving haughtiness, and tramped the lawn.

With a shock it was revealed to him: "Gosh, I wonder if she was right—if she was partly right?" Overwork must have flayed him to abnormal sensitiveness; it was one of the few times in his life when he had queried his eternal excellence; and he perceived the summer night, smelled the wet grass. Then: "I don't care! I've pulled it off. We're going to have our spree. And for Paul, I'd do anything."

## II

They were buying their Maine tackle at Ijams Brothers', the Sporting Goods Mart, with the help of Willis Ijams, fellow member of the Boosters' Club. Babbitt was completely mad. He trumpeted and danced. He muttered to Paul, "Say, this is pretty good, eh? To be buying the stuff, eh? And good old Willis Ijams himself coming down on the floor to wait on us! Say, if those fellows that are getting their kit for the North Lakes knew we were going clear up to Maine, they'd have a fit, eh? . . . Well, come on, Brother Ijams—Willis, I mean. Here's your chance! We're a couple of easy marks! Whee! Let me at it! I'm going to buy out the store!"

He gloated on fly-rods and gorgeous rubber hip-boots, on tents with celluloid windows and folding chairs and ice-boxes. He simple-heartedly wanted to buy all of them. It was the Paul whom he was always vaguely protecting who kept him from his drunken desires.

But even Paul lightened when Willis Ijams, a salesman with poetry and diplomacy, discussed flies. "Now, of course, you boys know," he said, "the great scrap is between dry flies and wet flies. Personally, I'm for dry flies. More sporting."

"That's so. Lots more sporting," fulminated Babbitt, who knew very little about flies either wet or dry.

"Now if you'll take my advice, Georgie, you'll stock up well on these pale evening dims, and silver sedges, and red ants. Oh, boy, there's a fly, that red ant!"

"You bet! That's what it is—a fly!" rejoiced Babbitt.

"Yes, sir, that red ant," said Ijams, "is a real honest-to-God *fly!*"

"Oh, I guess ole Mr. Trout won't come a-hustling when I drop one of those red ants on the water!" asserted Babbitt, and his thick wrists made a rapturous motion of casting.

"Yes, and the landlocked salmon will take it, too," said Ijams, who had never seen a landlocked salmon.

"Salmon! Trout! Say, Paul, can you see Uncle George with his khaki pants on haulin' 'em in, some morning 'bout seven? Whee!"

## III

They were on the New York express, incredibly bound for Maine, incredibly without their families. They were free, in a man's world, in the smoking-compartment of the Pullman.

Outside the car window was a glaze of darkness stippled with the gold of infrequent mysterious lights. Babbitt was immensely conscious, in the sway and authoritative clatter of the train, of going, of going on. Leaning toward Paul he grunted, "Gosh, pretty nice to be hiking, eh?"

The small room, with its walls of ocher-colored steel, was filled mostly with the sort of men he classified as the Best Fellows You'll Ever Meet—Real Good Mixers. There were four of them on the long seat; a fat man with a shrewd fat face, a knife-edged man in a green velour hat, a very young young man with an imitation amber cigarette-holder, and Babbitt. Facing them, on two movable leather chairs, were Paul and a lanky, old-fashioned man, very cunning, with wrinkles bracketing his mouth. They all read newspapers or trade journals, boot-and-shoe journals, crockery journals, and waited for the joys of conversation. It was the very young man, now making his first journey by Pullman, who began it.

"Say, gee, I had a wild old time in Zenith!" he gloried. "Say, if a fellow knows the ropes there he can have as wild a time as he can in New York!"

"Yuh, I bet you simply raised the old Ned. I figured you were a bad man when I saw you get on the train!" chuckled the fat one.

The others delightedly laid down their papers.

"Well, that's all right now! I guess I seen some things in the Arbor you never seen!" complained the boy.

"Oh, I'll bet you did! I bet you lapped up the malted milk like a reg'lar little devil!"

Then, the boy having served as introduction, they ignored him and charged into real talk. Only Paul, sitting by himself, reading at a serial story in a newspaper, failed to join them, and all but Babbitt regarded him as a snob, an eccentric, a person of no spirit.

Which of them said which has never been determined, and does not matter, since they all had the same ideas and expressed them always with the same ponderous and brassy assurance. If it was not Babbitt who was delivering any given verdict, at least he was beaming on the chancellor who did deliver it.

"At that, though," announced the first, "they're selling quite some booze in Zenith. Guess they are everywhere. I don't know how you fellows feel about prohibition, but the way it strikes me is that it's a mighty beneficial thing for the poor zob that hasn't got any will-power but for fellows like us, it's an infringement of personal liberty."

"That's a fact. Congress has got no right to interfere with a fellow's personal liberty," contended the second.

A man came in from the car, but as all the seats were full he stood up while he smoked his cigarette. He was an Outsider; he was not one of the Old Families of the smoking-compartment. They looked upon him bleakly and, after trying to appear at ease by examining his chin in the mirror, he gave it up and went out in silence.

"Just been making a trip through the South. Business conditions not very good down there," said one of the council.

"Is that a fact! Not very good, eh?"

"No, didn't strike me they were up to normal."

"Not up to normal, eh?"

"No, I wouldn't hardly say they were."

The whole council nodded sagely and decided, "Yump, not hardly up to snuff."

"Well, business conditions ain't what they ought to be out West, neither, not by a long shot."

"That's a fact. And I guess the hotel business feels it. That's one good thing, though: these hotels that've been charging five bucks a day—yes, and maybe six-seven!—for a rotten room are going to be darn glad to get four, and maybe give you a little service."

"That's a fact. Say, uh, speaknubout hotels, I hit the St. Francis at San Francisco for the first time, the other day, and say, it certainly is a first-class place."

"You're right, brother! The St. Francis is a swell place—absolutely A1."

That's a fact. I'm right with you. It's a first-class place."

"Yuh, but say, any of you fellows ever stay at the Rippleton, in Chicago? I don't want to knock—I believe in boosting wherever you can—but say, of all the rotten dumps that pass 'emselves off as first-class hotels, that's the worst. I'm going to *get* those guys, one of these days, and I told 'em so. You know how I am—well, maybe you don't know, but I'm accustomed to first-class accommodations, and I'm perfectly willing to pay a reasonable price. I got into Chicago late the other night, and the Rippleton's near the station —I'd never been there before, but I says to the taxi-driver—I always believe in taking a taxi when you get in late; may cost a little more money, but, gosh, it's worth it when you got to be up early next morning and out selling a lot of crabs—and I said to him, 'Oh, just drive me over to the Rippleton.'

"Well, we got there, and I breezed up to the desk and said to the clerk, 'Well, brother, got a nice room with bath for Cousin Bill?' Saaaay! You'd 'a' thought I'd sold him a second, or asked him to work on Yom Kippur! He hands me the cold-boiled stare and yaps, 'I dunno, friend, I'll see,' and he ducks behind the rigamajig they keep track of the rooms on. Well, I guess he called up the Credit Association and the American Security League to see if I was all right—he certainly took long enough—or maybe he just went to sleep; but finally he comes out and looks at me like it hurts him, and croaks, 'I think I can let you have a room with bath.' 'Well, that's awful nice of you—sorry to trouble you—how much 'll it set me back?' I says, real sweet. 'It'll cost you seven bucks a day, friend,' he says.

"Well, it was late, and anyway, it went down on my expense-account—gosh, if I'd been paying it instead of the firm, I'd 'a' tramped the streets all night before I'd 'a' let any hick tavern stick me seven great big round dollars, believe me! So I lets it go at that. Well, the clerk wakes a nice young bell-hop—fine lad—not a day over seventy-nine years old—fought at the Battle of Gettysburg and doesn't know it's over yet—thought I was one of the Confederates, I guess, from the way he looked at me—and Rip van Winkle took me up to something—I found out afterwards they called it a room, but first I thought there'd been some mistake—I thought they were putting me in the Salvation Army collection-box! At seven *per* each and every *diem!* Gosh!"

"Yuh, I've heard the Rippleton was pretty cheesy. Now, when I go to

Chicago I always stay at the Blackstone or the La Salle—first-class places."

"Say, any of you fellows ever stay at the Birchdale at Terre Haute? How is it?"

"Oh, the Birchdale is a first-class hotel."

(Twelve minutes of conference on the state of hotels in South Bend, Flint, Dayton, Tulsa, Wichita, Fort Worth, Winona, Erie, Fargo, and Moose Jaw.)

"Speaknubout prices," the man in the velour hat observed, fingering the elk-tooth on his heavy watch-chain, "I'd like to know where they get this stuff about clothes coming down. Now, you take this suit I got on." He pinched his trousers-leg. "Four years ago I paid forty-two fifty for it, and it was real sure-'nough value. Well, here the other day I went into a store back home and asked to see a suit, and the fellow yanks out some hand-me-downs that, honest, I wouldn't put on a hired man. Just out of curiosity I asks him, 'What you charging for that junk?' 'Junk,' he says, 'what d' you mean junk? That's a swell piece of goods, all wool—' Like hell! It was nice vegetable wool, right off the Ole Plantation! 'It's all wool,' he says, 'and we get sixty-seven ninety for it.' 'Oh, you do, do you!' I says. 'Not from me you don't,' I says, and I walks right out on him. You bet! I says to the wife, 'Well,' I said, 'as long as your strength holds out and you can go on putting a few more patches on papa's pants, we'll just pass up buying clothes.'"

"That's right, brother. And just look at collars, frinstance—"

"Hey! Wait!" the fat man protested. "What's the matter with collars? I'm selling collars! D' you realize the cost of labor on collars is still two hundred and seven per cent. above—"

They voted that if their old friend the fat man sold collars, then the price of collars was exactly what it should be; but all other clothing was tragically too expensive. They admired and loved one another now. They went profoundly into the science of business, and indicated that the purpose of manufacturing a plow or a brick was so that it might be sold. To them, the Romantic Hero was no longer the knight, the wandering poet, the cowpuncher, the aviator, nor the brave young district attorney, but the great sales-manager, who had an Analysis of Merchandizing Problems on his glass-topped desk, whose title of nobility was "Go-getter," and who devoted himself and all his young samurai to the cosmic purpose of Selling—not of selling anything in particular, for or to anybody in particular, but pure Selling.

The shop-talk roused Paul Riesling. Though he was a player of violins and an interestingly unhappy husband, he was also a very able salesman of tar-roofing. He listened to the fat man's remarks on "the value of house-organs and bulletins as a method of jazzing-up the Boys out on the road;" and he himself offered one or two excellent thoughts on the use of two-cent stamps on circulars. Then he committed an offense against the holy law of the Clan of Good Fellows. He became highbrow.

They were entering a city. On the outskirts they passed a steel-mill which flared in scarlet and orange flame that licked at the cadaverous stacks, at the iron-sheathed walls and sullen converters.

"My Lord, look at that—beautiful!" said Paul.

"You bet it's beautiful, friend. That's the Shelling-Horton Steel Plant, and they tell me old John Shelling made a good three million bones out of munitions during the war!" the man with the velour hat said reverently.

"I didn't mean—I mean it's lovely the way the light pulls that picturesque yard, all littered with junk, right out of the darkness," said Paul.

They stared at him, while Babbitt crowed, "Paul there has certainly got one great little eye for picturesque places and quaint sights and all that stuff. 'D of been an author or something if he hadn't gone into the roofing line."

Paul looked annoyed. (Babbitt sometimes wondered if Paul appreciated his loyal boosting.) The man in the velour hat grunted, "Well, personally, I think Shelling-Horton keep their works awful dirty. Bum routing. But I don't suppose there's any law against calling 'em 'picturesque' if it gets you that way!"

Paul sulkily returned to his newspaper and the conversation logically moved on to trains.

"What time do we get into Pittsburg?" asked Babbitt.

"Pittsburg? I think we get in at—no, that was last year's schedule—wait a minute—let's see—got a time-table right here."

"I wonder if we're on time?"

"Yuh, sure, we must be just about on time."

"No, we aren't—we were seven minutes late, last station."

"Were we? Straight? Why, gosh, I thought we were right on time."

"No, we're about seven minutes late."

"Yuh, that's right; seven minutes late."

The porter entered—a negro in white jacket with brass buttons.

"How late are we, George?" growled the fat man.

"'Deed, I don't know, sir. I think we're about on time," said the porter, folding towels and deftly tossing them up on the rack above the washbowls. The council stared at him gloomily and when he was gone they wailed:

"I don't know what's come over these niggers, nowadays. They never give you a civil answer."

"That's a fact. They're getting so they don't have a single bit of respect for you. The old-fashioned coon was a fine old cuss—he knew his place—but these young dinges don't want to be porters or cotton-pickers. Oh, no! They got to be lawyers and professors and Lord knows what all! I tell you, it's becoming a pretty serious problem. We ought to get together and show the black man, yes, and the yellow man, his place. Now, I haven't got one particle of race-prejudice. I'm the first to be glad when a nigger succeeds—so long as he stays where he belongs and doesn't try to usurp the rightful authority and business ability of the white man."

"That's the i.! And another thing we got to do," said the man with the velour hat (whose name was Koplinsky), "is to keep these damn foreigners out of the country. Thank the Lord, we're putting a limit on immigration. These Dagoes and Hunkies have got to learn that this is a white man's country, and they ain't wanted here. When we've assimilated the foreigners we got here now and learned 'em the principles of Americanism and turned 'em into regular folks, why then maybe we'll let in a few more."

"You bet. That's a fact," they observed, and passed on to lighter topics. They rapidly reviewed motor-car prices, tire-mileage, oil-stocks, fishing, and the prospects for the wheat-crop in Dakota.

But the fat man was impatient at this waste of time. He was a veteran traveler and free of illusions. Already he had asserted that he was "an old he-one." He leaned forward, gathered in their attention by his expression of sly humor, and grumbled, "Oh, hell, boys, let's cut out the formality and get down to the stories!"

They became very lively and intimate.

Paul and the boy vanished. The others slid forward on the long seat, unbuttoned their vests, thrust their feet up on the chairs, pulled the stately brass cuspidors nearer, and ran the green window-shade down on its little trolley, to shut them in from the uncomfortable strangeness of night. After each bark of laughter they cried, "Say, jever hear the one about—" Babbitt was expansive and virile. When the train stopped at an important station, the four men walked up and down the cement platform, under the vast smoky train-shed roof, like a stormy sky, under the elevated footways, beside crates of ducks and sides of beef, in the mystery of an unknown city. They strolled abreast, old friends and well content. At the long-drawn "Alllll aboarrrrrd"—like a mountain call at dusk—they hastened back into the smoking-compartment, and till two of the morning continued the droll tales, their eyes damp with cigar-smoke and laughter. When they parted they shook hands, and chuckled, "Well, sir, it's been a great session. Sorry to bust it up. Mighty glad to met you."

Babbitt lay awake in the close hot tomb of his Pullman berth, shaking with remembrance of the fat man's limerick about the lady who wished to be wild. He raised the shade; he lay with a puffy arm tucked between his head and the skimpy pillow, looking out on the sliding silhouettes of trees, and village lamps like exclamation-points. He was very happy.

# 11

They had four hours in New York between trains. The one thing Babbitt wished to see was the Pennsylvania Hotel, which had been built since his last visit. He stared up at it, muttering, "Twenty-two hundred rooms and twenty-two hundred baths! That's got everything in the world beat. Lord, their turnover must be—well, suppose price of rooms is four to eight dollars a day, and I suppose maybe some ten and—four times twenty-two hundred —say six times twenty-two hundred—well, anyway, with restaurants and everything, say summers between eight and fifteen thousand a day. Every day! I never thought I'd see a thing like that! Some town! Of course the average fellow in Zenith has got more Individual Initiative than the fourflushers here, but I got to hand it to New York. Yes, sir, town, you're all right—some ways. Well, old Paulski, I guess we've seen everything that's worth while. How'll we kill the rest of the time? Movie?"

But Paul desired to see a liner. "Always wanted to go to Europe—and, by thunder, I will, too, some day before I pass out," he sighed.

From a rough wharf on the North River they stared at the stern of the *Aquitania* and her stacks and wireless antennæ lifted above the dock-house which shut her in.

"By golly," Babbitt droned, "wouldn't be so bad to go over to the Old Country and take a squint at all these ruins, and the place where Shakespeare was born. And think of being able to order a drink whenever you wanted one! Just range up to a bar and holler out loud, 'Gimme a cocktail, and darn the police!' Not bad at all. What juh like to see, over there, Paulibus?"

Paul did not answer. Babbitt turned. Paul was standing with clenched fists, head drooping, staring at the liner as in terror. His thin body, seen against the summer-glaring planks of the wharf, was childishly meager.

Again, "What would you hit for on the other side, Paul?"

Scowling at the steamer, his breast heaving, Paul whispered, "Oh, my God!" While Babbitt watched him anxiously he snapped, "Come on, let's get out of this," and hastened down the wharf, not looking back.

"That's funny," considered Babbitt. "The boy didn't care for seeing the ocean boats after all. I thought he'd be interested in 'em."

## II

Though he exulted, and made sage speculations about locomotive horse-power, as their train climbed the Maine mountain-ridge and from the summit he looked down the shining way among the pines; though he remarked, "Well, by golly!" when he discovered that the station at Katadumcook, the end of the line, was an aged freight-car; Babbitt's moment of impassioned release came when they sat on a tiny wharf on Lake Sunasquam, awaiting the launch from the hotel. A raft had floated down the lake; between the logs and the shore, the water was transparent, thin-looking, flashing with minnows. A guide in black felt hat with trout-flies in the band, and flannel shirt of a peculiarly daring blue, sat on a log and whittled and was silent. A dog, a good country dog, black and woolly gray, a dog rich in leisure and in meditation, scratched and grunted and slept. The thick sunlight was lavish on the bright water, on the rim of gold-green balsam boughs, the silver birches and tropic ferns, and across the lake it burned on the sturdy shoulders of the mountains. Over everything was a holy peace.

Silent, they loafed on the edge of the wharf, swinging their legs above the water. The immense tenderness of the place sank into Babbitt, and he murmured, "I'd just like to sit here—the rest of my life—and whittle—and sit. And never hear a typewriter. Or Stan Graff fussing in the 'phone. Or Rone and Ted scrapping. Just sit. Gosh!"

He patted Paul's shoulder. "How does it strike you, old snoozer?"

"Oh, it's darn good, Georgie. There's something sort of eternal about it."

For once, Babbitt understood him.

### III

Their launch rounded the bend; at the head of the lake, under a mountain slope, they saw the little central dining-shack of their hotel and the crescent of squat log cottages which served as bedrooms. They landed, and endured the critical examination of the habitués who had been at the hotel for a whole week. In their cottage, with its high stone fireplace, they hastened, as Babbitt expressed it, to "get into some regular he-togs." They came out; Paul in an old gray suit and soft white shirt; Babbitt in khaki shirt and vast and flapping khaki trousers. It was excessively new khaki; his rimless spectacles belonged to a city office; and his face was not tanned but a city pink. He made a discordant noise in the place. But with infinite satisfaction he slapped his legs and crowed, "Say, this is getting back home, eh?"

They stood on the wharf before the hotel. He winked at Paul and drew from his back pocket a plug of chewing-tobacco, a vulgarism forbidden in the Babbitt home. He took a chew, beaming and wagging his head as he tugged at it. "Um! Um! Maybe I haven't been hungry for a wad of eating-tobacco! Have some?"

They looked at each other in a grin of understanding. Paul took the plug, gnawed at it. They stood quiet, their jaws working. They solemnly spat, one after the other, into the placid water. They stretched voluptuously, with lifted arms and arched backs. From beyond the mountains came the shuffling sound of a far-off train. A trout leaped, and fell back in a silver circle. They sighed together.

### IV

They had a week before their families came. Each evening they planned to get up early and fish before breakfast. Each morning they lay abed till the breakfast-bell, pleasantly conscious that there were no efficient wives to rouse them. The mornings were cold; the fire was kindly as they dressed.

Paul was distressingly clean, but Babbitt reveled in a good sound dirtiness, in not having to shave till his spirit was moved to it. He treasured every grease spot and fish-scale on his new khaki trousers.

All morning they fished unenergetically, or tramped the dim and aqueous-lighted trails among rank ferns and moss sprinkled with crimson bells. They slept all afternoon, and till midnight played stud-poker with the guides. Poker was a serious business to the guides. They did not gossip; they shuffled the thick greasy cards with a deft ferocity menacing to the "sports;" and Joe Paradise, king of guides, was sarcastic to loiterers who halted the game even to scratch.

At midnight, as Paul and he blundered to their cottage over the pungent wet grass, and pine-roots confusing in the darkness, Babbitt rejoiced that he did not have to explain to his wife where he had been all evening.

They did not talk much. The nervous loquacity and opinionation of the Zenith Athletic Club dropped from them. But when they did talk they slipped into the naïve intimacy of college days. Once they drew their canoe up to the bank of Sunasquam Water, a stream walled in by the dense green of the hardhack. The sun roared on the green jungle but in the shade was sleepy peace, and the water was golden and rippling. Babbitt drew his hand through the cool flood, and mused:

"We never thought we'd come to Maine together!"

"No. We've never done anything the way we thought we would. I expected to live in Germany with my granddad's people, and study the fiddle."

"That's so. And remember how I wanted to be a lawyer and go into politics? I still think I might have made a go of it. I've kind of got the gift of the gab—anyway, I can think on my feet, and make some kind of a spiel on most anything, and of course that's the thing you need in politics. By golly, Ted's going to law-school, even if I didn't! Well— I guess it's worked out all right. Myra's been a fine wife. And Zilla means well, Paulibus."

"Yes. Up here, I figure out all sorts of plans to keep her amused. I kind of feel life is going to be different, now that we're getting a good rest and can go back and start over again."

"I hope so, old boy." Shyly: "Say, gosh, it's been awful nice to sit around and loaf and gamble and act regular, with you along, you old horse-thief!"

"Well, you know what it means to me, Georgie. Saved my life."

The shame of emotion overpowered them; they cursed a little, to prove they were good rough fellows; and in a mellow silence, Babbitt whistling while Paul hummed, they paddled back to the hotel.

### v

Though it was Paul who had seemed overwrought, Babbitt who had been the protecting big brother, Paul became clear-eyed and merry, while Babbitt sank into irritability. He uncovered layer on layer of hidden weariness. At first he had played nimble jester to Paul and for him sought amusements; by the end of the week Paul was nurse, and Babbitt accepted favors with the condescension one always shows a patient nurse.

The day before their families arrived, the women guests at the hotel bubbled, "Oh, isn't it nice! You must be so excited;" and the proprieties compelled Babbitt and Paul to look excited. But they went to bed early and grumpy.

When Myra appeared she said at once, "Now, we want you boys to go on playing around just as if we weren't here."

The first evening, he stayed out for poker with the guides, and she said in placid merriment, "My! You're a regular bad one!" The second evening, she groaned sleepily, "Good heavens, are you going to be out every single night?" The third evening, he didn't play poker.

He was tired now in every cell. "Funny! Vacation doesn't seem to have done me a bit of good," he lamented. "Paul's frisky as a colt, but I swear, I'm crankier and nervouser than when I came up here."

He had three weeks of Maine. At the end of the second week he began to feel calm, and interested in life. He planned an expedition to climb Sachem Mountain, and wanted to camp overnight at Box Car Pond. He was curiously weak, yet cheerful, as though he had cleansed his veins of poisonous energy and was filling them with wholesome blood.

He ceased to be irritated by Ted's infatuation with a waitress (his seventh tragic affair this year); he played catch with Ted, and with pride taught him to cast a fly in the pine-shadowed silence of Skowtuit Pond.

At the end he sighed, "Hang it, I'm just beginning to enjoy my vacation. But, well, I feel a lot better. And it's going to be one great year! Maybe the Real Estate Board will elect me president, instead of some fuzzy old-fashioned faker like Chan Mott."

On the way home, whenever he went into the smoking-compartment he felt guilty at deserting his wife and angry at being expected to feel guilty, but each time he triumphed, "Oh, this is going to be a great year, a great old year!"

# 12

All the way home from Maine, Babbitt was certain that he was a changed man. He was converted to serenity. He was going to cease worrying about business. He was going to have more "interests"—theaters, public affairs, reading. And suddenly, as he finished an especially heavy cigar, he was going to stop smoking.

He invented a new and perfect method. He would buy no tobacco; he would depend on borrowing it; and, of course, he would be ashamed to borrow often. In a spasm of righteousness he flung his cigar-case out of the smoking-compartment window. He went back and was kind to his wife about nothing in particular; he admired his own purity, and decided, "Absolutely simple. Just a matter of will-power." He started a magazine serial about a scientific detective. Ten miles on, he was conscious that he desired to smoke. He ducked his head, like a turtle going into its shell; he appeared uneasy; he skipped two pages in his story and didn't know it. Five miles later, he leaped up and sought the porter. "Say, uh, George, have you got a—" The porter looked patient. "Have you got a time-table?" Babbitt finished. At the next stop he went out and bought a cigar. Since it was to be his last before he reached Zenith, he finished it down to an inch stub.

Four days later he again remembered that he had stopped smoking, but he was too busy catching up with his office-work to keep it remembered.

## II

Baseball, he determined, would be an excellent hobby. "No sense a man's working his fool head off. I'm going out to the Game three times a week. Besides, fellow ought to support the home team."

He did go and support the team, and enhance the glory of Zenith, by yelling "Attaboy!" and "Rotten!" He performed the rite scrupulously. He wore a cotton handkerchief about his collar; he became sweaty; he opened his mouth in a wide loose grin; and drank lemon soda out of a bottle. He went to the Game three times a week, for one week. Then he compromised on watching the *Advocate-Times* bulletin-board. He stood in the thickest and steamiest of the crowd, and as the boy up on the lofty platform recorded the achievements of Big Bill Bostwick, the pitcher, Babbitt remarked to complete strangers, "Pretty nice! Good work!" and hastened back to the office.

He honestly believed that he loved baseball. It is true that he hadn't, in twenty-five years, himself played any baseball except back-lot catch with Ted —very gentle, and strictly limited to ten minutes. But the game was a custom of his clan, and it gave outlet for the homicidal and sides-taking instincts which Babbitt called "patriotism" and "love of sport."

As he approached the office he walked faster and faster, muttering, "Guess better hustle." All about him the city was hustling, for hustling's sake. Men in motors were hustling to pass one another in the hustling traffic. Men were hustling to catch trolleys, with another trolley a minute behind, and to leap from the trolleys, to gallop across the sidewalk, to hurl themselves into buildings, into hustling express elevators. Men in dairy lunches were hustling to gulp down the food which cooks had hustled to fry. Men in barber shops were snapping, "Jus' shave me once over. Gotta hustle." Men were feverishly getting rid of visitors in offices adorned with the signs, "This Is My Busy Day" and "The Lord Created the World in Six Days—You Can Spiel All You Got to Say in Six Minutes." Men who had made five thousand, year before last, and ten thousand last year, were urging on nerve-yelping bodies and parched brains so that they might make twenty thousand this year; and the men who had broken down immediately after making their twenty thousand dollars were hustling to catch trains, to hustle through the vacations which the hustling doctors had ordered.

Among them Babbitt hustled back to his office, to sit down with nothing much to do except see that the staff looked as though they were hustling.

## III

Every Saturday afternoon he hustled out to his country club and hustled through nine holes of golf as a rest after the week's hustle.

In Zenith it was as necessary for a Successful Man to belong to a country club as it was to wear a linen collar. Babbitt's was the Outing Golf and Country Club, a pleasant gray-shingled building with a broad porch, on a daisy-starred cliff above Lake Kennepoose. There was another, the Tonawanda Country Club, to which belonged Charles McKelvey, Horace Updike, and the other rich men who lunched not at the Athletic but at the Union Club. Babbitt explained with frequency, "You couldn't hire me to join the Tonawanda, even if I did have a hundred and eighty bucks to throw away on the initiation fee. At the Outing we've got a bunch of real human fellows, and the finest lot of little women in town—just as good at joshing as the men— but at the Tonawanda there's nothing but these would-be's in New York get-ups, drinking tea! Too much dog altogether. Why, I wouldn't join the Tonawanda even if they— I wouldn't join it on a bet!"

When he had played four or five holes, he relaxed a bit, his tobacco-fluttering heart beat more normally, and his voice slowed to the drawling of his hundred generations of peasant ancestors.

IV

At least once a week Mr. and Mrs. Babbitt and Tinka went to the movies. Their favorite motion-picture theater was the Château, which held three thousand spectators and had an orchestra of fifty pieces which played Arrangements from the Operas and suites portraying a Day on the Farm, or a Four-alarm Fire. In the stone rotunda, decorated with crown-embroidered velvet chairs and almost medieval tapestries, parrakeets sat on gilded lotos columns.

With exclamations of "Well, by golly!" and "You got to go some to beat this dump!" Babbitt admired the Château. As he stared across the thousands of heads, a gray plain in the dimness, as he smelled good clothes and mild perfume and chewing-gum, he felt as when he had first seen a mountain and realized how very, very much earth and rock there was in it.

He liked three kinds of films: pretty bathing girls with bare legs; policemen or cowboys and an industrious shooting of revolvers; and funny fat men who ate spaghetti. He chuckled with immense, moist-eyed sentimentality at interludes portraying puppies, kittens, and chubby babies; and he wept at deathbeds and old mothers being patient in mortgaged cottages. Mrs. Babbitt preferred the pictures in which handsome young women in elaborate frocks moved through sets ticketed as the drawing-rooms of New York millionaires. As for Tinka, she preferred, or was believed to prefer, whatever her parents told her to.

All his relaxations—baseball, golf, movies, bridge, motoring, long talks with Paul at the Athletic Club, or at the Good Red Beef and Old English Chop House—were necessary to Babbitt, for he was entering a year of such activity as he had never known.

# 13

It was by accident that Babbitt had his opportunity to address the S. A. R. E. B.

The S. A. R. E. B., as its members called it, with the universal passion for mysterious and important-sounding initials, was the State Association of Real Estate Boards; the organization of brokers and operators. It was to hold its annual convention at Monarch, Zenith's chief rival among the cities of the state. Babbitt was an official delegate; another was Cecil Rountree, whom Babbitt admired for his picaresque speculative building, and hated for his social position, for being present at the smartest dances on Royal Ridge. Rountree was chairman of the convention program-committee.

Babbitt had growled to him, "Makes me tired the way these doctors and profs and preachers put on lugs about being 'professional men.' A good realtor has to have more knowledge and finesse than any of 'em."

"Right you are! I say: Why don't you put that into a paper, and give it at the S. A. R. E. B.?" suggested Rountree.

"Well, if it would help you in making up the program— Tell you: the way I look at it is this: First place, we ought to insist that folks call us 'realtors' and not 'real-estate men.' Sounds more like a reg'lar profession. Second place— What is it distinguishes a profession from a mere trade, business, or occupation? What is it? Why, it's the public service and the skill, the trained skill, and the knowledge and, uh, all that, whereas a fellow that merely goes out for the jack, he never considers the—public service and trained skill and so on. Now as a professional—"

"Rather! That's perfectly bully! Perfectly corking! Now you write it in a paper," said Rountree, as he rapidly and firmly moved away.

## II

However accustomed to the literary labors of advertisements and correspondence, Babbitt was dismayed on the evening when he sat down to prepare a paper which would take a whole ten minutes to read.

He laid out a new fifteen-cent school exercise-book on his wife's collapsible sewing-table, set up for the event in the living-room. The household had been bullied into silence; Verona and Ted requested to disappear, and Tinka threatened with "If I hear one sound out of you—if you holler for a glass of water one single solitary time— You better not, that's all!" Mrs. Babbitt sat over by the piano, making a nightgown and gazing with respect while Babbitt wrote in the exercise-book, to the rhythmical wiggling and squeaking of the sewing-table.

When he rose, damp and jumpy, and his throat dusty from cigarettes, she marveled, "I don't see how you can just sit down and make up things right out of your own head!"

"Oh, it's the training in constructive imagination that a fellow gets in modern business life."

He had written seven pages, whereof the first page set forth:

(1) a profession

(2) Not just Trade

(3) ~~Skill + Vision~~

(3) Shd be called "realtor" + not just real est man

The other six pages were rather like the first.

For a week he went about looking important. Every morning, as he dressed, he thought aloud: "Jever stop to consider, Myra, that before a town can have buildings or prosperity or any of those things, some realtor has got to sell 'em the land? All civilization starts with him. Jever realize that?" At the Athletic Club he led unwilling men aside to inquire, "Say, if you had to read a paper before a big convention, would you start in with the funny stories or just kind of scatter 'em all through?" He asked Howard Littlefield for a "set of statistics about real-estate sales; something good and impressive," and Littlefield provided something exceedingly good and impressive.

But it was to T. Cholmondeley Frink that Babbitt most often turned. He caught Frink at the club every noon, and demanded, while Frink looked hunted and evasive, "Say, Chum—you're a shark on this writing stuff—how would you put this sentence, see here in my manuscript—manuscript—now where the deuce is that?—oh, yes, here. Would you say 'We ought not also to alone think?' or 'We ought also not to think alone?' or—"

One evening when his wife was away and he had no one to impress, Babbitt forgot about Style, Order, and the other mysteries, and scrawled off what he really thought about the real-estate business and about himself, and he found the paper written. When he read it to his wife she yearned, "Why, dear, it's splendid; beautifully written, and so clear and interesting, and such splendid ideas! Why, it's just—it's just splendid!"

Next day he cornered Chum Frink and crowed, "Well, old son, I finished it last evening! Just lammed it out! I used to think you writing-guys must have a hard job making up pieces, but Lord, it's a cinch. Pretty soft for you fellows; you certainly earn your money easy! Some day when I get ready to retire, guess I'll take to writing and show you boys how to do it. I always used to think I could write better stuff, and more punch and originality, than all this stuff you see printed, and now I'm doggone sure of it!"

He had four copies of the paper typed in black with a gorgeous red title, had them bound in pale blue manilla, and affably presented one to old Ira Runyon, the managing editor of the *Advocate-Times,* who said yes, indeed yes, he was very glad to have it, and he certainly would read it all through—as soon as he could find time.

Mrs. Babbitt could not go to Monarch. She had a women's-club meeting. Babbitt said that he was very sorry.

III

Besides the five official delegates to the convention—Babbitt, Rountree, W. A. Rogers, Alvin Thayer, and Elbert Wing—there were fifty unofficial delegates, most of them with their wives.

They met at the Union Station for the midnight train to Monarch. All of them, save Cecil Rountree, who was such a snob that he never wore badges, displayed celluloid buttons the size of dollars and lettered "We zoom for Zenith." The official delegates were magnificent with silver and magenta ribbons. Martin Lumsen's little boy Willy carried a tasseled banner inscribed "Zenith the Zip City—Zeal, Zest and Zowie—1,000,000 in 1935." As the delegates arrived, not in taxicabs but in the family automobile driven by the oldest son or by Cousin Fred, they formed impromptu processions through the station waiting-room.

It was a new and enormous waiting-room, with marble pilasters, and frescoes depicting the exploration of the Chaloosa River Valley by Père Emile Fauthoux in 1740. The benches were shelves of ponderous mahogany; the news-stand a marble kiosk with a brass grill. Down the echoing spaces of the hall the delegates paraded after Willy Lumsen's banner, the men waving their cigars, the women conscious of their new frocks and strings of beads, all singing to the tune of Auld Lang Syne the official City Song, written by Chum Frink:

> Good old Zenith,
> Our kin and kith,
> Wherever we may be,
> Hats in the ring,
> We blithely sing
> Of thy Prosperity.

Warren Whitby, the broker, who had a gift of verse for banquets and birthdays, had added to Frink's City Song a special verse for the realtors' convention:

> Oh, here we come,
> The fellows from
> Zenith, the Zip Citee.
> We wish to state
> In real estate
> There's none so live as we.

Babbitt was stirred to hysteric patriotism. He leaped on a bench, shouting to the crowd:

"What's the matter with Zenith?"

"She's all right!"

"What's best ole town in the U. S. A.?"

"Zeeeeeen-ith!"

The patient poor people waiting for the midnight train stared in unenvious wonder—Italian women with shawls, old weary men with broken shoes, roving road-wise boys in suits which had been flashy when they were new but which were faded now and wrinkled.

Babbitt perceived that as an official delegate he must be more dignified. With Wing and Rogers he tramped up and down the cement platform beside the waiting Pullmans. Motor-driven baggage-trucks and red-capped porters carrying bags sped down the platform with an agreeable effect of activity. Arc-lights glared and stammered overhead. The glossy yellow sleeping-cars shone impressively. Babbitt made his voice to be measured and lordly; he thrust out his abdomen and rumbled, "We got to see to it that the convention lets the Legislature understand just where they get off in this matter of taxing realty transfers." Wing uttered approving grunts and Babbitt swelled —gloated—

The blind of a Pullman compartment was raised, and Babbitt looked into an unfamiliar world. The occupant of the compartment was Lucile Mc-Kelvey, the pretty wife of the millionaire contractor. Possibly, Babbitt thrilled, she was going to Europe! On the seat beside her was a bunch of orchids and violets, and a yellow paper-bound book which seemed foreign. While he stared, she picked up the book, then glanced out of the window as though she was bored. She must have looked straight at him, and he had met her, but she gave no sign. She languidly pulled down the blind, and he stood still, a cold feeling of insignificance in his heart.

But on the train his pride was restored by meeting delegates from Sparta, Pioneer, and other smaller cities of the state, who listened respectfully when, as a magnifico from the metropolis of Zenith, he explained politics and the value of a Good Sound Business Administration. They fell joyfully into shop-talk, the purest and most rapturous form of conversation:

"How'd this fellow Rountree make out with this big apartment-hotel he was going to put up? Whadde do? Get out bonds to finance it?" asked a Sparta broker.

"Well, I'll tell you," said Babbitt. "Now if I'd been handling it—"

"So," Elbert Wing was droning, "I hired this shop-window for a week, and put up a big sign, 'Toy Town for Tiny Tots,' and stuck in a lot of doll houses and some dinky little trees, and then down at the bottom, 'Baby Likes This Dollydale, but Papa and Mama Will Prefer Our Beautiful Bungalows,' and you know, that certainly got folks talking, and first week we sold—"

The trucks sang "lickety-lick, lickety-lick" as the train ran through the factory district. Furnaces spurted flame, and power-hammers were clanging.

Red lights, green lights, furious white lights rushed past, and Babbitt was important again, and eager.

### IV

He did a voluptuous thing: he had his clothes pressed on the train. In the morning, half an hour before they reached Monarch, the porter came to his berth and whispered, "There's a drawing-room vacant, sir. I put your suit in there." In tan autumn overcoat over his pajamas, Babbitt slipped down the green-curtain-lined aisle to the glory of his first private compartment. The porter indicated that he knew Babbitt was used to a man-servant; he held the ends of Babbitt's trousers, that the beautifully sponged garment might not be soiled, filled the bowl in the private washroom, and waited with a towel.

To have a private washroom was luxurious. However enlivening a Pullman smoking-compartment was by night, even to Babbitt it was depressing in the morning, when it was jammed with fat men in woolen undershirts, every hook filled with wrinkled cottony shirts, the leather seat piled with dingy toilet-kits, and the air nauseating with the smell of soap and toothpaste. Babbitt did not ordinarily think much of privacy, but now he reveled in it, reveled in his valet, and purred with pleasure as he gave the man a tip of a dollar and a half.

He rather hoped that he was being noticed as, in his newly pressed clothes, with the adoring porter carrying his suit-case, he disembarked at Monarch.

He was to share a room at the Hotel Sedgwick with W. A. Rogers, that shrewd, rustic-looking Zenith dealer in farm-lands. Together they had a noble breakfast, with waffles, and coffee not in exiguous cups but in large pots. Babbitt grew expansive, and told Rogers about the art of writing; he gave a bell-boy a quarter to fetch a morning newspaper from the lobby, and sent to Tinka a post-card: "Papa wishes you were here to bat round with him."

### V

The meetings of the convention were held in the ballroom of the Allen House. In an anteroom was the office of the chairman of the executive committee. He was the busiest man in the convention; he was so busy that he got nothing done whatever. He sat at a marquetry table, in a room littered with crumpled paper and, all day long, town-boosters and lobbyists and orators who wished to lead debates came and whispered to him, whereupon he looked vague, and said rapidly, "Yes, yes, that's a fine idea; we'll do that," and instantly forgot all about it, lighted a cigar and forgot that too, while the telephone rang mercilessly and about him men kept beseeching, "Say, Mr. Chairman—say, Mr. Chairman!" without penetrating his exhausted hearing.

In the exhibit-room were plans of the new suburbs of Sparta, pictures of the new state capitol, at Galop de Vache, and large ears of corn with the label, "Nature's Gold, from Shelby County, the Garden Spot of God's Own Country."

The real convention consisted of men muttering in hotel bedrooms or in groups amid the badge-spotted crowd in the hotel-lobby, but there was a show of public meetings.

The first of them opened with a welcome by the mayor of Monarch. The pastor of the First Christian Church of Monarch, a large man with a long damp frontal lock, informed God that the real-estate men were here now.

The venerable Minnemagantic realtor, Major Carlton Tuke, read a paper in which he denounced coöperative stores. William A. Larkin of Eureka gave a comforting prognosis of "The Prospects for Increased Construction," and reminded them that plate-glass prices were two points lower.

The convention was on.

The delegates were entertained, incessantly and firmly. The Monarch Chamber of Commerce gave them a banquet, and the Manufacturers' Association an afternoon reception, at which a chrysanthemum was presented to each of the ladies, and to each of the men a leather bill-fold inscribed "From Monarch the Mighty Motor Mart."

Mrs. Crosby Knowlton, wife of the manufacturer of Fleetwing Automobiles, opened her celebrated Italian garden and served tea. Six hundred real-estate men and wives ambled down the autumnal paths. Perhaps three hundred of them were quietly inconspicuous; perhaps three hundred vigorously exclaimed, "This is pretty slick, eh?" surreptitiously picked the late asters and concealed them in their pockets, and tried to get near enough to Mrs. Knowlton to shake her lovely hand. Without request, the Zenith delegates (except Rountree) gathered round a marble dancing nymph and sang "Here we come, the fellows from Zenith, the Zip Citee."

It chanced that all the delegates from Pioneer belonged to the Brotherly and Protective Order of Elks, and they produced an enormous banner lettered: "B. P. O. E.—Best People on Earth—Boost Pioneer, Oh Eddie." Nor was Galop de Vache, the state capital, to be slighted. The leader of the Galop de Vache delegation was a large, reddish, roundish man, but active. He took off his coat, hurled his broad black felt hat on the ground, rolled up his sleeves, climbed upon the sundial, spat, and bellowed:

"We'll tell the world, and the good lady who's giving the show this afternoon, that the bonniest burg in this man's state is Galop de Vache. You boys can talk about your zip, but jus' lemme murmur that old Galop has the largest proportion of home-owning citizens in the state; and when folks own their homes, they ain't starting labor-troubles, and they're raising kids instead of raising hell! Galop de Vache! The town for homey folks! The town that eats 'em alive oh, Bosco! We'll—tell—the—world!"

The guests drove off; the garden shivered into quiet. But Mrs. Crosby Knowlton sighed as she looked at a marble seat warm from five hundred summers of Amalfi. On the face of a winged sphinx which supported it some one had drawn a mustache in lead-pencil. Crumpled paper napkins were dumped among the Michaelmas daisies. On the walk, like shredded lovely

flesh, were the petals of the last gallant rose. Cigarette stubs floated in the
goldfish pool, trailing an evil stain as they swelled and disintegrated, and
beneath the marble seat, the fragments carefully put together, was a smashed
teacup.

## VI

As he rode back to the hotel Babbitt reflected, "Myra would have enjoyed
all this social agony." For himself he cared less for the garden party than
for the motor tours which the Monarch Chamber of Commerce had arranged. Indefatigably he viewed water-reservoirs, suburban trolley-stations,
and tanneries. He devoured the statistics which were given to him, and marveled to his roommate, W. A. Rogers, "Of course this town isn't a patch on
Zenith; it hasn't got our outlook and natural resources; but did you know—I
nev' did till to-day—that they manufactured seven hundred and sixty-three
million feet of lumber last year? What d' you think of that!"

He was nervous as the time for reading his paper approached. When he
stood on the low platform before the convention, he trembled and saw only
a purple haze. But he was in earnest, and when he had finished the formal
paper he talked to them, his hands in his pockets, his spectacled face a flashing disk, like a plate set up on edge in the lamplight. They shouted "That's
the stuff!" and in the discussion afterward they referred with impressiveness
to "our friend and brother, Mr. George F. Babbitt." He had in fifteen minutes changed from a minor delegate to a personage almost as well known
as that diplomat of business, Cecil Rountree. After the meeting, delegates
from all over the state said, "Hower you, Brother Babbitt?" Sixteen complete
strangers called him "George," and three men took him into corners to confide, "Mighty glad you had the courage to stand up and give the Profession
a real boost. Now I've always maintained—"

Next morning, with tremendous casualness, Babbitt asked the girl at the
hotel news-stand for the newspapers from Zenith. There was nothing in the
*Press*, but in the *Advocate-Times*, on the third page— He gasped. They had
printed his picture and a half-column account. The heading was "Sensation
at Annual Land-men's Convention. G. F. Babbitt, Prominent Ziptown Realtor, Keynoter in Fine Address."

He murmured reverently, "I guess some of the folks on Floral Heights
will sit up and take notice now, and pay a little attention to old Georgie!"

## VII

It was the last meeting. The delegations were presenting the claims of
their several cities to the next year's convention. Orators were announcing
that "Galop de Vache, the Capital City, the site of Kremer College and of
the Upholtz Knitting Works, is the recognized center of culture and high-
class enterprise;" and that "Hamburg, the Big Little City with the Logical
Location, where every man is open-handed and every woman a heaven-born
hostess, throws wide to you her hospitable gates."

In the midst of these more diffident invitations, the golden doors of the ballroom opened with a blatting of trumpets, and a circus parade rolled in. It was composed of the Zenith brokers, dressed as cowpunchers, bareback riders, Japanese jugglers. At the head was big Warren Whitby, in the bearskin and gold-and-crimson coat of a drum-major. Behind him, as a clown, beating a bass drum, extraordinarily happy and noisy, was Babbitt.

Warren Whitby leaped on the platform, made merry play with his baton, and observed, "Boyses and girlses, the time has came to get down to cases. A dyed-in-the-wool Zenithite sure loves his neighbors, but we've made up our minds to grab this convention off our neighbor burgs like we've grabbed the condensed-milk business and the paper-box business and—"

J. Harry Barmhill, the convention chairman, hinted, "We're grateful to you, Mr. Uh, but you must give the other boys a chance to hand in their bids now."

A fog-horn voice blared, "In Eureka we'll promise free motor rides through the prettiest country—"

Running down the aisle, clapping his hands, a lean bald young man cried, "I'm from Sparta! Our Chamber of Commerce has wired me they've set aside eight thousand dollars, in real money, for the entertainment of the convention!"

A clerical-looking man rose to clamor, "Money talks! Move we accept the bid from Sparta!"

It was accepted.

### VIII

The Committee on Resolutions was reporting. They said that Whereas Almighty God in his beneficent mercy had seen fit to remove to a sphere of higher usefulness some thirty-six realtors of the state the past year, Therefore it was the sentiment of this convention assembled that they were sorry God had done it, and the secretary should be, and hereby was, instructed to spread these resolutions on the minutes, and to console the bereaved families by sending them each a copy.

A second resolution authorized the president of the S. A. R. E. B. to spend fifteen thousand dollars in lobbying for sane tax measures in the State Legislature. This resolution had a good deal to say about Menaces to Sound Business and clearing the Wheels of Progress from ill-advised and shortsighted obstacles.

The Committee on Committees reported, and with startled awe Babbitt learned that he had been appointed a member of the Committee on Torrens Titles.

He rejoiced, "I said it was going to be a great year! Georgie, old son, you got big things ahead of you! You're a natural-born orator and a good mixer and— Zowie!"

IX

There was no formal entertainment provided for the last evening. Babbitt had planned to go home, but that afternoon the Jered Sassburgers of Pioneer suggested that Babbitt and W. A. Rogers have tea with them at the Catalpa Inn.

Teas were not unknown to Babbitt—his wife and he earnestly attended them at least twice a year—but they were sufficiently exotic to make him feel important. He sat at a glass-covered table in the Art Room of the Inn, with its painted rabbits, mottoes lettered on birch bark, and waitresses being artistic in Dutch caps; he ate insufficient lettuce sandwiches, and was lively and naughty with Mrs. Sassburger, who was as smooth and large-eyed as a cloak-model. Sassburger and he had met two days before, so they were calling each other "Georgie" and "Sassy."

Sassburger said prayerfully, "Say, boys, before you go, seeing this is the last chance, I've *got it*, up in my room, and Miriam here is the best little mixologist in the Stati Unidos, like us Italians say."

With wide flowing gestures, Babbitt and Rogers followed the Sassburgers to their room. Mrs. Sassburger shrieked, "Oh, how terrible!" when she saw that she had left a chemise of sheer lavender crêpe on the bed. She tucked it into a bag, while Babbitt giggled, "Don't mind us; we're a couple o' little divvils!"

Sassburger telephoned for ice, and the bell-boy who brought it said, prosaically and unprompted, "Highball glasses or cocktail?" Miriam Sassburger mixed the cocktails in one of those dismal, nakedly white water-pitchers which exist only in hotels. When they had finished the first round she proved by intoning "Think you boys could stand another—you got a dividend coming" that, though she was but a woman, she knew the complete and perfect rite of cocktail-drinking.

Outside, Babbitt hinted to Rogers, "Say, W. A., old rooster, it comes over me that I could stand it if we didn't go back to the lovin' wives, this handsome *Abend*, but just kind of stayed in Monarch and threw a party, heh?"

"George, you speak with the tongue of wisdom and sagashiteriferousness. El Wing's wife has gone on to Pittsburg. Let's see if we can't gather him in."

At half-past seven they sat in their room, with Elbert Wing and two up-state delegates. Their coats were off, their vests open, their faces red, their voices emphatic. They were finishing a bottle of corrosive bootlegged whisky and imploring the bell-boy, "Say, son, can you get us some more of this embalming fluid?" They were smoking large cigars and dropping ashes and stubs on the carpet. With windy guffaws they were telling stories. They were, in fact, males in a happy state of nature.

Babbitt sighed, "I don't know how it strikes you hellions, but personally I like this busting loose for a change, and kicking over a couple of mountains and climbing up on the North Pole and waving the aurora borealis around."

The man from Sparta, a grave, intense youngster, babbled, "Say! I guess

I'm as good a husband as the run of the mill, but God, I do get so tired of going home every evening, and nothing to see but the movies. That's why I go out and drill with the National Guard. I guess I got the nicest little wife in my burg, but— Say! Know what I wanted to do as a kid? Know what I wanted to do? Wanted to be a big chemist. Tha's what I wanted to do. But Dad chased me out on the road selling kitchenware, and here I'm settled down—settled for *life*—not a chance! Oh, who the devil started this funeral talk? How 'bout 'nother lil drink? 'And a-noth-er drink wouldn' do 's 'ny harmmmmmmmm.'"

"Yea. Cut the sob-stuff," said W. A. Rogers genially. "You boys know I'm the village songster? Come on now—sing up:

> Said the old Obadiah to the young Obadiah,
> 'I am dry, Obadiah, I am dry.'
> Said the young Obadiah to the old Obadiah,
> 'So am I, Obadiah, so am I.'"

## X

They had dinner in the Moorish Grillroom of the Hotel Sedgwick. Somewhere, somehow, they seemed to have gathered in two other comrades: a manufacturer of fly-paper and a dentist. They all drank whisky from tea-cups, and they were humorous, and never listened to one another, except when W. A. Rogers "kidded" the Italian waiter.

"Say, Gooseppy," he said innocently, "I want a couple o' fried elephants' ears."

"Sorry, sir, we haven't any."

"Huh? No elephants' ears? What do you know about that!" Rogers turned to Babbitt. "Pedro says the elephants' ears are all out!"

"Well, I'll be switched!" said the man from Sparta, with difficulty hiding his laughter.

"Well, in that case, Carlo, just bring me a hunk o' steak and a couple o' bushels o' French fried potatoes and some peas," Rogers went on. "I suppose back in dear old sunny It' the Eyetalians get their fresh garden peas out of the can."

"No, sir, we have very nice peas in Italy."

"Is that a fact! Georgie, do you hear that? They get their fresh garden peas out of the garden, in Italy! By golly, you live and learn, don't you, Antonio, you certainly do live and learn, if you live long enough and keep your strength. All right, Garibaldi, just shoot me in that steak, with about two printers'-reams of French fried spuds on the promenade deck, *comprehenez-vous*, Michelovitch Angeloni?"

Afterward Elbert Wing admired, "Gee, you certainly did have that poor Dago going, W. A. He couldn't make you out at all!"

In the *Monarch Herald*, Babbitt found an advertisement which he read aloud, to applause and laughter:

Old Colony Theatre

Shake the Old Dogs to the
### WROLLICKING WRENS
The bonniest bevy of beauteous
bathing babes in burlesque.
Pete Menutti and his
Oh, Gee, Kids.

This is the straight steer, Benny, the painless chicklets of the Wrollick-
ing Wrens are the cuddlingest bunch that ever hit town. Steer the feet,
get the card board, and twist the pupils to the PDQest show ever. You
will get 111% on your kale in this fun-fest. The Calroza Sisters are sure
some lookers and will give you a run for your gelt. Jock Silbersteen is
one of the pepper lads and slips you a dose of real laughter. Shoot the
up and down to Jackson and West for graceful tappers. They run 1-2
under the wire. Provin and Adams will blow the blues in their laugh
skit "Hootch Mon!" Something doing, boys. Listen to what the Hep
Bird twitters.

"Sounds like a juicy show to me. Let's all take it in," said Babbitt.

But they put off departure as long as they could. They were safe while
they sat here, legs firmly crossed under the table, but they felt unsteady;
they were afraid of navigating the long and slippery floor of the grillroom
under the eyes of the other guests and the too-attentive waiters.

When they did venture, tables got in their way, and they sought to cover
embarrassment by heavy jocularity at the coat-room. As the girl handed out
their hats, they smiled at her, and hoped that she, a cool and expert judge,
would feel that they were gentlemen. They croaked at one another, "Who
owns the bum lid?" and "You take a good one, George; I'll take what's left,"
and to the check-girl they stammered, "Better come along, sister! High, wide,
and fancy evening ahead!" All of them tried to tip her, urging one another,
"No! Wait! Here! I got it right here!" Among them, they gave her three
dollars.

XI

Flamboyantly smoking cigars they sat in a box at the burlesque show, their
feet up on the rail, while a chorus of twenty daubed, worried, and inextin-
guishably respectable grandams swung their legs in the more elementary
chorus-evolutions, and a Jewish comedian made vicious fun of Jews. In the
entr'actes they met other lone delegates. A dozen of them went in taxicabs
out to Bright Blossom Inn, where the blossoms were made of dusty paper
festooned along a room low and stinking, like a cow-stable no longer wisely
used.

Here, whisky was served openly, in glasses. Two or three clerks, who on
pay-day longed to be taken for millionaires, sheepishly danced with tele-
phone-girls and manicure-girls in the narrow space between the tables. Fan-

tastically whirled the professionals, a young man in sleek evening-clothes and a slim mad girl in emerald silk, with amber hair flung up as jaggedly as flames. Babbitt tried to dance with her. He shuffled along the floor, too bulky to be guided, his steps unrelated to the rhythm of the jungle music, and in his staggering he would have fallen, had she not held him with supple kindly strength. He was blind and deaf from prohibition-era alcohol; he could not see the tables, the faces. But he was overwhelmed by the girl and her young pliant warmth.

When she had firmly returned him to his group, he remembered, by a connection quite untraceable, that his mother's mother had been Scotch, and with head thrown back, eyes closed, wide mouth indicating ecstasy, he sang, very slowly and richly, "Loch Lomond."

But that was the last of his mellowness and jolly companionship. The man from Sparta said he was a "bum singer," and for ten minutes Babbitt quarreled with him, in a loud, unsteady, heroic indignation. They called for drinks till the manager insisted that the place was closed. All the while Babbitt felt a hot raw desire for more brutal amusements. When W. A. Rogers drawled, "What say we go down the line and look over the girls?" he agreed savagely. Before they went, three of them secretly made appointments with the professional dancing girl, who agreed "Yes, yes, sure, darling" to everything they said, and amiably forgot them.

As they drove back through the outskirts of Monarch, down streets of small brown wooden cottages of workmen, characterless as cells, as they rattled across warehouse-districts which by drunken night seemed vast and perilous, as they were borne toward the red lights and violent automatic pianos and the stocky women who simpered, Babbitt was frightened. He wanted to leap from the taxicab, but all his body was a murky fire, and he groaned, "Too late to quit now," and knew that he did not want to quit.

There was, they felt, one very humorous incident on the way. A broker from Minnemagantic said, "Monarch is a lot sportier than Zenith. You Zenith tightwads haven't got any joints like these here." Babbitt raged, "That's a dirty lie! Snothin' you can't find in Zenith. Believe me, we got more houses and hootch-parlors an' all kinds o' dives than any burg in the state."

He realized they were laughing at him; he desired to fight; and forgot it in such musty unsatisfying experiments as he had not known since college.

In the morning, when he returned to Zenith, his desire for rebellion was partly satisfied. He had retrograded to a shame-faced contentment. He was irritable. He did not smile when W. A. Rogers complained, "Ow, what a head! I certainly do feel like the wrath of God this morning. Say! I know what was the trouble! Somebody went and put alcohol in my booze last night."

Babbitt's excursion was never known to his family, nor to any one in Zenith save Rogers and Wing. It was not officially recognized even by himself. If it had any consequences, they have not been discovered.

# 14

This autumn a Mr. W. G. Harding, of Marion, Ohio, was appointed President of the United States, but Zenith was less interested in the national campaign than in the local election. Seneca Doane, though he was a lawyer and a graduate of the State University, was candidate for mayor of Zenith on an alarming labor ticket. To oppose him the Democrats and Republicans united on Lucas Prout, a mattress-manufacturer with a perfect record for sanity. Mr. Prout was supported by the banks, the Chamber of Commerce, all the decent newspapers, and George F. Babbitt.

Babbitt was precinct-leader on Floral Heights, but his district was safe and he longed for stouter battling. His convention paper had given him the beginning of a reputation for oratory, so the Republican-Democratic Central Committee sent him to the Seventh Ward and South Zenith, to address small audiences of workmen and clerks, and wives uneasy with their new votes. He acquired a fame enduring for weeks. Now and then a reporter was present at one of his meetings, and the headlines (though they were not very large) indicated that George F. Babbitt had addressed Cheering Throng, and Distinguished Man of Affairs had pointed out the Fallacies of Doane. Once, in the rotogravure section of the Sunday *Advocate-Times*, there was a photograph of Babbitt and a dozen other business men, with the caption "Leaders of Zenith Finance and Commerce Who Back Prout."

He deserved his glory. He was an excellent campaigner. He had faith; he was certain that if Lincoln were alive, he would be electioneering for Mr. W. G. Harding—unless he came to Zenith and electioneered for Lucas Prout. He did not confuse audiences by silly subtleties; Prout represented honest industry, Seneca Doane represented whining laziness, and you could take your choice. With his broad shoulders and vigorous voice, he was obviously a Good Fellow; and, rarest of all, he really liked people. He almost liked common workmen. He wanted them to be well paid, and able to afford high rents—though, naturally, they must not interfere with the reasonable profits of stockholders. Thus nobly endowed, and keyed high by the discovery that he was a natural orator, he was popular with audiences, and he raged through the campaign, renowned not only in the Seventh and Eighth Wards but even in parts of the Sixteenth.

## II

Crowded in his car, they came driving up to Turnverein Hall, South Zenith—Babbitt, his wife, Verona, Ted, and Paul and Zilla Riesling. The hall was over a delicatessen shop, in a street banging with trolleys and smelling of onions and gasoline and fried fish. A new appreciation of Babbitt filled all of them, including Babbitt.

"Don't know how you keep it up, talking to three bunches in one evening. Wish I had your strength," said Paul; and Ted exclaimed to Verona, "The old man certainly does know how to kid these roughnecks along!"

Men in black sateen shirts, their faces new-washed but with a hint of grime under their eyes, were loitering on the broad stairs up to the hall. Babbitt's party politely edged through them and into the whitewashed room, at the front of which was a dais with a red-plush throne and a pine altar painted watery blue, as used nightly by the Grand Masters and Supreme Potentates of innumerable lodges. The hall was full. As Babbitt pushed through the fringe standing at the back, he heard the precious tribute, "That's him!" The chairman bustled down the center aisle with an impressive, "The speaker? All ready, sir! Uh—let's see—what was the name, sir?"

Then Babbitt slid into a sea of eloquence:

"Ladies and gentlemen of the Sixteenth Ward, there is one who cannot be with us here to-night, a man than whom there is no more stalwart Trojan in all the political arena—I refer to our leader, the Honorable Lucas Prout, standard-bearer of the city and county of Zenith. Since he is not here, I trust that you will bear with me if, as a friend and neighbor, as one who is proud to share with you the common blessing of being a resident of the great city of Zenith, I tell you in all candor, honesty, and sincerity how the issues of this critical campaign appear to one plain man of business—to one who, brought up to the blessings of poverty and of manual labor, has, even when Fate condemned him to sit at a desk, yet never forgotten how it feels, by heck, to be up at five-thirty and at the factory with the ole dinner-pail in his hardened mitt when the whistle blew at seven, unless the owner sneaked in ten minutes on us and blew it early! (Laughter.) To come down to the basic and fundamental issues of this campaign, the great error, insincerely promulgated by Seneca Doane—"

There were workmen who jeered—young cynical workmen, for the most part foreigners, Jews, Swedes, Irishmen, Italians—but the older men, the patient, bleached, stooped carpenters and mechanics, cheered him; and when he worked up to his anecdote of Lincoln their eyes were wet.

Modestly, busily, he hurried out of the hall on delicious applause, and sped off to his third audience of the evening. "Ted, you better drive," he said. "Kind of all in after that spiel. Well, Paul, how'd it go? Did I get 'em?"

"Bully! Corking! You had a lot of pep."

Mrs. Babbitt worshiped, "Oh, it was fine! So clear and interesting, and such nice ideas. When I hear you orating I realize I don't appreciate how profoundly you think and what a splendid brain and vocabulary you have. Just—splendid."

But Verona was irritating. "Dad," she worried, "how do you know that public ownership of utilities and so on and so forth will always be a failure?"

Mrs. Babbitt reproved, "Rone, I should think you could see and realize that when your father's all worn out with orating, it's no time to expect him to explain these complicated subjects. I'm sure when he's rested he'll be glad to explain it to you. Now let's all be quiet and give Papa a chance to

get ready for his next speech. Just think! Right now they're gathering in
Maccabee Temple, and *waiting* for us!"

III

Mr. Lucas Prout and Sound Business defeated Mr. Seneca Doane and Class
Rule, and Zenith was again saved. Babbitt was offered several minor appointments to distribute among poor relations, but he preferred advance information about the extension of paved highways, and this a grateful administra
tion gave to him. Also, he was one of only nineteen speakers at the dinner
with which the Chamber of Commerce celebrated the victory of righteousness.

His reputation for oratory established, at the dinner of the Zenith Real
Estate Board he made the Annual Address. The *Advocate-Times* reported
this speech with unusual fullness:

"One of the livest banquets that has recently been pulled off occurred
last night in the annual Get-Together Fest of the Zenith Real Estate Board,
held in the Venetian Ball Room of the O'Hearn House. Mine host Gil
O'Hearn had as usual done himself proud and those assembled feasted on
such an assemblage of plates as could be rivaled nowhere west of New York,
if there, and washed down the plenteous feed with the cup which inspired
but did not inebriate in the shape of cider from the farm of Chandler Mott,
president of the board and who acted as witty and efficient chairman.

"As Mr. Mott was suffering from slight infection and sore throat, G. F.
Babbitt made the principal talk. Besides outlining the progress of Torrensing
real estate titles, Mr. Babbitt spoke in part as follows:

" 'In rising to address you, with my impromptu speech carefully tucked into
my vest pocket, I am reminded of the story of the two Irishmen, Mike and
Pat, who were riding on the Pullman. Both of them, I forgot to say, were
sailors in the Navy. It seems Mike had the lower berth and by and by he
heard a terrible racket from the upper, and when he yelled up to find out
what the trouble was, Pat answered, "Shure an' bedad an' how can I ever
get a night's sleep at all, at all? I been trying to get into this darned little
hammock ever since eight bells!"

" 'Now, gentlemen, standing up here before you, I feel a good deal like
Pat, and maybe after I've spieled along for a while, I may feel so darn small
that I'll be able to crawl into a Pullman hammock with no trouble at all,
at all!

" 'Gentlemen, it strikes me that each year at this annual occasion when
friend and foe get together and lay down the battle-ax and let the waves of
good-fellowship waft them up the flowery slopes of amity, it behooves us,
standing together eye to eye and shoulder to shoulder as fellow-citizens of
the best city in the world, to consider where we are both as regards ourselves
and the common weal.

" 'It is true that even with our 361,000, or practically 362,000, population,
there are, by the last census, almost a score of larger cities in the United

States. But, gentlemen, if by the next census we do not stand at least tenth, then I'll be the first to request any knocker to remove my shirt and to eat the same, with the compliments of G. F. Babbitt, Esquire! It may be true that New York, Chicago, and Philadelphia will continue to keep ahead of us in size. But aside from these three cities, which are notoriously so overgrown that no decent white man, nobody who loves his wife and kiddies and God's good out-o'-doors and likes to shake the hand of his neighbor in greeting, would want to live in them—and let me tell you right here and now, I wouldn't trade a high-class Zenith acreage development for the whole length and breadth of Broadway or State Street!—aside from these three, it's evident to any one with a head for facts that Zenith is the finest example of American life and prosperity to be found anywhere.

"'I don't mean to say we're perfect. We've got a lot to do in the way of extending the paving of motor boulevards, for, believe me, it's the fellow with four to ten thousand a year, say, and an automobile and a nice little family in a bungalow on the edge of town, that makes the wheels of progress go round!

"'That's the type of fellow that's ruling America to-day; in fact, it's the ideal type to which the entire world must tend, if there's to be a decent, well-balanced, Christian, go-ahead future for this little old planet! Once in a while I just naturally sit back and size up this Solid American Citizen, with a whale of a lot of satisfaction.

"'Our Ideal Citizen—I picture him first and foremost as being busier than a bird-dog, not wasting a lot of good time in day-dreaming or going to sassiety teas or kicking about things that are none of his business, but putting the zip into some store or profession or art. At night he lights up a good cigar, and climbs into the little old 'bus, and maybe cusses the carburetor, and shoots out home. He mows the lawn, or sneaks in some practice putting, and then he's ready for dinner. After dinner he tells the kiddies a story, or takes the family to the movies, or plays a few fists of bridge, or reads the evening paper, and a chapter or two of some good lively Western novel if he has a taste for literature, and maybe the folks next-door drop in and they sit and visit about their friends and the topics of the day. Then he goes happily to bed, his conscience clear, having contributed his mite to the prosperity of the city and to his own bank-account.

"'In politics and religion this Sane Citizen is the canniest man on earth; and in the arts he invariably has a natural taste which makes him pick out the best, every time. In no country in the world will you find so many re-productions of the Old Masters and of well-known paintings on parlor walls as in these United States. No country has anything like our number of phono-graphs, with not only dance records and comic but also the best operas, such as Verdi, rendered by the world's highest-paid singers.

"'In other countries, art and literature are left to a lot of shabby bums living in attics and feeding on booze and spaghetti, but in America the successful writer or picture-painter is indistinguishable from any other decent business man; and I, for one, am only too glad that the man who has the rare skill to season his message with interesting reading matter and who shows both purpose and pep in handling his literary wares has a chance to drag down his fifty thousand bucks a year, to mingle with the biggest executives on terms of perfect equality, and to show as big a house and as swell a car as any Captain of Industry! But, mind you, it's the appreciation of the Regular Guy who I have been depicting which has made this possible, and you got to hand as much credit to him as to the authors themselves.

" 'Finally, but most important, our Standardized Citizen, even if he is a bachelor, is a lover of the Little Ones, a supporter of the hearthstone which is the basic foundation of our civilization, first, last, and all the time, and the thing that most distinguishes us from the decayed nations of Europe.

" 'I have never yet toured Europe—and as a matter of fact, I don't know that I care to such an awful lot, as long as there's our own mighty cities and mountains to be seen—but, the way I figure it out, there must be a good many of our own sort of folks abroad. Indeed, one of the most enthusiastic Rotarians I ever met boosted the tenets of one-hundred-per-cent pep in a burr that smacked o' bonny Scotland and all ye bonny braes o' Bobby Burns. But same time, one thing that distinguishes us from our good brothers, the hustlers over there, is that they're willing to take a lot off the snobs and journalists and politicians, while the modern American business man knows how to talk right up for himself, knows how to make it good and plenty clear that he intends to run the works. He doesn't have to call in some high-brow hired-man when it's necessary for him to answer the crooked critics of the sane and efficient life. He's not dumb, like the old-fashioned merchant. He's got a vocabulary and a punch.

" 'With all modesty, I want to stand up here as a representative business man and gently whisper, "Here's our kind of folks! Here's the specifications of the Standardized American Citizen! Here's the new generation of Americans: fellows with hair on their chests and smiles in their eyes and adding-machines in their offices. We're not doing any boasting, but we like ourselves first-rate, and if you don't like us, look out—better get under cover before the cyclone hits town!"

" 'So! In my clumsy way I have tried to sketch the Real He-man, the fellow with Zip and Bang. And it's because Zenith has so large a proportion of such men that it's the most stable, the greatest of our cities. New York also has its thousands of Real Folks, but New York is cursed with unnumbered foreigners. So are Chicago and San Francisco. Oh, we have a golden roster of cities—Detroit and Cleveland with their renowned factories, Cincinnati with its great machine-tool and soap products, Pittsburg and Birmingham with their steel, Kansas City and Minneapolis and Omaha that open their bountiful gates on the bosom of the ocean-like wheatlands, and countless other magnificent sister-cities, for, by the last census, there were no less than sixty-eight glorious American burgs with a population of over one hundred thousand! And all these cities stand together for power and purity, and against foreign ideas and communism—Atlanta with Hartford, Rochester with Denver, Milwaukee with Indianapolis, Los Angeles with Scranton, Portland,

Maine, with Portland, Oregon. A good live wire from Baltimore or Seattle or Duluth is the twin-brother of every like fellow booster from Buffalo or Akron, Fort Worth or Oskaloosa!

" 'But it's here in Zenith, the home for manly men and womanly women and bright kids, that you find the largest proportion of these Regular Guys, and that's what sets it in a class by itself; that's why Zenith will be remembered in history as having set the pace for a civilization that shall endure when the old time-killing ways are gone forever and the day of earnest efficient endeavor shall have dawned all round the world!

" 'Some time I hope folks will quit handing all the credit to a lot of motheaten, mildewed, out-of-date, old, European dumps, and give proper credit to the famous Zenith spirit, that clean fighting determination to win Success that has made the little old Zip City celebrated in every land and clime, wherever condensed milk and pasteboard cartons are known! Believe me, the world has fallen too long for these worn-out countries that aren't producing anything but bootblacks and scenery and booze, that haven't got one bathroom per hundred people, and that don't know a loose-leaf ledger from a slip-cover; and it's just about time for some Zenithite to get his back up and holler for a show-down!

" 'I tell you, Zenith and her sister-cities are producing a new type of civilization. There are many resemblances between Zenith and these other burgs, and I'm darn glad of it! The extraordinary, growing, and sane standardization of stores, offices, streets, hotels, clothes, and newspapers throughout the United States shows how strong and enduring a type is ours.

" 'I always like to remember a piece that Chum Frink wrote for the newspapers about his lecture-tours. It is doubtless familiar to many of you, but if you will permit me, I'll take a chance and read it. It's one of the classic poems, like "If" by Kipling, or Ella Wheeler Wilcox's "The Man Worth While"; and I always carry this clipping of it in my note-book:

*When I am out upon the road, a poet with a pedler's load, I mostly sing a hearty song, and take a chew and hike along, a-handing out my samples fine of Cheero Brand of sweet sunshine, and peddling optimistic pokes and stable lines of japes and jokes to Lyceums and other folks, to Rotarys, Kiwanis' Clubs, and feel I ain't like other dubs. And then old Major Silas Satan, a brainy cuss who's always waitin', he gives his tail a lively quirk, and gets in quick his dirty work. He fills me up with mullygrubs; my hair the backward way he rubs; he makes me lonelier than a hound, on Sunday when the folks ain't round. And then b' gosh, I would prefer to never be a lecturer, a-ridin' round in classy cars and smoking fifty-cent cigars, and never more I want to roam; I simply want to be back home, a-eatin' flap-jacks, hash, and ham, with folks who savvy whom I am!*

*But when I get that lonely spell, I simply seek the best hotel, no matter in what town I be—St. Paul, Toledo, or K.C., in Washington, Schenectady, in Louisville or Albany. And at that inn it hits my dome that I again am right at home. If I should stand a lengthy spell in front of that first-class*

*hotel, that to the drummers loves to cater, across from some big film theayter;*
*if I should look around and buzz, and wonder in what town I was, I swear*
*that I could never tell! For all the crowd would be so swell, in just the same*
*fine sort of jeans they wear at home, and all the queens with spiffy bonnets*
*on their beans, and all the fellows standing round a-talkin' always, I'll be*
*bound, the same good jolly kind of guff, 'bout autos, politics and stuff and*
*baseball players of renown that Nice Guys talk in my home town!*

*Then when I entered that hotel, I'd look around and say, "Well, well!"*
*For there would be the same news-stand, same magazines and candies grand,*
*same smokes of famous standard brand, I'd find at home, I'll tell! And when*
*I saw the jolly bunch come waltzing in for eats at lunch, and squaring up in*
*natty duds to platters large of French Fried spuds, why then I'd stand right*
*up and bawl, "I've never left my home at all!" And all replete I'd sit me*
*down beside some guy in derby brown upon a lobby chair of plush, and*
*murmur to him in a rush, "Hello, Bill, tell me, good old scout, how is your*
*stock a-holdin' out?" Then we'd be off, two solid pals, a-chatterin' like giddy*
*gals of flivvers, weather, home, and wives, lodge-brothers then for all our*
*lives! So when Sam Satan makes you blue, good friend, that's what I'd up*
*and do, for in these States where'er you roam, you never leave your home*
*sweet home.*

" 'Yes, sir, these other burgs are our true partners in the great game of
vital living. But let's not have any mistake about this. I claim that Zenith
is the best partner and the fastest-growing partner of the whole caboodle.
I trust I may be pardoned if I give a few statistics to back up my claims. If
they are old stuff to any of you, yet the tidings of prosperity, like the good
news of the Bible, never become tedious to the ears of a real hustler, no
matter how oft the sweet story is told! Every intelligent person knows that
Zenith manufactures more condensed milk and evaporated cream, more
paper boxes, and more lighting-fixtures, than any other city in the United
States, if not in the world. But it is not so universally known that we also
stand second in the manufacture of package-butter, sixth in the giant realm
of motors and automobiles, and somewhere about third in cheese, leather
findings, tar roofing, breakfast food, and overalls!

" 'Our greatness, however, lies not alone in punchful prosperity but equally
in that public spirit, that forward-looking idealism and brotherhood, which
has marked Zenith ever since its foundation by the Fathers. We have a right,
indeed we have a duty toward our fair city, to announce broadcast the facts
about our high schools, characterized by their complete plants and the finest
school-ventilating systems in the country, bar none; our magnificent new
hotels and banks and the paintings and carved marble in their lobbies; and
the Second National Tower, the second highest business building in any inland city in the entire country. When I add that we have an unparalleled
number of miles of paved streets, bathrooms, vacuum cleaners, and all the
other signs of civilization; that our library and art museum are well supported and housed in convenient and roomy buildings; that our park-system

is more than up to par, with its handsome driveways adorned with grass, shrubs, and statuary, then I give but a hint of the all-round unlimited greatness of Zenith!

" 'I believe, however, in keeping the best to the last. When I remind you that we have one motor car for every five and seven-eights persons in the city, then I give a rock-ribbed practical indication of the kind of progress and braininess which is synonymous with the name Zenith!

" 'But the way of the righteous is not all roses. Before I close I must call your attention to a problem we have to face, this coming year. The worst menace to sound government is not the avowed socialists but a lot of cowards who work under cover—the long-haired gentry who call themselves "liberals" and "radicals" and "non-partisan" and "intelligentsia" and God only knows how many other trick names! Irresponsible teachers and professors constitute the worst of this whole gang, and I am ashamed to say that several of them are on the faculty of our great State University! The U. is my own Alma Mater, and I am proud to be known as an alumni, but there are certain instructors there who seem to think we ought to turn the conduct of the nation over to hoboes and roustabouts.

" 'Those profs are the snakes to be scotched—they and all their milk-and-water ilk! The American business man is generous to a fault, but one thing he does demand of all teachers and lecturers and journalists: if we're going to pay them our good money, they've got to help us by selling efficiency and whooping it up for rational prosperity! And when it comes to these blab-mouth, fault-finding, pessimistic, cynical University teachers, let me tell you that during this golden coming year it's just as much our duty to bring influence to have those cusses fired as it is to sell all the real estate and gather in all the good shekels we can.

" 'Not till that is done will our sons and daughters see that the ideal of American manhood and culture isn't a lot of cranks sitting around chewing the rag about their Rights and their Wrongs, but a God-fearing, hustling, successful, two-fisted Regular Guy, who belongs to some church with pep and piety to it, who belongs to the Boosters or the Rotarians or the Kiwanis, to the Elks or Moose or Red Men or Knights of Columbus or any one of a score of organizations of good, jolly, kidding, laughing, sweating, upstanding, lend-a-handing Royal Good Fellows, who plays hard and works hard, and whose answer to his critics is a square-toed boot that'll teach the grouches and smart alecks to respect the He-man and get out and root for Uncle Samuel, U.S.A.!' "

### IV

Babbitt promised to become a recognized orator. He entertained a Smoker of the Men's Club of the Chatham Road Presbyterian Church with Irish, Jewish, and Chinese dialect stories.

But in nothing was he more clearly revealed as the Prominent Citizen than in his lecture on "Brass Tacks Facts on Real Estate," as delivered before the class in Sales Methods at the Zenith Y.M.C.A.

The *Advocate-Times* reported the lecture so fully that Vergil Gunch said to Babbitt, "You're getting to be one of the classiest spellbinders in town. Seems 's if I couldn't pick up a paper without reading about your well-known eloquence. All this guff ought to bring a lot of business into your office. Good work! Keep it up!"

"Go on, quit your kidding," said Babbitt feebly, but at this tribute from Gunch, himself a man of no mean oratorical fame, he expanded with delight and wondered how, before his vacation, he could have questioned the joys of being a solid citizen.

# 15

His march to greatness was not without disastrous stumbling.

Fame did not bring the social advancement which the Babbitts deserved. They were not asked to join the Tonawanda Country Club nor invited to the dances at the Union. Himself, Babbitt fretted, he didn't "care a fat hoot for all these highrollers, but the wife would kind of like to be Among Those Present." He nervously awaited his university class-dinner and an evening of furious intimacy with such social leaders as Charles McKelvey the millionaire contractor, Max Kruger the banker, Irving Tate the tool-manufacturer, and Adelbert Dobson the fashionable interior decorator. Theoretically he was their friend, as he had been in college, and when he encountered them they still called him "Georgie," but he didn't seem to encounter them often, and they never invited him to dinner (with champagne and a butler) at their houses on Royal Ridge.

All the week before the class-dinner he thought of them. "No reason why we shouldn't become real chummy now!"

II

Like all true American diversions and spiritual outpourings, the dinner of the men of the Class of 1896 was thoroughly organized. The dinner-committee hammered like a sales-corporation. Once a week they sent out reminders:

TICKLER NO. 3

Old man, are you going to be with us at the livest Friendship Feed the alumni of the good old U have ever known? The alumnæ of '08 turned out 60% strong. Are we boys going to be beaten by a bunch of skirts? Come on, fellows, let's work up some real genuine enthusiasm and all boost together for the snappiest dinner yet! Elegant eats, short ginger-talks, and memories shared together of the brightest, gladdest days of life.

The dinner was held in a private room at the Union Club. The club was a dingy building, three pretentious old dwellings knocked together, and the entrance-hall resembled a potato cellar, yet the Babbitt who was free of the magnificence of the Athletic Club entered with embarrassment. He nodded to the doorman, an ancient proud negro with brass buttons and a blue tail-coat, and paraded through the hall, trying to look like a member.

Sixty men had come to the dinner. They made islands and eddies in the hall; they packed the elevator and the corners of the private dining-room. They tried to be intimate and enthusiastic. They appeared to one another exactly as they had in college—as raw youngsters whose present mustaches, baldnesses, paunches, and wrinkles were but jovial disguises put on for the evening. "You haven't changed a particle!" they marveled. The men whom they could not recall they addressed, "Well, well, great to see you again, old man. What are you— Still doing the same thing?"

Some one was always starting a cheer or a college song, and it was always thinning into silence. Despite their resolution to be democratic they divided into two sets: the men with dress-clothes and the men without. Babbitt (extremely in dress-clothes) went from one group to the other. Though he was, almost frankly, out for social conquest, he sought Paul Riesling first. He found him alone, neat and silent.

Paul sighed, "I'm no good at this handshaking and 'well, look who's here' bunk."

"Rats now, Paulibus, loosen up and be a mixer! Finest bunch of boys on earth! Say, you seem kind of glum. What's matter?"

"Oh, the usual. Run-in with Zilla."

"Come on! Let's wade in and forget our troubles."

He kept Paul beside him, but worked toward the spot where Charles Mc-Kelvey stood warming his admirers like a furnace.

McKelvey had been the hero of the Class of '96; not only football captain and hammer-thrower but debater, and passable in what the State University considered scholarship. He had gone on, had captured the construction-company once owned by the Dodsworths, best-known pioneer family of Zenith. He built state capitols, skyscrapers, railway terminals. He was a heavy-shouldered, big-chested man, but not sluggish. There was a quiet humor in his eyes, a syrup-smooth quickness in his speech, which intimidated politicians and warned reporters; and in his presence the most intelligent scientist or the most sensitive artist felt thin-blooded, unworldly, and a little shabby. He was, particularly when he was influencing legislatures or hiring labor-spies, very easy and lovable and gorgeous. He was baronial; he was a peer in the rapidly crystallizing American aristocracy, inferior only to the haughty Old Families. (In Zenith, an Old Family is one which came to town before 1840.) His power was the greater because he was not hindered by scruples, by either the vice or the virtue of the older Puritan tradition.

McKelvey was being placidly merry now with the great, the manufacturers and bankers, the land-owners and lawyers and surgeons who had chauffeurs and went to Europe. Babbitt squeezed among them. He liked McKelvey's smile as much as the social advancement to be had from his favor. If in Paul's company he felt ponderous and protective, with McKelvey he felt slight and adoring.

He heard McKelvey say to Max Kruger, the banker, "Yes, we'll put up Sir Gerald Doak." Babbitt's democratic love for titles became a rich relish. "You know, he's one of the biggest iron-men in England, Max. Horribly well-off. . . . Why, hello, old Georgie! Say, Max, George Babbitt is getting fatter than I am!"

The chairman shouted, "Take your seats, fellows!"

"Shall we make a move, Charley?" Babbitt said casually to McKelvey.

"Right. Hello, Paul! How's the old fiddler? Planning to sit anywhere special, George? Come on, let's grab some seats. Come on, Max. Georgie, I read about your speeches in the campaign. Bully work!"

After that, Babbitt would have followed him through fire. He was enormously busy during the dinner, now bumblingly cheering Paul, now approaching McKelvey with "Hear you're going to build some piers in Brooklyn," now noting how enviously the failures of the class, sitting by themselves in a weedy group, looked up to him in his association with the nobility, now warming himself in the Society Talk of McKelvey and Max Kruger. They spoke of a "jungle dance" for which Mona Dodsworth had decorated her house with thousands of orchids. They spoke, with an excellent imitation of casualness, of a dinner in Washington at which McKelvey had met a Senator, a Balkan princess, and an English major-general. McKelvey called the princess "Jenny," and let it be known that he had danced with her.

Babbitt was thrilled, but not so weighted with awe as to be silent. If he was not invited by them to dinner, he was yet accustomed to talking with bank-presidents, congressmen, and clubwomen who entertained poets. He was bright and referential with McKelvey:

"Say, Charley, juh remember in Junior year how we chartered a sea-going hack and chased down to Riverdale, to the big show Madame Brown used to put on? Remember how you beat up that hick constabule that tried to run us in, and we pinched the pants-pressing sign and took and hung it on Prof. Morrison's door? Oh, gosh, those were the days!"

Those, McKelvey agreed, were the days.

Babbitt had reached "It isn't the books you study in college but the friendships you make that counts" when the men at head of the table broke into song. He attacked McKelvey:

"It's a shame, uh, shame to drift apart because our, uh, business activities lie in different fields. I've enjoyed talking over the good old days. You and Mrs. McKelvey must come to dinner some night."

Vaguely, "Yes, indeed—"

"Like to talk to you about the growth of real estate out beyond your

Grantsville warehouse. I might be able to tip you off to a thing or two, possibly."

"Splendid! We must have dinner together, Georgie. Just let me know. And it will be a great pleasure to have your wife and you at the house," said McKelvey, much less vaguely.

Then the chairman's voice, that prodigious voice which once had roused them to cheer defiance at rooters from Ohio or Michigan or Indiana, whooped, "Come on, you wombats! All together in the long yell!" Babbitt felt that life would never be sweeter than now, when he joined with Paul Riesling and the newly recovered hero, McKelvey, in:

> Baaaaaattle-ax
> Get an ax,
> Bal-ax,
> Get-nax,
> Who, who? The U.!
> Hooroo!

### III

The Babbitts invited the McKelveys to dinner, in early December, and the McKelveys not only accepted but, after changing the date once or twice, actually came.

The Babbitts somewhat thoroughly discussed the details of the dinner, from the purchase of a bottle of champagne to the number of salted almonds to be placed before each person. Especially did they mention the matter of the other guests. To the last Babbitt held out for giving Paul Riesling the benefit of being with the McKelveys. "Good old Charley would like Paul and Verg Gunch better than some highfalutin' Willy boy," he insisted, but Mrs. Babbitt interrupted his observations with, "Yes—perhaps— I think I'll try to get some Lynnhaven oysters," and when she was quite ready she invited Dr. J. T. Angus, the oculist, and a dismally respectable lawyer named Maxwell, with their glittering wives.

Neither Angus nor Maxwell belonged to the Elks or to the Athletic Club; neither of them had ever called Babbitt "brother" or asked his opinions on carburetors. The only "human people" whom she invited, Babbitt raged, were the Littlefields; and Howard Littlefield at times became so statistical that Babbitt longed for the refreshment of Gunch's, "Well, old lemon-pie-face, what's the good word?"

Immediately after lunch Mrs. Babbitt began to set the table for the seven-thirty dinner to the McKelveys, and Babbitt was, by order, home at four. But they didn't find anything for him to do, and three times Mrs. Babbitt scolded, "Do please try to keep out of the way!" He stood in the door of the garage, his lips drooping, and wished that Littlefield or Sam Doppelbrau or somebody would come along and talk to him. He saw Ted sneaking about the corner of the house.

"What's the matter, old man?" said Babbitt.

"Is that you, thin, owld one? Gee, Ma certainly is on the warpath! I told her Rone and I would jus' soon not be let in on the fiesta to-night, and she bit me. She says I got to take a bath, too. But, say, the Babbitt men will be some lookers to-night! Little Theodore in a dress-suit!"

"The Babbitt men!" Babbitt liked the sound of it. He put his arm about the boy's shoulder. He wished that Paul Riesling had a daughter, so that Ted might marry her. "Yes, your mother is kind of rouncing round, all right," he said, and they laughed together, and sighed together, and dutifully went in to dress.

The McKelveys were less than fifteen minutes late.

Babbitt hoped that the Doppelbraus would see the McKelveys' limousine, and their uniformed chauffeur, waiting in front.

The dinner was well cooked and incredibly plentiful, and Mrs. Babbitt had brought out her grandmother's silver candlesticks. Babbitt worked hard. He was good. He told none of the jokes he wanted to tell. He listened to the others. He started Maxwell off with a resounding, "Let's hear about your trip to the Yellowstone." He was laudatory, extremely laudatory. He found opportunities to remark that Dr. Angus was a benefactor to humanity, Maxwell and Howard Littlefield profound scholars, Charles McKelvey an inspiration to ambitious youth, and Mrs. McKelvey an adornment to the social circles of Zenith, Washington, New York, Paris, and numbers of other places.

But he could not stir them. It was a dinner without a soul. For no reason that was clear to Babbitt, heaviness was over them and they spoke laboriously and unwillingly.

He concentrated on Lucile McKelvey, carefully not looking at her blanched lovely shoulder and the tawny silken band which supported her frock.

"I suppose you'll be going to Europe pretty soon again, won't you?" he invited.

"I'd like awfully to run over to Rome for a few weeks."

"I suppose you see a lot of pictures and music and curios and everything there."

"No, what I really go for is: there's a little *trattoria* on the Via della Scrofa where you get the best *fettuccine* in the world."

"Oh, I— Yes. That must be nice to try that. Yes."

At a quarter to ten McKelvey discovered with profound regret that his wife had a headache. He said blithely, as Babbitt helped him with his coat, "We must lunch together some time, and talk over the old days."

When the others had labored out, at half-past ten, Babbitt turned to his wife, pleading, "Charley said he had a corking time and we must lunch— said they wanted to have us up to the house for dinner before long."

She achieved, "Oh, it's just been one of those quiet evenings that are often so much more enjoyable than noisy parties where everybody talks at once and doesn't really settle down to—nice quiet enjoyment."

But from his cot on the sleeping-porch he heard her weeping, slowly, without hope.

### IV

For a month they watched the social columns, and waited for a return dinner-invitation.

As the hosts of Sir Gerald Doak, the McKelveys were headlined all the week after the Babbitts' dinner. Zenith ardently received Sir Gerald (who had come to America to buy coal). The newspapers interviewed him on prohibition, Ireland, unemployment, naval aviation, the rate of exchange, tea-drinking *versus* whisky-drinking, the psychology of American women, and daily life as lived by English county families. Sir Gerald seemed to have heard of all those topics. The McKelveys gave him a Singhalese dinner, and Miss Elnora Pearl Bates, society editor of the *Advocate-Times*, rose to her highest lark-note. Babbitt read aloud at breakfast-table:

'Twixt the original and Oriental decorations, the strange and delicious food, and the personalities both of the distinguished guests, the charming hostess and the noted host, never has Zenith seen a more recherche affair than the Ceylon dinner-dance given last evening by Mr. and Mrs. Charles McKelvey to Sir Gerald Doak. Methought as we—fortunate one!—were privileged to view that fairy and foreign scene, nothing at Monte Carlo or the choicest ambassadorial sets of foreign capitals could be more lovely. It is not for nothing that Zenith is in matters social rapidly becoming known as the choosiest inland city in the country.

Though he is too modest to admit it, Lord Doak gives a cachet to our smart quartier such as it has not received since the ever-memorable visit of the Earl of Sittingbourne. Not only is he of the British peerage, but he is also, on dit, a leader of the British metal industries. As he comes from Nottingham, a favorite haunt of Robin Hood, though now, we are informed by Lord Doak, a live modern city of 275,573 inhabitants, and important lace as well as other industries, we like to think that perhaps through his veins runs some of the blood, both virile red and bonny blue, of that earlier lord o' the good greenwood, the roguish Robin.

The lovely Mrs. McKelvey never was more fascinating than last evening in her black net gown relieved by dainty bands of silver and at her exquisite waist a glowing cluster of Aaron Ward roses.

Babbitt said bravely, "I hope they don't invite us to meet this Lord Doak guy. Darn sight rather just have a nice quiet little dinner with Charley and the Missus."

At the Zenith Athletic Club they discussed it amply. "I s'pose we'll have to call McKelvey 'Lord Chaz' from now on," said Sidney Finkelstein.

"It beats all get-out," meditated that man of data, Howard Littlefield, "how hard it is for some people to get things straight. Here they call this fellow 'Lord Doak' when it ought to be 'Sir Gerald.'"

Babbitt marveled, "Is that a fact! Well, well! 'Sir Gerald,' eh? That's what you call um, eh? Well, sir, I'm glad to know that."

Later he informed his salesmen, "It's funnier 'n a goat the way some folks that, just because they happen to lay up a big wad, go entertaining famous foreigners, don't have any more idea 'n a rabbit how to address 'em so's to make 'em feel at home!"

That evening, as he was driving home, he passed McKelvey's limousine and saw Sir Gerald, a large, ruddy, pop-eyed, Teutonic Englishman whose dribble of yellow mustache gave him an aspect sad and doubtful. Babbitt drove on slowly, oppressed by futility. He had a sudden, unexplained, and horrible conviction that the McKelveys were laughing at him.

He betrayed his depression by the violence with which he informed his wife, "Folks that really tend to business haven't got the time to waste on a bunch like the McKelveys. This society stuff is like any other hobby; if you devote yourself to it, you get on. But I like to have a chance to visit with you and the children instead of all this idiotic chasing round."

They did not speak of the McKelveys again.

V

It was a shame, at this worried time, to have to think about the Overbrooks.

Ed Overbrook was a classmate of Babbitt who had been a failure. He had a large family and a feeble insurance business out in the suburb of Dorchester. He was gray and thin and unimportant. He had always been gray and thin and unimportant. He was the person whom, in any group, you forgot to introduce, then introduced with extra enthusiasm. He had admired Babbitt's good-fellowship in college, had admired ever since his power in real estate, his beautiful house and wonderful clothes. It pleased Babbitt, though it bothered him with a sense of responsibility. At the class-dinner he had seen poor Overbrook, in a shiny blue serge business-suit, being diffident in a corner with three other failures. He had gone over and been cordial: "Why, hello, young Ed! I hear you're writing all the insurance in Dorchester now. Bully work!"

They recalled the good old days when Overbrook used to write poetry. Overbrook embarrassed him by blurting, "Say, Georgie, I hate to think of how we been drifting apart. I wish you and Mrs. Babbitt would come to dinner some night."

Babbitt boomed, "Fine! Sure! Just let me know. And the wife and I want to have you at the house." He forgot it, but unfortunately Ed Overbrook did not. Repeatedly he telephoned to Babbitt, inviting him to dinner. "Might as well go and get it over," Babbitt groaned to his wife. "But don't it simply amaze you the way the poor fish doesn't know the first thing about social etiquette? Think of him 'phoning me, instead of his wife sitting down and writing us a regular bid! Well, I guess we're stuck for it. That's the trouble with all this class-brother hooptedoodle."

He accepted Overbrook's next plaintive invitation, for an evening two weeks off. A dinner two weeks off, even a family dinner, never seems so appalling, till the two weeks have astoundingly disappeared and one comes dismayed to the ambushed hour. They had to change the date, because of their own dinner to the McKelveys, but at last they gloomily drove out to the Overbrooks' house in Dorchester.

It was miserable from the beginning. The Overbrooks had dinner at six-thirty, while the Babbitts never dined before seven. Babbitt permitted himself to be ten minutes late. "Let's make it as short as possible. I think we'll duck out quick. I'll say I have to be at the office extra early to-morrow," he planned.

The Overbrook house was depressing. It was the second story of a wooden two-family dwelling; a place of baby-carriages, old hats hung in the hall, cabbage-smell, and a Family Bible on the parlor table. Ed Overbrook and his wife were as awkward and threadbare as usual, and the other guests were two dreadful families whose names Babbitt never caught and never desired to catch. But he was touched, and disconcerted, by the tactless way in which Overbrook praised him: "We're mighty proud to have old George here to-night! Of course you've all read about his speeches and oratory in the papers —and the boy's good-looking, too, eh?—but what I always think of is back in college, and what a great old mixer he was, and one of the best swimmers in the class."

Babbitt tried to be jovial; he worked at it; but he could find nothing to interest him in Overbrook's timorousness, the blankness of the other guests, or the drained stupidity of Mrs. Overbrook, with her spectacles, drab skin, and tight-drawn hair. He told his best Irish story, but it sank like soggy cake. Most bleary moment of all was when Mrs. Overbrook, peering out of her fog of nursing eight children and cooking and scrubbing, tried to be conversational.

"I suppose you go to Chicago and New York right along, Mr. Babbitt," she prodded.

"Well, I get to Chicago fairly often."

"It must be awfully interesting. I suppose you take in all the theaters."

"Well, to tell the truth, Mrs. Overbrook, thing that hits me best is a great big beefsteak at a Dutch restaurant in the Loop!"

They had nothing more to say. Babbitt was sorry, but there was no hope; the dinner was a failure. At ten, rousing out of the stupor of meaningless talk, he said as cheerily as he could, " 'Fraid we got to be starting, Ed. I've got a fellow coming to see me early to-morrow." As Overbrook helped him with his coat, Babbitt said, "Nice to rub up on the old days! We must have lunch together, P.D.Q."

Mrs. Babbitt sighed, on their drive home, "It was pretty terrible. But how Mr. Overbrook does admire you!"

"Yep. Poor cuss! Seems to think I'm a little tin archangel, and the best-looking man in Zenith."

"Well, you're certainly not that but— Oh, Georgie, you don't suppose we have to invite them to dinner at our house now, do we?"

"Ouch! Gaw, I hope not!"

"See here, now, George! You didn't say anything about it to Mr. Overbrook, did you?"

"No! Gee! No! Honest, I didn't! Just made a bluff about having him to lunch some time."

"Well. . . . Oh, dear. . . . I don't want to hurt their feelings. But I don't see how I could stand another evening like this one. And suppose somebody like Dr. and Mrs. Angus came in when we had the Overbrooks there, and thought they were friends of ours!"

For a week they worried, "We really ought to invite Ed and his wife, poor devils!" But as they never saw the Overbrooks, they forgot them, and after a month or two they said, "That really was the best way, just to let it slide. It wouldn't be kind to *them* to have them here. They'd feel so out of place and hard-up in our home."

They did not speak of the Overbrooks again.

# 16

The certainty that he was not going to be accepted by the McKelveys made Babbitt feel guilty and a little absurd. But he went more regularly to the Elks; at a Chamber of Commerce luncheon he was oratorical regarding the wickedness of strikes; and again he saw himself as a Prominent Citizen.

His clubs and associations were food comfortable to his spirit.

Of a decent man in Zenith it was required that he should belong to one, preferably two or three, of the innumerous "lodges" and prosperity-boosting lunch-clubs; to the Rotarians, the Kiwanis, or the Boosters; to the Oddfellows, Moose, Masons, Red Men, Woodmen, Owls, Eagles, Maccabees, Knights of Pythias, Knights of Columbus, and other secret orders characterized by a high degree of heartiness, sound morals, and reverence for the Constitution. There were four reasons for joining these orders: It was the thing to do. It was good for business, since lodge-brothers frequently became customers. It gave to Americans unable to become Geheimräte or Commendatori such unctuous honorifics as High Worthy Recording Scribe and Grand Hoogow to add to the commonplace distinctions of Colonel, Judge, and Professor. And it permitted the swaddled American husband to stay away from home for one evening a week. The lodge was his piazza, his pavement café. He could shoot pool and talk man-talk and be obscene and valiant.

Babbitt was what he called a "joiner" for all these reasons.

Behind the gold and scarlet banner of his public achievements was the dun background of office-routine: leases, sales-contracts, lists of properties to rent. The evenings of oratory and committees and lodges stimulated him like brandy, but every morning he was sandy-tongued. Week by week he accumulated nervousness. He was in open disagreement with his outside salesman, Stanley Graff; and once, though her charms had always kept him nickeringly polite to her, he snarled at Miss McGoun for changing his letters.

But in the presence of Paul Riesling he relaxed. At least once a week they fled from maturity. On Saturday they played golf, jeering, "As a golfer, you're a fine tennis-player," or they motored all Sunday afternoon, stopping at village lunchrooms to sit on high stools at a counter and drink coffee from thick cups. Sometimes Paul came over in the evening with his violin, and even Zilla was silent as the lonely man who had lost his way and forever crept down unfamiliar roads spun out his dark soul in music.

## II

Nothing gave Babbitt more purification and publicity than his labors for the Sunday School.

His church, the Chatham Road Presbyterian, was one of the largest and richest, one of the most oaken and velvety, in Zenith. The pastor was the Reverend John Jennison Drew, M.A., D.D., LL.D. (The M.A. and the D.D. were from Elbert University, Nebraska, the LL.D. from Waterbury College, Oklahoma.) He was eloquent, efficient, and versatile. He presided at meetings for the denunciation of unions or the elevation of domestic service, and confided to the audiences that as a poor boy he had carried newspapers. For the Saturday edition of the *Evening Advocate* he wrote editorials on "The Manly Man's Religion" and "The Dollars and Sense Value of Christianity," which were printed in bold type surrounded by a wiggly border. He often said that he was "proud to be known as primarily a business man" and that he certainly was not going to "permit the old Satan to monopolize all the pep and punch." He was a thin, rustic-faced young man with gold spectacles and a bang of dull brown hair, but when he hurled himself into oratory he glowed with power. He admitted that he was too much the scholar and poet to imitate the evangelist, Mike Monday, yet he had once awakened his fold to new life, and to larger collections, by the challenge, "My brethren, the real cheap skate is the man who won't lend to the Lord!"

He had made his church a true community center. It contained everything but a bar. It had a nursery, a Thursday evening supper with a short bright missionary lecture afterward, a gymnasium, a fortnightly motion-picture show, a library of technical books for young workmen—though, unfortunately, no young workman ever entered the church except to wash the windows or repair the furnace—and a sewing-circle which made short little pants for the children of the poor while Mrs. Drew read aloud from earnest novels.

Though Dr. Drew's theology was Presbyterian, his church-building was gracefully Episcopalian. As he said, it had the "most perdurable features of those noble ecclesiastical monuments of grand Old England which stand as symbols of the eternity of faith, religious and civil." It was built of cheery iron-spot brick in an improved Gothic style, and the main auditorium had indirect lighting from electric globes in lavish alabaster bowls.

On a December morning when the Babbitts went to church, Dr. John Jennison Drew was unusually eloquent. The crowd was immense. Ten brisk young ushers, in morning coats with white roses, were bringing folding chairs up from the basement. There was an impressive musical program, conducted by Sheldon Smeeth, educational director of the Y.M.C.A., who also sang the offertory. Babbitt cared less for this, because some misguided person had taught young Mr. Smeeth to smile, smile, smile while he was singing, but with all the appreciation of a fellow-orator he admired Dr. Drew's sermon. It had the intellectual quality which distinguished the Chatham Road congregation from the grubby chapels on Smith Street.

"At this abundant harvest-time of all the year," Dr. Drew chanted, "when, though stormy the sky and laborious the path to the drudging wayfarer, yet the hovering and bodiless spirit swoops back o'er all the labors and desires of the past twelve months, oh, then it seems to me there sounds behind all our apparent failures the golden chorus of greeting from those passed happily on; and lo! on the dim horizon we see behind dolorous clouds the mighty mass of mountains—mountains of melody, mountains of mirth, mountains of might!"

"I certainly do like a sermon with culture and thought in it," meditated Babbitt.

At the end of the service he was delighted when the pastor, actively shaking hands at the door, twittered, "Oh, Brother Babbitt, can you wait a jiffy? Want your advice."

"Sure, doctor! You bet!"

"Drop into my office. I think you'll like the cigars there." Babbitt did like the cigars. He also liked the office, which was distinguished from other offices only by the spirited change of the familiar wall-placard to "This is the Lord's Busy Day." Chum Frink came in, then William W. Eathorne.

Mr. Eathorne was the seventy-year-old president of the First State Bank of Zenith. He still wore the delicate patches of side-whiskers which had been the uniform of bankers in 1870. If Babbitt was envious of the Smart Set of the McKelveys, before William Washington Eathorne he was reverent. Mr. Eathorne had nothing to do with the Smart Set. He was above it. He was the great-grandson of one of the five men who founded Zenith, in 1792, and he was of the third generation of bankers. He could examine credits, make loans, promote or injure a man's business. In his presence Babbitt breathed quickly and felt young.

The Reverend Dr. Drew bounced into the room and flowered into speech:

"I've asked you gentlemen to stay so I can put a proposition before you. The Sunday School needs bucking up. It's the fourth largest in Zenith, but there's no reason why we should take anybody's dust. We ought to be first.

I want to request you, if you will, to form a committee of advice and publicity for the Sunday School; look it over and make any suggestions for its betterment, and then, perhaps, see that the press gives us some attention—give the public some really helpful and constructive news instead of all these murders and divorces."

"Excellent," said the banker.

Babbitt and Frink were enchanted to join him.

### III

If you had asked Babbitt what his religion was, he would have answered in sonorous Boosters'-Club rhetoric, "My religion is to serve my fellow men, to honor my brother as myself, and to do my bit to make life happier for one and all." If you had pressed him for more detail, he would have announced, "I'm a member of the Presbyterian Church, and naturally, I accept its doctrines." If you had been so brutal as to go on, he would have protested, "There's no use discussing and arguing about religion; it just stirs up bad feeling."

Actually, the content of his theology was that there was a supreme being who had tried to make us perfect, but presumably had failed; that if one was a Good Man he would go to a place called Heaven (Babbitt unconsciously pictured it as rather like an excellent hotel with a private garden), but if one was a Bad Man, that is, if he murdered or committed burglary or used cocaine or had mistresses or sold non-existent real estate, he would be punished. Babbitt was uncertain, however, about what he called "this business of Hell." He explained to Ted, "Of course I'm pretty liberal; I don't exactly believe in a fire-and-brimstone Hell. Stands to reason, though, that a fellow can't get away with all sorts of Vice and not get nicked for it, see how I mean?"

Upon this theology he rarely pondered. The kernel of his practical religion was that it was respectable, and beneficial to one's business, to be seen going to services; that the church kept the Worst Elements from being still worse; and that the pastor's sermons, however dull they might seem at the time of taking, yet had a voodooistic power which "did a fellow good—kept him in touch with Higher Things."

His first investigations for the Sunday School Advisory Committee did not inspire him.

He liked the Busy Folks' Bible Class, composed of mature men and women and addressed by the old-school physician, Dr. T. Atkins Jordan, in a sparkling style comparable to that of the more refined humorous after-dinner speakers, but when he went down to the junior classes he was disconcerted. He heard Sheldon Smeeth, educational director of the Y.M.C.A. and leader of the church-choir, a pale but strenuous young man with curly hair and a smile, teaching a class of sixteen-year-old boys. Smeeth lovingly admonished them, "Now, fellows, I'm going to have a Heart to Heart Talk Evening at my house next Thursday. We'll get off by ourselves and be frank

about our Secret Worries. You can just tell old Sheldy anything, like all the
fellows do at the Y. I'm going to explain frankly about the horrible practises
a kiddy falls into unless he's guided by a Big Brother, and about the perils
and glory of Sex." Old Sheldy beamed damply; the boys looked ashamed;
and Babbitt didn't know which way to turn his embarrassed eyes.

Less annoying but also much duller were the minor classes which were
being instructed in philosophy and Oriental ethnology by earnest spinsters.
Most of them met in the highly varnished Sunday School room, but there
was an overflow to the basement, which was decorated with varicose water-
pipes and lighted by small windows high up in the oozing wall. What Babbitt
saw, however, was the First Congregational Church of Catawba. He was
back in the Sunday School of his boyhood. He smelled again that polite
stuffiness to be found only in church parlors; he recalled the case of drab
Sunday School books: "Hetty, a Humble Heroine" and "Josephus, a Lad of
Palestine;" he thumbed once more the high-colored text-cards which no boy
wanted but no boy liked to throw away, because they were somehow sacred;
he was tortured by the stumbling rote of thirty-five years ago, as in the vast
Zenith church he listened to:

"Now, Edgar, you read the next verse. What does it mean when it says
it's easier for a camel to go through a needle's eye? What does this teach
us? Clarence! Please don't wiggle so! If you had studied your lesson you
wouldn't be so fidgety. Now, Earl, what is the lesson Jesus was trying to teach
his disciples? The one thing I want you to especially remember, boys, is the
words, 'With God all things are possible.' Just think of that always—Clarence, *please* pay attention—just say 'With God all things are possible' whenever you feel discouraged, and, Alec, will you read the next verse; if you'd
pay attention you wouldn't lose your place!"

Drone—drone—drone—gigantic bees that boomed in a cavern of drowsiness—

Babbitt started from his open-eyed nap, thanked the teacher for "the privilege of listening to her splendid teaching," and staggered on to the next
circle.

After two weeks of this he had no suggestions whatever for the Reverend
Dr. Drew.

Then he discovered a world of Sunday School journals, an enormous and
busy domain of weeklies and monthlies which were as technical, as practical
and forward-looking, as the real-estate columns or the shoe-trade magazines.
He bought half a dozen of them at a religious book-shop and till after midnight he read them and admired.

He found many lucrative tips on "Focusing Appeals," "Scouting for New
Members," and "Getting Prospects to Sign up with the Sunday School." He
particularly liked the word "prospects," and he was moved by the rubric:

"The moral springs of the community's life lie deep in its Sunday Schools
—its schools of religious instruction and inspiration. Neglect now means loss
of spiritual vigor and moral power in years to come. . . . Facts like the above,

followed by a straight-arm appeal, will reach folks who can never be laughed or jollied into doing their part."

Babbitt admitted, "That's so. I used to skin out of the ole Sunday School at Catawba every chance I got, but same time, I wouldn't be where I am to-day, maybe, if it hadn't been for its training in—in moral power. And all about the Bible. Great literature. Have to read some of it again, one of these days."

How scientifically the Sunday School could be organized he learned from an article in the *Westminster Adult Bible Class:*

"The second vice-president looks after the fellowship of the class. She chooses a group to help her. These become ushers. Every one who comes gets a glad hand. No one goes away a stranger. One member of the group stands on the doorstep and invites passers-by to come in."

Perhaps most of all Babbitt appreciated the remarks by William H. Ridgway in the *Sunday School Times:*

"If you have a Sunday School class without any pep and get-up-and-go in it, that is, without interest, that is uncertain in attendance, that acts like a fellow with the spring fever, let old Dr. Ridgway write you a prescription. Rx. Invite the Bunch for Supper."

The Sunday School journals were as well rounded as they were practical. They neglected none of the arts. As to music the *Sunday School Times* advertised that C. Harold Lowden, "known to thousands through his sacred compositions," had written a new masterpiece, "entitled 'Yearning for You.' The poem, by Harry D. Kerr, is one of the daintiest you could imagine and the music is indescribably beautiful. Critics are agreed that it will sweep the country. May be made into a charming sacred song by substituting the hymn words, 'I Heard the Voice of Jesus Say.'"

Even manual training was adequately considered. Babbitt noted an ingenious way of illustrating the resurrection of Jesus Christ:

"Model for Pupils to Make. Tomb with Rolling Door.—Use a square covered box turned upside down. Pull the cover forward a little to form a groove at the bottom. Cut a square door, also cut a circle of cardboard to more than cover the door. Cover the circular door and the tomb thickly with stiff mixture of sand, flour and water and let it dry. It was the heavy circular stone over the door the women found 'rolled away' on Easter morning. This is the story we are to 'Go—tell.'"

In their advertisements the Sunday School journals were thoroughly efficient. Babbitt was interested in a preparation which "takes the place of exercise for sedentary men by building up depleted nerve tissue, nourishing the brain and the digestive system." He was edified to learn that the selling of Bibles was a hustling and strictly competitive industry, and as an expert on hygiene he was pleased by the Sanitary Communion Outfit Company's announcement of "an improved and satisfactory outfit throughout, including highly polished beautiful mahogany tray. This tray eliminates all noise, is lighter and more easily handled than others and is more in keeping with the furniture of the church than a tray of any other material."

IV

He dropped the pile of Sunday School journals.

He pondered, "Now, there's a real he-world. Corking!

"Ashamed I haven't sat in more. Fellow that's an influence in the community—shame if he doesn't take part in a real virile hustling religion. Sort of Christianity Incorporated, you might say.

"But with all reverence.

"Some folks might claim these Sunday School fans are undignified and unspiritual and so on. Sure! Always some skunk to spring things like that! Knocking and sneering and tearing-down—so much easier than building up. But me, I certainly hand it to these magazines. They've brought ole George F. Babbitt into camp, and that's the answer to the critics!

"The more manly and practical a fellow is, the more he ought to lead the enterprising Christian life. Me for it! Cut out this carelessness and boozing and— Rone! Where the devil you been? This is a fine time o' night to be coming in!"

# 17

There are but three or four old houses in Floral Heights, and in Floral Heights an old house is one which was built before 1880. The largest of these is the residence of William Washington Eathorne, president of the First State Bank.

The Eathorne Mansion preserves the memory of the "nice parts" of Zenith as they appeared from 1860 to 1900. It is a red brick immensity with gray sandstone lintels and a roof of slate in courses of red, green, and dyspeptic yellow. There are two anemic towers, one roofed with copper, the other crowned with castiron ferns. The porch is like an open tomb; it is supported by squat granite pillars above which hang frozen cascades of brick. At one side of the house is a huge stained-glass window in the shape of a keyhole.

But the house has an effect not at all humorous. It embodies the heavy dignity of those Victorian financiers who ruled the generation between the pioneers and the brisk "sales-engineers" and created a somber oligarchy by gaining control of banks, mills, land, railroads, mines. Out of the dozen contradictory Zeniths which together make up the true and complete Zenith, none is so powerful and enduring yet none so unfamiliar to the citizens as the small, still, dry, polite, cruel Zenith of the William Eathornes; and for that tiny hierarchy the other Zeniths unwittingly labor and insignificantly die.

Most of the castles of the testy Victorian tetrarchs are gone now or decayed into boarding-houses, but the Eathorne Mansion remains virtuous and aloof, reminiscent of London, Back Bay, Rittenhouse Square. Its marble steps are scrubbed daily, the brass plate is reverently polished, and the lace curtains are as prim and superior as William Washington Eathorne himself.

With a certain awe Babbitt and Chum Frink called on Eathorne for a meeting of the Sunday School Advisory Committee; with uneasy stillness they followed a uniformed maid through catacombs of reception-rooms to the library. It was as unmistakably the library of a solid old banker as Eathorne's side-whiskers were the side-whiskers of a solid old banker. The books were most of them Standard Sets, with the correct and traditional touch of dim blue, dim gold, and glossy calf-skin. The fire was exactly correct and traditional; a small, quiet, steady fire, reflected by polished fire-irons. The oak desk was dark and old and altogether perfect; the chairs were gently supercilious.

Eathorne's inquiries as to the healths of Mrs. Babbitt, Miss Babbitt, and the Other Children were softly paternal, but Babbitt had nothing with which to answer him. It was indecent to think of using the "How's tricks, ole socks?" which gratified Vergil Gunch and Frink and Howard Littlefield—men who till now had seemed successful and urbane. Babbitt and Frink sat politely, and politely did Eathorne observe, opening his thin lips just wide enough to dismiss the words, "Gentlemen, before we begin our conference—you may have felt the cold in coming here—so good of you to save an old man the journey—shall we perhaps have a whisky toddy?"

So well trained was Babbitt in all the conversation that befits a Good Fellow that he almost disgraced himself with "Rather than make trouble, and always providin' there ain't any enforcement officers hiding in the waste-basket—" The words died choking in his throat. He bowed in flustered obedience. So did Chum Frink.

Eathorne rang for the maid.

The modern and luxurious Babbitt had never seen any one ring for a servant in a private house, except during meals. Himself, in hotels, had rung for bell-boys, but in the house you didn't hurt Matilda's feelings; you went out in the hall and shouted for her. Nor had he, since prohibition, known any one to be casual about drinking. It was extraordinary merely to sip his toddy and not cry, "Oh, maaaaan, this hits me right where I live!" And always, with the ecstasy of youth meeting greatness, he marveled, "That little fuzzy-face there, why, he could make me or break me! If he told my banker to call my loans—! Gosh! That quarter-sized squirt! And looking like he hadn't got a single bit of hustle to him! I wonder— Do we Boosters throw too many fits about pep?"

From this thought he shuddered away, and listened devoutly to Eathorne's ideas on the advancement of the Sunday School, which were very clear and very bad.

Diffidently Babbitt outlined his own suggestions:

"I think if you analyze the needs of the school, in fact, going right at it as if it was a merchandizing problem, of course the one basic and fundamental need is growth. I presume we're all agreed we won't be satisfied till we build up the biggest darn Sunday School in the whole state, so the Chatham Road Presbyterian won't have to take anything off anybody. Now about jazzing up the campaign for prospects: they've already used contesting teams, and given prizes to the kids that bring in the most members. And they made a mistake there: the prizes were a lot of folderols and doodads like poetry books and illustrated Testaments, instead of something a real live kid would want to work for, like real cash or a speedometer for his motor cycle. Course I suppose it's all fine and dandy to illustrate the lessons with these decorated book-marks and blackboard drawings and so on, but when it comes down to real he-hustling, getting out and drumming up customers—or members, I mean, why, you got to make it worth a fellow's while.

"Now, I want to propose two stunts: First, divide the Sunday School into four armies, depending on age. Everybody gets a military rank in his own army according to how many members he brings in, and the duffers that lie down on us and don't bring in any, they remain privates. The pastor and superintendent rank as generals. And everybody has got to give salutes and all the rest of that junk, just like a regular army, to make 'em feel it's worth while to get rank.

"Then, second: Course the school has its advertising committee, but, Lord, nobody ever really works good—nobody works well just for the love of it. The thing to do is to be practical and up-to-date, and hire a real paid press-agent for the Sunday School—some newspaper fellow who can give part of his time."

"Sure, you bet!" said Chum Frink.

"Think of the nice juicy bits he could get in!" Babbitt crowed. "Not only the big, salient, vital facts, about how fast the Sunday School—and the collection—is growing, but a lot of humorous gossip and kidding: about how some blowhard fell down on his pledge to get new members, or a good time the Sacred Trinity class of girls had at their wieniewurst party. And on the side, if he had time, the press-agent might even boost the lessons themselves—do a little advertising for all the Sunday Schools in town, in fact. No use being hoggish toward the rest of 'em, providing we can keep the bulge on 'em in membership. Frinstance, he might get the papers to— Course I haven't got a literary training like Frink here, and I'm just guessing how the pieces ought to be written, but take frinstance, suppose the week's lesson is about Jacob; well, the press-agent might get in something that would have a fine moral, and yet with a trick headline that'd get folks to read it—say like: *Jake Fools the Old Man; Makes Getaway with Girl and Bankroll.* See how I mean? That'd get their interest! Now, course, Mr. Eathorne, you're conservative, and maybe you feel these stunts would be undignified, but honestly, I believe they'd bring home the bacon."

Eathorne folded his hands on his comfortable little belly and purred like an aged pussy:

"May I say, first, that I have been very much pleased by your analysis of the situation, Mr. Babbitt. As you surmise, it's necessary in My Position to be conservative, and perhaps endeavor to maintain a certain standard of dignity. Yet I think you'll find me somewhat progressive. In our bank, for example, I hope I may say that we have as modern a method of publicity and advertising as any in the city. Yes, I fancy you'll find us oldsters quite cognizant of the shifting spiritual values of the age. Yes, oh yes. And so, in fact, it pleases me to be able to say that though personally I might prefer the sterner Presbyterianism of an earlier era—"

Babbitt finally gathered that Eathorne was willing.

Chum Frink suggested as part-time press-agent one Kenneth Escott, reporter on the *Advocate-Times*.

They parted on a high plane of amity and Christian helpfulness.

Babbitt did not drive home, but toward the center of the city. He wished to be by himself and exult over the beauty of intimacy with William Washington Eathorne.

II

A snow-blanched evening of ringing pavements and eager lights.

Great golden lights of trolley-cars sliding along the packed snow of the roadway. Demure lights of little houses. The belching glare of a distant foundry, wiping out the sharp-edged stars. Lights of neighborhood drug stores where friends gossiped, well pleased, after the day's work.

The green light of a police-station, and greener radiance on the snow; the drama of a patrol-wagon—gong beating like a terrified heart, headlights scorching the crystal-sparkling street, driver not a chauffeur but a policeman proud in uniform, another policeman perilously dangling on the step at the back, and a glimpse of the prisoner. A murderer, a burglar, a coiner cleverly trapped?

An enormous graystone church with a rigid spire; dim light in the Parlors, and cheerful droning of choir-practise. The quivering green mercury-vapor light of a photo-engraver's loft. Then the storming lights of down-town; parked cars with ruby tail-lights; white arched entrances to movie theaters, like frosty mouths of winter caves; electric signs—serpents and little dancing men of fire; pink-shaded globes and scarlet jazz music in a cheap up-stairs dance-hall; lights of Chinese restaurants, lanterns painted with cherry-blossoms and with pagodas, hung against lattices of lustrous gold and black. Small dirty lamps in small stinking lunchrooms. The smart shopping-district, with rich and quiet light on crystal pendants and furs and suave surfaces of polished wood in velvet-hung reticent windows. High above the street, an unexpected square hanging in the darkness, the window of an office where some one was working late, for a reason unknown and stimulating. A man meshed in bankruptcy, an ambitious boy, an oil-man suddenly become rich?

The air was shrewd, the snow was deep in uncleared alleys, and beyond the city, Babbitt knew, were hillsides of snow-drift among wintry oaks, and the curving ice-enchanted river.

He loved his city with passionate wonder. He lost the accumulated weariness of business-worry and expansive oratory; he felt young and potential. He was ambitious. It was not enough to be a Vergil Gunch, an Orville Jones.

No. "They're bully fellows, simply lovely, but they haven't got any finesse." No. He was going to be an Eathorne; delicately rigorous, coldly powerful. "That's the stuff. The wallop in the velvet mitt. Not let anybody get fresh with you. Been getting careless about my diction. Slang. Colloquial. Cut it out. I was first-rate at rhetoric in college. Themes on— Anyway, not bad. Had too much of this hooptedoodle and good-fellow stuff. I— Why couldn't I organize a bank of my own some day? And Ted succeed me!"

He drove happily home, and to Mrs. Babbitt he was a William Washington Eathorne, but she did not notice it.

## III

Young Kenneth Escott, reporter on the *Advocate-Times*, was appointed press-agent of the Chatham Road Presbyterian Sunday School. He gave six hours a week to it. At least he was paid for giving six hours a week. He had friends on the *Press* and the *Gazette* and he was not (officially) known as a press-agent. He procured a trickle of insinuating items about neighborliness and the Bible, about class-suppers, jolly but educational, and the value of the Prayer-life in attaining financial success.

The Sunday School adopted Babbitt's system of military ranks. Quickened by this spiritual refreshment, it had a boom. It did not become the largest school in Zenith—the Central Methodist Church kept ahead of it by methods which Dr. Drew scored as "unfair, undignified, un-American, ungentlemanly, and unchristian"—but it climbed from fourth place to second, and there was rejoicing in heaven, or at least in that portion of heaven included in the parsonage of Dr. Drew, while Babbitt had much praise and good repute.

He had received the rank of colonel on the general staff of the school. He was plumply pleased by salutes on the street from unknown small boys; his ears were tickled to ruddy ecstasy by hearing himself called "Colonel;" and if he did not attend Sunday School merely to be thus exalted, certainly he thought about it all the way there.

He was particularly pleasant to the press-agent, Kenneth Escott; he took him to lunch at the Athletic Club and had him at the house for dinner.

Like many of the cocksure young men who forage about cities in apparent contentment and who express their cynicism in supercilious slang, Escott was shy and lonely. His shrewd starveling face broadened with joy at dinner, and he blurted, "Gee whillikins, Mrs. Babbitt, if you knew how good it is to have home eats again!"

Escott and Verona liked each other. All evening they "talked about ideas." They discovered that they were Radicals. True, they were sensible about it. They agreed that all communists were criminals; that this *vers libre* was tommyrot; and that while there ought to be universal disarmament, of course Great Britain and the United States must, on behalf of oppressed small nations, keep a navy equal to the tonnage of all the rest of the world. But they were so revolutionary that they predicted (to Babbitt's irritation) that there would some day be a Third Party which would give trouble to the Republicans and Democrats.

Escott shook hands with Babbitt three times, at parting.

Babbitt mentioned his extreme fondness for Eathorne.

Within a week three newspapers presented accounts of Babbitt's sterling labors for religion, and all of them tactfully mentioned William Washington Eathorne as his collaborator.

Nothing had brought Babbitt quite so much credit at the Elks, the Athletic Club, and the Boosters'. His friends had always congratulated him on his oratory, but in their praise was doubt, for even in speeches advertising the city there was something highbrow and degenerate, like writing poetry. But now Orville Jones shouted across the Athletic dining-room, "Here's the new director of the First State Bank!" Grover Butterbaugh, the eminent wholesaler of plumbers' supplies, chuckled, "Wonder you mix with common folks, after holding Eathorne's hand!" And Emil Wengert, the jeweler, was at last willing to discuss buying a house in Dorchester.

## IV

When the Sunday School campaign was finished, Babbitt suggested to Kenneth Escott, "Say, how about doing a little boosting for Doc Drew personally?"

Escott grinned. "You trust the doc to do a little boosting for himself, Mr. Babbitt! There's hardly a week goes by without his ringing up the paper to say if we'll chase a reporter up to his Study, he'll let us in on the story about the swell sermon he's going to preach on the wickedness of short skirts, or the authorship of the Pentateuch. Don't you worry about him. There's just one better publicity-grabber in town, and that's this Dora Gibson Tucker that runs the Child Welfare and the Americanization League, and the only reason she's got Drew beaten is because she has got *some* brains!"

"Well, now Kenneth, I don't think you ought to talk that way about the doctor. A preacher has to watch his interests, hasn't he? You remember that in the Bible about—about being diligent in the Lord's business, or something?"

"All right, I'll get something in if you want me to, Mr. Babbitt, but I'll have to wait till the managing editor is out of town, and then blackjack the city editor."

Thus it came to pass that in the Sunday *Advocate-Times*, under a picture of Dr. Drew at his earnestest, with eyes alert, jaw as granite, and rustic lock flamboyant, appeared an inscription—a wood-pulp tablet conferring twenty-four hours' immortality:

The Rev. Dr. John Jennison Drew, M.A., pastor of the beautiful Chatham Road Presbyterian Church in lovely Floral Heights, is a wizard soul-winner. He holds the local record for conversions. During his shepherdhood an average of almost a hundred sin-weary persons per year have declared their resolve to lead a new life and have found a harbor of refuge and peace.

Everything zips at the Chatham Road Church. The subsidiary organizations are keyed to the top-notch of efficiency. Dr. Drew is especially keen on good congregational singing. Bright cheerful hymns are used at every meeting, and the special Sing Services attract lovers of music and professionals from all parts of the city.

On the popular lecture platform as well as in the pulpit Dr. Drew is a renowned word-painter, and during the course of the year he receives literally scores of invitations to speak at varied functions both here and elsewhere.

v

Babbitt let Dr. Drew know that he was responsible for this tribute. Dr. Drew called him "brother," and shook his hand a great many times.

During the meetings of the Advisory Committee, Babbitt had hinted that he would be charmed to invite Eathorne to dinner, but Eathorne had murmured, "So nice of you—old man, now—almost never go out." Surely Eathorne would not refuse his own pastor. Babbitt said boyishly to Drew:

"Say, doctor, now we've put this thing over, strikes me it's up to the dominie to blow the three of us to a dinner!"

"Bully! You bet! Delighted!" cried Dr. Drew, in his manliest way. (Some one had once told him that he talked like the late President Roosevelt.)

"And, uh, say, doctor, be sure and get Mr. Eathorne to come. Insist on it. It's, uh— I think he sticks around home too much for his own health."

Eathorne came.

It was a friendly dinner. Babbitt spoke gracefully of the stabilizing of educational value of bankers to the community. They were, he said, the pastors of the fold of commerce. For the first time Eathorne departed from the topic of Sunday Schools, and asked Babbitt about the progress of his business. Babbitt answered modestly, almost filially.

A few months later, when he had a chance to take part in the Street Traction Company's terminal deal, Babbitt did not care to go to his own bank for a loan. It was rather a quiet sort of deal and, if it had come out, the Public might not have understood. He went to his friend Mr. Eathorne; he was welcomed, and received the loan as a private venture; and they both profited in their pleasant new association.

After that, Babbitt went to church regularly, except on spring Sunday mornings which were obviously meant for motoring. He announced to Ted, "I tell you, boy, there's no stronger bulwark of sound conservatism than the evangelical church, and no better place to make friends who'll help you to gain your rightful place in the community than in your own church-home!"

# 18

Though he saw them twice daily, though he knew and amply discussed every detail of their expenditures, yet for weeks together Babbitt was no more conscious of his children than of the buttons on his coat-sleeves.

The admiration of Kenneth Escott made him aware of Verona.

She had become secretary to Mr. Gruensberg of the Gruensberg Leather Company; she did her work with the thoroughness of a mind which reveres details and never quite understands them; but she was one of the people who give an agitating impression of being on the point of doing something desperate—of leaving a job or a husband—without ever doing it. Babbitt was so hopeful about Escott's hesitant ardors that he became the playful parent. When he returned from the Elks he peered coyly into the living-room and gurgled, "Has our Kenny been here to-night?" He never credited Verona's protest, "Why, Ken and I are just good friends, and we only talk about Ideas. I won't have all this sentimental nonsense, that would spoil everything."

It was Ted who most worried Babbitt.

With conditions in Latin and English but with a triumphant record in manual training, basket-ball, and the organization of dances, Ted was struggling through his Senior year in the East Side High School. At home he was interested only when he was asked to trace some subtle ill in the ignition system of the car. He repeated to his tut-tutting father that he did not wish to go to college or law-school, and Babbitt was equally disturbed by this "shiftlessness" and by Ted's relations with Eunice Littlefield, next door.

Though she was the daughter of Howard Littlefield, that wrought-iron fact-mill, that horse-faced priest of private ownership, Eunice was a midge in the sun. She danced into the house, she flung herself into Babbitt's lap when he was reading, she crumpled his paper, and laughed at him when he adequately explained that he hated a crumpled newspaper as he hated a broken sales-contract. She was seventeen now. Her ambition was to be a cinema actress. She did not merely attend the showing of every "feature film;" she also read the motion-picture magazines, those extraordinary symptoms of the Age of Pep—monthlies and weeklies gorgeously illustrated with portraits of young women who had recently been manicure girls, not very skilful manicure girls, and who, unless their every grimace had been arranged by a director, could not have acted in the Easter cantata of the Central Methodist Church; magazines reporting, quite seriously, in "interviews" plastered with pictures of riding-breeches and California bungalows, the views on sculpture and international politics of blankly beautiful, suspiciously beautiful young men; outlining the plots of films about pure prostitutes and kind-hearted train-robbers; and giving directions for making bootblacks into Celebrated Scenario Authors overnight.

These authorities Eunice studied. She could, she frequently did, tell whether it was in November or December, 1905, that Mack Harker, the renowned screen cowpuncher and badman, began his public career, as chorus man in "Oh, You Naughty Girlie." On the wall of her room, her father reported, she had pinned up twenty-one photographs of actors. But the signed portrait of the most graceful of the movie heroes she carried in her young bosom.

Babbitt was bewildered by this worship of new gods, and he suspected that Eunice smoked cigarettes. He smelled the cloying reek from up-stairs, and heard her giggling with Ted. He never inquired. The agreeable child dismayed him. Her thin and charming face was sharpened by bobbed hair; her skirts were short, her stockings were rolled, and, as she flew after Ted, above the caressing silk were glimpses of soft knees which made Babbitt uneasy, and wretched that she should consider him old. Sometimes, in the veiled life of his dreams, when the fairy child came running to him she took on the semblance of Eunice Littlefield.

Ted was motor-mad as Eunice was movie-mad.

A thousand sarcastic refusals did not check his teasing for a car of his own. However lax he might be about early rising and the prosody of Vergil, he was tireless in tinkering. With three other boys he bought a rheumatic Ford chassis, built an amazing racer-body out of tin and pine, went skidding round corners in the perilous craft, and sold it at a profit. Babbitt gave him a motorcycle, and every Saturday afternoon, with seven sandwiches and a bottle of Coca-Cola in his pockets, and Eunice perched eerily on the rumble seat, he went roaring off to distant towns.

Usually Eunice and he were merely neighborhood chums, and quarreled with a wholesome and violent lack of delicacy; but now and then, after the color and scent of a dance, they were silent together and a little furtive, and Babbitt was worried.

Babbitt was an average father. He was affectionate, bullying, opinionated, ignorant, and rather wistful. Like most parents, he enjoyed the game of waiting till the victim was clearly wrong, then virtuously pouncing. He justified himself by croaking, "Well, Ted's mother spoils him. Got to be somebody who tells him what's what, and me, I'm elected the goat. Because I try to bring him up to be a real, decent, human being and not one of these sapheads and lounge-lizards, of course they all call me a grouch!"

Throughout, with the eternal human genius for arriving by the worst possible routes at surprisingly tolerable goals, Babbitt loved his son and warmed to his companionship and would have sacrificed everything for him —if he could have been sure of proper credit.

II

Ted was planning a party for his set in the Senior Class.

Babbitt meant to be helpful and jolly about it. From his memory of high-school pleasures back in Catawba he suggested the nicest games: Going to Boston, and charades with stewpans for helmets, and word-games in which you were an Adjective or a Quality. When he was most enthusiastic he discovered that they weren't paying attention; they were only tolerating him. As for the party, it was as fixed and standardized as a Union Club Hop. There was to be dancing in the living-room, a noble collation in the dining-room, and in the hall two tables of bridge for what Ted called "the poor old dumb-bells that you can't get to dance hardly more 'n half the time."

Every breakfast was monopolized by conferences on the affair. No one listened to Babbitt's bulletins about the February weather or to his throat-clearing comments on the headlines. He said furiously, "If I may be *permitted* to interrupt your engrossing private *conversation*— Juh hear what I *said?*"

"Oh, don't be a spoiled baby! Ted and I have just as much right to talk as you have!" flared Mrs. Babbitt.

On the night of the party he was permitted to look on, when he was not helping Matilda with the Vecchia ice cream and the *petits fours*. He was deeply disquieted. Eight years ago, when Verona had given a high-school party, the children had been featureless gabies. Now they were men and women of the world, very supercilious men and women; the boys condescended to Babbitt, they wore evening-clothes, and with hauteur they accepted cigarettes from silver cases. Babbitt had heard stories of what the Athletic Club called "goings-on" at young parties; of girls "parking" their corsets in the dressing-room, of "cuddling" and "petting," and a presumable increase in what was known as Immorality. To-night he believed the stories. These children seemed bold to him, and cold. The girls wore misty chiffon, coral velvet, or cloth of gold, and around their dipping bobbed hair were shining wreaths. He had it, upon urgent and secret inquiry, that no corsets were known to be parked upstairs; but certainly these eager bodies were not stiff with steel. Their stockings were of lustrous silk, their slippers costly and unnatural, their lips carmined and their eyebrows penciled. They danced cheek to cheek with the boys, and Babbitt sickened with apprehension and unconscious envy.

Worst of them all was Eunice Littlefield, and maddest of all the boys was Ted. Eunice was a flying demon. She slid the length of the room; her tender shoulders swayed; her feet were deft as a weaver's shuttle; she laughed, and enticed Babbitt to dance with her.

Then he discovered the annex to the party.

The boys and girls disappeared occasionally, and he remembered rumors of their drinking together from hip-pocket flasks. He tiptoed round the house, and in each of the dozen cars waiting in the street he saw the points of light from cigarettes, from each of them heard high giggles. He wanted to denounce them but (standing in the snow, peering round the dark corner) he did not dare. He tried to be tactful. When he had returned to the front hall he coaxed the boys, "Say, if any of you fellows are thirsty, there's some dandy ginger ale."

"Oh! Thanks!" they condescended.

He sought his wife, in the pantry, and exploded, "I'd like to go in there and throw some of those young pups out of the house! They talk down to me like I was the butler! I'd like to—"

"I know," she sighed; "only everybody says, all the mothers tell me, unless you stand for them, if you get angry because they go out to their cars to have a drink, they won't come to your house any more, and we wouldn't want Ted left out of things, would we?"

He announced that he would be enchanted to have Ted left out of things, and hurried in to be polite, lest Ted be left out of things.

But, he resolved, if he found that the boys were drinking, he would—well, he'd "hand 'em something that would surprise 'em." While he was trying to be agreeable to large-shouldered young bullies he was earnestly sniffing at them. Twice he caught the reek of prohibition-time whisky, but then, it was only twice—

Dr. Howard Littlefield lumbered in.

He had come, in a mood of solemn parental patronage, to look on. Ted and Eunice were dancing, moving together like one body. Littlefield gasped. He called Eunice. There was a whispered duologue, and Littlefield explained to Babbitt that Eunice's mother had a headache and needed her. She went off in tears. Babbitt looked after them furiously. "That little devil! Getting Ted into trouble! And Littlefield, the conceited old gas-bag, acting like it was Ted that was the bad influence!"

Later he smelled whisky on Ted's breath.

After the civil farewell to the guests, the row was terrific, a thorough Family Scene, like an avalanche, devastating and without reticences. Babbitt thundered, Mrs. Babbitt wept, Ted was unconvincingly defiant, and Verona in confusion as to whose side she was taking.

For several months there was coolness between the Babbitts and the Littlefields, each family sheltering their lamb from the wolf-cub next door. Babbitt and Littlefield still spoke in pontifical periods about motors and the senate, but they kept bleakly away from mention of their families. Whenever Eunice came to the house she discussed with pleasant intimacy the fact that she had been forbidden to come to the house; and Babbitt tried, with no success whatever, to be fatherly and advisory with her.

### III

"Gosh all fishhooks!" Ted wailed to Eunice, as they wolfed hot chocolate, lumps of nougat, and an assortment of glacé nuts, in the mosaic splendor of the Royal Drug Store, "it gets me why Dad doesn't just pass out from being so poky. Every evening he sits there, about half-asleep, and if Rone or I say, 'Oh, come on, let's do something,' he doesn't even take the trouble to think about it. He just yawns and says, 'Naw, this suits me right here.' He doesn't know there's any fun going on anywhere. I suppose he must do some thinking, same as you and I do, but gosh, there's no way of telling it. I don't believe that outside of the office and playing a little bum golf on Saturday he knows there's anything in the world to do except just keep sitting there—sitting there every night—not wanting to go anywhere—not wanting to do anything—thinking us kids are crazy—sitting there—Lord!"

#### IV

If he was frightened by Ted's slackness, Babbitt was not sufficiently frightened by Verona. She was too safe. She lived too much in the neat little airless room of her mind. Kenneth Escott and she were always under foot. When they were not at home, conducting their cautiously radical courtship over sheets of statistics, they were trudging off to lectures by authors and Hindu philosophers and Swedish lieutenants.

"Gosh," Babbitt wailed to his wife, as they walked home from the Fogartys' bridge-party, "it gets me how Rone and that fellow can be so poky. They sit there night after night, whenever he isn't working, and they don't know there's any fun in the world. All talk and discussion—Lord! Sitting there—sitting there—night after night—not wanting to do anything—thinking I'm crazy because I like to go out and play a fist of cards—sitting there—gosh!"

Then round the swimmer, bored by struggling through the perpetual surf of family life, new combers swelled.

#### V

Babbitt's father- and mother-in-law, Mr. and Mrs. Henry T. Thompson, rented their old house in the Bellevue district and moved to the Hotel Hatton, that glorified boarding-house filled with widows, red-plush furniture, and the sound of ice-water pitchers. They were lonely there, and every other Sunday evening the Babbitts had to dine with them, on fricasseed chicken, discouraged celery, and cornstarch ice cream, and afterward sit, polite and restrained, in the hotel lounge, while a young woman violinist played songs from the German via Broadway.

Then Babbitt's own mother came down from Catawba to spend three weeks.

She was a kind woman and magnificently uncomprehending. She congratulated the convention-defying Verona on being a "nice, loyal home-body without all these Ideas that so many girls seem to have nowadays;" and when Ted filled the differential with grease, out of pure love of mechanics and filthiness, she rejoiced that he was "so handy around the house and helping his father and all, and not going out with the girls all the time and trying to pretend he was a society fellow."

Babbitt loved his mother, and sometimes he rather liked her, but he was annoyed by her Christian Patience, and he was reduced to pulpiness when she discoursed about a quite mythical hero called "Your Father":

"You won't remember it, Georgie, you were such a little fellow at the time—my, I remember just how you looked that day, with your goldy brown curls and your lace collar, you always were such a dainty child, and kind of puny and sickly, and you loved pretty things so much and the red tassels on your little bootees and all—and Your Father was taking us to church and a man stopped us and said 'Major'—so many of the neighbors used to call Your Father 'Major;' of course he was only a private in The War but everybody knew that was because of the jealousy of his captain and he ought to have been a high-ranking officer, he had that natural ability to command that so very, very few men have—and this man came out into the road and held up his hand and stopped the buggy and said, 'Major,' he said, 'there's a lot of the folks around here that have decided to support Colonel Scanell for congress, and we want you to join us. Meeting people the way you do in the store, you could help us a lot.'

"Well, Your Father just looked at him and said, 'I certainly shall do nothing of the sort. I don't like his politics,' he said. Well, the man—Captain Smith they used to call him, and heaven only knows why, because he hadn't the shadow or vestige of a right to be called 'Captain' or any other title—this Captain Smith said, 'We'll make it hot for you if you don't stick by your friends, Major.' Well, you know how Your Father was, and this Smith knew it too; he knew what a Real Man he was, and he knew Your Father knew the political situation from A to Z, and he ought to have seen that here was one man he couldn't impose on, but he went on trying to and hinting and trying till Your Father spoke up and said to him, 'Captain Smith,' he said, 'I have a reputation around these parts for being one who is amply qualified to mind his own business and let other folks mind theirs!' and with that he drove on and left the fellow standing there in the road like a bump on a log!"

Babbitt was most exasperated when she revealed his boyhood to the children. He had, it seemed, been fond of barley-sugar; had worn the "loveliest little pink bow in his curls" and corrupted his own name to "Goo-goo." He heard (though he did not officially hear) Ted admonishing Tinka, "Come on now, kid; stick the lovely pink bow in your curls and beat it down to breakfast, or Goo-goo will jaw your head off."

Babbitt's half-brother, Martin, with his wife and youngest baby, came down from Catawba for two days. Martin bred cattle and ran the dusty general-store. He was proud of being a freeborn independent American of the good old Yankee stock; he was proud of being honest, blunt, ugly, and disagreeable. His favorite remark was "How much did you pay for that?" He regarded Verona's books, Babbitt's silver pencil, and flowers on the table as citified extravagances, and said so. Babbitt would have quarreled with him but for his gawky wife and the baby, whom Babbitt teased and poked fingers at and addressed:

"I think this baby's a bum, yes, sir, I think this little baby's a bum, he's a bum, yes, sir, he's a bum, that's what he is, he's a bum, this baby's a bum, he's nothing but an old bum, that's what he is—a bum!"

All the while Verona and Kenneth Escott held long inquiries into epistemology; Ted was a disgraced rebel; and Tinka, aged eleven, was demanding that she be allowed to go to the movies thrice a week, "like all the girls."

Babbitt raged, "I'm sick of it! Having to carry three generations. Whole damn bunch lean on me. Pay half of mother's income, listen to Henry T., listen to Myra's worrying, be polite to Mart, and get called an old grouch for trying to help the children. All of 'em depending on me and picking on me and not a damn one of 'em grateful! No relief, and no credit, and no help from anybody. And to keep it up for—good Lord, how long?"

He enjoyed being sick in February; he was delighted by their consternation that he, the rock, should give way.

He had eaten a questionable clam. For two days he was languorous and petted and esteemed. He was allowed to snarl "Oh, let me alone!" without reprisals. He lay on the sleeping-porch and watched the winter sun slide along the taut curtains, turning their ruddy khaki to pale blood red. The shadow of the draw-rope was dense black, in an enticing ripple on the canvas. He found pleasure in the curve of it, sighed as the fading light blurred it. He was conscious of life, and a little sad. With no Vergil Gunches before whom to set his face in resolute optimism, he beheld, and half admitted that he beheld, his way of life as incredibly mechanical. Mechanical business—a brisk selling of badly built houses. Mechanical religion—a dry, hard church, shut off from the real life of the streets, inhumanly respectable as a top-hat. Mechanical golf and dinner-parties and bridge and conversation. Save with Paul Riesling, mechanical friendships—back-slapping and jocular, never daring to essay the test of quietness.

He turned uneasily in bed.

He saw the years, the brilliant winter days and all the long sweet afternoons which were meant for summery meadows, lost in such brittle pretentiousness. He thought of telephoning about leases, of cajoling men he hated, of making business calls and waiting in dirty anterooms—hat on knee, yawning at fly-specked calendars, being polite to office-boys.

"I don't hardly want to go back to work," he prayed. "I'd like to— I don't know."

But he was back next day, busy and of doubtful temper.

# 19

The Zenith Street Traction Company planned to build car-repair shops in the suburb of Dorchester, but when they came to buy the land they found it held, on options, by the Babbitt-Thompson Realty Company. The purchasing-agent, the first vice-president, and even the president of the Traction Company protested against the Babbitt price. They mentioned their duty toward stockholders, they threatened an appeal to the courts, though somehow the appeal to the courts was never carried out and the officials found it wiser to compromise with Babbitt. Carbon copies of the correspondence are in the company's files, where they may be viewed by any public commission.

Just after this Babbitt deposited three thousand dollars in the bank, the purchasing-agent of the Street Traction Company bought a five thousand dollar car, the first vice-president built a home in Devon Woods, and the president was appointed minister to a foreign country.

To obtain the options, to tie up one man's land without letting his neighbor know, had been an unusual strain on Babbitt. It was necessary to introduce rumors about planning garages and stores, to pretend that he wasn't taking any more options, to wait and look as bored as a poker-player at a time when the failure to secure a key-lot threatened his whole plan. To all this was added a nerve-jabbing quarrel with his secret associates in the deal. They did not wish Babbitt and Thompson to have any share in the deal except as brokers. Babbitt rather agreed. "Ethics of the business—broker ought to strictly represent his principles and not get in on the buying," he said to Thompson.

"Ethics, rats! Think I'm going to see that bunch of holy grafters get away with the swag and us not climb in?" snorted old Henry.

"Well, I don't like to do it. Kind of double-crossing."

"It ain't. It's triple-crossing. It's the public that gets double-crossed. Well, now we've been ethical and got it out of our systems, the question is where we can raise a loan to handle some of the property for ourselves, on the Q. T. We can't go to our bank for it. Might come out."

"I could see old Eathorne. He's close as the tomb."

"That's the stuff."

Eathorne was glad, he said, to "invest in character," to make Babbitt the loan and see to it that the loan did not appear on the books of the bank. Thus certain of the options which Babbitt and Thompson obtained were on parcels of real estate which they themselves owned, though the property did not appear in their names.

In the midst of closing this splendid deal, which stimulated business and public confidence by giving an example of increased real-estate activity, Babbitt was overwhelmed to find that he had a dishonest person working for him.

The dishonest one was Stanley Graff, the outside salesman.

For some time Babbitt had been worried about Graff. He did not keep his word to tenants. In order to rent a house he would promise repairs which the owner had not authorized. It was suspected that he juggled inventories of furnished houses so that when the tenant left he had to pay for articles which had never been in the house and the price of which Graff put into his pocket. Babbitt had not been able to prove these suspicions, and though he had rather planned to discharge Graff he had never quite found time for it.

Now into Babbitt's private room charged a red-faced man, panting, "Look here! I've come to raise particular merry hell, and unless you have that fellow pinched, I will!"

"What's— Calm down, o' man. What's trouble?"

"Trouble! Huh! Here's the trouble—"

"Sit down and take it easy! They can hear you all over the building!"

"This fellow Graff you got working for you, he leases me a house. I was in yesterday and signs the lease, all O.K., and he was to get the owner's signature and mail me the lease last night. Well, and he did. This morning I comes down to breakfast and the girl says a fellow had come to the house right after the early delivery and told her he wanted an envelope that had been mailed by mistake, big long envelope with 'Babbitt-Thompson' in the corner of it. Sure enough, there it was, so she lets him have it. And she describes the fellow to me, and it was this Graff. So I 'phones to him and he, the poor fool, he admits it! He says after my lease was all signed he got a better offer from another fellow and he wanted my lease back. Now what you going to do about it?"

"Your name is—?"

"William Varney—W. K. Varney."

"Oh, yes. That was the Garrison house." Babbitt sounded the buzzer. When Miss McGoun came in, he demanded, "Graff gone out?"

"Yes, sir."

"Will you look through his desk and see if there is a lease made out to Mr. Varney on the Garrison house?" To Varney: "Can't tell you how sorry I am this happened. Needless to say, I'll fire Graff the minute he comes in. And of course your lease stands. But there's one other thing I'd like to do. I'll tell the owner not to pay us the commission but apply it to your rent. No! Straight! I want to. To be frank, this thing shakes me up bad. I suppose I've always been a Practical Business Man. Probably I've told one or two fairy stories in my time, when the occasion called for it—you know: sometimes you have to lay things on thick, to impress boneheads. But this is the first time I've ever had to accuse one of my own employees of anything more dishonest than pinching a few stamps. Honest, it would hurt me if we profited by it. So you'll let me hand you the commission? Good!"

## II

He walked through the February city, where trucks flung up a spattering of slush and the sky was dark above dark brick cornices. He came back miserable. He, who respected the law, had broken it by concealing the Federal crime of interception of the mails. But he could not see Graff go to jail and his wife suffer. Worse, he had to discharge Graff, and this was a part of office routine which he feared. He liked people so much, he so much wanted them to like him, that he could not bear insulting them.

Miss McGoun dashed in to whisper, with the excitement of an approaching scene, "He's here!"

"Mr. Graff? Ask him to come in."

He tried to make himself heavy and calm in his chair, and to keep his eyes expressionless. Graff stalked in—a man of thirty-five, dapper, eye-glassed, with a foppish mustache.

"Want me?" said Graff.

"Yes. Sit down."

Graff continued to stand, grunting, "I suppose that old nut Varney has been in to see you. Let me explain about him. He's a regular tightwad, and he sticks out for every cent, and he practically lied to me about his ability to pay the rent—I found that out just after we signed up. And then another fellow comes along with a better offer for the house, and I felt it was my duty to the firm to get rid of Varney, and I was so worried about it I skun up there and got back the lease. Honest, Mr. Babbitt, I didn't intend to pull anything crooked. I just wanted the firm to have all the commis—"

"Wait now, Stan. This may all be true, but I've been having a lot of complaints about you. Now I don't s'pose you ever mean to do wrong, and I think if you just get a good lesson that'll jog you up a little, you'll turn out a first-class realtor yet. But I don't see how I can keep you on."

Graff leaned against the filing-cabinet, his hands in his pockets, and laughed. "So I'm fired! Well, old Vision and Ethics, I'm tickled to death! But I don't want you to think you can get away with any holier-than-thou stuff. Sure I've pulled some raw stuff—a little of it—but how could I help it, in this office?"

"Now, by God, young man—"

"Tut, tut! Keep the naughty temper down, and don't holler, because everybody in the outside office will hear you. They're probably listening right now. Babbitt, old dear, you're crooked in the first place and a damn skinflint in the second. If you paid me a decent salary I wouldn't have to steal pennies off a blind man to keep my wife from starving. Us married just five months, and her the nicest girl living, and you keeping us flat broke all the time, you damned old thief, so you can put money away for your saphead of a son and your wishywashy fool of a daughter! Wait, now! You'll by God take it, or I'll bellow so the whole office will hear it! And crooked— Say, if I told the prosecuting attorney what I know about this last Street Traction option steal, both you and me would go to jail, along with some nice, clean, pious, high-up traction guns!"

"Well, Stan, looks like we were coming down to cases. That deal— There was nothing crooked about it. The only way you can get progress is for the broad-gauged men to get things done; and they got to be rewarded—"

"Oh, for Pete's sake, don't get virtuous on me! As I gather it, I'm fired. All right. It's a good thing for me. And if I catch you knocking me to any other firm, I'll squeal all I know about you and Henry T. and the dirty little lickspittle deals that you corporals of industry pull off for the bigger and brainier crooks, and you'll get chased out of town. And me—you're right, Babbitt, I've been going crooked, but now I'm going straight, and the first step will be to get a job in some office where the boss doesn't talk about Ideals. Bad luck, old dear, and you can stick your job up the sewer!"

Babbitt sat for a long time, alternately raging, "I'll have him arrested," and yearning "I wonder— No, I've never done anything that wasn't necessary to keep the Wheels of Progress moving."

Next day he hired in Graff's place Fritz Weilinger, the salesman of his most injurious rival, the East Side Homes and Development Company, and thus at once annoyed his competitor and acquired an excellent man. Young Fritz was a curly-headed, merry, tennis-playing youngster. He made customers welcome to the office. Babbitt thought of him as a son, and in him had much comfort.

### III

An abandoned race-track on the outskirts of Chicago, a plot excellent for factory sites, was to be sold, and Jake Offutt asked Babbitt to bid on it for him. The strain of the Street Traction deal and his disappointment in Stanley Graff had so shaken Babbitt that he found it hard to sit at his desk and concentrate. He proposed to his family, "Look here, folks! Do you know who's going to trot up to Chicago for a couple of days—just week-end; won't lose but one day of school—know who's going with that celebrated business-ambassador, George F. Babbitt? Why, Mr. Theodore Roosevelt Babbitt!"

"Hurray!" Ted shouted, and "Oh, maybe the Babbitt men won't paint that lil ole town red!"

And, once away from the familiar implications of home, they were two men together. Ted was young only in his assumption of oldness, and the only realms, apparently, in which Babbitt had a larger and more grown-up knowledge than Ted's were the details of real estate and the phrases of politics. When the other sages of the Pullman smoking-compartment had left them to themselves, Babbitt's voice did not drop into the playful and otherwise offensive tone in which one addresses children but continued its overwhelming and monotonous rumble, and Ted tried to imitate it in his strident tenor:

"Gee, dad, you certainly did show up that poor boot when he got flip about the League of Nations!"

"Well, the trouble with a lot of these fellows is, they simply don't know what they're talking about. They don't get down to facts. . . . What do you think of Ken Escott?"

"I'll tell you, dad: it strikes me Ken is a nice lad; no special faults except he smokes too much; but slow, Lord! Why, if we don't give him a shove the poor dumb-bell never will propose! And Rone just as bad. Slow."

"Yes, I guess you're right. They're slow. They haven't either one of 'em got our pep."

"That's right. They're slow. I swear, dad, I don't know how Rone got into our family! I'll bet, if the truth were known, you were a bad old egg when you were a kid!"

"Well, I wasn't so slow!"

"I'll bet you weren't! I'll bet you didn't miss many tricks!"

"Well, when I was out with the girls I didn't spend all the time telling 'em about the strike in the knitting industry!"

They roared together, and together lighted cigars.

"What are we going to do with 'em?" Babbitt consulted.

"Gosh, I don't know. I swear, sometimes I feel like taking Ken aside and putting him over the jumps and saying to him, 'Young fella me lad, are you going to marry young Rone, or are you going to talk her to death? Here you are getting on toward thirty, and you're only making twenty or twenty-five a week. When you going to develop a sense of responsibility and get a raise? If there's anything that George F. or I can do to help you, call on us, but show a little speed, anyway!' "

"Well, at that, it might not be so bad if you or I talked to him, except he might not understand. He's one of these highbrows. He can't come down to cases and lay his cards on the table and talk straight out from the shoulder, like you or I can."

"That's right, he's like all these highbrows."

"That's so, like all of 'em."

"That's a fact."

They sighed, and were silent and thoughtful and happy.

The conductor came in. He had once called at Babbitt's office, to ask about houses. "H' are you, Mr. Babbitt! We going to have you with us to Chicago? This your boy?"

"Yes, this is my son Ted."

"Well now, what do you know about that! Here I been thinking you were a youngster yourself, not a day over forty, hardly, and you with this great big fellow!"

"Forty? Why, brother, I'll never see forty-five again!"

"Is that a fact! Wouldn't hardly 'a' thought it!"

"Yes, sir, it's a bad give-away for the old man when he has to travel with a young whale like Ted here!"

"You're right, it is." To Ted: "I suppose you're in college now."

Proudly, "No, not till next fall. I'm just kind of giving the diff'rent colleges the once-over now."

As the conductor went on his affable way, huge watch-chain jingling against his blue chest, Babbitt and Ted gravely considered colleges. They arrived at Chicago late at night; they lay abed in the morning, rejoicing, "Pretty nice not to have to get up and get down to breakfast, heh?" They were staying at the modest Eden Hotel, because Zenith business men always stayed at the Eden, but they had dinner in the brocade and crystal Versailles Room of the Regency Hotel. Babbitt ordered Blue Point oysters with cocktail sauce, a tremendous steak with a tremendous platter of French fried potatoes, two pots of coffee, apple pie with ice cream for both of them and, for Ted, an extra piece of mince pie.

"Hot stuff! Some feed, young fella!" Ted admired.

"Huh! You stick around with me, old man, and I'll show you a good time!"

They went to a musical comedy and nudged each other at the matrimonial jokes and the prohibition jokes; they paraded the lobby, arm in arm, between acts, and in the glee of his first release from the shame which dissevers fathers and sons Ted chuckled, "Dad, did you ever hear the one about the three milliners and the judge?"

When Ted had returned to Zenith, Babbitt was lonely. As he was trying to make alliance between Offutt and certain Milwaukee interests which wanted the race-track plot, most of his time was taken up in waiting for telephone calls. . . . Sitting on the edge of his bed, holding the portable telephone, asking wearily, "Mr. Sagen not in yet? Didn' he leave any message for me? All right, I'll hold the wire." Staring at a stain on the wall, reflecting that it resembled a shoe, and being bored by this twentieth discovery that it resembled a shoe. Lighting a cigarette; then, bound to the telephone with no ash-tray in reach, wondering what to do with this burning menace and anxiously trying to toss it into the tiled bathroom. At last, on the telephone, "No message, eh? All right, I'll call up again."

One afternoon he wandered through snow-rutted streets of which he had never heard, streets of small tenements and two-family houses and marooned cottages. It came to him that he had nothing to do, that there was nothing he wanted to do. He was bleakly lonely in the evening, when he dined by himself at the Regency Hotel. He sat in the lobby afterward, in a plush chair bedecked with the Saxe-Coburg arms, lighting a cigar and looking for some one who would come and play with him and save him from thinking. In the chair next to him (showing the arms of Lithuania) was a half-familiar man, a large red-faced man with pop eyes and a deficient yellow mustache. He seemed kind and insignificant, and as lonely as Babbitt himself. He wore a tweed suit and a reluctant orange tie.

It came to Babbitt with a pyrotechnic crash. The melancholy stranger was Sir Gerald Doak.

Instinctively Babbitt rose, bumbling, "How 're you, Sir Gerald? 'Member we met in Zenith, at Charley McKelvey's? Babbitt's my name—real estate."

"Oh! How d' you do." Sir Gerald shook hands flabbily.

Embarrassed, standing, wondering how he could retreat, Babbitt maundered, "Well, I suppose you been having a great trip since we saw you in Zenith."

"Quite. British Columbia and California and all over the place," he said doubtfully, looking at Babbitt lifelessly.

"How did you find business conditions in British Columbia? Or I suppose maybe you didn't look into 'em. Scenery and sport and so on?"

"Scenery? Oh, capital. But business conditions— You know, Mr. Babbitt, they're having almost as much unemployment as we are." Sir Gerald was speaking warmly now.

"So? Business conditions not so doggone good, eh?"

"No, business conditions weren't at all what I'd hoped to find them."

"Not good, eh?"

"No, not—not really good."

"That's a darn shame. Well— I suppose you're waiting for somebody to take you out to some big shindig, Sir Gerald."

"Shindig? Oh. Shindig. No, to tell you the truth, I was wondering what the deuce I could do this evening. Don't know a soul in Tchicahgo. I wonder if you happen to know whether there's a good theater in this city?"

"Good? Why say, they're running grand opera right now! I guess maybe you'd like that."

"Eh? Eh? Went to the opera once in London. Covent Garden sort of thing. Shocking! No, I was wondering if there was a good cinema—movie."

Babbitt was sitting down, hitching his chair over, shouting, "Movie? Say, Sir Gerald, I supposed of course you had a raft of dames waiting to lead you out to some soirée—"

"God forbid!"

"—but if you haven't, what do you say you and me go to a movie? There's a peach of a film at the Grantham: Bill Hart in a bandit picture."

"Right-o! Just a moment while I get my coat."

Swollen with greatness, slightly afraid lest the noble blood of Nottingham change its mind and leave him at any street corner, Babbitt paraded with Sir Gerald Doak to the movie palace and in silent bliss sat beside him, trying not to be too enthusiastic, lest the knight despise his adoration of six-shooters and broncos. At the end Sir Gerald murmured, "Jolly good picture, this. So awfully decent of you to take me. Haven't enjoyed myself so much for weeks. All these Hostesses—they never let you go to the cinema!"

"The devil you say!" Babbitt's speech had lost the delicate refinement and all the broad A's with which he had adorned it, and become hearty and natural. "Well, I'm tickled to death you liked it, Sir Gerald."

They crawled past the knees of fat women into the aisle; they stood in the lobby waving their arms in the rite of putting on overcoats. Babbitt hinted, "Say, how about a little something to eat? I know a place where we could get a swell rarebit, and we might dig up a little drink—that is, if you ever touch the stuff."

"Rather! But why don't you come to my room? I've some Scotch—not half bad."

"Oh, I don't want to use up all your hootch. It's darn nice of you, but— You probably want to hit the hay."

Sir Gerald was transformed. He was beefily yearning. "Oh really, now; I haven't had a decent evening for so long! Having to go to all these dances. No chance to discuss business and that sort of thing. Do be a good chap and come along. Won't you?"

"Will I? You bet! I just thought maybe— Say, by golly, it does do a fellow good, don't it, to sit and visit about business conditions, after he's been to these balls and masquerades and banquets and all that society stuff. I often feel that way in Zenith. Sure, you bet I'll come."

"That's awfully nice of you." They beamed along the street. "Look here, old chap, can you tell me, do American cities always keep up this dreadful social pace? All these magnificent parties?"

"Go on now, quit your kidding! Gosh, you with court balls and functions and everything—"

"No, really, old chap! Mother and I—Lady Doak, I should say, we usually play a hand of bezique and go to bed at ten. Bless my soul, I couldn't keep up your beastly pace! And talking! All your American women, they know so much—culture and that sort of thing. This Mrs. McKelvey—your friend—"

"Yuh, old Lucile. Good kid."

"—she asked me which of the galleries I liked best in Florence. Or was it in Firenze? Never been in Italy in my life! And primitives. Did I like primitives. Do you know what the deuce a primitive is?"

"Me? I should say not! But I know what a discount for cash is."

"Rather! So do I, by George! But primitives!"

"Yuh! Primitives!"

They laughed with the sound of a Boosters' luncheon.

Sir Gerald's room was, except for his ponderous and durable English bags, very much like the room of George F. Babbitt; and quite in the manner of Babbitt he disclosed a huge whisky flask, looked proud and hospitable, and chuckled, "Say, when, old chap."

It was after the third drink that Sir Gerald proclaimed, "How do you Yankees get the notion that writing chaps like Bertrand Shaw and this Wells represent us? The real business England, we think those chaps are traitors. Both our countries have their comic Old Aristocracy—you know, old county families, hunting people and all that sort of thing—and we both have our wretched labor leaders, but we both have a backbone of sound business men who run the whole show."

"You bet. Here's to the real guys!"

"I'm with you! Here's to ourselves!"

It was after the fourth drink that Sir Gerald asked humbly, "What do you think of North Dakota mortgages?" but it was not till after the fifth that Babbitt began to call him "Jerry," and Sir Gerald confided, "I say, do you mind if I pull off my boots?" and ecstatically stretched his knightly feet, his poor, tired, hot, swollen feet out on the bed.

After the sixth, Babbitt irregularly arose. "Well, I better be hiking along. Jerry, you're a regular human being! I wish to thunder we'd been better acquainted in Zenith. Lookit. Can't you come back and stay with me a while?"

"So sorry—must go to New York to-morrow. Most awfully sorry, old boy. I haven't enjoyed an evening so much since I've been in the States. Real talk. Not all this social rot. I'd never have let them give me the beastly title—and I didn't get it for nothing, eh?—if I'd thought I'd have to talk to women about primitives and polo! Goodish thing to have in Nottingham, though; annoyed the mayor most frightfully when I got it; and of course the missus likes it. But nobody calls me 'Jerry' now—" He was almost weeping. "—and nobody in the States has treated me like a friend till to-night! Good-by, old chap, good-by! Thanks awfully!"

"Don't mention it, Jerry. And remember whenever you get to Zenith, the latch-string is always out."

"And don't forget, old boy, if you ever come to Nottingham, Mother and I will be frightfully glad to see you. I shall tell the fellows in Nottingham your ideas about Visions and Real Guys—at our next Rotary Club luncheon."

### IV

Babbitt lay abed at his hotel, imagining the Zenith Athletic Club asking him, "What kind of a time d'you have in Chicago?" and his answering, "Oh, fair; ran around with Sir Gerald Doak a lot;" picturing himself meeting Lucile McKelvey and admonishing her, "You're all right, Mrs. Mac, when you aren't trying to pull this highbrow pose. It's just as Gerald Doak says to me in Chicago—oh, yes, Jerry's an old friend of mine—the wife and I are thinking of running over to England to stay with Jerry in his castle, next year—and he said to me, 'Georgie, old bean, I like Lucile first-rate, but you and me, George, we got to make her get over this highty-tighty hooptediddle way she's got."

But that evening a thing happened which wrecked his pride.

### V

At the Regency Hotel cigar-counter he fell to talking with a salesman of pianos, and they dined together. Babbitt was filled with friendliness and well-being. He enjoyed the gorgeousness of the dining-room: the chandeliers, the looped brocade curtains, the portraits of French kings against panels of gilded oak. He enjoyed the crowd: pretty women, good solid fellows who were "liberal spenders."

He gasped. He stared, and turned away, and stared again. Three tables off, with a doubtful sort of woman, a woman at once coy and withered, was Paul Riesling, and Paul was supposed to be in Akron, selling tar-roofing. The woman was tapping his hand, mooning at him and giggling. Babbitt felt that he had encountered something involved and harmful. Paul was talking with the rapt eagerness of a man who is telling his troubles. He was concentrated on the woman's faded eyes. Once he held her hand and once, blind to the other guests, he puckered his lips as though he was pretending to kiss her. Babbitt had so strong an impulse to go to Paul that he could feel his body uncoiling, his shoulders moving, but he felt, desperately, that he must be diplomatic, and not till he saw Paul paying the check did he bluster to the piano-salesman, "By golly—friend of mine over there—'scuse me second—just say hello to him."

He touched Paul's shoulder, and cried, "Well, when did you hit town?"

Paul glared up at him, face hardening. "Oh, hello, George. Thought you'd gone back to Zenith." He did not introduce his companion. Babbitt peeped at her. She was a flabbily pretty, weakly flirtatious woman of forty-two or three, in an atrocious flowery hat. Her rouging was thorough but unskilful.

"Where you staying, Paulibus?"

The woman turned, yawned, examined her nails. She seemed accustomed to not being introduced.

Paul grumbled, "Campbell Inn, on the South Side."

"Alone?" It sounded insinuating.

"Yes! Unfortunately!" Furiously Paul turned toward the woman, smiling with a fondness sickening to Babbitt. "May! Want to introduce you. Mrs. Arnold, this is my old—acquaintance, George Babbitt."

"Pleasmeech," growled Babbitt, while she gurgled, "Oh, I'm very pleased to meet any friend of Mr. Riesling's, I'm sure."

Babbitt demanded, "Be back there later this evening, Paul? I'll drop down and see you."

"No, better— We better lunch together to-morrow."

"All right, but I'll see you to-night, too, Paul. I'll go down to your hotel, and I'll wait for you!"

# 20

He sat smoking with the piano-salesman, clinging to the warm refuge of gossip, afraid to venture into thoughts of Paul. He was the more affable on the surface as secretly he became more apprehensive, felt more hollow. He was certain that Paul was in Chicago without Zilla's knowledge, and that he was doing things not at all moral and secure. When the salesman yawned that he had to write up his orders, Babbitt left him, left the hotel, in leisurely calm. But savagely he said "Campbell Inn!" to the taxi-driver. He sat agitated on the slippery leather seat, in that chill dimness which smelled of dust and perfume and Turkish cigarettes. He did not heed the snowy lake-front, the dark spaces and sudden bright corners in the unknown land south of the Loop.

The office of the Campbell Inn was hard, bright, new; the night clerk harder and brighter. "Yep?" he said to Babbitt.

"Mr. Paul Riesling registered here?"

"Yep."

"Is he in now?"

"Nope."

"Then if you'll give me his key, I'll wait for him."

"Can't do that, brother. Wait down here if you wanna."

Babbitt had spoken with the deference which all the Clan of Good Fellows give to hotel clerks. Now he said with snarling abruptness:

"I may have to wait some time. I'm Riesling's brother-in-law. I'll go up to his room. D' I look like a sneak-thief?"

His voice was low and not pleasant. With considerable haste the clerk took down the key, protesting, "I never said you looked like a sneak-thief. Just rules of the hotel. But if you want to—"

On his way up in the elevator Babbitt wondered why he was here. Why shouldn't Paul be dining with a respectable married woman? Why had he lied to the clerk about being Paul's brother-in-law? He had acted like a child. He must be careful not to say foolish dramatic things to Paul. As he settled down he tried to look pompous and placid. Then the thought— Suicide. He'd been dreading that, without knowing it. Paul would be just the person to do something like that. He must be out of his head or he wouldn't be confiding in that—that dried-up hag.

Zilla (oh, damn Zilla! how gladly he'd throttle that nagging fiend of a woman!)—she'd probably succeeded at last, and driven Paul crazy.

Suicide. Out there in the lake, way out, beyond the piled ice along the shore. It would be ghastly cold to drop into the water to-night.

Or—throat cut—in the bathroom—

Babbitt flung into Paul's bathroom. It was empty. He smiled, feebly.

He pulled at his choking collar, looked at his watch, opened the window to stare down at the street, looked at his watch, tried to read the evening paper lying on the glass-topped bureau, looked again at his watch. Three minutes had gone by since he had first looked at it.

And he waited for three hours.

He was sitting fixed, chilled, when the doorknob turned. Paul came in glowering.

"Hello," Paul said. "Been waiting?"

"Yuh, little while."

"Well?"

"Well what? Just thought I'd drop in to see how you made out in Akron."

"I did all right. What difference does it make?"

"Why, gosh, Paul, what are you sore about?"

"What are you butting into my affairs for?"

"Why, Paul, that's no way to talk! I'm not butting into nothing. I was so glad to see your ugly old phiz that I just dropped in to say howdy."

"Well, I'm not going to have anybody following me around and trying to boss me. I've had all of that I'm going to stand!"

"Well, gosh, I'm not—"

"I didn't like the way you looked at May Arnold, or the snooty way you talked."

"Well, all right then! If you think I'm a buttinsky, then I'll just butt in! I don't know who your May Arnold is, but I know doggone good and well that you and her weren't talking about tar-roofing, no, nor about playing the violin, neither! If you haven't got any moral consideration for yourself, you ought to have some for your position in the community. The idea of your going around places gawping into a female's eyes like a love-sick pup! I can understand a fellow slipping once, but I don't propose to see a fellow that's been as chummy with me as you have getting started on the downward path and sneaking off from his wife, even as cranky a one as Zilla, to go woman-chasing—"

"Oh, you're a perfectly moral little husband!"

"I am, by God! I've never looked at any woman except Myra since I've been married—practically—and I never will! I tell you there's nothing to immorality. It don't pay. Can't you see, old man, it just makes Zilla still crankier?"

Slight of resolution as he was of body, Paul threw his snow-beaded overcoat on the floor and crouched on a flimsy cane chair. "Oh, you're an old blowhard, and you know less about morality than Tinka, but you're all right, Georgie. But you can't understand that— I'm through. I can't go Zilla's hammering any longer. She's made up her mind that I'm a devil, and— Reg'lar Inquisition. Torture. She enjoys it. It's a game to see how sore she can make me. And me, either it's find a little comfort, any comfort, anywhere, or else do something a lot worse. Now this Mrs. Arnold, she's not so young, but she's a fine woman and she understands a fellow, and she's had her own troubles."

"Yea! I suppose she's one of these hens whose husband 'doesn't understand her'!"

"I don't know. Maybe. He was killed in the war."

Babbitt lumbered up, stood beside Paul patting his shoulder, making soft apologetic noises.

"Honest, George, she's a fine woman, and she's had one hell of a time. We manage to jolly each other up a lot. We tell each other we're the dandiest pair on earth. Maybe we don't believe it, but it helps a lot to have somebody with whom you can be perfectly simple, and not all this discussing—explaining—"

"And that's as far as you go?"

"It is not! Go on! Say it!"

"Well, I don't—I can't say I like it, but—" With a burst which left him feeling large and shining with generosity, "it's none of my darn business! I'll do anything I can for you, if there's anything I can do."

"There might be. I judge from Zilla's letters that 've been forwarded from Akron that she's getting suspicious about my staying away so long. She'd be perfectly capable of having me shadowed, and of coming to Chicago and busting into a hotel dining-room and bawling me out before everybody."

"I'll take care of Zilla. I'll hand her a good fairy-story when I get back to Zenith."

"I don't know—I don't think you better try it. You're a good fellow, but I don't know that diplomacy is your strong point." Babbitt looked hurt, then irritated. "I mean with women! With women, I mean. Course they got to go some to beat you in business diplomacy, but I just mean with women. Zilla may do a lot of rough talking, but she's pretty shrewd. She'd have the story out of you in no time."

"Well, all right, but—" Babbitt was still pathetic at not being allowed to play Secret Agent. Paul soothed:

"Course maybe you might tell her you'd been in Akron and seen me there."

"Why, sure, you bet! Don't I have to go look at that candy-store property in Akron? Don't I? Ain't it a shame I have to stop off there when I'm so anxious to get home? Ain't it a regular shame? I'll say it is! I'll say it's a doggone shame!"

"Fine. But for glory hallelujah's sake don't go putting any fancy fixings on the story. When men lie they always try to make it too artistic, and that's why women get suspicious. And— Let's have a drink, Georgie. I've got some gin and a little vermouth."

The Paul who normally refused a second cocktail took a second now, and a third. He became red-eyed and thick-tongued. He was embarrassingly jocular and salacious.

In the taxicab Babbitt incredulously found tears crowding into his eyes.

II

He had not told Paul of his plan but he did stop at Akron, between trains, for the one purpose of sending to Zilla a postcard with "Had to come here for the day, ran into Paul." In Zenith he called on her. If for public appearances Zilla was over-coiffed, over-painted, and resolutely corseted, for private misery she wore a filthy blue dressing-gown and torn stockings thrust into streaky pink satin mules. Her face was sunken. She seemed to have but half as much hair as Babbitt remembered, and that half was stringy. She sat in a rocker amid a debris of candy-boxes and cheap magazines, and she sounded dolorous when she did not sound derisive. But Babbitt was exceedingly breezy:

"Well, well, Zil, old dear, having a good loaf while hubby's away? That's the idea! I'll bet a hat Myra never got up till ten, while I was in Chicago. Say, could I borrow your thermos—just dropped in to see if I could borrow your thermos bottle. We're going to have a toboggan party—want to take some coffee *mit*. Oh, did you get my card from Akron, saying I'd run into Paul?"

"Yes. What was he doing?"

"How do you mean?" He unbuttoned his overcoat, sat tentatively on the arm of a chair.

"You know how I mean!" She slapped the pages of a magazine with an irritable clatter. "I suppose he was trying to make love to some hotel waitress or manicure girl or somebody."

"Hang it, you're always letting on that Paul goes round chasing skirts. He doesn't, in the first place, and if he did, it would prob'ly be because you keep hinting at him and dinging at him so much. I hadn't meant to, Zilla, but since Paul is away, in Akron—"

"He really is in Akron? I know he has some horrible woman that he writes to in Chicago."

"Didn't I tell you I saw him in Akron? What 're you trying to do? Make me out a liar?"

"No, but I just— I get so worried."

"Now, there you are! That's what gets me! Here you love Paul, and yet you plague him and cuss him out as if you hated him. I simply can't understand why it is that the more some folks love people, the harder they try to make 'em miserable."

"You love Ted and Rone—I suppose—and yet you nag them."

"Oh. Well. That. That's different. Besides, I don't nag 'em. Not what you'd call nagging. But zize saying: Now, here's Paul, the nicest, most sensitive critter on God's green earth. You ought to be ashamed of yourself the way you pan him. Why, you talk to him like a washerwoman. I'm surprised you can act so doggone common, Zilla!"

She brooded over her linked fingers. "Oh, I know. I do go and get mean sometimes, and I'm sorry afterwards. But, oh, Georgie, Paul is so aggravating! Honestly, I've tried awfully hard, these last few years, to be nice to him, but just because I used to be spiteful—or I seemed so; I wasn't, really, but I used to speak up and say anything that came into my head—and so he made up his mind that everything was my fault. Everything can't always be my fault, can it? And now if I get to fussing, he just turns silent, oh, so dreadfully silent, and he won't look at me—he just ignores me. He simply isn't human! And he deliberately keeps it up till I bust out and say a lot of things I don't mean. So silent— Oh, you righteous men! How wicked you are! How rotten wicked!"

They thrashed things over and over for half an hour. At the end, weeping drably, Zilla promised to restrain herself.

Paul returned four days later, and the Babbitts and Rieslings went festively to the movies and had chop suey at a Chinese restaurant. As they walked to the restaurant through a street of tailor shops and barber shops, the two wives in front, chattering about cooks, Babbitt murmured to Paul, "Zil seems a lot nicer now."

"Yes, she has been, except once or twice. But it's too late now. I just— I'm not going to discuss it, but I'm afraid of her. There's nothing left. I don't ever want to see her. Some day I'm going to break away from her. Somehow."

# 21

The International Organization of Boosters' Clubs has become a world-force for optimism, manly pleasantry, and good business. Chapters are to be found now in thirty countries. Nine hundred and twenty of the thousand chapters, however, are in the United States.

None of these is more ardent than the Zenith Boosters' Club.

The second March lunch of the Zenith Boosters was the most important of the year, as it was to be followed by the annual election of officers. There was agitation abroad. The lunch was held in the ballroom of the O'Hearn House. As each of the four hundred Boosters entered he took from a wall-board a huge celluloid button announcing his name, his nickname, and his business. There was a fine of ten cents for calling a Fellow Booster by any-thing but his nickname at a lunch, and as Babbitt jovially checked his hat the air was radiant with shouts of "Hello, Chet!" and "How're you, Shorty!" and "Top o' the mornin', Mac!"

They sat at friendly tables for eight, choosing places by lot. Babbitt was with Albert Boos the merchant tailor, Hector Seybolt of the Little Sweetheart Condensed Milk Company, Emil Wengert the jeweler, Professor Pumphrey of the Riteway Business College, Dr. Walter Gorbutt, Roy Teegarten the photographer, and Ben Berkey the photo-engraver. One of the merits of the Boosters' Club was that only two persons from each department of business were permitted to join, so that you at once encountered the Ideals of other occupations, and realized the metaphysical oneness of all occupations—plumbing and portrait-painting, medicine and the manufacture of chewing-gum.

Babbitt's table was particularly happy to-day, because Professor Pumphrey had just had a birthday, and was therefore open to teasing.

"Let's pump Pump about how old he is!" said Emil Wengert.

"No, let's paddle him with a dancing-pump!" said Ben Berkey.

But it was Babbitt who had the applause, with "Don't talk about pumps to that guy! The only pump he knows is a bottle! Honest, they tell me he's starting a class in home-brewing at the ole college!"

At each place was the Boosters' Club booklet, listing the members. Though the object of the club was good-fellowship, yet they never lost sight of the importance of doing a little more business. After each name was the mem-ber's occupation. There were scores of advertisements in the booklet, and on one page the admonition: "There's no rule that you have to trade with your Fellow Boosters, but get wise, boy—what's the use of letting all this good money get outside of our happy fambly?" And at each place, to-day, there was a present; a card printed in artistic red and black:

## SERVICE AND BOOSTERISM

Service finds its finest opportunity and development only in its broadest and deepest application and the consideration of its perpetual action upon reaction. I believe the highest type of Service, like the most pro-gressive tenets of ethics, senses unceasingly and is motived by active adherence and loyalty to that which is the essential principle of Boost-erism—Good Citizenship in all its factors and aspects.

DAD PETERSEN.

Compliments of Dadbury Petersen Advertising Corp.
"Ads, not Fads, at Dad's"

The Boosters all read Mr. Petersen's aphorism and said they understood it perfectly.

The meeting opened with the regular weekly "stunts." Retiring President Vergil Gunch was in the chair, his stiff hair like a hedge, his voice like a brazen gong of festival. Members who had brought guests introduced them publicly. "This tall red-headed piece of misinformation is the sporting editor of the *Press*," said Willis Ijams; and H. H. Hazen, the druggist, chanted, "Boys, when you're on a long motor tour and finally get to a romantic spot or scene and draw up and remark to the wife, 'This is certainly a romantic place,' it sends a glow right up and down your vertebræ. Well, my guest to-day is from such a place, Harper's Ferry, Virginia, in the beautiful Southland, with memories of good old General Robert E. Lee and of that brave soul, John Brown who, like every good Booster, goes marching on—"

There were two especially distinguished guests: the leading man of the "Bird of Paradise" company, playing this week at the Dodsworth Theater, and the mayor of Zenith, the Hon. Lucas Prout.

Vergil Gunch thundered, "When we manage to grab this celebrated Thespian off his lovely aggregation of beautiful actresses—and I got to admit I butted right into his dressing-room and told him how the Boosters appreciated the high-class artistic performance he's giving us—and don't forget that the treasurer of the Dodsworth is a Booster and will appreciate our patronage —and when on top of that we yank Hizzonor out of his multifarious duties at City Hall, then I feel we've done ourselves proud, and Mr. Prout will now say a few words about the problems and duties—"

By rising vote the Boosters decided which was the handsomest and which the ugliest guest, and to each of them was given a bunch of carnations, donated, President Gunch noted, by Brother Booster H. G. Yeager, the Jennifer Avenue florist.

Each week, in rotation, four Boosters were privileged to obtain the pleasures of generosity and of publicity by donating goods or services to four fellow-members, chosen by lot. There was laughter, this week, when it was announced that one of the contributors was Barnabas Joy, the undertaker. Everybody whispered, "I can think of a coupla good guys to be buried if his donation is a free funeral!"

Through all these diversions the Boosters were lunching on chicken croquettes, peas, fried potatoes, coffee, apple pie, and American cheese. Gunch did not lump the speeches. Presently he called on the visiting secretary of the Zenith Rotary Club, a rival organization. The secretary had the distinction of possessing State Motor Car License Number 5.

The Rotary secretary laughingly admitted that wherever he drove in the state so low a number created a sensation, and "though it was pretty nice to have the honor, yet traffic cops remembered it only too darn well, and sometimes he didn't know but what he'd almost as soon have just plain B56,876 or something like that. Only let any doggone Booster try to get Number 5 away from a live Rotarian next year, and watch the fur fly! And if they'd permit him, he'd wind up by calling for a cheer for the Boosters and Rotarians and the Kiwanis all together!"

Babbitt sighed to Professor Pumphrey, "Be pretty nice to have as low a number as that! Everybody 'd say, 'He must be an important guy!' Wonder how he got it? I'll bet he wined and dined the superintendent of the Motor License Bureau to a fare-you-well!"

Then Chum Frink addressed them:

"Some of you may feel that it's out of place here to talk on a strictly highbrow and artistic subject, but I want to come out flatfooted and ask you boys to O.K. the proposition of a Symphony Orchestra for Zenith. Now, where a lot of you make your mistake is in assuming that if you don't like classical music and all that junk, you ought to oppose it. Now, I want to confess that, though I'm a literary guy by profession, I don't care a rap for all this long-haired music. I'd rather listen to a good jazz band any time than to some piece by Beethoven that hasn't any more tune to it than a bunch of fighting cats, and you couldn't whistle it to save your life! But that isn't the point. Culture has become as necessary an adornment and advertisement for a city to-day as pavements or bank-clearances. It's Culture, in theaters and art-galleries and so on, that brings thousands of visitors to New York every year and, to be frank, for all our splendid attainments we haven't yet got the Culture of a New York or Chicago or Boston—or at least we don't get the credit for it. The thing to do then, as a live bunch of go-getters, is to *capitalize Culture*; to go right out and grab it.

"Pictures and books are fine for those that have the time to study 'em, but they don't shoot out on the road and holler 'This is what little old Zenith can put up in the way of Culture.' That's precisely what a Symphony Orchestra does do. Look at the credit Minneapolis and Cincinnati get. An orchestra with first-class musickers and a swell conductor—and I believe we ought to do the thing up brown and get one of the highest-paid conductors on the market, providing he ain't a Hun—it goes right into Beantown and New York and Washington; it plays at the best theaters to the most cultured and moneyed people; it gives such class-advertising as a town can get in no other way; and the guy who is so short-sighted as to crab this orchestra proposition is passing up the chance to impress the glorious name of Zenith on some big New York millionaire that might—that might establish a branch factory here!

"I could also go into the fact that for our daughters who show an interest in highbrow music and may want to teach it, having an A1 local organization is of great benefit, but let's keep this on a practical basis, and I call on you good brothers to whoop it up for Culture and a World-beating Symphony Orchestra!"

They applauded.

To a rustle of excitement President Gunch proclaimed, "Gentlemen, we will now proceed to the annual election of officers." For each of the six offices, three candidates had been chosen by a committee. The second name among the candidates for vice-president was Babbitt's.

He was surprised. He looked self-conscious. His heart pounded. He was still more agitated when the ballots were counted and Gunch said, "It's a pleasure to announce that Georgie Babbitt will be the next assistant gavel-wielder. I know of no man who stands more stanchly for common sense and enterprise than good old George. Come on, let's give him our best long yell!"

As they adjourned, a hundred men crushed in to slap his back. He had never known a higher moment. He drove away in a blur of wonder. He lunged into his office, chuckling to Miss McGoun, "Well, I guess you better congratulate your boss! Been elected vice-president of the Boosters!"

He was disappointed. She answered only, "Yes— Oh, Mrs. Babbitt's been trying to get you on the 'phone." But the new salesman, Fritz Weilinger, said, "By golly, chief, say, that's great, that's perfectly great! I'm tickled to death! Congratulations!"

Babbitt called the house, and crowed to his wife, "Heard you were trying to get me, Myra. Say, you got to hand it to little Georgie, this time! Better talk careful! You are now addressing the vice-president of the Boosters' Club!"

"Oh, Georgie—"

"Pretty nice, huh? Willis Ijams is the new president, but when he's away, little ole Georgie takes the gavel and whoops 'em up and introduces the speakers—no matter if they're the governor himself—and—"

"George! Listen!"

"—it puts him in solid with big men like Doc Dilling and—"

"George! Paul Riesling—"

"Yes, sure, I'll 'phone Paul and let him know about it right away."

"Georgie! *Listen!* Paul's in jail. He shot his wife, he shot Zilla, this noon. She may not live."

# 22

He drove to the City Prison, not blindly, but with unusual fussy care at corners, the fussiness of an old woman potting plants. It kept him from facing the obscenity of fate.

The attendant said, "Naw, you can't see any of the prisoners till three-thirty—visiting-hour."

It was three. For half an hour Babbitt sat looking at a calendar and a clock on a whitewashed wall. The chair was hard and mean and creaky. People went through the office and, he thought, stared at him. He felt a belligerent defiance which broke into a wincing fear of this machine which was grinding Paul—Paul—

Exactly at half-past three he sent in his name.

The attendant returned with "Riesling says he don't want to see you."

"You're crazy! You didn't give him my name! Tell him it's George wants to see him, George Babbitt."

"Yuh, I told him, all right, all right! He said he didn't want to see you."

"Then take me in anyway."

"Nothing doing. If you ain't his lawyer, if he don't want to see you, that's all there is to it."

"But, my *God*— Say, let me see the warden."

"He's busy. Come on, now, you—" Babbitt reared over him. The attendant hastily changed to a coaxing "You can come back and try to-morrow. Probably the poor guy is off his nut."

Babbitt drove, not at all carefully or fussily, sliding viciously past trucks, ignoring the truckmen's curses, to the City Hall; he stopped with a grind of wheels against the curb, and ran up the marble steps to the office of the Hon. Mr. Lucas Prout, the mayor. He bribed the mayor's doorman with a dollar; he was instantly inside, demanding, "You remember me, Mr. Prout? Babbitt—vice-president of the Boosters—campaigned for you? Say, have you heard about poor Riesling? Well, I want an order on the warden or whatever you call um of the City Prison to take me back and see him. Good. Thanks."

In fifteen minutes he was pounding down the prison corridor to a cage where Paul Riesling sat on a cot, twisted like an old beggar, legs crossed, arms in a knot, biting at his clenched fist.

Paul looked up blankly as the keeper unlocked the cell, admitted Babbitt, and left them together. He spoke slowly: "Go on! Be moral!"

Babbitt plumped on the couch beside him. "I'm not going to be moral! I don't care what happened! I just want to do anything I can. I'm glad Zilla got what was coming to her."

Paul said argumentatively, "Now, don't go jumping on Zilla. I've been thinking; maybe she hasn't had any too easy a time. Just after I shot her— I didn't hardly mean to, but she got to deviling me so I went crazy, just for a second, and pulled out that old revolver you and I used to shoot rabbits with, and took a crack at her. Didn't hardly mean to— After that, when I was trying to stop the blood— It was terrible what it did to her shoulder, and she had beautiful skin— Maybe she won't die. I hope it won't leave her skin all scarred. But just afterward, when I was hunting through the bathroom for some cotton to stop the blood, I ran onto a little fuzzy yellow duck we hung on the tree one Christmas, and I remembered she and I'd been awfully happy then— Hell. I can't hardly believe it's me here." As Babbitt's arm tightened about his shoulder, Paul sighed, "I'm glad you came. But I thought maybe you'd lecture me, and when you've committed a murder, and been brought here and everything—there was a big crowd outside the apartment house, all staring, and the cops took me through it— Oh, I'm not going to talk about it any more."

But he went on, in a monotonous, terrified insane mumble. To divert him Babbitt said, "Why, you got a scar on your cheek."

"Yes. That's where the cop hit me. I suppose cops get a lot of fun out of lecturing murderers, too. He was a big fellow. And they wouldn't let me help carry Zilla down to the ambulance."

"Paul! Quit it! Listen: she won't die, and when it's all over you and I'll go off to Maine again. And maybe we can get that May Arnold to go along. I'll go up to Chicago and ask her. Good woman, by golly. And afterwards I'll see that you get started in business out West somewhere, maybe Seattle —they say that's a lovely city."

Paul was half smiling. It was Babbitt who rambled now. He could not tell whether Paul was heeding, but he droned on till the coming of Paul's lawyer, P. J. Maxwell, a thin, busy, unfriendly man who nodded at Babbitt and hinted, "If Riesling and I could be alone for a moment—"

Babbitt wrung Paul's hands, and waited in the office till Maxwell came pattering out. "Look, old man, what can I do?" he begged.

"Nothing. Not a thing. Not just now," said Maxwell. "Sorry. Got to hurry. And don't try to see him. I've had the doctor give him a shot of morphine, so he'll sleep."

It seemed somehow wicked to return to the office. Babbitt felt as though he had just come from a funeral. He drifted out to the City Hospital to inquire about Zilla. She was not likely to die, he learned. The bullet from Paul's huge old .44 army revolver had smashed her shoulder and torn upward and out.

He wandered home and found his wife radiant with the horrified interest we have in the tragedies of our friends. "Of course Paul isn't altogether to blame, but this is what comes of his chasing after other women instead of bearing his cross in a Christian way," she exulted.

He was too languid to respond as he desired. He said what was to be said about the Christian bearing of crosses, and went out to clean the car. Dully, patiently, he scraped linty grease from the drip-pan, gouged at the mud caked on the wheels. He used up many minutes in washing his hands; scoured them with gritty kitchen soap; rejoiced in hurting his plump knuckles. "Damn soft hands—like a woman's. Aah!"

At dinner, when his wife began the inevitable, he bellowed, "I forbid any of you to say a word about Paul! I'll 'tend to all the talking about this that's necessary, hear me? There's going to be one house in this scandal-mongering town to-night that isn't going to spring the holier-than-thous. And throw those filthy evening papers out of the house!"

But he himself read the papers, after dinner.

Before nine he set out for the house of Lawyer Maxwell. He was received without cordiality. "Well?" said Maxwell.

"I want to offer my services in the trial. I've got an idea. Why couldn't I go on the stand and swear I was there, and she pulled the gun first and he wrestled with her and the gun went off accidentally?"

"And perjure yourself?"

"Huh? Yes, I suppose it would be perjury. Oh— Would it help?"

"But, my dear fellow! Perjury!"

"Oh, don't be a fool! Excuse me, Maxwell; I didn't mean to get your goat.

I just mean: I've known and you've known many and many a case of perjury, just to annex some rotten little piece of real estate, and here where it's a case of saving Paul from going to prison, I'd perjure myself black in the face."

"No. Aside from the ethics of the matter, I'm afraid it isn't practicable. The prosecutor would tear your testimony to pieces. It's known that only Riesling and his wife were there at the time."

"Then, look here! Let me go on the stand and swear—and this would be the God's truth—that she pestered him till he kind of went crazy."

"No. Sorry. Riesling absolutely refuses to have any testimony reflecting on his wife. He insists on pleading guilty."

"Then let me get up and testify something—whatever you say. Let me do *something!*"

"I'm sorry, Babbitt, but the best thing you can do—I hate to say it, but you could help us most by keeping strictly out of it."

Babbitt, revolving his hat like a defaulting poor tenant, winced so visibly that Maxwell condescended:

"I don't like to hurt your feelings, but you see we both want to do our best for Riesling, and we mustn't consider any other factor. The trouble with you, Babbitt, is that you're one of these fellows who talk too readily. You like to hear your own voice. If there were anything for which I could put you in the witness-box, you'd get going and give the whole show away. Sorry. Now I must look over some papers— So sorry."

## II

He spent most of the next morning nerving himself to face the garrulous world of the Athletic Club. They would talk about Paul; they would be lip-licking and rotten. But at the Roughnecks' Table they did not mention Paul. They spoke with zeal of the coming baseball season. He loved them as he never had before.

## III

He had, doubtless from some story-book, pictured Paul's trial as a long struggle, with bitter arguments, a taut crowd, and sudden and overwhelming new testimony. Actually, the trial occupied less than fifteen minutes, largely filled with the evidence of doctors that Zilla would recover and that Paul must have been temporarily insane. Next day Paul was sentenced to three years in the State Penitentiary and taken off—quite undramatically, not hand-cuffed, merely plodding in a tired way beside a cheerful deputy sheriff— and after saying good-by to him at the station Babbitt returned to his office to realize that he faced a world which, without Paul, was meaningless.

# 23

---

He was busy, from March to June. He kept himself from the bewilderment of thinking. His wife and the neighbors were generous. Every evening he played bridge or attended the movies, and the days were blank of face and silent.

In June, Mrs. Babbitt and Tinka went East, to stay with relatives, and Babbitt was free to do—he was not quite sure what.

All day long after their departure he thought of the emancipated house in which he could, if he desired, go mad and curse the gods without having to keep up a husbandly front. He considered, "I could have a reg'lar party tonight; stay out till two and not do any explaining afterwards. Cheers!" He telephoned to Vergil Gunch, to Eddie Swanson. Both of them were engaged for the evening, and suddenly he was bored by having to take so much trouble to be riotous.

He was silent at dinner, unusually kindly to Ted and Verona, hesitating but not disapproving when Verona stated her opinion of Kenneth Escott's opinion of Dr. John Jennison Drew's opinion of the opinions of the evolutionists. Ted was working in a garage through the summer vacation, and he related his daily triumphs: how he had found a cracked ball-race, what he had said to the Old Grouch, what he had said to the foreman about the future of wireless telephony.

Ted and Verona went to a dance after dinner. Even the maid was out. Rarely had Babbitt been alone in the house for an entire evening. He was restless. He vaguely wanted something more diverting than the newspaper comic strips to read. He ambled up to Verona's room, sat on her maidenly blue and white bed, humming and grunting in a solid-citizen manner as he examined her books: Conrad's "Rescue," a volume strangely named "Figures of Earth," poetry (quite irregular poetry, Babbitt thought) by Vachel Lindsay, and essays by H. L. Mencken—highly improper essays, making fun of the church and all the decencies. He liked none of the books. In them he felt a spirit of rebellion against niceness and solid-citizenship. These authors—and he supposed they were famous ones, too—did not seem to care about telling a good story which would enable a fellow to forget his troubles. He sighed. He noted a book, "The Three Black Pennies," by Joseph Hergesheimer. Ah, that was something like it! It would be an adventure story, maybe about counterfeiting—detectives sneaking up on the old house at night. He tucked the book under his arm, he clumped down-stairs and solemnly began to read, under the piano-lamp:

"A twilight like blue dust sifted into the shallow fold of the thickly wooded hills. It was early October, but a crisping frost had already stamped the maple trees with gold, the Spanish oaks were hung with patches of wine red, the sumach was brilliant in the darkening underbrush. A pattern of wild geese, flying low and unconcerned above the hills, wavered against the serene ashen evening. Howat Penny, standing in the comparative clearing of a road, decided that the shifting regular flight would not come close enough for a shot. . . . He had no intention of hunting the geese. With the drooping of day his keenness had evaporated; an habitual indifference strengthened, permeating him. . . ."

There it was again: discontent with the good common ways. Babbitt laid down the book and listened to the stillness. The inner doors of the house were open. He heard from the kitchen the steady drip of the refrigerator, a rhythm demanding and disquieting. He roamed to the window. The summer evening was foggy and, seen through the wire screen, the street lamps were crosses of pale fire. The whole world was abnormal. While he brooded, Verona and Ted came in and went up to bed. Silence thickened in the sleeping house. He put on his hat, his respectable derby, lighted a cigar, and walked up and down before the house, a portly, worthy, unimaginative figure, humming "Silver Threads among the Gold." He casually considered, "Might call up Paul." Then he remembered. He saw Paul in a jailbird's uniform, but while he agonized he didn't believe the tale. It was part of the unreality of this fog-enchanted evening.

If she were here Myra would be hinting, "Isn't it late, Georgie?" He tramped in forlorn and unwanted freedom. Fog hid the house now. The world was uncreated, a chaos without turmoil or desire.

Through the mist came a man at so feverish a pace that he seemed to dance with fury as he entered the orb of glow from a street-lamp. At each step he brandished his stick and brought it down with a crash. His glasses on their broad pretentious ribbon banged against his stomach. Babbitt incredulously saw that it was Chum Frink.

Frink stopped, focused his vision, and spoke with gravity:

"There's another fool. George Babbitt. Lives for renting howshes—houses. Know who I am? I'm traitor to poetry. I'm drunk. I'm talking too much. I don't care. Know what I could 've been? I could 've been a Gene Field or a James Whitcomb Riley. Maybe a Stevenson. I could 've. Whimsies. 'Magination. Lissen. Lissen to this. Just made it up:

Glittering summery meadowy noise
Of beetles and bums and respectable boys.

Hear that? Whimzh—whimsy. I made that up. *I* don't know what it means! Beginning good verse. Chile's Garden Verses. And whadi write? Tripe! Cheer-up poems. All tripe! Could have written— Too late!"

He darted on with an alarming plunge, seeming always to pitch forward yet never quite falling. Babbitt would have been no more astonished and no less had a ghost skipped out of the fog carrying his head. He accepted Frink with vast apathy; he grunted, "Poor boob!" and straightway forgot him.

He plodded into the house, deliberately went to the refrigerator and rifled it. When Mrs. Babbitt was at home, this was one of the major household crimes. He stood before the covered laundry tubs, eating a chicken leg and half a saucer of raspberry jelly, and grumbling over a clammy cold boiled potato. He was thinking. It was coming to him that perhaps all life as he knew it and vigorously practised it was futile; that heaven as portrayed by the Reverend Dr. John Jennison Drew was neither probable nor very interesting; that he hadn't much pleasure out of making money; that it was of doubtful worth to rear children merely that they might rear children who would rear children. What was it all about? What did he want?

He blundered into the living-room, lay on the davenport, hands behind his head.

What did he want? Wealth? Social position? Travel? Servants? Yes, but only incidentally.

"I give it up," he sighed.

But he did know that he wanted the presence of Paul Riesling; and from that he stumbled into the admission that he wanted the fairy girl—in the flesh. If there had been a woman whom he loved, he would have fled to her, humbled his forehead on her knees.

He thought of his stenographer, Miss McGoun. He thought of the prettiest of the manicure girls at the Hotel Thornleigh barber shop. As he fell asleep on the davenport he felt that he had found something in life, and that he had made a terrifying, thrilling break with everything that was decent and normal.

II

He had forgotten, next morning, that he was a conscious rebel, but he was irritable in the office and at the eleven o'clock drive of telephone calls and visitors he did something he had often desired and never dared: he left the office without excuses to those slave-drivers his employees, and went to the movies. He enjoyed the right to be alone. He came out with a vicious determination to do what he pleased.

As he approached the Roughnecks' Table at the club, everybody laughed.

"Well, here's the millionaire!" said Sidney Finkelstein.

"Yes, I saw him in his Locomobile!" said Professor Pumphrey.

"Gosh, it must be great to be a smart guy like Georgie!" moaned Vergil Gunch. "He's probably stolen all of Dorchester. I'd hate to leave a poor little defenseless piece of property lying around where he could get his hooks on it!"

They had, Babbitt perceived, "something on him." Also, they "had their kidding clothes on." Ordinarily he would have been delighted at the honor implied in being chaffed, but he was suddenly touchy. He grunted, "Yuh, sure; maybe I'll take you guys on as office boys!" He was impatient as the jest elaborately rolled on to its dénouement.

"Of course he may have been meeting a girl," they said, and "No, I think he was waiting for his old roommate, Sir Jerusalem Doak."

He exploded, "Oh, spring it, spring it, you boneheads! What's the great joke?"

"Hurray! George is peeved!" snickered Sidney Finkelstein, while a grin went round the table. Gunch revealed the shocking truth: He had seen Babbitt coming out of a motion-picture theater—at noon!

They kept it up. With a hundred variations, a hundred guffaws, they said that he had gone to the movies during business-hours. He didn't so much mind Gunch, but he was annoyed by Sidney Finkelstein, that brisk, lean, red-headed explainer of jokes. He was bothered, too, by the lump of ice in his glass of water. It was too large; it spun round and burned his nose when he tried to drink. He raged that Finkelstein was like that lump of ice. But he won through; he kept up his banter till they grew tired of the superlative jest and turned to the great problems of the day.

He reflected, "What's the matter with me to-day? Seems like I've got an awful grouch. Only they talk so darn much. But I better steer careful and keep my mouth shut."

As they lighted their cigars he mumbled, "Got to get back," and on a chorus of "If you *will* go spending your mornings with lady ushers at the movies!" he escaped. He heard them giggling. He was embarrassed. While he was most bombastically agreeing with the coat-man that the weather was warm, he was conscious that he was longing to run childishly with his troubles to the comfort of the fairy child.

III

He kept Miss McGoun after he had finished dictating. He searched for a topic which would warm her office impersonality into friendliness.

"Where you going on your vacation?" he purred.

"I think I'll go up-state to a farm do you want me to have the Siddons lease copied this afternoon?"

"Oh, no hurry about it. . . . I suppose you have a great time when you get away from us cranks in the office."

She rose and gathered her pencils. "Oh, nobody's cranky here I think I can get it copied after I do the letters."

She was gone. Babbitt utterly repudiated the view that he had been trying to discover how approachable was Miss McGoun. "Course! knew there was nothing doing!" he said.

IV

Eddie Swanson, the motor-car agent who lived across the street from Babbitt, was giving a Sunday supper. His wife Louetta, young Louetta who loved jazz in music and in clothes and laughter, was at her wildest. She cried, "We'll have a real party!" as she received the guests. Babbitt had uneasily felt that to many men she might be alluring; now he admitted that to himself she was overwhelmingly alluring. Mrs. Babbitt had never quite approved of Louetta; Babbitt was glad that she was not here this evening.

He insisted on helping Louetta in the kitchen: taking the chicken croquettes from the warming-oven, the lettuce sandwiches from the ice-box. He held her hand, once, and she depressingly didn't notice it. She caroled, "You're a good little mother's-helper, Georgie. Now trot in with the tray and leave it on the side-table."

He wished that Eddie Swanson would give them cocktails; that Louetta would have one. He wanted— Oh, he wanted to be one of these Bohemians you read about. Studio parties. Wild lovely girls who were independent. Not necessarily bad. Certainly not! But not tame, like Floral Heights. How he'd ever stood it all these years—

Eddie did not give them cocktails. True, they supped with mirth, and with several repetitions by Orville Jones of "Any time Louetta wants to come sit on my lap I'll tell this sandwich to beat it!" but they were respectable, as befitted Sunday evening. Babbitt had discreetly preëmpted a place beside Louetta on the piano bench. While he talked about motors, while he listened with a fixed smile to her account of the film she had seen last Wednesday, while he hoped that she would hurry up and finish her description of the plot, the beauty of the leading man, and the luxury of the setting, he studied her. Slim waist girdled with raw silk, strong brows, ardent eyes, hair parted above a broad forehead—she meant youth to him and a charm which saddened. He thought of how valiant a companion she would be on a long motor tour, exploring mountains, picnicking in a pine grove high above a valley. Her frailness touched him; he was angry at Eddie Swanson for the incessant family bickering. All at once he identified Louetta with the fairy girl. He was startled by the conviction that they had always had a romantic attraction for each other.

"I suppose you're leading a simply terrible life, now you're a widower," she said.

"You bet! I'm a bad little fellow and proud of it. Some evening you slip Eddie some dope in his coffee and sneak across the road and I'll show you how to mix a cocktail," he roared.

"Well, now, I might do it! You never can tell!"

"Well, whenever you're ready, you just hang a towel out of the attic window and I'll jump for the gin!"

Every one giggled at this naughtiness. In a pleased way Eddie Swanson stated that he would have a physician analyze his coffee daily. The others were diverted to a discussion of the more agreeable recent murders, but Babbitt drew Louetta back to personal things:

"That's the prettiest dress I ever saw in my life."

"Do you honestly like it?"

"Like it? Why, say, I'm going to have Kenneth Escott put a piece in the paper saying that the swellest dressed woman in the U. S. is Mrs. E. Louetta Swanson."

"Now, you stop teasing me!" But she beamed. "Let's dance a little. George, you've got to dance with me."

Even as he protested, "Oh, you know what a rotten dancer I am!" he was lumbering to his feet.

"I'll teach you. I can teach anybody."

Her eyes were moist, her voice was jagged with excitement. He was convinced that he had won her. He clasped her, conscious of her smooth warmth, and solemnly he circled in a heavy version of the one-step. He bumped into only one or two people. "Gosh, I'm not doing so bad; hittin' 'em up like a regular stage dancer!" he gloated; and she answered busily, "Yes—yes—I told you I could teach anybody—*don't take such long steps!*"

For a moment he was robbed of confidence; with fearful concentration he sought to keep time to the music. But he was enveloped again by her enchantment. "She's got to like me; I'll make her!" he vowed. He tried to kiss the lock beside her ear. She mechanically moved her head to avoid it, and mechanically she murmured, "Don't!"

For a moment he hated her, but after the moment he was as urgent as ever. He danced with Mrs. Orville Jones, but he watched Louetta swooping down the length of the room with her husband. "Careful! You're getting foolish!" he cautioned himself, the while he hopped and bent his solid knees in dalliance with Mrs. Jones, and to that worthy lady rumbled, "Gee, it's hot!" Without reason, he thought of Paul in that shadowy place where men never dance. "I'm crazy to-night; better go home," he worried, but he left Mrs. Jones and dashed to Louetta's lovely side, demanding, "The next is mine."

"Oh, I'm so hot; I'm not going to dance this one."

"Then," boldly, "come out and sit on the porch and get all nice and cool."

"Well—"

In the tender darkness, with the clamor in the house behind them, he resolutely took her hand. She squeezed his once, then relaxed.

"Louetta! I think you're the nicest thing I know!"

"Well, I think you're very nice."

"Do you? You got to like me! I'm so lonely!"

"Oh, you'll be all right when your wife comes home."

"No, I'm always lonely."

She clasped her hands under her chin, so that he dared not touch her. He sighed:

"When I feel punk and—" He was about to bring in the tragedy of Paul, but that was too sacred even for the diplomacy of love. "—when I get tired out at the office and everything, I like to look across the street and think of you. Do you know I dreamed of you, one time!"

"Was it a nice dream?"

"Lovely!"

"Oh, well, they say dreams go by opposites! Now I must run in."

She was on her feet.

"Oh, don't go in yet! Please, Louetta!"

"Yes, I must. Have to look out for my guests."

"Let 'em look out for 'emselves!"

"I couldn't do that." She carelessly tapped his shoulder and slipped away.

But after two minutes of shamed and childish longing to sneak home he was snorting, "Certainly I wasn't trying to get chummy with her! Knew there was nothing doing, all the time!" and he ambled in to dance with Mrs. Orville Jones, and to avoid Louetta, virtuously and conspicuously.

# 24

His visit to Paul was as unreal as his night of fog and questioning. Unseeing he went through prison corridors stinking of carbolic acid to a room lined with pale yellow settees pierced in rosettes, like the shoe-store benches he had known as a boy. The guard let in Paul. Above his uniform of linty gray, Paul's face was pale and without expression. He moved timorously in response to the guard's commands; he meekly pushed Babbitt's gifts of tobacco and magazines across the table to the guard for examination. He had nothing to say but "Oh, I'm getting used to it" and "I'm working in the tailor shop; the stuff hurts my fingers."

Babbitt knew that in this place of death Paul was already dead. And as he pondered on the train home something in his own self seemed to have died: a loyal and vigorous faith in the goodness of the world, a fear of public disfavor, a pride in success. He was glad that his wife was away. He admitted it without justifying it. He did not care.

## II

Her card read "Mrs. Daniel Judique." Babbitt knew of her as the widow of a wholesale paper-dealer. She must have been forty or forty-two but he thought her younger when he saw her in the office, that afternoon. She had come to inquire about renting an apartment, and he took her away from the unskilled girl accountant. He was nervously attracted by her smartness. She was a slender woman, in a black Swiss frock dotted with white, a cool-looking graceful frock. A broad black hat shaded her face. Her eyes were lustrous, her soft chin of an agreeable plumpness, and her cheeks an even rose. Babbitt wondered afterward if she was made up, but no man living knew less of such arts.

She sat revolving her violet parasol. Her voice was appealing without being coy. "I wonder if you can help me?"

"Be delighted."

"I've looked everywhere and— I want a little flat, just a bedroom, or perhaps two, and sitting-room and kitchenette and bath, but I want one that really has some charm to it, not these dingy places or these new ones with terrible gaudy chandeliers. And I can't pay so dreadfully much. My name's Tanis Judique."

"I think maybe I've got just the thing for you. Would you like to chase around and look at it now?"

"Yes. I have a couple of hours."

In the new Cavendish Apartments, Babbitt had a flat which he had been holding for Sidney Finkelstein, but at the thought of driving beside this agreeable woman he threw over his friend Finkelstein, and with a note of gallantry he proclaimed, "I'll let you see what I can do!"

He dusted the seat of the car for her, and twice he risked death in showing off his driving.

"You do know how to handle a car!" she said.

He liked her voice. There was, he thought, music in it and a hint of culture, not a bouncing giggle like Louetta Swanson's.

He boasted, "You know, there's a lot of these fellows that are so scared and drive so slow that they get in everybody's way. The safest driver is a fellow that knows how to handle his machine and yet isn't scared to speed up when it's necessary, don't you think so?"

"Oh, yes!"

"I bet you drive like a wiz."

"Oh, no—I mean—not really. Of course, we had a car—I mean, before my husband passed on—and I used to make believe drive it, but I don't think any woman ever learns to drive like a man."

"Well, now, there's some mighty good woman drivers."

"Oh, of course, these women that try to imitate men, and play golf and everything, and ruin their complexions and spoil their hands!"

"That's so. I never did like these mannish females."

"I mean—of course, I admire them, dreadfully, and I feel so weak and useless beside them."

"Oh, rats now! I bet you play the piano like a wiz."

"Oh, no—I mean—not really."

"Well, I'll bet you do!" He glanced at her smooth hands, her diamond and ruby rings. She caught the glance, snuggled her hands together with a kittenish curving of slim white fingers which delighted him, and yearned:

"I do love to play—I mean—I like to drum on the piano, but I haven't had any real training. Mr. Judique used to say I would 've been a good pianist if I'd had any training, but then, I guess he was just flattering me."

"I'll bet he wasn't! I'll bet you've got temperament."

"Oh— Do you like music, Mr. Babbitt?"

"You bet I do! Only I don't know 's I care so much for all this classical stuff."

"Oh, I do! I just love Chopin and all those."

"Do you, honest? Well, of course, I go to lots of these highbrow concerts, but I do like a good jazz orchestra, right up on its toes, with the fellow that plays the bass fiddle spinning it around and beating it up with the bow."

"Oh, I know. I do love good dance music. I love to dance, don't you, Mr. Babbitt?"

"Sure, you bet. Not that I'm very darn good at it, though."

"Oh, I'm sure you are. You ought to let me teach you. I can teach anybody to dance."

"Would you give me a lesson some time?"

"Indeed I would."

"Better be careful, or I'll be taking you up on that proposition. I'll be coming up to your flat and making you give me that lesson."

"Ye-es." She was not offended, but she was non-committal. He warned himself, "Have some sense now, you chump! Don't go making a fool of yourself again!" and with loftiness he discoursed:

"I wish I could dance like some of these young fellows, but I'll tell you: I feel it's a man's place to take a full, you might say, a creative share in the world's work and mold conditions and have something to show for his life, don't you think so?"

"Oh, I do!"

"And so I have to sacrifice some of the things I might like to tackle, though I do, by golly, play about as good a game of golf as the next fellow!"

"Oh, I'm sure you do. . . . Are you married?"

"Uh—yes. . . . And, uh, of course official duties—I'm the vice-president of the Boosters' Club, and I'm running one of the committees of the State Association of Real Estate Boards, and that means a lot of work and responsibility—and practically no gratitude for it."

"Oh, I know! Public men never do get proper credit."

They looked at each other with a high degree of mutual respect, and at the Cavendish Apartments he helped her out in a courtly manner, waved his hand at the house as though he were presenting it to her, and ponderously ordered the elevator boy to "hustle and get the keys." She stood close to him in the elevator, and he was stirred but cautious.

It was a pretty flat, of white woodwork and soft blue walls. Mrs. Judique gushed with pleasure as she agreed to take it, and as they walked down the hall to the elevator she touched his sleeve, caroling, "Oh, I'm so glad I went to you! It's such a privilege to meet a man who really Understands. Oh! The flats *some* people have showed me!"

He had a sharp instinctive belief that he could put his arm around her, but he rebuked himself and with excessive politeness he saw her to the car, drove her home. All the way back to his office he raged:

"Glad I had some sense for once. . . . Curse it, I wish I'd tried. She's a darling! A corker! A reg'lar charmer! Lovely eyes and darling lips and that trim waist—never get sloppy, like some women. . . . No, no, no! She's a real cultured lady. One of the brightest little women I've met these many moons. Understands about Public Topics and— But, darn it, why didn't I try? . . . Tanis!"

### III

He was harassed and puzzled by it, but he found that he was turning toward youth, as youth. The girl who especially disturbed him—though he had never spoken to her—was the last manicure girl on the right in the

Pompeian Barber Shop. She was small, swift, black-haired, smiling. She was nineteen, perhaps, or twenty. She wore thin salmon-colored blouses which exhibited her shoulders and her black-ribboned camisoles.

He went to the Pompeian for his fortnightly hair-trim. As always, he felt disloyal at deserting his neighbor, the Reeves Building Barber Shop. Then, for the first time, he overthrew his sense of guilt. "Doggone it, I don't have to go here if I don't want to! I don't own the Reeves Building! These barbers got nothing on me! I'll doggone well get my hair cut where I doggone well want to! Don't want to hear anything more about it! I'm through standing by people—unless I want to. It doesn't get you anywhere. I'm through!"

The Pompeian Barber Shop was in the basement of the Hotel Thornleigh, largest and most dynamically modern hotel in Zenith. Curving marble steps with a rail of polished brass led from the hotel-lobby down to the barber shop. The interior was of black and white and crimson tiles, with a sensational ceiling of burnished gold, and a fountain in which a massive nymph forever emptied a scarlet cornucopia. Forty barbers and nine manicure girls worked desperately, and at the door six colored porters lurked to greet the customers, to care reverently for their hats and collars, to lead them to a place of waiting where, on a carpet like a tropic isle in the stretch of white stone floor, were a dozen leather chairs and a table heaped with magazines.

Babbitt's porter was an obsequious gray-haired negro who did him an honor highly esteemed in the land of Zenith—greeted him by name. Yet Babbitt was unhappy. His bright particular manicure girl was engaged. She was doing the nails of an overdressed man and giggling with him. Babbitt hated him. He thought of waiting, but to stop the powerful system of the Pompeian was inconceivable, and he was instantly wafted into a chair.

About him was luxury, rich and delicate. One votary was having a violet-ray facial treatment, the next an oil shampoo. Boys wheeled about miraculous electrical massage-machines. The barbers snatched steaming towels from a machine like a howitzer of polished nickel and disdainfully flung them away after a second's use. On the vast marble shelf facing the chairs were hundreds of tonics, amber and ruby and emerald. It was flattering to Babbitt to have two personal slaves at once—the barber and the bootblack. He would have been completely happy if he could also have had the manicure girl. The barber snipped at his hair and asked his opinion of the Havre de Grace races, the baseball season, and Mayor Prout. The young negro bootblack hummed "The Camp Meeting Blues" and polished in rhythm to his tune, drawing the shiny shoe-rag so taut at each stroke that it snapped like a banjo string. The barber was an excellent salesman. He made Babbitt feel rich and important by his manner of inquiring, "What is your favorite tonic, sir? Have you time to-day, sir, for a facial massage? Your scalp is a little tight; shall I give you a scalp massage?"

Babbitt's best thrill was in the shampoo. The barber made his hair creamy with thick soap, then (as Babbitt bent over the bowl, muffled in towels) drenched it with hot water which prickled along his scalp, and at last ran the water ice-cold. At the shock, the sudden burning cold on his skull, Babbitt's heart thumped, his chest heaved, and his spine was an electric wire. It was a sensation which broke the monotony of life. He looked grandly about the shop as he sat up. The barber obsequiously rubbed his wet hair and bound it in a towel as in a turban, so that Babbitt resembled a plump pink calif on an ingenious and adjustable throne. The barber begged (in the manner of one who was a good fellow yet was overwhelmed by the splendors of the calif), "How about a little Eldorado Oil Rub, sir? Very beneficial to the scalp, sir. Didn't I give you one the last time?"

He hadn't, but Babbitt agreed, Well, all right."

With quaking eagerness he saw that his manicure girl was free.

"I don't know, I guess I'll have a manicure after all," he droned, and excitedly watched her coming, dark-haired, smiling, tender, little. The manicuring would have to be finished at her table, and he would be able to talk to her without the barber listening. He waited contentedly, not trying to peep at her, while she filed his nails and the barber shaved him and smeared on his burning cheeks all the interesting mixtures which the pleasant minds of barbers have devised through the revolving ages. When the barber was done and he sat opposite the girl at her table, he admired the marble slab of it, admired the sunken set bowl with its tiny silver taps, and admired himself for being able to frequent so costly a place. When she withdrew his wet hand from the bowl, it was so sensitive from the warm soapy water that he was abnormally aware of the clasp of her firm little paw. He delighted in the pinkness and glossiness of her nails. Her hands seemed to him more adorable than Mrs. Judique's thin fingers, and more elegant. He had a certain ecstasy in the pain when she gnawed at the cuticle of his nails with a sharp knife. He struggled not to look at the outline of her young bosom and her shoulders, the more apparent under a film of pink chiffon. He was conscious of her as an exquisite thing, and when he tried to impress his personality on her he spoke as awkwardly as a country boy at his first party:

"Well, kinda hot to be working to-day."

"Oh, yes, it is hot. You cut your own nails, last time, didn't you!"

"Ye-es, guess I must 've."

"You always ought to go to a manicure."

"Yes, maybe that's so. I—"

"There's nothing looks so nice as nails that are looked after good. I always think that's the best way to spot a real gent. There was an auto salesman in here yesterday that claimed you could always tell a fellow's class by the car he drove, but I says to him, 'Don't be silly,' I says; 'the wisenheimers grab a look at a fellow's nails when they want to tell if he's a tinhorn or a real gent!'"

"Yes, maybe there's something to that. Course, that is—with a pretty kiddy like you, a man can't help coming to get his mitts done."

"Yeh, I may be a kid, but I'm a wise bird, and I know nice folks when I see um—I can read character at a glance—and I'd never talk so frank with a fellow if I couldn't see he was a nice fellow."

She smiled. Her eyes seemed to him as gentle as April pools. With great seriousness he informed himself that "there were some roughnecks who would think that just because a girl was a manicure girl and maybe not awful well educated, she was no good, but as for him, he was a democrat, and understood people," and he stood by the assertion that this was a fine girl, a good girl—but not too uncomfortably good. He inquired in a voice quick with sympathy:

"I suppose you have a lot of fellows who try to get fresh with you."

"Say, gee, do I! Say, listen, there's some of these cigar-store sports that think because a girl's working in a barber shop, they can get away with anything. The things they saaaaaay! But, believe me, I know how to hop those birds! I just give um the north and south and ask um, 'Say, who do you think you're talking to?' and they fade away like love's young nightmare and oh, don't you want a box of nail-paste? It will keep the nails as shiny as when first manicured, harmless to apply and lasts for days."

"Sure, I'll try some. Say— Say, it's funny; I've been coming here ever since the shop opened and—" With arch surprise. "—I don't believe I know your name!"

"Don't you? My, that's funny! I don't know yours!"

"Now you quit kidding me! What's the nice little name?"

"Oh, it ain't so darn nice. I guess it's kind of kike. But my folks ain't kikes. My papa's papa was a nobleman in Poland, and there was a gentleman in here one day, he was kind of a count or something—"

"Kind of a no-account, I guess you mean!"

"Who's telling this, smarty? And he said he knew my papa's papa's folks in Poland and they had a dandy big house. Right on a lake!" Doubtfully, "Maybe you don't believe it?"

"Sure. No. Really. Sure I do. Why not? Don't think I'm kidding you, honey, but every time I've noticed you I've said to myself, 'That kid has Blue Blood in her veins!'"

"Did you, honest?"

"Honest I did. Well, well, come on—now we're friends—what's the darling little name?"

"Ida Putiak. It ain't so much-a-much of a name. I always say to Ma, I say, 'Ma, why didn't you name me Dolores, or something with some class to it?'"

"Well, now, I think it's a scrumptious name. Ida!"

"I bet I know *your* name!"

"Well, now, not necessarily. Of course— Oh, it isn't so specially well known."

"Aren't you Mr. Sondheim that travels for the Krackajack Kitchen Kutlery Ko.?"

"I am not! I'm Mr. Babbitt, the real-estate broker!"

"Oh, excuse me! Oh, of course. You mean here in Zenith."

"Yep." With the briskness of one whose feelings have been hurt.

"Oh, sure. I've read your ads. They're swell."

"Um, well— You might have read about my speeches."

"Course I have! I don't get much time to read but— I guess you think I'm an awfully silly little nit!"

"I think you're a little darling!"

"Well— There's one nice thing about this job. It gives a girl a chance to meet some awfully nice gentlemen and improve her mind with conversation, and you get so you can read a guy's character at the first glance."

"Look here, Ida; please don't think I'm getting fresh—" He was hotly reflecting that it would be humiliating to be rejected by this child, and dangerous to be accepted. If he took her to dinner, if he were seen by censorious friends— But he went on ardently: "Don't think I'm getting fresh if I suggest it would be nice for us to go out and have a little dinner together some evening."

"I don't know as I ought to but— My gentleman-friend's always wanting to take me out. But maybe I could to-night."

IV

There was no reason, he assured himself, why he shouldn't have a quiet dinner with a poor girl who would benefit by association with an educated and mature person like himself. But, lest some one see them and not understand, he would take her to Biddlemeier's Inn, on the outskirts of the city. They would have a pleasant drive, this hot lonely evening, and he might hold her hand—no, he wouldn't even do that. Ida was complaisant; her bare shoulders showed it only too clearly; but he'd be hanged if he'd make love to her merely because she expected it.

Then his car broke down; something had happened to the ignition. And he *had* to have the car this evening! Furiously he tested the spark-plugs, stared at the commutator. His angriest glower did not seem to stir the sulky car, and in disgrace it was hauled off to a garage. With a renewed thrill he thought of a taxicab. There was something at once wealthy and interestingly wicked about a taxicab.

But when he met her, on a corner two blocks from the Hotel Thornleigh, she said, "A taxi? Why, I thought you owned a car!"

"I do. Of course I do! But it's out of commission to-night."

"Oh," she remarked, as one who had heard that tale before.

All the way out to Biddlemeier's Inn he tried to talk as an old friend, but he could not pierce the wall of her words. With interminable indignation she narrated her retorts to "that fresh head-barber" and the drastic things she would do to him if he persisted in saying that she was "better at gassing than at hoof-paring."

At Biddlemeirer's Inn they were unable to get anything to drink. The head-waiter refused to understand who George F. Babbitt was. They sat steaming before a vast mixed grill, and made conversation about baseball. When he tried to hold Ida's hand she said with bright friendliness, "Careful! That fresh waiter is rubbering." But they came out into a treacherous summer night, the air lazy and a little moon above transfigured maples.

"Let's drive some other place, where we can get a drink and dance!" he demanded.

"Sure, some other night. But I promised Ma I'd be home early to-night."

"Rats! It's too nice to go home."

"I'd just love to, but Ma would give me fits."

He was trembling. She was everything that was young and exquisite. He put his arm about her. She snuggled against his shoulder, unafraid, and he was triumphant. Then she ran down the steps of the Inn, singing, "Come on, Georgie, we'll have a nice drive and get cool."

It was a night of lovers. All along the highway into Zenith, under the low and gentle moon, motors were parked and dim figures were clasped in revery. He held out hungry hands to Ida, and when she patted them he was grateful. There was no sense of struggle and transition; he kissed her and simply she responded to his kiss, they two behind the stolid back of the chauffeur.

Her hat fell off, and she broke from his embrace to reach for it.

"Oh, let it be!" he implored.

"Huh? My hat? Not a chance!"

He waited till she had pinned it on, then his arm sank about her. She drew away from it, and said with maternal soothing, "Now, don't be a silly boy! Mustn't make Ittle Mama scold! Just sit back, dearie, and see what a swell night it is. If you're a good boy, maybe I'll kiss you when we say nighty-night. Now give me a cigarette."

He was solicitous about lighting her cigarette and inquiring as to her comfort. Then he sat as far from her as possible. He was cold with failure. No one could have told Babbitt that he was a fool with more vigor, precision, and intelligence than he himself displayed. He reflected that from the standpoint of the Rev. Dr. John Jennison Drew he was a wicked man, and from the standpoint of Miss Ida Putiak, an old bore who had to be endured as the penalty attached to eating a large dinner.

"Dearie, you aren't going to go and get peevish, are you?"

She spoke pertly. He wanted to spank her. He brooded, "I don't have to take anything off this gutter-pup! Darn immigrant! Well, let's get it over as quick as we can, and sneak home and kick ourselves for the rest of the night."

He snorted, "Huh? Me peevish? Why, you baby, why should I be peevish? Now, listen, Ida; listen to Uncle George. I want to put you wise about this scrapping with your head-barber all the time. I've had a lot of experience with employees, and let me tell you it doesn't pay to antagonize—"

At the drab wooden house in which she lived he said good-night briefly and amiably, but as the taxicab drove off he was praying "Oh, my God!"

# 25

He awoke to stretch cheerfully as he listened to the sparrows, then to remember that everything was wrong; that he was determined to go astray, and not in the least enjoying the process. Why, he wondered, should he be in rebellion? What was it all about? "Why not be sensible; stop all this idiotic running around, and enjoy himself with his family, his business, the fellows at the club?" What was he getting out of rebellion? Misery and shame—the shame of being treated as an offensive small boy by a ragamuffin like Ida Putiak! And yet— Always he came back to "And yet." Whatever the misery, he could not regain contentment with a world which, once doubted, became absurd.

Only, he assured himself, he was "through with this chasing after girls."

By noontime he was not so sure even of that. If in Miss McGoun, Louetta Swanson, and Ida he had failed to find the lady kind and lovely, it did not prove that she did not exist. He was hunted by the ancient thought that somewhere must exist the not impossible she who would understand him, value him, and make him happy.

## II

Mrs. Babbitt returned in August.

On her previous absences he had missed her reassuring buzz and of her arrival he had made a fête. Now, though he dared not hurt her by letting a hint of it appear in his letters, he was sorry that she was coming before he had found himself, and he was embarrassed by the need of meeting her and looking joyful.

He loitered down to the station; he studied the summer-resort posters, lest he have to speak to acquaintances and expose his uneasiness. But he was well trained. When the train clanked in he was out on the cement platform, peering into the chair-cars, and as he saw her in the line of passengers moving toward the vestibule he waved his hat. At the door he embraced her, and announced, "Well, well, well, well, by golly, you look fine, you look fine." Then he was aware of Tinka. Here was something, this child with her absurd little nose and lively eyes, that loved him, believed him great, and as he clasped her, lifted and held her till she squealed, he was for the moment come back to his old steady self.

Tinka sat beside him in the car, with one hand on the steering-wheel, pretending to help him drive, and he shouted back to his wife, "I'll bet the kid will be the best chuffer in the family! She holds the wheel like an old professional!"

All the while he was dreading the moment when he would be alone with his wife and she would patiently expect him to be ardent.

### III

There was about the house an unofficial theory that he was to take his vacation alone, to spend a week or ten days in Catawba, but he was nagged by the memory that a year ago he had been with Paul in Maine. He saw himself returning; finding peace there, and the presence of Paul, in a life primitive and heroic. Like a shock came the thought that he actually could go. Only, he couldn't, really; he couldn't leave his business, and "Myra would think it sort of funny, his going way off there alone. Course he'd decided to do whatever he darned pleased, from now on, but still—to go way off to Maine!"

He went, after lengthy meditations.

With his wife, since it was inconceivable to explain that he was going to seek Paul's spirit in the wilderness, he frugally employed the lie prepared over a year ago and scarcely used at all. He said that he had to see a man in New York on business. He could not have explained even to himself why he drew from the bank several hundred dollars more than he needed, nor why he kissed Tinka so tenderly, and cried, "God bless you, baby!" From the train he waved to her till she was but a scarlet spot beside the brown bulkier presence of Mrs. Babbitt, at the end of a steel and cement aisle ending in vast barred gates. With melancholy he looked back at the last suburb of Zenith.

All the way north he pictured the Maine guides: simple and strong and daring, jolly as they played stud-poker in their unceiled shack, wise in wood-craft as they tramped the forest and shot the rapids. He particularly remembered Joe Paradise, half Yankee, half Indian. If he could but take up a backwoods claim with a man like Joe, work hard with his hands, be free and noisy in a flannel shirt, and never come back to this dull decency!

Or, like a trapper in a Northern Canada movie, plunge through the forest, make camp in the Rockies, a grim and wordless caveman! Why not? He *could* do it! There'd be enough money at home for the family to live on till Verona was married and Ted self-supporting. Old Henry T. would look out for them. Honestly! Why *not?* Really *live*—

He longed for it, admitted that he longed for it, then almost believed that he was going to do it. Whenever common sense snorted, "Nonsense! Folks don't run away from decent families and partners; just simply don't do it, that's all!" then Babbitt answered pleadingly, "Well, it wouldn't take any more nerve than for Paul to go to jail and—Lord, how I'd like to do it! Moccasins—six-gun—frontier town—gamblers—sleep under the stars—be a regular man, with he-men like Joe Paradise—gosh!"

So he came to Maine, again stood on the wharf before the camp-hotel, again spat heroically into the delicate and shivering water, while the pines rustled, the mountains glowed, and a trout leaped and fell in a sliding circle. He hurried to the guides' shack as to his real home, his real friends, long-missed. They would be glad to see him. They would stand up and shout,

"Why, here's Mr. Babbitt! He ain't one of these ordinary sports! He's a real guy!"

In their boarded and rather littered cabin the guides sat about the greasy table playing stud-poker with greasy cards: half a dozen wrinkled men in old trousers and easy old felt hats. They glanced up and nodded. Joe Paradise, the swart aging man with the big mustache, grunted, "How do. Back again?"

Silence, except for the clatter of chips.

Babbitt stood beside them, very lonely. He hinted, after a period of highly concentrated playing, "Guess I might take a hand, Joe."

"Sure. Sit in. How many chips you want? Let's see; you were here with your wife, last year, wa'n't you?" said Joe Paradise.

That was all of Babbitt's welcome to the old home.

He played for half an hour before he spoke again. His head was reeking with the smoke of pipes and cheap cigars, and he was weary of pairs and four-flushes, resentful of the way in which they ignored him. He flung at Joe:

"Working now?"

"Nope."

"Like to guide me for a few days?"

"Well, jus' soon. I ain't engaged till next week."

Only thus did Joe recognize the friendship Babbitt was offering him. Babbitt paid up his losses and left the shack rather childishly. Joe raised his head from the coils of smoke like a seal rising from surf, grunted, "I'll come 'round t'morrow," and dived down to his three aces.

Neither in his voiceless cabin, fragrant with planks of new-cut pine, nor along the lake, nor in the sunset clouds which presently eddied behind the lavender-misted mountains, could Babbitt find the spirit of Paul as a reassuring presence. He was so lonely that after supper he stopped to talk with an ancient old lady, a gasping and steadily discoursing old lady, by the stove in the hotel-office. He told her of Ted's presumable future triumphs in the State University and of Tinka's remarkable vocabulary till he was homesick for the home he had left forever.

Through the darkness, through that Northern pine-walled silence, he blundered down to the lake-front and found a canoe. There were no paddles in it but with a board, sitting awkwardly amidships and poking at the water rather than paddling, he made his way far out on the lake. The lights of the hotel and the cottages became yellow dots, a cluster of glow-worms at the base of Sachem Mountain. Larger and ever more imperturbable was the mountain in the star-filtered darkness, and the lake a limitless pavement of black marble. He was dwarfed and dumb and a little awed, but that insignificance freed him from the pomposities of being Mr. George F. Babbitt of Zenith; saddened and freed his heart. Now he was conscious of the presence of Paul, fancied him (rescued from prison, from Zilla and the brisk exactitudes of the tar-roofing business) playing his violin at the end of the canoe. He vowed, "I will go on! I'll never go back! Now that Paul's out of it, I don't want to see any of those damn people again! I was a fool to get sore

because Joe Paradise didn't jump up and hug me. He's one of these woods-
men; too wise to go yelping and talking your arm off like a cityman. But get
him back in the mountains, out on the trail—! That's real living!"

## IV

Joe reported at Babbitt's cabin at nine the next morning. Babbitt greeted
him as a fellow caveman:

"Well, Joe, how d' you feel about hitting the trail, and getting away from
these darn soft summerites and these women and all?"

"All right, Mr. Babbitt."

"What do you say we go over to Box Car Pond—they tell me the shack there
isn't being used—and camp out?"

"Well, all right, Mr. Babbitt, but it's nearer to Skowtuit Pond, and you can
get just about as good fishing there."

"No, I want to get into the real wilds."

"Well, all right."

"We'll put the old packs on our backs and get into the woods and really
hike."

"I think maybe it would be easier to go by water, through Lake Chogue.
We can go all the way by motor boat—flat-bottom boat with an Evinrude."

"No, sir! Bust up the quiet with a chugging motor? Not on your life! You
just throw a pair of socks in the old pack, and tell 'em what you want for
eats. I'll be ready soon 's you are."

"Most of the sports go by boat, Mr. Babbitt. It's a long walk."

"Look here, Joe: are you objecting to walking?"

"Oh, no, I guess I can do it. But I haven't tramped that far for sixteen years.
Most of the sports go by boat. But I can do it if you say so—I guess." Joe
walked away in sadness.

Babbitt had recovered from his touchy wrath before Joe returned. He pictured him as warming up and telling the most entertaining stories. But Joe
had not yet warmed up when they took the trail. He persistently kept behind
Babbitt, and however much his shoulders ached from the pack, however
sorely he panted, Babbitt could hear his guide panting equally. But the trail
was satisfying: a path brown with pine-needles and rough with roots, among
the balsams, the ferns, the sudden groves of white birch. He became credulous again, and rejoiced in sweating. When he stopped to rest he chuckled,
"Guess we're hitting it up pretty good for a couple o' old birds, eh?"

"Uh-huh," admitted Joe.

"This is a mighty pretty place. Look, you can see the lake down through
the trees. I tell you, Joe, you don't appreciate how lucky you are to live in
woods like this, instead of a city with trolleys grinding and typewriters clack-
ing and people bothering the life out of you all the time! I wish I knew the
woods like you do. Say, what's the name of that little red flower?"

Rubbing his back, Joe regarded the flower resentfully. "Well, some folks
call it one thing and some calls it another. I always just call it Pink Flower."

Babbitt blessedly ceased thinking as tramping turned into blind plodding. He was submerged in weariness. His plump legs seemed to go on by themselves, without guidance, and he mechanically wiped away the sweat which stung his eyes. He was too tired to be consciously glad as, after a sun-scourged mile of corduroy tote-road through a swamp where flies hovered over a hot waste of brush, they reached the cool shore of Box Car Pond. When he lifted the pack from his back he staggered from the change in balance, and for a moment could not stand erect. He lay beneath an ample-bosomed maple tree near the guest-shack, and joyously felt sleep running through his veins.

He awoke toward dusk, to find Joe efficiently cooking bacon and eggs and flapjacks for supper, and his admiration of the woodsman returned. He sat on a stump and felt virile.

"Joe, what would you do if you had a lot of money? Would you stick to guiding, or would you take a claim 'way back in the woods and be independent of people?"

For the first time Joe brightened. He chewed his cud a second, and bubbled, "I've often thought of that! If I had the money, I'd go down to Tinker's Falls and open a swell shoe store."

After supper Joe proposed a game of stud-poker but Babbitt refused with brevity, and Joe contentedly went to bed at eight. Babbitt sat on the stump, facing the dark pond, slapping mosquitoes. Save the snoring guide, there was no other human being within ten miles. He was lonelier than he had ever been in his life. Then he was in Zenith.

He was worrying as to whether Miss McGoun wasn't paying too much for carbon paper. He was at once resenting and missing the persistent teasing at the Roughnecks' Table. He was wondering what Zilla Riesling was doing now. He was wondering whether, after the summer's maturity of being a garageman, Ted would "get busy" in the university. He was thinking of his wife. "If she would only—if she wouldn't be so darn satisfied with just settling down— No! I won't! I won't go back! I'll be fifty in three years. Sixty in thirteen years. I'm going to have some fun before it's too late. I don't care! I will!"

He thought of Ida Putiak, of Louetta Swanson, of that nice widow—what was her name?—Tanis Judique?—the one for whom he'd found the flat. He was enmeshed in imaginary conversations. Then:

"Gee, I can't seem to get away from thinking about folks!"

Thus it came to him merely to run away was folly, because he could never run away from himself.

That moment he started for Zenith. In his journey there was no appearance of flight, but he was fleeing, and four days afterward he was on the Zenith train. He knew that he was slinking back not because it was what he longed to do but because it was all he could do. He scanned again his discovery that he could never run away from Zenith and family and office, because in his own brain he bore the office and the family and every street and disquiet and illusion of Zenith.

"But I'm going to—oh, I'm going to start something!" he vowed, and he tried to make it valiant.

# 26

As he walked through the train, looking for familiar faces, he saw only one person whom he knew, and that was Seneca Doane, the lawyer who, after the blessings of being in Babbitt's own class at college and of becoming a corporation-counsel, had turned crank, had headed farmer-labor tickets and fraternized with admitted socialists. Though he was in rebellion, naturally Babbitt did not care to be seen talking with such a fanatic, but in all the Pullmans he could find no other acquaintance, and reluctantly he halted. Seneca Doane was a slight, thin-haired man, rather like Chum Frink except that he hadn't Frink's grin. He was reading a book called "The Way of All Flesh." It looked religious to Babbitt, and he wondered if Doane could possibly have been converted and turned decent and patriotic.

"Why, hello, Doane," he said.

Doane looked up. His voice was curiously kind. "Oh! How do, Babbitt."

"Been away, eh?"

"Yes, I've been in Washington."

"Washington, eh? How's the old Government making out?"

"It's— Won't you sit down?"

"Thanks. Don't care if I do. Well, well! Been quite a while since I've had a good chance to talk to you, Doane. I was, uh— Sorry you didn't turn up at the last class-dinner."

"Oh—thanks."

"How's the unions coming? Going to run for mayor again?"

Doane seemed restless. He was fingering the pages of his book. He said "I might" as though it didn't mean anything in particular, and he smiled.

Babbitt liked that smile, and hunted for conversation: "Saw a bang-up cabaret in New York: the 'Good-Morning Cutie' bunch at the Hotel Minton."

"Yes, they're pretty girls. I danced there one evening."

"Oh. Like dancing?"

"Naturally. I like dancing and pretty women and good food better than anything else in the world. Most men do."

"But gosh, Doane, I thought you fellows wanted to take all the good eats and everything away from us."

"No. Not at all. What I'd like to see is the meetings of the Garment Workers held at the Ritz, with a dance afterward. Isn't that reasonable?"

"Yuh, might be good idea, all right. Well— Shame I haven't seen more of you, recent years. Oh, say, hope you haven't held it against me, my bucking you as mayor, going on the stump for Prout. You see, I'm an organization Republican, and I kind of felt—"

"There's no reason why you shouldn't fight me. I have no doubt you're good for the Organization. I remember—in college you were an unusually liberal, sensitive chap. I can still recall your saying to me that you were going to be a lawyer, and take the cases of the poor for nothing, and fight the rich. And I remember I said I was going to be one of the rich myself, and buy paintings and live at Newport. I'm sure you inspired us all."

"Well. . . . Well. . . . I've always aimed to be liberal." Babbitt was enormously shy and proud and self-conscious; he tried to look like the boy he had been a quarter-century ago, and he shone upon his old friend Seneca Doane as he rumbled, "Trouble with a lot of these fellows, even the live wires and some of 'em that think they're forward-looking, is they aren't broad-minded and liberal. Now, I always believe in giving the other fellow a chance, and listening to his ideas."

"That's fine."

"Tell you how I figure it: A little opposition is good for all of us, so a fellow, especially if he's a business man and engaged in doing the work of the world, ought to be liberal."

"Yes—"

"I always say a fellow ought to have Vision and Ideals. I guess some of the fellows in my business think I'm pretty visionary, but I just let 'em think what they want to and go right on—same as you do. . . . By golly, this is nice to have a chance to sit and visit and kind of, you might say, brush up on our ideals."

"But of course we visionaries do rather get beaten. Doesn't it bother you?"

"Not a bit! Nobody can dictate to me what I think!"

"You're the man I want to help me. I want you to talk to some of the business men and try to make them a little more liberal in their attitude toward poor Beecher Ingram."

"Ingram? But, why, he's this nut preacher that got kicked out of the Congregationalist Church, isn't he, and preaches free love and sedition?"

This, Doane explained, was indeed the general conception of Beecher Ingram, but he himself saw Beecher Ingram as a priest of the brotherhood of man, of which Babbitt was notoriously an upholder. So would Babbitt keep his acquaintances from hounding Ingram and his forlorn little church?

"You bet! I'll call down any of the boys I hear getting funny about Ingram," Babbitt said affectionately to his dear friend Doane.

Doane warmed up and became reminiscent. He spoke of student days in Germany, of lobbying for single tax in Washington, of international labor conferences. He mentioned his friends, Lord Wycombe, Colonel Wedgwood, Professor Piccoli. Babbitt had always supposed that Doane associated only with the I. W. W., but now he nodded gravely, as one who knew Lord Wycombes by the score, and he got in two references to Sir Gerald Doak. He felt daring and idealistic and cosmopolitan.

Suddenly, in his new spiritual grandeur, he was sorry for Zilla Riesling, and understood her as these ordinary fellows at the Boosters' Club never could.

## II

Five hours after he had arrived in Zenith and told his wife how hot it was in New York, he went to call on Zilla. He was buzzing with ideas and forgiveness. He'd get Paul released; he'd do things, vague but highly benevolent things, for Zilla; he'd be as generous as his friend Seneca Doane.

He had not seen Zilla since Paul had shot her, and he still pictured her as buxom, high-colored, lively, and a little blowsy. As he drove up to her boarding-house, in a depressing back street below the wholesale district, he stopped in discomfort. At an upper window, leaning on her elbow, was a woman with the features of Zilla, but she was bloodless and aged, like a yellowed wad of old paper crumpled into wrinkles. Where Zilla had bounced and jiggled, this woman was dreadfully still.

He waited half an hour before she came into the boarding-house parlor. Fifty times he opened the book of photographs of the Chicago World's Fair of 1893, fifty times he looked at the picture of the Court of Honor.

He was startled to find Zilla in the room. She wore a black streaky gown which she had tried to brighten with a girdle of crimson ribbon. The ribbon had been torn and patiently mended. He noted this carefully, because he did not wish to look at her shoulders. One shoulder was lower than the other; one arm she carried in contorted fashion, as though it were paralyzed; and behind a high collar of cheap lace there was a gouge in the anemic neck which had once been shining and softly plump.

"Yes?" she said.

"Well, well, old Zilla! By golly, it's good to see you again!"

"He can send his messages through a lawyer."

"Why, rats, Zilla, I didn't come just because of him. Came as an old friend."

"You waited long enough!"

"Well, you know how it is. Figured you wouldn't want to see a friend of his for quite some time and— Sit down, honey! Let's be sensible. We've all of us done a bunch of things that we hadn't ought to, but maybe we can sort of start over again. Honest, Zilla, I'd like to do something to make you both happy. Know what I thought to-day? Mind you, Paul doesn't know a thing about this—doesn't know I was going to come see you. I got to thinking: Zilla's a fine, big-hearted woman, and she'll understand that, uh, Paul's had his lesson now. Why wouldn't it be a fine idea if you asked the governor to pardon him? Believe he would, if it came from you. No! Wait! Just think how good you'd feel if you were generous."

"Yes, I wish to be generous." She was sitting primly, speaking icily. "For that reason I wish to keep him in prison, as an example to evil-doers. I've gotten religion, George, since the terrible thing that man did to me. Sometimes I used to be unkind, and I wished for worldly pleasures, for dancing and the theater. But when I was in the hospital the pastor of the Pentecostal Communion Faith used to come to see me, and he showed me, right from the prophecies written in the Word of God, that the Day of Judgment is coming and all the members of the older churches are going straight to eternal damnation, because they only do lip-service and swallow the world, the flesh, and the devil—"

For fifteen wild minutes she talked, pouring out admonitions to flee the wrath to come, and her face flushed, her dead voice recaptured something of the shrill energy of the old Zilla. She wound up with a furious:

"It's the blessing of God himself that Paul should be in prison now, and torn and humbled by punishment, so that he may yet save his soul, and so other wicked men, these horrible chasers after women and lust, may have an example."

Babbitt had itched and twisted. As in church he dared not move during the sermon so now he felt that he must seem attentive, though her screeching denunciations flew past him like carrion birds.

He sought to be calm and brotherly:

"Yes, I know, Zilla. But gosh, it certainly is the essence of religion to be charitable, isn't it? Let me tell you how I figure it: What we need in the world is liberalism, liberality, if we're going to get anywhere. I've always believed in being broad-minded and liberal—"

"You? Liberal?" It was very much the old Zilla. "Why, George Babbitt, you're about as broad-minded and liberal as a razor-blade!"

"Oh, I am, am I! Well, just let me tell you, just—let—me—tell—you, I'm as by golly liberal as you are religious, anyway! *You religious!*"

"I am so! Our pastor says I sustain him in the faith!"

"I'll bet you do! With Paul's money! But just to show you how liberal I am, I'm going to send a check for ten bucks to this Beecher Ingram, because a lot of fellows are saying the poor cuss preaches sedition and free love, and they're trying to run him out of town."

"And they're right! They ought to run him out of town! Why, he preaches —if you can call it preaching—in a theater, in the House of Satan! You don't know what it is to find God, to find peace, to behold the snares that the devil spreads out for our feet. Oh, I'm so glad to see the mysterious purposes of God in having Paul harm me and stop my wickedness—and Paul's getting his, good and plenty, for the cruel things he did to me, and I hope he *dies* in prison!"

Babbitt was up, hat in hand, growling, "Well, if that's what you call being at peace, for heaven's sake just warn me before you go to war, will you?"

### III

Vast is the power of cities to reclaim the wanderer. More than mountains or the shore-devouring sea, a city retains its character, imperturbable, cynical, holding behind apparent changes its essential purpose. Though Babbitt had deserted his family and dwelt with Joe Paradise in the wilderness, though he had become a liberal, though he had been quite sure, on the night before he reached Zenith, that neither he nor the city would be the same again, ten days after his return he could not believe that he had ever been away. Nor was it at all evident to his acquaintances that there was a new George F. Babbitt, save that he was more irritable under the incessant chaffing at the Athletic Club, and once, when Vergil Gunch observed that Seneca Doane ought to be hanged, Babbitt snorted, "Oh, rats, he's not so bad."

At home he grunted "Eh?" across the newspaper to his commentatory wife, and was delighted by Tinka's new red tam o'shanter, and announced, "No class to that corrugated iron garage. Have to build me a nice frame one."

Verona and Kenneth Escott appeared really to be engaged. In his news-paper Escott had conducted a pure-food crusade against commission-houses. As a result he had been given an excellent job in a commission-house, and he was making a salary on which he could marry, and denouncing irresponsible reporters who wrote stories criticizing commission-houses without knowing what they were talking about.

This September Ted had entered the State University as a freshman in the College of Arts and Sciences. The university was at Mohalis, only fifteen miles from Zenith, and Ted often came down for the week-end. Babbitt was worried. Ted was "going in for" everything but books. He had tried to "make" the football team as a light half-back, he was looking forward to the basket-ball season, he was on the committee for the Freshman Hop, and (as a Zenithite, an aristocrat among the yokels) he was being "rushed" by two fraternities. But of his studies Babbitt could learn nothing save a mumbled, "Oh, gosh, these old stiffs of teachers just give you a lot of junk about litera-ture and economics."

One week-end Ted proposed, "Say, Dad, why can't I transfer over from the College to the School of Engineering and take mechanical engineering? You always holler that I never study, but honest, I would study there."

"No, the Engineering School hasn't got the standing the College has," fretted Babbitt.

"I'd like to know how it hasn't! The Engineers can play on any of the teams!"

There was much explanation of the "dollars-and-cents value of being known as a college man when you go into the law," and a truly oratorical account of the lawyer's life. Before he was through with it, Babbitt had Ted a United States Senator.

Among the great lawyers whom he mentioned was Seneca Doane.

"But, gee whiz," Ted marveled, "I thought you always said this Doane was a reg'lar nut!"

"That's no way to speak of a great man! Doane's always been a good friend of mine—fact I helped him in college—I started him out and you might say inspired him. Just because he's sympathetic with the aims of Labor, a lot of chumps that lack liberality and broad-mindedness think he's a crank, but let me tell you there's mighty few of 'em that rake in the fees he does, and he's a friend of some of the strongest, most conservative men in the world —like Lord Wycombe, this, uh, this big English nobleman that's so well known. And you now, which would you rather do: be in with a lot of greasy mechanics and laboring-men, or chum up to a real fellow like Lord Wycombe, and get invited to his house for parties?"

"Well—gosh," sighed Ted.

The next week-end he came in joyously with, "Say, Dad, why couldn't I take mining engineering instead of the academic course? You talk about standing—maybe there isn't much in mechanical engineering, but the Miners, gee, they got seven out of eleven in the new elections to Nu Tau Tau!"

# 27

The strike which turned Zenith into two belligerent camps, white and red, began late in September with a walk-out of telephone girls and linemen, in protest against a reduction of wages. The newly formed union of dairy-products workers went out, partly in sympathy and partly in demand for a forty-four hour week. They were followed by the truck-drivers' union. Industry was tied up, and the whole city was nervous with talk of a trolley strike, a printers' strike, a general strike. Furious citizens, trying to get telephone calls through strike-breaking girls, danced helplessly. Every truck that made its way from the factories to the freight-stations was guarded by a policeman, trying to look stoical beside the scab driver. A line of fifty trucks from the Zenith Steel and Machinery Company was attacked by strikers— rushing out from the sidewalk, pulling drivers from the seats, smashing carburetors and commutators, while telephone girls cheered from the walk, and small boys heaved bricks.

The National Guard was ordered out. Colonel Nixon, who in private life was Mr. Caleb Nixon, secretary of the Pullmore Tractor Company, put on a long khaki coat and stalked through crowds, a .44 automatic in hand. Even Babbitt's friend, Clarence Drum the shoe merchant—a round and merry man who told stories at the Athletic Club, and who strangely resembled a Victorian pug-dog—was to be seen as a waddling but ferocious captain, with his belt tight about his comfortable little belly, and his round little mouth petulant as he piped to chattering groups on corners. "Move on there now! I can't have any of this loitering!"

Every newspaper in the city, save one, was against the strikers. When mobs raided the news-stands, at each was stationed a militiaman, a young, embarrassed citizen-soldier with eye-glasses, bookkeeper or grocery-clerk in private life, trying to look dangerous while small boys yelped, "Get onto de tin soldier!" and striking truck-drivers inquired tenderly, "Say, Joe, when I was fighting in France, was you in camp in the States or was you doing Swede exercises in the Y.M.C.A.? Be careful of that bayonet, now, or you'll cut yourself!"

There was no one in Zenith who talked of anything but the strike, and no one who did not take sides. You were either a courageous friend of Labor, or you were a fearless supporter of the Rights of Property; and in either case you were belligerent, and ready to disown any friend who did not hate the enemy.

A condensed-milk plant was set afire—each side charged it to the other—and the city was hysterical.

And Babbitt chose this time to be publicly liberal.

He belonged to the sound, sane, right-thinking wing, and at first he agreed that the Crooked Agitators ought to be shot. He was sorry when his friend, Seneca Doane, defended arrested strikers, and he thought of going to Doane and explaining about these agitators, but when he read a broadside alleging that even on their former wages the telephone girls had been hungry, he was troubled. "All lies and fake figures," he said, but in a doubtful croak.

For the Sunday after, the Chatham Road Presbyterian Church announced a sermon by Dr. John Jennison Drew on "How the Saviour Would End Strikes." Babbitt had been negligent about church-going lately, but he went to the service, hopeful that Dr. Drew really did have the information as to what the divine powers thought about strikes. Beside Babbitt in the large, curving, glossy, velvet-upholstered pew was Chum Frink.

Frink whispered, "Hope the doc gives the strikers hell! Ordinarily, I don't believe in a preacher butting into political matters—let him stick to straight religion and save souls, and not stir up a lot of discussion—but at a time like this, I do think he ought to stand right up and bawl out those plug-uglies to a fare-you-well!"

"Yes—well—" said Babbitt.

The Rev. Dr. Drew, his rustic bang flopping with the intensity of his poetic and sociologic ardor, trumpeted:

"During the untoward series of industrial dislocations which have—let us be courageous and admit it boldly—throttled the business life of our fair city these past days, there has been a great deal of loose talk about scientific prevention of scientific—*scientific!* Now, let me tell you that the most unscientific thing in the world is science! Take the attacks on the established fundamentals of the Christian creed which were so popular with the 'scientists' a generation ago. Oh, yes, they were mighty fellows, and great poo-bahs of criticism! They were going to destroy the church; they were going to prove the world was created and has been brought to its extraordinary level of morality and civilization by blind chance. Yet the church stands just as firmly to-day as ever, and the only answer a Christian pastor needs make to the long-haired opponents of his simple faith is just a pitying smile!

"And now these same 'scientists' want to replace the natural condition of free competition by crazy systems which, no matter by what high-sounding names they are called, are nothing but a despotic paternalism. Naturally,

I'm not criticizing labor courts, injunctions against men proven to be striking unjustly, or those excellent unions in which the men and the boss get together. But I certainly am criticizing the systems in which the free and fluid motivation of independent labor is to be replaced by cooked-up wage-scales and minimum salaries and government commissions and labor federations and all that poppycock.

"What is not generally understood is that this whole industrial matter isn't a question of economics. It's essentially and only a matter of Love, and of the practical application of the Christian religion! Imagine a factory —instead of committees of workmen alienating the boss, the boss goes among them smiling, and they smile back, the elder brother and the younger. Brothers, that's what they must be, loving brothers, and then strikes would be as inconceivable as hatred in the home!"

It was at this point that Babbitt muttered, "Oh, rot!"

"Huh?" said Chum Frink.

"He doesn't know what he's talking about. It's just as clear as mud. It doesn't mean a darn thing."

"Maybe, but—"

Frink looked at him doubtfully, through all the service kept glancing at him doubtfully, till Babbitt was nervous.

## II

The strikers had announced a parade for Tuesday morning, but Colonel Nixon had forbidden it, the newspapers said. When Babbitt drove west from his office at ten that morning, he saw a drove of shabby men heading toward the tangled, dirty district beyond Court House Square. He hated them, because they were poor, because they made him feel insecure. "Damn loafers! Wouldn't be common workmen if they had any pep," he complained. He wondered if there was going to be a riot. He drove toward the starting-point of the parade, a triangle of limp and faded grass known as Moore Street Park, and halted his car.

The park and streets were buzzing with strikers, young men in blue denim shirts, old men with caps. Through them, keeping them stirred like a boiling pot, moved the militiamen. Babbitt could hear the soldiers' monotonous orders: "Keep moving—move on, 'bo—keep your feet warm!" Babbitt admired their stolid good temper. The crowd shouted, "Tin soldiers," and "Dirty dogs —servants of the capitalists!" but the militiamen grinned and answered only, "Sure, that's right. Keep moving, Billy!"

Babbitt thrilled over the citizen-soldiers, hated the scoundrels who were obstructing the pleasant ways of prosperity, admired Colonel Nixon's striding contempt for the crowd; and as Captain Clarence Drum, that rather puffing shoe-dealer, came raging by, Babbitt respectfully clamored, "Great work, Captain! Don't let 'em march!" He watched the strikers filing from the park. Many of them bore posters with "They can't stop our peacefully walking." The militiamen tore away the posters, but the strikers fell in behind their leaders and straggled off, a thin unimpressive trickle between steel-glinting lines of soldiers. Babbitt saw with disappointment that there wasn't going to be any violence, nothing interesting at all. Then he gasped.

Among the marchers, beside a bulky young workman, was Seneca Doane, smiling, content. In front of him was Professor Brockbank, head of the history department in the State University, an old man and white-bearded, known to come from a distinguished Massachusetts family.

"Why, gosh," Babbitt marveled, "a swell like him in with the strikers? And good ole Senny Doane! They're fools to get mixed up with this bunch. They're parlor socialists! But they have got nerve. And nothing in it for them, not a cent! And—I don't know 's *all* the strikers look like such tough nuts. Look just about like anybody else to me!"

The militiamen were turning the parade down a side street.

"They got just as much right to march as anybody else! They own the streets as much as Clarence Drum or the American Legion does!" Babbitt grumbled. "Of course, they're—they're a bad element, but— Oh, rats!"

At the Athletic Club, Babbitt was silent during lunch, while the others fretted, "I don't know what the world's coming to," or solaced their spirits with "kidding."

Captain Clarence Drum came swinging by, splendid in khaki.

"How's it going, Captain?" inquired Vergil Gunch.

"Oh, we got 'em stopped. We worked 'em off on side streets and separated 'em and they got discouraged and went home."

"Fine work. No violence."

"Fine work nothing!" groaned Mr. Drum. "If I had my way, there'd be a whole lot of violence, and I'd start it, and then the whole thing would be over. I don't believe in standing back and wet-nursing these fellows and letting the disturbances drag on. I tell you these strikers are nothing in God's world but a lot of bomb-throwing socialists and thugs, and the only way to handle 'em is with a club! That's what I'd do; beat up the whole lot of 'em!"

Babbitt heard himself saying, "Oh, rats, Clarence, they look just about like you and me, and I certainly didn't notice any bombs."

Drum complained, "Oh, you didn't, eh? Well, maybe you'd like to take charge of the strike! Just tell Colonel Nixon what innocents the strikers are! He'd be glad to hear about it!" Drum strode on, while all the table stared at Babbitt.

"What's the idea? Do you want us to give those hell-hounds love and kisses, or what?" said Orville Jones.

"Do you defend a lot of hoodlums that are trying to take the bread and butter away from our families?" raged Professor Pumphrey.

Vergil Gunch intimidatingly said nothing. He put on sternness like a mask; his jaw was hard, his bristly short hair seemed cruel, his silence was a ferocious thunder. While the others assured Babbitt that they must have misunderstood him, Gunch looked as though he had understood only too well. Like a robed judge he listened to Babbitt's stammering:

"No, sure; course they're a bunch of toughs. But I just mean— Strikes me it's bad policy to talk about clubbing 'em. Cabe Nixon doesn't. He's got the fine Italian hand. And that's why he's colonel. Clarence Drum is jealous of him."

"Well," said Professor Pumphrey, "you hurt Clarence's feelings, George. He's been out there all morning getting hot and dusty, and no wonder he wants to beat the tar out of those sons of guns!"

Gunch said nothing, and watched; and Babbitt knew that he was being watched.

### III

As he was leaving the club Babbitt heard Chum Frink protesting to Gunch, "—don't know what's got into him. Last Sunday Doc Drew preached a corking sermon about decency in business and Babbitt kicked about that, too. Near 's I can figure out—"

Babbitt was vaguely frightened.

### IV

He saw a crowd listening to a man who was talking from the rostrum of a kitchen-chair. He stopped his car. From newspaper pictures he knew that the speaker must be the notorious free-lance preacher, Beecher Ingram, of whom Seneca Doane had spoken. Ingram was a gaunt man with flamboyant hair, weather-beaten cheeks, and worried eyes. He was pleading:

"—if those telephone girls can hold out, living on one meal a day, doing their own washing, starving and smiling, you big hulking men ought to be able—"

Babbitt saw that from the sidewalk Vergil Gunch was watching him. In vague disquiet he started the car and mechanically drove on, while Gunch's hostile eyes seemed to follow him all the way.

### V

"There's a lot of these fellows," Babbitt was complaining to his wife, "that think if workmen go on strike they're a regular bunch of fiends. Now, of course, it's a fight between sound business and the destructive element, and we got to lick the stuffin's out of 'em when they challenge us, but doggoned if I see why we can't fight like gentlemen and not go calling 'em dirty dogs and saying they ought to be shot down."

"Why, George," she said placidly, "I thought you always insisted that all strikers ought to be put in jail."

"I never did! Well, I mean— Some of 'em, of course. Irresponsible leaders. But I mean a fellow ought to be broad-minded and liberal about things like—"

"But dearie, I thought you always said these so-called 'liberal' people were the worst of—"

"Rats! Woman never can understand the different definitions of a word.

Depends on how you mean it. And it don't pay to be too cocksure about anything. Now, these strikers: Honest, they're not such bad people. Just foolish. They don't understand the complications of merchandizing and profit, the way we business men do, but sometimes I think they're about like the rest of us, and no more hogs for wages than we are for profits."

"George! If people were to hear you talk like that—of course I *know* you; I remember what a wild crazy boy you were; I know you don't mean a word you say—but if people that didn't understand you were to hear you talking, they'd think you were a regular socialist!"

"What do I care what anybody thinks? And let me tell you right now—I want you to distinctly understand I never was a wild crazy kid, and when I say a thing, I mean it, and I stand by it and— Honest, do you think people would think I was too liberal if I just said the strikers were decent?"

"Of course they would. But don't worry, dear; I know you don't mean a word of it. Time to trot up to bed now. Have you enough covers for to-night?"

On the sleeping-porch he puzzled, "She doesn't understand me. Hardly understand myself. Why can't I take things easy, way I used to?

"Wish I could go out to Senny Doane's house and talk things over with him. No! Suppose Verg Gunch saw me going in there!

"Wish I knew some really smart woman, and nice, that would see what I'm trying to get at, and let me talk to her and— I wonder if Myra's right? Could the fellows think I've gone nutty just because I'm broad-minded and liberal? Way Verg looked at me—"

# 28

Miss McGoun came into his private office at three in the afternoon with "Lissen, Mr. Babbitt; there's a Mrs. Judique on the 'phone—wants to see about some repairs, and the salesmen are all out. Want to talk to her?"

"All right."

The voice of Tanis Judique was clear and pleasant. The black cylinder of the telephone-receiver seemed to hold a tiny animated image of her: lustrous eyes, delicate nose, gentle chin.

"This is Mrs. Judique. Do you remember me? You drove me up here to the Cavendish Apartments and helped me find such a nice flat."

"Sure! Bet I remember! What can I do for you?"

"Why, it's just a little— I don't know that I ought to bother you, but the janitor doesn't seem to be able to fix it. You know my flat is on the top floor, and with these autumn rains the roof is beginning to leak, and I'd be awfully glad if—"

"Sure! I'll come up and take a look at it." Nervously, "When do you expect to be in?"

"Why, I'm in every morning."

"Be in this afternoon, in an hour or so?"

"Ye-es. Perhaps I could give you a cup of tea. I think I ought to, after all your trouble."

"Fine! I'll run up there soon as I can get away."

He meditated, "Now there's a woman that's got refinement, savvy, *class!* 'After all your trouble—give you a cup of tea.' She'd appreciate a fellow. I'm a fool, but I'm not such a bad cuss, get to know me. And not so much a fool as they think!"

The great strike was over, the strikers beaten. Except that Vergil Gunch seemed less cordial, there were no visible effects of Babbitt's treachery to the clan. The oppressive fear of criticism was gone, but a diffident loneliness remained. Now he was so exhilarated that, to prove he wasn't, he droned about the office for fifteen minutes, looking at blue-prints, explaining to Miss McGoun that this Mrs. Scott wanted more money for her house—had raised the asking-price—raised it from seven thousand to eighty-five hundred —would Miss McGoun be sure and put it down on the card—Mrs. Scott's house—raise. When he had thus established himself as a person unemotional and interested only in business, he sauntered out. He took a particularly long time to start his car; he kicked the tires, dusted the glass of the speedometer, and tightened the screws holding the wind-shield spot-light.

He drove happily off toward the Bellevue district, conscious of the presence of Mrs. Judique as of a brilliant light on the horizon. The maple leaves had fallen and they lined the gutters of the asphalted streets. It was a day of pale gold and faded green, tranquil and lingering. Babbitt was aware of the meditative day, and of the barrenness of Bellevue—blocks of wooden houses, garages, little shops, weedy lots. "Needs pepping up; needs the touch that people like Mrs. Judique could give a place," he ruminated, as he rattled through the long, crude, airy streets. The wind rose, enlivening, keen, and in a blaze of well-being he came to the flat of Tanis Judique.

She was wearing, when she flutteringly admitted him, a frock of black chiffon cut modestly round at the base of her pretty throat. She seemed to him immensely sophisticated. He glanced at the cretonnes and colored prints in her living-room, and gurgled, "Gosh, you've fixed the place nice! Takes a clever woman to know how to make a home, all right!"

"You really like it? I'm so glad! But you've neglected me, scandalously. You promised to come some time and learn to dance."

Rather unsteadily, "Oh, but you didn't mean it seriously!"

"Perhaps not. But you might have tried!"

"Well, here I've come for my lesson, and you might just as well prepare to have me stay for supper!"

They both laughed in a manner which indicated that of course he didn't mean it.

"But first I guess I better look at that leak."

She climbed with him to the flat roof of the apartment-house—a detached world of slatted wooden walks, clothes-lines, water-tank in a penthouse. He poked at things with his toe, and sought to impress her by being learned about copper gutters, the desirability of passing plumbing pipes through a lead collar and sleeve and flashing them with copper, and the advantages of cedar over boiler-iron for roof-tanks.

"You have to know so much, in real estate!" she admired.

He promised that the roof should be repaired within two days. "Do you mind my 'phoning from your apartment?" he asked.

"Heavens, no!"

He stood a moment at the coping, looking over a land of hard little bunga-lows with abnormally large porches, and new apartment-houses, small, but brave with variegated brick walls and terra-cotta trimmings. Beyond them was a hill with a gouge of yellow clay like a vast wound. Behind every apartment-house, beside each dwelling, were small garages. It was a world of good little people, comfortable, industrious, credulous.

In the autumnal light the flat newness was mellowed, and the air was a sun-tinted pool.

"Golly, it's one fine afternoon. You get a great view here, right up Tanner's Hill," said Babbitt.

"Yes, isn't it nice and open."

"So darn few people appreciate a View."

"Don't you go raising my rent on that account! Oh, that was naughty of me! I was just teasing. Seriously though, there are so few who respond—who react to Views. I mean—they haven't any feeling of poetry and beauty."

"That's a fact, they haven't," he breathed, admiring her slenderness and the absorbed, airy way in which she looked toward the hill, chin lifted, lips smiling. "Well, guess I'd better telephone the plumbers, so they'll get on the job first thing in the morning."

When he had telephoned, making it conspicuously authoritative and gruff and masculine, he looked doubtful, and sighed, "S'pose I'd better be—"

"Oh, you must have that cup of tea first!"

"Well, it would go pretty good, at that."

It was luxurious to loll in a deep green rep chair, his legs thrust out before him, to glance at the black Chinese telephone stand and the colored photo-graph of Mount Vernon which he had always liked so much, while in the tiny kitchen—so near—Mrs. Judique sang "My Creole Queen." In an intoler-able sweetness, a contentment so deep that he was wistfully discontented, he saw magnolias by moonlight and heard plantation darkies crooning to the banjo. He wanted to be near her, on pretense of helping her, yet he wanted to remain in this still ecstasy. Languidly he remained.

When she bustled in with the tea he smiled up at her. "This is awfully nice!" For the first time, he was not fencing; he was quietly and securely friendly; and friendly and quiet was her answer: "It's nice to have you here. You were so kind, helping me to find this little home."

They agreed that the weather would soon turn cold. They agreed that prohibition was prohibitive. They agreed that art in the home was cultural. They agreed about everything. They even became bold. They hinted that these modern young girls, well, honestly, their short skirts were short. They were proud to find that they were not shocked by such frank speaking. Tanis ventured, "I know you'll understand—I mean—I don't quite know how to say it, but I do think that girls who pretend they're bad by the way they dress really never go any farther. They give away the fact that they haven't the instincts of a womanly woman."

Remembering Ida Putiak, the manicure girl, and how ill she had used him, Babbitt agreed with enthusiasm; remembering how ill all the world had used him, he told of Paul Riesling, of Zilla, of Seneca Doane, of the strike:

"See how it was? Course I was as anxious to have those beggars licked to a standstill as anybody else, but gosh, no reason for not seeing their side. For a fellow's own sake, he's got to be broad-minded and liberal, don't you think so?"

"Oh, I do!" Sitting on the hard little couch, she clasped her hands beside her, leaned toward him, absorbed him; and in a glorious state of being appreciated he proclaimed:

"So I up and said to the fellows at the club, 'Look here,' I—"

"Do you belong to the Union Club? I think it's—"

"No; the Athletic. Tell you: Course they're always asking me to join the Union, but I always say, 'No, sir! Nothing doing!' I don't mind the expense but I can't stand all the old fogies."

"Oh, yes, that's so. But tell me: what did you say to them?"

"Oh, you don't want to hear it. I'm probably boring you to death with my troubles! You wouldn't hardly think I was an old duffer; I sound like a kid!"

"Oh, you're a boy yet. I mean—you can't be a day over forty-five."

"Well, I'm not—much. But by golly I begin to feel middle-aged sometimes; all these responsibilities and all."

"Oh, I know!" Her voice caressed him; it cloaked him like warm silk. "And I feel lonely, so lonely, some days, Mr. Babbitt."

"We're a sad pair of birds! But I think we're pretty darn nice!"

"Yes, I think we're lots nicer than most people I know!" They smiled. "But please tell me what you said at the Club."

"Well, it was like this: Course Seneca Doane is a friend of mine—they can say what they want to, they can call him anything they please, but what most folks here don't know is that Senny is the bosom pal of some of the biggest statesmen in the world—Lord Wycombe, frinstance—you know, this big British nobleman. My friend Sir Gerald Doak told me that Lord Wycombe is one of the biggest guns in England—well, Doak or somebody told me."

"Oh! Do you know Sir Gerald? The one that was here, at the McKelveys'?"

"Know him? Well, say, I know him just well enough so we call each other George and Jerry, and we got so pickled together in Chicago—"

"That must have been fun. But—" She shook a finger at him. "—I can't have you getting pickled! I'll have to take you in hand!"

"Wish you would! . . . Well, zize saying: You see I happen to know what a big noise Senny Doane is outside of Zenith, but of course a prophet hasn't got any honor in his own country, and Senny, darn his old hide, he's so blame modest that he never lets folks know the kind of an outfit he travels with when he goes abroad. Well, during the strike Clarence Drum comes pee-rading up to our table, all dolled up fit to kill in his nice lil cap'n's uniform, and somebody says to him, 'Busting the strike, Clarence?'

"Well, he swells up like a pouter-pigeon and he hollers, so 's you could hear him way up in the reading-room, 'Yes, sure; I told the strike-leaders where they got off, and so they went home.'

" 'Well,' I says to him, 'glad there wasn't any violence.'

" 'Yes,' he says, 'but if I hadn't kept my eye skinned there would 've been. All those fellows had bombs in their pockets. They're reg'lar anarchists.'

" 'Oh, rats, Clarence,' I says, 'I looked 'em all over carefully, and they didn't have any more bombs 'n a rabbit,' I says. 'Course,' I says, 'they're foolish, but they're a good deal like you and me, after all.'

"And then Vergil Gunch or somebody—no, it was Chum Frink—you know, this famous poet—great pal of mine—he says to me, 'Look here,' he says, 'do you mean to say you advocate these strikes?' Well, I was so disgusted with a fellow whose mind worked that way that I swear, I had a good mind to not explain at all—just ignore him—"

"Oh, that's so wise!" said Mrs. Judique.

"—but finally I explains to him: 'If you'd done as much as I have on Chamber of Commerce committees and all,' I says, 'then you'd have the right to talk! But same time,' I says, 'I believe in treating your opponent like a gentleman!' Well, sir, that held 'em! Frink—Chum I always call him —he didn't have another word to say. But at that, I guess some of 'em kind o' thought I was too liberal. What do you think?"

"Oh, you were so wise. And courageous! I love a man to have the courage of his convictions!"

"But do you think it was a good stunt? After all, some of these fellows are so darn cautious and narrow-minded that they're prejudiced against a fellow that talks right out in meeting."

"What do you care? In the long run they're bound to respect a man who makes them think, and with your reputation for oratory you—"

"What do you know about my reputation for oratory?"

"Oh, I'm not going to tell you everything I know! But seriously, you don't realize what a famous man you are."

"Well— Though I haven't done much orating this fall. Too kind of bothered by this Paul Riesling business, I guess. But— Do you know, you're the first person that's really understood what I was getting at, Tanis— Listen to me, will you! Fat nerve I've got, calling you Tanis!"

"Oh, do! And shall I call you George? Don't you think it's awfully nice when two people have so much—what shall I call it?—so much analysis that they can discard all these stupid conventions and understand each other and become acquainted right away, like ships that pass in the night?"

"I certainly do! I certainly do!"

He was no longer quiescent in his chair; he wandered about the room, he dropped on the couch beside her. But as he awkwardly stretched his hand toward her fragile, immaculate fingers, she said brightly, "Do give me a cigarette. Would you think poor Tanis was dreadfully naughty if she smoked?"

"Lord, no! I like it!"

He had often and weightily pondered flappers smoking in Zenith restaurants, but he knew only one woman who smoked—Mrs. Sam Doppelbrau, his flighty neighbor. He ceremoniously lighted Tanis's cigarette, looked for a place to deposit the burnt match, and dropped it into his pocket.

"I'm sure you want a cigar, you poor man!" she crooned.

"Do you mind one?"

"Oh, no! I love the smell of a good cigar; so nice and—so nice and like a man. You'll find an ash-tray in my bedroom, on the table beside the bed, if you don't mind getting it."

He was embarrassed by her bedroom: the broad couch with a cover of violet silk, mauve curtains striped with gold, Chinese Chippendale bureau, and an amazing row of slippers, with ribbon-wound shoe-trees, and primrose stockings lying across them. His manner of bringing the ash-tray had just the right note of easy friendliness, he felt. "A boob like Verg Gunch would try to get funny about seeing her bedroom, but I take it casually." He was not casual afterward. The contentment of companionship was gone, and he was restless with desire to touch her hand. But whenever he turned toward her, the cigarette was in his way. It was a shield between them. He waited till she should have finished, but as he rejoiced at her quick crushing of its light on the ash-tray she said, "Don't you want to give me another cigarette?" and hopelessly he saw the screen of pale smoke and her graceful tilted hand again between them. He was not merely curious now to find out whether she would let him hold her hand (all in the purest friendship, naturally), but agonized with need of it.

On the surface appeared none of all this fretful drama. They were talking cheerfully of motors, of trips to California, of Chum Frink. Once he said delicately, "I do hate these guys—I hate these people that invite themselves to meals, but I seem to have a feeling I'm going to have supper with the lovely Mrs. Tanis Judique to-night. But I suppose you probably have seven dates already."

"Well, I was thinking some of going to the movies. Yes, I really think I ought to get out and get some fresh air."

She did not encourage him to stay, but never did she discourage him. He considered, "I better take a sneak! She *will* let me stay—there *is* something doing—and I mustn't get mixed up with—I mustn't—I've got to beat it." Then, "No, it's too late now."

Suddenly, at seven, brushing her cigarette away, brusquely taking her hand:

"Tanis! Stop teasing me! You know we— Here we are, a couple of lonely birds, and we're awful happy together. Anyway I am! Never been so happy! Do let me stay! I'll gallop down to the delicatessen and buy some stuff—cold chicken maybe—or cold turkey—and we can have a nice little supper, and afterwards, if you want to chase me out, I'll be good and go like a lamb."

"Well—yes—it would be nice," she said.

Nor did she withdraw her hand. He squeezed it, trembling, and blundered toward his coat. At the delicatessen he bought preposterous stores of food, chosen on the principle of expensiveness. From the drug store across the street he telephoned to his wife, "Got to get a fellow to sign a lease before he leaves town on the midnight. Won't be home till late. Don't wait up for me. Kiss Tinka good-night." He expectantly lumbered back to the flat.

"Oh, you bad thing, to buy so much food!" was her greeting, and her voice was gay, her smile acceptant.

He helped her in the tiny white kitchen; he washed the lettuce, he opened the olive bottle. She ordered him to set the table, and as he trotted into the living-room, as he hunted through the buffet for knives and forks, he felt utterly at home.

"Now the only other thing," he announced, "is what you're going to wear. I can't decide whether you're to put on your swellest evening gown, or let your hair down and put on short skirts and make-believe you're a little girl."

"I'm going to dine just as I am, in this old chiffon rag, and if you can't stand poor Tanis that way, you can go to the club for dinner!"

"Stand you!" He patted her shoulder. "Child, you're the brainiest and the loveliest and finest woman I've ever met! Come now, Lady Wycombe, if you'll take the Duke of Zenith's arm, we will proambulate in to the magnolious feed!"

"Oh, you do say the funniest, nicest things!"

When they had finished the picnic supper he thrust his head out of the window and reported, "It's turned awful chilly, and I think it's going to rain. You don't want to go to the movies."

"Well—"

"I wish we had a fireplace! I wish it was raining like all get-out to-night, and we were in a funny little old-fashioned cottage, and the trees thrashing like everything outside, and a great big log fire and—I'll tell you! Let's draw this couch up to the radiator, and stretch our feet out, and pretend it's a wood-fire."

"Oh, I think that's pathetic! You big child!"

But they did draw up to the radiator, and propped their feet against it— his clumsy black shoes, her patent-leather slippers. In the dimness they talked of themselves; of how lonely she was, how bewildered he, and how wonderful that they had found each other. As they fell silent the room was stiller than a country lane. There was no sound from the street save the whir of motor-tires, the rumble of a distant freight-train. Self-contained was the room, warm, secure, insulated from the harassing world.

He was absorbed by a rapture in which all fear and doubting were smoothed away; and when he reached home, at dawn, the rapture had mellowed to contentment serene and full of memories.

# 29

The assurance of Tanis Judique's friendship fortified Babbitt's self-approval. At the Athletic Club he became experimental. Though Vergil Gunch was silent, the others at the Roughnecks' Table came to accept Babbitt as having, for no visible reason, "turned crank." They argued windily with him, and he was cocky, and enjoyed the spectacle of his interesting martyrdom. He even praised Seneca Doane. Professor Pumphrey said that was carrying a joke too far; but Babbitt argued, "No! Fact! I tell you he's got one of the keenest intellects in the country. Why, Lord Wycombe said that—"

"Oh, who the hell is Lord Wycombe? What you always lugging him in for? You been touting him for the last six weeks!" protested Orville Jones.

"George ordered him from Sears-Roebuck. You can get those English highmuckamucks by mail for two bucks apiece," suggested Sidney Finkelstein.

"That's all right now! Lord Wycombe, he's one of the biggest intellects in English political life. As I was saying: Of course I'm conservative myself, but I appreciate a guy like Senny Doane because—"

Vergil Gunch interrupted harshly, "I wonder if you are so conservative? I find I can manage to run my own business without any skunks and reds like Doane in it!"

The grimness of Gunch's voice, the hardness of his jaw, disconcerted Babbitt, but he recovered and went on till they looked bored, then irritated, then as doubtful as Gunch.

II

He thought of Tanis always. With a stir he remembered her every aspect. His arms yearned for her. "I've found her! I've dreamed of her all these years and now I've found her!" he exulted. He met her at the movies in the morning; he drove out to her flat in the late afternoon or on evenings when he was believed to be at the Elks. He knew her financial affairs and advised her about them, while she lamented her feminine ignorance, and praised his masterfulness, and proved to know much more about bonds than he did. They had remembrances, and laughter over old times. Once they quarreled, and he raged that she was as "bossy" as his wife and far more whining when he was inattentive. But that passed safely.

Their high hour was a tramp on a ringing December afternoon, through snow-drifted meadows down to the icy Chaloosa River. She was exotic in an astrachan cap and a short beaver coat; she slid on the ice and shouted, and he panted after her, rotund with laughter. . . . Myra Babbitt never slid on the ice.

He was afraid that they would be seen together. In Zenith it is impossible to lunch with a neighbor's wife without the fact being known, before nightfall, in every house in your circle. But Tanis was beautifully discreet. However appealingly she might turn to him when they were alone, she was gravely detached when they were abroad, and he hoped that she would be taken for a client. Orville Jones once saw them emerging from a movie theater, and Babbitt bumbled, "Let me make you 'quainted with Mrs. Judique. Now here's a lady who knows the right broker to come to, Orvy!" Mr. Jones, though he was a man censorious of morals and of laundry machinery, seemed satisfied.

His predominant fear—not from any especial fondness for her but from the habit of propriety—was that his wife would learn of the affair. He was certain that she knew nothing specific about Tanis, but he was also certain that she suspected something indefinite. For years she had been bored by anything more affectionate than a farewell kiss, yet she was hurt by any slackening in his irritable periodic interest, and now he had no interest; rather, a revulsion. He was completely faithful—to Tanis. He was distressed by the sight of his wife's slack plumpness, by her puffs and billows of flesh, by the tattered petticoat which she was always meaning and always forgetting to throw away. But he was aware that she, so long attuned to him, caught all his repulsions. He elaborately, heavily, jocularly tried to check them. He couldn't.

They had a tolerable Christmas. Kenneth Escott was there, admittedly engaged to Verona. Mrs. Babbitt was tearful and called Kenneth her new son. Babbitt was worried about Ted, because he had ceased complaining of the State University and become suspiciously acquiescent. He wondered what the boy was planning, and was too shy to ask. Himself, Babbitt slipped away on Christmas afternoon to take his present, a silver cigarette-box, to Tanis. When he returned Mrs. Babbitt asked, much too innocently, "Did you go out for a little fresh air?"

"Yes, just lil drive," he mumbled.

After New Year's his wife proposed, "I heard from my sister to-day, George. She isn't well. I think perhaps I ought to go stay with her for a few weeks."

Now, Mrs. Babbitt was not accustomed to leave home during the winter except on violently demanding occasions, and only the summer before, she had been gone for weeks. Nor was Babbitt one of the detachable husbands who take separations casually. He liked to have her there; she looked after his clothes; she knew how his steak ought to be cooked; and her clucking made him feel secure. But he could not drum up even a dutiful "Oh, she doesn't really need you, does she?" While he tried to look regretful, while he felt that his wife was watching him, he was filled with exultant visions of Tanis.

"Do you think I'd better go?" she said sharply.

"You've got to decide, honey; I can't."

She turned away, sighing, and his forehead was damp.

Till she went, four days later, she was curiously still, he cumbrously affectionate. Her train left at noon. As he saw it grow small beyond the train-shed he longed to hurry to Tanis.

"No, by golly, I won't do that!" he vowed. "I won't go near her for a week!" But he was at her flat at four.

### III

He who had once controlled or seemed to control his life in a progress unimpassioned but diligent and sane was for that fortnight borne on a current of desire and very bad whisky and all the complications of new acquaintances, those furious new intimates who demand so much more attention than old friends. Each morning he gloomily recognized his idiocies of the evening before. With his head throbbing, his tongue and lips stinging from cigarettes, he incredulously counted the number of drinks he had taken, and groaned, "I got to quit!" He had ceased saying, "I *will* quit!" for however resolute he might be at dawn, he could not, for a single evening, check his drift.

He had met Tanis's friends; he had, with the ardent haste of the Midnight People, who drink and dance and rattle and are ever afraid to be silent, been adopted as a member of her group, which they called "The Bunch." He first met them after a day when he had worked particularly hard and when he hoped to be quiet with Tanis and slowly sip her admiration.

From down the hall he could hear shrieks and the grind of a phonograph. As Tanis opened the door he saw fantastic figures dancing in a haze of cigarette smoke. The tables and chairs were against the wall.

"Oh, isn't this dandy!" she gabbled at him. "Carrie Nork had the loveliest idea. She decided it was time for a party, and she 'phoned the Bunch and told 'em to gather round. . . . George, this is Carrie."

"Carrie" was, in the less desirable aspects of both, at once matronly and spinsterish. She was perhaps forty; her hair was an unconvincing ash-blond; and if her chest was flat, her hips were ponderous. She greeted Babbitt with a giggling "Welcome to our little midst! Tanis says you're a real sport."

He was apparently expected to dance, to be boyish and gay with Carrie, and he did his unforgiving best. He towed her about the room, bumping into other couples, into the radiator, into chair-legs cunningly ambushed. As he danced he surveyed the rest of the Bunch: A thin young woman who looked capable, conceited, and sarcastic. Another woman whom he could never quite remember. Three overdressed and slightly effeminate young men—soda-fountain clerks, or at least born for that profession. A man of his own age, immovable, self-satisfied, resentful of Babbitt's presence.

When he had finished his dutiful dance Tanis took him aside and begged,

"Dear, wouldn't you like to do something for me? I'm all out of booze, and the Bunch want to celebrate. Couldn't you just skip down to Healey Hanson's and get some?"

"Sure," he said, trying not to sound sullen.

"I'll tell you: I'll get Minnie Sonntag to drive down with you." Tanis was pointing to the thin, sarcastic young woman.

Miss Sonntag greeted him with an astringent "How d'you do, Mr. Babbitt. Tanis tells me you're a very prominent man, and I'm honored by being allowed to drive with you. Of course I'm not accustomed to associating with society people like you, so I don't know how to act in such exalted circles!"

Thus Miss Sonntag talked all the way down to Healey Hanson's. To her jibes he wanted to reply "Oh, go to the devil!" but he never quite nerved himself to that reasonable comment. He was resenting the existence of the whole Bunch. He had heard Tanis speak of "darling Carrie" and "Min Sonntag—she's so clever—you'll adore her," but they had never been real to him. He had pictured Tanis as living in a rose-tinted vacuum, waiting for him, free of all the complications of a Floral Heights.

When they returned he had to endure the patronage of the young soda-clerks. They were as damply friendly as Miss Sonntag was dryly hostile. They called him "Old Georgie" and shouted, "Come on now, sport; shake a leg" . . . boys in belted coats, pimply boys, as young as Ted and as flabby as chorus-men, but powerful to dance and to mind the phonograph and smoke cigarettes and patronize Tanis. He tried to be one of them; he cried "Good work, Pete!" but his voice creaked.

Tanis apparently enjoyed the companionship of the dancing darlings; she bridled to their bland flirtation and casually kissed them at the end of each dance. Babbitt hated her, for the moment. He saw her as middle-aged. He studied the wrinkles in the softness of her throat, the slack flesh beneath her chin. The taut muscles of her youth were loose and drooping. Between dances she sat in the largest chair, waving her cigarette, summoning her callow admirers to come and talk to her. ("She thinks she's a blooming queen!" growled Babbitt.) She chanted to Miss Sonntag, "Isn't my little studio sweet?" ("Studio, rats! It's a plain old-maid-and-chow-dog flat! Oh, God, I wish I was home! I wonder if I can't make a getaway now?")

His vision grew blurred, however, as he applied himself to Healey Hanson's raw but vigorous whisky. He blended with the Bunch. He began to rejoice that Carrie Nork and Pete, the most nearly intelligent of the nimble youths, seemed to like him; and it was enormously important to win over the surly older man, who proved to be a railway clerk named Fulton Bemis.

The conversation of the Bunch was exclamatory, high-colored, full of references to people whom Babbitt did not know. Apparently they thought very comfortably of themselves. They were the Bunch, wise and beautiful and amusing; they were Bohemians and urbanites, accustomed to all the luxuries of Zenith: dance-halls, movie-theaters, and road-houses; and in a cynical superiority to people who were "slow" or "tightwad" they cackled:

"Oh, Pete, did I tell you what that dub of a cashier said when I came in late yesterday? Oh, it was per-fect-ly priceless!"

"Oh, but wasn't T. D. stewed! Say, he was simply ossified! What did Gladys say to him?"

"Think of the nerve of Bob Bickerstaff trying to get us to come to his house! Say, the nerve of him! Can you beat it for nerve? Some nerve I call it!"

"Did you notice how Dotty was dancing? Gee, wasn't she the limit!"

Babbitt was to be heard sonorously agreeing with the once-hated Miss Minnie Sonntag that persons who let a night go by without dancing to jazz music were crabs, pikers, and poor fish; and he roared "You bet!" when Mrs. Carrie Nork gurgled, "Don't you love to sit on the floor? It's so Bohemian!" He began to think extremely well of the Bunch. When he mentioned his friends Sir Gerald Doak, Lord Wycombe, William Washington Eathorne, and Chum Frink, he was proud of their condescending interest. He got so thoroughly into the jocund spirit that he didn't much mind seeing Tanis drooping against the shoulder of the youngest and milkiest of the young men, and he himself desired to hold Carrie Nork's pulpy hand, and dropped it only because Tanis looked angry.

When he went home, at two, he was fully a member of the Bunch, and all the week thereafter he was bound by the exceedingly straitened conventions, the exceedingly wearing demands, of their life of pleasure and freedom. He had to go to their parties; he was involved in the agitation when everybody telephoned to everybody else that she hadn't meant what she'd said when she'd said that, and anyway, why was Pete going around saying she'd said it?"

Never was a Family more insistent on learning one another's movements than were the Bunch. All of them volubly knew, or indignantly desired to know, where all the others had been every minute of the week. Babbitt found himself explaining to Carrie or Fulton Bemis just what he had been doing that he should not have joined them till ten o'clock, and apologizing for having gone to dinner with a business acquaintance.

Every member of the Bunch was expected to telephone to every other member at least once a week. "Why haven't you called me up?" Babbitt was asked accusingly, not only by Tanis and Carrie but presently by new ancient friends, Jennie and Capitolina and Toots.

If for a moment he had seen Tanis as withering and sentimental, he lost that impression at Carrie Nork's dance. Mrs. Nork had a large house and a small husband. To her party came all of the Bunch, perhaps thirty-five of them when they were completely mobilized. Babbitt, under the name of "Old Georgie," was now a pioneer of the Bunch, since each month it changed half its membership and he who could recall the prehistoric days of a fortnight ago, before Mrs. Absolom, the food-demonstrator, had gone to Indianapolis, and Mac had "got sore at" Minnie, was a venerable leader and able to condescend to new Petes and Minnies and Gladyses.

At Carrie's, Tanis did not have to work at being hostess. She was dignified and sure, a clear fine figure in the black chiffon frock he had always loved;

and in the wider spaces of that ugly house Babbitt was able to sit quietly with her. He repented of his first revulsion, mooned at her feet, and happily drove her home. Next day he bought a violent yellow tie, to make himself young for her. He knew, a little sadly, that he could not make himself beautiful; he beheld himself as heavy, hinting of fatness, but he danced, he dressed, he chattered, to be as young as she was . . . as young as she seemed to be.

## IV

As all converts, whether to a religion, love, or gardening, find as by magic that though hitherto these hobbies have not seemed to exist, now the whole world is filled with their fury, so, once he was converted to dissipation, Babbitt discovered agreeable opportunities for it everywhere.

He had a new view of his sporting neighbor, Sam Doppelbrau. The Doppelbraus were respectable people, industrious people, prosperous people, whose ideal of happiness was an eternal cabaret. Their life was dominated by suburban bacchanalia of alcohol, nicotine, gasoline, and kisses. They and their set worked capably all the week, and all week looked forward to Saturday night, when they would, as they expressed it, "throw a party;" and the thrown party grew noisier and noisier up to Sunday dawn, and usually included an extremely rapid motor expedition to nowhere in particular.

One evening when Tanis was at the theater, Babbitt found himself being lively with the Doppelbraus, pledging friendship with men whom he had for years privily denounced to Mrs. Babbitt as a "rotten bunch of tin-horns that I wouldn't go out with, not if they were the last people on earth." That evening he had sulkily come home and poked about in front of the house, chipping off the walk the ice-clots, like fossil footprints, made by the steps of passers-by during the recent snow. Howard Littlefield came up snuffling.

"Still a widower, George?"

"Yump. Cold again to-night."

"What do you hear from the wife?"

"She's feeling fine, but her sister is still pretty sick."

"Say better come in and have dinner with us to-night, George."

"Oh—oh, thanks. Have to go out."

Suddenly he could not endure Littlefield's recitals of the more interesting statistics about totally uninteresting problems. He scraped at the walk and grunted.

Sam Doppelbrau appeared.

"Evenin', Babbitt. Working hard?"

"Yuh, lil exercise."

"Cold enough for you to-night?"

"Well, just about."

"Still a widower?"

"Uh-huh."

"Say, Babbitt, while she's away— I know you don't care much for boozefights, but the Missus and I'd be awfully glad if you could come in some night. Think you could stand a good cocktail for once?"

"Stand it? Young fclla, I bet old Uncle George can mix the best cocktail in these United States!"

"Hurray! That's the way to talk! Look here: There's some folks coming to the house to-night, Louetta Swanson and some other live ones, and I'm going to open up a bottle of pre-war gin, and maybe we'll dance a while. Why don't you drop in and jazz it up a little, just for a change?"

"Well— What time they coming?"

He was at Sam Doppelbrau's at nine. It was the third time he had entered the house. By ten he was calling Mr. Doppelbrau "Sam, old hoss."

At eleven they all drove out to the Old Farm Inn. Babbitt sat in the back of Doppelbrau's car with Louetta Swanson. Once he had timorously tried to make love to her. Now he did not try; he merely made love; and Louetta dropped her head on his shoulder, told him what a nagger Eddie was, and accepted Babbitt as a decent and well-trained libertine.

With the assistance of Tanis's Bunch, the Doppelbraus, and other companions in forgetfulness, there was not an evening for two weeks when he did not return home late and shaky. With his other faculties blurred he yet had the motorist's gift of being able to drive when he could scarce walk; of slowing down at corners and allowing for approaching cars. He came wambling into the house. If Verona and Kenneth Escott were about, he got past them with a hasty greeting, horribly aware of their level young glances, and hid himself up-stairs. He found when he came into the warm house that he was hazier than he had believed. His head whirled. He dared not lie down. He tried to soak out the alcohol in a hot bath. For the moment his head was clearer but when he moved about the bathroom his calculations of distance were wrong, so that he dragged down the towels, and knocked over the soapdish with a clatter which, he feared, would betray him to the children. Chilly in his dressing-gown he tried to read the evening paper. He could follow every word; he seemed to take in the sense of things; but a minute afterward he could not have told what he had been reading. When he went to bed his brain flew in circles, and he hastily sat up, struggling for self-control. At last he was able to lie still, feeling only a little sick and dizzy—and enormously ashamed. To hide his "condition" from his own children! To have danced and shouted with people whom he despised! To have said foolish things, sung idiotic songs, tried to kiss silly girls! Incredulously he remembered that he had by his roaring familiarity with them laid himself open to the patronizing of youths whom he would have kicked out of his office; that by dancing too ardently he had exposed himself to rebukes from the rattiest of withering women. As it came relentlessly back to him he snarled, "I hate myself! God how I hate myself!" But, he raged, "I'm through! No more! Had enough, plenty!"

He was even surer about it the morning after, when he was trying to be grave and paternal with his daughters at breakfast. At noontime he was less sure. He did not deny that he had been a fool; he saw it almost as clearly as at midnight; but anything, he struggled, was better than going back to a life of barren heartiness. At four he wanted a drink. He kept a whisky flask in his desk now, and after two minutes of battle he had his drink. Three drinks later he began to see the Bunch as tender and amusing friends, and by six he was with them . . . and the tale was to be told all over.

Each morning his head ached a little less. A bad head for drinks had been his safeguard, but the safeguard was crumbling. Presently he could be drunk at dawn, yet not feel particularly wretched in his conscience—or in his stomach—when he awoke at eight. No regret, no desire to escape the toil of keeping up with the arduous merriment of the Bunch, was so great as his feeling of social inferiority when he failed to keep up. To be the "livest" of them was as much his ambition now as it had been to excel at making money, at playing golf, at motor-driving, at oratory, at climbing to the McKelvey set. But occasionally he failed.

He found that Pete and the other young men considered the Bunch too austerely polite and the Carrie who merely kissed behind doors too embarrassingly monogamic. As Babbitt sneaked from Floral Heights down to the Bunch, so the young gallants sneaked from the proprieties of the Bunch off to "times" with bouncing young women whom they picked up in department stores and at hotel coatrooms. Once Babbitt tried to accompany them. There was a motor car, a bottle of whisky, and for him a grubby shrieking cash-girl from Parcher and Stein's. He sat beside her and worried. He was apparently expected to "jolly her along," but when she sang out, "Hey, leggo, quit crushing me cootie-garage," he did not quite know how to go on. They sat in the back room of a saloon, and Babbitt had a headache, was confused by their new slang, looked at them benevolently, wanted to go home, and had a drink—a good many drinks.

Two evenings after, Fulton Bemis, the surly older man of the Bunch, took Babbitt aside and grunted, "Look here, it's none of my business, and God knows I always lap up my share of the hootch, but don't you think you better watch yourself? You're one of these enthusiastic chumps that always overdo things. D' you realize you're throwing in the booze as fast as you can, and you eat one cigarette right after another? Better cut it out for a while."

Babbitt tearfully said that good old Fult was a prince, and yes, he certainly would cut it out, and thereafter he lighted a cigarette and took a drink and had a terrific quarrel with Tanis when she caught him being affectionate with Carrie Nork.

Next morning he hated himself that he should have sunk into a position where a fifteenth-rater like Fulton Bemis could rebuke him. He perceived that, since he was making love to every woman possible, Tanis was no longer his one pure star, and he wondered whether she had ever been anything more to him than A Woman. And if Bemis had spoken to him, were other people talking about him? He suspiciously watched the men at the Athletic Club that noon. It seemed to him that they were uneasy. They had been talking about him then? He was angry. He became belligerent. He not only defended Seneca Doane but even made fun of the Y.M.C.A. Vergil Gunch was rather brief in his answers.

Afterward Babbitt was not angry. He was afraid. He did not go to the next lunch of the Boosters' Club but hid in a cheap restaurant, and, while he munched a ham-and-egg sandwich and sipped coffee from a cup on the arm of his chair, he worried.

Four days later, when the Bunch were having one of their best parties, Babbitt drove them to the skating-rink which had been laid out on the Chaloosa River. After a thaw the streets had frozen in smooth ice. Down those wide endless streets the wind rattled between the rows of wooden houses, and the whole Bellevue district seemed a frontier town. Even with skid chains on all four wheels, Babbitt was afraid of sliding, and when he came to the long slide of a hill he crawled down, both brakes on. Slewing round a corner came a less cautious car. It skidded, it almost raked them with its rear fenders. In relief at their escape the Bunch—Tanis, Minnie Sonntag, Pete, Fulton Bemis—shouted "Oh, baby," and waved their hands to the agitated other driver. Then Babbitt saw Professor Pumphrey laboriously crawling up hill, afoot, staring owlishly at the revelers. He was sure that Pumphrey recognized him and saw Tanis kiss him as she crowed, "You're such a good driver!"

At lunch next day he probed Pumphrey with "Out last night with my brother and some friends of his. Gosh, what driving! Slippery 's glass. Thought I saw you hiking up the Bellevue Avenue Hill."

"No, I wasn't—I didn't see you," said Pumphrey, hastily, rather guiltily.

Perhaps two days afterward Babbitt took Tanis to lunch at the Hotel Thornleigh. She who had seemed well content to wait for him at her flat had begun to hint with melancholy smiles that he must think but little of her if he never introduced her to his friends, if he was unwilling to be seen with her except at the movies. He thought of taking her to the "ladies' annex" of the Athletic Club, but that was too dangerous. He would have to introduce her and, oh, people might misunderstand and— He compromised on the Thornleigh.

She was unusually smart, all in black: small black tricorne hat, short black caracul coat, loose and swinging, and austere high-necked black velvet frock at a time when most street costumes were like evening gowns. Perhaps she was too smart. Every one in the gold and oak restaurant of the Thornleigh was staring at her as Babbitt followed her to a table. He uneasily hoped that the head-waiter would give them a discreet place behind a pillar, but they were stationed on the center aisle. Tanis seemed not to notice her admirers; she smiled at Babbitt with a lavish "Oh, isn't this nice! What a peppy-looking orchestra!" Babbitt had difficulty in being lavish in return, for two tables away he saw Vergil Gunch. All through the meal Gunch watched them, while Babbitt watched himself being watched and lugubriously tried to keep from spoiling Tanis's gaiety. "I felt like a spree to-day," she rippled. "I love the Thornleigh, don't you? It's so live and yet so—so refined."

He made talk about the Thornleigh, the service, the food, the people he recognized in the restaurant, all but Vergil Gunch. There did not seem to be anything else to talk of. He smiled conscientiously at her fluttering jests; he agreed with her that Minnie Sonntag was "so hard to get along with," and young Pete "such a silly lazy kid, really just no good at all." But he himself had nothing to say. He considered telling her his worries about Gunch, but—"oh, gosh, it was too much work to go into the whole thing and explain about Verg and everything."

He was relieved when he put Tanis on a trolley; he was cheerful in the familiar simplicities of his office.

At four o'clock Vergil Gunch called on him.

Babbitt was agitated, but Gunch began in a friendly way:

"How's the boy? Say, some of us are getting up a scheme we'd kind of like to have you come in on."

"Fine, Verg. Shoot."

"You know during the war we had the Undesirable Element, the Reds and walking delegates and just the plain common grouches, dead to rights, and so did we for quite a while after the war, but folks forget about the danger and that gives these cranks a chance to begin working underground again, especially a lot of these parlor socialists. Well, it's up to the folks that do a little sound thinking to make a conscious effort to keep bucking these fellows. Some guy back East has organized a society called the Good Citizens' League for just that purpose. Of course the Chamber of Commerce and the American Legion and so on do a fine work in keeping the decent people in the saddle, but they're devoted to so many other causes that they can't attend to this one problem properly. But the Good Citizens' League, the G.C.L., they stick right to it. Oh, the G.C.L. has to have some other ostensible purposes—frinstance here in Zenith I think it ought to support the park-extension project and the City Planning Committee—and then, too, it should have a social aspect, being made up of the best people—have dances and so on, especially as one of the best ways it can put the kibosh on cranks is to apply this social boycott business to folks big enough so you can't reach 'em otherwise. Then if that don't work, the G.C.L. can finally send a little delegation around to inform folks that get too flip that they got to conform to decent standards and quit shooting off their mouths so free. Don't it sound like the organization could do a great work? We've already got some of the strongest men in town, and of course we want you in. How about it?"

Babbitt was uncomfortable. He felt a compulsion back to all the standards he had so vaguely yet so desperately been fleeing. He fumbled:

"I suppose you'd especially light on fellows like Seneca Doane and try to make 'em—"

"You bet your sweet life we would! Look here, old Georgie: I've never for one moment believed you meant it when you've defended Doane, and the strikers and so on, at the Club. I knew you were simply kidding those poor galoots like Sid Finkelstein. . . . At least I certainly hope you were kidding!"

"Oh, well—sure— Course you might say—" Babbitt was conscious of how feeble he sounded, conscious of Gunch's mature and relentless eye. "Gosh, you know where I stand! I'm no labor agitator! I'm a business man, first, last, and all the time! But—but honestly, I don't think Doane means so badly, and you got to remember he's an old friend of mine."

"George, when it comes right down to a struggle between decency and the security of our homes on the one hand, and red ruin and those lazy dogs plotting for free beer on the other, you got to give up even old friendships. 'He that is not with me is against me.'"

"Ye-es, I suppose—"

"How about it? Going to join us in the Good Citizens' League?"

"I'll have to think it over, Verg."

"All right, just as you say." Babbitt was relieved to be let off so easily, but Gunch went on: "George, I don't know what's come over you; none of us do; and we've talked a lot about you. For a while we figured out you'd been upset by what happened to poor Riesling, and we forgave you for any fool things you said, but that's old stuff now, George, and we can't make out what's got into you. Personally, I've always defended you, but I must say it's getting too much for me. All the boys at the Athletic Club and the Boosters' are sore, the way you go on deliberately touting Doane and his bunch of hell-hounds, and talking about being liberal—which means being wishy-washy— and even saying this preacher guy Ingram isn't a professional free-love artist. And then the way you been carrying on personally! Joe Pumphrey says he saw you out the other night with a gang of totties, all stewed to the gills, and here to-day coming right into the Thornleigh with a—well, she may be all right and a perfect lady, but she certainly did look like a pretty gay skirt for a fellow with his wife out of town to be taking to lunch. Didn't look well. What the devil has come over you, George?"

"Strikes me there's a lot of fellows that know more about my personal business than I do myself!"

"Now don't go getting sore at me because I come out flat-footed like a friend and say what I think instead of tattling behind your back, the way a whole lot of 'em do. I tell you, George, you got a position in the community, and the community expects you to live up to it. And— Better think over joining the Good Citizens' League. See you about it later."

He was gone.

That evening Babbitt dined alone. He saw all the Clan of Good Fellows peering through the restaurant window, spying on him. Fear sat beside him, and he told himself that to-night he would not go to Tanis's flat; and he did not go . . . till late.

# 30

The summer before, Mrs. Babbitt's letters had crackled with desire to return to Zenith. Now they said nothing of returning, but a wistful "I suppose everything is going on all right without me" among her dry chronicles of weather and sicknesses hinted to Babbitt that he hadn't been very urgent about her coming. He worried it:

"If she were here, and I went on raising Cain like I been doing, she'd have a fit. I got to get hold of myself. I got to learn to play around and yet not make a fool of myself. I can do it, too, if folks like Verg Gunch 'll let me alone, and Myra 'll stay away. But—poor kid, she sounds lonely. Lord, I don't want to hurt her!"

Impulsively he wrote that they missed her, and her next letter said happily that she was coming home.

He persuaded himself that he was eager to see her. He bought roses for the house, he ordered squab for dinner, he had the car cleaned and polished. All the way home from the station with her he was adequate in his accounts of Ted's success in basket-ball at the university, but before they reached Floral Heights there was nothing more to say, and already he felt the force of her stolidity, wondered whether he could remain a good husband and still sneak out of the house this evening for half an hour with the Bunch. When he had housed the car he blundered upstairs, into the familiar talcum-scented warmth of her presence, blaring, "Help you unpack your bag?"

"No, I can do it."

Slowly she turned, holding up a small box, and slowly she said, "I brought you a present, just a new cigar-case. I don't know if you'd care to have it—"

She was the lonely girl, the brown appealing Myra Thompson, whom he had married, and he almost wept for pity as he kissed her and besought, "Oh, honey, honey, *care* to have it? Of course I do! I'm awful proud you brought it to me. And I needed a new case badly."

He wondered how he would get rid of the case he had bought the week before.

"And you really are glad to see me back?"

"Why, you poor kiddy, what you been worrying about?"

"Well, you didn't seem to miss me very much."

By the time he had finished his stint of lying they were firmly bound again. By ten that evening it seemed improbable that she had ever been away. There was but one difference: the problem of remaining a respectable husband, a Floral Heights husband, yet seeing Tanis and the Bunch with frequency. He had promised to telephone to Tanis that evening, and now it was melodramatically impossible. He prowled about the telephone, impulsively thrusting out a hand to lift the receiver, but never quite daring to risk it. Nor could he find a reason for slipping down to the drug store on Smith Street, with its telephone-booth. He was laden with responsibility till he threw it off with the speculation: "Why the deuce should I fret so about not being able to 'phone Tanis? She can get along without me. I don't owe her anything. She's a fine girl, but I've given her just as much as she has me. . . . Oh, damn these women and the way they get you all tied up in complications!"

II

For a week he was attentive to his wife, took her to the theater, to dinner at the Littlefields'; then the old weary dodging and shifting began, and at least two evenings a week he spent with the Bunch. He still made pretense of going to the Elks and to committee-meetings but less and less did he trouble to have his excuses interesting, less and less did she affect to believe them. He was certain that she knew he was associating with what Floral Heights called "a sporty crowd," yet neither of them acknowledged it. In matrimonial geography the distance between the first mute recognition of a break and the admission thereof is as great as the distance between the first naïve faith and the first doubting.

As he began to drift away he also began to see her as a human being, to like and dislike her instead of accepting her as a comparatively movable part of the furniture, and he compassionated that husband-and-wife relation which, in twenty-five years of married life, had become a separate and real entity. He recalled their high lights: the summer vacation in Virginia meadows under the blue wall of the mountains; their motor tour through Ohio, and the exploration of Cleveland, Cincinnati, and Columbus; the birth of Verona; their building of this new house, planned to comfort them through a happy old age—chokingly they had said that it might be the last home either of them would ever have. Yet his most softening remembrance of these dear moments did not keep him from barking at dinner, "Yep, going out f' few hours. Don't sit up for me."

He did not dare now to come home drunk, and though he rejoiced in his return to high morality and spoke with gravity to Pete and Fulton Bemis about their drinking, he prickled at Myra's unexpressed criticisms and sulkily meditated that a "fellow couldn't ever learn to handle himself if he was always bossed by a lot of women."

He no longer wondered if Tanis wasn't a bit worn and sentimental. In contrast to the complacent Myra he saw her as swift and air-borne and radiant, a fire-spirit tenderly stooping to the hearth, and however pitifully he brooded on his wife, he longed to be with Tanis.

Then Mrs. Babbitt tore the decent cloak from her unhappiness and the astounded male discovered that she was having a small determined rebellion of her own.

### III

They were beside the fireless fire-place, in the evening.

"Georgie," she said, "you haven't given me the list of your household expenses while I was away."

"No, I— Haven't made it out yet." Very affably: "Gosh, we must try to keep down expenses this year."

"That's so. I don't know where all the money goes to. I try to economize, but it just seems to evaporate."

"I suppose I oughtn't to spend so much on cigars. Don't know but what I'll cut down my smoking, maybe cut it out entirely. I was thinking of a good way to do it, the other day: start on these cubeb cigarettes, and they'd kind of disgust me with smoking."

"Oh, I do wish you would! It isn't that I care, but honestly, George, it is so bad for you to smoke so much. Don't you think you could reduce the amount? And George—I notice now, when you come home from these lodges and all, that sometimes you smell of whisky. Dearie, you know I don't worry so much about the moral side of it, but you have a weak stomach and you can't stand all this drinking."

"Weak stomach, hell! I guess I can carry my booze about as well as most folks!"

"Well, I do think you ought to be careful. Don't you see, dear, I don't want you to get sick."

"Sick, rats! I'm not a baby! I guess I ain't going to get sick just because maybe once a week I shoot a highball! That's the trouble with women. They always exaggerate so."

"George, I don't think you ought to talk that way when I'm just speaking for your own good."

"I know, but gosh all fishhooks, that's the trouble with women! They're always criticizing and commenting and bringing things up, and then they say it's 'for your own good'!"

"Why, George, that's not a nice way to talk, to answer me so short."

"Well, I didn't mean to answer short, but gosh, talking as if I was a kindergarten brat, not able to tote one highball without calling for the St. Mary's ambulance! A find idea you must have of me!"

"Oh, it isn't that; it's just—I don't want to see you get sick and— My, I didn't know it was so late! Don't forget to give me those household accounts for the time while I was away."

"Oh, thunder, what's the use of taking the trouble to make 'em out now? Let's just skip 'em for that period."

"Why, George Babbitt, in all the years we've been married we've never failed to keep a complete account of every penny we've spent!"

"No. Maybe that's the trouble with us."

"What in the world do you mean?"

"Oh, I don't mean anything, only— Sometimes I get so darn sick and tired of all this routine and the accounting at the office and expenses at home and fussing and stewing and fretting and wearing myself out worrying over a lot of junk that doesn't really mean a doggone thing, and being so careful and— Good Lord, what do you think I'm made for? I could have been a darn good orator, and here I fuss and fret and worry—"

"Don't you suppose I ever get tired of fussing? I get so bored with ordering three meals a day, three hundred and sixty-five days a year, and ruining my eyes over that horrid sewing-machine, and looking after your clothes and Rone's and Ted's and Tinka's and everybody's, and the laundry, and darning socks, and going down to the Piggly Wiggly to market, and bringing my basket home to save money on the cash-and-carry and—*everything!*"

"Well, gosh," with a certain astonishment, "I suppose maybe you do! But talk about— Here I have to be in the office every single day, while you can go out all afternoon and see folks and visit with the neighbors and do any blinkin' thing you want to!"

"Yes, and a fine lot of good that does me! Just talking over the same old things with the same old crowd, while you have all sorts of interesting people coming in to see you at the office."

"Interesting! Cranky old dames that want to know why I haven't rented their dear precious homes for about seven times their value, and bunch of old crabs panning the everlasting daylights out of me because they don't receive every cent of their rentals by three P.M. on the second of the month! Sure! Interesting! Just as interesting as the smallpox!"

"Now, George, I will not have you shouting at me that way!"

"Well, it gets my goat the way women figure out that a man doesn't do a darn thing but sit on his chair and have lovey-dovey conferences with a lot of classy dames and give 'em the glad eye!"

"I guess you manage to give them a glad enough eye when they do come in."

"What do you mean? Mean I'm chasing flappers?"

"I should hope not—at your age!"

"Now you look here! You may not believe it— Of course all you see is fat little Georgie Babbitt. Sure! Handy man around the house! Fixes the furnace when the furnace-man doesn't show up, and pays the bills, but dull, awful dull! Well, you may not believe it, but there's some women that think old George Babbitt isn't such a bad scout! They think he's not so bad-looking, not so bad that it hurts anyway, and he's got a pretty good line of guff, and some even think he shakes a darn wicked Walkover at dancing!"

"Yes." She spoke slowly. "I haven't much doubt that when I'm away you manage to find people who properly appreciate you."

"Well, I just mean—" he protested, with a sound of denial. Then he was angered into semi-honesty. "You bet I do! I find plenty of folks, and doggone nice ones, that don't think I'm a weak-stomached baby!"

"That's exactly what I was saying! You can run around with anybody you please, but I'm supposed to sit here and wait for you. You have the chance to get all sorts of culture and everything, and I just stay home—"

"Well, gosh almighty, there's nothing to prevent your reading books and going to lectures and all that junk, is there?"

"George, I *told* you, I won't have you shouting at me like that! I don't know what's come over you. You never used to speak to me in this cranky way."

"I didn't mean to sound cranky, but gosh, it certainly makes me sore to get the blame because you don't keep up with things."

"I'm going to! Will you help me?"

"Sure. Anything I can do to help you in the culture-grabbing line—yours to oblige, G. F. Babbitt."

"Very well then, I want you to go to Mrs. Mudge's New Thought meeting with me, next Sunday afternoon."

"Mrs. Who's which?"

"Mrs. Opal Emerson Mudge. The field-lecturer for the American New Thought League. She's going to speak on 'Cultivating the Sun Spirit' before the League of the Higher Illumination, at the Thornleigh."

"Oh, punk! New Thought! Hashed thought with a poached egg! 'Cultivating the—' It sounds like 'Why is a mouse when it spins?' That's a fine spiel for a good Presbyterian to be going to, when you can hear Doc Drew!"

"Reverend Drew is a scholar and a pulpit orator and all that, but he hasn't got the Inner Ferment, as Mrs. Mudge calls it; he hasn't any inspiration for the New Era. Women need inspiration now. So I want you to come, as you promised."

IV

The Zenith branch of the League of the Higher Illumination met in the smaller ballroom at the Hotel Thornleigh, a refined apartment with pale green walls and plaster wreaths of roses, refined parquet flooring, and ultra-refined frail gilt chairs. Here were gathered sixty-five women and ten men. Most of the men slouched in their chairs and wriggled, while their wives sat rigidly at attention, but two of them—red-necked, meaty men—were as respectably devout as their wives. They were newly rich contractors who, having bought houses, motors, hand-painted pictures, and gentlemanliness, were now buying a refined ready-made philosophy. It had been a toss-up with them whether to buy New Thought, Christian Science, or a good stand-ard high-church model of Episcopalianism.

In the flesh, Mrs. Opal Emerson Mudge fell somewhat short of a prophetic aspect. She was pony-built and plump, with the face of a haughty Pekingese, a button of a nose, and arms so short that, despite her most indignant endeavors, she could not clasp her hands in front of her as she sat on the platform waiting. Her frock of taffeta and green velvet, with three strings of glass beads, and large folding eye-glasses dangling from a black ribbon, was a triumph of refinement.

Mrs. Mudge was introduced by the president of the League of the Higher Illumination, an oldish young woman with a yearning voice, white spats, and a mustache. She said that Mrs. Mudge would now make it plain to the simplest intellect how the Sun Spirit could be cultivated, and they who had been thinking about cultivating one would do well to treasure Mrs. Mudge's words, because even Zenith (and everybody knew that Zenith stood in the van of spiritual and New Thought progress) didn't often have the opportunity to sit at the feet of such an inspiring Optimist and Metaphysical Seer as Mrs. Opal Emerson Mudge, who had lived the Life of Wider Usefulness through Concentration, and in the Silence found those Secrets of Mental Control and the Inner Key which were immediately going to transform and bring Peace, Power, and Prosperity to the unhappy nations; and so, friends, would they for this precious gem-studded hour forget the Illusions of the Seeming Real, and in the actualization of the deep-lying Veritas pass, along with Mrs. Opal Emerson Mudge, to the Realm Beautiful.

If Mrs. Mudge was rather pudgier than one would like one's swamis, yogis, seers, and initiates, yet her voice had the real professional note. It was refined and optimistic; it was overpoweringly calm; it flowed on relentlessly, without one comma, till Babbitt was hypnotized. Her favorite word was "always," which she pronounced ollllle-ways. Her principal gesture was a pontifical but thoroughly ladylike blessing with two stubby fingers.

She explained about this matter of Spiritual Saturation:

"There are those—"

Of "those" she made a linked sweetness long drawn out; a far-off delicate call in a twilight minor. It chastely rebuked the restless husbands, yet brought them a message of healing.

"There are those who have seen the rim and outer seeming of the Logos there are those who have glimpsed and in enthusiasm possessed themselves of some segment and portion of the Logos there are those who thus flicked but not penetrated and radioactivated by the Dynamis go always to and fro assertative that they possess and are possessed of the Logos and the Metaphysikos but this word I bring you this concept I enlarge that those that are not utter are not even inceptive and that holiness is in its definitive essence always always always whole-iness and—"

It proved that the Essence of the Sun Spirit was Truth, but its Aura and Effluxion were Cheerfulness:

"Face always the day with the dawn-laugh with the enthusiasm of the initiate who perceives that all works together in the revolutions of the Wheel and who answers the strictures of the Soured Souls of the Destructionists with a Glad Affirmation—"

It went on for about an hour and seven minutes.

At the end Mrs. Mudge spoke with more vigor and punctuation:

"Now let me suggest to all of you the advantages of the Theosophical and Pantheistic Oriental Reading Circle, which I represent. Our object is to unite all the manifestations of the New Era into one cohesive whole—New Thought, Christian Science, Theosophy, Vedanta, Bahaism, and the other sparks from the one New Light. The subscription is but ten dollars a year, and for this mere pittance the members receive not only the monthly magazine, *Pearls of Healing*, but the privilege of sending right to the president,

our revered Mother Dobbs, any questions regarding spiritual progress, matrimonial problems, health and well-being questions, financial difficulties,
and—"

They listened to her with adoring attention. They looked genteel. They
looked ironed-out. They coughed politely, and crossed their legs with quietness, and in expensive linen handkerchiefs they blew their noses with a
delicacy altogether optimistic and refined.

As for Babbitt, he sat and suffered.

When they were blessedly out in the air again, when they drove home
through a wind smelling of snow and honest sun, he dared not speak. They
had been too near to quarreling, these days. Mrs. Babbitt forced it:

"Did you enjoy Mrs. Mudge's talk?"

"Well I— What did you get out of it?"

"Oh, it starts a person thinking. It gets you out of a routine of ordinary
thoughts."

"Well, I'll hand it to Opal she isn't ordinary, but gosh— Honest, did that
stuff mean anything to you?"

"Of course I'm not trained in metaphysics, and there was lots I couldn't
quite grasp, but I did feel it was inspiring. And she speaks so readily. I do
think you ought to have got something out of it."

"Well, I didn't! I swear, I was simply astonished, the way those women
lapped it up! Why the dickens they want to put in their time listening to
all that blaa when they—"

"It's certainly better for them than going to roadhouses and smoking and
drinking!"

"I don't know whether it is or not! Personally I don't see a whole lot of
difference. In both cases they're trying to get away from themselves—most
everybody is, these days, I guess. And I'd certainly get a whole lot more out
of hoofing it in a good lively dance, even in some dive, than sitting looking
as if my collar was too tight, and feeling too scared to spit, and listening to
Opal chewing her words."

"I'm sure you do! You're very fond of dives. No doubt you saw a lot of
them while I was away!"

"Look here! You been doing a hell of a lot of insinuating and hinting
around lately, as if I were leading a double life or something, and I'm damn
sick of it, and I don't want to hear anything more about it!"

"Why, George Babbitt! Do you realize what you're saying? Why, George,
in all our years together you've never talked to me like that!"

"It's about time then!"

"Lately you've been getting worse and worse, and now, finally, you're cursing and swearing at me and shouting at me, and your voice so ugly and
hateful— I just shudder!"

"Oh, rats, quit exaggerating! I wasn't shouting, or swearing either."

"I wish you could hear your own voice! Maybe you don't realize how it
sounds. But even so— You never used to talk like that. You simply *couldn't*
talk this way if something dreadful hadn't happened to you."

His mind was hard. With amazement he found that he wasn't particularly sorry. It was only with an effort that he made himself more agreeable: "Well, gosh, I didn't mean to get sore."

"George, do you realize that we can't go on like this, getting farther and farther apart, and you ruder and ruder to me? I just don't know what's going to happen."

He had a moment's pity for her bewilderment; he thought of how many deep and tender things would be hurt if they really "couldn't go on like this." But his pity was impersonal, and he was wondering, "Wouldn't it maybe be a good thing if— Not a divorce and all that, o' course, but kind of a little more independence?"

While she looked at him pleadingly he drove on in a dreadful silence.

# 31

When he was away from her, while he kicked about the garage and swept the snow off the running-board and examined a cracked hose-connection, he repented, he was alarmed and astonished that he could have flared out at his wife, and thought fondly how much more lasting she was than the flighty Bunch. He went in to mumble that he was "sorry, didn't mean to be grouchy," and to inquire as to her interest in movies. But in the darkness of the movie theater he brooded that he'd "gone and tied himself up to Myra all over again." He had some satisfaction in taking it out on Tanis Judique. "Hang Tanis anyway! Why'd she gone and got him into these mix-ups and made him all jumpy and nervous and cranky? Too many complications! Cut 'em out!"

He wanted peace. For ten days he did not see Tanis nor telephone to her, and instantly she put upon him the compulsion which he hated. When he had stayed away from her for five days, hourly taking pride in his resoluteness and hourly picturing how greatly Tanis must miss him, Miss McGoun reported, "Mrs. Judique on the 'phone. Like t' speak t' you 'bout some repairs."

Tanis was quick and quiet:

"Mr. Babbitt? Oh, George, this is Tanis. I haven't seen you for weeks— days, anyway. You aren't sick, are you?"

"No, just been terribly rushed. I, uh, I think there'll be a big revival of building this year. Got to, uh, got to work hard."

"Of course, my man! I want you to. You know I'm terribly ambitious for you; much more than I am for myself. I just don't want you to forget poor Tanis. Will you call me up soon?"

"Sure! Sure! You bet!"

"Please do. I sha'n't call you again."

He meditated, "Poor kid! . . . But gosh, she oughtn't to 'phone me at the office. . . . She's a wonder—sympathy—'ambitious for me.' . . . But gosh, I won't be made and compelled to call her up till I get ready. Darn these women, the way they make demands! It'll be one long old time before I see her! . . . But gosh, I'd like to see her to-night—sweet little thing. . . . Oh, cut that, son! Now you've broken away, be wise!"

She did not telephone again, nor he, but after five more days she wrote to him:

> Have I offended you? You must know, dear, I didn't mean to. I'm so lonely and I need somebody to cheer me up. Why didn't you come to the nice party we had at Carrie's last evening I remember she invited you. Can't you come around here to-morrow Thur evening? I shall be alone and hope to see you.

His reflections were numerous:

"Doggone it, why can't she let me alone? Why can't women ever learn a fellow hates to be bulldozed? And they always take advantage of you by yelling how lonely they are.

"Now that isn't nice of you, young fella. She's a fine, square, straight girl, and she does get lonely. She writes a swell hand. Nice-looking stationery. Plain. Refined. I guess I'll have to go see her. Well, thank God, I got till to-morrow night free of her, anyway.

"She's nice but— Hang it, I won't be *made* to do things! I'm not married to her. No, nor by golly going to be!

"Oh, rats, I suppose I better go see her."

### II

Thursday, the to-morrow of Tanis's note, was full of emotional crises. At the Roughnecks' Table at the club, Verg Gunch talked of the Good Citizens' League and (it seemed to Babbitt) deliberately left him out of the invitations to join. Old Mat Penniman, the general utility man at Babbitt's office, had Troubles, and came in to groan about them: his oldest boy was "no good," his wife was sick, and he had quarreled with his brother-in-law. Conrad Lyte also had Troubles, and since Lyte was one of his best clients, Babbitt had to listen to them. Mr. Lyte, it appeared, was suffering from a peculiarly interesting neuralgia, and the garage had overcharged him. When Babbitt came home, everybody had Troubles: his wife was simultaneously thinking about discharging the impudent new maid, and worried lest the maid leave; and Tinka desired to denounce her teacher.

"Oh, quit fussing!" Babbitt fussed. "You never hear me whining about my Troubles, and yet if you had to run a real-estate office— Why, to-day I found Miss Bannigan was two days behind with her accounts, and I pinched my finger in my desk, and Lyte was in and just as unreasonable as ever."

He was so vexed that after dinner, when it was time for a tactful escape to Tanis, he merely grumped to his wife, "Got to go out. Be back by eleven, should think."

"Oh! You're going out again?"

"Again! What do you mean 'again'! Haven't hardly been out of the house for a week!"

"Are you—are you going to the Elks?"

"Nope. Got to see some people."

Though this time he heard his own voice and knew that it was curt, though she was looking at him with wide-eyed reproach, he stumped into the hall, jerked on his ulster and fur-lined gloves, and went out to start the car.

He was relieved to find Tanis cheerful, unreproachful, and brilliant in a frock of brown net over gold tissue. "You poor man, having to come out on a night like this! It's terribly cold. Don't you think a small highball would be nice?"

"Now, by golly, there's a woman with savvy! I think we could more or less stand a highball if it wasn't too long a one—not over a foot tall!"

He kissed her with careless heartiness, he forgot the compulsion of her demands, he stretched in a large chair and felt that he had beautifully come home. He was suddenly loquacious; he told her what a noble and misunderstood man he was, and how superior to Pete, Fulton Bemis, and the other men of their acquaintance; and she, bending forward, chin in charming hand, brightly agreed. But when he forced himself to ask, "Well, honey, how's things with *you*," she took his duty-question seriously, and he discovered that she too had Troubles:

"Oh, all right but— I did get so angry with Carrie. She told Minnie that I told her that Minnie was an awful tightwad, and Minnie told me Carrie had told her, and of course I told her I hadn't said anything of the kind, and then Carrie found Minnie had told me, and she was simply furious because Minnie had told me, and of course I was just boiling because Carrie had told her I'd told her, and then we all met up at Fulton's—his wife is away—thank heavens!—oh, there's the dandiest floor in his house to dance on —and we were all of us simply furious at each other and— Oh, I do hate that kind of a mix-up, don't you? I mean—it's so lacking in refinement, but— And Mother wants to come and stay with me for a whole month, and of course I do love her, I suppose I do, but honestly, she'll cramp my style something dreadful—she never can learn not to comment, and she always wants to know where I'm going when I go out evenings, and if I lie to her she always spies around and ferrets around and finds out where I've been, and then she looks like Patience on a Monument till I could just scream. And oh, I *must* tell you— You know I *never* talk about myself; I just hate people who do, don't you? But— I feel so stupid to-night, and I know I must be boring you with all this but— What would you do about Mother?"

He gave her facile masculine advice. She was to put off her mother's stay. She was to tell Carrie to go to the deuce. For these valuable revelations she thanked him, and they ambled into the familiar gossip of the Bunch. Of what a sentimental fool was Carrie. Of what a lazy brat was Pete. Of how nice Fulton Bemis could be—"course lots of people think he's a regular old grouch when they meet him because he doesn't give 'em the glad hand the first crack out of the box, but when they get to know him, he's a corker."

But as they had gone conscientiously through each of these analyses before, the conversation staggered. Babbitt tried to be intellectual and deal with General Topics. He said some thoroughly sound things about Disarmament, and broad-mindedness and liberalism; but it seemed to him that General Topics interested Tanis only when she could apply them to Pete, Carrie, or themselves. He was distressingly conscious of their silence. He tried to stir her into chattering again, but silence rose like a gray presence and hovered between them.

"I, uh—" he labored. "It strikes me—it strikes me that unemployment is lessening."

"Maybe Pete will get a decent job, then."

Silence.

Desperately he essayed, "What's the trouble, old honey? You seem kind of quiet to-night."

"Am I? Oh, I'm not. But—do you really care whether I am or not?"

"Care? Sure! Course I do!"

"Do you really?" She swooped on him, sat on the arm of his chair.

He hated the emotional drain of having to appear fond of her. He stroked her hand, smiled up at her dutifully, and sank back.

"George, I wonder if you really like me at all?"

"Course I do, silly."

"Do you really, precious? Do you care a bit?"

"Why certainly! You don't suppose I'd be here if I didn't!"

"Now see here, young man, I won't have you speaking to me in that huffy way!"

"I didn't mean to sound huffy. I just—" In injured and rather childish tones: "Gosh almighty, it makes me tired the way everybody says I sound huffy when I just talk natural! Do they expect me to sing it or something?"

"Who do you mean by 'everybody'? How many other ladies have you been consoling?"

"Look here now, I won't have this hinting!"

Humbly: "I know, dear. I was only teasing. I know it didn't mean to talk huffy—it was just tired. Forgive bad Tanis. But say you love me, say it!"

"I love you. . . . Course I do."

"Yes, you do!" cynically. "Oh, darling, I don't mean to be rude but— I get so lonely. I feel so useless. Nobody needs me, nothing I can do for anybody. And you know, dear, I'm so active—I could be if there was something to do. And I *am* young, aren't I! I'm not an old thing! I'm not old and stupid, am I?"

He had to assure her. She stroked his hair, and he had to look pleased under that touch, the more demanding in its beguiling softness. He was impatient. He wanted to flee out to a hard, sure, unemotional man-world.

Through her delicate and caressing fingers she may have caught something of his shrugging distaste. She left him—he was for the moment buoyantly relieved—she dragged a footstool to his feet and sat looking beseechingly up at him. But as in many men the cringing of a dog, the flinching of a frightened child, rouse not pity but a surprised and jerky cruelty, so her humility only annoyed him. And he saw her now as middle-aged, as beginning to be old. Even while he detested his own thoughts, they rode him. She was old, he winced. Old! He noted how the soft flesh was creasing into webby folds beneath her chin, below her eyes, at the base of her wrists. A patch of her throat had a minute roughness like the crumbs from a rubber eraser. Old! She was younger in years than himself, yet it was sickening to have her yearning up at him with rolling great eyes—as if, he shuddered, his own aunt were making love to him.

He fretted inwardly, "I'm through with this asinine fooling around. I'm going to cut her out. She's a darn decent nice woman, and I don't want to hurt her, but it'll hurt a lot less to cut her right out, like a good clean surgical operation."

He was on his feet. He was speaking urgently. By every rule of self-esteem, he had to prove to her, and to himself, that it was her fault.

"I suppose maybe I'm kind of out of sorts to-night, but honest, honey, when I stayed away for a while to catch up on work and everything and figure out where I was at, you ought to have been cannier and waited till I came back. Can't you see, dear, when you *made* me come, I—being about an average bull-headed chump—my tendency was to resist? Listen, dear, I'm going now—"

"Not for a while, precious! No!"

"Yep. Right now. And then sometime we'll see about the future."

"What do you mean, dear, 'about the future'? Have I done something I oughtn't to? Oh, I'm so dreadfully sorry!"

He resolutely put his hands behind him. "Not a thing, God bless you, not a thing. You're as good as they make 'em. But it's just— Good Lord, do you realize I've got things to do in the world? I've got a business to attend to and, you might not believe it, but I've got a wife and kids that I'm awful fond of!" Then only during the murder he was committing was he able to feel nobly virtuous. "I want us to be friends but, gosh, I can't go on this way feeling I *got* to come up here every so often—"

"Oh, darling, darling, and I've always told you, so carefully, that you were absolutely free. I just wanted you to come around when you were tired and wanted to talk to me, or when you could enjoy our parties—"

She was so reasonable, she was so gently right! It took him an hour to make his escape, with nothing settled and everything horribly settled. In a barren freedom of icy Northern wind he sighed, "Thank God that's over! Poor Tanis, poor darling decent Tanis! But it is over. Absolute! I'm free!"

# 32

His wife was up when he came in. "Did you have a good time?" she sniffed.

"I did not. I had a rotten time! Anything else I got to explain?"

"George, how can you speak like— Oh, I don't know what's come over you!"

"Good Lord, there's nothing come over me! Why do you look for trouble all the time?" He was warning himself, "Careful! Stop being so disagreeable. Course she feels it, being left alone here all evening." But he forgot his warning as she went on:

"Why do you go out and see all sorts of strange people? I suppose you'll say you've been to another committee-meeting this evening!"

"Nope. I've been calling on a woman. We sat by the fire and kidded each other and had a whale of a good time, if you want to know!"

"Well— From the way you say it, I suppose it's my fault you went there! I probably sent you!"

"You did!"

"Well, upon my word—"

"You hate 'strange people' as you call 'em. If you had your way, I'd be as much of an old stick-in-the-mud as Howard Littlefield. You never want to have anybody with any git to 'em at the house; you want a bunch of old stiffs that sit around and gas about the weather. You're doing your level best to make me old. Well, let me tell you, I'm not going to have—"

Overwhelmed she bent to his unprecedented tirade, and in answer she mourned:

"Oh, dearest, I don't think that's true. I don't mean to make you old, I know. Perhaps you're partly right. Perhaps I am slow about getting acquainted with new people. But when you think of all the dear good times we have, and the supper-parties and the movies and all—"

With true masculine wiles he not only convinced himself that she had injured him but, by the loudness of his voice and the brutality of his attack, he convinced her also, and presently he had her apologizing for his having spent the evening with Tanis. He went up to bed well pleased, not only the master but the martyr of the household. For a distasteful moment after he had lain down he wondered if he had been altogether just. "Ought to be ashamed, bullying her. Maybe there is her side to things. Maybe she hasn't had such a bloomin' hectic time herself. But I don't care! Good for her to get waked up a little. And I'm going to keep free. Of her and Tanis and the fellows at the club and everybody. I'm going to run my own life!"

## II

In this mood he was particularly objectionable at the Boosters' Club lunch next day. They were addressed by a congressman who had just returned from an exhaustive three-months study of the finances, ethnology, political systems, linguistic divisions, mineral resources, and agriculture of Germany, France, Great Britain, Italy, Austria, Czechoslovakia, Jugoslavia, and Bulgaria. He told them all about those subjects, together with three funny stories about European misconceptions of America and some spirited words on the necessity of keeping ignorant foreigners out of America.

"Say, that was a mighty informative talk. Real he-stuff," said Sidney Finkelstein.

But the disaffected Babbitt grumbled, "Four-flusher! Bunch of hot air! And what's the matter with the immigrants? Gosh, they aren't all ignorant, and I got a hunch we're all descended from immigrants ourselves."

"Oh, you make me tired!" said Mr. Finkelstein.

Babbitt was aware that Dr. A. I. Dilling was sternly listening from across the table. Dr. Dilling was one of the most important men in the Boosters'. He was not a physician but a surgeon, a more romantic and sounding occupation. He was an intense large man with a boiling of black hair and a thick black mustache. The newspapers often chronicled his operations; he was professor of surgery in the State University; he went to dinner at the very best houses on Royal Ridge; and he was said to be worth several hundred thousand dollars. It was dismaying to Babbitt to have such a person glower at him. He hastily praised the congressman's wit, to Sidney Finkelstein, but for Dr. Dilling's benefit.

## III

That afternoon three men shouldered into Babbitt's office with the air of a Vigilante committee in frontier days. They were large, resolute, big-jawed men, and they were all high lords in the land of Zenith—Dr. Dilling the surgeon, Charles McKelvey the contractor, and, most dismaying of all, the white-bearded Colonel Rutherford Snow, owner of the *Advocate-Times*. In their whelming presence Babbitt felt small and insignificant.

"Well, well, great pleasure, have chairs, what c'n I do for you?" he babbled.

They neither sat nor offered observations on the weather.

"Babbitt," said Colonel Snow, "we've come from the Good Citizens' League. We've decided we want you to join. Vergil Gunch says you don't care to, but I think we can show you a new light. The League is going to combine with the Chamber of Commerce in a campaign for the Open Shop, so it's time for you to put your name down."

In his embarrassment Babbitt could not recall his reasons for not wishing to join the League, if indeed he had ever definitely known them, but he was passionately certain that he did not wish to join, and at the thought of their forcing him he felt a stirring of anger against even these princes of commerce.

"Sorry, Colonel, have to think it over a little," he mumbled.

McKelvey snarled, "That means you're not going to join, George?"

Something black and unfamiliar and ferocious spoke from Babbitt: "Now, you look here, Charley! I'm damned if I'm going to be bullied into joining anything, not even by you plutes!"

"We're not bullying anybody," Dr. Dilling began, but Colonel Snow thrust him aside with, "Certainly we are! We don't mind a little bullying, if it's necessary. Babbitt, the G.C.L. has been talking about you a good deal. You're supposed to be a sensible, clean, responsible man; you always have been; but here lately, for God knows what reason, I hear from all sorts of sources that you're running around with a loose crowd, and what's a whole lot worse, you've actually been advocating and supporting some of the most dangerous elements in town, like this fellow Doane."

"Colonel, that strikes me as my private business."

"Possibly, but we want to have an understanding. You've stood in, you and your father-in-law, with some of the most substantial and forward-looking interests in town, like my friends of the Street Traction Company, and my papers have given you a lot of boosts. Well, you can't expect the decent citizens to go on aiding you if you intend to side with precisely the people who are trying to undermine us."

Babbitt was frightened, but he had an agonized instinct that if he yielded in this he would yield in everything. He protested:

"You're exaggerating, Colonel. I believe in being broad-minded and liberal, but, of course, I'm just as much agin the cranks and blatherskites and labor unions and so on as you are. But fact is, I belong to so many organizations now that I can't do 'em justice, and I want to think it over before I decide about coming into the G.C.L."

Colonel Snow condescended, "Oh, no, I'm not exaggerating! Why the doctor here heard you cussing out and defaming one of the finest types of Republican congressmen, just this noon! And you have entirely the wrong idea about 'thinking over joining.' We're not begging you to join the G.C.L.—we're permitting you to join. I'm not sure, my boy, but what if you put it off it'll be too late. I'm not sure we'll want you then. Better think quick—better think quick!"

The three Vigilantes, formidable in their righteousness, stared at him in a taut silence. Babbitt waited through. He thought nothing at all, he merely waited, while in his echoing head buzzed, "I don't want to join—I don't want to join—I don't want to."

"All right. Sorry for you!" said Colonel Snow, and the three men abruptly turned their beefy backs.

### IV

As Babbitt went out to his car that evening he saw Vergil Gunch coming down the block. He raised his hand in salutation, but Gunch ignored it and crossed the street. He was certain that Gunch had seen him. He drove home in sharp discomfort.

His wife attacked at once: "Georgie dear, Muriel Frink was in this afternoon, and she says that Chum says the committee of this Good Citizens' League especially asked you to join and you wouldn't. Don't you think it would be better? You know all the nicest people belong, and the League stands for—"

"I know what the League stands for! It stands for the suppression of free speech and free thought and everything else! I don't propose to be bullied and rushed into joining anything, and it isn't a question of whether it's a good league or a bad league or what the hell kind of a league it is; it's just a question of my refusing to be told I got to—"

"But dear, if you don't join, people might criticize you."

"Let 'em criticize!"

"But I mean *nice* people!"

"Rats, I— Matter of fact, this whole League is just a fad. It's like all these other organizations that start off with such a rush and let on they're going to change the whole works, and pretty soon they peter out and everybody forgets all about 'em!"

"But if it's *the* fad now, don't you think you—"

"No, I don't! Oh, Myra, please quit nagging me about it. I'm sick of hearing about the confounded G.C.L. I almost wish I'd joined it when Verg first came around, and got it over. And maybe I'd 've come in to-day if the committee hadn't tried to bullyrag me, but, by God, as long as I'm a free-born independent American cit—"

"Now, George, you're talking exactly like the German furnace-man."

"Oh, I am, am I! Then, I won't talk at all!"

He longed, that evening, to see Tanis Judique, to be strengthened by her sympathy. When all the family were up-stairs he got as far as telephoning to her apartment-house, but he was agitated about it and when the janitor answered he blurted, "Nev' mind—I'll call later," and hung up the receiver.

## v

If Babbitt had not been certain about Vergil Gunch's avoiding him, there could be little doubt about William Washington Eathorne, next morning. When Babbitt was driving down to the office he overtook Eathorne's car, with the great banker sitting in anemic solemnity behind his chauffeur. Babbitt waved and cried, "Mornin'!" Eathorne looked at him deliberately, hesitated, and gave him a nod more contemptuous than a direct cut.

Babbitt's partner and father-in-law came in at ten:

"George, what's this I hear about some song and dance you gave Colonel Snow about not wanting to join the G.C.L.? What the dickens you trying to do? Wreck the firm? You don't suppose these Big Guns will stand your bucking them and springing all this 'liberal' poppycock you been getting off lately, do you?"

"Oh, rats, Henry T., you been reading bum fiction. There ain't any such a thing as these plots to keep folks from being liberal. This is a free country. A man can do anything he wants to."

"Course th' ain't any plots. Who said they was? Only if folks get an idea you're scatter-brained and unstable, you don't suppose they'll want to do business with you, do you? One little rumor about your being a crank would do more to ruin this business than all the plots and stuff that these fool storywriters could think up in a month of Sundays."

That afternoon, when the old reliable Conrad Lyte, the merry miser, Conrad Lyte, appeared, and Babbitt suggested his buying a parcel of land in the new residential section of Dorchester, Lyte said hastily, too hastily, "No, no, don't want to go into anything new just now."

A week later Babbitt learned, through Henry Thompson, that the officials of the Street Traction Company were planning another real-estate coup, and that Sanders, Torrey and Wing, not the Babbitt-Thompson Company, were to handle it for them.

"I figure that Jake Offutt is kind of leery about the way folks are talking about you. Of course Jake is a rock-ribbed old die-hard, and he probably advised the Traction fellows to get some other broker. George, you got to do something!" trembled Thompson.

And, in a rush, Babbitt agreed. All nonsense the way people misjudged him, but still— He determined to join the Good Citizens' League the next time he was asked, and in furious resignation he waited. He wasn't asked. They ignored him. He did not have the courage to go to the League and beg in, and he took refuge in a shaky boast that he had "gotten away with bucking the whole city. Nobody could dictate to *him* how he was going to think and act!"

He was jarred as by nothing else when the paragon of stenographers, Miss McGoun, suddenly left him, though her reasons were excellent—she needed a rest, her sister was sick, she might not do any more work for six months. He was uncomfortable with her successor, Miss Havstad. What Miss Havstad's given name was, no one in the office ever knew. It seemed improbable that she had a given name, a lover, a powder-puff, or a digestion. She was so impersonal, this slight, pale, industrious Swede, that it was vulgar to think of her as going to an ordinary home to eat hash. She was a perfectly oiled and enameled machine, and she ought, each evening, to have been dusted off and shut in her desk beside her too-slim, too-frail pencil points. She took dictation swiftly, her typing was perfect, but Babbitt became jumpy when he tried to work with her. She made him feel puffy, and at his best-beloved daily jokes she looked gently inquiring. He longed for Miss McGoun's return, and thought of writing to her.

Then he heard that Miss McGoun had, a week after leaving him, gone over to his dangerous competitors, Sanders, Torrey and Wing.

He was not merely annoyed; he was frightened. "Why did she quit, then?" he worried. "Did she have a hunch my business is going on the rocks? And it was Sanders got the Street Traction deal. Rats—sinking ship!"

Gray fear loomed always by him now. He watched Fritz Weilinger, the young salesman, and wondered if he too would leave. Daily he fancied slights. He noted that he was not asked to speak at the annual Chamber of Commerce dinner. When Orville Jones gave a large poker party and he was not invited, he was certain that he had been snubbed. He was afraid to go to lunch at the Athletic Club, and afraid not to go. He believed that he was spied on; that when he left the table they whispered about him. Everywhere he heard the rustling whispers: in the offices of clients, in the bank when he made a deposit, in his own office, in his own home. Interminably he wondered what They were saying of him. All day long in imaginary conversations he caught them marveling, "Babbitt? Why, say, he's a regular anarchist! You got to admire the fellow for his nerve, the way he turned liberal and, by golly, just absolutely runs his life to suit himself, but say, he's dangerous, that's what he is, and he's got to be shown up."

He was so twitchy that when he rounded a corner and chanced on two acquaintances talking—whispering—his heart leaped, and he stalked by like an embarrassed schoolboy. When he saw his neighbors Howard Littlefield and Orville Jones together, he peered at them, went indoors to escape their spying, and was miserably certain that they had been whispering—plotting —whispering.

Through all his fear ran defiance. He felt stubborn. Sometimes he decided that he had been a very devil of a fellow, as bold as Seneca Doane; sometimes he planned to call on Doane and tell him what a revolutionist he was, and never got beyond the planning. But just as often, when he heard the soft whispers enveloping him he wailed, "Good Lord, what have I done? Just played with the Bunch, and called down Clarence Drum about being such a high-and-mighty sodger. Never catch *me* criticizing people and trying to make them accept *my* ideas!"

He could not stand the strain. Before long he admitted that he would like to flee back to the security of conformity, provided there was a decent and creditable way to return. But, stubbornly, he would not be forced back; he would not, he swore, "eat dirt."

Only in spirited engagements with his wife did these turbulent fears rise to the surface. She complained that he seemed nervous, that she couldn't understand why he did not want to "drop in at the Littlefields'" for the evening. He tried, but he could not express to her the nebulous facts of his rebellion and punishment. And, with Paul and Tanis lost, he had no one to whom he could talk. "Good Lord, Tinka is the only real friend I have, these days," he sighed, and he clung to the child, played floor-games with her all evening.

He considered going to see Paul in prison, but, though he had a pale curt note from him every week, he thought of Paul as dead. It was Tanis for whom he was longing.

"I thought I was so smart and independent, cutting Tanis out, and I need her, Lord how I need her!" he raged. "Myra simply can't understand. All she sees in life is getting along by being just like other folks. But Tanis, she'd tell me I was all right."

Then he broke, and one evening, late, he did run to Tanis. He had not dared to hope for it, but she was in, and alone. Only she wasn't Tanis. She was a courteous, brow-lifting, ice-armored woman who looked like Tanis. She said, "Yes, George, what is it?" in even and uninterested tones, and he crept away, whipped.

His first comfort was from Ted and Eunice Littlefield.

They danced in one evening when Ted was home from the university, and Ted chuckled, "What's this I hear from Euny, dad? She says her dad says you raised Cain by boosting old Seneca Doane. Hot dog! Give 'em fits! Stir 'em up! This old burg is asleep!" Eunice plumped down on Babbitt's lap, kissed him, nestled her bobbed hair against his chin, and crowed, "I think you're lots nicer than Howard. Why is it," confidentially, "that Howard is such an old grouch? The man has a good heart, and honestly, he's awfully bright, but he never will learn to step on the gas, after all the training I've given him. Don't you think we could do something with him, dearest?"

"Why, Eunice, that isn't a nice way to speak of your papa," Babbitt observed, in the best Floral Heights manner, but he was happy for the first time in weeks. He pictured himself as the veteran liberal strengthened by the loyalty of the young generation. They went out to rifle the ice-box. Babbitt gloated, "If your mother caught us at this, we'd certainly get our come-uppance!" and Eunice became maternal, scrambled a terrifying number of eggs for them, kissed Babbitt on the ear, and in the voice of a brooding abbess marveled, "It beats the devil why feminists like me still go on nursing these men!"

Thus stimulated, Babbitt was reckless when he encountered Sheldon Smeeth, educational director of the Y.M.C.A. and choir-leader of the Chatham Road Church. With one of his damp hands Smeeth imprisoned Babbitt's thick paw while he chanted, "Brother Babbitt, we haven't seen you at church very often lately. I know you're busy with a multitude of details, but you mustn't forget your dear friends at the old church home."

Babbitt shook off the affectionate clasp—Sheldy liked to hold hands for a long time—and snarled, "Well, I guess you fellows can run the show without me. Sorry, Smeeth; got to beat it. G'day."

But afterward he winced, "If that white worm had the nerve to try to drag me back to the Old Church Home, then the holy outfit must have been doing a lot of talking about me, too."

He heard them whispering—whispering—Dr. John Jennison Drew, Cholmondeley Frink, even William Washington Eathorne. The independence seeped out of him and he walked the streets alone, afraid of men's cynical eyes and the incessant hiss of whispering.

# 33

He tried to explain to his wife, as they prepared for bed, how objectionable was Sheldon Smeeth, but all her answer was, "He has such a beautiful voice —so spiritual. I don't think you ought to speak of him like that just because you can't appreciate music!" He saw her then as a stranger; he stared bleakly at this plump and fussy woman with the broad bare arms, and wondered how she had ever come here.

In his chilly cot, turning from aching side to side, he pondered of Tanis. "He'd been a fool to lose her. He had to have somebody he could really talk to. He'd—oh, he'd *bust* if he went on stewing about things by himself. And Myra, useless to expect her to understand. Well, rats, no use dodging the issue. Darn shame for two married people to drift apart after all these years; darn rotten shame; but nothing could bring them together now, as long as he refused to let Zenith bully him into taking orders—and he was by golly not going to let anybody bully him into anything, or wheedle him or coax him either!"

He woke at three, roused by a passing motor, and struggled out of bed for a drink of water. As he passed through the bedroom he heard his wife groan. His resentment was night-blurred; he was solicitous in inquiring, "What's the trouble, hon?"

"I've got—such a pain down here in my side—oh, it's just—it tears at me."

"Bad indigestion? Shall I get you some bicarb?"

"Don't think—that would help. I felt funny last evening and yesterday, and then—oh!—it passed away and I got to sleep and— That auto woke me up."

Her voice was laboring like a ship in a storm. He was alarmed.

"I better call the doctor."

"No, no! It'll go away. But maybe you might get me an ice-bag."

He stalked to the bathroom for the ice-bag, down to the kitchen for ice. He felt dramatic in this late-night expedition, but as he gouged the chunk of ice with the dagger-like pick he was cool, steady, mature; and the old friendliness was in his voice as he patted the ice-bag into place on her groin, rumbling, "There, there, that'll be better now." He retired to bed, but he did not sleep. He heard her groan again. Instantly he was up, soothing her, "Still pretty bad, honey?"

"Yes, it just gripes me, and I can't get to sleep."

Her voice was faint. He knew her dread of doctors' verdicts and he did not inform her, but he creaked down-stairs, telephoned to Dr. Earl Patten, and waited, shivering, trying with fuzzy eyes to read a magazine, till he heard the doctor's car.

The doctor was youngish and professionally breezy. He came in as though it were sunny noontime. "Well, George, little trouble, eh? How is she now?"

he said busily as, with tremendous and rather irritating cheerfulness, he tossed his coat on a chair and warmed his hands at a radiator. He took charge of the house. Babbitt felt ousted and unimportant as he followed the doctor up to the bedroom, and it was the doctor who chuckled, "Oh, just little stomach-ache" when Verona peeped through her door, begging, "What is it, Dad, what is it?"

To Mrs. Babbitt the doctor said with amiable belligerence, after his examination, "Kind of a bad old pain, eh? I'll give you something to make you sleep, and I think you'll feel better in the morning. I'll come in right after breakfast." But to Babbitt, lying in wait in the lower hall, the doctor sighed, "I don't like the feeling there in her belly. There's some rigidity and some inflammation. She's never had her appendix out, has she? Um. Well, no use worrying, I'll be here first thing in the morning, and meantime she'll get some rest. I've given her a hypo. Good night."

Then was Babbitt caught up in the black tempest.

Instantly all the indignations which had been dominating him and the spiritual dramas through which he had struggled became pallid and absurd before the ancient and overwhelming realities, the standard and traditional realities, of sickness and menacing death, the long night, and the thousand steadfast implications of married life. He crept back to her. As she drowsed away in the tropic languor of morphia, he sat on the edge of her bed, holding her hand, and for the first time in many weeks her hand abode trustfully in his.

He draped himself grotesquely in his toweling bathrobe and a pink and white couch-cover, and sat lumpishly in a wing-chair. The bedroom was uncanny in its half-light, which turned the curtains to lurking robbers, the dressing-table to a turreted castle. It smelled of cosmetics, of linen, of sleep. He napped and woke, napped and woke, a hundred times. He heard her move and sigh in slumber; he wondered if there wasn't some officious brisk thing he could do for her, and before he could quite form the thought he was asleep, racked and aching. The night was infinite. When dawn came and the waiting seemed at an end, he fell asleep, and was vexed to have been caught off his guard, to have been aroused by Verona's entrance and her agitated "Oh, what _is_ it, Dad?"

His wife was awake, her face sallow and lifeless in the morning light, but now he did not compare her with Tanis; she was not merely A Woman, to be contrasted with other women, but his own self, and though he might criticize her and nag her, it was only as he might criticize and nag himself, interestedly, unpatronizingly, without the expectation of changing—or any real desire to change—the eternal essence.

With Verona he sounded fatherly again, and firm. He consoled Tinka, who satisfactorily pointed the excitement of the hour by wailing. He ordered early breakfast, and wanted to look at the newspaper, and felt somehow heroic and useful in not looking at it. But there were still crawling and totally unheroic hours of waiting before Dr. Patten returned.

"Don't see much change," said Patten. "I'll be back about eleven, and if you don't mind, I think I'll bring in some other world-famous pill-pedler for consultation, just to be on the safe side. Now George, there's nothing you can do. I'll have Verona keep the ice-bag filled—might as well leave that on, I guess—and you, you better beat it to the office instead of standing around her looking as if you were the patient. The nerve of husbands! Lot more neurotic than the women! They always have to horn in and get all the credit for feeling bad when their wives are ailing. Now have another nice cup of coffee and git!"

Under this derision Babbitt became more matter-of-fact. He drove to the office, tried to dictate letters, tried to telephone and, before the call was answered, forgot to whom he was telephoning. At a quarter after ten he returned home. As he left the down-town traffic and sped up the car, his face was as grimly creased as the mask of tragedy.

His wife greeted him with surprise. "Why did you come back, dear? I think I feel a little better. I told Verona to skip off to her office. Was it wicked of me to go and get sick?"

He knew that she wanted petting, and she got it, joyously. They were curiously happy when he heard Dr. Patten's car in front. He looked out of the window. He was frightened, With Patten was an impatient man with turbulent black hair and a hussar mustache—Dr. A. I. Dilling, the surgeon. Babbitt sputtered with anxiety, tried to conceal it, and hurried down to the door.

Dr. Patten was profusely casual: "Don't want to worry you, old man, but I thought it might be a good stunt to have Dr. Dilling examine her." He gestured toward Dilling as toward a master.

Dilling nodded in his curtest manner and strode up-stairs. Babbitt tramped the living-room in agony. Except for his wife's confinements there had never been a major operation in the family, and to him surgery was at once a miracle and an abomination of fear. But when Dilling and Patten came down again he knew that everything was all right, and he wanted to laugh, for the two doctors were exactly like the bearded physicians in a musical comedy, both of them rubbing their hands and looking foolishly sagacious.

Dr. Dilling spoke:

"I'm sorry, old man, but it's acute appendicitis. We ought to operate. Of course you must decide, but there's no question as to what has to be done."

Babbitt did not get all the force of it. He mumbled, "Well, I suppose we could get her ready in a couple o' days. Probably Ted ought to come down from the university, just in case anything happened."

Dr. Dilling growled, "Nope. If you don't want peritonitis to set in, we'll have to operate right away. I must advise it strongly. If you say go ahead, I'll 'phone for the St. Mary's ambulance at once, and we'll have her on the table in three-quarters of an hour."

"I—I— Of course, I suppose you know what— But great God, man, I can't get her clothes ready and everything in two seconds, you know! And in her state, so wrought-up and weak—"

"Just throw her hair-brush and comb and tooth-brush in a bag; that's all she'll need for a day or two," said Dr. Dilling, and went to the telephone.

Babbitt galloped desperately up-stairs. He sent the frightened Tinka out of the room. He said gaily to his wife, "Well, old thing, the doc thinks maybe we better have a little operation and get it over. Just take a few minutes—not half as serious as a confinement—and you'll be all right in a jiffy."

She gripped his hand till the fingers ached. She said patiently, like a cowed child, "I'm afraid—to go into the dark, all alone!" Maturity was wiped from her eyes; they were pleading and terrified. "Will you stay with me? Darling, you don't have to go to the office now, do you? Could you just go down to the hospital with me? Could you come see me this evening—if everything's all right? You won't have to go out this evening, will you?"

He was on his knees by the bed. While she feebly ruffled his hair, he sobbed, he kissed the lawn of her sleeve, and swore, "Old honey, I love you more than anything in the world! I've kind of been worried by business and everything, but that's all over now, and I'm back again."

"Are you really? George, I was thinking, lying here, maybe it would be a good thing if I just *went*. I was wondering if anybody really needed me. Or wanted me. I was wondering what was the use of my living. I've been getting so stupid and ugly—"

"Why, you old humbug! Fishing for compliments when I ought to be packing your bag! Me, sure, I'm young and handsome and a regular village cut-up and—" He could not go on. He sobbed again; and in muttered incoherencies they found each other.

As he packed, his brain was curiously clear and swift. He'd have no more wild evenings, he realized. He admitted that he would regret them. A little grimly he perceived that this had been his last despairing fling before the paralyzed contentment of middle-age. Well, and he grinned impishly, "it was one doggone good party while it lasted!" And—how much was the operation going to cost? "I ought to have fought that out with Dilling. But no, damn it, I don't care how much it costs!"

The motor ambulance was at the door. Even in his grief the Babbitt who admired all technical excellences was interested in the kindly skill with which the attendants slid Mrs. Babbitt upon a stretcher and carried her downstairs. The ambulance was a huge, suave, varnished, white thing. Mrs. Babbitt moaned, "It frightens me. It's just like a hearse, just like being put in a hearse. I want you to stay with me."

"I'll be right up front with the driver," Babbitt promised.

"No, I want you to stay inside with me." To the attendants: "Can't he be inside?"

"Sure, ma'am, you bet. There's a fine little camp-stool in there," the older attendant said, with professional pride.

He sat beside her in that traveling cabin with its cot, its stool, its active little electric radiator, and its quite unexplained calendar, displaying a girl eating cherries, and the name of an enterprising grocer. But as he flung out

his hand in hopeless cheerfulness it touched the radiator, and he squealed:
"Ouch! Jesus!"

"Why, George Babbitt, I won't have you cursing and swearing and blaspheming!"

"I know, awful sorry but— Gosh all fishhooks, look how I burned my hand! Gee whiz, it hurts! It hurts like the mischief! Why, that damn radiator is hot as—it's hot as—it's hotter 'n the hinges of Hades! Look! You can see the mark!"

So, as they drove up to St. Mary's Hospital, with the nurses already laying out the instruments for an operation to save her life, it was she who consoled him and kissed the place to make it well, and though he tried to be gruff and mature, he yielded to her and was glad to be babied.

The ambulance whirled under the hooded carriage-entrance of the hospital, and instantly he was reduced to a zero in the nightmare succession of cork-floored halls, endless doors open on old women sitting up in bed, an elevator, the anesthetizing room, a young interne contemptuous of husbands. He was permitted to kiss his wife; he saw a thin dark nurse fit the cone over her mouth and nose; he stiffened at a sweet and treacherous odor; then he was driven out, and on a high stool in a laboratory he sat dazed, longing to see her once again, to insist that he had always loved her, had never for a second loved anybody else or looked at anybody else. In the laboratory he was conscious only of a decayed object preserved in a bottle of yellowing alcohol. It made him very sick, but he could not take his eyes from it. He was more aware of it than of waiting. His mind floated in abeyance, coming back always to that horrible bottle. To escape it he opened the door to the right, hoping to find a sane and business-like office. He realized that he was looking into the operating-room; in one glance he took in Dr. Dilling, strange in white gown and bandaged head, bending over the steel table with its screws and wheels, then nurses holding basins and cotton sponges, and a swathed thing, just a lifeless chin and a mound of white in the midst of which was a square of sallow flesh with a gash a little bloody at the edges, protruding from the gash a cluster of forceps like clinging parasites.

He shut the door with haste. It may be that his frightened repentance of the night and morning had not eaten in, but this dehumanizing interment of her who had been so pathetically human shook him utterly, and as he crouched again on the high stool in the laboratory he swore faith to his wife . . . to Zenith . . . to business efficiency . . . to the Boosters' Club . . . to every faith of the Clan of Good Fellows.

Then a nurse was soothing, "All over! Perfect success! She'll come out fine! She'll be out from under the anesthetic soon, and you can see her."

He found her on a curious tilted bed, her face an unwholesome yellow but her purple lips moving slightly. Then only did he really believe that she was alive. She was muttering. He bent, and heard her sighing, "Hard get real maple syrup for pancakes." He laughed inexhaustibly; he beamed on the nurse and proudly confided, "Think of her talking about maple syrup! By golly, I'm going to go and order a hundred gallons of it, right from Vermont!"

II

She was out of the hospital in seventeen days. He went to see her each afternoon, and in their long talks they drifted back to intimacy. Once he hinted something of his relations to Tanis and the Bunch, and she was inflated by the view that a Wicked Woman had captivated her poor George.

If once he had doubted his neighbors and the supreme charm of the Good Fellows, he was convinced now. You didn't, he noted, "see Seneca Doane coming around with any flowers or dropping in to chat with the Missus," but Mrs. Howard Littlefield brought to the hospital her priceless wine jelly (flavored with real wine); Orville Jones spent hours in picking out the kind of novels Mrs. Babbitt liked—nice love stories about New York millionaires and Wyoming cowpunchers; Louetta Swanson knitted a pink bed-jacket; Sidney Finkelstein and his merry brown-eyed flapper of a wife selected the prettiest nightgown in all the stock of Parcher and Stein.

All his friends ceased whispering about him, suspecting him. At the Athletic Club they asked after her daily. Club members whose names he did not know stopped him to inquire, "How's your good lady getting on?" Babbitt felt that he was swinging from bleak uplands down into the rich warm air of a valley pleasant with cottages.

One noon Vergil Gunch suggested, "You planning to be at the hospital about six? The wife and I thought we'd drop in." They did drop in. Gunch was so humorous that Mrs. Babbitt said he must "stop making her laugh because honestly it was hurting her incision." As they passed down the hall Gunch demanded amiably, "George, old scout, you were soreheaded about something, here a while back. I don't know why, and it's none of my business. But you seem to be feeling all hunky-dory again, and why don't you come join us in the Good Citizens' League, old man? We have some corking times together, and we need your advice."

Then did Babbitt, almost tearful with joy at being coaxed instead of bullied, at being permitted to stop fighting, at being able to desert without injuring his opinion of himself, cease utterly to be a domestic revolutionist. He patted Gunch's shoulder, and next day he became a member of the Good Citizens' League.

Within two weeks no one in the League was more violent regarding the wickedness of Seneca Doane, the crimes of labor unions, the perils of immigration, and the delights of golf, morality, and bank-accounts than was George F. Babbitt.

# 34

The Good Citizens' League had spread through the country, but nowhere was it so effective and well esteemed as in cities of the type of Zenith, commercial cities of a few hundred thousand inhabitants, most of which—though not all—lay inland, against a background of cornfields and mines and of small towns which depended upon them for mortgage-loans, table-manners, art, social philosophy and millinery.

To the League belonged most of the prosperous citizens of Zenith. They were not all of the kind who called themselves "Regular Guys." Besides these hearty fellows, these salesmen of prosperity, there were the aristocrats, that is, the men who were richer or had been rich for more generations: the presidents of banks and of factories, the land-owners, the corporation lawyers, the fashionable doctors, and the few young-old men who worked not at all but, reluctantly remaining in Zenith, collected luster-ware and first editions as though they were back in Paris. All of them agreed that the working-classes must be kept in their place; and all of them perceived that American Democracy did not imply any equality of wealth, but did demand a wholesome sameness of thought, dress, painting, morals, and vocabulary.

In this they were like the ruling-class of any other country, particularly of Great Britain, but they differed in being more vigorous and in actually trying to produce the accepted standards which all classes, everywhere, desire, but usually despair of realizing.

The longest struggle of the Good Citizens' League was against the Open Shop—which was secretly a struggle against all union labor. Accompanying it was an Americanization Movement, with evening classes in English and history and economics, and daily articles in the newspapers, so that newly arrived foreigners might learn that the true-blue and one hundred per cent. American way of settling labor-troubles was for workmen to trust and love their employers.

The League was more than generous in approving other organizations which agreed with its aims. It helped the Y.M.C.A. to raise a two-hundred-thousand-dollar fund for a new building. Babbitt, Vergil Gunch, Sidney Finkelstein, and even Charles McKelvey told the spectators at movie theaters how great an influence for manly Christianity the "good old Y." had been in their own lives; and the hoar and mighty Colonel Rutherford Snow, owner of the *Advocate-Times,* was photographed clasping the hand of Sheldon Smeeth of the Y.M.C.A. It is true that afterward, when Smeeth lisped, "You must come to one of our prayer-meetings," the ferocious Colonel bellowed, "What the hell would I do that for? I've got a bar of my own," but this did not appear in the public prints.

The League was of value to the American Legion at a time when certain of the lesser and looser newspapers were criticizing that organization of veterans of the Great War. One evening a number of young men raided the Zenith Socialist Headquarters, burned its records, beat the office staff, and agreeably dumped desks out of the window. All of the newspapers save the *Advocate-Times* and the *Evening Advocate* attributed this valuable but perhaps hasty direct-action to the American Legion. Then a flying squadron from the Good Citizens' League called on the unfair papers and explained that no ex-soldier could possibly do such a thing, and the editors saw the light, and retained their advertising. When Zenith's lone Conscientious Objector came home from prison and was righteously run out of town, the newspapers referred to the perpetrators as an "unidentified mob."

## II

In all the activities and triumphs of the Good Citizens' League Babbitt took part, and completely won back to self-respect, placidity, and the affection of his friends. But he began to protest, "Gosh, I've done my share in cleaning up the city. I want to tend to business. Think I'll just kind of slacken up on this G.C.L. stuff now."

He had returned to the church as he had returned to the Boosters' Club. He had even endured the lavish greeting which Sheldon Smeeth gave him. He was worried lest during his late discontent he had imperiled his salvation. He was not quite sure there was a Heaven to be attained, but Dr. John Jennison Drew said there was, and Babbitt was not going to take a chance.

One evening when he was walking past Dr. Drew's parsonage he impulsively went in and found the pastor in his study.

"Jus' minute—getting 'phone call," said Dr. Drew in business-like tones, then, aggressively, to the telephone: "'Lo—'lo! This Berkey and Hannis? Reverend Drew speaking. Where the dickens is the proof for next Sunday's calendar? Huh? Y' ought to have it here. Well, I can't help it if they're *all* sick! I got to have it to-night. Get an A.D.T. boy and shoot it up here quick."

He turned, without slackening his briskness. "Well, Brother Babbitt, what c'n I do for you?"

"I just wanted to ask— Tell you how it is, dominie: Here a while ago I guess I got kind of slack. Took a few drinks and so on. What I wanted to ask is: How is it if a fellow cuts that all out and comes back to his senses? Does it sort of, well, you might say, does it score against him in the long run?"

The Reverend Dr. Drew was suddenly interested. "And, uh, brother—the other things, too? Women?"

"No, practically, you might say, practically not at all."

"Don't hesitate to tell me, brother! That's what I'm here for. Been going on joy-rides? Squeezing girls in cars?" The reverend eyes glistened.

"No—no—"

"Well, I'll tell you. I've got a deputation from the Don't Make Prohibition a Joke Association coming to see me in a quarter of an hour, and one from the Anti-Birth-Control Union at a quarter of ten." He busily glanced at his watch. "But I can take five minutes off and pray with you. Kneel right down by your chair, brother. Don't be ashamed to seek the guidance of God."

Babbitt's scalp itched and he longed to flee, but Dr. Drew had already flopped down beside his desk-chair and his voice had changed from rasping efficiency to an unctuous familiarity with sin and with the Almighty. Babbitt also knelt, while Drew gloated:

"O Lord, thou seest our brother here, who has been led astray by manifold temptations. O Heavenly Father, make his heart to be pure, as pure as a little child's. Oh, let him know again the joy of a manly courage to abstain from evil—"

Sheldon Smeeth came frolicking into the study. At the sight of the two men he smirked, forgivingly patted Babbitt on the shoulder, and knelt beside him, his arm about him, while he authorized Dr. Drew's imprecations with moans of "Yes, Lord! Help our brother, Lord!"

Though he was trying to keep his eyes closed, Babbitt squinted between his fingers and saw the pastor glance at his watch as he concluded with a triumphant, "And let him never be afraid to come to Us for counsel and tender care, and let him know that the church can lead him as a little lamb."

Dr. Drew sprang up, rolled his eyes in the general direction of Heaven, chucked his watch into his pocket, and demanded, "Has the deputation come yet, Sheldy?"

"Yep, right outside," Sheldy answered, with equal liveliness; then, caressingly, to Babbitt, "Brother, if it would help, I'd love to go into the next room and pray with you while Dr. Drew is receiving the brothers from the Don't Make Prohibition a Joke Association."

"No—no thanks—can't take the time!" yelped Babbitt, rushing toward the door.

Thereafter he was often seen at the Chatham Road Presbyterian Church, but it is recorded that he avoided shaking hands with the pastor at the door.

III

If his moral fiber had been so weakened by rebellion that he was not quite dependable in the more rigorous campaigns of the Good Citizens' League nor quite appreciative of the church, yet there was no doubt of the joy with which Babbitt returned to the pleasures of his home and of the Athletic Club, the Boosters, the Elks.

Verona and Kenneth Escott were eventually and hesitatingly married. For the wedding Babbitt was dressed as carefully as was Verona; he was crammed into the morning coat he wore to teas thrice a year; and with a certain relief, after Verona and Kenneth had driven away in a limousine, he returned to the house, removed the morning coat, sat with his aching feet up on the davenport, and reflected that his wife and he could have the living-room to themselves now, and not have to listen to Verona and Kenneth worrying, in a cultured collegiate manner, about minimum wages and the Drama League.

But even this sinking into peace was less consoling than his return to being one of the best-loved men in the Boosters' Club.


IV


President Willis Ijams began that Boosters' Club luncheon by standing quiet and staring at them so unhappily that they feared he was about to announce the death of a Brother Booster. He spoke slowly then, and gravely:

"Boys, I have something shocking to reveal to you; something terrible about one of our own members."

Several Boosters, including Babbitt, looked disconcerted.

"A knight of the grip, a trusted friend of mine, recently made a trip up-state, and in a certain town, where a certain Booster spent his boyhood, he found out something which can no longer be concealed. In fact, he discovered the inward nature of a man whom we have accepted as a Real Guy and as one of us. Gentlemen, I cannot trust my voice to say it, so I have written it down."

He uncovered a large blackboard and on it, in huge capitals, was the legend:

George Follansbee Babbitt—oh you Folly!

The Boosters cheered, they laughed, they wept, they threw rolls at Babbitt, they cried, "Speech, speech! Oh you Folly!"

President Ijams continued:

"That, gentlemen, is the awful thing Georgie Babbitt has been concealing all these years, when we thought he was just plain George F. Now I want you to tell us, taking it in turn, what you've always supposed the F. stood for."

Flivver, they suggested, and Frog-face and Flathead and Farinaceous and Freezone and Flapdoodle and Foghorn. By the joviality of their insults Babbitt knew that he had been taken back to their hearts, and happily he rose.

"Boys, I've got to admit it. I've never worn a wrist-watch, or parted my name in the middle, but I will confess to 'Follansbee.' My only justification is that my old dad—though otherwise he was perfectly sane, and packed an awful wallop when it came to trimming the City Fellers at checkers—named me after the family doc, old Dr. Ambrose Follansbee. I apologize, boys. In my next what-d'you-call-it I'll see to it that I get named something really practical—something that sounds swell and yet is good and virile—something, in fact, like that grand old name so familiar to every household—that bold and almost overpowering name, Willis Jimjams Ijams!"

He knew by the cheer that he was secure again and popular; he knew that he would no more endanger his security and popularity by straying from the Clan of Good Fellows.


V


Henry Thompson dashed into the office, clamoring, "George! Big news! Jake Offutt says the Traction Bunch are dissatisfied with the way Sanders,

Torrey and Wing handled their last deal, and they're willing to dicker with us!"

Babbitt was pleased in the realization that the last scar of his rebellion was healed, yet as he drove home he was annoyed by such background thoughts as had never weakened him in his days of belligerent conformity. He discovered that he actually did not consider the Traction group quite honest. "Well, he'd carry out one more deal for them, but as soon as it was practicable, maybe as soon as old Henry Thompson died, he'd break away from all association with them. He was forty-eight; in twelve years he'd be sixty; he wanted to leave a clean business to his grandchildren. Course there was a lot of money in negotiating for the Traction people, and a fellow had to look at things in a practical way, only—" He wriggled uncomfortably. He wanted to tell the Traction group what he thought of them. "Oh, he couldn't do it, not now. If he offended them this second time, they would crush him. But—"

He was conscious that his line of progress seemed confused. He wondered what he would do with his future. He was still young; was he through with all adventuring? He felt that he had been trapped into the very net from which he had with such fury escaped and, supremest jest of all, been made to rejoice in the trapping.

"They've licked me; licked me to a finish!" he whimpered.

The house was peaceful, that evening, and he enjoyed a game of pinochle with his wife. He indignantly told the Tempter that he was content to do things in the good old-fashioned way. The day after, he went to see the purchasing-agent of the Street Traction Company and they made plans for the secret purchase of lots along the Evanston Road. But as he drove to his office he struggled, "I'm going to run things and figure out things to suit my-self—when I retire."

## VI

Ted had come down from the University for the week-end. Though he no longer spoke of mechanical engineering and though he was reticent about his opinion of his instructors, he seemed no more reconciled to college, and his chief interest was his wireless telephone set.

On Saturday evening he took Eunice Littlefield to a dance at Devon Woods. Babbitt had a glimpse of her, bouncing in the seat of the car, brilliant in a scarlet cloak over a frock of thinnest creamy silk. The two had not returned when the Babbitts went to bed, at half-past eleven. At a blurred indefinite time of late night Babbitt was awakened by the ring of the telephone and gloomily crawled down-stairs. Howard Littlefield was speaking:

"George, Euny isn't back yet. Is Ted?"

"No—at least his door is open—"

"They ought to be home. Eunice said the dance would be over at midnight. What's the name of those people where they're going?"

"Why, gosh, tell the truth, I don't know, Howard. It's some classmate of

Ted's, out in Devon Woods. Don't see what we can do. Wait, I'll skip up and ask Myra if she knows their name."

Babbitt turned on the light in Ted's room. It was a brown boyish room; disordered dresser, worn books, a high-school pennant, photographs of basket-ball teams and baseball teams. Ted was decidedly not there.

Mrs. Babbitt, awakened, irritably observed that she certainly did not know the name of Ted's host, that it was late, that Howard Littlefield was but little better than a born fool, and that she was sleepy. But she remained awake and worrying while Babbitt, on the sleeping-porch, struggled back into sleep through the incessant soft rain of her remarks. It was after dawn when he was aroused by her shaking him and calling "George! George!" in something like horror.

"Wha— wha— what is it?"

"Come here quick and see. Be quiet!"

She led him down the hall to the door of Ted's room and pushed it gently open. On the worn brown rug he saw a froth of rose-colored chiffon lingerie; on the sedate Morris chair a girl's silver slipper. And on the pillows were two sleepy heads—Ted's and Eunice's.

Ted woke to grin, and to mutter with unconvincing defiance, "Good morning! Let me introduce my wife—Mrs. Theodore Roosevelt Eunice Littlefield Babbitt, Esquiress."

"Good God!" from Babbitt, and from his wife a long wailing, "You've gone and—"

"We got married last evening. Wife! Sit up and say a pretty good morning to mother-in-law."

But Eunice hid her shoulders and her charming wild hair under the pillow.

By nine o'clock the assembly which was gathered about Ted and Eunice in the living-room included Mr. and Mrs. George Babbitt, Dr. and Mrs. Howard Littlefield, Mr. and Mrs. Kenneth Escott, Mr. and Mrs. Henry T. Thompson, and Tinka Babbitt, who was the only pleased member of the inquisition.

A crackling shower of phrases filled the room:

"At their age—" "Ought to be annulled—" "Never heard of such a thing in—" "Fault of both of them and—" "Keep it out of the papers—" "Ought to be packed off to school—" "Do something about it at once, and what I say is—" "Damn good old-fashioned spanking—"

Worst of them all was Verona. "*Ted!* Some way *must* be found to make you under*stand* how dreadfully *serious* this is, instead of standing *around* with that silly foolish *smile* on your face!"

He began to revolt. "Gee whittakers, Rone, you got married yourself, didn't you?"

"That's entirely different."

"You bet it is! They didn't have to work on Eu and me with a chain and tackle to get us to hold hands!"

"Now, young man, we'll have no more flippancy," old Henry Thompson ordered. "You listen to me."

"You listen to Grandfather!" said Verona.

"Yes, listen to your Grandfather!" said Mrs. Babbitt.

"Ted, you listen to Mr. Thompson!" said Howard Littlefield.

"Oh, for the love o' Mike, I am listening!" Ted shouted. "But you look here, all of you! I'm getting sick and tired of being the corpse in this post mortem! If you want to kill somebody, go kill the preacher that married us! Why, he stung me five dollars, and all the money I had in the world was six dollars and two bits. I'm getting just about enough of being hollered at!"

A new voice, booming, authoritative, dominated the room. It was Babbitt. "Yuh, there's too darn many putting in their oar! Rone, you dry up. Howard and I are still pretty strong, and able to do our own cussing. Ted, come into the dining-room and we'll talk this over."

In the dining-room, the door firmly closed, Babbitt walked to his son, put both hands on his shoulders. "You're more or less right. They all talk too much. Now what do you plan to do, old man?"

"Gosh, dad, are you really going to be human?"

"Well, I— Remember one time you called us 'the Babbitt men' and said we ought to stick together? I want to. I don't pretend to think this isn't serious. The way the cards are stacked against a young fellow to-day, I can't say I approve of early marriages. But you couldn't have married a better girl than Eunice; and way I figure it, Littlefield is darn lucky to get a Babbitt for a son-in-law! But what do you plan to do? Course you could go right ahead with the U., and when you'd finished—"

"Dad, I can't stand it any more. Maybe it's all right for some fellows. Maybe I'll want to go back some day. But me, I want to get into mechanics. I think I'd get to be a good inventor. There's a fellow that would give me twenty dollars a week in a factory right now."

"Well—" Babbitt crossed the floor, slowly, ponderously, seeming a little old. "I've always wanted you to have a college degree." He meditatively stamped across the floor again. "But I've never— Now, for heaven's sake, don't repeat this to your mother, or she'd remove what little hair I've got left, but practically, I've never done a single thing I've wanted to in my whole life! I don't know 's I've accomplished anything except just get along. I figure out I've made about a quarter of an inch out of a possible hundred rods. Well, maybe you'll carry things on further. I don't know. But I do get a kind of sneaking pleasure out of the fact that you knew what you wanted to do and did it. Well, those folks in there will try to bully you, and tame you down. Tell 'em to go to the devil! I'll back you. Take your factory job, if you want to. Don't be scared of the family. No, nor all of Zenith. Nor of yourself, the way I've been. Go ahead, old man! The world is yours!"

Arms about each other's shoulders, the Babbitt men marched into the living-room and faced the swooping family.

# Arrowsmith

# 1

The driver of the wagon swaying through forest and swamp of the Ohio wilderness was a ragged girl of fourteen. Her mother they had buried near the Monongahela—the girl herself had heaped with torn sods the grave beside the river of the beautiful name. Her father lay shrinking with fever on the floor of the wagon-box, and about him played her brothers and sisters, dirty brats, tattered brats, hilarious brats.

She halted at the fork in the grassy road, and the sick man quavered, "Emmy, ye better turn down towards Cincinnati. If we could find your Uncle Ed, I guess he'd take us in."

"Nobody ain't going to take us in," she said. "We're going on jus' long as we can. Going West! They's a whole lot of new things I aim to be seeing!"

She cooked the supper, she put the children to bed, and sat by the fire, alone.

That was the great-grandmother of Martin Arrowsmith.

## II

Cross-legged in the examining-chair in Doc Vickerson's office, a boy was reading "Gray's Anatomy." His name was Martin Arrowsmith, of Elk Mills, in the state of Winnemac.

There was a suspicion in Elk Mills—now, in 1897, a dowdy red-brick village, smelling of apples—that this brown-leather adjustable seat which Doc Vickerson used for minor operations, for the infrequent pulling of teeth and for highly frequent naps, had begun life as a barber's chair. There was also a belief that its proprietor must once have been called Doctor Vickerson, but for years he had been only The Doc, and he was scurfier and much less adjustable than the chair.

Martin was the son of J. J. Arrowsmith, who conducted the New York Clothing Bazaar. By sheer brass and obstinacy he had, at fourteen, become the unofficial, also decidedly unpaid, assistant to the Doc, and while the Doc was on a country call he took charge—though what there was to take charge of, no one could ever make out. He was a slender boy, not very tall; his hair and restless eyes were black, his skin unusually white, and the contrast gave him an air of passionate variability. The squareness of his head and a reasonable breadth of shoulders saved him from any appearance of effeminacy or of that querulous timidity which artistic young gentlemen call Sensitiveness. When he lifted his head to listen, his right eyebrow, slightly higher than the left, rose and quivered in his characteristic expression of energy, of independence, and a hint that he could fight, a look of impertinent inquiry which had been known to annoy his teachers and the Sunday School superintendent.

Martin was, like most inhabitants of Elk Mills before the Slavo-Italian immigration, a Typical Pure-bred Anglo-Saxon American, which means that he was a union of German, French, Scotch, Irish, perhaps a little Spanish, conceivably a little of the strains lumped together as "Jewish," and a great deal of English, which is itself a combination of Primitive Britain, Celt, Phoenician, Roman, German, Dane, and Swede.

It is not certain that, in attaching himself to Doc Vickerson, Martin was entirely and edifyingly controlled by a desire to become a Great Healer. He did awe his Gang by bandaging stone-bruises, dissecting squirrels, and explaining the astounding and secret matters to be discovered at the back of the physiology, but he was not completely free from an ambition to command such glory among them as was enjoyed by the son of the Episcopalian minister, who could smoke an entire cigar without becoming sick. Yet this afternoon he read steadily at the section on the lymphatic system, and he muttered the long and perfectly incomprehensible words in a hum which made drowsier the dusty room.

It was the central room of the three occupied by Doc Vickerson, facing on Main Street above the New York Clothing Bazaar. On one side of it was the foul waiting-room, on the other, the Doc's bedroom. He was an aged widower; for what he called "female fixings" he cared nothing; and the bedroom with its tottering bureau and its cot of frowsy blankets was cleaned only by Martin, in not very frequent attacks of sanitation.

This central room was at once business office, consultation-room, operating-theater, living-room, poker den, and warehouse for guns and fishing-tackle. Against a brown plaster wall was a cabinet of zoological collections and medical curiosities, and beside it the most dreadful and fascinating object known to the boy-world of Elk Mills—a skeleton with one gaunt gold tooth. On evenings when the Doc was away, Martin would acquire prestige among the trembling Gang by leading them into the unutterable darkness and scratching a sulfur match on the skeleton's jaw.

On the wall was a home-stuffed pickerel on a home-varnished board. Beside the rusty stove, a sawdust-box cuspidor rested on a slimy oilcloth worn through to the threads. On the senile table was a pile of memoranda of debts which the Doc was always swearing he would "collect from those dead-beats right now," and which he would never, by any chance, at any time, collect from any of them. A year or two—a decade or two—a century or two—they were all the same to the plodding doctor in the bee-murmuring town.

The most unsanitary corner was devoted to the cast-iron sink, which was oftener used for washing eggy breakfast plates than for sterilizing instruments. On its ledge were a broken test-tube, a broken fishhook, an unlabeled and forgotten bottle of pills, a nail-bristling heel, a frayed cigar-butt, and a rusty lancet stuck in a potato.

The wild raggedness of the room was the soul and symbol of Doc Vickerson; it was more exciting than the flat-faced stack of shoe-boxes in the New York Bazaar: it was the lure to questioning and adventure for Martin Arrowsmith.

III

The boy raised his head, cocked his inquisitive brow. On the stairway was the cumbersome step of Doc Vickerson. The Doc was sober! Martin would not have to help him into bed.

But it was a bad sign that the Doc should first go down the hall to his bedroom. The boy listened sharply. He heard the Doc open the lower part of the washstand, where he kept his bottle of Jamaica rum. After a long gurgle the invisible Doc put away the bottle and decisively kicked the doors shut. Still good. Only one drink. If he came into the consultation-room at once, he would be safe. But he was still standing in the bedroom. Martin sighed as the washstand doors were hastily opened again, as he heard another gurgle and a third.

The Doc's step was much livelier when he loomed into the office, a gray mass of a man with a gray mass of mustache, a form vast and unreal and undefined, like a cloud taking for the moment a likeness of humanity. With the brisk attack of one who wishes to escape the discussion of his guilt, the Doc rumbled while he waddled toward his desk-chair:

"What you doing here, young fella? What you doing here? I knew the cat would drag in something if I left the door unlocked." He gulped slightly; he smiled to show that he was being humorous—people had been known to misconstrue the Doc's humor.

He spoke more seriously, occasionally forgetting what he was talking about:

"Reading old Gray? That's right. Physician's library just three books: 'Gray's Anatomy' and Bible and Shakespeare. Study. You may become great doctor. Locate in Zenith and make five thousand dollars year—much as United States Senator! Set a high goal. Don't let things slide. Get training. Go college before go medical school. Study. Chemistry. Latin. Knowledge! I'm plug doc—got chick nor child—nobody—old drunk. But you—leadin' physician. Make five thousand dollars year.

"Murray woman's got endocarditis. Not thing I can do for her. Wants somebody hold her hand. Road's damn' disgrace. Culvert's out, beyond the grove. 'Sgrace.

"Endocarditis and—

"Training, that's what you got t' get. Fundamentals. Know chemistry. Biology. I nev' did. Mrs. Reverend Jones thinks she's got gastric ulcer. Wants to go city for operation. Ulcer, hell! She and the Reverend both eat too much.

"Why they don't repair that culvert— And don't be a booze-hoister like me, either. And get your basic science. I'll splain."

The boy, normal village youngster though he was, given to stoning cats and to playing pom-pom-pullaway, gained something of the intoxication of treasure-hunting as the Doc struggled to convey his vision of the pride of learning, the universality of biology, the triumphant exactness of chemistry. A fat old man and dirty and unvirtuous was the Doc; his grammar was doubtful, his vocabulary alarming, and his references to his rival, good Dr. Needham, were scandalous; yet he invoked in Martin a vision of making chemicals explode with much noise and stink and of seeing animalcules that no boy in Elk Mills had ever beheld.

The Doc's voice was thickening; he was sunk in his chair, blurry of eye and lax of mouth. Martin begged him to go to bed, but the Doc insisted:

"Don't need nap. No. Now you lissen. You don't appreciate but— Old man now. Giving you all I've learned. Show you collection. Only museum in whole county. Scientif' pioneer."

A hundred times had Martin obediently looked at the specimens in the brown, crackly-varnished bookcase: the beetles and chunks of mica; the embryo of a two-headed calf, the gallstones removed from a respectable lady whom the Doc enthusiastically named to all visitors. The Doc stood before the case, waving an enormous but shaky forefinger.

"Looka that butterfly. Name is *porthesia chrysorrhoea*. Doc Needham couldn't tell you that! He don't know what butterflies are called! He don't care if you get trained. Remember that name now?" He turned on Martin. "You payin' attention? You interested? *Huh?* Oh, the devil! Nobody wants to know about my museum—not a person. Only one in county but— I'm an old failure."

Martin asserted, "Honest, it's slick!"

"Look here! Look here! See that? In the bottle? It's an appendix. First one ever took out 'round here. I did it! Old Doc Vickerson, he did the first 'pendectomy in *this* neck of the woods, you bet! And first museum. It ain't— so big—but it's start. I haven't put away money like Doc Needham, but I started first c'lection—I started it!"

He collapsed in a chair, groaning, "You're right. Got to sleep. All in." But as Martin helped him to his feet he broke away, scrabbled about on his desk, and looked back doubtfully. "Want to give you something—start your training. And remember the old man. Will anybody remember the old man?"

He was holding out the beloved magnifying glass which for years he had used in botanizing. He watched Martin slip the lens into his pocket, he sighed, he struggled for something else to say, and silently he lumbered into his bedroom.

# 2

The state of Winnemac is bounded by Michigan, Ohio, Illinois, and Indiana, and like them it is half Eastern, half Midwestern. There is a feeling of New England in its brick and sycamore villages, its stable industries, and a tradi-

tion which goes back to the Revolutionary War. Zenith, the largest city in
the state, was founded in 1792. But Winnemac is Midwestern in its fields
of corn and wheat, its red barns and silos, and, despite the immense antiquity
of Zenith, many counties were not settled till 1860.

The University of Winnemac is at Mohalis, fifteen miles from Zenith.
There are twelve thousand students; beside this prodigy Oxford is a tiny
theological school and Harvard a select college for young gentlemen. The
University has a baseball field under glass; its buildings are measured by the
mile; it hires hundreds of young Doctors of Philosophy to give rapid instruction in Sanskrit, navigation, accountancy, spectacle-fitting, sanitary engineering, Provençal poetry, tariff schedules, rutabaga-growing, motor-car designing,
the history of Voronezh, the style of Matthew Arnold, the diagnosis of *myo-
hypertrophia kymoparalytica*, and department-store advertising. Its president
is the best money-raiser and the best after-dinner speaker in the United
States; and Winnemac was the first school in the world to conduct its extension courses by radio.

It is not a snobbish rich-man's college, devoted to leisurely nonsense. It
is the property of the people of the state, and what they want—or what they
are told they want—is a mill to turn out men and women who will lead
moral lives, play bridge, drive good cars, be enterprising in business, and
occasionally mention books, though they are not expected to have time to
read them. It is a Ford Motor Factory, and if its products rattle a little, they
are beautifully standardized, with perfectly interchangeable parts. Hourly
the University of Winnemac grows in numbers and influence, and by 1950
one may expect it to have created an entirely new world-civilization, a civilization larger and brisker and purer.

## II

In 1904, when Martin Arrowsmith was an Arts and Science Junior preparing for medical school, Winnemac had but five thousand students yet it
was already brisk.

Martin was twenty-one. He still seemed pale, in contrast to his black
smooth hair, but he was a respectable runner, a fair basket-ball center, and
a savage hockey-player. The co-eds murmured that he "looked so romantic,"
but as this was before the invention of sex and the era of petting-parties, they
merely talked about him at a distance, and he did not know that he could
have been a hero of amours. For all his stubbornness he was shy. He was
not entirely ignorant of caresses but he did not make an occupation of them.
He consorted with men whose virile pride it was to smoke filthy corncob
pipes and to wear filthy sweaters.

The University had become his world. For him Elk Mills did not exist.
Doc Vickerson was dead and buried and forgotten; Martin's father and
mother were dead, leaving him only enough money for his arts and medical
courses. The purpose of life was chemistry and physics and the prospect of
biology next year.

His idol was Professor Edward Edwards, head of the department of chemistry, who was universally known as "Encore." Edwards' knowledge of the history of chemistry was immense. He could read Arabic, and he infuriated his fellow chemists by asserting that the Arabs had anticipated all their researches. Himself, Professor Edwards never did researches. He sat before fires and stroked his collie and chuckled in his beard.

This evening Encore was giving one of his small and popular At Home's. He lolled in a brown-corduroy Morris chair, being quietly humorous for the benefit of Martin and half a dozen other fanatical young chemists, and baiting Dr. Norman Brumfit, the instructor in English. The room was full of heartiness and beer and Brumfit.

Every university faculty must have a Wild Man to provide thrills and to shock crowded lecture-rooms. Even in so energetically virtuous an institution as Winnemac there was one Wild Man, and he was Norman Brumfit. He was permitted, without restriction, to speak of himself as immoral, agnostic and socialistic, so long as it was universally known that he remained pure, Presbyterian, and Republican. Dr. Brumfit was in form, tonight. He asserted that whenever a man showed genius, it could be proved that he had Jewish blood. Like all discussions of Judaism at Winnemac, this led to the mention of Max Gottlieb, professor of bacteriology in the medical school.

Professor Gottlieb was the mystery of the University. It was known that he was a Jew, born and educated in Germany, and that his work on immunology had given him fame in the East and in Europe. He rarely left his small brown weedy house except to return to his laboratory, and few students outside of his classes had ever identified him, but everyone had heard of his tall, lean, dark aloofness. A thousand fables fluttered about him. It was believed that he was the son of a German prince, that he had immense wealth, that he lived as sparsely as the other professors only because he was doing terrifying and costly experiments which probably had something to do with human sacrifice. It was said that he could create life in the laboratory, that he could talk to the monkeys which he inoculated, that he had been driven out of Germany as a devil-worshiper or an anarchist, and that he secretly drank real champagne every evening at dinner.

It was the tradition that faculty-members did not discuss their colleagues with students, but Max Gottlieb could not be regarded as anybody's colleague. He was impersonal as the chill northeast wind. Dr. Brumfit rattled:

"I'm sufficiently liberal, I should assume, toward the claims of science, but with a man like Gottlieb— I'm prepared to believe that he knows all about material forces, but what astounds me is that such a man can be blind to the vital force that creates all others. He says that knowledge is worthless unless it is proven by rows of figures. Well, when one of you scientific sharks can take the genius of a Ben Jonson and measure it with a yardstick, then I'll admit that we literary chaps, with our doubtless absurd belief in beauty and loyalty and the world o' dreams, are off on the wrong track!"

Martin Arrowsmith was not exactly certain what this meant and he enthusiastically did not care. He was relieved when Professor Edwards from the midst of his beardedness and smokiness made a sound curiously like "Oh, hell!" and took the conversation away from Brumfit. Ordinarily Encore would have suggested, with amiable malice, that Gottlieb was a "crape-hanger" who wasted time destroying the theories of other men instead of making new ones of his own. But tonight, in detestation of such literary playboys as Brumfit, he exalted Gottlieb's long, lonely, failure-burdened effort to synthesize antitoxin, and his diabolic pleasure in disproving his own contentions as he would those of Ehrlich or Sir Almroth Wright. He spoke of Gottlieb's great book, "Immunology," which had been read by seven-ninths of all the men in the world who could possibly understand it—the number of these being nine.

The party ended with Mrs. Edwards' celebrated doughnuts. Martin tramped toward his boarding-house through a veiled spring night. The discussion of Gottlieb had roused him to a reasonless excitement. He thought of working in a laboratory at night, alone, absorbed, contemptuous of academic success and of popular classes. Himself, he believed, he had never seen the man, but he knew that Gottlieb's laboratory was in the Main Medical Building. He drifted toward the distant medical campus. The few people whom he met were hurrying with midnight timidity. He entered the shadow of the Anatomy Building, grim as a barracks, still as the dead men lying up there in the dissecting-room. Beyond him was the turreted bulk of the Main Medical Building, a harsh and blurry mass, high up in its dark wall a single light. He started. The light had gone out abruptly, as though an agitated watcher were trying to hide from him.

On the stone steps of the Main Medical, two minutes after, appeared beneath the arc-light a tall figure, ascetic, self-contained, apart. His swart cheeks were gaunt, his nose high-bridged and thin. He did not hurry, like the belated home-bodies. He was unconscious of the world. He looked at Martin and through him; he moved away, muttering to himself, his shoulders stooped, his long hands clasped behind him. He was lost in the shadows, himself a shadow.

He had worn the threadbare top-coat of a poor professor, yet Martin remembered him as wrapped in a black velvet cape with a silver star arrogant on his breast.

III

On his first day in medical school, Martin Arrowsmith was in a high state of superiority. As a medic he was more picturesque than other students, for medics are reputed to know secrets, horrors, exhilarating wickednesses. Men from the other departments go to their rooms to peer into their books. But also as an academic graduate, with a training in the basic sciences, he felt superior to his fellow medics, most of whom had but a high-school diploma, with perhaps one year in a ten-room Lutheran college among the cornfields.

For all his pride, Martin was nervous. He thought of operating, of making a murderous wrong incision; and with a more immediate, macabre fear, he thought of the dissecting-room and the stony, steely Anatomy Building. He had heard older medics mutter of its horrors: of corpses hanging by hooks, like rows of ghastly fruit, in an abominable tank of brine in the dark basement; of Henry the janitor, who was said to haul the cadavers out of the brine, to inject red lead into their veins, and to scold them as he stuffed them on the dumb-waiter.

There was prairie freshness in the autumn day but Martin did not heed. He hurried into the slate-colored hall of the Main Medical, up the wide stairs to the office of Max Gottlieb. He did not look at passing students, and when he bumped into them he grunted in confused apology. It was a portentous hour. He was going to specialize in bacteriology; he was going to discover enchanting new germs; Professor Gottlieb was going to recognize him as a genius, make him an assistant, predict for him— He halted in Gottlieb's private laboratory, a small, tidy apartment with racks of cotton-corked test-tubes on the bench, a place unimpressive and unmagical save for the constant-temperature bath with its tricky thermometer and electric bulbs. He waited till another student, a stuttering gawk of a student, had finished talking to Gottlieb, dark, lean, impassive at his desk in a cubbyhole of an office, then he plunged.

If in the misty April night Gottlieb had been romantic as a cloaked horseman, he was now testy and middle-aged. Near at hand, Martin could see wrinkles beside the hawk eyes. Gottlieb had turned back to his desk, which was heaped with shabby note-books, sheets of calculations, and a marvelously precise chart with red and green curves descending to vanish at zero. The calculations were delicate, minute, exquisitely clear; and delicate were the scientist's thin hands among the papers. He looked up, spoke with a hint of German accent. His words were not so much mispronounced as colored with a warm unfamiliar tint.

"Vell? Yes?"

"Oh, Professor Gottlieb, my name is Arrowsmith. I'm a medic freshman, Winnemac B.A. I'd like awfully to take bacteriology this fall instead of next year. I've had a lot of chemistry—"

"No. It is not time for you."

"Honest, I know I could do it now."

"There are two kinds of students that the gods give me. One kind they dump on me like a bushel of potatoes. I do not like potatoes, and the potatoes they do not ever seem to have great affection for me, but I take them and teach them to kill patients. The other kind—they are very few!—they seem for some reason that is not at all clear to me to wish a liddle bit to become scientists, to work with bugs and make mistakes. Those, ah, those, I seize them, I denounce them, I teach them right away the ultimate lesson of science, which is to wait and doubt. Of the potatoes, I demand nothing; of the foolish ones like you, who think I could teach them something, I demand everything. No. You are too young. Come back next year."

"But honestly, with my chemistry—"

"Have you taken physical chemistry?"

"No, sir, but I did pretty well in organic."

"Organic chemistry! Puzzle chemistry! Stink chemistry! Drugstore chemistry! Physical chemistry is power, it is exactness, it is life. But organic chemistry—that is a trade for pot-washers. No. You are too young. Come back in a year."

Gottlieb was absolute. His talon fingers waved Martin to the door, and the boy hastened out, not daring to argue. He slunk off in misery. On the campus he met that jovial historian of chemistry, Encore Edwards, and begged, "Say, Professor, tell me, is there any value for a doctor in organic chemistry?"

"Value? Why, it seeks the drugs that allay pain! It produces the paint that slicks up your house, it dyes your sweetheart's dress—and maybe, in these degenerate days, her cherry lips! Who the dickens has been talking scandal about my organic chemistry?"

"Nobody. I was just wondering," Martin complained, and he drifted to the College Inn where, in an injured and melancholy manner, he devoured an enormous banana-split and a bar of almond chocolate, as he meditated:

"I want to take bacteriology. I want to get down to the bottom of this disease stuff. I'll learn some physical chemistry. I'll show old Gottlieb, damn him! Some day I'll discover the germ of cancer or something, and then he'll look foolish in the face! . . . Oh, Lord, I hope I won't take sick, first time I go into the dissecting-room. . . . I want to take bacteriology—now!"

He recalled Gottlieb's sardonic face; he felt and feared his quality of dynamic hatred. Then he remembered the wrinkles, and he saw Max Gottlieb not as a genius but as a man who had headaches, who became agonizingly tired, who could be loved.

"I wonder if Encore Edwards knows as much as I thought he did? What *is* Truth?" he puzzled.

IV

Martin was jumpy on his first day of dissecting. He could not look at the inhumanly stiff faces of the starveling gray men lying on the wooden tables. But they were so impersonal, these lost old men, that in two days he was, like the other medics, calling them "Billy" and "Ike" and "the Parson," and regarding them as he had regarded animals in biology. The dissecting-room itself was impersonal: hard cement floor, walls of hard plaster between wire-glass windows. Martin detested the reek of formaldehyde; that and some dreadful subtle other odor seemed to cling about him outside the dissecting-room; but he smoked cigarettes to forget it, and in a week he was exploring arteries with youthful and altogether unholy joy.

His dissecting partner was the Reverend Ira Hinkley, known to the class by a similar but different name.

Ira was going to be a medical missionary. He was a man of twenty-nine, a graduate of Pottsburg Christian College and of the Sanctification Bible and Missions School. He had played football; he was as strong and nearly as large as a steer, and no steer ever bellowed more enormously. He was a bright and happy Christian, a romping optimist who laughed away sin and doubt, a joyful Puritan who with annoying virility preached the doctrine of his tiny sect, the Sanctification Brotherhood, that to have a beautiful church was almost as damnable as the debaucheries of card-playing.

Martin found himself viewing "Billy," their cadaver—an undersized, blotchy old man with a horrible little red beard on his petrified, vealy face— as a machine, fascinating, complex, beautiful, but a machine. It damaged his already feeble belief in man's divinity and immortality. He might have kept his doubts to himself, revolving them slowly as he dissected out the nerves of the mangled upper arm, but Ira Hinkley would not let him alone. Ira believed that he could bring even medical students to bliss, which, to Ira, meant singing extraordinarily long and unlovely hymns in a chapel of the Sanctification Brotherhood.

"Mart, my son," he roared, "do you realize that in this, what some might call a sordid task, we are learning things that will enable us to heal the bodies and comfort the souls of countless lost unhappy folks?"

"Huh! Souls. I haven't found one yet in old Billy. Honest, do you believe that junk?"

Ira clenched his fist and scowled, then belched with laughter, slapped Martin distressingly on the back, and clamored, "Brother, you've got to do better than that to get Ira's goat! You think you've got a lot of these fancy Modern Doubts. You haven't—you've only got indigestion. What you need is exercise and faith. Come on over to the Y.M.C.A. and I'll take you for a swim and pray with you. Why, you poor skinny little agnostic, here you have a chance to see the Almighty's handiwork, and all you grab out of it is a feeling that you're real smart. Buck up, young Arrowsmith. You don't know how funny you are, to a fellow that's got a serene faith!"

To the delight of Clif Clawson, the class jester, who worked at the next table, Ira chucked Martin in the ribs, patted him, very painfully, upon the head, and amiably resumed work, while Martin danced with irritation.

v

In college Martin had been a "barb"—he had not belonged to a Greek Letter secret society. He had been "rushed," but he had resented the condescension of the aristocracy of men from the larger cities. Now that most of his Arts classmates had departed to insurance offices, law schools, and banks, he was lonely, and tempted by an invitation from Digamma Pi, the chief medical fraternity.

Digamma Pi was a lively boarding-house with a billiard table and low prices. Rough and amiable noises came from it at night, and a good deal of singing about When I Die Don't Bury Me at All; yet for three years Digams had won the valedictory and the Hugh Loizeau Medal in Experimental Surgery. This autumn the Digams elected Ira Hinkley, because they had been gaining a reputation for dissipation—girls were said to have been smuggled in late at night—and no company which included the Reverend

Mr. Hinkley could possibly be taken by the Dean as immoral, which was an advantage if they were to continue comfortably immoral.

Martin had prized the independence of his solitary room. In a fraternity, all tennis rackets, trousers, and opinions are held in common. When Ira found that Martin was hesitating, he insisted, "Oh, come on in! Digam needs you. You do study hard—I'll say that for you—and think what a chance you'll have to influence The Fellows for good."

(On all occasions, Ira referred to his classmates as The Fellows, and frequently he used the term in prayers at the Y.M.C.A.)

"I don't want to influence anybody. I want to learn the doctor trade and make six thousand dollars a year."

"My boy, if you only knew how foolish you sound when you try to be cynical! When you're as old as I am, you'll understand that the glory of being a doctor is that you can teach folks high ideals while you soothe their tortured bodies."

"Suppose they don't want my particular brand of high ideals?"

"Mart, have I got to stop and pray with you?"

"No! Quit! Honestly, Hinkley, of all the Christians I ever met you take the rottenest advantages. You can lick anybody in the class, and when I think of how you're going to bully the poor heathen when you get to be a missionary, and make the kids put on breeches, and marry off all the happy lovers to the wrong people, I could bawl!"

The prospect of leaving his sheltered den for the patronage of the Reverend Mr. Hinkley was intolerable. It was not till Angus Duer accepted election to Digamma Pi that Martin himself came in.

Duer was one of the few among Martin's classmates in the academic course who had gone on with him to the Winnemac medical school. Duer had been the valedictorian. He was a silent, sharp-faced, curly-headed, rather handsome young man, and he never squandered an hour or a good impulse. So brilliant was his work in biology and chemistry that a Chicago surgeon had promised him a place in his clinic. Martin compared Angus Duer to a razor blade on a January morning; he hated him, was uncomfortable with him, and envied him. He knew that in biology Duer had been too busy passing examinations to ponder, to get any concept of biology as a whole. He knew that Duer was a tricky chemist, who neatly and swiftly completed the experiments demanded by the course and never ventured on original experiments which, leading him into a confused land of wondering, might bring him to glory or disaster. He was sure that Duer cultivated his manner of chill efficiency to impress instructors. Yet the man stood out so bleakly from a mass of students who could neither complete their experiments nor ponder nor do anything save smoke pipes and watch football-practice that Martin loved him while he hated him, and almost meekly he followed him into Digamma Pi.

Martin, Ira Hinkley, Angus Duer, Clif Clawson, the meaty class jester, and one "Fatty" Pfaff were initiated into Digamma Pi together. It was a noisy and rather painful performance, which included smelling asafetida. Martin was bored, but Fatty Pfaff was in squeaking, billowing, gasping terror.

Fatty was of all the new Freshmen candidates the most useful to Digamma Pi. He was planned by nature to be a butt. He looked like a distended hot-water bottle; he was magnificently imbecile; he believed everything, he knew nothing, he could memorize nothing; and anxiously he forgave the men who got through the vacant hours by playing jokes upon him. They persuaded him that mustard plasters were excellent for colds—solicitously they gathered about him, affixed an enormous plaster to his back, and afterward fondly removed it. They concealed the ear of a cadaver in his nice, clean, new pocket handkerchief when he went to Sunday supper at the house of a girl cousin in Zenith. . . . At supper he produced the handkerchief with a flourish.

Every night when Fatty retired he had to remove from his bed a collection of objects which thoughtful house-mates had stuffed between the sheets— soap, alarm clocks, fish. He was the perfect person to whom to sell useless things. Clif Clawson, who combined a brisk huckstering with his jokes, sold to Fatty for four dollars a History of Medicine which he had bought, second-hand, for two, and while Fatty never read it, never conceivably could read it, the possession of the fat red book made him feel learned. But Fatty's greatest beneficence to Digamma was his belief in spiritualism. He went about in terror of spooks. He was always seeing them emerging at night from the dissecting-room windows. His classmates took care that he should behold a great many of them flitting about the halls of the fraternity.

### VI

Digamma Pi was housed in a residence built in the expansive days of 1885. The living-room suggested a recent cyclone. Knife-gashed tables, broken Morris chairs, and torn rugs were flung about the room, and covered with backless books, hockey shoes, caps, and cigarette stubs. Above, there were four men to a bedroom, and the beds were iron double-deckers, like steerage.

For ash-trays the Digams used sawed skulls, and on the bedroom walls were anatomical charts, to be studied while dressing. In Martin's room was a complete skeleton. He and his roommates had trustingly bought it from a salesman who came out from a Zenith surgical supply house. He was such a genial and sympathetic salesman; he gave them cigars and told G. U. stories and explained what prosperous doctors they were all going to be. They bought the skeleton gratefully, on the installment plan. . . . Later the salesman was less genial.

Martin roomed with Clif Clawson, Fatty Pfaff, and an earnest second-year medic named Irving Watters.

Any psychologist desiring a perfectly normal man for use in demonstrations could not have done better than to have engaged Irving Watters. He was always and carefully dull; smilingly, easily, dependably dull. If there was any cliché which he did not use, it was because he had not yet heard it. He believed in morality—except on Saturday evenings; he believed in the Episcopal Church—but not the High Church; he believed in the Constitution, Darwinism, systematic exercise in the gymnasium, and the genius of the president of the university.

Among them, Martin most liked Clif Clawson. Clif was the clown of the fraternity-house, he was given to raucous laughter, he clogged and sang meaningless songs, he even practiced on the cornet, yet he was somehow a good fellow and solid, and Martin, in his detestation of Ira Hinkley, his fear of Angus Duer, his pity for Fatty Pfaff, his distaste for the amiable dullness of Irving Watters, turned to the roaring Clif as to something living and experimenting. At least Clif had reality; the reality of a plowed field, of a steaming manure-pile. It was Clif who would box with him; Clif who—though he loved to sit for hours smoking, grunting, magnificently loafing—could be persuaded to go for a five-mile walk.

And it was Clif who risked death by throwing baked beans at the Reverend Ira Hinkley at supper, when Ira was bulkily and sweetly corrective.

In the dissecting-room Ira was maddening enough with his merriment at such of Martin's ideas as had not been accepted in Pottsburg Christian College, but in the fraternity-house he was a moral pest. He never ceased trying to stop their profanity. After three years on a backwoods football team he still believed with unflinching optimism that he could sterilize young men by administering reproofs, with the nickering of a lady Sunday School teacher and the delicacy of the charging elephant.

Ira also had statistics about Clean Living.

He was full of statistics. Where he got them did not matter to him; figures in the daily papers, in the census report, or in the Miscellany Column of the *Sanctification Herald* were equally valid. He announced at supper table, "Clif, it's a wonder to me how as bright a fella as you go on sucking that dirty old pipe. D'you realize that 67.9 per cent of all women who go to the operating table have husbands who smoke tobacco?"

"What the devil would they smoke?" demanded Clif.

"Where'd you get those figures?" from Martin.

"They came out at a medical convention in Philadelphia in 1902," Ira condescended. "Of course I don't suppose it'll make any difference to a bunch of wise galoots like you that some day you'll marry a nice bright little woman and ruin her life with your vices. Sure, keep right on—fine brave virile bunch! A poor weakling preacher like me wouldn't dare do anything so brave as smoke a pipe!"

He left them triumphantly, and Martin groaned, "Ira makes me want to get out of medicine and be an honest harness maker."

"Aw, gee now, Mart," Fatty Pfaff complained, "you oughtn't to cuss Ira out. He's awful sincere."

"Sincere? Hell! So is a cockroach!"

Thus they jabbered, while Angus Duer watched them in a superior silence that made Martin nervous. In the study of the profession to which he had looked forward all his life he found irritation and vacuity as well as serene wisdom; he saw no one clear path to Truth but a thousand paths to a thousand truths far-off and doubtful.

# 3

John A. Robertshaw, John Aldington Robertshaw, professor of physiology in the medical school, was rather deaf, and he was the only teacher in the University of Winnemac who still wore mutton-chop whiskers. He came from Back Bay; he was proud of it and let you know about it. With three other Brahmins he formed in Mohalis a Boston colony which stood for sturdy sweetness and decorously shaded light. On all ocasions he remarked, "When I was studying with Ludwig in Germany—" He was too absorbed in his own correctness to heed individual students, and Clif Clawson and the other young men technically known as "hell-raisers" looked forward to his lectures on physiology.

They were held in an amphitheater whose seats curved so far around that the lecturer could not see both ends at once, and while Dr. Robertshaw, continuing to drone about blood circulation, was peering to the right to find out who was making that outrageous sound like a motor horn, far over on the left Clif Clawson would rise and imitate him, with sawing arm and stroking of imaginary whiskers. Once Clif produced the masterpiece of throwing a brick into the sink beside the platform, just when Dr. Robertshaw was working up to his annual climax about the effect of brass bands on the intensity of the knee-jerk.

Martin had been reading Max Gottlieb's scientific papers—as much of them as he could read, with their morass of mathematical symbols—and from them he had a conviction that experiments should be something dealing with the foundations of life and death, with the nature of bacterial infection, with the chemistry of bodily reactions. When Robertshaw chirped about fussy little experiments, standard experiments, maiden-aunt experiments, Martin was restless. In college he had felt that prosody and Latin Composition were futile, and he had looked forward to the study of medicine as illumination. Now, in melancholy worry about his own unreasonableness, he found that he was developing the same contempt for Robertshaw's rules of the thumb—and for most of the work in anatomy.

The professor of anatomy, Dr. Oliver O. Stout, was himself an anatomy, a dissection-chart, a thinly covered knot of nerves and blood vessels and bones. Stout had precise and enormous knowledge; in his dry voice he could repeat more facts about the left little toe than you would have thought anybody would care to learn regarding the left little toe.

No discussion at the Digamma Pi supper table was more violent than the incessant debate over the value to a doctor, a decent normal doctor who made a good living and did not worry about reading papers at medical associations, of remembering anatomical terms. But no matter what they thought, they all ground at learning the lists of names which enable a man to crawl through examinations and become an Educated Person, with a market value of five dollars an hour. Unknown sages had invented rimes which enabled them to memorize. At supper—the thirty piratical Digams sitting at a long and spotty table, devouring clam chowder and beans and codfish balls and banana layer-cake—the Freshmen earnestly repeated after a senior:

> On old Olympus' topmost top
> A fat-eared German viewed a hop.

Thus by association with the initial letters they mastered the twelve cranial nerves: olfactory, optic, oculomotor, trochlear, and the rest. To the Digams it was the world's noblest poem, and they remembered it for years after they had become practicing physicians and altogether forgotten the names of the nerves themselves.

### II

In Dr. Stout's anatomy lectures there were no disturbances, but in his dissecting-room were many pleasantries. The mildest of them was the insertion of a fire-cracker in the cadaver on which the two virginal and unhappy co-eds worked. The real excitement during Freshman year was the incident of Clif Clawson and the pancreas.

Clif had been elected class president, for the year, because he was so full of greetings. He never met a classmate in the hall of Main Medical without shouting, "How's your vermiform appendix functioning this morning?" or "I bid thee a lofty greeting, old pediculosis." With booming decorum he presided at class meetings (indignant meetings to denounce the proposal to let the "aggies" use the North Side Tennis Courts), but in private life he was less decorous.

The terrible thing happened when the Board of Regents were being shown through the campus. The Regents were the supreme rulers of the University; they were bankers and manufacturers and pastors of large churches; to them even the president was humble. Nothing gave them more interesting thrills than the dissecting-room of the medical school. The preachers spoke morally of the effect of alcohol on paupers, and the bankers of the disrespect for savings-accounts which is always to be seen in the kind of men who insist on becoming cadavers. In the midst of the tour, led by Dr. Stout and the umbrella-carrying secretary of the University, the plumpest and most educational of all the bankers stopped near Clif Clawson's dissecting-table, with his derby hat reverently held behind him, and into that hat Clif dropped a pancreas.

Now a pancreas is a damp and disgusting thing to find in your new hat, and when the banker did so find one, he threw down the hat and said that the students of Winnemac had gone to the devil. Dr. Stout and the secretary comforted him; they cleaned the derby and assured him that vengeance should be done on the man who could put a pancreas in a banker's hat.

Dr. Stout summoned Clif, as president of the Freshmen. Clif was pained. He assembled the class, he lamented that any Winnemac Man could place a pancreas in a banker's hat, and he demanded that the criminal be manly enough to stand up and confess.

Unfortunately the Reverend Ira Hinkley, who sat between Martin and Angus Duer, had seen Clif drop the pancreas. He growled, "This is outrageous! I'm going to expose Clawson, even if he is a frat-brother of mine."

Martin protested, "Cut it out. You don't want to get him fired?"

"He ought to be!"

Angus Duer turned in his seat, looked at Ira, and suggested, "Will you kindly shut up?" and, as Ira subsided, Angus became to Martin more admirable and more hateful than ever.

### III

When he was depressed by a wonder as to why he was here, listening to a Professor Robertshaw, repeating verses about fat-eared Germans, learning the trade of medicine like Fatty Pfaff or Irving Watters, then Martin had relief in what he considered debauches. Actually they were extremely small debauches; they rarely went beyond too much lager in the adjacent city of Zenith, or the smiles of a factory girl parading the sordid back avenues, but to Martin, with his pride in taut strength, his joy in a clear brain, they afterward seemed tragic.

His safest companion was Clif Clawson. No matter how much bad beer he drank, Clif was never much more intoxicated than in his normal state. Martin sank or rose to Clif's buoyancy, while Clif rose or sank to Martin's speculativeness. As they sat in a back-room, at a table glistening with beer-glass rings, Clif shook his finger and babbled, "You're only one 'at gets me, Mart. You know with all the hell-raising, and all the talk about bein' c'mmercial that I pull on these high boys like Ira Stinkley, I'm jus' sick o' c'mmercialism an' bunk as you are."

"Sure. You bet," Martin agreed with alcoholic fondness. "You're jus' like me. My God, do you get it—dough-face like Irving Watters or heartless climber like Angus Duer, and then old Gottlieb! Ideal of research! Never bein' content with what *seems* true! Alone, not carin' a damn, square-toed as a captain on the bridge, working all night, getting to the bottom of things!"

"Thash stuff. That's my idee, too. Lez have 'nother beer. Shake you for it!" observed Clif Clawson.

Zenith, with its saloons, was fifteen miles from Mohalis and the University of Winnemac; half an hour by the huge, roaring, steel interurban trolleys, and to Zenith the medical students went for their forays. To say that one had "gone into town last night" was a matter for winks and leers. But with Angus Duer, Martin discovered a new Zenith.

At supper Duer said abruptly, "Come into town with me and hear a concert."

For all his fancied superiority to the class, Martin was illimitably ignorant of literature, of painting, of music. That the bloodless and acquisitive Angus Duer should waste time listening to fiddlers was astounding to him. He discovered that Duer had enthusiasm for two composers, called Bach and Beethoven, presumably Germans, and that he himself did not yet comprehend all the ways of the world. On the interurban, Duer's gravity loosened, and he cried, "Boy, if I hadn't been born to carve up innards, I'd have been a great musician! Tonight I'm going to lead you right into Heaven!"

Martin found himself in a confusion of little chairs and vast gilded archs, of polite but disapproving ladies with programs in their laps, unromantic musicians making unpleasant noises below and, at last, incomprehensible beauty, which made for him pictures of hills and deep forests, then suddenly became achingly long-winded. He exulted, "I'm going to have 'em all—the fame of Max Gottlieb—I mean his ability—and the lovely music and lovely women— Golly! I'm going to do big things. And see the world. . . . Will this piece never quit?"

### IV

It was a week after the concert that he rediscovered Madeline Fox.

Madeline was a handsome, high-colored, high-spirited, opinionated girl whom Martin had known in college. She was staying on, ostensibly to take a graduate course in English, actually to avoid going back home. She considered herself a superb tennis player; she played it with energy and voluble swoopings and large lack of direction. She believed herself to be a connoisseur of literature; the fortunates to whom she gave her approval were Hardy, Meredith, Howells, and Thackeray, none of whom she had read for five years. She had often reproved Martin for his inappreciation of Howells, for wearing flannel shirts, and for his failure to hand her down from street-cars in the manner of a fiction hero. In college, they had gone to dances together, though as a dancer Martin was more spirited than accurate, and his partners sometimes had difficulty in deciding just what he was trying to dance. He liked Madeline's tall comeliness and her vigor; he felt that with her energetic culture she was somehow "good for him." During this year, he had scarcely seen her. He thought of her late in the evenings, and planned to telephone to her, and did not telephone. But as he became doubtful about medicine he longed for her sympathy, and on a Sunday afternoon of spring he took her for a walk along the Chaloosa River.

From the river bluffs the prairie stretches in exuberant rolling hills. In the long barley fields, the rough pastures, the stunted oaks and brilliant birches, there is the adventurousness of the frontier, and like young plainsmen they tramped the bluffs and told each other they were going to conquer the world.

He complained, "These damn' medics—"

"Oh, Martin, do you think 'damn' is a nice word?" said Madeline.

He did think it was a very nice word indeed, and constantly useful to a busy worker, but her smile was desirable.

"Well—these darn' studes, they aren't trying to learn science; they're simply learning a trade. They just want to get the knowledge that'll enable them to cash in. They don't talk about saving lives but about 'losing cases'— losing dollars! And they wouldn't even mind losing cases if it was a sensational operation that'd advertise 'em! They make me sick! How many of 'em do you find that're interested in the work Ehrlich is doing in Germany—yes, or that Max Gottlieb is doing right here and now! Gottlieb's just taken an awful fall out of Wright's opsonin theory."

"Has he, really?"

"*Has* he! I should say he had! And do you get any of the medics stirred up about it? You do not! They say, 'Oh, sure, science is all right in its way; helps a doc to treat his patients,' and then they begin to argue about whether they can make more money if they locate in a big city or a town, and is it better for a young doc to play the good-fellow and lodge game, or join the church and look earnest. You ought to hear Irve Watters. He's just got one idea: the fellow that gets ahead in medicine, is he the lad that knows his pathology? Oh, no; the bird that succeeds is the one that gets an office on a northeast corner, near a trolley car junction, with a 'phone number that'll be easy for patients to remember! Honest! He said so! I swear, when I graduate I believe I'll be a ship's doctor. You see the world that way, and at least you aren't racing up and down the boat trying to drag patients away from some rival doc that has an office on another deck!"

"Yes, I know; it's dreadful the way people don't have ideals about their work. So many of the English grad students just want to make money teaching, instead of enjoying scholarship the way I do."

It was disconcerting to Martin that she should seem to think that she was a superior person quite as much as himself, but he was even more disconcerted when she bubbled:

"At the same time, Martin, one does have to be practical, doesn't one! Think how much more money—no, I mean how much more social position and power for doing good a successful doctor has than one of these scientists that just putter, and don't know what's going on in the world. Look at a surgeon like Dr. Loizeau, riding up to the hospital in a lovely car with a chauffeur in uniform, and all his patients simply worshiping him, and then your Max Gottlieb—somebody pointed him out to me the other day, and he had on a dreadful old suit, and I certainly thought he could stand a hair-cut."

Martin turned on her with fury, statistics, vituperation, religious zeal, and confused metaphors. They sat on a crooked old-fashioned rail-fence where over the sun-soaked bright plantains the first insects of spring were humming. In the storm of his fanaticism she lost her airy Culture and squeaked, "Yes, I see now, I see," without stating what it was she saw. "Oh, you do have a fine mind and such fine—such integrity."

"Honest? Do you think I have?"

"Oh, indeed I do, and I'm sure you're going to have a wonderful future.

And I'm so glad you aren't commercial, like the others. Don't mind what they say!"

He noted that Madeline was not only a rare and understanding spirit but also an extraordinarily desirable woman—fresh color, tender eyes, adorable slope from shoulder to side. As they walked back, he perceived that she was incredibly the right mate for him. Under his training she would learn the distinction between vague "ideals" and the hard sureness of science. They paused on the bluff, looking down at the muddy Chaloosa, a springtime Western river wild with floating branches. He yearned for her; he regretted the casual affairs of a student and determined to be a pure and extremely industrious young man, to be, in fact, "worthy of her."

"Oh, Madeline," he mourned, "you're so darn' lovely!"

She glanced at him, timidly.

He caught her hand; in a desperate burst he tried to kiss her. It was very badly done. He managed only to kiss the point of her jaw, while she struggled and begged, "Oh, don't!" They did not acknowledge, as they ambled back into Mohalis, that the incident had occurred, but there was softness in their voices and without impatience now she heard his denunciation of Professor Robertshaw as a phonograph, and he listened to her remarks on the shallowness and vulgarity of Dr. Norman Brumfit, that sprightly English instructor. At her boarding-house she sighed, "I wish I could ask you to come in, but it's almost suppertime and— Will you call me up some day?"

"You bet I will!" said Martin, according to the rules for amorous discourse in the University of Winnemac.

He raced home in adoration. As he lay in his narrow upper bunk at midnight, he saw her eyes, now impertinent, now reproving, now warm with trust in him. "I love her! I *love* her! I'll 'phone her— Wonder if I dare call her up as early as eight in the morning?"

But at eight he was too busy studying the lacrimal apparatus to think of ladies' eyes. He saw Madeline only once, and in the publicity of her boarding-house porch, crowded with co-eds, red cushions, and marshmallows, before he was hurled into hectic studying for the year's final examinations.


v


At examination-time, Digamma Pi fraternity showed its value to urgent seekers after wisdom. Generations of Digams had collected test-papers and preserved them in the sacred Quiz Book; geniuses for detail had labored through the volume and marked with red pencil the problems most often set in the course of years. The Freshmen crouched in a ring about Ira Hinkley in the Digam living-room, while he read out the questions they were most likely to get. They writhed, clawed their hair, scratched their chins, bit their fingers, and beat their temples in the endeavor to give the right answer before Angus Duer should read it to them out of the textbook.

In the midst of their sufferings they had to labor with Fatty Pfaff.

Fatty had failed in the mid-year anatomical, and he had to pass a special quiz before he could take the finals. There was a certain fondness for him in Digamma Pi; Fatty was soft, Fatty was superstitious, Fatty was an imbecile, yet they had for him the annoyed affection they might have had for a second-hand motor or a muddy dog. All of them worked on him; they tried to lift him and thrust him through the examination as through a trap-door. They panted and grunted and moaned at the labor, and Fatty panted and moaned with them.

The night before his special examination they kept him at it till two, with wet towels, black coffee, prayer, and profanity. They repeated lists—lists—lists to him; they shook their fists in his mournful red round face and howled, "Damn you, *will* you remember that the bicuspid valve is the SAME as the mitral valve and NOT another one?" They ran about the room, holding up their hands and wailing, "Won't he never remember nothing about nothing?" and charged back to purr with fictive calm, "Now no use getting fussed, Fatty. Take it easy. Just listen to this, quietly, will yuh, and try," coaxingly, "do try to remember *one* thing, anyway!"

They led him carefully to bed. He was so filled with facts that the slightest jostling would have spilled them.

When he awoke at seven, with red eyes and trembling lips, he had forgotten everything he had learned.

"There's nothing for it," said the president of Digamma Pi. "He's got to have a crib, and take his chance on getting caught with it. I thought so. I made one out for him yesterday. It's a lulu. It'll cover enough of the questions so he'll get through."

Even the Reverend Ira Hinkley, since he had witnessed the horrors of the midnight before, went his ways ignoring the crime. It was Fatty himself who protested: "Gee, I don't like to cheat. I don't think a fellow that can't get through an examination had hardly ought to be allowed to practice medicine. That's what my Dad said."

They poured more coffee into him and (on the advice of Clif Clawson, who wasn't exactly sure what the effect might be but who was willing to learn) they fed him a potassium bromide tablet. The president of Digamma, seizing Fatty with some firmness, growled, "I'm going to stick this crib in your pocket—look, here in your breast pocket, behind your handkerchief."

"I won't use it. I don't care if I fail," whimpered Fatty.

"That's all right, but you keep it there. Maybe you can absorb a little information from it through your lungs, for God knows—" The president clenched his hair. His voice rose, and in it was all the tragedy of night watches and black draughts and hopeless retreats. "—God knows you can't take it in through your head!"

They dusted Fatty, they stood him right side up, and pushed him through the door, on his way to Anatomy Building. They watched him go: a balloon on legs, a sausage in corduroy trousers.

"Is it possible he's going to be honest?" marveled Clif Clawson.

"Well, if he is, we better go up and begin packing his trunk. And this ole frat'll never have another goat like Fatty," grieved the president.

They saw Fatty stop, remove his handkerchief, mournfully blow his nose—and discover a long thin slip of paper. They saw him frown at it, tap it on his knuckles, begin to read it, stuff it back into his pocket, and go on with a more resolute step.

They danced hand in hand about the living-room of the fraternity, piously assuring one another, "He'll use it—it's all right—he'll get through or get hanged!"

He got through.

## VI

Digamma Pi was more annoyed by Martin's restless doubtings than by Fatty's idiocy, Clif Clawson's raucousness, Angus Duer's rasping, or the Reverend Ira Hinkley's nagging.

During the strain of study for examinations Martin was peculiarly vexing in regard to "laying in the best quality medical terms like the best quality sterilizers—not for use but to impress your patients." As one, the Digams suggested, "Say, if you don't like the way we study medicine, we'll be tickled to death to take up a collection and send you back to Elk Mills, where you won't be disturbed by all us lowbrows and commercialists. Look here! We don't tell you how you ought to work. Where do you get the idea you got to tell us? Oh, turn it off, will you!"

Angus Duer observed, with sour sweetness, "We'll admit we're simply carpenters, and you're a great investigator. But there's several things you might turn to when you finish science. What do you know about architecture? How's your French verbs? How many big novels have you ever read? Who's the premier of Austro-Hungary?"

Martin struggled, "I don't pretend to know anything—except I do know what a man like Max Gottlieb means. He's got the right method, and all these other hams of profs, they're simply witch doctors. You think Gottlieb isn't religious, Hinkley. Why, his just being in a lab is a prayer. Don't you idiots realize what it means to have a man like that here, making new concepts of life? Don't you—"

Clif Clawson, with a chasm of yawning, speculated, "Praying in the lab! I'll bet I get the pants took off me, when I take bacteriology, if Pa Gottlieb catches me praying during experiment hours!"

"Damn it, listen!" Martin wailed. "I tell you, you fellows are the kind that keep medicine nothing but guess-work diagnosis, and here you have a man—"

So they argued for hours, after their sweaty fact-grinding.

When the others had gone to bed, when the room was a muck-heap of flung clothing and weary young men snoring in iron bunks, Martin sat at the splintery long pine study-table, worrying. Angus Duer glided in, demanding, "Look here, old son. We're all sick of your crabbing. If you think medicine is rot, the way we study it, and if you're so confoundedly honest, why don't you get out?"

He left Martin to agonize, "He's right. I've got to shut up or get out. Do I really mean it? What *do* I want? What *am* I going to do?"

<br>

VII

Angus Duer's studiousness and his reverence for correct manners were alike offended by Clif's bawdy singing, Clif's howling conversation, Clif's fondness for dropping things in people's soup, and Clif's melancholy inability to keep his hands washed. For all his appearance of nerveless steadiness, during the tension of examination-time Duer was as nervous as Martin, and one evening at supper, when Clif was bellowing, Duer snapped, "Will you kindly not make so much racket?"

"I'll make all the damn' racket I damn' please!" Clif asserted, and a feud was on.

Clif was so noisy thereafter that he almost became tired of his own noise. He was noisy in the living-room, he was noisy in the bath, and with some sacrifice he lay awake pretending to snore. If Duer was quiet and book-wrapped, he was not in the least timid; he faced Clif with the eye of a magistrate, and cowed him. Privily Clif complained to Martin, "Darn him, he acts like I was a worm. Either he or me has got to get out of Digam, that's a cinch, and it won't be me!"

He was ferocious and very noisy about it, and it was he who got out. He said that the Digams were a "bunch of bum sports; don't even have a decent game of poker," but he was fleeing from the hard eyes of Angus Duer. And Martin resigned from the fraternity with him, planned to room with him the coming autumn.

Clif's blustering rubbed Martin as it did Duer. Clif had no reticences; when he was not telling slimy stories he was demanding, "How much chuh pay for those shoes—must think you're a Vanderbilt!" or "D'I see you walking with that Madeline Fox femme—what chuh tryin' to do?" But Martin was alienated from the civilized, industrious, nice young men of Digamma Pi, in whose faces he could already see prescriptions, glossy white sterilizers, smart enclosed motors, and glass office-signs in the best gilt lettering. He preferred a barbarian loneliness, for next year he would be working with Max Gottlieb, and he could not be bothered.

That summer he spent with a crew installing telephones in Montana.

He was a lineman in the wire-gang. It was his job to climb the poles, digging the spurs of his leg-irons into the soft and silvery pine, to carry up the wire, lash it to the glass insulators, then down and to another pole.

They made perhaps five miles a day; at night they drove into little rickety wooden towns. Their retiring was simple—they removed their shoes and rolled up in a horse-blanket. Martin wore overalls and a flannel shirt. He looked like a farm-hand. Climbing all day long, he breathed deep, his eyes cleared of worry, and one day he experienced a miracle.

He was atop a pole and suddenly, for no clear cause, his eyes opened and he saw; as though he had just awakened he saw that the prairie was vast, that the sun was kindly on rough pasture and ripening wheat, on the old horses, the easy, broad-beamed, friendly horses, and on his red-faced jocose companions; he saw that the meadow larks were jubilant, and blackbirds shining by little pools, and with the living sun all life was living. Suppose the Angus Duers and Irving Watterses were tight tradesmen. What of it? "I'm *here!*" he gloated.

The wire-gang were as healthy and as simple as the west wind; they had no pretentiousness; though they handled electrical equipment they did not, like medics, learn a confusion of scientific terms and pretend to the farmers that they were scientists. They laughed easily and were content to be themselves, and with them Martin was content to forget how noble he was. He had for them an affection such as he had for no one at the University save Max Gottlieb.

He carried in his bag one book, Gottlieb's "Immunology." He could often get through half a page of it before he bogged down in chemical formulae. Occasionally, on Sundays or rainy days, he tried to read it, and longed for the laboratory; occasionally he thought of Madeline Fox, and became certain that he was devastatingly lonely for her. But week slipped into careless and robust week, and when he awoke in a stable, smelling the sweet hay and the horses and the lark-ringing prairie that crept near to the heart of these shanty towns, he cared only for the day's work, the day's hiking, westward toward the sunset.

So they straggled through the Montana wheatland, whole duchies of wheat in one shining field, through the cattle-country and the sagebrush desert, and suddenly, staring at a persistent cloud, Martin realized that he beheld the mountains.

Then he was on a train; the wire-gang were already forgotten; and he was thinking only of Madeline Fox, Clif Clawson, Angus Duer, and Max Gottlieb.

# 4

Professor Max Gottlieb was about to assassinate a guinea pig with anthrax germs, and the bacteriology class were nervous.

They had studied the forms of bacteria, they had handled Petri dishes and platinum loops, they had proudly grown on potato slices the harmless red cultures of *Bacillus prodigiosus*, and they had come now to pathogenic germs and the inoculation of a living animal with swift disease. These two beady-eyed guinea pigs, chittering in a battery jar, would in two days be stiff and dead.

Martin had an excitement not free from anxiety. He laughed at it, he remembered with professional scorn how foolish were the lay visitors to the laboratory, who believed that sanguinary microbes would leap upon them from the mysterious centrifuge, from the benches, from the air itself. But he was conscious that in the cotton-plugged test-tube between the instrument-bath and the bichloride jar on the demonstrator's desk were millions of fatal anthrax germs.

The class looked respectful and did not stand too close. With the flair of technique, the sure rapidity which dignified the slightest movement of his hands, Dr. Gottlieb clipped the hair on the belly of a guinea pig held by the assistant. He soaped the belly with one flicker of a hand-brush, he shaved it and painted it with iodine.

(And all the while Max Gottlieb was recalling the eagerness of his first students, when he had just returned from working with Koch and Pasteur, when he was fresh from enormous beer seidels and Korpsbrüder and ferocious arguments. Passionate, beautiful days! *Die goldene Zeit!* His first classes in America, at Queen City College had been awed by the sensational discoveries in bacteriology; they had crowded about him reverently; they had longed to know. Now the class was a mob. He looked at them—Fatty Pfaff in the front row, his face vacant as a doorknob; the co-eds emotional and frightened; only Martin Arrowsmith and Angus Duer visibly intelligent. His memory fumbled for a pale blue twilight in Munich, a bridge and a waiting girl, and the sound of music.)

He dipped his hands in the bichloride solution and shook them—a quick shake, fingers down, like the fingers of a pianist above the keys. He took a hypodermic needle from the instrument-bath and lifted the test-tube. His voice flowed indolently, with German vowels and blurred W's:

"This, gentlemen, iss a twenty-four-hour culture of *Bacillus anthracis*. You will note, I am sure you will have noted already, that in the bottom of the tumbler there was cotton to keep the tube from being broken. I cannot advise breaking tubes of anthrax germs and afterwards getting the hands into the culture. You *might* merely get anthrax boils—"

The class shuddered.

Gottlieb twitched out the cotton plug with his little finger, so neatly that the medical students who had complained, "Bacteriology is junk; urinalysis and blood tests are all the lab stuff we need to know," now gave him something of the respect they had for a man who could do card tricks or remove an appendix in seven minutes. He agitated the mouth of the tube in the Bunsen burner, droning, "Every time you take the plug from a tube, flame the mouth of the tube. Make that a rule. It is a necessity of the technique, and technique, gentlemen, is the beginning of all science. It iss also the least-known thing in science."

The class was impatient. Why didn't he get on with it, on to the entertainingly dreadful moment of inoculating the pig?

(And Max Gottlieb, glancing at the other guinea pig in the prison of its battery jar, meditated, "Wretched innocent! Why should I murder him, to teach *Dummköpfe*? It would be better to experiment on that fat young man.")

He thrust the syringe into the tube, he withdrew the piston dextrously with his index finger, and lectured:

"Take one half c.c. of the culture. There are two kinds of M.D.'s—those to whom c.c. means cubic centimeter and those to whom it means compound cathartic. The second kind are more prosperous."

(But one cannot convey the quality of it: the thin drawl, the sardonic amiability, the hiss of the S's, the D's turned into blunt and challenging T's.)

The assistant held the guinea pig close; Gottlieb pinched up the skin of the belly and punctured it with a quick down thrust of the hypodermic needle. The pig gave a little jerk, a little squeak, and the co-eds shuddered. Gottlieb's wise fingers knew when the peritoneal wall was reached. He pushed home the plunger of the syringe. He said quietly, "This poor animal will now soon be dead as Moses." The class glanced at one another uneasily. "Some of you will think that it does not matter; some of you will think, like Bernard Shaw, that I am an executioner and the more monstrous because I am cool about it; and some of you will not think at all. This difference in philosophy iss what makes life interesting."

While the assistant tagged the pig with a tin disk in its ear and restored it to the battery jar, Gottlieb set down its weight in a note-book, with the time of inoculation and the age of the bacterial culture. These notes he reproduced on the blackboard, in his fastidious script, murmuring, "Gentlemen, the most important part of living is not the living but pondering upon it. And the most important part of experimentation is not doing the experiment but making notes, ve-ry accurate *quantitative* notes—in ink. I am told that a great many clever people feel they can keep notes in their heads. I have often observed with pleasure that such persons do not have heads in which to keep their notes. This iss very good, because thus the world never sees their results and science is not encumbered with them. I shall now inoculate the second guinea pig, and the class will be dismissed. Before the next lab hour I shall be glad if you will read Pater's 'Marius the Epicurean,' to derife from it the calmness which is the secret of laboratory skill."

II

As they bustled down the hall, Angus Duer observed to a brother Digam, "Gottlieb is an old laboratory plug; he hasn't got any imagination; he sticks here instead of getting out into the world and enjoying the fight. But he certainly is handy. Awfully good technique. He might have been a first-rate surgeon, and made fifty thousand dollars a year. As it is, I don't suppose he gets a cent over four thousand!"

Ira Hinkley walked alone, worrying. He was an extraordinarily kindly man, this huge and bumbling parson. He reverently accepted everything, no matter how contradictory to everything else, that his medical instructors told him, but this killing of animals—he hated it. By a connection not evident to him he remembered that the Sunday before, in the slummy chapel where he preached during his medical course, he had exalted the sacrifice of the martyrs and they had sung of the blood of the lamb, the fountain filled with blood drawn from Emmanuel's veins, but this meditation he lost, and he lumbered toward Digamma Pi in a fog of pondering pity.

Clif Clawson, walking with Fatty Pfaff, shouted, "Gosh, ole pig certainly did jerk when Pa Gottlieb rammed that needle home!" and Fatty begged, "Don't! Please!"

But Martin Arrowsmith saw himself doing the same experiment and, as he remembered Gottlieb's unerring fingers, his hands curved in imitation.

III

The guinea pigs grew drowsier and drowsier. In two days they rolled over, kicked convulsively, and died. Full of dramatic expectation, the class re-assembled for the necropsy. On the demonstrator's table was a wooden tray, scarred from the tacks which for years had pinned down the corpses. The guinea pigs were in a glass jar, rigid, their hair ruffled. The class tried to remember how nibbling and alive they had been. The assistant stretched out one of them with thumb-tacks. Gottlieb swabbed its belly with a cotton wad soaked in lysol, slit it from belly to neck, and cauterized the heart with a red-hot spatula—the class quivered as they heard the searing of the flesh. Like a priest of diabolic mysteries, he drew out the blackened blood with a pipette. With the distended lungs, the spleen and kidneys and liver, the assistant made wavy smears on glass slides which were stained and given to the class for examination. The students who had learned to look through the microscope without having to close one eye were proud and professional, and all of them talked of the beauty of identifying the bacillus, as they twiddled the brass thumbscrews to the right focus and the cells rose from cloudiness to sharp distinctness on the slides before them. But they were uneasy, for Gottlieb remained with them that day, stalking behind them, saying nothing, watching them always, watching the disposal of the remains of the guinea pigs, and along the benches ran nervous rumors about a bygone student who had died from anthrax infection in the laboratory.

IV

There was for Martin in these days a quality of satisfying delight; the zest of a fast hockey game, the serenity of the prairie, the bewilderment of great music, and a feeling of creation. He woke early and thought contentedly of the day; he hurried to his work, devout, unseeing.

The confusion of the bacteriological laboratory was ecstasy to him—the students in shirt-sleeves, filtering nutrient gelatine, their fingers gummed from the crinkly gelatine leaves; or heating media in an autoclave like a silver howitzer. The roaring Bunsen flames beneath the hot-air ovens, the steam from the Arnold sterilizers rolling to the rafters, clouding the windows, were to Martin lovely with activity, and to him the most radiant things in the world were rows of test-tubes filled with watery serum and plugged with cotton singed to a coffee brown, a fine platinum loop leaning in a shiny test-glass, a fantastic hedge of tall glass tubes mysteriously connecting jars, or a bottle rich with gentian violet stain.

He had begun, perhaps in youthful imitation of Gottlieb, to work by him-self in the laboratory at night. . . . The long room was dark, thick dark, but for the gas-mantle behind his microscope. The cone of light cast a gloss on the bright brass tube, a sheen on his black hair, as he bent over the eye-piece. He was studying trypanosomes from a rat—an eight-branched rosette stained with polychrome methylene blue; a cluster of organisms delicate as a narcissus, with their purple nuclei, their light blue cells, and the thin lines of the flagella. He was excited and a little proud; he had stained the germs perfectly, and it is not easy to stain a rosette without breaking the petal shape. In the darkness, a step, the weary step of Max Gottlieb, and a hand on Martin's shoulder. Silently Martin raised his head, pushed the microscope toward him. Bending down, a cigarette stub in his mouth—the smoke would have stung the eyes of any human being—Gottlieb peered at the preparation.

He adjusted the gas light a quarter inch, and mused, "Splendid! You have craftsmanship. Oh, there is an art in science—for a few. You Americans, so many of you—all full with ideas, but you are impatient with the beautiful dullness of long labors. I see already—and I watch you in the lab before—perhaps you may try the trypanosomes of sleeping sickness. They are very, very interesting, and very, very ticklish to handle. It is quite a nice disease. In some villages in Africa, fifty per cent of the people have it, and it is in-variably fatal. Yes, I think you might work on the bugs."

Which, to Martin, was getting his brigade in battle.

"I shall have," said Gottlieb, "a little sandwich in my room at midnight. If you should happen to work so late, I should be very pleast if you would come to have a bite."

Diffidently, Martin crossed the hall to Gottlieb's immaculate laboratory at midnight. On the bench were coffee and sandwiches, curiously small and excellent sandwiches, foreign to Martin's lunch-room taste.

Gottlieb talked till Clif had faded from existence and Angus Duer seemed but an absurd climber. He summoned forth London laboratories, dinners on frosty evenings in Stockholm, walks on the Pincio with sunset behind the dome of San Pietro, extreme danger and overpowering disgust from excreta-smeared garments in an epidemic at Marseilles. His reserve slipped from him and he talked of himself and of his family as though Martin were a con-temporary.

The cousin who was a colonel in Uruguay and the cousin, a rabbi, who was tortured in a pogrom in Moscow. His sick wife—it might be cancer. The three children—the youngest girl, Miriam, she was a good musician, but the boy, the fourteen-year-old, he was a worry; he was saucy, he would not study. Himself, he had worked for years on the synthesis of antibodies; he was at present in a blind alley, and at Mohalis there was no one who was inter-ested, no one to stir him, but he was having an agreeable time massacring the opsonin theory, and that cheered him.

"No, I have done nothing except be unpleasant to people that claim too much, but I have dreams of real discoveries some day. And— No. Not five times in five years do I have students who understand craftsmanship and precision and maybe some big imagination in hypotheses. I t'ink perhaps you may have them. If I can help you— So!

"I do not t'ink you will be a good doctor. Good doctors are fine—often they are artists—but their trade, it is not for us lonely ones that work in labs. Once, I took an M.D. label. In Heidelberg that was—Herr Gott, back in 1875! I could not get much interested in bandaging legs and looking at tongues. I was a follower of Helmholtz—what a wild blithering young fellow! I tried to make researches into the physics of sound—I was bad, most unbelievable, but I learned that in this wale of tears there is nothing certain but the quantitative method. And I was a chemist—a fine stink-maker was I. And so into biology and much trouble. It has been good. I have found one or two things. And if sometimes I feel an exile, cold— I had to get out of Germany one time for refusing to sing *Die Wacht am Rhein* and trying to kill a cavalry captain—he was a stout fellow—I had to choke him—you see I am boasting, but I was a lifely *Kerl* thirty years ago! Ah! So!

"There is but one trouble of a philosophical bacteriologist. Why should we destroy these amiable pathogenic germs? Are we too sure, when we regard these oh, most unbeautiful young students attending Y.M.C.A.'s and singing dinkle-songs and wearing hats with initials burned into them—iss it worth while to protect them from the so elegantly functioning *Bacillus typhosus* with its lovely flagella? You know, once I asked Dean Silva would it not be better to let loose the pathogenic germs on the world, and so solve all economic questions. But he did not care for my met'od. Oh, well, he is older than I am; he also gives, I hear, some dinner parties with bishops and judges present, all in nice clothes. He would know more than a German Jew who loves Father Nietzsche and Father Schopenhauer (but damn him, he was teleological-minded!) and Father Koch and Father Pasteur and Brother Jacques Loeb and Brother Arrhenius. Ja! I talk foolishness. Let us go look at your slides and so good night."

When he had left Gottlieb at his stupid brown little house, his face as reticent as though the midnight supper and all the rambling talk had never happened, Martin ran home altogether drunk.

## 5

Though bacteriology was all of Martin's life now, it was the theory of the University that he was also studying pathology, hygiene, surgical anatomy, and enough other subjects to swamp a genius.

Clif Clawson and he lived in a large room with flowered wall-paper, piles of filthy clothes, iron beds, and cuspidors. They made their own breakfasts; they dined on hash at the Pilgrim Lunch Wagon or the Dew Drop Inn. Clif was occasionally irritating; he hated open windows; he talked of dirty socks; he sang "Some Die of Diabetes" when Martin was studying; and he was altogether unable to say anything directly. He had to be humorous. He remarked, "Is it your combobulatory concept that we might now feed the old faces?" or "How about ingurgitating a few calories?" But he had for Martin a charm that could not be accounted for by cheerfulness, his shrewdness, his vague courage. The whole of Clif was more than the sum of his various parts.

In the joy of his laboratory work Martin thought rarely of his recent associates in Digamma Pi. He occasionally protested that the Reverend Ira Hinkley was a village policeman and Irving Watters a plumber, that Angus Duer would walk to success over his grandmother's head, and that for an idiot like Fatty Pfaff to practice on helpless human beings was criminal, but mostly he ignored them and ceased to be a pest. And when he had passed his first triumphs in bacteriology and discovered how remarkably much he did not know, he was curiously humble.

If he was less annoying in regard to his classmates, he was more so in his classrooms. He had learned from Gottlieb the trick of using the word "control" in reference to the person or animal or chemical left untreated during an experiment, as a standard for comparison; and there is no trick more infuriating. When a physician boasted of his success with this drug or that electric cabinet, Gottlieb always snorted, "Where was your control? How many cases did you have under identical conditions, and how many of them did not get the treatment?" Now Martin began to mouth it—control, control, control, where's your control? where's your control?—till most of his fellows and a few of his instructors desired to lynch him.

He was particularly tedious in materia medica.

The professor of materia medica, Dr. Lloyd Davidson, would have been an illustrious shopkeeper. He was very popular. From him a future physician could learn that most important of all things: the proper drugs to give a patient, particularly when you cannot discover what is the matter with him. His classes listened with zeal, and memorized the sacred hundred and fifty favorite prescriptions. (He was proud that this was fifty more than his predecessor had required.)

But Martin was rebellious. He inquired, and publicly, "Dr. Davidson, how do they know ichthyol is good for erysipelas? Isn't it just rotten fossil fish—isn't it like the mummy-dust and puppy-ear stuff they used to give in the olden days?"

"How do they know? Why, my critical young friend, because thousands of physicians have used it for years and found their patients getting better, and that's how they know!"

"But honest, Doctor, wouldn't the patients maybe have gotten better anyway? Wasn't it maybe a *post hoc, propter hoc?* Have they ever experimented on a whole slew of patients together, with controls?"

"Probably not—and until some genius like yourself, Arrowsmith, can herd together a few hundred people with exactly identical cases of erysipelas, it probably never will be tried! Meanwhile I trust that you other gentlemen, who perhaps lack Mr. Arrowsmith's profound scientific attainments and the power to use such handy technical terms as 'control,' will, merely on my feeble advice, continue to use ichthyol!"

But Martin insisted, "Please, Dr. Davidson, what's the use of getting all these prescriptions by heart, anyway? We'll forget most of 'em, and besides, we can always look 'em up in the book."

Davidson pressed his lips together, then:

"Arrowsmith, with a man of your age I hate to answer you as I would a three-year-old boy, but apparently I must. Therefore, you will learn the properties of drugs and the contents of prescriptions *because I tell you to!* If I did not hesitate to waste the time of the other members of this class, I would try to convince you that my statements may be accepted, not on my humble authority, but because they are the conclusions of wise men—men wiser or certainly a little older than you, my friend—through many ages. But as I have no desire to indulge in fancy flights of rhetoric and eloquence, I shall merely say that you will accept, and you will study, and you will memorize, because I tell you to!"

Martin considered dropping his medical course and specializing in bacteriology. He tried to confide in Clif, but Clif had become impatient of his fretting, and he turned again to the energetic and willowy Madeline Fox.

II

Madeline was at once sympathetic and sensible. Why not complete his medical course, then see what he wanted to do?

They tramped, they skated, they skied, they went to the University Dramatic Society play. Madeline's widowed mother had come to live with her, and they had taken a top-floor flat in one of the tiny apartment-houses which were beginning to replace the expansive old wooden houses of Mohalis. The flat was full of literature and decoration: a bronze Buddha from Chicago, a rubbing of Shakespeare's epitaph, a set of Anatole France in translation, a photograph of Cologne cathedral, a wicker tea-table with a samovar whose operation no one in the University understood, and a souvenir post-card album. Madeline's mother was a Main Street dowager duchess. She was stately and white-haired but she attended the Methodist Church. In Mohalis she was flustered by the chatter of the students; she longed for her home-town, for the church sociables and the meetings of the women's club—they were studying Education this year and she hated to lose all the information about university ways.

With a home and a chaperone, Madeline began to "entertain": eight-o'clock parties with coffee, chocolate cake, chicken salad, and word-games.

She invited Martin, but he was jealous of his evenings, beautiful evenings of research. The first affair to which she enticed him was her big New Year's Party in January. They "did advertisements"—guessed at tableaux representing advertising pictures; they danced to the phonograph; and they had not merely a lap-supper but little tables excessively covered with doilies.

Martin was unaccustomed to such elegance. Though he had come in sulky unwillingness, he was impressed by the supper, by the frocks of the young women; he realized that his dancing was rusty, and he envied the senior who could do the new waltz called the "Boston." There was no strength, no grace, no knowledge, that Martin Arrowsmith did not covet, when consciousness of it had pierced through the layers of his absorption. If he was but little greedy for possessions, he was hungry for every skill.

His reluctant wonder at the others was drowned in his admiration for Madeline. He had known her as a jacketed outdoor girl, but this was an exquisite indoor Madeline, slender in yellow silk. She seemed to him a miracle of tact and ease as she bullied her guests into an appearance of merriment. She had need of tact, for Dr. Norman Brumfit was there, and it was one of Dr. Brumfit's evenings to be original and naughty. He pretended to kiss Madeline's mother, which vastly discomforted the poor lady; he sang a strongly improper Negro song containing the word hell; he maintained to a group of women graduate students that George Sand's affairs might perhaps be partially justified by their influence on men of talent; and when they looked shocked, he pranced a little, and his eye-glasses glittered.

Madeline took charge of him. She trilled, "Dr. Brumfit, you're terribly learned and so on and so forth, and sometimes in English classes I'm simply scared to death of you, but other times you're nothing but a bad small boy, and I won't have you teasing the girls. You can help me bring in the sherbet, that's what you can do."

Martin adored her. He hated Brumfit for the privilege of disappearing with her into the closet-like kitchen of the flat. Madeline! She was the one person who understood him! Here, where everyone snatched at her and Dr. Brumfit beamed on her with almost matrimonial fondness, she was precious, she was something he must have.

On pretense of helping her set the tables, he had a moment with her, and whimpered, "Lord, you're so lovely!"

"I'm glad you think I'm a wee bit nice." She, the rose and the adored of all the world, gave him her favor.

"Can I come call on you tomorrow evening?"

"Well, I— Perhaps."

### III

It cannot be said, in this biography of a young man who was in no degree a hero, who regarded himself as a seeker after truth yet who stumbled and slid back all his life and bogged himself in every obvious morass, that Martin's intentions toward Madeline Fox were what is called "honorable." He was not a Don Juan, but he was a poor medical student who would have to

wait for years before he could make a living. Certainly he did not think of
proposing marriage. He wanted—like most poor and ardent young men in
such a case, he wanted all he could get.

As he raced toward her flat, he was expectant of adventure. He pictured
her melting; he felt her hand glide down his cheek. He warned himself,
"Don't be a fool now! Probably nothing doing at all. Don't go get all worked
up and then be disappointed. She'll probably cuss you out for something
you did wrong at the party. She'll probably be sleepy and wish you hadn't
come. Nothing!" But he did not for a second believe it.

He rang, he saw her opening the door, he followed her down the meager
hall, longing to take her hand. He came into the over-bright living-room—and
he found her mother, solid as a pyramid, permanent-looking as sunless
winter.

But of course Mother would obligingly go, and leave him to conquest.
Mother did not.

In Mohalis, the suitable time for young men callers to depart is ten o'clock,
but from eight till a quarter after eleven Martin did battle with Mrs. Fox;
talked to her in two languages, an audible gossip and a mute but furious
protest, while Madeline—she was present; she sat about and looked pretty.
In an equally silent tongue Mrs. Fox answered him, till the room was thick
with their antagonism, while they seemed to be discussing the weather, the
University, and the trolley service into Zenith.

"Yes, of course, some day I guess they'll have a car every twenty minutes,"
he said weightily.

("Darn her, why doesn't she go to bed? Cheers! She's doing up her knitting. Nope. Damn it! She's taking another ball of wool.")

"Oh, yes, I'm sure they'll have to have better service," said Mrs. Fox.

("Young man, I don't know much about you, but I don't believe you're
the right kind of person for Madeline to go with. Anyway, it's time you
went home.")

"Oh, yes, sure, you bet. Lot better service."

("I know I'm staying too long, and I know you know it, but I don't care!")

It seemed impossible that Mrs. Fox should endure his stolid persistence.
He used thought-forms, will-power, and hypnotism, and when he rose, defeated, she was still there, extremely placid. They said good-by not too
warmly. Madeline took him to the door; for an exhilarating half-minute he
had her alone.

"I wanted so much—I wanted to talk to you!"

"I know. I'm sorry. Some time!" she muttered.

He kissed her. It was a tempestuous kiss, and very sweet.

IV

Fudge parties, skating parties, sleighing parties, a literary party with the
guest of honor a lady journalist who did the social page for the Zenith *Advocate-Times*—Madeline leaped into an orgy of jocund but extraordinarily

tiring entertainments, and Martin obediently and smolderingly followed her. She appeared to have trouble in getting enough men, and to the literary evening Martin dragged the enraged Clif Clawson. Clif grumbled, "This is the damnedest zoo of sparrows I ever did time in," but he bore off treasure—he had heard Madeline call Martin by her favorite name of "Martykins." That was very valuable. Clif called him Martykins. Clif told others to call him Martykins. Fatty Pfaff and Irving Watters called him Martykins. And when Martin wanted to go to sleep, Clif croaked:

"Yuh, you'll probably marry her. She's a dead shot. She can hit a smart young M.D. at ninety paces. Oh, you'll have one fine young time going on with science after that skirt sets you at tonsil-snatching. . . . She's one of these literary birds. She knows all about lite'ature except maybe how to read. . . . She's not so bad-looking, now. She'll get fat, like her Ma."

Martin said that which was necessary, and he concluded, "She's the only girl in the graduate school that's got any pep. The others just sit around and talk, and she gets up the best parties—"

"Any kissing parties?"

"Now you look here! I'll be getting sore, first thing you know! You and I are roughnecks, but Madeline Fox—she's like Angus Duer, some ways. I realize all the stuff we're missing: music and literature, yes, and decent clothes, too—no harm to dressing well—"

"That's just what I was tellin' you! She'll have you all dolled up in a Prince Albert and a boiled shirt, diagnosing everything as rich-widowitis. How you can fall for that four-flushing dame— *Where's your control?*"

Clif's opposition stirred him to consider Madeline not merely with a sly and avaricious interest but with a dramatic conviction that he longed to marry her.

v

Few women can for long periods keep from trying to Improve their men, and to Improve means to change a person from what he is, whatever that may be, into something else. Girls like Madeline Fox, artistic young women who do not work at it, cannot be restrained from Improving for more than a day at a time. The moment the urgent Martin showed that he was stirred by her graces, she went at his clothes—his corduroys and soft collars and eccentric old gray felt hat—at his vocabulary and his taste in fiction, with new and more patronizing vigor. Her sketchy way of saying, "Why, of course everybody knows that Emerson was the greatest thinker" irritated him the more in contrast to Gottlieb's dark patience.

"Oh, let me alone!" he hurled at her. "You're the nicest thing the Lord ever made, when you stick to things you know about, but when you spring your ideas on politics and chemotherapy— Darn it, quit bullying me! I guess you're right about slang. I'll cut out all this junk about 'feeding your face' and so on. But I will not put on a hard-boiled collar! I won't!"

He might never have proposed to her but for the spring evening on the roof.

She used the flat roof of her apartment-house as a garden. She had set out one box of geraniums and a cast-iron bench like those once beheld in cemetery plots; she had hung up two Japanese lanterns—they were ragged and they hung crooked. She spoke with scorn of the other inhabitants of the apartment-house, who were "so prosaic, so conventional, that they never came up to this darling hidey-place." She compared her refuge to the roof of a Moorish palace, to a Spanish patio, to a Japanese garden, to a "pleasaunce of old Provençal." But to Martin it seemed a good deal like a plain roof. He was vaguely ready for a quarrel, that April evening when he called on Madeline and her mother sniffily told him that she was to be found on the roof.

"Damned Japanese lanterns. Rather look at liver-sections," he grumbled, as he trudged up the curving stairs.

Madeline was sitting on the funereal iron bench, her chin in her hands. For once she did not greet him with flowery excitement but with a non-committal "Hello." She seemed spiritless. He felt guilty for his scoffing; he suddenly saw the pathos in her pretense that this stretch of tar-paper and slatted walks was a blazing garden. As he sat beside her he piped, "Say, that's a dandy new strip of matting you've put down."

"It is not! It's mangy!" She turned toward him. She wailed, "Oh, Mart, I'm so sick of myself, tonight. I'm always trying to make people think I'm somebody. I'm not. I'm a bluff."

"What is it, dear?"

"Oh, it's lots. Dr. Brumfit, hang him—only he was right—he as good as told me that if I don't work harder I'll have to get out of the graduate school. I'm not doing a thing, he said, and if I don't have my Ph.D., then I won't be able to land a nice job teaching English in some swell school, and I'd better land one, too, because it doesn't look to poor Madeline as if anybody was going to marry her."

His arm about her, he blared, "I know exactly who—"

"No, I'm not fishing. I'm almost honest, tonight. I'm no good, Mart. I tell people how clever I am. And I don't suppose they believe it. Probably they go off and laugh at me!"

"They do not! If they did— I'd like to see anybody that tried laughing—"

"It's awfully sweet and dear of you, but I'm not worth it. The poetic Madeline. With her ree-fined vocabulary! I'm a—I'm a—Martin, I'm a tin-horn sport! I'm everything your friend Clif thinks I am. Oh, you needn't tell me. I know what he thinks. And—I'll have to go home with Mother, and I can't stand it, dear, I can't stand it! I won't go back! That town! Never anything doing! The old tabbies, and the beastly old men, always telling the same old jokes. I won't!"

Her head was in the hollow of his arm; she was weeping, hard; he was stroking her hair, not covetously now but tenderly, and he was whispering:

"Darling! I almost feel as if I dared to love you. You're going to marry me and— Take me couple more years to finish my medical course and couple in hospital, then we'll be married and— By thunder, with you helping me,

I'm going to climb to the top! Be big surgeon! We're going to have everything!"

"Dearest, do be wise. I don't want to keep you from your scientific work—"

"Oh. Well. Well, I would like to keep up *some* research. But thunder, I'm not just a lab-cat. Battle o' life. Smashing your way through. Competing with real men in real he-struggle. If I can't do that and do some scientific work too, I'm no good. Course while I'm with Gottlieb, I want to take advantage of it, but afterward— Oh, Madeline!"

Then was all reasoning lost in a blur of nearness to her.

### VI

He dreaded the interview with Mrs. Fox; he was certain that she would demand, "Young man, how do you expect to support my Maddy? And you use bad language." But she took his hand and mourned, "I hope you and my baby will be happy. She's a dear good girl, even if she is a little flighty sometimes, and I know you're nice and kind and hard-working. I shall pray you'll be happy—oh, I'll pray so hard! You young people don't seem to think much of prayer, but if you knew how it helped me— Oh, I'll petition for your sweet happiness!"

She was weeping; she kissed Martin's forehead with the dry, soft, gentle kiss of an old woman, and he was near to weeping with her.

At parting Madeline whispered, "Boy, I don't care a bit, myself, but Mother would love it if we went to church with her. Don't you think you could, just once?"

The astounded world, the astounded and profane Clif Clawson, had the spectacle of Martin in shiny pressed clothes, a painful linen collar, and an arduously tied scarf, accompanying Mrs. Fox and the chastely chattering Madeline to the Mohalis Methodist Church, to hear the Reverend Dr. Myron Schwab discourse on "The One Way to Righteousness."

They passed the Reverend Ira Hinkley, and Ira gloated with a holy gloating at Martin's captivity.

### VII

For all his devotion to Max Gottlieb's pessimistic view of the human intellect, Martin had believed that there was such a thing as progress, that events meant something, that people could learn something, that if Madeline had once admitted she was an ordinary young woman who occasionally failed, then she was saved. He was bewildered when she began improving him more airily than ever. She complained of his vulgarity and what she asserted to be his slack ambition. "You think it's terribly smart of you to feel superior. Sometimes I wonder if it isn't just laziness. You like to day-dream around labs. Why should *you* be spared the work of memorizing your materia medica and so on and so forth? All the others have to do it. No, I won't kiss you. I want you to grow up and listen to reason."

In fury at her badgering, in desire for her lips and forgiving smile, he was whirled through to the end of the term.

A week before examinations, when he was trying to spend twenty-four hours a day in making love to her, twenty-four in grinding for examinations, and twenty-four in the bacteriological laboratory, he promised Clif that he would spent that summer vacation with him, working as a waiter in a Canadian hotel. He met Madeline in the evening, and with her walked through the cherry orchard on the Agricultural Experiment Station grounds.

"You know what I think of your horrid Clif Clawson," she complained. "I don't suppose you care to hear my opinion of him."

"I've had your opinion, my beloved." Martin sounded mature, and not too pleasant.

"Well, I can tell you right now you haven't had my opinion of your being a waiter! For the life of me I can't understand why you don't get some gentlemanly job for vacation, instead of hustling dirty dishes. Why couldn't you work on a newspaper, where you'd have to dress decently and meet nice people?"

"Sure. I might edit the paper. But since you say so, I won't work at all this summer. Fool thing to do, anyway. I'll go to Newport and play golf and wear a dress suit every night."

"It wouldn't hurt you any! I do respect honest labor. It's like Burns says. But waiting on table! Oh, Mart, why are you so proud of being a roughneck? Do stop being smart, for a minute. Listen to the night. And smell the cherry blossoms. . . . Or maybe a great scientist like you, that's so superior to ordinary people, is too good for cherry blossoms!"

"Well, except for the fact that every cherry blossom has been gone for weeks now, you're dead right."

"Oh, they have, have they! They may be faded but— Will you be so good as to tell me what that pale white mass is up there?"

"I will. It looks to me like a hired-man's shirt."

"Martin Arrowsmith, if you think for one moment that I'm ever going to marry a vulgar, crude, selfish, microbe-grubbing smart aleck—"

"And if you think I'm going to marry a dame that keeps nag-nag-naggin' and jab-jab-jabbin' at me all day long—"

They hurt each other; they had pleasure in it; and they parted forever, twice they parted forever, the second time very rudely, near a fraternity-house where students were singing heart-breaking summer songs to a banjo.

In ten days, without seeing her again, he was off with Clif to the North Woods, and in his sorrow of losing her, his longing for her soft flesh and for her willingness to listen to him, he was only a little excited that he should have led the class in bacteriology, and that Max Gottlieb should have appointed him undergraduate assistant for the coming year.

# 6

The waiters at Nokomis Lodge, among the Ontario pines, were all of them university students. They were not supposed to appear at the Lodge dances —they merely appeared, and took the prettiest girls away from the elderly and denunciatory suitors in white flannels. They had to work but seven hours a day. The rest of the time they fished, swam, and tramped the shadowy trails, and Martin came back to Mohalis placid—and enormously in love with Madeline.

They had written to each other, politely, regretfully, and once a fortnight; then passionately and daily. For the summer she had been dragged to her home town, near the Ohio border of Winnemac, a town larger than Martin's native Elk Mills but more sun-baked, more barren with little factories. She sighed, in a huge loose script dashing all over the page:

> Perhaps we shall never see each other again but I do want you to know how much I prize all the talks we had together about science & ideals & education, etc.—I certainly appreciate them here when I listen to these stick in the muds going on, oh, it is too dreadful, about their automobiles & how much they have to pay their maids and so on & so forth. You gave me so much but I did give you something didn't I? I cant always be in the wrong can I?

"My dear, my little girl!" he lamented. " 'Can't always be in the wrong'! You poor kid, you poor dear kid!"

By midsummer they were firmly re-engaged and, though he was slightly disturbed by the cashier, a young and giggling Wisconsin school-teacher with ankles, he so longed for Madeline that he lay awake thinking of giving up his job and fleeing to her caresses—lay awake for minutes at a time.

The returning train was torturingly slow, and he dismounted at Mohalis fevered with visions of her. Twenty minutes after, they were clinging together in the quiet of her living-room. It is true that twenty minutes after that, she was sneering at Clif Clawson, at fishing, and at all school-teachers, but to his fury she yielded in tears.

## II

His Junior year was a whirlwind. To attend lectures on physical diagnosis, surgery, neurology, obstetrics, and gynecology in the morning, with hospital demonstrations in the afternoon; to supervise the making of media and the sterilization of glassware for Gottlieb; to instruct a new class in the use of microscope and filter and autoclave; to read a page now and then of scientific German or French; to see Madeline constantly; to get through it all he drove himself to hysterical hurrying, and in the dizziest of it he began his first original research—his first lyric, his first ascent of unexplored mountains.

He had immunized rabbits to typhoid, and he believed that if he mixed serum taken from these immune animals with typhoid germs, the germs would die. Unfortunately—he felt—the germs grew joyfully. He was troubled; he was sure that his technique had been clumsy; he performed his experiment over and over, working till midnight, waking at dawn to ponder on his notes. (Though in letters to Madeline his writing was an inconsistent scrawl, in his laboratory notes it was precise.) When he was quite sure that Nature was persisting in doing something she ought not to, he went guiltily to Gottlieb, protesting, "The darn' bugs ought to die in this immune serum, but they don't. There's something wrong with the theories."

"Young man, do you set yourself up against science?" grated Gottlieb, flapping the papers on his desk. "Do you feel competent, huh, to attack the dogmas of immunology?"

"I'm sorry, sir. I can't help what the dogma is. Here's my protocols. Honestly, I've gone over and over the stuff, and I get the same results, as you can see. I only know what I observe."

Gottlieb beamed. "I give you, my boy, my episcopal blessings! That is the way! Observe what you observe, and if it does violence to all the nice correct views of science—out they go! I am very pleast, Martin. But now find out the Why, the underneath principle."

Ordinarily, Gottlieb called him "Arrowsmith" or "You" or "Uh." When he was furious he called him, or any other student, "Doctor." It was only in high moments that he honored him with "Martin," and the boy trotted off blissfully, to try to find (but never to succeed in finding) the Why that made everything so.

III

Gottlieb had sent him into Zenith, to the huge Zenith General Hospital, to secure a strain of meningococcus from an interesting patient. The bored reception clerk—who was interested only in obtaining the names, business addresses, and religions of patients, and did not care who died or who spat on the beautiful blue and white linoleum or who went about collecting meningococci, so long as the addresses were properly entered—loftily told him to go up to Ward D. Through the long hallways, past numberless rooms from which peered yellow-faced old women sitting up in bed in linty nightgowns, Martin wandered, trying to look important, hoping to be taken for a doctor, and succeeding only in feeling extraordinarily embarrassed.

He passed several nurses rapidly, half nodding to them, in the manner (or what he conceived to be the manner) of a brilliant young surgeon who is about to operate. He was so absorbed in looking like a brilliant young surgeon that he was completely lost, and discovered himself in a wing filled with private suites. He was late. He had no more time to go on being impressive. Like all males, he hated to confess ignorance by asking directions, but grudgingly he stopped at the door of a bedroom in which a probationer nurse was scrubbing the floor.

She was a smallish and slender probationer, muffled in a harsh blue denim dress, an enormous white apron, and a turban bound about her head with an elastic—a uniform as grubby as her pail of scrub-water. She peered up with the alert impudence of a squirrel.

"Nurse," he said, "I want to find Ward D."

Lazily, "Do you?"

"I do! If I can interrupt your work—"

"Doesn't matter. The damn' superintendent of nurses put me at scrubbing, and we aren't ever *supposed* to scrub floors, because she caught me smoking a cigarette. She's an old terror. If she found a child like you wandering around here, she'd drag you out by the ear."

"My *dear* young woman, it may interest you to know—"

"Oh! 'My dear young woman, it may—' Sounds exactly like our old prof, back home."

Her indolent amusement, her manner of treating him as though they were a pair of children making tongues at each other in a railroad station, was infuriating to the earnest young assistant of Professor Gottlieb.

"I am Dr. Arrowsmith," he snorted, "and I've been informed that even probationers learn that the first duty of a nurse is to stand when addressing doctors! I wish to find Ward D, to take a strain of—*it may interest you to know!*—a very dangerous microbe, and if you will kindly direct me—"

"Oh, gee, I've been getting fresh again. I don't seem to get along with this military discipline. All right. I'll stand up." She did. Her every movement was swiftly smooth as the running of a cat. "You go back, turn right, then left. I'm sorry I was fresh. But if you saw some of the old muffs of doctors that a nurse has to be meek to— Honestly, Doctor—if you *are* a doctor—"

"I don't see that I need to convince you!" he raged, as he stalked off. All the way to Ward D he was furious at her veiled derision. He was an eminent scientist, and it was outrageous that he should have to endure impudence from a probationer—a singularly vulgar probationer, a thin and slangy young woman apparently from the West. He repeated his rebuke: "I don't see that I need to convince you." He was proud of himself for having been lofty. He pictured himself telling Madeline about it, concluding, "I just said to her quietly, 'My dear young woman, I don't know that you are the person to whom I have to explain my mission here,' I said, and she wilted."

But her image had not wilted, when he had found the intern who was to help him and had taken the spinal fluid. She was before him, provocative, enduring. He had to see her again, and convince her— "Take a better man than she is, better man than I've ever met, to get away with being insulting to *me!*" said the modest young scientist.

He had raced back to her room and they were staring at each other before it came to him that he had not worked out the crushing things he was going to say. She had risen from her scrubbing. She had taken off her turban, and her hair was silky and honey-colored, her eyes were blue, her face childish.

There was nothing of the slavey in her. He could imagine her running down hillsides, shinning up a stack of straw.

"Oh," she said gravely. "I didn't mean to be rude then. I was just— Scrubbing makes me bad-tempered. I thought you were awfully nice, and I'm sorry I hurt your feelings, but you did seem so young for a doctor."

"I'm not. I'm a medic. I was showing off."

"So was I!"

He felt an instant and complete comradeship with her, a relation free from the fencing and posing of his struggle with Madeline. He knew that this girl was of his own people. If she was vulgar, jocular, unreticent, she was also gallant, she was full of laughter at humbugs, she was capable of a loyalty too casual and natural to seem heroic. His voice was lively, though his words were only:

"Pretty hard, this training for nursing, I guess."

"Not so awful, but it's just as romantic as being a hired girl—that's what we call 'em in Dakota."

"Come from Dakota?"

"I come from the most enterprising town—three hundred and sixty-two inhabitants—in the entire state of North Dakota—Wheatsylvania. Are you in the U. medic school?"

To a passing nurse, the two youngsters would have seemed absorbed in hospital business. Martin stood at the door, she by her scrubbing pail. She had reassumed her turban; its bagginess obscured her bright hair.

"Yes, I'm a Junior medic in Mohalis. But— I don't know. I'm not much of a medic. I like the lab side. I think I'll be a bacteriologist, and raise Cain with some of the fool theories of immunology. And I don't think much of the bed-side manner."

"I'm glad you don't. You get it here. You ought to hear some of the docs that are the sweetest old pussies with their patients—the way they bawl out the nurses. But labs—they seem sort of real. I don't suppose you can bluff a bacteria—what is it?—bacterium?"

"No, they're— What do they call you?"

"Me? Oh, it's an idiotic name—Leora Tozer."

"What's the matter with Leora? It's fine."

Sound of mating birds, sound of spring blossoms dropping in the tranquil air, the bark of sleepy dogs at midnight; who is to set them down and make them anything but hackneyed? And as natural, as conventional, as youthfully gauche, as eternally beautiful and authentic as those ancient sounds was the talk of Martin and Leora in that passionate half-hour when each found in the other a part of his own self, always vaguely missed, discovered now with astonished joy. They rattled like hero and heroine of a sticky tale, like sweat-shop operatives, like bouncing rustics, like prince and princess. Their words were silly and inconsequential, heard one by one, yet taken together they were as wise and important as the tides or the sounding wind.

He told her that he admired Max Gottlieb, that he had crossed her North Dakota on a train, and that he was an excellent hockey-player. She told him

that she "adored" vaudeville, that her father, Andrew Jackson Tozer, was
born in the East (by which she meant Illinois), and that she didn't particularly care for nursing. She had no especial personal ambition; she had
come here because she liked adventure. She hinted, with debonair regret,
that she was not too popular with the superintendent of nurses; she meant
to be good but somehow she was always dragged into rebellions connected
with midnight fudge or elopements. There was nothing heroic in her story
but from her placid way of telling it he had an impression of gay courage.

He interrupted with an urgent, "When can you get away from the hospital
for dinner? Tonight?"

"Why—"

"Please!"

"All right."

"When can I call for you?"

"Do you think I ought to— Well, seven."

All the way back to Mohalis he alternately raged and rejoiced. He informed himself that he was a moron to make this long trip into Zenith twice
in one day; he remembered that he was engaged to a girl called Madeline
Fox; he worried the matter of unfaithfulness; he asserted that Leora Tozer
was merely an imitation nurse who was as illiterate as a kitchen wench and
as impertinent as a newsboy; he decided, several times he decided, to telephone her and free himself from the engagement.

He was at the hospital at a quarter to seven.

He had to wait for twenty minutes in a reception-room like that of an
undertaker. He was in a panic. What was he doing here? She'd probably be
agonizingly dull, through a whole long dinner. Would he even recognize her,
in mufti? Then he leaped up. She was at the door. Her sulky blue uniform
was gone; she was childishly slim and light in a princess frock that was a
straight line from high collar and soft young breast to her feet. It seemed
natural to tuck her hand under his arm as they left the hospital. She moved
beside him with a little dancing step, shyer now than she had been in the
dignity of her job but looking up at him with confidence.

"Glad I came?" he demanded.

She thought it over. She had a trick of gravely thinking over obvious questions; and gravely (but with the gravity of a child, not the ponderous gravity
of a politician or an office-manager) she admitted, "Yes, I am glad. I was
afraid you'd go and get sore at me because I was so fresh, and I wanted to
apologize and— I liked your being so crazy about your bacteriology. I think
I'm a little crazy, too. The interns here—they come bothering around a lot,
but they're so sort of—so sort of *soggy*, with their new stethoscopes and their
brand-new dignity. Oh—" Most gravely of all: "Oh, gee, yes, I'm glad you
came. . . . Am I an idiot to admit it?"

"You're a darling to admit it." He was a little dizzy with her. He pressed
her hand with his arm.

"You won't think I let every medic and doctor pick me up, will you?"

"Leora! And you don't think I try and pick up every pretty girl I meet? I liked—I felt somehow we two could be chums. Can't we? Can't we?"

"I don't know. We'll see. Where are we going for dinner?"

"The Grand Hotel."

"We are not! It's terribly expensive. Unless you're awfully rich. You aren't, are you?"

"No, I'm not. Just enough money to get through medic school. But I want—"

"Let's go to the Bijou. It's a nice place, and it isn't expensive."

He remembered how often Madeline Fox had hinted that it would be a tasty thing to go to the Grand, Zenith's most resplendent hotel, but that was the last time he thought of Madeline that evening. He was absorbed in Leora. He found in her a casualness, a lack of prejudice, a directness, surprising in the daughter of Andrew Jackson Tozer. She was feminine but undemanding; she was never Improving and rarely shocked; she was neither flirtatious nor cold. She was indeed the first girl to whom he had ever talked without self-consciousness. It is doubtful if Leora herself had a chance to say anything, for he poured out his every confidence as a disciple of Gottlieb. To Madeline, Gottlieb was a wicked old man who made fun of the sanctities of Marriage and Easter lilies, to Clif, he was a bore, but Leora glowed as Martin banged the table and quoted his idol: "Up to the present, even in the work of Ehrlich, most research has been largely a matter of trial and error, the empirical method, which is the opposite of the scientific method, by which one seeks to establish a general law governing a group of phenomena so that he may predict what will happen."

He intoned it reverently, staring across the table at her, almost glaring at her. He insisted, "Do you see where he leaves all these detail-grubbing, machine-made researchers buzzing in the manure heap just as much as he does the commercial docs? Do you get him? Do you?"

"Yes, I think I do. Anyway, I get your enthusiasm for him. But please don't bully me so!"

"Was I bullying? I didn't mean to. Only, when I get to thinking about the way most of these damned profs don't even know what he's up to—"

Martin was off again, and if Leora did not altogether understand the relation of the synthesis of antibodies to the work of Arrhenius, yet she listened with comfortable pleasure in his zeal, with none of Madeline Fox's gently corrective admonitions.

She had to warn him that she must be at the hospital by ten.

"I've talked too much! Lord, I hope I haven't bored you," he blurted.

"I loved it."

"And I was so technical, and so noisy— Oh, I *am* a chump!"

"I like having you trust me. I'm not 'earnest,' and I haven't any brains whatever, but I do love it when my menfolks think I'm intelligent enough to hear what they really think and— Good night!"

They dined together twice in two weeks, and only twice in that time, though she telephoned to him, did Martin see his honest affianced, Madeline.

He came to know all of Leora's background. Her bed-ridden grand-aunt in Zenith, who was her excuse for coming so far to take hospital training. The hamlet of Wheatsylvania, North Dakota; one street of shanties with the red grain-elevators at the end. Her father, Andrew Jackson Tozer, sometimes known as Jackass Tozer; owner of the bank, of the creamery, and an elevator, therefore the chief person in town; pious at Wednesday evening prayer-meeting, fussing over every penny he gave to Leora or her mother. Bert Tozer, her brother; squirrel teeth, a gold eye-glass chain over his ear, cashier and all the rest of the staff in the one-room bank owned by his father. The chicken salad and coffee suppers at the United Brethren Church; German Lutheran farmers singing ancient Teutonic hymns; the Hollanders, the Bohemians and Poles. And round about the village, the living wheat, arched above by tremendous clouds. He saw Leora, always an "odd child," doing obediently enough the flat household tasks but keeping snug the belief that some day she would find a youngster with whom, in whatever danger or poverty, she would behold all the colored world.

It was at the end of her hesitating effort to make him see her childhood that he cried, "Darling, you don't have to tell me about you. I've always known you. I'm not going to let you go, no matter what. You're going to marry me—"

They said it with clasping hands, confessing eyes, in that blatant restaurant. Her first words were:

"I want to call you 'Sandy.' Why do I? I don't know why. You're as unsandy as can be, but somehow 'Sandy' means you to me and— Oh, my dear, I do like you!"

Martin went home engaged to two girls at once.

## IV

He had promised to see Madeline the next morning.

By any canon of respectable behavior he should have felt like a low dog; he assured himself that he must feel like a low dog; but he could not bring it off. He thought of Madeline's pathetic enthusiasms: her "Provençal pleasaunce" and the limp-leather volumes of poetry which she patted with fond finger-tips; of the tie she had bought for him, and her pride in his hair when he brushed it like the patent-leather heroes in magazine illustrations. He mourned that he had sinned against loyalty. But his agitation broke against the solidity of his union with Leora. Her companionship released his soul. Even when, as advocate for Madeline, he pleaded that Leora was a trivial young woman who probably chewed gum in private and certainly was careless about her nails in public, her commonness was dear to the commonness that was in himself, valid as ambition or reverence, an earthy base to her gaiety as it was to his nervous scientific curiosity.

He was absent-minded in the laboratory, that fatal next day. Gottlieb had twice to ask him whether he had prepared the new batch of medium, and Gottlieb was an autocrat, sterner with his favorites than with the ruck of students. He snarled, "Arrowsmith, you are a moon-calf! My God, am I to spend my life with *Dummköpfe*? I cannot be always alone, Martin! Are you going to fail me? Two, three days now you haf not been keen about work."

Martin went off mumbling, "I love that man!" In his tangled mood he catalogued Madeline's pretenses, her nagging, her selfishness, her fundamental ignorance. He worked himself up to a state of virtue in which it was agreeably clear to him that he must throw Madeline over, entirely as a rebuke. He went to her in the evening prepared to blaze out at her first complaining, to forgive her finally, but to break their engagement and make life resolutely simple again.

She did not complain.

She ran to him. "Dear, you're so tired—your eyes look tired. Have you been working frightfully hard? I've been so sorry you couldn't come 'round, this week. Dear, you mustn't kill yourself. Think of all the years you have ahead to do splendid things in. No, don't talk. I want you to rest. Mother's gone to the movies. Sit here. See, I'll make you so comfy with these pillows. Just lean back—go to sleep if you want to—and I'll read you 'The Crock of Gold.' You'll love it."

He was determined that he would not love it and, as he probably had no sense of humor whatever, it is doubtful whether he appreciated it, but its differentness aroused him. Though Madeline's voice was shrill and cornfield-ish after Leora's lazy softness, she read so eagerly that he was sick ashamed of his intention to hurt her. He saw that it was she, with her pretenses, who was the child, and the detached and fearless Leora who was mature, mistress of a real world. The reproofs with which he had planned to crush her vanished.

Suddenly she was beside him, begging, "I've been so lonely for you, all week!"

So he was a traitor to both women. It was Leora who had intolerably roused him; it was really Leora whom he was caressing now; but it was Madeline who took his hunger to herself, and when she whimpered, "I'm so glad you're glad to be here," he could say nothing. He wanted to talk about Leora, to shout about Leora, to exult in her, his woman. He dragged out a few sound but unimpassioned flatteries; he observed that Madeline was a handsome young woman and a sound English scholar; and while she gaped with disappointment at his lukewarmness, he got himself away, at ten. He had finally succeeded very well indeed in feeling like a low dog.

He hastened to Clif Clawson.

He had told Clif nothing about Leora. He resented Clif's probable scoffing. He thought well of himself for the calmness with which he came into their room. Clif was sitting on the small of his back, shoeless feet upon the study table, reading a Sherlock Holmes story which rested on the powerful volume of Osler's Medicine which he considered himself to be reading.

"Clif! Want a drink. Tired. Let's sneak down to Barney's and see if we can rustle one."

"Thou speakest as one having tongues and who putteth the speed behind

the ole rhombencephalon comprising the cerebellum and the medulla ob-
longata."

"Oh, cut out the cuteness! I'm in a bad temper."

"Ah, the laddie has been having a scrap with his chaste lil Madeline! Was
she horrid to ickly Martykins? All right. I'll quit. Come on. Yoicks for the
drink."

He told three new stories about Professor Robertshaw, all of them scurrilous and most of them untrue, on their way, and he almost coaxed Martin
into cheerfulness. "Barney's" was a poolroom, a tobacco shop and, since Mohalis was dry by local option, an admirable blind-pig. Clif and the hairy-
handed Barney greeted each other in a high and worthy manner:

"The benisons of eventide to you, Barney. May your circulation proceed
unchecked and particularly the dorsal carpal branch of the ulnar artery, in
which connection, comrade, Prof. Dr. Col. Egbert Arrowsmith and I would
fain trifle with another bottle of that renowned strawberry pop."

"Gosh, Clif, you cer'nly got a swell line of jaw-music. If I ever need a' arm
amputated when you get to be a doc, I'll come around and let you talk it
off. Strawberry pop, gents?"

The front room of Barney's was an impressionistic painting in which a
pool-table, piles of cigarettes, chocolate bars, playing cards, and pink sporting
papers were jumbled in chaos. The back room was simpler: cases of sweet
and thinly flavored soda, a large ice-box, and two small tables with broken
chairs. Barney poured, from a bottle plainly marked Ginger Ale, two glasses
of powerful and appallingly raw whisky, and Clif and Martin took them to
the table in the corner. The effect was swift. Martin's confused sorrows
turned to optimism. He told Clif that he was going to write a book exposing
idealism, but what he meant was that he was going to do something clever
about his dual engagement. He had it! He would invite Leora and Madeline
to lunch together, tell them the truth, and see which of them loved him.
He whooped, and had another whisky; he told Clif that he was a fine fellow,
and Barney that he was a public benefactor, and unsteadily he retired to the
telephone, which was shut off from public hearing in a closet.

At the Zenith General Hospital he got the night superintendent, and the
night superintendent was a man frosty and suspicious. "This is no time to
be calling up a probationer! Half-past eleven! Who are you, anyway?"

Martin checked the "I'll damn' soon tell you who I am!" which was his
natural reaction, and explained that he was speaking for Leora's invalid
grand-aunt, that the poor old lady was very low, and if the night superintendent cared to take upon himself the murder of a blameless gentlewoman—

When Leora came to the telephone he said quickly, and soberly now,
feeling as though he had come from the menace of thronging strangers into
the security of her presence:

"Leora? Sandy. Meet me Grand lobby tomorrow, twelve-thirty. Must! Important! Fix 't somehow—your aunt's sick."

"All right, dear. G' night," was all she said.

It took him long minutes to get an answer from Madeline's flat, then Mrs. Fox's voice sounded, sleepily, quaveringly:

"Yes, yes?"

" 'S Martin."

"Who is it? Who is it? What is it? Are you calling the Fox apartment?"

"Yes, yes! Mrs. Fox, it's Martin Arrowsmith speaking."

"Oh, oh, my dear! The 'phone woke me out of a sound sleep, and I couldn't make out what you were saying. I was so frightened. I thought maybe it was a telegram or something. I thought perhaps something had happened to Maddy's brother. What is it, dear? Oh, I do hope nothing's happened!"

Her confidence in him, the affection of this uprooted old woman bewildered in a strange land, overcame him; he lost all his whisky-colored feeling that he was a nimble fellow, and in a melancholy way, with all the weight of life again upon him, he sighed that no, nothing had happened, but he'd forgotten to tell Madeline something—so shor—so sorry call so late—could he speak Mad just minute—

Then Madeline was bubbling, "Why, Marty dear, what is it? I do hope nothing has happened! Why, dear, you just left here—"

"Listen, d-dear. Forgot to tell you. There's a—there's a great friend of mine in Zenith that I want you to meet—"

"Who is he?"

"You'll see tomorrow. Listen, I want you come in and meet—come meet um at lunch. Going," with ponderous jocularity, "going to blow you all to a swell feed at the Grand—"

"Oh, how nice!"

"—so I want you to meet me at the eleven-forty interurban, at College Square. Can you?"

Vaguely, "Oh, I'd love to but—I have an eleven o'clock, and I don't like to cut it, and I promised May Harmon to go shopping with her—she's looking for some kind of shoes that you can wear with her pink crêpe de chine but that you can walk in—and we sort of thought maybe we might lunch at Ye Kollege Karavanserai—and I'd half planned to go to the movies with her or somebody, Mother says that new Alaska film is simply dandy, she saw it tonight, and I thought I might go see it before they take it off, though Heaven knows I ought to come right home and study and not go anywhere at all—"

"Now *listen!* It's important. Don't you trust me? Will you come or not?"

"Why, of course I trust you, dear. All right, I'll try to be there. The eleven-forty?"

"Yes."

"At College Square? Or at Bluthman's Book Shop?"

"*At College Square!*"

Her gentle "I trust you" and her wambling "I'll try to" were warring in his ears as he plunged out of the suffocating cell and returned to Clif.

"What's the grief?" Clif wondered. "Wife passed away? Or did the Giants win in the ninth? Barney, our wandering-boy-tonight looks like a necropsy. Slip him another strawberry pop, quick. Say, Doctor, I think you better call a physician."

"Oh, shut up," was all Martin had to say, and that without conviction. Before telephoning he had been full of little brightnesses; he had praised Clif's pool-playing and called Barney "old *Cimex lectularius*"; but now, while the affectionate Clif worked on him, he sat brooding save when he grumbled (with a return of self-satisfaction), "If you knew all the troubles I have—all the doggone mess a fellow can get into—*you'd* feel down in the mouth!"

Clif was alarmed. "Look here, old socks. If you've gotten in debt, I'll raise the cash, somehow. If it's— Been going a little too far with Madeline?"

"You make me sick! You've got a dirty mind. I'm not worthy to touch Madeline's hand. I regard her with nothing but respect."

"The hell you do! But never mind, if you say so. Gosh, wish there was *something* I could do for you. Oh! Have 'nother shot! Barney! Come a-runnin'!"

By several drinks Martin was warmed into a hazy carelessness, and Clif solicitously dragged him home after he had desired to fight three large academic sophomores. But in the morning he awoke with a crackling skull and a realization that he was going to face Leora and Madeline at lunch.

v

His half-hour journey with Madeline into Zenith seemed a visible and oppressing thing, like a tornado cloud. He had not merely to get through each minute as it came; the whole grim thirty minutes were present at the same time. While he was practicing the tactful observation he was going to present two minutes from now, he could still hear the clumsy thing he had said two minutes before. He fought to keep her attention from the "great friend of his" whom they were to meet. With fatuous beaming he described a night at Barney's; without any success whatever he tried to be funny; and when Madeline lectured him on the evils of liquor and the evils of association with immoral persons, he was for once relieved. But he could not side-track her.

"Who is this man we're going to see? What are you so mysterious about? Oh, Martykins, is it a joke? Aren't we going to meet anybody? Did you just want to run away from Mama for a while and we have a bat at the Grand together? Oh, what fun! I've always wanted to lunch at the Grand. Of course I do think it's too sort of rococo, but still, it is impressive, and— Did I guess it, darling?"

"No, there's someone— Oh, we're going to meet somebody, all right!"

"Then why don't you tell me who he is? Honestly, Mart, you make me impatient."

"Well, I'll tell you. It isn't a Him; it's a Her."

"Oh!"

"It's— You know my work takes me to the hospitals, and some of the nurses at Zenith General have been awfully helpful." He was panting. His eyes ached. Since the torture of the coming lunch was inevitable, he wondered why he should go on trying to resist his punishment. "Especially there's one nurse there who's a wonder. She's learned so much about the care of the sick, and she puts me onto a lot of good stunts, and she seems like a nice girl—Miss Tozer, her name is—I think her first name is Lee or something like that—and she's so—her father is one of the big men in North Dakota— awfully rich—big banker—I guess she just took up nursing to do her share in the world's work." He had achieved Madeline's own tone of poetic uplift. "I thought you two might like to know each other. You remember you were saying how few girls there are in Mohalis that really appreciate—appreciate ideals."

"Ye-es." Madeline gazed at something far away and, whatever it was, she did not like it. "I shall be ver' pleased to meet her, of course. Any friend of yours— Oh, Mart! I do hope you don't flirt; I hope you don't get too friendly with all these nurses. I don't know anything about it, of course, but I keep hearing how some of these nurses are regular man-hunters."

"Well, let me tell you right now, Leora isn't!"

"No, I'm sure, but— Oh, Martykins, you won't be silly and let these nurses just amuse themselves with you? I mean, for your own sake. They have such an advantage. Poor Madeline, she wouldn't be allowed to go hanging around men's rooms learning—things, and you think you're so psychological, Mart, but honestly, any smart woman can twist you around her finger."

"Well, I guess I can take care of myself!"

"Oh, I mean—I don't mean— But I do hope this Tozer person— I'm sure I shall like her, if you do, but— I am your own true love, aren't I, always!"

She, the proper, ignored the passengers as she clasped his hand. She sounded so frightened that his anger at her reflections on Leora turned into misery. Incidentally, her thumb was gouging painfully into the back of his hand. He tried to look tender as he protested, "Sure—sure—gosh, honest, Mad, look out. That old duffer across the aisle is staring at us."

For whatever infidelities he might ever commit he was adequately pun-ished before they had reached the Grand Hotel.

The Grand was, in 1907, the best hotel in Zenith. It was compared by traveling salesmen to the Parker House, the Palmer House, the West Hotel. It has been humbled since by the supercilious modesty of the vast Hotel Thornleigh; dirty now is its tessellated floor and all the wild gilt tarnished, and in its ponderous leather chairs are torn seams and stogie ashes and horse-dealers. But in its day it was the proudest inn between Chicago and Pittsburgh; an oriental palace, the entrance a score of brick Moorish arches, the lobby towering from a black and white marble floor, up past gilt iron balconies, to the green, pink, pearl, and amber skylight seven stories above.

They found Leora in the lobby, tiny on an enormous couch built round a pillar. She stared at Madeline, quiet, waiting. Martin perceived that Leora was unusually sloppy—his own word. It did not matter to him how clumsily her honey-colored hair was tucked under her black hat, a characterless little mush-room of a hat, but he did see and resent the contrast between her shirtwaist, with the third button missing, her checked skirt, her unfortunate bright brown bolero jacket, and Madeline's sleekness of blue serge. The resentment was not toward Leora. Scanning them together (not haughtily, as the choosing and lofty male, but anxiously) he was more irritated than ever by Madeline. That she should be better dressed was an affront. His affection flew to guard Leora, to wrap and protect her.

And all the while he was bumbling:

"—thought you two girls ought to know each other—Miss Fox, want t' make you 'quainted with Miss Tozer—little celebration—lucky dog have two Queens of Sheba—"

And to himself, "Oh, hell!"

While they murmured nothing in particular to each other he herded them into the famous dining-room of the Grand. It was full of gilt chandeliers, red plush chairs, heavy silverware, and aged Negro retainers with gold and green waistcoats. Round the walls ran select views of Pompeii, Venice, Lake Como, and Versailles.

"Swell room!" chirped Leora.

Madeline had looked as though she intended to say the same thing in longer words, but she considered the frescoes all over again and explained, "Well, it's very large—"

He was ordering, with agony. He had appropriated four dollars for the orgy, strictly including the tip, and his standard of good food was that he must spend every cent of the four dollars. While he wondered what "Purée St. Germain" could be, and the waiter hideously stood watching behind his shoulder, Madeline fell to. She chanted with horrifying politeness:

"Mr. Arrowsmith tells me you are a nurse, Miss—Tozer."

"Yes, sort of."

"Do you find it interesting?"

"Well—yes—yes, I think it's interesting."

"I suppose it must be wonderful to relieve suffering. Of course my work— I'm taking my Doctor of Philosophy degree in English—" She made it sound as though she were taking her earldom—"it's rather dry and detached. I have to master the growth of the language and so on and so forth. With your practical training, I suppose you'd find that rather stupid."

"Yes, it must be—no, it must be very interesting."

"Do you come from Zenith, Miss—Tozer?"

"No, I come from— Just a little town. Well, hardly a town. . . . North Dakota."

"Oh! North Dakota!"

"Yes. . . . Way West."

"Oh, yes. . . . Are you staying East for some time?" It was precisely what a much-resented New York cousin had once said to Madeline.

"Well, I don't— Yes, I guess I may be here quite some time."

"Do you, uh, do you find you like it here?"

"Oh, yes, it's pretty nice. These big cities— So much to see."

" 'Big'? Well, I suppose it all depends on the point of view, *doesn't* it? I always think of New York as big but— Of course— Do you find the contrast to North Dakota interesting?"

"Well, of course it's different."

"Tell me what North Dakota's like. I've always wondered about these Western states." It was Madeline's second plagiarism of her cousin. "What is the general impression it makes on you?"

"I don't think I know just how you mean."

"I mean what is the general effect? The—*impression.*"

"Well, it's got lots of wheat and lots of Swedes."

"But I mean— I suppose you're all terribly virile and energetic, compared with us Easterners."

"I don't— Well, yes, maybe."

"Have you met lots of people in Zenith?"

"Not so *awfully* many."

"Oh, have you met Dr. Birchall, that operates in your hospital? He's such a nice man, and not just a good surgeon but frightfully talented. He sings won-derfully, and he comes from the most frightfully nice family."

"No, I don't think I've met him yet," Leora bleated.

"Oh, you must. And he plays the slickest—the most gorgeous game of tennis. He always goes to all these millionaire parties on Royal Ridge. Fright-fully smart."

Martin now first interrupted. "Smart? Him? He hasn't got any brains whatever."

"My dear child, I didn't mean 'smart' in that sense!" He sat alone and helpless while she again turned on Leora and ever more brightly inquired whether Leora knew this son of a corporation lawyer and that famous débu-tante, this hatshop and that club. She spoke familiarly of what were known as the Leaders of Zenith Society, the personages who appeared daily in the society columns of the *Advocate-Times*, the Cowxes and Van Antrims and Dodsworths. Martin was astonished by the familiarity; he remembered that she had once gone to a charity ball in Zenith but he had not known that she was so intimate with the peerage. Certainly Leora had appallingly never heard of these great ones, nor ever attended the concerts, the lectures, the recitals at which Madeline apparently spent all her glittering evenings.

Madeline shrugged a little, then, "Well— Of course with the fascinating doctors and everybody that you meet in the hospital, I suppose you'd find lectures frightfully tame. Well—" She dismissed Leora and looked patroniz-ingly at Martin. "Are you planning some more work on the what-is-it with rabbits?"

He was grim. He could do it now, if he got it over quickly. "Madeline! Brought you two together because— Don't know whether you cotton to each other or not, but I wish you could, because I've—I'm not making any ex-cuses for myself. I couldn't help it. I'm engaged to both of you, and I want to know—"

Madeline had sprung up. She had never looked quite so proud and fine.

She stared at them, and walked away, wordless. She came back, she touched Leora's shoulder, and quietly kissed her. "Dear, I'm sorry for you. You've got a job! You poor baby!" She strode away, her shoulders straight.

Hunched, frightened, Martin could not look at Leora.

He felt her hand on his. He looked up. She was smiling, easy, a little mocking. "Sandy, I warn you that I'm never going to give you up. I suppose you're as bad as She says; I suppose I'm foolish—I'm a hussy. But you're mine! I warn you it isn't a bit of use your getting engaged to somebody else again. I'd tear her eyes out! Now don't think so well of yourself! I guess you're pretty selfish. But I don't care. You're mine!"

He said brokenly many things beautiful in their commonness.

She pondered, "I do feel we're nearer together than you and Her. Perhaps you like me better because you can bully me—because I tag after you and She never would. And I know your work is more important to you than I am, maybe more important than you are. But I am stupid and ordinary and She isn't. I simply admire you frightfully (Heaven knows why, but I do), while She has sense enough to make you admire Her and tag after Her."

"No! I swear it isn't because I can bully you, Leora—I swear it isn't—I don't think it is. Dearest, don't *don't* think she's brighter than you are. She's glib but— Oh, let's stop talking! I've found you! My life's begun!"

# 7

The difference between Martin's relations to Madeline and to Leora was the difference between a rousing duel and a serene comradeship. From their first evening, Leora and he depended on each other's loyalty and liking, and certain things in his existence were settled forever. Yet his absorption in her was not stagnant. He was always making discoveries about the observations of life which she kept incubating in her secret little head while she made smoke rings with her cigarettes and smiled silently. He longed for the girl Leora; she stirred him, and with gay frank passion she answered him; but to another, sexless Leora he talked more honestly than to Gottlieb or his own worried self, while with her boyish nod or an occasional word she encouraged him to confidence in his evolving ambition and disdains.

## II

Digamma Pi fraternity was giving a dance. It was understood among the anxiously whispering medics that so cosmopolitan was the University of Winnemac becoming that they were expected to wear the symbols of respectability known as "dress-suits." On the solitary and nervous occasion when Martin had worn evening clothes he had rented them from the Varsity Pantorium, but he must own them, now that he was going to introduce Leora to the world as his pride and flowering. Like two little old people, absorbed in each other and diffidently exploring new, unwelcoming streets of the city where their alienated children live, Martin and Leora edged into the garnished magnificence of Benson, Hanley and Koch's, the loftiest department store in Zenith. She was intimidated by the luminous cases of mahogany and plate glass, by the opera hats and lustrous mufflers and creamy riding breeches. When he had tried on a dinner suit and come out for her approval, his long brown tie and soft-collared shirt somewhat rustic behind the low evening waistcoat, and when the clerk had gone to fetch collars, she wailed:

"Darn it, Sandy, you're too grand for me. I just simply can't get myself to fuss over my clothes, and here you're going to go and look so spiffy I won't have a chance with you."

He almost kissed her.

The clerk, returning, warbled, "I think, Modom, you'll find that your husband will look vurry nice indeed in these wing collars."

Then, while the clerk sought ties, he did kiss her, and she sighed:

"Oh, gee you're one of these people that get ahead. I never thought I'd have to live up to a man with a dress-suit and a come-to-Heaven collar. Oh, well, I'll tag!"

### III

For the Digamma Ball, the University Armory was extremely decorated. The brick walls were dizzy with bunting, spotty with paper chrysanthemums and plaster skulls and wooden scalpels ten feet long.

In six years at Mohalis, Martin had gone to less than a score of dances, though the refined titillations of communal embracing were the chief delight of the co-educational university. When he arrived at the Armory, with Leora timorously brave in a blue crêpe de chine made in no recognized style, he did not care whether he had a single two-step, though he did achingly desire to have the men crowd in and ask Leora, admire her and make her welcome. Yet he was too proud to introduce her about, lest he seem to be begging his friends to dance with her. They stood alone, under the balcony, disconsolately facing the vastness of the floor, while beyond them flashed the current of dancers, beautiful, formidable, desirable. Leora and he had assured each other that, for a student affair, dinner jacket and black waistcoat would be the thing, as stated in the Benson, Hanley and Koch Chart of Correct Gents' Wearing Apparel, but he grew miserable at the sight of voluptuous white waistcoats, and when that embryo famous surgeon, Angus Duer, came by, disdainful as a greyhound and pushing on white gloves (which are the whitest, the most superciliously white objects on earth), then Martin felt himself a hobbledehoy.

"Come on, *we'll* dance," he said, as though it were a defiance to all Angus Duers.

He very much wanted to go home.

He did not enjoy the dance, though she waltzed easily and himself not too badly. He did not even enjoy having her in his arms. He could not believe that she was in his arms. As they revolved he saw Duer join a brilliance of pretty girls and distinguished-looking women about the great Dr. Silva, dean of the medical school. Angus seemed appallingly at home, and he waltzed off with the prettiest girl, sliding, swinging, deft. Martin tried to hate him as a fool, but he remembered that yesterday Angus had been elected to the honorary society of Sigma Xi.

Leora and he crept back to the exact spot beneath the balcony where they had stood before, to their den, their one safe refuge. While he tried to be nonchalant and talk up to his new clothes, he was cursing the men he saw go by laughing with girls, ignoring his Leora.

"Not many here yet," he fussed. "Pretty soon they'll all be coming, and then you'll have lots of dances."

"Oh, I don't mind."

("God, won't somebody come and ask the poor kid?")

He fretted over his lack of popularity among the dancing-men of the medical school. He wished Clif Clawson were present—Clif liked any sort of assembly, but he could not afford dress-clothes. Then, rejoicing as at sight of the best-beloved, he saw Irving Watters, that paragon of professional normality, wandering toward them, but Watters passed by, merely nodding. Thrice Martin hoped and desponded, and now all his pride was gone. If Leora could be happy—

"I wouldn't care a hoot if she fell for the gabbiest fusser in the whole U., and gave me the go-by all evening. Anything to let her have a good time! If I could coax Duer over— No, that's one thing I couldn't stand: crawling to that dirty snob— I will!"

Up ambled Fatty Pfaff, just arrived. Martin pounced on him lovingly. "H'lo, old Fat! You a stag tonight? Meet my friend Miss Tozer."

Fatty's bulbous eyes showed approval of Leora's cheeks and amber hair. He heaved, "Pleasedmeetch—dance starting—have the honor?" in so flattering a manner that Martin could have kissed him.

That he himself stood alone through the dance did not occur to him. He leaned against a pillar and gloated. He felt gorgeously unselfish. . . . That various girl wallflowers were sitting near him, waiting to be asked, did not occur to him either.

He saw Fatty introduce Leora to a decorative pair of Digams, one of whom begged her for the next. Thereafter she had more invitations than she could take. Martin's excitement cooled. It seemed to him that she clung too closely to her partners, that she followed their steps too eagerly. After the fifth dance he was agitated. "Course! *She's* enjoying herself! Hasn't got time to notice that I just stand here—yes, by thunder, and hold her scarf! Sure! Fine for her. Fact I might like a little dancing myself— And the way she grins and gawps at that fool Brindle Morgan, the—the—the damnedest— Oh, you and I are going to have a talk, young woman! And those hounds trying to pinch her off me—the one thing I've ever loved! Just because they dance better than I can, and spiel a lot of foolishness— And that damn' orchestra playing that damn' peppery music— And she falling for all their damn' cheap compliments and— You and I are going to have one lovely little understanding!"

When she next returned to him, besieged by three capering medics, he muttered to her, "Oh, it doesn't *matter* about *me!*"

"Would you like this one? *Course* you shall have it!" She turned to him fully; she had none of Madeline's sense of having to act for the benefit of observers. Through a strained eternity of waiting, while he glowered, she babbled of the floor, the size of the room, and her "dandy partners." At the sound of the music he held out his arms.

"No," she said. "I want to talk to you." She led him to a corner and hurled at him, "Sandy, this is the last time I'm going to stand for your looking jealous. Oh, I know! See here! If we're going to stick together—and we are! —I'm going to dance with just as many men as I want to, and I'm going to be just as foolish with 'em as I want to. Dinners and those things—I suppose I'll always go on being a clam. Nothing to say. But I love dancing, and I'm going to do exactly what I want to, and if you had any sense whatever, you'd know I don't care a hang for anybody but you. Yours! Absolute. No matter what fool things you do—and they'll probably be a plenty. So when you go and get jealous on me again, you sneak off and get rid of it. Aren't you ashamed of yourself!"

"I wasn't jealous— Yes, I was. Oh, I can't help it! I love you so much. I'd be one fine lover, now wouldn't I, if I never got jealous!"

"All right. Only you've got to keep it under cover. Now we'll finish the dance."

He was her slave.

IV

It was regarded as immoral, at the University of Winnemac, to dance after midnight, and at that hour the guests crowded into the Imperial Cafeteria. Ordinarily it closed at eight, but tonight it kept open till one, and developed a spirit of almost lascivious mirth. Fatty Pfaff did a jig, another humorous student, with a napkin over his arm, pretended to be a waiter, and a girl (but she was much disapproved) smoked a cigarette.

At the door Clif Clawson was waiting for Martin and Leora. He was in his familiar shiny gray suit, with a blue flannel shirt.

Clif assumed that he was the authority to whom all of Martin's friends must be brought for judgment. He had not met Leora. Martin had confessed his double engagement; he had explained that Leora was unquestionably the most gracious young woman on earth; but as he had previously used up all of his laudatory adjectives and all of Clif's patience on the subject of Madeline, Clif failed to listen, and prepared to dislike Leora as another siren of morality.

He eyed her now with patronizing enmity. He croaked at Martin, behind her back, "Good-looking kid, I will say that for her—what's wrong with her?"

When they had brought their own sandwiches and coffee and mosaic cake from the long counter, Clif rasped:

"Well, it's grand of a couple of dress-suit swells like you to assassinate with me 'mid the midmosts of sartorials and Sassiety. Gosh, it's fierce I had to miss the select pleasures of an evening with Anxious Duer and associated highboys, and merely play a low game of poker—in which Father deftly removed the sum of six simolea, point ten, from the foregathered bums and yahoos. Well, Leory, I suppose you and Martykins here have now ratiocinated all these questions of polo and, uh, Monte Carlo and so on."

She had an immense power of accepting people as they were. While Clif waited, leering, she placidly investigated the inside of a chicken sandwich and assented, "Um-huh."

"Good boy! I thought you were going to pull that 'If you are a roughneck, I don't see why you think you've got to boast about it' stuff that Mart springs on me!"

Clif turned into a jovial and (for him) unusually quiet companion. . . . Ex-farmhand, ex-book-agent, ex-mechanic, he had so little money yet so scratching a desire to be resplendent that he took refuge in pride in poverty, pride in being offensive. Now, when Leora seemed to look through his boasting, he liked her as quickly as had Martin, and they buzzed with gaiety. Martin was warmed to benevolence toward mankind, including Angus Duer, who was at the end of the room at a table with Dean Silva and his silvery women. Without plan, Martin sprang up, raced down the room. Holding out his hand he clamored:

"Angus, old man, want to congratulate you on getting Sigma Xi. That's fine."

Duer regarded the outstretched hand as though it was an instrument which he had seen before but whose use he could not quite remember. He picked it up and shook it tentatively. He did not turn his back; he was worse than rude—he looked patient.

"Well, good luck," said Martin, chilled and shaky.

"Very good of you. Thanks."

Martin returned to Leora and Clif, to tell them the incident as a cosmic tragedy. They agreed that Angus Duer was to be shot. In the midst of it Duer came past, trailing after Dean Silva's party, and nodded to Martin, who glared back, feeling noble and mature.

At parting, Clif held Leora's hand and urged, "Honey, I think a lot of Mart, and one time I was afraid the old kid was going to get tied up to—to parties that would turn him into a hand-shaker. I'm a hand-shaker myself. I know less about medicine than Prof Robertshaw. But this boob has some conscience to him, and I'm so darn' glad he's playing around with a girl that's real folks and— Oh, listen at me fallin' all over my clumsy feet! But I just mean I hope you won't mind Uncle Clif saying he does by golly like you a lot!"

It was almost four when Martin returned from taking Leora home and sagged into bed. He could not sleep. The aloofness of Angus Duer racked him as an insult to himself, as somehow an implied insult to Leora, but his boyish rage had passed into a bleaker worry. Didn't Duer, for all his snobbishness and shallowness, have something that he himself lacked? Didn't Clif, with his puppy-dog humor, his speech of a vaudeville farmer, his suspicion of fine manners as posing, take life too easily? Didn't Duer know how to control and drive his hard little mind? Wasn't there a technique of manners as there was of experimentation. . . . Gottlieb's fluent bench-technique versus the clumsy and podgy hands of Ira Hinkley. . . . Or was all this inquiry a treachery, a yielding to Duer's own affected standard?

He was so tired that behind his closed eyelids were flashes of fire. His whirling mind flew over every sentence he had said or heard that night, till round his twisting body there was fevered shouting.

V

As he grumped across the medical campus next day, he came unexpectedly upon Angus and he was smitten with the guiltiness and embarrassment one has toward a person who has borrowed money and probably will not return it. Mechanically he began to blurt "Hello," but he checked it in a croak, scowled, and stumbled on.

"Oh, Mart," Angus called. He was dismayingly even. "Remember speaking to me last evening? It struck me when I was going out that you looked huffy. I was wondering if you thought I'd been rude. I'm sorry if you did. Fact is, I had a rotten headache. Look. I've got four tickets for 'As It Listeth,' in Zenith, next Friday evening—original New York cast! Like to see it? And I noticed you were with a peach, at the dance. Suppose she might like to go along with us, she and some friend of hers?"

"Why—gosh—I'll 'phone her—darn' nice of you to ask us—"

It was not till melancholy dusk, when Leora had accepted and promised to bring with her a probationer-nurse named Nelly Byers, that Martin began to brood:

"Wonder if he did have a headache last night?

"Wonder if somebody *gave* him the tickets?

"Why didn't he ask Dad Silva's daughter to go with us? Does he think Leora is some tart I've picked up?

"Sure, he never really quarrels with anybody—wants to keep us all friendly, so we'll send him surgical patients some day when we're hick G. P.'s and he's a Great and Only.

"Why did I crawl down so meekly?

"I don't care! If Leora enjoys it— Me personally, I don't care two hoots for all this trotting around— Though of course it isn't so bad to see pretty women in fine clothes, and be dressed as good as anybody— Oh, I don't *know!*"

In the slightly Midwestern city of Zenith, the appearance of a play "with the original New York cast" was an event. (What play it was did not much matter.) The Dodsworth Theatre was splendid with the aristocracy from the big houses on Royal Ridge. Leora and Nelly Byers admired the bloods—graduates of Yale and Harvard and Princeton, lawyers and bankers, motor-manufacturers and inheritors of real estate, virtuosi of golf, familiars of New York—who with their shrill and glistening women occupied the front rows. Miss Byers pointed out the Dodsworths, who were often mentioned in *Town Topics*.

Leora and Miss Byers bounced with admiration of the hero when he refused the governorship; Martin worried because the heroine was prettier than Leora; and Angus Duer (who gave an appearance of knowing all about plays without having seen more than half a dozen in his life) admitted that the set depicting "Jack Vanduzen's Camp in the Adirondacks: Sunset, the Next Day" was really very nice.

Martin was in a mood of determined hospitality. He was going to give them supper and that was all there was to it. Miss Byers explained that they had to be in the hospital by a quarter after eleven, but Leora said lazily, "Oh, I don't care. I'll slip in through a window. If you're there in the morning, the Old Cat can't prove you got in late." Shaking her head at this lying wickedness, Miss Byers fled to a trolley car, while Leora, Angus, and Martin strolled to Epstein's Alt Nuremberg Café for beer and Swiss cheese sandwiches flavored by the sight of German drinking mottos and papier-mâché armor.

Angus was studying Leora, looking from her to Martin, watching their glances of affection. That a keen young man should make a comrade of a girl who could not bring him social advancement, that such a thing as the boy and girl passion between Martin and Leora could exist, was probably inconceivable to him. He decided that she was conveniently frail. He gave Martin a refined version of a leer, and set himself to acquiring her for his own uses.

"I hope you enjoyed the play," he condescended to her.

"Oh, yes—"

"Jove, I envy you two. Of course I understand why girls fall for Martin here, with his romantic eyes, but a grind like me, I have to go on working without a single person to give me sympathy. Oh, well, I deserve it for being shy of women."

With unexpected defiance from Leora: "When anybody says that, it means they're not shy, and they despise women."

"Despise them? Why, child, honestly, I long to be a Don Juan. But I don't know how. Won't you give me a lesson?" Angus's aridly correct voice had become lulling; he concentrated on Leora as he would have concentrated on dissecting a guinea pig. She smiled at Martin now and then to say, "Don't be jealous, idiot. I'm magnificently uninterested in this conceited hypnotist." But she was flustered by Angus's sleek assurance, by his homage to her eyes and wit and reticence.

Martin twitched with jealousy. He blurted that they must be going—Leora really had to be back— The trolleys ran infrequently after midnight and they walked to the hospital through hollow and sounding streets. Angus and Leora kept up a high-strung chatter, while Martin stalked beside them, silent, sulky, proud of being sulky. Skittering through a garage alley they came out on the mass of Zenith General Hospital, a block long, five stories of bleak windows with infrequent dim blotches of light. No one was about. The first floor was but five feet from the ground, and they lifted Leora up to the limestone ledge of a half-open corridor window. She slid in, whispering, "G' night! Thanks!"

Martin felt empty, dissatisfied. The night was full of a chill mournfulness. A light was suddenly flickering in a window above them, and there was a woman's scream breaking down into moans. He felt the tragedy of parting —that in the briefness of life he should lose one moment of her living presence.

"I'm going in after her; see she gets there safe," he said.

The frigid edge of the stone sill bit his hands, but he vaulted, thrust up his knee, crawled hastily through the window. Ahead of him, in the cork-floored hallway lit only by a tiny electric globe, Leora was tiptoeing toward a flight of stairs. He ran after her, on his toes. She squeaked as he caught her arm.

"We got to say good night better than that!" he grumbled. "With that damn' Duer—"

"Sssssh! They'd simply murder me if they caught you here. Do you want to get me fired?"

"Would you care, if it was because of me?"

"Yes—no—well— But they'd probably fire you from medic school, my lad. If—" His caressing hands could feel her shiver with anxiety. She peered along the corridor, and his quickened imagination created sneaking forms, eyes peering from doorways. She sighed, then, resolutely: "We can't talk here. We'll slip up to my room—roommate's away for the week. Stand there, in the shadow. If nobody's in sight upstairs, I'll come back."

He followed her to the floor above, to a white door, then breathlessly inside. As he closed the door he was touched by this cramped refuge, with its camp-beds and photographs from home and softly wrinkled linen. He clasped her, but with hand against his chest she forbade him, as she mourned:

"You were jealous again! How can you distrust me so? With that fool! Women not like him? They wouldn't have a chance! Likes himself too well. And then you jealous!"

"I wasn't— Yes, I was, but I don't dare! To have to sit there and grin like a hyena, with him between us, when I wanted to talk to you, to kiss you! All right! Probably I'll always be jealous. It's you that have got to trust me. I'm not easy-going; never will be. Oh, trust me—"

Their profound and unresisted kiss was the more blind in memory of that barren hour with Angus. They forgot that the superintendent of nurses might dreadfully come bursting in; they forgot that Angus was waiting. "Oh, curse Angus—let him go home!" was Martin's only reflection, as his eyes closed and his long loneliness vanished.

"Good night, dear love—my love forever," he exulted.

In the still ghostliness of the hall, he laughed as he thought of how irritably Angus must have marched away. But from the window he discovered Angus huddled on the stone steps, asleep. As he touched the ground, he whistled, but stopped short. He saw bursting from the shadow a bulky man, vaguely in a porter's uniform, who was shouting:

"I've caught yuh! Back you come into the hospital, and we'll find out what you've been up to!"

They closed. Martin was wiry, but in the watchman's clasp he was smothered. There was a reek of dirty overalls, of unbathed flesh. Martin kicked his shins, struck at his boulder of red cheek, tried to twist his arm. He broke loose, started to flee, and halted. The struggle, in its contrast to the aching sweetness of Leora, had infuriated him. He faced the watchman, raging.

From the awakened Angus, suddenly appearing beside him, there was a thin sound of disgust. "Oh, come *on*! Let's get out of this. Why do you dirty your hands on scum like him?"

The watchman bellowed, "Oh, I'm scum, am I? I'll show you!"

He collared Angus and slapped him.

Under the sleepy street-lamp, Martin saw a man go mad. It was not the unfeeling Angus Duer who stared at the watchman; it was a killer, and his eyes were the terrible eyes of the killer, speaking to the least experienced a message of death. He gasped only, "He dared to touch me!" A pen-knife was somehow in his hands, he had leaped at the watchman, and he was busily and earnestly endeavoring to cut his throat.

As Martin tried to hold them he heard the agitated pounding of a policeman's night stick on the pavement. Martin was slim but he had pitched hay and strung telephone wire. He hit the watchman, judiciously, beside the left ear, snatched Angus's wrist, and dragged him away. They ran up an alley, across a courtyard. They came to a thoroughfare as an owl trolley glowed and rattled round the corner; they ran beside it, swung up on the steps, and were safe.

Angus stood on the back platform, sobbing. "My God, I wish I'd killed him! He laid his filthy hands on me! Martin! Hold me here on the car. I thought I'd got over that. Once when I was a kid I tried to kill a fellow— God, I wish I'd cut that filthy swine's throat!"

As the trolley came into the center of the city, Martin coaxed, "There's an all-night lunch up Oberlin Avenue where we can get some white mule. Come on. It'll straighten you up."

Angus was shaky and stumbling—Angus the punctilious. Martin led him into the lunch-room where, between catsup bottles, they had raw whisky in granite-like coffee cups. Angus leaned his head on his arm and sobbed, careless of stares, till he had drunk himself into obliteration, and Martin steered him home. Then to Martin, in his furnished room with Clif snoring, the evening became incredible and nothing more incredible than Angus Duer. "Well, he'll be a good friend of mine now, for always. Fine!"

Next morning, in the hall of the Anatomy Building, he saw Angus and rushed toward him. Angus snapped, "You were frightfully stewed last night, Arrowsmith. If you can't handle your liquor better than that, you better cut it out entirely."

He walked on, clear-eyed, unruffled.

# 8

And always Martin's work went on—assisting Max Gottlieb, instructing bacteriological students, attending lectures and hospital demonstrations—sixteen merciless hours to the day. He stole occasional evenings for original research or for peering into the stirring worlds of French and German bacteriological publications; he went proudly now and then to Gottlieb's cottage where, against rain-smeared brown wall-paper, were Blake drawings and a signed portrait of Koch. But the rest was nerve-gnawing.

Neurology, O.B., internal medicine, physical diagnosis; always a few pages more than he could drudge through before he fell asleep at his rickety study-table.

Memorizing of gynecology, of ophthalmology, till his mind was burnt raw.

Droning afternoons of hospital demonstrations, among stumbling students barked at by tired clinical professors.

The competitive exactions of surgery on dogs, in which Angus Duer lorded it with impatient perfection.

Martin admired the professor of internal medicine, T. J. H. Silva, known as "Dad" Silva, who was also dean of the medical faculty. He was a round little man with a little crescent of mustache. Silva's god was Sir William Osler, his religion was the art of sympathetic healing, and his patriotism was accurate physical diagnosis. He was a Doc Vickerson of Elk Mills, grown wiser and soberer and more sure. But Martin's reverence for Dean Silva was counterbalanced by his detestation for Dr. Roscoe Geake, professor of otolaryngology.

Roscoe Geake was a peddler. He would have done well with oil stock. As an otolaryngologist he believed that tonsils had been placed in the human organism for the purpose of providing specialists with closed motors. A physician who left the tonsils in any patient was, he felt, foully and ignorantly overlooking his future health and comfort—the physician's future health and comfort. His earnest feeling regarding the nasal septum was that it never hurt any patient to have part of it removed, and if the most hopeful examination could find nothing the matter with the patient's nose and throat except that he was smoking too much, still, in any case, the enforced rest after an operation was good for him. Geake denounced this cant about Letting Nature Alone. Why, the average well-to-do man appreciated attention! He really didn't think much of his specialists unless he was operated on now and then—just a little and not very painfully. Geake had one classic annual address in which, winging far above otolaryngology, he evaluated all medicine, and explained to grateful healers like Irving Watters the method of getting suitable fees:

"Knowledge is the greatest thing in the medical world but it's no good whatever unless you can sell it, and to do this you must first impress your personality on the people who have the dollars. Whether a patient is a new or an old friend, you must always use *salesmanship* on him. Explain to him, also to his stricken and anxious family, the hard work and thought you are giving to his case, and so make him feel that the good you have done him, or intend to do him, is even greater than the fee you plan to charge. Then, when he gets your bill, he will not misunderstand or kick."

II

There was, as yet, no vision in Martin of serene spaciousness of the mind. Beyond doubt he was a bustling young man, and rather shrill. He had no uplifted moments when he saw himself in relation to the whole world—if indeed he realized that there was a deal of the world besides himself. His friend Clif was boorish, his beloved Leora was rustic, however gallant she might be, and he himself wasted energy in hectic busyness and in astonishment at dullness. But if he had not ripened, yet he was close to earth, he did hate pretentiousness, he did use his hands, and he did seek iron actualities with a curiosity inextinguishable.

And at infrequent times he perceived the comedy of life; relaxed for a gorgeous hour from the intensity wearing to his admirers. Such was the hour before Christmas vacation when Roscoe Geake rose to glory.

It was announced in the *Winnemac Daily News* that Dr. Geake had been called from the chair of otolaryngology to the vice-presidency of the puissant New Idea Medical Instrument and Furniture Company of Jersey City. In celebration he gave a final address to the entire medical school on "The Art and Science of Furnishing the Doctor's Office."

He was a neatly finished person, Geake, eye-glassed and enthusiastic and fond of people. He beamed on his loving students and cried:

"Gentlemen, the trouble with too many doctors, even those splendid old pioneer war-horses who through mud and storm, through winter's chill blast and August's untempered heat, go bringing cheer and surcease from pain to the world's humblest, yet even these old Nestors not so infrequently settle down in a rut and never shake themselves loose. Now that I am leaving this field where I have labored so long and happily, I want to ask every man jack of you to read, before you begin to practice medicine, not merely your Rosenau and Howell and Gray, but also, as a preparation for being that which all good citizens must be, namely, practical men, a most valuable little manual of modern psychology, 'How to Put Pep in Salesmanship,' by Grosvenor A. Bibby. For don't forget, gentlemen, and this is my last message to you, the man worth while is not merely the man who takes things with a smile but also the man who's trained in philosophy, *practical* philosophy, so that instead of day-dreaming and spending all his time talking about 'ethics,' splendid though they are, and 'charity,' glorious virtue though that be, yet he never forgets that unfortunately the world judges a man by the amount of good hard cash he can lay away. The graduates of the University of Hard Knocks judge a physician as they judge a business man, not merely by his alleged 'high ideals' but by the horsepower he puts into carrying them out— and making them pay! And from a scientific standpoint, don't overlook the fact that the impression of properly remunerated competence which you make on a patient is of just as much importance, in these days of the new psychology, as the drugs you get into him or the operations he lets you get away with. The minute he begins to see that other folks appreciate and reward your skill, that minute he must begin to feel your power and so to get well.

"Nothing is more important in inspiring him than to have such an office that as soon as he steps into it, you have begun to sell him the idea of being properly cured. I don't care whether a doctor has studied in Germany, Munich, Baltimore, and Rochester. I don't care whether he has all science at his finger-tips, whether he can instantly diagnose with a considerable degree of accuracy the most obscure ailment, whether he has the surgical technique of a Mayo, a Crile, a Blake, an Ochsner, a Cushing. If he has a dirty old office, with hand-me-down chairs and a lot of second-hand magazines, then the patient isn't going to have confidence in him; he is going to resist the treatment—and the doctor is going to have difficulty in putting over and collecting an adequate fee.

"To go far below the surface of this matter into the fundamental philosophy and esthetics of office-furnishing for the doctor, there are today two warring schools, the Tapestry School and the Aseptic School, if I may venture to so denominate and conveniently distinguish them. Both of them have their merits. The Tapestry School claims that luxurious chairs for waiting patients, handsome hand-painted pictures, a bookcase jammed with the world's best literature in expensively bound sets, together with cut-glass vases and potted palms, produce an impression of that opulence which can come only from sheer ability and knowledge. The Aseptic School, on the other hand, maintains that what the patient wants is that appearance of scrupulous hygiene which can be produced only by furnishing the outer waiting-room as well as the inner offices in white-painted chairs and tables, with merely a Japanese print against a gray wall.

"But, gentlemen, it seems obvious to me, so obvious that I wonder it has not been brought out before, that the ideal reception-room is a combination of these two schools! Have your potted palms and handsome pictures—to the practical physician they are as necessary a part of his working equipment as a sterilizer or a Baumanometer. But so far as possible have everything in sanitary-looking white—and think of the color-schemes you can evolve, or the good wife for you, if she be one blessed with artistic tastes! Rich golden or red cushions, in a Morris chair enameled the purest white! A floor-covering of white enamel, with just a border of delicate rose! Recent and unspotted numbers of expensive magazines, with art covers, lying on a white table! Gentlemen, there is the idea of imaginative salesmanship which I wish to leave with you; there is the gospel which I hope to spread in my fresh field of endeavor, the New Idea Instrument Company of Jersey City, where at any time I shall be glad to see and shake by the hand any and all of you."

III

Through the storm of his Christmas examinations, Martin had an intensified need of Leora. She had been summoned home to Dakota, perhaps for months, on the ground that her mother was unwell, and he had, or thought he had, to see her daily. He must have slept less than four hours a night. Grinding at examinations on the interurban car, he dashed in to her, looking up to scowl when he thought of the lively interns and the men patients whom she met in the hospital, scorning himself for being so primitive, and worrying all over again. To see her at all, he had to wait for hours in the lobby, or walk up and down in the snow outside till she could slip to a window and peep out. When they were together, they were completely absorbed. She had a genius for frank passion; she teased him, tantalized him, but she was tender and unafraid.

He was sick lonely when he saw her off at the Union Station.

His examination papers were competent but, save in bacteriology and internal medicine, they were sketchy. He turned emptily to the laboratory for vacation time.

He had so far displayed more emotion than achievement in his tiny original researches. Gottlieb was patient. "It iss a fine system, this education. All what we cram into the students, not Koch and two dieners could learn. Do not worry about the research. We shall do it yet." But he expected Martin to perform a miracle or two in the whole fortnight of the holidays and Martin had no stomach with which to think. He played in the laboratory; he spent his time polishing glassware, and when he transplanted cultures from his rabbits, his notes were incomplete.

Gottlieb was instantly grim. "*Wass giebt es dann?* Do you call these notes? Always when I praise a man must he stop working? Do you think that you are a Theobald Smith or a Novy that you should sit and meditate? You have the ability of Pfaff!"

For once, Martin was impenitent. He mumbled to himself, as Gottlieb stamped out like a Grand Duke, "Rats, I've got *some* rest coming to me.

Gosh, most fellows, why, they go to swell homes for vacation, and have dances and fathers and everything. If Leora was here, we'd go to a show tonight."

He viciously seized his cap (a soggy and doubtful object), sought Clif Clawson, who was spending the vacation in sleeping between poker games at Barney's, and outlined a project of going into town and getting drunk. It was executed so successfully that during vacation it was repeated whenever he thought of the coming torture-wheel of uninspiring work, whenever he realized that it was only Gottlieb and Leora who held him here. After vacation, in late January, he found that whisky relieved him from the frenzy of work, from the terror of loneliness—then betrayed him and left him the more weary, the more lonely. He felt suddenly old; he was twenty-four now, he reminded himself, and a schoolboy, his real work not even begun. Clif was his refuge; Clif admired Leora and would listen to his babbling of her.

But Clif and Martin came to the misfortune of Founder's Day.

## IV

January thirtieth, the birthday of the late Dr. Warburton Stonedge, founder of the medical department of Winnemac, was annually celebrated by a banquet rich in fraternalism and speeches and large lack of wine. All the faculty reserved their soundest observations for the event, and all the students were expected to be present.

This year it was held in the large hall of the University Y.M.C.A., a moral apartment with red wall paper, portraits of whiskered alumni who had gone out to be missionaries, and long thin pine boxes intended to resemble exposed oak beams. About the famous guests—Dr. Rouncefield the Chicago surgeon, a diabetes specialist from Omaha, a Pittsburgh internist—stood massed the faculty members. They tried to look festal, but they were worn and nervous after four months of school. They had wrinkles and tired eyes. They were all in business suits, mostly unpressed. They sounded scientific and interested; they used words like phlebarteriectasia and hepatocholangio-enterostomy, and they asked the guests, "So you just been in Rochester? What's, uh, what're Charley and Will doing in orthopedics?" But they were full of hunger and melancholy. It was half-past seven, and they who did not normally dine at seven, dined at six-thirty.

Upon this seedy gaiety entered a splendor, a tremendous black-bearded personage, magnificent of glacial shirt-bosom, vast of brow, wild-eyed with genius or with madness. In a marvelous great voice, with a flavor of German accent, he inquired for Dr. Silva, and sailed into the dean's group like a frigate among fishing-smacks.

"Who the dickens is that?" wondered Martin.

"Let's edge in and find out," said Clif, and they clung to the fast increasing knot about Dean Silva and the mystery, who was introduced as Dr. Benoni Carr, the pharmacologist.

They heard Dr. Carr, to the pale admiration of the school-bound assistant professors, boom genially of working with Schmiedeberg in Germany on the isolation of dihydroxypentamethylendiamin, of the possibilities of chemotherapy, of the immediate cure of sleeping sickness, of the era of scientific healing. "Though I am American-born, I have the advantage of speaking German from a child, and so perhaps I can better understand the work of my dear friend Ehrlich. I saw him receive a decoration from His Imperial Highness the Kaiser. Dear old Ehrlich, he was like a child!"

There was at this time (but it changed curiously in 1914 and 1915) an active Germanophile section of the faculty. They bent before this tornado of erudition. Angus Duer forgot that he was Angus Duer; and Martin listened with excited stimulation. Benoni Carr had all of Gottlieb's individuality, all his scorn of machine-made teachers, all his air of a great world which showed Mohalis as provincial, with none of Gottlieb's nervous touchiness. Martin wished Gottlieb were present; he wondered whether the two giants would clash.

Dr. Carr was placed at the speakers' table, near the dean. Martin was astonished to see the eminent pharmacologist, after a shocked inspection of the sour chicken and mishandled salad which made up most of the dinner, pour something into his water glass from a huge silver flask—and pour that something frequently. He became boisterous. He leaned across two men to slap the indignant dean on the shoulder; he contradicted his neighbors; he sang a stanza of "I'm Bound Away for the Wild Missourai."

Few phenomena at the dinner were so closely observed by the students as the manners of Dr. Benoni Carr.

After an hour of strained festivity, when Dean Silva had risen to announce the speakers, Carr lumbered to his feet and shouted, "Let's not have any speeches. Only fools make speeches. Wise men sing songs. Whoopee! Oh, tireolee, oh, tireolee, oh, tireolee a lady! You profs are the bunk!"

Dean Silva was to be seen beseeching him, then leading him out of the room, with the assistance of two professors and a football tackle, and in the hush of a joyful horror Clif grunted to Martin:

"Here's where I get mine! And the damn' fool promised to stay sober!"

"Huh?"

"I might of known he'd show up stewed and spill the beans. Oh, maybe the dean won't hand me hell proper!"

He explained. Dr. Benoni Carr was born Benno Karkowski. He had graduated from a medical school which gave degrees in two years. He had read vastly, but he had never been in Europe. He had been "spieler" in medicine shows, chiropodist, spiritualist medium, esoteric teacher, head of sanitariums for the diversion of neurotic women. Clif had encountered him in Zenith, when they were both drunk. It was Clif who had told Dean Silva that the celebrated pharmacologist, just back from Europe, was in Zenith for a few days and perhaps might accept an invitation—

The dean had thanked Clif ardently.

The banquet ended early, and there was inadequate attention to Dr. Rouncefield's valuable address on the Sterilization of Catgut.

Clif sat up worrying, and admitting the truth of Martin's several observations. Next day—he had a way with women when he deigned to take the trouble—he pumped the dean's girl secretary, and discovered his fate. There had been a meeting of a faculty committee; the blame for the Benoni Carr outrage had been placed on Clif; and the dean had said all the things Clif had imagined, with a number which he had not possessed the talent to conceive. But the dean was not going to summon him at once; he was going to keep him waiting in torture, then execute him in public.

"Good-by, old M.D. degree! Rats, I never thought much of the doctor business. Guess I'll be a bond salesman," said Clif to Martin. He strolled away, he went to the dean, and remarked:

"Oh, Dean Silva, I just dropped in to tell you I've decided to resign from the medic school. Been offered a big job in, uh, in Chicago, and I don't think much of the way you run the school, anyway. Too much memorizing and too little real spirit of science. Good luck, Doc. So long."

"Gggggg—" said Dean Silva.

Clif moved into Zenith, and Martin was left alone. He gave up the double room at the front of his boarding-house for a hall-room at the rear, and in that narrow den he sat and mourned in a desolation of loneliness. He looked out on a vacant lot in which a tattered advertisement of pork and beans flapped on a leaning billboard. He saw Leora's eyes and heard Clif's comfortable scoffing, and the quiet was such as he could not endure.

# 9

The persistent yammer of a motor horn drew Martin to the window of the laboratory, a late afternoon in February. He looked down on a startling roadster, all streamlines and cream paint, with enormous headlights. He slowly made out that the driver, a young man in coffee-colored loose motor coat and hectic checked cap and intense neckwear, was Clif Clawson, and that Clif was beckoning.

He hastened down, and Clif cried:

"Oh, boy! How do you like the boat? Do you diagnose this suit? Scotch heather—honest! Uncle Clif has nabbed off a twenty-five-buck-a-week job *with* commissions, selling autos. Boy, I was lost in your old medic school. I can sell anything to anybody. In a year I'll be making eighty a week. Jump in, old son. I'm going to take you in to the Grand and blow you to the handsomest feed you ever stuffed into your skinny organism."

The thirty-eight miles an hour at which Clif drove into Zenith was, in 1908, dismaying speed. Martin discovered a new Clif. He was as noisy as ever, but more sure, glowing with schemes for immediately acquiring large sums of money. His hair, once bushy and greasy in front, tending to stick out jaggedly behind, was sleek now, and his face had the pinkness of massage. He stopped at the fabulous Grand Hotel with a jar of brakes; before he left the car he changed his violent yellow driving-gauntlets for a pair of gray gloves with black stitching, which he immediately removed as he paraded through the lobby. He called the coat-girl "Sweetie," and at the dining-room door he addressed the head-waiter:

"Ah, Gus, how's the boy, how's the boy feeling tonight? How's the mucho famoso majordomoso? Gus, want to make you 'quainted with Dr. Arrowsmith. Any time the doc comes here I want you to shake a leg and hand him out that well-known service, my boy, and give him anything he wants, and if he's broke, you charge it to me. Now, Gus, I want a nice little table for two, with garage and hot and cold water, and wouldst fain have thy advice, Gustavus, on the oysters and hore duffers and all the ingredients fair of a Maecenan feast."

"Yes, sir, right this way, Mr. Clawson," breathed the head-waiter.

Clif whispered to Martin, "I've got him like that in two weeks! You watch my smoke!"

While Clif was ordering, a man stopped beside their table. He resembled an earnest traveling-man who liked to get back to his suburban bungalow every Saturday evening. He was beginning to grow slightly bald, slightly plump. His rimless eye-glasses, in the midst of a round smooth face, made him seem innocent. He stared about as though he wished he had someone with whom to dine. Clif darted up, patted the man's elbow, and bawled:

"Ah, there, Babski, old boy. Feeding with anybody? Come join the Sporting Gents' Association."

"All right, be glad to. Wife's out of town," said the man.

"Shake hands with Dr. Arrowsmith. Mart, meet George F. Babbitt, the hoch-gecelebrated Zenith real-estate king. Mr. Babbitt has just adorned his thirty-fourth birthday by buying his first benzine buggy from yours truly and beg to remain as always."

It was, at least on the part of Clif and Mr. Babbitt, a mirthful affair, and when Martin had joined them in cocktails, St. Louis beer, and highballs, he saw that Clif was the most generous person now living, and Mr. George F. Babbitt a companion of charm.

Clif explained how certain he was—apparently his distinguished medical training had something to do with it—to be president of a motor factory, and Mr. Babbitt confided:

"You fellows are a lot younger than I am, eight-ten years, and you haven't learned yet, like I have, that where the big pleasure is, is in Ideals and Service and a Public Career. Now just between you and me and the gatepost, my vogue doesn't lie in real estate but in oratory. Fact, one time I planned to study law and go right in for politics. Just between ourselves, and I don't want this to go any farther, I've been making some pretty good affiliations lately—been meeting some of the rising young Republican politicians. Of course a fellow has got to start in modestly, but I may say, *sotto voce*, that

I expect to run for alderman next fall. It's practically only a step from that to mayor and then to governor of the state, and if I find the career suits me, there's no reason why in ten or twelve years, say in 1918 or 1920, I shouldn't have the honor of representing the great state of Winnemac in Washington D. C.!"

In the presence of a Napoleon like Clif and a Gladstone like George F. Babbitt, Martin perceived his own lack of power and business skill, and when he had returned to Mohalis he was restless. Of his poverty he had rarely thought, but now, in contrast to Clif's rich ease, his own shabby clothes and his pinched room seemed shameful.

## II

A long letter from Leora, hinting that she might not be able to return to Zenith, left him the more lonely. Nothing seemed worth doing. In that listless state he was mooning about the laboratory during elementary bacteriology demonstration hour, when Gottlieb sent him to the basement to bring up six male rabbits for inoculation. Gottlieb was working eighteen hours a day on new experiments; he was jumpy and testy; he gave orders like insults. When Martin came dreamily back with six females instead of males, Gottlieb shrieked at him, "You are the worst fool that was ever in this lab!"

The groundlings, second-year men who were not unmindful of Martin's own scoldings, tittered like small animals, and jarred him into raging, "Well, I couldn't make out what you said. And it's the first time I ever fell down. I won't stand your talking to me like that!"

"You will stand anything I say! Clumsy! You can take your hat and get out!"

"You mean I'm fired as assistant?"

"I am glad you haf enough intelligence to understand that, no matter how wretchet I talk!"

Martin flung away. Gottlieb suddenly looked bewildered and took a step toward Martin's retreating back. But the class, the small giggling animals, they stood delighted, hoping for more, and Gottlieb shrugged, glared them into terror, sent the least awkward of them for the rabbits, and went on, curiously quiet.

And Martin, at Barney's dive, was hotly drinking the first of the whiskys which sent him wandering all night, by himself. With each drink he admitted that he had an excellent chance to become a drunkard, and with each he boasted that he did not care. Had Leora been nearer than Wheatsylvania, twelve hundred miles away, he would have fled to her for salvation. He was still shaky next morning, and he had already taken a drink to make it possible to live through the morning when he received the note from Dean Silva bidding him report to the office at once.

The dean lectured:

"Arrowsmith, you've been discussed a good deal by the faculty council of late. Except in one or two courses—in my own I have no fault to find—you have been very inattentive. Your marks have been all right, but you could do still better. Recently you have also been drinking. You have been seen in places of very low repute, and you have been intimate with a man who took it upon himself to insult me, the Founder, our guests, and the University. Various faculty members have complained of your superior attitude—making fun of our courses right out in class! But Dr. Gottlieb has always warmly defended you. He insisted that you have a real flair for investigative science. Last night, however, he admitted that you had recently been impertinent to him. Now unless you immediately turn over a new leaf, young man, I shall have to suspend you for the rest of the year and, if that doesn't do the work, I shall have to ask for your resignation. And I think it might be a good thing for your humility—you seem to have the pride of the devil, young man!—it might be a good idea for you to see Dr. Gottlieb and start off your reformation by apologizing—"

It was the whisky spoke, not Martin:

"I'm damned if I will! He can go to the devil! I've given him my life, and then he tattles on me—"

"That's absolutely unfair to Dr. Gottlieb. He merely—"

"Sure. He merely let me down. I'll see him in hell before I'll apologize, after the way I've worked for him. And as for Clif Clawson that you were hinting at—him 'take it on himself to insult anybody'? He just played a joke, and you went after his scalp. I'm glad he did it!"

Then Martin waited for the words that would end his scientific life.

The little man, the rosy, pudgy, good little man, he stared and hummed and spoke softly:

"Arrowsmith, I could fire you right now, of course, but I believe you have good stuff in you. I decline to let you go. Naturally, you're suspended, at least till you come to your senses and apologize to me and to Gottlieb." He was fatherly; almost he made Martin repent; but he concluded, "And as for Clawson, his 'joke' regarding this Benoni Carr person—and why I never looked the fellow up is beyond me, I suppose I was too busy—his 'joke,' as you call it, was the action either of an idiot or a blackguard, and until you are able to perceive that fact, I don't think you will be ready to come back to us."

"All right," said Martin, and left the room.

He was very sorry for himself. The real tragedy, he felt, was that though Gottlieb had betrayed him and ended his career, ended the possibility of his mastering science and of marrying Leora, he still worshiped the man.

He said good-by to no one in Mohalis save his landlady. He packed, and it was a simple packing. He stuffed his books, his notes, a shabby suit, his inadequate linen, and his one glory, the dinner clothes, into his unwieldy imitation-leather bag. He remembered with drunken tears the hour of buying the dinner jacket.

Martin's money, from his father's tiny estate, came in bi-monthly checks from the bank at Elk Mills. He had now but six dollars.

In Zenith he left his bag at the interurban trolley station and sought Clif, whom he found practicing eloquence over a beautiful pearl-gray motor hearse, in which a beer-fed undertaker was jovially interested. He waited, sitting hunched and twisted on the steel running-board of a limousine. He resented but he was too listless to resent greatly the stares of the other salesmen and the girl stenographers.

Clif dashed up, bumbling, "Well, well, how's the boy? Come out and catchum little drink."

"I could use one."

Martin knew that Clif was staring at him. As they entered the bar of the Grand Hotel, with its paintings of lovely but absent-minded ladies, its mirrors, its thick marble rail along a mahogany bar, he blurted:

"Well, I got mine, too. Dad Silva's fired me, for general footlessness. I'm going to bum around a little and then get some kind of a job. God, but I'm tired and nervous! Say, can you lend me some money?"

"You bet. All I've got. How much you want?"

"Guess I'll need a hundred dollars. May drift around quite some time."

"Golly, I haven't got that much, but prob'ly I can raise it at the office. Here, sit down at this table and wait for me."

How Clif obtained the hundred dollars has never been explained, but he was back with it in a quarter-hour. They went on to dinner, and Martin had much too much whisky. Clif took him to his own boarding-house—which was decidedly less promissory of prosperity than Clif's clothes—firmly gave him a cold bath to bring him to, and put him to bed. Next morning he offered to find a job for him, but Martin refused and left Zenith by the northbound train at noon.

Always, in America, there remains from pioneer days a cheerful pariahdom of shabby young men who prowl causelessly from state to state, from gang to gang, in the power of the Wanderlust. They wear black sateen shirts, and carry bundles. They are not permanently tramps. They have home towns to which they return, to work quietly in the factory or the section-gang for a year—for a week—and as quietly to disappear again. They crowd the smoking cars at night; they sit silent on benches in filthy stations; they know all the land yet of it they know nothing, because in a hundred cities they see only the employment agencies, the all-night lunches, the blind-pigs, the scabrous lodging-houses. Into that world of voyageurs Martin vanished. Drinking steadily, only half-conscious of whither he was going, of what he desired to do, shamefully haunted by Leora and Clif and the swift hands of Gottlieb, he flitted from Zenith to the city of Sparta, across to Ohio, up into Michigan, west to Illinois. His mind was a shambles. He could never quite remember, afterward, where he had been. Once, it is clear, he was soda-fountain clerk in a Minnemagantic drug-store. Once he must have been, for a week, dishwasher in the stench of a cheap restaurant. He wandered by freight trains, on blind baggages, on foot. To his fellow prospectors he was known as "Slim," the worst-tempered and most restless of all their company.

After a time a sense of direction began to appear in his crazy drifting. He was instinctively headed westward, and to the west, toward the long prairie dusk, Leora was waiting. For a day or two he stopped drinking. He woke up feeling not like the sickly hobo called "Slim," but like Martin Arrowsmith, and he pondered, with his mind running clear, "Why shouldn't I go back? Maybe this hasn't been so bad for me. I was working too hard. I was pretty high-strung. Blew up. Like to, uh— Wonder what happened to my rabbits? . . . Will they ever let me do research again?"

But to return to the University before he had seen Leora was impossible. His need of her was an obsession, making the rest of earth absurd and worthless. He had, with blurry cunning, saved most of the hundred dollars he had taken from Clif; he had lived—very badly, on grease-swimming stews and soda-reeking bread—by what he earned along the way. Suddenly, on no particular day, in no particular town in Wisconsin, he stalked to the station, bought a ticket to Wheatsylvania, North Dakota, and telegraphed to Leora, "Coming 2:43 tomorrow Wednesday Sandy."

III

He crossed the wide Mississippi into Minnesota. He changed trains at St. Paul; he rolled into gusty vastnesses of snow, cut by thin lines of fence-wire. He felt free, in release from the little fields of Winnemac and Ohio, in relaxation from the shaky nerves of midnight study and midnight booziness. He remembered his days of wire-stringing in Montana and regained that careless peace. Sunset was a surf of crimson, and by night, when he stepped from the choking railroad coach and tramped the platform at Sauk Center, he drank the icy air and looked up to the vast and solitary winter stars. The fan of the Northern Lights frightened and glorified the sky. He returned to the coach with the energy of that courageous land. He nodded and gurgled in brief smothering sleep; he sprawled on the seat and talked with friendly fellow vagrants; he drank bitter coffee and ate enormously of buckwheat cakes at a station restaurant; and so, changing at anonymous towns, he came at last to the squatty shelters, the two wheat-elevators, the cattle-pen, the oil-tank, and the red box of a station with its slushy platform, which composed the outskirts of Wheatsylvania. Against the station, absurd in a huge coonskin coat, stood Leora. He must have looked a little mad as he stared at her from the vestibule, as he shivered with the wind. She lifted to him her two open hands, childish in red mittens. He ran down, he dropped his awkward bag on the platform and, unaware of the gaping furry farmers, they were lost in a kiss.

Years after, in a tropic noon, he remembered the freshness of her windcooled cheeks.

The train was gone, pounding out of the tiny station. It had stood like a dark wall beside the platform, protecting them, but now the light from the snowfields glared in on them and left them exposed and self-conscious.

"What—what's happened?" she fluttered. "No letters. I was so frightened."

"Off bumming. The dean suspended me—being fresh to profs. D' y' care?"

"Course not, if you wanted to—"

"I've come to marry you."

"I don't see how we can, dearest, but— All right. There'll be a lovely row with Dad." She laughed. "He's always so surprised and *hurt* when anything happens that he didn't plan out. It'll be nice to have you with me in the scrap, because you aren't supposed to know that he expects to plan out everything for everybody and— Oh, Sandy, I've been so lonely for you! Mother isn't really a bit sick, not the least bit, but they go on keeping me here. I think probably somebody hinted to Dad that folks were saying he must be broke, if his dear little daughter had to go off and learn nursing, and he hasn't worried it all out yet—it takes Andrew Jackson Tozer about a year to worry out anything. Oh, Sandy! You're here!"

After the clatter and jam of the train, the village seemed blankly empty. He could have walked around the borders of Wheatsylvania in ten minutes. Probably to Leora one building differed from another—she appeared to distinguish between the general store of Norblom and that of Frazier & Lamb— but to Martin the two-story wooden shacks creeping aimlessly along the wide Main Street were featureless and inappreciable. Then "There's our house, end of the next block," said Leora, as they turned the corner at the feed and implement store, and in a panic of embarrassment Martin wanted to halt. He saw a storm coming: Mr. Tozer denouncing him as a failure who desired to ruin Leora, Mrs. Tozer weeping.

"Say—say—say—have you told 'em about me?" he stammered.

"Yes. Sort of. I said you were a wonder in medic school, and maybe we'd get married when you finished your internship, and then when your wire came, they wanted to know why you were coming, and why it was you wired from Wisconsin, and what color necktie you had on when you were sending the wire, and I couldn't make 'em understand I didn't know. They discussed it. Quite a lot. They do discuss things. All through supper. Solemn. Oh, Sandy, do curse and swear some at meals."

He was in a funk. Her parents, formerly amusing figures in a story, became oppressively real in sight of the wide, brown, porchy house. A large plate-glass window with a colored border had recently been cut through the wall, as a sign of prosperity, and the garage was new and authoritative.

He tagged after Leora, expecting the blast. Mrs. Tozer opened the door, and stared at him plaintively—a thin, faded, unhumorous woman. She bowed as though he was not so much unwelcome as unexplained and doubtful.

"Will you show Mr. Arrowsmith his room, Ory, or shall I?" she peeped.

It was the kind of house that has a large phonograph but no books, and if there were any pictures, as beyond hope there must have been, Martin never remembered them. The bed in his room was lumpy but covered with a chaste figured spread, and the flowery pitcher and bowl rested on a cover embroidered in red with lambs, frogs, water lilies, and a pious motto.

He took as long as he could in unpacking things which needed no unpacking, and hesitated down the stairs. No one was in the parlor, which smelled of furnace-heat and balsam pillows; then, from nowhere apparent, Mrs. Tozer was there, worrying about him and trying to think of something polite to say.

"Did you have a comfortable trip on the train?"

"Oh, yes, it was— Well, it was pretty crowded."

"Oh, was it crowded?"

"Yes, there were a lot of people traveling."

"Were there? I suppose— Yes. Sometimes I wonder where all the people can be going that you see going places all the time. Did you—was it very cold in the Cities—in Minneapolis and St. Paul?"

"Yes, it was pretty cold."

"Oh, was it cold?"

Mrs. Tozer was so still, so anxiously polite. He felt like a burglar taken for a guest, and intensely he wondered where Leora could be. She came in serenely, with coffee and a tremendous Swedish coffee-ring voluptuous with raisins and glistening brown sugar, and she had them talking, almost easily, about the coldness of winter and the value of Fords when into the midst of all this brightness slid Mr. Andrew Jackson Tozer, and they drooped again to politeness.

Mr. Tozer was as thin and undistinguished and sun-worn as his wife, and like her he peered, he kept silence and fretted. He was astonished by everything in the world that did not bear on his grain elevator, his creamery, his tiny bank, the United Brethren Church, and the careful conduct of an Overland car. It was not astounding that he should have become almost rich, for he accepted nothing that was not natural and convenient to Andrew Jackson Tozer.

He hinted a desire to know whether Martin "drank," how prosperous he was, and how he could possibly have come all this way from the urbanities of Winnemac. (The Tozers were born in Illinois, but they had been in Dakota since childhood, and they regarded Wisconsin as the farthest, most perilous rim of the Eastern horizon.) They were so blank, so creepily polite, that Martin was able to avoid such unpleasant subjects as being suspended. He dandled an impression that he was an earnest young medic who in no time at all would be making large and suitable sums of money for the support of their Leora, but as he was beginning to lean back in his chair he was betrayed by the appearance of Leora's brother.

Bert Tozer, Albert R. Tozer, cashier and vice-president of the Wheatsylvania State Bank, auditor and vice-president of the Tozer Grain and Storage Company, treasurer and vice-president of the Star Creamery, was not in the least afflicted by the listening dubiousness of his parents. Bertie was a very articulate and modern man of affairs. He had buck teeth, and on his eyeglasses was a gold chain leading to a dainty hook behind his left ear. He believed in town-boosting, organized motor tours, Boy Scouts, baseball, and the hanging of I.W.W.'s; and his most dolorous regret was that Wheatsylvania was too small—as yet—to have a Y.M.C.A. or a Commercial Club. Plunging in beside him was his fiancée, Miss Ada Quist, daughter of the feed and implement store. Her nose was sharp, but not so sharp as her voice or the suspiciousness with which she faced Martin.

"This Arrowsmith?" demanded Bert. "Huh! Well, guess you're glad to be out here in God's country!"

"Yes, it's fine—"

"Trouble with the Eastern states is, they haven't got the git, or the room to grow. You ought to see a real Dakota harvest! Look here, how come you're away from school this time of year?"

"Why—"

"I know all about school-terms. I went to business college in Grand Forks. How come you can get away now?"

"I took a little lay-off."

"Leora says you and her are thinking of getting married."

"We—"

"Got any cash outside your school-money?"

"I have not!"

"Thought so! How juh expect to support a wife?"

"I suppose I'll be practicing medicine some day."

"Some day! Then what's the use of talking about being engaged till you can support a wife?"

"That," interrupted Bert's lady-love, Miss Ada Quist, "that's just what I said, Ory!" She seemed to speak with her pointed nose as much as with her button of a mouth. "If Bert and I can wait, I guess other people can!"

Mrs. Tozer whimpered, "Don't be too hard on Mr. Arrowsmith, Bertie. I'm sure he wants to do the right thing."

"I'm not being hard on anybody! I'm being sensible. If Pa and you would tend to things instead of standing around fussing, I wouldn't have to butt in. I don't believe in interfering with anybody else's doings, or anybody interfering with mine. Live and let live and mind your own business is my motto, and that's what I said to Alec Ingleblad the other day when I was in there having a shave and he was trying to get funny about our holding so many mortgages, but I'll be blamed if I'm going to allow a fellow that I don't know anything about to come snooping around My Sister till I find out something about his prospects!"

Leora crooned, "Bertie, lamb, your tie is climbing your collar again."

"Yes and *you*, Ory," shrieked Bert, "if it wasn't for me you'd have married Sam Petchek, two years ago!"

Bert further said, with instances and illustrations, that she was light-minded, and as for nursing— *Nursing!*

She said that Bert was what he was, and tried to explain to Martin the matter of Sam Petchek. (It has never yet been altogether explained.)

Ada Quist said that Leora did not care if she broke her dear parents' hearts and ruined Bert's career.

Martin said, "Look here, I—" and never got farther.

Mr. and Mrs. Tozer said they were all to be calm, and of course Bert didn't mean— But really, it was true; they had to be sensible, and how Mr. Arrowsmith could expect to support a wife—

The conference lasted till nine-thirty, which, as Mr. Tozer pointed out, was everybody's bedtime, and except for the five-minute discussion as to whether Miss Ada Quist was to stay to supper, and the debate on the saltiness of this last cornbeef, they clave faithfully to the inquiry as to whether Martin and Leora were engaged. All persons interested, which apparently did not include Martin and Leora, decided that they were not. Bert ushered Martin upstairs. He saw to it that the lovers should not have a chance for a good-night kiss; and until Mr. Tozer called down the hall, at seven minutes after ten, "You going to stay up and chew the rag the whole blessed night, Bert?" he made himself agreeable by sitting on Martin's bed, looking derisively at his shabby baggage, and demanding the details of his parentage, religion, politics, and attitude toward the horrors of card-playing and dancing.

At breakfast they all hoped that Martin would stay one more night in their home—plenty of room.

Bert stated that Martin would come down-town at ten and be shown the bank, creamery, and wheat elevator.

But at ten Martin and Leora were on the eastbound train. They got out at the county seat, Leopolis, a vast city of four thousand population, with a three-story building. At one that afternoon they were married, by the German Lutheran pastor. His study was a bareness surrounding a large, rusty wood-stove, and the witnesses, the pastor's wife and an old German who had been shoveling walks, sat on the wood-box and looked drowsy. Not till they had caught the afternoon train for Wheatsylvania did Martin and Leora escape from the ghostly apprehension which had haunted them all day. In the fetid train, huddled close, hands locked, innocently free of the alienation which the pomposity of weddings sometimes casts between lovers, they sighed, "Now what are we going to do—what *are* we going to do?"

At the Wheatsylvania station they were met by the whole family, rampant.

Bert had suspected elopement. He had searched half a dozen towns by long-distance telephone, and got through to the county clerk just after the license had been granted. It did not soften Bert's mood to have the clerk remark that if Martin and Leora were of age, there was nothing he could do, and he didn't "care a damn who's talking—I'm running this office!"

Bert had come to the station determined to make Martin perfect, even as Bert Tozer was perfect, and to do it right now.

It was a dreadful evening in the Tozer mansion.

Mr. Tozer said, with length, that Martin had undertaken responsibilities.

Mrs. Tozer wept, and said that she hoped Ory had not, for certain reasons, *had* to be married—

Bert said that if such was the case, he'd kill Martin—

Ada Quist said that Ory could now see what came of pride and boasting about going off to her old Zenith—

Mr. Tozer said that there was one good thing about it, anyway: Ory could see for herself that they couldn't let her go back to nursing school and get into more difficulties—

Martin from time to time offered remarks to the effect that he was a good young man, a wonderful bacteriologist, and able to take care of *his* wife; but no one save Leora listened.

Bert further propounded (while his father squeaked, "Now don't be *too* hard on the boy,") that if Martin *thought* for one single *second* that he was going to get one red *cent* out of the Tozers because he'd gone and butted *in* where nobody'd *invited* him, he, Bert, wanted to *know* about it, that was all, he certainly wanted to *know* about it!

And Leora watched them, turning her little head from one to another. Once she came over to press Martin's hand. In the roughest of the storm, when Martin was beginning to glare, she drew from a mysterious pocket a box of very bad cigarettes, and lighted one. None of the Tozers had discovered that she smoked. Whatever they thought about her sex morals, her infidelity to United Brethrenism, and her general dementia, they had not suspected that she could commit such an obscenity as smoking. They charged on her, and Martin caught his breath savagely.

During these fulminations Mr. Tozer had somehow made up his mind. He could at times take the lead away from Bert, whom he considered useful but slightly indiscreet, and unable to grasp the "full value of a dollar." (Mr. Tozer valued it at one dollar and ninety, but the progressive Bert at scarce more than one-fifty.) Mr. Tozer mildly gave orders:

They were to stop "scrapping." They had no proof that Martin was necessarily a bad match for Ory. They would see. Martin would return to medical school at once, and be a good boy and get through as quickly as he could and begin to earn money. Ory would remain at home and behave herself—and she certainly would never act like a Bad Woman again, and smoke cigarettes. Meantime Martin and she would have no, uh, relations. (Mrs. Tozer looked embarrassed, and the hungrily attentive Ada Quist tried to blush.) They could write to each other once a week, but that was all. They would in no way, uh, act as though they were married till he gave permission.

"Well?" he demanded.

Doubtless Martin should have defied them and with his bride in his arms have gone forth into the night. But it seemed only a moment to graduation, to beginning his practice. He had Leora now, forever. For her, he must be sensible. He would return to work, and be Practical. Gottlieb's ideals of science? Laboratories? Research? Rot!

"All right," he said.

It did not occur to him that their abstention from love began tonight; it did not come to him till, holding out his hands to Leora, smiling with virtue at having determined to be prudent, he heard Mr. Tozer cackling, "Ory, you go on up to bed now—in your own room!"

That was his bridal night; tossing in his bed, ten yards from her.

Once he heard a door open, and thrilled to her coming. He waited, taut. She did not come. He peeped out, determined to find her room. His deep feeling about his brother-in-law suddenly increased. Bert was parading the hall, on guard. Had Bert been more formidable, Martin might have killed him, but he could not face that buck-toothed and nickering righteousness.

He lay and resolved to curse them all in the morning and go off with Leora, but with the coming of the three-o'clock depression he perceived that with him she would probably starve, that he was disgraced, that it was not at all certain he would not become a drunkard.

"Poor kid, I'm not going to spoil her life. God, I do love her! I'm going back, and the way I'm going to work— Can I stand this?"

That was his bridal night and the barren dawn.

Three days later he was walking into the office of Dr. Silva, dean of the Winnemac Medical School.

# 10

Dean Silva's secretary looked up delightedly, she hearkened with anticipation. But Martin said meekly, "Please, could I see the dean?" and meekly he waited, in the row of oak chairs beneath the Dawson Hunziker pharmaceutical calendar.

When he had gone solemnly through the ground-glass door to the dean's office, he found Dr. Silva glowering. Seated, the little man seemed large, so domed was his head, so full his rounding mustache.

"Well, sir!"

Martin pleaded, "I'd like to come back, if you'll let me. Honest, I do apologize to you, and I'll go to Dr. Gottlieb and apologize—though honest, I can't lay down on Clif Clawson—"

Dr. Silva bounced up from his chair, bristling. Martin braced himself. Wasn't he welcome? Had he no home, anywhere? He could not fight. He had no more courage. He was so tired after the drab journey, after restraining himself from flaring out at the Tozers. He was so tired! He looked wistfully at the dean.

The little man chuckled, "Never mind, boy. It's all right! We're glad you're back. Bother the apologies! I just wanted you to do whatever'd buck you up. It's good to have you back! I believed in you, and then I thought perhaps we'd lost you. Clumsy old man!"

Martin was sobbing, too weak for restraint, too lonely and too weak, and Dr. Silva soothed, "Let's just go over everything and find out where the trouble was. What can I do? Understand, Martin, the thing I want most in life is to help give the world as many good physicians, great healers, as I can. What started your nervousness? Where have you been?"

When Martin came to Leora and his marriage, Silva purred, "I'm delighted! She sounds like a splendid girl. Well, we must try and get you into Zenith General for your internship, a year from now, and make you able to support her properly."

Martin remembered how often, how astringently, Gottlieb had sneered at "dese merry vedding or jail bells." He went away Silva's disciple; he went away to study furiously; and the brilliant insanity of Max Gottlieb's genius vanished from his faith.


## II

Leora wrote that she had been dropped from the school of nursing for over-absence and for being married. She suspected that it was her father who had informed the hospital authorities. Then, it appeared, she had secretly sent for a shorthand book and, on pretense of helping Bert, she was using the typewriter in the bank, hoping that by next autumn she could join Martin and earn her own living as a stenographer.

Once he offered to give up medicine, to take what work he could find and send for her. She refused.

Though in his service to Leora and to the new god, Dean Silva, he had become austere, denying himself whisky, learning page on page of medicine with a frozen fury, he was always in a vacuum of desire for her, and always he ran the last block to his boarding-house, looking for a letter from her. Suddenly he had a plan. He had tasted shame—this one last shame would not matter. He would flee to her in Easter vacation; he would compel Tozer to support her while she studied stenography in Zenith; he would have her near him through the last year. He paid Clif the borrowed hundred, when the bi-monthly check came from Elk Mills, and calculated his finances to the penny. By not buying the suit he distressingly needed, he could manage it. Then for a month and more he had but two meals a day, and of those meals one was bread and butter and coffee. He washed his own linen in the bath-tub and, except for occasional fiercely delightful yieldings, he did not smoke.

His return to Wheatsylvania was like his first flight, except that he talked less with fellow tramps, and all the way, between uneasy naps in the red-plush seats of coaches, he studied the bulky books of gynecology and internal medicine. He had written certain instructions to Leora. He met her on the edge of Wheatsylvania and they had a moment's talk, a resolute kiss.

News spreads not slowly in Wheatsylvania. There is a certain interest in other people's affairs, and the eyes of citizens of whose existence Martin did not know had followed him from his arrival. When the culprits reached the bone-littered castle of the Tozer ogres, Leora's father and brother were already there, and raging. Old Andrew Jackson cried out upon them. He said that conceivably it may not have been insane in Martin to have "run away from school once, but to go and sneak back this second time was absolutely plumb crazy." Through his tirade, Martin and Leora smiled confidently.

From Bert, "By God, sir, this is too much!" Bert had been reading fiction. "I object to the use of profanity, but when you come and annoy My Sister a second time, all I can say is, by God, sir, this is too blame much!"

Martin looked meditatively out of the window. He noticed three people strolling the muddy street. They all viewed the Tozer house with hopeful interest. Then he spoke steadily:

"Mr. Tozer, I've been working hard. Everything has gone fine. But I've decided I don't care to live without my wife. I've come to take her back. Legally, you can't prevent me. I'll admit, without any argument, I can't support her yet, if I stay in the University. She's going to study stenography. She'll be supporting herself in a few months, and meanwhile I expect you to be decent enough to send her money."

"This *is* too much," said Tozer, and Bert carried it on: "Fellow not only practically ruins a girl but comes and demands that we support her for him!"

"All right. Just as you want. In the long run it'll be better for her and for me and for you if I finish medic school and have my profession, but if you won't take care of her, I'll chuck school, I'll go to work. Oh, I'll support her, all right! Only you'll never see her again. If you go on being idiots, she and I will leave here on the night train for the Coast, and that'll be the end." For the first time in his centuries of debate with the Tozers, he was melodramatic. He shook his fist under Bert's nose. "And if you try to prevent our going, God help you! And the way this town will laugh at you! . . . How about it, Leora? Are you ready to go away with me—forever?"

"Yes," she said.

They discussed it, greatly. Tozer and Bert struck attitudes of defense. They couldn't, they said, be bullied by anybody. Also, Martin was an Adventurer, and how did Leora know he wasn't planning to live on the money they sent her? In the end they crawled. They decided that this new, mature Martin, this new, hard-eyed Leora were ready to throw away everything for each other.

Mr. Tozer whined a good deal, and promised to send her seventy dollars a month till she should be prepared for office-work.

At the Wheatsylvania station, looking from the train window, Martin realized that this anxious-eyed, lip-puckering Andrew Jackson Tozer did love his daughter, did mourn her going.

### III

He found for Leora a room on the frayed northern edge of Zenith, miles nearer Mohalis and the University than her hospital had been; a square white and blue room, with blotchy but shoulder-wise chairs. It looked out on breezy, stubbly waste land reaching to distant glittering railroad tracks. The landlady was a round German woman with an eye for romance. It is doubtful if she ever believed that they were married. She was a good woman.

Leora's trunk had come. Her stenography books were primly set out on her little table and her pink felt slippers were arranged beneath the white iron bed. Martin stood with her at the window, mad with the pride of proprietorship. Suddenly he was so weak, so tired, that the mysterious cement which holds cell to cell seemed dissolved, and he felt that he was collapsing. But with knees rigidly straightening, his head back, his lips tight across his teeth, he caught himself, and cried, "Our first home!"

That he should be with her, quiet, none disturbing, was intoxication.

The commonplace room shone with peculiar light; the vigorous weeds and rough grass of the waste land were radiant under the April sun, and sparrows were cheeping.

"Yes," said Leora, with voice, then hungry lips.

IV

Leora attended the Zenith University of Business Administration and Finance, which title indicated that it was a large and quite reasonably bad school for stenographers, bookkeepers, and such sons of Zenith brewers and politicians as were unable to enter even state universities. She trotted daily to the car-line, a neat, childish figure with note-books and sharpened pencils, to vanish in the horde of students. It was six months before she had learned enough stenography to obtain a place in an insurance office.

Till Martin graduated they kept that room, their home, ever dearer. No one was so domestic as these birds of passage. At least two evenings a week Martin dashed in from Mohalis and studied there. She had a genius for keeping out of his way, for not demanding to be noticed, so that, while he plunged into his books as he never had done in Clif's rustling, grunting, expectorating company, he had ever the warm, half-conscious feeling of her presence. Sometimes, at midnight, just as he began to realize that he was hungry, he would find that a plate of sandwiches had by silent magic appeared at his elbow. He was none the less affectionate because he did not comment. She made him secure. She shut out the world that had pounded at him.

On their walks, at dinner, in the dissolute and deliciously wasteful quarter-hour when they sat on the edge of the bed with comforters wrapped about them and smoked an inexcusable cigarette before breakfast, he explained his work to her, and when her own studying was done, she tried to read whichever of his books was not in use. Knowing nothing, never learning much, of the actual details of medicine, yet she understood—better it may be than Angus Duer—his philosophy and the basis of his work. If he had given up Gottlieb-worship and his yearning for the laboratory as for a sanctuary, if he had resolved to be a practical and wealth-mastering doctor, yet something of Gottlieb's spirit remained. He wanted to look behind details and impressive-sounding lists of technical terms for the causes of things, for general rules which might reduce the chaos of dissimilar and contradictory symptoms to the orderliness of chemistry.

Saturday evening they went solemnly to the motion pictures—one- and two-reel films with Cowboy Billy Anderson and a girl later to be famous as Mary Pickford—and solemnly they discussed the non-existent plots as they returned, unconscious of other people on the streets; but when they walked into the country on a Sunday (with four sandwiches and a bottle of ginger ale in his threadbare pockets), he chased her up-hill and down-gully, and they lost their solemnity in joyous childishness. He intended, when he came to her room in the evening, to catch the owl-car to Mohalis and be near his work when he woke in the morning. He was resolute about it, always, and she admired his efficiency, but he never caught the car. The crew of the six o'clock morning interurban became used to a pale, quick-moving young man who sat hunched in a back seat, devouring large red books, absently gnawing a rather dreadful doughnut. But in this young man there was none of the heaviness of workers dragged out of bed at dawn for another gray and futile day of labor. He appeared curiously determined, curiously content.

It was all so much easier, now that he was partly freed from the tyrannical honesty of Gottliebism, from the unswerving quest for causes which, as it drove through layer below layer, seemed ever farther from the bottommost principles, from the intolerable strain of learning day by day how much he did not know. It warmed him to escape from Gottlieb's ice-box into Dean Silva's neighborly world.

Now and then he saw Gottlieb on the campus. They bowed in embarrassment and passed in haste.

v

There seemed to be no division between his Junior and Senior years. Because of the time he had lost, he had to remain in Mohalis all summer. The year and a half from his marriage to his graduation was one whirling bewilderment, without seasons or dates.

When he had, as they put it, "cut out his nonsense and buckled down to work," he had won the admiration of Dr. Silva and all the Good Students, especially Angus Duer and the Reverend Ira Hinkley. Martin had always announced that he did not care for their approbation, for the applause of commonplace drudges, but now that he had it, he prized it. However much he scoffed, he was gratified when he was treated as a peer by Angus, who spent the summer as extern in the Zenith General Hospital, and who already had the unapproachable dignity of a successful young surgeon.

Through that hot summer Martin and Leora labored, panting, and when they sat in her room, over their books and a stout pot of beer, neither their costumes nor their language had the decorum which one ought to expect from a romantic pair devoted to science and high endeavor. They were not very modest. Leora came to use, in her casual way, such words, such ancient Anglo-Saxon monosyllables, as would have dismayed Angus or Bert Tozer. On their evenings off they went economically to an imitation Coney Island beside a scummy and stinking lake, and with grave pleasure they ate Hot Dogs, painstakingly they rode the scenic railway.

Their chief appetizer was Clif Clawson. Clif was never willingly alone or silent except when he was asleep. It is probable that his success in motor-salesmanship came entirely from his fondness for the enormous amounts of bright conversation which seem necessary in that occupation. How much of his attention to Martin and Leora was friendliness and how much of it was due to his fear of being alone cannot be determined, but certainly he enter-

tained them and drew them out of themselves, and never seemed offended
by the surly unwillingness with which Martin was sometimes guilty of greeting him.

He would come roaring up to the house in a motor, the muffler always cut
out. He would shout at their window, "Come on, you guys! Come out of it!
Shake a leg! Lez have a little drive and get cooled off, and then I'll buy you
a feed."

That Martin had to work, Clif never comprehended. There was small
excuse for Martin's occasional brutality in showing his annoyance but, now
that he was fulfilled in Leora and quite thoroughly and selfishly careless as
to what hungry need others might have of himself, now that he was in a rut
of industry and satisfied companionship, he was bored by Clif's unchanging
flood of heavy humor. It was Leora who was courteous. She had heard rather
too often the seven jokes which, under varying guises, made up all of Clif's
humor and philosophy, but she could sit for hours looking amiable while
Clif told how clever he was at selling, and she sturdily reminded Martin that
they would never have a friend more loyal or generous.

But Clif went to New York, to a new motor agency, and Martin and Leora
were more completely and happily dependent on each other than ever before.

Their last agitation was removed by the complacence of Mr. Tozer. He
was cordial now in all his letters, however much he irritated them by the
parental advice with which he penalized them for every check he sent.

VI

None of the hectic activities of Senior year—neurology and pediatrics,
practical work in obstetrics, taking of case-histories in the hospitals, attendance on operations, dressing wounds, learning not to look embarrassed when
charity patients called one "Doctor"—was quite so important as the discussion of "What shall we do after graduation?"

Is it necessary to be an intern for more than a year? Shall we remain
general practitioners all our lives, or work toward becoming specialists?
Which specialties are the best—that is, the best paid? Shall we settle in the
country or in the city? How about going West? What about the army medical corps; salutes, riding-boots, pretty women, travel?

This discussion they harried in the corridors of Main Medical, at the hospital, at lunch-rooms; and when Martin came home to Leora he went
through it all again, very learnedly, very explanatorily. Almost every evening
he "reached a decision" which was undecided again by morning.

Once when Dr. Loizeau, professor of surgery, had operated before a clinic
which included several renowned visiting doctors—the small white figure of
the surgeon below them, slashing between life and death, dramatic as a great
actor taking his curtain-call—Martin came away certain that he was for surgery. He agreed then with Angus Duer, who had just won the Hugh Loizeau
Medal in Experimental Surgery, that the operator was the lion, the eagle,
the soldier among doctors. Angus was one of the few who knew without

wavering precisely what he was going to do: after his internship he was to join the celebrated Chicago clinic headed by Dr. Rouncefield, the eminent abdominal surgeon. He would, he said briefly, be making twenty thousand a year as a surgeon within five years.

Martin explained it all to Leora. Surgery. Drama. Fearless nerves. Adoring assistants. Save lives. Science in devising new techniques. Make money—not be commercial, of course, but provide Leora with comforts. To Europe—they two together—gray London. Viennese cafés. Leora was useful to him during his oration. She blandly agreed; and the next evening, when he sought to prove that surgery was all rot and most surgeons merely good carpenters, she agreed more amiably than ever.

Next to Angus, and the future medical missionary, Ira Hinkley, Fatty Pfaff was the first to discover what his future was. He was going to be an obstetrician—or, as the medical students called it technically, a "baby-snatcher." Fatty had the soul of a midwife; he sympathized with women in their gasping agony, sympathized honestly and almost tearfully, and he was magnificent at sitting still and drinking tea and waiting. During his first obstetrical case, when the student with him was merely nervous as they fidgeted by the bed in the hard desolation of the hospital room, Fatty was terrified, and he longed as he had never longed for anything in his flabby yet wistful life to comfort this gray-faced, straining, unknown woman, to take her pains on himself.

While the others drifted, often by chance, often through relatives, into their various classes, Martin remained doubtful. He admired Dean Silva's insistence on the physician's immediate service to mankind, but he could not forget the cool ascetic hours in the laboratory. Toward the end of Senior year, decision became necessary, and he was moved by a speech in which Dean Silva condemned too much specialization and pictured the fine old country doctor, priest and father of his people, sane under open skies, serene in self-conquest. On top of this came urgent letters from Mr. Tozer, begging Martin to settle in Wheatsylvania.

Tozer loved his daughter, apparently, and more or less liked Martin, and he wanted them near him. Wheatsylvania was a "good location," he said: solid Scandinavian and Dutch and German and Bohemian farmers who paid their bills. The nearest doctor was Hesselink, at Groningen, nine and a half miles away, and Hesselink had more than he could do. If they would come, he would help Martin buy his equipment: he would even send him a check now and then during his two-year hospital internship. Martin's capital was practically gone. Angus Duer and he had received appointments to Zenith General Hospital, where he would have an incomparable training, but Zenith General gave its interns, for the first year, nothing but board and room, and he had feared that he could not take the appointment. Tozer's offer excited him. All night Leora and he sat up working themselves into enthusiasm about the freedom of the West, about the kind hearts and friendly hands of the pioneers, about the heroism and usefulness of country doctors, and this time they reached a decision which remained decided.

They would settle in Wheatsylvania.

If he ached a little for research and Gottlieb's divine curiosity—well, he would be such a country doctor as Robert Koch! He would not degenerate into a bridge-playing, duck-hunting drone. He would have a small laboratory of his own. So he came to the end of the year and graduated, looking rather flustered in his cap and gown. Angus stood first and Martin seventh in the class. He said good-by, with lamentations and considerable beer; he found a room for Leora nearer to the hospital; and he emerged as Martin L. Arrowsmith, M.D., house physician in the Zenith General Hospital.

# 11

The Boardman Box Factory was afire. All South Zenith was agitated by the glare on the low-hung clouds, the smell of scorched timber, the infernal bells of charging fire-apparatus. Miles of small wooden houses west of the factory were threatened, and shawled women, tousled men in trousers over night-shirts, tumbled out of bed and came running with a thick mutter of footsteps in the night-chilled streets.

With professional calmness, firemen in helmets were stoking the dripping engines. Policemen tramped in front of the press of people, swinging their clubs, shouting, "Get back there, you!" The fire-line was sacred. Only the factory-owner and the reporters were admitted. A crazy-eyed factory-hand was stopped by a police sergeant.

"My tools are in there!" he shrieked.

"That don't make no never-minds," bawled the strutting sergeant. "Nobody can't get through here!"

But one got through. They heard the blang-blang-blang of a racing ambulance, incessant, furious, defiant. Without orders, the crowd opened, and through them, almost grazing them, slid the huge gray car. At the back, haughty in white uniform, nonchalant on a narrow seat, was The Doctor—Martin Arrowsmith.

The crowd admired him, the policemen sprang to receive him.

"Where's the fireman got hurt?" he snapped.

"Over in that shed," cried the police sergeant, running beside the ambulance.

"Drive over closer. Nev' mind the smoke!" Martin barked at the driver.

A lieutenant of firemen led him to a pile of sawdust on which was huddled an unconscious youngster, his face bloodless and clammy.

"He got a bad dose of smoke from the green lumber and keeled over. Fine kid. Is he a goner?" the lieutenant begged.

Martin knelt by the man, felt his pulse, listened to his breathing.

Brusquely opening a black bag, he gave him a hypodermic of strychnin and held a vial of ammonia to his nose. "He'll come around. Here, you two, getum into the ambulance—hustle!"

The police sergeant and the newest probationer patrolman sprang together, and together they mumbled, "All right, Doc."

To Martin came the chief reporter of the *Advocate-Times*. In years he was only twenty-nine, but he was the oldest and perhaps the most cynical man in the world. He had interviewed senators; he had discovered graft in charity societies and even in prize-fights. There were fine wrinkles beside his eyes, he rolled Bull Durham cigarettes constantly, and his opinion of man's honor and woman's virtue was but low. Yet to Martin, or at least to The Doctor, he was polite.

"Will he pull through, Doc?" he twanged.

"Sure, I think so. Suffocation. Heart's still going."

Martin yelped the last words from the step at the back of the ambulance as it went bumping and rocking through the factory yard, through the bitter smoke, toward the shrinking crowd. He owned and commanded the city, he and the driver. They ignored traffic regulations, they disdained the people, returning from theaters and movies, who dotted the streets which unrolled before the flying gray hood. Let 'em get out of the way! The traffic officer at Chickasaw and Twentieth heard them coming, speeding like the Midnight Express—urrrrrr—blang-blang-blang-blang—and cleared the noisy corner. People were jammed against the curb, threatened by rearing horses and backing motors, and past them hurled the ambulance, blang-blang-blang-blang, with The Doctor holding a strap and swinging easily on his perilous seat.

At the hospital the hall-man cried, "Shooting case in the Arbor, Doc."

"All right. Wait'll I sneak in a drink," said Martin placidly.

On the way to his room he passed the open door of the hospital laboratory, with its hacked bench, its lifeless rows of flasks and test-tubes.

"Huh! That stuff! Poking 'round labs! This is real sure-enough life," he exulted, and he did not permit himself to see the vision of Max Gottlieb waiting there, so gaunt, so tired, so patient.

## II

The six interns in Zenith General, including Martin and Angus Duer, lived in a long dark room with six camp beds, and six bureaus fantastic with photographs and ties and undarned socks. They spent hours sitting on their beds, arguing surgery versus internal medicine, planning the dinners which they hoped to enjoy on their nights off, and explaining to Martin, as the only married man, the virtues of the various nurses with whom, one by one, they fell in love.

Martin found the hospital routine slightly dull. Though he developed the Intern's Walk, that quick corridor step with the stethoscope conspicuous in the pocket, he did not, he could not, develop the bedside manner. He was sorry for the bruised, yellowed, suffering patients, always changing as to individuals and never changing as a mass of drab pain, but when he had thrice dressed a wound, he had had enough; he wanted to go on to new experiences. Yet the ambulance work outside the hospital was endlessly stimulating to his pride.

The Doctor, and The Doctor alone, was safe by night in the slum called "the Arbor." His black bag was a pass. Policemen saluted him, prostitutes bowed to him without mockery, saloon-keepers called out, "Evenin', Doc," and hold-up men stood back in doorways to let him pass. Martin had power, the first obvious power in his life. And he was led into incessant adventure.

He took a bank-president out of a dive; he helped the family conceal the disgrace; he irritably refused their bribe; and afterward, when he thought of how he might have dined with Leora, he was sorry he had refused it. He broke into hotel-rooms reeking with gas and revived would-be suicides. He drank Trinidad rum with a Congressman who advocated prohibition. He attended a policeman assaulted by strikers, and a striker assaulted by policemen. He assisted at an emergency abdominal operation at three o'clock in the morning. The operating-room—white tile walls and white tile floor and glittering frosted-glass skylight—seemed lined with fire-lit ice, and the large incandescents glared on the glass instrument cases, the cruel little knives. The surgeon, in long white gown, white turban, and pale orange rubber gloves, made his swift incision in the square of yellowish flesh exposed between towels, cutting deep into layers of fat, and Martin looked on unmoved as the first blood menacingly followed the cut. And a month after, during the Chaloosa River flood, he worked for seventy-six hours, with half-hours of sleep in the ambulance or on a police-station table.

He landed from a boat at what had been the second story of a tenement and delivered a baby on the top floor; he bound up heads and arms for a line of men; but what gave him glory was the perfectly foolhardy feat of swimming the flood to save five children marooned and terrified on a bobbing church pew. The newspapers gave him large headlines, and when he had returned to kiss Leora and sleep twelve hours, he lay and thought about research with salty self-defensive scorn.

"Gottlieb, the poor old impractical fusser! I'd like to see him swim that current!" jeered Dr. Arrowsmith to Martin.

But on night duty, alone, he had to face the self he had been afraid to uncover, and he was homesick for the laboratory, for the thrill of uncharted discoveries, the quest below the surface and beyond the moment, the search for fundamental laws which the scientist (however blasphemously and colloquially he may describe it) exalts above temporary healing as the religious exalts the nature and terrible glory of God above pleasant daily virtues. With this sadness there was envy that he should be left out of things, that others should go ahead of him, ever surer in technique, more widely aware of the phenomena of biological chemistry, more deeply daring to explain laws at which the pioneers had but fumbled and hinted.

In his second year of internship, when the thrills of fires and floods and murder became as obvious a routine as bookkeeping, when he had seen the strangely few ways in which mankind can contrive to injure themselves and slaughter one another, when it was merely wearing to have to live up to the pretentiousness of being The Doctor, Martin tried to satisfy and perhaps kill his guilty scientific lust by voluntary scrabbling about the hospital laboratory, correlating the blood counts in pernicious anemia. His trifling with the drug of research was risky. Amid the bustle of operations he began to picture the rapt quietude of the laboratory. "I better cut this out," he said to Leora, "if I'm going to settle down in Wheatsylvania and 'tend to business and make a living—and I by golly am!"

Dean Silva often came to the hospital on consultations. He passed through the lobby one evening when Leora, returned from the office where she was a stenographer, was meeting Martin for dinner. Martin introduced them, and the little man held her hand, purred at her, and squeaked, "Will you children give me the pleasure of taking you to dinner? My wife has deserted me. I am a lone and misanthropic man."

He trotted between them, round and happy. Martin and he were not student and teacher, but two doctors together, for Dean Silva was one pedagogue who could still be interested in a man who no longer sat at his feet. He led the two starvelings to a chop-house and in a settle-walled booth he craftily stuffed them with roast goose and mugs of ale.

He concentrated on Leora, but his talk was of Martin:

"Your husband must be an Artist Healer, not a picker of trifles like these laboratory men."

"But Gottlieb's no picker of trifles," insisted Martin.

"No-o. But with him— It's a difference of one's gods. Gottlieb's gods are the cynics, the destroyers—crapehangers, the vulgar call 'em: Diderot and Voltaire and Elser; great men, wonder-workers, yet men that had more fun destroying other people's theories than creating their own. But my gods now, they're the men who took the discoveries of Gottlieb's gods and turned them to the use of human beings—made them come alive!

"All credit to the men who invented paint and canvas, but there's more credit, eh? to the Raphaels and Holbeins who used those discoveries! Laënnec and Osler, those are the men! It's all very fine, this business of pure research: seeking the truth, unhampered by commercialism or fame-chasing. Getting to the bottom. Ignoring consequences and practical uses. But do you realize if you carry that idea far enough, a man could justify himself for doing nothing but count the cobblestones on Warehouse Avenue—yes, and justify himself for torturing people just to see how they screamed—and then sneer at a man who was making millions of people well and happy!

"No, no! Mrs. Arrowsmith, this lad Martin is a passionate fellow, not a drudge. He must be passionate on behalf of mankind. He's chosen the highest calling in the world, but he's a feckless, experimental devil. You must keep him at it, my dear, and not let the world lose the benefit of his passion."

After this solemnity Dad Silva took them to a musical comedy and sat between them, patting Martin's shoulder, patting Leora's arm, choking with delight when the comedian stepped into the pail of whitewash. In midnight volubility Martin and Leora sputtered their affection for him, and saw their Wheatsylvania venture as glory and salvation.

But a few days before the end of Martin's internship and their migration to North Dakota, they met Max Gottlieb on the street.

Martin had not seen him for more than a year; Leora never. He looked worried and ill. While Martin was agonizing as to whether to pass with a bow, Gottlieb stopped.

"How is everything, Martin?" he said cordially. But his eyes said, "Why have you never come back to me?"

The boy stammered something, nothing, and when Gottlieb had gone by, stooped and moving as in pain, he longed to run after him.

Leora was demanding, "Is that the Professor Gottlieb you're always talking about?"

"Yes. Say! How does he strike you?"

"I don't— Sandy, he's the greatest man I've ever seen! I don't know how I know, but he is! Dr. Silva is a darling, but that was a *great* man! I wish—I wish we were going to see him again. There's the first man I ever laid eyes on that I'd leave you for, if he wanted me. He's so—oh, he's like a sword—no, he's like a brain walking. Oh, Sandy, he looked so wretched. I wanted to cry. I'd black his shoes!"

"God! So would I!"

But in the bustle of leaving Zenith, the excitement of the journey to Wheatsylvania, the scramble of his state examinations, the dignity of being a Practicing Physician, he forgot Gottlieb, and on that Dakota prairie radiant in early June, with meadow larks on every fence post, he began his work.

# 12

At the moment when Martin met him on the street, Gottlieb was ruined.

Max Gottlieb was a German Jew, born in Saxony in 1850. Though he took his medical degree, at Heidelberg, he was never interested in practicing medicine. He was a follower of Helmholtz, and youthful researches in the physics of sound convinced him of the need of the quantitative method in the medical sciences. Then Koch's discoveries drew him into biology. Always an elaborately careful worker, a maker of long rows of figures, always realizing the presence of uncontrollable variables, always a vicious assailant of what he considered slackness or lie or pomposity, never too kindly to well-intentioned stupidity, he worked in the laboratories of Koch, of Pasteur, he followed the early statements of Pearson in biometrics, he drank beer and wrote vitriolic letters, he voyaged to Italy and England and Scandinavia, and casually, between two days, he married (as he might have bought a coat or hired a housekeeper) the patient and wordless daughter of a Gentile merchant.

Then began a series of experiments, very important, very undramatic-sounding, very long, and exceedingly unappreciated. Back in 1881 he was confirming Pasteur's results in chicken cholera immunity and, for relief and pastime, trying to separate an enzyme from yeast. A few years later, living on the tiny inheritance from his father, a petty banker, and quite carelessly and cheerfully exhausting it, he was analyzing critically the ptomain theory of disease, and investigating the mechanism of the attenuation of virulence of microorganisms. He got thereby small fame. Perhaps he was over-cautious, and more than the devil or starvation he hated men who rushed into publication unprepared.

Though he meddled little in politics, considering them the most repetitious and least scientific of human activities, he was a sufficiently patriotic German to hate the Junkers. As a youngster he had a fight or two with ruffling subalterns; once he spent a week in jail; often he was infuriated by discriminations against Jews: and at forty he went sadly off to the America which could never become militaristic or anti-Semitic—to the Hoagland Laboratory in Brooklyn, then to Queen City University as professor of bacteriology.

Here he made his first investigation of toxin-anti-toxin reactions. He announced that antibodies, excepting antitoxin, had no relation to the immune state of an animal, and while he himself was being ragingly denounced in the small but hectic world of scientists, he dealt calmly and most brutally with Yersin's and Marmorek's theories of sera.

His dearest dream, now and for years of racking research, was the artificial production of antitoxin—its production *in vitro*. Once he was prepared to publish, but he found an error and rigidly suppressed his notes. All the while he was lonely. There was apparently no one in Queen City who regarded him as other than a cranky Jew catching microbes by their little tails and leering at them—no work for a tall man at a time when heroes were building bridges, experimenting with Horseless Carriages, writing the first of the poetic Compelling Ads, and selling miles of calico and cigars.

In 1899 he was called to the University of Winnemac, as professor of bacteriology in the medical school, and here he drudged on for a dozen years. Not once did he talk of results of the sort called "practical"; not once did he cease warring on the *post hoc propter hoc* conclusions which still make up most medical lore; not once did he fail to be hated by his colleagues, who were respectful to his face, uncomfortable in feeling his ironic power, but privily joyous to call him Mephisto, Diabolist, Killjoy, Pessimist, Destructive Critic, Flippant Cynic, Scientific Bounder Lacking in Dignity and Seriousness, Intellectual Snob, Pacifist, Anarchist, Atheist, Jew. They said, with reason, that he was so devoted to Pure Science, to art for art's sake, that he would rather have people die by the right therapy than be cured by the wrong. Having built a shrine for humanity, he wanted to kick out of it all mere human beings.

The total number of his papers, in a brisk scientific realm where really clever people published five times a year, was not more than twenty-five in thirty years. They were all exquisitely finished, all easily reduplicated and checked by the doubtfulest critics.

At Mohalis he was pleased by large facilities for work, by excellent assistants, endless glassware, plenty of guinea pigs, enough monkeys; but he was bored by the round of teaching, and melancholy again in a lack of understanding friends. Always he sought someone to whom he could talk without suspicion or caution. He was human enough, when he meditated upon the exaltation of doctors bold through ignorance, of inventors who were but tinkers magnified, to be irritated by his lack of fame in America, even in Mohalis, and to complain not too nobly.

He had never dined with a duchess, never received a prize, never been interviewed, never produced anything which the public could understand, nor experienced anything since his schoolboy amours which nice people could regard as romantic. He was, in fact, an authentic scientist.

He was of the great benefactors of humanity. There will never, in any age, be an effort to end the great epidemics or the petty infections which will not have been influenced by Max Gottlieb's researches, for he was not one who tagged and prettily classified bacteria and protozoa. He sought their chemistry, the laws of their existence and destruction, basic laws for the most part unknown after a generation of busy biologists. Yet they were right who called him "pessimist," for this man who, as much as any other, will have been the cause of reducing infectious diseases to almost-zero often doubted the value of reducing infectious diseases at all.

He reflected (it was an international debate in which he was joined by a few and damned by many) that half a dozen generations nearly free from epidemics would produce a race so low in natural immunity that when a great plague, suddenly springing from almost-zero to a world-smothering cloud, appeared again, it might wipe out the world entire, so that the measures to save lives to which he lent his genius might in the end be the destruction of all human life.

He meditated that if science and public hygiene did remove tuberculosis and the other major plagues, the world was grimly certain to become so overcrowded, to become such a universal slave-packed shambles, that all beauty and ease and wisdom would disappear in a famine-driven scamper for existence. Yet these speculations never checked his work. If the future became overcrowded, the future must by birth-control or otherwise look to itself. Perhaps it would, he reflected. But even this drop of wholesome optimism was lacking in his final doubts. For he doubted all progress of the intellect and the emotions, and he doubted, most of all, the superiority of divine mankind to the cheerful dogs, the infallibly graceful cats, the unmoral and unagitated and irreligious horses, the superbly adventuring sea-gulls.

While medical quacks, manufacturers of patent medicines, chewing-gum salesmen, and high priests of advertising lived in large houses, attended by servants, and took their sacred persons abroad in limousines, Max Gottlieb dwelt in a cramped cottage whose paint was peeling, and rode to his laboratory on an ancient and squeaky bicycle. Gottlieb himself protested rarely. He was not so unreasonable—usually—as to demand both freedom and the fruits of popular slavery. "Why," he once said to Martin, "should the world pay me for doing what I want and what they do not want?"

If in his house there was but one comfortable chair, on his desk were letters, long, intimate, and respectful, from the great ones of France and Germany, Italy and Denmark, and from scientists whom Great Britain so much valued that she gave them titles almost as high as those with which she rewarded distillers, cigarette-manufacturers, and the owners of obscene newspapers.

But poverty kept him from fulfillment of his summer longing to sit beneath the poplars by the Rhine or the tranquil Seine, at a table on whose checkered cloth were bread and cheese and wine and dusky cherries, those ancient and holy simplicities of all the world.

## II

Max Gottlieb's wife was thick and slow-moving and mute; at sixty she had not learned to speak easy English; and her German was of the small-town bourgeois, who pay their debts and over-eat and grow red. If he was not confidential with her, if at table he forgot her in long reflections, neither was he unkind or impatient, and he depended on her housekeeping, her warming of his old-fashioned nightgown. She had not been well of late. She had nausea and indigestion, but she kept on with her work. Always you heard her old slippers slapping about the house.

They had three children, all born when Gottlieb was over thirty-eight: Miriam, the youngest, an ardent child who had a touch at the piano, an instinct about Beethoven, and hatred for the "ragtime" popular in America; an older sister who was nothing in particular; and their boy Robert—Robert Koch Gottlieb. He was a wild thing and a distress. They sent him, with anxiety over the cost, to a smart school near Zenith, where he met the sons of manufacturers and discovered a taste for fast motors and eccentric clothes, and no taste whatever for studying. At home he clamored that his father was a "tightwad." When Gottlieb sought to make it clear that he was a poor man, the boy answered that out of his poverty he was always sneakingly spending money on his researches—he had no right to do that and shame his son—let the confounded University provide him with material!

## III

There were few of Gottlieb's students who saw him and his learning as anything but hurdles to be leaped as quickly as possible. One of the few was Martin Arrowsmith.

However harshly he may have pointed out Martin's errors, however loftily he may have seemed to ignore his devotion, Gottlieb was as aware of Martin as Martin of him. He planned vast things. If Martin really desired his help (Gottlieb could be as modest personally as he was egotistic and swaggering in competitive science), he would make the boy's career his own. During Martin's minute original research, Gottlieb rejoiced in his willingness to abandon conventional—and convenient—theories of immunology and in the exasperated carefulness with which he checked results. When Martin for unknown reasons became careless, when he was obviously drinking too much, obviously mixed up in some absurd personal affair, it was tragic hunger for friends and flaming respect for excellent work which drove Gottlieb to snarl at him. Of the apologies demanded by Silva he had no notion. He would have raged—

He waited for Martin to return. He blamed himself: "Fool! There was a fine spirit. You should have known one does not use a platinum loop for shoveling coal." As long as he could (while Martin was dish-washing and wandering on improbable trains between impossible towns), he put off the appointment of a new assistant. Then all his wistfulness chilled to anger. He considered Martin a traitor, and put him out of his mind.

## IV

It is possible that Max Gottlieb was a genius. Certainly he was mad as any genius. He did, during the period of Martin's internship in Zenith General, a thing more preposterous than any of the superstitions at which he scoffed.

He tried to become an executive and a reformer! He, the cynic, the anarch, tried to found an Institution, and he went at it like a spinster organizing a league to keep small boys from learning naughty words.

He conceived that there might, in this world, be a medical school which should be altogether scientific, ruled by exact quantitative biology and chemistry, with spectacle-fitting and most of surgery ignored, and he further conceived that such an enterprise might be conducted at the University of Winnemac! He tried to be practical about it; oh, he was extremely practical and plausible!

"I admit we should not be able to turn out doctors to cure village belly-aches. And ordinary physicians are admirable and altogether necessary—perhaps. But there are too many of them already. And on the 'practical' side, you gif me twenty years of a school that is precise and cautious, and we shall cure diabetes, maybe tuberculosis and cancer, and all these arthritis things that the carpenters shake their heads at them and call them 'rheumatism.' So!"

He did not desire the control of such a school, nor any credit. He was too busy. But at a meeting of the American Academy of Sciences he met one Dr. Entwisle, a youngish physiologist from Harvard, who would make an excellent dean. Entwisle admired him, and sounded him on his willingness to be called to Harvard. When Gottlieb outlined his new sort of medical school, Entwisle was fervent. "Nothing I'd like so much as to have a chance at a place like that," he fluttered, and Gottlieb went back to Mohalis triumphant. He was the more assured because (though he sardonically refused it) he was at this time offered the medical deanship of the University of West Chippewa.

So simple, or so insane, was he that he wrote to Dean Silva politely bidding him step down and hand over his school—his work, his life—to an unknown teacher in Harvard! A courteous old gentleman was Dad Silva, a fit disciple of Osler, but this incredible letter killed his patience. He replied that while he could see the value of basic research, the medical school belonged to the people of the state, and its task was to provide them with immediate and practical attention. For himself, he hinted, if he ever believed that the school would profit by his resignation he would go at once, but he needed a rather broader suggestion than a letter from one of his own subordinates!

Gottlieb retorted with spirit and indiscretion. He damned the People of the State of Winnemac. Were they, in their present condition of nincompoopery, worth any sort of attention? He unjustifiably took his demand over Silva's head to that great orator and patriot, Dr. Horace Greeley Truscott, president of the University.

President Truscott said, "Really, I'm too engrossed to consider chimerical schemes, however ingenious they may be."

"You are too busy to consider anything but selling honorary degrees to millionaires for gymnasiums," remarked Gottlieb.

Next day he was summoned to a special meeting of the University Council. As head of the medical department of bacteriology, Gottlieb was a member of this all-ruling body, and when he entered the long Council Chamber, with its gilt ceiling, its heavy maroon curtains, its somber paintings of pioneers, he started for his usual seat, unconscious of the knot of whispering members, meditating on far-off absorbing things.

"Oh, uh, Professor Gottlieb, will you please sit down there at the far end of the table?" called President Truscott.

Then Gottlieb was aware of tensions. He saw that out of the seven members of the Board of Regents, the four who lived in or near Zenith were present. He saw that sitting beside Truscott was not the dean of the academic department but Dean Silva. He saw that however easily they talked, they were looking at him through the mist of their chatter.

President Truscott announced, "Gentlemen, this joint meeting of the Council and the regents is to consider charges against Professor Max Gottlieb preferred by his dean and by myself."

Gottlieb suddenly looked old.

"These charges are: Disloyalty to his dean, his president, his regents and to the State of Winnemac. Disloyalty to recognized medical and scholastic ethics. Insane egoism. Atheism. Persistent failure to collaborate with his colleagues, and such inability to understand practical affairs as makes it dangerous to let him conduct the important laboratories and classes with which we have entrusted him. Gentlemen, I shall now prove each of these points, from Professor Gottlieb's own letters to Dean Silva."

He proved them.

The chairman of the Board of Regents suggested, "Gottlieb, I think it would simplify things if you just handed us your resignation and permitted us to part in good feeling, instead of having the unpleasant—"

"I'm damned if I will resign!" Gottlieb was on his feet, a lean fury. "Because you all haf schoolboy minds, golf-links minds, you are twisting my expression, and perfectly accurate expression, of a sound revolutionary ideal, which would personally to me be of no value or advantage whatefer, into a desire to steal promotions. That fools should judge honor—!" His long forefinger was a fish-hook, reaching for President Truscott's soul. "No! I will not resign! You can cast me out!"

"I'm afraid, then, we must ask you to leave the room while we vote." The president was very suave, for so large and strong and hearty a man.

Gottlieb rode his wavering bicycle to the laboratory. It was by telephone message from a brusque girl clerk in the president's office that he was informed that "his resignation had been accepted."

He agonized, "Discharge me? They couldn't! I'm the chief glory, the only glory, of this shopkeepers' school!" When he comprehended that apparently they very much had discharged him, he was shamed that he should have given them a chance to kick him. But the really dismaying thing was that he should by an effort to be a politician have interrupted the sacred work.

He required peace and a laboratory, at once.

They'd see what fools they were when they heard that Harvard had called him!

He was eager for the mellower ways of Cambridge and Boston. Why had he remained so long in raw Mohalis? He wrote to Dr. Entwisle, hinting that he was willing to hear an offer. He expected a telegram. He waited a week, then had a long letter from Entwisle admitting that he had been premature in speaking for the Harvard faculty. Entwisle presented the faculty's compliments and their hope that some time they might have the honor of his presence, but as things were now—

Gottlieb wrote to the University of West Chippewa that, after all, he was willing to think about their medical deanship . . . and had answer that the place was filled, that they had not greatly liked the tone of his former letter, and they did not "care to go into the matter further."

At sixty-one, Gottlieb had saved but a few hundred dollars—literally a few hundred. Like any bricklayer out of work, he had to have a job or go hungry. He was no longer a genius impatient of interrupted creation but a shabby schoolmaster in disgrace.

He prowled through his little brown house, fingering papers, staring at his wife, staring at old pictures, staring at nothing. He still had a month of teaching—they had dated ahead the resignation which they had written for him—but he was too dispirited to go to the laboratory. He felt unwanted, almost unsafe. His ancient sureness was broken into self-pity. He waited from delivery to delivery for the mail. Surely there would be aid from somebody who knew what he was, what he meant. There were many friendly letters about research, but the sort of men with whom he corresponded did not listen to intercollegiate faculty tattle nor know of his need.

He could not, after the Harvard mischance and the West Chippewa rebuke, approach the universities or the scientific institutes, and he was too proud to write begging letters to the men who revered him. No, he would be business-like! He applied to a Chicago teachers' agency, and received a stilted answer promising to look about and inquiring whether he would care to take the position of teacher of physics and chemistry in a suburban high school.

Before he had sufficiently recovered from his fury to be able to reply, his household was overwhelmed by his wife's sudden agony.

She had been unwell for months. He had wanted her to see a physician, but she had refused, and all the while she was stolidly terrified by the fear that she had cancer of the stomach. Now when she began to vomit blood, she cried to him for help. The Gottlieb who scoffed at medical credos, at "carpenters" and "pill mongers," had forgotten what he knew of diagnosis, and when he was ill, or his family, he called for the doctor as desperately as any backwoods layman to whom illness was the black malignity of unknown devils.

In unbelievable simplicity he considered that, as his quarrel with Silva was not personal, he could still summon him, and this time he was justified. Silva came, full of excessive benignity, chuckling to himself, "When he's got something the matter, he doesn't run for Arrenhius or Jacques Loeb, but for me!" Into the meager cottage the little man brought strength, and Gottlieb gazed down on him trustingly.

Mrs. Gottlieb was suffering. Silva gave her morphine. Not without satisfaction he learned that Gottlieb did not even know the dose. He examined her—his pudgy hands had the sensitiveness if not the precision of Gottlieb's skeleton fingers. He peered about the airless bedroom: the dark green curtains, the crucifix on the dumpy bureau, the color-print of a virtuously voluptuous maiden. He was bothered by an impression of having recently been in the room. He remembered. It was the twin of the doleful chamber of a German grocer whom he had seen during a consultation a month ago.

He spoke to Gottlieb not as to a colleague or an enemy but as a patient, to be cheered.

"Don't think there's any tumorous mass. As of course you know, Doctor, you can tell such a lot by the differences in the shape of the lower border of the ribs, and by the surface of the belly during deep breathing."

"Oh, yesss."

"I don't think you need to worry in the least. We'd better hustle her off to the University Hospital, and we'll give her a test meal and get her X-rayed and take a look for Boas-Oppler bugs."

She was taken away, heavy, inert, carried down the cottage steps. Gottlieb was with her. Whether or not he loved her, whether he was capable of ordinary domestic affection, could not be discovered. The need of turning to Dean Silva had damaged his opinion of his own wisdom. It was the final affront, more subtle and more enervating than the offer to teach chemistry to children. As he sat by her bed, his dark face was blank, and the wrinkles which deepened across that mask may have been sorrow, may have been fear. . . . Nor is it known how, through the secure and uninvaded years, he had regarded his wife's crucifix, which Silva had spied on their bureau—a gaudy plaster crucifix on a box set with gilded shells.

Silva diagnosed it as probable gastric ulcer, and placed her on treatment, with light and frequent meals. She improved, but she remained in the hospital for four weeks, and Gottlieb wondered: Are these doctors deceiving us? Is it really cancer, which by Their mystic craft They are concealing from me who know naught?

Robbed of her silent assuring presence on which night by weary night he had depended, he fretted over his daughters, despaired at their noisy piano-practice, their inability to manage the slattern maid. When they had gone to bed he sat alone in the pale lamplight, unmoving, not reading. He was bewildered. His haughty self was like a robber baron fallen into the hands of rebellious slaves, stooped under a filthy load, the proud eye rheumy and patient with despair, the sword hand chopped off, obscene flies crawling across the gnawed wrist.

It was at this time that he encountered Martin and Leora on the street in Zenith.

He did not look back when they had passed him, but all that afternoon he brooded on them. "That girl, maybe it was she that stole Martin from me—from science! No! He was right. One sees what happens to the fools like me!"

On the day after Martin and Leora had started for Wheatsylvania, singing, Gottlieb went to Chicago to see the teachers' agency.

The firm was controlled by a Live Wire who had once been a county superintendent of schools. He was not much interested. Gottlieb lost his temper: "Do you make an endeavor to find positions for teachers, or do you merely send out circulars to amuse yourself? Haf you looked up my record? Do you know who I am?"

The agent roared, "Oh, we know about you, all right, all right! I didn't when I first wrote you, but— You seem to have a good record as a laboratory man, thought I don't see that you've produced anything of the slightest use in medicine. We had hoped to give you a chance such as you nor nobody else ever had. John Edtooth, the Oklahoma oil magnate, has decided to found a university that for plant and endowment and individuality will beat anything that's ever been pulled off in education—biggest gymnasium in the world, with an ex-New York Giant for baseball coach! We thought maybe we might work you in on the bacteriology or the physiology—I guess you could manage to teach that, too, if you boned up on it. But we've been making some inquiries. From some good friends of ours, down Winnemac way. And we find that you're not to be trusted with a position of real responsibility. Why, they fired you for general incompetence! But now that you've had your lesson— Do you think you'd be competent to teach Practical Hygiene in Edtooth University?"

Gottlieb was so angry that he forgot to speak English, and as all his cursing was in student German, in a creaky dry voice, the whole scene was very funny indeed to the cackling bookkeeper and the girl stenographers. When he went from that place Max Gottlieb walked slowly, without purpose, and in his eyes were senile tears.

# 13

No one in the medical world had ever damned more heartily than Gottlieb the commercialism of certain large pharmaceutical firms, particularly Dawson T. Hunziker & Co., Inc., of Pittsburgh. The Hunziker Company was an old and ethical house which dealt only with reputable doctors—or practically only with reputable doctors. It furnished excellent antitoxins for diphtheria and tetanus, as well as the purest of official preparations, with the plainest and most official-looking labels on the swaggeringly modest brown bottles. Gottlieb had asserted that they produced doubtful vaccines, yet he returned from Chicago to write to Dawson Hunziker that he was no longer interested in teaching, and he would be willing to work for them on half time if he might use their laboratories, on possibly important research, for the rest of the day.

When the letter had gone he sat mumbling. He was certainly not altogether sane. "Education! Biggest gymnasium in the world! Incapable of responsibility. Teaching I can do no more. But Hunziker will laugh at me. I haf told the truth about him and I shall haf to— Dear Gott, what shall I do?"

Into this still frenzy, while his frightened daughters peered at him from doorways, hope glided.

The telephone rang. He did not answer it. On the third irascible burring he took up the receiver and grumbled, "Yes, yes, vot iss it?"

A twanging nonchalant voice: "This M. C. Gottlieb?"

"This is Dr. Gottlieb!"

"Well, I guess you're the party. Hola wire. Long distance wants yuh."

Then, "Professor Gottlieb? This is Dawson Hunziker speaking. From Pittsburgh. My dear fellow, we should be delighted to have you join our staff."

"I— But—"

"I believe you have criticized the pharmaceutical houses—oh, we read the newspaper clippings very efficiently!—but we feel that when you come to us and understand the Spirit of the Old Firm better, you'll be enthusiastic. I hope, by the way, I'm not interrupting something."

Thus, over certain hundreds of miles, from the gold and blue drawing-room of his Sewickley home, Hunziker spoke to Max Gottlieb sitting in his patched easy chair, and Gottlieb grated with a forlorn effort at dignity:

"No, it iss all right."

"Well—we shall be glad to offer you five thousand dollars a year, for a starter, and we shan't worry about the half-time arrangement. We'll give you all the space and technicians and material you need, and you just go ahead and ignore us, and work out whatever seems important to you. Our only request is that if you do find any serums which are of real value to the world, we shall have the privilege of manufacturing them, and if we lose money on 'em, it doesn't matter. We like to make money, if we can do it honestly, but our chief purpose is to serve mankind. Of course if the serums pay, we shall be only too delighted to give you a generous commission. Now about practical details—"

## II

Gottlieb, the placidly virulent hater of religious rites, had a religious-seeming custom.

Often he knelt by his bed and let his mind run free. It was very much like prayer, though certainly there was no formal invocation, no consciousness of a Supreme Being—other than Max Gottlieb. This night, as he knelt, with the wrinkles softening in his drawn face, he meditated, "I was asinine that I should ever scold the commercialists! This salesman fellow, he has his feet on the ground. How much more aut'entic the worst counter-jumper than frightened professors! Fine dieners! Freedom! No teaching of imbeciles! *Du Heiliger!*"

But he had no contract with Dawson Hunziker.

## III

In the medical periodicals the Dawson Hunziker Company published full-page advertisements, most starchy and refined in type, announcing that Professor Max Gottlieb, perhaps the most distinguished immunologist in the world, had joined their staff.

In his Chicago clinic, one Dr. Rouncefield chuckled, "That's what becomes of these super-highbrows. Pardon me if I seem to grin."

In the laboratories of Ehrlich and Roux, Bordet and Sir David Bruce, sorrowing men wailed, "How could old Max have gone over to that damned pill-peddler? Why didn't he come to us? Oh, well, if he didn't want to—*Voilà!* He is dead."

In the village of Wheatsylvania, in North Dakota, a young doctor protested to his wife, "Of all the people in the world! I wouldn't have believed it! Max Gottlieb falling for those crooks!"

"I don't care!" said his wife. "If he's gone into business, he had some good reason for it. I told you, I'd leave you for—"

"Oh, well," sighingly, "give and forgive. I learned a lot from Gottlieb and I'm grateful for— God, Leora, I wish *he* hadn't gone wrong!"

And Max Gottlieb, with his three young and a pale, slow-moving wife, was arriving at the station in Pittsburgh, tugging a shabby wicker bag, an immigrant bundle, and a Bond Street dressing-case. From the train he had stared up at the valiant cliffs, down to the smoke-tinged splendor of the river, and his heart was young. Here was fiery enterprise, not the flat land and flat minds of Winnemac. At the station-entrance every dingy taxicab seemed radiant to him, and he marched forth a conqueror.

## IV

In the Dawson Hunziker building, Gottlieb found such laboratories as he had never planned, and instead of student assistants he had an expert who himself had taught bacteriology, as well as three swift technicians, one of them German-trained. He was received with acclaim in the private office of Hunziker, which was remarkably like a minor cathedral. Hunziker was bald and business-like as to skull but tortoise-spectacled and sentimental of eye. He stood up at his Jacobean desk, gave Gottlieb a Havana cigar, and told him that they had awaited him pantingly.

In the enormous staff dining-room Gottlieb found scores of competent young chemists and biologists who treated him with reverence. He liked them. If they talked too much of money—of how much this new tincture of cinchona ought to sell, and how soon their salaries would be increased—yet they were free of the careful pomposities of college instructors. As a young-ster, the cap-tilted young Max had been a laughing man, and now in gusty arguments his laughter came back.

His wife seemed better; his daughter Miriam found an excellent piano teacher; the boy Robert entered college that autumn; they had a spacious though decrepit house; the relief from the droning and the annually re-peated, inevitable routine of the classroom was exhilarating; and Gottlieb had never in his life worked so well. He was unconscious of everything outside of his laboratory and a few theaters and concert-halls.

Six months passed before he realized that the young technical experts resented what he considered his jolly thrusts at their commercialism. They were tired of his mathematical enthusiasms and some of them viewed him as an old bore, muttered of him as a Jew. He was hurt, for he liked to be merry with fellow workers. He began to ask questions and to explore the Hunziker building. He had seen nothing of it save his laboratory, a corridor or two, the dining-room, and Hunziker's office.

However abstracted and impractical, Gottlieb would have made an excel-lent Sherlock Holmes—if anybody who would have made an excellent Sherlock Holmes would have been willing to be a detective. His mind burned through appearances to actuality. He discovered now that the Dawson Hunziker Com-pany was quite all he had asserted in earlier days. They did make excellent antitoxins and ethical preparations, but they were also producing a new "can-cer remedy" manufactured from the orchid, pontifically recommended and possessing all the value of mud. And to various billboard-advertising beauty companies they sold millions of bottles of a complexion-cream guaranteed to turn a Canadian Indian guide as lily-fair as the angels. This treasure cost six cents a bottle to make and a dollar over the counter, and the name of Dawson Hunziker was never connected with it.

It was at this time that Gottlieb succeeded in his masterwork after twenty years of seeking. He produced antitoxin in the test-tube, which meant that it would be possible to immunize against certain diseases without tediously making sera by the inoculation of animals. It was a revolution, the revolution, in immunology . . . if he was right.

He revealed it at a dinner for which Hunziker had captured a general, a college president, and a pioneer aviator. It was an expansive dinner, with admirable hock, the first decent German wine Gottlieb had drunk in years. He twirled the slender green glass affectionately; he came out of his dreams and became excited, gay, demanding. They applauded him, and for an hour he was a Great Scientist. Of them all, Hunziker was most generous in his praise. Gottlieb wondered if someone had not tricked this good bald man into intrigues with the beautifiers.

Hunziker summoned him to the office next day. Hunziker did his summoning very well indeed (unless it happened to be merely a stenographer). He sent a glossy morning-coated male secretary, who presented Mr. Hunziker's compliments to the much less glossy Dr. Gottlieb, and hinted with the delicacy of a lilac bud that if it was quite altogether convenient, if it would not in the least interfere with Dr. Gottlieb's experiments, Mr. Hunziker would be flattered to see him in the office at a quarter after three.

When Gottlieb rambled in, Hunziker motioned the secretary out of existence and drew up a tall Spanish chair.

"I lay awake half the night thinking about your discovery, Dr. Gottlieb. I've been talking to the technical director and sales-manager and we feel it's the time to strike. We'll patent your method of synthesizing antibodies and immediately put them on the market in large quantities, with a great big advertising campaign—you know—not circus it, of course strictly high-class ethical advertising. We'll start with anti-diphtheria serum. By the way, when you receive your next check you'll find we've raised your honorarium to seven thousand a year." Hunziker was a large purring pussy, now, and Gottlieb death-still. "Need I say, my dear fellow, that if there's the demand I anticipate, you will have exceedingly large commissions coming!"

Hunziker leaned back with a manner of "How's that for glory, my boy?"

Gottlieb spoke nervously: "I do not approve of patenting serological processes. They should be open to all laboratories. And I am strongly against premature production or even announcement. I think I am right, but I must check my technique, perhaps improve it—be *sure*. Then, I should think there should be no objection to market production, but in ve-ry small quantities and in fair competition with others, not under patents, as if this was a dinglebat toy for the Christmas tradings!"

"My dear fellow, I quite sympathize. Personally I should like nothing so much as to spend my whole life in just producing one priceless scientific discovery, without consideration of mere profit. But we have our duty toward the stockholders of the Dawson Hunziker Company to make money for them. Do you realize that they have—and many of them are poor widows and orphans—invested their Little All in our stock, and that we must keep faith? I am helpless; I am but their Humble Servant. And on the other side: I think we've treated you rather well, Dr. Gottlieb, and we've given you complete freedom. And we intend to go on treating you well! Why, man, you'll be rich; you'll be one of us! I don't like to make any demands, but on this point it's my duty to insist, and I shall expect you at the earliest possible moment to start manufacturing—"

Gottlieb was sixty-two. The defeat at Winnemac had done something to his courage. . . . And he had no contract with Hunziker.

He protested shakily, but as he crawled back to his laboratory it seemed impossible for him to leave this sanctuary and face the murderous brawling world, and quite as impossible to tolerate a cheapened and ineffective imitation of his antitoxin. He began, that hour, a sordid strategy which his old proud self would have called inconceivable; he began to equivocate, to put off announcement and production till he should have "cleared up a few points," while week on week Hunziker became more threatening. Meantime he prepared for disaster. He moved his family to a smaller house, and gave up every luxury, even smoking.

Among his economies was the reduction of his son's allowance.

Robert was a square-rigged, swart, tempestuous boy, arrogant where there seemed to be no reason for arrogance, longed for by the anemic, milky sort of girls, yet ever supercilious to them. While his father was alternately proud and amiably sardonic about his own Jewish blood, the boy conveyed to his classmates in college that he was from pure and probably noble German stock. He was welcomed, or half welcomed, in a motoring, poker-playing, country-club set, and he had to have more money. Gottlieb missed twenty dollars from his desk. He who ridiculed conventional honor had the honor, as he had the pride, of a savage old squire. A new misery stained his incessant bitterness at having to deceive Hunziker. He faced Robert with, "My boy, did you take the money from my desk?"

Few youngsters could have faced that jut of his hawk nose, the red-veined rage of his sunken eyes. Robert spluttered, then shouted:

"Yes, I did! And I've got to have some more! I've got to get some clothes and stuff. It's your fault. You bring me up to train with a lot of fellows that have all the cash in the world, and then you expect me to dress like a hobo!"

"Stealing—"

"Rats! What's stealing! You're always making fun of these preachers that talk about Sin and Truth and Honesty and all those words that've been used so much they don't mean a darn' thing and— I don't care! Daws Hunziker, the old man's son, he told me his dad said you could be a millionaire, and then you keep us strapped like this, and Mom sick— Let me tell you, back in Mohalis Mom used to slip me a couple of dollars almost every week and— I'm tired of it! If you're going to keep me in rags, I'm going to cut out college!"

Gottlieb stormed, but there was no force in it. He did not know, all the next fortnight, what his son was going to do, what himself was going to do.

Then, so quietly that not till they had returned from the cemetery did they realize her passing, his wife died, and the next week his oldest daughter ran off with a worthless laughing fellow who lived by gambling.

Gottlieb sat alone. Over and over he read the Book of Job. "Truly the Lord hath smitten me and my house," he whispered. When Robert came in, mumbling that he would be good, the old man lifted to him a blind face, unhearing. But as he repeated the fables of his fathers it did not occur to him to believe them, or to stoop in fear before their God of Wrath—or to gain ease by permitting Hunziker to defile his discovery.

He arose, in time, and went silently to his laboratory. His experiments were as careful as ever, and his assistants saw no change save that he did not lunch in hall. He walked blocks away, to a vile restaurant at which he could save thirty cents a day.

v

Out of the dimness which obscured the people about him, Miriam emerged.

She was eighteen, the youngest of his brood, squat, and in no way comely save for her tender mouth. She had always been proud of her father, understanding the mysterious and unreasoning compulsions of his science, but she had been in awe till now, when he walked heavily and spoke rarely. She dropped her piano lessons, discharged the maid, studied the cook-book, and prepared for him the fat crisp dishes that he loved. Her regret was that she had never learned German, for he dropped now and then into the speech of his boyhood.

He eyed her, and at length: "So! One is with me. Could you endure the poverty if I went away—to teach chemistry in a high school!"

"Yes. Of course. Maybe I could play the piano in a movie theater."

He might not have done it without her loyalty, but when Dawson Hunziker next paraded into the laboratory, demanding, "Now look here. We've fussed long enough. We got to put your stuff on the market," then Gottlieb answered, "No. If you wait till I have done all I can—maybe one year, probably three—you shall have it. But not till I am sure. No."

Hunziker went off huffily, and Gottlieb prepared for sentence.

Then the card of Dr. A. DeWitt Tubbs, Director of the McGurk Institute of Biology, of New York, was brought to him.

Gottlieb knew of Tubbs. He had never visited McGurk but he considered it, next to Rockefeller and McCormick, the soundest and freest organization for pure scientific research in the country, and if he had pictured a Heavenly laboratory in which good scientists might spend eternity in happy and thoroughly impractical research, he would have devised it in the likeness of McGurk. He was mildly pleased that its director should have called on him.

Dr. A. DeWitt Tubbs was tremendously whiskered on all visible spots save his nose and temples and the palms of his hands, short but passionately whiskered, like a Scotch terrier. Yet they were not comic whiskers; they were the whiskers of dignity; and his eyes were serious, his step an earnest trot, his voice a piping solemnity.

"Dr. Gottlieb, this is a great pleasure. I have heard your papers at the Academy of Sciences but, to my own loss, I have hitherto failed to have an introduction to you."

Gottlieb tried not to sound embarrassed.

Tubbs looked at the assistants, like a plotter in a political play, and hinted, "May we have a talk—"

Gottlieb led him to his office, overlooking a vast bustle of side-tracks, of curving rails and brown freight-cars, and Tubbs urged:

"It has come to our attention, by a curious chance, that you are on the eve of your most significant discovery. We all wondered, when you left academic work, at your decision to enter the commercial field. We wished that you had cared to come to us."

"You would have taken me in? I needn't at all have come here?"

"Naturally! Now from what we hear, you are not giving your attention to the commercial side of things, and that tempts us to wonder whether you could be persuaded to join us at McGurk. So I just sprang on a train and ran down here. We should be delighted to have you become a member of the institute, and chief of the Department of Bacteriology and Immunology. Mr. McGurk and I desire nothing but the advancement of science. You would, of course, have absolute freedom as to what researches you thought it best to pursue, and I think we could provide as good assistance and material as would be obtainable anywhere in the world. In regard to salary— permit me to be business-like and perhaps blunt, as my train leaves in one hour—I don't suppose we could equal the doubtless large emolument which the Hunziker people are able to pay you, but we can go to ten thousand dollars a year—"

"Oh, my God, do not talk of the money! I shall be wit' you in New York one week from today. You see," said Gottlieb, "I haf no contract here!"

# 14

All afternoon they drove in the flapping buggy across the long undulations of the prairie. To their wandering there was no barrier, neither lake nor mountain nor factory-bristling city, and the breeze about them was flowing sunshine.

Martin cried to Leora, "I feel as if all the Zenith dust and hospital lint were washed out of my lungs. Dakota. Real man's country. Frontier. Opportunity. America!"

From the thick swale the young prairie chickens rose. As he watched them sweep across the wheat, his sun-drowsed spirit was part of the great land, and he was almost freed of the impatience with which he had started out from Wheatsylvania.

"If you're going driving, don't forget that supper is six o'clock sharp," Mrs. Tozer had said, smiling to sugar-coat it.

On Main Street, Mr. Tozer waved to them and shouted, "Be back by six. Supper at six o'clock sharp."

Bert Tozer ran out from the bank, like a country schoolmaster skipping from a one-room schoolhouse, and cackled, "Say, you folks better not forget to be back at six o'clock for supper or the Old Man'll have a fit. He'll expect you for supper at six o'clock sharp, and when he says six o'clock *sharp*, he means six o'clock *sharp*, and not five minutes *past* six!"

"Now that," observed Leora, "is funny, because in my twenty-two years in Wheatsylvania I remember three different times when supper was as late as seven minutes after six. Let's get out of this, Sandy. . . . I wonder were we so wise to live with the family and save money?"

Before they had escaped from the not very extensive limits of Wheatsylvania they passed Ada Quist, the future Mrs. Bert Tozer, and through the lazy air they heard her voice slashing: "Better be home by six."

Martin would be heroic. "We'll by golly get back when we're by golly good and ready!" he said to Leora; but on them both was the cumulative dread of the fussing voices, beyond every breezy prospect was the order, "Be back at six sharp"; and they whipped up to arrive at eleven minutes to six, as Mr. Tozer was returning from the creamery, full thirty seconds later than usual.

"Glad to see you among us," he said. "Hustle now and get that horse in the livery stable. Supper's at six—sharp!"

Martin survived it sufficiently to sound domestic when he announced at the supper-table:

"We had a bully drive. I'm going to like it here. Well, I've loafed for a day and a half, and now I've got to get busy. First thing is, I must find a location for my office. What is there vacant, Father Tozer?"

Mrs. Tozer said brightly, "Oh, I have such a nice idea, Martin. Why can't we fix up an office for you out in the barn? It'd be so handy to the house, for you to get to meals on time, and you could keep an eye on the house if the girl was out and Ory and I went out visiting or to the Embroidery Circle."

"In the barn!"

"Why, yes, in the old harness room. It's partly ceiled, and we could put in some nice tar paper or even beaver board."

"Mother Tozer, what the dickens do you think I'm planning to do? I'm not a hired man in a livery stable, or a kid looking for a place to put his birds' eggs! I was thinking of opening an office as a physician!"

Bert made it all easy: "Yuh, but you aren't much of a physician yet. You're just getting your toes in."

"I'm one hell of a good physician! Excuse me for cussing, Mother Tozer, but— Why, nights in the hospital, I've held hundreds of lives in my hand! I intend—"

"Look here, Mart," said Bertie. "As we're putting up the money—I don't want to be a tightwad but after all, a dollar is a dollar—if we furnish the dough, we've got to decide the best way to spend it."

Mr. Tozer looked thoughtful and said helplessly, "That's so. No sense taking a risk, with the blame' farmers demanding all the money they can get for their wheat and cream, and then deliberately going to work and not paying the interest on their loans. I swear, it don't hardly pay to invest in mortgages any longer. No sense putting on lugs. Stands to reason you can look at a fellow's sore throat or prescribe for an ear-ache just as well in a nice simple little office as in some fool place all fixed up like a Moorhead saloon. Mother will see you have a comfortable corner in the barn—"

Leora intruded: "Look here, Papa. I want you to lend us one thousand dollars, outright, to use as we see fit." The sensation was immense. "We'll pay you six per cent—no, we won't; we'll pay you five; that's enough."

"And mortgages bringing six, seven, and eight!" Bert quavered.

"Five's enough. And we want our own say, absolute, as to how we use it—to fit up an office or anything else."

Mr. Tozer began, "That's a foolish way to—"

Bert took it away from him: "Ory, you're crazy! I suppose we'll have to lend you some money, but you'll blame well come to us for it from time to time, and you'll blame well take our advice—"

Leora rose. "Either you do what I say, just exactly what I say, or Mart and I take the first train and go back to Zenith, and I mean it! Plenty of places open for him there, with a big salary, so we won't have to be dependent on anybody!"

There was much conversation, most of which sounded like all the rest of it. Once Leora started for the stairs, to go up and pack; once Martin and she stood waving their napkins as they shook their fists, the general composition remarkably like the Laocoön.

Leora won.

They settled down to the most solacing fussing.

"Did you bring your trunk up from the depot?" asked Mr. Tozer.

"No sense leaving it there—paying two bits a day storage!" fumed Bert.

"I got it up this morning," said Martin.

"Oh, yes, Martin had it brought up this morning," agreed Mrs. Tozer.

"You had it brought? Didn't you bring it up yourself?" agonized Mr. Tozer.

"No. I had the fellow that runs the lumberyard haul it up for me," said Martin.

"Well, gosh almighty, you could just as well've put it on a wheelbarrow and brought it up yourself and saved a quarter!" said Bert.

"But a doctor has to keep his dignity," said Leora.

"Dignity, rats! Blame sight more dignified to be seen shoving a wheel-barrow than smoking them dirty cigarettes all the time!"

"Well, anyway— Where'd you put it?" asked Mr. Tozer.

"It's up in our room," said Martin.

"Where'd you think we better put it when it's unpacked? The attic is awful' full," Mr. Tozer submitted to Mrs. Tozer.

"Oh, I think Martin could get it in there."

"Why couldn't he put it in the barn?"

"Oh, not a nice new trunk like that!"

"What's the matter with the barn?" said Bert. "It's all nice and dry. Seems a shame to waste all that good space in the barn, now that you've gone and decided he mustn't have his dear little office there!"

"Bertie," from Leora, "I know what we'll do. You seem to have the barn on your brain. You move your old bank there, and Martin'll take the bank building for his office."

"That's entirely different—"

"Now there's no sense you two showing off and trying to be smart," protested Mr. Tozer. "Do you ever hear your mother and I scrapping and fussing like that? When do you think you'll have your trunk unpacked, Mart?" Mr. Tozer could consider barns and he could consider trunks but his was not a brain to grasp two such complicated matters at the same time.

"I can get it unpacked tonight, if it makes any difference—"

"Well, I don't suppose it really makes any special difference, but when you start to *do* a thing—"

"Oh, what difference does it make whether he—"

"If he's going to look for an office, instead of moving right into the barn, he can't take a month of Sundays getting unpacked and—"

"Oh, good Lord, I'll get it done tonight—"

"And I think we can get it in the attic—"

"I tell you it's jam full already—"

"We'll go take a look at it after supper—"

"Well now, I tell you when I tried to get that duck-boat in—"

Martin probably did not scream, but he heard himself screaming. The free and virile land was leagues away and for years forgotten.

II

To find an office took a fortnight of diplomacy, and of discussion brightening three meals a day, every day. (Not that office-finding was the only thing the Tozers mentioned. They went thoroughly into every moment of Martin's day; they commented on his digestion, his mail, his walks, his shoes that needed cobbling, and whether he had yet taken them to the farmer-trapper-cobbler, and how much the cobbling ought to cost, and the presumable theology, politics, and marital relations of the cobbler.)

Mr. Tozer had from the first known the perfect office. The Norbloms lived above their general store, and Mr. Tozer knew that the Norbloms were thinking of moving. There was indeed nothing that was happening or likely to happen in Wheatsylvania which Mr. Tozer did not know and explain. Mrs. Norblom was tired of keeping house, and she wanted to go to Mrs. Beeson's boarding house (to the front room, on the right as you went along the up-stairs hall, the room with the plaster walls and the nice little stove that Mrs. Beeson bought from Otto Krag for seven dollars and thirty-five cents—no, seven and a quarter it was).

They called on the Norbloms and Mr. Tozer hinted that "it might be nice for the Doctor to locate over the store, if the Norbloms were thinking of making any change—"

The Norbloms stared at each other, with long, bleached, cautious, Scandinavian stares, and grumbled that they "didn't *know*—of course it was the finest location in town—" Mr. Norblom admitted that if, against all probability, they ever considered moving, they would probably ask twenty-five dollars a month for the flat, unfurnished.

Mr. Tozer came out of the international conference as craftily joyful as any Mr. Secretary Tozer or Lord Tozer in Washington or London:

"Fine! Fine! We made him commit himself! Twenty-five, he says. That means, when the time's ripe, we'll offer him eighteen and close for twenty-one-seventy-five. If we just handle him careful, and give him time to go see Mrs. Beeson and fix up about boarding with her, we'll have him just where we want him!"

"Oh, if the Norbloms can't make up their minds, then let's try something else," said Martin. "There's a couple of vacant rooms behind the *Eagle* office."

"What? Go chasing around, after we've given the Norbloms reason to think we're serious, and make enemies of 'em for life? Now that would be a fine way to start building up a practice, wouldn't it! And I must say I wouldn't blame the Norbloms one bit for getting wild if you let 'em down like that. This ain't Zenith, where you can go yelling around expecting to get things done in two minutes!"

Through a fortnight, while the Norbloms agonized over deciding to do what they had long ago decided to do, Martin waited, unable to begin work. Until he should open a certified and recognizable office, most of the village did not regard him as a competent physician but as "that son-in-law of Andy Tozer's." In the fortnight he was called only once: for the sick-headache of Miss Agnes Ingleblad, aunt and housekeeper of Alec Ingleblad the barber. He was delighted, till Bert Tozer explained:

"Oh, so *she* called you in, eh? She's always doctorin' around. There ain't a thing the matter with her, but she's always trying out the latest stunt. Last time it was a fellow that come through here selling pills and liniments out of a Ford, and the time before that it was a faith-healer, crazy loon up here at Dutchman's Forge, and then for quite a spell she doctored with an osteopath in Leopolis—though I tell you there's something to this osteopathy—they cure a lot of folks that you regular docs can't seem to find out what's the matter with 'em, don't you think so?"

Martin remarked that he did not think so.

"Oh, you docs!" Bert crowed in his most jocund manner, for Bert could be very joky and bright. "You're all alike, especially when you're just out of school and think you know it all. You can't see any good in chiropractic or electric belts or bone-setters or anything, because they take so many good dollars away from you."

Then behold the Dr. Martin Arrowsmith who had once infuriated Angus Duer and Irving Watters by his sarcasm on medical standards upholding to a lewdly grinning Bert Tozer the benevolence and scientific knowledge of all doctors; proclaiming that no medicine had ever (at least by any Winnemac graduate) been prescribed in vain nor any operation needlessly performed.

He saw a good deal of Bert now. He sat about the bank, hoping to be called on a case, his fingers itching for bandages. Ada Quist came in with frequency and Bert laid aside his figuring to be coy with her:

"You got to be careful what you even think about, when the doc is here, Ade. He's been telling me what a whale of a lot of neurology and all that mind-reading stuff he knows. How about it, Mart? I'm getting so scared that I've changed the combination on the safe."

"Heh!" said Ada. "He may fool some folks but he can't fool me. Anybody can learn things in books, but when it comes to practicing 'em— Let me tell you, Mart, if you ever have one-tenth of the savvy that old Dr. Winter of Leopolis has, you'll live longer than I expect!"

Together they pointed out that for a person who felt his Zenith training had made him so "gosh-awful' smart that he sticks up his nose at us poor hicks of dirt-farmers," Martin's scarf was rather badly tied.

All of his own wit and some of Ada's Bert repeated at the supper table.

"You oughtn't to ride the boy so hard. Still, that was pretty cute about the necktie—I guess Mart does think he's some punkins," chuckled Mr. Tozer.

Leora took Martin aside after supper. "Darlin', can you stand it? We'll have our own house, soon as we can. Or shall we vamoose?"

"I'm by golly going to stand it!"

"Um. Maybe. Dear, when you hit Bertie, do be careful—they'll hang you."

He ambled to the front porch. He determined to view the rooms behind the *Eagle* office. Without a retreat in which to be safe from Bert he could not endure another week. He could not wait for the Norbloms to make up their minds, though they had become to him dread and eternal figures whose enmity would crush him; prodigious gods shadowing this Wheatsylvania which was the only perceptible world.

He was aware, in the late sad light, that a man was tramping the plank walk before the house, hesitating and peering at him. The man was one Wise, a Russian Jew known to the village as "Wise the Polack." In his shack near the railroad he sold silver stock and motor-factory stock, bought and sold farmlands and horses and muskrat hides. He called out, "That you, Doc?"

"Yup!"

Martin was excited. A patient!

"Say, I wish you'd walk down a ways with me. Couple things I'd like to talk to you about. Or say, come on over to my place and sample some new cigars I've got." He emphasized the word "cigars." North Dakota was, like Mohalis, theoretically dry.

Martin was pleased. He had been sober and industrious so long now!

Wise's shack was a one-story structure, not badly built, half a block from Main Street, with nothing but the railroad track between it and open wheat country. It was lined with pine, pleasant-smelling under the stench of old pipe-smoke. Wise winked—he was a confidential, untrustworthy wisp of a man—and murmured, "Think you could stand a little jolt of first-class Kentucky bourbon?"

"Well, I wouldn't get violent about it."

Wise pulled down the sleazy window-shades and from a warped drawer of his desk brought up a bottle out of which they both drank, wiping the mouth of the bottle with circling palms. Then Wise, abruptly:

"Look here, Doc. You're not like these hicks; you understand that sometimes a fellow gets mixed up in crooked business he didn't intend to. Well, make a long story short, I guess I've sold too much mining stock, and they'll be coming down on me. I've got to be moving—curse it—hoped I could stay settled for couple of years, this time. Well, I hear you're looking for an office. This place would be ideal. Ideal! Two rooms at the back besides this one. I'll rent it to you, furniture and the whole shooting-match, for fifteen dollars a month, if you'll pay me one year in advance. Oh, this ain't phony. Your brother-in-law knows all about my ownership."

Martin tried to be very business-like. Was he not a young doctor who would soon be investing money, one of the most Substantial Citizens in Wheatsylvania? He returned home, and under the parlor lamp, with its green daisies on pink glass, the Tozers listened acutely, Bert stooping forward with open mouth.

"You'd be safe renting it for a year, but that ain't the point," said Bert.

"It certainly isn't! Antagonize the Norbloms, now that they've almost made up their minds to let you have their place? Make me a fool, after all the trouble I've taken?" groaned Mr. Tozer.

They went over it and over it till almost ten o'clock, but Martin was resolute, and the next day he rented Wise's shack.

For the first time in his life he had a place utterly his own, his and Leora's.

In his pride of possession this was the most lordly building on earth, and every rock and weed and doorknob was peculiar and lovely. At sunset he sat on the back stoop (a very interesting and not too broken soap-box) and from the flamboyant horizon the open country flowed across the thin band of the railroad to his feet. Suddenly Leora was beside him, her arm round his neck, and he hymned all the glory of their future:

"Know what I found in the kitchen here? A dandy old auger, hardly rusty a bit, and I can take a box and make a test-tube rack . . . of my own!"

# 15

With none of the profane observations on "medical peddlers" which had annoyed Digamma Pi, Martin studied the catalogue of the New Idea Instrument and Furniture Company, of Jersey City. It was a handsome thing. On the glossy green cover, in red and black, were the portraits of the president, a round quippish man who loved all young physicians; the general manager, a cadaverous scholarly man who surely gave all his laborious nights and days to the advancement of science; and the vice-president, Martin's former preceptor, Dr. Roscoe Geake, who had a lively, eye-glassed, forward-looking modernity all his own. The cover also contained, in surprisingly small space, a quantity of poetic prose, and the inspiring promise:

> Doctor, don't be buffaloed by the unenterprising. No reason why YOU should lack the equipment which impresses patients, makes practice easy, and brings honor and riches. All the high-class supplies which distinguish the Leaders of the Profession from the Dubs are within YOUR reach right NOW by the famous New Idea Financial System: "Just a little down and the rest FREE—out of the increased earnings which New Idea apparatus will bring you!"

Above, in a border of laurel wreaths and Ionic capitals, was the challenge:

> Sing not the glory of soldiers or explorers or statesmen for who can touch the doctor—wise, heroic, uncontaminated by common greed. Gentlemen, we salute you humbly and herewith offer you the most up-to-the-jiffy catalogue ever presented by any surgical supply house.

The back cover, though it was less glorious with green and red, was equally arousing. It presented illustrations of the Bindledorf Tonsillectomy Outfit and of an electric cabinet, with the demand:

> Doctor, are you sending your patients off to specialists for tonsil removal or to sanitoriums for electric, etc., treatment? If so, you are losing the chance to show yourself one of the distinguished powers in the domain of medical advancement in your locality, and losing a lot of big fees. Don't you WANT to be a high-class practitioner? Here's the Open Door.
>
> The Bindledorf Outfit is not only useful but exquisitely beautiful, adorns and gives class to any office. We guarantee that by the installation of a Bindledorf Outfit and a New Idea Panaceatic Electro-Therapeutic Cabinet (see details on pp. 34 and 97) you can increase your income from a thousand to ten thousand annually and please patients more than by the most painstaking plugging.

When the Great Call sounds, Doctor, and it's time for you to face your reward, will you be satisfied by a big Masonic funeral and tributes from Grateful Patients if you have failed to lay up provision for the kiddies, and faithful wife who has shared your tribulations?

You may drive through blizzard and August heat, and go down into the purple-shadowed vale of sorrow and wrestle with the ebon-cloaked Powers of Darkness for the lives of your patients, but that heroism is incomplete without Modern Progress, to be obtained by the use of a Bindledorf Tonsillectomy Outfit and the New Idea Panaceatic Cabinet, to be obtained on small payment down, rest on easiest terms known in history of medicine!

## II

This poetry of passion Martin neglected, for his opinion of poetry was like his opinion of electric cabinets, but excitedly he ordered a steel stand, a sterilizer, flasks, test-tubes, and a white-enameled mechanism with enchanting levers and gears which transformed it from examining-chair to operating-table. He yearned over the picture of a centrifuge while Leora was admiring the "stunning seven-piece Reception Room fumed oak set, upholstered in genuine Barcelona Longware Leatherette, will give your office the class and distinction of any high-grade New York specialist's."

"Aw, let 'em sit on plain chairs," Martin grunted.

In the attic Mrs. Tozer found enough seedy chairs for the reception-room, and an ancient bookcase which, when Leora had lined it with pink fringed paper, became a noble instrument-cabinet. Till the examining-chair should arrive, Martin would use Wise's lumpy couch, and Leora busily covered it with white oilcloth. Behind the front room of the tiny office-building were two cubicles, formerly bedroom and kitchen. Martin made them into consultation-room and laboratory. Whistling, he sawed out racks for the glassware and turned the oven of a discarded kerosene stove into a hot-air oven for sterilizing glassware.

"But understand, Lee, I'm not going to go monkeying with any scientific research. I'm through with all that."

Leora smiled innocently. While he worked she sat outside in the long wild grass, sniffing the prairie breeze, her hands about her ankles, but every quarter-hour she had to come in and admire.

Mr. Tozer brought home a package at suppertime. The family opened it, babbling. After supper Martin and Leora hastened with the new treasure to the office and nailed it in place. It was a plate-glass sign; on it in gold letters, "M. Arrowsmith, M.D." They looked up, arms about each other, squealing softly, and in reverence he grunted, "There—by—jiminy!"

They sat on the back stoop, exulting in freedom from Tozers. Along the railroad bumped a freight train with a cheerful clanking. The fireman waved to them from the engine, a brakeman from the platform of the red caboose. After the train there was silence but for the crickets and a distant frog.

"I've never been so happy," he murmured.

III

He had brought from Zenith his own Ochsner surgical case. As he laid out the instruments he admired the thin, sharp, shining bistoury, the strong tenotome, the delicate curved needles. With them was a dental forceps. Dad Silva had warned his classes, "Don't forget the country doctor often has to be not only physician but dentist, yes, and priest, divorce lawyer, blacksmith, chauffeur, and road engineer, and if you are too lily-handed for those trades, don't get out of sight of a trolley line and a beauty parlor." And the first patient whom Martin had in the new office, the second patient in Wheatsylvania, was Nils Krag, the carpenter, roaring with an ulcerated tooth. This was a week before the glass sign was up, and Martin rejoiced to Leora, "Begun already! You'll see 'em tumbling in now."

They did not see them tumbling in. For ten days Martin tinkered at his hot-air oven or sat at his desk, reading and trying to look busy. His first joy passed into fretfulness, and he could have yelped at the stillness, the inactivity.

Late one afternoon, when he was in a melancholy way preparing to go home, into the office stamped a grizzled Swedish farmer who grumbled, "Doc, I got a fish-hook caught in my thumb and it's all swole." To Arrowsmith, intern in Zenith General Hospital with its out-patient clinic treating hundreds a day, the dressing of a hand had been less important than borrowing a match, but to Dr. Arrowsmith of Wheatsylvania it was a hectic operation, and the farmer a person remarkable and very charming. Martin shook his left hand violently and burbled, "Now if there's anything, you just 'phone me—you just 'phone me."

There had been, he felt, a rush of admiring patients sufficient to justify them in the one thing Leora and he longed to do, the thing about which they whispered at night: the purchase of a motor car for his country calls.

They had seen the car at Frazier's store.

It was a Ford, five years old, with torn upholstery, a gummy motor, and springs made by a blacksmith who had never made springs before. Next to the chugging of the gas engine at the creamery, the most familiar sound in Wheatsylvania was Frazier's closing the door of his Ford. He banged it flatly at the store, and usually he had to shut it thrice again before he reached home.

But to Martin and Leora, when they had tremblingly bought the car and three new tires and a horn, it was the most impressive vehicle on earth. It was their own; they could go when and where they wished.

During his summer at a Canadian hotel Martin had learned to drive the Ford station wagon, but it was Leora's first venture. Bert had given her so many directions that she had refused to drive the family Overland. When she first sat at the steering wheel, when she moved the hand-throttle with her little finger and felt in her own hands all this power, sorcery enabling her to go as fast as she might desire (within distinct limits), she transcended human strength, she felt that she could fly like the wild goose—and then in a stretch of sand she killed the engine.

Martin became the demon driver of the village. To ride with him was to sit holding your hat, your eyes closed, waiting for death. Apparently he accelerated for corners, to make them more interesting. The sight of anything on the road ahead, from another motor to a yellow pup, stirred in him a frenzy which could be stilled only by going up and passing it. The village adored, "The Young Doc is quite some driver, all right." They waited, with amiable interest, to hear that he had been killed. It is possible that half of the first dozen patients who drifted into his office came because of awe at his driving . . . the rest because there was nothing serious the matter, and he was nearer than Dr. Hesselink at Groningen.

### IV

With his first admirers he developed his first enemies.

When he met the Norbloms on the street (and in Wheatsylvania it is difficult not to meet everyone on the street every day), they glared. Then he antagonized Pete Yeska.

Pete conducted what he called a "drug store," devoted to the sale of candy, soda water, patent medicines, fly paper, magazines, washing-machines, and Ford accessories, yet Pete would have starved if he had not been postmaster also. He alleged that he was a licensed pharmacist but he so mangled prescriptions that Martin burst into the store and addressed him piously.

"You young docs make me sick," said Pete. "I was putting up prescriptions when you was in the cradle. The old doc that used to be here sent everything to me. My way o' doing things suits me, and I don't figure on changing it for you or any other half-baked young string-bean."

Thereafter Martin had to purchase drugs from St. Paul, overcrowd his tiny laboratory, and prepare his own pills and ointments, looking in a homesick way at the rarely used test-tubes and the dust gathering on the bell glass of his microscope, while Pete Yeska joined with the Norbloms in whispering, "This new doc here ain't any good. You better stick to Hesselink."

### V

So blank, so idle, had been the week that when he heard the telephone at the Tozers', at three in the morning, he rushed to it as though he were awaiting a love message.

A hoarse and shaky voice: "I want to speak to the doctor."

"Yuh—yuh— 'S the doctor speaking."

"This is Henry Novak, four miles northeast, on the Leopolis road. My little girl, Mary, she has a terrible sore throat. I think maybe it is croup and she look awful and— Could you come right away?"

"You bet. Be right there."

Four miles—he would do it in eight minutes.

He dressed swiftly, dragging his worn brown tie together, while Leora beamed over the first night call. He furiously cranked the Ford, banged and clattered past the station and into the wheat prairie. When he had gone six miles by the speedometer, slackening at each rural box to look for the owner's name, he realized that he was lost. He ran into a farm driveway and stopped under the willows, his headlight on a heap of dented milk-cans, broken harvester wheels, cordwood, and bamboo fishing-poles. From the barn dashed a woolly anomalous dog, barking viciously, leaping up at the car.

A frowsy head protruded from a ground-floor window. "What you want?" screamed a Scandinavian voice.

"This is The Doctor. Where does Henry Novak live?"

"Oh! The Doctor! Dr. Hesselink?"

"No! Dr. Arrowsmith."

"Oh. Dr. Arrowsmith. From Wheatsylvania? Um. Well, you went right near his place. You yoost turn back one mile and turn to the right by the brick schoolhouse, and it's about forty rods up the road—the house with a cement silo. Somebody sick by Henry's?"

"Yuh—yuh—girl's got croup—thanks—"

"Yoost keep to the right. You can't miss it."

Probably no one who has listened to the dire "you can't miss it" has ever failed to miss it.

Martin swung the Ford about, grazing a slashed chopping-block; he rattled up the road, took the corner that side of the schoolhouse instead of this, ran half a mile along a boggy trail between pastures, and stopped at a farmhouse. In the surprising fall of silence, cows were to be heard feeding, and a white horse, startled in the darkness, raised its head to wonder at him. He had to arouse the house with wild squawkings of his horn, and an irate farmer who bellowed, "Who's there? I've got a shotgun!" sent him back to the country road.

It was forty minutes from the time of the telephone call when he rushed into a furrowed driveway and saw on the doorstep, against the lamplight, a stooped man who called, "The Doctor? This is Novak."

He found the child in a newly finished bedroom of white plastered walls and pale varnished pine. Only an iron bed, a straight chair, a chromo of St. Anne, and a shadeless hand-lamp on a rickety stand broke the staring shininess of the apartment, a recent extension of the farmhouse. A heavy-shouldered woman was kneeling by the bed. As she lifted her wet red face, Novak urged:

"Don't cry now; he's here!" And to Martin: "The little one is pretty bad but we done all we could for her. Last night and tonight we steam her throat, and we put her here in our own bedroom!"

Mary was a child of seven or eight. Martin found her lips and finger-tips blue, but in her face no flush. In the effort to expel her breath she writhed into terrifying knots, then coughed up saliva dotted with grayish specks. Martin worried as he took out his clinical thermometer and gave it a professional-looking shake.

It was, he decided, laryngeal croup or diphtheria. Probably diphtheria. No time now for bacteriological examination, for cultures and leisurely precision. Silva the healer bulked in the room, crowding out Gottlieb the inhuman perfectionist. Martin leaned nervously over the child on the tousled bed, absent-mindedly trying her pulse again and again. He felt helpless without the equipment of Zenith General, its nurses and Angus Duer's sure advice. He had a sudden respect for the lone country doctor.

He had to make a decision, irrevocable, perhaps perilous. He would use diphtheria antitoxin. But certainly he could not obtain it from Pete Yeska's in Wheatsylvania.

Leopolis?

"Hustle up and get me Blassner, the druggist at Leopolis, on the 'phone," he said to Novak, as calmly as he could contrive. He pictured Blassner driving through the night, respectfully bringing the antitoxin to The Doctor. While Novak bellowed into the farm-line telephone in the dining-room, Martin waited—waited—staring at the child; Mrs. Novak waited for him to do miracles; the child's tossing and hoarse gasping became horrible; and the glaring walls, the glaring lines of pale yellow woodwork, hypnotized him into sleepiness. It was too late for anything short of antitoxin or tracheotomy. Should he operate; cut into the wind-pipe that she might breathe? He stood and worried; he drowned in sleepiness and shook himself awake. He had to do something, with the mother kneeling there, gaping at him, beginning to look doubtful.

"Get some hot cloths—towels, napkins—and keep 'em around her neck. I wish to God he'd get that telephone call!" he fretted.

As Mrs. Novak, padding on thick slippered feet, brought in the hot cloths, Novak appeared with a blank "Nobody sleeping at the drug store, and Blassner's house-line is out of order."

"Then listen. I'm afraid this may be serious. I've got to have antitoxin. Going to drive t' Leopolis and get it. You keep up these hot applications and— Wish we had an atomizer. And room ought to be moister. Got 'n alcohol stove? Keep some water boiling in here. No use of medicine. B' right back."

He drove the twenty-four miles to Leopolis in thirty-seven minutes. Not once did he slow down for a cross-road. He defied the curves, the roots thrusting out into the road, though always one dark spot in his mind feared a blow-out and a swerve. The speed, the casting away of all caution, wrought in him a high exultation, and it was blessed to be in the cool air and alone, after the strain of Mrs. Novak's watching. In his mind all the while was the page in Osler regarding diphtheria, the very picture of the words: "In severe cases the first dose should be from 8,000—" No. Oh, yes: "—from 10,000 to 15,000 units."

He regained confidence. He thanked the god of science for antitoxin and for the gas motor. It was, he decided, a Race with Death.

"I'm going to do it—going to pull it off and save that poor kid!" he rejoiced.

He approached a grade crossing and hurled toward it, ignoring possible trains. He was aware of a devouring whistle, saw sliding light on the rails, and brought up sharp. Past him, ten feet from his front wheels, flung the Seattle Express like a flying volcano. The fireman was stoking, and even in the thin clearness of coming dawn the glow from the fire-box was appalling on the under side of the rolling smoke. Instantly the apparition was gone and Martin sat trembling, hands trembling on the little steering-wheel, foot trembling like St. Vitus's dance on the brake. "That was an awful' close thing!" he muttered, and thought of a widowed Leora, abandoned to Tozers. But the vision of the Novak child, struggling for each terrible breath, overrode all else. "Hell! I've killed the engine!" he groaned. He vaulted over the side, cranked the car, and dashed into Leopolis.

To Crynssen County, Leopolis with its four thousand people was a metropolis, but in the pinched stillness of the dawn it was a tiny graveyard: Main Street a sandy expanse, the low shops desolate as huts. He found one place astir; in the bleak office of the Dakota Hotel the night clerk was playing poker with the 'bus-driver and the town policeman.

They wondered at his hysterical entrance.

"Dr. Arrowsmith, from Wheatsylvania. Kid dying from diphtheria. Where's Blassner live? Jump in my car and show me."

The constable was a lanky old man, his vest swinging open over a collarless shirt, his trousers in folds, his eyes resolute. He guided Martin to the home of the druggist, he kicked the door, then, standing with his lean and bristly visage upraised in the cold early light, he bawled, "Ed! Hey, you, Ed! Come out of it!"

Ed Blassner grumbled from the up-stairs window. To him, death and furious doctors had small novelty. While he drew on his trousers and coat he was to be heard discoursing to his drowsy wife on the woes of druggists and the desirability of moving to Los Angeles and going into real estate. But he did have diphtheria antitoxin in his shop, and sixteen minutes after Martin's escape from being killed by a train he was speeding to Henry Novak's.

## VI

The child was still alive when he came brusquely into the house.

All the way back he had seen her dead and stiff. He grunted "Thank God!" and angrily called for hot water. He was no longer the embarrassed cub doctor but the wise and heroic physician who had won the Race with Death, and in the peasant eyes of Mrs. Novak, in Henry's nervous obedience, he read his power.

Swiftly, smoothly, he made intravenous injection of the antitoxin, and stood expectant.

The child's breathing did not at first vary, as she choked in the labor of expelling her breath. There was a gurgle, a struggle in which her face blackened, and she was still. Martin peered, incredulous. Slowly the Novaks began to glower, shaky hands at their lips. Slowly they knew the child was gone.

In the hospital, death had become indifferent and natural to Martin. He had said to Angus, he had heard nurses say one to another, quite cheerfully, "Well, fifty-seven has just passed out." Now he raged with desire to do the impossible. She *couldn't* be dead. He'd do something— All the while he was groaning, "I should've operated—I should have." So insistent was the thought that for a time he did not realize that Mrs. Novak was clamoring, "She is dead? Dead?"

He nodded, afraid to look at the woman.

"You killed her, with that needle thing! And not even tell us, so we could call the priest!"

He crawled past her lamentations and the man's sorrow and drove home, empty of heart.

"I shall never practice medicine again," he reflected.

"I'm through," he said to Leora. "I'm no good. I should of operated. I can't face people, when they know about it. I'm through. I'll go get a lab job—Dawson Hunziker or some place."

Salutary was the tartness with which she protested, "You're the most conceited man that ever lived! Do you think you're the only doctor that ever lost a patient? I know you did everything you could." But he went about next day torturing himself, the more tortured when Mr. Tozer whined at supper, "Henry Novak and his woman was in town today. They say you ought to have saved their girl. Why didn't you give your mind to it and manage to cure her somehow? Ought to tried. Kind of too bad, because the Novaks have a lot of influence with all these Pole and Hunky farmers."

After a night when he was too tired to sleep, Martin suddenly drove to Leopolis.

From the Tozers he had heard almost religious praise of Dr. Adam Winter of Leopolis, a man of nearly seventy, the pioneer physician of Crynssen County, and to this sage he was fleeing. As he drove he mocked furiously his melodramatic Race with Death, and he came wearily into the dust-whirling Main Street. Dr. Winter's office was above a grocery, in a long "block" of bright red brick stores with an Egyptian cornice—of tin. The darkness of the broad hallway was soothing after the prairie heat and incandescence. Martin had to wait till three respectful patients had been received by Dr. Winter, a hoary man with a sympathetic bass voice, before he was admitted to the consultation-room.

The examining-chair was of doubtful superiority to that once used by Doc Vickerson of Elk Mills, and sterilizing was apparently done in a wash-bowl, but in a corner was an electric therapeutic cabinet with more electrodes and pads than Martin had ever seen.

He told the story of the Novaks, and Winter cried, "Why, Doctor, you did everything you could have and more too. Only thing is, next time, in a crucial case, you better call some older doctor in consultation—not that you need his advice, but it makes a hit with the family, it divides the responsibility, and keeps 'em from going around criticizing. I, uh, I frequently have the honor of being called by some of my younger colleagues. Just wait. I'll 'phone the editor of the *Gazette* and give him an item about the case."

When he had telephoned, Dr. Winter shook hands ardently. He indicated his electric cabinet. "Got one of those things yet? Ought to, my boy. Don't know as I use it very often, except with the cranks that haven't anything the matter with 'em, but say, it would surprise you how it impresses folks. Well, Doctor, welcome to Crynssen County. Married? Won't you and your wife come take dinner with us some Sunday noon? Mrs. Winter will be real pleased to meet you. And if I ever can be of service to you in a consultation— I only charge a very little more than my regular fee, and it looks so well, talking the case over with an older man."

Driving home, Martin fell into vain and wicked boasting:

"You bet I'll stick to it! At worst, I'll never be as bad as that snuffling old fee-splitter!"

Two weeks after, the *Wheatsylvania Eagle*, a smeary four-page rag, reported:

Our enterprising contemporary, the *Leopolis Gazette*, had as follows last week to say of one of our townsmen who we recently welcomed to our midst.

"Dr. M. Arrowsmith of Wheatsylvania is being congratulated, we are informed by our valued pioneer local physician, Dr. Adam Winter, by the medical fraternity all through the Pony River Valley, there being no occupation or profession more unselfishly appreciative of each other's virtues than the medical gentlemen, on the courage and enterprise he recently displayed in addition to his scientific skill.

"Being called to attend the little daughter of Henry Norwalk of near Delft the well-known farmer and finding the little one near death with diphtheria he made a desperate attempt to save it by himself bringing antitoxin from Blassner our ever popular druggist, who had on hand a full and fresh supply. He drove out and back in his gasoline chariot, making the total distance of 48 miles in 79 minutes.

"Fortunately our ever alert policeman, Joe Colby, was on the job and helped Dr. Arrowsmith find Mr. Blassner's bungalow on Red River Avenue and this gentleman rose from bed and hastened to supply the doctor with the needed article but unfortunately the child was already too low to be saved but it is by such incidents of pluck and quick thinking as well as knowledge which make the medical profession one of our greatest blessings."

Two hours after this was published, Miss Agnes Ingleblad came in for another discussion of her non-existent ailments, and two days later Henry Novak appeared, saying proudly:

"Well, Doc, we all done what we could for the poor little girl, but I guess I waited too long calling you. The woman is awful' cut up. She and I was reading that piece in the *Eagle* about it. We showed it to the priest. Say,

Doc, I wish you'd take a look at my foot. I got kind of a rheumatic pain in the ankle."

# 16

When he had practiced medicine in Wheatsylvania for one year, Martin was an inconspicuous but not discouraged country doctor. In summer Leora and he drove to the Pony River for picnic suppers and a swim, very noisy, splashing, and immodest; through autumn he went duck-hunting with Bert Tozer, who became nearly tolerable when he stood at sunset on a pass between two slews; and with winter isolating the village in a sun-blank desert of snow, they had sleigh-rides, card-parties, "sociables" at the churches.

When Martin's flock turned to him for help, their need and their patient obedience made them beautiful. Once or twice he lost his temper with jovial villagers who bountifully explained to him that he was less aged than he might have been; once or twice he drank too much whisky at poker parties in the back room of the Co-operative Store; but he was known as reliable, skillful, and honest—and on the whole he was rather less distinguished than Alec Ingleblad the barber, less prosperous than Nils Krag the carpenter, and less interesting to his neighbors than the Finnish garageman.

Then one accident and one mistake made him famous for full twelve miles about.

He had gone fishing, in the spring. As he passed a farmhouse a woman ran out shrieking that her baby had swallowed a thimble and was choking to death. Martin had for surgical kit a large jack-knife. He sharpened it on the farmer's oilstone, sterilized it in the tea-kettle, operated on the baby's throat, and saved its life.

Every newspaper in the Pony River Valley had a paragraph, and before this sensation was over he cured Miss Agnes Ingleblad of her desire to be cured.

She had achieved cold hands and a slow circulation, and he was called at midnight. He was soggily sleepy, after two country drives on muddy roads, and in his torpor he gave her an overdose of strychnin, which so shocked and stimulated her that she decided to be well. It was so violent a change that it made her more interesting than being an invalid—people had of late taken remarkably small pleasure in her symptoms. She went about praising Martin, and all the world said, "I hear this Doc Arrowsmith is the only fellow Agnes ever doctored with that's done her a mite of good."

He gathered a practice small, sound, and in no way remarkable. Leora and he moved from the Tozers' to a cottage of their own, with a parlor-dining-room which displayed a nickeled stove on bright, new, pleasant-smelling linoleum, and a golden-oak sideboard with a souvenir match-holder from Lake Minnetonka. He bought a small Roentgen ray outfit; and he was made a director of the Tozer bank. He became too busy to long for his days of scientific research, which had never existed, and Leora sighed:

"It's fierce, being married. I did expect I'd have to follow you out on the road and be a hobo, but I never expected to be a Pillar of the Community. Well, I'm too lazy to look up a new husband. Only I warn you: when you become the Sunday School superintendent, you needn't expect me to play the organ and smile at the cute jokes you make about Willy's not learning his Golden Text."

## II

So did Martin stumble into respectability.

In the autumn of 1912, when Mr. Debs, Mr. Roosevelt, Mr. Wilson, and Mr. Taft were campaigning for the presidency, when Martin Arrowsmith had lived in Wheatsylvania for a year and a half, Bert Tozer became a Prominent Booster. He returned from the state convention of the Modern Woodmen of America with notions. Several towns had sent boosting delegations to the convention, and the village of Groningen had turned out a motor procession of five cars, each with an enormous pennant, "Groningen for White Men and Black Dirt."

Bert came back clamoring that every motor in town must carry a Wheatsylvania pennant. He had bought thirty of them, and they were on sale at the bank at seventy-five cents apiece. This, Bert explained to everyone who came into the bank, was exactly cost-price, which was within eleven cents of the truth. He came galloping at Martin, demanding that he be the first to display a pennant.

"I don't want one of those fool things flopping from my 'bus," protested Martin. "What's the idea, anyway?"

"What's the *idea*? To advertise your own town, of course!"

"What is there to advertise? Do you think you're going to make strangers believe Wheatsylvania is a metropolis like New York or Jimtown by hanging a dusty rag behind a secondhand tin Lizzie?"

"You never did have any patriotism! Let me tell you, Mart, if you don't put on a banner I'll see to it that everybody in town notices it!"

While the other rickety cars of the village announced to the world, or at least to several square miles of the world, that Wheatsylvania was the "Wonder Town of Central N. D.," Martin's clattering Ford went bare; and when his enemy Norblom remarked, "I like to see a fellow have some public spirit and appreciate the place he gets his money outa," the citizenry nodded and spat, and began to question Martin's fame as a worker of miracles.

## III

He had intimates—the barber, the editor of the *Eagle*, the garageman—to whom he talked comfortably of hunting and the crops, and with whom he played poker. Perhaps he was too intimate with them. It was the theory of Crynssen County that it was quite all right for a young professional man to take a timely drink providing he kept it secret and made up for it by yearning over the clergy of the neighborhood. But with the clergy Martin was brief, and his drinking and poker he never concealed.

If he was bored by the United Brethren minister's discourse on doctrine, on the wickedness of movies, and the scandalous pay of pastors, it was not at all because he was a distant and supersensitive young man but because he found more savor in the garageman's salty remarks on the art of remembering to ante in poker.

Through all the state there were celebrated poker players, rustic-looking men with stolid faces, men who sat in shirt-sleeves, chewing tobacco; men whose longest remark was "By me," and who delighted to plunder the gilded and condescending traveling salesmen. When there was news of a "big game on," the county sports dropped in silently and went to work—the sewing-machine agent from Leopolis, the undertaker from Vanderheide's Grove, the bootlegger from St. Luke, the red fat man from Melody who had no known profession.

Once (still do men tell of it gratefully, up and down the Valley), they played for seventy-two unbroken hours, in the office of the Wheatsylvania garage. It had been a livery-stable; it was littered with robes and long whips, and the smell of horses mingled with the reek of gasoline.

The players came and went, and sometimes they slept on the floor for an hour or two, but they were never less than four in the game. The stink of cheap feeble cigarettes and cheap powerful cigars hovered about the table like a malign spirit; the floor was scattered with stubs, matches, old cards, and whisky bottles. Among the warriors were Martin, Alec Ingleblad the barber, and a highway engineer, all of them stripped to flannel undershirts, not moving for hour on hour, ruffling their cards, eyes squinting and vacant.

When Bert Tozer heard of the affair, he feared for the good fame of Wheatsylvania, and to everyone he gossiped about Martin's evil ways and his own patience. Thus it happened that while Martin was at the height of his prosperity and credit as a physician, along the Pony River Valley sinuated the whispers that he was a gambler, that he was a "drinking man," that he never went to church; and all the godly enjoyed mourning, "Too bad to see a decent young man like that going to the dogs."

Martin was as impatient as he was stubborn. He resented the well-meant greetings: "You ought to leave a little hooch for the rest of us to drink, Doc," or "I s'pose you're too busy playing poker to drive out to the house and take a look at the woman." He was guilty of an absurd and boyish tactlessness when he heard Norblom observing to the postmaster, "A fellow that calls himself a doctor just because he had luck with that fool Agnes Ingleblad, he hadn't ought to go getting drunk and disgracing—"

Martin stopped. "Norblom! You talking about me?"

The storekeeper turned slowly. "I got more important things to do 'n talk about you," he cackled.

As Martin went on he heard laughter.

He told himself that these villagers were generous; that their snooping was in part an affectionate interest, and inevitable in a village where the most absorbing event of the year was the United Brethren Sunday School picnic on Fourth of July. But he could not rid himself of twitchy discomfort at their unending and maddeningly detailed comments on everything. He felt as though the lightest word he said in his consultation-room would be megaphoned from flapping ear to ear all down the country roads.

He was contented enough in gossiping about fishing with the barber, nor was he condescending to meteorologicomania, but except for Leora he had no one with whom he could talk of his work. Angus Duer had been cold, but Angus had his teeth into every change of surgical technique, and he was an acrid debater. Martin saw that, unless he struggled, not only would he harden into timid morality under the pressure of the village, but be fixed in a routine of prescriptions and bandaging.

He might find a stimulant in Dr. Hesselink of Groningen.

He had seen Hesselink only once, but everywhere he heard of him as the most honest practitioner in the Valley. On impulse Martin drove down to call on him.

Dr. Hesselink was a man of forty, ruddy, tall, broad-shouldered. You knew immediately that he was careful and that he was afraid of nothing, however much he might lack in imagination. He received Martin with no vast ebullience, and his stare said, "Well, what do you want? I'm a busy man."

"Doctor," Martin chattered, "do you find it hard to keep up with medical developments?"

"No. Read the medical journals."

"Well, don't you—gosh, I don't want to get sentimental about it, but don't you find that without contact with the Big Guns you get mentally lazy—sort of lacking in inspiration?"

"I do not! There's enough inspiration for me in trying to help the sick."

To himself Martin was protesting, "All right, if you don't want to be friendly, go to the devil!" But he tried again:

"I know. But for the game of the thing, for the pleasure of increasing medical knowledge, how can you keep up if you don't have anything but routine practice among a lot of farmers?"

"Arrowsmith, I may do you an injustice, but there's a lot of you young practitioners who feel superior to the farmers, that are doing their own jobs better than you are. You think that if you were only in the city with libraries and medical meetings and everything, you'd develop. Well, I don't know of anything to prevent your studying at home! You consider yourself so much better educated than these rustics, but I notice you say 'gosh' and 'Big Guns' and that sort of thing. How much do you read? Personally, I'm extremely well satisfied. My people pay me an excellent living wage, they appreciate my work, and they honor me by election to the schoolboard. I find that a good many of these farmers think a lot harder and squarer than the swells I meet in the city. Well! I don't see any reason for feeling superior, or lonely either!"

"Hell, I don't!" Martin mumbled. As he drove back he raged at Hesselink's superiority about not feeling superior, but he stumbled into uncomfortable meditation. It was true; he was half-educated. He was supposed to be a college graduate but he knew nothing of economics, nothing of history, nothing of music or painting. Except in hasty bolting for examinations he had read no poetry save that of Robert Service, and the only prose besides medical journalism at which he looked nowadays was the baseball and murder news in the Minneapolis papers and Wild West stories in the magazines.

He reviewed the "intelligent conversation" which, in the desert of Wheatsylvania, he believed himself to have conducted at Mohalis. He remembered that to Clif Clawson it had been pretentious to use any phrase which was not as colloquial and as smutty as the speech of a truck-driver, and that his own discourse had differed from Clif's largely in that it had been less fantastic and less original. He could recall nothing save the philosophy of Max Gottlieb, occasional scoldings of Angus Duer, one out of ten among Madeline Fox's digressions, and the councils of Dad Silva which was above the level of Alec Ingleblad's barber-shop.

He came home hating Hesselink but by no means loving himself; he fell upon Leora and, to her placid agreement, announced that they were "going to get educated, if it kills us." He went at it as he had gone at bacteriology.

He read European history aloud at Leora, who looked interested or at least forgiving; he worried the sentences in a copy of "The Golden Bowl" which an unfortunate school-teacher had left at the Tozers'; he borrowed a volume of Conrad from the village editor and afterward, as he drove the prairie roads, he was marching into jungle villages—sun helmets, orchids, lost temples of obscene and dog-faced deities, secret and sun-scarred rivers. He was conscious of his own mean vocabulary. It cannot be said that he became immediately and conspicuously articulate, yet it is possible that in those long intense evenings of reading with Leora he advanced a step or two toward the tragic enchantments of Max Gottlieb's world—enchanting sometimes and tragic always.

But in becoming a schoolboy again he was not so satisfied as Dr. Hesselink.

IV

Gustaf Sondelius was back in America.

In medical school, Martin had read of Sondelius, the soldier of science. He held reasonable and lengthy degrees, but he was a rich man and eccentric, and neither toiled in laboratories nor had a decent office and a home and a lacy wife. He roamed the world fighting epidemics and founding institutions and making inconvenient speeches and trying new drinks. He was a Swede by birth, a German by education, a little of everything by speech, and his clubs were in London, Paris, Washington, and New York. He had been heard of from Batoum and Fuchau, from Milan and Bechuanaland, from Antofagasta and Cape Romanzoff. Manson on Tropical Diseases mentions Sondelius's admirable method of killing rats with hydrocyanic acid gas, and *The Sketch* once mentioned his atrocious system in baccarat.

Gustaf Sondelius shouted, in high places and low, that most diseases could be and must be wiped out; that tuberculosis, cancer, typhoid, the plague, influenza, were an invading army against which the world must mobolize—literally; that public health authorities must supersede generals and oil kings. He was lecturing through America, and his exclamatory assertions were syndicated in the press.

Martin sniffed at most newspaper articles touching on science or health but Sondelius's violence caught him, and suddenly he was converted, and it was an important thing for him, that conversion.

He told himself that however much he might relieve the sick, essentially he was a business man, in rivalry with Dr. Winter of Leopolis and Dr. Hesselink of Groningen; that though they might be honest, honesty and healing were less their purpose than making money; that to get rid of avoidable disease and produce a healthy population would be the worst thing in the world for them; and that they must all be replaced by public health officials.

Like all ardent agnostics, Martin was a religious man. Since the death of his Gottlieb-cult he had unconsciously sought a new passion, and he found it now in Gustaf Sondelius's war on disease. Immediately he became as annoying to his patients as he had once been to Digamma Pi.

He informed the farmers at Delft that they had no right to have so much tuberculosis.

This was infuriating, because none of their rights as American citizens was better established, or more often used, than the privilege of being ill. They fumed, "Who does he think he is? We call him in for doctoring, not for bossing. Why, the damn' fool said we ought to burn down our houses—said we were committing a crime if we had the con. here! Won't stand for nobody talking to me like that!"

Everything became clear to Martin—too clear. The nation must make the best physicians autocratic officials, at once, and that was all there was to it. As to how the officials were to become perfect executives, and how people were to be persuaded to obey them, he had no suggestions but only a beautiful faith. At breakfast he scolded, "Another idiotic day of writing prescriptions for bellyaches that ought never to have happened! If I could only get into the Big Fight, along with men like Sondelius! It makes me tired!"

Leora murmured, "Yes, darling. I'll promise to be good. I won't have any little bellyaches or T.B. or anything, so please don't lecture me!"

Even in his irritability he was gentle, for Leora was with child.

v

Their baby was coming in five months. Martin promised to it everything he had missed.

"He's going to have a real education!" he gloated, as they sat on the porch in spring twilight. "He'll learn all this literature and stuff. We haven't done much ourselves—here we are, stuck in this two-by-twice crossroads for the rest of our lives—but maybe we've gone a little beyond our dads, and he'll go way beyond us."

He was worried, for all his flamboyance. Leora had undue morning sickness. Till noon she dragged about the house, pea-green and tousled and hollow-faced. He found a sort of maid, and came home to help, to wipe the dishes and sweep the front walk. All evening he read to her, not history now and Henry James but "Mrs. Wiggs of the Cabbage Patch," which both of them esteemed a very fine tale. He sat on the floor by the grubby second-hand couch on which she lay in her weakness; he held her hand and crowed:

"Golly, we— No, not 'golly.' Well, what *can* you say except 'golly'? Anyway: Some day we'll save up enough money for a couple months in Italy and all those places. All those old narrow streets and old castles! There must be scads of 'em that are couple hundred years old or older! And we'll take the boy . . . Even if he turns out to be a girl, darn him! . . . And he'll learn to chatter Wop and French and everything like a regular native, and his dad and mother'll be so proud! Oh, we'll be a fierce pair of old birds! We never did have any more morals 'n a rabbit, either of us, and probably when we're seventy we'll sit out on the doorstep and smoke pipes and snicker at all the respectable people going by, and tell each other scandalous stories about 'em till they want to take a shot at us, and our boy—he'll wear a plug hat and have a chauffeur—he won't dare to recognize us!"

Trained now to the false cheerfulness of the doctor, he shouted, when she was racked and ghastly with the indignity of morning sickness, "There, that's fine, old girl! Wouldn't be making a good baby if you weren't sick. Everybody is." He was lying, and he was nervous. Whenever he thought of her dying, he seemed to die with her. Barren of her companionship, there would be nothing he wanted to do, nowhere to go. What would be the worth of having all the world if he could not share it to her, if she was not there—

He denounced Nature for her way of tricking human beings, by every gay device of moonlight and white limbs and reaching loneliness, into having babies, then making birth as cruel and clumsy and wasteful as she could. He was abrupt and jerky with patients who called him into the country. With their suffering he was sympathetic as he had never been, for his eyes had opened to the terrible beauty of pain, but he must not go far from Leora's need.

Her morning sickness turned into pernicious vomiting. Suddenly, while she was torn and inhuman with agony, he sent for Dr. Hesselink, and that horrible afternoon when the prairie spring was exuberant outside the windows of the poor iodoform-reeking room, they took the baby from her, dead.

Had it been possible, he might have understood Hesselink's success then, have noted that gravity and charm, that pity and sureness, which made people entrust their lives to him. Not cold and blaming was Hesselink now, but an older and wiser brother, very compassionate. Martin saw nothing. He was not a physician. He was a terrified boy, less useful to Hesselink than the dullest nurse.

When he was certain that Leora would recover, Martin sat by her bed, coaxing, "We'll just have to make up our minds we never can have a baby now, and so I want— Oh, I'm no good! And I've got a rotten temper. But to you, I want to be everything!"

She whispered, scarce to be heard:

"He would have been such a sweet baby. Oh, I know! I saw him so often. Because I knew he was going to be like you, when you were a baby." She tried to laugh. "Perhaps I wanted him because I could boss him. I've never had anybody that would let me boss him. So if I can't have a real baby, I'll have to bring you up. Make you a great man that everybody will wonder at, like your Sondelius. . . . Darling, I worried so about your worrying—"

He kissed her, and for hours they sat together, unspeaking, eternally understanding, in the prairie twilight.

# 17

---

Dr. Coughlin of Leopolis had a red mustache, a large heartiness, and a Maxwell which, though it was three years old this May and deplorable as to varnish, he believed to be the superior in speed and beauty of any motor in Dakota.

He came home in high cheerfulness, rode the youngest of his three children pickaback, and remarked to his wife:

"Tessie, I got a swell idea."

"Yes, and you got a swell breath, too. I wish you'd quit testing that old Spirits Frumentus bottle at the drug store!"

"'At a girl! But honest, listen!"

"I will not!" She bussed him heartily. "Nothing doing about driving to Los Angeles this summer. Too far, with all the brats squalling."

"Sure. All right. But I mean: Let's pack up and light out and spend a week touring 'round the state. Say tomorrow or next day. Got nothing to keep me now except that obstetrical case, and we'll hand that over to Winter."

"All right. We can try out the new thermos bottles!"

Dr. Coughlin, his lady, and the children started at four in the morning. The car was at first too well arranged to be interesting, but after three days, as he approached you on the flat road that without an inch of curving was slashed for leagues through the grassy young wheat, you saw the doctor in his khaki suit, his horn-rimmed spectacles, and white linen boating hat; his wife in a green flannel blouse and a lace boudoir cap. The rest of the car was slightly confused. While you motored by you noticed a canvas Egyptian Water Bottle, mud on wheels and fenders, a spade, two older children leaning perilously out and making tongues at you, the baby's diapers hanging on a line across the tonneau, a torn copy of *Snappy Stories*, seven lollypop sticks, a jack, a fish-rod, and a rolled tent.

Your last impression was of two large pennants labeled "Leopolis, N. D.," and "Excuse Our Dust."

The Coughlins had agreeable adventures. Once they were stuck in a mud-hole. To the shrieking admiration of the family, the doctor got them out by making a bridge of fence rails. Once the ignition ceased and, while they awaited a garageman summoned by telephone, they viewed a dairy farm with an electrical milking machine. All the way they were broadened by travel, and discovered the wonders of the great world: the movie theater at Roundup, which had for orchestra not only a hand-played piano but also a violin; the black fox farm at Melody; and the Severance water-tower, which was said to be the tallest in Central North Dakota.

Dr. Coughlin "dropped in to pass the time of day," as he said, with all the doctors. At St. Luke he had an intimate friend in Dr. Tromp—at least they had met twice, at the annual meetings of the Pony River Valley Medical Association. When he told Tromp how bad they had found the hotels, Tromp looked uneasy and conscientious, and sighed, "If the wife could fix it up somehow, I'd like to invite you all to stay with us tonight."

"Oh, don't want to impose on you. Sure it wouldn't be any trouble?" said Coughlin.

After Mrs. Tromp had recovered from her desire to call her husband aside and make unheard but vigorous observations, and after the oldest Tromp boy had learned that "it wasn't nice for a little gentleman to kick his wee guests that came from so far, far away," they were all very happy. Mrs. Coughlin and Mrs. Tromp bewailed the cost of laundry soap and butter, and exchanged recipes for pickled peaches, while the men, sitting on the edge of the porch, their knees crossed, eloquently waving their cigars, gave themselves up to the ecstasy of shop-talk:

"Say, Doctor, how do you find collections?"

(It was Coughlin speaking—or it might have been Tromp.)

"Well, they're pretty good. These Germans pay up first rate. Never send 'em a bill, but when they've harvested they come in and say, 'How much do I owe you, Doctor?'"

"Yuh, the Germans are pretty good pay."

"Yump, they certainly are. Not many dead-beats among the Germans."

"Yes, that's a fact. Say, tell me, Doctor, what do you do with your jaundice cases?"

"Well, I'll tell you, Doctor: if it's a persistent case I usually give ammonium chlorid."

"Do you? I've been giving ammonium chlorid but here the other day I see a communication in the *Journal of the* A.M.A. where a fellow was claiming it wasn't any good."

"Is that a fact! Well, well! I didn't see that. Hum. Well. Say, Doctor, do you find you can do much with asthma?"

"Well now, Doctor, just in confidence, I'm going to tell you something that may strike you as funny, but I believe that foxes' lungs are fine for asthma, and T.B. too. I told that to a Sioux City pulmonary specialist one time and he laughed at me—said it wasn't scientific—and I said to him, 'Hell!' I said, 'scientific!' I said, 'I don't know if it's the latest fad and wrinkle in science or not,' I said, 'but I get results, and that's what I'm looking for 's results!' I said. I tell you a plug G.P. may not have a lot of letters after his name, but he sees a slew of mysterious things that he can't explain, and I swear I believe most of these damn' alleged scientists could learn a whale of a lot from the plain country practitioners, let me tell you!"

"Yuh, that's a fact. Personally I'd rather stay right here in the country and be able to do a little hunting and take it easy than be the classiest specialist in the cities. One time I kind of figured on becoming an X-ray specialist—place in New York where you can take the whole course in eight weeks—and maybe settling in Butte or Sioux Falls, but I figured that even if I got to making eight-ten thousand a year, 'twouldn't hardly mean more than three thousand does here and so— And a fellow has to consider his duty to his old patients."

"That's so. . . . Say, Doctor, say, what sort of fellow is McMinturn, down your way?"

"Well, I don't like to knock any fellow practitioner, and I suppose he's well intentioned, but just between you and me he does too confounded much guesswork. Now you take you and me, we apply *science* to a case, instead of taking a chance and just relying on experience and going off half-cocked. But McMinturn, he doesn't know enough. And *say*, that wife of his, she's a caution—she's got the meanest tongue in four counties, and the way she chases around drumming up business for Mac— Well, I suppose that's their way of doing business."

"Is old Winter keeping going?"

"Oh, yes, in a sort of way. You know how he is. Of course he's about twenty years behind the times, but he's a great hand-holder—keep some fool woman in bed six weeks longer than he needs to, and call around twice a day and chin with her—absolutely unnecessary."

"I suppose you get your biggest competition from Silzer, Doctor?"

"Don't you believe it, Doctor! He isn't beginning to do the practice he lets on to. Trouble with Silzer is, he's too brash—shoots off his mouth too much—likes to hear himself talk. Oh, say, by the way, have you run into this new fellow—will been located here about two years now—at Wheatsylvania—Arrowsmith?"

"No, but they say he's a good bright young fellow."

"Yes, they claim he's a brainy man—very well-informed—and I hear his wife is a nice brainy little woman."

"I hear Arrowsmith hits it up too much though—likes his booze awful' well."

"Yes, so they say. Shame, for a nice hustling young fellow. I like a nip myself, now and then, but a Drinking Man—! Suppose he's drunk and gets called out on a case! And a fellow from down there was telling me Arrowsmith is great on books and study, but he's a freethinker—never goes to church."

"Is that a fact! Hm. Great mistake for any doctor to not identify himself with some good solid religious denomination, whether he believes the stuff or not. I tell you a priest or a preacher can send you an awful lot of business."

"You bet he can! Well, this fellow said Arrowsmith was always arguing with the preachers—he told some Reverend that everybody ought to read this immunologist Max Gottlieb, and this Jacques Loeb—you know—the fellow that, well, I don't recall just exactly what it was, but he claimed he could create living fishes out of chemicals."

"Sure! There you got it! That's the kind of delusions these laboratory fellows get unless they have some practical practice to keep 'em well balanced. Well, if Arrowsmith falls for that kind of fellow, no wonder people don't trust him."

"That's so. Hm. Well, it's too bad Arrowsmith goes drinking and helling around and neglecting his family and his patients. I can see his finish. Shame. Well—wonder what time o' night it's getting to be?"

## II

Bert Tozer wailed, "Mart, what you been doing to Dr. Coughlin of Leopolis? Fellow told me he was going around saying you were a booze-hoister and so on."

"Did he? People do sort of keep an eye on one another around here, don't they?"

"You bet your life they do, and that's why I tell you you ought to cut out the poker and the booze. You don't see *me* needing any liquor, do you?"

Martin more desperately than ever felt the whole county watching him. He was not a praise-eater; he was not proud that he should feel misplaced; but however sturdily he struggled he saw himself outside the picture of Wheatsylvania and trudging years of country practice.

Suddenly, without planning it, forgetting in his admiration for Sondelius and the health war his pride of the laboratory, he was thrown into a research problem.

## III

There was blackleg among the cattle in Crynssen County. The state veterinarian had been called and Dawson Hunziker vaccine had been injected, but the disease spread. Martin heard the farmers wailing. He noted that the injected cattle showed no inflammation nor rise in temperature. He was roused by a suspicion that the Hunziker vaccine had insufficient living organisms, and he went yelping on the trail of his hypothesis.

He obtained (by misrepresentations) a supply of the vaccine and tested it in his stuffy closet of a laboratory. He had to work out his own device for growing anaerobic cultures, but he had been trained by the Gottlieb who remarked, "Any man dat iss unable to build a filter out of toot'-picks, if he has to, would maybe better buy his results along with his fine equipment." Out of a large fruit-jar and a soldered pipe Martin made his apparatus.

When he was altogether sure that the vaccine did not contain living black-leg organisms, he was much more delighted than if he had found that good Mr. Dawson Hunziker was producing honest vaccine.

With no excuse and less encouragement he isolated blackleg organisms from sick cattle and prepared an attenuated vaccine of his own. It took much time. He did not neglect his patients but certainly he failed to appear in the stores, at the poker games. Leora and he dined on a sandwich every evening and hastened to the laboratory, to heat the cultures in the improvised water-bath, an ancient and leaky oatmeal-cooker with an alcohol lamp. The Martin who had been impatient of Hesselink was of endless patience as he watched his results. He whistled and hummed, and the hours from seven to mid-night were a moment. Leora, frowning placidly, the tip of her tongue at the corner of her mouth, guarded the temperature like a good little watchdog.

After three efforts with two absurd failures, he had a vaccine which satis-fied him, and he injected a stricken herd. The blackleg stopped, which was for Martin the end and the reward, and he turned his notes and supply of vaccine over to the state veterinarian. For others, it was not the end. The veterinarians of the county denounced him for intruding on their right to save or kill cattle; the physicians hinted, "That's the kind of monkey-business that ruins the dignity of the profession. I tell you Arrowsmith's a medical nihilist and a notoriety-seeker, that's what he is. You mark my words, instead of his sticking to decent regular practice, you'll be hearing of his opening a quack sanitarium, one of these days!"

He commented to Leora:

"Dignity, hell! If I had my way I'd be doing research—oh, not this cold detached stuff of Gottlieb but really practical work—and then I'd have some fellow like Sondelius take my results and jam 'em down people's throats, and I'd make them and their cattle and their tabby-cats healthy whether they wanted to be or not, that's what I'd do!"

In this mood he read in his Minneapolis paper, between a half column on the marriage of the light middleweight champion and three lines devoted to the lynching of an I.W.W. agitator, the announcement:

> Gustave Sundelios, well-known authority on cholera prevention, will give an address on "Heroes of Health" at the University summer school next Friday evening.

He ran into the house gloating, "Lee! Sondelius going to lecture in Min-neapolis. I'm going! Come on! We'll hear him and have a bat and every-thing!"

"No, you run down by yourself. Be fine for you to get away from the town and the family and me for a while. I'll go down with you in the fall. Honestly. If I'm not in the way, maybe you can manage to have a good long talk with Dr. Sondelius."

"Fat chance! The big city physicians and the state health authorities will be standing around him ten deep. But I'm going."

IV

The prairie was hot, the wheat rattled in a weary breeze, the day-coach was gritty with cinders. Martin was cramped by the hours of slow riding. He drowsed and smoked and meditated. "I'm going to forget medicine and everything else," he vowed. "I'll go up and talk to somebody in the smoker and tell him I'm a shoe-salesman."

He did. Unfortunately his confidant happened to be a real shoe-salesman, with a large curiosity as to what firm Martin represented, and he returned to the day coach with a renewed sense of injury. When he reached Minneapolis, in mid-afternoon, he hastened to the University and besought a ticket to the Sondelius lecture before he had even found a hotel, though not before he had found the long glass of beer which he had been picturing for a hundred miles.

He had an informal but agreeable notion of spending his first evening of freedom in dissipation. Somewhere he would meet a company of worthies who would succor him with laughter and talk and many drinks—not too many drinks, of course—and motor very rapidly to Lake Minnetonka for a moonlight swim. He began his search for the brethren by having a cocktail at a hotel bar and dinner in a Hennepin Avenue restaurant. Nobody looked at him, nobody seemed to desire a companion. He was lonely for Leora, and all his state of grace, all his earnest and simple-hearted devotion to carousal, degenerated into sleepiness.

As he turned and turned in his hotel bed he lamented, "And probably the Sondelius lecture will be rotten. Probably he's simply another Roscoe Geake."

V

In the hot night desultory students wandered up to the door of the lecture-hall, scanned the modest Sondelius poster, and ambled away. Martin was half minded to desert with them, and he went in sulkily. The hall was a third full of summer students and teachers, and men who might have been doctors or school-principals. He sat at the back, fanning with his straw hat, disliking the man with side-whiskers who shared the row with him, disapproving of Gustaf Sondelius, and as to himself having no good opinions whatever.

Then the room was charged with vitality. Down the central aisle, ineffectively attended by a small fussy person, thundered a man with a smile, a broad brow, and a strawpile of curly flaxen hair—a Newfoundland dog of a man. Martin sat straight. He was strengthened to endure even the depressing man with side-whiskers as Sondelius launched out, in a musical bellow with Swedish pronunciation and Swedish singsong:

"The medical profession can have but one desire: to destroy the medical profession. As for the laymen, they can be sure of but one thing: nine-tenths of what they know about health is not so, and with the other tenth they do nothing. As Butler shows in 'Erewhon'—the swine stole that idea from me, too, maybe thirty years before I ever got it—the only crime for w'ich we should hang people is having toobercoolosis."

"Umph!" grunted the studious audience, doubtful whether it was fitting to be amused, offended, bored, or edified.

Sondelius was a roarer and a playboy, but he knew incantations. With him Martin watched the heroes of yellow fever, Reed, Agramonte, Carroll, and Lazear; with him he landed in a Mexican port stilled with the plague and famished beneath the virulent sun; with him rode up the mountain trails to a hill town rotted with typhus; with him, in crawling August, when babies were parched skeletons, fought an ice trust beneath the gilt and blunted sword of the law.

"That's what I want to do! Not just tinker at a lot of worn-out bodies but make a new world!" Martin hungered. "Gosh, I'd follow him through fire! And the way he lays out the crapehangers that criticize public health results! If I could only manage to meet him and talk to him for a couple o' minutes—"

He lingered after the lecture. A dozen people surrounded Sondelius on the platform; a few shook hands; a few asked questions; a doctor worried, "But how about the danger of free clinics and all those things drifting into socialism?" Martin stood back till Sondelius had been deserted. A janitor was closing the windows, very firmly and suggestively. Sondelius looked about, and Martin would have sworn that the Great Man was lonely. He shook hands with him, and quaked:

"Sir, if you aren't due some place, I wonder if you'd like to come out and have a—a—"

Sondelius loomed over him in solar radiance and rumbled, "Have a drink? Well, I think maybe I would. How did the joke about the dog and his fleas go tonight? Do you think they liked it?"

"Oh, sure, you bet."

The warrior who had been telling of feeding five thousand Tatars, of receiving a degree from a Chinese university and refusing a decoration from quite a good Balkan king, looked affectionately on his band of one disciple and demanded, "Was it all right—was it? Did they like it? So hot tonight, and I been lecturing nine time a week—Des Moines, Fort Dodge, LaCrosse, Elgin, Joliet [but he pronounced it Zho-lee-ay] and—I forget. Was it all right? Did they like it?"

"Simply corking! Oh, they just ate it up! Honestly, I've never enjoyed anything so much in my life!"

The prophet crowed, "Come! I buy a drink. As a hygienist, I war on alcohol. In excessive quantities it is almost as bad as coffee or even ice cream soda. But as one who is fond of talking, I find a nice long whisky and soda a great solvent of human idiocy. Is there a cool place with some Pilsener here in Detroit—no; where am I tonight?—Minneapolis?"

"I understand there's a good beer-garden. And we can get the trolley right near here."

Sondelius stared at him. "Oh, I have a taxi waiting."

Martin was abashed by this luxury. In the taxi-cab he tried to think of the proper things to say to a celebrity.

"Tell me, Doctor, do they have city health boards in Europe?"

Sondelius ignored him. "Did you see that girl going by? What ankles! What shoulders! Is it good beer at the beer-garden? Have they any decent cognac? Do you know Courvoisier 1865 cognac? Oof! Lecturing! I swear I will give it up. And wearing dress clothes a night like this! You know, I mean all the crazy things I say in my lectures, but let us now forget being earnest, let us drink, let us sing 'Der Graf von Luxemburg,' let us detach exquisite girls from their escorts, let us discuss the joys of 'Die Meistersinger,' which only I appreciate!"

In the beer-garden the tremendous Sondelius discoursed of the Cosmos Club, Halle's investigation of infant mortality, the suitability of combining benedictine and apple-jack, Biarritz, Lord Haldane, the Doane-Buckley method of milk examination, George Gissing, and *homard thermidor*. Martin looked for a connection between Sondelius and himself, as one does with the notorious or with people met abroad. He might have said, "I think I met a man who knows you," or "I have had the pleasure of reading all your articles," but he fished with "Did you ever run into the two big men in my medical school—Winnemac—Dean Silva and Max Gottlieb?"

"Silva? I don't remember. But Gottlieb—you know him? Oh!" Sondelius waved his mighty arms. "The greatest! The spirit of science! I had the pleasure to talk with him at McGurk. He would not sit here bawling like me! He makes me like a circus clown! He takes all my statements about epidemiology and shows me I am a fool! Ho, ho, ho!" He beamed, and was off on a denunciation of high tariff.

Each topic had its suitable refreshment. Sondelius was a fantastic drinker, and zinc-lined. He mixed Pilsener, whisky, black coffee, and a liquid which the waiter asserted to be absinthe. "I should go to bed at midnight," he lamented, "but it is a cardinal sin to interrupt good talk. Yoost tempt me a little! I am an easy one to be tempted! But I must have five hours' sleep. Absolute! I lecture in—it's some place in Iowa—tomorrow evening. Now that I am past fifty, I cannot get along with three hours as I used to, and yet I have found so many new things that I want to talk about."

He was more eloquent than ever; then he was annoyed. A surly-looking man at the next table listened and peered, and laughed at them. Sondelius dropped from Haffkine's cholera serum to an irate:

"If that fellow stares at me some more, I am going over and kill him! I am a peaceful man, now that I am not so young, but I do not like starers. I will go and argue with him. I will yoost hit him a little!"

While the waiters came rushing, Sondelius charged the man, threatened him with enormous fists, then stopped, shook hands repeatedly, and brought him back to Martin.

"This is a born countryman of mine, from Gottenborg. He is a carpenter. Sit down, Nilsson, sit down and have a drink. Herumph! vai-ter!"

The carpenter was a socialist, a Swedish Seventh Day Adventist, a ferocious arguer, and fond of drinking aquavit. He denounced Sondelius as an aristocrat, he denounced Martin for his ignorance of economics, he denounced the waiter concerning the brandy; Sondelius and Martin and the waiter answered with vigor; and the conversation became admirable. Presently they were turned out of the beer-garden and the three of them crowded into the still waiting taxicab, which shook to their debating. Where they went, Martin could never trace. He may have dreamed the whole tale. Once they were apparently in a roadhouse on a long street which must have been University Avenue; once in a saloon on Washington Avenue South, where three tramps were sleeping at the end of the bar; once in the carpenter's house, where an unexplained man made coffee for them.

Wherever they might be, they were at the same time in Moscow and Curaçao and Murwillumbah. The carpenter created communistic states, while Sondelius, proclaiming that he did not care whether he worked under socialism or an emperor so long as he could bully people into being well, annihilated tuberculosis and by dawn had cancer fleeing.

They parted at four, tearfully swearing to meet again, in Minnesota or Stockholm, in Rio or on the southern seas, and Martin started for Wheatsylvania to put an end to all this nonsense of allowing people to be ill.

And the great god Sondelius had slain Dean Silva, as Silva had slain Gottlieb, Gottlieb had slain "Encore" Edwards the playful chemist, Edwards had slain Doc Vickerson, and Vickerson had slain the minister's son who had a real trapeze in his barn.

# 18

Dr. Woestijne of Vanderheide's Grove acted in spare time as Superintendent of Health for Crynssen County, but the office was not well paid and it did not greatly interest him. When Martin burst in and offered to do all the work for half the pay, Woestijne accepted with benevolence, assuring him that it would have a great effect on his private practice.

It did. It almost ruined his private practice.

There was never an official appointment. Martin signed Woestijne's name (spelling it in various interesting ways, depending on how he felt) to papers, and the Board of County Commissioners recognized Martin's limited power, but the whole thing was probably illegal.

There was small science and considerably less heroism in his first furies as a health officer, but a great deal of irritation for his fellow-townsmen. He poked into yards, he denounced Mrs. Beeson for her reeking ash-barrels, Mr. Norblom for piling manure on the street, and the schoolboard for the school ventilation and lack of instruction in tooth-brushing. The citizens had formerly been agitated by his irreligion, his moral looseness, and his lack of local patriotism, but when they were prodded out of their comfortable and probably beneficial dirt, they exploded.

Martin was honest and appallingly earnest, but if he had the innocence of the dove he lacked the wisdom of the serpent. He did not make them understand his mission; he scarce tried to make them understand. His authority, as Woestijne's *alter ego*, was imposing on paper but feeble in action, and it was worthless against the stubbornness which he aroused.

He advanced from garbage-spying to a drama of infection.

The community at Delft had a typhoid epidemic which slackened and continually reappeared. The villagers believed that it came from a tribe of squatters six miles up the creek, and they considered lynching the offenders, as a practical protest and an interesting break in wheat-farming. When Martin insisted that in six miles the creek would purify any waste and that the squatters were probably not the cause, he was amply denounced.

"He's a fine one, he is, to go around blatting that we'd ought to have more health precautions! Here we go and show him where there's some hell-hounds that ought to be shot, and them only Bohunks anyway, and he doesn't do a darn' thing but shoot a lot of hot air about germicidal effect or whatever the fool thing is," remarked Kaes, the wheat-buyer at the Delft elevator.

Flashing through the county, not neglecting but certainly not enlarging his own practice, Martin mapped every recent case of typhoid within five miles of Delft. He looked into milk-routes and grocery deliveries. He discovered that most of the cases had appeared after the visits of an itinerant seamstress, a spinster virtuous and almost painfully hygienic. She had had typhoid four years before.

"She's a chronic carrier of the bugs. She's got to be examined," he announced.

He found her sewing at the house of an old farmer-preacher.

With modest indignation she refused to be examined, and as he went away she could be heard weeping at the insult, while the preacher cursed him from the doorstep. He returned with the township police officer and had the seamstress arrested and confined in the segregation ward of the county poor-farm. In her discharges he found billions of typhoid bacilli.

The frail and decent body was not comfortable in the board-lined white-washed ward. She was shamed and frightened. She had always been well beloved, a gentle, shabby, bright-eyed spinster who brought presents to the babies, helped the overworked farmwives to cook dinner, and sang to the children in her thin sparrow voice. Martin was reviled for persecuting her. "He wouldn't dare pick on her if she wasn't so poor," they said, and they talked of a jail-delivery.

Martin fretted. He called upon the seamstress at the poor-farm, he tried to make her understand that there was no other place for her, he brought her magazines and sweets. But he was firm. She could not go free. He was convinced that she had caused at least one hundred cases of typhoid, with nine deaths.

The county derided him. Cause typhoid now, when she had been well for four years? The County Commissioners and the County Board of Health called Dr. Hesselink in from the next county. He agreed with Martin and his maps. Every meeting of the Commissioners was a battle now, and it was uncertain whether Martin would be ruined or throned.

Leora saved him and the seamstress. "Why not take up a collection to send her off to some big hospital where she can be treated, or where they can keep her if she can't be cured?" said she.

The seamstress entered a sanitarium—and was amiably forgotten by everybody for the rest of her life—and his recent enemies said of Martin, "He's mighty smart, and right on the job." Hesselink drove over to inform him, "You did pretty well this time, Arrowsmith. Glad to see you're settling down to business."

Martin was slightly cocky, and immediately bounded after a fine new epidemic. He was so fortunate as to have a case of small-pox and several which he suspected. Some of these lay across the border in Mencken County, Hesselink's domain, and Hesselink laughed at him. "It's probably all chicken-pox, except your one case. Mighty rarely you get small-pox in summer," he chuckled, while Martin raged up and down the two counties, proclaiming the scourge, imploring everyone to be vaccinated, thundering, "There's going to be all hell let loose here in ten or fifteen days!"

But the United Brethren parson, who served chapels in Wheatsylvania and two other villages, was an anti-vaccinationist and he preached against it. The villages sided with him. Martin went from house to house, beseeching them, offering to treat them without charge. As he had never taught them to love him and follow him as a leader, they questioned, they argued long and easily on doorsteps, they cackled that he was drunk. Though for weeks his strongest draft had been the acrid coffee of the countryside, they peeped one to another that he was drunk every night, that the United Brethren minister was about to expose him from the pulpit.

And ten dreadful days went by and fifteen, and all but the first case did prove to be chicken-pox. Hesselink gloated and the village roared and Martin was the butt of the land.

He had only a little resented their gossip about his wickedness, only in evenings of slow depression had he meditated upon fleeing from them, but at their laughter he was black furious.

Leora comforted him with cool hands. "It'll pass over," she said. But it did not pass.

By autumn it had become such a burlesque epic as peasants love through all the world. He had, they mirthfully related, declared that anybody who kept hogs would die of small-pox; he had been drunk for a week, and diagnosed everything from gall-stones to heart-burn as small-pox. They greeted him, with no meaning of offense in their snickering, "Got a pimple on my chin, Doc. What is 't—small-pox?"

More terrible than their rage is the people's laughter, and if it rends tyrants, with equal zest it pursues the saint and wise man and befouls their treasure.

When the neighborhood suddenly achieved a real epidemic of diphtheria and Martin shakily preached antitoxin, one-half of them remembered his failure to save Mary Novak and the other half clamored, "Oh, give us a rest! You got epidemics on the brain!" That a number of children quite adequately died did not make them relinquish their comic epic.

Then it was that Martin came home to Leora and said quietly, "I'm licked. I've got to get out. Nothing more I can do here. Take years before they'd trust me again. They're so damned *humorous*! I'm going to go get a real job —public health."

"I'm so glad! You're too good for them here. We'll find some big place where they'll appreciate your work."

"No, that's not fair. I've learned a little something. I've failed here. I've antagonized too many people. I didn't know how to handle them. We could stick it out, and I would, except that life is short and I think I'm a good worker in some ways. Been worrying about being a coward, about running away, 'turning my—' What is it? '—turning my hand from the plow.' I don't care now! By God, I know what I can do! Gottlieb saw it! And I want to get to work. On we go. All right?"

"Of course!"

II

He had read in the *Journal of the American Medical Association* that Gustaf Sondelius was giving a series of lectures at Harvard. He wrote asking whether he knew of a public health appointment. Sondelius answered, in a profane and blotty scrawl, that he remembered with joy their Minneapolis vacation, that he disagreed with Entwisle of Harvard about the nature of metathrombin, that there was an excellent Italian restaurant in Boston, and that he would inquire among his health-official friends as to a position.

Two days later he wrote that Dr. Almus Pickerbaugh, Director of Public Health in the city of Nautilus, Iowa, was looking for a second-in-command, and would probably be willing to send particulars.

Leora and Martin swooped on an almanac.

"Gosh! Sixty-nine thousand people in Nautilus! Against three hundred and sixty-six here—no, wait, it's three hundred and sixty-seven now, with that new baby of Pete Yeska's that the dirty swine called in Hesselink for. People! People that can talk! Theaters! Maybe concerts! Leora, we'll be like a pair of kids let loose from school!"

He telegraphed for details, to the enormous interest of the station agent, who was also telegraph operator.

The mimeographed form which was sent to him said that Dr. Pickerbaugh required an assistant who would be the only full-time medical officer besides Pickerbaugh himself, as the clinic and school doctors were private physicians working part-time. The assistant would be epidemiologist, bacteriologist, and manager of the office clerks, the nurses, and the lay inspectors of dairies and sanitation. The salary would be twenty-five hundred dollars a year—against the fifteen or sixteen hundred Martin was making in Wheatsylvania.

Proper recommendations were desired.

Martin wrote to Sondelius, to Dad Silva, and to Max Gottlieb, now at the McGurk Institute in New York.

Dr. Pickerbaugh informed him, "I have received very pleasant letters from Dean Silva and Dr. Sondelius about you, but the letter from Dr. Gottlieb is quite remarkable. He says you have rare gifts as a laboratory man. I take great pleasure in offering you the appointment; kindly wire."

Not till then did Martin completely realize that he was leaving Wheatsylvania—the tedium of Bert Tozer's nagging—the spying of Pete Yeska and the Norbloms—the inevitability of turning, as so many unchanging times he had turned, south from the Leopolis road at the Two Mile Grove and following again that weary, flat, unbending trail—the superiority of Dr. Hesselink and the malice of Dr. Coughlin—the round which left him no time for his dusty laboratory—leaving it all for the achievement and splendor of the great city of Nautilus.

"Leora, we're going! We're really going!"

### III

Bert Tozer said:

"You know by golly there's folks that would call you a traitor, after all we've done for you, even if you did pay back the thousand, to let some other doc come in here and get all that influence away from the Family."

Ada Quist said:

"I guess if you ain't any too popular with the folks around here you'll have one fine time in a big city like Nautilus! Well Bert and me are going to get married next year and when you two swells make a failure of it I suppose we'll have to take care of you at our house when you come sneaking back do you think we could get your house at the same rent you paid for it oh Bert why couldn't we take Mart's office instead it would save money well I've always said since we were in school together you couldn't stand a decent regular life Ory."

Mr. Tozer said:

"I simply can't understand it, with everything going so nice. Why, you'd be making three-four thousand a year some day, if you just stuck to it. Haven't we tried to treat you nice? I don't like to have my little girl go away and leave me alone, now I'm getting on in years. And Bert gets so cranky with me and Mother, but you and Ory would always kind of listen to us. Can't you fix it somehow so you could stay?"

Pete Yeska said:

"Doc, you could of knocked me down with a feather when I heard you were going! Course you and me have scrapped about this drug business, but Lord! I been kind of half thinking about coming around some time and offering you a partnership and let you run the drug end to suit yourself, and we could get the Buick agency, maybe, and work up a nice little business. I'm real sorry you're going to leave us. . . . Well, come back some day and we'll take a shot at the ducks, and have a good laugh about that bull you made over the small-pox. I never will forget that! I was saying to the old woman just the other day, when she had an ear-ache, 'Ain't got small-pox, have yuh, Bess!' "

Dr. Hesselink said:

"Doctor, what's this I hear? You're not going away? Why, you and I were just beginning to bring medical practice in this neck of the woods up to where it ought to be, so I drove over tonight— Huh? We panned you? Ye-es, I suppose we did, but that doesn't mean we didn't appreciate you. Small place like here or Groningen, you have to roast your neighbors to keep busy. Why, Doctor, I've been watching you develop from an unlicked cub to a real upstanding physician, and now you're going away—you don't know how I feel!"

Henry Novak said:

"Why, Doc, you ain't going to *leave* us? And we got a new baby coming, and I said to the woman, just the other day, 'It's a good thing we got a doctor that hands you out the truth and not all this guff we used to get from Doc Winter.' "

The wheat-buyer at Delft said:

"Doc, what's this I hear? You ain't going *away?* A fellow told me you was and I says to him, 'Don't be more of a damn' fool than the Lord meant you to be,' I says. But I got to worrying about it, and I drove over and— Doc, I fire off my mouth pretty easy, I guess. I was agin you in the typhoid epidemic, when you said that seamstress was carrying the sickness around, and then you showed me up good. Doc, if you'd like to be state senator, and if you'll stay—I got quite a little influence—believe me, I'll get out and work my shirt off for you!"

Alec Ingleblad said:

"You're a lucky guy!"

All the village was at the train when they left for Nautilus.

For a hundred autumn-blazing miles Martin mourned his neighbors. "I feel like getting off and going back. Didn't we used to have fun playing Five Hundred with the Fraziers! I hate to think of the kind of doctor they may get. I swear, if some quack settles there or if Woestijne neglects the health work again, I'll go back and run 'em both out of business! And be kind of fun to be state senator, some ways."

But as evening thickened and nothing in all the rushing world existed save the yellow Pintsch gas globes above them in the long car, they saw ahead of them great Nautilus, high honor and achievement, the making of a radiant model city and the praise of Sondelius—perhaps even of Max Gottlieb.

# 19

Midmost of the black-soiled Iowa plain, watered only by a shallow and insignificant creek, the city of Nautilus bakes and rattles and glistens. For hundreds of miles the tall corn springs in a jungle of undeviating rows, and the stranger who sweatily trudges the corn-walled roads is lost and nervous with the sense of merciless growth.

Nautilus is to Zenith what Zenith is to Chicago.

With seventy thousand people, it is a smaller Zenith but no less brisk. There is one large hotel to compare with the dozen in Zenith, but that one is as busy and standardized and frenziedly modern as its owner can make it. The only authentic difference between Nautilus and Zenith is that in both cases all the streets look alike but in Nautilus they do not look alike for so many miles.

The difficulty in defining its quality is that no one has determined whether it is a very large village or a very small city. There are houses with chauffeurs and Bacardi cocktails, but on August evenings all save a few score burghers sit in their shirt-sleeves on front porches. Across from the ten-story office building, in which a little magazine of the New Prose is published by a young woman who for five months lived in the cafés of Montparnasse, is an old frame mansion comfortable with maples, and a line of Fords and lumber-wagons in which the overalled farmers have come to town.

Iowa has the richest land, the lowest illiteracy rate, the largest percentages of native-born whites and motor-car owners, and the most moral and forward-looking cities of all the States, and Nautilus is the most Iowan city in Iowa. One out of every three persons above the age of sixty has spent a winter in California, and among them are the champion horseshoe pitcher of Pasadena and the woman who presented the turkey which Miss Mary Pickford, the cinema princess, enjoyed at her Christmas dinner in 1912.

Nautilus is distinguished by large houses with large lawns and by an astounding quantity of garages and lofty church spires. The fat fields run up to the edge of the city, and the scattered factories, the innumerable railroad side-tracks, and the scraggly cottages for workmen are almost amid the corn. Nautilus manufactures steel windmills, agricultural implements, including the celebrated Daisy Manure Spreader, and such corn-products as Maize Mealies, the renowned breakfast-food. It makes brick, it sells groceries wholesale, and it is the headquarters of the Cornbelt Co-operative Insurance Company.

One of its smallest but oldest industries is Mugford Christian College, which has two hundred and seventeen students, and sixteen instructors, of whom eleven are ministers of the Church of Christ. The well-known Dr. Tom

Bissex is football coach, health director, and professor of hygiene, chemistry, physics, French, and German. Its shorthand and piano departments are known far beyond the limits of Nautilus, and once, though that was some years ago, Mugford held the Grinnell College baseball team down to a score of eleven to five. It has never been disgraced by squabbles over teaching evolutionary biology—it never has thought of teaching biology at all.

## II

Martin left Leora at the Sims House, the old-fashioned, second-best hotel in Nautilus, to report to Dr. Pickerbaugh, Director of the Department of Public Health.

The department was on an alley, in a semi-basement at the back of that large graystone fungus, the City Hall. When he entered the drab reception-office he was highly received by the stenographer and the two visiting nurses. Into the midst of their flutterings—"Did you have a good trip, Doctor? Dr. Pickerbaugh didn't hardly expect you till tomorrow, Doctor. Is Mrs. Arrowsmith with you, Doctor?"—charged Pickerbaugh, thundering welcomes.

Dr. Almus Pickerbaugh was forty-eight. He was a graduate of Mugford College and of the Wassau Medical School. He looked somewhat like President Roosevelt, with the same squareness and the same bristly mustache, and he cultivated the resemblance. He was a man who never merely talked: he either bubbled or made orations.

He received Martin with four "Well's," which he gave after the manner of a college cheer; he showed him through the Department, led him into the Director's private office, gave him a cigar, and burst the dam of manly silence:

"Doctor, I'm delighted to have a man with your scientific inclinations. Not that I should consider myself entirely without them. In fact I make it a regular practice to set aside a period for scientific research, without a certain amount of which even the most ardent crusade for health methods would scarcely make much headway."

It sounded like the beginning of a long seminar. Martin settled in his chair. He was doubtful about his cigar, but he found that it helped him to look more interested.

"But with me, I admit, it's a matter of temperament. I have often hoped that, without any desire whatever for mere personal aggrandizement, the powers above may yet grant me the genius to become at once the Roosevelt and the Longfellow of the great and universally growing movement for public health measures is your cigar too mild, Doctor? or perhaps it would be better to say the Kipling of public health rather than the Longfellow, because despite the beautiful passages and high moral atmosphere of the Sage of Cambridge, his poetry lacked the swing and punch of Kipling.

"I assume you agree with me, or you will when you had had an opportunity to see the effect our work has on the city, and the success we have in selling the idea of Better Health, that what the world needs is a really in-

spired, courageous, overtowering leader—say a Billy Sunday of the movement
—a man who would know how to use sensationalism properly and wake the
people out of their sloth. Sometimes the papers, and I can only say they
flatter me when they compare me with Billy Sunday, the greatest of all
evangelists and Christian preachers—sometimes they claim that I'm too sensational. Huh! If they only could understand it, trouble is I can't be sensational
enough! Still, I try, I try, and— Look here. Here's a placard, it was painted by
my daughter Orchid and the poetry is my own humble effort, and let me
tell you it gets quoted around everywhere:

> You can't get health
> By a pussyfoot stealth,
> So let's every health-booster
> Crow just like a rooster.

"Then there's another—this is a minor thing; it doesn't try to drive home
general abstract principles, but it'd surprise you the effect it's had on careless
housewives, who of course don't mean to neglect the health of their little
ones and merely need instruction and a little pep put into them, and when
they see a card like this, it makes 'em think:

> Boil the milk bottles or by gum
> You better buy your ticket to Kingdom Come.

"I've gotten quite a lot of appreciation in my small way for some of these
things that didn't hardly take me five minutes to dash off. Some day when
you get time, glance over this volume of clippings—just to show you, Doctor,
what you can do if you go at the Movement in the up-to-date and scientific
manner. This one, about the temperance meeting I addressed in Des Moines
—say, I had that hall, and it was jam-pack-full, lifting right up on their feet
when I proved by statistics that ninety-three per cent of all insanity is caused
by booze! Then this—well, it hasn't anything to do with health, directly,
but it'll just indicate the opportunity you'll have here to get in touch with
all the movements for civic weal."

He held out a newspaper clipping in which, above a pen-and-ink caricature
portraying him with large mustached head on a tiny body, was the headline:

DOC PICKERBAUGH BANNER BOOSTER

OF EVANGELINE COUNTY LEADS BIG

GO-TO-CHURCH DEMONSTRATION HERE

Pickerbaugh looked it over, reflecting, "That was a dandy meeting! We
increased church attendance here seventeen per cent! Oh, Doctor, you went
to Winnemac and had your internship in Zenith, didn't you? Well, this
might interest you then. It's from the *Zenith Advocate-Times*, and it's by
Chum Frink, who, I think you'll agree with me, ranks with Eddie Guest and
Walt Mason as the greatest, as they certainly are the most popular, of all our
poets, showing that you can bank every time on the literary taste of the
American Public. Dear old Chum! That was when I was in Zenith to address

the national convention of Congregational Sunday-schools, I happen to be a Congregationalist myself, on 'The Morality of A 1 Health.' So Chum wrote this poem about me:"

> Zenith welcomes with high hurraw
> A friend in Almus Pickerbaugh,
> The two-fisted fightin' poet doc
> Who stands for health like Gibraltar's rock.
> He's jammed with figgers and facts and fun,
> The plucky old, lucky old son—of—a—gun!

For a moment the exuberant Dr. Pickerbaugh was shy.

"Maybe it's kind of immodest in me to show that around. And when I read a poem with such originality and swing, when I find a genu-ine vest-pocket masterpiece like this, then I realize that I'm not a poet at all, no matter how much my jingles may serve to jazz up the Cause of Health. My brain-children may teach sanitation and do their little part to save thousands of dear lives, but they aren't literature, like what Chum Frink turns out. No, I guess I'm nothing but just a plain scientist in an office.

"Still, you'll readily see how one of these efforts of mine, just by having a good laugh and a punch and some melody in it, does gild the pill and make careless folks stop spitting on the sidewalks, and get out into God's great outdoors and get their lungs packed full of ozone and lead a real hairy-chested he-life. In fact you might care to look over the first number of a little semi-yearly magazine I'm just starting—I know for a fact that a number of newspaper editors are going to quote from it and so carry on the good work as well as boost my circulation."

He handed to Martin a pamphlet entitled *Pickerbaugh Pickings*.

In verse and aphorism, *Pickings* recommended good health, good roads, good business, and the single standard of morality. Dr. Pickerbaugh backed up his injunctions with statistics as impressive as those the Reverend Ira Hinkley had once used at Digamma Pi. Martin was edified by an item which showed that among all families divorced in Ontario, Tennessee, and Southern Wyoming in 1912, the appalling number of fifty-three per cent of the husbands drank at least one glass of whisky daily.

Before this warning had sunk in, Pickerbaugh snatched *Pickings* from him with a boyish, "Oh, you won't want to read any more of my rot. You can look it over some future time. But this second volume of my clippings may perhaps interest you, just as a hint of what a fellow can do."

While he considered the headlines in the scrapbook, Martin realized that Dr. Pickerbaugh was vastly better known than he had realized. He was exposed as the founder of the first Rotary Club in Iowa; superintendent of the Jonathan Edwards Congregational Sunday School of Nautilus; president of the Moccasin Ski and Hiking Club, of the West Side Bowling Club, and the 1912 Bull Moose and Roosevelt Club; organizer and cheer-leader of a Joint Picnic of the Woodmen, Moose, Elks, Masons, Odd Fellows, Turnverein, Knights of Columbus, B'nai B'rith, and the Y.M.C.A.; and winner of the prizes both for reciting the largest number of Biblical texts and for dancing the best Irish jig at the Harvest Moon Soiree of the Jonathan Edwards Bible Class for the Grown-ups.

Martin read of him as addressing the Century Club of Nautilus on "A Yankee Doctor's Trip Through Old Europe," and the Mugford College Alumni Association on "Wanted: A Man-sized Feetball Coach for Old Mugford." But outside of Nautilus as well, there were loud alarums of his presence.

He had spoken at the Toledo Chamber of Commerce Weekly Luncheon on "More Health—More Bank Clearings." He had edified the National Interurban Trolley Council, meeting at Wichita, on "Health Maxims for Trolley Folks." Seven thousand, six hundred Detroit automobile mechanics had listened to his observations on "Health First, Safety Second, and Booze Nowhere A-tall." And in a great convention at Waterloo he had helped organize the first regiment in Iowa of the Anti-rum Minute Men.

The articles and editorials regarding him, in newspapers, house organs, and one rubber-goods periodical, were accompanied by photographs of himself, his buxom wife, and his eight bounding daughters, depicted in Canadian winter costumes among snow and icicles, in modest but easy athletic costumes, playing tennis in the backyard, and in costumes of no known genus whatever, frying bacon against a background of Northern Minnesota pines.

Martin felt strongly that he would like to get away and recover.

He walked back to the Sims House. He realized that to a civilized man the fact that Pickerbaugh advocated any reform would be sufficient reason for ignoring it.

When he had gone thus far, Martin pulled himself up, cursed himself for what he esteemed his old sin of superiority to decent normal people. . . . Failure. Disloyalty. In medical school, in private practice, in his bullying health administration. Now again?

He urged, "This pep and heartiness stuff of Pickerbaugh's is exactly the thing to get across to the majority of people the scientific discoveries of the Max Gottliebs. What do I care how much Pickerbaugh gases before conventions of Sunday School superintendents and other morons, as long as he lets me alone and lets me do my work in the lab and dairy inspection?"

He pumped up enthusiasm and came quite cheerfully and confidently into the shabby, high-ceilinged hotel bedroom where Leora sat in a rocker by the window.

"Well?" she said.

"It's fine—gave me fine welcome. And they want us to come to dinner tomorrow evening."

"What's he like?"

"Oh, he's awfully optimistic—he puts things over—he— Oh, Leora, am I going to be a sour, cranky, unpopular, rotten failure again?"

His head was buried in her lap and he clung to her affection, the one reality in a world of chattering ghosts.

### III

When the maples fluttered beneath their window in the breeze that sprang up with the beginning of twilight, when the amiable citizens of Nautilus had driven home to supper in their shaky Fords, Leora had persuaded him that Pickerbaugh's flamboyance would not interfere with his own work, that in any case they would not remain in Nautilus forever, that he was impatient, and that she loved him dearly. So they descended to supper, an old-fashioned Iowa supper with corn fritters and many little dishes which were of interest after the loving but misinformed cooking of Leora, and they went to the movies and held hands and were not ill content.

The next day Dr. Pickerbaugh was busier and less buoyant. He gave Martin a notion of the details of his work.

Martin had thought of himself, freed from tinkering over cut fingers and ear-aches, as spending ecstatic days in the laboratory, emerging only to battle with factory-owners who defied sanitation. But he found that it was impossible to define his work, except that he was to do a little of everything that Pickerbaugh, the press, or any stray citizen of Nautilus might think of.

He was to placate voluble voters who came in to complain of everything from the smell of sewer-gas to the midnight beer parties of neighbors; he was to dictate office correspondence to the touchy stenographer, who was not a Working Girl but a Nice Girl Who Was Working; to give publicity to the newspapers; to buy paper-clips and floor-wax and report-blanks at the lowest prices; to assist, in need, the two part-time physicians in the city clinic; to direct the nurses and the two sanitary inspectors; to scold the Garbage Removal Company; to arrest—or at least to jaw at—all public spitters; to leap into a Ford and rush out to tack placards on houses in which were infectious diseases; to keep a learned implacable eye on epidemics from Vladivostok to Patagonia, and to prevent (by methods not very clearly outlined) their coming in to slay the yeomanry and even halt the business activities of Nautilus.

But there was a little laboratory work: milk tests, Wassermanns for private physicians, the making of vaccines, cultures in suspected diphtheria.

"I get it," said Leora, as they dressed for the dinner at Pickerbaugh's. "Your job will only take about twenty-eight hours a day, and the rest of the time you're perfectly welcome to spend in research, unless somebody interrupts you."

### IV

The home of Dr. and Mrs. Almus Pickerbaugh, on the steeple-prickly West Side, was a Real Old-fashioned Home. It was a wooden house with towers, swings, hammocks, rather mussy shade trees, a rather mangy lawn, a rather damp arbor, and an old carriage-house with a line of steel spikes along the ridge pole. Over the front gate was the name: UNEEDAREST.

Martin and Leora came into a shambles of salutations and daughters.

The eight girls, from pretty Orchid aged nineteen to the five-year-old twins, surged up in a tidal wave of friendly curiosity and tried to talk all at once.

Their hostess was a plump woman with an air of worried trustfulness. Her conviction that everything was all right was constantly struggling with her knowledge that a great many things seemed to be all wrong. She kissed Leora while Pickerbaugh was pump-handling Martin. Pickerbaugh had a way of pressing his thumb into the back of your hand which was extraordinarily cordial and painful.

He immediately drowned out even his daughters by an oration on the Home Nest:

"Here you've got an illustration of Health in the Home. Look at these great strapping girls, Arrowsmith! Never been sick a day in their lives—practically—and though Mother does have her sick-headaches, that's to be attributed to the early neglect of her diet, because while her father, the old deacon—and a fine upstanding gentleman of the old school he was, too, if there ever was one, and a friend of Nathaniel Mugford, to whom more than any other we owe not only the foundation of Mugford College but also the tradition of integrity and industry which have produced our present prosperity—BUT he had no knowledge of diet or sanitation, and I've always thought—"

The daughters were introduced as Orchid, Verbena, Daisy, Jonquil, Hibisca, Narcissa, and the twins, Arbuta and Gladiola.

Mrs. Pickerbaugh sighed:

"I suppose it would be dreadfully conventional to call them My Jewels—I do so hate these conventional phrases that everybody uses, don't you?—but that's what they really are to their mother, and the Doctor and I have sometimes wished— Of course when we'd started giving them floral names we had to keep it up, but if we'd started with jewels, just think of all the darling names we might have used, like Agate and Cameo and Sardonyx and Beryl and Topaz and Opal and Esmeralda and Chrysoprase—it *is* Chrysoprase, isn't it, not Chrysalis? Oh, well, many people have congratulated us on their names as it is. You know the girls are getting quite famous—their pictures in so many papers, and we have a Pickerbaugh Ladies' Baseball Team all our own—only the Doctor has to play on it now, because I'm beginning to get a little stout."

Except by their ages, it was impossible to tell the daughters apart. They were all bouncing, all blond, all pretty, all eager, all musical, and not merely pure but clamorously clean-minded. They all belonged to the Congregational Sunday School, and to either the Y.W.C.A. or the Camp Fire Girls; they were all fond of picnicking; and they could all of them, except the five-year-old twins, quote practically without error the newest statistics showing the evils of alcohol.

"In fact," said Dr. Pickerbaugh, "*we* think they're a very striking brood of chickabiddies."

"They certainly are!" quivered Martin.

"But best of all, they are able to help me put over the doctrine of the

*Mens Sana* in the *Corpus Sano*. Mrs. Pickerbaugh and I have trained them to sing together, both in the home and publicly, and as an organization we call them the Healthette Octette."

"Really?" said Leora, when it was apparent that Martin had passed beyond speech.

"Yes, and before I get through with it I hope to popularize the name Healthette from end to end of this old nation, and you're going to see bands of happy young women going around spreading their winged message into every dark corner. Healthette Bands! Beautiful and pure-minded and enthusiastic and good basket-ball players! I tell you, *they'll* make the lazy and willful stir their stumps! They'll shame the filthy livers and filthy talkers into decency! I've already worked out a poem-slogan for the Healthette Bands. Would you like to hear it?"

> Winsome young womanhood wins with a smile
> Boozers, spitters, and gamblers from things that are vile.
> Our parents and teachers have explained the cause of life,
> So against the evil-minded we'll also make strife.
> We'll shame them, reclaim them, from bad habits, you bet!
> Better watch out, Mr. Loafer, I am a Healthette!

"But of course an even more important Cause is—and I was one of the first to advocate it—having a Secretary of Health and Eugenics in the cabinet at Washington—"

On the tide of this dissertation they were swept through a stupendous dinner. With a hearty "Nonsense, nonsense, man, of course you want a second helping—this is Hospitality Hall!" Pickerbaugh so stuffed Martin and Leora with roast duck, candied sweet potatoes, and mince pie that they became dangerously ill and sat glassy-eyed. But Pickerbaugh himself did not seem to be affected. While he carved and gobbled, he went on discoursing till the dining-room, with its old walnut buffet, its Hoffmann pictures of Christ, and its Remington pictures of cowpunchers, seemed to vanish, leaving him on a platform beside a pitcher of ice-water.

Not always was he merely fantastic. "Dr. Arrowsmith, I tell you we're lucky men to be able to get a living out of doing our honest best to make the people in a he-town like this well and vital. I could be pulling down eight or ten thousand a year in private practice, and I've been told I could make more than that in the art of advertising, yet I'm glad, and my dear ones are glad with me, to take a salary of four thousand. Think of our having a job where we've got nothing to sell but honesty and decency and the brotherhood o' man!"

Martin perceived that Pickerbaugh meant it, and the shame of the realization kept him from leaping up, seizing Leora, and catching the first freight train out of Nautilus.

After dinner the younger daughters desired to love Leora, in swarms. Martin had to take the twins on his knees and tell them a story. They were remarkably heavy twins, but no heavier than the labor of inventing a plot.

Before they went to bed, the entire Healthette Octette sang the famous
Health Hymn (written by Dr. Almus Pickerbaugh) which Martin was to
hear on so many bright and active public occasions in Nautilus. It was set
to the tune of "The Battle Hymn of the Republic," but as the twins' voices
were energetic and extraordinarily shrill, it had an effect all its own:

Oh, are you out for happiness or are you out for pelf?
You owe it to the grand old flag to cultivate yourself,
To train the mind, keep clean the streets, and ever guard your health.
> Then we'll all go marching on.

> A healthy mind in A clean body,
> A healthy mind in A clean body,
> A healthy mind in A clean body,
> > The slogan for one and all.

As a bedtime farewell, the twins then recited, as they had recently recited
at the Congregational Festival, one of their father's minor lyrics:

> What does little birdie say
> On the sill at break o' day?
> "Hurrah for health in Nautilus
> For Pa and Ma and all of us,
> > Hurray, hurray, hurray!"

"There, my popsywopsies, up to bed we go!" said Mrs. Pickerbaugh.
"Don't you think, Mrs. Arrowsmith, they're natural-born actresses? They're
not afraid of any audience, and the way they throw themselves into it—
perhaps not Broadway, but the more refined theaters in New York would
just love them, and maybe they've been sent to us to elevate the drama.
Upsy go."

During her absence the others gave a brief musical program.

Verbena, the second oldest, played Chaminade. ("Of course we all love
music, and popularize it among the neighbors, but Verby is perhaps the
only real musical genius in the family.") But the unexpected feature was
Orchid's cornet solo.

Martin dared not look at Leora. It was not that he was sniffily superior
to cornet solos, for in Elk Mills, Wheatsylvania, and surprisingly large portions of Zenith, cornet solos were done by the most virtuous females. But
he felt that he had been in a madhouse for dozens of years.

"I've never been so drunk in my life. I wish I could get at a drink and
sober up," he agonized. He made hysterical and completely impractical plans
for escape. Then Mrs. Pickerbaugh, returning from the still audible twins,
sat down at the harp.

While she played, a faded woman and thickish, she fell into a great dreaming, and suddenly Martin had a picture of her as a gay, good, dove-like
maiden who had admired the energetic young medical student, Almus Pickerbaugh. She must have been a veritable girl of the late eighties and the

early nineties, the naïve and idyllic age of Howells, when young men were pure, when they played croquet and sang Swanee River; a girl who sat on a front porch enchanted by the sweetness of lilacs, and hoped that when Almus and she were married they would have a nickel-plated baseburner stove and a son who would become a missionary or a millionaire.

For the first time that evening, Martin managed to put a respectable heartiness into his "Enjoyed that s' much." He felt victorious, and somewhat recovered from his weakness.

But the evening's orgy was only begun.

They played word-games, which Martin hated and Leora did very badly indeed. They acted charades, at which Pickerbaugh was tremendous. The sight of him on the floor in his wife's fur coat, being a seal on an ice-floe, was incomparable. Then Martin, Orchid, and Hibisca (aged twelve) had to present a charade, and there were complications.

Orchid was as full of simple affections, of smilings and pattings and bouncings, as her younger sisters, but she was nineteen and not altogether a child. Doubtless she was as pure-minded and as devoted to Clean and Wholesome Novels as Dr. Pickerbaugh stated, and he stated it with frequency, but she was not unconscious of young men, even though they were married.

She planned to enact the word *doleful*, with a beggar asking a dole, and a corncrib full. As they skipped upstairs to dress, she hugged Martin's arm, frisked beside him, and murmured, "Oh, Doctor, I'm so glad Daddy has you for assistant—somebody that's young and good-looking. Oh, was that dreadful of me? But I mean: you look so athletic and everything, and the other assistant director—don't tell Daddy I said so, but he was an old crank!"

He was conscious of brown eyes and unshadowed virginal lips. As Orchid put on her agreeably loose costume as a beggar, he was also conscious of ankles and young bosom. She smiled at him, as one who had long known him, and said loyally, "We'll show 'em! I know you're a dan-dy actor!"

When they bustled downstairs, as she did not take his arm, he took hers, and he pressed it slightly and felt alarmed and relinquished it with emphasis.

Since his marriage he had been so absorbed in Leora, as lover, as companion, as helper, that till this hour his most devastating adventure had been a glance at a pretty girl in a train. But the flushed young gaiety of Orchid disturbed him. He wanted to be rid of her, he hoped that he would not be altogether rid of her, and for the first time in years he was afraid of Leora's eyes.

There were acrobatic feats later, and a considerable prominence of Orchid, who did not wear stays, who loved dancing, and who praised Martin's feats in the game of "Follow the Leader."

All the daughters save Orchid were sent to bed, and the rest of the fête consisted of what Pickerbaugh called "a little quiet scientific conversation by the fireside," made up of his observations on good roads, rural sanitation, Ideals in politics, and methods of letter filing in health departments. Through this placid hour, or it may have been an hour and a half, Martin saw that Orchid was observing his hair, his jaw, his hands, and he had, and dismissed, and had again a thought about the innocent agreeableness of holding her small friendly paw.

He also saw that Leora was observing both of them, and he suffered a good deal, and had practically no benefit whatever from Pickerbaugh's notes on the value of disinfectants. When Pickerbaugh predicted for Nautilus, in fifteen years, a health department thrice as large, with many full-time clinic and school physicians and possibly Martin as director (Pickerbaugh himself having gone off to mysterious and interesting activities in a Larger Field), Martin merely croaked, "Yes, that's be—be fine," while to himself he was explaining, "Damn that girl, I wish she wouldn't shake herself at me."

At half-past eight he had pictured his escape as life's highest ecstasy; at twelve he took leave with nervous hesitation.

They walked to the hotel. Free from the sight of Orchid, brisk in the coolness, he forgot the chit and pawed again the problem of his work in Nautilus.

"Lord, I don't know whether I can do it. To work under that gas-bag, with his fool pieces about boozers—"

"They weren't so bad," protested Leora.

"Bad? Why, he's probably the worst poet that ever lived, and he certainly knows less about epidemiology than I thought any one man could ever learn, all by himself. But when it comes to this—what was it Clif Clawson used to call it?—by the way, wonder what's ever become of Clif; haven't heard from him for a couple o' years—when it comes to this 'overpowering Christian Domesticity'— Oh, let's hunt for a blind-pig and sit around with the nice restful burglars."

She insisted, "I thought his poems were kind of cute."

"Cute! What a word!"

"It's no worse than the cuss-words you're always using! But the cornet yowling by that awful oldest daughter— Ugh!"

"Well, now she played darn' well!"

"Martin, the cornet is the kind of an instrument my brother would play. And you so superior about the doctor's poetry and my saying 'cute'! You're just as much a backwoods hick as I am, and maybe more so!"

"Why, gee, Leora, I never knew you to get sore about nothing before! And can't you understand how important— You see, a man like Pickerbaugh makes all public health work simply ridiculous by his circusing and his ignorance. If he said that fresh air was a good thing, instead of making me open my windows it'd make me or any other reasonable person close 'em. And to use the word 'science' in those flop-eared limericks or whatever you call 'em—it's sacrilege!"

"Well, if you want to *know*, Martin Arrowsmith, I'll have no more of these high jinks with that Orchid girl! Practically hugging her when you came downstairs, and then mooning at her all evening! I don't mind your cursing and being cranky and even getting drunk, in a reasonable sort of way, but ever since the lunch when you told me and that Fox woman, 'I hope you girls won't mind, but I just happen to remember that I'm engaged to both of you'— You're mine, and I won't have any trespassers. I'm a cavewoman, and you'd better learn it, and as for that Orchid, with her simper and her stroking your arm and her great big absurd feet— Orchid! She's no orchid! She's a bachelor's button!"

"But, honest, I don't even remember which of the eight she was."

"Huh! Then you've been making love to all of 'em, that's why. Drat her! Well, I'm not going to go on scrapping about it. I just wanted to warn you, that's all."

At the hotel, after giving up the attempt to find a short, jovial, convincing way of promising that he would never flirt with Orchid, he stammered, "If you don't mind, I think I'll stay down and walk a little more. I've got to figure this health department business out."

He sat in the Sims House office—singularly dismal it was, after midnight, and singularly smelly.

"That fool Pickerbaugh! I wish I'd told him right out that we know hardly anything about the epidemiology of tuberculosis, for instance.

"Just the same, she's a darling child. Orchid! She's like an orchid—no, she's too healthy. Be a great kid to go hunting with. Sweet. And she acted as if I were her own age, not an old doctor. I'll be good, oh, I'll be good, but— I'd like to kiss her once, *good!* She likes me. Those darling lips, like—like rosebuds!

"Poor Leora. I nev' was so astonished in my life. Jealous. Well, she's got a right to be! No woman ever stood by a man like— Lee, sweet, can't you see, idiot, if I skipped round the corner with seventeen billion Orchids, it'd be you I loved, and never anybody but you!

"I can't go round singing Healthette Octette Pantalette stuff. Even if it did instruct people, which it don't. Be almost better to let 'em die than have to live and listen to—

"Leora said I was a 'backwoods hick.' Let me tell you, young woman, as it happens I am a Bachelor of Arts, and you may recall the kind of books the 'backwoods hick' was reading to you last winter, and even Henry James and everybody and— Oh, she's right. I am. I do know how to make pipets and agar, but— And yet some day I want to travel like Sondelius—

"Sondelius! God! If it were he I was working for, instead of Pickerbaugh, I'd slave for him—

"Or does he pull the bunk, too?

"Now that's just what I mean. That kind of phrase. 'Pull the bunk'! Horrible!

"Hell! I'll use any kind of phrase I want to! I'm not one of your social climbers like Angus. The way Sondelius cusses, for instance, and yet he's used to all those highbrows—

"And I'll be so busy here in Nautilus that I won't even be able to go on reading. Still— I don't suppose they read much, but there must be quite a few of these rich men here that know about nice houses. Clothes. Theaters. That stuff.

"Rats!"

He wandered to an all-night lunch-wagon, where he gloomily drank coffee. Beside him, seated at the long shelf which served as table, beneath the noble red-glass window with a portrait of George Washington, was a policeman who, as he gnawed a Hamburger sandwich, demanded:

"Say, ain't you this new doctor that's come to assist Pickerbaugh? Seen you at City Hall."

"Yes. Say, uh, say, how does the city like Pickerbaugh? How do you like him? Tell me honestly, because I'm just starting in, and, uh— You get me."

With his spoon held inside the cup by a brawny thumb, the policeman gulped his coffee and proclaimed, while the greasy friendly cook of the lunch-wagon nodded in agreement:

"Well, if you want the straight dope, he hollers a good deal, but he's one awful brainy man. He certainly can sling the Queen's English, and jever hear one of his poems? They're darn' bright. I'll tell you: There's some people say Pickerbaugh pulls the song and dance too much, but way I figure it, course maybe for you and me, Doctor, it'd be all right if he just looked after the milk and the garbage and the kids' teeth. But there's a lot of careless, ignorant, foreign slobs that need to be jollied into using their konks about these health biznai, so's they won't go getting sick with a lot of these infectious diseases and pass 'em on to the rest of us, and believe me, old Doc Pickerbaugh is the boy that gets the idea into their noodles!

"Yes, sir, he's a great old coot—he ain't a clam like some of these docs. Why, say, one day he showed up at the St. Patrick picnic, even if he is a dirty Protestant, and him and Father Costello chummed up like two old cronies, and darn' if he didn't wrestle a fellow half his age, and awful' near throw him, yes, you bet he did, he certainly give that young fellow a run for his money all right! We fellows on the Force all like him, and we have to grin, the way he comes around and soft-soaps us into doing a lot of health work that by law we ain't hardly supposed to do, you might say, instead of issuing a lot of fool orders. You bet. He's a real guy."

"I see," said Martin, and as he returned to the hotel he meditated:

"But think of what Gottlieb would say about him.

"Damn Gottlieb! Damn everybody except Leora!

"I'm not going to fail here, way I did in Wheatsylvania.

"Some day Pickerbaugh will get a bigger job— Huh! He's just the kind of jollying fourflusher that *would* climb! But anyway, I'll have my training then, and maybe I'll make a real health department here.

"Orchid said we'd go skating this winter—

"*Damn* Orchid!"

# 20

Martin found in Dr. Pickerbaugh a generous chief. He was eager to have Martin invent and clamor about his own Causes and Movements. His scientific knowledge was rather thinner than that of the visiting nurses, but he had little jealousy, and he demanded of Martin only the belief that a rapid and noisy moving from place to place is the means (and possibly the end) of Progress.

In a two-family house on Social Hill, which is not a hill but a slight swelling in the plain, Martin and Leora found an upper floor. There was a simple pleasantness in these continuous lawns, these wide maple-shaded streets, and a joy in freedom from the peering whispers of Wheatsylvania.

Suddenly they were being courted by the Nice Society of Nautilus.

A few days after their arrival Martin was summoned to the telephone to hear a masculine voice rasping:

"Hello. Martin? I bet you can't guess who this is!"

Martin, very busy, restrained his desire to observe, "You win—g' by!" and he buzzed, with the cordiality suitable to a new Assistant Director:

"No, I'm afraid I can't."

"Well, make a guess."

"Oh—Clif Clawson?"

"Nope. Say, I see you're looking fine. Oh, I guess I've got you guessing this time! Go on! Have another try!"

The stenographer was waiting to take letters, and Martin had not yet learned to become impersonal and indifferent in her presence. He said with a perceptible tartness:

"Oh, I suppose it's President Wilson. Look here—"

"Well, Mart, it's Irve Watters! What do you know about that!"

Apparently the jester expected large gratification, but it took ten seconds for Martin to remember who Irving Watters might be. Then he had it: Watters, the appalling normal medical student whose faith in the good, the true, the profitable, had annoyed him at Digamma Pi. He made his response as hearty as he could:

"Well, well, what you doing here, Irve?"

"Why, I'm settled here. Been here ever since internship. And got a nice little practice, too. Look, Mart, Mrs. Watters and I want you and your wife—I believe you are married, aren't you?—to come up to the house for dinner, tomorrow evening, and I'll put you onto all the local slants."

The dread of Watters's patronage enabled Martin to lie vigorously:

"Awfully sorry—awfully sorry—got a date for tomorrow evening and the next evening."

"Then come have lunch with me tomorrow at the Elks' Club, and you and your wife take dinner with us Sunday noon."

Hopelessly, "I don't think I can make it for lunch but— Well, we'll dine with you Sunday."

It is one of the major tragedies that nothing is more discomforting than the hearty affection of the Old Friends who never were friends. Martin's imaginative dismay at being caught here by Watters was not lessened when Leora and he reluctantly appeared on Sunday at one-thirty and were by a fury of Old Friendship dragged back into the days of Digamma Pi.

Watters's house was new, and furnished in a highly built-in and leaded-glass manner. He had in three years of practice already become didactic and incredibly married; he had put on weight and infallibility; and he had learned many new things about which to be dull. Having been graduated a year earlier than Martin and having married an almost rich wife, he was kind and hospitable with an emphasis which aroused a desire to do homicide. His conversation was a series of maxims and admonitions:

"If you stay with the Department of Public Health for a couple of years and take care to meet the right people, you'll be able to go into very lucrative practice here. It's a fine town—prosperous—so few dead beats.

"You want to join the country club and take up golf. Best opportunity in the world to meet the substantial citizens. I've picked up more than one high-class patient there.

"Pickerbaugh is a good active man and a fine booster but he's got a bad socialistic tendency. These clinics—outrageous—the people that go to them that can afford to pay! Pauperize people. Now this may startle you—oh, you had a lot of crank notions when you were in school, but you aren't the only one that does some thinking for himself!—sometimes I believe it'd be better for the general health situation if there weren't any public health departments at all, because they get a lot of people into the habit of going to free clinics instead of to private physicians, and cut down the earnings of the doctors and reduce their number, so there are less of us to keep a watchful eye on sickness.

"I guess by this time you've gotten over the funny ideas you used to have about being practical—'commercialism' you used to call it. You can see now that you've got to support your wife and family, and if you don't, nobody else is going to.

"Any time you want a straight tip about people here, you just come to me. Pickerbaugh is a crank—he won't give you the right dope—the people you want to tie up with are the good, solid, conservative, successful business men."

Then Mrs. Watters had her turn. She was meaty with advice, being the daughter of a prosperous person, none other than Mr. S. A. Peaseley, the manufacturer of the Daisy Manure Spreader.

"You haven't any children?" she sobbed at Leora. "Oh, you must! Irving and I have two, and you don't know what an interest they are to us, and they keep us so young."

Martin and Leora looked at each other pitifully.

After dinner, Irving insisted on their recalling the "good times we used to have together at the dear old U." He took no denial. "You always want to make folks think you're eccentric, Mart. You pretend you haven't any college patriotism, but I know better—I know you're showing off—you admire the old place and our profs just as much as anybody. Maybe I know you better than you do yourself! Come on, now; let's give a long cheer and sing 'Winnemac, Mother of Brawny Men.'"

And, "Don't be silly; of course you're going to sing," said Mrs. Watters, as she marched to the piano, with which she dealt in a firm manner.

When they had politely labored through the fried chicken and brick ice cream, through the maxims, gurglings, and memories, Martin and Leora went forth and spoke in tongues:

"Pickerbaugh must be a saint, if Watters roasts him. I begin to believe he has sense enough to come in when it rains."

In their common misery they forgot that they had been agitated by a girl named Orchid.

II

Between Pickerbaugh and Irving Watters, Martin was drafted into many of the associations, clubs, lodges, and "causes" with which Nautilus foamed; into the Chamber of Commerce, the Moccasin Ski and Hiking Club, the Elks' Club, the Odd Fellows, and the Evangeline County Medical society. He resisted, but they said in a high hurt manner, "Why, my boy, if you're going to be a public official, and if you have the slightest appreciation of their efforts to make you welcome here—"

Leora and he found themselves with so many invitations that they, who had deplored the dullness of Wheatsylvania, complained now that they could have no quiet evenings at home. But they fell into the habit of social ease, of dressing, of going places without nervous anticipation. They modernized their rustic dancing; they learned to play bridge, rather badly, and tennis rather well; and Martin, not by virtue and heroism but merely by habit, got out of the way of resenting the chirp of small talk.

Probably they were never recognized by their hostesses as pirates, but considered a Bright Young Couple who, since they were protégés of Pickerbaugh, must be earnest and forward-looking, and who, since they were patronized by Irving and Mrs. Watters, must be respectable.

Watters took them in hand and kept them there. He had so thick a rind that it was impossible for him to understand that Martin's frequent refusals of his invitations could conceivably mean that he did not wish to come. He detected traces of heterodoxy in Martin, and with affection, diligence, and an extraordinarily heavy humor he devoted himself to the work of salvation. Frequently he sought to entertain other guests by urging, "Come on now, Mart, let's hear some of those crazy ideas of yours!"

His friendly zeal was drab compared with that of his wife. Mrs. Watters had been reared by her father and by her husband to believe that she was the final fruit of the ages, and she set herself to correct the barbarism of the Arrowsmiths. She rebuked Martin's damns, Leora's smoking, and both their theories of bidding at bridge. But she never nagged. To have nagged would have been to admit that there were persons who did not acknowledge her sovereignty. She merely gave orders, brief, humorous, and introduced by a strident "Now don't be silly," and she expected that to settle the matter.

Martin groaned, "Oh, Lord, between Pickerbaugh and Irve, it's easier to become a respectable member of society than to go on fighting."

But Watters and Pickerbaugh were not so great a compulsion to respectability as the charms of finding himself listened to in Nautilus as he never had been in Wheatsylvania, and of finding himself admired by Orchid.

### III

He had been seeking a precipitation test for the diagnosis of syphilis which should be quicker and simpler than the Wassermann. His slackened fingers and rusty mind were becoming used to the laboratory and to passionate hypotheses when he was dragged away to help Pickerbaugh in securing publicity. He was coaxed into making his first speech: an address on "What the Laboratory Teaches about Epidemics" for the Sunday Afternoon Free Lecture Course of the Star of Hope Universalist Church.

He was flustered when he tried to prepare his notes, and on the morning of the affair he was chill as he remembered the dreadful thing he would do this day, but he was desperate with embarrassment when he came up to the Star of Hope Church.

People were crowding in; mature, responsible people. He quaked, "They're coming to hear *me*, and I haven't got a darn' thing to say to 'em!" It made him feel the more ridiculous that they who presumably wished to listen to him should not be aware of him, and that the usher, profusely shaking hands at the Byzantine portal, should bluster, "You'll find plenty room right up the side aisles, young man."

"I'm the speaker for the afternoon."

"Oh, oh, yes, oh, yes, Doctor. Right round to the Bevis Street entrance, if you please, Doctor."

In the parlors he was unctuously received by the pastor and a committee of three, wearing morning clothes and a manner of Christian intellectuality.

They held his hand in turn, they brought up rustling women to meet him, they stood about him in a polite and twittery circle, and dismayingly they expected him to say something intelligent. Then, suffering, ghastly frightened, dumb, he was led through an arched doorway into the auditorium. Millions of faces were staring at his apologetic insignificance—faces in the curving lines of pews, faces in the low balcony, eyes which followed him and doubted him and noted that his heels were run down.

The agony grew while he was prayed over and sung over.

The pastor and the lay chairman of the Lecture Course opened with suitable devotions. While Martin trembled and tried to look brazenly at the massed people who were looking at him, while he sat nude and exposed and unprotected on the high platform, the pastor made announcement of the Thursday Missionary Supper and the Little Lads' Marching Club. They sang a brief cheerful hymn or two—Martin wondering whether to sit or stand —and the chairman prayed that "our friend who will address us today may have power to put his Message across." Through the prayer Martin sat with his forehead in his hand, feeling foolish, and raving, "I guess this is the proper attitude—they're all gawping at me—gosh, won't he ever quit?—oh, damn it, now what was that point I was going to make about fumigation?— oh, Lord, he's winding up and I've got to shoot!"

Somehow, he was standing by the reading-desk, holding it for support, and his voice seemed to be going on, producing reasonable words. The blur of faces cleared and he saw individuals. He picked out a keen old man and tried to make him laugh and marvel.

He found Leora, toward the back, nodding to him, reassuring him. He dared to look away from the path of faces directly in front of him. He glanced at the balcony—

The audience perceived a young man who was being earnest about sera and vaccines but, while his voice buzzed on, that churchly young man had noted two silken ankles distinguishing the front row of the balcony, had discovered that they belonged to Orchid Pickerbaugh and that she was flashing down admiration.

At the end Martin had the most enthusiastic applause ever known—all lecturers, after all lectures, are gratified by that kind of applause—and the chairman said the most flattering things ever uttered, and the audience went out with the most remarkable speed ever witnessed, and Martin discovered himself holding Orchid's hand in the parlors while she warbled, in the most adorable voice ever heard, "Oh, Dr. Arrowsmith, you were just wonderful! Most of these lecturers are old stuffs, but you put it right over! I'm going to do a dash home and tell Dad. He'll be so tickled!"

Not till then did he find that Leora had made her way to the parlors and was looking at them like a wife.

As they walked home Leora was eloquently silent.

"Well, did you like my spiel?" he said, after a suitable time of indignant waiting.

"Yes, it wasn't bad. It must have been awfully hard to talk to all those stupid people."

"Stupid? What d'you mean by 'stupid'? They got me splendidly. They were fine."

"Were they? Well anyway, thank Heaven, you won't have to keep up this silly gassing. Pickerbaugh likes to hear himself talk too well to let you in on it very often."

"I didn't mind it. Fact, don't know but what it's a good thing to have to express myself publicly now and then. Makes you think more lucidly."

"As for instance the nice, lovely, lucid politicians!"

"Now you look here, Lee! Of course we know your husband is a mutt, and no good outside the laboratory, but I do think you might *pretend* to be a little enthusiastic over the first address he's ever made—the very first he's ev-er tackled—when it went off so well."

"Why, silly, I was enthusiastic. I applauded a lot. I thought you were terribly smart. It's just— There's other things I think you can do better. What shall we do tonight; have a cold snack at home or go to the cafeteria?"

Thus was he reduced from hero to husband, and he had all the pleasures of inappreciation.

He thought about his indignities the whole week, but with the coming of winter there was a fever of dully sprightly dinners and safely wild bridge and their first evening at home, their first opportunity for secure and comfortable quarreling, was on Friday. They sat down to what he announced as "getting back to some real reading, like physiology and a little of this fellow Arnold Bennett—nice quiet reading," but which consisted of catching up on the news notes in the medical journals.

He was restless. He threw down his magazine. He demanded:

"What're you going to wear at Pickerbaugh's snow picnic tomorrow?"

"Oh, I haven't— I'll find something."

"Lee, I want to ask you: Why the devil did you say I talked too much at Dr. Strafford's last evening? I know I've got most of the faults going, but I didn't know talking too much was one of 'em."

"It hasn't been, till now."

" 'Till now'!"

"You look here, Sandy Arrowsmith! You've been pouting like a bad brat, all week. What's the matter with you?"

"Well, I— Gosh, it makes me tired! Here everybody is so enthusiastic about my Star of Hope spiel—that note in the *Morning Frontiersman*, and Pickerbaugh says Orchid said it was a corker—and you never so much as peep!"

"Didn't I applaud? But— It's just that I hope you aren't going to keep up this drooling."

"You do, do you! Well, let me tell you I *am* going to keep it up! Not that I'm going to talk a lot of hot air. I gave 'em straight science, last Sunday, and they ate it up. I hadn't realized it isn't necessary to be mushy, to hold an audience. And the amount of good you can do! Why, I got across more Health Instruction and ideas about the value of the lab in that three-quarters of an hour than— I don't care for being a big gun but it's fine to have people where they have to listen to what you've got to say and can't butt in, way they did in Wheatsylvania. You bet I'm going to keep up what you so politely call my damn' fool drooling—"

"Sandy, it may be all right for some people, but not for you. I can't tell you—that's one reason why I haven't said more about your talk—I can't tell you how astonished I am to hear you, who're always sneering at what you call sentimentality, simply weeping over the Dear Little Tots!"

"I never said that—never used the phrase and you know it. And by God! *You* talk about sneering! Just let me tell you that the Public Health Movement, by correcting early faults in children, by looking after their eyes and tonsils and so on, can save millions of lives and make a future generation—"

"I know it! I love children much more than you do! But I mean all this ridiculous simpering—"

"Well, gosh, somebody has to do it. You can't work with people till you educate 'em. There's where old Pick, even if he is an imbecile, does such good work with his poems and all that stuff. Prob'ly be a good thing if I could write 'em—golly, wonder if I couldn't learn to?"

"They're horrible!"

"Now there's a fine consistency for you! The other evening you called 'em 'cute.' "

"I don't have to be consistent. I'm a mere woman. You, Martin Arrowsmith, you'd be the first to tell me so. And for Dr. Pickerbaugh they're all right, but not for you. You belong in a laboratory, finding out things, not advertising them. Do you remember once in Wheatsylvania for five minutes you almost thought of joining a church and being a Respectable Citizen? Are you going on for the rest of your life, stumbling into respectability and having to be dug out again? Will you never learn you're a barbarian?"

"By God, I am! And—what was that other lovely thing you called me?— I'm also, soul of my soul, a damn' backwoods hick! And a fine lot you help! When I want to settle down to a decent and useful life and not go 'round antagonizing people, you, the one that ought to believe in me, you're the first one to crab!"

"Maybe Orchid Pickerbaugh would help you better."

"She probably would! Believe me, she's a darling, and she did appreciate my spiel at the church, and if you think I'm going to sit up all night listening to you sneering at my work and my friends— I'm going to have a hot bath. Good *night!*"

In the bath he gasped that it was impossible he should have been quarreling with Leora. Why! She was the only person in the world, besides Gottlieb and Sondelius and Clif Clawson—by the way, where was Clif? still in New York? didn't Clif owe him a letter? but anyway— He was a fool to have lost his temper, even if she was so stubborn that she wouldn't adjust her opinions, couldn't see that he had a gift for influencing people. Nobody would ever stand by him as she had, and he loved her—

He dried himself violently; he dashed in with repentances; they told each other that they were the most reasonable persons living; they kissed with eloquence; and then Leora reflected:

"Just the same, my lad, I'm not going to help you fool yourself. You're not a booster. You're a lie-hunter. Funny, you'd think to hear about these lie-hunters, like Professor Gottlieb and your old Voltaire, they couldn't be fooled. But maybe they were like you: always trying to get away from the tiresome truth, always hoping to settle down and be rich, always selling their souls to the devil and then going and doublecrossing the poor devil. I think— I think—" She sat up in bed, holding her temples in the labor of articulation.

"You're different from Professor Gottlieb. He never makes mistakes or wastes time on—"

"He wasted time at Hunziker's nostrum factory all right, and his title is 'Doctor,' not 'Professor,' if you *must* give him a—"

"If he went to Hunziker's he had some good reason. He's a genius; he couldn't be wrong. Or could he, even he? But *anyway*: you, Sandy, you have to stumble every so often; have to learn by making mistakes. I will say one thing: you learn from your crazy mistakes. But I get a little tired, sometimes, watching you rush up and put your neck in every noose—like being a blinking orator or yearning over your Orchid."

"Well, by golly! After I come in here trying to make peace! It's a good thing *you* never make any mistakes! But one perfect person in a household is enough!"

He banged into bed. Silence. Soft sounds of "Mart—*Sandy!*" He ignored her, proud that he could be hard with her, and so fell asleep. At breakfast, when he was ashamed and eager, she was curt.

"I don't care to discuss it," she said.

In that wry mood they went on Saturday afternoon to the Pickerbaughs' snow picnic.

### IV

Dr. Pickerbaugh owned a small log cabin in a scanty grove of oaks among the hillocks north of Nautilus. A dozen of them drove out in a bob-sled filled with straw and blue woolly robes. The sleigh bells were exciting and the children leaped out to run beside the sled.

The school physician, a bachelor, was attentive to Leora; twice he tucked her in, and that, for Nautilus, was almost compromising. In jealousy Martin turned openly and completely to Orchid.

He grew interested in her not for the sake of disciplining Leora but for her own rosy sweetness. She was wearing a tweed jacket, with a tam, a flamboyant scarf, and the first breeches any girl had dared to display in Nautilus. She patted Martin's knee, and when they rode behind the sled on a perilous toboggan, she held his waist, resolutely.

She was calling him "Dr. Martin" now, and he had come to a warm "Orchid."

At the cabin there was a clamor of disembarkation. Together Martin and Orchid carried in the hamper of food; together they slid down the hillocks on skiis. When their skiis were entangled, they rolled into a drift, and as she clung to him, unafraid and unembarrassed, it seemed to him that in the roughness of tweeds she was but the softer and more wonderful—eyes fearless, cheeks brilliant as she brushed the coating of wet snow from them, flying legs of a slim boy, shoulders adorable in their pretense of sturdy boyishness—

But "I'm a sentimental fool! Leora was right!" he snarled at himself. "I thought you had some originality! And poor little Orchid—she'd be shocked if she knew how sneak-minded you are!"

But poor little Orchid was coaxing, "Come on, Dr. Martin, let's shoot off that high bluff. We're the only ones that have any pep."

"That's because we're the only young ones."

"It's because you're so young. I'm dreadfully old. I just sit and moon when you rave about your epidemics and things."

He saw that, with her infernal school physician, Leora was sliding on a distant slope. It may have been pique and it may have been relief that he was licensed to be alone with Orchid, but he ceased to speak to her as though she were a child and he a person laden with wisdom; ceased to speak to her as though he were looking over his shoulder. They raced to the high bluff. They skied down it and fell; they had one glorious swooping slide, and wrestled in the snow.

They returned to the cabin together, to find the others away. She stripped off her wet sweater and patted her soft blouse. They ferreted out a thermos of hot coffee, and he looked at her as though he was going to kiss her, and she looked back at him as though she did not mind. As they laid out the food they hummed with the intimacy of understanding, and when she trilled, "Now hurry up, lazy one, and put those cups on that horrid old table," it was as one who was content to be with him forever.

They said nothing compromising, they did not hold hands, and as they rode home in the electric snow-flying darkness, though they sat shoulder by shoulder he did not put his arms about her except when the bob-sled slewed on sharp corners. If Martin was exalted with excitement, it was presumably caused by the wholesome exercises of the day. Nothing happened and nobody looked uneasy. At parting all their farewells were cheery and helpful.

And Leora made no comments, though for a day or two there was about her a chill air which the busy Martin did not investigate.

# 21

Nautilus was one of the first communities in the country to develop the Weeks habit, now so richly grown that we have Correspondence School Week, Christian Science Week, Osteopathy Week, and Georgia Pine Week.

A Week is not merely a week.

If an aggressive, wide-awake, live-wire, and go-ahead church or chamber of commerce or charity desires to improve itself, which means to get more money, it calls in those few energetic spirits who run any city, and proclaims a Week. This consists of one month of committee meetings, a hundred columns of praise for the organization in the public prints, and finally a day or two on which athletic persons flatter inappreciative audiences in churches or cinema theaters, and the prettiest girls in town have the pleasure of being allowed to talk to male strangers on the street corners, apropos of giving them extremely undecorative tags in exchange for the smallest sums which those strangers think they must pay if they are to be considered gentlemen.

The only variation is the Weeks in which the object is not to acquire money immediately by the sale of tags but by general advertising to get more of it later.

Nautilus had held a Pep Week, during which a race of rapidly talking men, formerly book-agents but now called Efficiency Engineers, went about giving advice to shopkeepers on how to get money away from one another more rapidly, and Dr. Almus Pickerbaugh addressed a prayer-meeting on "The Pep of St. Paul, the First Booster." It had held a Gladhand Week, when everybody was supposed to speak to at least three strangers daily, to the end that infuriated elderly traveling salesmen were back-slapped all day long by hearty and powerful unknown persons. There had also been an Old Home Week, a Write to Mother Week, a We Want Your Factory in Nautilus Week, an Eat More Corn Week, a Go to Church Week, a Salvation Army Week, and an Own Your Own Auto Week.

Perhaps the bonniest of all was Y. Week, to raise eighty thousand dollars for a new Y.M.C.A. building.

On the old building were electric signs, changed daily, announcing "You Must Come Across," "Young Man Come Along" and "Your Money Creates 'Appiness." Dr. Pickerbaugh made nineteen addresses in three days, comparing the Y.M.C.A. to the Crusaders, the Apostles, and the expeditions of Dr. Cook—who, he believed, really had discovered the North Pole. Orchid sold three hundred and nineteen Y. tags, seven of them to the same man, who afterward made improper remarks to her. She was rescued by a Y.M.C.A. secretary, who for a considerable time held her hand to calm her.

No organization could rival Almus Pickerbaugh in the invention of Weeks.

He started in January with a Better Babies Week, and a very good Week it was, but so hotly followed by Banish the Booze Week, Tougher Teeth Week, and Stop the Spitter Week that people who lacked his vigor were heard groaning, "My health is being ruined by all this fretting over health."

During Clean-up Week, Pickerbaugh spread abroad a new lyric of his own composition:

> Germs come by stealth
> And ruin health,
> So listen, pard,
> Just drop a card
> To some man who'll clean up your yard
> And that will hit the old germs hard.

Swat the Fly Week brought him, besides the joy of giving prizes to the children who had slaughtered the most flies, the inspiration for two verses. Posters admonished:

> Sell your hammer and buy a horn,
> But hang onto the old fly-swatter.
> If you don't want disease sneaking into the Home
> Then to kill the fly you gotter!

It chanced that the Fraternal Order of Eagles were holding a state convention at Burlington that week, and Pickerbaugh telegraphed to them:

> Just mention fly-prevention
> At the good old Eagles' convention.

This was quoted in ninety-six newspapers, including one in Alaska, and waving the clippings Pickerbaugh explained to Martin, "Now you see the way a fellow can get the truth across, if he goes at it right."

Three Cigars a Day Week, which Pickerbaugh invented in midsummer, was not altogether successful, partly because an injudicious humorist on a local newspaper wanted to know whether Dr. Pickerbaugh really expected all babes in arms to smoke as many as three cigars a day, and partly because the cigar-manufacturers came around to the Department of Health with strong remarks about Common Sense. Nor was there thorough satisfaction in Can the Cat and Doctor the Dog Week.

With all his Weeks, Pickerbaugh had time to preside over the Program Committee of the State Convention of Health Officers and Agencies.

It was he who wrote the circular letter sent to all members:

Brother Males and Shemales:

Are you coming to the Health Bee? It will be the livest Hop-to-it that this busy lil ole planet has ever see. And it's going to be Practical. We'll kiss out on all these glittering generalities and get messages from men as kin talk, so we can lug a think or two (2) home wid us.

Luther Botts, the famous community-sing leader, will be there to put Wim an Wigor neverything into the program. John F. Zeisser, M.A., M.D., nall the rest of the alphabet (part your hair Jack and look cute, the ladies sure love you) will unlimber a coupla key-notes. (On your tootsies, fellers, thar she blows!) From time to time, if the brakes hold, we will, or shall in the infinitive, hie oursellufs from wherein we are at to thither, and grab a lunch with Wild Wittles.

Do it sound like a good show? It do! Barber, you're next. Let's have those cards saying you're coming.

This created much enthusiasm and merriment. Dr. Feesons of Clinton wrote to Pickerbaugh:

I figure it was largely due to your snappy come-on letter that we pulled such an attendance and with all modesty I think we may say it was the best health convention ever held in the world. I had to laugh at one old hen, Bostonian or somepun, who was howling that your letter was "undignified"! Can you beat it! I think people as hypercritical and

lacking in humor as her should be treated with the dignified contempt
they deserve, the damn fool!

## II

Martin was enthusiastic during Better Babies Week. Leora and he weighed
babies, examined them, made out diet charts, and in each child saw the
baby they could never have. But when it came to More Babies Week, then
he was argumentative. He believed, he said, in birth-control. Pickerbaugh
answered with theology, violence, and the example of his own eight beauties.

Martin was equally unconvinced by Anti-Tuberculosis Week. He liked his
windows open at night and he disliked men who spat tobacco juice on sidewalks, but he was jarred by hearing these certainly esthetic and possibly
hygienic reforms proposed with holy frenzy and bogus statistics.

Any questioning of his fluent figures about tuberculosis, any hint that the
cause of decline in the disease may have been natural growth of immunity
and not the crusades against spitting and stale air, Pickerbaugh regarded as
a criticism of his honesty in making such crusades. He had the personal
touchiness of most propagandists; he believed that because he was sincere,
therefore his opinions must always be correct. To demand that he be accurate in his statements, to quote Raymond Pearl's dictum: "As a matter
of objective scientific fact, extremely little is known about why the mortality
from tuberculosis has declined"—this was to be a scoundrel who really liked
to befoul the pavements.

Martin was so alienated that he took an anti-social and probably vicious
joy in discovering that though the death-rate in tuberculosis certainly had
decreased during Pickerbaugh's administration in Nautilus, it had decreased
at the same rate in most villages of the district, with no speeches about
spitting, no Open Your Windows parades.

It was fortunate for Martin that Pickerbaugh did not expect him to take
much share in his publicity campaigns but rather to be his substitute in the
office during them. They stirred in Martin the most furious and complicated
thoughts that had ever afflicted him.

Whenever he hinted criticism, Pickerbaugh answered, "What if my statistics aren't always exact? What if my advertising, my jollying of the public,
does strike some folks as vulgar? It all does good; it's all on the right side.
No matter what methods we use, if we can get people to have more fresh
air and cleaner yards and less alcohol, we're justified."

To himself, a little surprised, Martin put it, "Yes, does it really matter?
Does truth matter—clean, cold, unfriendly truth, Max Gottlieb's truth?
Everybody says, 'Oh, you mustn't tamper with the truth,' and everybody
is furious if you hint that they themselves are tampering with it. Does anything matter, except making love and sleeping and eating and being flattered?

"I think truth does matter to me, but if it does, isn't the desire for scientific precision simply my hobby, like another man's excitement about his
golf? Anyway, I'm going to stick by Pickerbaugh."

To the defense of his chief he was the more impelled by the attitude of Irving Watters and such other physicians as attacked Pickerbaugh because they feared that he really would be successful, and reduce their earnings. But all the while Martin was weary of unchecked statistics.

He estimated that according to Pickerbaugh's figures on bad teeth, careless motoring, tuberculosis, and seven other afflictions alone, every person in the city had a one hundred and eighty per cent chance of dying before the age of sixteen, and he could not startle with much alarm when Pickerbaugh shouted, "Do you realize that the number of people who died from yaws in Pickens County, Mississippi, last year alone, was twenty-nine and that they might all have been saved, yes, sir, *saved*, by a daily cold shower?"

For Pickerbaugh had the dreadful habit of cold showers, even in winter, though he might have known that nineteen men between the ages of seventeen and forty-two died of cold showers in twenty-two years in Milwaukee alone.

To Pickerbaugh the existence of "variables," a word which Martin now used as irritatingly as once he had used "control," was without significance. That health might be determined by temperature, heredity, profession, soil, natural immunity, or by anything save health-department campaigns for increased washing and morality, was to him inconceivable.

"Variables! Huh!" Pickerbaugh snorted. "Why, every enlightened man in the public service *knows* enough about the causes of disease—matter now of acting on that knowledge."

When Martin sought to show that they certainly knew very little about the superiority of fresh air to warmth in schools, about the hygienic dangers of dirty streets, about the real danger of alcohol, about the value of face-masks in influenza epidemics, about most of the things they tub-thumped in their campaigns, Pickerbaugh merely became angry, and Martin wanted to resign, and saw Irving Watters again, and returned to Pickerbaugh with new zeal, and was in general as agitated and wretched as a young revolutionist discovering the smugness of his leaders.

He came to question what Pickerbaugh called "the proven practical value" of his campaigns as much as the accuracy of Pickerbaugh's biology. He noted how bored were most of the newspapermen by being galvanized into a new saving of the world once a fortnight, and how incomparably bored was the Man in the Street when the nineteenth pretty girl in twenty days had surged up demanding that he buy a tag to support an association of which he had never heard.

But more dismaying was the slimy trail of the dollar which he beheld in Pickerbaugh's most ardent eloquence.

When Martin suggested that all milk should be pasteurized, that certain tenements known to be tuberculosis-breeders should be burnt down instead of being fumigated in a fiddling useless way, when he hinted that these attacks would save more lives than ten thousand sermons and ten years of parades by little girls carrying banners and being soaked by the rain, then Pickerbaugh worried, "No, no, Martin, don't think we could do that. Get so much opposition from the dairymen and the landlords. Can't accomplish anything in this work unless you keep from offending people."

When Pickerbaugh addressed a church or the home circle he spoke of "the value of health in making life more joyful," but when he addressed a business luncheon he changed it to "the value in good round dollars and cents of having workmen who are healthy and sober, and therefore able to work faster at the same wages." Parents' associations he enlightened upon "the saving in doctors' bills of treating the child before maladjustments go too far," but to physicians he gave assurance that public health agitation would merely make the custom of going regularly to doctors more popular.

To Martin, he spoke of Pasteur, George Washington, Victor Vaughan, and Edison as his masters, but in asking the business men of Nautilus—the Rotary Club, the Chamber of Commerce, the association of wholesalers—for their divine approval of more funds for his department, he made it clear that they were his masters and lords of all the land, and fatly, behind cigars, they accepted their kinghood.

Gradually Martin's contemplation moved beyond Almus Pickerbaugh to all leaders, of armies or empires, of universities or churches, and he saw that most of them were Pickerbaughs. He preached to himself, as Max Gottlieb had once preached to him, the loyalty of dissent, the faith of being very doubtful, the gospel of not bawling gospels, the wisdom of admitting the probable ignorance of one's self and of everybody else, and the energetic acceleration of a Movement for going very slow.

III

A hundred interruptions took Martin out of his laboratory. He was summoned into the reception-room of the department to explain to angry citizens why the garage next door to them should smell of gasoline; he went back to his cubbyhole to dictate letters to school-principals about dental clinics; he drove out to Swede Hollow to see what attention the food and dairy inspector had given to the slaughter-houses; he ordered a family in Shantytown quarantined; and escaped at last into the laboratory.

It was well lighted, convenient, well stocked. Martin had little time for anything but cultures, blood-tests, and Wassermanns for the private physicians of the city, but the work rested him, and now and then he struggled over a precipitation test which was going to replace Wassermanns and make him famous.

Pickerbaugh apparently believed that this research would take six weeks; Martin had hoped to do it in two years; and with the present interruptions it would require two hundred, by which time the Pickerbaughs would have eradicated syphilis and made the test useless.

To Martin's duties was added the entertainment of Leora in the strange city of Nautilus.

"Do you manage to keep busy all day?" he encouraged her, and, "Any place you'd like to go this evening?"

She looked at him suspiciously. She was as easily and automatically contented by herself as a pussy cat, and he had never before worried about her amusement.

IV

The Pickerbaugh daughters were always popping into Martin's laboratory. The twins broke test-tubes, and made doll tents out of filter paper. Orchid lettered the special posters for her father's Weeks, and the laboratory, she said, was the quietest place in which to work. While Martin stood at his bench he was conscious of her, humming at a table in the corner. They talked, tremendously, and he listened with fatuous enthusiasm to opinions which, had Leora produced them, he would have greeted with "That's a damn' silly remark!"

He held a clear, claret-red tube of hemolyzed blood up to the light, thinking half of its color and half of Orchid's ankles as she bent over the table, absurdly patient with her paint-brushes, curling her legs in a fantastic knot.

Abruptly he asked her, "Look here, honey. Suppose you—suppose a kid like you were to fall in love with a married man. What d'you think she ought to do? Be nice to him? Or chuck him?"

"Oh, she ought to chuck him. No matter how much she suffered. Even if she liked him terribly. Because even if she liked him, she oughtn't to wrong his wife."

"But suppose the wife never knew, or maybe didn't care?" He had stopped his pretense of working; he was standing before her, arms akimbo, dark eyes demanding.

"Well, if she didn't know— But it isn't that. I believe marriages really and truly are made in Heaven, don't you? Some day Prince Charming will come, the perfect lover—" She was so young, her lips were so young, so very sweet! "—and of course I want to keep myself for him. It would spoil everything if I made light of love before my Hero came."

But her smile was caressing.

He pictured them thrown together in a lonely camp. He saw her parroted moralities forgotten. He went through a change as definite as religious conversion or the coming of insane frenzy in war; the change from shamed reluctance to be unfaithful to his wife, to a determination to take what he could get. He began to resent Leora's demand that she, who had eternally his deepest love, should also demand his every wandering fancy. And she did demand it. She rarely spoke of Orchid, but she could tell (or nervously he thought she could tell) when he had spent an afternoon with the child. Her mute examination of him made him feel illicit. He who had never been unctuous was profuse and hearty as he urged her, "Been home all day? Well, we'll just skip out after dinner and take in a movie. Or shall we call up somebody and go see 'em? Whatever you'd like."

He heard his voice being flowery, and he hated it and knew that Leora was not cajoled. Whenever he drifted into one of his meditations on the superiority of his brand of truth to Pickerbaugh's, he snarled, "You're a fine bird to think about truth, you liar!"

He paid, in fact, an enormous price for looking at Orchid's lips, and no amount of anxiety about the price kept him from looking at them.

In early summer, two months before the outbreak of the Great War in Europe, Leora went to Wheatsylvania for a fortnight with her family. Then she spoke:

"Sandy, I'm not going to ask you any questions when I come back, but I hope you won't look as foolish as you've been looking lately. I don't think that bachelor's button, that ragweed, that lady idiot of yours is worth our quarreling Sandy darling, I do want you to be happy, but unless I up and die on you some day, I'm not going to be hung up like an old cap. I warn you. Now about ice. I've left an order for a hundred pounds a week, and if you want to get your own dinners sometimes—"

When she had gone, nothing immediately happened, though a good deal was always about to happen. Orchid had the flapper's curiosity as to what a man was likely to do, but she was satisfied by exceedingly small thrills.

Martin swore, that morning of June, that she was a fool and a flirt, and he "hadn't the slightest intention of going near her." No! He would call on Irving Watters in the evening, or read, or have a walk with the school-clinic dentist.

But at half-past eight he was loitering toward her house.

If the elder Pickerbaughs were there— Martin could hear himself saying, "Thought I'd just drop by, Doctor, and ask you what you thought about—" Hang it! Thought about what? Pickerbaugh never thought about anything.

On the low front steps he could see Orchid. Leaning over her was a boy of twenty, one Charley, a clerk.

"Hello, Father in?" he cried, with a carelessness on which he could but pride himself.

"I'm terribly sorry; he and Mama won't be back till eleven. Won't you sit down and cool off a little?"

"Well—" He did sit down, firmly, and tried to make youthful conversation, while Charley produced sentiments suitable, in Charley's opinion, to the aged Dr. Arrowsmith, and Orchid made little purry interested sounds, an art in which she was very intelligent.

"Been, uh, been seeing many of the baseball games?" said Martin.

"Oh, been getting in all I can," said Charley. "How's things going at City Hall? Been nailing a lot of cases of small-pox and winkulus pinkulus and all those fancy diseases?"

"Oh, keep busy," grunted old Dr. Arrowsmith.

He could think of nothing else. He listened while Charley and Orchid giggled cryptically about things which barred him out and made him feel a hundred years old: references to Mamie and Earl, and a violent "Yeh, that's all right, but any time you see me dancing with her you just tell me about it, will yuh!" At the corner, Verbena Pickerbaugh was yelping, and observing, "Now you quit!" to persons unknown.

"Hell! It isn't worth it! I'm going home," Martin sighed, but at the moment Charley screamed, "Well, ta, ta, be good; gotta toddle along."

He was left to Orchid and peace and a silence rather embarrassing.

"It's so nice to be with somebody that has brains and doesn't always try to flirt, like Charley," said Orchid.

He considered, "Splendid! She's going to be just a nice good girl. And I've come to my senses. We'll just have a little chat and I'll go home."

She seemed to have moved nearer. She whispered at him, "I was so lonely, especially with that horrid slangy boy, till I heard your step on the walk. I knew it the second I heard it."

He patted her hand. As his pats were becoming more ardent than might have been expected from the assistant and friend of her father, she withdrew her hand, clasped her knees, and began to chatter.

Always it had been so in the evenings when he had drifted to the porch and found her alone. She was ten times more incalculable than the most complex woman. He managed to feel guilty toward Leora without any of the reputed joys of being guilty.

While she talked he tried to discover whether she had any brains whatever. Apparently she did not have enough to attend a small Midwestern denominational college. Verbena was going to college this autumn, but Orchid, she explained, thought she "ought to stay home and help Mama take care of the chickabiddies."

"Meaning," Martin reflected, "that she can't even pass the Mugford entrance exams!" But his opinion of her intelligence was suddenly enlarged as she whimpered, "Poor little me, prob'ly I'll always stay here in Nautilus, while you—oh, with your knowledge and your frightfully strong will-power, I know you're going to conquer the world!"

"Nonsense, I'll never conquer any world, but I do hope to pull off a few good health measures. Honestly, Orchid honey, do you think I have much will-power?"

The full moon was spacious now behind the maples. The seedy Pickerbaugh domain was enchanted; the tangled grass was a garden of roses, the ragged grape-arbor a shrine to Diana, the old hammock turned to fringed cloth of silver, the bad-tempered and sputtering lawn-sprinkler a fountain, and over all the world was the proper witchery of moonstruck love. The little city, by day as noisy and busy as a pack of children, was stilled and forgotten. Rarely had Martin been inspired to perceive the magic of a perfect hour, so absorbed was he ever in irascible pondering, but now he was caught, and lifted in rapture.

He held Orchid's quiet hand—and was lonely for Leora.

The belligerent Martin who had carried off Leora had not thought about romance, because in his clumsy way he had been romantic. The Martin who, like a returned warrior scented and enfeebled, yearned toward a girl in the moonlight, now desirously lifted his face to romance and was altogether unromantic.

He felt the duty of making love. He drew her close, but when she sighed,

"Oh, please don't," there was in him no ruthlessness and no conviction with which to go on. He considered the moonlight again, but also he considered being at the office early in the morning, and he wondered if he could without detection slip out his watch and see what time it was. He managed it. He stooped to kiss her good-night, and somehow didn't quite kiss her, and found himself walking home.

As he went, he was ruthless and convinced enough regarding himself. He had never, he raged, however stumbling he might have been, expected to find himself a little pilferer of love, a peeping, creeping area-sneak, and not even successful in his sneaking, less successful than the soda-clerks who swanked nightly with the virgins under the maples. He told himself that Orchid was a young woman of no great wisdom, a sigher and drawer-out of her M's and O's, but once he was in his lonely flat he longed for her, thought of miraculous and completely idiotic ways of luring her here tonight, and went to bed yearning, "Oh, Orchid—"

Perhaps he had paid too much attention to moonlight and soft summer, for quite suddenly, one day when Orchid came swarming all over the laboratory and perched on the bench with a whisk of stockings, he stalked to her, masterfully seized her wrists, and kissed her as she deserved to be kissed.

He immediately ceased to be masterful. He was frightened. He stared at her wanly. She stared back, shocked, eyes wide, lips uncertain.

"Oh!" she profoundly said.

Then, in a tone of immense interest and some satisfaction:

"Martin—oh—my dear—do you think you ought to have done that?"

He kissed her again. She yielded and for a moment there was nothing in the universe, neither he nor she, neither laboratory nor fathers nor wives nor traditions, but only the intensity of their being together.

Suddenly she babbled, "I know there's lots of conventional people that would say we'd done wrong, and perhaps I'd have thought so, one time, but— Oh, I'm terribly glad I'm liberal! Of course I wouldn't hurt dear Leora or do anything *really* wrong for the world, but isn't it wonderful that with so many bourgeois folks all around, we can rise above them and realize the call that strength makes to strength and— But I've simply *got* to be at the Y.W.C.A. meeting. There's a woman lawyer from New York that's going to tell us about the Modern Woman's Career."

When she had gone Martin viewed himself as a successful lover. "I've won her," he gloated. . . . Probably never has gloating been so shakily and badly done.

That evening, when he was playing poker in his flat with Irving Watters, the school-clinic dentist, and a young doctor from the city clinic, the telephone bell summoned him to an excited but saccharine:

"This is Orchid. Are you glad I called up?"

"Oh, yes, yes, mighty glad you called up." He tried to make it at once amorously joyful, and impersonal enough to beguile the three coatless, beer-swizzling, grinning doctors.

"Are you doing anything this evening, Marty?"

"Just, uh, couple fellows here for a little game cards."

"Oh!" It was acute. "Oh, then you— I was such a baby to call you up, but Daddy is away and Verbena and everybody, and it was such a lovely evening, and I just thought— *Do* you think I'm an awful little silly?"

"No—no—sure not."

"I'm so glad you don't. I'd hate it if I thought you thought I was just a silly to call you up. You don't, do you?"

"No—no—course not. Look, I've got to—"

"I know. I mustn't keep you. But I just wanted you to tell me whether you thought I was a silly to—"

"No! Honest! Really!"

Three fidgety minutes later, deplorably aware of masculine snickers from behind him, he escaped. The poker-players said all the things considered suitable in Nautilus: "Oh, you little Don Jewen!" and "Can you beat it—his wife only gone for a week!" and "Who is she, Doctor? Go on, you tightwad, bring her up here!" and "Say, I know who it is; it's that little milliner on Prairie Avenue."

Next noon she telephoned from a drug store that she had lain awake all night, and on profound contemplation decided that they "mustn't ever do that sort of thing again"—and would he meet her at the corner of Crimmins Street and Missouri Avenue at eight, so that they might talk it all over?

In the afternoon she telephoned and changed the tryst to half-past eight.

At five she called him up just to remind him—

In the laboratory that day Martin transplanted cultures no more. He was too confusedly human to be a satisfactory experimenter, too coldly thinking to be a satisfactory sinful male, and all the while he longed for the sure solace of Leora.

"I can go as far as I like with her tonight.

"But she's a brainless man-chaser.

"All the better. I'm tired of being a punk philosopher.

"I wonder if these other lucky lovers that you read about in all this fiction and poetry feel as glum as I do?

"I will *not* be middle-aged and cautious and monogamic and moral! It's against my religion. I demand the right to be free—

"Hell! These free souls that have to slave at being free are just as bad as their Methodist dads. I have enough sound natural immorality in me so I can afford to be moral. I want to keep my brain clear for work. I won't want it blurred by dutifully running around trying to kiss everybody I can.

"Orchid is too easy. I hate to give up the right of being a happy sinner, but my way was so straight, with just Leora and my work, and I'm not going to mess it. God help any man that likes his work and his wife! He's beaten from the beginning."

He met Orchid at eight-thirty, and the whole matter was unkind. He was equally distasteful of the gallant Martin of two days ago and the prosy cautious Martin of tonight. He went home desolately ascetic, and longed for Orchid all the night.

A week later Leora returned from Wheatsylvania.

He met her at the station.

"It's all right," he said. "I feel a hundred and seven years old. I'm a respectable, moral young man, and Lord how I'd hate it, if it wasn't for my precipitation test and you and— *Why* do you always lose your trunk check? I suppose I am a bad example for others, giving up so easily. No, no, darling, can't you *see*; that's the transportation check the conductor gave you!"

# 22

This summer Pickerbaugh had shouted and hand-shaken his way through a brief Chautauqua tour in Iowa, Nebraska, and Kansas. Martin realized that though he seemed, in contrast to Gustaf Sondelius, an unfortunately articulate and generous lout, he was destined to be ten times better known in America than Sondelius could ever be, a thousand times better known than Max Gottlieb.

He was a correspondent of many of the nickel-plated Great Men whose pictures and sonorous aphorisms appeared in the magazines: the advertising men who wrote little books about Pep and Optimism, the editor of the magazine which told clerks how to become Goethes and Stonewall Jacksons by studying correspondence-courses and never touching the manhood-rotting beer, and the cornfield sage who was equally an authority on finance, peace, biology, editing, Peruvian ethnology, and making oratory pay. These intellectual rulers recognized Pickerbaugh as one of them; they wrote quippish letters to him: and when he answered he signed himself "Pick," in red pencil.

The *Onward March Magazine*, which specialized in biographies of Men Who Have Made Good, had an account of Pickerbaugh among its sketches of the pastor who built his own beautiful Neo-Gothic church out of tin cans, the lady who had in seven years kept 2,698 factory-girls from leading lives of shame, and the Oregon cobbler who had taught himself to read Sanskrit, Finnish, and Esperanto.

"Meet Ol' Doc Almus Pickerbaugh, a he-man whom Chum Frink has hailed as 'the two-fisted, fighting poet doc,' a scientist who puts his remarkable discoveries right over third base, yet who, as a reg'lar old-fashioned Sunday-school superintendent, rebukes the atheistic so-called scientists that are menacing the foundations of our religion and liberties by their smart-aleck cracks at everything that is noble and improving," chanted the chronicler.

Martin was reading this article, trying to realize that it was actually exposed in a fabulous New York magazine, with a million circulation, when Pickerbaugh summoned him.

"Mart," he said, "do you feel competent to run this Department?"

"Why, uh—"

"Do you think you can buck the Interests and keep a clean city all by yourself?"

"Why, uh—"

"Because it looks as if I were going to Washington, as the next congressman from this district!"

"Really?"

"Looks that way. Boy, I'm going to take to the whole nation the Message I've tried to ram home here!"

Martin got out quite a good "I congratulate you." He was so astonished that it sounded fervent. He still had a fragment of his boyhood belief that congressmen were persons of intelligence and importance.

"I've just been in conference with some of the leading Republicans of the district. Great surprise to me. Ha, ha, ha! Maybe they picked me because they haven't anybody else to run this year. Ha, ha, ha!"

Martin also laughed. Pickerbaugh looked as though that was not exactly the right response, but he recovered and caroled on:

"I said to them, 'Gentlemen, I must warn you that I am not sure I possess the rare qualifications needful in a man who shall have the high privilege of laying down, at Washington, the rules and regulations for the guidance, in every walk of life, of this great nation of a hundred million people. However, gentlemen,' I said, 'the impulse that prompts me to consider, in all modesty, your unexpected and probably undeserved honor is the fact that it seems to me that what Congress needs is more forward-looking scientists to plan and more genu-ine trained business men to execute the improvements demanded by our evolving commonwealth, and also the possibility of persuading the Boys there at Washington of the pre-eminent and crying need of a Secretary of Health who shall completely control—'"

But no matter what Martin thought about it, the Republicans really did nominate Pickerbaugh for Congress.

## II

While Pickerbaugh went out campaigning, Martin was in charge of the Department, and he began his reign by getting himself denounced as a tyrant and a radical.

There was no more sanitary and efficient dairy in Iowa than that of old Klopchuk, on the outskirts of Nautilus. It was tiled and drained and excellently lighted; the milking machines were perfect; the bottles were super-boiled; and Klopchuk welcomed inspectors and the tuberculin test. He had fought the dairymen's union and kept his dairy open-shop by paying more than the union scale. Once, when Martin attended a meeting of the Nautilus Central Labor Council as Pickerbaugh's representative, the secretary of the council confessed that there was no plant which they would so like to unionize and which they were so unlikely to unionize as Klopchuk's Dairy.

Now Martin's labor sympathies were small. Like most laboratory men, he believed that the reason why workmen found less joy in sewing vests or in pulling a lever than he did in a long research was because they were an inferior race, born lazy and wicked. The complaint of the unions was the one thing to convince him that at last he had found perfection.

Often he stopped at Klopchuk's merely for the satisfaction of it. He noted but one thing which disturbed him: a milker had a persistent sore throat. He examined the man, made cultures, and found hemolytic streptococcus. In a panic he hurried back to the dairy, and after cultures he discovered that there was streptococcus in the udders of three cows.

When Pickerbaugh had saved the health of the nation through all the smaller towns in the congressional district and had returned to Nautilus, Martin insisted on the quarantine of the infected milker and the closing of the Klopchuk Dairy till no more infection should be found.

"Nonsense! Why, that's the cleanest place in the city," Pickerbaugh scoffed. "Why borrow trouble? There's no sign of an epidemic of strep."

"There darn' well will be! Three cows infected. Look at what's happened in Boston and Baltimore, here recently. I've asked Klopchuk to come in and talk it over."

"Well, you know how busy I am, but—"

Klopchuk appeared at eleven, and to Klopchuk the affair was tragic. Born in a gutter in Poland, starving in New York, working twenty hours a day in Vermont, in Ohio, in Iowa, he had made this beautiful thing, his dairy.

Seamed, drooping, twirling his hat, almost in tears, he protested, "Dr. Pickerbaugh, I do everything the doctors say is necessary. I know dairies! Now comes this young man and he says because one of my men has a cold, I kill little children with diseased milk! I tell you, this is my life, and I would sooner hang myself than send out one drop of bad milk. The young man has some wicked reason. I have asked questions. I find he is a great friend from the Central Labor Council. Why, he go to their meetings! And they want to break me!"

To Martin the trembling old man was pitiful, but he had never before been accused of treachery. He said grimly:

"You can take up the personal charges against me later, Dr. Pickerbaugh. Meantime I suggest you have in some expert to test my results; say Long of Chicago or Brent of Minneapolis or somebody."

"I—I—I—" The Kipling and Billy Sunday of health looked as distressed as Klopchuk. "I'm sure our friend here doesn't really mean to make charges against you, Mart. He's overwrought, naturally. Can't we just treat the fellow that has the strep infection and not make everybody uncomfortable?"

"All right, if you want a bad epidemic here, toward the end of your campaign!"

"You know cussed well I'd do anything to avoid— Though I want you to distinctly understand it has nothing to do with my campaign for Congress!

It's simply that I owe my city the most scrupulous performance of duty in safeguarding it against disease, and the most fearless enforcement—"

At the end of his oratory Pickerbaugh telegraphed to Dr. J. C. Long, the Chicago bacteriologist.

Dr. Long looked as though he had made the train journey in an ice-box. Martin had never seen a man so free from the poetry and flowing philanthropy of Almus Pickerbaugh. He was slim, precise, lipless, lapless, and eye-glassed, and his hair was parted in the middle. He coolly listened to Martin, coldly listened to Pickerbaugh, icily heard Klopchuk, made his inspection, and reported, "Dr. Arrowsmith seems to know his business perfectly, there is certainly a danger here, I advise closing the dairy, my fee is one hundred dollars, thank you no I shall not stay to dinner I must catch the evening train."

Martin went home to Leora snarling, "That man was just as lovable as a cucumber salad, but my God, Lee, with his freedom from bunk he's made me wild to get back to research; away from all these humanitarians that are so busy hollering about loving the dear people that they let the people die! I hated him, but— Wonder what Max Gottlieb's doing this evening? The old German crank! I'll bet—I'll bet he's talking music or something with some terrible highbrow bunch. Wouldn't you like to see the old coot again? You know, just couple minutes. D'I ever tell you about the time I made the dandy stain of the trypanosomes— Oh, did I?"

He assumed that with the temporary closing of the dairy the matter was ended. He did not understand how hurt was Klopchuk. He knew that Irving Watters, Klopchuk's physician, was unpleasant when they met, grumbling, "What's the use going on being an alarmist, Mart?" But he did not know how many persons in Nautilus had been trustily informed that this fellow Arrowsmith was in the pay of labor-union thugs.

### III

Two months before, when Martin had been making his annual inspection of factories, he had encountered Clay Tredgold, the president (by inheritance) of the Steel Windmill Company. He had heard that Tredgold, an elaborate but easy-spoken man of forty-five, moved as one clad in purple on the loftiest planes of Nautilus society. After the inspection Tredgold urged, "Sit down, Doctor; have a cigar and tell me all about sanitation."

Martin was wary. There was in Tredgold's affable eye a sardonic flicker. "What d'you want to know about sanitation?"

"Oh, all about it."

"The only thing I know is that your men must like you. Of course you haven't enough wash-bowls in that second-floor toilet room, and the whole lot of 'em swore you were putting in others immediately. If they like you enough to lie against their own interests, you must be a good boss, and I think I'll let you get away with it—till my next inspection! Well, got to hustle."

Tredgold beamed on him. "My dear man, I've been pulling that dodge on Pickerbaugh for three years. I'm glad to have seen you. And I think I really may put in some more bowls—just before your next inspection. Good-by!"

After the Klopchuk affair, Martin and Leora encountered Clay Tredgold and that gorgeous slim woman, his wife, in front of a motion-picture theater.

"Give you a lift, Doctor?" cried Tredgold.

On the way he suggested, "I don't know whether you're dry, like Pickerbaugh, but if you'd like I'll run you out to the house and present you with the noblest cocktail conceived since Evangeline County went dry. Does it sound reasonable?"

"I haven't heard anything so reasonable for years," said Martin.

The Tredgold house was on the highest knoll (fully twenty feet above the general level of the plain) in Ashford Grove, which is the Back Bay of Nautilus. It was a Colonial structure, with a sun-parlor, a white-paneled hall, and a blue and silver drawing-room. Martin tried to look casual as they were wafted in on Mrs. Tredgold's chatter, but it was the handsomest house he had ever entered.

While Leora sat on the edge of her chair in the manner one likely to be sent home, and Mrs. Tredgold sat forward like a hostess, Tredgold flourished the cocktail-shaker and performed courtesies:

"How long you been here now, Doctor?"

"Almost a year."

"Try that. Look here, it strikes me you're kind of different from Salvation Pickerbaugh."

Martin felt that he ought to praise his chief but, to Leora's gratified amazement, he sprang up and ranted in something like Pickerbaugh's best manner:

"Gentlemen of the Steel Windmill Industries, than which there is no other that has so largely contributed to the prosperity of our commonwealth, while I realize that you are getting away with every infraction of the health laws that the inspector doesn't catch you at, yet I desire to pay a tribute to your high respect for sanitation, patriotism, and cocktails, and if I only had an assistant more earnest than young Arrowsmith, I should, with your permission, become President of the United States."

Tredgold clapped. Mrs. Tredgold asserted, "If that isn't exactly like Dr. Pickerbaugh!" Leora looked proud, and so did her husband.

"I'm glad you're free from this socialistic clap-trap of Pickerbaugh's," said Tredgold.

The assumption roused something sturdy and defensive in Martin:

"Oh, I don't care a hang how socialistic he is—whatever that means. Don't know anything about socialism. But since I've gone and given an imitation of him—I suppose it was probably disloyal—I must say I'm not very fond of oratory that's so full of energy it hasn't any room for facts. But mind you, Tredgold, it's partly the fault of people like your Manufacturers' Association.

You encourage him to rant. I'm a laboratory man—or rather, I sometimes wish I were. I like to deal with exact figures."

"So do I. I was keen on mathematics in Williams," said Tredgold.

Instantly Martin and he were off on education, damning the universities for turning out graduates like sausages. Martin found himself becoming confidential about "variables," and Tredgold proclaimed that he had not wanted to take up the ancestral factory, but to specialize in astronomy.

Leora was confessing to the friendly Mrs. Tredgold how cautiously the wife of an assistant director has to economize and with that caressing voice of hers Mrs. Tredgold comforted, "I know. I was horribly hard-up after Dad died. Have you tried the little Swedish dressmaker on Crimmins Street, two doors from the Catholic church? She's awfully clever, and so cheap."

Martin had found, for the first time since marriage, a house in which he was altogether happy; Leora had found, in a woman with the easy smartness which she had always feared and hated, the first woman to whom she could talk of God and the price of toweling. They came out from themselves and were not laughed at.

It was at midnight, when the charms of bacteriology and toweling were becoming pallid, that outside the house sounded a whooping, wheezing motor horn, and in lumbered a ruddy fat man who was introduced as Mr. Schlemihl, president of the Cornbelt Insurance Company of Nautilus.

Even more than Clay Tredgold was he a leader of the Ashford Grove aristocracy, but, while he stood like an invading barbarian in the blue and silver room, Schlemihl was cordial:

"Glad meet yuh, Doctor. Well, say, Clay, I'm tickled to death you've found another highbrow to gas with. Me, Arrowsmith, I'm simply a poor old insurance salesman. Clay is always telling me what an illiterate boob I am. Look here, Clay darling, do I get a cocktail or don't I? I seen your lights! I seen you in here telling what a smart guy you are! Come on! *Mix!*"

Tredgold mixed, extensively. Before he had finished, young Monte Mugford, great-grandson of the sainted but side-whiskered Nathaniel Mugford who had founded Mugford College, also came in, uninvited. He wondered at the presence of Martin, found him human, told him he was human, and did his rather competent best to catch up on the cocktails.

Thus it happened that at three in the morning Martin was singing to a commendatory audience the ballad he had learned from Gustaf Sondelius:

> She'd a dark and a roving eye,
> And her hair hung down in ringlets,
> A nice girl, a decent girl,
> But one of the rakish kind.

At four, the Arrowsmiths had been accepted by the most desperately Smart Set of Nautilus, and at four-thirty they were driven home, at a speed neither legal nor kind, by Clay Tredgold.

IV

There was in Nautilus a country club which was the axis of what they called Society, but there was also a tribe of perhaps twelve families in the Ashford Grove section who, though they went to the country club for golf, condescended to other golfers, kept to themselves, and considered themselves as belonging more to Chicago than to Nautilus. They took turns in entertaining one another. They assumed that they were all welcome at any party given by any'of them, and to none of their parties was anyone outside the Group invited except migrants from larger cities and occasional free lances like Martin. They were a tight little garrison in a heathen town.

The members of the Group were very rich, and one of them, Montgomery Mugford, knew something about his great-grandfather. They lived in Tudor manor houses and Italian villas so new that the scarred lawns had only begun to grow. They had large cars and larger cellars, though the cellars contained nothing but gin, whisky, vermouth, and a few sacred bottles of rather sweet champagne. Everyone in the Group was familiar with New York—they stayed at the St. Regis or the Plaza and went about buying clothes and discovering small smart restaurants—and five of the twelve couples had been in Europe; had spent a week in Paris, intending to go to art galleries and actually going to the more expensive fool-traps of Montmartre.

In the Group Martin and Leora found themselves welcomed as poor relations. They were invited to choric dinners, to Sunday lunches at the country club. Whatever the event, it always ended in rapidly motoring somewhere, having a number of drinks, and insisting that Martin again "give that imitation of Doc Pickerbaugh."

Besides motoring, drinking, and dancing to the Victrola, the chief diversion of the Group was cards. Curiously, in this completely unmoral set, there were no flirtations; they talked with considerable freedom about "sex," but they all seemed monogamic, all happily married or afraid to appear unhappily married. But when Martin knew them better he heard murmurs of husbands having "times" in Chicago, of wives picking up young men in New York hotels, and he scented furious restlessness beneath their superior sexual calm.

It is not known whether Martin ever completely accepted as a gentleman-scholar the Clay Tredgold who was devoted to everything about astronomy except studying it, or Monte Mugford as the highly descended aristocrat, but he did admire the Group's motor cars, shower baths, Fifth Avenue frocks, tweed plus-fours, and houses somewhat impersonally decorated by daffodillic young men from Chicago. He discovered sauces and old silver. He began to consider Leora's clothes not merely as convenient coverings, but as a possible expression of charm, and irritably he realized how careless she was.

In Nautilus, alone, rarely saying much about herself, Leora had developed an intense mute little life of her own. She belonged to a bridge club, and she went solemnly by herself to the movies, but her ambition was to know

France and it engrossed her. It was an old desire, mysterious in source and long held secret, but suddenly she was sighing:

"Sandy, the one thing I want to do, maybe ten years from now, is to see Touraine and Normandy and Carcassonne. Could we, do you think?"

Rarely had Leora asked for anything. He was touched and puzzled as he watched her reading books on Brittany, as he caught her, over a highly simplified French grammar, breathing "J'ay—j'aye—damn it, whatever it is!"

He crowed, "Lee, dear, if you want to go to France— Listen! Some day we'll shoot over there with a couple of knapsacks on our backs, and we'll see that ole country from end to end!"

Gratefully yet doubtfully: "You know if you got bored, Sandy, you could go see the work at the Pasteur Institute. Oh, I would like to tramp, just once, between high plastered walls, and come to a foolish little café and watch the men with funny red sashes and floppy blue pants go by. Really, do you think maybe we could?"

Leora was strangely popular in the Ashford Grove Group, though she possessed nothing of what Martin called their "elegance." She always had at least one button missing. Mrs. Tredgold, best natured as she was least pious of women, adopted her complete.

Nautilus had always doubted Clara Tredgold. Mrs. Almus Pickerbaugh said that she "took no part in any movement for the betterment of the city." For years she had seemed content to grow her roses, to make her startling hats, to almond-cream her lovely hands, and listen to her husband's improper stories—and for years she had been a lonely woman. In Leora she perceived an interested casualness equal to her own. The two women spent afternoons sitting on the sun-porch, reading, doing their nails, smoking cigarettes, saying nothing, trusting each other.

With the other women of the Group Leora was never so intimate as with Clara Tredgold, but they liked her, the more because she was a heretic whose vices, her smoking, her indolence, her relish of competent profanity, disturbed Mrs. Pickerbaugh and Mrs. Irving Watters. The Group rather approved all unconventionalities—except such economic unconventionalities as threatened their easy wealth. Leora had tea, or a cocktail, alone with nervous young Mrs. Monte Mugford, who had been the lightest-footed debutante in Des Moines four years before and who hated now the coming of her second baby; and it was to Leora that Mrs. Schlemihl, though publicly she was rompish and serene with her porker of a husband, burst out, "If that man would only quit pawing me—reaching for me—slobbering on me! I hate it here! I *will* have my winter in New York—alone!"

The childish Martin Arrowsmith, so unworthy of Leora's old quiet wisdoms, was not content with her acceptance by the Group. When she appeared with a hook unfastened or her hair like a crow's nest, he worried, and said things about her "sloppiness" which he later regretted.

"Why can't you take a little time to make yourself attractive? God knows you haven't anything else to do! Great Jehoshaphat, can't you even sew on buttons?"

But Clara Tredgold laughed, "Leora, I do think you have the sweetest back, but do you mind if I pin you up before the others come?"

It happened after a party which lasted till two, when Mrs. Schlemihl had worn the new frock from Lucile's and Jack Brundidge (by day vice-president and sales-manager of the Maize Mealies Company) had danced what he belligerently asserted to be a Finnish polka, that when Martin and Leora were driving home in a borrowed Health Department car he snarled, "Lee, why can't you ever take any trouble with what you wear? Here this morning—or yesterday morning—you were going to mend that blue dress, and as far as I can figure out you haven't done a darn' thing the whole day but sit around and read, and then you come out with that ratty embroidery—"

"Will you stop the car!" she cried.

He stopped it, astonished. The headlights made ridiculously important a barbed-wire fence, a litter of milkweeds, a bleak reach of gravel road.

She demanded, "Do you want me to become a harem beauty? I could. I could be a floosey. But I've never taken the trouble. Oh, Sandy, I won't go on fighting with you. Either I'm the foolish sloppy wife that I am, or I'm nothing. What do you want? Do you want a real princess like Clara Tredgold, or do you want me, that don't care a hang where we go or what we do as long as we stand by each other? You do such a lot of worrying. I'm tired of it. Come on now. What do you want?"

"I don't want anything but you. But can't you understand— I'm not just a climber—I want us both to be equal to anything we run into. I certainly don't see why we should be inferior to this bunch, in *anything*. Darling, except for Clara, maybe, they're nothing but rich bookkeepers! But we're real soldiers of fortune. Your France that you love so much—some day we'll go there, and the French President will be at the N.P. depot to meet us! Why should we let anybody do anything better than we can? Technique!"

They talked for an hour in that drab place, between the poisonous lines of barbed wire.

Next day, when Orchid came into his laboratory and begged, with the wistfulness of youth, "Oh, Dr. Martin, aren't you ever coming to the house again?" he kissed her so briskly, so cheerfully, that even a flapper could perceive that she was unimportant.

### v

Martin realized that he was likely to be the next Director of the Department. Pickerbaugh had told him, "Your work is very satisfactory. There's only one thing you lack, my boy: enthusiasm for getting together with folks and giving a long pull and a strong pull, all together. But perhaps that'll come to you when you have more responsibility."

Martin sought to acquire a delight in giving long strong pulls all together, but he felt like a man who has been dragooned into wearing yellow tights at a civic pageant.

"Gosh, I may be up against it when I become Director," he fretted. "I wonder if there's people who become what's called 'successful' and then hate it? Well, anyway, I'll start a decent system of vital statistics in the department before they get me. I won't lay down! I'll fight! I'll make myself succeed!"

# 23

It may have been a yearning to give one concentrated dose of inspiration so powerful that no citizen of Nautilus would ever again dare to be ill, or perhaps Dr. Pickerbaugh desired a little reasonable publicity for his congressional campaign, but certainly the Health Fair which the good man organized was overpowering.

He got an extra appropriation from the Board of Aldermen; he bullied all the churches and associations into co-operation; he made the newspapers promise to publish three columns of praise each day.

He rented the rather dilapidated wooden "tabernacle" in which the Reverend Mr. Billy Sunday, an evangelist, had recently wiped out all the sin in the community. He arranged for a number of novel features. The Boy Scouts were to give daily drills. There was a W.C.T.U. booth at which celebrated clergymen and other physiologists would demonstrate the evils of alcohol. In a bacteriology booth, the protesting Martin (in a dinky white coat) was to do jolly things with test-tubes. An anti-nicotine lady from Chicago offered to kill a mouse every half-hour by injecting ground-up cigarette paper into it. The Pickerbaugh twins, Arbuta and Gladiola, now aged six, were to show the public how to brush its teeth, and in fact they did, until a sixty-year-old farmer of whom they had lovingly inquired, "Do you brush your teeth daily?" made thunderous answer, "No, but I'm going to paddle your bottoms daily, and I'm going to start in right now."

None of these novelties was so stirring as the Eugenic Family, who had volunteered to give, for a mere forty dollars a day, an example of the benefits of healthful practices.

They were father, mother, and five children, all so beautiful and powerful that they had recently been presenting refined acrobatic exhibitions on the Chautauqua Circuit. None of them smoked, drank, spit upon pavements, used foul language, or ate meat. Pickerbaugh assigned to them the chief booth on the platform once sacerdotally occupied by the Reverend Mr. Sunday.

There were routine exhibits: booths with charts and banners and leaflets. The Pickerbaugh Healthette Octette held song recitals, and daily there were lectures, most of them by Pickerbaugh or by his friend Dr. Bissex, football coach and professor of hygiene and most other subjects in Mugford College.

A dozen celebrities, including Gustaf Sondelius and the governor of the state, were invited to come and "give their messages," but it happened, unfortunately, that none of them seemed able to get away that particular week.

The Health Fair opened with crowds and success. There was a slight misunderstanding the first day. The Master Bakers' Association spoke strongly to Pickerbaugh about the sign "Too much pie makes pyorrhea" on the diet booth. But the thoughtless and prosperity-destroying sign was removed at once, and the Fair was thereafter advertised in every bakery in town.

The only unhappy participant, apparently, was Martin. Pickerbaugh had fitted up for him an exhibition laboratory which, except that it had no running water and except that the fire laws forbade his using any kind of a flame, was exactly like a real one. All day long he poured a solution of red ink from one test-tube into another, with his microscope carefully examined nothing at all, and answered the questions of persons who wished to know how you put bacterias to death once you had caught them swimming about.

Leora appeared as his assistant, very pretty and demure in a nurse's costume, very exasperating as she chuckled at his low cursing. They found one friend, the fireman on duty, a splendid person with stories about pet cats in the fire-house and no tendency to ask questions in bacteriology. It was he who showed them how they could smoke in safety. Behind the Clean Up and Prevent Fires exhibit, consisting of a miniature Dirty House with red arrows to show where a fire might start and an extremely varnished Clean House, there was an alcove with a broken window which would carry off the smoke of their cigarettes. To this sanctuary Martin, Leora, and the bored fireman retired a dozen times a day, and thus wore through the week.

One other misfortune occured. The detective sergeant coming in not to detect but to see the charming spectacle of the mouse dying in agony from cigarette paper, stopped before the booth of the Eugenic Family, scratched his head, hastened to the police station, and returned with certain pictures. He growled to Pickerbaugh:

"Hm. That Eugenic Family. Don't smoke or booze or anything?"

"Absolutely! And look at their perfect health."

"Hm. Better keep an eye on 'em. I won't spoil your show, Doc—we fellows at City Hall had all ought to stick together. I won't run 'em out of town till after the Fair. But they're the Holton gang. The man and woman ain't married, and only one of the kids is theirs. They've done time for selling licker to the Indians, but their specialty, before they went into education, used to be the badger game. I'll detail a plain-clothes man to keep 'em straight. Fine show you got here, Doc. Ought to give this city a lasting lesson in the value of up-to-date health methods. Good luck! Say, have you picked your secretary yet, for when you get to Congress? I've got a nephew that's a crackajack stenographer and a bright kid and knows how to keep his mouth shut about stuff that don't concern him. I'll send him around to have a talk with you. So long."

But, except that once he caught the father of the Eugenic Family relieving the strain of being publicly healthy by taking a long, gurgling, ecstatic drink from a flask, Pickerbaugh found nothing wrong in their conduct, till Saturday. There was nothing wrong with anything, till then.

Never had a Fair been such a moral lesson, or secured so much publicity. Every newspaper in the congressional district gave columns to it, and all the accounts, even in the Democractic papers, mentioned Pickerbaugh's campaign.

Then, on Saturday, the last day of the Fair, came tragedy.

There was terrific rain, the roof leaked without restraint, and the lady in charge of the Healthy Housing Booth, which also leaked, was taken home threatened with pneumonia. At noon, when the Eugenic Family were giving a demonstration of perfect vigor, their youngest blossom had an epileptic fit, and before the excitement was over, upon the Chicago anti-nicotine lady as she triumphantly assassinated a mouse charged an anti-vivisection lady, also from Chicago.

Round the two ladies and the unfortunate mouse gathered a crowd. The anti-vivisection lady called the anti-nicotine lady a murderer, a wretch, and an atheist, all of which the anti-nicotine lady endured, merely weeping a little and calling for the police. But when the anti-vivisection lady wound up, "And as for your pretensions to know anything about science, you're no scientist at all!" then with a shriek the anti-nicotine lady leaped from her platform, dug her fingers into the anti-vivisection lady's hair, and observed with distinctness, "I'll show you whether I know anything about science!"

Pickerbaugh tried to separate them. Martin, standing happily with Leora and their friend the fireman on the edge, distinctly did not. Both ladies turned on Pickerbaugh and denounced him, and when they had been removed he was the center of a thousand chuckles, in decided danger of never going to Congress.

At two o'clock, when the rain had slackened, when the after-lunch crowd had come in and the story of the anti ladies was running strong, the fireman retired behind the Clean Up and Prevent Fires exhibit for his hourly smoke. He was a very sleepy and unhappy little fireman; he was thinking about the pleasant fire-house and the unending games of pinochle. He dropped the match, unextinguished, on the back porch of the model Clean House. The Clean House had been so handsomely oiled that it was like kindling soaked in kerosene. It flared up, and instantly the huge and gloomy Tabernacle was hysterical with flames. The crowd rushed toward the exits.

Naturally, most of the original exits of the Tabernacle had been blocked by booths. There was a shrieking panic, and children were being trampled.

Almus Pickerbaugh was neither a coward nor slothful. Suddenly, coming from nowhere, he was marching through the Tabernacle at the head of his eight daughters, singing "Dixie," his head up, his eyes terrible, his arms wide in pleading. The crowd weakly halted. With the voice of a clipper captain he unsnarled them and ushered them safely out, then charged back into the spouting flames.

The rain-soaked building had not caught. The fireman, with Martin and the head of the Eugenic Family, was beating the flames. Nothing was destroyed save the Clean House, and the crowd which had fled in agony came back in wonder. Their hero was Pickerbaugh.

Within two hours the Nautilus papers vomited specials which explained that not merely had Pickerbaugh organized the greatest lesson in health ever seen, but he had also, by his courage and his power to command, saved hundreds of people from being crushed, which latter was probably the only completely accurate thing that has been said about Dr. Almus Pickerbaugh in ten thousand columns of newspaper publicity.

Whether to see the Fair, Pickerbaugh, the delightful ravages of a disaster, or another fight between the anti ladies, half the city struggled into the Tabernacle that evening, and when Pickerbaugh took the platform for his closing lecture he was greeted with frenzy. Next day, when he galloped into the last week of his campaign, he was overlord of all the district.

## II

His opponent was a snuffy little lawyer whose strength lay in his training. He had been state senator, lieutenant governor, county judge. But the Democratic slogan, "Pickerbaugh the Pick-up Candidate," was drowned in the admiration for the hero of the health fair. He dashed about in motors, proclaiming, "I am not running because I want office, but because I want the chance to take to the whole nation my ideals of health." Everywhere was plastered:

For Congress

**PICKERBAUGH**

The two-fisted fighting poet doc

Just elect him for a term
And all through the nation he'll swat the germ.

Enormous meetings were held. Pickerbaugh was ample and vague about his Policies. Yes, he was opposed to our entering the European War, but he assured them, he certainly did assure them, that he was for using every power of our Government to end this terrible calamity. Yes, he was for high tariff, but it must be so adjusted that the farmers in his district could buy everything cheaply. Yes, he was for high wages for each and every workman, but he stood like a rock, like a boulder, like a moraine, for protecting the prosperity of all manufacturers, merchants, and real-estate owners.

While this larger campaign thundered, there was proceeding in Nautilus a smaller and much defter campaign, to re-elect as mayor one Mr. Pugh, Pickerbaugh's loving chief. Mr. Pugh sat nicely at desks, and he was pleasant and promissory to everybody who came to see him; clergymen, gamblers, G.A.R. veterans, circus advance-agents, policemen, and ladies of reasonable virtue— everybody except perhaps socialist agitators, against whom he staunchly protected the embattled city. In his speeches Pickerbaugh commended Pugh for "that firm integrity and ready sympathy with which His Honor had backed up every movement for the public weal," and when Pickerbaugh (quite honestly) begged, "Mr. Mayor, if I go to Congress you must appoint Arrowsmith in my place; he knows nothing about politics but he's incorruptible," then Pugh gave his promise, and amity abode in that land. . . . Nobody said anything at all about Mr. F. X. Jordan.

F. X. Jordan was a contractor with a generous interest in politics. Picker-baugh called him a grafter, and the last time Pugh had been elected—it had been on a Reform Platform, though since that time the reform had been coaxed to behave itself and be practical—both Pugh and Pickerbaugh had denounced Jordan as a "malign force." But so kindly was Mayor Pugh that in the present election he said nothing that could hurt Mr. Jordan's feelings, and in return what could Mr. Jordan do but speak forgivingly about Mr. Pugh to the people in blind-pigs and houses of ill fame?

On the evening of the election, Martin and Leora were among the company awaiting the returns at the Pickerbaughs'. They were confident. Martin had never been roused by politics, but he was stirred now by Pickerbaugh's twitchy pretense of indifference, by the telephoned report from the newspaper office, "Here's Willow Grove township—Pickerbaugh leading, two to one!" by the crowds which went past the house howling, "Pickerbaugh, Pickerbaugh, Pickerbaugh!"

At eleven the victory was certain, and Martin, his bowels weak with unconfidence, realized that he was now Director of Public Health, with responsibility for seventy thousand lives.

He looked wistfully toward Leora and in her still smile found assurance.

Orchid had been airy and distant with Martin all evening, and dismayingly chatty and affectionate with Leora. Now she drew him into the back parlor and "So I'm going off to Washington—and you don't care a bit!" she said, her eyes blurred and languorous and undefended. He held her, muttering, "You darling child, I can't let you go!" As he walked home he thought less of being Director than of Orchid's eyes.

In the morning he groaned, "Doesn't anybody ever learn anything? Must I watch myself and still be a fool, all my life? Doesn't any story ever end?"

He never saw her afterward, except on the platform of the train.

Leora surprisingly reflected, after the Pickerbaughs had gone, "Sandy dear, I know how you feel about losing your Orchid. It's sort of Youth going. She really is a peach. Honestly, I can appreciate how you feel, and sympathize with you—I mean, of course, providin' you aren't ever going to see her again."

III

Over the *Nautilus Cornfield's* anouncement was the vigorous headline:

### ALMUS PICKERBAUGH WINS
First Scientist Ever Elected
to Congress

Side-kick of Darwin and Pasteur
Gives New Punch to Steering
Ship of State

Pickerbaugh's resignation was to take effect at once; he was, he explained, going to Washington before his term began, to study legislative methods and start his propaganda for the creation of a national Secretaryship of Health. There was a considerable struggle over the appointment of Martin in his stead. Klopchuk the dairyman was bitter; Irving Watters whispered to fellow doctors that Martin was likely to extend the socialistic free clinics; F. X. Jordan had a sensible young doctor as his own candidate. It was the Ashford Grove Group, Tredgold, Schlemihl, Monte Mugford, who brought it off.

Martin went to Tredgold worrying, "Do the people want me? Shall I fight Jordan or get out?"

Tredgold said balmily, "Fight? What about? I own a good share of the bank that's lent various handy little sums to Mayor Pugh. You leave it to me."

Next day Martin was appointed, but only as Acting Director, with a salary of thirty-five hundred instead of four thousand.

That he had been put in by what he would have called "crooked politics" did not occur to him.

Mayor Pugh called him in and chuckled:

"Doc, there's been a certain amount of opposition to you, because you're pretty young and not many folks know you. I haven't any doubt I can give you the full appointment later—if we find you're competent and popular. Meantime you better avoid doing anything brash. Just come and ask my advice. I know this town and the people that count better than you do."

IV

The day of Pickerbaugh's leaving for Washington was made a fiesta. At the Armory, from twelve to two, the Chamber of Commerce gave to everybody who came a lunch of hot wienies, doughnuts, and coffee, with chewing gum for the women and, for the men, Schweinhügel's Little Dandy Nautilus-made Cheroots.

The train left at three-fifty-five. The station was, to the astonishment of innocent passengers gaping from the train windows, jammed with thousands.

By the rear platform, on a perilous packing box, Mayor Pugh held forth. The Nautilus Silver Cornet Band played three patriotic selections, then Pickerbaugh stood on the platform, his family about him. As he looked on the crowd, tears were in his eyes.

"For once," he stammered, "I guess I can't make a speech. D-darn it, I'm all choked up! I meant to orate a lot, but all I can say is—I love you all, I'm mighty grateful, I'll represent you my level best, neighbors! God bless you!"

The train moved out, Pickerbaugh waving as long as he could see them.

And Martin to Leora, "Oh, he's a fine old boy. He— No, I'm hanged if he is! The world's always letting people get away with assininities because they're kind-hearted. And here I've sat back like a coward, not saying a word, and watched 'em loose that wind-storm on the whole country. Oh, curse it, isn't anything in the world simple? Well, let's go to the office, and I'll begin to do things conscientiously and all wrong."

# 24

It cannot be said that Martin showed any large ability for organization, but under him the Department of Public Health changed completely. He chose as his assistant Dr. Rufus Ockford, a lively youngster recommended by Dean Silva of Winnemac. The routine work, examination of babies, quarantines, anti-tuberculosis placarding, went on as before.

Inspection of plumbing and food was perhaps more thorough, because Martin lacked Pickerbaugh's buoyant faith in the lay inspectors, and one of them he replaced, to the considerable displeasure of the colony of Germans in the Homedale district. Also he gave thought to the killing of rats and fleas, and he regarded the vital statistics as something more than a recording of births and deaths. He had notions about their value which were most amusing to the health department clerk. He wanted a record of the effect of race, occupation, and a dozen other factors upon the disease rate.

The chief difference was that Martin and Rufus Ockford found themselves with plenty of leisure. Martin estimated that Pickerbaugh must have used half his time in being inspirational and eloquent.

He made his first mistake in assigning Ockford to spend part of the week in the free city clinic, in addition to the two half-time physicians. There was fury in the Evangeline County Medical Society. At a restaurant, Irving Watters came over to Martin's table.

"I hear you've increased the clinic staff," said Dr. Watters.

"Yuh."

"Thinking of increasing it still more?"

"Might be a good idea."

"Now you see here, Mart. As you know, Mrs. Watters and I have done everything in our power to make you and Leora welcome. Glad to do anything I can for a fellow alumnus of old Winnemac. But at the same time, there are limits, you know! Not that I've got any objection to your providing free clinical facilities. Don't know but what it's a good thing to treat the damn', lazy, lousy pauper-class free, and keep the D.B.'s off the books of the regular physicians. But same *time*, when you begin to make a practice of encouraging a lot of folks, that can afford to pay, to go and get free treatment, and practically you attack the integrity of the physicians of this city, that have been giving God knows how much of their time to charity—"

Martin answered neither wisely nor competently: "Irve, sweetheart, you can go straight to hell!"

After that hour, when they met there was nothing said between them.

Without disturbing his routine work, he found himself able to sink blissfully into the laboratory. At first he merely tinkered, but suddenly he was in full cry, oblivious of everything save his experiment.

He was playing with cultures isolated from various dairies and various people, thinking mostly of Klopchuk and streptococcus. Accidentally he discovered the lavish production of hemolysin in sheep's blood as compared with the blood of other animals. Why should streptococcus dissolve the red blood corpuscles of sheep more easily than those of rabbits?

It is true that a busy health-department bacteriologist has no right to waste the public time in being curious, but the irresponsible sniffing beagle in Martin drove out the faithful routineer.

He neglected the examination of an ominously increasing number of tubercular sputums; he set out to answer the question of the hemolysin. He wanted the streptococcus to produce its blood-destroying poison in twenty-four-hour cultures.

He beautifully and excitedly failed, and sat for hours meditating. He tried a six-hour culture. He mixed the supernatant fluid from a centrifugated culture with a suspension of red blood corpuscles and placed it in the incubator. When he returned, two hours after, the blood cells were dissolved.

He telephoned to Leora: "Lee! Got something! C'n you pack up sandwich and come down here f'r evening?"

"Sure," said Leora.

When she appeared he explained to her that his discovery was accidental, that most scientific discoveries were accidental, and that no investigator, however great, could do anything more than see the value of his chance results.

He sounded mature and rather angry.

Leora sat in the corner, scratching her chin, reading a medical journal. From time to time she reheated coffee, over a doubtful Bunsen flame. When the office staff arrived in the morning they found something that had but rarely occurred during the régime of Almus Pickerbaugh: the Director of the Department was transplanting cultures, and on a long table was his wife, asleep.

Martin blared at Dr. Ockford, "Get t' hell out of this, Rufus, and take charge of the department for today—I'm out—I'm dead—and oh, say, get Leora home and fry her a couple o' eggs, and you might bring me a Denver sandwich from the Sunset Trail Lunch, will you?"

"You bet, chief," said Ockford.

Martin repeated his experiment, testing the cultures for hemolysin after two, four, six, eight, ten, twelve, fourteen, sixteen, and eighteen hours of incubation. He discovered that the maximum production of hemolysin occurred between four and ten hours. He began to work out the formula of production—and he was desolate. He fumed, raged, sweated. He found that his mathematics was childish, and all his science rusty. He pottered with chemistry, he ached over his mathematics, and slowly he began to assemble his results. He believed that he might have a paper for the *Journal of Infectious Diseases*.

Now Almus Pickerbaugh had published scientific papers—often. He had published them in the *Midwest Medical Quarterly*, of which he was one of fourteen editors. He had discovered the germ of epilepsy and the germ of cancer—two entirely different germs of cancer. Usually it took him a fortnight to make the discovery, write the report, and have it accepted. Martin lacked this admirable facility.

He experimented, he re-experimented, he cursed, he kept Leora out of bed, he taught her to make media, and was ill-pleased by her opinions on agar. He was violent to the stenographer; not once could the pastor of the Jonathan Edwards Congregational Church get him to address the Bible Class; and still for months his paper was not complete.

The first to protest was His Honor the Mayor. Returning from an extremely agreeable game of chemin de fer with F. X. Jordan, taking a short cut through the alley behind the City Hall, Mayor Pugh saw Martin at two in the morning drearily putting test-tubes into the incubator, while Leora sat in a corner smoking. Next day he summoned Martin, and protested.

"Doc, I don't want to butt in on your department—my specialty is never butting in—but it certainly strikes me that after being trained by a seventy-horse-power booster like Pickerbaugh, you ought to know that it's all damn' foolishness to spend so much time in the laboratory, when you can hire an A1 laboratory fellow for thirty bucks a week. What you ought to be doing is jollying along these sobs that are always panning the administration. Get out and talk to the churches and clubs, and help me put across the ideas that we stand for."

"Maybe he's right," Martin considered. "I'm a rotten bacteriologist. Probably I never will get this experiment together. My job here is to keep tobacco-chewers from spitting. Have I the right to waste the tax-payers' money on anything else?"

But that week he read, as an announcement issued by the McGurk Institute of Biology of New York, that Dr. Max Gottlieb had synthesized antibodies *in vitro*.

He pictured the saturnine Gottlieb not at all enjoying the triumph but, with locked door, abusing the papers for their exaggerative reports of his work; and as the picture became sharp Martin was like a subaltern stationed in a desert isle when he learns that his old regiment is going off to an agreeable Border war.

Then the McCandless fury broke.

## II

Mrs. McCandless had once been a "hired girl"; then nurse, then confidante, then wife to the invalid Mr. McCandless, wholesale grocer and owner of real estate. When he died she inherited everything. There was a suit, of course, but she had an excellent lawyer.

She was a grim, graceless, shady, mean woman, yet a nymphomaniac. She was not invited into Nautilus society, but in her unaired parlor, on the mildewed couch, she entertained seedy, belching, oldish married men, a young policeman to whom she often lent money, and the contractor-politician, F. X. Jordan.

She owned, in Swede Hollow, the filthiest block of tenements in Nautilus. Martin had made a tuberculosis map of these tenements, and in conferences with Dr. Ockford and Leora he denounced them as murder-holes. He wanted to destroy them, but the police power of the Director of Public Health was vague. Pickerbaugh had enjoyed the possession of large power only because he never used it.

Martin sought a court decision for the demolition of the McCandless tenements. Her lawyer was also the lawyer of F. X. Jordan, and the most eloquent witness against Martin was Dr. Irving Watters. But it chanced, because of the absence of the proper judge, that the case came before an ignorant and honest person who quashed the injunction secured by Mrs. McCandless's lawyer and instructed the Department of Public Health that it might use such methods as the city ordinances provided for emergencies.

That evening Martin grumbled to young Ockford, "You don't suppose for a moment, do you, Rufus, that McCandless and Jordan won't appeal the case? Let's get rid of the tenements while it's comparatively legal, heh?"

"You bet, chief," said Ockford, and, "Say, let's go out to Oregon and start practice when we get kicked out. Well, we can depend on our sanitary inspector, anyway. Jordan seduced his sister, here 'bout six years back."

At dawn a gang headed by Martin and Ockford, in blue overalls, joyful and rowdyish, invaded the McCandless tenements, drove the tenants into the street, and began to tear down the flimsy buildings. At noon, when lawyers appeared and the tenants were in new flats commandeered by Martin, the wreckers set fire to the lower stories, and in half an hour the buildings had been annihilated.

F. X. Jordan came to the scene after lunch. A filthy Martin and a dusty Ockford were drinking coffee brought by Leora.

"Well, boys," said Jordan, "you've put it all over us. Only if you ever pull this kind of stunt again, use dynamite and save a lot of time. You know, I like you boys—I'm sorry for what I've got to do to you. But may the saints help you, because it's just a question of time when I learn you not to monkey with the buzz-saw."

### III

Clay Tredgold admired their amateur arson and rejoiced, "Fine! I'm going to back you up in everything the D.P.H. does."

Martin was not too pleased by the promise, for Tredgold's set were somewhat exigent. They had decided that Martin and Leora were free spirits like themselves, and amusing, but they had also decided, long before the Arrowsmiths had by coming to Nautilus entered into authentic existence, that the Group had a monopoly of all Freedom and Amusingness, and they expected the Arrowsmiths to appear for cocktails and poker every Saturday and Sunday evening. They could not understand why Martin should desire to spend his time in a laboratory, drudging over something called "streptolysin," which had nothing to do with cocktails, motors, steel windmills, or insurance.

On an evening perhaps a fortnight after the destruction of the McCandless tenements, Martin was working late in the laboratory. He wasn't even doing experiments which might have diverted the Group—causing bacterial colonies to cloud liquids, or making things change color. He was merely sitting at a table, looking at logarithmic tables. Leora was not there, and he was mumbling, "Confound her, why did she have to go and be sick today?"

Tredgold and Schlemihl and their wives were bound for the Old Farmhouse Inn. They had telephoned to Martin's flat and learned where he was. From the alley behind City Hall they could peer in and see him, dreary and deserted.

"We'll take the old boy out and brighten him up. First, let's rush home and shake up a few cocktails and bring 'em down to surprise him," was Tredgold's inspiration.

Tredgold came into the laboratory, a half-hour later, with much clamor.

"This is a nice way to put in a moonlit spring evening, young Narrowsmith! Come on, we'll all go out and dance a little. Grab your hat."

"Gosh, Clay, I'd like to, but honestly I can't. I've got to work; simply got to."

"Rats! Don't be silly. You've been working too hard. Here—look what Father's brought. Be reasonable. Get outside of a nice long cocktail and you'll have a new light on things."

Martin was reasonable up to that point, but he did not have a new light. Tredgold would not take No. Martin continued to refuse, affectionately, then a bit tartly. Outside, Schlemihl pressed down the button of the motor horn and held it, producing a demanding, infuriating yawp which made Martin cry, "For God's sake go out and make 'em quit that, will you, and let me alone! I've got to work, I told you!"

Tredgold stared a moment. "I certainly shall! I'm not accustomed to force my attentions on people. Pardon me for disturbing you!"

By the time Martin sulkily felt that he must apologize, the car was gone. Next day and all the week, he waited for Tredgold to telephone, and Tredgold waited for him to telephone, and they fell into a circle of dislike. Leora and Clara Tredgold saw each other once or twice, but they were uncomfortable, and a fortnight later, when the most prominent physician in town dined with the Tredgolds and attacked Martin as a bumptious and narrowvisioned young man, both the Tredgolds listened and agreed.

Opposition to Martin developed all at once.

Various physicians were against him, not only because of the enlarged clinics, but because he rarely asked their help and never their advice. Mayor Pugh considered him tactless. Klopchuk and F. X. Jordan were assailing him as crooked. The reporters disliked him for his secrecy and occasional brusqueness. And the Group had ceased to defend him. Of all these forces Martin was more or less aware, and behind them he fancied that doubtful business men, sellers of impure ice-cream and milk, owners of unsanitary shops and dirty tenements, men who had always hated Pickerbaugh but who had feared to attack him because of his popularity, were gathering to destroy the entire Department of Public Health. . . . He appreciated Pickerbaugh in those days, and loved soldier-wise the Department.

There came from Mayor Pugh a hint that he would save trouble by resigning. He would not resign. Neither would he go to the citizens begging for support. He did his work, and leaned on Leora's assurance, and tried to ignore his detractors. He could not.

News-items and three-line editorial squibs dug at his tyranny, his ignorance, his callowness. An old woman died after treatment at the clinic, and the coroner hinted that it had been the fault of "our almighty health-officer's pet cub assistant." Somewhere arose the name "the Schoolboy Czar" for Martin, and it stuck.

In the gossip at luncheon clubs, in discussions at the Parents' and Teachers' Association, in one frank signed protest sent to the Mayor, Martin was blamed for too strict an inspection of milk, for insufficiently strict inspection of milk; for permitting garbage to lie untouched, for persecuting the over-worked garbage collectors; and when a case of small-pox appeared in the Bohemian section, there was an opinion that Martin had gone out personally and started it.

However vague the citizens were as to the nature of his wickedness, once they lost faith in him they lost it completely and with joy, and they welcomed an apparently spontaneously generated rumor that he had betrayed his benefactor, their beloved Dr. Pickerbaugh, by seducing Orchid.

At this interesting touch of immorality, he had all the fashionable churches against him. The pastor of the Jonathan Edwards Church touched up a sermon about Sin in High Places by a reference to "one who, while like a Czar he pretends to be safeguarding the city from entirely imaginary dangers, yet winks at the secret vice rampant in hidden places; who allies himself with the forces of graft and evil and the thugs who batten on honest but deluded Labor; one who cannot arise, a manly man among men, and say, 'I have a clean heart and clean hands.'"

It is true that some of the delighted congregation thought that this referred to Mayor Pugh, and others applied it to F. X. Jordan, but wise citizens saw that it was a courageous attack on that monster of treacherous lewdness, Dr. Arrowsmith.

In all the city there were exactly two ministers who defended him: Father Costello of the Irish Catholic Church and Rabbi Rovine. They were, it happened, very good friends, and not at all friendly with the pastor of the Jonathan Edwards Church. They bullied their congregations; each of them asserted, "People come sneaking around with criticisms of our new Director of Health. If you want to make charges, make them openly. I will not listen to cowardly hints. And let me tell you that this city is lucky in having for health-officer a man who is honest and who actually knows something!"

But their congregations were poor.

Martin realized that he was lost. He tried to analyze his unpopularity.

"It isn't just Jordan's plotting and Tredgold's grousing and Pugh's weak spine. It's my own fault. I can't go out and soft-soap the people and get their permission to help keep them well. And I won't tell them what a hell of an important thing my work is—that I'm the one thing that saves the whole lot of 'em from dying immediately. Apparently an official in a democratic state has to do those things. Well, I don't! But I've got to think up something or they'll emasculate the whole Department."

One inspiration he did have. If Pickerbaugh were here, he could crush, or lovingly smother, the opposition. He remembered Pickerbaugh's farewell: "Now, my boy, even if I'm way off there in Washington, this Work will be as close to my heart as it ever was, and if you should really need me, you just send for me and I'll drop everything and come."

Martin wrote hinting that he was very much needed.

Pickerbaugh replied by return mail—good old Pickerbaugh!—but the reply was, "I cannot tell you how grieved I am that I cannot for the moment possibly get away from Washington but am sure that in your earnestness you exaggerate strength of opposition, write me freely, at any time."

"That's my last shot," Martin said to Leora. "I'm done. Mayor Pugh will fire me, just as soon as he comes back from his fishing trip. I'm a failure again, darling."

"You're not a failure, and you must eat some of this nice steak, and what shall we do now—time for us to be moving on, anyway—I hate staying in one place," said Leora.

"I don't know what we'll do. Maybe I could get a job at Hunziker's. Or go back to Dakota and try to work up a practice. What I'd like is to become a farmer and get me a big shot-gun and drive every earnest Christian citizen off the place. But meantime I'm going to stick here. I might win yet—with just a couple of miracles and a divine intervention. Oh, God, I am so tired! Are you coming back to the lab with me this evening? Honest, I'll quit early —before eleven, maybe."

He had completed his paper on the streptolysin research, and he took a day off to go to Chicago and talk it over with an editor of the *Journal of Infectious Diseases*. As he left Nautilus he was confused. He had caught himself rejoicing that he was free of Wheatsylvania and bound for great Nautilus. Time bent back, progress was annihilated, and he was mazed with futility.

The editor praised his paper, accepted it, and suggested only one change. Martin had to wait for his train. He remembered that Angus Duer was in Chicago, with the Rouncefield Clinic—a private organization of medical specialists, sharing costs and profits.

The clinic occupied fourteen rooms in a twenty-story building constructed (or so Martin certainly remembered it) of marble, gold, and rubies. The clinic reception-room, focused on a vast stone fireplace, was like the drawing-room of an oil magnate, but it was not a place of leisure. The young woman at the door demanded Martin's symptoms and address. A page in buttons sped with his name to a nurse, who flew to the inner offices. Before Angus appeared, Martin had to wait a quarter-hour in a smaller, richer, still more abashing reception-room. By this time he was so awed that he would have permitted the clinic surgeons to operate on him for any ill which at the moment they happened to fancy.

In medical school and Zenith General Hospital, Angus Duer had been efficient enough, but now he was ten times as self-assured. He was cordial; he invited Martin to step out for a dish of tea as though he almost meant it; but beside him Martin felt young, rustic, inept.

Angus won him by pondering, "Irving Watters? He was Digam? I'm not sure I remember him. Oh, yes—he was one of these boneheads that are the curse of every profession."

When Martin had sketched his conflict at Nautilus, Angus suggested, "You better come join us here at Rouncefield, as pathologist. Our pathologist is leaving in a few weeks. You could do the job, all right. You're getting thirty-five hundred a year now? Well, I think I could get you forty-five hundred, as a starter, and some day you'd become a regular member of the clinic and get in on all the profits. Let me know if you want it. Rouncefield told me to dig up a man."

With this resource and with an affection for Angus, Martin returned to Nautilus and open war. When Mayor Pugh returned he did not discharge Martin, but he appointed over him, as full Director, Pickerbaugh's friend, Dr. Bissex, the football coach and health director of Mugford College.

Dr. Bissex first discharged Rufus Ockford, which took five minutes, went out and addressed a Y.M.C.A. meeting, then bustled in and invited Martin to resign.

"I will like hell!" said Martin. "Come on, be honest, Bissex. If you want to fire me, do it, but let's have things straight. I won't resign, and if you do fire me I think I'll take it to the courts, and maybe I can turn enough light on you and His Honor and Frank Jordan to keep you from taking all the guts out of the work here."

"Why, Doctor, what a way to talk! Certainly I won't fire you," said Bissex, in the manner of one who has talked to difficult students and to lazy football teams. "Stay with us as long as you like. Only, in the interests of economy, I reduce your salary to eight hundred dollars a year!"

"All right, reduce and be damned," said Martin.

It sounded particularly fine and original when he said it, but less so when Leora and he found that, with their rent fixed by their lease, they could not by whatever mean economies live on less than a thousand a year.

Now that he was free from responsibility he began to form his own faction, to save the Department. He gathered Rabbi Rovine, Father Costello, Ockford, who was going to remain in town and practice, the secretary of the Labor Council, a banker who regarded Tredgold as "fast," and that excellent fellow the dentist of the school clinic.

"With people like that behind me, I can do something," he gloated to Leora. "I'm going to stick by it. I'm not going to have the D.P.H. turned into a Y.M.C.A. Bissex has all of Pickerbaugh's mush without his honesty and vigor. I can beat him! I'm not much of an executive, but I was beginning to visualize a D.P.H. that would be solid and not gaseous—that would save kids and prevent epidemics. I won't give it up. You watch me!"

His committee made representations to the Commercial Club, and for a time they were certain that the chief reporter of the *Frontiersman* was going to support them, "as soon as he could get his editor over being scared of a row." But Martin's belligerency was weakened by shame, for he never had enough money to meet his bills, and he was not used to dodging irate grocers, receiving dunning letters, standing at the door arguing with impertinent bill-collectors. He, who had been a city dignitary a few days before, had to endure, "Come on now, you pay up, you dead beat, or I'll get a cop!" When the shame had grown to terror, Dr. Bissex suddenly reduced his salary another two hundred dollars.

Martin stormed into the mayor's office to have it out, and found F. X. Jordan sitting with Pugh. It was evident that they both knew of the second reduction and considered it an excellent joke.

He reassembled his committee. "I'm going to take this into the courts," he raged.

"Fine," said Father Costello; and Rabbi Rovine: "Jenkins, that radical lawyer, would handle the case free."

The wise banker observed, "You haven't got anything to take into the courts till they discharge you without cause. Bissex has a legal right to reduce your salary all he wants to. The city regulations don't fix the salary for anybody except the Director and the inspectors. You haven't a thing to say."

With a melodramatic flourish Martin protested, "And I suppose I haven't a thing to say if they wreck the Department!"

"Not a thing, if the city doesn't care."

"Well, I care! I'll starve before I'll resign!"

"You'll starve if you don't resign, and your wife, too. Now here's my plan," said the banker. "You go into private practice here—I'll finance your getting an office and so on—and when the time comes, maybe in five or ten years from now, we'll all get together again and have you put in as full Director."

"Ten years of waiting—in *Nautilus?* Nope. I'm licked. I'm a complete failure—at thirty-two! I'll resign. I'll wander on," said Martin.

"I know I'm going to love Chicago," said Leora.

IV

He wrote to Angus Duer. He was appointed pathologist in the Rouncefield Clinic. But, Angus wrote, "they could not at the moment see their way clear to pay him forty-five hundred a year, though they were glad to go to twenty-five hundred."

Martin accepted.

V

When the Nautilus papers announced that Martin had resigned, the good
citizens chuckled, "Resigned? He got kicked out, that's what happened." One
of the papers had an innocent squib:

> Probably a certain amount of hypocrisy is inevitable in us sinful hu-
> man critters, but when a public official tries to pose as a saint while
> indulging in every vice, and tries to cover up his gross ignorance and
> incompetence by pulling political wires, and makes a holy show of him-
> self by not even doing a first-class job of wire-pulling, then even the
> cussedest of us old scoundrels begins to holler for the meat-ax.

Pickerbaugh wrote to Martin from Washington:

> I greatly regret to hear that you have resigned your post. I cannot
> tell you how disappointed I am, after all the pains I took in breaking
> you in and making you acquainted with my ideals. Bissex informs me
> that, because of crisis in city finances, he had to reduce your salary
> temporarily. Well personally I would rather work for the D.P.H. for
> nothing a year and earn my keep by being a night watchman than give up
> the fight for everything that is decent and constructive. I am sorry. I had
> a great liking for you, and your defection, your going back to private
> practice merely for commercial gain, your selling out for what I presume
> is a very high emolument, is one of the very greatest blows I have re-
> cently had to sustain.

VI

As they rode up to Chicago Martin thought aloud:
"I never knew I could be so badly licked. I never want to see a laboratory
or a public health office again. I'm done with everything but making money.
"I suppose this Rouncefield Clinic is probably nothing but a gilded boob-
trap—scare the poor millionaire into having all the fancy kinds of examinations and treatments the traffic will bear. I hope it is! I expect to be a com-
mercial-group doctor the rest of my life. I hope I have the sense to be!
"All wise men are bandits. They're loyal to their friends, but they despise
the rest. Why not, when the mass of people despise them if they *aren't*
bandits? Angus Duer had the sense to see this from the beginning, way back
in medic school. He's probably a perfect technician as a surgeon, but he
knows you get only what you grab. Think of the years it's taken me to learn
what he savvied all the time!
"Know what I'll do? I'll stick to the Rouncefield Clinic till I'm making
maybe thirty thousand a year, and then I'll get Ockford and start my own
clinic, with myself as internist and head of the whole shooting-match, and
collect every cent I can.
"All right, if what people want is a little healing and a lot of tapestry, they
shall have it—and pay for it.

"I never thought I could be such a failure—to become a commercialist and not want to be anything else. And I don't want to be anything else, believe me! I'm through!"

# 25

Then for a year with each day longer than a sleepless night, yet the whole year speeding without events or seasons or eagerness, Martin was a faithful mechanic in that most competent, most clean and brisk and visionless medical factory, the Rouncefield Clinic. He had nothing of which to complain. The clinic did, perhaps, give over-many roentgenological examinations to socially dislocated women who needed children and floor-scrubbing more than pretty little skiagraphs; they did, perhaps, view all tonsils with too sanguinary a gloom; but certainly no factory could have been better equipped or more gratifyingly expensive, and none could have routed its raw human material through so many processes so swiftly. The Martin Arrowsmith who had been supercilious toward Pickerbaughs and old Dr. Winters had for Rouncefield and Angus Duer and the other keen taut specialists of the clinic only the respect of the poor and uncertain for the rich and shrewd.

He admired Angus's firmness of purpose and stability of habit.

Angus had a swim or a fencing lesson daily; he swam easily and fenced like a still-faced demon. He was in bed before eleven-thirty; he never took more than one drink a day; and he never read anything or said anything which would not contribute to his progress as a Brilliant Young Surgeon. His underlings knew that Dr. Duer would not fail to arrive precisely on time, precisely well dressed, absolutely sober, very cool, and appallingly unpleasant to any nurse who made a mistake or looked for a smile.

Martin would without fear have submitted to the gilded and ardent tonsil-snatcher of the clinic, would have submitted to Angus for abdominal surgery or to Rouncefield for any operation of the head or neck, providing he was himself quite sure the operation was necessary, but he was never able to rise to the clinic's lyric faith that any portions of the body without which people could conceivably get along should certainly be removed at once.

The real flaw in his year of Chicago was that through all his working day he did not live. With quick hands, and one-tenth of his brain, he made blood counts, did urinalyses and Wassermanns and infrequent necropsies, and all the while he was dead, in a white-tiled coffin. Amid the blattings of Pickerbaugh and the peepings of Wheatsylvania, he had lived, had fought his environment. Now there was nothing to fight.

After hours, he almost lived. Leora and he discovered the world of book-shops and print-shops and theaters and concerts. They read novels and history and travel; they talked, at dinners given by Rouncefield or Angus, to journalists, engineers, bankers, merchants. They saw a Russian play, and heard Mischa Elman, and read Gottlieb's beloved Rabelais. Martin learned to flirt without childishness, and Leora went for the first time to a hairdresser and to a manicure, and began her lessons in French. She had called Martin a "lie-hunter," a "truth-seeker." They decided now, talking it over in their tight little two-and-quarter room flat, that most people who called themselves "truth-seekers"—persons who scurry about chattering of Truth as though it were a tangible separable thing, like houses or salt or bread—did not so much desire to find Truth as to cure their mental itch. In novels, these truth-seekers quested the "secret of life" in laboratories which did not seem to be provided with Bunsen flames or reagents, or they went, at great expense and much discomfort from hot trains and undesirable snakes, to Himalayan monasteries, to learn from unaseptic sages that the Mind can do all sorts of edifying things if one will but spend thirty or forty years in eating rice and gazing on one's navel.

To these high matters Martin responded, "Rot!" He insisted that there is no Truth but only many truths; that Truth is not a colored bird to be chased among the rocks and captured by its tail, but a skeptical attitude toward life. He insisted that no one could expect more than, by stubbornness or luck, to have the kind of work he enjoyed and an ability to become better acquainted with the facts of that work than the average job-holder.

His mechanistic philosophy did not persuade him that he was progressing adequately. When he tried to match himself with the experts of the clinic or with their professional friends, he was even more uncomfortable than he had been under the disconcerting scorn of Dr. Hesselink of Groningen. At clinic luncheons he met surgeons from London, New York, Boston; men with limousines and social positions and the offensive briskness of the man who has numerous engagements, or the yet more offensive quietness of the person who is amused by his inferiors; master technicians, readers of papers at medical congresses, executives and controllers, unafraid to operate before a hundred peering doctors, or to give well-bred and exceedingly final orders to subordinates; captain-generals of medicine, never doubting themselves; great priests and healers; men mature and wise and careful and blandly cordial.

In their winged presences, Max Gottlieb seemed an aged fusser, Gustaf Sondelius a mountebank, and the city of Nautilus unworthy of passionate warfare. As their suave courtesy smothered him, Martin felt like a footman.

In long hours of increasing frankness and lucidity he discussed with Leora the question of "What is this Martin Arrowsmith and whither is he going?" and he admitted that the sight of the Famous Surgeons disturbed his ancient faith that he was somehow a superior person. It was Leora who consoled him:

"I've got a lovely description for your dratted Famous Surgeons. You know how polite and important they are, and they smile so carefully? Well, don't you remember you once said that Professor Gottlieb called all such people like that 'men of measured merriment'?"

He caught up the phrase; they sang it together; and they made of it a beating impish song:

"Men of measured merriment! Men of measured merriment! Damn the great executives, the men of measured merriment, damn the men with careful smiles, damn the men that run the shops, oh, damn their measured merriment, the men with measured merriment, oh, damn their measured merriment, and DAMN their careful smiles!"

## II

While Martin developed in a jagged way from the boy of Wheatsylvania to mature man, his relations to Leora developed from loyal boy-and-girl adventurousness to lasting solidity. They had that understanding of each other known only to married people, a few married people, wherein for all their differences they were as much indissoluble parts of a whole as are the eye and hand. Their identification did not mean that they dwelt always in rosy bliss. Because he was so intimately fond of her and so sure of her, because anger and eager hot injustices are but ways of expressing trust, Martin was irritated by her and querulous with her as he would not have endured being with any other woman, any charming Orchid.

He stalked out now and then after a quarrel, disdaining to answer her, and for hours he left her alone, enjoying the knowledge that he was hurting her, that she was alone, waiting, perhaps weeping. Because he loved her and also was fond of her, he was annoyed when she was less sleek, less suave, than the women he encountered at Angus Duer's.

Mrs. Rouncefield was a worthy old waddler—beside her, Leora was shining and exquisite. But Mrs. Duer was of amber and ice. She was a rich young woman, she dressed with distinction, she spoke with finishing-school mock-melodiousness, she was ambitious, and she was untroubled by the possession of a heart or a brain. She was, indeed, what Mrs. Irving Watters believed herself to be.

In the simple gorgeousness of the Nautilus smart set, Mrs. Clay Tredgold had petted Leora and laughed at her if she lacked a shoe-buckle or split an infinitive, but the gold-slippered Mrs. Duer was accustomed to sneer at carelessness with the most courteous and unresentable and unmistakable sneers.

As they returned by taxicab from the Duers', Martin flared:

"Don't you ever learn anything? I remember once in Nautilus we stopped on a country road and talked till—oh, darn' near dawn, and you were going to be so energetic, but here we are again tonight, with just the same thing—Good God, couldn't you even take the trouble to notice that you had a spot of soot on your nose tonight? Mrs. Duer noticed it, all right! Why are you so sloppy? Why can't you take a little care? And why can't you make an effort, anyway, to have something to say? You just sit there at dinner—you just sit and look healthy! Don't you want to help me? Mrs. Duer will probably help Angus to become president of the American Medical Association, in about

twenty years, and by that time I suppose you'll have me back in Dakota as
assistant to Hesselink!"

Leora had been snuggling beside him in the unusual luxury of a taxicab.
She sat straight now, and when she spoke she had lost the casual independence with which she usually regarded life:

"Dear, I'm awfully sorry. I went out this afternoon, I went out and had a
facial massage, so as to look nice for you, and then I knew you like conversation, so I got my little book about modern painting that I bought and I
studied it terribly hard, but tonight I just couldn't seem to get the conversation around to modern painting—"

He was sobbing, with her head on his shoulder, "Oh, you poor, scared,
bullied kid, trying to be grown-up with these dollar-chasers!"

### III

After the first daze of white tile and bustling cleverness at the Rouncefield Clinic, Martin had the desire to tie up a few loose knots of his streptolysin research.

When Angus Duer discovered it he hinted, "Look here, Martin, I'm glad
you're keeping on with your science, but if I were you I wouldn't, I think,
waste too much energy on mere curiosity. Dr. Rouncefield was speaking about
it the other day. We'd be glad to have you do all the research you want, only
we'd like it if you went at something practical. Take for instance: if you could
make a tabulation of the blood-counts in a couple of hundred cases of appendicitis and publish it, that'd get somewhere, and you could sort of bring
in a mention of the clinic, and we'd all receive a little credit—and inciden-
tally maybe we could raise you to three thousand a year then."

This generosity had the effect of extinguishing Martin's desire to do any
research whatever.

Angus is right. What he means is: as a scientist I'm finished. I am. I'll
never try to do anything original again."

It was at this time, when Martin had been with the clinic for a year, that
his streptolysin paper was published in the *Journal of Infectious Diseases.*
He gave reprints to Rouncefield and to Angus. They said extremely nice
things which showed that they had not read the paper, and again they suggested his tabulating blood-counts.

He also sent a reprint to Max Gottlieb, at the McGurk Institute of
Biology.

Gottlieb wrote to him, in that dead-black spider-web script:

Dear Martin:

I have read your paper with great pleasure. The curves of the relation
of hemolysin production to age of culture are illuminating. I have spoken about you to Tubbs. When are you coming to us—to me? Your
laboratory and diener are waiting for you here. The last thing I want to
be is a mystic, but I feel when I see your fine engraved letterhead of

a clinic and a Rouncefield that you should be tired of trying to be a good citizen and ready to come back to work. We shall be glad, & Dr. Tubbs, if you can come.

Truly yours,

M. Gottlieb.

"I'm simply going to adore New York," said Leora.

# 26

The McGurk Building. A sheer wall, thirty blank stories of glass and limestone, down in the pinched triangle whence New York rules a quarter of the world.

Martin was not overwhelmed by his first hint of New York; after a year in the Chicago Loop, Manhattan seemed leisurely. But when from the elevated railroad he beheld the Woolworth Tower, he was exalted. To him architecture had never existed; buildings were larger or smaller bulks containing more or less interesting objects. His most impassioned architectural comment had been, "There's a cute bungalow; be nice place to live." Now he pondered, "Like to see that tower every day—clouds and storms behind it and everything—so sort of satisfying."

He came along Cedar Street, among thunderous trucks portly with wares from all the world; came to the bronze doors of the McGurk Building and a corridor of intemperately colored terra-cotta, with murals of Andean Indians, pirates booming up the Spanish Main, guarded gold-trains, and the stout walls of Cartagena. At the Cedar Street end of the corridor, a private street, one block long, was the Bank of the Andes and Antilles (Ross McGurk chairman of the board), in whose gold-crusted sanctity red-headed Yankee exporters drew drafts on Quito, and clerks hurled breathless Spanish at bulky women. A sign indicated, at the Liberty Street end, "Passenger Offices, Mc-Gurk Line, weekly sailings for the West Indies and South America."

Born to the prairies, never far from the sight of the cornfields, Martin was conveyed to blazing lands and portentous enterprises.

One of the row of bronze-barred elevators was labeled "Express to McGurk Institute." He entered it proudly, feeling himself already a part of the godly association. They rose swiftly, and he had but half-second glimpses of ground glass doors with the signs of mining companies, lumber companies, Central American railroad companies.

The McGurk Institute is probably the only organization for scientific research in the world which is housed in an office building. It has the twenty-ninth and thirtieth stories of the McGurk Building, and the roof is devoted to its animal house and to tiled walks along which (above a world of stenog-

raphers and bookkeepers and earnest gentlemen who desire to sell Better-
bilt Garments to the golden dons of the Argentine) saunter rapt scientists
dreaming of osmosis in Spirogyra.

Later, Martin was to note that the reception-room of the Institute was
smaller, yet more forbiddingly polite, in its white paneling and Chippendale
chairs, than the lobby of the Rouncefield Clinic, but now he was unconscious
of the room, of the staccato girl attendant, of everything except that he was
about to see Max Gottlieb, for the first time in five years.

At the door of the laboratory he stared hungrily.

Gottlieb was thin-cheeked and dark as ever, his hawk nose bony, his fierce
eyes demanding, but his hair had gone gray, the flesh round his mouth was
sunken, and Martin could have wept at the feebleness with which he rose.
The old man peered down at him, his hand on Martin's shoulder, but he
said only:

"Ah! Dis is good. . . . Your laboratory is three doors down the hall. . . .
But I object to one thing in the good paper you send me. You say, 'The
regularity of the rate at which the streptolysin disappears suggests that an
equation may be found—'"

"But it can, sir!"

"Then why did you not make the equation?"

"Well— I don't know. I wasn't enough of a mathematician."

"Then you should not have published till you knew your math!"

"I— Look, Dr. Gottlieb, do you really think I know enough to work here?
I want terribly to succeed."

"Succeed? I have heard that word. It is English? Oh, yes, it is a word that
liddle schoolboys use at the University of Winnemac. It means passing examinations. But there are no examinations to pass here. . . . Martin, let us
be clear. You know something of laboratory technique; you have heard about
dese bacilli; you are not a good chemist, and mathematics—pfui!—most terrible! But you have curiosity and you are stubborn. You do not accept rules.
Therefore I t'ink you will either make a very good scientist or a very bad
one, and if you are bad enough, you will be popular with the rich ladies
who rule this city, New York, and you can gif lectures for a living or even
become, if you get to be plausible enough, a college president. So anyvay, it
will be interesting."

Half an hour later they were arguing ferociously, Martin asserting that the
whole world ought to stop warring and trading and writing and get straightway into laboratories to observe new phenomena; Gottlieb insisting that
there were already too many facile scientists, that the one thing necessary was
the mathematical analysis (and often the destruction) of phenomena already
observed.

It sounded bellicose, and all the while Martin was blissful with the certainty that he had come home.

The laboratory in which they talked (Gottlieb pacing the floor, his long
arms fantastically knotted behind his thin back; Martin leaping on and off
tall stools) was not in the least remarkable—a sink, a bench with racks of

numbered test-tubes, a microscope, a few note-books and hydrogen-ion charts, a grotesque series of bottles connected by glass and rubber tubes on an ordinary kitchen table at the end of the room—yet now and then during his tirades Martin looked about reverently.

Gottlieb interrupted their debate: "What work do you want to do here?"

"Why, sir, I'd like to help you, if I can. I suppose you're cleaning up some things on the synthesis of antibodies."

"Yes, I t'ink I can bring immunity reactions under the mass action law. But you are not to help me. You are to do your own work. What do you want to do? This is not a clinic, wit' patients going through so neat in a row!"

"I want to find a hemolysin for which there's an antibody. There isn't any for streptolysin. I'd like to work with staphylolysin. Would you mind?"

"I do not care what you do—if you just do not steal my staph cultures out of the ice-box, and if you will look mysterious all the time, so Dr. Tubbs, our Director, will t'ink you are up to something big. So! I haf only one suggestion: when you get stuck in a problem, I have a fine collection of detective stories in my office. But no. Should I be serious—this once, when you are just come?

"Perhaps I am a crank, Martin. There are many who hate me. There are plots against me—oh, you t'ink I imagine it, but you shall see! I make many mistakes. But one thing I keep always pure: the religion of a scientist.

"To be a scientist—it is not just a different job, so that a man should choose between being a scientist and being an explorer or a bond-salesman or a physician or a king or a farmer. It is a tangle of ver-y obscure emotions, like mysticism, or wanting to write poetry; it makes its victim all different from the good normal man. The normal man, he does not care much what he does except that he should eat and sleep and make love. But the scientist is intensely religious—he is so religious that he will not accept quarter-truths, because they are an insult to his faith.

"He wants that everything should be subject to inexorable laws. He is equal opposed to the capitalists who t'ink their silly money-grabbing is a system, and to liberals who t'ink man is not a fighting animal; he takes both the American booster and the European aristocrat, and he ignores all their blithering. Ignores it! All of it! He hates the preachers who talk their fables, but he iss not too kindly to the anthropologists and historians who can only make guesses, yet they have the nerf to call themselves scientists! Oh, yes, he is a man that all nice good-natured people should naturally hate!

"He speaks no meaner of the ridiculous faith-healers and chiropractors than he does of the doctors that want to snatch our science before it is tested and rush around hoping they heal people, and spoiling all the clues with their footsteps; and worse than the men like hogs, worse than the imbeciles who have not even heard of science, he hates pseudo-scientists, guess-scientists—like these pycho-analysts; and worse than those comic dream-scientists he hates the men that are allowed in a clean kingdom like biology but know only one text-book and how to lecture to nincompoops all so popular! He is the only real revolutionary, the authentic scientist, because he alone knows how liddle he knows.

"He must be heartless. He lives in a cold, clear light. Yet dis is a funny t'ing: really, in private, he is not cold nor heartless—so much less cold than the Professional Optimists. The world has always been ruled by the Philanthropists: by the doctors that want to use therapeutic methods they do not understand, by the soldiers that want something to defend their country against, by the preachers that yearn to make everybody listen to them, by the kind manufacturers that love their workers, by the eloquent statesmen and soft-hearted authors—and see once what a fine mess of hell they haf made of the world! Maybe now it is time for the scientist, who works and searches and never goes around howling how he loves everybody!

"But once again always remember that not all the men who work at science are scientists. So few! The rest—secretaries, press-agents, camp-followers! To be a scientist is like being a Goethe: it is born in you. Sometimes I t'ink you have a liddle of it born in you. If you haf, there is only one t'ing—no, there is two t'ings you must do: work twice as hard as you can, and keep people from using you. I will try to protect you from Success. It is all I can do. So. . . . I should wish, Martin, that you will be very happy here. May Koch bless you!"

II

Five rapt minutes Martin spent in the laboratory which was to be his—smallish but efficient, the bench exactly the right height, a proper sink with pedal taps. When he had closed the door and let his spirit flow out and fill that minute apartment with his own essence, he felt secure.

No Pickerbaugh or Rouncefield could burst in here and drag him away to be explanatory and plausible and public; he would be free to work, instead of being summoned to the package-wrapping and dictation of breezy letters which men call work.

He looked out of the broad window above his bench and saw that he did have the coveted Woolworth Tower, to keep and gloat on. Shut in to a joy of precision, he would nevertheless not be walled out from flowing life. He had, to the north, not the Woolworth Tower alone but the Singer Building, the arrogant magnificence of the City Investing Building. To the west, tall ships were riding, tugs were bustling, all the world went by. Below his cliff, the streets were feverish. Suddenly he loved humanity as he loved the decent, clean rows of test-tubes, and he prayed then the prayer of the scientist:

"God give me unclouded eyes and freedom from haste. God give me a quiet and relentless anger against all pretense and all pretentious work and all work left slack and unfinished. God give me a restlessness whereby I may neither sleep nor accept praise till my observed results equal my calculated results or in pious glee I discover and assault my error. God give me strength not to trust to God!"

III

He walked all the way up to their inconsiderable hotel in the Thirties, and all the way the crowds stared at him—this slim, pale, black-eyed, beaming young man who thrust among them, half-running, seeing nothing yet in a blur seeing everything: gallant buildings, filthy streets, relentless traffic, soldiers of fortune, fools, pretty women, frivolous shops, windy sky. His feet raced to the tune of "I've found my work, I've found my work, I've found my work!"

Leora was awaiting him—Leora whose fate it was ever to wait for him in creaky rocking-chairs in cheapish rooms. As he galloped in she smiled, and all her thin, sweet body was illumined. Before he spoke she cried:

"Oh, Sandy, I'm so glad!"

She interrupted his room-striding panegyrics on Max Gottlieb, on the Mc-Gurk Institute, on New York, on the charms of staphylolysin, by a meek "Dear, how much are they going to pay you?"

He stopped with a bump. "Gosh! I forgot to ask!"

"Oh!"

"Now you look here! This isn't a Rouncefield Clinic! I hate these buzzards that can't see anything but making money—"

"I know, Sandy. Honestly, I don't care. I was just wondering what kind of a flat we'll be able to afford, so I can begin looking for it. Go on. Dr. Gottlieb said—"

It was three hours after, at eight, when they went to dinner.

IV

The city of magic was to become to Martin neither a city nor any sort of magic but merely a route: their flat, the subway, the Institute, a favorite inexpensive restaurant, a few streets of laundries and delicatessens and movie theaters. But tonight it was a fog of wonder. They dined at the Brevoort, of which Gustaf Sondelius had told him. This was in 1916, before the country had become wholesome and sterile, and the Brevoort was a tumult of French uniforms, caviar, Louis, dangling neckties, Nuits St. Georges, illustrators, Grand Marnier, British Intelligence officers, brokers, conversation, and Martell, V.O.

"It's a fine crazy bunch," said Martin. "Do you realize we can stop being respectable now? Irving Watters isn't watching us, or Angus! Would we be too insane if we had a bottle of champagne?"

He awoke next day to fret that there must be a trick somewhere, as there had been in Nautilus, in Chicago. But as he set to work he seemed to be in a perfect world. The Institute deftly provided all the material and facilities he could desire—animals, incubators, glassware, cultures, media—and he had a thoroughly trained technician—"garçon" they called him at the Institute. He really was let alone; he really was encouraged to do individual work; he really was associated with men who thought not in terms of poetic posters

or of two-thousand-dollar operations but of colloids and sporulation and elec-
trons, and of the laws and energies which governed them.

On his first day there came to greet him the head of the Department of
Physiology, Dr. Rippleton Holabird.

Holabird seemed, though Martin had found his name starred in physiologi-
cal journals, too young and too handsome to be the head of a department:
a tall, slim, easy man with a trim mustache. Martin had been reared in the
school of Clif Clawson; he had not realized, till he heard Dr. Holabird's
quick greeting, that a man's voice may be charming without effeminacy.

Holabird guided him through the two floors of the Institute, and Martin
beheld all the wonders of which he had ever dreamed. If it was not so large,
McGurk ranked in equipment with Rockefeller, Pasteur, McCormick, Lister.
Martin saw rooms for sterilizing glass and preparing media, for glass-blowing,
for the polariscope and the spectroscope, and a steel-and-cement-walled
combustion-chamber. He saw a museum of pathology and bacteriology to
which he longed to add. There was a department of publications, whence
were issued the Institute reports, and the *American Journal of Geographic
Pathology*, edited by the Director, Dr. Tubbs; there was a room for photography, a glorious library, an aquarium for the Department of Marine Biology,
and (Dr. Tubbs's own idea) a row of laboratories which visiting foreign
scientists were invited to use as their own. A Belgian biologist and a Portuguese bio-chemist were occupying guest laboratories now, and once, Martin
thrilled to learn, Gustaf Sondelius had been here.

Then Martin saw the Berkeley-Saunders centrifuge.

The principle of the centrifuge is that of the cream-separator. It collects
as sediment the solids scattered through a liquid, such as bacteria in a solution. Most centrifuges are hand- or water-power contrivances the size of a
large cocktail-shaker, but this noble implement was four feet across, electri-
cally driven, the central bowl enclosed in armor plate fastened with levers
like a submarine hatch, the whole mounted on a cement pillar.

Holabird explained, "There're only three of these in existence. They're
made by Berkeley-Saunders in England. You know the normal speed, even
for a good centrifuge, is about four thousand revolutions a minute. This does
twenty thousand a minute—fastest in the world. Eh?"

"Jove, they do give you the stuff to work with!" gloated Martin. (He really
did, under Holabird's handsome influence, say Jove, not Gosh.)

"Yes, McGurk and Tubbs are the most generous men in the scientific
world. I think you'll find it very pleasant to be here, Doctor."

"I know I will—shall. And Jove, it's awfully nice of you to take me around
this way."

"Can't you see how much I'm enjoying my chance to display my knowl-
edge? There's no form of egotism so agreeable and so safe as being a cicerone.
But we still have the real wonder of the Institute for to behold, Doctor.
Down this way."

The real wonder of the Institute had nothing visible to do with science.
It was the Hall, in which lunched the staff, and in which occasional scien-

tific dinners were given, with Mrs. McGurk as hostess. Martin gasped and his head went back as his glance ran from glistening floor to black and gold ceiling. The Hall rose the full height of the two floors of the Institute. Clinging to the soaring wall, above the dais on which lunched the Director and the seven heads of departments, was a carved musicians'-gallery. Against the oak paneling of the walls were portraits of the pontiffs of science, in crimson robes, with a vast mural by Maxfield Parrish, and above all was an electrolier of a hundred globes.

"Gosh—*Jove!*" said Martin. "I never knew there was such a room!"

Holabird was generous. He did not smile. "Oh, perhaps it's almost too gorgeous. It's Capitola's pet creation—Capitola is Mrs. Ross McGurk, wife of the founder; she's really an awfully nice woman but she does love Movements and Associations. Terry Wickett, one of the chemists here, calls this 'Bonanza Hall.' Yet it does inspire you when you come in to lunch all tired and grubby. Now let's go call on the Director. He told me to bring you in."

After the Babylonian splendor of the Hall, Martin expected to find the office of Dr. A. DeWitt Tubbs fashioned like a Roman bath, but it was, except for a laboratory bench at one end, the most rigidly business-like apartment he had ever seen.

Dr. Tubbs was an earnest man, whiskered like a terrier, very scholarly, and perhaps the most powerful American exponent of co-operation in science, but he was also a man of the world, fastidious of boots and waistcoats. He had graduated from Harvard, studied on the Continent, been professor of pathology in the University of Minnesota, president of Hartford University, minister to Venezuela, editor of the *Weekly Statesman* and president of the Sanity League, finally Director of McGurk.

He was a member both of the American Academy of Arts and Letters and of the Academy of Sciences. Bishops, generals, liberal rabbis, and musical bankers dined with him. He was one of the Distinguished Men to whom the newspapers turned for authoritative interviews on all subjects.

You realized before he had talked to you for ten minutes that here was one of the few leaders of mankind who could discourse on any branch of knowledge, yet could control practical affairs and drive stumbling mankind on to sane and reasonable ideals. Though a Max Gottlieb might in his research show a certain talent, yet his narrowness, his sour and antic humor, kept him from developing the broad view of education, politics, commerce, and all other noble matters which marked Dr. A. DeWitt Tubbs.

But the Director was as cordial to the insignificant Martin Arrowsmith as though Martin were a visiting senator. He shook his hand warmly; he unbent in a smile; his baritone was mellow.

"Dr. Arrowsmith, I trust we shall do more than merely say you are welcome here; I trust we shall show you how welcome you are! Dr. Gottlieb tells me that you have a natural aptitude for cloistered investigation but that you have been looking over the fields of medical practice and public health before you settled down to the laboratory. I can't tell you how wise I consider you to have made that broad preliminary survey. Too many would-be scientists lack the tutored vision which comes from co-ordinating all mental domains."

Martin was dazed to discover that he had been making a broad survey.

"Now you'll doubtless wish to take some time, perhaps a year or more, in getting into your stride, Dr. Arrowsmith. I shan't ask you for any reports. So long as Dr. Gottlieb feels that you yourself are satisfied with your progress, I shall be content. Only if there is anything in which I can advise you, from a perhaps somewhat longer career in science, please believe that I shall be delighted to be of aid, and I am quite sure the same obtains with Dr. Holabird here, though he really ought to be jealous, because he is one of our youngest workers—in fact I call him my *enfant terrible*—but you, I believe, are only thirty-three, and you quite put the poor fellow's nose out!"

Holabird merrily suggested, "Oh, no, Doctor, it's been put out long ago. You forget Terry Wickett. He's under forty."

"Oh. *Him!*" murmured Dr. Tubbs.

Martin had never heard a man disposed of so poisonously with such politeness. He saw that in Terry Wickett there might be a serpent even in this paradise.

"Now," said Dr. Tubbs, "perhaps you might like to glance around my place here. I pride myself on keeping our card-indices and letter-files as unimaginatively as though I were an insurance agent. But there is a certain exotic touch in these charts." He trotted across the room to show a nest of narrow drawers filled with scientific blue-prints.

Just what they were charts of, he did not say, nor did Martin ever learn.

He pointed to the bench at the end of the room, and laughingly admitted:

"You can see there what an inefficient fellow I really am. I keep asserting that I have given up all the idyllic delights of pathological research for the less fascinating but so very important and fatiguing cares of the directorship. Yet such is the weakness of *genus homo* that sometimes, when I ought to be attending to practical details, I become obsessed by some probably absurd pathological concept, and so ridiculous am I that I can't wait to hasten down the hall to my regular laboratory—I must always have a bench at hand and an experiment going on. Oh, I'm afraid I'm not the moral man that I pose as being in public! Here I am married to executive procedure, and still I hanker for my first love, Milady Science!"

"I think it's fine you still have an itch for it," Martin ventured.

He was wondering just what experiments Dr. Tubbs had been doing lately. The bench seemed rather unused.

"And now, Doctor, I want you to meet the real Director of the Institute —my secretary, Miss Pearl Robbins."

Martin had already noticed Miss Robbins. You could not help noticing Miss Robbins. She was thirty-five and stately, a creamy goddess. She rose to shake hands—a firm, competent grasp—and to cry in her glorious contralto, "Dr. Tubbs is so complimentary only because he knows that otherwise I wouldn't give him his afternoon tea. We've heard so much about your cleverness from Dr. Gottlieb that I'm almost afraid to welcome you, Dr. Arrowsmith, but I do want to."

Then, in a glow, Martin stood in his laboratory looking at the Woolworth Tower. He was dizzy with these wonders—his own wonders, now! In Rippleton Holabird, so gaily elegant yet so distinguished, he hoped to have a friend. He found Dr. Tubbs somewhat sentimental, but he was moved by his kindness and by Miss Robbins's recognition. He was in a haze of future glory when his door was banged open by a hard-faced, red-headed, soft-shirted man of thirty-six or -eight.

"Arrowsmith?" the intruder growled. "My name is Wickett, Terry Wickett. I'm a chemist. I'm with Gottlieb. Well, I noticed the Holy Wren was showing you the menagerie."

"Dr. Holabird?"

"Him. . . . Well, you must be more or less intelligent, if Pa Gottlieb let you in. How's it starting? Which kind are you going to be? One of the polite birds that uses the Institute for social climbing and catches him a rich wife, or one of the roughnecks like me and Gottlieb?"

Terry Wickett's croak was as irritating a sound as Martin had ever heard. He answered in a voice curiously like that of Rippleton Holabird:

"I don't think you need to worry. I happen to be married already!"

"Oh, don't let that fret you, Arrowsmith. Divorces are cheap, in this man's town. Well, did the Holy Wren show you Gladys the Tart?"

"Huh?"

"Gladys the Tart, or the Galloping Centrifuge."

"Oh. You mean the Berkeley-Saunders?"

"I do, soul of my soul. Whajuh think of it?"

"It's the finest centrifuge I've ever seen. Dr. Holabird said—"

"Hell, he ought to say something! He went and got old Tubbs to buy it. He just loves it, Holy Wren does."

"Why not? It's the fastest—"

"Sure. Speediest centrifuge in the whole *Vereinigen*, and made of the best toothpick steel. The only trouble is, it always blows out fuses, and it spatters the bugs so that you need a gas-mask if you're going to use it. . . . And did you love dear old Tubbsy and the peerless Pearl?"

"I did!"

"Fine. Of course Tubbs is an illiterate jackass but still, at that, he hasn't got persecution-mania, like Gottlieb."

"Look here, Wickett—is it Dr. Wickett?"

"Uh-huh. . . . M.D., Ph.D., but a first-rate chemist just the same."

"Well, Dr. Wickett, it seems to me a shame that a man of your talents should have to associate with idiots like Gottlieb and Tubbs and Holabird. I've just left a Chicago clinic where everybody is nice and sensible. I'd be glad to recommend you for a job there!"

"Wouldn't be so bad. At least I'd avoid all the gassing at lunch in Bonanza Hall. Well, sorry I got your goat, Arrowsmith, but you look all right to me."

"Thanks!"

Wickett grinned obscenely—red-headed, rough-faced, wiry—and snorted, "By the way, did Holabird tell you about being wounded in the first month of the war, when he was a field marshal or a hospital orderly or something in the British Army?"

"He did not! He didn't mention the war!"

"He will! Well, Brer Arrowsmith, I look forward to many happy, happy years together, playing at the feet of Pa Gottlieb. So long. My lab is right next to yours."

"Fool!" Martin decided, and, "Well, I can stand him as long as I can fall back on Gottlieb and Holabird. But— The conceited idiot! Gosh, so Holabird was in the war! Invalided out, I guess. I certainly got back at Wickett on that! 'Did he tell you about his being a jolly old hero in the blinkin' war?' he said, and I came right back at him, 'I'm sorry to displease you,' I said, 'but Dr. Holabird did not mention the war.' The idiot! Well, I won't let him worry me."

And indeed, as Martin met the staff at lunch, Wickett was the only one whom he did not find courteous, however brief their greetings. He did not distinguish among them; for days most of the twenty researchers remained a blur. He confused Dr. Yeo, head of the Department of Biology, with the carpenter who had come to put up shelves.

The staff sat in Hall at two long tables, one on the dais, one below: tiny insect groups under the massy ceiling. They were not particularly noble of aspect, these possible Darwins and Huxleys and Pasteurs. None of them were wide-browed Platos. Except for Rippleton Holabird and Max Gottlieb and perhaps Martin himself, they looked like lunching grocers: brisk featureless young men; thick mustached elders; and wimpish little men with spectacles, men whose collars did not meet. But there was a steady calm about them; there was, Martin believed, no anxiety over money in their voices nor any restlessness of envy and scandalous gossip. They talked gravely or frivolously of their work, the one sort of work that, since it becomes part of the chain of discovered fact, is eternal, however forgotten the worker's name.

As Martin listened to Terry Wickett (rude and slangy as ever, referring to himself as "the boy chemist," speaking of "this gaudy Institute" and "our trusting new lil brother, Arrowsmith") debating with a slight thin-bearded man—Dr. William T. Smith, assistant in bio-chemistry—the possibility of increasing the effects of all enzymes by doses of X-rays, as he heard one associate-member vituperate another for his notions of cell-chemistry and denounce Ehrlich as "the Edison of medical science," Martin perceived new avenues of exciting research; he stood on a mountain, and unknown valleys, craggy tantalizing paths, were open to his feet.

v

Dr. and Mrs. Rippleton Holabird invited them to dinner, a week after their coming.

As Holabird's tweeds made Clay Tredgold's smartness seem hard and pretentious, so his dinner revealed Angus Duer's affairs in Chicago as mechanical and joyless and a little anxious. Everyone whom Martin met at the Holabirds' flat was a Somebody, though perhaps a minor Somebody: a goodish editor or a rising ethnologist; and all of them had Holabird's graceful casualness.

The provincial Arrowsmiths arrived on time, therefore fifteen minutes early. Before the cocktails appeared, in old Venetian glass, Martin demanded, "Doctor, what problems are you getting after now in your physiology?"

Holabird was transformed into an ardent boy. With a deprecatory "Would you really like to hear about 'em—you needn't be polite, you know!" he dashed into an exposition of his experiments, drawing sketches on the blank spaces in newspaper advertisements, on the back of a wedding invitation, on the fly-leaf of a presentation novel, looking at Martin apologetically, learned yet gay.

"We're working on the localization of brain functions. I think we've gone beyond Bolton and Flechsig. Oh, it's jolly exciting, exploring the brain. Look here!"

His swift pencil was sketching the cerebrum; the brain lived and beat under his fingers.

He threw down the paper. "I say, it's a shame to inflict my hobbies on you. Besides, the others are coming. Tell me, how is your work going? Are you comfortable at the Institute? Do you find you like people?"

"Everybody except— To be frank, I'm jarred by Wickett."

Generously, "I know. His manner is slightly aggressive. But you mustn't mind him; he's really an extraordinarily gifted bio-chemist. He's a bachelor —gives up everything for his work. And he doesn't really mean half the rude things he says. He detests me, among others. Has he mentioned me?"

"Why, not especially—"

"I have a feeling he goes around saying that I talk about my experiences in the war, which really isn't quite altogether true."

"Yes," in a burst, "he did say that."

"I do rather wish he wouldn't. So sorry to have offended him by going and getting wounded. I'll remember and not do it again! Such a fuss for a war record as insignificant as mine! What happened was: when the war broke out in '14 I was in England, studying under Sherrington. I pretended to be a Canadian and joined up with the medical corps and got mine within three weeks and got hoofed out, and that was the end of my magnificent career! Here's somebody arriving."

His easy gallantry won Martin complete. Leora was equally captivated by Mrs. Holabird, and they went home from the dinner in new enchantment.

So began for them a white light of happiness. Martin was scarce more blissful in his undisturbed work than in his life outside the laboratory.

All the first week he forgot to ask what his salary was to be. Then it became a game to wait till the end of the month. Evenings, in little restaurants, Leora and he would speculate about it. The Institute would surely not pay him less than the twenty-five hundred dollars a year he had received at the Rouncefield Clinic, but on evenings when he was tired it dropped to fifteen hundred, and one evening when they had Burgundy he raised it to thirty-five hundred.

When his first monthly check came, neat in a little sealed envelope, he dared not look at it. He took it home to Leora. In their hotel room they stared at the envelope as though it was likely to contain poison. Martin opened it shakily; he stared, and whispered, "Oh, those decent people! They're paying me—this is for four hundred and twenty dollars—they're paying me five thousand a year!"

Mrs. Holabird, a white kitten of a woman, helped Leora find a three-room flat with a spacious living-room, in an old house near Gramercy Park, and helped her furnish it with good bits, second-hand. When Martin was permitted to look he cried, "I hope we stay here for fifty years!"

This was the Grecian isle where they found peace. Presently they had friends: the Holabirds, Dr. Billy Smith—the thin-bearded bio-chemist, who had an intelligent taste in music and German beer—an anatomist whom Martin met at a Winnemac alumni dinner, and always Max Gottlieb.

Gottlieb had found his own serenity. In the Seventies he had a brown small flat, smelling of tobacco and leather books. His son Robert had graduated from City College and gone bustlingly into business. Miriam kept up her music while she guarded her father—a dumpling of a girl, holy fire behind the deceptive flesh. After an evening of Gottlieb's acrid doubting, Martin was inspired to hasten to the laboratory and attempt a thousand new queries into the laws of micro-organisms, a task which usually began with blasphemously destroying all the work he had recently done.

Even Terry Wickett became more tolerable. Martin perceived that Wickett's snarls were partly a Clif Clawson misconception of humor, but partly a resentment, as great as Gottlieb's, of the morphological scientists who ticket things with the nicest little tickets, who name things and rename them and never analyze them. Wickett often worked all night; he was to be seen in shirt-sleeves, his sulky red hair rumpled, sitting with a stop-watch before a constant temperature bath for hours. Now and then it was a relief to have the surly intentness of Wickett instead of the elegance of Rippleton Holabird, which demanded from Martin so much painful elegance in turn, at a time when he was sunk beyond sounding in his experimentation.

# 27

His work began fumblingly. There were days when, for all the joy of it, he dreaded lest Tubbs stride in and bellow, "What are you doing here? You're the wrong Arrowsmith! Get out!"

He had isolated twenty strains of staphylococcus germs and he was testing them to discover which of them was most active in producing a hemolytic, a blood-disintegrating toxin, so that he might produce an antitoxin.

There were picturesque moments when, after centrifuging, the organisms lay in coiling cloudy masses at the bottoms of the tubes; or when the red corpuscles were completely dissolved and the opaque brick-red liquid turned to the color of pale wine. But most of the processes were incomparably tedious: removing samples of the culture every six hours, making salt suspensions of corpuscles in small tubes, recording the results.

He never knew they were tedious.

Tubbs came in now and then, found him busy, patted his shoulder, said something which sounded like French and might even have been French, and gave vague encouragement; while Gottlieb imperturbably told him to go ahead, and now and then stirred him by showing his own note-books (they were full of figures and abbreviations, stupid-seeming as invoices of calico) or by speaking of his own work, in a vocabulary as heathenish as Tibetan magic:

"Arrhenius and Madsen have made a contribution toward bringing immunity reactions under the mass action law, but I hope to show that antigen-antibody combinations occur in stoicheiometric proportions when certain variables are held constant."

"Oh, yes, I see," said Martin; and to himself: "Well, I darn' near a quarter understand that! Oh, Lord, if they'll only give me a little time and not send me back to tacking up diphtheria posters!"

When he had obtained a satisfactory toxin, Martin began his effort to find an antitoxin. He made vast experiments with no results. Sometimes he was certain that he had something, but when he rechecked his experiments he was bleakly certain that he hadn't. Once he rushed into Gottlieb's laboratory with the announcement of the antitoxin, whereupon with affection and several discomforting questions and the present of a box of real Egyptian cigarettes, Gottlieb showed him that he had not considered certain dilutions.

With all his amateurish fumbling, Martin had one characteristic without which there can be no science: a wide-ranging, sniffing, snuffling, undignified, unself-dramatizing curiosity, and it drove him on.

## II

While he puttered his insignificant way through the early years of the Great European War, the McGurk Institute had a lively existence under its placid surface.

Martin may not have learned much in the matter of antibodies but he did learn the secret of the Institute, and he saw that behind all its quiet industriousness was Capitola McGurk, the Great White Uplifter.

Capitola, Mrs. Ross McGurk, had been opposed to woman suffrage—until she learned that women were certain to get the vote—but she was a complete controller of virtuous affairs. Ross McGurk had bought the Institute not only to glorify himself but to divert Capitola and keep her itching fingers out of his shipping and mining and lumber interests, which would not too well have borne the investigations of a Great White Uplifter.

Ross McGurk was at the time a man of fifty-four, second generation of California railroad men; a graduate of Yale; big, suave, dignified, cheerful, unscrupulous. Even in 1908, when he had founded the Institute, he had had too many houses, too many servants, too much food, and no children, because Capitola considered "that sort of thing detrimental to women with large responsibilities." In the Institute he found each year more satisfaction, more excuse for having lived.

When Gottlieb arrived, McGurk went up to look him over. McGurk had bullied Dr. Tubbs now and then; Tubbs was compelled to scurry to his office as though he were a messenger boy; yet when he saw the saturnine eyes of Gottlieb, McGurk looked interested; and the two men, the bulky, clothes-conscious, powerful, reticent American and the cynical, simple, power-despising European, became friends. McGurk would slip away from a conference affecting the commerce of a whole West Indian island to sit on a high stool, silent, and watch Gottlieb work.

"Some day when I quit hustling and wake up, I'm going to become your garçon, Max," said McGurk, and Gottlieb answered, "I don't know—you haf imagination, Ross, but I t'ink you are too late to get a training in reality. Now if you do not mind eating at Childs's, we will avoid your very expostulatory Regal Hall, and I shall invite you to lunch."

But Capitola did not join their communion.

Gottlieb's arrogance had returned, and with Capitola McGurk he needed it. She had such interesting little problems for her husband's pensioners to attack. Once, in excitement, she visited Gottlieb's laboratory to tell him that large numbers of persons die of cancer, and why didn't he drop this anti-whatever-it-was and find a cure for cancer, which would be ever so nice for all of them.

But her real grievance arose when, after Rippleton Holabird had agreed to give midnight supper on the roof of the Institute to one of her most intellectual dinner-parties, she telephoned to Gottlieb, merely asking, "Would it be too much trouble for you to go down and open your lab, so we can all enjoy just a tiny peep at it?" and he answered:

"It would! Good night!"

Capitola protested to her husband. He listened—at least he seemed to listen—and remarked:

"Cap, I don't mind your playing the fool with the footmen. They've got to stand it. But if you get funny with Max, I'll simply shut up the whole Institute, and then you won't have anything to talk about at the Colony Club. And it certainly does beat the deuce that a man worth thirty million dollars—at least a fellow that's got that much—can't find a clean pair of pajamas. No, I *won't* have a valet! Oh, please now, Capitola, please quit being high-minded and let me go to sleep, will you!"

But Capitola was uncontrollable, especially in the matter of the monthly dinners which she gave at the Institute.

III

The first of the McGurk Scientific Dinners which Martin and Leora witnessed was a particularly important and explanatory dinner, because the guest of honor was Major-General Sir Isaac Mallard, the London surgeon, who was in America with a British War Mission. He had already beautifully let himself be shown through the Institute; he had been Sir Isaac'd by Dr. Tubbs and every researcher except Terry Wickett; he remembered meeting Rippleton Holabird in London, or said he remembered; and he admired Gladys the Centrifuge.

The dinner began with one misfortune in that Terry Wickett, who hitherto could be depended upon to stay decently away now appeared, volunteering to the wife of an ex-ambassador, "I simply couldn't duck this spread, with dear Sir Isaac coming. Say, if I hadn't told you, you wouldn't hardly think my dress-suit was rented, would you! Have you noticed that Sir Isaac is getting so he doesn't tear the carpet with his spurs any more? I wonder if he still kills all his mastoid patients?"

There was vast music, vaster food; there were uncomfortable scientists explaining to golden cooing ladies, in a few words, just what they were up to and what in the next twenty years they hoped to be up to; there were the cooing ladies themselves, observing in tones of pretty rebuke, "But I'm afraid you haven't yet made it as clear as you might." There were the cooing ladies' husbands—college graduates, manipulators of oil stocks or of corporation law —who sat ready to give to anybody who desired it their opinion that while antitoxins might be racy, what we really needed was a good substitute for rubber.

There was Rippleton Holabird, being charming.

And in the pause of the music, there suddenly was Terry Wickett, saying to quite an important woman, one of Capitola's most useful friends, "Yes, his name is spelled G-o-t-t-l-i-e-b but it's pronounced Gottdamn."

But such outsiders as Wickett and such silent riders as Martin and Leora and such totally absent members as Max Gottlieb were few, and the dinner waxed magnificently to a love-feast when Dr. Tubbs and Sir Isaac Mallard paid compliments to each other, to Capitola, to the sacred soil of France, to brave little Belgium, to American hospitality, to British love of privacy, and to the extremely interesting things a young man with a sense of co-operation might do in modern science.

The guests were conducted through the Institute. They inspected the marine biology aquarium, the pathological museum, and the animal house, at sight of which one sprightly lady demanded of Wickett, "Oh, the poor little guinea pigs and darling rabbicks! Now honestly, Doctor, don't you think it would be ever so much nicer if you let them go free, and just worked with your test-tubes?"

A popular physician, whose practice was among rich women, none of them west of Fifth Avenue, said to the sprightly lady, "I think you're absolutely right. I never have to kill any poor wee little beasties to get my knowledge!"

With astounding suddenness Wickett took his hat and went away.

The sprightly lady said, "You see, he didn't dare stand up to a real argument. Oh, Dr. Arrowsmith, of course I know how wonderful Ross McGurk and Dr. Tubbs and all of you are, but I must say I'm disappointed in your laboratories. I'd expected there'd be such larky retorts and electric furnaces and everything but, honestly, I don't see a single thing that's interesting, and I do think all you clever people ought to do *something* for us, now that you've coaxed us all the way down here. Can't you or somebody create life out of turtle eggs, or whatever it is? Oh, please do! Pretty please! Or at least, do put on one of these cunnin' dentist coats that you wear."

Then Martin also went rapidly away, accompanied by a furious Leora, who in the taxicab announced that she had desired to taste the champagne-cup which she had observed on the buffet, and that her husband was little short of a fool.

IV

Thus, however satisfying his work, Martin began to wonder about the perfection of his sanctuary; to wonder why Gottlieb should be so insulting at lunch to neat Dr. Sholtheis, the industrious head of the Department of Epidemiology, and why Dr. Sholtheis should endure the insults; to wonder why Dr. Tubbs, when he wandered into one's laboratory, should gurgle, "The one thing for you to keep in view in all your work is the ideal of co-operation"; to wonder why so ardent a physiologist as Rippleton Holabird should all day long be heard conferring with Tubbs instead of sweating at his bench.

Holabird had, five years before, done one bit of research which had taken his name into scientific journals throughout the world: he had studied the effect of the extirpation of the anterior lobes of a dog's brain on its ability to find its way through the laboratory. Martin had read of that research before he had thought of going to McGurk; on his arrival he was thrilled to have it chronicled by the master himself; but when he had heard Holabird refer to it a dozen times he was considerably less thrilled, and he speculated whether all his life Holabird would go on being "the man—*you* remember—the chap that did the big stunt, whatever it was, with locomotion in dogs or something."

Martin speculated still more as he perceived that all his colleagues were secretly grouped in factions.

Tubbs, Holabird, and perhaps Tubbs's secretary, Pearl Robbins, were the ruling caste. It was murmured that Holabird hoped some day to be made Assistant Director, an office which was to be created for him. Gottlieb, Terry Wickett, and Dr. Nicholas Yeo, that long-mustached and rustic biologist whom Martin had first taken for a carpenter, formed an independent faction of their own, and however much he disliked the boisterous Wickett, Martin was dragged into it.

Dr. William Smith, with his little beard and a notion of mushrooms formed in Paris, kept to himself. Dr. Sholtheis, who had been born to a synagogue in Russia but who was now the most zealous high-church Episcopalian in Yonkers, was constantly in his polite small way trying to have his scientific work commended by Gottlieb. In the Department of Bio-Physics, the good-natured chief was reviled and envied by his own assistant. And in the whole Institute there was not one man who would, in all states of liquor, assert that the work of any other scientist anywhere was completely sound, or that there was a single one of his rivals who had not stolen ideas from him. No rocking-chair clique on a summer-hotel porch, no knot of actors, ever whispered more scandal or hinted more warmly of complete idiocy in their confrères than did these uplifted scientists.

But these discoveries Martin could shut out by closing his door, and he had that to do now which deafened him to the mutters of intrigue.

v

For once Gottlieb did not amble into his laboratory but curtly summoned him. In a corner of Gottlieb's office, a den opening from his laboratory, was Terry Wickett, rolling a cigarette and looking sardonic.

Gottlieb observed, "Martin, I haf taken the privilege of talking you over with Terry, and we concluded that you haf done well enough now so it is time you stop puttering and go to work."

"I thought I was working, sir!"

All the wide placidness of his halcyon days was gone; he saw himself driven back to Pickerbaughism.

Wickett intruded, "No, you haven't. You've just been showing that you're a bright boy who might work if he only knew something."

While Martin turned on Wickett with a "Who the devil are you?" expression, Gottlieb went on:

"The fact is, Martin, you can do nothing till you know a little mathematics. If you are not going to be a cookbook bacteriologist, like most of them, you must be able to handle some of the fundamentals of science. All living things are physico-chemical machines. Then how can you make progress if you do not know physical chemistry, and how can you know physical chemistry without much mathematics?"

"Yuh," said Wickett, "you're lawn-mowing and daisy-picking, not digging."

Martin faced them. "But rats, Wickett, a man can't know everything. I'm a bacteriologist, not a physicist. Strikes me a fellow ought to use his insight, not just a chest of tools, to make discoveries. A good sailor could find his way at sea even if he didn't have instruments, and a whole *Lusitania*-ful of junk wouldn't make a good sailor out of a dub. Man ought to develop his brain, not depend on tools."

"Ye-uh, but if there were charts and quadrants in existence, a sailor that cruised off without 'em would be a chump!"

For half an hour Martin defended himself, not too politely, before the gem-like Gottlieb, the granite Wickett. All the while he knew that he was sickeningly ignorant.

They ceased to take interest. Gottlieb was looking at his note-books, Wickett was clumping off to work. Martin glared at Gottlieb. The man meant so much that he could be furious with him as he would have been with Leora, with his own self.

"I'm sorry you think I don't know anything," he raged, and departed with the finest dramatic violence. He slammed into his own laboratory, felt freed, then wretched. Without volition, like a drunken man, he stormed to Wickett's room, protesting, "I suppose you're right. My physical chemistry is nix, and my math rotten. What am I going to do—what am I going to do?"

The embarrassed barbarian grumbled, "Well, for Pete's sake, Slim, don't worry. The old man and I were just egging you on. Fact is, he's tickled to death about the careful way you're starting in. About the math—probably you're better off than the Holy Wren and Tubbs right now; you've forgotten all the math you ever knew, and they never knew any. Gosh all fishhooks! Science is supposed to mean Knowledge—from the Greek, a handsome language spoken by the good old booze-hoisting Hellenes—and the way most of the science boys resent having to stop writing little jeweled papers or giving teas and sweat at getting some knowledge certainly does make me a grand booster for the human race. My own math isn't any too good, Slim, but if you'd like to have me come around evenings and tutor you— Free, I mean!"

Thus began the friendship between Martin and Terry Wickett; thus began a change in Martin's life whereby he gave up three or four hours of wholesome sleep each night to grind over matters which everyone is assumed to know, and almost everyone does not know.

He took up algebra; found that he had forgotten most of it; cursed over the competition of the indefatigable A and the indolent B who walk from Y to Z; hired a Columbia tutor; and finished the subject, with a spurt of something like interest in regard to quadratic equations, in six weeks . . . while Leora listened, watched, waited, made sandwiches, and laughed at the tutor's jokes.

By the end of his first nine months at McGurk, Martin had reviewed trigonometry and analytic geometry and he was finding differential calculus romantic. But he made the mistake of telling Terry Wickett how much he knew.

Terry croaked, "Don't trust math too much, son," and he so confused him with references to the thermo-dynamical derivation of the mass action law, and to the oxidation reduction potential, that he stumbled again into raging humility, again saw himself an impostor and a tenth-rater.

He read the classics of physical science: Copernicus and Galileo, Lavoisier, Newton, LaPlace, Descartes, Faraday. He became completely bogged in Newton's "Fluxions"; he spoke of Newton to Tubbs and found that the illustrious Director knew nothing about him. He cheerfully mentioned this to Terry, and was shockingly cursed for his conceit as a "nouveau cultured," as a "typical enthusiastic convert," and so returned to the work whose end is satisfying because there is never an end.

His life did not seem edifying nor in any degree amusing. When Tubbs peeped into his laboratory he found a humorless young man going about his tests of hemolytic toxins, with no apparent flair for the Real Big Thing in Science, which was co-operation and being efficient. Tubbs tried to set him straight with "Are you quite sure you're following a regular demarked line in your work?"

It was Leora who bore the real tedium.

She sat quiet (a frail child, only up to one's shoulder, not nine minutes older than at marriage, nine years before), or she napped inoffensively, in the long living-room of their flat, while he worked over his dreary digit-infested books till one, till two, and she politely awoke to let him worry at her, "But look here now, I've got to keep up my research at the same time. God, I am so tired!"

She dragged him away for an illegal five-day walk on Cape Cod, in March. He sat between the Twin Lights at Chatham, and fumed, "I'm going back and tell Terry and Gottlieb they can go to the devil with their crazy physical chemistry. I've had enough, now I've done math," and she commented, "Yes, I certainly would—though isn't it funny how Dr. Gottlieb always seems to be right?"

He was so absorbed in staphylolysin and in calculus that he did not realize the world was about to be made safe for democracy. He was a little dazed when America entered the war.

VI

Dr. Tubbs dashed to Washington to offer the services of the Institute to the War Department.

All the members of the staff, except Gottlieb and two others who declined to be so honored, were made officers and told to run out and buy nice uniforms.

Tubbs became a Colonel, Rippleton Holabird a Major, Martin and Wickett and Billy Smith were Captains. But the garçons had no military rank whatever, nor any military duties except the polishing of brown riding-boots and leather puttees, which the several warriors wore as pleased their fancies or their legs. And the most belligerent of all, Miss Pearl Robbins, she who at tea heroically slaughtered not only German men but all their women and viperine children, was wickedly unrecognized and had to make up a uniform for herself.

The only one of them who got nearer to the front than Liberty Street was Terry Wickett, who suddenly asked for leave, was transferred to the artillery, and sailed off to France.

He apologized to Martin: "I'm ashamed of chucking my work like this, and I certainly don't want to kill Germans—I mean not any more'n I want to kill most people—but I never could resist getting into a big show. Say, Slim, keep an eye on Pa Gottlieb, will you? This has hit him bad. He's got a bunch of nephews and so on in the German army, and the patriots like Big Foot Pearl will give an exhibit of idealism by persecuting him. So long, Slim, take care y'self."

Martin had vaguely protested at being herded into the army. The war was to him chiefly another interruption to his work, like Pickerbaughism, like earning his living at Wheatsylvania. But when he had gone strutting forth in uniform, it was so enjoyable that for several weeks he was a standard patriot. He had never looked so well, so taut and erect, as in khaki. It was enchanting to be saluted by privates, quite as enchanting to return the salute in the dignified, patronizing, all-comrades-together splendor which Martin shared with the other doctors, professors, lawyers, brokers, authors, and former socialist intellectuals who were his fellow-officers.

But in a month the pleasures of being a hero became mechanical, and Martin longed for soft shirts, easy shoes, and clothes with reasonable pockets. His puttees were a nuisance to wear and an inferno to put on; his collar pinched his neck and jabbed his chin; and it was wearing on a man who sat up till three, on the perilous duty of studying calculus, to be snappy at every salute.

Under the martinet eye of Col. Director Dr. A. DeWitt Tubbs he had to wear his uniform, at least recognizable portions of it, at the Institute, but by evening he slipped into the habit of sneaking into citizen clothes, and when he went with Leora to the movies he had an agreeable feeling of being Absent Without Leave, of risking at every street corner arrest by the Military Police and execution at dawn.

Unfortunately no M.P. ever looked at him. But one evening when in an estimable and innocent manner he was looking at the remains of a gunman who had just been murdered by another gunman, he realized that Major Rippleton Holabird was standing by, glaring. For once the Major was unpleasant:

"Captain, does it seem to you that this is quite playing the game, to wear mufti? We, unfortunately, with our scientific work, haven't the privilege of joining the Boys who are up against the real thing, but we are under orders just as if we were in the trenches—where *some* of us would so much like to be again! Captain, I trust I shall never again see you breaking the order about being in uniform, or—uh—"

Martin blurted to Leora, later:

"I'm sick of hearing about his being wounded. Nothing that I can see to prevent his going back to the trenches. Wound's all right now. I want to be patriotic, but my patriotism is chasing antitoxins, doing my job, not wearing a particular kind of pants and a particular set of ideas about the Germans. Mind you, I'm anti-German all right—I think they're probably just as bad as we are. Oh, let's go back and do some more calculus. . . . Darling, my working nights doesn't bore you too much, does it?"

Leora had cunning. When she could not be enthusiastic, she could be unannoyingly silent.

At the Institute Martin perceived that he was not the only defender of his country who was not comfortable in the garb of heroes. The most dismal of the staff-members was Dr. Nicholas Yeo, the Yankee sandy-mustached head of the Department of Biology.

Yeo had put on Major's uniform, but he never felt neighborly with it. (He knew he was a Major, because Col. Dr. Tubbs had told him he was, and he knew that this was a Major's uniform, because the clothing salesman said so.) He walked out of the McGurk Building in a melancholy, deprecatory way, with one breeches leg bulging over his riding-boots; and however piously he tried, he never remembered to button his blouse over the violet-flowered shirts which, he often confided, you could buy ever so cheap on Eighth Avenue.

But Major Dr. Yeo had one military triumph. He hoarsely explained to Martin, as they were marching to the completely militarized dining-hall:

"Say, Arrowsmith, do you ever get balled up about this saluting? Darn it, I never can figure out what all these insignia mean. One time I took a Salvation Army Lieutenant for a Y.M.C.A. General, or maybe he was a Portygee. But I've got the idea now!" Yeo laid his finger beside his large nose, and produced wisdom: "Whenever I see any fellow in uniform that looks older than I am, I salute him—my nephew, Ted, has drilled me so I salute swell now—and if he don't salute back, well, Lord, I just think about my work and don't fuss. If you look at it scientifically, this military life isn't so awful' hard after all!"

### VII

Always, in Paris or in Bonn, Max Gottlieb had looked to America as a land which, in its freedom from Royalist tradition, in its contact with the realities of cornfields and blizzards and town-meetings, had set its face against the puerile pride of war. He believed that he had ceased to be a German, now, and become a countryman of Lincoln.

The European War was the one thing, besides his discharge from Winnemac, which had ever broken his sardonic serenity. In the war he could see no splendor nor hope, but only crawling tragedy. He treasured his months of work and good talk in France, in England, in Italy; he loved his French and English and Italian friends as he loved his ancient *Korpsbrüder*, and very well indeed beneath his mocking did he love the Germans with whom he had drudged and drunk.

His sister's sons—on home-craving vacations he had seen them, in babyhood, in boyhood, in ruffling youngmanhood—went out with the Kaiser's colors in 1914; one of them became an Oberst, much decorated, one existed insignificantly, and one was dead and stinking in ten days. This he sadly endured, as later he endured his son Robert's going out as an American lieutenant, to fight his own cousins. What struck down this man to whom abstractions and scientific laws were more than kindly flesh was the mania of hate which overcame the unmilitaristic America to which he had emigrated in protest against Junkerdom.

Incredulously he perceived women asserting that all Germans were babykillers, universities barring the language of Heine, orchestras outlawing the music of Beethoven, professors in uniform bellowing at clerks, and the clerks never protesting.

It is uncertain whether the real hurt was to his love for America or to his egotism, that he should have guessed so grotesquely; it is curious that he who had so denounced the machine-made education of the land should yet have been surprised when it turned blithely to the old, old, mechanical mockeries of war.

When the Institute sanctified the war, he found himself regarded not as the great and impersonal immunologist but as a suspect German Jew.

True, the Terry who went off to the artillery did not look upon him dourly, but Major Rippleton Holabird became erect and stiff when they passed in the corridor. When Gottlieb insisted to Tubbs at lunch, "I am villing to admit every virtue of the French—I am very fond of that so individual people—but on the theory of probabilities I suggest that there must be some good Germans out of sixty millions," then Col. Dr. Tubbs commanded, "In this time of world tragedy, it does not seem to me particularly becoming to try to be flippant, Dr. Gottlieb!"

In shops and on the elevated trains, little red-faced sweaty people when they heard his accent glared at him, and growled one to another, "There's one of them damn' barb'rous well-poisoning Huns!" and however contemptuous he might be, however much he strove for ignoring pride, their nibbling reduced him from arrogant scientist to an insecure, raw-nerved, shrinking old man.

And once a hostess who of old time had been proud to know him, a hostess whose maiden name was Straufnabel and who had married into the famous old Anglican family of Rosemont, when Gottlieb bade her "*Auf Wiedersehen*" cried out upon him, "Dr. Gottlieb, I'm very sorry, but the use of that disgusting language is not permitted in this house!"

He had almost recovered from the anxieties of Winnemac and the Hunziker factory; he had begun to expand, to entertain people—scientists, musicians, talkers. Now he was thrust back into himself. With Terry gone, he trusted only Miriam and Martin and Ross McGurk; and his deep-set wrinkle-lidded eyes looked ever on sadness.

But he could still be tart. He suggested that Capitola ought to have in the window of her house a Service Flag with a star for every person at the Institute who had put on uniform.

She took it quite seriously, and did it.

VIII

The military duties of the McGurk staff did not consist entirely in wearing uniforms, receiving salutes, and listening to Col. Dr. Tubbs's luncheon lectures on "the part America will inevitably play in the reconstruction of a Democratic Europe."

They prepared sera; the assistant in the Department of Bio-Physics was inventing electrified wire entanglements; Dr. Billy Smith, who six months before had been singing *Student Lieder* at Lüchow's, was working on poison gas to be used against all singers of *Lieder*; and to Martin was assigned the manufacture of lipovaccine, a suspension of finely ground typhoid and para-typhoid organisms in oil. It was a greasy job, and dull. Martin was faithful enough about it, and gave to it almost every morning, but he blasphemed more than usual and he unholily welcomed scientific papers in which lipovac-cines were condemned as inferior to ordinary salt solutions.

He was conscious of Gottlieb's sorrowing and tried to comfort him.

It was Martin's most pitiful fault that he was not very kind to shy people and lonely people and stupid old people; he was not cruel to them, he simply was unconscious of them or so impatient of their fumbling that he avoided them. Whenever Leora taxed him with it he grumbled:

"Well, but— I'm too much absorbed in my work, or in doping stuff out, to waste time on morons. And it's a good thing. Most people above the grade of hog do so much chasing around after a lot of vague philanthropy that they never get anything done—and most of your confounded shy people get spiritually pauperized. Oh, it's so much easier to be good-natured and purring and self-congratulatory and generally footless than it is to pound ahead and keep yourself strictly for your own work, the work that gets some-where. Very few people have the courage to be decently selfish—not answer letters—and demand the right to work. If they had their way, these sentimen-talists would've had a Newton—yes, or probably a Christ!—giving up every-thing they did for the world to address meetings and listen to the troubles of cranky old maids. Nothing takes so much courage as to keep hard and clear-headed."

And he hadn't even that courage.

When Leora had made complaint, he would be forcibly kind to all sorts of alarmed stray beggars for a day or two, then drift back into his absorption. There were but two people whose unhappiness could always pierce him: Leora and Gottlieb.

Though he was busier than he had known anyone could ever be, with lipovaccines in the morning, physical chemistry in the evening and, at all sorts of intense hours between, the continuation of his staphylolysin research, he gave what time he could to seeking out Gottlieb and warming his vanity by reverent listening.

Then his research wiped out everything else, made him forget Gottlieb and Leora and all his briskness about studying, made him turn his war work over to others, and confounded night and day in one insane flaming blur as he realized that he had something not unworthy of a Gottlieb, something at the mysterious source of life.

# 28

Captain Martin Arrowsmith, M.R.C., came home to his good wife Leora, wailing, "I'm so rotten tired, and I feel kind of discouraged. I haven't accomplished a darn' thing in this whole year at McGurk. Sterile. No good. And I'm hanged if I'll study calculus this evening. Let's go to the movies. Won't even change to regular human clothes. Too tired."

"All right, honey," said Leora. "But let's have dinner here. I bought a wonderful ole fish this afternoon."

Through the film Martin gave his opinion, as a captain and as a doctor, that it seemed improbable a mother should not know her daughter after an absence of ten years. He was restless and rational, which is not a mood in which to view the cinema. When they came blinking out of that darkness lit only from the shadowy screen, he snorted, "I'm going back to the lab. I'll put you in a taxi."

"Oh, let the beastly thing go for one night."

"Now that's unfair! I haven't worked late for three or four nights now!"

"Then take me along."

"Nope. I have a hunch I may be working all night."

Liberty Street, as he raced along it, was sleeping below its towers. It was McGurk's order that the elevator to the Institute should run all night, and indeed three or four of the twenty staff-members did sometimes use it after respectable hours.

That morning Martin had isolated a new strain of staphylococcus bacteria from the gluteal carbuncle of a patient in the Lower Manhattan Hospital, a carbuncle which was healing with unusual rapidity. He had placed a bit of the pus in broth and incubated it. In eight hours a good growth of bacteria had appeared. Before going wearily home he had returned the flask to the incubator.

He was not particularly interested in it, and now, in his laboratory, he removed his military blouse, looked down to the lights on the blue-black river, smoked a little, thought what a dog he was not to be gentler to Leora, and damned Bert Tozer and Pickerbaugh and Tubbs and anybody else who was handy to his memory before he absent-mindedly wavered to the incubator, and found that the flask, in which there should have been a perceptible cloudy growth, had no longer any signs of bacteria—of staphylococci.

"Now what the hell!" he cried. "Why, the broth's as clear as when I seeded it! Now what the— Think of this fool accident coming up just when I was going to start something new!"

He hastened from the incubator, in a closet off the corridor, to his laboratory and, holding the flask under a strong light, made certain that he had seen aright. He fretfully prepared a slide from the flask contents and examined it under the microscope. He discovered nothing but shadows of what had been bacteria: thin outlines, the form still there but the cell substance gone; minute skeletons on an infinitesimal battlefield.

He raised his head from the microscope, rubbed his tired eyes, reflectively rubbed his neck—his blouse was off, his collar on the floor, his shirt open at the throat. He considered:

"Something funny here. This culture was growing all right, and now it's committed suicide. Never heard of bugs doing that before. I've hit something! What caused it? Some chemical change? Something organic?"

Now in Martin Arrowsmith there were no decorative heroisms, no genius for amours, no exotic wit, no edifyingly borne misfortunes. He presented neither picturesque elegance nor a moral message. He was full of hasty faults and of perverse honesty; a young man often unkindly, often impolite. But he had one gift: a curiosity whereby he saw nothing as ordinary. Had he been an acceptable hero, like Major Rippleton Holabird, he would have chucked the contents of the flask into the sink, avowed with pretty modesty, "Silly! I've made some error!" and gone his ways. But Martin, being Martin, walked prosaically up and down his laboratory, snarling, "Now there was some *cause* for that, and I'm going to find out what it was."

He did have one romantic notion: he would telephone to Leora and tell her that splendor was happening, and she wasn't to worry about him. He fumbled down the corridor, lighting matches, trying to find electric switches.

At night all halls are haunted. Even in the smirkingly new McGurk Building there had been a bookkeeper who committed suicide. As Martin groped he was shakily conscious of feet padding behind him, of shapes which leered from doorways and insolently vanished, of ancient bodiless horrors, and when he found the switch he rejoiced in the blessing and security of sudden light that recreated the world.

At the Institute telephone switchboard he plugged in wherever it seemed reasonable. Once he thought he was talking to Leora, but it proved to be a voice, sexless and intolerant, which said "Nummer pleeeeeze" with a taut alertness impossible to anyone so indolent as Leora. Once it was a voice which slobbered, "Is this Sarah?" then, "I don't want *you!* Ring off, will yuh!" Once a girl pleaded, "Honestly, Billy, I did try to get there but the boss came in at five and he said—"

As for the rest it was only a burring; the sound of seven million people hungry for sleep or love or money.

He observed, "Oh, rats, I guess Lee'll have gone to bed by now," and felt his way back to the laboratory.

A detective, hunting the murderer of bacteria, he stood with his head back, scratching his chin, scratching his memory for like cases of microorganisms committing suicide or being slain without perceptible cause. He rushed up-stairs to the library, consulted the American and English authorities and, laboriously, the French and German. He found nothing.

He worried lest there might, somehow, have been no living staphylococci in the pus which he had used for seeding the broth—none there to die. At a hectic run, not stopping for lights, bumping corners and sliding on the too perfect tile floor, he skidded down the stairs and galloped through the corridors to his room. He found the remains of the original pus, made a smear on a glass slide, and stained it with gentian-violet, nervously dribbling out one drop of the gorgeous dye. He sprang to the microscope. As he bent over the brass tube and focused the objective, into the gray-lavender circular field of vision rose to existence the grape-like clusters of staphylococcus germs, purple dots against the blank plane.

"Staph in it, all right!" he shouted.

Then he forgot Leora, war, night, weariness, success, everything, as he charged into preparations for an experiment, his first great experiment. He paced furiously, rather dizzy. He shook himself into calmness and settled down at a table, among rings and spirals of cigarette smoke, to list on small sheets of paper all the possible causes of suicide in the bacteria—all the questions he had to answer and the experiments which should answer them.

It might be that alkali in an improperly cleaned flask had caused the clearing of the culture. It might be some anti-staph substance existing in the pus, or something liberated by the staphylococci themselves. It might be some peculiarity of this particular broth.

Each of these had to be tested.

He pried open the door of the glass-storeroom, shattering the lock. He took new flasks, cleaned them, plugged them with cotton, and placed them in the hot-air oven to sterilize. He found other batches of broth—as a matter of fact he stole them, from Gottlieb's private and highly sacred supply in the ice-box. He filtered some of the clarified culture through a sterile porcelain filter, and added it to his regular staphylococcus strains.

And, perhaps most important of all, he discovered that he was out of cigarettes.

Incredulously he slapped each of his pockets, and went the round and slapped them all over again. He looked into his discarded military blouse; had a cheering idea about having seen cigarettes in a drawer; did not find them; and brazenly marched into the room where hung the aprons and jackets of the technicians. Furiously he pilfered pockets, and found a dozen beautiful cigarettes in a wrinkled and flattened paper case.

To test each of the four possible causes of the flask's clearing he prepared and seeded with bacteria a series of flasks under varying conditions, and set them away in the incubator at body temperature. Till the last flask was put away, his hand was steady, his worn face calm. He was above all nervousness, free from all uncertainty, a professional going about his business.

By this time it was six o'clock of a fine wide August morning, and as he ceased his swift work, as taut nerves slackened, he looked out of his lofty window and was conscious of the world below: bright roofs, jubilant towers, and a high-decked Sound steamer swaggering up the glossy river.

He was completely fagged; he was, like a surgeon after a battle, like a reporter during an earthquake, perhaps a little insane; but sleepy he was not. He cursed the delay involved in the growth of the bacteria, without which he could not discover the effect of the various sorts of broths and bacterial strains, but choked his impatience.

He mounted the noisy slate stairway to the lofty world of the roof. He listened at the door of the Institute's animal house. The guinea pigs, awake and nibbling, were making a sound like that of a wet cloth rubbed on glass in window-cleaning. He stamped his foot, and in fright they broke out in their strange sound of fear, like the cooing of doves.

He marched violently up and down, refreshed by the soaring sky, till he was calmed to hunger. Again he went pillaging. He found chocolate belonging to an innocent technician; he even invaded the office of the Director and in the desk of the Diana-like Pearl Robbins unearthed tea and a kettle (as well as a lip-stick, and a love-letter beginning "My Little Ickles"). He made himself a profoundly bad cup of tea, then, his whole body dragging, returned to his table to set down elaborately, in a shabby, nearly-filled note-book, every step of his experiment.

After seven he worked out the operation of the telephone switchboard and called the Lower Manhattan Hospital. Could Dr. Arrowsmith have some more pus from the same carbuncle? What? It'd healed? Curse it! No more of that material.

He hesitated over waiting for Gottlieb's arrival, to tell him of the discovery, but determined to keep silence till he should have determined whether it was an accident. Eyes wide, too wrought up to sleep in the subway, he fled uptown to tell Leora. He had to tell someone! Waves of fear, doubt, certainty, and fear again swept over him; his ears rang and his hands trembled.

He rushed up to the flat; he bawled "Lee! Lee!" before he had unlocked the door. And she was gone.

He gaped. The flat breathed emptiness. He searched it again. She had slept there, she had had a cup of coffee, but she had vanished.

He was at once worried lest there had been an accident, and furious that she should not have been here at the great hour. Sullenly he made breakfast for himself. . . . It is strange that excellent bacteriologists and chemists should scramble eggs so waterily, should make such bitter coffee and be so casual about dirty spoons. . . . By the time he had finished the mess he was ready to believe that Leora had left him forever. He quavered, "I've neglected her a lot." Sluggishly, an old man now, he started for the Institute, and at the entrance to the subway he met her.

She wailed, "I was so worried! I couldn't get you on the 'phone. I went clear down to the Institute to see what'd happened to you."

He kissed her, very competently, and raved, "God, woman, I've got it! The real big stuff! I've found something, not a chemical you put in I mean, that eats bugs—dissolves 'em—kills 'em. May be a big new step in therapeutics. Oh, no, rats, I don't suppose it really is. Prob'ly just another of my bulls."

She sought to reassure him but he did not wait. He dashed down to the subway, promising to telephone to her. By ten, he was peering into his incubator.

There was a cloudy appearance of bacteria in all the flasks except those in which he had used broth from the original alarming flask. In these, the mysterious murderer of germs had prevented the growth of the new bacteria which he had introduced.

"Great stuff," he said.

He returned the flasks to the incubator, recorded his observations, went again to the library, and searched handbooks, bound proceedings of societies, periodicals in three languages. He had acquired a reasonable scientific French and German. It is doubtful whether he could have bought a drink or asked the way to the Kursaal in either language, but he understood the universal Hellenistic scientific jargon, and he pawed through the heavy books, rubbing his eyes, which were filled with salty fire.

He remembered that he was an army officer and had lipovaccine to make this morning. He went to work, but he was so twitchy that he ruined the batch, called his patient garçon a fool, and after this injustice sent him out for a pint of whisky.

He had to have a confidant. He telephoned to Leora, lunched with her expensively, and asserted, "It still looks as if there were something to it." He was back in the Institute every hour that afternoon, glancing at his flasks, but between he tramped the streets, creaking with weariness, drinking too much coffee.

Every five minutes it came to him, as a quite new and ecstatic idea, "Why don't I go to sleep?" then he remembered, and groaned, "No, I've got to keep going and watch every step. Can't leave it, or I'll have to begin all over again. But I'm so sleepy! Why don't I go to sleep?"

He dug down, before six, into a new layer of strength, and at six his examination showed that the flasks containing the original broth still had no growth of bacteria, and the flasks which he had seeded with the original pus had, like the first eccentric flask, after beginning to display a good growth of bacteria cleared up again under the slowly developing attack of the unknown assassin.

He sat down, drooping with relief. He had it! He stated in the conclusions of his first notes:

"I have observed a principle, which I shall temporarily call the X Principle, in pus from a staphylococcus infection, which checks the growth of several strains of staphylococcus, and which dissolves the staphylococci from the pus in question."

When he had finished, at seven, his head was on his notebook and he was asleep.

He awoke at ten, went home, ate like a savage, slept again, and was in the laboratory before dawn. His next rest was an hour that afternoon, sprawled on his laboratory table, with his garçon on guard; the next, a day and a half later, was eight hours in bed, from dawn till noon.

But in dreams he was constantly upsetting a rack of test-tubes or breaking a flask. He discovered an X Principle which dissolved chairs, tables, human beings. He went about smearing it on Bert Tozers and Dr. Bissexes and fiendishly watching them vanish, but accidentally he dropped it on Leora and saw her fading, and he woke screaming to find the real Leora's arms about him, while he sobbed, "Oh, I couldn't do anything without you! Don't ever leave me! I do love you so, even if this damned work does keep me tied up. Stay with me!"

While she sat by him on the frowsy bed, gay in her gingham, he went to sleep, to wake up three hours later and start off for the Institute, his eyes blood-glaring and set. She was ready for him with strong coffee, waiting on him silently, looking at him proudly, while he waved his arms, babbling:

"Gottlieb better not talk any more about the importance of new observations! The X Principle may not just apply to staph. Maybe you can sic it on any bug—cure any germ disease by it. Bug that lives on bugs! Or maybe it's a chemical principle, an enzyme. Oh, I don't know. But I will!"

As he bustled to the Institute he swelled with the certainty that after years of stumbling he had arrived. He had visions of his name in journals and textbooks; of scientific meetings cheering him. He had been an unknown among the experts of the Institute, and now he pitied all of them. But when he was back at his bench the grandiose aspirations faded and he was the sniffing, snuffling beagle, the impersonal worker. Before him, supreme joy of the investigator, new mountain-passes of work opened, and in him was new power.

II

For a week Martin's life had all the regularity of an escaped soldier in the enemy's country, with the same agitation and the same desire to prowl at night. He was always sterilizing flasks, preparing media of various hydrogen-ion concentrations, copying his old notes into a new book lovingly labeled "X Principle, Staph," and adding to it further observations. He tried, elaborately, with many flasks and many reseedings, to determine whether the X Principle would perpetuate itself indefinitely, whether when it was transmitted from tube to new tube of bacteria it would reappear, whether, growing by cell-division automatically, it was veritably a germ, a sub-germ infecting germs.

During the week Gottlieb occasionally peered over his shoulder, but Martin was unwilling to report until he should have proof, and one good night's sleep, and perhaps even a shave.

When he was sure that the X Principle did reproduce itself indefinitely, so that in the tenth tube it grew to have as much effect as in the first, then he solemnly called on Gottlieb and laid before him his results, with his plans for further investigation.

The old man tapped his thin fingers on the report, read it intently, looked up and, not wasting time in congratulations, vomited questions:

Have you done dis? Why have you not done dat? At what temperature is the activity of the Principle at its maximum? Is its activity manifested on agar-solid medium?

"This is my plan for new work. I think you'll find it includes most of your suggestions."

"Huh!" Gottlieb ran through it and snorted, "Why have you not planned to propagate it on dead staph? That is most important of all."

"Why?"

Gottlieb flew instantly to the heart of the jungle in which Martin had struggled for many days: "Because that will show whether you are dealing with a living virus."

Martin was humbled, but Gottlieb beamed:

"You haf a big thing. Now do not let the Director know about this and get enthusiastic too soon. I am glad, Martin!"

There was that in his voice which sent Martin swanking down the corridor, back to work—and to not sleeping.

What the X Principle was—chemical or germ—he could not determine, but certainly the original Principle flourished. It could be transmitted indefinitely; he determined the best temperature for it and found that it did not propagate on dead staphylococcus. When he added a drop containing the Principle to a growth of staphylococcus which was a gray film on the solid surface of agar, the drop was beautifully outlined by bare patches, as the enemy made its attack, so that the agar slant looked like moth-eaten beeswax. But within a fortnight one of the knots of which Gottlieb warned him appeared.

Wary of the hundreds of bacteriologists who would rise to slay him once his paper appeared, he sought to make sure that his results could be confirmed. At the hospital he obtained pus from many boils, of the arms, the legs, the back; he sought to reduplicate his results—and failed, complete. No X Principle appeared in any of the new boils, and sadly he went to Gottlieb.

The old man meditated, asked a question or two, sat hunched in his cushioned chair, and demanded:

"What kind of a carbuncle was the original one?"

"Gluteal."

"Ah, den the X Principle may be present in the intestinal contents. Look for it, in people with boils and without."

Martin dashed off. In a week he had obtained the Principle from intestinal contents and from other gluteal boils, finding an especial amount in boils which were "healing of themselves"; and he transplanted his new Principle, in a heaven of triumph, of admiration for Gottlieb. He extended his investigation to the intestinal group of organisms and discovered an X Principle against the colon bacillus. At the same time he gave some of the original Principle to a doctor in the Lower Manhattan Hospital for the treatment of boils, and from him had excited reports of cures, more excited inquiries as to what this mystery might be.

With these new victories he went parading in to Gottlieb, and suddenly he was being trounced:

"Oh! So! Beautiful! You let a doctor try it before you finished your research? You want fake reports of cures to get into the newspapers, to be telegraphed about places, and have everybody in the world that has a pimple come tumbling in to be cured, so you will never be able to work? You want to be a miracle man, and not a scientist? You do not want to complete things? You wander off monkey-skipping and flap-doodeling with colon bacillus before you have finish with staph—before you haf really begun your work—before you have found what is the *nature* of the X Principle? Get out of my office! You are a—a—a college president! Next I know you will be dining with Tubbs, and get your picture in the papers for a smart cure-vendor!"

Martin crept out, and when he met Billy Smith in the corridor and the little chemist twittered, "Up to something big? Haven't seen you lately," Martin answered in the tone of Doc Vickerson's assistant in Elk Mills:

"Oh—no—gee—I'm just grubbing along, I guess."

### III

As sharply and quite as impersonally as he would have watched the crawling illness of an infected guinea pig, Martin watched himself, in the madness of overwork, drift toward neurasthenia. With considerable interest he looked up the symptoms of neurasthenia, saw one after another of them twitch at him, and casually took the risk.

From an irritability which made him a thoroughly impossible person to live with, he passed into a sick nervousness in which he missed things for which he reached, dropped test-tubes, gasped at sudden footsteps behind him. Dr. Yeo's croaking voice became to him a fever, an insult, and he waited with his whole body clenched, muttering, "Shut up—shut up—oh, shut *up!*" when Yeo stopped to talk to someone outside his door.

Then he was obsessed by the desire to spell backward all the words which snatched at him from signs.

As he stood dragging out his shoulder on a subway strap, he pored over the posters, seeking new words to spell backward. Some of them were remarkably agreeable: No Smoking became a jaunty and agreeable "gnikoms on," and Broadway was tolerable as "yawdaorb," but he was displeased by his attempts on Punch, Health, Rough; while Strength, turning into "htgnerts" was abominable.

When he had to return to his laboratory three times before he was satisfied that he had closed the window, he sat down, coldly, informed himself that he was on the edge, and took council as to whether he dared go on. It was not very good council: he was so glorified by his unfolding work that his self could not be taken seriously.

At last Fear closed in on him.

It began with childhood's terror of the darkness. He lay awake dreading burglars; footsteps in the hall were a creeping cutthroat; an unexplained scratching on the fire-escape was a murderer with an automatic in his fist. He beheld it so clearly that he had to spring from bed and look timorously out, and when in the street below he did actually see a man standing still, he was cold with panic.

Every sky glow was a fire. He was going to be trapped in his bed, be smothered, die writhing.

He knew absolutely that his fears were absurd, and that knowledge did not at all keep them from dominating him.

He was ashamed at first to acknowledge his seeming cowardice to Leora. Admit that he was crouching like a child? But when he had lain rigid, almost screaming, feeling the cord of an assassin squeezing his throat, till the safe dawn brought back a dependable world, he muttered of "insomnia" and after that, night on night, he crept into her arms and she shielded him from the horrors, protected him from garroters, kept away the fire.

He made a checking list of the favorite neurasthenic fears: agoraphobia, claustrophobia, pyrophobia, anthropophobia, and the rest, ending with what he asserted to be "the most fool, pretentious, witch-doctor term of the whole bloomin' lot," namely, siderodromophobia, the fear of a railway journey. The first night, he was able to check against pyrophobia, for at the vaudeville with Leora, when on the stage a dancer lighted a brazier, he sat waiting for the theater to take fire. He looked cautiously along the row of seats (raging at himself the while for doing it), he estimated his chance of reaching an exit, and became easy only when he had escaped into the street.

It was when anthropophobia set in, when he was made uneasy by people who walked too close to him, that, sagely viewing his list and seeing how many phobias were now checked, he permitted himself to rest.

He fled to the Vermont hills for a four-day tramp—alone, that he might pound on the faster. He went at night, by sleeper, and was able to make the most interesting observations of siderodromophobia.

He lay in a lower berth, the little pillow wadded into a lump. He was annoyed by the waving of his clothes as they trailed from the hanger beside him, at the opening of the green curtains. The window-shade was up six inches; it left a milky blur across which streaked yellow lights, emphatic in the noisy darkness of his little cell. He was shivering with anxiety. Whenever he tried to relax, he was ironed back into apprehension. When the train stopped between stations and from the engine came a questioning, fretful whistle, he was aghast with certainty that something had gone wrong—a bridge was out, a train was ahead of them; perhaps another was coming just behind them, about to smash into them at sixty miles an hour—

He imagined being wrecked, and he suffered more than from the actual occurrence, for he pictured not one wreck but half a dozen, with assorted miseries. . . . The flat wheel just beneath him—surely it shouldn't pound like that—why hadn't the confounded man with the hammer detected it at the last big station?—the flat wheel cracking; the car lurching, falling, being dragged on its side. . . . A collision, a crash, the car instantly a crumpled, horrible heap, himself pinned in the telescoped berth, caught between seat and seat. Shrieks, death groans, the creeping flames. . . . The car turning, falling, plumping into a river on its side; himself trying to crawl through a window as the water seeped about his body. . . . Himself standing by the wrenched car, deciding whether to keep away and protect his sacred work or go back, rescue people, and be killed.

So real were the visions that he could not endure lying here, waiting. He reached for the berth light, and could not find the button. In agitation he tore a match-box from his coat pocket, scratched a match, snapped on the light. He saw himself, under the sheets, reflected in the polished wooden ceiling of his berth like a corpse in a coffin. Hastily he crawled out, with trousers and coat over his undergarments (he had somehow feared to show so much trust in the train as to put on pajamas), and with bare disgusted feet he paddled up to the smoking compartment.

The porter was squatting on a stool, polishing an amazing pile of shoes.

Martin longed for his encouraging companionship, and ventured, "Warm night."

"Uh-huh," said the porter.

Martin curled on the chill leather seat of the smoking compartment, profoundly studying a brass wash-bowl. He was conscious that the porter was disapproving, but he had comfort in calculating that the man must make this run thrice a week, tens of thousands of miles yearly, apparently without being killed, and there might be a chance of their lasting till morning.

He smoked till his tongue was raw and till, fortified by the calmness of the porter, he laughed at the imaginary catastrophes. He staggered sleepily to his berth.

Instantly he was tense again, and he lay awake till dawn.

For four days he tramped, swam in cold brooks, slept under trees or in straw stacks, and came back (but by day) with enough reserve of energy to support him till his experiment should have turned from overwhelming glory into sane and entertaining routine.


# 29


When the work on the X Principle had gone on for six weeks, the Institute staff suspected that something was occurring, and they hinted to Martin that he needed their several assistances. He avoided them. He did not desire to be caught in any of the log-rolling factions, though for Terry Wickett, still in France, and for Terry's rough compulsion to honesty he was sometimes lonely.

How the Director first heard that Martin was finding gold is not known.

Dr. Tubbs was tired of being a Colonel—there were too many Generals in New York—and for two weeks he had not had an Idea which would revolutionize even a small part of the world. One morning he burst in, whiskers alive, and reproached Martin:

"What is this mysterious discovery you're making, Arrowsmith? I've asked Dr. Gottlieb, but he evades me; he says you want to be sure, first. I must know about it, not only because I take a very friendly interest in your work but because I am, after all, your Director!"

Martin felt that his one ewe lamb was being snatched from him but he could see no way to refuse. He brought out his note-books and the agar slants with their dissolved patches of bacilli. Tubbs gasped, assaulted his whiskers, did a moment of impressive thinking, and clamored:

"Do you mean to say you think you've discovered an infectious disease of bacteria, and you haven't told me about it? My dear boy, I don't believe you quite realize that you may have hit on the supreme way to kill pathogenic bacteria. . . . And you didn't tell me!"

"Well, sir, I wanted to make certain—"

"I admire your caution, but you must understand, Martin, that the basic aim of this Institution is the conquest of disease, not making pretty scientific notes! You *may* have hit on one of the discoveries of a generation; the sort of thing that Mr. McGurk and I are looking for. . . . If your results are confirmed. . . . I shall ask Dr. Gottlieb's opinion."

He shook Martin's hand five or six times and bustled out. Next day he called Martin to his office, shook his hand some more, told Pearl Robbins that they were honored to know him, then led him to a mountain top and showed him all the kingdoms of the world:

"Martin, I have some plans for you. You have been working brilliantly, but without a complete vision of broader humanity. Now the Institute is organized on the most flexible lines. There are no set departments, but only units formed about exceptional men like our good friend Gottlieb. If any new man has the real right thing, we'll provide him with every facility, instead of letting him merely plug along doing individual work. I have given your results the most careful consideration, Martin; I have talked them over with Dr. Gottlieb—though I must say he does not altogether share my enthusiasm about immediate practical results. And I have decided to submit to the Board of Trustees a plan for a Department of Microbic Pathology, with you as head! You will have an assistant—a real trained Ph.D.—and more room and technicians, and you will report to me directly, talk things over with me daily, instead of with Gottlieb. You will be relieved of all war work, by my order—though you can retain your uniform and everything. And your salary will be, I should think, if Mr. McGurk and the other Trustees confirm me, ten thousand a year instead of five.

"Yes, the best room for you would be that big one on the upper floor, to the right of the elevators. That's vacant now. And your office across the hall.

"And all the assistance you require. Why, my boy, you won't need to sit up nights using your hands in this wasteful way, but just think things out and take up possible extensions of the work—cover all the possible fields. We'll extend this to everything! We'll have scores of physicians in hospitals helping us and confirming our results and widening our efforts. . . . We might have a weekly council of all these doctors and assistants, with you and me jointly presiding. . . . If men like Koch and Pasteur had only had such a system, how much more *scope* their work might have had! Efficient universal *co-operation*—that's the thing in science today—the time of this silly, jealous, fumbling individual research has gone by.

"My boy, we may have found the real thing—another salvarsan! We'll publish together! We'll have the whole world talking! Why, I lay awake last night thinking of our magnificent opportunity! In a few months we may be curing not only staph infections but typhoid, dysentery! Martin, as your colleague, I do not for a moment wish to detract from the great credit which is yours, but I must say that if you had been more closely allied with Me you would have extended your work to practical proofs and results long before this."

Martin wavered back to his room, dazzled by the view of a department of his own, assistants, a cheering world—and ten thousand a year. But his work seemed to have been taken from him, his own self had been taken from him; he was no longer to be Martin, and Gottlieb's disciple, but a Man of Measured Merriment, Dr. Arrowsmith, Head of the Department of Microbic Pathology, who would wear severe collars and make addresses and never curse.

Doubts enfeebled him. Perhaps the X Principle would develop only in the test-tube; perhaps it had no large value for human healing. He wanted to know—to *know*.

Then Rippleton Holabird burst in on him:

"Martin, my dear boy, the Director has just been telling me about your discovery and his splendid plans for you. I want to congratulate you with all my heart, and to welcome you as a fellow department-head—and you so young—only thirty-four, isn't it? What a magnificent future! Think, Martin" —Major Holabird discarded his dignity, sat astride a chair—"think of all you have ahead! If this work really pans out, there's no limit to the honors that'll come to you, you lucky young dog! Acclaim by scientific societies, any professorship you might happen to want, prizes, the biggest men begging to consult you, a ripping place in society!

"Now listen, old boy: Perhaps you know how close I am to Dr. Tubbs, and I see no reason why you shouldn't come in with us, and we three run things here to suit ourselves. Wasn't it simply too decent of the Director to be so eager to recognize and help you in every way! So cordial—and so helpful. Now you really understand him. And the three of us— Some day we might be able to erect a superstructure of co-operative science which would control not only McGurk but every institute and every university scientific department in the country, and so produce really efficient research. When Dr. Tubbs retires, I have—I'm speaking with the most complete confidence—I have some reason to suppose that the Board of Trustees will consider me as his successor. Then, old boy, if this work succeeds, you and I can do things together!

"To be ever so frank, there are very few men in our world (think of poor old Yeo!) who combine presentable personalities with first-rate achievement, and if you'll just get over some of your abruptness and your unwillingness to appreciate big executives and charming women (because, thank God, you do wear your clothes well—when you take the trouble!) why, you and I can become the dictators of science throughout the whole country!"

Martin did not think of an answer till Holabird had gone.

He perceived the horror of the shrieking bawdy thing called Success, with its demand that he give up quiet work and parade forth to be pawed by every blind devotee and mud-spattered by every blind enemy.

He fled to Gottlieb as to the wise and tender father, and begged to be saved from Success and Holabirds and A. DeWitt Tubbses and their hordes of address-making scientists, degree-hunting authors, pulpit orators, popular surgeons, valeted journalists, sentimental merchant princes, literary politicians, titled sportsmen, statesmenlike generals, interviewed senators, sententious bishops.

Gottlieb was worried:

"I knew Tubbs was up to something idealistic and nasty when he came purring to me, but I did not t'ink he would try to turn you into a megaphone all so soon in one day! I will gird up my loins and go oud to battle with the forces of publicity!"

He was defeated.

"I have let you alone, Dr. Gottlieb," said Tubbs, "but, hang it, I am the Director! And I must say that, perhaps owing to my signal stupidity, I fail to see the horrors of enabling Arrowsmith to cure thousands of suffering persons and to become a man of weight and esteem!"

Gottlieb took it to Ross McGurk.

"Max, I love you like a brother, but Tubbs is the Director, and if he feels he needs this Arrowsmith (Is he the thin young fellow I see around your lab?) then I have no right to stop him. I've got to back him up the same as I would the master of one of our ships," said McGurk.

Not till the Board of Trustees, which consisted of McGurk himself, the president of the University of Wilmington, and three professors of science in various universities, should meet and give approval, would Martin be a department-head. Meantime Tubbs demanded:

"Now, Martin, you must hasten and publish your results. Get right to it. In fact you should have done it before this. Throw your material together as rapidly as possible and send a note in to the Society for Experimental Biology and Medicine, to be published in their next proceedings."

"But I'm not ready to publish! I want to have every loophole plugged up before I announce anything whatever!"

"Nonsense! That attitude is old-fashioned. This is no longer an age of parochialism but of competition, in art and science just as much as in commerce—co-operation with your own group, but with those outside it, competition to the death! Plug up the holes thoroughly, later, but we can't have somebody else stealing a march on us. Remember you have your name to make. The way to make it is by working with me—toward the greatest good for the greatest number."

As Martin began his paper, thinking of resigning but giving it up because Tubbs seemed to him at least better than the Pickerbaughs, he had a vision of a world of little scientists, each busy in a roofless cell. Perched on a cloud, watching them, was the divine Tubbs, a glory of whiskers, ready to blast any of the little men who stopped being earnest and wasted time on speculation about anything which he had not assigned to them. Back of their welter of coops, unseen by the tutelary Tubbs, the lean giant figure of Gottlieb stood sardonic on a stormy horizon.

Literary expression was not easy to Martin. He delayed with his paper, while Tubbs became irritable and whipped him on. The experiments had ceased; there were misery and pen-scratching and much tearing of manuscript paper in Martin's particular roofless cell.

For once he had no refuge in Leora. She cried:

"Why not? Ten thousand a year would be awfully nice, Sandy. Gee! We've always been so poor, and you do like nice flats and things. And to boss your own department— And you could consult Dr. Gottlieb just the same. He's a department-head, isn't he, and yet he keeps independent of Dr. Tubbs. Oh, I'm for it!"

And slowly, under the considerable increase in respect given to him at Institute lunches, Martin himself was "for it."

"We could get one of those new apartments on Park Avenue. Don't suppose they cost more than three thousand a year," he meditated. "Wouldn't be so bad to be able to entertain people there. Not that I'd let it interfere with my work. . . . Kind of nice."

It was still more kind of nice, however agonizing in the taking, to be recognized socially.

Capitola McGurk, who hitherto had not perceived him except as an object less interesting than Gladys the Centrifuge, telephoned: ". . . Dr. Tubbs so enthusiastic and Ross and I are so pleased. Be delighted if Mrs. Arrowsmith and you could dine with us next Thursday at eight-thirty."

Martin accepted the royal command.

It was his conviction that after glimpses of Angus Duer and Rippleton Holabird he had seen luxury, and understood smart dinner parties. Leora and he went without too much agitation to the house of Ross McGurk, in the East Seventies, near Fifth Avenue. The house did, from the street, seem to have an unusual quantity of graystone gargoyles and carven lintels and bronze grills, but it did not seem large.

Inside, the vaulted stone hallway opened up like a cathedral. They were embarrassed by the footmen, awed by the automatic elevator, oppressed by a hallway full of vellum folios and Italian chests and a drawing-room full of water-colors, and reduced to rusticity by Capitola's queenly white satin and pearls.

There were eight or ten Persons of Importance, male and female, looking insignificant but bearing names as familiar as Ivory Soap.

Did one give his arm to some unknown lady and "take her in," Martin wondered. He rejoiced to find that one merely straggled into the dining-room under McGurk's amiable basso herding.

The dining-room was gorgeous and very hideous, in stamped leather and hysterias of gold, with collections of servants watching one's use of asparagus forks. Martin was seated (it is doubtful if he ever knew that he was the guest of honor) between Capitola McGurk and a woman of whom he could learn only that she was the sister of a countess.

Capitola leaned toward him in her great white splendor.

"Now, Dr. Arrowsmith, just what is this you are discovering?"

"Why, it's—uh—I'm trying to figure—"

"Dr. Tubbs tells us that you have found such wonderful new ways of controlling disease." Her L's were a melody of summer rivers, her R's the trill of birds in the brake. "Oh, what—*what* could be more beau-tiful than relieving this sad old world of its burden of illness! But just precisely what *is* it that you're doing?"

"Why, it's awfully early to be sure but— You see, it's like this. You take certain bugs like staph—"

"Oh, how interesting science is, but how frightfully difficult for simple people like me to grasp! But we're all so humble. We're just waiting for scientists like you to make the world secure for friendship—"

Then Capitola gave all her attention to her other man. Martin looked straight ahead and ate and suffered. The sister of the countess, a sallow and stringy woman, was glowing at him. He turned with unhappy meekness (noting that she had one more fork than he, and wondering where he had got lost).

She blared, "You are a scientist, I am told."

"Ye-es."

"The trouble with scientists is that they do not understand beauty. They are so cold."

Rippleton Holabird would have made pretty mirth, but Martin could only quaver, "No, I don't think that's true," and consider whether he dared drink another glass of champagne.

When they had been herded back to the drawing-room, after masculine but achingly elaborate passings of the port, Capitola swooped on him with white devouring wings:

"Dear Dr. Arrowsmith, I really didn't get a chance at dinner to ask you just exactly *what* you are doing. . . . Oh! Have you seen my dear little children at the Charles Street settlement? I'm sure ever so many of them will become the most fascinating scientists. You must come lecture to them."

That night he fretted to Leora, "Going to be hard to keep up this twittering. But I suppose I've got to learn to enjoy it. Oh, well, think how nice it'll be to give some dinners of our own, with real people, Gottlieb and everybody, when I'm a department-head."

Next morning Gottlieb came slowly into Martin's room. He stood by the window; he seemed to be avoiding Martin's eyes. He sighed, "Something sort of bad perhaps not altogether bad—has happened."

"What is it, sir? Anything I can do?"

"It does not apply to me. To you."

Irritably Martin thought, "Is he going into all this danger-of-rapid-success stuff again? I'm getting tired of it!"

Gottlieb ambled toward him. "It iss a pity, Martin, but you are not the discoverer of the X Principle."

"Wh-what—"

"Someone else has done it."

"They have not! I've searched all the literature, and except for Twort, not one person has even hinted at anticipating— Why, good Lord, Dr. Gottlieb, it would mean that all I've done, all these weeks, has just been waste, and I'm a fool—"

"Vell. Anyvay. D'Hérelle of the Pasteur Institute has just now published in the *Comptes Rendus, Académie des Sciences,* a report—it is your X Principle, absolute. Only he calls it 'bacteriophage.' So."

"Then I'm—"

In his mind Martin finished it, "Then I'm not going to be a department-head or famous or anything else. I'm back in the gutter." All strength went out of him and all purpose, and the light of creation faded to dirty gray.

"Now of course," said Gottlieb, "you could claim to be co-discoverer and spend the rest of your life fighting to get recognized. Or you could forget it, and write a nice letter congratulating D'Hérelle, and go back to work."

Martin mourned, "Oh, I'll go back to work. Nothing else to do. I guess Tubbs'll chuck the new department now. I'll have time to really finish my research—maybe I've got some points that D'Hérelle hasn't hit on—and I'll publish it to corroborate him. . . . Damn him! . . . Where is his report? . . . I suppose you're glad that I'm saved from being a Holabird."

"I ought to be. It is a sin against my religion that I am not. But I am getting old. And you are my friend. I am sorry you are not to have the fun of being pretentious and successful—for a while. . . . Martin, it iss nice that you will corroborate D'Hérelle. That is science: to work and not to care—too much—if somebody else gets the credit. . . . Shall I tell Tubbs about D'Hérelle's priority, or will you?"

Gottlieb straggled away, looking back a little sadly.

Tubbs came in to wail, "If you had only published earlier, as I told you, Dr. Arrowsmith! You have really put me in a most embarrassing position before the Board of Trustees. Of course there can be no question now of a new department."

"Yes," said Martin vacantly.

He carefully filed away the beginnings of his paper and turned to his bench. He stared at a shining flask till it fascinated him like a crystal ball. He pondered:

"Wouldn't have been so bad if Tubbs had let me alone. Damn these old men, damn these Men of Measured Merriment, these Important Men that come and offer you honors. Money. Decorations. Titles. Want to make you windy with authority. Honors! If you get 'em, you become pompous, and then when you're used to 'em, if you lose 'em you feel foolish.

"So I'm not going to be rich. Leora, poor kid, she won't have her new dresses and flat and everything. We— Won't be so much fun in the lil old flat, now. Oh, quit whining!

"I wish Terry were here.

"I love that man Gottlieb. He might have gloated—

"Bacteriophage, the Frenchman calls it. Too long. Better just call it *phage*. Even got to take his name for it, for my own X Principle! Well, I had a lot of fun, working all those nights. Working—"

He was coming out of his trance. He imagined the flask filled with staph-clouded broth. He plodded into Gottlieb's office to secure the journal containing D'Hérelle's report, and read it minutely, enthusiastically.

"There's a man, there's a scientist!" he chuckled.

On his way home he was planning to experiment on the Shiga dysentery bacillus with phage (as henceforth he called the X Principle), planning to volley questions and criticisms at D'Hérelle, hoping that Tubbs would not discharge him for a while, and expanding with relief that he would not have to do his absurd premature paper on phage, that he could be lewd and soft-collared and easy, not judicious and spied-on and weighty.

He grinned, "Gosh, I'll bet Tubbs was disappointed! He'd figured on signing all my papers with me and getting the credit. Now for this Shiga experiment— Poor Lee, she'll have to get used to my working nights, I guess."

Leora kept to herself what she felt about it—or at least most of what she felt.

# 30

For a year broken only by Terry Wickett's return after the Armistice, and by the mockeries of that rowdy intelligence, Martin was in a grind of drudgery. Week on week he toiled at complicated phage experiments. His work—his hands, his technique—became more adept, and his days more steady, less fretful.

He returned to his evening studying. He went from mathematics into physical chemistry; began to understand the mass action law; became as sarcastic as Terry about what he called the "bedside manner" of Tubbs and Holabird; read much French and German; went canoeing on the Hudson on Sunday afternoons; and had a bawdy party with Leora and Terry to celebrate the day when the Institute was purified by the sale of Holabird's pride, Gladys the Centrifuge.

He suspected that Dr. Tubbs, now magnificent with the ribbon of the Legion of Honor, had retained him in the Institute only because of Gottlieb's intervention. But it may be that Tubbs and Holabird hoped he would again blunder into publicity-bringing miracles, for they were both polite to him at lunch—polite and wistfully rebuking, and full of meaty remarks about publishing one's discoveries early instead of dawdling.

It was more than a year after Martin's anticipation by D'Hérelle when Tubbs appeared in the laboratory with suggestions:

"I've been thinking, Arrowsmith," said Tubbs.

He looked it.

"D'Hérelle's discovery hasn't aroused the popular interest I thought it would. If he'd only been here with us, I'd have seen to it that he got the proper attention. Practically no newspaper comment at all. Perhaps we can still do something. As I understand it, you've been going along with what Dr. Gottlieb would call 'fundamental research.' I think it may now be time for you to use phage in practical healing. I want you to experiment with phage in pneumonia, plague, perhaps typhoid, and when your experiments get going, make some practical tests in collaboration with the hospitals. Enough of all this mere frittering and vanity. Let's really *cure* somebody!"

Martin was not free from a fear of dismissal if he refused to obey. And he was touched as Tubbs went on:

"Arrowsmith, I suspect you sometimes feel I lack a sense of scientific precision when I insist on practical results. I— Somehow I don't see the really noble and transforming results coming out of this Institute that we ought to be getting, with our facilities. I'd like to do something big, my boy, something fine for poor humanity, before I pass on. Can't you give it to me? Go cure the plague!"

For once Tubbs was a tired smile and not an earnestness of whiskers.

That day, concealing from Gottlieb his abandonment of the quest for the fundamental nature of phage, Martin set about fighting pneumonia, before attacking the Black Death. And when Gottlieb learned of it, he was absorbed in certain troubles of his own.

Martin cured rabbits of pleuro-pneumonia by the injection of phage, and by feeding them with it he prevented the spread of pneumonia. He found that phage-produced immunity could be as infectious as a disease.

He was pleased with himself, and expected pleasure from Tubbs, but for weeks Tubbs did not heed him. He was off on a new enthusiasm, the most virulent of his whole life: he was organizing the League of Cultural Agencies.

He was going to standardize and co-ordinate all mental activities in America, by the creation of a bureau which should direct and pat and gently rebuke and generally encourage chemistry and batik-making, poetry and Arctic exploration, animal husbandry and Bible study, Negro spirituals and business-letter writing. He was suddenly in conference with conductors of symphony orchestras, directors of art-schools, owners of itinerant Chautauquas, liberal governors, ex-clergymen who wrote tasty philosophy for news-paper syndicates, in fact all the proprietors of American intellectuality—particularly including a millionaire named Minnigen who had recently been elevating the artistic standards of the motion pictures.

Tubbs was all over the Institute inviting the researchers to join him in the League of Cultural Agencies with its fascinating committee-meetings and dinners. Most of them grunted, "The Old Man is erupting again," and forgot him, but one ex-major went out every evening to confer with serious ladies who wore distinguished frocks, who sobbed over "the loss of spiritual and intellectual horse-power through lack of co-ordination," and who went home in limousines.

There were rumors. Dr. Billy Smith whispered that he had gone in to see Tubbs and heard McGurk shouting at him, "Your job is to run this shop and not work for that land-stealing, four-flushing, play-producing son of evil, Pete Minnigen!"

The morning after, when Martin ambled to his laboratory, he discovered a gasping, a muttering, a shaking in the corridors, and incredulously he heard:

"Tubbs has resigned!"

"No!"

"They say he's gone to his League of Cultural Agencies. This fellow Min-nigen has given the League a scad of money, and Tubbs is to get twice the salary he had here!"

## II

Instantly, for all but the zealots like Gottlieb, Terry, Martin, and the bio-physics assistant, research was halted. There was a surging of factions, a be-nevolent and winning buzz of scientists who desired to be the new Director of the Institute.

Rippleton Holabird, Yeo the carpenter-like biologist, Gillingham the joky chief in bio-physics, Aaron Sholtheis the neat Russian Jewish High Church Episcopalian, all of them went about with expressions of modest willingness. They were affectionate with everybody they met in the corridors, however violent they were in private discussions. Added to them were no few out-siders, professors and researchers in other institutes, who found it necessary to come and confer about rather undefined matters with Ross McGurk.

Terry remarked to Martin, "Probably Pearl Robbins and your garçon are pitching horseshoes for the Directorship. My garçon ain't—the only reason, though, is because I've just murdered him. At that, I think Pearl would be the best choice. She's been Tubbs's secretary so long that she's learned all his ignorance about scientific technique."

Rippleton Holabird was the most unctuous of the office seekers, and the most hungry. The war over, he missed his uniform and his authority. He urged Martin:

"You know how I've always believed in your genius, Martin, and I know how dear old Gottlieb believes in you. If you would get Gottlieb to back me, to talk to McGurk— Of course in taking the Directorship I would be making a sacrifice, because I'd have to give up my research, but I'd be willing because I feel, really, that somebody with a Tradition ought to carry on the control. Tubbs is backing me, and if Gottlieb did—I'd see that it was to Gottlieb's advantage. I'd give him a lot more floor-space!"

Through the Institute it was vaguely known that Capitola was advocating the election of Holabird as "the only scientist here who is also a gentleman." She was seen sailing down corridors, a frigate, with Holabird a sloop in her wake.

But while Holabird beamed, Nicholas Yeo looked secret and satisfied.

The whole Institute fluttered on the afternoon when the Board of Trustees met in the Hall, for the election of a Director. They were turned from investigators into boarding-school girls. The Board debated, or did something annoying, for draining hours.

At four, Terry Wickett hastened to Martin with, "Say, Slim, I've got a straight tip that They've elected Silva, dean of the Winnemac medical school. That's your shop, isn't it? Wha's like?"

"He's a fine old— No! He and Gottlieb hate each other. Lord! Gottlieb'll resign, and I'll have to get out. Just when my work's going nice!"

At five, past doors made of attentive eyes, the Board of Trustees marched to the laboratory of Max Gottlieb.

Holabird was heard saying bravely, "Of course with me, I wouldn't give my research up for any administrative job." And Pearl Robbins informed Terry, "Yes, it's true—Mr. McGurk himself just told me—the Board has elected Dr. Gottlieb the new Director."

"Then they're fools," said Terry. "He'll refuse it, with wilence. 'Dot dey should ask me to go monkey-skipping mit committee meetings!' Fat chance!"

When the Board had gone, Martin and Terry flooded into Gottlieb's laboratory and found the old man standing by his bench, more erect than they had seen him for years.

"Is it true—they want you to be Director?" panted Martin.

"Yes, they have asked me."

"But you'll refuse? You won't let 'em gum up your work!"

"Vell. . . . I said my real work must go on. They consent I should appoint an Assistant Director to do the detail. You see— Of course nothing must interfere with my immunology, but dis gives me the chance to do big t'ings and make a free scientific institute for all you boys. And those fools at Winnemac that laughed at my idea of a real medical school, now maybe they will see— Do you know who was my rival for Director—do you know who it was, Martin? It was that man Silva! Ha!"

In the corridor Terry groaned, "*Requiescat in pace.*"

### III

To the dinner in Gottlieb's honor (the only dinner that ever was given in Gottlieb's honor) there came not only the men of impressive but easy affairs who attend all dinners of honor, but the few scientists whom Gottlieb admired.

He appeared late, rather shaky, escorted by Martin. When he reached the speakers' table, the guests rose to him, shouting. He peered at them, he tried to speak, he held out his long arms as if to take them all in, and sank down sobbing.

There were cables from Europe; ardent letters from Tubbs and Dean Silva bewailing their inability to be present; telegrams from college presidents; and all of these were read to admiring applause.

But Capitola murmured, "Just the same, we shall miss dear Dr. Tubbs. He was so forward-looking. Don't play with your fork, Ross."

So Max Gottlieb took charge of the McGurk Institute of Biology, and in a month that Institute became a shambles.

IV

Gottlieb planned to give only an hour a day to business. As Assistant Director he appointed Dr. Aaron Sholtheis, the epidemiologist, the Yonkers churchman and dahlia-fancier. Gottlieb explained to Martin that, though of course Sholtheis was a fool, yet he was the only man in sight who combined at least a little scientific ability with a willingness to endure the routine and pomposity and compromises of executive work.

By continuing his ancient sneers at all bustling managers, Gottlieb obviously felt that he excused himself for having become a manager.

He could not confine his official work to an hour a day. There were too many conferences, too many distinguished callers, too many papers which needed his signature. He was dragged into dinner-parties; and the long, vague, palavering luncheons to which a Director has to go, and the telephoning to straighten out the dates of these tortures, took nervous hours. Each day his executive duties crawled into two hours or three or four, and he raged, he became muddled by complications of personnel and economy, he was ever more autocratic, more testy; and the loving colleagues of the Institute, who had been soothed or bullied into surface peace by Tubbs, now jangled openly.

While he was supposed to radiate benevolence from the office recently occupied by Dr. A. DeWitt Tubbs, Gottlieb clung to his own laboratory and to his narrow office as a cat clings to its cushion under a table. Once or twice he tried to sit and look impressive in the office of the Director, but he fled from that large clean vacuity and from Miss Robbins's snapping typewriter to his own den that smelled not of forward-looking virtue but only of cigarettes and old papers.

To McGurk, as to every scientific institution, came hundreds of farmers and practical nurses and suburban butchers who had paid large fares from Oklahoma or Oregon to get recognition for the unquestionable cures which they had discovered: oil of Mississippi catfish which saved every case of tuberculosis, arsenic pastes guaranteed to cure all cancers. They came with letters and photographs amid the frayed clean linen in their shabby suit-cases—at any opportunity they would stoop over their bags and hopefully bring out testimonials from their Pastors; they begged for a chance to heal humanity, and for themselves only enough money to send The Girl to musical conservatory. So certain, so black-crapely beseeching were they that no reception-clerk could be trained to keep them all out.

Gottlieb found them seeping into his office. He was sorry for them. They did take his working hours, they did scratch his belief that he was hardhearted, but they implored him with such wretched timorousness that he could not get rid of them without making promises, and admitting afterward that to have been more cruel would have been less cruel.

It was the Important People to whom he was rude.

The Directorship devoured enough time and peace to prevent Gottlieb from going on with the ever more recondite problems of his inquiry into the nature of specificity, and his inquiry prevented him from giving enough attention to the Institute to keep it from falling to pieces. He depended on Sholtheis, passed decisions on to him, but Sholtheis, since in any case Gottlieb would get all the credit for a successful Directorship, kept up his own scientific work and passed the decisions to Miss Pearl Robbins, so that the actual Director was the handsome and jealous Pearl.

There was no craftier or crookeder Director in the habitable world. Pearl enjoyed it. She so warmly and modestly assured Ross McGurk of the merits of Gottlieb and of her timorous devotion to him, she so purred to the flattery of Rippleton Holabird, she so blandly answered the hoarse hostility of Terry Wickett by keeping him from getting materials for his work, that the Institute reeled with intrigue.

Yeo was not speaking to Sholtheis. Terry threatened Holabird to "paste him one." Gottlieb constantly asked Martin for advice, and never took it. Joust, the vulgar but competent bio-physicist, lacking the affection which kept Martin and Terry from reproaching the old man, told Gottlieb that he was a "rotten Director and ought to quit," and was straightway discharged and replaced by a muffin.

Max Gottlieb had ever discoursed to Martin of "the jests of the gods." Among these jests Martin had never beheld one so pungent as this whereby the pretentiousness and fussy unimaginativeness which he had detested in Tubbs should have made him a good manager, while the genius of Gottlieb should have made him a feeble tyrant; the jest that the one thing worse than a too managed and standardized institution should be one that was not managed and standardized at all. He would once have denied it with violence, but nightly now he prayed for Tubbs's return.

If the business of the Institute was not more complicated thereby, certainly its placidity was the more disturbed by the appearance of Gustaf Sondelius, who had just returned from a study of sleeping sickness in Africa and who noisily took one of the guest laboratories.

Gustaf Sondelius, the soldier of preventive medicine whose lecture had sent Martin from Wheatsylvania to Nautilus, had remained in his gallery of heroes as possessing a little of Gottlieb's perception, something of Dad Silva's steady kindliness, something of Terry's tough honesty though none of his scorn of amenities, and with these a spicy, dripping richness altogether his own. It is true that Sondelius did not remember Martin. Since their evening in Minneapolis he had drunk and debated and flamboyantly ridden to obscure but vinous destinations with too many people. But he was made to remember, and in a week Sondelius and Terry and Martin were to be seen tramping and dining, or full of topics and gin at Martin's flat.

Sondelius's wild flaxen hair was almost gray, but he had the same bull shoulders, the same wide brow, and the same tornado of plans to make the world aseptic, without neglecting to enjoy a few of the septic things before they should pass away.

His purpose was, after finishing his sleeping sickness report, to found a school of tropical medicine in New York.

He besieged McGurk and the wealthy Mr. Minnigen who was Tubbs's new patron, and in and out of season he besieged Gottlieb.

He adored Gottlieb and made noises about it. Gottlieb admired his courage and his hatred of commercialism, but his presence Gottlieb could not endure. He was flustered by Sondelius's hilarity, his compliments, his bounding optimism, his inaccuracy, his boasting, his oppressive bigness. It may be that Gottlieb resented the fact that though Sondelius was only eleven years younger—fifty-eight to Gottlieb's sixty-nine—he seemed thirty years younger, half a century gayer.

When Sondelius perceived this grudgingness he tried to overcome it by being more noisy and complimentary and enthusiastic than ever. On Gottlieb's birthday he gave him a shocking smoking-jacket of cherry and mauve velvet, and when he called at Gottlieb's flat, which was often, Gottlieb had to put on the ghastly thing and sit humming while Sondelius assaulted him with roaring condemnations of mediocre soup and mediocre musicians. . . . That Sondelius gave up surprisingly decorative dinner-parties for these calls, Gottlieb never knew.

Martin turned to Sondelius for courage as he turned to Terry for concentration. Courage and concentration were needed, in these days of an Institute gone insane, if a man was to do his work.

And Martin was doing it.

v

After a consultation with Gottlieb and a worried conference with Leora about the danger of handling the germs, he had gone on to bubonic plague, to the possibilities of preventing it and curing it with phage.

To have heard him asking Sondelius about his experience in plague epidemics, one would have believed that Martin found the Black Death delightful. To have beheld him infecting lean snaky rats with the horror, all the while clucking to them and calling them pet names, one would have known him mad.

He found that rats fed with phage failed to come down with plague; that after phage-feeding, *Bacillus pestis* disappeared from carrier rats which, without themselves being killed thereby, harbored and spread chronic plague; and that, finally, he could cure the disease. He was as absorbed and happy and nervous as in the first days of the X Principle. He worked all night. . . . At the microscope, under a lone light, fishing out with a glass pipette drawn fine as a hair one single plague bacillus.

To protect himself from infection by the rat-fleas he wore, while he worked with the animals, rubber gloves, high leather boots, straps about his sleeves. These precautions thrilled him, and to the others at McGurk they had something of the esoteric magic of the alchemists. He became a bit of a hero and a good deal of a butt. No more than hearty business men in offices or fussy old men in villages are researchers free from the tedious vice of jovial commenting. The chemists and biologists called him "The Pest," refused to come to his room, and pretended to avoid him in the corridors.

As he went fluently on from experiment to experiment, as the drama of science obsessed him, he thought very well of himself and found himself taken seriously by the others. He published one cautious paper on phage in plague, which was mentioned in numerous scientific journals. Even the harassed Gottlieb was commendatory, though he could give but little attention and no help. But Terry Wickett remained altogether cool. He showed for Martin's somewhat brilliant work only enough enthusiasm to indicate that he was not jealous; he kept poking in to ask whether, with his new experimentation, Martin was continuing his quest for the fundamental nature of all phage, and his study of physical chemistry.

Then Martin had such an assistant as has rarely been known, and that assistant was Gustaf Sondelius.

Sondelius was discouraged regarding his school of tropical medicine. He was looking for new trouble. He had been through several epidemics, and he viewed plague with affectionate hatred. When he understood Martin's work he gloated, "Hey, Yesus! Maybe you got the t'ing that will be better than Yersin or Haffkine or anybody! Maybe you cure all the world of plague—the poor devils in India—millions of them. Let me in!"

He became Martin's collaborator; unpaid, tireless, not very skillful, valuable in his buoyancy. As well as Martin he loved irregularity; by principle he never had his meals at the same hours two days in succession, and by choice he worked all night and made poetry, rather bad poetry, at dawn.

Martin had always been the lone prowler. Possibly the thing he most liked in Leora was her singular ability to be cheerfully non-existent even when she was present. At first he was annoyed by Sondelius's disturbing presence, however interesting he found his fervors about plague-bearing rats (whom Sondelius hated not at all but whom, with loving zeal, he had slaughtered by the million, with a romantic absorption in traps and poison gas). But the Sondelius who was raucous in conversation could be almost silent at work. He knew exactly how to hold the animals while Martin did intrapleural injections; he made cultures of *Bacillus pestis*; when Martin's technician had gone home at but a little after midnight (the garçon liked Martin and thought well enough of science, but he was prejudiced in favor of six hours' daily sleep and sometimes seeing his wife and children in Harlem), then Sondelius cheerfully sterilized glassware and needles, and lumbered up to the animal house to bring down victims.

The change whereby Sondelius was turned from Martin's master to his slave was so unconscious, and Sondelius, for all his Pickerbaughian love of sensationalism, cared so little about mastery or credit, that neither of them considered that there had been a change. They borrowed cigarettes from each other; they went out at the most improbable hours to have flap-jacks and coffee at an all-night lunch; and together they handled test-tubes charged with death.

# 31

From Yunnan in China, from the clattering bright bazaars, crept something invisible in the sun and vigilant by dark, creeping, sinister, ceaseless; creeping across the Himalayas, down through walled market-places, across a desert, along hot yellow rivers, into an American missionary compound—creeping, silent, sure; and here and there on its way a man was black and stilled with plague.

In Bombay a new dock-guard, unaware of things, spoke boisterously over his family rice of a strange new custom of the rats.

Those princes of the sewer, swift to dart and turn, had gone mad. They came out on the warehouse floor, ignoring the guard, springing up as though (the guard said merrily) they were trying to fly, and straightway falling dead. He had poked at them, but they did not move.

Three days later that dock-guard died of the plague.

Before he died, from his dock a ship with a cargo of wheat steamed off to Marseilles. There was no sickness on it all the way; there was no reason why at Marseilles it should not lie next to a tramp steamer, nor why that steamer, pitching down to Montevideo with nothing more sensational than a discussion between the supercargo and the second officer in the matter of a fifth ace, should not berth near the S.S. *Pendown Castle*, bound for the island of St. Hubert to add cocoa to its present cargo of lumber.

On the way to St. Hubert, a Goanese seedie boy and after him the mess-room steward on the *Pendown Castle* died of what the skipper called influenza. A greater trouble was the number of rats which, ill satisfied with lumber as diet, scampered up to the food-stores, then into the forecastle, and for no reason perceptible died on the open decks. They danced comically before they died, and lay in the scuppers stark and ruffled.

So the *Pendown Castle* came to Blackwater, the capital and port of St. Hubert.

It is a little isle of the southern West Indies, but St. Hubert supports a hundred thousand people—English planters and clerks, Hindu road-makers, Negro cane-hands, Chinese merchants. There is history along its sands and peaks. Here the buccaneers careened their ships; here the Marquess of Wimsbury, when he had gone mad, took to repairing clocks and bade his slaves burn all the sugar-cane.

Hither that peasant beau, Gaston Lopo, brought Madame de Merlemont, and dwelt in fashionableness till the slaves whom he had often relished to lash came on him shaving, and straightway the lather was fantastically smeared with blood.

Today, St. Hubert is all sugar-cane and Ford cars, oranges and plantains and the red and yellow pods of cocoa, bananas and rubber trees and jungles of bamboo, Anglican churches and tin chapels, colored washerwomen busy at the hollows in the roots of silk-cotton trees, steamy heat and royal palms and the immortelle that fills the valleys with crimson; today it is all splendor and tourist dullness and cabled cane-quotations, against the unsparing sun.

Blackwater, flat and breathless town of tin-roofed plaster houses and incandescent bone-white roads, of salmon-red hibiscus and balconied stores whose dark depths open without barrier from the stifling streets, has the harbor to one side and a swamp to the other. But behind it are the Penrith Hills, on whose wholesome and palm-softened heights is Government House, looking to the winking sails.

Here lived in bulky torpor His Excellency the Governor of St. Hubert, Colonel Sir Robert Fairlamb.

Sir Robert Fairlamb was an excellent fellow, a teller of messroom stories, one who in a heathen day never smoked till the port had gone seven times round; but he was an execrable governor and a worried governor. The man whose social rank was next to his own—the Hon. Cecil Eric George Twyford, a lean, active, high-nosed despot who owned and knew rod by snake-writhing rod some ten thousand acres of cane in St. Swithin's Parish—Twyford said that His Excellency was a "potty and snoring fool," and versions of the opinion came not too slowly to Fairlamb. Then, to destroy him complete, the House of Assembly, which is the St. Hubert legislature, was riven by the feud of Kellett the Red Leg and George William Vertigan.

The Red Legs were a tribe of Scotch-Irish poor whites who had come to St. Hubert as indentured servants two hundred years before. Most of them were still fishermen and plantation-foremen, but one of them, Kellett, a man small-mouthed and angry and industrious, had risen from office-boy to owner of a shipping company, and while his father still spread his nets on the beach at Point Carib, Kellett was the scourge of the House of Assembly and a hound for economy—particularly any economy which would annoy his fellow legislator, George William Vertigan.

George William, who was sometimes known as "Old Jeo Wm" and sometimes as "The King of the Ice House" (that enticing and ruinous bar), had been born behind a Little Bethel in Lancashire. He owned The Blue Bazaar, the hugest stores in St. Hubert; he caused tobacco to be smuggled into Venezuela; he was as full of song and incaution and rum as Kellett the Red Leg was full of figures and envy and decency.

Between them, Kellett and George William split the House of Assembly. There could be, to a respectable person, no question as to their merits: Kellett the just and earnest man of domesticity whose rise was an inspiration to youth; George William the gambler, the lusher, the smuggler, the liar, the seller of shoddy cottons, a person whose only excellence was his cheap good nature.

Kellett's first triumph in economy was to pass an ordinance removing the melancholy Cockney (a player of oboes) who was the official rat-catcher of St. Hubert.

George William Vertigan insisted in debate, and afterward privily to Sir Robert Fairlamb, that rats destroy food and perhaps spread disease, and His Excellency must veto the bill. Sir Robert was troubled. He called in The Surgeon General, Dr. R. E. Inchcape Jones (but he preferred to be called Mister, not Doctor).

Dr. Inchcape Jones was a thin, tall, fretful, youngish man, without bowels. He had come out from Home only two years before, and he wanted to go back Home, to that particular part of Home represented by tennis-teas in Surrey. He remarked to Sir Robert that rats and their ever faithful fleas do carry diseases—plague and infectious jaundice and rat-bite fever and possibly leprosy—but these diseases did not and therefore could not exist in St. Hubert, except for leprosy, which was a natural punishment of outlandish Native Races. In fact, noted Inchcape Jones, nothing did exist in St. Hubert except malaria, dengue, and a general beastly dullness, and if Red Legs like Kellett longed to die of plague and rat-bite fever, why should decent people object?

So by the sovereign power of the House of Assembly of St. Hubert, and of His Excellency the Governor, the Cockney rat-catcher and his jiggling young colored assistant were commanded to cease to exist. The rat-catcher became a chauffeur. He drove Canadian and American tourists, who stopped over at St. Hubert for a day or two between Barbados and Trinidad, along such hill-trails as he considered most easy to achieve with a second-hand motor, and gave them misinformation regarding the flowers. The rat-catcher's assistant became a respectable smuggler and leader of a Wesleyan choir. And as for the rats themselves, they flourished, they were glad in the land, and each female produced from ten to two hundred offspring every year.

They were not often seen by day. "The rats aren't increasing; the cats kill 'em," said Kellett the Red Leg. But by darkness they gamboled in the warehouses and in and out of the schooners along the quay. They ventured countryward, and lent their fleas to a species of ground squirrels which were plentiful about the village of Carib.

A year and a half after the removal of the rat-catcher, when the *Pendown Castle* came in from Montevideo and moored by the Councillor Pier, it was observed by ten thousand glinty small eyes among the piles.

As a matter of routine, certainly not as a thing connected with the deaths from what the skipper had called influenza, the crew of the *Pendown Castle* put rat-shields on the mooring hawsers, but they did not take up the gang-plank at night, and now and then a rat slithered ashore to find among its kin in Blackwater more unctuous fare than hardwood lumber. The *Pendown* sailed amiably for home, and from Avonmouth came to Surgeon General Inchcape Jones a cable announcing that the ship was held, that others of the crew had died . . . and died of plague.

In the curt cablegram the word seemed written in bone-scorching fire.

Two days before the cable came, a Blackwater lighterman had been smitten by an unknown ill, very unpleasant, with delirium and buboes. Inchcape Jones said that it could not be plague, because there never was plague in St. Hubert. His confrère, Stokes, retorted that perhaps it couldn't be plague, but it damn' well *was* plague.

Dr. Stokes was a wiry, humorless man, the parish medical officer of St. Swithin Parish. He did not remain in the rustic reaches of St. Swithin, where he belonged, but snooped all over the island, annoying Inchcape Jones. He was an M.B. of Edinburgh; he had served in the African bush; he had had blackwater fever and cholera and most other reasonable afflictions; and he had come to St. Hubert only to recover his red blood corpuscles and to disturb the unhappy Inchcape Jones. He was not a nice man; he had beaten Inchcape Jones at tennis, with a nasty, unsporting serve—the sort of serve you'd expect from an American.

And this Stokes, rather a bounder, a frightful bore, fancied himself as an amateur bacteriologist! It was a bit thick to have him creeping about the docks, catching rats, making cultures from the bellies of their fleas, and barg-ing in—sandy-headed and red-faced, thin and unpleasant—to insist that they bore plague.

"My dear fellow, there's always some *Bacillus pestis* among rats," said Inchcape Jones, in a kindly but airy way.

When the lighterman died, Stokes irritatingly demanded that it be openly admitted that the plague had come to St. Hubert.

"Even if it was plague, which is not certain," said Inchcape Jones, "there's no reason to cause a row and frighten everybody. It was a sporadic case. There won't be any more."

There was more, immediately. In a week three other water-front workers and a fisherman at Point Carib were down with something which, even Inchcape Jones acknowledged, was uncomfortably like the description of plague in "Manson's Tropical Diseases": "a prodromal stage characterized by depression, anorexia, aching of the limbs," then the fever, the vertigo, the haggard features, the bloodshot and sunken eyes, the buboes in the groin. It was not a pretty disease. Inchcape Jones ceased being chattery and ever so jolly about picnics, and became almost as grim as Stokes. But publicly he still hoped and denied and St. Hubert did not know . . . did not know.

## II

To drinking men and wanderers, the pleasantest place in the rather dull and tin-roofed town of Blackwater is the bar and restaurant called the Ice House.

It is on the floor above the Kellett Shipping Agency and the shop where the Chinaman who is supposed to be a graduate of Oxford sells carved tortoise, and cocoanuts in the horrible likeness of a head shrunken by head-hunters. Except for the balcony, where one lunches and looks down on squatting breech-clouted Hindu beggars, and unearthly pearl-pale English children at games in the savannah, all of the Ice House is a large and dreaming dimness wherein you are but half conscious of Moorish grills, a touch of gilt on white-painted walls, a heavy, amazingly long mahogany bar, slot machines, and marble-topped tables beyond your own.

Here, at the cocktail-hour, are all the bloodless, sun-helmeted white rulers of St. Hubert who haven't quite the caste to belong to the Devonshire Club: the shipping-office clerks, the merchants who have no grandfathers, the secretaries to the Inchcape Joneses, the Italians and Portuguese who smuggle into Venezuela.

Calmed by rum swizzles, those tart and commanding apéritifs which are made in their deadly perfection only by the twirling swizzle-sticks of the darkies at the Ice House bar, the exiles become peaceful, and have another swizzle, and grow certain again (as for twenty-four hours, since the last cocktail-hour, they have not been certain) that next year they will go Home. Yes, they will taper off, take exercise in the dawn coolness, stop drinking, become strong and successful, and go Home . . . the Lotus Eaters, tears in their eyes when in the dimness of the Ice House they think of Piccadilly or the heights of Quebec, of Indiana or Catalonia or the clogs of Lancashire. . . . They never go Home. But always they have new reassuring cocktail-hours at the Ice House, until they die, and the other lost men come to their funerals and whisper one to another that they *are* going Home.

Now of the Ice House, George William Vertigan, owner of The Blue Bazaar, was unchallenged monarch. He was a thick, ruddy man, the sort of Englishman one sees in the Midlands, the sort that is either very Non-Conformist or very alcoholic, and George William was not Non-Conformist. Each day from five to seven he was tilted against the bar, never drunk, never altogether sober, always full of melody and kindliness; the one man who did not long for Home, because outside the Ice House he remembered no home.

When it was whispered that a man had died of something which might be plague, George William announced to his court that if it were true, it would serve Kellett the Red Leg jolly well right. But everyone knew that the West Indian climate prevented plague.

The group, quivering on the edge of being panicky, were reassured.

It was two nights afterward that there writhed into the Ice House a rumor that George William Vertigan was dead.

III

No one dared speak of it, whether in the Devonshire Club or the Ice House or the breeze-fluttered, sea-washed park where the Negroes gather after working hours, but they heard, almost without hearing, of this death—and this—and another. No one liked to shake hands with his oldest friend; everyone fled from everyone else, though the rats loyally stayed with them; and through the island galloped the Panic, which is more murderous than its brother, the Plague.

Still there was no quarantine, no official admission. Inchcape Jones vomited feeble proclamations on the inadvisability of too-large public gatherings, and wrote to London to inquire about Haffkine's prophylactic, but to Sir Robert Fairlamb he protested, "Honestly, there's only been a few deaths, and I think it's all passed over. As for these suggestions of Stokes that we burn the village of Carib, merely because they've had several cases—why, it's barbarous! And it's been conveyed to me that if we were to establish a quarantine, the merchants would take the strongest measures against the administration. It would ruin the tourist and export business."

But Stokes of St. Swithin's secretly wrote to Dr. Max Gottlieb, Director of the McGurk Institute, that the plague was ready to flare up and consume all the West Indies, and would Dr. Gottlieb do something about it?

# 32

There may have been in the shadowy heart of Max Gottlieb a diabolic insensibility to divine pity, to suffering humankind; there may have been mere resentment of the doctors who considered his science of value only as it was handy to advertising their business of healing; there may have been the obscure and passionate and unscrupulous demand of genius for privacy. Certainly he who had lived to study the methods of immunizing mankind against disease had little interest in actually using those methods. He was like a fabulous painter, so contemptuous of popular taste that after a lifetime of creation he should destroy everything he had done, lest it be marred and mocked by the dull eyes of the crowd.

The letter from Dr. Stokes was not his only intimation that plague was striding through St. Hubert, that tomorrow it might be leaping to Barbados, to the Virgin Islands . . . to New York. Ross McGurk was an emperor of the new era, better served than any cloistered satrap of old. His skippers looked in at a hundred ports; his railroads penetrated jungles; his correspondents whispered to him of the next election in Colombia, of the Cuban cane-crop, of what Sir Robert Fairlamb had said to Dr. R. E. Inchcape Jones on his bungalow porch. Ross McGurk, and after him Max Gottlieb, knew better than did the Lotus Eaters of the Ice House how much plague there was in St. Hubert.

Yet Gottlieb did not move, but pondered the unknown chemical structure of antibodies, interrupted by questions as to whether Pearl Robbins had enough pencils, whether it would be quite all right for Dr. Holabird to receive the Lettish scientific mission this afternoon, so that Dr. Sholtheis might attend the Anglican Conference on the Reservation of the Host.

He was assailed by inquirers: public health officials, one Dr. Almus Pickerbaugh, a congressman who was said to be popular in Washington, Gustaf Sondelius, and a Martin Arrowsmith who could not (whether because he was too big or too small) quite attain Gottlieb's concentrated indifference.

It was rumored that Arrowsmith of McGurk had something which might eradicate plague. Letters demanded of Gottlieb, "Can you stand by, with the stuff of salvation in your hands, and watch thousands of these unfortunate people dying in St. Hubert, and what is more, are you going to let the dreaded plague gain a foothold in the Western hemisphere? My dear man, this is the time to come out of your scientific reverie and act!"

Then Ross McGurk, over a comfortable steak, hinted, not too diffidently, that this was the opportunity for the Institute to acquire world-fame.

Whether it was the compulsion of McGurk or the demands of the public-spirited, or whether Gottlieb's own imagination aroused enough to visualize the far-off misery of the blacks in the canefields, he summoned Martin and remarked:

"It comes to me that there is pneumonic plague in Manchuria and bubonic in St. Hubert, in the West Indies. If I could trust you, Martin, to use the phage with only half your patients and keep the others as controls, under normal hygienic conditions but without the phage, then you could make an absolute determination of its value, as complete as what we have of mosquito transmission of yellow fever, and then I would send you down to St. Hubert. What do you t'ink?"

Martin swore by Jacques Loeb that he would observe test conditions; he would determine forever the value of phage by the contrast between patients treated and untreated, and so, perhaps, end all plague forever; he would harden his heart and keep clear his eyes.

"We will get Sondelius to go along," said Gottlieb. "He will do the big boom-boom and so bring us the credit in the newspapers which, I am now told, a Director must obtain."

Sondelius did not merely consent—he insisted.

Martin had never seen a foreign country—he could not think of Canada, where he had spent a vacation as hotel-waiter, as foreign to him. He could not comprehend that he was really going to a place of palm trees and brown faces and languid Christmas Eves. He was busy (while Sondelius was out ordering linen suits and seeking a proper new sun helmet) making anti-plague phage on a large scale: a hundred liters of it, sealed in tiny ampules. He felt like the normal Martin, but conferences and powers were considering him.

There was a meeting of the Board of Trustees to advise Martin and Sondelius as to their methods. For it the President of the University of Wilmington gave up a promising interview with a millionaire alumnus, Ross McGurk gave up a game of golf, and one of the three university scientists arrived by aeroplane. Called in from the laboratory, a rather young man in a wrinkled soft collar, dizzy still with the details of Erlenmeyer flasks, infusorial earth, and sterile filters, Martin was confronted by the Men of Measured Merriment, and found that he was no longer concealed in the invisibility of insignificance but regarded as a leader who was expected not only to produce miracles but to explain beforehand how important and mature and miraculous he was.

He was shy before the spectacled gravity of the five Trustees as they sat, like a Supreme Court, at the dais table in Bonanza Hall—Gottlieb a little removed, also trying to look grave and supreme. But Sondelius rolled in, enthusiastic and tremendous, and suddenly Martin was not shy, nor was he respectful to his one-time master in public health.

Sondelius wanted to exterminate all the rodents in St. Hubert, to enforce a quarantine, to use Yersin's serum and Haffkine's prophylactic, and to give Martin's phage to everybody in St. Hubert, all at once, all with everybody.

Martin protested. For the moment it might have been Gottlieb speaking.

He knew, he flung at them, that humanitarian feeling would make it impossible to use the poor devils of sufferers as mere objects of experiment, but he must have at least a few real test cases, and he was damned, even before the Trustees he was damned, if he would have his experiment so mucked up by multiple treatment that they could never tell whether the cures were due to Yersin or Haffkine or phage or none of them.

The Trustees adopted his plan. After all, while they desired to save humanity, wasn't it better to have it saved by a McGurk representative than by Yersin or Haffkine or the outlandish Sondelius?

It was agreed that if Martin could find in St. Hubert a district which was comparatively untouched by the plague, he should there endeavor to have test cases, one half injected with phage, one half untreated. In the badly afflicted districts, he might give the phage to everyone, and if the disease slackened unusually, that would be a secondary proof.

Whether the St. Hubert government, since they had not asked for aid, would give Martin power to experiment and Sondelius police authority, the Trustees did not know. The Surgeon General, a chap named Inchcape Jones, had replied to their cables: "No real epidemic not need help." But McGurk promised that he would pull his numerous wires to have the McGurk Commission (Chairman, Martin Arrowsmith, B.A., M.D.) welcomed by the authorities.

Sondelius still insisted that in this crisis mere experimentation was heartless, yet he listened to Martin's close-reasoned fury with enthusiasm which this bull-necked eternal child had for anything which sounded new and preferably true. He did not, like Almus Pickerbaugh, regard a difference of scientific opinion as an attack on his character.

He talked of going on his own, independent of Martin and McGurk, but he was won back when the Trustees murmured that though they really did wish the dear man wouldn't fool with sera, they would provide him with apparatus to kill all the rats he wanted.

Then Sondelius was happy:

"And you watch me! I am the captain-general of rat-killers! I yoost walk into a warehouse and the rats say, 'There's that damn' old Uncle Gustaf— what's the use?' and they turn up their toes and die! I am yoost as glad I have you people behind me, because I am broke—I went and bought some oil stock that don't look so good now—and I shall need a lot of hydrocyanic acid gas. Oh, those rats! You watch me! Now I go and telegraph I can't keep a lecture engagement next week—huh! me to lecture to a women's college, me that can talk rat-language and know seven beautiful deadly kind of traps!"

## II

Martin had never known greater peril than swimming a flood as a hospital intern. From waking to midnight he was too busy making phage and receiving unsolicited advice from all the Institute staff to think of the dangers of a plague epidemic, but when he went to bed, when his brain was still revolving with plans, he pictured rather too well the chance of dying, unpleasantly.

When Leora received the idea that he was going off to a death-haunted isle, to a place of strange ways and trees and faces (a place, probably, where they spoke funny languages and didn't have movies or tooth-paste), she took the notion secretively away with her, to look at it and examine it, precisely as she often stole little foods from the table and hid them and meditatively ate them at odd hours of the night, with the pleased expression of a bad child. Martin was glad that she did not add to his qualms by worrying. Then, after three days, she spoke:

"I'm going with you."

"You are not!"

"Well. . . . I am!"

"It's not safe."

"Silly! Of course it is. You can shoot your nice old phage into me, and then I'll be absolutely all right. Oh, I have a husband who cures things, I have! I'm going to blow in a lot of money for thin dresses, though I bet St. Hubert isn't any hotter than Dakota can be in August."

"Listen! Lee, darling! Listen! I do think the phage will immunize against the plague—you bet I'll be mighty well injected with it myself!—but I don't *know*, and even if it were practically perfect, there'd always be some people it wouldn't protect. You simply can't go, sweet. Now I'm terribly sleepy—"

Leora seized his lapels, as comic fierce as a boxing kitten, but her eyes were not comic, nor her wailing voice; age-old wail of the soldiers' women:

"Sandy, don't you know I haven't any life outside of you? I might've had, but honestly, I've been glad to let you absorb me. I'm a lazy, useless, ignorant scut, except as maybe I keep you comfortable. If you were off there, and I didn't know you were all right, or if you died and somebody else cared for your body that I've loved so—haven't I loved it, dear?—I'd go mad. I mean it—can't you see I mean it—I'd go mad! It's just—I'm you, and I got to be with you. And I *will* help you! Make your media and everything. You know how often I've helped you. Oh, I'm not much good at McGurk, with all your awful' complicated jiggers, but I did help you at Nautilus—I *did* help you, didn't I?—and maybe in St. Hubert"—her voice was the voice of women in midnight terror—"maybe you won't find anybody that can help you even my little bit, and I'll cook and everything—"

"Darling, don't make it harder for me. Going to be hard enough in any case—"

"Damn you, Sandy Arrowsmith, don't you dare use those old stuck-up expressions that husbands have been drooling out to wives forever and ever! I'm not a wife, any more'n you're a husband. You're a rotten husband! You neglect me absolutely. The only time you know what I've got on is when some doggone button slips—and how they can pull off when a person has gone over 'em and sewed 'em all on again is simply beyond me!—and then you bawl me out. But I don't care. I'd rather have you than any decent husband. . . . Besides. I'm going."

Gottlieb opposed it, Sondelius roared about it, Martin worried about it, but Leora went, and—his only act of craftiness as Director of the Institute—Gottlieb made her "Secretary and Technical Assistant to the McGurk Plague and Bacteriophage Commission to the Lesser Antilles," and blandly gave her a salary.

### III

The day before the Commission sailed, Martin insisted that Sondelius take his first injection of phage. He refused.

"No, I will not touch it till you get converted to humanity, Martin, and give it to everybody in St. Hubert. And you will! Wait till you see them suffering by the thousand. You have not seen such a thing. Then you will forget science and try to save everybody. You shall not inject me till you will inject all my Negro friends down there too."

That afternoon Gottlieb called Martin in. He spoke with hesitation:

"You're off for Blackwater tomorrow."

"Yes, sir."

"Hm. You may be gone some time. I— Martin, you are my oldest friend in New York, you and the good Miriam. Tell me: At first you and Terry t'ought I should not take up the Directorship. Don't you now t'ink I was wise?"

Martin stared, then hastily he lied and said that which was comforting and expected.

"I am glad you t'ink so. You have known so long what I have tried to do.

I haf faults, but I t'ink I begin to see a real scientific note coming into the Institute at last, after the popoolarity-chasing of Tubbs and Holabird. . . . I wonder how I can discharge Holabird, that pants-presser of science? If only he dit not know Capitola so well—socially, they call it! But anyway—

"There are those that said Max Gottlieb could not do the child job of running an institution. Huh! Buying note-books! Hiring women that sweep floors! Or no—the floors are swept by women hired by the superintendent of the building, *nicht wahr?* But anyway—

"I did not make a rage when Terry and you doubted. I am a great fellow for allowing everyone his opinion. But it pleases me—I am very fond of you two boys—the only real sons I have—" Gottlieb laid his withered hand on Martin's arm. "It pleases me that you see now I am beginning to make a real scientific Institute. Though I have enemies. Martin, you would t'ink I was joking if I told you the plotting against me—

"Even Yeo. I t'ought he was my friend. I t'ought he was a real biologist. But just today he comes to me and says he cannot get enough sea-urchins for his experiments. As if I could make sea-urchins out of thin air! He said I keep him short of all materials. Me! That have always stood for— I do not care what they *pay* scientists, but always I have stood, against that fool Silva and all of them, all my enemies—

"You do not know how many enemies I have, Martin! They do not dare show their faces. They smile to me, but they whisper— I will show Holabird —always he plot against me and try to win over Pearl Robbins, but she is a good girl, she knows what I am doing, but—"

He looked perplexed; he peered at Martin as though he did not quite recognize him, and begged:

"Martin, I grow old—not in years—it is a lie I am over seventy—but I have my worries. Do you mind if I give you advice as I have done so often, so many years? Though you are not a schoolboy now in Queen City—no, at Winnemac it was. You are a man and you are a genuine worker. But—

"Be sure you do not let anything, not even your own good kind heart, spoil your experiment at St. Hubert. I do not make funniness about humanitarianism as I used to; sometimes now I t'ink the vulgar and contentious human race may yet have as much grace and good taste as the cats. But if this is to be, there must be knowledge. So many men, Martin, are kind and neighborly; so few have added to knowledge. You have the chance! You may be the man who ends all plague, and maybe old Max Gottlieb will have helped, too, *hein*, maybe?

"You must not be just a good doctor at St. Hubert. You must pity, oh, so much the generation after generation yet to come that you can refuse to let yourself indulge in pity for the men you will see dying.

"Dying. . . . It will be peace.

"Let nothing, neither beautiful pity nor fear of your own death, keep you from making this plague experiment complete. And as my friend— If you do this, something will yet have come out of my Directorship. If but one fine thing could come, to justify me—"

When Martin came sorrowing into his laboratory he found Terry Wickett waiting.

"Say, Slim," Terry blurted, "just wanted to butt in and suggest, now for St. Gottlieb's sake keep your phage notes complete and up-to-date, and keep 'em in ink!"

"Terry, it looks to me as if you thought I had a fine chance of not coming back with the notes myself."

"Aw, what's biting you!" said Terry feebly.

#### IV

The epidemic in St. Hubert must have increased, for on the day before the McGurk Commission sailed, Dr. Inchcape Jones declared that the island was quarantined. People might come in, but no one could leave. He did this despite the fretting of the Governor, Sir Robert Fairlamb, and the protests of the hotel-keepers who fed on tourists, the ex-rat-catchers who drove the same, Kellett the Red Leg who sold them tickets, and all the other representatives of sound business in St. Hubert.

#### V

Besides his ampules of phage and his Luer syringes for injection, Martin made personal preparations for the tropics. He bought, in seventeen minutes, a Palm Beach suit, two new shirts, and, as St. Hubert was a British possession and as he had heard that all Britishers carry canes, a stick which the shop-keeper guaranteed to be as good as genuine malacca.

#### VI

They started, Martin and Leora and Gustaf Sondelius, on a winter morning, on the six-thousand-ton steamer *St. Buryan* of the McGurk Line, which carried machinery and flour and codfish and motors to the Lesser Antilles and brought back molasses, cocoa, avacados, Trinidad asphalt. A score of winter tourists made the round trip, but only a score, and there was little handkerchief-waving.

The McGurk Line pier was in South Brooklyn, in a district of brown anonymous houses. The sky was colorless above dirty snow. Sondelius seemed well content. As they drove upon a wharf littered with hides and boxes and disconsolate steerage passengers, he peered out of their crammed taxicab and announced that the bow of the *St. Buryan*—all they could see of it— reminded him of the Spanish steamer he had taken to the Cape Verde Isles. But to Martin and Leora, who had read of the drama of departure, of stewards darting with masses of flowers, dukes and divorcées being interviewed, and bands playing "The Star-spangled Banner," the *St. Buryan* was unromantic and its ferry-like casualness was discouraging.

Only Terry came to see them off, bringing a box of candy for Leora.

Martin had never ridden a craft larger than a motor launch. He stared up at the black wall of the steamer's side. As they mounted the gangplank he was conscious that he was cutting himself off from the safe, familiar land, and he was embarrassed by the indifference of more experienced-looking passengers, staring down from the rail. Aboard, it seemed to him that the forward deck looked like the backyard of an old-iron dealer, that the *St. Buryan* leaned too much to one side, and that even in the dock she swayed undesirably.

The whistle snorted contemptuously; the hawsers were cast off. Terry stood on the pier till the steamer, with Martin and Leora and Sondelius above him, their stomachs pressed against the rail, had slid past him, then he abruptly clumped away.

Martin realized that he was off for the perilous sea and the perilous plague; that there was no possibility of leaving the ship till they should reach some distant island. This narrow deck, with its tarry lines between planks, was his only home. Also, in the breeze across the wide harbor he was beastly cold, and in general God help him!

As the *St. Buryan* was warped out into the river, as Martin was suggesting to his Commission, "How about going down-stairs and seeing if we can raise a drink?" there was the sound of a panicky taxicab on the pier, the sight of a lean, tall figure running—but so feebly, so shakily—and they realized that it was Max Gottlieb, peering for them, tentatively raising his thin arm in greeting, not finding them in the line at the rail, and turning sadly away.

### VII

As representatives of Ross McGurk and his various works, evil and benevolent, they had the two suites de luxe on the boat deck.

Martin was cold off snow-blown Sandy Hook, sick off Cape Hatteras, and tired and relaxed between; with him Leora was cold, and in a ladylike manner she was sick, but she was not at all tired. She insisted on conveying information to him, from the West Indian guide-book which she had earnestly bought.

Sondelius was conspicuously all over the ship. He had tea with the Captain, scouse with the fo'c'sle, and intellectual conferences with the Negro missionary in the steerage. He was to be heard—always he was to be heard: singing on the promenade deck, defending Bolshevism against the boatswain, arguing oil-burning with the First Officer, and explaining to the bar steward how to make a gin sling. He held a party for the children in the steerage, and he borrowed from the First Officer a volume of navigation to study between parties.

He gave flavor to the ordinary cautious voyage of the *St. Buryan*, but he made a mistake. He was courteous to Miss Gwilliam; he tried to cheer her on a seemingly lonely adventure.

Miss Gwilliam came from one of the best families in her section of New Jersey; her father was a lawyer and a church-warden, her grandfather had been a solid farmer. That she had not married, at thirty-three, was due entirely to the preference of modern young men for jazz-dancing hussies; and she was not only a young lady of delicate reservations but also a singer; in fact, she was going to the West Indies to preserve the wonders of primitive art for reverent posterity in the native ballads she would collect and sing to a delighted public—if only she learned how to sing.

She studied Gustaf Sondelius. He was a silly person, not in the least like the gentlemanly insurance-agents and office-managers she was accustomed to meet at the country club, and what was worse, he did not ask her opinions on art and good form. His stories about generals and that sort of people could be discounted as lies, for did he not associate with grimy engineers? He needed some of her gentle but merry chiding.

When they stood together at the rail and he chanted in his ludicrous up-and-down Swedish sing-song that it was a fine evening, she remarked, "Well, Mr. Roughneck, have you been up to something smart again today? Or have you been giving somebody else a chance to talk, for once?"

She was placidly astonished when he clumped away with none of the obedient reverence which any example of cultured American womanhood has a right to expect from all males, even foreigners.

Sondelius came to Martin lamenting, "Slim—if I may call you so, like Terry—I think you and your Gottlieb are right. There is no use saving fools. It's a great mistake to be natural. One should always be a stuffed shirt, like old Tubbs. Then one would have respect even from artistic New Jersey spinsters. . . . How strange is conceit! That I who have been cursed and beaten by so many Great Ones, who was once led out to be shot in a Turkish prison, should never have been annoyed by them as by this smug wench. Ah, smugness! That is the enemy!"

Apparently he recovered from Miss Gwilliam. He was seen arguing with the ship's doctor about sutures in Negro skulls, and he invented a game of deck cricket. But one evening when he sat reading in the "social hall," stooped over, wearing betraying spectacles and his mouth puckered, Martin walked past the window and incredulously saw that Sondelius was growing old.

VIII

As he sat by Leora in a deck-chair, Martin studied her, really looked at her pale profile, after years when she had been a matter of course. He pondered on her as he pondered on phage; he weightily decided that he had neglected her, and weightily he started right in to be a good husband.

"Now I have a chance to be human, Lee, I realize how lonely you must have been in New York."

"But I haven't."

"Don't be foolish! Of course you've been lonely! Well, when we get back, I'll take a little time off every day and we'll—we'll have walks and go to the movies and everything. And I'll send you flowers, every morning. Isn't it a relief to just sit here! But I do begin to think and realize how I've prob'ly neglected— Tell me, honey, has it been too terribly dull?"

"Hunka. Really."

"No, but *tell* me."

"There's nothing to tell."

"Now hang it, Leora, here when I *do* have the first chance in eleven thousand years to think about you, and I come right out frankly and admit how slack I've been— And planning to send you flowers—"

"You look here, Sandy Arrowsmith! Quit bullying me! You want the luxury of harrowing yourself by thinking what a poor, bawling, wretched, story-book wife I am. You're working up to become perfectly miserable if you can't enjoy being miserable. . . . It would be terrible, when we got back to New York, if you did get on the job and devoted yourself to showing me a good time. You'd go at it like a bull. I'd have to be so dratted grateful for the flowers every day—the days you didn't forget!—and the way you'd sling me off to the movies when I wanted to stay home and snooze—"

"Well, by thunder, of all the—"

"No, please! You're dear and good, but you're so bossy that I've always got to be whatever *you* want, even if it's lonely. But— Maybe I'm lazy. I'd rather just snoop around than have to work at being well-dressed and popular and all those jobs. I fuss over the flat—hang it, wish I'd had the kitchen repainted while we're away, it's a *nice* little kitchen—and I make believe read my French books, and go out for a walk, and look in the windows, and eat an ice cream soda, and the day slides by. Sandy, I do love you awful' much; if I could, I'd be as ill-treated as the dickens, so you could enjoy it, but I'm no good at educated lies, only at easy little ones like the one I told you last week—I said I hadn't eaten any candy and didn't have a stomach-ache, and I'd eaten half a pound and I was sick as a pup. . . . Gosh, I'm a good wife I am!"

They rolled from gray seas to purple and silver. By dusk they stood at the rail, and he felt the spaciousness of the sea, of life. Always he had lived in his imagination. As he had blundered through crowds, an inconspicuous young husband trotting out to buy cold roast beef for dinner, his brain-pan had been wide as the domed sky. He had seen not the streets, but micro-organisms large as jungle monsters, miles of flasks cloudy with bacteria, himself giving orders to his garçon, Max Gottlieb awesomely congratulating him. Always his dreams had clung about his work. Now, no less passionately, he awoke to the ship, the mysterious sea, the presence of Leora, and he cried to her, in the warm tropic winter dusk:

"Sweet, this is only the first of our big hikes! Pretty soon, if I'm successful in St. Hubert, I'll begin to count in science, and we'll go abroad, to your France and England and Italy and everywhere!"

"Can we, do you think? Oh, Sandy! Going *places!*"

## IX

He never knew it but for an hour, in their cabin half-lighted from the lamps in their sitting-room beyond, she watched him sleeping.

He was not handsome; he was grotesque as a puppy napping on a hot afternoon. His hair was ruffled, his face was deep in the crumpled pillow he had encircled with both his arms. She looked at him, smiling, with the stretched corners of her lips like tiny flung arrows.

"I do love him so when he's frowsy! Don't you see, Sandy, I was wise to come! You're so worn out. *It* might get you, and nobody but me could nurse you. Nobody knows all your cranky ways—about how you hate prunes and everything. Night and day I'll nurse you—the least whisper and I'll be awake. And if you need ice bags and stuff— And I'll *have* ice, too, if I have to sneak into some millionaire's house and steal it out of his highballs! My dear!"

She shifted the electric fan so that it played more upon him, and on soft toes she crept into their stiff sitting-room. It did not contain much save a round table, a few chairs, and a Sybaritic glass and mahogany wall-cabinet whose purpose was never discovered.

"It's so sort of— Aah! Pinched. I guess maybe I ought to fix it up somehow."

But she had no talent for the composing of chairs and pictures which brings humanness into a dead room. Never in her life had she spent three minutes in arranging flowers. She looked doubtful, she smiled and turned out the light, and slipped in to him.

She lay on the coverlet of her berth, in the tropic languidness, a slight figure in a frivolous nightgown. She thought, "I like a small bedroom, because Sandy is nearer and I don't get so scared by things. What a dratted bully the man is! Some day I'm going to up and say to him: 'You go to the devil!' I will so! Darling, we will hike off to France together, just you and I, won't we!"

She was asleep, smiling, so thin a little figure—

# 33

Misty mountains they saw, and on their flanks the palm-crowned fortifications built of old time against the pirates. In Martinique were white-faced houses like provincial France, and a boiling market full of colored women with kerchiefs ultramarine and scarlet. They passed hot St. Lucia, and Saba that is all one lone volcano. They devoured paw-paws and breadfruit and avocados, bought from coffee-colored natives who came alongside in nervous small boats; they felt the languor of the isles, and panted before they approached Barbados.

Just beyond was St. Hubert.

None of the tourists had known of the quarantine. They were raging that the company should have taken them into danger. In the tepid wind they felt the plague.

The skipper reassured them, in a formal address. Yes, they would stop at Blackwater, the port of St. Hubert, but they would anchor far out in the harbor; and while the passengers bound for St. Hubert would be permitted to go ashore, in the port-doctor's launch, no one in St. Hubert would be allowed to leave—nothing from that pest-hole would touch the steamer except the official mail, which the ship's surgeon would disinfect.

(The ship's surgeon was wondering, the while, how you disinfected mail—let's see—sulfur burning in the presence of moisture, wasn't it?)

The skipper had been trained in oratory by arguments with wharf-masters, and the tourists were reassured. But Martin murmured to his Commission, "I hadn't thought of that. Once we go ashore, we'll be practically prisoners till the epidemic's over—if it ever does get over—prisoners with the plague around us."

"Why, of course!" said Sondelius.

## II

They left Bridgetown, the pleasant port of Barbados, by afternoon. It was late night, with most of the passengers asleep, when they arrived at Blackwater. As Martin came out on the damp and vacant deck, it seemed unreal, harshly unfriendly, and of the coming battleground he saw nothing but a few shore lights beyond uneasy water.

About their arrival there was something timorous and illicit. The ship's surgeon ran up and down, looking disturbed; the captain could be heard growling on the bridge; the First Officer hastened up to confer with him and disappeared below again; and there was no one to meet them. The steamer waited, rolling in a swell, while from the shore seemed to belch a hot miasma.

"And here's where we're going to land and *stay!*" Martin grunted to Leora, as they stood by their bags, their cases of phage, on the heaving, black-shining deck near the top of the accommodation-ladder.

Passengers came out in dressing-gowns, chattering, "Yes, this must be the place, those lights there. Must be fierce. *What?* Somebody going ashore? Oh, sure, those two doctors. Well, they got nerve. I certainly don't envy them!"

Martin heard.

From shore a pitching light made toward the ship, slid round the bow, and sidled to the bottom of the accommodation-ladder. In the haze of a lantern held by a steward at the foot of the steps, Martin could see a smart covered launch, manned by darky sailors in naval uniform and glazed black straw hats with ribbons, and commanded by a Scotch-looking man with some sort of a peaked uniform cap over a civilian jacket.

The captain clumped down the swinging steps beside the ship. While the launch bobbed, its wet canvas top glistening, he had a long and complaining conference with the commander of the launch, and received a pouch of mail, the only thing to come aboard.

The ship's surgeon took it from the captain with aversion, grumbling, "Now where can I get a barrel to disinfect these darn' letters in?"

Martin and Leora and Sondelius waited, without option.

They had been joined by a thin woman in black whom they had not seen all the trip—one of the mysterious passengers who are never noticed till they come on deck at landing. Apparently she was going ashore. She was pale, her hands twitching.

The captain shouted at them, "All right—all right—all right! You can go now. Hustle, please. I've got to get on. . . . Damn' nuisance."

The *St. Buryan* had not seemed large or luxurious, but it was a castle, steadfast among storms, its side a massy wall, as Martin crept down the swaying stairs, thinking all at once, "We're in for it; like going to the scaffold —they lead you along—no chance to resist," and, "You're letting your imagination run away with you; quit it now!" and, "Is it too late to make Lee stay behind, on the steamer?" and an agonized, "Oh, Lord, are the stewards handling that phage carefully?" Then he was on the tiny square platform at the bottom of the accommodation-ladder, the ship's side was high above him, lit by the round ports of cabins, and someone was helping him into the launch.

As the unknown woman in black came aboard, Martin saw in lantern light how her lips tightened once, then her whole face went blank, like one who waited hopelessly.

Leora squeezed his hand, hard, as he helped her in.

He muttered, while the steamer whistled, "Quick! You can still go back! You must!"

"And leave the pretty launch? Why, Sandy! Just look at the elegant engine it's got! . . . Gosh, I'm scared blue!"

As the launch sputtered, swung round, and headed for the filtering of lights ashore, as it bowed its head and danced to the swell, the sandy-headed official demanded of Martin:

"You're the McGurk Commission?"

"Yes."

"Good." He sounded pleased yet cold, a busy voice and humorless.

"Are you the port-doctor?" asked Sondelius.

"No, not exactly. I'm Dr. Stokes, of St. Swithin's Parish. We're all of us almost everything, nowadays. The port-doctor— In fact he died couple of days ago."

Martin grunted. But his imagination had ceased to agitate him.

"You're Dr. Sondelius, I imagine. I know your work in Africa, in German East—was out there myself. And you're Dr. Arrowsmith? I read your plague phage paper. Much impressed. Now I have just the chance to say before we go ashore— You'll both be opposed. Inchcape Jones, the S.G., has lost his head. Running in circles, lancing buboes—afraid to burn Carib, where most of the infection is. Arrowsmith, I have a notion of what you may want to do experimentally. If Inchcape balks, you come to me in my parish—if I'm still alive. Stokes, my name is. . . . Damn it, boy, what *are* you doing? Trying to drift clear down to Venezuela? . . . Inchcape and H.E. are so afraid that they won't even cremate the bodies—some religious prejudice among the blacks—obee or something."

"I see," said Martin.

"How many cases plague you got now?" said Sondelius.

"Lord knows. Maybe a thousand. And ten million rats. . . . I'm so sleepy! . . . Well, welcome, gentlemen—" He flung out his arms in a dry hysteria. "Welcome to the Island of Hesperides!"

Out of darkness Blackwater swung toward them, low flimsy barracks on a low swampy plain stinking of slimy mud. Most of the town was dark, dark and wickedly still. There was no face along the dim waterfront—warehouses, tram station, mean hotels—and they ground against a pier, they went ashore, without attention from customs officials. There were no carriages, and the hotel-runners who once had pestered tourists landing from the *St. Buryan*, whatever the hour, were dead now or hidden.

The thin mysterious woman passenger vanished, staggering with her suitcase—she had said no word, and they never saw her again. The Commission, with Stokes and the harbor-police who had manned the launch, carried the baggage (Martin weaving with a case of the phage) through the rutty balconied streets to the San Marino Hotel.

Once or twice faces, disembodied things with frightened lips, stared at them from alley-mouths; and when they came to the hotel, when they stood before it, a weary caravan laden with bags and boxes, the bulging-eyed manageress peered from a window before she would admit them.

As they entered, Martin saw under a street light the first stirring of life: a crying woman and a bewildered child following an open wagon in which were heaped a dozen stiff bodies.

"And I might have saved all of them, with phage," he whispered to himself.

His forehead was cold, yet it was greasy with sweat as he babbled to the manageress of rooms and meals, as he prayed that Leora might not have seen the Things in that slow creaking wagon.

"I'd have choked her before I let her come, if I'd known," he was shuddering.

The woman apologized, "I must ask you gentlemen to carry your things up to your rooms. Our boys— They aren't here any more."

What became of the walking stick which, in such pleased vanity, Martin had bought in New York, he never knew. He was too busy guarding the cases of phage, and worrying, "Maybe this stuff would save everybody."

Now Stokes of St. Swithin's was a reticent man and hard, but when they had the last bag upstairs, he leaned his head against a door, cried, "My God, Arrowsmith, I'm so glad you've got here," and broke from them, running. . . . One of the Negro harbor-police, expressionless, speaking the English of the Antilles with something of the accent of Piccadilly, said, "Sar, have you any other command for I? If you permit, we boys will now go home. Sar, on the table is the whisky Dr. Stokes have told I to bring."

Martin stared. It was Sondelius who said, "Thank you very much, boys. Here's a quid between you. Now get some sleep."

They saluted and were not.

Sondelius made the novices as merry as he could for half an hour.

Martin and Leora woke to a broiling, flaring, green and crimson morning, yet ghastly still; awoke and realized that about them was a strange land, as yet unseen, and before them the work that in distant New York had seemed dramatic and joyful and that stank now of the charnel house.

### III

A sort of breakfast was brought to them by a Negress who, before she would enter, peeped fearfully at them from the door.

Sondelius rumbled in from his room, in an impassioned silk dressing-gown. If ever, spectacled and stooped, he had looked old, now he was young and boisterous.

"Hey, ya, Slim, I think we get some work here! Let me at those rats! This Inchcape—to try to master them with strychnin! A noble melon! Leora, when you divorce Martin, you marry me, heh? Give me the salt. Yey, I sleep fine!"

The night before, Martin had scarce looked at their room. Now he was diverted by what he considered its foreignness: the lofty walls of wood painted a watery blue, the wide furnitureless spaces, the bougainvillaea at the window, and in the courtyard the merciless heat and rattling metallic leaves of palmettoes.

Beyond the courtyard walls were the upper stories of a balconied Chinese shop and the violent-colored skylight of The Blue Bazaar.

He felt that there should be a clamor from this exotic world, but there was only a rebuking stillness, and even Sondelius became dumb, though he had his moment. He waddled back to his room, dressed himself in surah silk last worn on the East Coast of Africa, and returned bringing a sun-helmet which secretly he had bought for Martin.

In linen jacket and mushroom helmet, Martin belonged more to the tropics than to his own harsh Northern meadows. But his pleasure in looking foreign was interrupted by the entrance of the Surgeon General, Dr. R. E. Inchcape Jones, lean but apple-cheeked, worried and hasty.

"Of course you chaps are welcome, but really, with all we have to do I'm afraid we can't give you the attention you doubtless expect," he said indignantly.

Martin sought for adequate answer. It was Sondelius who spoke of a non-existent cousin who was a Harley Street specialist, and who explained that all they wanted was a laboratory for Martin and, for himself, a chance to slaughter rats. How many times, in how many lands, had Gustaf Sondelius flattered pro-consuls and persuaded the heathen to let themselves be saved!

Under his hands the Surgeon General became practically human; he looked as though he really thought Leora was pretty; he promised that he might perhaps let Sondelius tamper with his rats. He would return that afternoon and conduct them to the house prepared for them, Penrith Lodge, on the safe secluded hills behind Blackwater. And (he bowed gallantly) he thought that Mrs. Arrowsmith would find the Lodge a topping bungalow, with three rather decent servants. The butler, though a colored chap, was an old mess-sergeant.

Inchcape Jones had scarce gone when at the door there was a pounding and it opened on Martin's classmate at Winnemac, Dr. the Rev. Ira Hinkley.

Martin had forgotten Ira, that bulky Christian who had tried to save him during otherwise dulcet hours of dissection. He recalled him confusedly. The man came in, vast and lumbering. His eyes were staring and altogether mad, and his voice was parched:

"Hello, Mart. Yump, it's old Ira. I'm in charge of all the chapels of the Sanctification Brotherhood here. Oh, Mart, if you only knew the wickedness of the natives, and the way they lie and sing indecent songs and commit all manner of vileness! And the Church of England lets them wallow in their sins! Only us to save them. I heard you were coming. I have been laboring, Mart. I've nursed the poor plague-stricken devils, and I've told them how hellfire is roaring about them. Oh, Mart, if you knew how my heart bleeds to see these ignorant fellows going unrepentant to eternal torture! After all these years I know you can't still be a scoffer. I come to you with open hands, begging you not merely to comfort the sufferers but to snatch their souls from the burning lakes of sulfur to which, in His everlasting mercy, the Lord of Hosts hath condemned those that blaspheme against His gospel, freely given—"

Again it was Sondelius who got Ira Hinkley out, not too discontented, while Martin could only splutter, "Now how do you suppose that maniac ever got here? This is going to be awful!"

Before Inchcape Jones returned, the Commission ventured out for their first sight of the town. . . . A Scientific Commission, yet all the while they were only boisterous Gustaf and doubtful Martin and casual Leora.

The citizens had been told that in bubonic plague, unlike pneumonic, there is no danger from direct contact with people developing the disease, so long as vermin were kept away, but they did not believe it. They were afraid of one another, and the more afraid of strangers. The Commission found a street dying with fear. House-shutters were closed, hot slatted patches in the sun; and the only traffic was an empty trolley-car with a frightened motorman who peered down at them and sped up lest they come aboard. Grocery shops and drugstores were open, but from their shady depths the shopkeepers looked out timidly, and when the Commission neared a fish-stall, the one customer fled, edging past them.

Once a woman, never explained, a woman with wild ungathered hair, ran by them shrieking, "My little boy—"

They came to the market, a hundred stalls under a long corrugated-iron roof, with stone pillars bearing the fatuous names of the commissioners who had built it—by voting bonds for the building. It should have been buzzing with jovial buyers and sellers, but in all the gaudy booths there were only one Negress with a row of twig besoms, one Hindu in gray rags squatting before his wealth of a dozen vegetables. The rest was emptiness, and a litter of rotted potatoes and scudding papers.

Down a grim street of coal yards, they found a public square, and here was the stillness not of sleep but of ancient death.

The square was rimmed with the gloom of mango trees, which shut out the faint-hearted breeze and cooped in the heat—stale lifeless heat, in whose misery the leering silence was the more dismaying. Through a break in the evil mangoes they beheld a plaster house hung with black crape.

"It's too hot to walk. Perhaps we'd better go back to the hotel," said Leora.

## IV

In the afternoon Inchcape Jones appeared with a Ford, whose familiarity made it the more grotesque in this creepy world, and took them to Penrith Lodge, on the cool hills behind Blackwater.

They traversed a packed native section of bamboo hovels and shops that were but unpainted, black-weathered huts, without doors, without windows, from whose recesses dark faces looked at them resentfully. They passed, at their colored driver's most jerky speed, a new brick structure in front of which stately Negro policemen with white gloves, white sun-helmets, and scarlet coats cut by white belts, marched with rifles at the carry.

Inchcape Jones sighed, "Schoolhouse. Turned it into pest-house. Hundred cases in there. Die every hour. Have to guard it—patients get delirious and try to escape."

After them trailed an odor of rotting.

Martin did not feel superior to humanity.

## V

With broad porches and low roof, among bright flamboyants and the cheerful sago palms, the bungalow of Penrith Lodge lay high on a crest, looking across the ugly flat of the town to the wash of sea. At its windows the reed jalousies whispered and clattered, and the high bare rooms were enlivened by figured Carib scarfs. . . . It had belonged to the port-doctor, dead these three days.

Inchcape Jones assured the doubtful Leora that she would nowhere else be so safe; the house was rat-proofed, and the doctor had caught the plague at the pier, had died without ever coming back to this well-beloved bungalow in which he, the professional bachelor, had given the most clamorous parties in St. Hubert.

Martin had with him sufficient equipment for a small laboratory, and he established it in a bedroom with gas and running water. Next to it was his and Leora's bedroom, then an apartment which Sondelius immediately made homelike by dropping his clothes and his pipe ashes all over it.

There were two colored maids and an ex-soldier butler, who received them and unpacked their bags as though the plague did not exist.

Martin was perplexed by their first caller. He was a singularly handsome young Negro, quick-moving, intelligent of eye. Like most white Americans, Martin had talked a great deal about the inferiority of Negroes and had learned nothing whatever about them. He looked questioning as the young man observed:

"My name is Oliver Marchand."

"Yes?"

"Dr. Marchand—I have my M.D. from Howard."

"Oh."

"May I venture to welcome you, Doctor? And may I ask before I hurry off— I have three cases from official families isolated at the bottom of the hill— oh, yes, in this crisis they permit a Negro doctor to practice even among the whites! But— Dr. Stokes insists that D'Hérelle and you are right in calling bacteriophage an organism. But what about Bordet's contention that it's an enzyme?"

Then for half an hour did Dr. Arrowsmith and Dr. Marchand, forgetting the plague, forgetting the more cruel plague of race-fear, draw diagrams.

Marchand sighed, "I must go, Doctor. May I help you in any way I can? It is a great privilege to know you."

He saluted quietly and was gone, a beautiful young animal.

"I never thought a Negro doctor— I wish people wouldn't keep showing me how much I don't know!" said Martin.

## VI

While Martin prepared his laboratory, Sondelius was joyfully at work, finding out what was wrong with Inchcape Jones's administration, which proved to be almost anything that could be wrong.

A plague epidemic today, in a civilized land, is no longer an affair of people dying in the streets and of drivers shouting "Bring out your dead." The fight against it is conducted like modern warfare, with telephones instead of foaming chargers. The ancient horror bears a face of efficiency. There are offices, card indices, bacteriological examinations of patients and of rats. There is, or should be, a lone director with superlegal powers. There are large funds, education of the public by placard and newspaper, brigades of rat-killers, a corps of disinfectors, isolation of patients lest vermin carry the germs from them to others.

In most of these particulars Inchcape Jones had failed. To have the existence of the plague admitted in the first place, he had had to fight the merchants controlling the House of Assembly, who had howled that a quarantine would ruin them, and who now refused to give him complete power and tried to manage the epidemic with a Board of Health, which was somewhat worse than navigating a ship during a typhoon by means of a committee.

Inchcape Jones was courageous enough, but he could not cajole people. The newspapers called him a tyrant, would not help win over the public to take precautions against rats and ground squirrels. He had tried to fumigate a few warehouses with sulfur dioxid, but the owners complained that the fumes stained fabrics and paint; and the Board of Health bade him wait—wait a little while—wait and see. He had tried to have the rats examined, to discover what were the centers of infection, but his only bacteriologists were the overworked Stokes and Oliver Marchand; and Inchcape Jones had often explained, at nice dinner-parties, that he did not trust the intelligence of Negroes.

He was nearly insane; he worked twenty hours a day; he assured himself that he was not afraid; he reminded himself that he had an honestly won D.S.O.; he longed to have someone besides a board of Red Leg merchants give him orders; and always in the blur of his sleepless brain he saw the hills of Surrey, his sisters in the rose-walk, and the basket-chairs and tea-table beside his father's tennis-lawn.

Then Sondelius, that crafty and often lying lobbyist, that unmoral soldier of the Lord, burst in and became dictator.

He terrified the Board of Health. He quoted his own experiences in Mongolia and India. He assured them that if they did not cease being politicians, the plague might cling in St. Hubert forever, so that they would no more have the amiable dollars of the tourists and the pleasures of smuggling.

He threatened and flattered, and told a story which they had never heard, even at the Ice House; and he had Inchcape Jones appointed dictator of St. Hubert.

Gustaf Sondelius stood extremely close behind the dictator.

He immediately started rat-killing. On a warrant signed by Inchcape Jones, he arrested the owner of a warehouse who had declared that he was not going to have *his* piles of cocoa ruined. He marched his policemen, stout black fellows trained in the Great War, to the warehouse, set them on guard, and pumped in hydrocyanic acid gas.

The crowd gathered beyond the police line, wondering, doubting. They could not believe that anything was happening, for the cracks in the warehouse walls had been adequately stuffed and there was no scent of gas. But the roof was leaky. The gas crept up through it, colorless, diabolic, and suddenly a buzzard circling above the roof tilted forward, fell slantwise, and lay dead among the watchers.

A man picked it up, goggling.

"Dead, right enough," everybody muttered. They looked at Sondelius, parading among his soldiers, with reverence.

His rat-crew searched each warehouse before pumping in the gas, lest someone be left in the place, but in the third one a tramp had been asleep, and when the doors were anxiously opened after the fumigation, there were not only thousands of dead rats but also a dead and very stiff tramp.

"Poor fella—bury him," said Sondelius.

There was no inquest.

Over a rum swizzle at the Ice House, Sondelius reflected, "I wonder how many men I murder, Martin? When I was disinfecting ships at Antofagasta, always afterward we find two or three stowaways. They hide too good. Poor fellas."

Sondelius arbitrarily dragged bookkeepers and porters from their work, to pursue the rats with poison, traps, and gas, or to starve them by concreting and screening stables and warehouses. He made a violent red and green rat map of the town. He broke every law of property by raiding shops for supplies. He alternately bullied and caressed the leaders of the House of Assembly. He called on Kellett, told stories to his children, and almost wept as he explained what a good Lutheran he was—and consistently (but not at Kellett's) he drank too much.

The Ice House, that dimmest and most peaceful among saloons, with its cool marble tables, its gilt-touched white walls, had not been closed, though only the oldest topers and the youngest bravos, fresh out from Home and agonizingly lonely for Peckham or Walthamstow, for Peel Park or the Cirencester High Street, were desperate enough to go there, and of the attendants there remained only one big Jamaica barman. By chance he was among them all the most divine mixer of the planter's punch, the New Orleans fizz, and the rum swizzle. His masterpieces Sondelius acclaimed, he alone placid among the scary patrons who came in now not to dream but to gulp and flee. After a day of slaughtering rats and disinfecting houses he sat with Martin, with Martin and Leora, or with whomever he could persuade to linger.

To Gustaf Sondelius, dukes and cobblers were alike remarkable, and Martin was sometimes jealous when he saw Sondelius turning to a cocoa-broker's clerk with the same smile he gave to Martin. For hours Sondelius talked, of Shanghai and epistemology and the painting of Nevinson; for hours he sang scurrilous lyrics of the Quarter, and boomed, "Yey, how I kill the rats at Kellett's wharf today! I don't t'ink one little swizzle would break down too many glomeruli in an honest man's kidneys."

He was cheerful, but never with the reproving and infuriating cheerfulness of an Ira Hinkley. He mocked himself, Martin, Leora, and their work. At home dinner he never cared what he ate (though he did care what he drank), which at Penrith Lodge was desirable, in view of Leora's efforts to combine the views of Wheatsylvania with the standards of West Indian servants and the absence of daily deliveries. He shouted and sang—and took precautions for working among rats and the agile fleas: the high boots, the strapped wrists, and the rubber neck-band which he had invented and which is known in every tropical supply shop today as the Sondelius Anti-vermin Neck Protector.

It happened that he was, without Martin or Gottlieb ever understanding it, the most brilliant as well as the least pompous and therefore least appreciated warrior against epidemics that the world has known.

Thus with Sondelius, though for Martin there were as yet but embarrassment and futility and the fear of fear.

# 34

To persuade the shopkeeping lords of St. Hubert to endure a test in which half of them might die, so that all plague might—perhaps—be ended forever, was impossible. Martin argued with Inchcape Jones, with Sondelius, but he had no favor, and he began to meditate a political campaign as he would have meditated an experiment.

He had seen the suffering of the plague and he had (though he still resisted) been tempted to forget experimentation, to give up the possible saving of millions for the immediate saving of thousands. Inchcape Jones, a little rested now under Sondelius's padded bullying and able to slip into a sane routine, drove Martin to the village of Carib, which, because of its pest of infected ground squirrels, was proportionately worse smitten than Blackwater.

They sped out of the capital by white shell roads agonizing to the sun-poisoned eyes; they left the dusty shanties of suburban Yamtown for a land cool with bamboo groves and palmettoes, thick with sugar-cane. From a hilltop they swung down a curving road to a beach where the high surf boomed in limestone caves. It seemed impossible that this joyous shore could be threatened by plague, the slimy creature of dark alleys.

The motor cut through a singing trade wind which told of clean sails and disdainful men. They darted on where the foam feathers below Point Carib and where, round that lone royal palm on the headland, the bright wind hums. They slipped into a hot valley, and came to the village of Carib and to creeping horror.

The plague had been dismaying in Blackwater; in Carib it was the end of all things. The rat-fleas had found fat homes in the ground squirrels which burrowed in every garden about the village. In Blackwater there had from the first been isolation of the sick, but in Carib death was in every house, and the village was surrounded by soldier police, with bayonets, who let no one come or go save the doctors.

Martin was guided down the stinking street of cottages palm-thatched and walled with cow-dung plaster on bamboo laths, cottages shared by the roosters and the goats. He heard men shrieking in delirium; a dozen times he saw that face of terror—sunken bloody eyes, drawn face, open mouth—which marks the Black Death; and once he beheld an exquisite girl child in coma on the edge of death, her tongue black and round her the scent of the tomb.

They fled away, to Point Carib and the trade wind, and when Inchcape Jones demanded, "After that sort of thing, can you really talk of experimenting?" then Martin shook his head, while he tried to recall the vision of Gottlieb and all their little plans: "half to get the phage, half to be sternly deprived."

It came to him that Gottlieb, in his secluded innocence, had not realized what it meant to gain leave to experiment amid the hysteria of an epidemic.

He went to the Ice House; he had a drink with a frightened clerk from Derbyshire; he regained the picture of Gottlieb's sunken, demanding eyes; and he swore that he would not yield to a compassion which in the end would make all compassion futile.

Since Inchcape Jones could not understand the need of experimentation, he would call on the Governor, Colonel Sir Robert Fairlamb.

II

Though Government House was officially the chief residence of St. Hubert, it was but a thatched bungalow a little larger than Martin's own Penrith Lodge. When he saw it, Martin felt more easy, and he ambled up to the broad steps, at nine of the evening, as though he were dropping in to call on a neighbor in Wheatsylvania.

He was stopped by a Jamaican man-servant of appalling courtesy.

He snorted that he was Dr. Arrowsmith, head of the McGurk Commission, and he was sorry but he must see Sir Robert at once.

The servant was suggesting, in his blandest and most annoying manner, that really Dr. Uh would do better to see the Surgeon General, when a broad red face and a broad red voice projected themselves over the veranda railing, with a rumble of, "Send him up, Jackson, and don't be a fool!"

Sir Robert and Lady Fairlamb were finishing dinner on the veranda, at a small round table littered with coffee and liqueurs and starred with candles. She was a slight, nervous insignificance; he was rather puffy, very flushed, undoubtedly courageous, and altogether dismayed; and at a time when no laundress dared go anywhere, his evening shirt was luminous.

Martin was in his now beloved linen suit, with a crumply soft shirt which Leora had been meanin' to wash.

Martin explained what he wanted to do—what he must do, if the world was ever to get over the absurdity of having plague.

Sir Robert listened so agreeably that Martin thought he understood, but at the end he bellowed:

"Young man, if I were commanding a division at the front, with a dud show, an awful show, going on, and a War Office clerk asked me to risk the whole thing to try out some precious little invention of his own, can you imagine what I'd answer? There isn't much I can do now—these doctor Johnnies have taken everything out of my hands—but as far as possible I shall certainly prevent you Yankee vivisectionists from coming in and using us as a lot of sanguinary—sorry, Evelyn—sanguinary corpses. Good night, sir!"

III

Thanks to Sondelius's crafty bullying, Martin was able to present his plan to a Special Board composed of the Governor, the temporarily suspended Board of Health, Inchcape Jones, several hearty members of the House of Assembly, and Sondelius himself, attending in the unofficial capacity which all over the world he had found useful for masking a cheerful tyranny. Sondelius even brought in the Negro doctor, Oliver Marchand, not on the ground that he was the most intelligent person on the island (which happened to be Sondelius's reason) but because he "represented the plantation hands."

Sondelius himself was as much opposed to Martin's unemotional experiments as was Fairlamb; he believed that all experiments should be, by devices not entirely clear to him, carried on in the laboratory without disturbing the conduct of agreeable epidemics, but he could never resist a drama like the innocent meeting of the Special Board.

The meeting was set for a week ahead . . . with scores dying every day. While he waited for it Martin manufactured more phage and helped Sondelius murder rats, and Leora listened to the midnight debates of the two men and tried to make them acknowledge that it had been wise to let her come. Inchcape Jones offered to Martin the position of Government bacteriologist, but he refused lest he be sidetracked.

The Special Board met in Parliament House, all of them trying to look not like their simple and domestic selves but like judges. With them appeared such doctors of the island as could find the time.

While Leora listened from the back of the room, Martin addressed them, not unaware of the spectacle of little Mart Arrowsmith of Elk Mills taken seriously by the rulers of a tropic isle headed by a Sir Somebody. Beside him stood Max Gottlieb, and in Gottlieb's power he reverently sought to explain that mankind has ever given up eventual greatness because some crisis, some war or election or loyalty to a Messiah which at the moment seemed weighty, has choked the patient search for truth. He sought to explain that he could—perhaps—save half of a given district, but that to test for all time the value of phage, the other half must be left without it . . . though, he craftily told them, in any case the luckless half would receive as much care as at present.

Most of the Board had heard that he possessed a magic cure for the plague which, for unknown and probably discreditable reasons, he was withholding, and they were not going to have it withheld. There was a great deal of discussion rather unconnected with what he had said, and out of it came only the fact that everybody except Stokes and Oliver Marchand was against him; Kellett was angry with this American, Sir Robert Fairlamb was beefily disapproving, and Sondelius admitted that though Martin was quite a decent young man, he was a fanatic.

Into their argument plunged a fury in the person of Ira Hinkley, missionary of the Sanctification Brotherhood.

Martin had not seen him since the first morning in Blackwater. He gaped as he heard Ira pleading:

"Gentlemen, I know almost the whole bunch of you are Church of England, but I beg you to listen to me, not as a minister but as a qualified doctor of medicine. Oh, the wrath of God is upon you— But I mean: I was a classmate of Arrowsmith in the States. I'm onto him! He was such a failure that he was suspended from medical school. A scientist! And his boss, this fellow Gottlieb, he was fired from the University of Winnemac for incompetence! I know 'em! Liars and fools! Scorners of righteousness! Has anybody but Arrowsmith himself told you he's a qualified scientist?"

The face of Sondelius changed from curiosity to stolid Scandinavian wrath. He arose and shouted:

"Sir Robert, this man is crazy! Dr. Gottlieb is one of the seven distinguished living scientists, and Dr. Arrowsmith is his representative! I announce my agreement with him, complete. As you must have seen from my work, I'm perfectly independent of him and entirely at your service, but I know his standing and I follow him, quite humbly."

The Special Board coaxed Ira Hinkley out, for the meanest of reasons— in St. Hubert the whites do not greatly esteem the holy ecstasies of Negroes in the Sanctification Brotherhood chapels—but they voted only to "give the matter their consideration," while still men died by the score each day, and in Manchuria as in St. Hubert they prayed for rest from the ancient clawing pain.

Outside, as the Special Board trudged away, Sondelius blared at Martin and the indignant Leora, "Yey, a fine fight!"

Martin answered, "Gustaf, you've joined me now. The first darn' thing you do, you come have a shot of phage."

"No. Slim, I said I will not have your phage till you give it to everybody. I mean it, no matter how much I make fools of your Board."

As they stood before Parliament House, a small motor possessing everything but comfort and power staggered up to them, and from it vaulted a man lean as Gottlieb and English as Inchcape Jones.

"You Dr. Arrowsmith? My name is Twyford, Cecil Twyford of St. Swithin's Parish. Tried to get here for the Special Board meeting, but my beastly foreman had to take the afternoon off and die of plague. Stokes has told me your plans. Quite right. All nonsense to go on having plague. Board refused? Sorry. Perhaps we can do something in St. Swithin's. Goo' day."

All evening Martin and Sondelius were full of language. Martin went to bed longing for the regularity of working all night and foraging for cigarettes at dawn. He could not sleep, because an imaginary Ira Hinkley was always bursting in on him.

Four days later he heard that Ira was dead.

Till he had sunk in coma, Ira had nursed and blessed his people, the humble colored congregation in the hot tin chapel which he had now turned into a pest-house. He staggered from cot to cot, under the gospel texts he had lettered on the white-washed wall, then he cried once, loudly, and dropped by the pine pulpit where he had joyed to preach.

### IV

One chance Martin did have. In Carib, where every third man was down with plague and one doctor to attend them all, he now gave phage to the entire village; a long strain of injections, not improved by the knowledge that one jaunty flea from any patient might bring him the plague.

The tedium of dread was forgotten when he began to find and make precise notes of a slackening of the epidemic, which was occurring nowhere except here at Carib.

He came home raving to Leora, "I'll show 'em! Now they'll let me try test conditions, and then when the epidemic's over we'll hustle home. It'll be lovely to be cold again! Wonder if Holabird and Sholtheis are any more friendly now? Be pretty good to see the little ole flat, eh?"

"Yes, won't it!" said Leora. "I wish I'd thought to have the kitchen painted while we're away. . . . I think I'll put that blue chair in the bedroom."

Though there was a decrease in the plague at Carib, Sondelius was worried, because it was the worst center for infected ground squirrels on the island. He made decisions quickly. One evening he explained certain things to Inch-cape Jones and Martin, rode down their doubts, and snorted:

"Only way to disinfect that place is to burn it—burn th' whole thing. Have it done by morning, before anybody can stop us."

With Martin as his lieutenant he marshaled his troop of rat-catchers—ruffians all of them, with high boots, tied jacket sleeves, and ebon visages of piracy. They stole food from shops, tents and blankets and camp-stoves from the Government military warehouse, and jammed their booty into motor trucks. The line of trucks roared down to Carib, the rat-catchers sitting atop, singing pious hymns.

They charged on the village, drove out the healthy, carried the sick on litters, settled them all in tents in a pasture up the valley, and after midnight they burned the town.

The troops ran among the huts, setting them alight with fantastic torches. The palm thatch sent up thick smoke, dead sluggish white with currents of ghastly black through which broke sudden flames. Against the glare the palmettoes were silhouetted. The solid-seeming huts were instantly changed into thin bamboo frameworks, thin lines of black slats, with the thatch falling in sparks. The flame lighted the whole valley; roused the terrified squawking birds, and turned the surf at Point Carib to bloody foam.

With such of the natives as had strength enough and sense enough, Sondelius's troops made a ring about the burning village, shouting insanely as they clubbed the fleeing rats and ground squirrels. In the flare of devastation

Sondelius was a fiend, smashing the bewildered rats with a club, shooting at them as they fled, and singing to himself all the while the obscene chantey of Bill the Sailor. But at dawn he was nursing the sick in the bright new canvas village, showing mammies how to use their camp-stoves, and in a benevolent way discussing methods of poisoning ground squirrels in their burrows.

Sondelius returned to Blackwater, but Martin remained in the tent village for two days, giving them the phage, making notes, directing the amateur nurses. He returned to Blackwater one mid-afternoon and sought the office of the Surgeon General, or what had been the office of the Surgeon General till Sondelius had come and taken it away from him.

Sondelius was there, at Inchcape Jones's desk, but for once he was not busy. He was sunk in his chair, his eyes bloodshot.

"Yey! We had a fine time with the rats at Carib, eh? How is my new tent willage?" he chuckled, but his voice was weak, and as he rose he staggered.

"What is it? What is it?"

"I t'ink— It's got me. Some flea got me. Yes," in a shaky but extremely interested manner, "I was yoost thinking I will go and quarantine myself. I have fever all right, and adenitis. My strength— Huh! I am almost sixty, but the way I can lift weights that no sailor can touch— And I could fight five rounds! Oh, my God, Martin, I am so weak! Not scared! No!"

But for Martin's arms he would have collapsed.

He refused to return to Penrith Lodge and Leora's nursing. "I who have isolated so many—it is my turn," he said.

Martin and Inchcape Jones found for Sondelius a meager clean cottage— the family had died there, all of them, but it had been fumigated. They procured a nurse and Martin himself attended the sick man, trying to remember that once he had been a doctor, who understood ice-bags and consolation. One thing was not to be had—mosquito netting—and only of this did Sondelius complain.

Martin bent over him, agonized to see how burning was his skin, how swollen his face and his tongue, how weak his voice as he babbled:

"Gottlieb is right about these jests of God. Yey! His best one is the tropics. God planned them so beautiful, flowers and sea and mountains. He made the fruit to grow so well that man need not work—and then He laughed, and stuck in volcanoes and snakes and damp heat and early senility and the plague and malaria. But the nastiest trick He ever played on man was inventing the flea."

His bloated lips widened, from his hot throat oozed a feeble croaking, and Martin realized that he was trying to laugh.

He became delirious, but between spasms he muttered, with infinite pain, tears in his eyes at his own weakness:

"I want you to see how an agnostic can die!

"I am not afraid, but yoost once more I would like to see Stockholm, and Fifth Avenue on the day the first snow falls and Holy Week at Sevilla. And one good last drunk! I am very peaceful, Slim. It hurts some, but life was a good game. And— I am a pious agnostic. Oh, Martin, give my people the phage! Save all of them— God, I did not think they could hurt me so!"

His heart had failed. He was still on his low cot.

v

Martin had an unhappy pride that, with all his love for Gustaf Sondelius, he could still keep his head, still resist Inchcape Jones's demand that he give the phage to everyone, still do what he had been sent to do.

"I'm not a sentimentalist; I'm a scientist!" he boasted.

They snarled at him in the streets now; small boys called him names and threw stones. They had heard that he was willfully withholding their salvation. The citizens came in committees to beg him to heal their children, and he was so shaken that he had ever to keep before him the vision of Gottlieb.

The panic was increasing. They who had at first kept cool could not endure the strain of wakening at night to see upon their windows the glow of the pile of logs on Admiral Knob, the emergency crematory where Gustaf Sondelius and his curly gray mop had been shoveled into the fire along with a crippled Negro boy and a Hindu beggar.

Sir Robert Fairlamb was a blundering hero, exasperating the sick while he tried to nurse them; Stokes remained the Rock of Ages—he had only three hours' sleep a night, but he never failed to take his accustomed fifteen minutes of exercise when he awoke; and Leora was easy in Penrith Lodge, helping Martin prepare phage.

It was the Surgeon General who went to pieces.

Robbed of his dependence on the despised Sondelius, sunk again in a mad planlessness, Inchcape Jones shrieked when he thought he was speaking low, and the cigarette which was ever in his thin hand shook so that the smoke quivered up in trembling spirals.

Making his tour, he came at night on a sloop by which a dozen Red Legs were escaping to Barbados, and suddenly he was among them, bribing them to take him along.

As the sloop stood out from Blackwater Harbor he stretched his arms toward his sisters and the peace of the Surrey hills, but as the few frightened lights of the town were lost, he realized that he was a coward and came up out of his madness, with his lean head high.

He demanded that they turn the sloop and take him back. They refused, howling at him, and locked him in the cabin. They were becalmed; it was two days before they reached Barbados, and by then the world would know that he had deserted.

Altogether expressionless, Inchcape Jones tramped from the sloop to a waterfront hotel in Barbados, and stood for a long time in a slatternly room smelling of slop-pails. He would never see his sisters and the cool hills. With the revolver which he had carried to drive terrified patients back into the isolation wards, with the revolver which he had carried at Arras, he killed himself.

VI

Thus Martin came to his experiment. Stokes was appointed Surgeon General, vice Inchcape Jones, and he made an illegal assignment of Martin to St. Swithin's Parish, as medical officer with complete power. This, and the concurrence of Cecil Twyford, made his experiment possible.

He was invited to stay at Twyford's. His only trouble was the guarding of Leora. He did not know what he would encounter in St. Swithin's, while Penrith Lodge was as safe as any place on the island. When Leora insisted that, during his experiment, the cold thing which had stilled the laughter of Sondelius might come to him and he might need her, he tried to satisfy her by promising that if there was a place for her in St. Swithin's, he would send for her.

Naturally, he was lying.

"Hard enough to see Gustaf go. By thunder she's not going to run risks!" he vowed.

He left her, protected by the maids and the soldier butler, with Dr. Oliver Marchand to look in when he could.

VII

In St. Swithin's Parish the cocoa and bamboo groves and sharp hills of southern St. Hubert gave way to unbroken canefields. Here Cecil Twyford, that lean abrupt man, ruled every acre and interpreted every law.

His place, Frangipani Court, was a refuge from the hot humming plain. The house was old and low, of thick stone and plaster walls; the paneled rooms were lined with the china, the portraits, and the swords of Twyfords for three hundred years; and between the wings was a walled garden dazzling with hibiscus.

Twyford led Martin through the low cool hall and introduced him to five great sons and to his mother, who, since his wife's death, ten years ago, had been mistress of the house.

"Have tea?" said Twyford. "Our American guest will be down in a moment."

He would not have thought of saying it, but he had sworn that since for generations Twyfords had drunk tea here at a seemly hour, no panic should prevent their going on drinking it at that hour.

When Martin came into the garden, when he saw the old silver on the wicker table and heard the quiet voices, the plague seemed conquered, and he realized that, four thousand miles southwest of the Lizard, he was in England.

They were seated, pleasant but not too comfortable, when the American guest came down and from the door stared at Martin as strangely as he stared in turn.

He beheld a woman who must be his sister. She was perhaps thirty to his thirty-seven, but in her slenderness, her paleness, her black brows and dusky hair, she was his twin; she was his self enchanted.

He could hear his voice croaking, "But you're my sister!" and she opened her lips, yet neither of them spoke as they bowed at introduction. When she sat down, Martin had never been so conscious of a woman's presence.

He learned, before evening, that she was Joyce Lanyon, widow of Roger Lanyon of New York. She had come to St. Hubert to see her plantations and had been trapped by the quarantine. He had tentatively heard of her dead husband as a young man of wealth and family; he seemed to remember having seen in *Vanity Fair* a picture of the Lanyons at Palm Beach.

She talked only of the weather, the flowers, but there was a rising gaiety in her which stirred even the dour Cecil Twyford. In the midst of her debonair insults to the hugest of the huge sons, Martin turned on her:

"You *are* my sister!"

"Obviously. Well, since you're a scientist— Are you a good scientist?"

"Pretty good."

"I've met your Mrs. McGurk. And Dr. Rippleton Holabird. Met 'em in Hessian Hook. You know it, don't you?"

"No, I— Oh, I've heard of it."

"You know. It's that renovated old part of Brooklyn where writers and economists and all those people, some of them almost as good as the very best, consort with people who are almost as smart as the very smartest. You know. Where they dress for dinner but all of them have heard about James Joyce. Dr. Holabird is frightfully charming, don't you think?"

"Why—"

"Tell me. I really mean it. Cecil has been explaining what you plan to do experimentally. Could I help you—nursing or cooking or something—or would I merely be in the way?"

"I don't know yet. If I can use you, I'll be unscrupulous enough!"

"Oh, don't be earnest like Cecil here, and Dr. Stokes! They have no sense of play. Do you like that man Stokes? Cecil adores him, and I suppose he's simply infested with virtues, but I find him so dry and thin and unappetizing. Don't you think he might be a little gayer?"

Martin gave up all chance of knowing her as he hurled:

"Look here! You said you found Holabird 'charming.' It makes me tired to have you fall for his scientific tripe and not appreciate Stokes. Stokes is hard—thank God!—and probably he's rude. Why not? He's fighting a world that bellows for fake charm. No scientist can go through his grind and not come out more or less rude. And I tell you Stokes was born a researcher. I wish we had him at McGurk. Rude? Wish you could hear him being rude to me!"

Twyford looked doubtful, his mother looked delicately shocked, and the five sons beefily looked nothing at all, while Martin raged on, trying to convey his vision of the barbarian, the ascetic, the contemptuous acolyte of science.

But Joyce Lanyon's lovely eyes were kind, and when she spoke she had lost something of her too-cosmopolitan manner of a diner-out:

"Yes. I suppose it's the difference between me, playing at being a planter, and Cecil."

After dinner he walked with her in the garden and sought to defend himself against he was not quite sure what, till she hinted:

"My dear man, you're so apologetic about never being apologetic! If you really must be my twin brother, do me the honor of telling me to go to the devil whenever you want to. I don't mind. Now about your Gottlieb, who seems to be so much of an obsession with you—"

"Obsession! Rats! He—"

They parted an hour after.

Least of all things Martin desired such another peeping, puerile, irritable restlessness as he had shared with Orchid Pickerbaugh, but as he went to bed in a room with old prints and a four-poster, it was disturbing to know that somewhere near him was Joyce Lanyon.

He sat up, aghast with truth. Was he going to fall in love with this desirable and quite useless young woman? (How lovely her shoulders, above black satin at dinner! She had a genius of radiant flesh; it made that of most women, even the fragile Leora, seem coarse and thick. There was a rosy glow behind it, as from an inner light.)

Did he really want Leora here, with Joyce Lanyon in the house? (Dear Leora, who was the source of life! Was she now, off there in Penrith Lodge, missing him, lying awake for him?)

How could he, even in the crisis of an epidemic, invite the formal Twyfords to invite Leora? (How honest was he? That afternoon he had recognized the rigid though kindly code of the Twyfords, but could he not set it aside by being frankly an Outlander?)

Suddenly he was out of bed, kneeling, praying to Leora.

# 35

The plague had only begun to invade St. Swithin's, but it was unquestionably coming, and Martin, with his power as official medical officer of the parish, was able to make plans. He divided the population into two equal parts. One of them, driven in by Twyford, was injected with plague phage, the other half was left without.

He began to succeed. He saw far-off India, with its annual four hundred thousand deaths from plague, saved by his efforts. He heard Max Gottlieb saying, "Martin, you haf done your experiment. I am very glat!"

The pest attacked the unphaged half of the parish much more heavily than those who had been treated. There did appear a case or two among those who had the phage, but among the others there were ten, then twenty, then thirty daily victims. These unfortunate cases he treated, giving the phage to alternate patients, in the somewhat barren almshouse of the parish, a whitewashed cabin the meaner against its vaulting background of banyans and breadfruit trees.

He could never understand Cecil Twyford. Though Twyford had considered his hands as slaves, though he had, in his great barony, given them only this barren almshouse, yet he risked his life now in nursing them, and the lives of all his sons.

Despite Martin's discouragement, Mrs. Lanyon came down to cook, and a remarkably good cook she was. She also made beds; she showed more intelligence than the Twyford men about disinfecting herself; and as she bustled about the rusty kitchen, in a gingham gown she had borrowed from a maid, she so disturbed Martin that he forgot to be gruff.

II

In the evening, while they returned by Twyford's rattling little motor to Frangipani Court, Mrs. Lanyon talked to Martin as one who had shared his work, but when she had bathed and powdered and dressed, he talked to her as one who was afraid of her. Their bond was their resemblance as brother and sister. They decided, almost irritably, that they looked utterly alike, except that her hair was more patent-leather than his and she lacked his impertinent, cocking eyebrow.

Often Martin returned to his patients at night, but once or twice Mrs. Lanyon and he fled, as much from the family stolidity of the Twyfords as from the thought of fever-scorched patients, to the shore of a rocky lagoon which cut far in from the sea.

They sat on a cliff, full of the sound of the healing tide. His brain was hectic with the memory of charts on the whitewashed broad planks of the almshouse, the sun cracks in the wall, the puffy terrified faces of black patients, how one of the Twyford sons had knocked over an ampule of phage, and how itchingly hot it had been in the ward. But to his intensity the lagoon breeze was cooling, and cooling the rustling tide. He perceived that Mrs. Lanyon's white frock was fluttering about her knees; he realized that she too was strained and still. He turned somberly toward her, and she cried:

"I'm so frightened and so lonely! The Twyfords are heroic, but they're stone. I'm so marooned!"

He kissed her, and she rested against his shoulder. The softness of her sleeve was agitating to his hand. But she broke away with:

"No! You don't really care a hang about me. Just curious. Perhaps that's a good thing for me—tonight."

He tried to assure her, to assure himself, that he did care with peculiar violence, but languor was over him; between him and her fragrance were the hospital cots, a great weariness, and the still face of Leora. They were silent together, and when his hand crept to hers they sat unimpassioned, comprehending, free to talk of what they would.

He stood outside her door, when they had returned to the house, and imagined her soft moving within.

"No," he raged. "Can't do it. Joyce—women like her—one of the million things I've given up for work and for Lee. Well. That's all there is to it then. But if I were here two weeks— Fool! She'd be furious if you knocked! But—"

He was aware of the dagger of light under her door; the more aware of it as he turned his back and tramped to his room.

### III

The telephone service in St. Hubert was the clumsiest feature of the island. There was no telephone at Penrith Lodge—the port-doctor had cheerfully been wont to get his calls through a neighbor. The central was now demoralized by the plague, and when for two hours Martin had tried to have Leora summoned, he gave up.

But he had triumphed. In three or four days he would drive to Penrith Lodge. Twyford had blankly assented to his suggestion that Leora be invited hither, and if she and Joyce Lanyon should become such friends that Joyce would never again turn to him in loneliness, he was willing, he was eager— he was almost eager.

### IV

When Martin left her at the Lodge, in the leafy gloom high on the Penrith Hills, Leora felt his absence. They had been so little apart since he had first come on her, scrubbing a hospital room in Zenith.

The afternoon was unending; each time she heard a creaking she roused with the hope that it was his step, and realized that he would not be coming, all the blank evening, the terrifying night; would not be here anywhere, not his voice nor the touch of his hand.

Dinner was mournful. Often enough she had dined alone when Martin was at the Institute, but then he had been returning to her some time before dawn—probably—and she had reflectively munched a snack on the corner of the kitchen table, looking at the funnies in the evening paper. Tonight she had to live up to the butler, who served her as though she were a dinner-party of twenty.

She sat on the porch, staring at the shadowy roofs of Blackwater below, sure that she felt a "miasm" writhing up through the hot darkness.

She knew the direction of St. Swithin's Parish—beyond that delicate glimmer of lights from palm huts coiling up the hills. She concentrated on it, wondering if by some magic she might not have a signal from him, but she could get no feeling of his looking toward her. She sat long and quiet. . . . She had nothing to do.

Her night was sleepless. She tried to read in bed, by an electric globe inside the misty little tent of the mosquito-netting, but there was a tear in the netting and the mosquitoes crept through. As she turned out the light and lay tense, unable to give herself over to sleep, unable to sink into security, while to her blurred eyes the half-seen folds of the mosquito netting seemed to slide about her, she tried to remember whether these mosquitoes might be carrying plague germs. She realized how much she had depended on Martin for such bits of knowledge, as for all philosophy. She recalled how annoyed he had been because she could not remember whether the yellow fever mosquito was *Anopheles* or *Stegomyia*—or was it *Aëdes?*—and suddenly she laughed in the night.

She was reminded that he had told her to give herself another injection of phage.

"Hang it, I forgot. Well, I must be sure to do that tomorrow."

"Do that t'morrow—do that t'morrow," buzzed in her brain, an irritating inescapable refrain, while she was suspended over sleep, conscious of how much she wanted to creep into his arms.

Next morning (and she did not remember to give herself another injection) the servants seemed twitchy, and her effort to comfort them brought out the news that Oliver Marchand, the doctor on whom they depended, was dead.

In the afternoon the butler heard that his sister had been taken off to the isolation ward, and he went down to Blackwater to make arrangements for his nieces. He did not return; no one ever learned what had become of him.

Toward dusk, when Leora felt as though a skirmish line were closing in on her, she fled into Martin's laboratory. It seemed filled with his jerky brimming presence. She kept away from the flasks of plague germs, but she picked up, because it was his, a half-smoked cigarette and lighted it.

Now there was a slight crack in her lips; and that morning, fumbling at dusting—here in the laboratory meant as a fortress against disease—a maid had knocked over a test-tube, which had trickled. The cigarette seemed dry enough, but in it there were enough plague germs to kill a regiment.

Two nights after, when she was so desperately lonely that she thought of walking to Blackwater, finding a motor, and fleeing to Martin, she woke with a fever, a headache, her limbs chilly. When the maids discovered her in the morning, they fled from the house. While lassitude flowed round her, she was left alone in the isolated house, with no telephone.

All day, all night, as her throat crackled with thirst, she lay longing for someone to help her. Once she crawled to the kitchen for water. The floor of the bedroom was an endless heaving sea, the hall a writhing dimness, and by the kitchen door she dropped and lay for an hour, whimpering.

"Got to—got to—can't remember what it was," her voice kept appealing to her cloudy brain.

Aching, fighting the ache, she struggled up, wrapped about her a shabby cloak which one of the maids had abandoned in flight, and in the darkness staggered out to find help. As she came to the highway she stumbled, and lay under the hedge, unmoving, like a hurt animal. On hands and knees she crawled back into the Lodge, and between times, as her brain went dark, she nearly forgot the pain in her longing for Martin.

She was bewildered; she was lonely; she dared not start on her long journey without his hand to comfort her. She listened for him—listened—tense with listening.

"You will come! I know you'll come and help me! I know. You'll come! Martin! Sandy! *Sandy!*" she sobbed.

Then she slipped down into the kindly coma. There was no more pain, and all the shadowy house was quiet but for her hoarse and struggling breath.

## V

Like Sondelius, Joyce Lanyon tried to persuade Martin to give the phage to everybody.

"I'm getting to be good and stern, with all you people after me. Regular Gottlieb. Nothing can make me do it, not if they tried to lynch me," he boasted.

He had explained Leora to Joyce.

"I don't know whether you two will like each other. You're so darn' different. You're awfully articulate, and you like these 'pretty people' that you're always talking about, but she doesn't care a hang for 'em. She sits back—oh, she never misses anything, but she never says much. Still, she's got the best instinct for honesty that I've ever known. I hope you two'll get each other. I was afraid to let her come here—didn't know what I'd find—but now I'm going to hustle to Penrith and bring her here today."

He borrowed Twyford's car and drove to Blackwater, up to Penrith, in excellent spirits. For all the plague, they could have a lively time in the evenings. One of the Twyford sons was not so solemn; he and Joyce, with Martin and Leora, could slip down to the lagoon for picnic suppers; they would sing—

He came up to Penrith Lodge bawling, "Lee! Leora! Come on! *Here* we are!"

The veranda, as he ran up on it, was leaf-scattered and dusty, and the front door was banging. His voice echoed in a desperate silence. He was uneasy. He darted in, found no one in the living-room, the kitchen, then hastened into their bedroom.

On the bed, across the folds of the torn mosquito netting, was Leora's body, very frail, quite still. He cried to her, he shook her, he stood weeping.

He talked to her, his voice a little insane, trying to make her understand that he had loved her and had left her here only for her safety—

There was rum in the kitchen, and he went out to gulp down raw full glasses. They did not affect him.

By evening he strode to the garden, the high and windy garden looking toward the sea, and dug a deep pit. He lifted her light stiff body, kissed it, and laid it in the pit. All night he wandered. When he came back to the house and saw the row of her little dresses with the lines of her soft body in them, he was terrified.

Then he went to pieces.

He gave up Penrith Lodge, left Twyford's, and moved into a room behind the Surgeon General's office. Beside his cot there was always a bottle.

Because death had for the first time been brought to him, he raged, "Oh, damn experimentation!" and, despite Stokes's dismay, he gave the phage to everyone who asked.

Only in St. Swithin's, since there his experiment was so excellently begun, did some remnant of honor keep him from distributing the phage universally; but the conduct of this experiment he turned over to Stokes.

Stokes saw that he was a little mad, but only once, when Martin snarled, "What do I care for your science?" did he try to hold Martin to his test.

Stokes himself, with Twyford, carried on the experiment and kept the notes Martin should have kept. By evening, after working fourteen or fifteen hours since dawn, Stokes would hasten to St. Swithin's by motor-cycle—he hated the joggling and the lack of dignity and he found it somewhat dangerous to take curving hill-roads at sixty miles an hour, but this was the quickest way, and till midnight he conferred with Twyford, gave him orders for the next day, arranged his clumsy annotations, and marveled at his grim meekness.

Meantime, all day, Martin injected a line of frightened citizens, in the Surgeon General's office in Blackwater. Stokes begged him at least to turn the work over to another doctor and take what interest he could in St. Swithin's, but Martin had a bitter satisfaction in throwing away all his significance, in helping to wreck his own purposes.

With a nurse for assistant, he stood in the bare office. File on file of people, black, white, Hindu, stood in an agitated cue a block long, ten deep, waiting dumbly, as for death. They crept up to the nurse beside Martin and in embarrassment exposed their arms, which she scrubbed with soap and water and dabbled with alcohol before passing them on to him. He brusquely pinched up the skin of the upper arm and jabbed it with the needle of the syringe, cursing at them for jerking, never seeing their individual faces. As they left him they fluttered with gratitude—"Oh, may God bless you, Doctor!"—but he did not hear.

Sometimes Stokes was there, looking anxious, particularly when in the cue he saw plantation-hands from St. Swithin's, who were supposed to remain in their parish under strict control, to test the value of the phage. Sometimes Sir Robert Fairlamb came down to beam and gurgle and offer his aid. . . . Lady Fairlamb had been injected first of all, and next to her a tattered kitchen wench, profuse with Hallelujah's.

After a fortnight when he was tired of the drama, he had four doctors making the injections, while he manufactured phage.

But by night Martin sat alone, tousled, drinking steadily, living on whisky and hate, freeing his soul and dissolving his body by hatred as once hermits dissolved theirs by ecstasy. His life was as unreal as the nights of an old drunkard. He had an advantage over normal cautious humanity in not caring whether he lived or died, he who sat with the dead, talking to Leora and Sondelius, to Ira Hinkley and Oliver Marchand, to Inchcape Jones and a shadowy horde of blackmen with lifted appealing hands.

After Leora's death he had returned to Twyford's but once, to fetch his baggage, and he had not seen Joyce Lanyon. He hated her. He swore that it was not her presence which had kept him from returning earlier to Leora, but he was aware that while he had been chattering with Joyce, Leora had been dying.

"Damn' glib society climber! Thank God I'll never see *her* again!"

He sat on the edge of his cot, in the constricted and airless room, his hair ruffled, his eyes blotched with red, a stray alley kitten, which he esteemed his only friend, asleep on his pillow. At a knock he muttered, "I can't talk to Stokes now. Let him do his own experiments. Sick of experiments!"

Sulkily, "Oh, come in!"

The door opened on Joyce Lanyon, cool, trim, sure.

"What do you want?" he grunted.

She stared at him; she shut the door; silently she straightened the litter of food, papers, and instruments on his table. She coaxed the indignant kitten to a mat, patted the pillow, and sat by him on the frowsy cot. Then:

"Please! I know what's happened. Cecil is in town for an hour and I wanted to bring— Won't it comfort you a little if you know how fond we are of you? Won't you let me offer you friendship?"

"I don't want anybody's friendship. I haven't any friends!"

He sat dumb, her hand on his, but when she was gone he felt a shiver of new courage.

He could not get himself to give up his reliance on whisky, and he could see no way of discontinuing the phage-injection of all who came begging for it, but he turned both injection and manufacture over to others, and went back to the most rigid observation of his experiment in St. Swithin's . . . blotted as it now was by the unphaged portion of the parish going in to Blackwater to receive the phage.

He did not see Joyce. He lived at the almshouse, but most evenings now he was sober.

## VI

The gospel of rat-extermination had spread through the island; everybody from five-year-old to hobbling grandam was out shooting rats and ground squirrels. Whether from phage or rat-killing or Providence, the epidemic paused, and six months after Martin's coming, when the West Indian May was broiling and the season of hurricanes was threatened, the plague had almost vanished and the quarantine was lifted.

St. Hubert felt safe in its kitchens and shops, and amid the roaring spring the island rejoiced as a sick man first delivered from pain rejoices at merely living and being at peace.

That chaffering should be abusive and loud in the public market, that lovers should stroll unconscious of all save themselves, that loafers should tell stories and drink long drinks at the Ice House, that old men should squat cackling in the shade of the mangoes, that congregations should sing together to the Lord—this was no longer ordinary to them nor stupid, but the bliss of paradise.

They made a festival of the first steamer's leaving. White and black, Hindu and Chink and Caribbee, they crowded the wharf, shouting, waving scarfs, trying not to weep at the feeble piping of what was left of the Blackwater Gold Medal Band; and as the steamer, the *St. Ia* of the McGurk Line, was warped out, with her captain at the rail of the bridge, very straight, saluting them with a flourish but his eyes so wet that he could not see the harbor, they felt that they were no longer jailed lepers but a part of the free world.

On that steamer Joyce Lanyon sailed. Martin said good-by to her at the wharf.

Strong of hand, almost as tall as he, she looked at him without flutter, and rejoiced, "You've come through. So have I. Both of us have been mad, trapped here the way we've been. I don't suppose I helped you, but I did try. You see, I'd never been trained in reality. You trained me. Good-by."

"Mayn't I come to see you in New York?"

"If you'd really like to."

She was gone, yet she had never been so much with him as through that tedious hour when the steamer was lost beyond the horizon, a line edged with silver wire. But that night, in panic, he fled up to Penrith Lodge and buried his cheek in the damp soil above the Leora with whom he had never had to fence and explain, to whom he had never needed to say, "Mayn't I come to see you?"

But Leora, cold in her last bed, unsmiling, did not answer him nor comfort him.

### VII

Before Martin took leave he had to assemble the notes of his phage experiment; add the observation of Stokes and Twyford to his own first precise figures.

As the giver of phage to some thousands of frightened islanders, he had become a dignitary. He was called, in the first issue of the *Blackwater Guardian* after the quarantine was raised, "the savior of all our lives." He was the universal hero. If Sondelius had helped to cleanse them, had Sondelius not been his lieutenant? If it was the intervention of the Lord, as the earnest old Negro who succeeded Ira Hinkley in the chapels of the Sanctification Brotherhood insisted, had not the Lord surely sent him?

No one heeded a wry Scotch doctor, diligent but undramatic through the epidemic, who hinted that plagues have been known to slacken and cease without phage.

When Martin was completing his notes he had a letter from the McGurk Institute, signed by Rippleton Holabird.

Holabird wrote that Gottlieb was "feeling seedy," that he had resigned the Directorship, suspended his own experimentation, and was now at home, resting. Holabird himself had been appointed Acting Director of the Institute, and as such he chanted:

The reports of your work in the letters from Mr. McGurk's agents which the quarantine authorities have permitted to get through to us apprize us far more than does your own modest report what a really sensational success you have had. You have done what few other men living could do, both established the value of bacteriophage in plague by tests on a large scale, and saved most of the unfortunate population. The Board of Trustees and I are properly appreciative of the glory which you have added, and still more will add when your report is published, to the name of McGurk Institute, and we are thinking, now that we may for some months be unable to have your titular chief, Dr. Gottlieb, working with us, of establishing a separate Department, with you as its head.

"Established the value—rats! I about half made the tests," sighed Martin, and: "Department! I've given too many orders here. Sick of authority. I want to get back to my lab and start all over again."

It came to him that now he would probably have ten thousand a year. . . . Leora would have enjoyed small extravagant dinners.

Though he had watched Gottlieb declining, it was a shock that he could be so unwell as to drop his work even for a few months.

He forgot his own self as it came to him that in giving up his experiment, playing the savior, he had been a traitor to Gottlieb and all that Gottlieb represented. When he returned to New York he would have to call on the old man and admit to him, to those sunken relentless eyes, that he did not have complete proof of the value of the phage.

If he could have run to Leora with his ten thousand a year—

VIII

He left St. Hubert three weeks after Joyce Lanyon.

The evening before his sailing, a great dinner with Sir Robert Fairlamb in the chair was given to him and to Stokes. While Sir Robert ruddily blurted compliments and Kellett tried to explain things, and all of them drank to him, standing, after the toast to the King, Martin sat lonely, considering that tomorrow he would leave these trusting eyes and face the harsh demands of Gottlieb, of Terry Wickett.

The more they shouted his glory, the more he thought about what unknown, tight-minded scientists in distant laboratories would say of a man who had had his chance and cast it away. The more they called him the giver of life, the more he felt himself disgraced and a traitor; and as he looked at Stokes he saw in his regard a pity worse than condemnation.

# 36

It happened that Martin returned to New York, as he had come, on the *St. Buryan*. The ship was haunted with the phantoms of Leora dreaming, of Sondelius shouting on the bridge.

And on the *St. Buryan* was the country-club Miss Gwilliam who had offended Sondelius.

She had spent the winter importantly making notes on native music in Trinidad and Caracas; at least in planning to make notes. She saw Martin come aboard at Blackwater, and pertly noted the friends who saw him off —two Englishmen, one puffy, one rangy, and a dry-looking Scotsman.

"Your friends all seem to be British," she enlightened him, when she had claimed him as an old friend.

"Yes."

"You've spent the winter here."

"Yes."

"Hard luck to be caught by the quarantine. But I *told* you you were silly to go ashore! You must have managed to pick up quite a little money practicing. But it must have been unpleasant, really."

"Ye-es, I suppose it was."

"I *told* you it would be! You ought to have come on to Trinidad. Such a fascinating island! And tell me, how is the Roughneck?"

"Who?"

"Oh, you know—that funny Swede that used to dance and everything."

"He is dead."

"Oh, I *am* sorry. You know, no matter what the others said, I never thought he was so bad. I'm sure he had quite a nice cultured mind, when he wasn't carousing around. Your wife isn't with you, is she?"

"No—she isn't with me. I must go down and unpack now."

Miss Gwilliam looked after him with an expression which said that the least people could do was to learn some manners.

## II

With the heat and the threat of hurricanes, there were few first-class passengers on the *St. Buryan*, and most of these did not count, because they were not jolly, decent Yankee tourists but merely South Americans. As tourists do when their minds have been broadened and enriched by travel, when they return to New Jersey or Wisconsin with the credit of having spent a whole six months in the West Indies and South America, the respectable remnant studied one another fastidiously, and noted the slim pale man who seemed so restless, who all day trudged round the deck, who after midnight was seen standing by himself at the rail.

"That guy looks awful' restless to me!" said Mr. S. Sanborn Hibble of Detroit to the charming Mrs. Dawson of Memphis, and she answered, with the wit which made her so popular wherever she went, "Yes, don't he. I reckon he must be in love!"

"Oh, I know him!" said Miss Gwilliam. "He and his wife were on the *St. Buryan* when I came down. She's in New York now. He's some kind of a doctor—not awful' successful I don't believe. Just between ourselves, I don't think much of him or of her either. They sat and looked stupid all the way down."

### III

Martin was itching to get his fingers on his test-tubes. He knew, as once he had guessed, that he hated administration and Large Affairs.

As he tramped the deck, his head cleared and he was himself. Angrily he pictured the critics who would soon be pecking at whatever final report he might make. For a time he hated the criticism of his fellow laboratory-grinds as he had hated their competition; he hated the need of forever looking over his shoulder at pursuers. But on a night when he stood at the rail for hours, he admitted that he was afraid of their criticism, and afraid because his experiment had so many loopholes. He hurled overboard all the polemics with which he had protected himself: "Men who never have had the experience of trying, in the midst of an epidemic, to remain calm and keep experimental conditions, do not realize in the security of their laboratories what one has to contend with."

Constant criticism was good, if only it was not spiteful, jealous, petty—

No, even then it might be good! Some men had to be what easy-going workers called "spiteful." To them the joyous spite of crushing the almost-good was more natural than creation. Why should a great house-wrecker, who could clear the cumbered ground, be set at trying to lay brick?

"All right!" he rejoiced. "Let 'em come! Maybe I'll anticipate 'em and publish a roast of my own work. I have got something, from the St. Swithin test, even if I did let things slide for a while. I'll take my tables to a biometrician. He may rip 'em up. Good! What's left, I'll publish."

He went to bed feeling that he could face the eyes of Gottlieb and Terry, and for the first time in weeks he slept without terror.

### IV

At the pier in Brooklyn, to the astonishment and slight indignation of Miss Gwilliam, Mr. S. Sanborn Hibble, and Mrs. Dawson, Martin was greeted by reporters who agreeably though vaguely desired to know what were these remarkable things he had been doing to some disease or other, in some island some place.

He was rescued from them by Rippleton Holabird, who burst through them with his hands out, crying, "Oh, my dear fellow! We know all that's happened. We grieve for you so, and we're so glad you were spared to come back to us."

Whatever Martin might, under the shadow of Max Gottlieb, have said about Holabird, now he wrung his hands and muttered, "It's good to be home."

Holabird (he was wearing a blue shirt with a starched blue collar, like an actor) could not wait till Martin's baggage had gone through the customs. He had to return to his duties as Acting Director of the Institute. He delayed only to hint that the Board of Trustees were going to make him full Director, and that certainly, my dear fellow, he would see that Martin had the credit and the reward he deserved.

When Holabird was gone, driving away in his neat coupé (he often explained that his wife and he could afford a chauffeur, but they preferred to spend the money on other things), Martin was conscious of Terry Wickett, leaning against a gnawed wooden pillar of the wharf-house, as though he had been there for hours.

Terry strolled up and snorted, "Hello, Slim. All O.K.? Lez shoot the stuff through the customs. Great pleasure to see the Director and you kissing."

As they drove through the summer-walled streets of Brooklyn, Martin inquired, "How's Holabird working out as Director? And how is Gottlieb?"

"Oh, the Holy Wren is no worse than Tubbs; he's even politer and more ignorant. . . . Me, you watch me! One of these days I'm going off to the woods—got a shack in Vermont—going to work there without having to produce results for the Director! They've stuck me in the Department of Biochemistry. And Gottlieb—" Terry's voice became anxious. "I guess he's pretty shaky— They've pensioned him off. Now look, Slim: I hear you're going to be a gilded department-head, and I'll never be anything but an associate member. Are you going on with me, or are you going to be one of the Holy Wren's pets—hero-scientist?"

"I'm with you, Terry, you old grouch." Martin dropped the cynicism which had always seemed proper between him and Terry. "I haven't got anybody else. Leora and Gustaf are gone and now maybe Gottlieb. You and I have got to stick together!"

"It's a go!"

They shook hands, they coughed gruffly, and talked of straw hats.

v

When Martin entered the Institute, his colleagues galloped up to shake hands and to exclaim, and if their praise was flustering, there is no time at which one can stomach so much of it as at home-coming.

Sir Robert Fairlamb had written to the Institute a letter glorifying him. The letter arrived on the same boat with Martin, and next day Holabird gave it out to the press.

The reporters, who had been only a little interested at his landing, came around for interviews, and while Martin was sulky and jerky Holabird took them in hand, so that the papers were able to announce that America, which was always rescuing the world from something or other, had gone and done it again. It was spread in the prints that Dr. Martin Arrowsmith was not only a powerful witch-doctor and possibly something of a laboratory-hand, but also a ferocious rat-killer, village-burner, Special Board addresser, and snatcher from death. There was at the time, in certain places, a doubt as to how benevolent the United States had been to its Little Brothers—Mexico, Cuba, Haiti, Nicaragua—and the editors and politicians were grateful to Martin for this proof of their sacrifice and tender watchfulness.

He had letters from the Public Health service; from an enterprising Mid-western college which desired to make him a Doctor of Civil Law; from medical schools and societies which begged him to address them. Editorials on his work appeared in the medical journals and the newspapers; and Con-gressman Almus Pickerbaugh telegraphed him from Washington, in what the Congressman may conceivably have regarded as verse: "They got to go some to get ahead of fellows that come from old Nautilus." And he was again invited to dinner at the McGurks', not by Capitola but by Ross McGurk, whose name had never had such a whitewashing.

He refused all invitations to speak, and the urgent organizations which had invited him responded with meekness that they understood how in-timidatingly busy Dr. Arrowsmith was, and if he ever *could* find the time, they would be most highly honored—

Rippleton Holabird was elected full Director now, in succession to Gott-lieb, and he sought to use Martin as the prize exhibit of the Institute. He brought all the visiting dignitaries, all the foreign Men of Measured Merri-ment, in to see him, and they looked pleased and tried to think up questions. Then Martin was made head of the new Department of Microbiology at twice his old salary.

He never did learn what was the difference between microbiology and bacteriology. But none of his glorification could he resist. He was still too dazed—he was the more dazed when he had seen Max Gottlieb.

VI

The morning after his return he had telephoned to Gottlieb's flat, had spoken to Miriam and received permission to call in the late afternoon.

All the way uptown he could hear Gottlieb saying, "You were my son! I gave you eferyt'ing I knew of truth and honor, and you haf betrayed me. Get out of my sight!"

Miriam met him in the hall, fretting, "I don't know if I should have let you come at all, Doctor."

"Why? Isn't he well enough to see people?"

"It isn't that. He doesn't really seem ill, except that he's feeble, but he doesn't know anyone. The doctors say it's senile dementia. His memory is gone. And he's just suddenly forgotten all his English. He can only speak

German, and I can't speak it, hardly at all. If I'd only studied it, instead of music! But perhaps it may do him good to have you here. He was always so fond of you. You don't know how he talked of you and the splendid experiment you've been doing in St. Hubert."

"Well, I—" He could find nothing to say.

Miriam led him into a room whose walls were dark with books. Gottlieb was sunk in a worn chair, his thin hand lax on the arm.

"Doctor, it's Arrowsmith, just got back!" Martin mumbled.

The old man looked as though he half understood; he peered at him, then shook his head and whimpered, "*Versteh' nicht.*" His arrogant eyes were clouded with ungovernable slow tears.

Martin understood that never could he be punished now and cleansed. Gottlieb had sunk into his darkness still trusting him.

VII

Martin closed his flat—their flat—with a cold swift fury, lest he yield to his misery in finding among Leora's possessions a thousand fragments which brought her back: the frock she had bought for Capitola McGurk's dinner, a petrified chocolate she had hidden away to munch illegally by night, a memorandum, "Get almonds for Sandy." He took a grimly impersonal room in a hotel, and sunk himself in work. There was nothing for him but work and the harsh friendship of Terry Wickett.

His first task was to check the statistics of his St. Swithin treatments and the new figures still coming in from Stokes. Some of them were shaky, some suggested that the value of phage certainly had been confirmed, but there was nothing final. He took his figures to Raymond Pearl the biometrician, who thought less of them than did Martin himself.

He had already made a report of his work to the Director and the Trustees of the Institute, with no conclusion except "the results await statistical analysis and should have this before they are published." But Holabird had run wild, the newspapers had reported wonders, and in on Martin poured demands that he send out phage; inquiries as to whether he did not have a phage for tuberculosis, for syphilis; offers that he take charge of this epidemic and that.

Pearl had pointed out that his agreeable results in first phaging the whole of Carib village must be questioned, because it was possible that when he began the curve of the disease had already passed its peak. With this and the other complications, viewing his hot work in St. Hubert as coldly as though it were the pretense of a man whom he had never seen, Martin decided that he had no adequate proof, and strode in to see the Director.

Holabird was gentle and pretty, but he sighed that if this conclusion were published, he would have to take back all the things he had said about the magnificence which, presumably, he had inspired his subordinate to accomplish. He was gentle and pretty, but firm; Martin was to suppress (Holabird did not say "suppress"—he said "leave to me for further consideration") the real statistical results, and issue the report with an ambiguous summary.

Martin was furious, Holabird delicately relentless. Martin hastened to Terry, declaring that he would resign—would denounce—would expose— Yes! He would! He no longer had to support Leora. He'd work as a drug-clerk. He'd go back right now and tell the Holy Wren—

"Hey! Slim! Wait a minute! Hold your horses!" observed Terry. "Just get along with Holy for a while, and we'll work out something we can do together and be independent. Meanwhile you have got your lab here, and you still have some physical chemistry to learn! And, uh— Slim, I haven't said anything about your St. Hubert stuff, but you know and I know you bunged it up badly. Can you come into court with clean hands, if you're going to indict the Holy One? Though I do agree that aside from being a dirty, lying, social-climbing, sneaking, power-grabbing hypocrite, he's all right. Hold on. We'll fix up something. Why, son, we've just been learning our science; we're just beginning to work."

Then Holabird published officially, under the Institute's seal, Martin's original report to the Trustees, with such quaint revisions as a change of "the results should have analysis" to "while statistical analysis would seem desirable, it is evident that this new treatment has accomplished all that had been hoped."

Again Martin went mad, again Terry calmed him; and with a hard fury unlike his eagerness of the days when he had known that Leora was waiting for him he resumed his physical chemistry.

He learned the involved mysteries of freezing-point determinations, osmotic pressure determinations, and tried to apply Northrop's generalizations on enzymes to the study of phage.

He became absorbed in mathematical laws which strangely predicted natural phenomena; his world was cold, exact, austerely materialistic, bitter to those who founded their logic on impressions. He was daily more scornful toward the counters of paving stones, the renamers of species, the compilers of irrelevant data. In his absorption the pleasant seasons passed unseen.

Once he raised his head in astonishment to perceive that it was spring; once Terry and he tramped two hundred miles through the Pennsylvania hills, by summer roads; but it seemed only a day later when it was Christmas, and Holabird was being ever so jolly and yuley about the Institute.

The absence of Gottlieb may have been good for Martin, since he no longer turned to the master for solutions in tough queries. When he took up diffusion problems, he began to develop his own apparatus, and whether it was from inborn ingenuity or merely from a fury of labor, he was so competent that he won from Terry the almost overwhelming praise: "Why, that's not so darn' bad, Slim!"

The sureness to which Max Gottlieb seems to have been born came to Martin slowly, after many stumblings, but it came. He desired a perfection of technique in the quest for absolute and provable fact; he desired as greatly as any Pater to "burn with a hard gem-like flame," and he desired not to

have ease and repute in the market-place, but rather to keep free of those
follies, lest they confuse him and make him soft.

Holabird was as much bewildered as Tubbs would have been by the ramifi-
cations of Martin's work. What did he think he was anyway—a bacteriologist
or a bio-physicist? But Holabird was won by the scientific world's reception
of Martin's first important paper, on the effect of X-rays, gamma rays, and
beta rays on the anti-Shiga phage. It was praised in Paris and Brussels and
Cambridge as much as in New York, for its insight and for "the clarity and
to perhaps be unscientifically enthusiastic, the sheer delight and style of its
presentation," as Professor Berkeley Wurtz put it; which may be indicated
by quoting the first paragraph of the paper:

> In a preliminary publication, I have reported a marked qualitative
> destructive effect of the radiations from radium emanations on Bacterio-
> phage-anti-Shiga. In the present paper it is shown that X-rays, gamma
> rays, and beta rays produce identical inactivating effects on this bacterio-
> phage. Furthermore, a quantitative relation is demonstrated to exist
> between this inactivation and the radiations that produce it. The results
> obtained from this quantitative study permit the statement that the per-
> centage of inactivation, as measured by determining the units of bac-
> teriophage remaining after irradiation by gamma and beta rays of a
> suspension of fixed virulence, is a function of the two variables, milli-
> curies and hours. The following equation accounts quantitatively for the
> experimental results obtained:

$$K = \frac{\lambda \log e \frac{u_0}{u}}{E_0(\varepsilon - \lambda t_1)}$$

When Director Holabird saw the paper—Yeo was vicious enough to take
it in and ask his opinion—he said, "Splendid, oh, I say, simply splendid! I've
just had the chance to skim through it, old boy, but I shall certainly read it
carefully, the first free moment I have."

# 37

Martin did not see Joyce Lanyon for weeks after his return to New York.
Once she invited him to dinner, but he could not come, and he did not
hear from her again.

His absorption in osmotic pressure determinations did not content him
when he sat in his prim hotel room and was reduced from Dr. Arrowsmith
to a man who had no one to talk to. He remembered how they had sat by

the lagoon in the tepid twilight; he telephoned asking whether he might come in for tea.

He knew in an unformulated way that Joyce was rich, but after seeing her in gingham, cooking in the kitchen of St. Swithin's almshouse, he did not grasp her position; and he was uncomfortable when, feeling dusty from the laboratory, he came to her great house and found her the soft-voiced mistress of many servants. Hers was a palace, and palaces, whether they are such very little ones as Joyce's, with its eighteen rooms, or Buckingham or vast Fontainebleau, are all alike; they are choked with the superfluities of pride, they are so complete that one does not remember small endearing charms, they are indistinguishable in their common feeling of polite and uneasy grandeur, they are therefore altogether tedious.

But amid the pretentious splendor which Roger Lanyon had accumulated, Joyce was not tedious. It is to be suspected that she enjoyed showing Martin what she really was, by producing footmen and too many kinds of sandwiches, and by boasting, "Oh, I never do know what they're going to give me for tea."

But she had welcomed him, crying, "You look so much better. I'm frightfully glad. Are you still my brother? I was a good cook at the almshouse, wasn't I!"

Had he been suave then and witty, she would not have been greatly interested. She knew too many men who were witty and well-bred, ivory smooth and competent to help her spend the four or five million dollars with which she was burdened. But Martin was at once a scholar who made osmotic pressure determinations almost interesting, a taut swift man whom she could fancy running or making love, and a lonely youngster who naïvely believed that here in her soft security she was still the girl who had sat with him by the lagoon, still the courageous woman who had come to him in a drunken room at Blackwater.

Joyce Lanyon knew how to make men talk. Thanks more to her than to his own articulateness, he made living the Institute, the members, their feuds, and the drama of coursing on the trail of a discovery.

Her easy life here had seemed tasteless after the risks of St. Hubert, and in his contempt for ease and rewards she found exhilaration.

He came now and then to tea, to dinner; he learned the ways of her house, her servants, the more nearly intelligent of her friends. He liked—and possibly he was liked by—some of them. With one friend of hers Martin had a state of undeclared war. This was Latham Ireland, an achingly well-dressed man of fifty, a competent lawyer who was fond of standing in front of fireplaces and being quietly clever. He fascinated Joyce by telling her that she was subtle, then telling her what she was being subtle about.

Martin hated him.

In midsummer Martin was invited for a week-end at Joyce's vast blossom-hid country house at Greenwich. She was half apologetic for its luxury; he was altogether unhappy.

The strain of considering clothes, of galloping out to buy white trousers when he wanted to watch the test-tubes in the constant-temperature bath, of trying to look easy in the limousine which met him at the station, and of deciding which servants to tip and how much and when, was dismaying to a simple man. He felt rustic when, after he had blurted, "Just a minute till I go up and unpack my suit-case," she said gently, "Oh, that will have been done for you."

He discovered that a valet had laid out for him to put on, that first evening, all the small store of underclothes he had brought, and had squeezed out on his brush a ribbon of tooth-paste.

He sat on the edge of his bed, groaning, "This is too rich for my blood!"

He hated and feared that valet, who kept stealing his clothes, putting them in places where they could not be found, then popping in menacingly when Martin was sneaking about the enormous room looking for them.

But his chief unhappiness was that there was nothing to do. He had no sport but tennis, at which he was too rusty to play with these chattering unidentified people who filled the house and, apparently with perfect willingness, worked at golf and bridge. He had met but few of the friends of whom they talked. They said, "You know dear old R. G.," and he said, "Oh, yes," but he never did know dear old R. G.

Joyce was as busily amiable as when they were alone at tea, and she found for him a weedy flapper whose tennis was worse than his own, but she had twenty guests—forty at Sunday lunch—and he gave up certain agreeable notions of walking with her in fresh lanes and, after excitedly saying this and that, perhaps kissing her. He had one moment with her. As he was going, she ordered, "Come here, Martin," and led him apart.

"You haven't really enjoyed it."

"Why, sure, course I—"

"Of course you haven't! And you despise us, rather, and perhaps you're partly right. I do like pretty people and gracious manners and good games, but I suppose they seem piffling after nights in a laboratory."

"No, I like 'em too. In a way. I like to look at beautiful women—at you! But— Oh, darn it, Joyce, I'm not up to it. I've always been poor and horribly busy. I haven't learned your games."

"But, Martin, you could, with the intensity you put into everything."

"Even getting drunk in Blackwater!"

"And I hope in New York, too! Dear Roger, he did have such an innocent, satisfying time getting drunk at class-dinners! But I mean: if you went at it, you could play bridge and golf—and talking—better than any of them. If you only knew how frightfully recent most of the ducal class in America are! And Martin: wouldn't it be good for you? Wouldn't you work all the better if you got away from your logarithmic tables now and then? And are you going to admit there's anything you can't conquer?"

"No, I—"

"Will you come to dinner on Tuesday week, just us two, and we'll fight it out?"

"Be glad to."

For a number of hours, on the train to Terry Wickett's vacation place in the Vermont hills, Martin was convinced that he loved Joyce Lanyon, and that he was going to attack the art of being amusing as he had attacked physical chemistry. Ardently, and quite humorlessly, as he sat stiffly in a stale Pullman chair-car with his feet up on his suit-case, he pictured himself wearing a club-tie (presumably first acquiring the tie and the club), playing golf in plus-fours, and being entertaining about dear old R. G. and incredibly witty about dear old Latham Ireland's aged Rolls-Royce.

But these ambitions he forgot as he came to Terry's proud proprietary shanty, by a lake among oaks and maples, and heard Terry's real theories of the decomposition of quinine derivatives.

Being perhaps the least sentimental of human beings, Terry had named his place "Birdies' Rest." He owned five acres of woodland, two miles from a railroad station. His shanty was a two-room affair of logs, with bunks for beds and oilcloth for table-linen.

"Here's the layout, Slim," said Terry. "Some day I'm going to figure out a way of making a lab here pay, by manufacturing sera or something, and I'll put up a couple more buildings on the flat by the lake, and have one absolutely independent place for science—two hours a day on the commercial end, and say about six for sleeping and a couple for feeding and telling dirty stories. That leaves—two and six and two make ten, if I'm any authority on higher math—that leaves fourteen hours a day for research (except when you got something special on), with no Director and no Society patrons and no Trustees that you've got to satisfy by making fool reports. Of course there won't be any scientific dinners with ladies in candy-box dresses, but I figure we'll be able to afford plenty of salt pork and corncob pipes, and your bed will be made perfectly—if you make it yourself. Huh? Lez go and have a swim."

Martin returned to New York with the not very compatible plans of being the best-dressed golfer in Greenwich and of cooking beef-stew with Terry at Birdies' Rest.

But the first of these was the more novel to him.

## II

Joyce Lanyon was enjoying a conversion. Her St. Hubert experiences and her natural variability had caused her to be dissatisfied with Roger's fast-motoring set.

She let the lady Maecenases of her acquaintance beguile her into several of their Causes, and she enjoyed them as she had enjoyed her active and entirely purposeless war work in 1917, for Joyce Lanyon was to some degree an Arranger, which was an epithet invented by Terry Wickett for Capitola McGurk.

An Arranger and even an Improver was Joyce, but she was not a Capitola; she neither waved a feathered fan and spoke spaciously, nor did she take out her sex-passion in talking. She was fine and occasionally gorgeous, with tiger in her, though she was as far from perfumed-boudoir and black-lingerie passion as she was from Capitola's cooing staleness. Hers was sheer straight white silk and cherished skin.

Behind all her reasons for valuing Martin was the fact that the only time in her life when she had felt useful and independent was when she had been an almshouse cook.

She might have drifted on, in her world of drifters, but for the interposition of Latham Ireland, the lawyer-dilettante-lover.

"Joy," he observed, "there seems to be an astounding quantity of that Dr. Arrowsmith person about the place. As your benign uncle—"

"Latham, my sweet, I quite agree that Martin is too aggressive, thoroughly unlicked, very selfish, rather a prig, absolutely a pedant, and his shirts are atrocious. And I rather think I shall marry him. I almost think I love him!"

"Wouldn't cyanide be a neater way of doing suicide?" said Latham Ireland.

### III

What Martin felt for Joyce was what any widowed man of thirty-eight would feel for a young and pretty and well-spoken woman who was attentive to his wisdom. As to her wealth, there was no problem at all. He was no poor man marrying money! Why, he was making ten thousand a year, which was eight thousand more than he needed to live on!

Occasionally he was suspicious of her dependence on luxury. With tremendous craft he demanded that instead of their dining in her Jacobean hall of state, she come with him on his own sort of party. She came, with enthusiasm. They went to abysmal Greenwich Village restaurants with candles, artistic waiters, and no food; or to Chinatown dives with food and nothing else. He even insisted on their taking the subway—though after dinner he usually forgot that he was being Spartan, and ordered a taxi-cab. She accepted it all without either wincing or too much gurgling.

She played tennis with him in the court on her roof; she taught him bridge, which, with his concentration and his memory, he soon played better than she and enjoyed astonishingly; she persuaded him that he had a leg and would look well in golf clothes.

He came to take her to dinner, on a serene autumn evening. He had a taxi waiting.

"Why don't we stick to the subway?" she said.

They were standing on her doorstep, in a blankly expensive and quite unromantic street off Fifth Avenue.

"Oh, I hate the rotten subway as much as you do! Elbows in my stomach never did help me much to plan experiments. I expect when we're married I'll enjoy your limousine."

"Is this a proposal? I'm not at all sure I'm going to marry you. Really, I'm *not!* You have no sense of ease!"

They were married the following January, in St. George's Church, and Martin suffered almost as much over the flowers, the bishop, the relatives with high-pitched voices, and the top hat which Joyce had commanded, as he did over having Rippleton Holabird wring his hand with a look of, "At last, dear boy, you have come out of barbarism and become One of Us."

Martin had asked Terry to be his best man. Terry had refused, and asserted that only with pain would he come to the wedding at all. The best man was Dr. William Smith, with his beard trimmed for the occasion, and distressing morning clothes and a topper which he had bought in London eleven years before, but both of them were safe in charge of a cousin of Joyce who was guaranteed to have extra handkerchiefs and to recognize the Wedding March. He had understood that Martin was Groton and Harvard, and when he discovered that he was Winnemac and nothing at all, he became suspicious.

In their stateroom on the steamer Joyce murmured, "Dear, you were brave! I didn't know what a damn' fool that cousin of mine was. Kiss me!"

Thenceforth . . . except for a dreadful second when Leora floated between them, eyes closed and hands crossed on her pale cold breast . . . they were happy and in each other found adventurous new ways.

### IV

For three months they wandered in Europe.

On the first day Joyce had said, "Let's have this beastly money thing over. I should think you are the least mercenary of men. I've put ten thousand dollars to your credit in London—oh, yes, and fifty thousand in New York —and if you'd like, when you have to do things for me, I'd be glad if you'd draw on it. No! Wait! Can't you see how easy and decent I want to make it all? You won't hurt me to save your own self-respect?"

### V

They really had, it seemed, to stay with the Principessa del Oltraggio (formerly Miss Lucy Deemy Bessy of Dayton), Madame des Basses Loges (Miss Brown of San Francisco), and the Countess of Marazion (who had been Mrs. Arthur Snaipe of Albany, and several things before that), but Joyce did go with him to see the great laboratories in London, Paris, Copenhagen. She swelled to perceive how Nobel-prize winners received Her Husband, knew of him, desired to be violent with him about phage, and showed him their work of years. Some of them were hasty and graceless, she thought. Her Man was prettier than any of them, and if she would but be patient with him, she could make him master polo and clothes and conversation . . . but of course go on with his science . . . a pity he could not have a knighthood, like one or two of the British scientists they met. But even in America there were honorary degrees. . . .

While she discovered and digested Science, Martin discovered Women.

## VI

Aware only of Madeline Fox and Orchid Pickerbaugh, who were Nice American Girls, of soon-forgotten ladies of the night, and of Leora who, in her indolence, her indifference to decoration and good fame, was neither woman nor wife but only her own self, Martin knew nothing whatever about Women. He had expected Leora to wait for him, to obey his wishes, to understand without his saying them all the flattering things he had planned to say. He was spoiled, and Joyce was not timorous about telling him so.

It was not for her to sit beaming and wordless while he and his fellow-researchers arranged the world. With many jolts he perceived that even outside the bedroom he had to consider the fluctuations and variables of his wife, as A Woman, and sometimes as A Rich Woman.

It was confusing to find that where Leora had acidly claimed sex-loyalty but had hummingly not cared in what manner he might say Good Morning, Joyce was indifferent as to how many women he might have fondled (so long as he did not insult her by making love to them in her presence) but did require him to say Good Morning as though he meant it. It was confusing to find how starkly she discriminated between his caresses when he was absorbed in her and his hasty interest when he wanted to go to sleep. She could, she said, kill a man who considered her merely convenient furniture, and she uncomfortably emphasized the "kill."

She expected him to remember her birthday, her taste in wine, her liking for flowers, and her objection to viewing the process of shaving. She wanted a room to herself; she insisted that he knock before entering; and she demanded that he admire her hats.

When he was so interested in the work at Pasteur Institute that he had a clerk telephone that he would not be able to meet her for dinner, she was tight-lipped with rage.

"Oh, you got to expect that," he reflected, feeling that he was being tactful and patient and penetrating.

It annoyed him, sometimes, that she would never impulsively start off on a walk with him. No matter how brief the jaunt, she must first go to her room for white gloves—placidly stand there drawing them on. . . . And in London she made him buy spats . . . and even wear them.

Joyce was not only an Arranger—she was a Loyalist. Like most American cosmopolites she revered the English peerage, adopted all their standards and beliefs—or what she considered their standards and beliefs—and treasured her encounters with them. Three and a half years after the War of 1914–18, she still said that she loathed all Germans, and the one complete quarrel between her and Martin occurred when he desired to see the laboratories in Berlin and Vienna.

But for all their differences it was a romantic pilgrimage. They loved fearlessly; they tramped through the mountains and came back to revel in vast bathrooms and ingenious dinners; they idled before cafés, and save when he fell silent as he remembered how much Leora had wanted to sit before cafés in France, they showed each other all the eagernesses of their minds.

Europe, her Europe, which she had always known and loved, Joyce offered to him on generous hands, and he who had ever been sensitive to warm colors and fine gestures—when he was not frenzied with work—was grateful to her and boyish with wonder. He believed that he was learning to take life easily and beautifully; he criticized Terry Wickett (but only to himself) for provincialism; and so in a golden leisure they came back to America and prohibition and politicians charging to protect the Steel Trust from the communists, to conversation about bridge and motors and to osmotic pressure determinations.

# 38

Director Rippleton Holabird had also married money, and whenever his colleagues hinted that since his first ardent work in physiology he had done nothing but arrange a few nicely selected flowers on the tables hewn out by other men, it was a satisfaction to him to observe that these rotters came down to the Institute by subway, while he drove elegantly in his coupé. But now Arrowsmith, once the poorest of them all, came by limousine with a chauffeur who touched his hat, and Holabird's coffee was salted.

There was a simplicity in Martin, but it cannot be said that he did not lick his lips when Holabird mooned at the chauffeur.

His triumph over Holabird was less than being able to entertain Angus Duer and his wife, on from Chicago; to introduce them to Director Holabird, to Salamon the king of surgeons, and to a medical baronet; and to have Angus gush, "Mart, do you mind my saying we're all awfully proud of you? Rouncefield was speaking to me about it the other day. 'It may be presumptuous,' he said, 'but I really feel that perhaps the training we tried to give Dr. Arrowsmith here in the Clinic did in some way contribute to his magnificent work in the West Indies and at McGurk.' What a lovely woman your wife is, old man! Do you suppose she'd mind telling Mrs. Duer where she got that frock?"

Martin had heard about the superiority of poverty to luxury, but after the lunch-wagons of Mohalis, after twelve years of helping Leora check the laundry and worry about the price of steak, after a life of waiting in the slush for trolleys, it was not at all dismaying to have a valet who produced shirts automatically; not at all degrading to come to meals which were always interesting, and, in the discretion of his car, to lean an aching head against softness and think how clever he was.

"You see, by having other people do the vulgar things for you, it saves your own energy for the things that only you can do," said Joyce.

Martin agreed, then drove to Westchester for a lesson in golf.

A week after their return from Europe, Joyce went with him to see Gottlieb. He fancied that Gottlieb came out of his brooding to smile on them.

"After all," Martin considered, "the old man did like beautiful things. If he'd had the chance, he might've liked a big Establishment, too, maybe."

Terry was surprisingly complaisant.

"I'll tell you, Slim—if you want to know. Personally I'd hate to have to live up to servants. But I'm getting old and wise. I figure that different folks like different things, and awful' few of 'em have the sense to come and ask me what they ought to like. But honest, Slim, I don't think I'll come to dinner. I've gone and bought a dress-suit—*bought* it!—got it in my room—damn' landlady keeps filling it with moth-balls—but I don't think I could stand listening to Latham Ireland being clever."

It was, however, Rippleton Holabird's attitude which most concerned Martin, for Holabird did not let him forget that unless he desired to drift off and be merely a ghostly Rich Woman's husband, he would do well to remember who was Director.

Along with the endearing manners which he preserved for Ross McGurk, Holabird had developed the remoteness, the inhuman quiet courtesy, of the Man of Affairs, and people who presumed on his old glad days he courteously put in their places. He saw the need of repressing insubordination, when Arrowsmith appeared in a limousine. He gave him one week after his return to enjoy the limousine, then blandly called on him in his laboratory.

"Martin," he sighed, "I find that our friend Ross McGurk is just a bit dissatisfied with the practical results that are coming out of the Institute and, to convince him, I'm afraid I really must ask you to put less emphasis on bacteriophage for the moment and take up influenza. The Rockefeller Institute has the right idea. They've utilized their best minds, and spent money magnificently, on such problems as pneumonia, meningitis, cancer. They've already lessened the terrors of meningitis and pneumonia, and yellow fever is on the verge of complete abolition through Noguchi's work, and I have no doubt that their hospital, with its enormous resources and splendidly co-operating minds, will be the first to find something to alleviate diabetes. Now, I understand, they're hot after the cause of influenza. They're not going to permit another great epidemic of it. Well, dear chap, it's up to us to beat them on the flu, and I've chosen you to represent us in the race."

Martin was at the moment hovering over a method of reproducing phage on dead bacteria, but he could not refuse, he could not risk being discharged. He was too rich! Martin the renegade medical student could flounder off and be a soda-clerk, but if the husband of Joyce Lanyon should indulge in such insanity, he would be followed by reporters and photographed at the soda handles. Still less could he chance becoming merely her supported husband—a butler of the boudoir.

He assented, not very pleasantly.

He began to work on the cause of influenza with a half-heartedness almost magnificent. In the hospitals he secured cultures from cases which might be influenza and might be bad colds—no one was certain just what the influenza symptoms were; nothing was clean cut. He left most of the work to his assistants, occasionally giving them sardonic directions to "put on another hundred tubes of the A medium—hell, make it another thousand!" and when he found that they were doing as they pleased, he was not righteous nor rebuking. If he did not guiltily turn his hand from the plow it was only because he never touched the plow. Once his own small laboratory had been as fussily neat as a New Hampshire kitchen. Now the several rooms under his charge were a disgrace, with long racks of abandoned test-tubes, many half-filled with mold, none of them properly labeled.

Then he had his idea. He began firmly to believe that the Rockefeller investigators had found the cause of flu. He gushed in to Holabird and told him so. As for himself, he was going back to his search for the real nature of phage.

Holabird argued that Martin must be wrong. If Holabird wanted the McGurk Institute—and the Director of McGurk Institute—to have the credit for capturing influenza, then it simply could not be possible that Rockefeller was ahead of them. He also said weighty things about phage. Its essential nature, he pointed out, was an academic question.

But Martin was by now too much of a scientific dialectician for Holabird, who gave up and retired to his den (or so Martin gloomily believed) to devise new ways of plaguing him. For a time Martin was again left free to wallow in work.

He found a means of reproducing phage on dead bacteria by a very complicated, very delicate use of partial oxygen-carbon dioxide tension—as exquisite as cameo-carving, as improbable as weighing the stars. His report stirred the laboratory world, and here and there (in Tokio, in Amsterdam, in Winnemac) enthusiasts believed he had proven that phage was a living organism; and other enthusiasts said, in esoteric language with mathematical formulae, that he was a liar and six kinds of a fool.

It was at this time, when he might have become a Great Man, that he pitched over most of his own work and some of the duties of being Joyce's husband to follow Terry Wickett, which showed that he lacked common sense, because Terry was still an assistant while he himself was head of a department.

Terry had discovered that certain quinine derivatives when introduced into the animal body slowly decompose into products which are highly toxic to bacteria but only mildly toxic to the body. There was hinted here a whole new world of therapy. Terry explained it to Martin, and invited him to collaborate. Buoyant with great things they got leave from Holabird—and from Joyce—and though it was winter they went off to Birdies' Rest, in the Vermont hills. While they snowshoed and shot rabbits, and all the long dark evenings while they lay on their bellies before the fire, they ranted and planned.

Martin had not been so long silk-wrapped that he could not enjoy gobbling salt pork after the northwest wind and the snow. It was not unpleasant to be free of thinking up new compliments for Joyce.

They had, they saw, to answer an interesting question: Do the quinine derivatives act by attaching themselves to the bacteria, or by changing the body fluids? It was a simple, clear, definite question which required for answer only the inmost knowledge of chemistry and biology, a few hundred animals on which to experiment, and perhaps ten or twenty or a million years of trying and failing.

They decided to work with the pneumococcus, and with the animal which should most nearly reproduce human pneumonia. This meant the monkey, and to murder monkeys is expensive and rather grim. Holabird, as Director, could supply them, but if they took him into confidence he would demand immediate results.

Terry meditated, " 'Member there was one of these Nobel-prize winners, Slim, one of these plumb fanatics that instead of blowing in the prize spent the whole thing on chimps and other apes, and he got together with another of those whiskery old birds, and they ducked up alleys and kept the anti-viv folks from prosecuting them, and settled the problem of the transfer of syphilis to lower animals? But we haven't got any Nobel Prize, I grieve to tell you, and it doesn't look to me—"

"Terry, I'll do it, if necessary! I've never sponged on Joyce yet, but I will now, if the Holy Wren holds out on us."

II

They faced Holabird in his office, sulkily, rather childishly, and they demanded the expenditure of at least ten thousand dollars for monkeys. They wished to start a research which might take two years without apparent results—possibly without any results. Terry was to be transferred to Martin's department as co-head, their combined salaries shared equally.

Then they prepared to fight.

Holabird stared, assembled his mustache, departed from his Diligent Director manner, and spoke:

"Wait a minute, if you don't mind. As I gather it, you are explaining to me that occasionally it's necessary to take some time to elaborate an experiment. I really must tell you that I was formerly a researcher in an Institute called McGurk, and learned several of these things all by myself! Hell, Terry, and you, Mart, don't be so egotistic! You're not the only scientists who like to work undisturbed! If you poor fish only knew how I long to get away from signing letters and get my fingers on a kymograph drum again! Those beautiful long hours of search for truth! And if you knew how I've fought the Trustees for the chance to keep you fellows free! All right. You shall have your monkeys. Fix up the joint department to suit yourselves. And work ahead as seems best. I doubt if in the whole scientific world there's two people that can be trusted as much as you two surly birds!"

Holabird rose, straight and handsome and cordial, his hand out. They sheepishly shook it and sneaked away, Terry grumbling, "He's spoiled my whole day! I haven't got a single thing to kick about! Slim, where's the catch? You can bet there is one—there always is!"

In a year of divine work, the catch did not appear. They had their monkeys, their laboratories and garçons, and their unbroken leisure; they began the most exciting work they had ever known, and decidedly the most nerve-jabbing. Monkeys are unreasonable animals; they delight in developing tuberculosis on no provocation whatever; in captivity they have a liking for epidemics; and they make scenes by cursing at their masters in seven dialects.

"They're so up-and-coming," sighed Terry. "I feel like lettin' 'em go and retiring to Birdies' Rest to grow potatoes. Why should we murder live-wires like them to save pasty-faced, big-bellied humans from pneumonia?"

Their first task was to determine with accuracy the tolerated dose of the quinine derivative, and to study its effects on the hearing and vision, and on the kidneys, as shown by endless determinations of blood sugar and blood urea. While Martin did the injections and observed the effect on the monkeys and lost himself in chemistry, Terry toiled (all night, all next day, then a drink and a frowsy nap and all night again) on new methods of synthesizing the quinine derivative.

This was the most difficult period of Martin's life. To work, staggering sleepy, all night, to drowse on a bare table at dawn and to breakfast at a greasy lunch-counter, these were natural and amusing, but to explain to Joyce why he had missed her dinner to a lady sculptor and a lawyer whose grandfather had been a Confederate General, this was impossible. He won a brief tolerance by explaining that he really had longed to kiss her good-night, that he did appreciate the basket of sandwiches which she had sent, and that he was about to remove pneumonia from the human race, a statement which he healthily doubted.

But when he had missed four dinners in succession; when she had raged, "Can you imagine how awful it was for Mrs. Thorn to be short a man at the last moment?" when she had wailed, "I didn't so much mind your rudeness on the other nights, but this evening when I had nothing to do and sat home alone and waited for you"—then he writhed.

Martin and Terry began to produce pneumonia in their monkeys and to treat them, and they had success which caused them to waltz solemnly down the corridor. They could save the monkeys from pneumonia invariably, when the infection had gone but one day, and most of them on the second day and the third.

Their results were complicated by the fact that a certain number of the monkeys recovered by themselves, and this they allowed for by simple-looking figures which took days of stiff, shoulder-aching sitting over papers . . . one wild-haired collarless man at a table, while the other walked among stinking cages of monkeys, clucking to them, calling them Bess and Rover, and grunting placidly, "Oh, you would bite me, would you, sweetheart!" and all the while, kindly but merciless as the gods, injecting them with the deadly pneumonia.

They came into a high upland where the air was thin with failures. They studied in the test-tube the break-down products of pneumococci—and failed. They constructed artificial body fluids (carefully, painfully, inadequately), they tried the effect of the derivative on germs in this artificial blood—and failed.

Then Holabird heard of their previous success, and came down on them with laurels and fury.

He understood, he said, that they had a cure for pneumonia. Very well! The Institute could do with the credit for curing that undesirable disease, and Terry and Martin would kindly publish their findings (mentioning Mc-Gurk) at once.

"We will not! Look here, Holabird!" snarled Terry, "I thought you were going to let us alone!"

"I have! Nearly a year! Till you should complete your research. And now you've completed it. It's time to let the world know what you're doing."

"If I did, the world would know a doggone sight more'n I do! Nothing doing, Chief. Maybe we can publish in a year from now."

"You'll publish now or—"

"All right, Holy. The blessed moment has arrived. I quit! And I'm so gentlemanly that I do it without telling you what I think of you!"

Thus was Terry Wickett discharged from McGurk. He patented the process of synthesizing his quinine derivative and retired to Birdies' Rest, to build a laboratory out of his small savings and spend a life of independent research supported by a restricted sale of sera and of his drug.

For Terry, wifeless and valetless, this was easy enough, but for Martin it was not simple.

### III

Martin assumed that he would resign. He explained it to Joyce. How he was to combine a town house and a Greenwich castle with flannel-shirt collaboration at Birdies' Rest he had not quite planned, but he was not going to be disloyal.

"Can you beat it! The Holy Wren fires Terry but doesn't dare touch me! I waited simply because I wanted to watch Holabird figure out what I'd do. And now—"

He was elucidating it to her in their—in her—car, on the way home from a dinner at which he had been so gaily charming to an important dowager that Joyce had crooned, "What a fool Latham Ireland was to say he couldn't be polite!"

"I'm free, by thunder at last I'm free, because I've worked up to something that's worth being free for!" he exulted.

She laid her fine hand on his, and begged, "Wait! I want to think. Please! Do be quiet a moment."

Then: "Mart, if you went on working with Mr. Wickett, you'd have to be leaving me constantly."

"Well—"

"I really don't think that would be quite nice—I mean especially now, because I fancy I'm going to have a baby."

He made a sound of surprise.

"Oh, I'm not going to do the weeping mother. And I don't know whether I'm glad or furious, though I do believe I'd like to have one baby. But it does complicate things, you know. And personally, I should be sorry if you left the Institute, which gives you a solid position, for a hole-and-corner existence. Dear, I have been fairly nice, haven't I? I really do like you, you know! I don't want you to desert me, and you would if you went off to this horrid Vermont place."

"Couldn't we get a little house near there, and spend part of the year?"

"Pos-sibly. But we ought to wait till this beastly job of bearing a Dear Little One is over, then think about it."

Martin did not resign from the Institute, and Joyce did not think about taking a house near Birdies' Rest to the extent of doing it.

# 39

With Terry Wickett gone, Martin returned to phage. He made a false start and did the worst work of his life. He had lost his fierce serenity. He was too conscious of the ordeal of a professional social life, and he could never understand that esoteric phenomenon, the dinner-party—the painful entertainment of people whom one neither likes nor finds interesting.

So long as he had had a refuge in talking to Terry, he had not been too irritated by well-dressed nonentities, and for a time he had enjoyed the dramatic game of making Nice People accept him. Now he was disturbed by reason.

Clif Clawson showed him how tangled his life had grown.

When he had first come to New York, Martin had looked for Clif, whose boisterousness had been his comfort among Angus Duers and Irving Watterses in medical school. Clif was not to be found, neither at the motor agency for which he had once worked nor elsewhere on Automobile Row. For fourteen years Martin had not seen him.

Then to his laboratory at McGurk was brought a black-and-red card:

CLIFFORD L. CLAWSON
(Clif)
TOP NOTCH GUARANTEED OIL INVESTMENTS

*Higham Block*
*Butte*

"Clif! Good old Clif! The best friend a man ever had! That time he lent me the money to get to Leora! Old Clif! By golly I need somebody like him, with Terry out of it and all these tea-hounds around me!" exulted Martin.

He dashed out and stopped abruptly, staring at a man who was, not softly, remarking to the girl reception-clerk:

"Well, sister, you scientific birds certainly do lay on the agony! Never struck a sweller layout than you got here, except in crook investment-offices— and I've never seen a nicer cutie than you anywhere. How 'bout lil dinner one of these beauteous evenings? I expect I'll parley-vous with thou full often now— I'm a great friend of Doc Arrowsmith. Fact I'm a doc myself—honest— real sawbones—went to medic school and everything. Ah! *Here's* the boy!"

Martin had not allowed for the changes of fourteen years. He was dismayed.

Clif Clawson, at forty, was gross. His face was sweaty, and puffy with pale flesh; his voice was raw; he fancied checked Norfolk jackets, tight across his swollen shoulders and his beefy hips.

He bellowed, while he belabored Martin's back:

"Well, well, well, well, well, well! Old Mart! Why, you old son of a gun! Why, you old son of a gun! Why, you damn' old chicken-thief! Say you skinny little runt, I'm a son of a gun if you look one day older'n when I saw you last in Zenith!"

Martin was aware of the bright leering of the once humble reception-clerk. He said, "Well, gosh, it certainly is good to see you," and hastened to get Clif into the privacy of his office.

"You look fine," he lied, when they were safe. "What you been doing with yourself? Leora and I did our best to look you up, when we first came to New York. Uh— Do you know about, uh, about her?"

"Yuh, I read about her passing away. Fierce luck. And about your swell work in the West Indies—where was it? I guess you're a great man now— famous plague-chaser and all that stuff, and world-renowned skee-entist. I don't suppose you remember your old friends now."

"Oh, don't be a chump! It's—it's—it's fine to see you."

"Well, I'm glad to observe you haven't got the *capitus enlargatus*, Mart. Golly, I says to meself says I, if I blew in and old Mart high-hatted me, I'd just about come nigh unto letting him hear the straight truth, after all the compliments he's been getting from the sassiety dames. I'm glad you've kept your head. I thought about writing you from Butte—been selling some bum oil-stock there and kind of got out quick to save the inspectors the trouble of looking over my books. 'Well,' I thought, 'I'll just sit down and write the whey-faced runt a letter, and make him feel good by telling him how tickled I am over his nice work.' But you know how it is—time kind of slips by. Well, this is excellentus! We'll have a chance to see a whole lot of each other now. I'm going in with a fellow on an investment stunt here in New York. Great pickings, old kid! I'll take you out and show you how to order a real feed, one of these days. Well, tell me what you been doing since you got back from the West Indies. I suppose you're laying your plans to try and get in as the boss or president or whatever they call it of this gecelebrated Institute."

"No—I, uh, well, I shouldn't much care to be Director. I prefer sticking to my lab. I— Perhaps you'd like to hear about my work on phage."

Rejoicing to discover something of which he could talk, Martin sketched his experiments.

Clif spanked his forehead with a spongy hand and shouted:

"Wait! Say, I've got an idea—and you can come right in on it. As I apperceive it, the dear old Gen. Public is just beginning to hear about this bac—what is it?—bacteriophage junk. Look here! Remember that old scoun drel Benoni Carr, that I introduced as a great pharmacologist at the medical banquet? Had din-din with him last eventide. He's running a sanitarium out on Long Island—slick idea, too—practically he's a bootlegger; gets a lot of high-rollers out there and let's 'em have all the hooch they want, on prescriptions, absolutely legal and water-tight! The parties they throw at that joint, dames and everything! Believe me, Uncle Clif is sore stricken with tootelus bootelus and is going to the Carr Sanitarium for what ails him! But now look: Suppose we got him or somebody to rig up a new kind of cure—call it phageotherapy—oh, it takes Uncle Clif to invent the names that claw in the bounteous dollars! Patients sit in a steam cabinet and eat tablets made of phage, with just a little strychnin to jazz up their hearts! Bran-new! Million in it! What-cha-think?"

Martin was almost feeble. "No. I'm afraid I'm against it."

"Why?"

"Well, I— Honestly, Clif, if you don't understand it, I don't know how I can explain the scientific attitude to you. You know—that's what Gottlieb used to call it—scientific attitude. And as I'm a scientist—least I hope I am— I couldn't— Well, to be associated with a thing like that—"

"But, you poor louse, don't you suppose I understand the scientific attitude? Gosh, I've seen a dissecting-room myself! Why, you poor crab, of course I wouldn't expect you to have your name associated with it! You'd keep in the background and slip us all the dope, and get a lot of publicity for phage in general so the Dee-ah People would fall easier, and we'd pull all the strong-arm work."

"But— I hope you're joking, Clif. If you weren't joking, I'd tell you that if anybody tried to pull a thing like that, I'd expose 'em and get 'em sent to jail, no matter who they were!"

"Well, gosh, if you feel that way about it—!"

Clif was peering over the fatty pads beneath his eyes. He sounded doubtful:

"I suppose you have the right to keep other guys from grabbing your own stuff. Well, all right, Mart. Got to be teloddeling. Tell you what you *might* do, though, if that don't hurt your tender conscience, too: you might invite old Clif up t' the house for dinner, to meet the new lil wifey that I read about in the sassiety journals. You might happen to remember, old bean, that there have been times when you were glad enough to let poor fat old Clif slip you a feed and a place to sleep!"

"Oh, I know. You bet there have! Nobody was ever decenter to me; nobody. Look. Where you staying? I'll find out from my wife what dates we have ahead, and telephone you tomorrow morning."

"So you let the Old Woman keep the work-sheet for you, huh? Well, I never butt into anybody's business. I'm staying at the Berrington Hotel, room 617—'member that, 617—and you might try and 'phone me before ten tomorrow. Say, that's one grand sweet song of a cutie you got on the door here. What cha think? How's chances on dragging her out to feed and shake a hoof with Uncle Clif?"

As primly as the oldest, most staid scientist in the Institute, Martin protested, "Oh, she belongs to very nice family. I don't think I should try it. Really, I'd rather you didn't."

Clif's gaze was sharp, for all its fattiness.

With excessive cordiality, with excessive applause when Clif remarked, "You better go back to work and put some salt on a coupla bacteria's tails," Martin guided him to the reception-room, safely past the girl clerk, and to the elevator.

For a long time he sat in his office and was thoroughly wretched.

He had for years pictured Clif Clawson as another Terry Wickett. He saw that Clif was as different from Terry as from Rippleton Holabird. Terry was rough, he was surly, he was colloquial, he despised many fine and gracious things, he offended many fine and gracious people, but these acerbities made up the haircloth robe wherewith he defended a devotion to such holy work as no cowled monk ever knew. But Clif—

"I'd do the world a service by killing that man!" Martin fretted. "Phageotherapy at a yegg sanitarium! I stand him only because I'm too much of a coward to risk his going around saying that 'in the days of my Success, I've gone back on my old friends.' (Success! Puddling at work! Dinners! Talking to idiotic women! Being furious because you weren't invited to the dinner to the Portuguese minister!) No. I'll 'phone Clif we can't have him at the house."

Over him came remembrance of Clif's loyalty in the old barren days, and Clif's joy to share with him every pathetic gain.

"Why *should* he understand my feeling about phage? Was his scheme any worse than plenty of reputable drug-firms? How much was I righteously offended, and how much was I sore because he didn't recognize the high social position of the rich Dr. Arrowsmith?"

He gave up the question, went home, explained almost frankly to Joyce what her probable opinion of Clif would be, and contrived that Clif should be invited to dinner with only the two of them.

"My dear Mart," said Joyce, "why do you insult me by hinting that I'm such a snob that I'll be offended by racy slang and by business ethics very much like those of dear Roger's grandpapa? Do you think I've never ventured out of the drawing-room? I thought you'd seen me outside it! I shall probably like your Clawson person very much indeed."

The day after Martin had invited him to dinner, Clif telephoned to Joyce:

"This Mrs. Arrowsmith? Well, say, this is old Clif."

"I'm afraid I didn't quite catch it."

"Clif! Old Clif!"

"I'm frightfully sorry but— Perhaps there's a bad connection."

"Why, it's Mr. *Clawson*, that's going to feed with you on—"

"Oh, of course. I *am* so sorry."

"Well, look: What I wanted to know is: Is this going to be just a homey grub-grabbing or a real soirée? In other words, honey, shall I dress natural or do I put on the soup-and-fish? Oh, I got 'em—swallow-tail and the whole dam' outfit!"

"I— Do you mean— Oh. Shall you dress for dinner? I think perhaps I would."

"Attaboy! I'll be there, dolled up like a new saloon. I'll show you folks the cutest lil line of jeweled studs you ever laid eyes on. Well, it's been a great pleezhure to meet Mart's Missus, and we will now close with singing 'Till We Meet Again' or 'Au Reservoir.'"

When Martin came home, Joyce faced him with, "Sweet, I can't do it! The man must be mad. Really, dear, you just take care of him and let me go to bed. Besides: you two won't want me—you'll want to talk over old times, and I'd only interfere. And with baby coming in two months now, I ought to go to bed early."

"Oh, Joy, Clif'd be awfully offended, and he's always been so decent to me and— And you've often asked me about my cub days. Don't you *want*," plaintively, "to hear about 'em?"

"Very well, dear. I'll try to be a little sunbeam to him, but I warn you I sha'n't be a success."

They worked themselves up to a belief that Clif would be raucous, would drink too much, and slap Joyce on the back. But when he appeared for dinner he was agonizingly polite and flowery—till he became slightly drunk. When Martin said "damn," Clif reproved him with, "Of course I'm only a hick, but I don't think a lady like the Princess here would like you to cuss."

And, "Well, I never expected a rube like young Mart to marry the real bon-ton article."

And, "Oh, maybe it didn't cost something to furnish this dining-room, oh, not a-tall!"

And, "Champagne, heh? Well, you're certainly doing poor old Clif proud. Your Majesty, just tell your High Dingbat to tell his valay to tell my secretary the address of your bootlegger, will you?"

In his cups, though he severely retained his moral and elegant vocabulary, Clif chronicled the jest of selling oil-wells unprovided with oil and of escaping before the law closed in; the cleverness of joining churches for the purpose of selling stock to the members; and the edifying experience of assisting Dr. Benoni Carr to capture a rich and senile widow for his sanitarium by promising to provide medical consultation from the spirit-world.

Joyce was silent through it all, and so superbly polite that everyone was wretched.

Martin struggled to make a liaison between them, and he had no elevating remarks about the strangeness of a man's boasting of his own crookedness, but he was coldly furious when Clif blundered:

"You said old Gottlieb was sort of down on his luck now."

"Yes, he's not very well."

"Poor old coot. But I guess you've realized by now how foolish you were when you used to fall for him like seven and a half brick. Honestly, Lady Arrowsmith, this kid used to think Pa Gottlieb was the cat's pajamas—begging your pardon for the slanguageness."

"What do you mean?" said Martin.

"Oh, I'm onto Gottlieb! Of course you know as well as I do that he always was a self-advertiser, getting himself talked about by confidin' to the whole *ops terrara* what a strict scientist he was, and putting on a lot of dog and emitting these wise cracks about philosophy and what fierce guys the regular docs were. But what's worse than— Out in San Diego I ran onto a fellow that used to be an instructor in botany in Winnemac, and he told me that with all this antibody stuff of his, Gottlieb never gave any credit to—well, he was some Russian that did most of it before and Pa Gottlieb stole all his stuff."

That in this charge against Gottlieb there was a hint of truth, that he knew the great god to have been at times ungenerous, merely increased the rage which was clenching Martin's fist in his lap.

Three years before, he would have thrown something, but he was an adaptable person. He had yielded to Joyce's training in being quietly instead of noisily disagreeable; and his only comment was "No, I think you're wrong, Clif. Gottlieb has carried the antibody work 'way beyond all the others."

Before the coffee and liqueurs had come into the drawing-room, Joyce begged, at her prettiest, "Mr. Clawson, do you mind awfully if I slip up to bed? I'm so frightfully glad to have had the opportunity of meeting one of my husband's oldest friends, but I'm not feeling very well, and I do think I'd be wise to have some rest."

"Madam the Princess, I noticed you were looking peeked."

"Oh! Well— Good-night!"

Martin and Clif settled in large chairs in the drawing-room, and tried to play at being old friends happy in meeting. They did not look at each other.

After Clif had cursed a little and told three sound smutty stories, to show that he had not been spoiled and that he had been elegant only to delight Joyce, he flung:

"Huh! So that is that, as the Englishers remark. Well, I could see your Old Lady didn't cotton to me. She was just as chummy as an iceberg. But gosh, I don't mind. She's going to have a kid, and of course women, all of 'em, get cranky when they're that way. But—"

He hiccuped, looked sage, and bolted his fifth cognac.

"But what I never could figure out— Mind you, I'm not criticizing the Old Lady. She's as swell as they make 'em. But what I can't understand is how after living with Leora, who was the real thing, you can stand a hoity-toity skirt like Joycey!"

Then Martin broke.

The misery of not being able to work, these months since Terry had gone, had gnawed at him.

"Look here, Clif. I won't have you discuss my wife. I'm sorry she doesn't please you, but I'm afraid that in this particular matter—"

Clif had risen, not too steadily, though his voice and his eyes were resolute.

"All right. I figured out you were going to high-hat me. Of course I haven't got a rich wife to slip me money. I'm just a plain old hobo. I don't belong in a place like this. Not smooth enough to be a butler. You are. All right. I wish you luck. And meanwhile you can go plumb to hell, my young friend!"

Martin did not pursue him into the hall.

As he sat alone he groaned, "Thank Heaven, that operation's over!"

He told himself that Clif was a crook, a fool, and a fat waster; he told himself that Clif was a cynic without wisdom, a drunkard without charm, and a philanthropist who was generous only because it larded his vanity. But these admirable truths did not keep the operation from hurting any more than it would have eased the removal of an appendix to be told that it was a bad appendix, an appendix without delicacy or value.

He had loved Clif—did love him and always would. But he would never see him again. Never!

The impertinence of that flabby blackguard to sneer at Gottlieb! His boorishness! Life was too short for—

"But hang it—yes, Clif is a tough, but so am I. He's a crook, but wasn't I a crook to fake my plague figures in St. Hubert—and the worse crook because I got praise for it?"

He bobbed up to Joyce's room. She was lying in her immense four-poster, reading "Peter Whiffle."

"Darling, it was all rather dreadful, wasn't it!" she said. "He's gone?"

"Yes. . . . He's gone. . . . I've driven out the best friend I ever had—practically. I let him go, let him go off feeling that he was a rotter and a failure. It would have been decenter to have killed him. Oh, why couldn't you have been simple and jolly with him? You were so confoundedly polite! He was uneasy and unnatural, and showed up worse than he really is. He's no tougher than—he's a lot better than the financiers who cover up their stuff by being suave. . . . Poor devil! I'll bet right now Clif's tramping in the rain, saying, 'The one man I ever loved and tried to do things for has turned against me, now he's—now he has a lovely wife. What's the use of ever being decent?' he's saying. . . . Why couldn't you be simple and chuck your high-falutin' manners for once?"

"See here! You disliked him quite as much as I did, and I will not have you blame it on me! You've grown beyond him. You that are always blaring about Facts—can't you face the fact? For once, at least, it's not my fault.

You may perhaps remember, my king of men, that I had the good sense to suggest that I shouldn't appear tonight; not meet him at all."

"Oh—well—yes—gosh—but— Oh, I suppose so. Well, anyway— It's over, and that's all there is to it."

"Darling, I do understand how you feel. But isn't it good it is over! Kiss me good-night."

"*But*"—Martin said to himself, as he sat feeling naked and lost and home-less, in the dressing-gown of gold dragon-flies on black silk which she had bought for him in Paris—"but if it'd been Leora instead of Joyce— Leora would've known Clif was a crook, and she'd've accepted it as a fact. (Talk about your facing facts!) She wouldn't've insisted on sitting as a judge. She wouldn't've said, 'This is different from me, so it's wrong.' She'd've said, 'This is different from me, so it's interesting.' Leora—"

He had a sharp, terrifying vision of her, lying there coffinless, below the mold in a garden on the Penrith Hills.

He came out of it to growl, "What was it Clif said? 'You're not her hus-band—you're her butler—you're too smooth.' He was right! The whole point is: I'm not allowed to see who I want to. I've been so clever that I've made myself the slave of Joyce and Holy Holabird."

He was always going to, but he never did see Clif Clawson again.

## II

It happened that both Joyce's and Martin's paternal grandfathers had been named John, and John Arrowsmith they called their son. They did not know it, but a certain John Arrowsmith, mariner of Bideford, had died in the mat-ter of the Spanish Armada, taking with him five valorous Dons.

Joyce suffered horribly, and renewed all of Martin's love for her (he did love pitifully this slim, brilliant girl).

"Death's a better game than bridge—you have no partner to help you!" she said, when she was grotesquely stretched on a chair of torture and in-dignity; when before they would give her the anesthetic, her face was green with agony.

John Arrowsmith was straight of back and straight of limb—ten good pounds he weighed at birth—and he was gay of eye when he had ceased to be a raw wrinkled grub and become a man-child. Joyce worshiped him, and Martin was afraid of him, because he saw that this minuscule aristocrat, this child born to the self-approval of riches, would some day condescend to him.

Three months after child-bearing, Joyce was more brisk than ever about putting and back-hand service and hats and Russian emigrés.

## III

For science Joyce had great respect and no understanding. Often she asked Martin to explain his work, but when he was glowing, making diagrams with his thumb-nail on the tablecloth, she would interrupt him with a gracious

"Darling—do you mind—just a second— Plinder, isn't there any more of the sherry?"

When she turned back to him, though her eyes were kind his enthusiasm was gone.

She came to his laboratory, asked to see his flasks and tubes, and begged him to bully her into understanding, but she never sat back watching for silent hours.

Suddenly, in his bogged floundering in the laboratory, he touched solid earth. He blundered into the effect of phage on the mutation of bacterial species—very beautiful, very delicate—and after plodding months when he had been a sane citizen, an almost good husband, an excellent bridge-player, and a rotten workman, he knew again the happiness of high taut insanity.

He wanted to work nights, every night. During his uninspired fumbling, there had been nothing to hold him at the Institute after five, and Joyce had become used to having him flee to her. Now he showed an inconvenient ability to ignore engagements, to snap at delightful guests who asked him to explain all about science, to forget even her and the baby.

"I've *got* to work evenings!" he said. "I can't be regular and easy about it when I'm caught by a big experiment, any more than you could be regular and easy and polite when you were gestating the baby."

"I know but— Darling, you get so nervous when you're working like this. Heavens, I don't care how much you offend people by missing engagements —well, after all, I wish you wouldn't, but I do know it may be unavoidable. But when you make yourself so drawn and trembly, are you gaining time in the long run? It's just for your own sake. Oh, I have it! Wait! You'll see what a scientist I am! No, I won't explain—not yet!"

Joyce had wealth and energy. A week later, flushed, slim, gallant, joyous, she said to him after dinner, "I've got a surprise for you!"

She led him to the unoccupied rooms over the garage, behind their house. In that week, using a score of workmen from the most immaculate and elaborate scientific supply-house in the country, she had created for him the best bacteriological laboratory he had ever seen—white-tile floor and enameled brick walls, ice-box and incubator, glassware and stains and microscope, a perfect constant-temperature bath—and a technician, trained in Lister and Rockefeller, who had his bedroom behind the laboratory and who announced his readiness to serve Dr. Arrowsmith day or night.

"There!" sang Joyce. "Now when you simply must work evenings, you won't have to go clear down to Liberty Street. You can duplicate your cultures, or whatever you call 'em. If you're bored at dinner—all right! You can slip out here afterward and work as late as ever you want. Is— Sweet, is it all right? Have I done it right? I tried so hard—I got the best men I could—"

While his lips were against hers he brooded, "To have done this for me! and to be so humble! . . . And now, curse it, I'll *never* be able to get away by myself!"

She so joyfully demanded his finding some fault that, to give her the novel pleasure of being meek, he suggested that the centrifuge was inadequate.

"You wait, my man!" she crowed.

Two evenings after, when they had returned from the opera, she led him to the cement-floored garage beneath his new laboratory, and in a corner, ready to be set up, was a second-hand but adequate centrifuge, a most adequate centrifuge, the masterpiece of the great firm of Berkeley-Saunders—in fact none other than Gladys, whose dismissal from McGurk for her sluttish ways had stirred Martin and Terry to go out and get bountifully drunk.

It was less easy for him, this time, to be grateful, but he worked at it.

IV

Through both the economico-literary and the Rolls-Royce sections of Joyce's set the rumor panted that there was a new diversion in an exhausted world—going out to Martin's laboratory and watching him work, and being ever so silent and reverent, except perhaps when Joyce murmured, "Isn't he adorable the way he teaches his darling bacteria to say 'Pretty Polly'!" or when Latham Ireland convulsed them by arguing that scientists had no sense of humor, or Sammy de Lembre burst out in his marvelous burlesque of jazz:

> Oh, Mistah Back-sil-lil-us, don't you gri-in at me;
> You mi-cro-bi-o-log-ic cuss, I'm o-on-to thee.
> When Mr. Dr. Arrowsmith's done looked at de clues,
> You'll sit in jail a-singin' dem Bac-ter-i-uh Blues.

Joyce's cousin from Georgia sparkled, "Mart is so cute with all those lil vases of his. But Ah can always get him so mad by tellin' him the trouble with *him* is, he don't go to church often enough!"

While Martin sought to concentrate.

They flocked from the house to his laboratory only once a week, which was certainly not enough to disturb a resolute man—merely enough to keep him constantly waiting for them.

When he sedately tried to explain this and that to Joyce, she said, "Did we bother you this evening? But they do admire you so."

He remarked, "Well," and went to bed.

V

R. A. Hopburn, the eminent patent-lawyer, as he drove away from the Arrowsmith-Lanyon mansion grunted at his wife:

"I don't mind a host throwing the port at you, if he thinks you're a chump, but I do mind his being bored at your daring to express any opinion whatever. . . . Didn't he look silly, out in his idiotic laboratory! . . . How the deuce do you suppose Joyce ever came to marry him?"

"I can't imagine."

"I can only think of one reason. Of course she may—"

"Now please don't be filthy!"

"Well, anyway— She who might have picked any number of well-bred, agreeable, intelligent chaps—and I *mean* intelligent, because this Arrowsmith person may know all about germs, but he doesn't know a symphony from a savory. . . . I don't think I'm too fussy, but I don't quite see why we should go to a house where the host apparently enjoys flatly contradicting you. . . . Poor devil, I'm really sorry for him; probably he doesn't even know when he's being rude."

"No. Perhaps. What hurts is to think of old Roger—so gay, so strong, real Skull and Bones—and to have this abrupt Outsider from the tall grass sitting in his chair, failing to appreciate his Pol Roger— What Joyce ever saw in him! Though he does have nice eyes and such funny strong hands—"

## VI

Joyce's busyness was on his nerves. Why she was so busy it was hard to ascertain; she had an excellent housekeeper, a noble butler, and two nurses for the baby. But she often said that she was never allowed to attain her one ambition: to sit and read.

Terry had once called her The Arranger, and though Martin resented it, when he heard the telephone bell he groaned, "Oh, Lord, there's The Arranger—wants me to come to tea with some high-minded hen."

When he sought to explain that he must be free from entanglements, she suggested, "Are you such a weak, irresolute, *little* man that the only way you can keep concentrated is by running away? Are you afraid of the big men who can do big work, and still stop and play?"

He was likely to turn abusive, particularly as to her definition of Big Men, and when he became hot and vulgar, she turned *grande dame*, so that he felt like an impertinent servant and was the more vulgar.

He was afraid of her then. He imagined fleeing to Leora, and the two of them, frightened little people, comforting each other and hiding from her in snug corners.

But often enough Joyce was his companion, seeking new amusements as surprises for him, and in their son they had a binding pride. He sat watching little John, rejoicing in his strength.

It was in early winter, after she had royally taken the baby South for a fortnight, that Martin escaped for a week with Terry at Birdies' Rest.

He found Terry tired and a little surly, after months of working absolutely alone. He had constructed beside the home cabin a shanty for laboratory, and a rough stable for the horses which he used in the preparation of his sera. Terry did not, as once he would have, flare into the details of his research, and not till evening, when they smoked before the rough fireplace of the cabin, loafing in chairs made of barrels cushioned with elk skin, could Martin coax him into confidences.

He had been compelled to give up much of his time to mere housework and the production of the sera which paid his expenses. "If you'd only been with me, I could have accomplished something." But his quinine derivative research had gone on solidly, and he did not regret leaving McGurk. He had found it impossible to work with monkeys; they were too expensive and too fragile to stand the Vermont winter; but he had contrived a method of using mice infected with pneumococcus and—

"Oh, what's the use of my telling you this, Slim? You're not interested, or you'd have been up here at work with me, months ago. You've chosen between Joyce and me. All right, but you can't have both."

Martin snarled, "I'm very sorry I intruded on you, Wickett," and slammed out of the cabin. Stumbling through the snow, blundering in darkness against stumps, he knew the agony of his last hour, the hour of failure.

"I've lost Terry, now (though I won't stand his impertinence!). I've lost everybody, and I've never really had Joyce. I'm completely alone. And I can only half work! I'm through! They'll never let me get to work again!"

Suddenly, without arguing it out, he knew that he was not going to give up. He floundered back to the cabin and burst in, crying, "You old grouch, we got to stick together!"

Terry was as much moved as he; neither of them was far from tears; and as they roughly patted each other's shoulders they growled, "Fine pair of fools, scrapping just because we're tired!"

"I will come and work with you, somehow!" Martin swore. "I'll get a six months' leave from the Institute, and have Joyce stay at some hotel near here, or do *something*. Gee! Back to real work. . . . *Work!* . . . Now tell me: When I come up here, what d'you say we—"

They talked till dawn.

# 40

Dr. and Mrs. Rippleton Holabird had invited only Joyce and Martin to dinner. Holabird was his most charming self. He admired Joyce's pearls, and when the squabs had been served he turned on Martin with friendly intensity:

"Now will Joyce and you listen to me most particularly? Things are happening, Martin, and I want you—no, Science wants you!—to take your proper part in them. I needn't, by the way, hint that this is absolutely confidential. Dr. Tubbs and his League of Cultural Agencies are beginning to accomplish marvels, and Colonel Minnigen has been extraordinarily liberal.

"They've gone at the League with exactly the sort of thoroughness and taking-it-slow that you and dear old Gottlieb have always insisted on. For four years now they've stuck to making plans. I happen to know that Dr. Tubbs and the council of the League have had the most wonderful conferences with college-presidents and editors and clubwomen and labor-leaders (the sound, sensible ones, of course) and efficiency-experts and the more advanced advertising-men and ministers, and all the other leaders of public thought.

"They've worked out elaborate charts classifying all intellectual occupations and interests, with the methods and materials and tools, and especially the goals—the aims, the ideals, the moral purposes—that are suited to each of them. Really tremendous! Why, a musician or an engineer, for example, could look at his chart and tell accurately whether he was progressing fast enough, at his age, and if not, just what his trouble was, and the remedy. With this basis, the League is ready to go to work and encourage all brain-workers to affiliate.

"McGurk Institute simply must get in on this co-ordination, which I regard as one of the greatest advances in thinking that has ever been made. We are at last going to make all the erstwhile chaotic spiritual activities of America really conform to the American ideal; we're going to make them as practical and supreme as the manufacture of cash-registers! I have certain reasons for supposing I can bring Ross McGurk and Minnigen together, now that the McGurk and Minnigen lumber interests have stopped warring, and if so I shall probably quit the Institute and help Tubbs guide the League of Cultural Agencies. Then we'll need a new Director of McGurk who will work with us and help us bring Science out of the monastery to serve Mankind."

By this time Martin understood everything about the League except what the League was trying to do.

Holabird went on:

"Now I know, Martin, that you've always rather sneered at Practicalness, but I have faith in you! I believe you've been too much under the influence of Wickett, and now that he's gone and you've seen more of life and of Joyce's set and mine, I believe I can coax you to take (oh! without in any way neglecting the severities of your lab work!) a broader view.

"I am authorized to appoint an Assistant Director, and I think I'm safe in saying he would succeed me as full Director. Sholtheis wants the place, and Dr. Smith and Yeo would leap at it, but I haven't yet found any of them that are quite Our Own Sort, and I offer it to you! I daresay in a year or two, you will be Director of McGurk Institute!"

Holabird was uplifted, as one giving royal favor. Mrs. Holabird was intense, as one present on an historical occasion and Joyce was ecstatic over the honor to her Man.

Martin stammered, "W-why, I'll have to think it over. Sort of unexpected—"

The rest of the evening Holabird so brimmingly enjoyed himself picturing an era in which Tubbs and Martin and he would rule, co-ordinate, standardize, and make useful the whole world of intelligence, from trousers-designing to poetry, that he did not resent Martin's silence. At parting he chanted, "Talk it over with Joyce, and let me have your decision tomorrow. By the way, I think we'll get rid of Pearl Robbins; she's been useful but now she considers herself indispensable. But that's a detail. . . . Oh, I do have faith in you, Martin, dear old boy! You've grown and calmed down, and you've widened your interests so much, this past year!"

In their car, in that moving curtained room under the crystal dome-light, Joyce beamed at him.

"Isn't it too wonderful, Mart! And I do feel Rippleton can bring it off. Think of your being Director, head of that whole great Institute, when just a few years ago you were only a cub there! But haven't I perhaps helped, just a little?"

Suddenly Martin hated the blue-and-gold velvet of the car, the cunningly hid gold box of cigarettes, all this soft and smothering prison. He wanted to be out beside the unseen chauffeur—His Own Sort!—facing the winter. He tried to look as though he were meditating, in an awed, appreciative manner, but he was merely being cowardly, reluctant to begin the slaughter. Slowly:

"Would you really like to see me Director?"

"Of course! All that— Oh, you know; I don't just mean the prominence and respect, but the power to accomplish good."

"Would you like to see me dictating letters, giving out interviews, buying linoleum, having lunch with distinguished fools, advising men about whose work I don't know a blame' thing?"

"Oh, don't be so superior! Someone has to do these things. And that'd be only a small part of it. Think of the opportunity of encouraging some youngster who wanted a chance to do splendid science!"

"And give up my own chance?"

"Why need you? You'd be head of your own department just the same. And even if you did give up— You are so stubborn! It's lack of imagination. You think that because you've started in on one tiny branch of mental activity, there's nothing else in the world. It's just as when I persuaded you that if you got out of your stinking laboratory once a week or so, and actually bent your powerful intellect to a game of golf, the world of science wouldn't immediately stop! No imagination! You're precisely like these business men you're always cursing because they can't see anything in life beyond their soap-factories or their banks!"

"And you really would have me give up my work—"

He saw that with all her eager complaisances she had never understood what he was up to, had not comprehended one word about the murderous effect of the directorship on Gottlieb.

He was silent again, and before they reached home she said only, "You know I'm the last person to speak of money, but really, it's you who have so often brought up the matter of hating to be dependent on me, and you know as Director you would make so much more that— Forgive me!"

She fled before him into her palace, into the automatic elevator.

He plodded up the stairs, grumbling, "Yes, it is the first chance I've had to really contribute to the expenses here. Sure! Willing to take her money, but not to do anything in return, and then call it 'devotion to science!' Well, I've got to decide right now—"

He did not go through the turmoil of deciding; he leaped to decision without it. He marched into Joyce's room, irritated by its snobbishness of discreet color. He was checked by the miserable way in which she sat brooding on the edge of her day couch, but he flung:

"I'm not going to do it, even if I have to leave the Institute—and Holabird will just about make me quit. I will not get buried in this pompous fakery of giving orders and—"

"Mart! Listen! Don't you want your son to be proud of you?"

"Um. Well— No, not if he's to be proud of me for being a stuffed shirt, a sideshow barker—"

"Please don't be vulgar."

"Why not? Matter of fact, I haven't been vulgar enough lately. What I ought to do is to go to Birdies' Rest right now, and work with Terry."

"I wish I had some way of showing you— Oh, for a 'scientist' you do have the most incredible blind-spots! I wish I could make you see just how weak and futile that is. The wilds! The simple life! The old argument. It's just the absurd, cowardly sort of thing these tired highbrows do that sneak off to some Esoteric Colony and think they're getting strength to conquer life, when they're merely running away from it."

"No. Terry has his place in the country only because he can live cheaper there. If we—if he could afford it, he'd probably be right here in town, with garçons and everything, like McGurk, but with no Director Holabird, by God—and no Director Arrowsmith!"

"Merely a cursing, ill-bred, intensely selfish Director Terry Wickett!"

"Now, by God, let me tell you—"

"Martin, do you need to emphasize your arguments by a 'by God' in every sentence, or have you a few other expressions in your highly scientific vocabulary?"

"Well, I have enough vocabulary to express the idea that I'm thinking of joining Terry."

"Look here, Mart. You feel so virtuous about wanting to go off and wear a flannel shirt and be peculiar and very, very pure. Suppose everybody argued that way. Suppose every father deserted his children whenever his nice little soul ached? Just what would become of the world? Suppose I were poor, and you left me, and I had to support John by taking in washing—"

"It'd probably be fine for you but fierce on the washing! No! I beg your pardon. That was an obvious answer. But— I imagine it's just that argument that's kept almost everybody, all these centuries, from being anything but a machine for digestion and propagation and obedience. The answer is that very few ever do, under any condition, willingly leave a soft bed for a shanty bunk in order to be pure, as you very properly call it, and those of us that are pioneers— Oh, this debate could go on forever! We could prove that I'm a hero or a fool or a deserter or anything you like, but the fact is I've suddenly seen I must go! I want my freedom to work, and I herewith quit whining about it and grab it. You've been generous to me. I'm grateful. But you've never been mine. Good-by."

"Darling, darling— We'll talk it over again in the morning, when you aren't so excited. . . . And an hour ago I was so proud of you!"

"All right. Good-night."

But before morning, taking two suit-cases and a bag of his roughest clothes, leaving for her a tender note which was the hardest thing he had ever written, kissing his son and muttering, "Come to me when you grow up, old man," he went to a cheap side-street hotel. As he stretched on the rickety iron bed, he grieved for their love. Before noon he had gone to the Institute, resigned, taken certain of his own apparatus and notes and books and materials, refused to answer a telephone call from Joyce, and caught a train for Vermont.

Cramped on the red-plush seat of the day-coach (he who of late had ridden in silken private cars), he grinned with the joy of no longer having to toil at dinner-parties.

He drove up to Birdies' Rest in a bob-sled. Terry was chopping wood, in a mess of chip-littered snow.

"Hello, Terry. Come for keeps."

"Fine, Slim. Say, there's a lot of dishes in the shack need washing."

II

He had become soft. To dress in the cold shanty and to wash in icy water was agony; to tramp for three hours through fluffy snow exhausted him. But the rapture of being allowed to work twenty-four hours a day without leaving an experiment at its juiciest moment to creep home for dinner, of plunging with Terry into arguments as cryptic as theology and furious as the indignation of a drunken man, carried him along, and he felt himself growing sinewy. Often he meditated on yielding to Joyce so far as to allow her to build a better laboratory for them, and more civilized quarters.

With only one servant, though, or two at the very most, and just a simple decent bathroom—

She had written, "You have been thoroughly beastly, and any attempt at reconciliation, if that is possible now, which I rather doubt, must come from you."

He answered, describing the ringing winter woods and not mentioning the platform word Reconciliation.

III

They wanted to study further the exact mechanism of the action of their quinine derivatives. This was difficult with the mice which Terry had contrived to use instead of monkeys, because of their size. Martin had brought with him strains of *Bacillus lepisepticus*, which causes a pleuro-pneumonia in rabbits, and their first labor was to discover whether their original compound was effective against this bacillus as well as against pneumococcus. Profanely they found that it was not; profanely and patiently they trudged into an infinitely complicated search for a compound that should be.

They earned their living by preparing sera which rather grudgingly they sold to physicians of whose honesty they were certain, abruptly refusing the popular drug-vendors. They thus received surprisingly large sums, and among all clever people it was believed that they were too coyly shrewd to be sincere.

Martin worried as much over what he considered his treachery to Clif Clawson as over his desertion of Joyce and John, but this worrying he did only when he could not sleep. Regularly, at three in the morning, he brought both Joyce and honest Clif to Birdies' Rest; and regularly, at six, when he was frying bacon, he forgot them.

Terry the barbarian, once he was free of the tittering and success-pawing of Holabird, was an easy campmate. Upper berth or lower was the same to him, and till Martin was hardened to cold and fatigue, Terry did more than his share of wood-cutting and supply-toting, and with great melody and skill he washed their clothes.

He had the genius to see that they two alone, shut up together season on season, would quarrel. He planned with Martin that the laboratory scheme should be extended to include eight (but never more!) maverick and un-domestic researchers like themselves, who should contribute to the expenses of the camp by manufacturing sera, but otherwise do their own independent work—whether it should be the structure of the atom, or a disproof of the results of Drs. Wickett and Arrowsmith. Two rebels, a chemist now caught in a drug-firm and a university professor, were coming next autumn.

"It's kind of a mis'able return to monasteries," grumbled Terry, "except that we're not trying to solve anything for anybody but our own fool selves. Mind you! When this place becomes a shrine, and a lot of cranks begin to creep in here, then you and I got to beat it, Slim. We'll move farther back in the woods, or if we feel too old for that, we'll take another shot at professor-ships or Dawson Hunziker or even the Rev. Dr. Holabird."

For the first time Martin's work began definitely to draw ahead of Terry's.

His mathematics and physical chemistry were now as sound as Terry's, his indifference to publicity and to flowery hangings as great, his industry as fanatical, his ingenuity in devising new apparatus at least comparable, and his imagination far more swift. He had less ease but more passion. He hurled out hypotheses like sparks. He began, incredulously, to comprehend his free-dom. He would yet determine the essential nature of phage; and as he be-came stronger and surer—and no doubt less human—he saw ahead of him innumerous inquiries into chemotherapy and immunity; enough adventures to keep him busy for decades.

It seemed to him that this was the first spring he had ever seen and tasted. He learned to dive into the lake, though the first plunge was an agony of fiery cold. They fished before breakfast, they supped at a table under the oaks, they tramped twenty miles on end, they had bluejays and squirrels for interested neighbors; and when they had worked all night, they came out to find serene dawn lifting across the sleeping lake.

Martin felt sun-soaked and deep of chest, and always he hummed.

And one day he peeped out, beneath his new horn-rimmed almost-middle-